praise for HUNGER'S BRIDES

Winner of the Writers Guild of Alberta
Georges Bugnet Award for Novel

A 2005 Kiriyama Prize Notable Book

Nominated for the Regional Commonwealth
Writers' Prize for Best First Book

Nominated for the City of Calgary W.O. Mitchell Book Prize

"*Hunger's Brides* is an instant collector's item." —*Toronto Star*

"This is an extraordinary debut, with depth of detail and narrative skill presented effortlessly throughout its staggering length. Highly recommended." —*Library Journal* (starred review)

"*Hunger's Brides* is a beautiful monster that resists, often with brilliance, the unforgiving logics of myopic inquisition." —*Calgary Herald*

"*Hunger's Brides* realizes its ambitions, taking the reader on a journey spanning 350 years and bringing to life one of the greatest literary figures of the 17th century." —*Publishing News* (UK)

"*Hunger's Brides*, one of the biggest gambles in Canadian publishing, is one of the most remarkable books in recent memory. . . . A taut, challenging novel of ideas. The dozen years Anderson spent on the book are readily apparent on each page. Even at over 1,300 pages . . . *Hunger's Brides* never feels too long. . . . Anderson's debut stands proudly alongside such works as Gabriel García Márquez's *One Hundred Years of Solitude* and Eduardo Galeano's Memory of Fire trilogy." —*Quill & Quire*

"Calgary writer Paul Anderson is after far more than an imagining of the hidden life of a writer. The novel attempts nothing less than an apocalyptic anatomizing of modernity. . . . Both the Juana and Gregory narratives contain some fine, memorable scenes, but what the author does with the Beulah sections is let language loose, and the result is startling, at times frightening and often beautiful. Everything and everyone Beulah encounters becomes raised to epiphany by the caustic intensity of her vision. . . . It becomes clear, through the verbal energy of these passages, that the greatest achievement of Anderson's novel (and perhaps its true subject) is in the evocation of the teeming, sordid pageant of Mesoamerica: its mythic, blood-soaked history, its geography of extremes, the holocaust of its cities and its people. Through Beulah's eyes, Mexico becomes emblematic of Western civilization, and what we have done to ourselves by inheriting the ethos of the conquistadors and becoming technological masters of the planet." —*The Globe and Mail*

"Like Molly Bloom on peyote. Anderson has an uncanny knack for writing believable female characters filled with both self-love and self-loathing. Sitting helplessly by while the remarkable Beulah tears her own heart out made for one of the most harrowing reading experiences I've had in a while. . . . Anderson writes as the best painters paint—with clarity, finesse and infinite suggestion. . . . All this beauty is worth the trip. The many trips." —*Vancouver Sun*

"The grace and the poetry of the presentation draw readers in and introduce them to the world of 17th-century Mexico—not just the Spanish world, but the Indian. It is, among other things, a short course in Mexican Indian mythology. It is also, at the beginning, the story of a brilliant little girl and the beloved grandfather who nurtures her intelligence. . . . An astoundingly beautiful book." —Canadian Press

"*Hunger's Brides* is one of those rare novels—there are no more than a handful of them in the modern history of the form—that will reshape our notions of what it is possible to do with fiction and history, with myth, legend and language; and, above all, with character. . . . And, as with every good novel—and *Hunger's Brides* is much more than simply good—this book will change your life." —*Winnipeg Free Press*

Paul Anderson

Hunger's Brides

A NOVEL OF THE BAROQUE

VINTAGE
CANADA

VINTAGE CANADA EDITION, 2005
COPYRIGHT © 2004 NEW SPECS INC.

Pages 1359–1360 constitute an extension of this copyright page. All rights reserved under
International and Pan-American Copyright Conventions. No part of this book may be reproduced in any form or by any electronic or mechanical means, including information storage
and retrieval systems, without permission in writing from the publisher, except by a reviewer,
who may quote brief passages in a review. Published in Canada by Vintage Canada, a division
of Random House of Canada Limited, Toronto. Originally published in hardcover in
Canada by Random House Canada, a division of Random House of Canada Limited,
Toronto, in 2004. Distributed by Random House of Canada Limited, Toronto.

Vintage Canada and colophon are registered trademarks of Random House of Canada Limited.

www.randomhouse.ca

LIBRARY AND ARCHIVES CANADA CATALOGUING IN PUBLICATION

Anderson, Paul (W. Paul)
    Hunger's brides: a novel of the Baroque / Paul Anderson.

ISBN 0-679-31200-5

    1. Juana Inés de la Cruz, Sor, 1648–1695—Fiction. I. Title.

PS8601.N44H85 2005   C813'.6   C2005-901321-4

THANKS TO . . .
(Canada)
Banff Centre for the Arts, Canada Council for the Arts, Alberta Foundation
for the Arts

(México)
Fondo Nacional para la Cultura y las Artes
Instituto Nacional de Bellas Artes

JACKET AND TEXT DESIGN: CS Richardson
TYPESETTING: Leah Springate

Printed and bound in the United States of America

10 9 8 7 6 5 4 3 2 1

for Satsuki

Contents

Hunger's Brides

This is the patent age of new inventions
For killing bodies, and for saving souls . . .

BYRON,
Don Juan

WHEN THE DOCUMENTS that have become this book came into my hands, my first thought was not of evening the score. I felt panic—and removed a manuscript about to implicate me in the carnage in that room. But as I began to see what a very small part I played in her story, dread and agitation gave way to relief. Then, to a certain indignation.

Beulah Limosneros had been a brilliantly accomplished protégée of mine, even as she spent her every spare moment researching the great seventeenth-century Mexican poet Sister Juana Inés de la Cruz (1648–1695). That Beulah became obsessed with Sor Juana is understandable. Of all the giants of world literature, her story is among the most captivating. A child prodigy who taught herself to read at three, she went from a farm in the wilds of Old Mexico to the very pinnacle of Spanish literature, emerging as the last great poet of its golden age. As a teenager she dazzled the New World's most sumptuous court and lived as an intimate of its vice-queen. Proto-feminist and slave owner, theologian and musical theorist, fabled beauty and nun—for twenty-five years she championed, against the unrelenting attacks of Church patriarchs, a woman's right to a life of the mind. Sor Juana defended also a nun's right to compose exquisitely sensuous and lucid poetry. And in doing so herself, she repeatedly defied her confessor, the Chief Censor for the Holy Inquisition. Her writing career unfolds between the mystery of a sudden flight from palace to cloister and the enigma of a final spiritual testament signed in blood.

A worthy research subject. But during Beulah's time with me, her notes, historical oddments and lyrical fabrications concerning Sor Juana came to look less and less like scholarship until, at the end, the work was more like a lurid cross between novel of ideas and tell-all biography. In this, my part was not so small. Now, with nothing but time on my hands, I've decided to edit and emend her unfinished manuscript. I've done it to set the record straight, perhaps to right a few wrongs.

At the outset, though, my intent had been to set her little pearl in such a way as to reveal all its eccentricities. Even she thought of it as baroque. Taking my cue from Beulah's own early work, I settled on the format of literary biography, finding this suited to my own, more modest, talents. I've extended the story's reach, however, to embrace not just Sor Juana but Beulah too. I have used every resource at my disposal and many that should not have been: Beulah's diary, her dream record, her diet journals.

And of course there was the manuscript itself: a mangy stack of papers of assorted sizes and colours, dog-eared, stained and spattered. Scripts ranging from scrawl to type to childlike printing that ignored the lines. Napkins, gas bills and manila envelopes. Clean white sheets started fresh in a full and fluid hand become by page's end a pinched and graphic twitching from which I could decipher only the occasional letter. The typed pages, a total of 457, were not necessarily the easiest: Beulah's hand would sometimes slip from ASDF to SDFG or even from JKL; to YUIO. I could read certain passages only by decoding painstakingly, letter by letter.

Overall, I've felt compelled to temper the wildness of her tone and the extremism of her conclusions, to bridge the gaps in her research and to abridge her lyrical flights. To draw just the occasional line between truth and fantasy. And then, to find an ending. The task has not been without its challenges, and not without its diversions. Yet my attempts to recreate myself with these materials would never have seen the light of day were it not for what I have found here. It is a sort of true-crime story, a document for an insatiable time.

But now I wonder if all this feels too impersonal. Perhaps knowing where it ends, with Beulah on her way to a sanatorium. Yes, a more intimate start.

Here, meanwhile, my own drama begins, with me making sense of retirement at forty-two. I'm sure I feel as many retirees do. We are like poets in exile on unfashionable islands. We are the tiny emperor appealing to history. We are the last living alchemist.

Getting up from the desk, I raise the blinds and stand a moment staring into the west. A sea of stone heaves up before these windows, a slab of Cambrian time. From the pilings beneath my feet, a wide trough slopes away deep and slow, then out to the Rockies' massive cresting. Most days I see a rib cage there, upthrust, transected by a glacial blade. It carves clean to the bone, laying bare a jagged spine of peaks that arches south along the broken curvature of the earth. This, it seems, is to be my consolation: to rediscover a landscape once lost to me. Days I spend walking the foothills above Cochrane, twenty-six miles from Calgary. My nights I spend quietly, in a vast, vaulted affair of varnished logs and endless windows euphemistically called a cabin by the former colleague who has lent it to me. My retreat stands like a cathedral on the last high tableland before the foothills. Below, a patchwork of leafless poplar, and thick spruce spilling in soft folds to the valley floor. The Bow snakes flat and white among the bluffs. Beneath the thinning ice the river quickens. The end of winter comes late up here.

I look out the north window at a pumpjack nodding away like a relentless rocking horse, while in the distance the wheels of justice grind slow and inhumanly fine. From where I now stand I see them— yoked, as Sor Juana might say, to the blind circlings of an ass.

So. A beginning.

Donald J. Gregory, Ph.D.
Cochrane, Alberta
May 9, 1995

Echo BOOK ONE

Some friendly promise in your face I view;
You stretch your arms, when I stretch mine to you,
Smile when I smile, and answer tears with tears . . .

OVID,
Metamorphoses[1]

CONTENTS

17th day of April, in the year of Our Lord 1695

A NUN OF THE HIERONYMITE ORDER slips out of the room to inform the Prioress, who will notify the Archbishop of Mexico. Who will in turn send word to the Viceroy of New Spain, and he finally to his monarch in Madrid. While I just stand by—raging, as Juana Inés de la Cruz lies stricken with plague. And I, Antonia Mora—betrayer, forger, *whore*—know exactly who to blame. Let the official record show that in these last, darkest days, Sor Juana Inés de la Cruz emerged from the safety of her seclusion and toiled unstintingly, impervious to the swelling pandemonium—with me, her oh-so-loyal secretary and companion at her side—ministering to the sick of this convent, even down to its servants and slaves.

The end began two months ago. Late February, 1695. It is become now a year to remember.

The first whispers sifted in like smoke: a strange pestilence, burning like a brushfire through the Indian population of nearby Xochimilco. Soon neighbours all across Mexico City were reminding each other of a terrible plague said to have reached the coast on a slave ship in from Africa last year. Killing hundreds, then vanishing. Leaving villages without a living soul. Fathers and husbands gone mad: home from a week's hunting to find their thresholds strewn with bloated bodies lying in the sun where dogs had turned away from them. Buzzards too sated to fly . . . rumours too horrible to be anything but true.

Here in the capital it has always started among the poor. This time is no different. Out of every ten Indians, it strikes nine and kills eight, depopulating an overcrowded slum in as little as a week. Among the Europeans, our city's densely packed religious communities offer up the ripest pickings. By the time the sickness takes hold in the convent of Jesús María, a few short blocks away, our own cloister is ablaze with tales—not so wild, it turns out—of nuns vomiting fire, of bodies swollen black, hunched, horridly misshapen.

All but a few here have succumbed to the rising hysteria, and I have felt it in me, in the pit of my stomach, a fluttering like young love. I have seen it wavering like firelight in my neighbours' eyes . . . and it is a temptation difficult to resist. I resist another day or two by writing this.

I write as she taught me, I write because she no longer can.

Three separate strains of disease, shipmates now ashore and travelling the same road.

Sometimes they attack simultaneously, but more often each culls its own prey—wolves dividing up a flock. The first favours the body's hollows and joints, spawning grotesque swellings at the neck, under the arms, between the legs. Death is slow but survival, if in a greatly diminished state, is at least a possibility.

The second—*el Dragón*, or so we in whispers now call it—covets the lungs, drawing from its tortured interlocutors carmine flames of arterial blood that scorch the air for several feet about the deathbed. *Llamas de carmina* everyone says, never red, never vermilion or scarlet. Carmine. What is it we sense in this tint just short of purple—the dye of the cloak that protects, or the mantle that none may resist?

How I wish I could ask her . . . this, and *trescientas cosas mas.*[2]

The third killer, the deadliest, we call *la Flojera*. The Lazy One. A name that chills me to my very soul. *La Flojera* fancies her meat predigested, liquefied. Savaging its victim's moist linings, her softest tissues . . . within hours a friend, a woman, is reduced to a moaning sac of overripe fruit leaking thin blood from her body's every opening.

Three nights ago, dark rites of propitiation for the deadly sins that surely brought on this plague flared into orgies of frenzied mortification. Chanting, flickering tapers, the swaying glow of censers . . . hairshirts black with blood and moonlight. Thirty nuns crawled that night on flayed knees over the convent patio, and with excoriated tongues licked its paving stones clean in the shape of a glistening cross.

We are the Brides of Christ, heads teeming with dreams of a lover resurrected as the plague claims us in our bloodied beds one by one.

It has been a consummation of appalling violence.

In this place of women, men now are everywhere, scuttling stooped and harried through the rooms and passageways, shovelling lime into now-vacant cells. Litter bearers and gravediggers, priests bending reluctantly to hear gasped confessions, handkerchiefs pressed to pale faces against the meaty stench. Any servants not yet stricken stay away. So few able-bodied women now remain that surgeons and priests do double duty supervising the labourers as they burn the dead women's garments.

Any man caught fondling a corpse or looting it of jewellery will be, by order of the Viceroy, drawn and quartered in the public square; and by order of the Archbishop, excommunicated from God. But we have discovered that neither decree is necessary. From best to worst, all of us have at last been delivered from sin.

It seems we have gone dead inside. Emotions, appetites, even the senses.

The screams echoing through these stone corridors are horror-filled and agonized—children's voices crying out for Lord and mother in equal measure, while we the living communicate in brief shouts, as though to the deaf.

We move, day and night, through a kind of roaring twilight welling up from the corners of our eyes. And *everywhere* now this sullen smudge of smoke fed on sodden cloth. In some insidious way it is indistinguishable from the drone of bottle flies buzzing above the jumble of unburied bodies beside the bonfires. Few of us notice anymore that everything, every surface—plaster, porcelain, stone, skin—glistens with a fatty sheen of suet and ash. Until the evenings, when by lamplight we all scrub furiously and wonder if the oily clinging of it will ever leave us.

Yesterday morning I struck an Indian full in the face for handling a body too roughly. Convent discipline verged on total breakdown. Mass hysteria, even violent madness, hovered about us, very near. . . .

Then, after the blackest night of all, just when it seems every last one of us must be taken, a clear morning breaks. An hour of eerie calm settles over this place. Though we cannot know it yet, the plague has withdrawn just as suddenly as it came.

There will be only one death today.

The stench too has lifted—and the flies, scattered now on a breeze that wafts the delicate fragrance of tangerines into Juana's cell. The nuns and novices who have assembled here, as though at a summons, exchange looks hungry for miracles. It is already beginning. They will say your body smelled of tangerines.

Oh yes, Juana, you've scripted your little dialogue with Greatness but do you know how I feel? To sit by and watch you—all these days and weeks. It didn't have to happen this way. This is my fault, my doing.

And now you watch me watching you play the sainted martyr. Ever the valiant sister: "Burning my body won't be so bad," you murmur. "Better here than on the Other Side. . . ."

Each time your beautiful eyes close, my heart leaps into my throat. Then they open once more.

"So, Antonia, it seems I won't have to lie next to Concepción after all, and listen to an eternity of her gossip."

You could have held back, not leaned so near—taken even a few hours' rest. The chaplain offered you his plague mask, and you just smiled.

I will not say good-bye to you. I will not be part of your chorus.

Oh, Juanita . . . look at you.

Leaf shadows play over the far wall as though reflecting off water. Juana turns her face towards the low window above her bed of planks. Rust-red daubs and handprints, violent smears along the whitewashed wall and windowsill above the bed. They appear to me now—in this one insane instant—grim as hieroglyphs, gay as a child's finger paints.

"Would you like me to bring your telescope?" I ask. Stupidly. I will either speak or lose my mind. "Mother Superior has kept it in her chambers." Juana shakes her head weakly, no, but I persist. "You were never forbidden to use it. Not officially."

"Yes, 'Tonia, that's true," she answers softly. Some of the novices in this vault-like room have never heard her voice. "And Galileo Galilei was never forbidden to write poetry. . . ."

To those who have known Juana the longest, to one who has just bathed her lingeringly . . . she has never been more beautiful. Pale as parchment, her body like a girl's, disincarnate, feather-light, unadulterated . . . purely and completely her own. The fever has left her now, its work done. Gone from her face are the lines these past days had etched there.

Through the low window, sunlight streams into her unflinching black eyes. Only now do I understand she is blind.

"I feel the sun. Is it a clear morning?" Juana asks.

"Yes it's clear . . . very clear."

"What can you see—can you see the volcanoes?"

"Yes, *mi amor*," I answer finally. "They are white and splendid. If I were that bird, that eagle soaring up there . . ."

I am not sure how to go on.

" . . . I could see your mother's hacienda."

"Others?" she asks.

"Can't you hear them, the *urracas?* And *there,* a parrot . . ." *You are doing this for me, to distract me.*

"And flowers?"

"Juanita, *hundreds!* The jacaranda trees are still blooming in the streets. *Y las flores de mandarín*—you must smell *them* at least. There are roses, too. . . ."

I look up at the women gathered about the bed. I think every last one—some weeping openly now—must know by heart Juana's lyric on the rose. Sister Eugenia looks decidedly unsteady, one of the few to be nursed back to health, and by Juana herself.

Then the Mother Prioress, our desiccated paragon of gravity, enters the cell. We make way as she approaches the bed.

"Sor Juana? Can you hear?" The Prioress leans nearer, putting out a hand to steady herself. "I've just received word. From the *Archbishop.* Juana . . . ? He says he wants you to leave the convent. For your own safety . . ."

Sor Juana Inés de la Cruz lies unmoving, eyes closed, her breath a stuttered rustling in her chest . . . then stirs, as the faintest hint of a smile caresses her dark lips.

JUANA INÉS
DE LA CRUZ

B. Limosneros, trans.

Rosa divina que en gentil cultura
eres, con tu fragrante sutileza,
magisterio purpureo en la belleza,
enseñanza nevada a la hermosura.

Amago de la humana arquitectura,
ejemplo de la vana gentileza,
en cuyo ser unió naturaleza
la cuna alegre y triste sepultura.

¡Cuán altiva en tu pompa, presumida,
soberbia, el riesgo de morir desdeñas,
y luego desmayada y encogida
de tu caduco ser das mustias señas,
con que con docta muerte y necia vida,
viviendo engañas y muriendo enseñas!

Rose, heaven's flower versed in grace,
from your subtle censers you dispense
on beauty, scarlet homilies,
snowy lessons in loveliness.

Frail emblem of our human framing,
prophetess of cultivation's ruin,
in whose chambers nature beds
the cradle's joys in sepulchral gloom.

So haughty in your youth, presumptuous bloom,
so archly death's approaches you disdained.
Yet even as blossoms fade and fray
to the tattered copes of our noon's collapse—
so through life's low masquerades and death's high craft,
your living veils all that your dying unmasks.

 took her maiden name, Ramírez de Santillana. She gave me *Juana* and *Inés*. The year was 1648: Isabel was beautiful, spectacularly pregnant again and still defiantly unwed. She took her confinement in what everyone called the cell, a hut of dry-laid fieldstone serving as tool shed and sometime way-station to any Dominicans stopping the night on their missions among the Indians. And so it was that even at my life's beginning, my cell was haunted by the Dominicans and their good works.

Of course I've heard it described. Gables thatched with dried agave spikes . . . in a child's imagination they loll like leathern tongues. From the ridgepole, the cane-stalk bassinet hangs just inside the door, at eye level set beyond the reach of snakes and scorpions. Walls left unmortared for ventilation, and in the evening breeze the slight basculations of the bassinet. If I have a memory all my own it's a modest one: of loose-chinked stone . . . a wall of shells pale as canvas, pegged in place by wands of light. And beyond, panes of jade vegetation and turquoise sky.

The shed stood at the upper reaches of Grandfather's hacienda in Nepantla. In the poetry of the ancient Mexicans, Nepantla means 'the unstable margins of things,' and according to family legend I'd surely have been raised there, in my shaky palace of shells, had not Grandfather, who was riding the fence line on a tour of inspection, glimpsed my seraphic head through the doorway. Naturally he relented, and ended his daughter's exile.

I'd one day learn that my mother's exile had been largely self-imposed, a dramatic gesture directed at my father because he was not there. Adults, it seemed, were complicated. And none more than she.

The chief thing, for me and for our *Siglo de Oro*'s latter, better half, was that she did emerge from our cell—either by Grandfather's leave or at his beseeching.[3] Whereupon she refused first the offer of his horse, then the offer of his help with the hollow-boned bundle of cherub she held.

She stalked down (here I imagine Grandfather riding meekly behind), little moved by the view. Just above the ranch house the path bends north over a hill. Straight ahead lay the city on the lake, its far shore a frail glitter in the distance. The bearish shoulders of Ajusco Hill would have blocked her view of the island where Mexico rests on the charred stones of the city it supplanted. For that is the custom of this place, to build on the ruins of the vanquished.

Below her lay the ranch house, a one-storey horseshoe barred to the west by a high corral of *ocotillo* thorns. Once down, she returned to running the hacienda, having handed me over ("fastened me," as she put it) to a wet nurse she called Sochee. In my version it was to preserve her figure; in Isabel's, to preserve her nipples from the predations of an infant cannibal. I once ventured to ask, If I was so much worse than my sisters, why was it that Xochitl never once complained? A question answered with the barest shrug, leaving me to conclude all on my own that a descendant of the Mexicas[†] could have no objection to nursing an infant of my sort.

[†] Meh-SHEE-ka(s)— the dominant nation of the people loosely called Aztecs, whence 'Mexican' and 'Mexico'

From about that time, the frequency of Father's visits dwindled to roughly once a year. He still came faithfully for the breaking of the yearlings but only on rare occasions now for the breeding of the mares. It seemed attending the birth of daughters was no longer in his routine. My sister Josefa told me, with malign satisfaction, that he used to come *much* more often before I was born. This only made it all the more like a royal visit for me, and not just because of his family's remote and lofty origins. There was the unmistakeable nobility of his bearing, there was the civility of his manners—and he was so *handsome*. With black, black hair, and a manly chin, and big soft brown eyes like a horse's—no wonder even the wildest ones bent to his wishes.

And tall, taller than Grandfather, even. When he stooped from the saddle to scoop us each up for a hug good-bye, it was like being lifted into heaven.

Then he was gone.

We caught our breath.

The seasons resumed their turning.

It was harvest time—I would have been nearly two—when I discovered the roof. I was in the courtyard confecting mud delicacies in the flower beds when there began a faint but incessant knocking at the great double doors. Eventually Xochitl hobbled over to open them for a dozen or so fieldworkers saddled under immense baskets of maize. Very quietly the first worker asked if *la patrona* was in, and when Xochitl shook her head, their faces brightened.

I had edged closer to determine for sure that these baskets, higher than each man's head and tapering to a point behind his knees, were indeed attached by straps—or was this some sort of centaur of the fields?

Xochitl waved them in. The baskets must have been crushingly heavy, to judge by how the straps cut into each brown shoulder. And still the men lingered at the door, asking after her, and very respectfully. Her health, her hip, her daughter Amanda, who was sleeping in the *rebozo* strapped to Xochitl's back.

Xochitl said to hurry up, before doña Isabel returned to find them all standing around.

"Yes, hurry up," I parroted, eager to see what might happen next with those baskets.

"You have taught her our tongue?" one asked.

"She learned. Same as Amanda."

"Doña Isabel does not mind?"

The first few men through the doors were all looking at me now.

"Go on up," Xochitl said more sternly, and drew the screen aside.

For over a year I had played in that courtyard with only a folding screen of woven straw between me and the sacred science of the stair. I had seen the ascending rectangles begin halfway up the wall and had—to the extent I noticed at all—thought them ornaments. It seemed my older sisters had not been interested; but then, they could go *outside* and wrestle for their lives with the coyotes and eagles and panthers and jaguars—and who knew what else—that we heard at night.

One by one the corn men lumbered up. Then, from down below where I swayed in wonder, I watched them turn and, from the topmost rectangle, step straight into the sky.

Xochitl shifted to block my ascent and redrew the screen, but the next day at siesta, I clambered up—with all the grace of a turtle, an indignity foisted on me by the thoughtless wretch who had built the steps so high.

At first all I took in was a wobbly carpet of cobs baking in the sun, and the hot, moist smell of the world as a drying oven. All I had known was the compound. I was splendidly unprepared for what I now saw.

Even a very short girl could see for nearly ten leagues[†] all around.   [†]twenty-five miles

To the southeast was a jumbled crust of sharp hills and spent craters like heaps of burnt sugar subsiding in a pan of caramel. To the southwest, as though warped on a loom, rough-woven panels of sugar cane stretched, and all through them the silver threading of irrigation ditches.

An Aztec feather-cape of greens fanned west and north—deep groves of limes and oranges, and blue-green plantations of what I eventually learned were Peruvian pineapple. Closer in, ranks of spindly papaya and the oily green oars of banana trees transplanted from the Philippines.

It may have been then that I had my earliest intimation of the links running from form to knowledge to power, for it was not long afterwards I began to draw. Maybe if I drew a thing I might learn to look for what I had not yet seen. And no sooner had I taken up my first piece of charcoal, than my eye found the pyramid in Popocatepetl. It took longer for my mind to trace the paradox hidden underneath: that volcanoes should mimic the simplest, stablest polyhedron, the pyramid—five sides to the cube's six. To picture that smouldering mass up there as *stable* was like a gentle tickling right behind the eyes.

For the next year I went up to the *azotea* every day, once I'd endured the first few spankings and then the dire injunctions to stay well back from the ledges.

Out onto the plain—as day after day I sketched their progress—the long dun caterpillars of aqueducts edged forth on their tiny arches . . . and on cold winter mornings I traced the little teapots of hot springs that riddled the join of plain and hill. Farther off stood a lonely tableland, and on it what Grandfather felt was certainly the ruined city of the House of Flowers. If only I looked hard enough I might make out the huge stained stones through the tangle of overgrowth . . . and then I would draw them for him.

I had discovered a world!—entire and new.

And now my old world was about to discover me. For I'd started trailing after my sister Josefa, who was not going out each day to wrestle jaguars after all, but to attend a school for girls. Though her teacher, Sister Ada, would not at first let me into the classroom, as I was only three, she indulged me, allowing me to look on through the window at their lessons of reading and writing. On the third day, as though by magic, a small bench of fresh white pine, sticky still with fragrant resins, stood under the low window. It was tranquil there beneath the arches, bees whirring among the bougainvillaea and geraniums, the gurgle of a little fountain echoing as from within a cave. . . . But I felt a great mystery about to be revealed. Far from nodding off as Sister Ada must have expected, I fairly bristled with concentration. The way my mouth was watering, one would have thought I was observing a lesson in cookery.

"I *must* learn to read," I pleaded that third day. "Please don't tell my mother—please?" Sister Ada consented not to tell for a little while, versed as she was in the attention span of three-year-olds. But when two more weeks had passed she insisted I ask my mother's permission, and in exchange she would find me a seat in the classroom, where I might learn a little of the alphabet. And what good would a seat inside do anyone spanked by Isabel? "No, no," I said, "I like your classes very well, but I can read now." She laughed—no, *brayed*. Which annoyed me, so I proceeded to treat her to samplings from the many little mottoes pinned up about the classroom walls. I had just the rudiments of reading but my memory was prodigious, and in combination these were enough to make her cross herself and go quite pallid. In our region, when one learns swiftly it's said, *The sorcerer has passed there.* Anyway her gesture was to me a very satisfactory form of applause. I thanked her for the lessons and left.

Grandfather was away in Mexico City visiting my aunt and her rich husband. A day or two later he returned with his latest trove of books and a few childish texts to serve me as primers, but he found it was too late for these.

That same week the parish priest made a rare visit to my mother. At its conclusion Padre Luis, himself a man of scant education, confided, "Your Juanita has much promise. God must have designed her for great exploits."

Isabel had little time for either priests or the Church. "Well then," she replied, "he should have *designed* her as a man."

From that day forward, Padre Luis went about suggesting, to anyone who would listen, that there was an unholy character to my hunger for learning. Priests.

I stopped eating cheese, though the *queso de campo* of the region— stringy and sharp and sour smelling—was a great favourite of mine. It was said that cheese made one stupid, and I already learned too slowly to appease my appetite. Though I missed the cheese sometimes, I did find that within a few months I could read nearly anything. Now when I needed to ask the meaning of an unfamiliar word, often only Grandfather could give it. If he was away for more than a week, we might spend an hour or two like this, with him helping me vanquish my collection of strange new foes.

First among the cherished memories of my childhood is that big sun face, round and tan, a thick red-grey ruff lining his jaw and tufting his chin. My *abuelo's* was the first serious portrait I sketched. His hair was reddish brown, the hairline high and well back from his temples, which lent a further roundness to the cheeks and forehead. His eyes were green, and clear as gems. After seeing him next to Father, I could no longer confidently call him tall; he was thick-set, with rounded shoulders. And down the years, to line up my sketches of him side by side was as if to chart the progress of ageing in the cinnamon bear.

Grandfather rented two haciendas from the Church. Ours in Nepantla, which Isabel ran, and another he looked after, higher up, just below the pass. In that house was a library I had only heard him speak of, but that shimmered in my mind as the real and true El Dorado. And it was from that great larder of books that Grandfather regularly restocked his shelf in Nepantla. Architectural studies, treatises on Euclid and Galen, and—still maddeningly inaccessible—the Latin poets. Virgil and Lucretius, Lucan and Catullus, Seneca and Juvenal. The names alone were as the metres of a mighty epic.

By the time I was five I had sworn an oath on the little ruby pricked from my thumb to learn Latin without delay. This was to be the first of my great failures, for as it turned out I would not master the godlike speech of Romans for almost ten years.

In translation, mercifully, was Ovid's *Metamorphoses,* and of course Grandfather's beloved *Iliad* and *Odyssey.* And the great classic of our Castilian tongue, Baltasar de Vitoria's *The Theatre of the Pagan Gods.* But the book he perhaps treasured most was by a soldier who fought under Cortés. *The True History of the Conquest of New Spain* is an old man's chronicle of the campaign, a story of the sufferings and deceptions inflicted on the common soldiers the author had fought beside as a youth.

"Books are powerful," Abuelo said. "This single book is why, *en mi opinión,* the many generations of us who followed Cortés have raised not a single monument to him."

Books *were* powerful, irresistible even: the scent of mildew they brought down from the mountains was for me like fresh bread, a bakery laid out between each set of covers.

Grandfather was a capable if reluctant farmer, but how he loved riding out over the land. Sometimes it was to El Dorado, or the land of Quivira, or the Seven Golden Cities of Cíbola, and then he would return to share out some of that fabled hoard: a legend, a rumour, a report he'd just read or heard.

"We live, Angelita, in the El Dorado of legends. *Sabes,* not so many years ago, on his way to a city on a lake, a man named Hernán Cortés—"

"Because he was courteous?" I asked, eager to show off.

"I doubt he was called Cortés for his courtesy. With his soldiers and a few horses, this Cortés was coming from the east, up from the sea. Sometimes they had to hack their way through the densest jungles they had ever seen. But as they worked their way upwards, he and his men began to climb through a cool forest of cedar and pine. Huge trees with growths hanging from them, like the beards of prophets. Yes, *feel*—but much longer than mine. Once at the pass, Cortés stood gasping in the thin air, satisfied he was now higher than any man had stood in Europe. Yet the peaks soared still a thousand *varas*[†] above their heads. He was surer than ever that it was indeed snow up there—though it was beyond belief, in such steamy latitudes as these. Can you see it, Juanita, the stubble on those lean wolf jaws of his? To confirm the marvel, he sent up ten men to fetch down ice."

[†]each roughly a yard

Grandfather neglected to add that they went also to fetch sulphur for their cannon; nor did he mention that Xochitl was from the pass and was his source for the story of the ice. She would one day tell me her people were greatly reassured by such a display of human curiosity from one rumoured to be the god FeatherSerpent returning from the East.

But they had never seen a curiosity quite like this.

"Just a few leagues from this hacienda—just there, beyond that next hill—Cortés came down from our sacred mountain to meet the Mexican Emperor. They met on the south shore of the lake that circled the imperial city . . . *great Tenochtitlan.*"

"Mexico," I said gravely.

"Yes, Angel, and here everything begins. See them: Cortés and Moctezuma[†] stand in the shadows of late afternoon, beside the longest of the stone causeways connecting the island to the land. This one, which we have now renamed the Calzada de San Antonio, is as straight as the horizon at sea on a still day. And wide enough to accommodate six carriages abreast! Before this day, the emperor's feet have never been allowed to touch the earth. Now, he stands ankle-deep in soft black mud. Into that mud he inserts the full length of his index finger. And what comes next stuns his attendants. He places it in his mouth. . . ."

[†]the variants Moctezuma, Montezuma and Moctehuzoma are standardized to Moctezuma here

Here was a gesture of grace, of surrender to *charys*, that Grandfather considered worthy of an Athenian—of old Pericles himself.

In a few weeks the great Moctezuma II, Regent of the Fifth Sun, incarnation of the war god BlueHummingbird who commanded a million men, would be taken prisoner in his own palace by a ragtag band of mercenaries. Iron clad, gold crazed, famished, reeking from the purulence of their wounds. Or so, listening to my grandfather, I imagined them. Locatable by their smell even through the stench of the dread Black Room, its every surface tarred in blood. There, stunned by their success, uncanny in its suddenness, they hold Moctezuma captive. Though captained by a lawyer (*¡un abogado!—¡imagínate, Juanita!*) they are in truth led and guided by a woman the Mexicas had sold to the Mayans as a slave. Now she has returned to bring her people, the chosen ones, a very different destiny.

"The unstable margins of things, indeed—eh, Angelina?"

The unstable margins of things. . . . The feature that gives Nepantla its name stands to the east: across the entire east, where the ground is heaved and rutted as by a titan's wheel of quakes and slides and lava floes. The country of my birth lies across the foothills of two white-tipped volcanoes. Iztaccihuatl and Popocatépetl. WhiteLady and SmokingStone. One dormant, the other murderously active. As the legend goes, they are lovers from rival tribes. She lies in a drowse of stone—struck down by a wizard's curse—while he, distraught, stands fuming over her, in a tower of ice and the black rock the Egyptians first called basalt.

Their slopes are the dark green of pine and cedar. After a rain in the afternoon, which falls as snow at the peaks, the fresh-glazed ice dazzles in the sun's decline, as the rains drift beyond them like a blue-black scrim. The effect is theatrical yet they are real—one deadly real—and from real stuff fashioned: rock, rain, ice, the very earth. Two immense actors up on the East's solitary dais. There in the setting sun they blaze up as if footlit by colossal lanterns. In autumn, when the rains come daily, rainbows are commonplace, prosaic as the tremors. And so it is not uncommon for them to be framed, quite perfectly, quite implausibly, under an immense rainbow. As though she has fallen in a bower of shimmering iris . . .

Ever since I can remember, ever since making a childish pledge to always live within sight of them, they *are* those lovers, more than they are mountains; they *are* that play, and the play can only be reality itself. This theatre has been my grandfather's gift to me.

I craved more time with him. But he took any excuse to be out, away from the place in Nepantla, which he conceded his daughter ran more ably than he ran the hacienda up in the pass. She could outwork any man, as Grandfather sometimes said to reassure himself. She was a force of nature, everywhere at once, startlingly so, like the first burgeoning of spring. Giving orders to Xochitl in the kitchen, riding out to the orchards and cornfields, butchering calves, fretting over lambs, shouting instructions to the *charros* as they bred the horses. All this, the work of a day.

Father's company, on the other hand, was too rare a delicacy to crave, which did not keep me from brooding on his absences. Grandfather one day referred to him as an adventurer, and this struck me as a calling of the highest sort. He was like a handsome ghost, a restless paladin of old whose occasional visits were so very vivid and memorable that all the rest seemed a fabrication. One spring day—I might have been four—felt particularly real. He had thrown open the portals and called in to all the girls to come out for horseback rides. They ran happily after him, but I'd been watching from the roof as he had put a fiery roan stallion, stamping and backing and screaming, through its paces. It was that horse he would now have us ride.

Josefa, and even María who was almost an adult, balked at being hoisted into a saddle that bore every sign of becoming a catapult. Though frightened I sprinted down from the roof, but by then there was Amanda, in my place, looking tiny and demure and being led about so placidly she might as well have been on the back of an enormous roan lamb.

I felt someone behind me at the door, and turned to find Isabel. In that proud face I thought I'd seen every variation on anger, but this one shaded swiftly into hurt. Which on her I had never seen and did not see for long before she turned away and walked across the courtyard to her room.

Father had seen her face too. So ended the children's rides, before my turn, as he thundered off on a long ride of his own.

Abuelo, for his part, stayed away for weeks sometimes. I came to think of men as a variety of migratory bird. Father on his noble and secret missions. Grandfather, reading, riding between the two haciendas, mending fences, tinkering with his little hydraulic projects—windmills, watering ponds, catchment basins.

It must have been the next spring, during one of those rare planetary conjunctions that brought Father and Abuelo to the hacienda at the same time. On the hill above the house Grandfather had recently installed a millpond to be replenished on windy days by the small windmill he'd had the workers build to his specifications. One morning he took me out with him right after breakfast. Though the ground in Nepantla was dry, he explained, the real problem was not the scarcity of water but rather the swiftness of its drainage. For this I must be wary of dry streambeds.

I knew this already.

"Imagine, Juanita, flash floods from a blue sky! Boulders, trunks and mud all washed down in massive swipes." This was dramatic even for him. "And so, in a way—no?—Time itself has gouged these ravines. As with an adze—there—in its fist. See how, between the arroyos, the high ground runs like roots? Are they not like the buttress roots of cypresses?"

I felt strangely anxious to know what he was leading up to.

Did I know that the people of this place once believed our volcano held up the sky? Here he included the heavens in the generous sweep of his arm. "They saw SmokingStone as a tree, rooted in the earth, its plumes of smoke and steam as branches supporting the heavens." His eyes met mine.

"We live, Angelina, in the Manoa of legends and—"

"I know, Abuelo, and you are its El Dorado."

He put his arm around me then. We looked out over the world he had helped me to see, that I still see as if through his eyes. The stage of the horizon and the forms beyond. The dry, grassy hills, the blond camber of their narrow spines. The orchards rising up from the ravines. Intersecting diagonals of deep green mango trees and avocados. Volcanoes that were lovers, who were really cypresses. . . .

"*Abuelito!*" I cried, eager to please him. "See how the hills are like snakes now?—see the diamonds on their backs, their green bellies."

He looked down at me as if surprised, and with a sober nod of that great head replied, "Why no, Juana Inés, I had not, until now."

And then he began to explain that we would be leaving Nepantla. The land was even richer up at the other hacienda. With my mother tending it, we would earn nearly as much as the two places combined.

"Abuelito, you're not leaving us?"

"No, no, child, not I." I should have guessed, then. "You'll like it up there. Just as much as here."

The message in all this was clear enough, I thought, with his parables of the tree, the mountain that changes yet abides: Permanence in change. I would soon read as much in Heraclitus. I wanted to shout, Of course I will love the other place, Abuelo—it has your library. Touched by his concern, I kept this to myself.

But that wasn't what he was trying to say at all.

Abuelo and I were looking back down at the ranch house. He was quiet a moment. A thread of mesquite smoke rose from the clay chimney pipe. A loose tissue of other such threads trailed up from the plain. Ewes bleated in the high corral of *ocotillo*; little red flowers budded among the thorns. There was the sweet scent of mesquite, and also of sage. And in the big laurel spreading its shade over the south wall a flock of *urracas* raised a castanet racket of the usual chatter. . . .

It was one of the rare times Abuelo talked to me of my father. "Did you know, child, that I was the one to introduce him to my daughter? With you here beside me now, how could I regret that miracle? I was up in the pass riding on a narrow trail when I met him. A natural horseman!" This was a thing Grandfather knew how to admire. "Your father is descended from the great Basque whalers. They crossed many times, you know, before Columbus ever thought of it." He found it deeply honourable that Father had come to America to restore his family's noble fortunes.

"It was always my great hope that they would marry. The love at first was obvious. But when your father did not come back for Isabel's lying-in this last time . . ."

Was that the time when Abuelo came to bring us down from the cell? Yes it was, and yes, my head was *very* angelic.

"I am not sure my daughter has yet abandoned her hopes. But never mention this. She would rather die than confess it."

The great current of his talk faltered then. Isabel called, and for once I skipped gladly down to the house. All that day I was in high spirits, playing on the patio with the others—my sisters and Amanda, and the younger children of some of the field hands. Usually I found such play difficult, though I loved to observe the others from the roof, admiring their capacity to invent new games on the spot, then enjoy those games well past the point when I might have stopped.

That day, Father was sitting at a table under the arches in the shade of the laurel. Beside his hand on the table rested a little *cántaro* of cool water, its top covered by a lace mantilla, its clay sides sweating in the heat. He himself had brought it from a journey to a land called Guadalajara. The flask was made of *barro comestible*, the speciality of potters in a village far to the west. One could *eat* the clay when the water was gone, a notion that enchanted me.

Even slouched in a chair, he seemed coiled to spring onto the back of a horse. He had a quick mind and was often amused by my little offerings, but the trick was holding his attention. I thought to ask him how the *cántaro* was able to keep the water so much cooler than the surrounding air. The thing was somehow to connect this to horses. Did he think, as I did, that by allowing the sides to sweat, like a horse, it dispensed its heat faster than the air could replace it? Or was there something about evaporation itself that cools? Since dogs didn't sweat in the heat but panted, were they panting sweat?

I was an idiot—what did he care about dogs?

But phantoms were perhaps formed of vapour after all, as was sometimes said. For when one entered a room did not everyone feel cold? So why oh why did I now stand before this one, flushed and sweating and babbling? I was about to ask, but my paladin of smoke was so *absorbed* in watching Josefa and Amanda playing with spinning tops beside me at the well. And yet I had no sooner observed the patterns being traced on the flagstones than—impelled by this madness of mine for hidden forms[4] —I called for some flour to be scattered there in order to better apprehend the effortless *motus* of the spherical form; whose impulse, persisting even when free and independent of its cause,[5] should—it seemed to me then—be mathematically describable. . . .

Exactly how I conveyed all this, I can't recall. He only blinked those great brown eyes at me and shook his head a little, like a horse adjusting to a bridle.

But later that day he did take me out for a short ride on his big roan. So I supposed I was partly successful. When he swung me down, I curtsied. "*Gracias, señor caballero.*"

"Oh, but it was my pleasure," he said and bowed. "And anyway, *señorita*, I owed you a ride. . . ."

He remembered. He remembered.

That night I lay awake well into the night, sitting up finally to watch the slopes of the volcano glisten in the moonlight and thinking about the geometry of pyramids. *We were going to the mountain. We were going to the library.* Perhaps Father would like it there. Enough to stay.

A wind was blowing from the west. A shutter was banging somewhere. I suppose I didn't realize how late it was. . . . All at once I had a
sort of childish revelation about the addition of pyramidal angles and
rushed out of bed to share it with him. Rather than take the long way
round through the arcades, I ran barefoot across the windy courtyard
to their room, in which I could see a light, and blundered in on a scene
not meant for my eyes. It was the first time I'd seen my mother that
way, yet I felt a shock of recognition as though finally seeing her as she
was. I couldn't have explained how, but I knew then that some of the
sounds I'd associated with the night were not from the fields or hills
but from her.

She was like a panther, beautiful and carnal and wild-eyed. She was
not ashamed, but this was no time for my nonsense. "Child!" she rasped,
"will you *never* learn your place?"

Will you never learn your place.

He reached out an arm to restrain her. It is my last image of him:
sweat drenched and lean, his eyes deep and blackened by lamplight, his
hair atangle, and even as he withdrew from her grasp his movements
were all fluid grace. He smiled gently, and shot me through with a look I
will never to my last day forget—a farrago of melancholy and regret.
Was there still a trace of that look in his eyes the next morning as he
turned in the saddle to cast one last glance over the slopes of the
Smoking Mountain? I like to imagine he was regretting bitterly even
then that he would not see me grown up. He was leaving, my phantom
pursuing a fantasy—wealth, glory, some goddess of Fortune. To be a
hidalgo in Spain, a latter-day *Conquistador* back from the New World,
and eligible at last to marry up to the station his family had fallen
from—with one of the stale and pasty virgins of his dusty Basque village.

He'd made up his mind. And looking into those rich, dark eyes, I
knew. I knew, and my mother did not; even as her soul merged with his,
she did not know. Even as it shattered like glass beneath the blows of a
hammer, she did not know. But I did, in that instant. And for this my
mother never quite forgave me.

After that night I ceased being a little girl in her eyes.

JUANA INÉS
DE LA CRUZ

F. J. Warnke, trans.

Que contiene una fantasía contenta con amor decente

Detente, sombra de mi bien esquivo,
imagen del hechizo que más quiero,
bella ilusión por quien alegre muero,
dulce ficción por quien penosa vivo.

Si al imán de tus gracias, atractivo,
sirve mi pecho de obediente acero,
¿para qué me enamoras lisonjero
si has de burlarme luego fugitivo?

Mas blasonar no puedes, satisfecho,
de que triunfa de mí tu tiranía:
que aunque dejas burlado el lazo estrecho
que tu forma fantástica ceñía,
poco importa burlar brazos y pecho
si te labra prisión mi fantasía.

In which she restrains a fantasy

Stay, elusive shadow that I cherish,
Image of the enchantment which I love,
Illusion fair for which I gladly perish,
Sweet fiction for whose sake in pain I live.

If my breast responds to your attractive graces
As to the magnet the obedient steel,
Why woo me with your flattering embraces,
To flee me later, mocking my appeal?

But you cannot in satisfaction boast
That your tyranny has triumphed over me:
Even if you escape the noose I fashioned
To bind the form of your evasive ghost,
It matters not to flee my arms impassioned,
If you're imprisoned in my fantasy.[6]

n leaving Nepantla I lost a father. During the slow, jolting journey up to our new home in the pass I recovered the twin I'd all but forgotten. Amanda and I were wordlessly skirmishing over who was to get the preferred seat, nearest the back of the mule cart. To settle this, naturally we needed to know who was older.

"Same," Xochitl said, ever the peacemaker.

"Not roughly," I insisted, "*exactly*."

"Same day."

No one had thought to mention this. There were so many more interesting things to talk about around our house.

The same *day*—I a month early, and Amanda, who was Xochitl's first, a week late.

"We're twins?" Amanda asked, excited, for many of the old stories Xochitl told involved twins.

No, there was more to it than that, which I at least knew. But it was typical of Xochitl's kindness that she seemed to share our regret.

So we alternated at the seat of choice. And within a day or two we were calling each other twin. It was our special joke but it expressed, too, all the wonder of a rediscovery that might never have happened at all. What if I'd ridden instead with María and Josefa up ahead in the first mule cart? What might my life have come to then?

Isabel drove the lead cart, a mantilla over her chestnut hair to shield it from the dust. My sisters rode next to her. Grandfather ranged back from their cart to circle ours before riding way up ahead, then back again. Our cavalry escort was looking nervous, I thought. Or else guilty about being the most comfortable among us: he sat a horse as easily as a rocking chair. Maybe he didn't want us to notice his delight to be bringing Isabel to take over his obligations at the hacienda up in the pass.

It must have been March when Father left, for the *ocotillo* corral wore a crest of red blossoms. By the time the rest of us were ready to leave Nepantla, it was already late fall.

All criss-crossed and scored, the road looked like a big ball of twine as it rolled and bumped away under us. To roll over it was to grapple with an unseen wrestler. The awning's noise and light and sudden shadow as it flopped and flapped were stunning, like being tossed in a blanket. But at least it fanned us. Closing my eyes, I tried to see myself lazing under an ostrich fan, on the deck of a barge on the Nile. The Nile in flood. The Nile in spate, the Nile in cataract . . .

This was clearly not working. At any other time I'd have been content to look for menageries in the clouds, as I often did up on the roof in Nepantla, but at least a roof consented to stand still. Grandfather, riding by, said I looked seasick. *Seasick*—I hadn't even been on a lake yet.

The seat next to the muleteer was heaped high with Isabel's dining room treasures—chairs, cutlery, lacquered sideboards. . . . So there was no room to ride on our little barge's upper decks—and anyway the driver was increasingly drunk on *pulque,* a ferment of the sweet sap of the maguey cactus.

To distract us, to distract me, for Amanda could sit still for hours, Xochitl had us trying to play a finger game with string. I was willing enough, but we had to reach out one hand or both to steady ourselves so often that the game fell apart. Just then the cart pitched, and a wheel dropped sickeningly into a hole before lurching out again. A small cry escaped Xochitl's lips. As soon as she could breathe, she called up to the driver, "Are you even awake, you idiot?" Her hip had never knitted properly after the accident, a fall from a horse, and the pain must have been awful.

However bad, the accident could not have been worse than the agony of birthing Amanda after it. It took *two days,* and had Xochitl not herself been a midwife, who can say how it might have turned out. But it did spell an end to her work in the fields and her life up in the pass. After the fall and the agonizing delivery, her hair had turned all but white. She wore it in a single lustrous plait, sometimes down her back, but when she worked in the kitchen, behind her head in a coil. Her face was the hue of oiled mahogany. To sketch it, I thought, one must begin with an arrangement of triangles: of her cheekbones, and chin; the black triangles of her eyes when she smiled; the sharp taper of her brows. Two triangles, base to base, formed her lips—the upper smaller, the lower quite full.

Isabel called her Sochee, but the X was a 'sh' and the end was like 'kettle,' only lighter. Like 'rattle'—it *was* a rattle, a faint rattling at the end. sho-CHITL. Since I could first speak I had been calling her Xochita.

The driver was now garrulously singing away.

"Xochita, what's *wrong* with him?"

"*Ye iuhqui itoch.*"

" . . . his rabbit . . . ?" I said. Amanda nodded expectantly. I knew the words but what did they mean?

"*Pulque,*" Xochitl said, "once was a sacred drink, offered to the Rabbit."

"God was a *rabbit?*"

"A double . . . a mask . . ."

And so it was said, sarcastically, that each drunkard had his own way of making the rabbit sacred. Some fight, some sing, some cry and quarrel. And some vomit, as this one had just now done.

Such is his rabbit. I was enchanted. And so, distracting me in a way the finger game never could have, Xochitl set Amanda and me to guessing at riddles and the meanings of old proverbs.

"What is a great blue-green jar scattered with popcorn?"

"The sky!" I said. But Amanda had called it out too, maybe a little ahead of me. "Another!"

"It is good to see you take an interest, Ixpetz. We should travel together more often."

"*Ixpetz?*"

"PolishedEye." Amanda answered.

"I *know,* but—"

"It is used," Xochitl said, "for someone quick to see into the turnings of things." By the light dancing in her eyes I could see she really *had* intended it to rhyme with Inés. My second name came from the Latin for 'lamb,' but Isabel used it whenever she was vexed. Which was usually. From then on Xochitl often said Ixpetz as a balm for the rasp in Inés.

"What about Amanda?" I said.

"That little one? *Cuicuitlauilli in tlalticpac.*"

"Nibbler . . . of earth . . . ?"

"A person who takes pains," Amanda said, "to learn a thing well."

Who learns by nibbling at the world. How lovely! NibbleTooth, that would be my name for her. And so, from that day forward we were to become PolishedEye and NibbleTooth, twins and riddlers and best friends.

She had blue-black hair, just like mine. Her skin was darker than mine, though paler than her mother's. Pale lips and a square little chin. Brown eyes, while mine were black like Isabel's. Always near her mother's side, Amanda had seemed so still I had thought her passive. But now I remembered times when at a nod from Xochitl she burst into a run across the courtyard with an explosive joy, like a foal frisking in new grass. As into a wind she ran, and as she ran the mask of her reserve tipped back like a little hat on a strap.

It now seemed to me that those times of play were always when Isabel had gone out. Grave, still, poised . . . Amanda was *watchful*, not passive.

"I have one," I said. "What dresses like a tree, is spiny, and leaves traces like a frightened squid?"

"What?"

"Books!" I felt my face flush. This one was not so successful as theirs. "Another, Xochita. Please?"

But instead it was Amanda who asked, grave and ominous, "Something seized in a black stone forest that dies on a white stone slab."

"Tell us. . . ." I shivered, expecting the worst.

"A head-louse we crush on our nail!"

"This one is nicer," said Xochitl, making a wry face. "What goes along the foothills, patting out tortillas with its palms?"

"A butterfly?"

Amanda nodded and smiled. She had known, and let me answer.

Blinking, Xochitl looked from Amanda to me, to Amanda again. "Daughters," she said gently, "you make my face wide."

"It means she's proud," said Amanda quietly. Indeed Xochitl's face was wide and smiling, and her eyes were very bright. And what else did I see there—relief?—but how could Amanda and I have been anything but the greatest of friends?

Amanda spoke our tongue hesitantly. In her mother's tongue she was another person—she had come to speak Nahuatl with a fluidity I now lacked. Our family's language, Castilian, was a sweet deep river of breath, clear water over a streambed of smooth even stones. Nahuatl in the ear was all soft clicks and snicks and collidings of teeth and tongue, like the secret language of sibyls. In the mouth, the canals of the cheeks, Nahuatl was rich, like *atole*—and thick like *pozole!*—yes, that was it, a thick stew. With chunks of the world bobbing in it like meat, and you wanted to *chew* it—but gingerly—anticipating a hardness, a stone or bone shard, against the molars, and . . .

But no, that wasn't quite it either. Until I had tasted *pulque* I would never quite find it. *Pulque*, which wrapped itself like a film, clinging, viscous, to the palate and molars and tongue. That was the sensation of Nahuatl in the mouth. Finding this new love right under my nose was like finding Amanda again.

More proverbs, more riddles.

If I was PolishedEye and Amanda NibbleTooth, what was Grand-father?

Xochitl barely hesitated. *He had achieved the four hundred,* he had accomplished many things.

And Xochitl herself? She shook her head. What about Isabel, then. *WoodenLips.*

What did that mean?—*one of firm words, who cannot be refuted.* Ah. Well. And Father?

No.

Please? No, it was not her place. But Amanda and I badgered her relentlessly. All right, enough.

Aca icuitlaxcoltzin quitlatalmachica.

What?

Aca icuitlaxcoltzin quitlatalmachica.

One who arranges his intestines artistically. I suspected she had used it ironically but I would put this away as a keepsake, in a quiet place, and work out its meaning myself one day.

Most of the heat had gone out of the afternoon. I watched the horizon for a while, the colour slowly draining back into the sky. I had glimpsed that a people's riddles were roads into its world, and our language the mask our face wears. And I now knew riddles to cure seasickness. It was a secret I wondered if the old Basque whalers knew, and if there was hidden somewhere a riddle in my father's leaving us.

The road rose and fell more steeply now. I caught a glimpse of two farmhands at the top of the last rise. "What about them," I said to Xochitl. "Is there a saying for them?"

She thought for a moment. "*Ompa onquiza'n tlalticpac.*"

"The world . . . spills out."

"For the poor, yes. Spills. From their pockets. And from the rags they wear, they themselves spill. . . ."

At nightfall we halted in the churchyard in Chimalhuacan. Everything in the carts was caked in a fard of fine white dust, including us, as though we had been made up for a play or some ceremony. Grandfather was on friendly terms with the priest here, which was sur-prising enough since he was always fuming about the priests he rented the haciendas from. But directly he finished his fulmination, he would cast a guilty eye my way to add, "Do not let that keep you from reading your Bible, Juanita. It is another El Dorado." The priest, Father Juan, was a distant relative and had baptized me. *Natural daughter of the Church.* That's what he put on my baptismal certificate, just as he had for María and Josefa.

We stayed a day to rest a little and bathe. Amanda and I set off exploring, leaving Josefa and María to wail about the state of their hair. We ducked into the church. It was built of a pinkish-brown *tezontle* cut from lava and rough as a file. Inside, it was dark and cold, with just a few candles shimmering on altars beneath shocks of fresh-cut flowers. As our eyes adjusted in the gloom, I saw the font where I was baptized. Above it a painting of John the Baptist.

† transept

We got as far as the *crucero*† when Amanda tugged hard at my sleeve—

"Cinteotl . . ." she whispered, backing away and pulling me with her. Seated on a rough wooden throne, not crucified but bleeding from scores of wounds—as from volleys of arrows—was a black Christ. Not black—the blood was black, the skin stained a deep mahogany like Xochitl's. His head was lowered, and in a gesture of great weariness the fingers of his left hand ran through a dust-brown wig of what must have been human hair.

But what Amanda stared at—almost *through*—was the ear of corn held upright in his other hand: as of a king, bloodied, with a sceptre of corn.

I let her drag me back up the aisle, and once she knew I would follow she ran like a deer. Only the stone wall at the west end of the churchyard made her stop and wait for me. The moment passed like the shadow of a cloud, and we burst into nervous laughter. Later we helped Father Juan plant some pine seedlings along the fence. One day, he said, they would grow and shelter the church from the wind. As we worked he told us of his plans to raise funds for a statue of Our Mother Coatlalocpeuh to stand guard at the church entrance.

Later that afternoon as Father Juan continued to work in the churchyard, Xochitl told us Cinteotl was the son of the Mother of the Corn. So was that Cinteotl or Christ all bloody in there?

"Maybe a double," she said, the triangles of her eyes narrowing as she watched Father Juan still digging in the churchyard. "Maybe ask *him.*"

We set out again the next day. From Chimalhuacan the road got smoother and rose only gradually. We were moving across the lower slopes of Popocatepetl and heading north towards Iztaccihuatl. The air was cooler, and we travelled mostly in the shade of the enormous pines and cedars that flanked the road, thicker at the base than our little cart was long. We persuaded Xochitl to let us take down the awning.

Leaning back against the corn sacks, Amanda and I rode quietly for a while, a little stunned by the great white peaks leaning in over the trees. From Nepantla they had been actors alone up on the stage of the horizon. Now they loomed like enormous attendants bent over three small creatures in a crate, or so it felt as we rolled along.

We had crossed over into a land of giants. Everything towered far above. The axis of this new country was the two volcanoes, so still as to make the sky around them race with clouds and wheeling birds. There were more birds here. Hawks and vultures, as there were back in Nepantla, but also falcons and eagles. Xochitl said we were just big enough now not to be carried off by one. She looked into my wide eyes and laughed. "And tomorrow, Ixpetz, you will have a sunburn on your chin from so much looking up." Her laugh—hup!—came out in a little swoop, pulling up. It made you want to laugh too. She was almost chatty, a real swallow's beak, maybe because the road was smoother, less painful for her hip.

Did I know the story about the volcanoes as lovers?

"Muchi oquicac in nacel!" I said. *Every one of my nits knows that one!* Even this earned a smile, and she looked younger by years. Amanda was just as wide-eyed as I was at the change in her. But this was Xochitl's land.

"Is it true, Xochita, what Grandfather said about Cortés sending men up there for ice?"

"The Speaker himself sent relays of runners every day."

"The Speaker?"

"Lord Moctezuma."

"Did they see each other, you think?"

"Who?"

"Cortés's men and Moctezuma's. Going for ice."

"Our people saw *them.* The Speaker was watching from the day their ships landed. He sent his artists to paint them. From hiding places all along the road."

"Someone told you?"

"I saw it. The ships and men. The horses . . ."

"You're not *that* old, Xochita."

She smiled again. "No, bold-tongue, in a book."

"You read *books*?"

"Ours, not yours. It was my family's place to keep the painted books. *Intlil, intlapal in ueuetque. . . .* [†] My ancestor was the wizard Ocelotl."

"Your ancestor was a *jaguar*?"

"There are limits, Ixpetz, even for the young."

"I'm sorry. . . ." I felt a flush rushing to my cheeks.

From the way she smiled I could tell she was not angry. "And *your* ancestor also, daughter," she said, squinting one eye at Amanda. "One bold tongue is enough."

Xochitl talked lightly on, her face mobile and relaxed, its triangles tilting this way and that. I snuggled in against Amanda to watch the mountains as we listened. The keeper of the painted books, it seemed, was himself part of that book, and in speaking it the keeper kindled a fire in the hearer's mind. Whereas the book itself was only the ashes of the fire the morning after, cool and delicate and precious, but not the same. To one who loved to sketch, how beautiful this notion of a book not written but painted.

"Up there—you see, near that big rock? There is a hidden opening. Some of the old wizards escaped through it and under the volcanoes, when the sea and fire descended on our people."[†] Her eyes scanned the hills. "Every few years now, early morning or dusk, one of the old ones is seen, wearing the ancient dress and speaking words of jade, the old songs of heart and blood. . . ."

She glanced around to get her bearings. As she looked away, my eyes followed the windings of the braid coiled tightly at her nape. The strands of grey and black through the thick white coils were like the graving lines of fine chisels in soft stone.

"Here the ground is holy," she said quietly. "The words are simple but we lose what it is like. . . ." She seemed reluctant to go on.

"What is it like, Mother?"

Her eyes had not left the mountains. I thought she wouldn't answer. I wondered where exactly she had fallen from the horse and if maybe she was remembering this.

"Here, Amanda, every step you take, you walk in halls of jade."

We lay back quietly, propped against each other and the sacks of maize. I was getting drowsy. The road wove in and out among those trees that had been too large to cut down and uproot. We watched the sky pivoting on its axis. Once, these volcanoes had *been* the East; now they could be in any direction at all.

I slept. And dreamed of being carried off on enormous wings . . . by a bird with an eagle's head and talons, and the long white neck of a swan.

I awoke just before Amanda did. A light rain tickled my face. The sun, not far above the western hills, seemed lower than we were, as if the last light rose past us to strike the peaks far above, still radiantly lit. Quietly we watched the soft rain beat traces of silver through the sunbeams where they slanted up among the boughs.

The trees were thinning. We were entering the town of Amecameca, less than a league from Grandfather's hacienda. María and Josefa were standing up in the lead cart, gawping shamelessly at the refinements of the largest settlement we had ever seen, and would traverse in under five minutes. Xochitl pointed out the school. "For girls like you." She looked at me with a crooked smile.

Then we were off the main road. The track bent sharply east. A gold light poured over our shoulders and cast ahead of us the shadow of a giant with two tiny heads—for Amanda and I were standing now, behind the driver. As we clung to his backrest, Xochitl clung grimly to our skirts to keep us from pitching headlong out. Across the ditch on the left and beyond a windbreak of oaks were orchard rows of apple and peach and pomegranate converging in the distance as they ran. Workers stopped and doffed their hats as Grandfather cantered grandly past. Close to the road, one woman squinted at Xochitl and waved with a little flutter.

I looked back. She stood there still, the sun setting red beside her through folds of road dust.

Closer to the house were plots of squash, and beans and tomatoes. We crossed a small stone bridge over a brook that fed the irrigation ditches. At the far end of the bridge stood a little guard post, empty now, as was the watchtower that topped the house. The house itself was framed by two tall African tulip trees, and in each orange blossom glowed the sunset's radiant echo.

As in Nepantla, the house was laid out on one floor. Here, though, the roof was not flat but shingled and pitched to shed rain—and, Grandfather promised, sometimes snow.

The western wall above the veranda was a pocked grey-white. The watchtower and the chapel belfry still blushed the softest rose in the faltering light. Workmen in white cotton breeches and shirts took form round the carts as if exhalations risen of the dusk. We heard the quiet murmurs, ". . . don Pedro . . . doña Isabel . . ." They formed a brigade to relay the sacks and tools to the sheds. No one questioned that Isabel should work beside the men. A woman went with a taper and lit the lanterns strung along the veranda. Amanda and I chafed to explore the house, which was still dark. We were not to go in until Josefa and María had safely swept it out, and they looked in no hurry even to start.

Grandfather was soon relinquishing his burdens to the men, but when one tried to help Xochitl she refused—a tight urgency in the shake of her head. I distinctly heard one man call her Mother in Nahuatl. I wanted to call out to them—She's not as old as she looks!—then bethought myself. It looked more like respect than consideration of her age. And I noticed the workers themselves were careful not to let this regard be noticed by don Pedro or his daughter.

It was full dark now and enthusiastically supported by my sisters, who were sick already of sweeping (though they'd hardly started), we begged to sleep around the firepit. Xochitl was in the kitchen struggling to bring enough order for breakfast in the morning. Isabel was back from the sheds and briskly sweeping out Grandfather's room.

Grandfather helped us light the fire, a fragrant heap of pine and mesquite, a waver of flame soon reflecting in eight black beady eyes over blankets pulled up to our chins—how chilly the nights were up here.

"A story please, Abuelo. *Please?*" He obliged us grandly and continued even after my sisters had nodded off, though weariness crumpled his great round face and bedraggled his big mane. In repayment for his putting my sisters to sleep, I offered to tell him about the wizard Ocelotl. But as I quickly realized that he knew much more than I, I asked instead the difference between priests and wizards. It was complicated, he said, but a priest has words and laws, and a wizard has visions. I wanted to go get Xochitl so they might tell us together about Ocelotl.

"It's late," Grandfather said. I didn't think she would mind. "*Mira, Angelita, que te lo cuenta.*" A warning in his tone stopped me. "This Martín Ocelotl, and his twin—"

"*Twin?*"

"And his twin, Andrés Mixcoatl, led an Indian uprising. It began right here in these mountains." The brothers were incarnations of the gods MirrorSmoke and FeatherSerpent, or so people here claimed. For this they fell afoul, Grandfather said, of a horror called the Inquisition and were finally condemned. Mixcoatl burned. "But Ocelotl . . ." he concluded mysteriously, "Ocelotl disappeared into the night."

He had his second wind. The firelight glowed softly on his face. Now there came tale after tale of golden cities and fiery mountains, blue hummingbirds and eagle knights, wizards and jaguars, curses and troths. Of the magic traps the Mexica wizards set for the Conquistadors, but who, not knowing Mexica magic, rode right on as if through gossamer.

Through half-lidded eyes I saw Amanda's eyes blinking, slow . . . close—flutter, stop. Then the threads unravelled and we were lofted up and up towards the mountains, Amanda and I, and softly stretched on sleep's stone ledges. By hummingbirds.

The next day we ran everywhere together, exploring. We scrambled up to the watchtower, and to our delight found a little bronze cannon, battered and so long out of use there was a nest in it. To the south, beyond the belfry of our chapel, faint blue smoke smudged up from the town. Beyond the house to the east bristled fields of maize, then what might be the grey-green of *agave*, and then a glimmer of water. From there, deep forest rose in ranks of pikes sharply up to the snow line. It felt like mid-morning, yet the sun had still not cleared the volcanoes. They were right there, right over us. That first day we must have stared up at them for an hour.

We had come up to get a commanding (even superior) view over the house, towards which our eyes finally condescended. I kept the sketch I made during those early days when it all seemed so new. The firepit around which we had slept stood near the centre, and next to it a well. A wide, shady arcade ran right around the courtyard, except for the main portal on the eastern side, between the kitchen and the library. At the four corners, full rain barrels bulged beneath waterspouts set in the eaves. On the north, near the kitchen, was a tiled basin in the shape of a cross.

The flower beds—roses, calla lilies, hyacinths—had run wild, and now nodded and buzzed and beamed along the colonnade from kitchen to dining room to what was now my bedroom, next to the watchtower steps at the northwest corner. From my bed, which Amanda and I had dragged under the window, I could see all but the tips of the volcanoes, so high were they, so close by.

I had expected a hard fight from my sisters for that room. But María found the volcanoes oppressive; Josefa *just shuddered* to imagine the sight of them at night. So instead they made a great show of their maturity by choosing to share the only room left. I applauded this. And, yes, it was the largest—fractionally. To one side of them was our mother's room, on the southwest corner next to the entrance to the chapel. To the other side was Grandfather's room, in the southeast corner next to the library.

The library, I resolved, would later be reconnoitred from every possible angle. Chins propped on our forearms, forearms on the sill, we had been kneeling on my bed under the window onto the courtyard.

"But Amanda," I said, "where do you and Xochita sleep?"

She led me at a dead run past the dining room and into the kitchen: beyond it hung two hammocks in the pantry's back corner. It seemed unprepossessing to me, cramped even. She was thrilled that she and Xochitl each had a window, and that the two afforded a cross-breeze (designed not for their pleasure but to keep the pantry cool and dry).

I kept this last observation to myself but resolved to take the matter up with Grandfather. "Let it alone, Angel. Amanda is happy."

And so I did. There was so much else to do.

Once we had settled in, the next order of business was to thwart the movement to put me in school. I had missed the first two months, and was certain to be made the butt of the cruellest pranks and jokes. Isabel surprised me by taking this seriously. Besides, I told Grandfather once she was out of earshot, there was not much chance of falling behind in only a year since apparently my classmates could not yet *read*. Here I let my head loll about like a boggled newborn, at which Grandfather laughed wheezily.

"I've been reading for *three years* already, Abuelo, did you know that?" My average was a book a week, and lately more like two. So that made over two hundred now, and I began to recite them for him in alphabetical order. Thus was the matter quickly settled.

And next fall was an eternity away. . . .

I was not quite as confident of my advantage as I let on. Through each siesta I read furiously while the others slept. Beside me, Grandfather snored his bliss for an hour in a hammock strung between the arcade's columns before the library door. I sat at a small table, his hammock beside me, an armspan away. Under one window, on the inside table, was a chess set. Reaching through the wrought-iron bars we could have played, my imaginary opponent and I, like contented prisoners whiling away the years. But I had a library to conquer, book by book. And so at the little table crowding the door, I sat—*stuck*. For this was the threshold I had not yet won Isabel's permission to cross.

"I said no, Inés. The library is a man's place. It is not for little girls too accustomed already to having their way." She had said this not even looking down, with me trotting alongside her on the way to the paddocks. "I don't care what he said. He spoils you." She was splendid, I had to admit, striding out in the sun, tucking that thick chestnut hair under her sombrero. In her riding boots she was almost as tall as I remembered Father, taller than Abuelo. I hadn't known anyone could cover so much ground just walking—it was a wonder she bothered with horses at all. She walked the way I talked—would she stop for a minute, wouldn't she care to explain?—we could negotiate. She laughed, then. A laugh deep like a man's. Warm. Brief. I couldn't remember ever making her laugh. I would try to be funnier the next time. But she still didn't stop or even look down.

Neverthless, that day and the next and until she stopped bothering to reply, I got some inkling of her reasons. Women and books had no place in this country; a woman's place was out in the world, in the fields and grain exchanges and stock markets, if she was prepared to fight for it. And if she wasn't, she would be at the mercy of men all her life. Not all the wishing or fighting in the world put women in libraries.

We would see about that. Time, I thought, was on my side. And since she had been so obliging about school, I laboured mightily at patience.

In the meantime, Grandfather brought me out each day a heaping tray of books to choose from—and a fine, adult selection, too. Each afternoon he shuffled through that doorway, and in his face was the quiet pride of a baker with a tray. In just that way did he place the books before me.

And through those days and weeks, it was as though I had broken open a vast garner. But I was no granary mouse. I ate like a calf, like a goat— everything at once. Herodotus, Sophocles, Aeschylus, Thucydides—here, at last I had reached the source of all learning. Our great poets, Lope de Vega and Góngora—the *early* Góngora, Grandfather stressed with a certain severity. Our Bible, of course, and now Juan de la Cruz[†] and his love lyrics to Christ.

[†]St. John of the Cross (canonized 1726)

And tales—of hungry picaroons erring through the Spanish countryside. While reading *Don Quixote*, I woke *mi abuelito* in the Hammock of the Sacred Nap almost every afternoon to protest the cruelties of

Cervantes, who, Grandfather conceded, had suffered sufficient indignities himself to know better.

This is probably why, the day I reached for Homer's *Iliad*, Grandfather placed his hand over mine. There was something we should talk about first. An attack by Apollo—*¡el emboscada más cobarde!*[†]—against Achilles' noble friend Patroklos. Though Abuelo sketched out for me just the barest outlines of that craven blow to the back—and from a *god*—his voice grew husky and tottery under the burden of Apollo's disgrace. So when the dark day again fell across those pages, I prodded his shoulder till he woke, and shared with him my outrage. No, Abuelo, you were right, this was not at all a thing for a god to do.

†the most cowardly ambush

For a week or two that first winter we puzzled together over a volume by an Italian, Pico della Mirandola, which I thought a marvellous sort of name. It was a treatise, Grandfather believed, on updating the hexachord to the octave, which he was very keen to read. This splendidly named *musicus* had written it in Latin, which my *abuelo* read easily. The trouble was that by inadvertence he'd purchased an Italian translation of an Italian who wrote in Latin.

At one point, we had fairly run the gamut when Grandfather sounded a note not far from fury. "Ut!" he sputtered. "This . . . this is finally and completely enough!"

I responded with a great severity of my own. "A terrible translation, no, Abuelo? That it should give two such scholars so much trouble?"

At this he coughed and patted my hand. "Yes, Angelita, a bad translation. That must be so."

By then an eternity had translated itself into a year. It was autumn and time to enrol in school, which brought me crashing to earth. I sat—dazed, in a sort of horological horror—in the forecourt of the school, under the motto Charity, Chastity and Grace. Just inside, Grandfather was arguing that I should be placed if not with the teenagers then in the third year at the very lowest.

Yes, don Pedro, but grandfathers were, after all, *expected* to think their little *nietas*[†] very precocious. "*Más, fiad, señor,* in our long experience with children." Since this would be my first year, I must of course begin with the beginners, but—*but*—they, the reverend sister teachers, would know just how to bring me along at a satisfactory pace.

†granddaughters

The fourth week ended prematurely, on the Wednesday afternoon, though it began exactly as had the others, and that was the problem.

With our ABCs. As ever, Sister Paula stood before the class and led us in the most maddening singsong sham of question and answer—this was the Socratic method she was playing with. How marvellous that we had somehow divined in under a month that A should stand for . . . Avocado! And were we sure? Oh yes, very.

So stubby were her legs, and arms to match, that she was forever treading on her rosary and then dipping her head to check herself, as though the beads were slung not at her waist but round her neck. And how she *exclaimed* over our sham right answers. My mind was invaded by the sketch of a pullet—pacing and bobbing and rearing back to crow, and stuntedly flapping and clapping over our great successes.

For weeks now, to quell the need to scream I would chant along under my breath. The chant ran on and on like this. Hard and quickly:

> *A* is for Aleph in Hebrew; it comes from Chaldaean. *B* is for Beta in Greek, a borrowing from Phoenician. *C* is for—can we name the capital of Chaldaea . . . ?

This question of the sorcerer's passing through Sister Paula's class-room that day, the precise wording of the hex I threw, has been taken up by those whose qualifications are beyond reproach. And I do not dispute that by the Wednesday of week four my ABCs had spiralled and rami-fied within me until I had perfected a whole new gamut. As an alterna-tive to Sister Paula's version, my solo began at M, for '*mi*,' of course, and for 'Mem' in Hebrew . . .

> Well <u>Mem</u> *is* interesting. Does it not look to you like the horns of an owl? Which is after all the al<u>m</u>ost universal symbol of *muerte y mortali-dad.*[†] Now, the Reverend Athanasius Kircher believes the alphabet is <u>m</u>odelled after for<u>m</u>s in nature, and yes, just like the hieroglyphs of Egypt—of which one of the clearest is—*precisely,* an owl! But a <u>M</u>ister Herodotus says a gentle<u>m</u>an na<u>m</u>ed Cadmus introduced the *entire alpha-bet* to Greece fro<u>m</u> Phoenicia. And we know the Phoenicians were <u>m</u>ariners and?—no?—why, *merchants* too. Yet this Cad<u>m</u>us brought back not only our *abecedario*[†] but also the *boustrophedon,* the lovely flow of our script fro<u>m</u> left to right, and down and back again—<u>m</u>uch like the tilling of your father's fields, is it not? And if we trace this now in ink, see all the little "<u>m</u>'s" lying on their sides—h<u>mmm</u>? Well, why *not* indeed?—<u>m</u>aybe

[†]death and mortality

[†]Spanish for the ABCs and also for the primer that teaches them

it *was* the same field in which Cadmus had sown the dragon's teeth. The very teeth which then sprouted up as men, if memory serves. Yes as enemies, unfortunately. And the Greeks—well, yes, right after Cadmus's funeral maybe, *quien sabe*—called this new marvel of the alphabet *stoicheia*. And surely felt it was minted expressly to convey *stoicism*—an invention the God of the Hebrews only imparted to Adam *after* the Fall. And here is the best part now: God still denied the *stoicheia* even to the seraphim, for after all—*angels never had to sit in school with so many SIX-YEAR-OLDS.*

I did not go on to the letter N. Sister Paula was in such a flap of crossing herself that she had come within one stub pinion of her own miraculous assumption.

My hexachord may not have run to exactly these words and notes that day, but whose childhood recollections are not coloured by the perceptions of others? Elders, adults like Sister Paula, should know to be more careful about exaggeration and its effects on children, and on the truly credulous. Her version of how the sorceress hexed her classroom has followed me for years, and it is greatly vexing that I can do so little against it.

When Grandfather brought me home that day, he described for Isabel the little Inquisition the sisters had held before releasing me. He was scandalized that their chief concern should be whether the others had been infected by my polluted lips.

"Infected?" he snorted. "Such a disease we should all hope to catch. . . ."

So that's what an Inquisition was. To calm Grandfather I told him I thought it might have been much worse. Still, this idea of pollution, infection, was unsettling. Just from my being near the younger girls? I was not so very different. I was good with facts, never forgot what things were or where they came from, and sometimes grasped even the whys. But I knew so little about *how* things were, how they *felt.*

And then, there were the books Grandfather had not let me see.

*G*he nuns had sent up a whirlwind of prayer as Grandfather escorted me home from school. *Hail Mary, full of grace, the Lord is with thee . . . Virgin serene, holy, pure and immaculate . . .*[7] Or so I recall, if not to the letter. Well, I might be different from the others in some ways, even if I was a little confused about how, but I *wasn't* polluted and I wasn't infected. Abuelo promised me I was not confused about that.

And I'd hardly begun to appreciate all the things the other children and I shared. They had a mother, for instance. And like me, they were subject to the arbitrary exercise of her power. I had won the good sisters' agreement to an early matriculation, only to discover I was still denied access to Abuelo's library.

"If you're quitting school," said Isabel, "it's because you're learning enough here. Are you or are you not learning enough here?"

Not that the argument was flawless. But what impressed me was that she had bothered to reason with me at all. And she didn't just sail off either, as if to say she had more important things to do than remonstrate with someone my size. She stood planted there, and under those long arching brows her black eyes beheld me evenly. This was important enough to settle here and now. What unnerved me was that I knew I had not yet understood *why*. She never went into the library. And as she stood facing me down, whatever her reason, it felt bigger than I was.

I flinched. Retreated. Gave way to her—*yet again*.

But there were other arrangements to try and titles to sample, laid out on Grandfather's book trays. Lycophron and Pythagoras; commentaries on the Cabbalists and their codes, on Galileo and other such 'moon-starers.' And, especially now, *novels*: tempting *picarescas* of young children running away from cruel mothers, of spurned knights throwing rings into reflecting wells, of wrongly accused brides vindicating their honour before the pitiful, shamed accusers, whom it took little effort to picture wearing nuns' habits. . . .

Sometimes I would close my eyes and choose at random from Grandfather's book tray. Once my hand fell upon a manual on the making of suits of armour, which, when ornamented with jewels and

pearls and precious metals, Grandfather said were among the most beautiful things ever fashioned by man's ingenuity or in his image. Among the
great European armourers were the Colmans and the legendary Jacobi
Topf. So icily beautiful were his designs, I had soon devoured the manual front to back.

How darkly fastidious, these black arts—all the intricacies in the flut-
ing, the roped and scalloped edges, the treatment of the surfaces—acid-
etched and russeted, blued and blacked. For the warhorse, the buff
armour of ox hide, and the chanfrons and crinnets without which its
lovely head might be severed at a single blow of an obsidian axe. So
impressed were the Conquistadors with the quilted Mexican armour,
they adopted it themselves. Though they did still cling to the kite-
shaped bucklers as if to the thread on which swung their lives.

Yet nothing prepared me for the annihilation of Melos.

Did Grandfather not see me reading Thucydides? How could anyone
forget *this*, Abuelo least of all. Yet he had forgotten, as he was beginning
to do, as I should have seen if I had been attentive enough to notice.
Then he did remember. He sat with me for over an hour, at first patting
me awkwardly on the shoulder, then pressing his forehead to mine.

These are old stories of course, but who among us may claim never to
have been wounded by one such as this, and a little changed inside? It is
that chapter in *The Peloponnesian War* when the mighty Athenian navy
stops at the small island of Melos to dictate terms. Terms the Melians so
gracefully contest in their final hours.

Each fine point, they turn this way and that, pleasantly—on both
sides, for the Athenian envoy too is a man of high reason. They are all
men like Thucydides, who stood by and watched, and was once an admiral himself. The fine, precise minds, the superb learning, these precious
things they shared.

"And all *for what?*" I asked Abuelo angrily. But I felt confusion too, that
a book by a historian two thousand years dead could loose such a flood
of feelings in me—wonder, fury and grief; the channels scored then have
never quite silted in. I know that chapter as though I'd written it, as the
one who watched them fall.

ATHENS: You know and we know, as practical men, that the question
of justice arises only between parties equal in strength, and that the
strong do what they can, and the weak submit.

MELOS: As you ignore justice and have made self-interest the basis of discussion, we must take the same ground, and we say that in our opinion it is in your interest to maintain a principle which is for the good of all—that anyone in danger should have just and equitable treatment and any advantage, even if not strictly his due, which he can secure by persuasion. This is your interest as much as ours, for your own fall would involve you in a crushing punishment that would be a lesson to the world.

ATHENS: Leave that danger to us to face. . . . We wish you to become our subjects with least trouble to ourselves, and we would like you to survive, in our interests as well as your own.

MELOS: It may be your interest to be our masters: how can it be ours to be your slaves?

ATHENS: By submitting you would avoid a terrible fate, and we should gain by not destroying you.

MELOS: Would you not agree to an arrangement under which we should keep out of the war, and be your friends instead of your enemies, but neutral?

ATHENS: No: your hostility injures us less than your friendship. That, to our subjects, is an illustration of weakness, while your hatred exhibits our power. . . .

MELOS: Surely then, if you are ready to risk so much to maintain your empire, and the enslaved peoples so much to escape from it, it would be criminal cowardice in us, who are still free, not to take any and every measure before submitting to slavery? . . . We trust that Heaven will not allow us to be worsted by Fortune, for in this quarrel we are right and you are wrong. . . . [8]

Thus spoke the last Melian emissary, before every man of Melos was slaughtered, every woman and child sold into bondage. Before every stone sacred to Melos was pulled to the ground. It was *terrible*—stupid and pitiless, the exercise of beautiful minds in a mindless, fatal cause. And then for trusting to heaven, for their faith in *right*, the Melians are held up to the scorn of all practical men. What real choice was left them? In the left hand, Athens holds slavery and criminal cowardice. In the right, annihilation.

"Yes, you are right, Angel, the Melians were very reasonable. But they were not realistic. There is no shame in surrender to a greatly superior force, or to Fortune, or God. There can be a kind of grace in this. Pericles saw this. Moctezuma saw. . . ."

I was sitting in the same chair as always, looking towards the library door, with the kitchen at my back. He had dragged the other chair to sit beside me now, so as to be able to look into my eyes and reason with me. His thin old leg, though not quite touching, felt warm next to mine. My face was hidden in my hands. I knew it was childish to cry like this. Gently he coaxed them down to the table, letting his big bony hand rest lightly across my wrists.

"But Socrates was an Athenian too, wasn't he, Abuelo? What about Plato's *Republic*—he proved to Thrasymachus that honour was necessary even among thieves. Socrates *proved* it."

"Yes. Yes he did. And resoundingly. But the Athenians had not read it."

"*Why?*"

"Because, Angelina, it would not be written for thirty more years."

"But Socrates was alive, he was a teacher. He and Thucydides both lived in Athens."

"It may be they never met."

"How big was Athens, then—bigger than Tenochtitlan?"

"No, no."

"Bigger than Mexico City now, or Seville?"

"Even smaller."

"Then how . . . ?"

They *had* to know each other. Aeschylus, Sophocles, Socrates, Pericles, Thucydides. These were Grandfather's heroes. They *were* Athens. How could they have become great all alone, all together, all at the same time? No. They influenced, *learned* from one another, as I learned from Abuelo. Athens made them, but they made each other great. Or else what was a city *for*? On Melos, Thucydides had somehow failed Athens. I sensed this, I knew this. But if he and Socrates had never had the chance to meet, or walk together, or know each other's hearts, then I must feel that their city had failed them first.

I could not have expressed it then, I was so hurt and shocked by something in it. Troubling enough that the envoys were so like-minded, so *gracious*. It would take years to understand, of course—yet how much more disturbing that in their golden age they were so much like us in ours. I wasn't ready to accept that they truly felt as we feel, but they spoke and thought like the very finest of us. This was not some wild-bearded tribe in Canaan—they could have been sitting at our table. Graciously, amiably. Terrible things happened, I knew. Earthquakes, floods . . . But here was the first, most terrible sense of a wrongness in the machinery of the world. A thing out of true. A bent cog that might be turning now in me.

The most bloodthirsty general of all the Tartars could have given the order to exterminate the Melians. But this was Thucydides, a *stratēgos*, one of the Ten. This was no earthquake, no eruption, no flood, such as we had here in this valley—our volcanoes were Necessity. *This* was only strategy. Navies do not inspire loyalty, though they might command it. . . .

"It was the greatness of Athens that inspired the states to follow her, wasn't it Abuelo?"

As I spoke, I kept my head bowed, ashamed of my hot, sticky face. I watched instead Grandfather's big hand where it lay over my wrists. Of vague surprise was that such a knobby, knuckly hand as his should be as pale as my wrists and palms. The skin was faintly spotted like an old pelt, and between the knuckles a pale, purplish-blue. The knuckle and index finger bulged out beyond the normal width, as if the finger of a bigger hand were sewn on and wrapped in a dressing. Much of the time his hand hovered a little, trembling, a soft patting that only occasionally brushed my skin—an ungainly bird uncertain where to light.

One thing above all others had badly shaken me. Even though Thucydides did not give that order, he would still have counselled it. Even if he did not counsel it, he had given orders like it during his own time as an admiral. *He knew.* Yet by the time he wrote, so many years later, he had seen in that hour not just the end of all that was Melos: for by then the great poets, the beautiful minds, were dead and Athens was broken. Euripedes in 406, Sophocles in 405. Socrates executed in 399, and Thucydides himself soon to be assassinated. Athens killed them both in a year, but not before he had seen his failure. He wrote with the same unsparing eyes, even then.

In all that time, he had still not learned mercy, even toward himself.

I saw an old man seeing this in exile, who had still not surrendered to grace, made peace with his lack of charity, and who used it to wound himself, knowingly. Mercilessly. And so wounded us.

"*He knew,*" I blubbered out. But for the first time in my life, words had failed me. I had not cried like this since my father left. "Abuelo, he knew it was wrong. *He* was—and still he didn't feel sorry."

Isabel had stopped on the way to the kitchen. She stood just behind Grandfather and asked what the fuss was about.

"Thucydides," he mumbled.

From the corner of my eye, I could see her shake her head. "I told you, the child is too young." Then she walked swiftly past us to the kitchen.

"Then I am too, Isabel," he called after her. "Too young."

† sausage

I had been staring at that pale *salchicha*† of a finger and trying not to look up at her. I fancied I saw a haplessness in it . . . like a little elephant trunk, that blank expanse just below the elephant's eyes where the trunk seems grafted on.

Grandfather's tone is what finally made me look up at him. His face was turned towards the light out in the courtyard. His head was tipped a little back, as if to keep the world from spilling from the delicate chalices of his eyes. I had never seen an adult cry, or even near to it. Amanda cried easily. Her chin would pull her upper lip down, which got all long over her teeth and rolled under them a little. This wasn't like that at all. It was quiet, and still.

After a moment he turned to me that big face of a medieval lion. I must not blame my mother, he said. *I must not, but I did.* There was something now I must never mention to anyone. Did I swear? he asked. His eyes were so beautiful then, green as wet grass. I'd have promised anything.

"Your mother has never learned to read."

"But . . . Abuelo . . ."

This seemed incredible. This was utterly mystifying. She was intelligent—that much I knew.

"Yes, Angelita, very intelligent. You are right. Something in the letters made her furious—physically sick, and furious. We tried for years. She jumbled everything. It was the most painful thing between us. Some of the worst moments of her life were at that desk in there. So try, *señorita*, to be more understanding. And a little thankful for what you have."

I have returned to Melos and Thucydides a dozen times at least since that day. And each time they reveal something new to me. The war ended in the defeat of Athens, and as the Melian envoy had foreseen, her fall served as a lesson to the world. For if right is only a question between equals, so also is loyalty. In the hour when Fortune ever so lightly tips the scales to Sparta, the confederacy under Athens must dissolve as if built upon a pedestal of sugar. The Spartan confederacy had held precisely when the Athenian did not: when the scales were tipped against them;

whereas Athens sued for peace at the first reversal. Six years after that, they violated, being practical men, the terms and principles of the treaty they had asked for. In 404 they surrendered completely. Sparta broke Athens, and the war broke Greece.

I have read the Athenian poets many times since then. I believe that the Athenian emissary, a practical man, was wrong about loyalty and right, and wrong about the message sparing Melos would have sent the confederate states. For already the greatest poets and dramatists of Athens had prepared the states to follow her in a show of mercy to Melos. Homer, they would have followed precisely *for* love of honour. Euripedes, in repugnance for savagery. Aristophanes, towards the pleasures of peace. Aeschylus, through the awe of suffering.[9] Most of all they would have followed Sophocles, who was already eighty, and had shown all Greece that to know the mind of any god, most especially Ananke,[†] was to earn her undying hatred.

[†] sometimes translated as Necessity

The Melians insisted on seeing right; Thucydides refused to see things as they might be. Athens betrayed herself by surrendering to expediency; Thucydides betrayed her by making it pass for necessity. He had made his sacrifices to an impostor. This is what I felt but could not find the words to say. Thucydides, more than anyone else except perhaps Grandfather, made a poet of me. How furious I was with him, so clear-eyed when I was not, so unsentimental where I could not be. So bent was he on opposing the *Iliad*'s cant of honour and glory—*he* would be the one to unmask it; he, for one, would not be gulled.

It seemed to me that day he was a kind of priest, with terrible, clear eyes. Eyes that had seen plagues and holocausts and exile, eyes that had watched Athens die and, themselves dying, had calmly watched his own executioner smile. . . .

So, in truth, I was not so very different from any child in each of the ages since the last ABCs were taught on Melos. After the last die had been shaken loose from the last pedestal, after the last Melian bone had been made dice, we learned our ABCs from Athens. Yes, we had learned also in the infancy of the world, but Athens was our first school.

To each generation since, the little building blocks, the dies, the primers.

And since that day at the little table outside Grandfather's library, I have had the most maddening time keeping it all straight: when a die is cast, is it to Fortune, or in the mould of Necessity? Keeping straight what came first, the roll of chance or the press of the stamp. And how it is that to set the dice upon someone is to oppress and tyrannize; and if it is our fate or only ill fortune to worship miscalculation and ignorance as imperatives.

Must this now forever be—*un dado, un datum, un desafío?*[†] Is it such good strategy to call these things pragmatism? And who are these pragmatists and men of action who follow *might* as noun, but will not hear of it as verb?

What is that moment in which a world conceives its own end? *When its inner poetry gives way to prose.* That must be what a poet is, I thought, what poets do. And this was another way for a child, not quite so young thereafter, to reverse the losses of that day. Of course these were childish things—of letters and blocks, and wizards and puzzles. But if priests had words and wizards had visions, *poets must be wizards with words.*

Real poets would never just find the might in *is*, but seek their being in 'might.' To make a place for vision here, for words of might—this seemed a fine thing then to do.

Here was the lesson Melos foresaw in Athens' fall, but since Thucydides we had lost the heart of it. This loss has been like a flaw pressed into a die, an error in type, that reproduces itself—inked and re-inked for each new run of primers. It is as one letter disfigured in the press, a die miscast by hazard so that never in the hundred generations since Melos have we read 'mercy' spelled aright.

Not long after, I sat down to be a poet.

> Yet in 'mercy?' and 'right!' combined,
> but for a miscast die,
> might one not rightly find
> (and who if not 'I')
> the anagram of a 'mightier cry!?' ... [10]

And in my scrawl I signed,
              A Junta I![†][11]

[†] 'a given, a datum, a dare'—Spanish synonyms for 'die'

[†] anagram for Juanita

hough I might find the wizardry of poetry a very fine thing, it had not yet spelled my entrance to the library. Eventually I grasped that I was jeopardizing a territorial agreement, delicately arrived at, wherein Grandfather had ceded to his daughter full sovereignty over the hacienda in exchange for remaining in perpetuity the library's uncontested patriarch and sole subject. What was extraordinary in this was that it appeared to have been arrived at in complete silence. As though a stern Jehovah had chiselled—neatly, so even a child could read—the new order onto tablets for us. No one was to enter there but he, not even to dust or tidy. Inwardly I could mock the rule, but for a time the silence cowed me.

Adults were becoming mystifying, more abstruse and difficult to read than any book. My father had been mystery itself, and Isabel was always elementally Isabel, but there was now Xochita and even Abuelo.

As in the case of our game of being twins: The morning after our arrival in Panoayan, Amanda and I'd swooped through the courtyard—PolishedEye and NibbleTooth, Ocelotl and Mixcoatl—shouting, "*Mellizas, mellizas! Cocoas, cocoas!*"[†] It was a joke no one else appreciated, but for us it was not mirth that made us laugh so, but rather purest delight. Xochitl told us to hush, which was startling enough. Around Isabel we never did much shouting, but when I caught sight of Grandfather glaring darkly at us—a thing I'd never seen him do—we fell silent. Which only made me all the more determined to make them see it one day for themselves, for instinctively I felt that anything that could give us so much joy must be true in some way more essential than fact.

Sometimes it seemed the adults barely talked of anything consequential at all, except *to* us or *through* us, or in glares. Here we had been endowed (some of us prodigally) with speech, and yet they insisted on making everyone around them read the garble in their silences. Why wasn't Amanda allowed to sit with us around the firepit? Xochitl would not say whose idea it had been—only that she didn't want Amanda 'bumblebeeing around.' And then there was school. No one had asked, let alone insisted, that *Amanda* go to school. This troubled me more than I let on, even to her. Some shape was sleeping there, something mute I

[†]*melliza*, Spanish for twin; *cocoa*, twin, snake or dragon in Nahuatl

did not want to disturb—during my month at school I'd found that what I missed most, felt most in danger of losing, was not the library at all. It was Amanda. The day Abuelo brought me home from Sister Paula's class, I swore a sacred oath that Amanda and I would make a school together in the fields and woods and hills. And I would tell her every little thing that was said at the firepit. As for the library, each day we would take with us one of the books I happened to be reading.

We always stayed out till the very last minute, till they took to ringing the chapel bell to call us in to lunch. When we did come in, it was through the kitchen, where we drank enormous quantities of cordials made from *horchata,* or beet, or tamarind, or hibiscus. After lunch Amanda would stay with Xochitl, while I went on to the little table outside the library door. There I would begin to read, and the pain of separation ebbed so quickly I had barely the time to feel guilty over it.

But each morning I awoke anxious to find her again. Days began early—often before dawn, with Amanda in my bedroom doorway, shifting her weight impatiently from foot to foot. We would stand a minute in the gathering light, nose to nose, knee to knee—and lock our hands hard, just for an instant. Then it was a sprint (I lost, I always lost) across the flagstones—icy under our bare soles—and up to the watchtower.

First we checked the bird's nest in the cannon barrel for eggs. But that year there was only the most delicate little cup of grass lined with blue-green down. Where had its architects gone? Next we snuggled under an old horse blanket up there that Father had used with the yearlings. By flapping it and waving it under their noses, he would gradually teach them not to shy. I was sure it still smelled of horses.

We waited.

On a clear morning it is as though the sun rising far to the east chisels WhiteLady's fall from a block of purest indigo. *Head thrown back—chin upthrust—soft heave of breast—knees demure . . .* I squinted up to see how a true poet would see her. Though SmokingStone was more spectacular, its white flint tip edged in keen fire, she was the one we watched, right above us.

The very instant the last pale rose had drained from El Popo's cone, we slapped and clattered barefoot down to the kitchen to find Xochitl grinding corn for tortillas. Soon we waited even that long only on the clearest mornings, for we were dawn's *cognoscentae* now. If the sky was at all cloudy, we were in the kitchen early enough to help with the cooking fire. Once the flames licked up, Amanda and I each took a kindling stick and with a little tremble of fire lit the lamps. Next we huffed and heaved in an armload of firewood, never forgetting to check the woodpile for scorpions first. Now we made a great show of helping Xochitl with the tortillas, so she might be free to make for us—Xochita, hurry *please*—a breakfast basket to take out into the fields.

We might go north then, through the orchards, or south past the paddocks. Very rarely west to the road. But almost always these days east through the cornfields, out along the river and past the little plot of maguey cactus. Though now it grew wild, it had been planted, Xochitl said, long before Cortés camped there—yes, right there—safe on open ground by the river. It is from this place that Panoayan takes its name: *Place of Maguey by Water.* That first night at the firepit Grandfather had been so excited to hear this, but when I made to call Xochitl out of the kitchen, I got another of those silences that made me—if just for a minute—never want to tell him anything again. But I couldn't stay quiet long. I was beginning to tell my own stories by the fire, constructed of the countless things I'd learned that day in the fields—rhymes and songs and plants and dances with Amanda. She had only to go through a dance once to remember it. From her mother, Amanda had to learn the dances mostly by ear—Xochitl's hip let her do little more than talk Amanda through the steps. She had the most wonderful grace with a gesture— the turn of a wrist, the tilt of her head. Amanda didn't talk much, at least compared with me. She didn't run on and on. She was quick with a story she'd learned, or a riddle. Dance was her great talent, but where she spoke most clearly was in the secret language of gifts. . . .

During a month of nights she made us each a heavy cotton satchel for the plants and flowers and rocks we collected in the woods. On each bag she had beaded a rabbit, mine green, hers blue. Some nights a flower on my pillow. Little dolls and polished stones, abandoned bird's nests— once, crickets in a cup.

A gift could be like a vision, a conjury delicate as glass. A gesture was like a magical symbol, like the corn, or a crown, but not stuck to an old hairpiece—a gesture was alive. And even, a little dangerous. Had I yet written a single poem like that?

All *I* knew were things from books. There were Grandfather's legends, but few new ones anymore. He seemed not to tell so many these days. Amanda did like the ones I made up. This intrigued her, that stories were not just learned but invented. And if I helped a bit, we could even write little songs together. To make it more interesting, she would have to find a line in Castilian[12] and I a line in Nahuatl. This one was for Xochitl.

> There are diamonds in the grass.
> There are serpents in the clouds.
> In the earth are halls of jade,
> and feathers in the temple.[13]

The next morning we recited it for her, and flushed with our great success went back to write another. For our reading and our poetry there was a shady place just beyond the cornfields, which were then in full bloom. It was like wading through the blue of the open sea, and we were giants whose feet touched bottom. A strip of trees ran between the corn and the plot of maguey, and there we would sit just above where the river ran closest. One of Abuelo's windmills perched on the riverbank near us, another at the far end of the field. Carrying out over the river and the cactus, the view to the mountains was clear and unbroken. After two years it still was hard not to stare at them.

To get us started I read her a page of verse I had laboured over that night. It began . . .

> In soft echoes are heard,
>   the bird;
> in flowing waters that sing,
>   the spring;
> in phrases' sweet shower,
>   the flower;
> in green-throated salute,
>   the shoot . . . [14]

I told her I had written it for her. What I meant was that I was *giving* it to her. She sat blinking at me for a moment. And then, as was our custom, she gave me something in return. She announced she was to learn to be a midwife, as her mother had been. The song she sang so gravely then she could not have learned overnight. I was struck by what a serious and grown-up affair this was, and that my tall swift twin was almost

a grown-up too. And if I didn't try very, very hard, I would never keep up
with her. . . .

My beloved child, my precious one,
here are the precepts, the principles
your father, your mother, Yohualtecutli, Yohualticitl, have laid down.
From your body, the middle of your body, I remove, I cut the
umbilical cord.

Know this, understand this:
Your home is not here.
You are the eagle, you are the jaguar,
you are the precious scarlet bird,
you are the precious golden bird of Tloque Nahuaque;[†]   [†]the Lord of Near
you are his serpent, you are his bird.   and Far
Only your nest is here.
Here you only break out of your shell,
here you only arrive, you only alight,
here you only come into the world.
Here like a plant, you sprout, you burst into bloom, you blossom.
Here like a fragment struck from a stone, chipped from a stone, you
are born.
Here you only have your cradle, your blanket, your pillow where you
lay your head.
This is only the place of arrival.

Where you belong is elsewhere:
You are pledged, you are promised, you are sent to the field of battle.
War is your destiny, your calling.
You shall provide drink,
you shall provide food,
you shall provide nourishment for the Sun, for the Lord of the Earth.
Your true home, your domain, your patrimony is the House of the
Sun in heaven where you shall shout the praises of, where you shall
amuse, the Everlastingly Resplendent One.
Perhaps you shall merit, perhaps you shall earn,
death by the obsidian knife in battle,
death by the obsidian knife in sacrifice . . . [15]

It was terrifying, and beautiful, like Aeschylus. This was the song for the newborn boy. The midwife first removes the cord. She takes the afterbirth and buries it in the earth in a corner of the house. She lays the cord out to dry in the sun. Later, if the boy is a warrior, he will carry it with him onto the field of battle. And if he falls it will be buried there.

I asked her the song for a girl. But Xochitl had said Amanda was not yet ready to learn it.

Amanda gave more, but that wasn't why I began to feel guilty. Jealousy I'd felt before. Of losing what I had. I'd felt it sometimes when Isabel would call Grandfather away from me for some reason. But this was new, this was envy. . . . The things Amanda could share with me seemed so much finer than mine—even *poetry* now. The only other thing I had left to offer was teaching Amanda to read. But books were *hard*—she had better understand that. Harder still was reading aloud before an auditor so very stern of late. I had been making her read Plutarch. Plutarch is a Greek who wrote a lot about Greece, which I had been trying so very patiently to teach her about. Plutarch is hard, even in Castilian. (And I was in no mood now to tell her how much trouble *he* had had learning to read Latin.)

There was a passage she kept stumbling over, right at the bottom of the page. Over and over, trying harder and harder to please me, her eyes almost as round and wide, for once, as mine. "No, don't look at me— read—no, you're trying too hard." She was almost *nine*. I was so frustrated because something delightful awaited, if only we could reach the top of the very next page. I had made a crown for her to wear, to mark the end of this difficult and profound and beautiful passage. And the crown was a very grand gesture—a wizardly conjury of my own, if she would only, please, *get there*.

†Bee-OH-shuh

"I *know* the names are Greek, but if you can't say 'Boeotia,'† how are we ever to read Hesiod?" It was as though she didn't even understand anymore what was coming out of her mouth. *Did* she?

"*Nympheutria—anakalypteria*[16]—tell me, Amanda: which is the bride's attendant, which is the unveiling gift?"

Would *I* have known, had I not just read it myself the night before? Well, today was not the day, either, for telling her I had no Greek at all.

"No, Amanda. *Nympheutria!* That's what they'd call *you*, if *I* were getting married. The unveiling thing is the—oh never mind, the *other* one."

Amanda cried easily. Silently, no sobs. Her neat head bent; then her eyes just gushed. She was quick to tears of tenderness, quick to tears of pity, or love—watching them netted one day like bright fish in her soft black hair was a moment of fascination. But she would never, *ever* be made to cry by something like this.

Over her face had fallen a mask of cold wood. How square the chin, how pale the lips, how very hard the wood.

It was the first day in two years I walked home alone.

As I approached the house, I saw two horsemen down by the paddocks and between them a long-horned black bull. It was almost as tall as the horses themselves and chafing at the tight tethers—two ropes bound to each rider's pommel. Isabel was sitting on the top rail of the corral and Abuelo had forgone his nap to stand with her and watch. The bull had been brought from Chimalhuacan. "Is he ours now?" I asked.

Isabel surprised me by answering first. "No, only for a week or two."

The bulls I'd seen were sullen, sluggish things. Freed of its tethers, this one moved swiftly around the corral, then stopped to hook one of its horns—lightly, now left, now right—against an upright, as if to test the firmness of its anchor. The older horseman glanced at Isabel then. The younger one had been stealing glances at her for a while. After a minute she climbed down and called to one of the workers to bring poles for braces.

Abuelo had held his silence until now. "This one," he told me proudly, first glancing at his daughter, "would be worthy of the finest corridas of Spain, not these butcheries here. True, the calves will be a little wild. . . ."

Just before dawn I awoke—and *there she was*, as always. But now Amanda waved over me a large white square of fine muslin, the sort Xochitl used for squeezing water from curd.

"Is this a truce?" Friends such as I did not deserve peace offerings.

"No, Ixpetz—I thought *you* would guess. Mother didn't know either. Look—*now* see? It's a *veil*."

Yes, Amanda, I saw. I did see at last.

We slipped out through the kitchen without even waiting for Xochitl to put food in our satchels.

On our way out to the fields, we went by the corral. Seeing us, the new arrival began to cut powerfully, quickly, back and forth across the enclosure. The bull still looked as if it could come right through the braced fence—or even over—if it saw something it wanted.

Amanda had already started towards our reading place. She hesitated, seemed about to say something, but then quietly came with me. As we picked flowers, she told me a little more of what she'd learned about midwifery from Xochitl. As the morning wore on, she grew more distracted. Soon it would be time to go in for lunch. She led me back to the shady spot past the cornfield. We sat. She was quiet, her eyes downcast. We sat. She looked up at me. Finally she said, "Have you given up?"

What an idiot I was—of course that's what she would think. I dug Plutarch out from under all that day's flowers and the wilted ones farther down. She must have seen my relief. She read, and for the first time in a while I was not stern at all. And she read *beautifully*, the whole of the lovely passage I had marked, which ends

> After veiling the bride they put on her head a crown of asparagus, for this plant yields the sweetest fruit from the harshest thorns . . . [17]

"The veil!" she said, delighted. "Wait . . ." She started digging in her own satchel for the muslin. "Wait, wait, I'll be your *attendant*, your . . . *Nympheutria!* Was that right?" She had closed her eyes to concentrate and opening them, looked up, the question in her eyes.

But as she opened them she saw that I, for once, had been the quicker. The crown was in my hands. It did look strange, I supposed. We didn't have asparagus, so I had taken agave spikes, cut them into long triangles and woven them into a slim crown. It was the best I could do. I had wanted *nopal*.[†]

[†] prickly pear

She looked at it a long while. "It's for you," I said. She nodded. She had understood all right. "Let me be *your* attendant for once, Nibble Tooth."

And I was. We plaited her hair. She wore a muslin veil, and an almost-asparagus crown. And I thought the bride, at her unveiling, very beautiful.

As I turned her around and pulled back her veil, her big almond eyes were full and danced like the light in a birdbath.

We missed lunch. As the bell tolled on, we chattered like *urracas* about crowns. "In Greece this could have been a laurel crown, for great feats of letters. You can read now, Amanda, really *read*. Plutarch is hard—but good, no?" The Greeks used crowns for everything. The crown of obsidion for generals raising sieges. "And no Greek woman not a virgin would be caught dead without her headpiece, also a kind of crown, like this—"

With my hands I showed her how it was—like a plane of holiness settled over the brow. Was it not like a rising into loveliness? Not quite an ascent into the sky but a surfacing . . .

"And the most beautiful thing—when the nuns in Mexico City take their vows, do you know they wear tall crowns of wildflowers? Wedding crowns like the asparagus—but for marrying *Christ*."

"Cinteotl?" she said, wide-eyed.

"Maybe, maybe not." I said, mysterious. "But listen to *this*, when a nun dies, she's buried wearing the same crown she wore as a girl, Nibble Tooth, as a bride. Isn't that lovely? Of course, the flowers would be a bit dry. . . ."

And as though the day were indeed blessed, Isabel had been busy with the cattle and had missed lunch herself.

The next morning at dawn, Amanda woke me wordlessly, an index finger to my lips. She led me out by the hand in my nightgown. It was a cold spring morning in the mountains. We weren't even dressed—we could see our breath. She was leading me towards the corral. A little nervously my eyes sought out the bull in the chill half light. I wanted to be sure it hadn't come through the fence. "Amanda . . ." I said, half complaining and chilly, in my bare feet. But Amanda wasn't looking at the bull, was almost casually looking *away* from him. Then I saw. My heart stopped.

The bull stood stock-still in the centre of the corral. Silent, solid, puffing gouts of steam, like the mountain itself. It shook its head now, wreathed in smoke, and glared at us with its small black eyes as through a green-wood fire. And around its horns was wound, in a long figure eight, a

  dark
    blue
      cornflower
        crown.

Green had been the colour of my envy that spring. Dark blue, the shade of its leaving.

My princess of the corn. She spoke to me in dance, in her love of swiftness, in the laughter she was so quick to cover with her hands. In the way the mask of all her wariness dropped away as she taught me a step.

We ran into the fields that day, and I could almost keep up with her. She stopped and waited for me. As always.

It was the next day that Xochitl told us about the special place.

How indignant we were. How could she have waited almost three years to tell us of it?

"Because you are almost women now." Xochitl smiled, her eyes a tilt of triangles. How easily we were mollified. But then perhaps she also knew how close Amanda truly was. Xochitl had waited "because the earth up there is jade. And because there are certain dangers. . . ."

I had come to think the word *danger* much abused by adults. There were, for example, the wild animals Isabel had once hinted that my sisters wrestled each day just beyond the portals in Nepantla. In the opposite sense, Abuelo was known to backtrack if he felt that his true tales of dangerous bandits or werewolves had brought them too vividly near our firepit. But this was not Xochitl's way, not the way among women. The special place was safe, but there were precautions to take along the path.

"To look big, walk close together."

As if Amanda and I might walk in any other fashion. "And make noise as you walk." She spoke now to me directly, and when I saw her eyes twinkling with this, I knew it really would be all right.

†pumas

Though *miztli*† often hunted during the day, jaguars rarely did, and there was a much better place for them, where the deer and the pigs came for salt. "Which is why—listen carefully now—you follow the south bank of the river, and do not follow the first stream up or the second. The third. Where it joins the river is a deep pool. There is a place to cross over. Then look to Iztaccihuatl. You see straight above you a line of waterfalls. The highest is at the snow line." We were to repeat it now for her. First me, then Amanda.

"It was a place for the women of our family," said Xochitl. "It is the Heart of the Earth, of the goddess of the earthquake. And of our grandmother, Toci. Among the men, only Ocelotl knew the way."

"His mist has not scattered," said Amanda, which meant he was respected. Xochitl nodded in approval and told us the Heart of the Earth was the jaguar's tutor. His pelt is on her throne.

"Did Ocelotl go there for visions?" I asked, casually.

She wasn't easily fooled.

"Could be, Ixpetz. But I think mostly he slept. Beside the spring you

will see the stones he used for his *temazcal*.[†] It is for my daughters now,   [†]sweat bath
who have made my hair white and my face very wide."

Just as we were turning to go, Xochitl called to us. "Here . . . There is
enough for breakfast and lunch. But when you look down to the hills and
the sun is two palm-widths above—start down. Never later."

We set out at a fast walk, which threatened at every step to break
into a trot. I held Amanda's hand tight to keep her from breaking away
altogether.

"Did you hear, Amanda? She didn't even tell us to keep it to ourselves!" Amanda nodded proudly. But if she had, I asked, wouldn't we
have been right to take it as a grievous insult? And wasn't it beautiful
about the Heart of the Earth, and . . .

And so we went as we would each time, to what became *our* special
place. East through the corn, shooing deer, which would cheekily stop
again after clearing the fence—a high fence whose lowest rails we ducked
through—in one soaring, effortless bound. So calmly they hung at the
top of their arc that it seemed they might nod off up there in the air.
They were like her, tense in stillness and in flight utterly at peace.

Ten minutes above the river, the path reared up more steeply. The
stream by which we had found our way slowly fell away to the left. For
half an hour we climbed a long incline of uniform width, pitched as
steeply as the stairs up to the hacienda's watchtower. On either side
sloped away banks of shale and what seemed almost to be coal but with
a glassy sheen. To our fancy, this incline appeared as a nose, one we followed to the place Amanda named *Ixayac*. Its Face.

The top of the incline ended in a sheer wall five times our height, but
up the surface of which a zigzag of handholds and footholds stood out
as clearly as rungs. Amanda scrambled up without hesitation, and I
clambered gratefully after her. This climb, I saw, was what would keep us
safe from anything on four legs following us.

We stood on a deep bench, the lower of two. Each of its brows sprouted
a score or so of stunted pines. The stream ran out of a thicket in front of
us and dropped away a little distance to the left. Amanda walked right up
to the edge where the stream fell. I inched up cautiously behind her. It
smashed and frayed and tumbled its way into a deep hollow of rubble
and shale. From there it ran more smoothly along the north cheek of the
incline before disappearing into the trees.

We sat down on the ledge. A stone's throw out from us, three grey rock doves flapped a broad arc across our field of view. Eventually I let my feet swing out into space, though not quite so freely as Amanda did. The world we looked out upon could have been another continent. But this *was* the other continent fixed in the imagination of the Europeans I had read. This was the great glittering lake they had seen or heard or dreamt about. It snaked its way north up the valley until it lost itself in the blue-grey of distance. And there was the white city on the lake, plotted, unlike any city in Europe, on a grid perfectly aligned to the cardinal directions and without defensive walls. Grandfather said Cortés's soldiers wept—as if they had had been overtaken by a dream of death and now stared out upon a warriors' heaven. A city without walls to defend or overcome . . . imagine it.

Just then, Amanda pointed out the small wedge of a falcon stooping on the doves. In three heartbeats it fell through them—an axe head splitting a block. In a tangle of esses, two doves flew on.

I had thought it far off, this place I'd read so much about. Before the Conquest, Tenochtitlan was a vast island city, an ivory eye—or, with its grid of streets, a white sunflower framed in leaves of an iridescent green. These were the *chinampas,* or floating gardens. The island was tethered to the shore by the mooring cables of long causeways running through shades of blue. The city was bone white, but its temples were painted in the gaudy hues of parrot plumes and jewels. And the pyramids of ruby and emerald and sapphire were as the flower's jewelled nectary. The pyramids were gone now and the *chinampas* much reduced, but the air was still clear enough to see the bell tower of what could only be the cathedral, and beside it the Viceroy's palace.

We sat on the ledge, swinging our feet, attempting little verses on what we saw. We decided there and then, like children nursing a candy, to make no further explorations until our next visit, so as to draw out the pleasure of discovery. After just an hour, we were ready to start down.

At the river we stopped to watch in wonder the enormous trout that converged at the bottom of the pool. There seemed to be a vent, some kind of spring at which they jostled and fed. And then it was dusk, which fell swiftly up the mountain. Amanda and I hurried through the cactus field, the richness of the day steeping quietly in us.

Near the hacienda stood a small enclosure, just back from the river where it winds through the cactus plot. Four bare poles under a thatch of maguey spikes, and a killing floor of smooth stone slabs. Incised in the floor was a channel to run blood straight into the water, which could be sluiced clean with just a bucket or two. The floor had always been here, and on it may once have stood an altar. It was useful now for slaughtering livestock so as not to attract scavengers to the house.

My heart sank to see Isabel look up as she and a workman butchered a lamb. This might befall a lamb if it were to break a leg, or perhaps come home late.

Isabel sent Amanda on to the house. I stood silently as they finished in the gloom. She had fetched up her skirts and tucked them between her thighs, and was plastered to her elbows in a black mud. I saw finally that it was blood, as she squatted there like some vengeful idol to the beauty of dusk.

She washed up, sending the workman ahead with the meat. She had not asked, and seemed not to listen to my mumbled evasions as to where we had been till such an hour. After administering a spanking with her customary efficiency and power she asked if I remembered yet. Grandfather's seventieth birthday. Which I must have known he attached significance to, and today of all days to leave him alone when he counted on me. . . .

I blurted, "If I was so late, why didn't *you* read for him?"

My ear rang and buzzed for an hour from a slap more impulsively delivered than the spanking.

"Come in when you've stopped."

That night I tossed and turned and ground my teeth—to be gone again, up to Ixayac—or anywhere. The place where my true life was. Not this, not here. This was not *my* life.

What kept me for so many hours so close to tears was not the ringing in my ear or even the humiliation. It was shame—scalding and caustic and vile. He *did* count on me.

"Angel, will you . . . ? My eyes are tired." And I would read for him—enchantingly, as any great actress would. That was our game. I had never thought of it as his needing me. Even though now, no matter how stunningly I read, how emphatically—how *loud,* I could never quite wake one of his eyes. The right. The one he kept turned away from me at the firepit. The truth was, he often just listened now, nodding sagely at the flames as I spoke.

That night dealt me a succession of confused dreams, and on each card the emblem of my guilt. Snake, horse, lion, falcon, *manatí.* Each appearance brief, each somehow me—a fugitive, a figure like Proteus wriggling through a thousand shapes to flee to Egypt with his sea calves. Or the daughter of Erysichthon—always unclean, no matter how many her guises.

I was still close to tears when I saw Xochitl the next morning.

"Two palm-widths above the horizon. Just like you told us, Xochita."

"Tell me about the trout."

I knew she asked this by way of consoling me. But how did she know they'd be there?

"As a girl I watched them," she said. "Just like you two. We had to practice a lot to spear them."

"You *speared* them?"

Amanda nodded. "They're quick."

"Yes, NibbleTooth, but also because they are not there."

"*After*, you mean?" I still didn't see.

"No—*then*. You see a fish. And there is a fish. But not there . . . over *here*." As she said this, she had turned up her right palm, now the left. "Not yet, eh, Ixpetz? Next time take a long stick. Our spears were higher than our arms could reach and straight. Put the stick in—"

"It bends!"

"Near the bottom, where the hot water comes, it bends more. The stick is straight. But not always. The fish is. But not there."

"Xochita, this is just *refraction*," I said, eager to explain.

"No, this is god."

"It's only *light*."

"Look more, Ixpetz. You will see the double you keep asking about."

She had never once given me a straight answer about any of this, nor had she ever been the one to bring it up.

"Sometimes we say *ixiptla*, sometimes mask. Or double. Or . . . twins."

"Why so many, Xochita, so many words?"

She made a funny face, the face of an insatiable child pleading for one more treat—a face just such as mine. "Maybe we were never sure we understood. Twins, doubles . . . Who can say, Ixpetz—*one* of them might be right."

How did she always manage it? She could make me want to laugh in the blink of an eye.

"Sometimes we say they are a couple. Like those two mountains."

"Maybe," I said, "the lovers are also between the fish."

"Maybe very good, Ixpetz."

"Fish," I said, trying not to smile.

"Fish."

"Not one fish."

"No."

"Not two."

"No."

"Here and there."

"Yes, Ixpetz. Near and far."

"Many masks—one face."

"Not one."

"Faceness—*face*. Only 'face.'"

"Ahh . . ."

"And we're needed, somehow."

"*We* bend the stick!" Amanda said.

"Very good, Nibble Tooth."

"But, Xochita, if you stand directly over the water," I said, "the stick . . ."

She shook her head sadly. "You think too much."

"That's no answer, Xochitita," I crooned. "Please?"

She thought about this. "In the world there is no such place. To stand."

"Above god," I added, hoping she might say more.

"Help me grind the corn—both of you. I am late again."

"I have a question."

"Grind."

Not even the poetry of Xochitl's reticence prepared us for this place beyond the trout pool that she had bequeathed to us. By the time we had started down I knew, and for once kept it to myself, that it was not to our maturity she had trusted. Such beauty kept its own secrets. We never told anyone.

We planned to go the very next day. But so many things, it seemed, had to happen before we could make our way back up to Ixayac, to discover the hot spring, the falcon nest, the plunge pool below the little waterfall. It seemed like years.

THE HUNT

*In which the editor
obtrudes, in anti-
quated fashion, with
some exposition.*

FROM HER NOTES it appears Beulah's researches began in earnest
after the first in a series of CBC radio broadcasts on the life of Sister
Juana Inés de la Cruz.

The first aired in the spring of 1990, toward the end of Beulah's
freshman year. Sor Juana had belonged to Beulah's private world for
almost as long as she could remember. When she was about twelve,
her father, a surgeon, brought home from Mexico a collection of the
nun's poetry. He himself had had to read her in grade school in Spain.
Possibly he hoped to encourage his daughter to keep up her
Spanish.[18] On the cover of that first poetry collection was a rich portrait in oils: a beautiful, elegant nun, seated at a writing desk before a
wall of impressive tomes. The collection became for Beulah a talisman
and a refuge. That her parents played up a casual physical resemblance
between this shining exemplar and their brilliant, volatile daughter
was perhaps innocent enough. A goad wrapped in a compliment. The
sort of thing parents do.

Colleagues had on more than one occasion mentioned Beulah
Limosneros to me. But in that freshman year she would have been
simply too gamine. As I later calculated, she'd turned seventeen barely
a week before classes began. Naturally I was curious. But when in 1992
I became her honours adviser it was only because Relkoff, the one real
poet on staff, had run afoul of the new department head and gone on
sabbatical to Ireland. Which left us to divide up his responsibilities.
Beulah fell to me.

When I saw her name on my class list that fall, I assumed she'd
enrolled in my seminar on early American literature to curry favour
with her new adviser. A notion of which I was quickly disabused.

She was at least two years younger than anyone in the room. She
spoke only rarely, but from the beginning her interventions were so
incisive that she seemed to preside over our discussions as a silent
moderator. Only part of the effect was owing to her unsettling physical
presence. She had turned nineteen by then, and was very much in
season.

She signed term papers with her student number. She was of course
alone in doing this. Metaphoric, quicksilver—a dash of sulphur—her

papers were like adventures in alchemy. I had no trouble matching them to her. For an undergraduate's, her style was perfectly unscholarly (which is to say, presumptuously confident). Yet, for the novelty of her ideas and her obvious mastery of the material, my colleagues had been handicapping her as our most promising aspirant in a long while.

One would set her a perfectly standard task for an undergraduate, say, a ten-page discussion of Anne Bradstreet and meanings of the number four in her "Four Elements," "Four Seasons," "Four Ages of Man," "Four Monarchies." Or, John Smith's Pocahontas—Saviour or Saved, Traitor or Translator? Both are decent enough topics. Instead, Beulah's first paper was on the use of poetic figures in a work of sub-atomic physics.

> . . . Charmed particles, anti-particles—with left-hand spin or right, strong forces and weak and sinister . . . like spells chanted over a cauldron, even as the stew of matter dematerializes. A language redolent of re-invested meanings, a charismatic language—'charismatic,' from the Indo-European *gher*, to desire, to yearn. With a ferry token for the wrothful Charon, the charmed traveller reaches out across the Straits of Messina, past the whirlpool of Charybdis, through the Greek *charizesthai*—to show favour, or invoke it, and finally up the beach over the more familiar *eukharistia* of simple gratitude. The basic eucharistic function of this language being to reinvest the material with meaning and therewith beseech divine favour: *charys* or grace.
>
> Grace, said by our poet physicists over a nervous meal of stew and figs, spread between the strands of Scylla and Charybdis . . .

After twenty pages of this, she pauses for a small excursus into Hawking's anthropic principle—much maligned by his colleagues precisely for being mythological and therefore unscientific. She stages a spirited defence of his physics from a poetic perspective. Then a spirited critique of his poetry from a quantum physics perspective. By page forty, you notice that all along she's been edging toward some thunderous megrim of her own—something scathing and strangely funny, her *misanthropic principle*.

In concluding (on about page fifty), she asks, "Why all these quantum leaps of metaphor? To make the work of physicists more accessible to the uninitiated? Or is it to reassure *themselves*, as though, without the primitive poetic charge, our seekers have not delved deeply enough into the charismatic mysteries?" She then compounds the unforgivable by asking a fourth consecutive question in her conclusion.

Can it be that our quantum physicists are only appealing, as so many before them, to a Muse to bless their poesy? Erato, say, or Polymathia or Polyhymnia. So much the better. If God does not play dice with the universe—she does not like doggerel, either.

But then, maybe the Muse dices physicists. By 1935 Einstein's doubts about a dice-playing God had badly shaken his quantum mechanical faith. Its most unbearable corollary was entanglement—instantaneous interaction at a distance. Interact with one particle in a spin-half pair and see its other half pirouette instantaneously, even half a galaxy away—snake eyes in the crapshoot of quantum fortunes. Time to call the pit boss. Time to call in Terpsichore.

At its root, Einstein's disenchantment is aesthetic. The free verse of such entanglements was intolerable to him *poetically*, offending his sense of order and elegance. And so the superb mind that had found nothing unthinkable balked, for once, at entanglement.[19]

Maybe it had just been far too long since the good professor was out before the moonrise, strolling arm in arm beneath the space-time canopy, to watch the spin-half pair of Castor and Pollux . . . enchanted double stars with club and lyre, dancing in the house of Gemini.

But now, entanglements in *Time*: who shall their Muse and poets be?

You can—and I did—quarrel with Beulah's conclusions, but the overall impression is of her playing your thin tune with her left hand, her own *étude* with the right, while balancing the globe on the tip of her nose as she rocks back and forth on a unicycle. Meanwhile, the true final line remains unstated: *But of course, my Misanthropic Principal, you must feel entirely free to give my little effort the grade you think it merits.*

It had started on the first day of class. I was favoured with my first private audience, outside office hours, of course, but she did knock. White tennis shoes, black jeans, long auburn hair gathered at her nape in a silver clasp, the arresting eyes I had not seen at close range. She wore a long-sleeved, white cotton turtleneck, and over it, in the manner of a smock, an extra-large men's T-shirt, short-sleeved, black.

She asked if I really intended to call John Smith to Anne
Bradstreet early American literature. Because I must realize it was not
early, not really American and not much of it literature. Do go on.
Third century—even the ninth—that was early. Or 1492, as the
beginning of the end.

"Your Americas, Professor, look like some Puritan's idea of New
England."

It was churlish of me, but I pointed out that had she done even the
most cursory research, she'd have seen what the course was to cover.

"Oh yes, your outline was fascinating."

"Thanks."

"It's like a course in prejudice."

The tone was playful, the eyes were not.

"It's Beulah something, isn't it?"

"Which makes you Professor *Somebody*, doesn't it."

I thought it a good moment to start over. The job really doesn't
have to be difficult.

"I meant no offence."

"Limosneros. Don't make it rhyme with rhinoceros. Please."

"I think I can manage."

"BYOOlah LeemosNEHRos—how's that?"

"Prejudices against what?"

"Let's see, Professor . . ." She used the long fingers of a small hand to
count the ways. "There's the *Lateeno*. The *Cath*olic. The *fee*-male . . .
Oh right, and the Baroque."

I glanced out the window, deciding if was I being called a hick,
bigot, Puritan or some fresh mix of the three.

I didn't get time to phrase the question. She'd swayed out, leaving
the door ajar. Ah, but they did keep us young. Beulah Limosneros, Day
One. The immediate effect: me deciding to change the course name for
the following year. Nothing wrong with it per se, aside from being
unexpectedly revealing. Her charges weren't fair, of course, not balanced, certainly, but neither were they wild shots in the dark, not
completely.

But then, I was still assuming she'd been working with just the
course outline, when by the first day of class she'd already skimmed
everything I'd ever published. Her paper on quantum physics arrived
on my desk a month later, and it was the perfect lure.

I'd come to a professional interest in literature late in life, while in France finishing up a doctorate in philosophy. From eight years at the summits of Scepticism and Empiricism—chez Ockham, Bacon, Descartes, Hume & *cie*—I had descended with a pressing wish to meet women. Ergo literature. The paper that changed the course of my academic career was only a lark. "James Fenimore Cooper and the Negative Way."

The short version: If you want to better understand the true, study the liar.

The long version: In radical mysticism, the negative way holds God to be unknowable, and goes from what can only be said inadequately to the great mystery of what cannot be said at all. A first dim step on that dark road is the attempt to say what God is *not*. Do this completely enough, and you are left with a cut-out of God, a template, a negative; list off all the false names and be left with the One True Name, and so on.

Though God is not of direct professional interest to sceptics, except of course as the anti-Christ, the method was promising.

James Fenimore Cooper, on the other hand, whose novels had been plunked down on my nightstand when I was a boy, was of enormous professional interest. He'd pretty much invented the myth of the American frontier and was singled out by Mark Twain as its biggest liar. Twain had done most of the heavy lifting. I did little more than list and categorize Cooper's techniques in the high art of falsification. My study ended with something wry about James Fenimore Cooper's great service to Truth, by exempting everything he touched from the need for serious inquiry. Looking for the authentic in his work was indeed to chase down the last of the Mohicans. I believe my unfortunate last line read, *If, however, someone were to come along equipped to lie about everything at once, the stars themselves might wink out.*

One winces to read this sort of thing now. It makes for a rather large target.[†] Yet the high road for my Cooper and the negative way was already paved and deliciously smooth. In those heady days of the late seventies, the knowability of Truth was becoming as problematical as God's had once been. And a quite elevated number of people found themselves preferring Truth's unknowability to its non-existence. Moreover, the smart-alecky tone was consonant with

[†] for future colleagues, of course, and other enemies—but now, a dozen years on, an undergraduate

postmodernism's sophomoric triumphalism, and therefore publishable. So the notion had legs, and I had my bailiwick: literature as *via negativa*.

A little string of publications followed.[20] It didn't hurt that my advanced studies had been in Paris under a French superstar (whom it would seem kindest to identify here as X.Z.). To the French, this meant I was at least capable of receiving culture, an imprimatur that turned out to be lofty enough for pretty much everyone else. For a while I pursued (against the grain, as it were) two careers, one in French, the other in English—sardonic sceptic in Europe, lyrical empiricist in America. I only moved back to Canada when I realized that I could accomplish the same results with a single paper for the two audiences. In fact, I could effect no other result, no matter what I wrote in either language.

Of course, the circle of researchers was tight and the topic obscure, but the conference sessions were often well attended. In Europe, the German sophisticate could indulge his own early childhood frontier fantasies. I came to call it the Karl May effect.[†] As for the French attendees, with me they could slum permissibly in a *petite cabane de bois*. This was an adult fantasy fully accessible only to the French, but the newcomer experienced it as a sort of lost weekend involving equal parts Rousseau, red Indian and maple syrup.

In America, on the other hand, the notions of literature as anti-truth, and Truth as poetic figure, brought a *je ne sais quoi* of European perversion to conferences that might otherwise have seemed exercises in parish civics.

The minute I started reading Beulah's paper on the poetry of physics, I saw that she had indeed done her research. I was mildly flattered that she was showing off for me. Rereading it three years later, I'm tempted to say I still had no idea what she was up to.[†] She was not hunting for higher grades, she was baiting a hook. And her timing was good.

At the same time, she had far bigger fish to concern herself with. In the first of many winding searches through the stacks of the university library tower, Beulah unearthed a little gem by Ermilio Abreu Gomez titled *La ruta de Sor Juana*, a work putting her on the nun's trail. Photos—of the poet's birthplace, the villages of her early period, the surrounding countryside—maps, portraits of her confessor and

[†]Karl May being Germany's over-the-top answer to Cooper. So when I called Beulah in to discuss her paper, it gave her a savage pleasure to tell me that May—thief, impostor, ex-convict, icon—was the best-loved author of Einstein's boyhood

[†]But then, I did keep a copy. I'll admit the paper was an extra-ordinary example of something

prelates, reproductions of diverse documents. All invaluable raw material. Beulah writes:

> . . . born, 1648, San Miguel de Nepantla. On slopes of volcano Popocatepetl . . . over 18,000 feet. Wet stormy summers. Snakes scorpions tarantulas flushed from crevices. Humid. Sheet lightning, distant rain. Houses low adobe, some whitewash. Claytiled red roofs. Low stone walls along roads into town.
>
> . . . Wisp of green, green whisper of river in the distance . . . spreading shade trees, moist grassy banks. Day skies pale blue sprouting wings— butterflies swallows hummingbirds hawks.
>
> Cirrus in the afternoon—cicadas dust and heat. Quick little lizards, tubular iguanas.
>
> Winter nights cold windy sky full of stars. Night owls and bats.
>
> . . . Playing, alone. Little girl, lovely, talk of the village. Mother tough independent beautiful. Diego the new lover—three more bastard children. Wicked tongues wagging. Diego's no farmer. No privacy for Isabel—whole village knows about her. Grasping sour Diego a pretender an extractor. Was he charming . . . ? What binds them together?
>
> What binds *us?* What is this thing?

If Beulah was searching out the thread of a connection to Sor Juana, she had only to begin with the Mexican poet's own self-analysis, written in 1691 in a letter of self-defence addressed to a bishop:

> From the moment I was first illuminated by the light of reason, my inclination toward letters has been so vehement that not even the admonitions of others . . . nor my own meditations have been sufficient to cause me to forswear this natural impulse that God placed in me . . . that inclination exploded in me like gunpowder. . . . [21]

Down through the years, much has been made of Sor Juana's voracious hunger for learning. And even a glance over the list of materials Beulah was to consult—and voluminously annotate—indicates that her own quest must have grown to consume as many as fourteen hours a day. Here, then, was that first incandescent thread, a connection Beulah was curiously slow to grasp and ultimately unable to defuse: an inclination to study that eventually went off like gunpowder.

Her first major obstacle, oddly enough, was on the library tower's tenth floor, in the Hispanic Studies area. The on-line catalogue had indicated several titles that should have been shelved alongside *La ruta de Sor Juana*. Finding almost none of them, she checked the catalogue again, but the books hadn't been signed out. So where were they?

Reading her journal entry for this day, I imagine her now, striding down the aisles, eyeing each student immured in a stack of books as the possible culprit, and in the process no doubt eliciting a few curious stares herself. She suspects that someone has made off with the whole section in order to hoard it in some out-of-the-way corner. Finally, exasperated, she goes to ask just what the hell is going on. A long-suffering librarian, maybe flinching just perceptibly, informs her the university has begun selling off some of its special-interest collections in the face of funding cutbacks. A powerful private university ("rich fascists") in the eastern United States is purchasing many of the rarest titles in the fields of Latin American history and culture. The library is slowly getting around to deleting them from the computer. Now the books can only be obtained through interlibrary loans, a process both expensive and slow.

Waiting impatiently for each new book to arrive, fuming at each fresh delay, Beulah hits upon a strategy—of going to a section, for example Mexican Colonial History, to look doggedly through every book index for some mention of Juana Inés de la Cruz, Sor / Sister.

Late one evening just before closing, her eye falls upon the following series of index entries:

Innocente IV, 58, 59, 76, 271
Inquisitio generalis, 63–64
Inquisitio specialis, 64–65

She pauses, tired but alert now, thoughts turning in narrowing circles around an as-yet indistinct point—then the sudden leap. *The Inquisition.* Excitedly she flips the book shut to discover she holds in her hands Medina's meticulously detailed *Historia de la Inquisición en México*. Beulah has just rounded the first sharp bend in the path. She has entered her labyrinth.

JUANA INÉS
DE LA CRUZ,

LOVE IS A
GREATER
LABYRINTH

B. Limosneros, trans.

ARIADNA:

Amo a Teseo, y temo de manera
su muerte, que me fuera más ligero
tormento si, muriendo yo primero,
los riesgos de su vida no temiera.

Mil veces mi temor lo considera
blandido sobre el cuello el duro acero,
y tantas veces yo del susto muero
cuantas presumo que él morir pudiera.

Y no es el mayor daño, si se advierte,
estar de tantos riesgos combatida,
que otro mal tengo que temer más fuerte:

que es pensar que con alma fementida,
en algún tiempo puede darme muerte,
a quien yo tantas veces doy la vida.

ARIADNE:

I *love* Theseus, and thus
his death do dread—the lighter
torment were to die first, no longer
to fear for his life's threats.

A thousand times does terror brandish
its icy steel against my throat;
just so many soft deaths do I know
in imagining he might perish.

But this brings not the greatest harm, in honesty—
to be embattled by so many menaces;
another must I fear with more intensity:

To think—O my soul is so perfidious!—
that he could at any moment murder me,
to whom I've so oft made my life the gift . . .

*G*he cart lurched up the track and away from Panoayan. A last shred of pride kept me from turning back and begging to be allowed to stay. I rode beside the muleteer, my back straight, my front crumbling.

One driver, three mules, a burro and a girl. I hardly recall a single feature of the roadside. Knowing I spoke Nahuatl, the driver asked me a polite question or two, to which I replied in monosyllables, hard as these had been for me to manage lately.

The one ray of light to reach through the clouds and down to me on that cart seat was that it was not the same muleskinner, drunk on *pulque*, who had driven us from Nepantla five years back, madly bawling away and singing. And vomiting. He had his way of making the Rabbit sacred. Mine was to work myself into an unholy fury: I was homesick. *I'd been away less than an hour.*

Away an hour and already so much to be thankful for. It was a different driver. No one saw me cry. And I didn't vomit. But then, riddles were a cure for seasickness, weren't they, and I now had a riddle to cross *oceans* with. For what a sight my ungrateful tears would have made—hadn't I demanded this very thing? Had I not vowed to Isabel that I would disguise myself as a boy and go to the Royal University? I would find my own teacher. Take classes! And among the towering racks of the New World's greatest library, stroll forever. This was what adventurers did— pursued their destiny, defied the risks, strove towards high exploits like giants storming heaven.[22] But with Amanda.

Not like this.

How I wanted to let Panoayan go now. Place of thorns, this El Dorado of loss—of pasts and precious jades, of tongues and riddles and *friends*. Josefa and María were right: these mountains were oppressive—suffocating. They might be the Heart of the Earth, a place of women's secrets, but that heart was cold now, and still. Or so I wanted mine to be in me. I was on my way to the city of Mexico, seat of empires. This was to be my life. I must make myself hard as iron and full of briars.

At the eastern shore the late sun loured on the lake with a light dulled to pewter. In the shallows, mats of flotsam heaved in a dance of woodblocks, reeds and corn husks. Up and down the shore, mounds of refuse stood slumped in squat pyramids—rags, cobs, potsherds and rinds, glass glints, strips of hide—as if built on the trash of an earlier tribe. That was the custom of this place, to build on what remains, and never, ever be free of it.

Back from the flat shore sprawled a midden of wattle huts and mud, endless mud and lurking dogs. In one hovel a woman in a greyish *huipil* nursed a dirty-cheeked infant while squatting and poking at a brazier. As if in its smoke she sought some small help in driving the flies away from the infant's mouth and eyes. This was a blouse such as Xochitl and Amanda wore. I had never seen one dirty. Outside, *macehuales*[†] lurched about drunk . . . dogs fought. For this, I was not yet hard enough.

[†]Nahuatl term for the lowborn

Was this really the lake I—and how many others—had dreamt of and conjured? It was not enough to leave home. Now I had to give up even my illusions of what we had seen from up at Ixayac. And everything Grandfather had taught me to see. . . .

This was not that blue-green eye into which *los conquistadores* had stared, and I had too—as down through the *oculus* of a vast underground cathedral. Over there, crouched beneath that rust sunset, was most certainly not the city of the white sunflower, its nectaries tall pyramids of cut gems. I had seen it *myself*, from Ixayac—seen this shore I now stood on. But then again, my eyes were not so very clear after all, and no longer was I his ray of pure white light.

I saw this shore become still more hideous as the light failed and a thick darkness gathered. For a few minutes more I could still have looked back to the volcanoes—the white chisel-tip edged in fire, her lover standing over her.

I would not. That beauty was behind me now.

But I would *never*—not dragged by four hundred mules—enter Mexico over this *calzada*. The old causeways the Mexica had built were as straight as dies—not these corruptions, as full of crooks and sags as an old stick. I would find a boat. The driver glared but said nothing. I guessed that he'd been planning to stop at a *pulquería*, and that a weakness for drink must surely be the chief hazard of mule-driving. Well, he might as soon talk sense to his mules as stop me getting down.

It was cold that night alone on the shore. But I was eleven now, and after all the brave talk, here was a thing the intrepid would never fear to do. I dragged my trunk down the beach. Any villager sober enough to see could have followed my trail to where I hid in a thicket. All that night I clutched tight to my chest a purse containing the fifty pesos Grandfather had left to me. It was a lot of money, and it was still his.

It was for our books.

Never had I imagined so many mosquitoes might exist in the world. Nor that all at once they would converge on me. At first light I was of a more subdued cast of mind. I climbed into the cargo canoe and went where the man gestured, up into the bow. He wrestled aboard the cedar trunk that carried my earthly attachments. There *were* books, quite a lot. By the time we had taken on two more passengers, weavers from Puebla and their huge bundles, the canoe seemed more awallow than afloat.

The boatman pushed off. Seeing the European girl in her one presentable dress and perched at the prow on her cedar trunk, they must have thought her the daughter of some Iberian grandee. One weaver whispered, glaring pointedly at my well-ballasted trunk, "*Aicnopilpan nemitiliztli. . . .*"

Among the poor is no life for kings.

To which I could not help but retort, "I'm not so rich, friends, but I hear my uncle over *there* is."

They were not much older than I, a couple already, or brother and sister. And once they had recovered from their embarrassment we laughed a little about their surprise and my rich uncle. They did not ask me how I had learned their tongue, and I liked this restraint and saw its dignity, and I liked them as they talked about their hopes for sales and how many days they might have to stay, and whether they would go back at all. Something passed between them then, and I surprised myself in resisting the impulse to ask about it.

We advanced alongside the causeway, though as the boatman paddled steadily on I was pleased to see us pulling away. I asked why there were even canoes *on* this shore anymore. He said the canals were still preferred for moving cargo within the city as long as the water was high. Few of the streets were paved, and after just two days of rain most became bogs to the heavy carriages.

As we talked, my eyes strayed once or twice to the white peaks behind the boatman. The sun had risen between them. I watched it go from gold to red and back to gold as it rose through the smoke plume of Popocatepetl. I decided there could be no real harm in speaking the

language of that country once in a while, though all of that was behind
me now. The weavers were excited and nervous, and glanced up past me
too: for what was behind me, in truth, was the city. As the conversation
died out, I turned to look, thinking I might as well get my bearings, since
I knew more about the canals of Venice than those of Mexico. I suppose
I was a little nervous too.

Again Mexico was closer than I knew. It filled the horizon—a canvas
stretched wide as a painted sail. The scene had just that quality of
grandeur and poise, of all the business of the world in suspension, stilled
in its detail and brushing. The sweep of streets, built up twice my height
above the water—hundreds, all running in parallels to the shore; the
gold light striking the blocks of the great houses, as if crates stacked for
off-loading from a single enormous wharf; smoky blue shadows between
the buildings; grey-black threads ravelling up into a coppice above the
chimneys. . . .

Right beside us, to the south, were the floating gardens, faintly undu-
lating. Around and amidst them worked scores of canoes, their sides
flashing like the wet bills of cormorants in the morning sun. These were
the farmers at their floating crops.

And all the furious activity at the entrance to the canal! Banging
and shouts, the clank of iron, and ringing steel. Horses and mules, the
clatter of carriages, a swarm of men and bundles. And half of these men
were black.

Africans . . .

Close now to the entrance, I saw that the Indians were ferrying bundles up from canal to cart, and the Africans down from cart to canal.
They were as two colonies, red and black, in a teeming mercantile
exchange of ant wares and formic delicacies. And I—I was bringing, high
in the holds of my belly, a whole colony of butterflies. . . .

We entered the canal.

My uncle was rich, one of New Spain's richest men; and he had half
the slaves in his charge out looking for me. The driver had not rushed to
a *pulquería*, after all, but had prudently gone to give Aunt María my views
on causeways. It was Aunt María herself who was waiting at the dock.

She stood looking very tall atop a flight of broad, shallow steps. She
stood tall, too, as the only woman in her generation of our family to have
conceived a child in wedlock, or to have achieved marriage at all. I had
met her just once, but there was no mistaking her. Hers was the cultivated

pallor of one whom luxury permits to evade the sun; her hair was a shade lighter than Isabel's deep chestnut, with glints of copper at her temples. And yet they were unmistakably sisters. Like Isabel's, her brows were black, but not so long, nor wide-spaced, nor arched. It was Aunt María's nose that was long and arched.

Isabel was beautiful. And her beauty was for me an annihilation—no matter how I held the mirror, all I could see were *her* traits. As a way to ward off that beauty, I had once in a poem made her nose 'aquaductile' in its straightness and strength of line.

But María's was truly aquiline and she, quite striking. In the prepossession of her nose, her pallor and the heavy blackness of her brows, there was the handsome brooding of a crow.

To see better, no doubt, for she seemed a little short-sighted, she had drawn back her white veil—veils were fashionable again, I learned, if only among gentlewomen recently landed from Europe. Which, of course, María was not. Around her neck hung a heavy silver chain and a thick crucifix inlaid with onyx. Otherwise she was dressed chin to heel in black shimmering silk.

She looked calm amidst the bustle of porters, and well she might: many of these men were her husband's slaves. But with a dozen running thither and yon looking for me, she had known exactly where to come. She had come alone, and she had driven herself in a light phaeton just right for two, hitched to a charcoal-grey horse. The carriage was spotless, unlike every other carriage or cart in sight. Uncle Juan, largely at his own expense, saw to it that at least one street running from his house to each of the southern and eastern canals was paved. And though the *tenayuca*[†] was rough, I think I could have enjoyed that first ride; as, in other circumstances, I think I could have liked her. But this was my jailer conducting me into exile.

[†]a paving of ovoid stones

And so began the first year of captivity. At least I was not made to walk to the gates.

"Isabel warned me you were willful."

That was all either of us said on the ride.

I had never seen before that day a house with three storeys, nor could I have imagined wanting one. The doors were tall and impressively carved, the grillwork at the windows heavy and elaborate. The frames of doors and windows alike were of a blond limestone, as was the lintel, whose ends were scrolls carved like the capital of Ionic columns. And in each of the scrolls' *oculi* I noted with grim satisfaction the ugly little face of a gargoyle.

The house itself stood as if cut from a quarry of dark grey slate. The grey was relieved only by a thin strip of blue and white tiles between each of the storeys, and another strip of tiling running under the eaves, with three more gargoyles as waterspouts. The way the sky was lowering, I wouldn't have to wait long to see them retching water.

In Panoayan I'd never thought much about the rain. There was always a big tree to sit beneath, and it was dry under the arcades. Here, the rain would add one more wall to those already keeping me in. Certainly I'd never associated rain with *moods*.

The first rule of this new life: We were never to go out alone.

Since Aunt María dragged poor Magda everywhere, this injunction was of little concern to my cousin. She was five years my senior, and with so little natural sparkle that her mother had undertaken to vigorously fossick the New World's largest city for marriage prospects. In my years in that house, and in a city thick with the scions of mining magnates, not a single one panned out.

I would never have imagined such an enormous house could so quickly become insufferably small. First, because it was only half a house. Uncle Juan's parents, a wizened little pair glimpsed only on the rarest occasions, had the whole of the opposing half. Which is to say that halfway to the back, on each floor, the corridor was blocked by a locked door built into a wooden divider. What's more, the courtyard was sectioned neatly in two by a heavy canvas, lashed at the sides to the handrails and columns of each storey's inner corridor and fastened at the top to a metal mesh, whose original purpose had been to keep out intruders and doves. So although the courtyard was technically open to the sky, the rain and light fell in tiny, cramped squares.

At ground level all this oppressive cloistering gave way to farce, for the canvas was tied down to buckles not only set in the flagstones but sunk even into the bottom of what must once have been a lovely fountain. I came to see in all this the letter of some arcane covenant on the sharing of family property, or the judgement of Solomon to halve the child. But not at first, when it just seemed laughable. At least once a week, one of the Indian servants was down scrubbing the greenish growth from our side of the canvas, and there were moments of true hilarity in watching her try to co-ordinate scrubbing motions with her counterpart—giggling and shouting instructions—on the other side of the bulging, bumping sheet. I had read of wedding nights in distant countries that might look thus.

And if all this were not enough to make me run for the doors, *our* half was a warehouse. The courtyard was choked with crates and bales, and the end of each corridor was stacked to the ceiling with inventories that seemed never to turn over. The secret path to vast fortunes was indeed perplexed and tortuous.

The next rule: We were to go to Mass twice a day, bent like porters under the heavy crucifixes assigned for the excursion. It was as if Aunt María hoped the three of us might be called from the pews to assist in the ceremonies. In churchly company, she would go to awkward lengths to trot out a near-complete store of the idioms of divine praise and favour, very much as I had done to practise Nahuatl. *God willing . . . Heaven be praised . . . If it be His will.* But in the cathedral itself she often freshened them, as if to prove her usage no mere formula: *Jesus be praised; if it be the will of Jesus Our Saviour; may the Son of God, Redeemer and Messiah, forbid . . .*

We were never to have friends over without notice.

In my case, this could never be anything but hypothetical, since I met no one on my own.

We were never to dress up as boys and go to the Royal University.

Never. It was not to be.

The Royal University was a preposterous idea for a girl. And dressing up as a boy . . . just this year someone in lascivious dress had been caught walking in the main square after curfew and discovered to be a man. After the trial, he was hanged in the square before a jeering mob.

And there would be a special penalty for sneaking out. Any domestics in a position to prevent me would be let go, nor would they find a place elsewhere if Aunt María had any say, and of course she had a very great deal of say.

This was coercion—*extortion.*

Good, we understood each other.

It was no hollow threat. Maybe this is why I never sought to know the servants, though we sometimes exchanged a word or two in Nahuatl. The better I knew them, the more I cared, and the more inescapable became my prison.

While most of the great houses used Africans, our house employed only Indians, and it was widely acknowledged that slaves were much better off than serfs. The Africans were hardier, more resistant to disease, less

numerous and often learned a trade. There were standards of fair treatment and there was a commission to appeal to. There was competition
for their services, and they could at least hope to save enough to one day
purchase their freedom. Some could hope to be freed by their holder.

An Indian was the property of the conquistadors. Or so it was at first.
The Conquest was privately financed. *Los conquistadores* had taken enormous risks and expected a return. "Return?" Abuelo had snorted. "Cortés
had all but stolen his ships! Was honour not a return, or service to the
Crown—was the greater glory of God not return enough?" A sneer was
not something that rode easily on Abuelo's broad face, but there it had
sat, like a moustache on a calf. From his lip the sneer had faded quickly
but not from his voice. Five hundred conquerors had been made
encomenderos by the Crown. The *encomienda* was the return on a capital
investment—New Spain divided among five hundred shareholders. But
they had not the faintest interest in land. Dumbfounded, I had asked if
I'd heard him right.

The conquerors of America had not the faintest interest in land.

Unless it was in Spain, of course. And even there, no peninsular
gentleman would ever let himself be seen at manual labour of any kind.
Horses, bulls and swords stood as the allowable exceptions. "Trans-
portable wealth. Liquid capital. Gold, Angelina." Gold and rents.

Every village in New Spain was for rent. Villagers from Panama to
Florida to California were subject to pay tribute as serfs and could be
rented like a house. A block of houses, rather, for they were rented out
together.

Their nickname, though, was *burritos*. Little beasts of burden. This
part Abuelo didn't teach me. I had to learn it in the city.

"Of course, Juanita, matters could not stand this way for long. Even
allowing for the depreciation of disease and death, let us say four percent
a year, the resource yielded a return out of all proportion to the outlay."
The conquistador's lease was redrafted to expire at death and the property reverted to the commonwealth. These days wealthy businessmen
rented villages from the Crown, or from landholders such as the Church.
The Church cared about land.

Paid a wage now, the Indians could be sent home at night to their own
districts, so did not even have to be fed and housed. For the past hundred years, the city administration had struggled to contain them in five
barrios, five blocks of rental properties. The Europeans were to live in

the centre and, above all, to keep the Indians away from the Africans, whose cults and superstitions were almost incurable.

So, too, proved the epidemic of *mestizaje*.[†] Passion leapt the barriers, life drove roots beneath them, opportunity sifted through every crack, and all made a mockery of the prophylaxis.

†mixing of races

In but one respect were the Indians envied by the other races: they were exempt from the jurisdiction of the Inquisition. So highly prized was the exemption that many of the light-skinned castes learned Nahuatl or the Mayan language so, if the need arose, they could pretend to be serfs.

The Inquisition had fetched a poor return on its investment in the Indians. Loving persuasion had proved so much more effective an evangelist, and harshness the very thing the Indians best resisted. Here was the first lesson Cortés learned, and at the urging of his translator he befriended Moctezuma. Indian resistance, on the other hand, was a fearsome thing. And here was Cortés's second lesson, taught in the siege of Tenochtitlan, where tens of thousands starved rather than surrender, where the women fought like Saracens, where the starving died with war axes in their hands.

The lake, too, had been a friend once, before the caravels and cannon. Yes there was steel, yes there was cavalry, but the single decisive engagement of the Conquest was a naval assault, on a white city on an island on a lake.

Now, there were sixty thousand *burritos* dredging out the canals and drainage ditches around the valley on any given day. But not the same sixty thousand. Many died too quickly to learn a trade or to acquire special skills. Many from the mountains had not learned to swim.

Water was not their element. But then, the lake was being drained.

As it was with the labourers, so it was with our house servants. It was not so much that they belonged nowhere else—they belonged *to* nowhere else. In Nepantla and Panoayan our field hands were rented from the Church; they came with the land. Yet I had never seen my mother, for all her faults, treat a field hand unfairly or speak to him cruelly. María, who on the canal dock had so clearly been Isabel's sister, was not like her at all.

This was Injustice.

I was permitted one monthly excursion of a personal nature, though never alone. I was allowed to buy books. This one right was never questioned, never threatened. So, whenever Uncle Juan requested my presence in the salon, I tried to go less grudgingly. Abuelo's fifty pesos were so much more money than I'd understood. And when the book-sellers learned whose granddaughter I was, fifty pesos became a hundred. I had known the bookmen's names for years, heard them listed many times in a roll call of thieves, and no doubt many were, but thieves with sentiments. Their sentimental gestures began to fill my shelves. My prison would have a library.

My room was on the third floor and was larger than mine in Panoayan. During the day at least, it was quiet on the third floor. The room faced east, with a view of the mountains, though I permitted myself only glimpses. The mornings were full of light and warmth and the afternoons dim and cool. But the most splendid feature by far was the bookshelves. They made almost the full circuit of the room. Though not ornate, they were well made, of a hardwood I didn't know, and built for this space. When I arrived they were also entirely bare of books.

The prisoner hadn't expected to find her cell so agreeable. Nor had I expected such a good first impression of Uncle Juan. I remembered imagining, years before and on no evidence whatever, that he and my grandfather had quarrelled. That was why Abuelo was making fewer visits to Mexico.

The day I arrived, Uncle Juan himself supervised my cedar trunk's precarious ascent, directing the porters to set their burden down next to the bookshelves. He seemed to have guessed about the books. His brusqueness with the porters bespoke a habit of command, but he thanked them—casually and very badly—in Nahuatl. The phrase he so blithely dismantled was *Tlazohcamati huel miac*. I looked hard to see if this was supposed to impress me, but though painful to my ear it tripped off his tongue like a stone worn smooth from a very long journey in one's shoe.

He said *Tasoca*, he had said it often, and I was impressed.

At the door he nodded, a little shyly. "The shelves will look better with books in them again." At that, he turned to go.

"I hope you didn't give up your office, Uncle."

His smile seemed faintly perplexed. "No, Juanita. We have offices near the palace. It's where I have to spend most of my time now."

And so it was. Not a month went by, it seemed, in which I saw him more than once—usually in the salon with his business associates, some of whom had literary tastes. For their entertainment I might be asked to improvise verses on a theme or rhyme scheme of their choosing. One or two of his regular visitors displayed a genuine interest. I eventually let them hear poems I was writing. Though it was not quite a pleasure, neither could I make the salon out to be a torture. Still, at the first opportunity I would excuse myself and go up to my room.

If I stood—at first, on a chair under my window, or then a small stack of books, or soon just stood—I could see down into the street. Once it happened that a neighbourhood urchin spotted my face up there, and we would exchange a sign or two from time to time. Over the years the faces changed and the number of urchins grew, as if the window had become a landmark; I came to believe their knowledge of the city was as intimate as ours had been of our woods.

Finally a small gang of more prosperous boys noticed me, and my window became the target of their affections. There were spectacular, manly throws of rotting fruit: the best results came with tomatoes. One time, for my entertainment, using fireworks I imagine, they blew up a watermelon in the street, an early instalment on the day they would find a catapult, or a cannon. I tried not to take umbrage—perhaps they were only practising for the theatre, which I hoped to visit one day too.

The nights were altogether different from the day's calm. The house was in the southeast barrio, and though land was indeed scarce in the centre, Uncle Juan had built here by choice, to be closer to the canals. It was an Indian barrio, well supplied with *pulque* concessions. Carefully supervised by Church and Crown, the trade in *pulque* remained one of Uncle Juan's more profitable businesses. Two thousand *arrobas*[†] a day, every day.

[†] fourteen thousand gallons

Eventually I grasped that some *pulquerías* also served as houses of prostitution. At daybreak, when the sun struck the wall above my bed well before there was brightness in the streets, the poor harlots could be seen doubled up against a wall—sleeping, I hoped, and not badly hurt. Sometimes there was more than one, sometimes they fought among themselves, or over clients—once over a little package that I couldn't make out, but which seemed precious to them. I could not keep from looking.

It must have been the starkest horror down in the beds of those canyons for someone with nowhere to turn, for even at the height of my room, the stillness was often rent by shouts and shrieks. The most brutal, grisly scenes of knives and cudgels and helplessness played themselves out under my lids. I could not keep from seeing myself huddled against just such a wall.

The night floated up on a tide of loneliness.

In that first year I was often terrified. Not so much of the streets themselves but of having nowhere to go.

I have become a light sleeper, I think from that time. When I did drift off, it was usually by snuffling my pillow, letting myself imagine it was Abuelo's shoulder. Drowsy, I could smell him. Mesquite from the firepit, and leather . . . warm wool, and the most delicious, very faint scent of rising dough.

It was only natural that I should wake in the night, having dreamt of him. Often the same dream: of him riding away on what I finally understood was Amanda's roan lamb. But he went west from Nepantla, not east, the direction my father had taken. Abuelo swaying on the back of a lamb as large as a camel didn't seem comical at all in a dream. When I awoke it felt as if he had just left the room.

One night something happened to make me wonder if as a young child I had often been afraid of the dark. I woke to screams. Coming from the streets three storeys down was a shrieking so terrible I couldn't get back to sleep at all. Lying there looking out at a quarter moon, I thought of a song we had learned from Xochitl. And of the time I first remembered hearing it. I was lying against her in a hammock, at night, in the storeroom behind the kitchen. . . .

There had been a jaguar killing cattle. It had come closer to the house than anyone expected, into the corral, with the horses. I have never forgotten the screaming of the horses. Abuelo awoke in great confusion, and in his undergarments had started up to the watchtower to load the cannon. "Father, come down!" shouted Isabel. She'd taken an instant to throw on a cloak, and had an arquebus in her hands. She fired into the night above the courtyard.

The sound was shattering, coming without warning over the terror in the corral. Grandfather teetered on the steps as though he might fall. I froze, and my sisters, too—they huddled together just outside their room, their nightgowns a pale smudge of starlight. Isabel went inside to reload and before we could rouse ourselves Xochitl had brought Abuelo a lantern. As she helped him down the steps, she whispered something to him. I had never seen them speak. Returned to his senses, he rushed— lantern high—after Isabel, who was already through the portals. Xochitl scooped me up, told María and Josefa to go back to bed, and took me to sleep with her. Amanda was already there in Xochitl's hammock.

Xochitl sang to us. We lay on either side of her, clutching at her breast, as we had at the beginning. She sang the song of the magical sleeping mat. A mat against the jaguar, Night, who mocks and taunts our vision, who is the mirror that multiplies each shadow until our eyes are filled with giants. She sang a charm against the giant wizards and bandits who wait at the crossroads under the cover of night.

> *Nomatca nehuatl*
> *niQuetzalcoatl,*
> *niMatl,*
> *ca nehuatl niyaotl*
> *nimoquequeloatzin*
> *Ye axcan yez:*
> *niquinmaahuiltiz nohueltihuan . . .*
>> Even I,
>> I, Quetzalcoatl,
>> I, Matl,
>> even as I am War,
>> who mocks all,
>> so it shall be now:
>> I will mock my sisters . . .

She sang us the song FeatherSerpent sang out to his sister, PreciousFeatherMat, where she fasted the four-year fast of penance with the mountain priests. The screaming had stopped, the shouts died out, and the gunshots. There was only Xochitl's voice now, its soft rattle and sway in our ears, its purr against our cheeks. Quetzalcoatl called to Quetzalpetlatl:

> *auh in ipan catca*
> *chalchiuhpetlatl,*
> *quetzalpetlatl,*
> *teocuitlapetlatl.*
>> There was he found,
>> on the mat of jade,
>> on the mat of quetzal,
>> on the mat of gold.

FeatherSerpent called out to his sister for protection and comfort, for he had been sickened and tricked by the jaguar, his adversary and twin. He had tasted now four times of the sacred *octli*,[†] and was intoxicated. In his vision, in his confusion he called his sister to his side, and she spent the night of intoxication with him, and brought him great comfort.

[†] *pulque*

And next to Xochitl in the hammock I slept. But before I fell asleep I knew she'd sung that song to me before. It felt as if I had heard it many times.

I remembered the song and the desolation of that night from our first weeks in Panoayan. I remembered it all those years later in Mexico City in a still unfamiliar room walled in by dark bookshelves, with screaming coming up from the streets.

The next night I sang the song to myself, and slept deeply. I dreamed I woke. Abuelo was sitting beside the bed, not discomforted by the absence of a chair there and amused that this should worry me. I saw him as clearly as when we sat together at the little table by the library. "Angelina, think . . . what do you really want with all your heart? Only ask it."

There was something in this, too, I had heard or felt before, and a few days later I found it in Kings. Solomon was in Gibeon making sacrifices to the God of his father, David. Well pleased, the God of David came to Solomon and asked him to name whatever he wanted.

Solomon asked neither riches nor honour but a wise and understanding heart, if he was to be given sovereignty over so great a people. He was granted what he asked, but also the riches and honour he did not seek.

I hadn't the faintest interest in riches, a good deal in honour, more still in understanding. What was the wisdom here that Abuelo was offering me? I read the passage again many times. It hurt—finally, in a good way—to be reminded of him, but I couldn't find it. I read all of Kings and Proverbs again, and the Song of Solomon. A mountain of wisdom was there, and passages of great beauty, but no special message that felt expressly for me. For the next several days I tried to be attentive to everything around me, which after all was only books, the household and the street. I thought again about Xochitl's song, the four-year fast, the four sips of *pulque*—had they got drunk on the fourth sip or the fifth? I remembered that FeatherSerpent had once travelled four years through the underworld with a big red dog. The two struggled together against giants and dragons, crossed deserts, brought back the bones of a lost race of men. But I couldn't find the wisdom there, and after a few weeks I slept better. And thought less about my dreams.

I found other escapes. A frequent one during those years was *The Nun-Ensign*. It was the most awful play, based on the true history of Catalina de Erauso, a nun who broke out of a convent and, disguised as a man, fled to South America to gamble, duel, court ladies and battle Indians. For her valour in the field, she was decorated with the military commission of ensign. She met the Pope as a woman (Catalina, that is), and eventually returned to Mexico, once again a man, and finished out her days as a muleskinner. Given my special experiences with them, I felt I might one day aspire to something similar. Skinning one could not be that difficult, once you let the *pulque* out.

If my destiny was to live out my life in a prison of books, I was equal to it. And much better books than *The Nun-Ensign* lay all around me, but fewer and fewer still unread, at least in Castilian. Teaching myself Latin now was urgent. I had sworn to learn it years ago—all the way back in Nepantla. My vow so fervently renewed, I became infuriated by my slow progress. The feature that most distinguished me from Isabel was a rather beautiful head of blue-black hair. It had been the envy of my sisters and now my cousin Magda, too. I remember Magda standing at the door to my room to watch me, as for the second time I cut a good length of it off. She found the experience satisfying, apparently, for I remember how she made a point of letting me see. Pausing dramatically until I looked at her, she glanced about the room, finally at the shelves, half filled almost with books. Her face was bloated like an invalid's, and gloating was its sickness.

She hated me. After that, I never doubted it.

I saw nothing in her life to gloat about. Well, she could stare however hideously she liked, but I pledged that if I hadn't learned Latin by such and such a date, I would crop it back farther still. *Better to have a head shorn of hair than one empty of learning.*[23] It took twenty sessions and three haircuts before I pronounced myself satisfied. Next, I vowed, would come Italian, then Greek, then Portuguese, then French. . . . At least one language a year. At such a rate, by the time I was eighteen I might be ready to contemplate learning Arabic. Ready to contemplate anything at all except the birthdays themselves, which were exactly twice as bad as they might have been. I only knew how to celebrate birthdays for two.

November twelfth.

And this next one, my fifteenth, would be incomparably worse. A girl's *Quinceañera* is her coming-out, our fondest tradition. It is when a woman begins to fulfil her destiny, takes her first soft step into womanhood.

I had been here four years.

María said she was willing to organize a *Quinceañera* for me. She was sure many of Magda's friends would come. Had I been willing to go to even a few *tertulias*† with Magda over the years, I might have had friends of my own to invite. María said this without evident malice, as if stating a fact, and it was. One that contained only part of the truth. Truer was the generosity of the offer. When I refused it, María said nothing. She stood just inside my room, her colour rising. I expected rage. What I saw was the wounding of her pride. And if it hadn't been for Amanda, if it hadn't been four years, if it hadn't been the *Quinceañera*, I might have accepted—apologized and thanked her for her offer.

Birthdays were the days I could not keep from looking at the mountains.

I knew that if Amanda and I were able to see the city from Ixayac, she could see me now. From here, if I let myself, I could see its face—and in it, hers—staring down at me. . . .

† parties, 'mixers'

We had run together every day to Ixayac and never told a soul. It was a holy place, our sacred place. And if I am ever to speak of it, there are things that must be said first. It was a year of pleasures so intense, I ached with them. And I had only to place my palm below Amanda's ribs and then my own to feel the same fluster of wings, settling there.

Then it ended. When I was not careful, when something slid. And then Xochitl finally said no to me, for the first time in my life. *No, Ixpetz*, that city is no place for Amanda, no place for any of her people—no. And even as she began to shake her head, I knew it to be true. I had not seen it before because I did not want to. Amanda, though, had. She had been watching the day come for years, drawing nearer—ever since the firepit. That was what Xochitl had meant by bumble-beeing around.

But Xochitl would have had to explain to Amanda *why*, and feel under her own palm, then, the fluster of her daughter's heart . . . settling.

I knew the exact moment Xochitl talked to her, about the firepit, about bumblebees: the afternoon of our first full day in Panoayan, when

Amanda and I came in dazed and excited from exploring. When we had each drunk two glasses of lime cordial. When I had gone off to the library.

Amanda knew from then on, and came with me anyway, ran with me everywhere, while I could afford to be blind. It was her most perfect gesture.

She let me have our childhood.

For four years now it had often been too painful even to think of her—the face of Ixayac or the mask of her hurt. I had made of it a hole in my memory but felt it now in my chest. In the weeks leading up to my *Quinceañera*, there opened in me a blackness I had never guessed at. It welled up from this hole in my chest, in a black tide leagues deep. It felt like the cries from the street, but the sounds were coming from me.

I could only just manage loneliness, not this. This floated up as mockery.

It mocked me to my face.

Didn't want to see? I hadn't seen because it was *inconvenient*. I must find—must *have* my destiny, so everything else must just fall into place as if preordained.

No, even this was too easy.

Exactly what hadn't I seen? Just what was it I didn't know? I did know that the Indians were not from the Indies. I knew about the Mexica. And I knew Xochitl was descended from the great Ocelotl. I knew he had dared to challenge Moctezuma with the truth, and had survived his prisons. I knew their empire was unbearably cruel, and I knew they had been lied to and starved and massacred. And I knew about the diseases that killed a million not-Indians a year for a hundred years. And I saw they were serfs now. I knew sixty thousand laboured without pay, or purpose or benefit or rest, or hope for release. And I saw to be a slave was to be better off. I knew what liberty was—it was what every Athenian had an inviolable right to. Unless he was a slave. And so I knew a little about justice—I knew at least this, I knew everything I needed to. And I knew better than Thucydides about necessity and false sacrifices and false goddesses like destiny and fortune. I knew Xochitl worked for us, and was wise and funny and had nursed me and sung for me in the night many times and raised me and taught me and was my mother. And I knew Amanda was Xochitl's daughter and my best friend and my twin—and this I knew with all my heart. I saw she was the best part of me, the part I could never be. I knew her gifts, I saw her grace. I knew she had let me stay a child for a little while longer, one day at a time. And I knew that although she had so much less time left and could run so much faster, she would always wait for me. This I saw every day we ran to Ixayac and never told a soul.

So what exactly couldn't I see? What didn't I know? What great night had so blinded my eyes and mocked me now?

I couldn't *see* Amanda was an Indian.

I didn't *know* she was my burro.

And now four years later how it mocked me to my face. All day, as my *Quinceañera* approached, and would not stop.

Give her a wise and understanding heart, to have sovereignty over a great people.

I tried to think of the other things I had learned and known and seen, and done—some of them fine, even in this place.

But they meant nothing to me.

And I thought, How do I defend myself from this, make learning my shining shield? Because it's *what* I know, my knowledge—my mind—my great *gift* that mocks. She was the best part of me—*my enemy is inside.* She does not know, she does not see?—she knows too much! She knows of the four-year fast, she knows of PreciousFeatherMat, she knows of the road of shame into the underworld, the nine levels of hell, knows about the wisdom of proverbs and the sacredness of a rabbit satchel. She knows all about rates of return and rates of depreciation, and loving persuasion and friendship. She knows of the harlots down in the street with nowhere to turn, she knows of Solomon's sword and his judgements. She knows too much. Divide the child.

She knows now what Amanda knew. She sees what Xochitl saw. Twins who could not both have a childhood—one could or neither. Two lifeless halves, one living whole. Decide. Divide.

And Xochitl allowed this out of love and the terrible purity of a wise and understanding heart. And Amanda heard Xochitl and gave herself up to this love, out of the most perfect and incomprehensible grace.

Then, when I thought I could bear no more, my *abuelo* came, the night of my fifteenth birthday.

He came twice in that month. Not in a shining vision, not as an

apparition from the beyond, but as a warmth and a voice so natural that
I knew both came from within. This, more than anything that he said,
helped close the hole in my chest. *My friend is inside me too.*

Twice that month he sat with me, and though he has never yet come
back except in dreams, I've always felt I knew where to find him. Both
times he said very little, which was a little unlike him. The first time he
began with a simple question. The second time he insulted me.

Who has the eyes of Thucydides now?

Hugeous jolt-head.

It was a month when things changed. Mercy was a beginning.

Uncle Juan came the morning after my birthday. As he glanced discreetly around at the books and papers scattered over the floor, I realized
he had not come fully into the room in four years.

"We may have to build you another bookshelf."

I didn't know what to say. I just stood by the window looking at him.

"Now that you're a woman of the world"—his smile held a trace of
irony but kindness too—"I have a business proposition for you." He was
a big man, soberly dressed, with a long, serious face. The forehead was
high, the jaw heavy and long. His hair was a pale, papery brown, singed
grey at the temples.

"Does it have to do with *pulque?*"

"Palaces."

"Palaces . . ."

"A competition of poetry. The incoming viceroy is its patron, I am its
sponsor. And still I have not been able to meet him. My friends think
you could do well. You don't have to win, just be among the last ten or
so. Be on the platform. The judges pick the last three, he picks the winner. I want him to see you."

"A business proposition."

"The finalists get a private audience with the Viceroy and his wife."

"Is that your prize or mine?"

"If you're a finalist, anything you ask."

Anything I ask . . . a little child who knows not how to go out or come in.

"Uncle Juan . . . you've been kind. Generous. But I don't want anything. Thank you. I don't want this."

He shrugged, his face showing no trace of irritation. "I just thought
you might enjoy the day. I know your grandfather would have. These
tourneys are quite an affair."

I saw how good my uncle was at his business. "And how would you know that, Uncle?"

"How? I knew the man."

"*Oh*. How well did you?"

"It may be hard for you to imagine a time before your birth, but he came here often then. María *is* his daughter. You haven't forgotten."

"No."

"I'm sorry to say this, Juana, but I think you have. He was a friend to me and a friend to my parents, who have few. He always tried very hard with María. He was always welcome in my house. He used to stay for weeks. Consulting archives . . . special collections at the Royal University. *There* was a man to talk with. You remember that, of course."

I remember.

"As soon as you could read, whenever he came to buy books it was always for the two of you. You were all he talked about. His best new stories were all about you. Your reading, your sketches. It wasn't always easy for María. Your mother of course had sketched as a child. There was a story he loved to tell about the two of you translating musical theories from—Italian, was it? Portuguese?"

"He told you?"

It was Italian, Uncle.

"You seem also to forget how you answered María when she tried to speak to you of him. You were not the only one hurt by his passing. Does it never enter your mind that some people are afraid of you? But no, never mind that. We're talking of him now. Don Pedro told me himself about your month at school with the nuns, the day of your ABCs."

"Sister Paula? You've known . . ." *Even this.*

"Yes, Juana, all this time. In his last few years it was obvious the books were no longer for him at all. He stayed only a few days. And very near the end he came for a single book. Do you remember what it was?"

"On falcons."

"He wasn't well. He left the next morning." After a moment Uncle Juan's face brightened. "But I know he liked it in here. So we were happy to give you this room, of course."

"What?"

"His room, Juanita, his bed. Only he ever slept here—how could you not know? María said she told you."

"No, she . . . I didn't."

"That woman of mine—what goes through her mind?" His features hardened. He turned and moved swiftly to the door.

"Uncle Juan?"

"Yes."

"Why do you think Abuelo would have liked the day?"

"We went to many bullfights together, Juanita."

"But . . ."

"Of course—I didn't say. Our poetry joust, it's in a bullring."

ARTS OF
ARMOURY

fter Uncle Juan left my room, *Abuelo's room*, it was sev-
eral hours before I could bring myself to look for
María. I had never felt such a violence—of four lonely
years—massed black like cliffs of hail. But she was
his daughter. The thought, however fleeting, had
only ever brought me displeasure. Now it was all I
could find to temper the cruelty of what she'd done—keeping Abuelo
from me, withholding the one small kindness that would have brought
comfort in that house. I might have had him with me through all those
nights, through that first year of sleeping afraid.

How the kind stroke withheld whets the edge of rage.

"*Why?*"

I found her in the salon where the light was good for the reading of
Bibles in mid-afternoon. A room of crucifixes, upholstered sofas—
sculpted, crested, inlaid, moulded—and one farthingale chair with the
upholstery removed for her holy lectures.

"Come in."

"What brings anyone to this?"

"Juan just left. Ask him."

"Nothing in the world dishonours Grandfather so much as pettiness—*Why?*"

The Bible lay open in her lap. Her right hand kept the page. Clutched
at the base, the onyx cross snapped left and right, spun in the fingers
of her left hand. Into her face had come a strange expression, almost of
reverie.

"Why . . . why . . . why," she asked.

"Petty cruelty and injustice."

At that, the cross stopped and her head swung to me. "Why?—
because you think you're *better*. Why?—because you're so much like her.
Why?—because having you in his room thinking you're better is like
seeing them in the library all over again."

"*Isabel?*"

"Yes, Isabel."

"You're *envious*—still?"

"*I could read.*"

"I see that, yes."

"Leaving so soon?"

"I'm nothing *like* her."

"More than you know. Much more like her than him."

"Why would I listen to *you?*"

"Don't go. I'll tell you, if you like."

"Give me one reason—"

"Give you? *Give?* You live in this house—all you do is take from us. What do you ever give in return? Juan asks one small thing of you."

"He *asks.* You hold the lives of your servants over my head."

"Wait—so clever, and still you haven't found the right question."

"Why take me in the first place? Why not send me back? Why the hideous threats? *And why put me in that room?*—if it's just to shame your-self and the man who gave you *life.*"

"Closer, Juana Inés, you're getting closer. . . . Ask why we never ques-tioned a single purchase of yours, when each book brings us closer to ruin."

"Whatever are you talking about? I've bought nothing on the Index."

"'The Index.' It's not just banned books, it's how *many.* What do you think attracts their suspicion in the first place? *Private collections,* Juana."

"Then why—"

"At last a question from you, Niece, I want to answer." She released her cross and placed her hand beside the other, on the Bible in her lap.

"Yes, we said nothing, Juana Inés. Because my father *was* better. Better than any of us. . . ."

I opened my mouth to answer. But all I wanted now was to be away from her, from here.

"And you, Niece, are not the only one around here with questions. Like the one I had for your uncle."

I paused at the door but did not look back.

"Can anyone in this house—I asked my dear noble husband—please tell me what they will make, when the day comes, of a creature like you?"

A creature like me.

I had started the fight but had no stomach to finish it. I sat at the edge of Abuelo's bed and stared at the bookshelves, more than half full again. And in each book was a face, filled with what I had not seen. I saw every-one around me knowing more about my life than I did. And what I did know was already sickening enough, the things and the people I seemed prepared to sacrifice.

Now came the discoveries of these past few hours, appalling me even as I quarrelled with María. How jealous I had been to keep Abuelo's memory for myself. And there were little things that wounded me in ways I couldn't understand at all. Isabel had sketched as a girl? I had been told this years ago and pushed it out of my mind. And how unaccountably painful it was to see her and Grandfather in the library through Aunt María's envious eyes. And to know, or know so late, that Abuelo had friends in this house, that he and Uncle Juan had gone to bullfights—many—together. And then to see my trips to the book shops in a new light. For it was dawning on me that Uncle Juan might have an arrangement with the booksellers to cover my purchases. I had been so proud of my haggling.

The day and the month after my fifteenth birthday were not always easier than the weeks before it, as I saw still more of what I had failed to see—here was a knowledge I did not seek—of the shapes and silences that lay among and between us, and that I had always shied from. These too were forms, with secret geometric formulas, with their own dark knowledge and power.

And there was a silence and secret shape in this grim half-house that I had never wanted to know about. It had nothing to do with me, I'd told myself. Let it be their affair. But their affairs and mine were not so separate as I liked to think, and if I, for the thousandth time, had been just a little more attentive to anyone other than myself, I would have seen that María (née Ramírez de Santillana), proud wife of the rich and powerful Juan de Mata, was afraid. The signs lay silently all about her, only waiting to be read. The crosses, the Masses, the bizarre formulas of piety, the endless reading of just one book.

Uncle Juan asked if I had never thought people might be afraid of me. I hadn't, and if this thought were not enormous enough, there was the mystery of *why*. That María might be one of those people hadn't occurred to me either. But it was true—she *was* afraid. With so many enormities to grapple with at once, I missed the obvious. She, at least, was not afraid of me for myself but because she feared something much more dangerous.

That night after our quarrel, when the house was quiet, I stood at the railing along the third-floor colonnade. Over the courtyard the stars were mapped in a mesh of fine-drawn wire, and as through a sieve darkness poured down over the flagstones.

After a time a servant went to the well to fill a bucket. She staggered with it back into the kitchen. The surface grew still again. Between kitchen and fountain, splashes gleamed dully on the flags. As I watched, it seemed as though each stone rested on the face of a gargoyle smiling into the earth as if behind a hand. As I walked back to my room, the voice of the blackness and mockery felt nearer by the instant. Inside, the charm of Abuelo's presence, fading like a scent, seemed frail magic against an enemy whose echoes had slipped in behind me. Frail magic, but it came from within and felt like all I had, these few words he had left me.

Who has the eyes of Thucydides now . . . ? he'd asked, smiling gently and sitting where there was no chair. And what he said next, I knew I had heard something like it before, but from my mother's lips. *You have the most wonderful eyes, Angelina, for seeing far. But none of us sees everything at once, no one can see near and far at the same time. Try for yourself. Hold up your finger. Like this . . .*

This was the month when my four years of confinement ended. But no, things were not always easier. For there came to me next a remembrance of a day not long after Abuelo and I had talked about Melos. . . .

Grandfather awoke from his afternoon nap tremendously refreshed— beaming. He climbed like a small bear down from the hammock and came to sit at the table. He glanced at the manual I had open before me—gave the impression it could have been on any topic at all, so keen was he to exercise his faculties. "Ah, Jacobi Topf. The very greatest of the armourers, Juanita. Greater even than the Colmans, without a doubt. Grace without ostentation, ornament but never at the cost of effectiveness." It gave him pleasure to see me looking into this again. And what, did I think, was the work of the great armourers—true art or mere craft? For in the armourer's *fabrica*,[†] who can fail to hear the echo of the Creation, feel the Hand that turned and piped our clays . . . ?

[†]workshop

The late-afternoon light slipped in through the columns and lit the wall beside us. Xochitl had swabbed out the courtyard; the wet slate cast up a soft glow into the library, warming the ceiling and tops of the shelves. His great sun face was washed clear as the first dawn. Even the tired right eye looked less bleared—if not emerald clear, then of gold-green marble.

The first few birds were coming for their evening bath in the stone basin. I had heard Isabel's horse canter by not long before. She would be coming in any minute.

"And is the armourer's art"—he was growing, by the minute, more passionate—"not the very echo of God's highest handiwork, for did not Jacobi Topf forge even the hardest metals in the image of Man?" Grandfather had turned towards the brightness in the courtyard and was fashioning, with those bony hands, some visor or knee-cop or pauldron of light.

"And is this art, Juanita, not a vessel of Man, even as the body is a vessel of the soul? And does not this armour, in shielding his flesh, act like our Church in guarding his soul?"

But no, not at all. I thought it a skill more like pottery. It was so *finicky*. All the plodding and plotting, the stickling—the *fussing*.

I had said this with a vehemence that surprised me and in a tone I would never normally take with him. Needing now to justify myself, I took pains over the next two days, went to lengths great even for me, to marshal my arguments. Yes, this was a craft, a trade like any other. I distilled for him its essential qualities. In the armourer's anxious measurements, he is like a tailor with his tape. And is he not the very image of a tinker with his tools and tins? His obedience to contour likens him to the upholsterer as much as to the sculptor. In his concerns with joints and articulations who can fail to see the maker of toys or the wright of mills and carts? Over the gussets see how he frets like a *sastra!*[†] In all the padding and plasters and unguents for blisters, why, he is like a nurse brawling with a cobbler.

[†]dressmaker

At any other time in my life then or since I would have deferred to him, for the sheer pleasure of hearing him again, to feel that river of his talk washing over me as it had so rarely done of late. But it was so soon after Melos, and I could find no beauty in the work of the armourers, not even Jacobi Topf.

"Then what is an artist, Angelina?" he said thoughtfully, a little crestfallen.

"But Abuelito," I replied, "an artist is like a wizard, like *Ocelotl*. Have you not told me as much yourself?"

He gave me a gentle smile. "And the craftsman . . . ?"

These years later, while I sat in the room I at last knew had been his, each detail of that afternoon returned to me with the force of a blow.

How gracelessly I had argued with him. He was only feeling fresh, he was only happy to be alive, he had only come to talk to me. And his vision was by far the more beautiful.

To be with him again in some way, I started a verse on the armourer's art—my own craft of make-believe. I had taken a view against his not from belief but because it *comforted me*. It made the icy beauty and power of the engravings before me less troubling.

I sat at the desk and wondered how to begin. I tried for the tone he himself might have taken.

> Such forgers of forges and foundries,
> Of tomes and poems such marvels!
> Of tottery pottery such prodigies
> we cobblers and scribblers and artisans are!
> With truth, ourselves to arm and furnish,
> we solace seek in arm'ry furnaces.
> For our eyes the visor of blinding burnish,
> for our minds the blade of glancing surfaces.
> Therewith at chinks in the ramparts
> we pry—all the keyholes of iron artifice
> try; so as by these lights to detect (at a glance!)
> —in art the highest or arts most black—
> the fussy craftsman's homely hand . . . [24]

I began the verse as a penance, but it came to me that this could be a prayer, as from a warrior on the eve of battle. He would have liked that. *But enough, Angelita, of all this shriving.* That's what he would have said. It is not such a crime to fail, though it is a sin if you cannot forgive yourself.

No, this was not the poem for him. I did not finish it. I should be drafting the lines that would win the poetry tourney—a *joust*, Uncle Juan had said, in a bullring. And how proud Abuelo would be if I did, I would make his face so *wide*, and wipe away a little of my thoughtlessness. Uncle Juan was right. Abuelo would have so enjoyed the day: coaching me on strategy, assessing the challengers, reading the judges' sober miens. Such a game he would have made of it, to make me feel safe. We would be knights of old, vying heart and soul for a handkerchief.

Since gaps in this account will not be tolerated by those whose offices are holy, I cannot forestall his dying much longer. But not yet, not . . . *yet*.

We had a bullring to visit. And I had a battle to join, under the standard of El Dorado, and an old lion as my counsellor.

He had been there before.

I'd have my shield of learning, my shining corselet of wit, and for sheer grace and quickness in the ring I'd have my twin with me: *Amanda, Princess of the Cornflowers.*

And only she, only she would lift my veil.

I had so wanted a spectacle.

To prepare for it, I let my mind turn to everything I had read about the sacrificing of bulls, bullocks, heifers, fatted calves, sea calves—oxen, bison even, and any and all contests against them. Herakles wrestling the white bull Phaëthon, forcing its mighty horns to the earth. And the white bull of Poseidon, father of the Minotaur—the Apis bulls of Memphis, the bull hunts of ancient Iberia—there was so much to know! I did know our Iberian bulls would rather die than run—even from armoured horses and knights keen for jousting. First lesson: *Die rather than run.* Well, maybe for the knight but surely not the bull. And which was I to be?

I saw how things would have to go. Down in the sand, pairs of combatants locked in mortal struggle. The last line of the contestant's poem rings out; all eyes turn to the Emperor. Thumb up, thumb down. The fanfares to rival Jericho, jugglers and jesters in the intermezzos. The day wears on, crowd favourites distinguish themselves—side bets, punters and touts. Fisticuffs in the aisles. The Maid battles on—quickness, grace, strategy, her arms . . .

The final pairing, the equal contest of noble adversaries—the bow, the curtsy—lord to lady, lady to lord. Acrostics and anagrams, reversible verses, triple echoes and *dobles entendidos.* Sonnet and gloss, eclogue and elegy, pyrotechnical panegyrics!

And then fireworks bursting across the sky like a thousand pomegranates launched by wild urchins—the booming of mortars now—for *there had been a tie.*

A tie.

Both are spared, both crowned—an unprecedented double laurel, and yet the bloodthirsty crowd *roars its approval down.* Then, soon, too soon . . . the lamentations at her early retirement from life in the ring. The encomiastic farewells, the tribute from her greatest adversary.

A quiet life, a lifelong friendship. People salute her in the street. She is allowed to walk in the street. She is walking with a friend.

She has a friend.

By the time the day came, I knew the tourney would not be as my imagination had painted it. Still, I told myself, it would be the most interesting thing to happen to me in years. The only thing. I might as well have been in my room for four years. Born of a vestal. Raised by wolves.

It turned out the bullring was available only because the Archbishop decided bullfights were not to be held during the festival of Guadalupe this year. The lake was high. It was the end of the rainy season and she was supposed to be our island city's protectress against the Flood. The Archbishop may have thought she needed to concentrate.

It wasn't even a real bullring.

Well, it was real, but not permanent, not an arena like the Roman Coliseum, but a rickety assemblage of wooden bleachers and scaffolding that could be dismantled in sections and stacked, then remounted at a day's notice. The carpenters had honed this to a fine art—indeed, many also built theatrical sets.

The contest was not decided on the sand, in pairings and jousts. There were four hundred contestants, an unheard-of number. I had only to do the arithmetic. It would have taken days. The poems were not improvised on the spot, on some whimsy of the Viceroy's—a theme, a metre, a style. Instead, we'd had two weeks to prepare. Two weeks?—I could have filled a book. And the theme was no noble fancy but rather Our Lady of Guadalupe. Now *there* was a surprise. The whole city was obsessed with Guadalupe, Guadalupe. . . .

But at least it was to be held in the Plaza del Volador. It was right next to the palace, but I didn't care so much about courtiers. No, I hoped I might see the Indian fliers who each day spun outwards on long ropes from a great whirling wheel five storeys in the air.

There *was* pageantry for our poetry joust. On the day of the city-wide invitation to contend in the tourney, we could hear the parade coming towards us, since ours was one of the few paved streets in our barrio. Sumptuous silver-trimmed carriages rumbled over the stones. There was even a sedan chair (I had never actually seen one) got up as Apollo's chariot, its sides emblazoned with gold and copper suns.

And such a dizzy cacophony! An intoxicate musical mob marched (out-of-step) drummed (off-beat) and intermittently blared (off-key)— effortless masters of this most intricate musical counterpoint. There were carriage bells and fifty church bells and a boys' choir. Up and down the block rose laughter and murmurs of wonder, exclamations and shouts of recognition as the menagerie passed: figures dressed head to foot as wild animals and unicorns and other fabulous beasts, spattered with mud to the knees. And as though driving them from the realm, there followed on his white charger a knight in a full suit of plate burnished black and gold-chased. As he passed abreast of me in the doorway, a smudged and weary-looking woman knelt in the street. Her male companion brusquely pulled her up—*it isn't really real.* Her face wore a quizzical look as she puzzled over the paradox. And somehow she did not look quite so tired.

A phalanx of soldiers now, brandishing halberds behind a troupe of Indian dancers, forty or so.

They shushed.

All the dancers wore bracelets and anklets thick with countless little shells, and as each *danzante* swished and whirled and bounded, the sound rose two-score multiplied. Swiftly there mounted among us the susurrus of a wind that surges and gusts along the oaks on a windy night at the hacienda. And to remember this I felt a kind of hush falling in me.

On they went with crowns of turquoises and bobbing quetzal plumes, precious cloaks embroidered in hieroglyphs, and feather capes of quetzal and heron. . . .

Next walked envoys of the religious orders and the Inquisition. A company of mummers and jesters scampered about with toy wands behind a knot of university scholars holding up True Learning's shining silver sceptres. Garish allegorical floats, and the indispensable dragon—*No hay procesión sin tarasca.*[†] Or that's what everybody said. This was my first one.

[†]No procession without a dragon or monster

Then came the parade marshal, the bearer of so great a burden of dignity it bowed his legs. He carried the silver mace of his office, and on a staff of solid silver *THE PLACARD.* For Saturday, twelve o'clock noon, on the eighth day of December, in the year of Our Lord sixteen hundred and sixty-three, the Placard announced the grand theme . . .

LITERARY PALAESTRA
AND POETICAL JOUST
IN WHICH
THE IMPERIAL, PONTIFICAL AND EVER AUGUST
MEXICAN ATHENS
proposes a design of the triumph of the
Most Holy Virgin of Guadalupe
to be sketched on a versical canvas in imperishable colours,
in which she treads upon the Dragon of sin, heresy and idolatry
and thereby abates the Great Flood sent to the Dragon's annihilation . . . [25]

As the marshal with the placard passed, it began lightly to rain, which served to remind us of the gravity of the theme. When the judging began two weeks later, a light rain was still falling. The Plaza del Volador seemed the sagest of choices now, since during the floods of 1629, it was one of only three plazas not to go under. Some of the lowest streets lay ankle-deep for five years thereafter. We all might hope Guadalupe was concentrating now.

I approached the plaza with Uncle Juan. We had to go the last four blocks on foot through streets so crowded as to be impassable by coach. I was peevish and glum, knowing this was not to be a real joust at all. But I was cheered to see a shop selling nothing but bullfighting gear, and the streets so festive. And there at the plaza entrance, beside the university gates and just above a little flight of steps, towered a massive bulletin:

SEGURO: AZAR DEL TOREO†

†CAUTION:
BULLFIGHT IN
PROGRESS

I laughed outright. Some wit had scratched in an *n* to make *TOREO* into *TORnEO*. They wanted a real tourney too. Caution: poetry hazard.

The bullring looked impressively large. The plaza itself seemed more riot than festival. Hundreds of vendors had spread out their wares with no hint of order or pattern. Thousands, now, milled through a square littered with trampled fruit, pottery and crushed straw hats.

The only clear route was in the shadow of the palace walls, where the guards permitted no commerce. Uncle Juan took me firmly by the arm; there was a great deal of intimate jostling and more than one impertinently placed hand before we reached the wall. This was becoming a very adult affair. Well, it's a borrowed dress anyway, I thought, but this was bravado, for however adult my body might look from the outside, I did not feel entirely sure of myself in a plaza full of unwashed men.

Exotic tapestries had been hung from the palace balconies, and I noticed something curious: running from the corner of our plaza to the main square was a narrow street with nothing but barber stalls, with their lancets and leeches and bloodletting basins, their whetstones and razors, their brushes and soaps.

Then we were inside the bullring and there *was* blood in the sand.

It was thrilling and disconcerting. For an instant I wondered if it might turn out as I'd imagined after all.

But as we were seated on the platform with all the luminaries to await the Viceroy's arrival, we were treated to a farce. Anticipating His Excellency's Excellent Lateness, the tournament secretary had thought to provide us with the same sort of diversion that preceded the bull-fights. It was that adventure of don Quixote in which the indomitable knight jousts with the furiously valiant Rinaldo for the legendary golden helmet of Mambrino. The great helm is, alas, a bronze barber's basin worn on a rainy day just such as this to preserve the hat of a barber not furiously valiant but today floridly fat. The barber's 'grey-dappled steed' was the most abject ass, infinitely worse than Sancho's, indeed of a class with the Knight of the Woeful Figure's own charger. Rozinante, the saddest *rozin*† ever bestrid. And this gave me a quiet moment. This was a wound barely closed. And as the ancient Rozinante lurched about drunkenly under the weight of don Quixote, I remembered this was just the sort of horse expended nowadays on fighting bulls. There came then into my mind the most heart-sickening image of that old jade swung up on the curved horns of a bull the size of a windmill, and with all the wind's irresistible power unstrung and gutted and slung to the ground.

†jade

So when I was given, next, a chance to laugh I took it gratefully. Enter don Quixote's Lady Dulcinea, a hairy-chested serving wench played by a bearded dwarf. Even Uncle Juan had tears running from his eyes. And now came the mighty Rinaldo, unhorsed and japing about under his barber basin as the old knight tried to run him through with a lance. Sancho, the realist, who fancied he saw a barber and no fighting knight, was trying anxiously to restrain his master.

"Leave hold, Sancho—hugeous jolt-head—thou eternal disbeliever . . ."

Hugeous jolt-head . . . eternal disbeliever . . .

I had woken Grandfather during this very section. I wanted to protest the cruel treatment Cervantes had yet again served up to the old Quixote. Why didn't Cervantes just let him go home? After only a hundred pages don Quixote already had so many fine stories, and true friends to tell them to.

"Read again, Angelina. Maybe you were too angry with Cervantes. Not every windmill is a giant, I know. And what looks like a funny adventure sometimes isn't, it's true. But as we look back, the same may sometimes be said of a disaster. Tell me when you've found it, and come and read. It has been too long since I read this myself. Now let me sleep another minute or two. . . ."

He didn't go back to sleep but, pretending to, watched me with a green squinty eye under the arm flung across his brow. So I found it, and nudged him. And as I read for him he lay back in the hammock and looked off into the west. Some while after I finished, he nodded and smiled. "There. Thank you, Angel—for do you know, I had forgotten the proverb, which is of course the very best part."

> . . . Let me tell thee, Sancho, it is the part of noble and generous spirits to pass by trifles. . . . 'Where one door shuts, another opens. . . .' Thus fortune, which last night deceived us with the false prospect of an adventure, this morning offers us a real one to make amends.[26]

I had not believed in the magic of this day, and had been only too ready to slide back into the gloom emanating from me as much as from that dark house. Unlike my great hero the nun-ensign, I had never even tried to free myself. I was the hugeous jolt-head. In that moment I felt Grandfather's presence for the second time, and the last—heard the husk of emotion in his voice, saw the big beaming face. And I was delighted to be in a crowd just like this, laughing till I cried like them.

The new Viceroy did look splendid riding into the ring and up to the platform on a jet black stallion caparisoned in pale green silks. The triumphal entry had been the Viceroy's idea, as an advent far more dramatic than in a university lecture theatre. For the first time, the finalists were all on the podium and the Viceroy himself read their poems aloud—then decided on the spot. Still . . . the ceremony I had in mind involved me in at least a *vuelta*† or two on that black stallion. I could ride him. I sat a horse passably well—I am my father's daughter after all.

†victory lap

Ten thousand people turned out, and three bishops. It was a lot, more than I could ever have imagined. Did one city really need three?

And never had I seen such an array of brilliant university gowns as on the platform that day, with its unsteady pulpit and the carved judges' chairs, each under its own canopy. I watched them all watching me up there along with them on the dais, and thought, Today the Royal University *has come to me*.

I took first place—and I did make a friend. Second prize went to a boy three or four years older than I. It created a sensation that 'children' should take the first two places, and the University's professor of poetry only the third. But the professor seemed so genuinely pleased for us that I liked him instantly. The boy, Carlos,[†] was vaguely descended from Góngora, the greatest poet of our language. Grandfather would have said the 'two greatest poets'—the greatest being the early Góngora, with the late as distant a second as all others came a distant third to him.

[†]Carlos de Sigüenza y Góngora, 1645–1700, mathematician, astronomer, historian, mythographer

We were at a reception at the parade marshal's house when I saw the other prize-winners again. It must have taken a cargo ship to supply textiles enough for all the dresses: velvets and satins and silks in crimson and violet and lemon. Jewels and pearls by the hod and barrow, and silver more plentiful than tin. Capes and plumed hats, jewelled swords—and spurs—silver spurs half the length of a man's forearm. The risk of a goring on a dance floor surely exceeded the rigours of the ring.

The courtyard was a delirious polyhedral arrangement of waist-high hedges, benches under fruit trees, stone paths in diagonals through flower beds. We were led in stately pomp towards the platform on the north side. Above us for three full storeys was a living green drapery of creepers abloom in fiery pinks and peach. I had no idea such a place might exist in this stone desert of a city. Like ours, this was another of the great houses with three tiers of colonnades running around a patio—but open to the sky, not barred like a prison window. *Here* was a courtyard and a fountain. Not a warehouse, not a half-fountain crushed like a tin prison cup.

I was standing on the dais with the officials and other finalists—of course, all men—and I wondered at the water pressure. This fountain squirted and gushed and sported and rolled as if the sprite of a fountain bathing in itself. We were, it was true, on the Alameda, just at the end of the aqueduct, but was there maybe a little wind-assisted pump somewhere? Such reflections on hydraulics soon leading me to notice that the soft jostle on the dais was just as intimate as in the plaza, and less impertinent only to the extent that similarly placed collisions were passed off here as accidents.

Moorish rugs were spread over that half of the dais protected by a canvas pavilion, open across the front and patterned upon the tents of distant Arabia. From the pavilion's corners, indeed from most of the courtyard columns, rich pennants, paper streamers and bunting drooped prettily. Throughout the patio, people posed studiedly under a fine, warm *llovizna*.[†] The evening sky had reached the palest blue edge of

[†]drizzle

grey. In that soft light the ladies gloried in their lambent fabrics; the men stood in quiet counterpoise in soft browns and blacks—charcoals and glosses and mattes. Among us at elbow height wobbled trays of chocolate and nutmeats borne by proud, puffing nymphs with beribboned hair. We were all at least half-aware of the beauty of the scene, and ennobled in a small way by our role in it. The rainfall blessed the women round the dais with sparkling curls and a hint of glaze on our lips, our cheeks, our wrists.

The glazing of our eyes was next effected by the speech makers.

When at last the quartet started up, I turned to Carlos, who had maintained a geometrically fixed distance from me all this time, and asked if the composer was Zarlino. I was quick to admit that I'd read a good deal of orchestral music but had heard next to nothing actually performed. Indeed it was, he said. Perhaps he might be permitted to escort me to a concert or two this month? He was home for all of December from the Jesuit seminary in Puebla.

This was all very quick. I would have to learn to be more careful about such easy openings. Coming up from just behind me was the other prize-winner (and to think I'd assumed the competition had ended), asking if I agreed with Zarlino, against Galilei, that music should have its own voice and not imitate the spoken word.

"My agreement, sir, might depend on the words spoken. In this past hour I find myself quite vehemently swayed towards Zarlino."

The conversation, as it must, turned to the competition. Carlos briefly feigned shock that a girl should be chosen, let alone a *doncella* of such tender years. (He was so much older.) But the professor remained so gracious that Carlos soon confided he was relieved not to have embarrassed the family and the name of Góngora, entirely. His true love was mathematics, and he would have the Chair of Mathematics one day.

To repay their grace I reminded them of what the Knight of the Woeful Figure had said about poetry prizes. "Always strive to carry off the second prize, for the first is forever awarded as a favour . . . the second going to the one who should have placed first—"

"Making third place, second," said the professor, smiling.

"And the first place, third," I continued.

"Which, as we know," Carlos said, "is in actuality second. . . ."

But such an unholy fuss was made when it became known that I had been born in the very year Miguel Sánchez published the first great work on our Virgin of Guadalupe. And had I not just won a great tourney taking her glory as its theme? Surely, said one fellow, this was a sign she had blessed the outcome herself.

It was Carlos who made the discovery. Just how old *was* I? he'd asked, that is, if he might presume. . . . So I was born in 1648! (Truly mathematics was his gift.) But what of it, don Carlos?

"Does the lady think it mere *coincidencia*?" he asked.

Here was an interesting word, I said (because it was new to me—and just as new was the sensation of being caught at a disadvantage). Had he meant the *coincidentia oppositorum*? But no, obviously he did not mean Guadalupe and I were opposites. Indeed he seemed to mean the reverse—but then what was the reverse of a union of opposites? A disunion of opposites, or a union of dissimilarities—or a complete nonrelation of perfect irrelevancies? Well, I couldn't stand there gaping forever, so I played for time.

"And where on earth, don Carlos, did you hear—"

"It has been newly employed," he said brusquely, "by a distinguished English scientist, Tomás Browne."

Fortunately he now went on to laboriously define it, which gained me the time I needed.

"But don Carlos, what can this new term possibly mean? To bring two events into conjunction precisely to say there is none? To say that what appears to mean something means nothing at all? Does your Englishman not offer to refute Superstition only at the cost of making Hazard his cult?"

Just such a conversation as I had dreamt of having one day in the capital . . .

I went on now rather eagerly—according to my information, English was a mere dialect, a gumbo of German and French, possessing a simplified lexicon improvised to communicate the rudimentary sentiments of global trade and the terse niceties of piracy.

"Which would make it, would it not, gentlemen, akin to the pidgin the Spanish use in the Philippines?"

England, its manners, its mercantile impulse, its rough tongue, creeps into many heated discussions here, for many of my fellow citizens are nervous about privateering, and about being cut off from Spain. Since the rout of our Armada, we spoke of the English, I imagined, much as the Romans had of the pirate fleets of the Vandals.

At this point we had attracted a small audience. It was the best part of the day, a real piratical free-for-all. People jumping in, flailing about, and whenever some fool or parlour wit would take my side, I'd change tacks, for the sheer fun of it. So thick was the spread of confusion that only Carlos seemed to notice, and smiled, I thought, a little wickedly.

"And after all," I said, on just such a tack, "there is our own debt to Latin. Few would think our Castilian the poorer for it."

"No great poetry," thundered some bluff wit in return, "has ever come from any *Protestant* country!"

"Was there not once word," I asked, "of a great flourishing on their stages at the same time as Spain's own best day?" I had heard of at least one great play—on the wizard Faustus, no less—and was distracted by a thought: how curious it was that such a character should take the name of 'one favoured by the augurs.'"

"But *señorita*, what notice should we take of their dramatists," Carlos said slyly, recalling me from my reverie, "when the English have closed their own theatres down?"

"*Señor*, do the Iberians not consider our Mexican culture to be a pidgin of like kind, precisely when they themselves have not produced a great poet for, what, a generation now? We should not be similarly complacent." He seemed prepared to agree so I tacked instead into rougher waters, arguing that any country capable of producing a great queen might just be ready to make one decent poet.

"Perhaps you'd care to amplify—"

"Well, yes, don Carlos, happily. Imagine, if you will, a great *pidgin* poet."

There was a gratifying moment of silence. Carlos nodded, appearing to consider this seriously. Then a thick-whiskered fellow said, "*Señorita*, you have the mind of a man."

"Ah, the mind of a man." I eyed them each in turn, taking my time. "A man, perhaps, *caballeros*. But *which* man . . ."

We were interrupted then, and I felt sorry Carlos was going back so soon to the seminary in Puebla. But we still had a month and there would be other receptions.

I did get to take home a glittering prize. A jewelled snuff box I couldn't wait to use.

As for the winning poem, I'm sorry it was not so good. Better than Carlos's but not much. Here in the city, craftiness and the contrivances of fashion counted for more than substance—*Art takes form, form takes substance, substance takes craft.* Or so it was said. How they worshipped at the shrines of their subtle framing devices. And at lines ending in unexpected rhymes, such as *urraca / saque / triquitraque / matraca. . . .* I would do many like this to earn my keep.

I was already a little sick of hearing about Guadalupe, but I owed her something better. One day I would write a poem for Carlos, for he had been truly passionate about her. If his poem had displayed slightly less skill, so also had it used less trickery than mine.

After just a few such experiences in the arena, I would come to feel that poetry written for the tastes of its time could almost never be great. We must write through our time, or even to it, but never *for* it. Poets must concern themselves with neither fashion nor even what people want, but with vision—raw and immediate—of what lies beyond our eyes. Beneath this, our great Dream of Common Sense.

But a poetry competition was not the place for such concerns, and this not quite the day for leaving the last childish things behind.

People were kind. "The Poetess, the Poetess!" they had cried as I left the ring, and again on my way to the carriage from the parade marshal's house. At the receptions that month, the gentlemen proved very attentive. Having Isabel's features and increasingly her form no longer seemed so terrible.

And I was out of my cave.

The boulder had been rolled back—the jar unsealed and Hope[†] broken free. I was determined Aunt María would never seal me in again.

[†]probable reference to Pandora

There were receptions and luncheons and balls for the Poetess to go to, and she would no longer be denied. In another fortnight the prize-winners were to have an audience with their majesties, the Viceroy and his German wife. A German. Here was a people that *elected* its emperors.

Her hair, they said, was of spun gold.

So much the better—but I was to meet my first *Goth.*

. . . tiende la vista a cuanto
alcanza a divisarse
desde este monte excelso
que es injuria de Atlante.
Mira aquestos ganados
que, inundando los valles,
de los prados fecundos
las esmeraldas pacen.

Mira en cándidos copos
la leche, que al cuajarse,
afrenta los jazmines
de la Aurora que nace.

Mira, de espigas rojas,
en los campos formarse
pajizos chamelotes
a las olas del aire.

Mira de esas montañas
los ricos minerales,
cuya preñez es oro,
rubíes y diamantes.

Mira, en el mar soberbio,
en conchas congelarse
el llanto de la Aurora
en perlas orientales.

Mira de esos jardines
los fecundos frutales,
de especies diferentes
dar frutos admirables.

Mira con verdes pinos
los montes coronarse:

con árboles que intentan
del Cielo ser Gigantes.

Escucha la armonía
de las canoras aves
que en coros diferentes
forman dulces discantes.

Mira de uno a otro Polo
los Reinos dilatarse,
dividiendo regiones
los brazos de los mares,

y mira cómo surcan
de las veleras naves
las ambiciosas proas
sus cerúleos cristales.

Mira entre aquellas grutas
diversos animales:
a unos, salir feroces;
a otros, huir cobardes.

Todo, bello Narciso,
sujeto a mi dictamen,
son posesiones mías,
son mis bienes dotales.

Y todo será Tuyo,
si Tú con pecho afable
depones lo severo
y llegas a adorarme.

. . . so let your gaze take in
all the land it surveys
from this lofty summit
that leaves Atlas in the shade.

See, into the valleys
those streams of cattle pour
to graze on the emeralds
that stud each valley floor.

See, like drifts of snow,
the curdled milk in jars
puts the jasmine to shame
with which dawn snuffs out stars.

See red-gold ears of grain
sending billows everywhere
like waves of watered silk
stirred by waves of the air.

Behold the rich ores
those swelling mountains hold:
how they teem with diamonds,
glow with rubies and gold.

See the leaping ocean
how the dawn's welling tears
are congealed in conch shells
and turn into pearls.

See, in those gardens,
how the fruit trees flourish;
behold the broad range
of rich fruits they nourish.

See how green crowns of pine
on high summits endeavour

to repeat the exploit
of the giants storming heaven.

Listen to the music
of all those singing birds.
In all of their choirs
sweet descants are heard.

See from pole to pole
realms spread far and wide.
Behold the many regions
which arms of sea divide,

and see the ambitious prows
of those swift-sailing ships—
how they cleave in their passage
the azure's crystal drift.

See amid those grottoes
creatures of every sort,
some timidly fleeing,
some bursting fiercely forth.

All this, fair Narcissus,
is mine to dispose of;
these are my possessions,
they accompany my love.

All is yours to enjoy
if you cease to be cold,
put severity aside
and love me heart and soul. . . .

JUANA INÉS
DE LA CRUZ,

"Echo, finding
Narcissus on a
mountaintop"

THE DIVINE
NARCISSUS

Alan Trueblood, trans.

t had turned out to be a fine day of jousting, after all, but what I missed in the bullring that day was spectacle, high drama. There was low comedy, and the high comedy of our English-pirate free-for-all. And low drama, for the two full minutes it took the Viceroy to look over every part of me before awarding his prize. No, I wanted colours and costumes and light—fireworks, fine voices and much finer poetry. *Ceremony.* I was not so very different from everyone else here. Juvenal was not mistaken in prescribing bread and circuses as the philtre for enthralling us.

Uncle Juan had largely financed the tournament, so as we rode back home from the parade marshal's house I gave him back the snuff box. I couldn't help asking if my victory had been paid for, since he'd paid for everything else. The carriage drew up before the house.

"You have done more for my standing with the new Viceroy in one day, Juana Inés, than my underwriting a dozen of these affairs."

He helped me down from the carriage, then walked quickly to the door. But once there, he paused to hold it open for me. There he stood: big and stocky, earnest and calm. And for no particular reason he struck me as brave, not in bluster and brandish of steel, but quietly, steadily brave. I liked him. As I brushed past, he held up a hand to detain me. "Oh—and Juana Inés, whatever else I may do," he said with a wry quirk of a smile, "I never tell a viceroy what poets he should like."

He did not posture or pretend. This was a business proposition, and while business was obviously good, I sensed it was also precarious. His network of alliances went to the top of both the *Cabildo* and the *Audiencia,* and into the lower echelons of the court. But one does not approach a viceroy with money. I was an asset now. I found I didn't mind. I had met a few of his associates at the house. Serious, earnest . . . if anything, a little preoccupied. Since they were much like him, I guessed that these were not just associates but friends. No posturers or hypocrites. I'm sure Uncle Juan knew these, too, and saw to their handling and care. What I liked is that he didn't have them at his house.

But he was not much of a family man. He seemed no more interested in poor Magda than he had been in me up till now. And there was something strained between him and Aunt María, who seemed more anxious with secrets all the time. His parents we hardly saw. I did have an intuition that the canvas dam across the courtyard and fountain had been more their idea than his, and that they might have preferred to get their water elsewhere. It arrived in the city all the way from Chapultepec springs via the aqueduct to the Alameda. The mains had been clay, then lead for a while; then someone somewhere in the city administration read a book of Roman history, and they were clay again (whose almost weekly repairs, in our neighbourhood at least, Uncle Juan paid for).

He also paid his debts, and he knew just what to get me. The Poetess and her escorts had been reserved a private box at the theatre. I *loved* the theatre—I just knew it, even though I'd never been. But I had read a hundred plays, made them burn like fire in my mind—*these* were our painted books.

He wouldn't come with us, being too serious for such things, but he did insist Aunt María and Magda go. It would do them good to get out. It would do Magda good.

They squeezed—parts of me—into another of Magda's old gowns. But it was of a lovely, sky-blue satin, which set off to advantage, I supposed, my black hair and black eyes. And then we were in the carriage, as the three of us had been on so many trips to the cathedral. I could not ride even a short way facing backwards without feeling ill, so as always María and Magda sat facing me. The ride was mercifully brief.

It was the single greatest thrill of my life to arrive for the first time at the theatre, ablaze with light, in a gleaming coach drawn by matched horses, steel tack flashing silver. As I stepped down I could hear the orchestra warming up above the shouts and cries of the coachmen jostling for position.

Inside, we met a group of Magda's friends, a girl and three young gentlemen. "Magda, why haven't we met your cousin before? You didn't tell us she was so beautiful . . . and that dress, what a splendid hue! You should try that colour yourself." Magda's evening was proving visibly less transcendent than mine.

Although the vicinity of the private boxes was perfectly dignified, looking down into the pit I could see why the public theatres were called *corrales*, and this one, El Coliseo, no less. I had not expected so much hooting. The idea of calling out to the players, warning them of an intrigue or ambush, well, that was perhaps the best part of the show. The *entractos* were also popular affairs and in parts delightful. There was a Mexica *mitote*[†] with ancient instruments, but I was glad it ended quickly as I had no intention of being homesick. Between acts one and two was a farcical skit that went over well, and a later interlude of ballads. The play itself was a local production stealing shamelessly from Ovid's version of the tale of Narcissus, and yet I was strangely fascinated.

Afterwards, in the milling and stir in the forecourt, I spotted a poster for last week's show: *The Nun-Ensign*. The awful play I had read a hundred times. This was my fellow prisoner and hero—fugitive nun, duellist and lady muleskinner. How I would have loved to see her just once outside my head.

On the way home all I could find to talk about was the play. Though I knew it to be no masterpiece, I was thrilled to hear for the first time poetic texts from the lips of trained actors, to see passions so nakedly expressed. On and on I chattered like a songbird between two ravens—countenances growing ever darker—about how certain lines seemed to weaken this effect or that, how the themes had been muddied, the symbols clumsily worked. I was talking now to work this out for myself, for during the slower moments in the theatre I'd had an idea for my own version of Echo and Narcissus. There'd be a prologue featuring two couples, one European, the other native Mexican. The Mexicans would be America and Occident. . . .

I would make Echo the brilliant angel who had fallen from Paradise— *then* rebelled. That was important. And at first sight of Narcissus it's as if she's always known him, who is after all as beautiful as any angel. In love, she takes him to a mountaintop and offers him a new paradise, a new world, if only she can tempt him to stay with her. . . .

I didn't have it all worked out. What little I did manage to say probably didn't make much sense to Magda and María anyway. But instead of looking bored or annoyed, they were watching me carefully. Thus encouraged, I even managed to find fault with Ovid's own vision of Narcissus, which had always seemed too harsh, simplistic. I saw Narcissus more as the victim of his yearnings for perfection, as Christlike—

"What?" croaked Aunt María, across from me, "What did you just say?" She leaned forward till her nose nearly touched my face.

[†] a traditional dances

"I said—"

"Is that what they teach young girls out in that godless countryside—to *blaspheme?*"

"I'm sorry, *Tia,*" I stammered, "but I didn't blas—"

"The Son of God, narcissistic! You heard her, Magda."

"She said it."

"I did *not.*"

"Did Isabel teach you to call your elders liars, too?"

"I was only trying to correct—I did *not* call Christ narcissistic. Narcissus, in his pain, was Christlike—there's nothing wrong with *saying* this. The teachings of the Greeks anticipate His Gospel. The Church has accepted—"

"What the Church teaches—at least here in this city, Juana Inés, is humility. Here, what we expect of ourselves is only the most careful soul-searching. Here in *our* city, we would never allow a child, still less a female child, to run riot through the pagan texts of antiquity *spouting blasphemies on the Passion!* Evidently you are one of those who have no respect for the Holy Office—"

"Have you ever *seen* an *auto,* Juana?" asked Magda suddenly.

"No," I said, grateful for what I thought was a change of subject. We had pulled up in front of the house but Aunt María, resting her hand on the handle, made no move to get down.

"We *have.* Several," she said coolly. "The effect has been lasting." She glanced at Magda. "Perhaps we may still broaden your marvellous education in some small way. You seem to enjoy riding in our carriage. Tomorrow I think we shall take you on a little tour. Magda has been a very enthusiastic student of our local history. There is much in this city you have yet to see. . . ."

In the morning, Aunt María wore her usual black silk, and a black veil. We all had on our heavy crosses. Magda's dress was of a purple velvet and suited her slight frame. Over her crucifix she wore a string of warped pearls of a fashion called *barruecas,* much prized in the city.

She was almost pretty. Her hair was a dark, flat brown. Her profile was not so prepossessing as her mother's. Her one unfortunate feature was her eyes: very small and deep-set, the irises so large as to leave scant room between her lids for the whites. The colour was an attractive one, a nut brown, but one could not help thinking of the polished pips of small, soft fruit, the cherimoya, perhaps, or the lychee from Cathay. Her nose was of a normal size but—between those tiny, beady eyes— betrayed a certain thickness at the bridge.

Sundays we usually ate little before mid-afternoon, but this day's break- fast was whipped chocolate, pork hocks and eggs fried in lard. As we left the house my escorts each carried a small assortment of fresh roses, out of season now and brought in at great expense from the south each year for Guadalupe's festival. Whites and yellows and reds ... the effect was quite gay. In the coach they insisted on sitting on my bench, on either side of me. It was my first inkling that this was not to be a ride like the others.

What they'd said was true: I liked the coach rides. I loved the horses, the rasp and chiselling of silver-shod hoofs over the flags. María had once confided her belief that their collection of coaches, gigs and car- riages was the finest in the New World. "We choose our things," she'd announced then, "on the basis of elegance, not vain show." The carriage cab was small and of a hardwood finished in black lacquer. The spokes were a lacquered grey. Inside, there *was* opulence: the walls were surfaced in the finest Chinese silk, deep brown and embroidered with gold dragons. The seats were thickly upholstered in velvet of a matching brown. The door handles, painted black outside, revealed themselves to be of bronze, as were the door bolts, gleaming and heavy. Fore and aft were sliding panels. The rear one was bolted shut, the one forward was open to allow communication with the driver. The heavy wooden side panels were drawn back for our tour.

We were not going to church.

When this dawned on me I was stunned, unable to imagine what might deflect Aunt María from the cathedral on a Sunday morning.

Aunt María and Cousin Magda were taking me over the route and to the stations of the last great *auto de fe* of 1649. Thirteen people burned at the stake, a hundred more in effigy.

Magda could only have been five or six at the time of the *auto*, yet fif- teen years later the sheer volume of ghastly detail she'd retained or had since learned was appalling. While I was to learn that to hear a story told can be more terrible than seeing the horror itself.

Our carriage had barely reached the corner when Aunt María said, "It started here. A neighbour came to tell us the Proclamation was being read through the streets. We rushed out of the house, Magda beside me, running on her chubby legs to keep up. Everyone was moving towards the *casas de la Inquisición,* where the processions began."

"I *remember* them," said Magda, in a tone of reminiscence. "Minstrels coming down the street in bright colours, trumpets blaring, fifes piping . . ."

"Every block or two," said Aunt María, "the procession would pause for the chief constable to dictate the Proclamation to the crier." He called out to all the nobles and their families an invitation to attend, wearing their finest, a general *auto de fe* on the eleventh of April.

Since I was now a noted Poetess, it might interest me to know that María had always preferred the Portuguese *'auto-<u>da</u>-fé.'*

"Our Castilian phrase means simply 'act of faith.' But for the Portuguese, Juana Inés, it means 'the act that *gives* faith.' We will give you some help with this today."

The coach clattered towards the Monastery of Santo Domingo. A light rain fell. The streets were quiet, with everyone at Mass at one of the fifty churches throughout the city. My aunt and cousin began to describe the days leading up to the *auto*, when at least thirty thousand celebrants made their way to the capital, swelling its population to four hundred thousand. The city's fifteen thousand carriages, most now in use at once, found room to pass only with difficulty even at three in the morning. All the plazas stood brightly lit, packed with people come to refresh themselves with glasses of *atole* or chocolate or *pulque*. On almost every corner Indian ladies were selling tortillas and tamales. Every inn in the capital was full. Each morning found thousands of revellers rolled up in blankets, asleep in the plazas and under the arcades, or in doorways and alleys.

Our carriage lurched to a halt beside the canal—we had nearly run down a beggar, a man of about fifty, with the aspect of a Gypsy or a Moor. Barefoot, in grimy rags, he carried a little bundle slung over his shoulder as if he were travelling, yet with nowhere to go, as he wandered back and forth across the road. The stench from the canal was overpowering. A carcass must be floating there, and the canal silted in. Magda and María had not brought the roses for colour or cheer but as nosegays. They fed at them now like ghastly hummingbirds.

Magda asked if I ever heard from my father, if I thought he might ever come back. It was the first word anyone in that house had ever spoken of him. I could not meet her gleaming, hateful eyes as she then turned to me and recounted the stories that were in circulation all that year of 1649—tales of new and hideously effective tortures and of the vast sums wasted on bribes to Inquisition officials . . . who were of course utterly incorruptible.

"Some of the accused had been turned in by their own children," said Magda, glancing past me at her mother. "Others by neighbours or in-laws or friends. They said the familiars of the Inquisition were everywhere gathering testimony."

Aunt María spoke, not turning from the window. "One neighbour whispered that the admiral of the Leeward Fleet had been arrested for Judaizing. Another said no it was the *proveedor general* of the Windward Fleet. His wife had grown so arrogant as to demand that all requests for appointments with her be made in writing."

"Mother even knew her a little, didn't you, Mother?" Before María could answer Magda exclaimed, "One woman was arrested—you know what for? Just smiling at the mention of the blessed Virgin!"

I remembered then that my cousin had been the one to serve me breakfast, and the pleasure she had taken. I felt my stomach lift as we lurched through a pothole. The closeness in the cab was becoming unbearable.

I caught a glimpse of the cathedral. We jarred over the rough paving for another two blocks, then turned east and came to a little square. María called for the driver to stop—we were getting out. *Gracias a Dios.* Aunt María held the door as I stepped down. Opposite us on the north side of the square was a small pink church built of the rough *tezontle* blocks I knew from the mountains. Early Mass had just let out, and over the heads of those streaming through the tall doors I could see a rose-coloured altar and pillars of pink marble spirals. The windows must have been stained in the same colour, for pale rose diagonals fell through the smoke in the nave.

The square looked festive at first. Indian musicians with their pipes and drums. A company of mummers calling to the passersby to gather round. Running the full length of the plaza's west side was a string of workshops, which I was surprised to see open. But then with Guadalupe's feast day coming on Wednesday, perhaps they were rushing to finish a special commission from the temple. Out in the open air, I looked about for the courage to tell María I'd had enough.

Occupying the entire block across the street to the east was an austere building with none of the flourishes for which the city's masons are noted. And it was towards that building we now walked. The iron gates were on the southwest corner. Two girls my age were giggling and flirting with the guards stiffly standing one to each side of the entrance. Overhead hung a banner on a silver staff, but angled in such a way that I could not read it until we were at the gates.

I had thought the building had three storeys; it was two—each no less than four times our height. I could see the banner's emblem now. It was a wooden cross, rough and unplaned, knots like the swellings of lesions all down its sides. Just inside the gates were several counters and offices arranged around a small patio, achingly bright in the sun. Running east and north were two long corridors. There was an impression of coolness. A cool draft of air flowed past my ankles. I thought of a deserted hospital.

A scribe scuttled by with an armload of heavy cases. Aunt María pointed out the warder with his keys heading down the eastern corridor. He had a blanket rolled under his arm.

Here were the Palaces of the Inquisition. In these palaces there were many rooms. He went to prepare a place in one.

I backed away.

They made no move to stop me. I walked blindly into the plaza. I could feel Magda and María close behind, one to each side. An Indian lady was selling herbs and cures, her white hair coiled at her nape just as Xochitl wore hers. This *curandera* clearly had faith in her exemption from the Holy Office's jurisdiction, and I was afraid for her. The mummers looked to be university students and though I did not stop, by the direction they were facing and by the twisting and clowning and groans, I knew their skit to parody what happened across the street. And I was afraid for them, too, but did not stop until I had passed the musicians and reached the workshops and stalls.

There was a little apothecary, with his stoppers and funnels, alembics and spouts. A printing press and bindery, its stamps and dies. Then a shop with inks, quills and papers for scribes. A candlemaker, and the smell of fats reducing in the back, and on tables his candles in ranks of white, black and green. Next door was the engraver, his vitriols and acids and etching tools in neat ranks on a shelf. Standing at a high bench with his heavy needles was the maker of awnings and sacks. Then a carpentry, with all the planks and rigging, screws and vises. Here was a supplier of surgical equipment: scalpels, forceps and specula, beaked masks.

Next door a Sunday crowd had gathered to watch a smith at his forge. Behind me the music drummed and piped jarringly to the hammering at the anvil. I could feel María and Magda standing close.

A row of humble craftsmen at their shops. Scents of pine and glue, solvents and printers' inks. I thought of Grandfather, tried to summon the feelings that being with him brought. I so wanted to lose myself in them now, to make an escape in my mind. Watching the farrier at his forge, it seemed he was indeed a prince among these journeymen. Young and narrow-hipped, bent to his anvil, he was cased in sweat like a warhorse, his naked torso armoured against flame and shards by a scorched apron of ox hide.

I took in all the terrible power of shoulder and veined forearm and yet the delicacy in his wrists as he angled the tongs and banked and rolled the hammer. *The art is in the wrists, Angelina.* Yes Grandfather, you were so very right, for smiths and armourers and the *jinete-matador*[†]—a kind of empathy in the wrist, to capture the very image of life. It is a craftsmanship of temper and temperance and temperature. Of edges, brittleness and breaking points, of heating, folding and collapse. A building up, a grasping, a hammering at stresses—relief, release, relaxation.

[†]knight-matador

Such a flurry of enterprise on a Sunday, special commissions for the Church. And now I understood, and knew what this place was. These were the busy, fussy craftsmen who forged the pears and branks and gags, who built the gambrils and gibbets and gallows, who raised the bleachers and rigged the scaffolding. Supplied the inks and quills, laid out the instruments and the restraints, saw meekly to the fit.

I knew all about this—for Grandfather I had distilled all the essential qualities. I wanted very much to find again comfort in these: measurement, contour, surface, articulation. . . . I tried hard to picture Abuelo's face, any face at all—even the mask of Amanda's features when she was hurt. I tried to make my thoughts fly straight, my eyes bend neither right nor left, to hold to all the faces I had lost, to solve the riddle hidden there. Fear was the riddle now, the thing I had not known.

Subdued, I took my place next to Magda in the cab, with María coming in after me. I made no protest. Only to be away from that music, that ringing, that craft. The horses' hooves rasped and chiselled over the flags.

 Five companies of the Soldiers of the Bramble were picketed all night around the square, to guard the Green Cross and the Palaces of the

Inquisition. The streets around them for once were bright with torch-light. The eleventh day of April, 1649.

The drama starts in the darkness two hours before dawn, as the Archbishop's carriage approaches the Holy Offices. The night's revellers, both afoot and in the many well-stocked carriages, pause in their debauches to cross themselves as the black carriage passes. Whispers of the Archbishop's arrival fly like startled swallows through the cells of the Inquisition's secret prison.

His Illustriousness, the Archbishop don Juan de Mañozca, *is* the Inquisition—forty years' service in the tribunals of the Holy and General Office, member in perpetuity of its Supreme Council and second only in rank to the Inquisitor General in Spain. It was Juan de Mañozca who in his younger days had brought the Holy Office to the wild slave port of Cartagena. It was the then famous don Juan de Mañozca who detected and grimly prosecuted the Great Complicity in Perú. And it is his nephew, Juan Sáenz de Mañozca, who under his famed tutor has risen to become the Inquisitor of this *auto*.

At the southwest corner the gates swing open. A young monk rushes to open the carriage door. The Archbishop, a lean and vigorous man of seventy, steps lightly out. He walks into the courtyard and down the eastern corridor. All is in readiness. The antiphon and hymns have been sung in the pink chapel, where a special Mass has been held for the Inquisitors before this final battle. The rosary was said at Prime. For the fourteen prisoners condemned to the stake, fourteen pairs of Jesuits have been sworn in. *For confession, a Dominican, for contrition, a Jesuit.*

In shifts they have begun to attend to the prisoners, exhorting the condemned to repent so as to receive absolution before death.

All the prisoners have been given breakfast. At the mouth of a passageway joining the prison to its outermost patio, the young Inquisitor, Sáenz de Mañozca, takes up position under his uncle's watchful eye. In the dim courtyard, lit by one or two torches and the first glow of a false dawn, the Inquisitor orders that the prisoners be brought out in single file. He reads out each sentence, and hands to the prisoners the costumes they are to wear in the coming day's production: for the condemned, the short *corozas*[†] and black *sambenitos* of sackcloth; for the reconciled, the tall *corozas* and yellow *sambenitos* with the double cross of Saint Andrew. To the penanced, he hands the same yellow sacks, but bearing a single cross.

[†] a stiff, peaked cap; a dunce cap

Those prisoners who will not stop protesting their innocence, the Archbishop orders gagged.

The vigilants out in the little plaza know it has begun when the bells of the cathedral begin to toll. And after them, all the bells of all the churches in the capital. A carillon—of discordant timbre and pitch and period—a tolling to make the hottest blood run cold. Sixteen familiars of the Inquisition come out first, ahead of three parish crosses draped in black. Next come the Indians with the exhumed remains of heretics who've fraudulently received a Christian burial and are now found out at last.

Behind them, others carry painted effigies. Father de Moedano's effigies are revered as the most lifelike. Some of his faces are of people dead for years, yet all who knew them see. His memory for heretics is remarkable.

Out into the bright morning stumble the condemned, sad jesters in their black sacking emblazoned with flames and devils, in their dunce caps painted with serpents. The women hold little green crosses.

But the onlookers have been expecting to see fourteen condemned prisoners, not thirteen.

During the night, Isabel Núñez has confessed and repented of her Judaizing. But this will not be known until ten days later, when she and another whore of Babylon—stripped to the waist—are each tied to the back of an ass and whipped through the streets. Two hundred lashes each.

Thirteen prisoners . . . The number raises a perplexed murmur all along the procession route to the amphitheatre. Scores of bleachers and platforms have been built and rented out along the way. By eight o'clock, the Procession of the Green Cross is within a few blocks of the plaza of the Indian fliers, the Plaza del Volador. The bullfights have been cancelled, the barbershops shuttered, the market stalls boarded.

The amphitheatre has been built to hold eighteen thousand. It covers the south, east and west; to the north it is open to the palace balconies and to a ructious mass of spectators unable to get seats. The total number in the square would exceed thirty thousand but for a hastily delivered order forbidding, on pain of excommunication, further entry into the desperately crowded square.

To the left, on the west side, is a grandstand constructed to accommodate the noble families of the realm and the officers of the Church, the most eminent being seated at the base. The various dignitaries, families and Inquisition officials can be seen retiring, throughout a long, hot day of sentencing, to comfortable lounges under the grandstand for the taking of rest and refreshments. The prisoners' dock is pyramidal, and the prisoners are distributed equitably. No side of the square is favoured. Between the dock and the grandstand is a large mahogany table to record the proceedings upon. The secretaries of the Holy Office sit in a row of heavy, carved chairs, each with its own canopy. Across from the table rise two pulpits for sermons and the reading of the edicts. Between these is a massive scaffold for the prisoners' sentences to be read from.

For the past hour, the armies of Christ Triumphant have driven the squadrons of Satan through the Plazuela del Marquez, then down the Calle de Mercaderes de San Agustín and up to the corner of the Calle del Arco. The Green Cross has at last reached the approaches of the square. Close behind the file of the condemned, and surrounded by the University's rectors, the warden of the Inquisition's prisons leads a white mule. On its back sways a lacquered chest inlaid with mother-of-pearl. It contains the charges against the condemned.

Here the situation gets out of hand.

Throughout the course of the procession, Tomas Trebino de Sobremonte has never ceased to trumpet his guiltlessness. Even knowing he is to burn alive, as the one unrepentant Judaizer, defiantly he swears through his metal gag to practise the law of Moses to the death. Wildly gesticulating, violently shaking his head, Trebino roars back his insolence to a crowd hurling fierce insults and exhortations to repent. As he makes his way through the streets, a hard-pressed company of infantry struggles to protect him from the incensed mob armed with paving stones and staves.

But when, still mouthing abominations, he nears the entrance to the square where thousands have been kneeling in hushed adoration of the Green Cross, the crowd closes in to silence him.

The soldiers panic, unwilling to die protecting a heretic. Yet the mob is so dense that they cannot get out of the way, and they fight back to save themselves. Before wading into the fray, the Archbishop sends someone through the empty back streets to the cathedral, with an order to silence the massive bells. The Archbishop waits. Each contingency and response has been anticipated—for the rigour of his forethought, the providence of his planning, he is rightly famed. Before long all the bells of the city fall silent and a languid stillness blankets the square, damping the fires of Christian fury.

The Archbishop, mounted on the back of his little mule, enters the sea of men and the waters part. At nine o'clock that morning, calmly, slowly, the Archbishop's venerable mule rounds the corner of the University with both troops and prisoners in tow. . . . Combatants in the everlasting war between God and Nature, Spirit and Flesh, they shuffle awkwardly down the little flight of steps and into the throng in the now silent plaza.

In reverence the crowd kneels until the Archbishop has taken up his station atop the scaffold. He sits under a black velvet baldachin, its coping adorned with gold brocade and golden fringes. The Inquisitors file in behind him.

By now the prisoners have occupied the dock. On the lowermost benches, Indians hold the effigies. Next, those prisoners to be penanced; above them, those to be reconciled. At the tip of the pyramid, and all around the uppermost rung, huddle the condemned, each between two Jesuits ceaselessly whispering.

Cloaked in shame in their sackcloth and dunce caps they sit, the bedraggled crew of a foundered ship, faces drained by insomnia, white with terror or fury.

The accused are prodded to stand. The crowd rises from its knees as the Archbishop sits—erect, without reclining—in a great white throne of marble. Behind him, the exchequer plants the Standard of the Faith. Before him stands an ebony table. Upon it a great book and a little brass bell. Visible beneath the table are glimpses of the Archbishop's sandalled feet.

Feet like fine brass.

All through the day of judgement he will toy absent-mindedly with a great key. It hangs on a thick golden chain in his left hand. From time to time his right hand reaches out and rings the little bell to accelerate the proceedings: time is short.

The Inquisitors settle onto cushions around his table, and throughout the proceedings are seen lounging like Persians, leonine eyes alert.

After the adoration of the Green Cross, still draped in black, after the reading of the Proclamation of the Faith, after the Bull conferring papal authority on the Holy Office of the Inquisition, the most profound silence reigns over the expectant multitude.

Each slow step rings out as the Dean of the Cathedral labours up to the pulpit. He salutes the Tribunal on his right, and glancing up at the Archbishop begins his sermon.

. . . Come hither; I will shew unto thee the judgement of the great whore that sitteth upon many waters . . .

The lacquered chest bearing the suits against the accused is brought forward. Four secretaries scuttle to and fro, conveying the heavy briefs to the pulpits, from which the charges are read in slow, rhythmic alternation. Three secretaries at a table sit scrabbling intently, quill hands lightly convulsed, to capture every nuance of the proceedings, just as they have done at interrogations.

. . . And I saw the dead, small and great, stand before God; and the books were opened . . .

Over the hushed plaza a little bell rings out with the sound of glass cracking in a flame. Then from a rostrum on the high scaffold at the centre of the amphitheatre, the sentences for each case are called out. Clasping the ceremonial black staff in front of his chest, the warden of the secret prisons brings each prisoner in turn to stand alone at the foot of the scaffold.

All eyes are on the Archbishop as he cants slightly forward to consult his notebook.

. . . And whosoever was not found written in the book of life was cast into the lake of fire . . .

First to be judged are the dead. Among them an eighty-year-old woman who lasted a full six months in prison. Her remains and effigy are consigned to the flames.

Now it is the turn of the living.

An exultant roar goes up as Tomas Trebino is sentenced first—to burn alive. Merciful, the Tribunal orders that the other twelve, before burning, be garrotted. From the prisoners' dock to the scaffold, the warden weaves back and forth like a shuttle.

. . . And upon her forehead was a name written, Mystery, <u>Babylon the Great</u>, the mother of harlots and abominations of the earth . . .

Among those condemned to die, it may be that one face at least, that of an old woman, is suffused with the peace of a loving god. The warden brings her, the last of the condemned, forward to hear her judgement. Ana de Carvajal staggers to the base of the scaffold. She is sixty-seven. Her breast cancer is so advanced, and she so wraithlike, that the heart-shaped tumour is visible beneath her *sambenito*.

She, too, is the Inquisition. In the *auto* of 1590, her father was burned in effigy. In 1596, her mother burned garrotted, her brother Luís burned alive. In the *auto* of 1601, when Ana was nineteen, the Holy Office reconciled her: but to lapse into the cult of the Pharisees was to be condemned to the flames.

Now, forty-eight years later, the Inquisition finds she has relapsed. At last her long wait is over.

. . . How much she hath glorified herself, and lived deliciously, so much torment and sorrow give her: for she saith in her heart, I sit a queen and am no widow, and shall see no sorrow . . .

Again the little bell rings. The warden brings forward the scores of the reconciled one by one. Since reconciliation comes at the price of confiscation of property, many in this group are wealthy. Among them are several women, and chief among these is Juana Enriquez, widely resented for the refinement of her manners and dress, for the luxury and glamour of her parties and balls, for her coaches and the bevies of servants that once followed her wherever she went.

Gone now the servants.

In yellow sackcloth before the scaffold she stands alone. She hears her fate read. Two hundred lashes. Confiscation of all estates. Banishment from the realm. Shrill cries of satisfaction rise from the crowd. Babylon, the Great, is fallen.

. . . And the kings of the earth, who have committed fornication and lived deliciously with her, shall bewail her, and lament for her, when they shall see the smoke of her burning . . .

Next, Simón Váez Sevilla: the richest man in the New World. At the foot of the scaffold, he stands in sackcloth, a green candle in his soft hands, a noose around his white neck: all behold the arrogant kingpin of a mercantile network of false converts spanning both oceans—*the whole globe*—from Malta to Manila.

Two hundred lashes. Confiscation. Banishment. Perpetual and irremissible prison. The crowd bellows another note in its paean to Apollo.

. . . For true and righteous are his judgements: for he hath judged the great whore, which did corrupt the earth with her fornication, and hath avenged the blood of his servants at her hand . . .

The condemned are led away through the jeering crowd to the *quemadero*, the burning ground. From the chapel, the last terrible strains of *De Miserere* die out.

The reconciled and the penanced are made to abjure their errors once more, to swear not to relapse, and to kiss a little iron cross thrust against their lips. The tension mounts; teasingly the black baize draped over the Green Cross falls away inch by inch in little tugs, as each sinner submits and returns to the bosom of the Church.

When at last the Green Cross stands clear of its black cloak of mourning, a great clamour of joy and triumph goes up, like the sound of many waters. Kettledrums, trumpet blasts, shouts—*Long live the Faith!*—the choir singing *Te Deum* now like larks, soldiers firing volleys into the air. . . .

The Archbishop's eyes are as a sheet of flame.

. . . And I saw an angel standing in the sun; and he cried with a loud voice, saying to all the fowls that fly in the midst of heaven, Come and gather yourselves together unto the supper of the great God . . . that ye may eat the flesh of kings . . .

An uncanny scene surrounds Tomas Trebino as they attempt to strap him to the back of an ass for the procession to the *quemadero*. The creature goes mad the instant it feels Trebino's weight. Braying wildly, it charges into the other animals brought to carry the condemned. One beast after another balks. The animals, normally docile, are so restive now that the prisoners, many of them aged, will have to walk to meet their death. It is an outrage to all aficionados, who for months to come, in taverns all over New Spain, will denounce this breach.

Only by firing repeatedly over the heads of the maddened crowd can Captain Mendoza's escort prevent the wildly ranting Trebino from being torn apart along the route.

He will not walk at all unless permitted to walk backwards. For a few steps he does, until his Jesuits call out for him to be carried.

The rest of the condemned, some silent, others crying or ceaselessly muttering—the satanic, half-mad citizens of Gog and Magog—crawl along the Alameda. For hours, hundreds of watchers have been clustering like pine cones in the branches of the giant trees that line the boulevard. Thousands more have scrambled up onto the piping of the aqueduct and squat like sagging rows of buzzards above the newly renovated Plaza de San Diego.

The stakes on scaffolds above the pyres are arranged over a rectangular area covered with lime. The shoddy construction also scandalizes many: the steps are narrow and unsteady; the arrangement of ropes and pegs on each stake does not allow the condemned to sit comfortably. It is a disgrace.

Eleven chests are stopped, eleven breaths. Eleven pairs of Jesuits may rest.

The last to mount and be strangled is Símon Montero. Hands bound behind his back, he does a little dance of contempt and clowns for the crowd, then feigns a stumble on the narrow steps to force his confessors to keep him from falling to his death.

"The carpentry," he cries out in the instant before his garrotting, "is better in Seville—"

The order is given to light the pyres. Silent Indians work the bellows.

. . . And he laid hold on the dragon, that old serpent, which is the Devil, and Satan, and bound him a thousand years . . . And cast him into the bottomless pit . . .

Tomas Trebino has also reached the terminus.

He falls silent, watching everything set alight around him. Effigies, chests of bones, strangled companions. Ana de Carvajal. Perhaps he has read Dante, and the scene is not without the slim comfort of some small precedent. His confessors mistake his silence for mortal terror. They remove his gag that he might repent. Instead the blasphemer launches into an attack on the poet of Revelations. Trebino exhorts John the Witness to join him in the fire, that the great saint might repent and confess his own crimes.

The executioner holds Tomas Trebino's head steady as they light his beard on fire.

Trebino struggles to look down through the flame. With his foot he drags a block of wood to the stake as if to say, *begin.*

On that day Nature in all her elements is forced to submit. Fire consumes him. Air receives the smoke. His charred bones are wrestled from the jaws of street curs and buried in shallow earth. His suet is scattered over the waters of a reeking canal.

His quintessence is consigned to oblivion.

In the suffocating closeness of the coach, our mingled perfumes ill mask the fetor of our bodies: María, Magda and I ride slowly home through the alleys of the New Jerusalem, covered in silence and ash.

Since I am not yet in a position of open defiance, soon enough I will oblige and give them an accounting of sorts. Gaps will not be tolerated. It is why the repeated questions, it is why the careful notes. It is a kind of fussiness, after all.

But the Inquisition is no conclave of rattled nuns. And it is not the want of charity, chastity and grace that the holy officers so fear and loathe but the slattern of Incontinence. Against her they are bulwark and bung, caisson and closter, dike and dam. This is the craft of clots and clods, of pears and branks and the surgeon's beaked mask.

These officers and learned doctors, these are the humble stop-gaps. Craft is enough, all is craft. The meekness that inherits the earth.

And who is their Jacobi Topf? Is he born, have we met somewhere, will we yet?

But gaps are everywhere . . . and lie in silent shapes just where there seems no gap at all. Their shrine and studio is memory. And how they shift and gape at this latest charge: that Uncle Juan's parents were secret Jews.

So differently now those days echo in my memory. For then, what Aunt María feared more even than my recklessness was her own daughter. Magda, the one who served the breakfast. And how unfathomably wise it was to dam the fountain, not comical at all. And the whimsy of finding Uncle Juan brave was not at all whimsical: for however sincere his efforts to be a good New Christian, he could never quite turn his back on the parents who would not abandon an older faith.

And is it true, as the holy officers now suggest, that my own father was one too? For it is among the Basques and Portuguese that the Inquisition finds so very many of its secret Judaizers. And indeed was there not a faint echo, in the *auto-da-fé* of 1656, of that great spectacle of 1649? The arrests began the following year and took place throughout the early 1650s. When Father rode away from us for the last time, I was five years old. It was the spring of 1654.

Did he stay away from us, so often, so long—and then abandon us— to keep us from harm? The Inquisition brought my childhood to an end during a carriage ride. It remains for me to know if they had already taken my father.

So many questions they have. I too have questions now. If it's an accounting they want, I too seek a settling of our accounts.

Magda asked about him. Did I think he was ever coming back? To be cruel, I thought, but perhaps to be doubly cruel. If she knew. And if she knew, it was because Aunt María did also. Grandfather had introduced my father to Isabel. But who introduced María to Uncle Juan? Were Juan and my father friends? My eldest sister and Magda were about the same age. . . .

How painful it can be to see where one has not looked, into places one has not dreamed of. How very differently I might have looked upon my aunt María, if I had grasped the worst of her fears. And what if I had known from the beginning that Uncle Juan had been my grandfather's friend? I liked him already—he might have become a second father to me. How I needed one then. And I would have feared, not pitied, Magda, had I known what she was. It is from her stock that the Inquisition's familiars are drawn.

Gaps will not be tolerated by the holy officers—gaps are all around us. I too was once frightened of them. But no longer. Yes, I will give them a reckoning of sorts. But for this, let there be another art, with eyes to see the gaps through lenses of clemency. With ears to hear their music, and hands to turn the instrument that plays it. Let there be others, too, for this work.

We will play on drums and spinets, on barrels and pins, on time's very axle. We march under the Ensign of the Trout with trident tongue. When they hear our chiming jingling tune of links and the gaps between, the holy armourers may find, as others have, that mail is lighter, suppler, stronger than plate. That each of us carries part of the score, and that we are all linked in surprising ways and strong. Strong despite ourselves, surprising in spite.

And even as night is the lace around each star, yet there is nothing frail in that dark. Of this night lace now may we fashion a shimmering net and cast it. And let us see if not a few fishers of souls are caught.

I sinned, Lord, but not because I have sinned
do I your clemency and love relinquish.
For my wrongs I tremble at being punished,
yet dream of being through your goodness pardoned.

I accuse myself, even as You have waited on me,
of being abhorrent in my ingratitude,
and so my sin of being all the viler,
for your being so worthy of all love.

Were it not for You, what would become of me?
And from myself, without You, who would deliver me
if your hand withheld its grace from me?
And but for me, my Lord, who would fail to love You?
And but for You, God, who would suffer me?
And to You, without You, my Lord, who would carry me?

LUÍS DE
CARVAJAL

"Heretic's Song"

B. Limosneros, trans.

The brother of Ana
de Carvajal, a
woman condemned
to the stake after a
forty-eight-year stay
of execution, wrote
at least one sonnet
while awaiting his
own sentence in the
Inquisition's secret
prisons. It is not
known whether the
heretic Luís de
Carvajal was
already a poet
before his trials, or
became one.

HALL OF
MIRRORS

DETECTIVES CURTIS AND GREEN have had to leave, after going to the trouble to sleuth out the location and then putting up with all the dust and switchbacks to get up here. It is a bright, spring day in the mountains. They left so soon. But they've got their work to do, their statements to take, their musical rides. I wasn't that sorry to see them go. I was afraid they might have heard I was going away for a while.

That night, she'd placed on her desk a box of journals, papers and a few souvenirs of our time together, carefully laid them out for me to find. Of this I'm certain now.

It is all such an infuriating, terrible *waste*. . . . Such a wrenchingly inadequate word, for a career, a life. I can call it a calamity, I can call it whatever I want, but the word changes nothing. This could have been prevented. This is not what advisers are for. This was my carelessness. And now I want to believe there is some way still to snatch something from the wreckage.

She sits by a window on the tenth floor of the library tower. Its book racks radiate out from the elevators that run up the tower core. The study carrels ring the floor, all along the windows. The views can be superb, but at least one person cares nothing for them: reflected in a window glass is a young woman poring over a volume in which her own ideal is depicted as being deeply fascinated with mirrors. But why should that matter to her so much?

What does Beulah see as she looks into the mirror, where the mind's images collide with those of the eye?

I sort through these journals and wonder where she lost her way. And try to find some evidence that it happened before we met.

. . . As a child she perches on a chair before the vanity in her mother's darkened bedroom and peers intently into a mirror, which consists of a fixed centrepiece and two side panels on hinges. By realigning the mirror's panels, she can create an infinite retrogression, an endless light relay of planar reflections curving gently away to a bottle-green dusk. To touch either panel even slightly is to launch a dragon's tail arcing through a two-dimensional sky, or to fold it up again just as suddenly, like a trick with cards. Amazed, she crouches there, indifferent to

the distant cries of other little girls playing hopscotch on the sidewalks or hobby horses on the lawns.

How many times has she longed to climb into the looking glass and
disappear, threading her way through its endless runs, its brittle windings and darkening alleys? To become a two-dimensional Alice exploring a wonderland where each thing flows to and from its opposite: left
hand into right, self into other—order from chaos, a candescence from
flesh.

Her journals also show that she felt grateful for the horrors mirrors
conceal.

Her research is unorthodox; its methods begin now to lead her
into a deep maze. And much of what she is on the verge of discovering about mazes she has already seen in a bedroom mirror: mystery,
concealment, deception, horror. Maybe it's in the library tower that
she first experiences the sensations that become both companion and
guide: a sudden tightening in the chest, a glimmering of shapes
falling into line on a distant horizon of the inner eye, the seashell
roar of the sea. . . .

At the next bend, her maze takes on the aspect of a funhouse: Sor
Juana Inés de la Cruz, too, has an abiding fascination with mirrors,
and Beulah—disoriented, a little at sea—is amazed by the happenstance of her discovery. She needn't have been.

Juana Ramírez was raised among the remnants of a people for
whom the mirror held great significance. Mexican cosmology, as
Beulah's research so vividly records, manages to be at once complex and
breathtakingly poetic. The night sky, the stars, the very concept of the
divine all partook of the demonic, the ravening and the terrible. No god
better exemplified this than Tezcatlipoca, one of the most haunting
visions of divinity ever conjured by the collective imagination.[28]

In the darkness of a night stalked by apparitions and spectres, people felt the Smoking Mirror particularly near. It was the jaguar, and it
waited at each crossroads. The god dwelt in his House of Mirrors—a
hall of concave, eerily reflective surfaces that enshrined a statue of
black obsidian. This statue, the Lord of the Mirror, was worshipped in
awe and cursed in despair as the master of inversions and sudden
reversals of fortune. Though possessed of a matchless power, typically
he chose to act through deception, misdirection and sleight of hand.
The statue's pectoral mirror was a scope through which Tezcatlipoca

could see others—into their very hearts—while himself remaining invisible. An obsidian mirror replaced one of his feet, torn off in some primordial combat with a demonic earth mother.

He was known also as Broken Face, He-who-causes-things-to-be-seen-in-a-mirror. The Smoking Mirror summoned visions and brought them rolling through smoke across vast stretches of space and time. To peer into it was an hallucinatory source of enchantment, terror, paralysis. . . .

His date marker in the Aztec calendar cycle was 1 Death.

Sor Juana certainly knew something of these legends. She may even have been marked by them. But her curiosity could just as easily have been purely intellectual, as of any seventeenth-century thinker reflecting the enthusiasms of her era. In seventeenth-century science, mirrors held renewed interest as refractors and reflectors of light. Newton fitted mirrors to his telescopes to improve upon Galileo's. For the philosophy of knowledge, a mirror's distortions were a troublesome source of altered perceptions—calling into question, in the age of Descartes, even man's faith in the data of his senses.

Finally, Sor Juana, a beautiful woman, could be permitted a little mirror-gazing.

I've been trying to show why Beulah needn't have read any great mystery into all this. To be fair, she was unlucky in a number of ways: in her adviser, evidently, but fatally so in her area of research, since it amplified so powerfully her own worst tendencies. The Baroque was besotted with myth and tricks of perception—the ceilings painted as if open to the sky, the cornices that turn out to be a painting, itself made to look like a sculpture, ad nauseam. . . .

Beulah was also right about certain things. About my distaste for all things baroque, obviously. She was even right about why. All my lofty reservations aside, in the Baroque's lack of restraint there is something offensively, dangerously . . . unchaste. To some of my former students and colleagues this will come as something of a howler. But had I been more forceful in impressing the dangers upon her earlier I might have saved a career, at the very least.

If the Renaissance was the first new budding on a branch the Middle Ages had thought barren, the Church's reactionary Counter-Reformation was a flask—a *fiasco*, slipped over that branch. The odd-shaped fruit of this suppression was the Baroque, like a pear grown into a bottle whose too-rich liqueur shocks the austere palate of the monk who uncorks it. An era of monstrous vitality and tension, of florid camouflage and violent contradictions—of unbridled licence and brutal censure. Of a craving that yields to disgust. And in Spanish America, it derived an added intensity from the systematic suppression of indigenous cultures.[29]

Yet as if by miracle, in the verses of Sor Juana Inés de la Cruz, the American Baroque[30] found by far its finest and most graceful expression: a grafting of Greco-Roman myth to contemporary politics; of aboriginal vocabularies to European forms. In the play *The Divine Narcissus*, for instance, Sor Juana wrote a dramatic poem of astonishing originality and daring.

> A nun writing in a convent cell at the end of the 17th century, Sor Juana treats Ovid's tale as allegory, with Narcissus as Christ, Echo as the fallen Angelic Nature (Satan), and Human Nature as Christ's own reflection in the spring. Echo, evil and jealous, afraid that Narcissus will fall in love with Human Nature, continually disturbs the reflecting surface with sin. Human Nature is so disfigured by the turbulence of sin that Christ is unable to see that what he loves in that image is really his own reflection, and thereby falls in love with it.[31]

Christ as Narcissus is so startling, even today, that it's easy to overlook the subtle portrait of Echo as Lucifer, the fallen star of morning. Sor Juana's creation, Echo, is an altogether human figure, who cannot endure the indifference of a self-absorbed young god and slowly wastes away. In the process, her gift of speech comes to seem a parody and punishment—and here is the Baroque in all its perverse splendour: the most passionate speeches of Sor Juana's Echo resonate clearly and beautifully of the Song of Solomon.

Sung, as it were, by Mephistopheles.

Our time is not without splendours of its own: according to one feminist reading of the Bible, the Song of Solomon (or the Song of Songs) is 'the Goddess's correction of Genesis.'[32] Oh my.

It is all such a distressing *mess*. And not just for its deplorable taste.[33] What we are facing is first and foremost a sickness of temperament. Out of this . . . mythomania, Beulah let herself be turned into yet another scholar projecting her own fetishes into the work. Mirrors, myth, the Baroque, and now the Goddess. It wasn't completely her fault, I'll admit. Such a mix would have been lethal to a saint. Here one has only to imagine a monstrously florid garden . . . myths, their reflections, distortions—twining, tangling—like so many limbs in a bathhouse, sending tendrils back and forth in time.

Today, though, it is no longer acceptable to judge these things by external, even eternal, standards. Today we must infiltrate the subject's *own* value system, probe from within the matrix of her influences. . . . Alas, this also means insinuating ourselves into her story.

All right, why did Beulah *freely choose* to give myth such a central place in her work? First off, it must be admitted that myths were vital to Sor Juana herself. Echo, Isis, Phaëthon, St. Catherine—these became emblems for her, not just of her work but of her very life. Today this must seem aberrant to us, even bizarre. It would be like Sylvia Plath fusing her identity with Ariel or Lazarus;[34] or T.S. Eliot at least half-seriously taking himself for the Fisher King. But Sor Juana was a child of her time.

She was also, arguably, the most mythologized mortal in human history.

During her own lifetime, on both sides of the Atlantic, she was hailed as the Mexican Athena, Sum of the Ten Sybils, Phoenix of America,[35] Pythoness of Delphi—to list just these. She was looked upon, from near and far, as a creature of fable, a beautiful monster. A freak of nature on a diabolical continent. Today we automatically filter out the hyperbole; the Baroque did not, indeed could not—the two arcs were not separable. It is impossible for us to imagine calling any-one—say, Sontag or Atwood—'Isis' without the ghost of a smile. Similarly with Simone Weil as St. Catherine, Anne Carson as Echo, Paglia as Lucifer, H. D. as Helen of Troy. . . . [36]

The paradox is that it makes Sor Juana an oddly modern figure, the prototype of larger-than-life fame. And in this one respect, her century is perhaps more modern than our own: the Baroque would have had no trouble comprehending, and then wildly embracing, our bizarre obsession with global celebrity.[37]

Modernity has been described as an annihilation, an abolition of the past.[38] In this, its self-absorption, the 'modern' is also apocalyptic (in a mumbling, minor key) in considering itself an end time. Which may be why Eliot, modernism's early theorist, saw a need to re-establish the importance of tradition in the poetic program—that the past is not dead. Beulah would have said this of myth. Neither was it for her quaint, in the postmodernist sense: an amusing theme park, a Chinatown in the shadow of skyscrapers, as it is in our home city.[39] Our century's most demoralizing discovery has been the methodical, technological and largely cynical exploitation of myth and archetype.[40] Here Beulah and I did not disagree. But she believed the genie could not be stuffed back—and should not be, since it derives its power from repression.[41]

And here was one of the things we disagreed upon, sometimes violently. It *can* be stuffed back into the bottle. It must. And manning the frontier between fiction and truth is decent, honest work—unspectacular, painstaking, and yes, occasionally tedious. But it is the Great Wall; because beyond it, the barbarian says things about us that should never be said or heard or known.

So, granted, there were reasons to take an interest in myths. But why in the world would she take it into her head to *modify* them?

Here she might point to Ovid. In fact, this Roman poet writing eight centuries after Homer has done more than anyone to shape our notions of what a Greek myth feels like. Sor Juana was just one in a long line of poets to follow him. A century or so after her death, Keats's concern, in reworking the great myths, was to bring them 'intimately alive' again, and in this might be found an echo of his medical training.[42] A more recent touchstone in this work of resuscitation was Camus, who wrote that myths exist for each new generation to breathe life into them—something he himself did so brilliantly for Sisyphus. The impulse, I believe, was to keep myth supple and vital, to keep it from ossifying into fixed meanings and museum pieces.[43]

But I think Sallust, the Roman historian, came closest to what Beulah was after. Her notes show she was enamoured of something Sallust once said of myth, bandied about as an epigraph for the two thousand years since: *These things never happened, but are always.*

I think it is in this 'always' that Beulah felt she could most closely approach her poet: taking up the same myths that had so impassioned and finally engulfed Sor Juana—and by turning them in her own hands, enter into them completely and step through the looking glass. Through the Smoking Mirror.

JUANA INÉS
DE LA CRUZ,

THE DIVINE
NARCISSUS

Alan Trueblood, trans.

... *Díganlo las edades que han pasado,*
díganlo las regiones que he corrido,
los suspiros que he dado,
de lágrimas los ríos que he vertido,
los trabajos, los hierros, las prisiones
que he padecido en tantas ocasiones.
      Una vez, por buscarle, me toparon
de la ciudad las guardas, y atrevidas,
no solo me quitaron
el manto, mas me dieron mil héridas
los centinelas de los altos muros,
teniéndose de mí por mal seguros.
¡Oh ninfas que habitais este flórido
y ameno prado, ansiosamente os ruego
que si acaso al querido
de mi alma encontrareis, de mi fuego
le noticeis, diciendo el agonía
con que de amor enferma el alma mía! ...

To this the ages passing testify,
the regions of the world I have traversed,
the sighs that I have heaved,
the flowing streams of tears my eyes have shed,
the toils, the chains, the prison bars
that left me branded with a thousand scars.
      The watchmen who went about the city
once found me as I sought him.
Not only did the keepers of the walls
despoil me of my veil—
they also smote me countless times,
as if in payment for unnumbered crimes.
      O nymphs who dwell amidst the bloom
that covers this fair meadow,
I charge you earnestly that if perchance
you come on the Beloved of my soul,
you tell him of the agony I feel
in this sick soul which he alone can heal ...

Within this cave,

listening attentively,

you may think you hear my story

in the frail echoes of bats in flight,

in the hollow patter of droplets on stone.

Pan surprised me in a glade.

Sleeping on a sun-lit rock.

I remember well the reek

the rancid wine made

beside that creek,

the screams

the whispers—

his

spiky whiskers,

the rank black fleece

between splayed fingers—

mine.

ECHO

As recast by B.
Limosneros . . .

There was pain—also mine—but pain he'd made, and laughter, his. There was rage—no shame, no fear. It's not that I was so dear to that hairy bleating fool, just a lazy, easy lay—not even pretty. Yet some say he did his best work on me that day. His ugly goat-seed nestled awhile then took. And somehow Iynx grew out of me, an elfin lynx-eyed beauty. A marvel to us both. In grace or looks like neither but most unlike her father, who'd stop by from time to time depending on the weather, amused to see child rearing child.

He smiled, said he came for conversation, called mine unequalled on all the island. If my tongue had been a sword . . . Still, I did what I could with words.

Him I never forgave, but Pan could play the pipes—that much I'll say. And there was more—of course the drinking problem, but he wasn't without talent, at least until Apollo, sly, wheedled away his gift to prophesy and Hermes stooped to lift—oh no, not steal!—while winy Pan, besotted, bent to kneel and, the barely stomached contents of a meal depositing, dropped his pipes beside a stream. . . . Poor Pan, too busy vomiting to notice Hermes scoop the miracle of reeds and peddle it to the god of wisdom, light and reason.

If music was my weakness—and Apollo's—it wasn't Iynx's. She'd wander off from glen to wooded glen, far from goats and flutes and men, learning forest lore in secrecy. Learning sorcery.

Enter Zeus. When Zeus wanted satisfaction he used my tongue. But not like that. His tastes were more refined, though not quite tame. Anyway, I was no longer young and he had always found me plain. Instead he used my storied tongue to divert the most jealous wife in history, already driven to distraction by his infidelities, by his passion to subvert. If I'd hated Hera half as much as Pan I might have had some fun, enjoyed the perks. Still, you couldn't bring yourself to pity Hera, not if you'd seen her with her ire up.

For instance once as she and Zeus indulged in another spate of lofty quibbling, this time over who feels more pleasure—woman or man—when they fornicate, she called upon a trembling Tiresias (who'd been for seven years a woman) to adjudicate their discordant concert of half-truth, spite and biases. Unlucky Tiresias sided with Zeus, saying the greater pleasure was hers. Hera in furious displeasure struck the mortal's eyes out for his lies.

A sorry Zeus, while unwilling to oppose her, gave Tiresias as a measure of recompense clearer sight within than others have without, and left the prophet with his heightened sense to walk the roads of Greece through endless night.

When one day Zeus appeared as a bull to my daughter, Iynx, she reacted with neither laughter nor aversion but circumspection, for his polymorphous appearances always accompanied some perversion or other. And when Zeus then sent me, her mother, to regale Hera with some drawn-out story, I still thought Iynx his quarry. Yet I had no cause to worry—Iynx, the budding sorceress, had quickly cast a spell and made Io, who was Hera's own priestess, the new object of Zeus's vicious tenderness. But so consumed was I by anxiety that my usually agile tongue stumbled over some unwonted infelicity and Hera grew suspicious. Soon she found Zeus toiling over Io in a shady wood. Not good at all. Not good.

Iynx, my chaste and clear-eyed child, for her reckless incantations Hera cast into exile as a wry-neck, a vulgar snake-bird condemned to long migrations. Io she turned into a piebald cow beating a trail to Egypt with a cloud of gadflies at her tail.

But my punishment was special, neat. The ugly body she let me keep, but the clever wagging tongue that'd made her laugh and weep, Hera now made to echo the last few words of whatever I heard anyone speak no matter how stupid, rash or weak.

So while Narcissus was making his way towards me in a zigzag peregrination, I was hiding in the Cretan woods avoiding insipid conversations. Sweet Narcissus . . . son of Leiriope, a violet-eyed nymph, and Cephisus, the river god, who'd caught her in his liquid coils and *ravished* her, I think's the word. Narcissus had his mother's eyes and his father's fluid grace. Few had seen so beautiful a face. Not since Apollo's ganymede, Hyacinthus—whose face was smashed in by a jealous West Wind one day, as the boy was learning to play with the sun god's golden . . . discus.

Narcissus was beautiful, yes, but like all rape seed, so hard of heart. Leiriope took her motherly misgivings to blind Tiresias, the boy's future course to chart. Would Narcissus grow old, content and tender-hearted? she asked. But the blind man's prophecy was just as sure as it was then obscure to her: Only if himself he never know, the seer answered sad and slow. (He'd just foreseen that he himself would lose both daughters to Apollo.)

Narcissus grew up a hunter and a collector. Starting out with butterflies, then on to trophy heads and trophy hides, then on again to the still-beating hearts of lovers. At Narcissus's latest departure on one of his hunting trips, a jilted pale Ameinius called with quivering lips after the arrogant archer, "May you never be able to love another, but only yourself in hell!"

Nemesis, resting in the cover of a nearby stand of ash, heard him well. . . .

So it was I heard them approaching one day with yells and shouts and vulgar speech. Narcissus and a group of louts, swinish and hirsute—Theban sea raiders on shore leave—with a brace of beautiful white Gabriel hounds, tall, graceful and unflagging in pursuit.

If you could have seen Narcissus then—what beauty! To see him was to love him. And love made no exceptions. Not even among ugly nymphs of a certain age and utterly lacking in discretion. The coiling of muscle beneath his golden hide, the cold-eyed serpentine grace as with bow and spear and net he plied his trade....

I followed him for days. Irises sprang up in the green bruises where he stepped or stopped to rest awhile on crushed meadow grasses—here a violet scar, another there. I wove a purple chaplet for my hair and followed still more closely as he got separated from the pack. As the baying of the hounds grew distant, Narcissus taken aback called out to his companions, "Wait an instant—wait for me!"

"Wait for me," I echoed.

"I'd wait for *you*," said he. A trace of pout—those sweet-petalled lips drooped as though in drought as he called after the unheeding group.

"I'd wait for you." *Forever.*

"Wait, come back!"

"Come . . ." I sighed.

"Who's here with me?" Narcissus called, still not knowing where to look.

"Back here, with me." *Forever.*

I could hear the hounds returning as he turned to me at last, but still he didn't see. "What *is* this?"

"Is this . . ." *My chance?* It was stupid and insane but they were coming back—now or never—I wouldn't get this chance again. I rushed forward and threw my eager arms around his neck.

"Is this some kind of trick? Are they playing a joke on me?" he said looking—anywhere but at me—for his ribald yokel friends to come running from the woods in glee.

"A joke, on me," I moaned.

"Let go of me. Let go!"

I saw disgust flood across his face. To him I was some grasping, mindless hag.

"Don't touch me," he cried, "leave me alone!"

"Don't leave me alone," I cried after him as he fled into the trees. "Touch me. . . ."

What else could I do but follow? And at each place he stopped to rest I swooped in, like some squawking crow raiding a still-warm nest, and pecked more purple flowers for my dark brow. But what hurts more than all the rest is how I trailed him lowing like some loathsome cow.

Just as he was rejoining his asinine companions at last, with much braying all round and slapping of sweaty backs, the Gabriel hounds started up a pure, white stag and started running it to ground.

"We've got it backed against the cliffs!" Narcissus cried, already having forgotten me.

At the foot of those colossal cliffs on whose brooding brow perched the palace of Cnossus—the Cretan seat of power—the white stag darted into a thick and tangled bower that had long concealed from nymphs and men what appeared to be the den of a bear or a lion. Surrounded on three sides, hard-pressed by hounds, the stag overcame its fright and in one bound leapt from leafy day to stony night—half a jump ahead of the fast-closing dogs, who unlike greyhounds hunted not just by sight alone but by their noses, and ahead too of the hunters flushed with blood lust, blinded to the danger.

Inside, it grew clear even as the light grew dim that this was no mere cave. The smooth walls in their stony regularity, the hidden turnings in their perverse ambiguities, the blind alleys and the forking paths all bore the stamp of an uncanny energy and plan. This lion's den must be the work of man.

Echoing from floor to roof all through these spiralling halls the clatter of cloven hooves, the deep baying of startled hounds reduced to a kind of yelping sound, the blaring calls of triton shells retreating, the amazed shouts and curses of bewildered men. I wondered with a shudder of fear if the Minotaur who'd stalked these passageways might still be near, but he'd been dead for years.

The din receded and dispersed, leaving me sifting the dying echoes, and leaving Narcissus with his jilted suitor's unflagging curse. Which in its cryptic drift carried him, the son of river god and water nymph, down towards the liquid core of things. Down to the heart of the labyrinth, to a chamber through whose lofty ceiling angled one broad shaft of sunlight—with just a glimpse of blue above the cliffs—a wondrous place that glittered with minerals, metallic veins, flakes of gold and crystal. And at the heart of that fabulous vault welled a clear and perfect spring never fouled by bird or man or animal. A spring of faultless royal blue— ultramarine where the sun shot through.

By threading a course along just those paths from which there came no echo, I made my own way to the silent place at the edge of the spring and found Narcissus kneeling. He had stripped to bathe and bent to drink from the spring, when in its convex, welling surface he found the face of his curse and prophecy.

That face wore now an expression of numb amazement. Perfect beauty ensnared in a faultless spring . . . among sharp, glittering pillars rising and falling to the faint shrill keening chatter—just audible now—of furious dog-headed bats. The blind rush of water up from soundless depths . . . the bright still coolness of the vault . . . I stood and stood—if only I could have stood and watched forever. Then he began to speak.

"O bright child—"

Bright Child, I murmured near silently. I longed to shout the words, but the only way to make him talk to me was not to let myself be heard.

"Bright child, I find the contents of my deepest fears disguised in your bright eyes. You strike a spark where all these years so many others, so despised, have left me strong and cold. Now you shudder when I try to hold you—don't flee, I give you power over me."

I give you power over me . . .

"In your eyes I see a love like mine invested in a brighter, better self. Yet though my love darkly mirrors yours, you seem to love without needing words . . . whereas my purest love for you is tainted as, shabbily, I yearn to be held by you, to be talked to."

To be held by you, talked to . . .

"O divine boy, for you must be divine, is this how you must love? Are you to love me without need, am I to love you without hope of love's reply?"

Without hope of love's reply . . .

"But don't you see? What you give I have no way of getting. And what you need I have no way of giving!"

No way of giving . . .

"So either I must love deluded, or without hope. Is this all you have to offer me—this cold and perfect love?"

Cold and perfect love . . .

"Has anyone been so cursed as to love with a love like mine? For this love surely is a curse: a love unreturned is worse, far worse than any kindred hatred. Why have you seduced me, O heartless boy, why waste my heart?"

Waste my heart . . .

"Your eyes like fevered suns devour me even as I bend to drink you in. But still you do not come, you will not bend. I try to slake my thirst in you, but your image will not yield. For you, I've killed all the other hungers once within me—even my love for Ceres, sweet goddess of the corn, my hope, my shield. Every other urge for food or drink have I purged, unable to think, to see straight. . . . I am poisoned by this thing, towards vileness urged."

I am poisoned by this thing . . .

"What cause have you to mock me, bright child, who inflicts his burning image on my depths? My beauty is not wanting—princes and goddesses and nymphs have wanted me. So what stands between us but this weightless veil—the thinnest veil of water . . . which I cannot lift or penetrate though I plunge my arms up to my chest, up to my eyes. A thin veil that in vain I try to rend in twain *as my arms cleave the azure's crystal drift,* but even as they do, it flows back again without a rift.[44] With all my fury I strike but glancing blows. Then your image glides back behind the veil and mocks me from below. How can you let such a slender thing come between us?"

Slender, a thing come between us . . .

"All oblique your gliding gaze even at its centre, while through a kind of haze I glimpse a garden sere and bleak because you will not enter. How I am deceived by those eyes, betrayed by this bright child who lay down with me!"

Bright Child . . . lay down with me . . .

"But couldn't we be friends at least? You reach out, yet do not touch me. *Some friendly promise in your face I view. You smile when I smile and answer tears with tears.* Your lips speak when I speak to you, but the words I cannot hear."

The words I cannot hear. . . . Witless fool I felt myself drawn blundering forward. He can't *hear* me, I told myself. I was about to spoil it all again. But even as I edged closer to the pool, in its convex, cool and silvered surface I saw his face bloated by tears. And in that face a flickering of troubled recognition, a sense of some tremendous mystery not yet revealed but just barely concealed beneath that lying reflection. Closer now, I could see him struggling with some clue, then the dawning knowledge of his fatal miscue, his misstep—even as the image of a sardonic, grinning bull seemed to surge up from the depths—

"No, not you! Is this the joke my fate has wrought? Is this my due? Is personality my fate? I am the one?—that one is you, the one I long to hate!"

As he struck at the pool with weak and hapless blows, I stepped forward to console him and broke the shaft of light that angled past his face. The surface of the pool below went black—

"Get back! Get back behind me. You foul the image."

Foul, the image . . .

"You have driven him away!"

Driven him away . . .

He turned to me, at last. He might at least have shown some gratitude. Still so sunk was he in his deluded visions—I could see him desperately eyeing my unruly waves of gorgon's hair, the chaplet bristling with sharp-petalled flowers, the sunlight on my burly shoulders, my ugliness—the recent object of his scorn—he sought anything that might have caused the appearance of those horns, anything to show the image he'd seen was not his own.

And in that instant, my dearest daughter, I would have given him anything, the whole wild sun-soaked world. But I couldn't speak unless spoken to, like some over-tutored child. What he needed then I could not give, and the only one who could have . . . lay dying beneath him in that spring.

The moment passed, the power of illusion crumbled. The face he turned back to his lover was filled with horror at how he had been humbled, with sorrow at how he'd been brought low. To become the freakish object of his own derision . . .

He sat desolate in his rage, beaten, before the surface of a brazen image he could not dispel, a visage now engraved upon his eyes.

And before *my* eyes my bronzed, exalted demigod, gone pale as marble, began to shatter as though some dark chisel had struck a secret fault. Yet even as cracks turned to shards, they started downward as frosted candlewax, to strike the pool as incandescent oil.

"*I've loved the shadow of what I am and in that love I burn.* A narcotic for my pain!" he uttered slowly. "Is this—my vain apocalypse—a vision or a prophecy? The better I know myself, the clearer it is to me how this must end."

My statuesque boy was turning to water before my eyes. Bright liquid poured into the spring from his lips, his eyes, his pores, his nose. I clutched at him—to keep him from melting away from me completely, to keep him from merging with the pool below. Startled from his liquid trance, he rose, reached high and broke from the tip of a stalactite a glittering slender lance. I could have stopped him. I was standing right there. But I stood rooted to the floor as he drove the crystal horn into his waxen breast . . . as his heart's precious blood flowed through the ultramarine in a violet flood.

This was my moment, my big chance. I could have mirrored his gesture, pulled the stony lance from his gory chest and plunged it into my own. But I still stood rooted to the ground. Did I love *myself* so much?

My moment passed.

After a time, I came to see myself for what I had become—a hollow oracle at the tomb of a dissipated superman, whose shade now contemplates *its* shade in the river Styx, while an abandoned universe goes crashing on the rocks.

My bones have turned to stone, my skin to scales of slate, my tongue to something I have grown to hate. And still they come with questions I can only echo and restate. So, daughter, you have come too late with yours. This is where I've gone. This is how it was. This is what's become of us.

> He, a river of amethyst
> I, a salted flood of petroglyphs
>   that flows
>   in archaic runes
>   to an echoic floor,
>   then dries—
> as all things do as each settles down to die—
>   another glittering
>   petrified ring
>   in the bole of God the tree.

Yet still the passion in her heart which drew,

Its food from bitter memory, lived and grew;

And sleepless sorrow made her body thin,

And wasting sickness shrivelled up her skin;

Till just a speaking skeleton was there.

Last stage of all, her voice was left alone,

And all her body's remnant turned to stone.

OVID,

Metamorphoses [45]

Isis BOOK TWO

I am that which is, has been, and shall be.

My veil no one has lifted.

The fruit I bore was the Sun. . . . [1]

CONTENTS

Contents

SHORTLY AFTER HER TWELFTH BIRTHDAY, in August of 1985, Beulah began to keep a diary. We might reasonably infer that it was a birthday gift since the first entry is dated September 2. With the series spread out before me, I notice all her subsequent journals were coil-bound notebooks, but the first was in a quarto format, bound in a fine burgundy leather. The volume's grown-up aspect is marred only slightly by *My Diary* printed on the front, and by the little lock of gilded tin—rather easily forced, as it turns out.

Once it is conceded that Beulah collected and made all of this available to me for some purpose, it follows that using one passage is as legitimate as using any other. I nevertheless find myself resisting. First because these early entries explain nothing; there can never be any unbreakable link drawn from biographical details to a particular work, career or psychology. This was one of the few topics on which I was confident Beulah and I were in agreement.

From problems of cause we pass to problems of content. The usual scruples about publishing any intimate document apply here. Moreover, several entries allude to acts that for the best of reasons remain taboo even in a permissive society. Permissive, yet one in which almost nothing remains of the private domain, and in which the public is inundated with denunciations, victim-scripts and the illicit, luridly exposed and confessed. More fatally, though, certain of these scripts have become stock items in publishing circles, almost a genre, and one recently coming in for a good deal of high-brow cynicism. For its practitioners, the most authentic horrors quickly lose their freshness even as the public appetite for them burgeons. So to air such things now amounts to a high-cost, low-yield venture in which everyone comes off the worse: the editor who opts to publish, the passé victim, the demonized malefactor and the media mavens moved to put their cynicism on display.

A few readers, of course, will claim that bowing to such scruples lets me suppress unflattering glimpses of myself or even incriminating evidence. So, *nota bene*, since I believe her journals constitute Exhibit A in my defence, I've decided to include virtually everything in her papers making significant mention of me.

NEEDY GIRL

Finally, there arise the inevitable questions as to veracity. It pains me to say this, but it is simply not possible for me to credit much of what Beulah has written.

Going at least as far back as 1985, she displayed a mania for weaving the events of her life into some vast, mythic struggle. Every windmill is a giant, every conflict with a parent or teacher, Armageddon. Regardless of what really took place she experienced it with a high quotient of pain. The mythologizing may well have been a tactic to make that pain meaningful and therefore more bearable. It may even have been the genesis of her obsessive interest in the myths surrounding her research subject.

Beulah herself seems to have taken pains to undermine the reliability of her accounts. At various junctures she has written little notes in the diary margins, often to an unspecified doctor. Which doctor?— there were several in her past. Was it a particular individual or did Beulah compile some arch-antagonist by taking features from several people? In a few cases, I *was* clearly the doctor in question. But this meant she had reread her early journals with me in mind, annotating them to goad or provoke, to repel or to draw me in.

The pen used for the marginalia is sometimes indistinguishable from that of the narration, but at other times the ink is of a different colour. She was aware—or even intended—that these passages would be read, which raises the question: Could entire journals be fictions— maybe even written after the fact and backdated? At what points does a testimony pass from the subjective through the fictive into the expressly counterfeit?

In light of the foregoing, in drawing from her diaries I've opted to include excerpts of three kinds: entries involving me, entries with dates coinciding with her research notes and her travel journals from Mexico, plus a few entries from before her researches formally began. This should suffice to give readers a flavour, and a chance to arrive at their own opinion on the legitimacy of my decision to use some materials while suppressing others.

[26 Dec 1985]
Always before it started he'd come in and say You're a needy little girl Beulah You know that don't you. I knew. Always when it was over smile

gone soft he'd say You can have anything you want You're going to have it all I promise you. Promise? He promised. But he doesn't come anymore.

20 Mar [19]89

Last night before I went out he said I could have it all just like he used to when I was little—if only I'd just get some help. Problems? They haven't seen anything yet.

31 Mar [19]89

They want me to See Someone again. Not just them this time. Everybody. It's all over school—the other mothers don't want their perfect little girls near me. We'll all go see Doctor Together—don't doctors' families get a discount, daddy? Discount daddy. We'll go as soon as the bruises go away. [. . .] Funny to hear him use those words. Eslut. I laughed in his face I couldn't help it what was I supposed to do him calling me an eslut? An estupid eslut. An especially estupid eslut. [. . .]

1 Apr [19]89

Goes away to Mexico now. A sudden little business trip thought he'd take in that medical conference after all. Or does he call it a composium? In daddy's absence there's been a little scrape with drugs—My daughter misses his steadying influence Officer. . . . So takin my tender age and solid family background n'all inta'count they decide to release me into the care of my doting mother.

   Today mummy and I have to have a real talk. Give her some credit she made the effort. Have I ever considered what effect all this was having on my brother? Leave Gavin the *fuck* out of this—Okay calm *down*. All right we won't talk about Gavin today. Let's talk about you. What'd I mean the other night ? [. . .] I couldn't know what I was saying. My father would never do anything to hurt me. He's a doctor.

17 Apr [1989]

I just couldn't figure it out why he did it kept thinking this wasn't like him. Another business-trip-guilt-gift from Mexico—does he think we all don't know why he *really* goes there? But not the usual airport gift-rack inspiration. So perfect . . . look at the binding it's hand-sewn he says feel the soft leather—THREE POETS OF THE BAROQUE: Louise Labé, *Gaspara Stampa, Juana Inés de la Cruz.*[2]

Thanks thank you it's beautiful. Really. Sorry for asking why are you giving me this? He looks at mummy for a second it all starts spilling out how I could still have it all, how I must know that, how I had everything beauty brains graduating not even seventeen in spite of all my—how if I would only get a little help talk some of these things out—he sees my face and stops. There's an inscription inside.

I couldn't remember ever seeing his handwriting. *I'm sorry for all the pain you've had to endure. Please know I love you like a daughter. Love Jonas.* Staring stupidly at him I still don't get it.

He wanted to say first of all my mother'd always wanted to tell—but he'd been against it. Now everyone knew it had been a mistake but mistakes happen. Right that's true. He hadn't wanted me to grow up feeling different—she says Beulah this is going to be terrible for you. What is?—*what?*

Jonas . . . tick tick tick . . . was not—I knew I *knew* then what she was going to say, this was too good to be true come on *say* it—*Jonas is not your real father*—it feels like a dream write it down circle it with stars—****not your natural father**** My unnatural father then? Don't—*please*—don't say anything for a minute—just one minute for Christ's sake. Your fath—Jonas thought we should wait and tell you when you were bigger.

I'm bigger.

Did I know he'd come to this country as a teenager? I knew. Enough that he was different—they never let up on him no matter how hard he'd tried to fit to learn their language perfectly he was always going to be some wog—Jonas, Joanie they called him Joanie Rhinoceros Joanie Rhino try to understand—shut up I wanted to *scream* shut the fuck up WHO IS MY FATHER?—

So then she wasn't my mother? Oh Beulah—of course I am. She always suspected I knew all along. I'd always known hadn't I it was a lie?—a white lie? *Yes inside me I have always known.* Jonas believes it's where your troubles started—troubles?—you know, your troubles with reality—My troubles with reality, how sweet daddy can I still call you that?—even though it was a white lie to protect me. Protect me. . . . It was why I'd been having these fantasies about—about *him*.

They said there was an accident when I was just a baby my father was killed—they tell you ok great news you've got a *real* father but the bad bad news is he's dead. They were so sorry. But it was time for the whole truth. They weren't lying now. They wouldn't lie about a thing like this. No no of course not, nothing but the truth so help them god keep their stories straight. Jonas was your father's best friend—so who needs enemies right?—*their* fathers were best friends back in Vigo. Jonas and Andy—his name's Andy?—Andrés—*my father's name is Andrés*—came over from Spain together as boys. They did everything together. Yes I can see that. Her face puffing up red like from a slap. Shut your dirty mouth—now *this* was more like it more like the old homestead—couldn't I just shut it and listen? What kind of 'accident' was this anyway? I look him right in the fucking face she starts to bawl. Beulah *please* they were like brothers. Sure Cain and Abel.

He worked like an animal Honey driving that truck he was always away starting to change starting to act strange. Then it got worse. When I got pregnant with you he . . . he didn't believe you were . . . *his*. Because of him. Because of that fucking hypocrite over there my own father couldn't believe I was really his little girl. He started drinking—oh Honey we were all so unhappy then. Mummy never ever drank at all before that time if it weren't for Jonas she would have gone out of her mind. Andy became so—she was afraid for all of us. She begged him to get help—*You* should get help Mummy get help getting all these people to get help.

There was an accident, with the truck. They say he'd been drinking—he was *ill*. In his mind. It wasn't just the drinking. Jonas says they've identified genes, genetic diseases. Mental diseases passed down from one generation to—*I know what genes are*. We want you to go for some tests. To the hospital. Just a few tests. Just for a few days. All my problems could be from—from *him*—specialists developing new therapies—I thought you said tests now it's therapy. You're trying to do the same to me as you did to him—blame the dead guy well I don't believe he *is* dead ok? I don't believe a fucking word. You want to put me where nobody will listen where nobody can hear me. But I can hurt you out here can't I? I want to hurt *you* now.

eX-daddy wanted me to stop this right this instant I shouldn't do this to my mother. We shouldn't do this to each other. We were a family.

8 [May 1989]
This man this great and famous [. . .] who did these things was not your daddy. You were someone else's little girl. And you took it all—because

your daddy could never do anything to hurt you but now he isn't your daddy [. . .] Your daddy would never do anything to hurt you but if he wasn't your daddy and he *had* hurt you it hurt so much still. But then he had a son a little boy of his own and it didn't hurt Gavin because your daddy could never do anything to hurt you. But Gavin cried and said they hurt him too but if that was true then your daddy and not your daddy could hurt when he loved you but hurt too when he didn't care. Or if they hurt it proved he didn't love you so you never wanted it to and if he loved you it proved it couldn't hurt not really. And if you loved him enough then maybe maybe it wouldn't if you could just believe hard enough he loved you. And maybe if he was not your daddy he had to do hurtful things but not hurt you to show he loved you because if it hurt he didn't care. He did these things [. . .] you were little but now you're big—

They only need you when you're small.

And now they want to tell the world you're crazy because of the crazy things you say.

They are trying to make me insane.

[10 May 1989]
Nine hundred eighty-two thousand four hundred twelve. Two hundred sixty nine thousand thirteen, five hundred twenty two thousand seven hundred seventeen . . .

4 Sept 1989
Rereading this now I have never in my whole life felt stronger but I know if not for her . . . with her as my guide I have learned to control my destiny. Under her protection I have learned to rule *them*.

Together we have learned to make sacrifices.

Mummy cried—so afraid for me she said but she was afraid *of* me. She pretends not to know what's happening but it wasn't my father's disease it was *his*. And now *I* know and I have never felt such

pure

clear

joy—

HE IS NOT MY FATHER. I will not eat his disease.

He tries to bully me screams at me to think of the children in Africa—good let's start thinking about the little children now—to stop being so ridiculous.

We have stopped being ridiculous.

He pretends to be furious but he is afraid too—it has been so *easy*. By August they'd have done anything to get rid of us. University? Of course. Money? No problem. My own place? Perhaps it was for the best. Hospital? No, not just now, but thanks for caring.

13 Apr 1990

... Fuck. I *deserve* this—am I such a child to let you slip to the floor like a forgotten doll? So sure you would be where I left you lying there so sure I could go back any time and pick you up. And now to have my nose rubbed in my own shit. Someone else comes along and finds you lying there, picks you up dusts you off and now a whole nation of cattle on couches steers on sectionals munching to the rhythm of the radio[3] knows more of you than I do.

You spoke to me once but I stopped hearing. You taught me secret things but I stopped learning. I'll find you. And if you'll only speak to me again I'll really listen and never stop. I will do anything, I will make sacrifices—if you'll just come back to me.

Talk to me.

Protect me.

I give you power over me.[4]

JUANA INÉS
DE LA CRUZ

B. Limosneros, trans.

World, in persecuting me, how do you profit?
How have I offended, in seeking
to earn beauty of the spirit
and not sell my soul for beauty?

     Never have I gain or lucre sought,
but instead find advantage in
putting my stock in richness of thought—
not wasting my thoughts on riches.

     I neither treasure the lovely lustre
that proves but the spoil of age,
nor covet wealth of counterfeit coinage;

     thinking it far better, by my lights,
to set aside the vanities of life
than spend a whole life in vain.

11 Feb [1993 Calgary]

HE'S STARTING TO TAKE CHANCES. Dinner for two. In public. Even
in the back, in a booth. Even in a French restaurant on a Thursday night.
Not that people looking at us—at me—would assume, not automatically.
But then he takes my hand and it's so obvious for anyone walking past . . .

Starched white tablecloth, peach polyester napkins folded in fans.
Reflections smear in the cutlery. I sit there like a stone. I can't help it,
can't move.

Cat got my tongue?—he didn't think he'd ever seen me looking nervous. I wasn't going to sit there like that all night was I? All these *people*—
nonsense, he smiles the winning smile, nobody was looking at us way
back here. A little wine wouldn't hurt tonight for once would it? And
where the hell *is* the waiter?

*Ayez l'obligeance de nous apporter une bouteille du Griotte-Chambertin. Le
'92, Monsieur? Non, le '91—bien evidemment. Ah oui, Monsieur.*

See that? sly prick tried to unload their '92 on us. At the same *price*.

See brave Doctor Gregory working so hard over the corpse of his
statue—plug the nose, seal the lips, puff.

Not to worry: he and Madeleine never came down here, never left
their neverland, northwest Calgary. She liked to call herself a north-
erner . . . their little joke. Yes, good one, Doctor. Sorry bad storyform to
talk about her. How was the research going?

He doesn't want to know. Yes he did—no *really*. Mr. Sincerity. Well . . .
just questions mostly. Questions were good, a very good sign. Such as?
Such as what her confessor is like. . . .

Yes? Go on, he was here to help—the brawny scholar paw reaches
out. Okay, she wrote poetry in Nahuatl too, so isn't she just possibly the
greatest Nahuatl poet—her time's greatest living writer in *two* languages?
I need to understand better what Isis means to her, and her poetry was
full of Greek and Egyptian myths yet only rarely Mexican, and what is it
to be consumed by knowledge—or need—or Mind—

Okayokay whoa slow down a bit. Now. Listen, there was something
we absolutely had to talk about. Absolutely, Don, then let's. I knew, didn't
I, that I could write just about anything for him—and yes we were only
talking about an honour's thesis—and I still had two months to cook

something up for grad school, but the time had come—pause for drrrummrollll—to say this was getting worrisome. What is? I surely had to know I hadn't presented him with a single topic even close to suitable. Unsuitable how? Don't be disingenuous. Be genuous then, Don, and tell me. Well for one thing, I knew purrfectly well none of this was what was meant by American literature. So Mexico is not America? or Mexico is just not literate. Very funny—but no one in the department was qualified to sit on my thesis committee. They didn't even read Spanish. But *he* does. Painfully, yes—which most certainly did not make him qualified to supervise on just any topic I could come up with.

No wait—I am studying under one of the leading authorities on early American literature but can't do research on the greatest American poet of the 16th, 17th, 18th—I don't know, Doctor Gregory, you tell *me* when to stop—Whitman, Dickinson, Eliot, Frost? Or is she better than everybody on the approved list of *any* American century? What is she then, *un*-American?

Come off it—fucking around with semantics wasn't going to make the rules go away. Okay semantics don't matter so what possible difference should the *language* make—it's all literature, after all. Maybe so, but this was still very plainly a project for romance studies or comparative lit—wake-up time, Beulah. The deadline for grad applications was the end of February, and here it was the eleventh already.

Yes happy Valentine's, *Profe*. A toast to our cupidity—don't be mean, Doctor Don, order us another beaujolly at eighty a bottle.

Be reasonable. He didn't make the rules. They just didn't have the resources anymore within the department for cross-disciplinary research or whatever this was to be. Christ, Beulah—you're up there every day. We cut to the bone five years ago. Anyway the kind of thing I seemed to be planning, if I could pull it off at all, needs to be under big names in big schools, not backwaters in the colonies. Go east, go south, go overseas, but go.

So why then is he back on the farm after gay Paris? Yes but, you see, at least he'd gone. A job, Beulah. That was all it was now. This little, he could do anywhere, even here. I should be thinking about my career.

Oh *that*—break new ground *carpe diem*, gut the fat bottom-feeding carp called opportunity. Like I give a fuck about jobs.

Yes well, that made two of us but I was about to lose a year. Which for a working sell-out like him or even a pure searcher like Beulah

Limosneros was still twelve long months. And anyway one could score all the points one wanted for my Sor Juana by making comparisons with someone like Anne Bradstreet—

Anne Bradstreet—are you *kidding?*—hello, class, my research paper is on Milton and Milton Acorn.

They aren't even in the same *galaxy.* And why does it only get to be his Pilgrim America? Quakers and shakers holding down the creaky palisade—Verily neighbours, let the dark night descend but not on our watch! We are the rock. Let the casements crack in this *casamatta,* house of godchild and lambslaughter, let the chasms yawn but we stand firm against the chaos—The greatest period in English literature is the Baroque, Don. Spenser Marlowe Shakespeare Donne Milton Marvell Jonson Dryden. Metaphysical?—why is it so hard to call a spade a mongrel? It's all myths and togas and fairies and fallen angels and ghosts and witches for almost two hundred years. Puritan *and* cavalier *and* metaphysical—the Baroque.

But that's why he took up early American lit in the first place, isn't it, Professor. The English can try to deny it—Mr. Bones in the closet—but Americans don't have to—right? Not with Dr. Donald J. Gregory holding down the fort. But if and only if we leave out Latin America. Then it's just Bradstreet and John Q-Fucking Smith's Pocahontas. Then Hawkeye and Chingachgook, soon Old Shatterhand—and on down the steep slippery slope to the joke.

If you can fix it, it ain't baroque.

The professorial smirk. Very good, Beulah, not to forget Tonto and Winnetou. And no he didn't think this whole thing was a joke, but weren't we supposed to be having a good time tonight?—and yes, Valentine's was nigh. Here try some of this fresh bread, come on eat while it was still warm, this was my fourth glass. Thought I said I never drank much. . . .

Turn on the charm, doctor Donald. Hot tap to the left cold to the right. Smile Don, feel the cheeks dimple, the laugh lines crinkle the intelligent eyes—oh yes, so blue, can't he just imagine the candlelight dancing in them now.

Sure she can, she can do this—flutter to his hand, smile perch and warble. We are not babybirds anymore. A little bread? Yes *please.* Bread on sideplate, spread napkin over lap, wedge baggie between thighs, no butter thanks. There. Just like she practised. Break off a piece, gently chew, wipe lips with napkin, dainty girl. Pretty bird. Palm wad into baggie, replace napkin, smile. Smile and repeat. As needed *ad infinitum* add *nauseam*.

Was that a smile?—we should have ordered appetizers right off. Okay, then, not Anne Bradstreet but how about Aphra Behn?

So living in Surinam for two years makes her American—but not Sor Juana?

Comparative lit, Beulah, not American. Ah. Think about it. Behn wasn't in her ballpark as a thinker, but she was versatile and prolific and gutsy and broke new ground for people like Dafoe—seminal in prose.

Did he say Seminole in pose, Cherokee in cheek and cheer, Delaware in all she did?

No really, consider it. Serially. Two famous women. Trailblazers. One goes from spying for King James to the poorhouse gates to woman of scandal. The other goes from palace to convent to living legend—forgotten five years after her death. Different choices, different lives, yet—

Bravo Don. But he's forgetting to mention the best part. Oh, what was that? With Aphra Bent in the picture, he won't have to be my thesis adviser. Beulah . . . try Stanwyck, she had her fingers in everyone's pie. This paleo-feminist white hat black hat stuff—making the world safe for the wailing eirenes of matriarchy—it just didn't cut it anymore, if it ever did. It was a ghetto now. It wasn't his fight, not his thing.

Not his thing—look at him—sandy ponytail white-water rafting gourmet cook / five years too young for the sixties, touches up his beard to bring out the grey in his gayParee *soixante-huit* goatee, tickly between my knees.

This is just women's work, is that it? Sappho, Sor Juana, St. Catherine— only a woman could be interested?

When he offered to be my thesis adviser . . . surely I could see this wasn't what he—look here was the waiter better get some food in us.

The waiting, the wine—I want to scream jets of spit spurting in the back of my mouth a tingling aching needling under each ear. Would I let him order for us both? See the garce's greasy smile. Something light, *please*, I'm not too—Nonsense. Let's see says the grand host connoisseur of the world of the senses and the mind. *Hurry.*

The Chateaubriand for two. Oh god, meat. *Rare* . . . the only way to have Chateaubriand.

Couldn't I see I didn't need him for a thesis adviser? I needed Erasmus, Leonardo maybe. Whole lifetimes were spent on a fraction of what I'd pretend to cover in two years. This was an exercise in anti-scholarship. To finish even in five I'd have to ransack the sources. Intellectual cannibalism the worst kind of dilettantism a vandal loose in the library.

So fucking what

So I had to understand this stuff went out of style with Blake—hell, Beulah, he was never *in*. Don't kid yourself this was the fashion business—you'd be rewriting the dead sea scrolls here. Another thing . . . Yes, mein Overseer? I could call this micro-history or social history or whatever but it was starting to smell like fiction—where was I getting all this data?

Call it thick description.

He'd had the distinct impression I was interested in scholarship. Discipline. No Don—just a spanking once in a while.

Seriously—right this minute I should please please assure him I didn't want to do *fiction*. Literary bodice rippers, windswept Heathcliffs, highbrow harlequins—kitchen sink Histories for entrepreneurial college gals.

Ah harlequins—*harlequins?*—what the fuck is philosophy, Doctor Don? but Muttonchop Realism, Victorian Self-Congratulation. All the learned societies shrinking into their starchy chastey labcotes—all the chesty strutting / the teenytiny cabinets of Sophiphiliac specialization / the pasty balding fratboys playing hide and seek in the haunty house of paradox. He isn't going to start calling literary criticism a *science* now? Not seriously.

So this was what he'd been sweating to save me from these past months? *Kitsch of the past*—the lisping diction, ye aulde oak-aged accents and lexical curiositie shoppes, the phony ironies.

Kitsch?—what is his transcendent truth of History but the kitsch of a bogus objectivity? And does he mean phony like *Richard III* or kitschy like poor anachronistic *Coriolanus* or the eh-historical *Iliad*?

And if you truly must have a justicayshun, Masta-Don—long in the tooth, yellow in the tusk—for all the pidgin dickshun, call it a translayshun.[5]

And who is he to be so highhorsed about lying—why didn't I say it *then*, why didn't I say it to his face?—Donald Gregory, the modern world's leading expert on the taxidermies of fable and heartless fib-relations. The wily stuffed fox, the walking liar's paradox. Gamekeeper gatekeeper Vegas liontamer on the American lit game farm. All to protect us from the wilderness inside. So hard you try, expert on the literary lie. You're more baroque than Donne, Don. Is that why you hate it so? Poor conflicted Donny playing po-mo mummy off against positivist daddy Popper, sownz like a rapper.

What was his po'pomo but the baroque with its heart torn out.

More wine, Beulah?

Stop playing the holy host, fucker.

Say, Beulah why not do this research of yours on the side?—sure, some of his best work comes on the side—right? Any more great ideas?

Is it Latin America he loathes? Why has he never once written about Poe and Faulkner who'd marked Latin America most, why is that, professor? praisesinger of Whitman and Hawthorne at Melville's expense, and always mentioning the Moby and the Mohican in the same tar-breath. And never once penning on Poe in all that time. Is it the *Private*, Donny's worst nightmare? Sticky private truths and private parts—*my Professor wants us to all go live in a quaker colony.*

Sssh, Beulah, hold it down. *I am fucker, I am—but just.* Alright yes, he found it annoying, all the fascinating heroines called Laura, all the fanci-fied butterflies, all the *Borges* cheap as borscht—So yeah, rooting out the lie down South meant going house to house. Was I satisfied? Sorry but surely I must see now how he could never effectively advise me. Oh but I could trust him. He wouldn't let me down. He'd have a word with the boys in Comp. Lit. for me. Or even Stanwyck, there was still time.

Promise, Don?

He promised—warm smile, takes my hands so cold so *chilly*—Beulah don't worry, just get a half-assed application in, plenty of time the whole summer to work everything out, to hammer away at this—hammer away at *me* you mean. Now could we please talk about something else?

Ahem . . . yes Sunday was Valentine's and yes he and Madeleine had plans—but how about Easter Break getting away for a day or two. . . .

All night long I sit for this just *sitting* there surrounded—stuffed faces chewing cud chaws of meat, the greasy smell of Prime Alberta Beef all night long sucking sucking—sucking up but not smiling at his little jokes afraid he'd see my teeth. Meat. My mouth filling with slick spit, the cologne smell from his perfect beard. God I hate your fucking face the arched brows—the playful sceptic eyes, blue complacent ruins—so co-conspiratorial.

Oh yes we share a special secret just you and me. He thinks they're his best feature. So sure of himself. Above any judgement but his own—how can he be so sure his good is good enough his bad is not too bad how can he be so sure his next fuck won't be his last.

Homo rectus the upright man.

Food the food finally comes. And do we need ground pepper, um, Miss? and I know I can't I couldn't eat could never swallowchoke this down with everyone watching. Him right there, watching my throat bobbing up and down a thick rat running down a hole.

Chew the meat. Chew the meat palm the wad into the napkin / slip the wad inside the bag don't ever let the rat down the hole. Chew the meat feel the greasy baggy swelling. Chew the meat feel the queasy gorge uplifting—chew the meat. Swallow swallow just the slickety spit / just keep it down keep from spewing out *wide* across the whole fucking ROOM.

Excuse m—no no fine, be right back—lunge humpbacked bent over the baggie shamble for the toilet / throat bobbing up bobbing down. They stop chewing to watch, jaws go slackstill drop, see the mashy topple inside their holes. Feel their filmy white eyes following. Mouth cheeks filling tingling with slippery spit. DON'T yet—

Ladies—welcome home / feel the cool still porcelain all around now, like marble, a tomb.

Old bag of skin mummy's age rinses little lady paws in sink. Startled eyes, still she hangs around washes each bony finger gleaming clean, watching. Out cunt. Out hurry up. OUT. Pick a stall / press warm meatbag against the eyes / behind the neck smear it cross the throat the heart hope to die / cross the chest the face the hair—cram it cram it all jam the little wads of mush / cuds of chaw into the yawing hole. No slow. Slow down stupid cow swallow don't chew swallow it whole hog—hog it all down hog it. Suck it swallow suck it—no teeth—don't chew—SWALLOW THE WORLD get it all down.

Coming. So come closer then. Don't rush now let it come cram don't chew / no hands look no ma—suck don't chew love this suckguzzle this all down almost—on your knees bitchdown feel the cold enamel still the fat throat / not yet don't rush too *late* too long oh god—help it up/come fingers down just a bit not too far *not too much.* Don't push let it come to shove—*farther*—now *now* shove all the way down *push till it comes.* AND

IT COMES a gut-heaving clearing voiding heave—again a beautiful wave she spills she jets her bilious guts up through a teary grin—and out and up and ALL ACROSS THE SKY—

In ribbons.

Waves wider-spaced wait for it pass the time join the last to the next a tiny thread don't ever let it end fill the time—how long has it been? will he ask will he see? is it all ruined now—think think of tonight. Fix it, fix it, make everything all right.

It's not all ruined—think.

The couple enters the Night clerk looks up they ask for one with two double beds he doesn't automatically assume. Room 327. Just watch her make everything all right. Watch her make him promise. He'll say anything. Promise. Make him say it. He does anything she says, he does nothing unless she says. He says Nobody ever fucks me like this. Say it again. He fumbles at her straps. She looks down—the body he loves the one she hates spills out like garbage splitting a bag. He turns down the sheets. From the bed she watches him undress pressed bluejeans folded over the chair sportscoat hung on the back. Clean white shorts thin legs knee-high black socks. Through a crack in the curtains light catches lunar pocks on his round hairy back a hairy golf ball—she finds this cute she finds this adorable—shorts off in one swift wriggle and kick he turns back to the bed. He is already excited. Everything is going to be all right. He walks like a man with a trophy, holding it out, a man bringing flowers. She is calm now. Calm and happy. She does not worry, everything will be all right. She *will* make him promise, her holy host on her tongue. Push it back through the gag in her gullet, fill her chest her lungs with it, feel the sweet storm of grain slap her crop, warm her belly, pluck her up.

But calmly, gently, now.

And when she has taken him prisoner, when she has taken his life in her mouth, when it is time when the time is right, she will bite right through it, will cut him off from his life.

And once it is over, she will walk slowly not hurrying to the toilet and lock it carefully. She will check, it is locked. Smile into the mirror, wipe the serum from her chin her lips, from throat to chest. Turn on both taps full sink then tub. And alone in her little cave of rushing welling water SeaCow will let it come SeaCow will let it run. There will be enough. She will get it all. And she will be calm and cold and still as stone, once more.

At last, sides aching from the tight twist of her quiet retching, lips and gums all warm and glowing, she goes to him gratefully, her knees weak, head pounding clear and fresh. He asks her drowsily Why do you always go in and run the water after? *La bucca dentata* smiles through blood-shot eyes, smiles unafraid now he will see her teeth and says I got it all didn't I. Last drop, sleepyhead smiles. You were pretty rough.

You know, for a minute there I thought you were about to

JUANA INÉS
DE LA CRUZ

B. Limonsneros, trans.

Este, que ves, engaño colorido,
que del arte ostentando los primores,
con falso silogismos de colores
es cauteloso engaño del sentido;
    este, en quien la lisonja ha pretendido
excusar de los años los horrores,
y venciendo del tiempo los rigores
triunfar de la vejez y del olvido,
    es un vano artificio del cuidado,
es una flor al viento delicada,
es un resguardo inútil para el hado:
    es una necia diligencia errada,
es un afán caduco y, bien mirado,
es cadáver, es polvo, es sombra, es nada.

She rejects the flattery visible in a portrait of herself

This painted semblance you so admire,
of an art flaunting its mastery
with false syllogisms of colour,
that smoothly mocks the eye;
    this face—in which flattery pretends
to still the horror of the racing hours,
to stay the hand of ravishing time,
and spare us ageing and oblivion—
    is only panic's thin disguise,
is a garland to bar the hurricane,
is a cry in the wilderness,
    is a token gesture made in vain,
is wasted toil and—through these eyes—
is Corpse. Dust. Shade. Nothingness.

I had forgotten this. Now the memory brings no pleasure.

Even here, he said, even in America, we serve the Sovereign of Two Worlds.

We were at the firepit, just the two of us, and had spent the day together reading. The air was crisp and cold that night—up from our lips drifted curls and waves of mist but we stayed late by the fire. There were too few such days, such nights.

Abuelo rarely spoke about the war. The House of Austria, stretched thin between Vienna and Madrid ... Turks and Moors to east and south, Bourbons and Protestants to west and north. Three hundred dukedoms and principalities tangled up in an impossible snarl of loyalties and betrayals. Catholic France sponsoring the Protestant Union, Lutheran Saxony fighting alongside the Catholic League. ... Four hundred armies swarming over Europe like locusts, like packs of dogs turning on each other. The populations of Europe slashed by a third in barely a generation, thirty years of war ...

"Half again as long as Troy, Angelina. And we fought for no better reasons ... every duke craving a kingdom, every king an empire. No wonder Homer went blind, straining to see to the end of it."

My grandfather volunteered in 1618. The truce with the low countries was expiring. Losing Portugal seemed just a matter of time. Everyone remembered that year, he said, for the comets. Three in the span of a few months, swords of flame over the horizon. This would be the Armageddon, the war to end the world. The important thing was to be fighting for the right side. They were just boys.

"No sooner had I survived the first campaign but I was *praying* for the war to end. The death, the rotting bread, the pestilence . . . Each Horseman had a season. Summers of war and fire—the cities went up like torches. Autumns of plague. And winters, winters were the harvest of the famine sown each spring, when the farmers were plucked from their planting and pressed into uniform.

"The land was exhausted anyway, not at all like here. Even when a field was sown, for every seed planted you were lucky to harvest six. One to replant, one to save, one to trade, the rest to armies and kings."

It grew worse.

He had always dreamt of travelling. He travelled, now. Through the Spanish possessions of Italy to Vienna they rode, thence to Bohemia, across Bavaria and through the Palatine. Then up the Spanish Road towards the low countries, the United Provinces. In Westphalia he had watched mobs begging offal from the slaughterhouses. In Prague thousands had simply starved ... tens of thousands more dying on battlefields and in *lazaretos*[†] all across the continent.

[†] 'lazarets,' stations of quarantine

"In '21 we thought it might be over, after White Mountain. There were such high hopes for the new king, though he was himself just a boy. I left in '24. Almost an old man already at thirty-five. And even then I was lucky ... Lucky not to have seen a thing like Magdeburg, where twenty thousand townspeople were massacred in a day."

What he said next surprised me, for I knew he considered it his great good fortune just to have survived.

"And yet, Angel ... I never fought under Spínola."[†] He lifted his chin just a little. "It would have been good to have served a prince in the field. But had I stayed for Breda, how many Magdeburgs might I have witnessed?"

[†] the ablest Spanish general, who laid siege to Breda and later pardoned its defenders

With the tip of his traveller's staff he raked at the embers. I was not sure I'd understood him, and went hunting for the lines of Sarpedon, Zeus's mortal son, to Glaucus.

> Glaucus, say why are we honor'd more
> Than other men of Lycia ...
> The shores of Xanthus ring of this: and shall we not exceed
> As much in merit as in noise? Come, be we great in deed
> As well as look, shine not in gold but in the flames of fight,
> That so our neat-arm'd Lycians may say: "See, these are right
> Our Kings, our Rulers: these deserve to eat and drink the best;
> These govern not ingloriously; these thus exceed the rest.
> Do more than they command to do. . . . [6]

When I had found this and read it for him, I saw I'd understood him well enough. He didn't speak for a moment, but I knew he would go on now.

"The whole way back I walked with a bloodied bandage around my head, and when I think of that walk I still hear the flies buzzing at one ear. Ahh," he said, "I see you hear them too. I walked back to my village, but the want and the sickness were too terrible there. Everyone was gone. I kept on, following the south bank down to the mouth of the Guadalquivir, stood up to my hips where the brown of the river ran to brine. My boots were more like sandals by then, but upside down, so worn were they at the soles. I went barefoot down the shore all the way to land's end, walking and thinking and arguing with the flies. I looked across the straits to Africa, past *el peñón de Calpe* to Mount Hacho, and past that one to where I was sure I glimpsed the Atlas range.[7]

"I stared at those mountains and thought hard about walking right down through Africa to land's end *there*. Angelina, I was standing at the pillars of Calpe and Abyla! Hardly a hundred years before, and for the two thousand before that, this had *been* the end of the world. But it felt in that instant as if its end lay not ahead but at my back—and I had escaped it.

"I unwrapped the bandage, and tossed it into the sea. I was not ready to be an old man quite yet. No, I would come to America and see for myself if the New World had an end *at all*. *Los Portugueses* were evasive as always. '*Tierra del fuego*' . . . ice and fire, seas of fog, earth disappearing into thin air. What was anyone to make of that, eh? But when a Portuguese[†] tells a Spaniard about the sea," Abuelo bent forward confidingly, his elbows on his knees, "you can be sure he is keeping the best parts to himself."

[†]Magellan

Nodding assent, I fed another stick to the fire as he talked. The flames roared up.

"Then I met my Beatriz on the boat across," he said, brightening, "a girl from the south bank, the village right next to mine. There was the end of one dream, but the beginning of a happier one. . . . And yet, and yet, who could ever have imagined it? That the horror I had volunteered for as a young man would not end until the year a certain granddaughter of mine was born."

"Me?"

"You, *mi hijita*, you. . . ."

How proud he was to have served, even an empire bankrupt and broken. Of all the epithets attaching to the Spanish king—Catholic Monarch, Planet King, &c.—the one my grandfather pronounced most proudly was this, *Soberano de los Dos Mundos*. So yes, proud, and sad, and with a fascination for the death of empires that stayed with him to the last day of his life.

Sovereign of the Two Worlds.

When I moved from my uncle's house to the Viceroy's court, so eager to serve, I wrote an elegy for a king, the young king my grandfather had served under. Courtiers who had known that king sniggered behind their handkerchiefs—even those who had been with him at the Alcázar[†] as he died. Even my friends smiled and thought me naïve, made excuses for me. *She is only seventeen.*

[†]the Royal Palace in Madrid

At the hour of his death, it is said, every eye in Madrid was dry. It is also said that just three people cried—Queen Mariana, and no one could name with any certainty the other two. One wag at our court averred that it was not three people but three *eyes*: the last shopkeeper in Madrid to extend the palace credit, and his one-eyed wife.

I weep for the king who dies unmourned, I wept for that one, Philip IV—to have presided at the ruin of Europe's greatest throne. I wept for the prince born to lead but never shown how, an Alexander without an Aristotle, unable to unravel the knot in the thread of his greatness. For the dying empire does not prepare its princes for this. Olivares did everything to keep him from the field, built for him a country pleasure palace, the envy of all Europe until Versailles. *El Palacio del Buen Retiro.*[†] A palace fit for our century of ten thousand comedies. Such merriments the comedians made on his retreats.

[†]Palace of the Good Retreat

Quevedo, for one. *Our king is like a hole. The more land they take from him, the greater he becomes.* I could never quite forgive Quevedo this one.

Philip was just sixteen when he ascended the throne. Planet King! they proclaimed him, that centrepiece about which all lesser bodies revolve like hungry courtiers tabled in their epicycles. Lesser bodies such as his future son-in-law, the young French Sun King, Louis XIV.

As I sat to write his elegy I thought of how he had been mocked, by history and by the stars. Forty years on, he must have seen this himself, as death approached, so elliptically. And seen also how he had been mocked by his own courtiers from the start. For, just a few years before the western Hapsburgs had acclaimed him Planet King, centre of the universe, the Hapsburg Emperor in Vienna had been studying astronomy. With Kepler.

Such a gift I have for seeing the emblems woven into other lives.

I could not forgive Quevedo, and yet within a year or two at court I was doing it also. I said things like this: *Louis did more for Copernicus than Galileo ever did—while Philip did for Ptolemy. Single-handedly.*

Did I really tell myself it made any difference that I was more than half in earnest—all the while knowing they would laugh twice as hard?

Philip IV. Who kept his dwarves like princes; kept by his princes a dwarf.

This was how I had come to serve the servants of the sovereign. Having forgotten all about my elegy and about the service of princes.

I may have forgotten this, but there is nothing wrong with my memory. Even to those closest to me I say the little that I can. It seems I have only to meet someone to find myself asked about my past. Yet I do not like to look back. Still less to have my childhood made the subject of my confessions.

Who is this Jesuit, Antonio Núñez de Miranda? Who comes to the palace yet is not of the palace, who does not live among us, yet is never far. Who confesses us all: the Vice-Queen, the Vice-King and most of his administration. All are a little afraid of him. He is not old, being of a generation hardly older than my father's. Small bones, small head, the skin dry as parchment, the stooped nodding walk . . . Maybe this is why so many say he seems ancient. They speak of his hatred of pride, of his humility . . . of the grey eyes meekly downcast, the thick lids heavy, as if in mirth—until opened wide the eyes blaze with rage, staring into yours. They speak of how it takes some getting used to.

This subtle man, among the most brilliant I have yet met, whose memory is uncanny, perfect, better even than my own. He has urged me to meditate on the past, and has listened to my confessions attentively. This soldier who bears no arms, yet is commanded by a general in Rome for whom he would gladly die. And yet with me, Father Núñez begins with none of the harshness and choler for which he is so well known. With not a little poetry, he speaks to me of Loyola, founder of the Company, son of a Basque nobleman born in the ancestral castle. Father Núñez speaks of how the young Loyola loved music, how he won his knighthood in the service of Antonio Manrique de Lara, Duke of Nájera and Viceroy of Navarre.

Ignatius Loyola, first General of the Company of Jesus, who wrote so movingly of his spiritual awakening, a man who until then cared only about martial exercises, with a *great and vain desire to win renown.*

Crippled in battle, Loyola lay for months on a convalescent's bed in an empty castle. Among the few works accessible to him were the writings of a certain monk. Over and over Loyola read them, absorbing the vision of this Cistercian who depicted the service of Christ as a holy order of chivalry and saw, in the lover of Christ, a chevalier plighted to the service of his liege.

Of course I am not told all of this at once. Father Núñez works patiently, over the weeks and months. In fact his greatest skill lies in what he does not say. He does not mention that the Manriques are Spain's greatest military family, nor that Rodrigo Manrique was Queen Isabela's great defender and first grandmaster of the Order of Santiago. My spiritual adviser gives no sign of knowing that the grandmaster's son wrote perhaps the finest poem of our language, at the death of his father. And so, only obliquely, does he remind me of my grandfather and what I have forgotten about service.

From his own purse, Father Núñez pays for my instruction in theology, since certain of my ideas in this area he deems dangerously inventive. The tutor he provides is merely the Dean of Theology at the Royal University. Father Núñez does this for me. He knows not a little about my childish dreams.

Who is this man who puts at my service his perfect memory of *my* memories? of a past of which it seems I've begun to speak so very freely. And asks me now, Who is it, Juana, *you* would serve, and how? Thus am I brought to ask myself a most curious question: *Where* best to serve, where to serve *best*—from a palace or a convent cell?

It would not have come to me of itself. And yet the question seems the sum of all the questions I have been asking myself. Have I come all this way from little Panoayan just to be a rhyming servant? What did I come so far to do? Write *comedies*? Is this truly *all*? he asks. What might a girl with such gifts not accomplish? Might she not also compose simple carols to console the hurt and the hungry?

Palace or convent. Solve the riddle, untangle the knot. Of course I do not use such childish terms, not openly, not at nineteen. But from what I remember of riddles, the solution often consists in finding false oppositions. Palace or convent—why it is hardly a choice at all. For each contains a library, does it not. Father Núñez only nods. Fate has fashioned for me a keeper who knows also how to turn the keys of silence.

He sits quietly across from me, as I tell myself we spend most of our days here cloistered from the men anyway, entertaining ourselves with plays and books and convent gossip. We knew that the Empress María lived in a convent in Madrid, a situation which nonetheless could not keep her from visiting half the capitals of Europe. Philip's true spiritual adviser was an abbess. His sister had entered a convent. He took half his meals there, the Queen almost all of hers. And it was common knowledge that the King's lovers—married or single, mothers or barren, it mattered not—were to enter a cloister as soon as he had finished with them. Just as a horse ridden by Philip was never to be ridden by another.

We women talked frequently of someone else as well. Christina of Sweden. Who had abdicated her throne for the Spanish Ambassador, the Count de Pimentel. Of course, the lover I still prefer to imagine at her side is Descartes. She travelled all over Europe, often dressed as a man, went anywhere, said anything she pleased—in eleven languages. Every year or so there was a new rumour that she planned to tour America. When she announced her intention to visit Madrid, every convent in Spain was put on alert, for Christina never failed to visit all the convents in her path, and liked nothing better than to lodge there, with all her train and baggage, parrots and monkeys. Female monkeys only. At first I thought this curious, but how else was one to lodge in convents, after all?

Her library in Sweden once exceeded fifty thousand volumes, but the number she took into exile to travel with was not inconsiderable.

Fourteen thousand.

Christina was the great sponsor of Descartes, Bernini, Scarlatti, Corelli; Christina was the Learned Queen, founder of the Arcadian Academy; but more, I see that Christina was the nun-ensign, my favourite heroine, one who embodied every fantasy I'd ever had, had lived adventures I'd not yet *dreamed* of having—

Nun-Empress.

It is Father Núñez himself who points this out to me.

He knows a good deal about our late King, too. He has come to know what I know, and a few things of his own. Of Philip, slave of lust, and his abiding fantasy to seduce a nun. The King grew so desperate to possess one sister in particular, he commanded her abbess to arrange an assignation. When she let him into the convent by a secret subterranean passageway, the King rushed in to find his prey awaiting him, stretched out on a slab, bled white, to all appearances dead by her own hand. Philip staggered out, horrified, whereupon she was revived and spirited to a new convent at the far frontiers of Spain. To protect her daughters, so far will Mother Church go. Yet is there a Lord to whom even she is but a handmaiden.

And so, again obliquely, am I reminded of more recent incidents at the palace. Things I would give anything to forget. Head or heart, heart or soul, soul or flesh. Palace or convent.

At this point I might have noticed my tendencies running away with me, for I decided now that really, for a woman, palace was to convent as *gallinero*[8] was to *caballerizo*†—cote to stall. Hardly a choice at all. Truly I had come far. From false opposition to false comparison to a choice between illusions. Perhaps what I was running away from was myself. Or perhaps I only thought myself an empress.

†as henhouse was to equerry

No, he insisted, the choice is real.

Who is this man to ask me to choose? I have dreaded just such choices all my life.

Choose—I chose, to reduce my choices to *which* convent, and even this was no choice at all. The convent of San José of the Discalced Carmelites. The most rigorous, of course. Teresa de Ávila's Order. He casually suggested one more lenient. This I chose to take as a challenge. And when I came to see that my choice was in fact a house of torment, I fought my way out again and came back to the palace, only to walk among the courtiers and ambassadors as if back from the dead. And it is true that I have returned from a place few return from. More strange even than the giant, is her revenant. If I felt monstrous in their eyes before, their scrutiny has become for me a purgatory.

Father Núñez admits to having made mistakes with me . . . such as letting me enter a convent too harsh for my temperament. While I may doubt this, he has become in other respects disarmingly candid. Father Núñez calls my position, now, untenable.

"The essential was to draw you out of the palace. Your friendship with the Vice-Queen will go on, but not as before."

He says this with such authority I cannot decide if I am being given my instructions or if he is conveying something the Vice-Queen has told him in confession. "Your haste in leaving her protection has embarrassed her. . . ."

He has manipulated me, allowed me to deceive myself, and makes no apologies.

"It is your soul I am concerned with."

"Only this?"

His eyes are no longer downcast, no longer heavy-lidded, not veiled and meek. He despises coquetry, I see. Fears it, perhaps. Now am I invited to find his candour chivalrous. "I am here, Juana Ramírez, to make war on you. To make war on the Evil in you and against the Enemy, for the dominion of your soul. And if only because I now consider you a house divided in all you do, I am optimistic of victory."

I thank him for the *mise en garde*.

To want the best for my soul *is* to want what is best for me. He says this very sincerely. There will be times ahead when I do not know whom to trust—this need in him, I can always trust. He means this, and I believe him. Thus am I encouraged to believe he loves me. And looking into his face I do believe. *He loves my soul.* Is this a small difference, I wonder, or an abyss?

"Should this seem harsh, Juana Inés, try to remember: Once I have beaten you, I will carry your soul to God. And if it helps, you may think, child, of a bright angel and a dark. . . ."

I am beginning to see that Father Núñez may one day be capable of cruelty.

"Only believe that it is not the bright one that I detest."

Quite openly he explains my options to me, which are few . . . for a penniless bastard from the hills with so few friends at the palace. Or, apparently, in any other quarter of our city. He observes that I entered the first convent with a certain urgency. Since I am soon to be out on the streets again, I should make a more practical choice this time. That is, if I am really so disinclined to the institution of marriage as seem the other women in my family. Were I prepared to alter my disposition, there are men whom he might persuade that a spotless virtue is not everything in an obedient wife.

Choose. How desperately I did not want to, and confessed to him instead. Until he knew enough of me to shape his questions perfectly, like a key.

Marriage in the world, or marriage *to* the world.

Sincerely, he asks how he may next serve my soul. He arranges for me to visit other, more lenient convents, assures me the problem of a nun's dowry might just be surmounted again.

The day goes agreeably, with cakes and teas. Everywhere he is well known, everywhere he is revered. I see that he confesses many of the prioresses. He sings to high heaven the praises of the nunnery of San Lorenzo as we leave. Towards the end of the day, he takes me to San Jerónimo, under the patronage of the widow Santa Paula and the learned virgins of the Holy Land, under the protection of Saint Jerome and the rule of Saint Augustine. It is a convent renowned for its programs of music and theatre, and for the quality of its library.

On the way back to the palace he takes me to a *recogimiento*. A place for prostitutes, a place of personal reflection and recollection, where the windows are bricked shut. To enhance concentration. Not just those on the outside, but those giving onto the courtyards, too. And the doors barred. My next step I really should take carefully. I will not be able to return to the palace after another fiasco. There are countries one does not return from twice.

He has to go away for a time. To Zacatecas. No, he does not know for how long. Not days, months maybe, at least a few weeks. He looks forward to hearing what my choice has been.

But I look so surprised. I need not. He leaves me in the hands of another. There is a book he has treasured since the days of his youth . . . He looks, for an instant—it's almost embarrassment. Reverend Father Antonio Núñez de Miranda claims to find a greatness in me. A beauty of the soul that for all his searching he does not find in himself. He brings out a book, but does not pass it to me. He says he leaves me to the care of a great companion, one who has also read the words of Sarpedon to Glaucus, for he has written that *with great gifts come the greatest responsibilities.*

Augustine. Our Holy Mother Church's greatest writer, greater even than Jerome. There is a saying. Who claims to have read all of Augustine . . . lies. But this, Juana Inés, I *have* read.

And these were the dishes wherein to me, hunger-starven for thee, they served up the sun and the moon. . . .

This book I have read many times, child, and offer it to you now as a guide. With chapped hands trembling as with ague, Father Núñez opens my fingers and places *The Confessions* in my hands.

I open the cover. And under his eyes take in the chapter titles as the parched take water, as the famished, bread. Adult Cruelty and Folly, The Attraction of Shows, A Twofold Prize, A Passion to Shine, A Year of Idleness, The Two Wills, The Anatomy of Evil, A Soul in Waste, The Wreckers, Faustus the Manichee, The Teacher as Seducer, The Death of a Friend, The Problem of Forgetting . . .

All the helpful titles, the edifying rubrics. But I had not read it yet. They were as the chapters of my own life. And as I read, the thirst only grew.

Here was a companion who had journeyed far. From the lands beyond the pillars of Calpe and Abyla. Who had lived a life in the world, yet married *to* the world. With his voice a secret in my ear I read of his boyhood among the Afri in Numidia, on the shores of Africa. His studies and dissipations in Carthage, capital of Roman Africa. His lusts. His lusts. Foaming over with lust in Rome and Milan. His years defending the heretical Manichees, his conversion to the Lord of *totus ubique*.[9] After the Vandal ransom of Rome, enemies on every side, for thirteen years he sat writing *City of God*. . . . To shore up the faith of the world *in* the world.

His mission and destiny were no less than this. I read of his reluctant accession to the bishopric, and even as the Vandals gathered at the walls of Hippo I watched as the Bishop sat quietly in the library, writing against time, writing to Saint Jerome in the desert in Egypt, putting the finishing touches upon *City of God, On Nature and Grace, On the Spirit and the Letter* . . .

Here was someone who had humour—*give me chastity and constancy— but not yet!* Who had discovered in the intimate connection of physical love the very source and wellspring of friendship. Who knew beauty— *too late I came to love thee, O thou Beauty both so ancient and so fresh* . . . who had tasted of the sweet joys of the secret mouth in the heart, probed the narrow entrance to the soul, who saw what it is to be in love with love, to know the horrors of going too far—and yet be unwilling to turn back.

Whence this monstrous state . . . ?

At the age of nineteen Augustine found and was forever changed by a single book, a pagan book since lost. Cicero's *Hortensius*, an exhortation to search for wisdom. And so in Augustine I had found someone who understood, as no one else, this craving for wisdom. Even wisdom in loss.

For the bare search for wisdom, even when it is not actually found, was prefer- able to finding treasures and earthly kingdoms. . . .

Here *is* a friend, to turn to when I no longer know whom to trust, a companion for a path in the desert on the road to *City of God*. Here is a soul that has greatness. A heart to serve, a spirit to sing praises, a hand to write them. *The Confessions*. The greatest of books. A meditation on greatness itself.

Had anyone delved more deeply into the mysteries of the mind? struggled more greatly to resist his greatness? surrendered to passion so utterly? remembered so completely—and survived it?

My infancy is dead long ago, yet I still live. . . .

Father Antonio Núñez de Miranda is a subtle man. And though I shall never know for certain how he intended to serve in giving it, this gift to a lonely spirit I do not forget, nor ever shall. To have such a friend, to swim in such intimate waters, to learn of even distant events and episodes in the life of our friend, these we do not simply hear or read, but know and feel and live as once before. To be given a great book is to be given a second life.

So a question now for the subtle man. To give, even in evil intent, a great book to one's enemy—so that he may see the truth of himself, so that the walls of his life may be pulled to the ground . . . can this truly be called an evil at all?

Tolle lege, tolle lege.[10] Augustine heard it spoken in the voice of a child. Take up and read. . . .

Perhaps, one day, I may yet hear it answered, in the small voice of a man.

JUANA INÉS
DE LA CRUZ

B. Limosneros, trans.

Prolix memory,
grant me surcease,
one instant's forgetting,
let these sufferings ease.

    Slacken the bonds
of all that is past,
lest one more twist
force them to snap.

    Surely you must see
how an end to my days
only liberates me
from all your tyrannies.

    Yet I seek not pity
in begging a respite,
but some other species
of torment in its stead.

    For can you think me
so brutal a beast
as to ask no more of life
than not to cease?

    You know too well,
as one to me so near,
that what I hold most dear
is what this life gives me to feel;

    and know too that forfeiting this,
I surrender all hope
of that love, that bliss
that for all eternity lives.

    For this alone, your clemency
do I kneel to implore:
not so that I survive—
but that hope's lease not expire.

    Is it not enough
that so long as you are near,
my absent Heaven's every trait
returns to flood my mind?

    A torrent of reminiscences—
her noble finesses,
her tongue's sweet cadences,
her tenderness . . .

    And is it not enough,
prolix memory . . . industrious bee,
that you extract, from glory's seasons
    past,
the present's draughts of agony . . . ?

PROMETHEUS

manda and I were planning to climb back to Ixayac that morning. We woke especially early, well before dawn. It was windy. There were no stars and no sign of the moon I had fallen asleep to. I smelled the smoke but half-asleep imagined it was Xochitl, already grilling tortillas. And then I knew that it wasn't, as Amanda and I climbed to the watchtower.

A vast wildfire seethed up the far north slope of Iztaccihuatl. Already it was turning the corner to the western face, not far from Ixayac. For a long while we couldn't tear ourselves from the sight of a conflagration rising over two thousand *varas* into the sky. Then Amanda shook my arm and we rushed down to find Xochitl standing in the kitchen, speaking rapidly in Nahuatl with three men, woodcutters on their way to warn the people of the town.

"Go get your mother," she said, which I did at a dead run but when I banged her door open I found her almost dressed.

"Wake your *abuelo*, Inés," Isabel said, without even glancing up. "And knock first." She looked at me now as she reached for her cloak. "Don't frighten him. Can you do that?"

I heard the evenness in her voice.

"*Sí, claro*," I said, and walked steadily to his room feeling very grown up.

When I brought Abuelo to the kitchen, everyone else was there. The workers were just outside, all crowded around the door. Isabel had gotten Amanda to translate as many of the details as the woodcutters seemed to possess. There had been lightning, but the men were not denying the possibility that they had sparked the fire themselves. Seeing Abuelo come in properly dressed, his hair neatly combed, Isabel seemed very close to giving me a smile.

"*Papá, buenos dias.* It's good you've come," Isabel said. "With this wind, your *molinos*† can be a great help to us now. The men will dig the trenches where you say. The woodsmen will stay and help. I'll ride in to warn the town and be back in two hours."

Grandfather was a colossus.

He set two men to fashioning leather buckets and two more men, extra mattocks. He directed the remaining workers, with such picks and

†windmills

mattocks as we already had, towards the places to start digging. Amanda stepped forward and I did too, though there were not yet implements enough to go around. "No, no," he said, "for you two I have the most important job of all. We need you up in the watchtower to look for spot fires, and any cinders on the roof—call out right away." Amanda and I would not have let ourselves be coddled. The spot fires I might have thought a ruse to keep us out of the way, but with almost no rain in a month, surely the shingles of the house and outbuildings really could catch fire. And from the tower, it was soon clear how true this was: the shingles were cracked like kindling beneath moss tinder-dry.

And there we spent the rest of the day, Ixayac close yet out of sight above us in the smoke. In the ochre light we could see both windmills where they stood above the river, one at each end of the maguey. Blades spinning dizzily in the rising wind, the nearer of the two stood just past the stand of evergreens where Amanda and I often went to read in the shade of a giant cedar. From the base of the windmill a ditch ran through our little strip of trees, then along the north side of the corn-fields and out to the orchards. Grandfather was fixing something at the far *molino*. From right beside him, a second ditch cut across the maguey, along the south side of the cornfields and into the watering troughs next to the paddocks. The air was increasingly thick with ash, smoke, and now dust.

The fieldhands worked in three parties, a half-dozen men in each—and so quickly that I realized the ditches they were excavating had already been there, filled with loose gravel and overgrown with grass or corn. This was not the first fire Grandfather had found a way to master here—and with the volcano smoking away above us, how could it be otherwise? By the time his daughter was back, a trench encircling the house had been linked up to the water troughs and was filling with water. From the well in the courtyard, workers were filling the leather buckets and passing them up to two men soaking down the roof.

Once the ditches had been scraped out, half the men set to work cutting down the blue-violet fields of corn. With so little rain this spring, the stalks and leaves were too dry, so near the house. The remaining men set up a brigade to relay up buckets of freshly dug earth for spreading over the rooftops—first of the house and chapel, then of the out-buildings. Now, a few splashes from a bucket every hour would be enough to keep things moist.

Maybe luck did come first to the well-prepared, or some days were simply luckier than others, for by nightfall it had begun to drizzle, then rain, then pour. But no one seemed to the think the day's work wasted, still less a shame.[11]

For three days straight the rain came down. During the hours when Amanda and I were normally out exploring, we did little else but read—at first from a frustrating volume of selections translated from Plutarch's *Moralia*. His other book, the parallel lives of Greek and Roman heroes, had been a great success with Amanda. And this new one started well enough with its wicked diatribes in the style of Menippus, and with fine touches in his advice to brides, but his dialogues on morals were mostly dull and though he'd been a priest at Delphi, his famous essay on the failure of the Oracles was left *out*. At least in the afternoons alone at the table outside the library—and evenings now, with the firepit rained out—I was free to pore over Reverend Athanasius Kircher's *Oedipus Aegyptiacus*. Egyptian Oedipus. I knew of the Greek Oedipus who had solved the deadly riddle of the Sphinx—and reading I found myself returning to something that had always puzzled me. How a riddle in Egypt had somehow become a monster in Greece. Had the other monsters, like the Chimera, begun as riddles too . . . ?

Ancient Egypt of the enigmatic forms . . . priests and priestesses with the heads of dogs or bulls or birds, like ibis-headed Thoth, inventor of writing and guide of souls into the western deserts. Avidly now I read about the teachings of a great sage who lived in the Egyptian desert at the time of Moses: Hermes Trismegistus, divine messenger! His secret texts had been only recently rediscovered but surely the riddles veiled therein contained great natural magic and the highest wisdom. If my excitement was burgeoning, Magister Kircher's was truly palpable. Reading him now was almost to be present as the greatest scholar of the modern world hailed his great forerunner: *I, Athanasius Kircher, and the new sages of Europe salute you from afar*. He was hopeful—on the verge, one could feel it—of recovering the most powerful Hermetic formulas. Light from darkness . . . attraction at a distance . . . a jar so tightly sealed as to exclude even air. . . . Was it really true that the Reverend Kircher had had himself lowered into Vesuvius to study its crater right after an eruption? How he would love Panoayan. Such marvels he could teach us. And what a master of decorum he must be to preserve the dignity of the cassock amidst such updrafts.

Clearly, great new discoveries were imminent: for to the classical instruments and faculties of mind, the new sages of Europe were now learning to couple close observation and measurement. And by the great Jesuit's shining example *I* was learning that the most powerful instrument of all, as Aristotle himself had said, was *admiratio*, the faculty of marvelling at the world—and surely I was acquiring some of this myself. From the Reverend's description it was child's play to construct a magic lantern, and through it project not just light but forms and likenesses. And what a sensation it created in our dining room when, after dinner one night, I projected my first image onto a sheet draped over the *aparador.*† I did not much care for Kircher's own first choice: a painted devil for terrifying sinners. An image of our volcano gouting beet juice turned out to be quite startling enough.

†sideboard, credenza

The best thing was, Reverend Kircher wasn't even dead, according to Abuelo. I had never read a living writer before—as far as I knew, but then I was fairly sure one couldn't tell the living from the dead just by reading them. How I would love to visit him one day.

The only trouble in imagining any such journey would be in keeping its real purpose from Amanda, who in the afternoons and evenings had Xochitl teaching her all the ancient songs and dances and medicines, and secrets only to be handed down directly from mother to daughter and never otherwise spoken of—potions, perhaps, or incantations and who knew what else. Whatever Amanda might feel about my afternoons and evenings, I was not the only one with a parallel life. I was determined at least to keep Egypt for myself. But somewhere on the road to Reverend Kircher's Rome I was bound to let something slip—for if building the lantern had been easy, leaving Amanda out of it had not been easy at all. Harder still to work at the harsh riddles of Hermes alone. She was good at riddles. We had always worked at them together.

And now the Greek had turned against me—as they will even when bringing gifts—for it was almost as if the Plutarch of the dull but harmless selections we had been reading had now forgotten Greece entirely, such was his new-found passion for *Egypt.* Suddenly this new Plutarch was running on—without the slightest discretion—about the proverbs of the Alexandrines and, worst of all, about Isis, *she who weeps,* a deity so august as to seem the sum of all the goddesses of Greece. I would have to find something else for us to read. Quickly.

It had been raining since dawn. The light was soft and grey, the air crisp. Snug under blankets and in rough woollen cloaks Amanda and I sat under the eaves, but in front of my room instead of the library, so as not to disturb Abuelo. Casually I mentioned that, like Plutarch, Hesiod was also from Boeotia.

"Place of Wild Oxen," Amanda said, instantly. After this auspicious beginning it would only be a matter of time before I persuaded her to try *Works and Days*.

When she agreed—reluctantly—to the change I ran for the book. Instead of walking the full circuit of the arcade I sprinted through the rain—not wanting to give her time to change her mind. The courtyard already lay mostly under water. The rain barrels were frothing and ful- minating as if they themselves had been dunked. I knew Amanda was watching, and to make her laugh I ran right under a waterspout to the library door, where I called in to ask Abuelo for the Hesiod. He didn't seem to be reading in there at all but was just sitting, chin propped on a hand, staring out the window at the rain. He turned to see me standing there dripping water.

"*Escuintle*," he chided, shaking his head. "You will catch your death."

He found *Works and Days* so quickly that I wondered if Hesiod wasn't a favourite of his. Shuffling back to the door he glanced down at the book, and then up at me with a sad little half-smile. "An excellent choice, Angelita. Your author would be at home in this weather." As I reached out, he straightened a little and stuck out his belly.

"*Espérate*. Dry off those hands first. Here, on my shirt. Now don't you dare run back across."

"*Sí, Abuelito,*" I said and for him I ran, chill and wet, the long way around.

"And dry yourself off before you start reading!" he called across the courtyard. "You're liable to be sitting out there all day."

I read to Amanda for a while, for the sheer pleasure of the words. The text was plain and strong, about hard work in the fields, about the cal- endar and crops and when to plant. It felt like a book about surviving hardship itself. Crops failing, and weather, and debt.

Just then, as a thunderclap stole the breath from my chest and the hail erupted, it happened I was reading—my voice rising more each instant— Hesiod's lines on surVIVING WINTER. North winds, frost, and hardship enough to *curve an old man like a wheel*. A hail of stones fell as big as avocado pits bounding crazily all about us like whole fields of grasshoppers startled underfoot. Then the hail and the rain just stopped.

The courtyard lay like a case of slate beneath a slurry of pearls, and in the air moved scents of tree sap and hail-mown grass. Cloud hung from the hills just as the breath did from our lips. Ice! We played in the hail like besotted jewellers, letting pearls stream from our fingers.

When we could no longer feel them, we skittered back to our rocking chairs and books and burrowed under the blankets. Amanda was clearly touched by Hesiod's plain words for life on the land, and intrigued, as I was, by the idea of the four ages and races of Man. But we needed to read something warmer. And yet if I were to switch books on her again . . .

I knew exactly how to do it.

"Wait now, NibbleTooth. Hesiod keeps talking about the gods' gift of good crops and bread, and he's told us twice about Pandora—which means what again?"

"Gift . . ."

"'*Universal* gift,' and yet he blames her for dragging Man down to the Age of Iron. The first Woman—*again*. But even so, that still meant Man had managed to drag himself down from Gold to Silver to Bronze without any help from her. And she was only created for this fellow Epimetheus[†] because Zeus'd ordered it. Looks to me like *this* was the afterthought. And now Hesiod has the gall to call her a plague on men who eat bread, which are like *tortillas* here—and what men eat those?"

"All men."

"She did not ask for that old jar, anyway, and who put the Spites in there in the first place? And she was the one who found the gift of Hope in a jar the men had thought empty. That reminds me, Helen is so famous for starting the Trojan War, but a certain poet was struck blind till he finally admitted she was never *in* Troy. Now Achilles, he made trouble without anyone's help, but he gets called a great warrior and Pandora a plague on men. Thetis wouldn't even have *had* Achilles if she hadn't been ravished by Peleus. What desperate tricks didn't she try, to stay out of trouble—fire, water, lion, snake, squid she changed into, anything to get away from him. Pandora, Helen, Thetis, Isi—I ask you, NibbleTooth, what of *their* hardship and grief, and what of poor Penelope, so many years without Odysseus? Well I'll tell you: *Grief* is a plague on the women who bake bread *for* men. Or tortillas. . . ."

[†] 'afterthought,' brother of Prometheus, 'forethought'

For some moments Amanda had been eyeing me suspiciously as I plunged on.

"Are these not like the stories your mother tells of CloudSerpent pursuing his sister? And did you know that Thetis rode dolphins?—which swim fast and chase really fast fish, very much as otters do, which reminds me of the seals of King Proteus of Egy—and amazing sea journeys and of another *great* book by Homer . . ."

Amanda sat angled toward me in the rocking chair. Under a mound of blankets all that could be seen were her hands holding Hesiod and—in the shortening intervals between the clouds of her breath—the grimace of exasperation pulling at a corner of her mouth as I myself ran out steam.

"You want to read something else now."

Disapproval, exasperation, but not anger. *Splendid.*

"Yes, NibbleTooth—the *Odyssey.*"

The weather cleared enough to see WhiteLady again, white as we had never seen her. She and Popocatepetl rose into the sky entirely cloaked in a light shawl of snow. Up one flank the fire track was an immense scald—steaming still from valley to treeline. It stopped at the northernmost edge of the western face. Ixayac was safe.

Surely we could go now.

As the weather cleared, Isabel rode out to inspect the damage. We had lost half the apple crop and all the vegetables to the hail, and the corn that we ourselves had cut down in the field nearest the house. Worse, Isabel had seen not one but two pumas. She made me promise to stay close to the house for another day or two.

Amanda and I did not get to the *Odyssey.* Even as the weather improved, I grew ill. I lay in my room, fussed and hovered over by Amanda, nursed by Xochitl on bitter infusions of herbs and a chicken stock seasoned with purplish *chipotle* peppers and lime. Of the first day I remember little but dreams and the lusty bawling of cattle pent close to the house. We seemed closer to Ithaca than Ixayac, so with a sigh I asked Xochitl, would she at least tell us something more about this place it seemed we would never get back to? Amanda was sitting at the end of the bed, Xochitl on a chair next to me, the bowl of broth in her lap. The shutters were closed. The whiteness of her hair glowed softly in the dim light.

"What have I told you two already?" she asked, testing us.

"It is a place for women," Amanda said. "The Heart of the Earth, Toci—"

"Goddess of the earthquake," I chimed in, "our grandmother."

"Good. You have not forgotten quite everything. But I did not tell you how."

"How . . . ?"

"It is as the moon, who waxes and wanes, that Toci instructs the Night. As she who is reborn in blood each month, she teaches the jaguar. As the warrior in childbirth, she wears his pelt on her throne. And in this she is also called Tlaelcuani, in licking the gore of birth from the child, and of love from the father."

"Filth . . ."

"Sip. There . . . Yes, Ixpetz. But the filth she eats is rarely her own. And it is she who gave women the *temazcal*. And tell me, did you find its walls still standing?"

"Xochita, we don't *know*," I said.

"How is that, did you not go up?"

"Yes, Mother," Amanda said, "but we didn't want to see everything at once."

The triangles of Xochita's eyes unfolded like little boxes.

"Hup!" There was that laugh we so rarely heard. Like a bird with a hiccup.

"You girls. I had forgotten how it is, to be so young. . . ." Though she'd said this with a smile, we were wounded. Xochita had told us about the special place only because we were almost women. Reading our expressions she added, "No, what you did was good, a sign of respect. Or am I mistaken."

"But it's been days and we still haven't seen anything!"

"You will soon, so lie back. Sip. More . . . good. Next to the hot spring you will see the walls of the sweat bath, where the midwife once went for her instruction. When I was a girl, two women of our village and the midwife climbed up there together at the full moon. They waited there almost a month, until their time.

Amanda nodded. What else had she already been told?

"But what did they do up there, Xochi, for all that time?"

There were baths to take, and medicines. Prayers and songs, for the midwife and the mother to offer to Cihuacoatl and Tlazolteotl, guardians of childbirth. There were readings to make of the baby's luck in the grains of thrown corn.

"Prophecy!—Tlazolteotl was a *wizard*."

"As the jaguar's tutor, she wears the skirt of black and red," Xochi answered, not exactly disagreeing. "It is why Ocelotl made the journey often. This climb, I made many times as a midwife. I was planning to go again for myself. For Amanda. But my luck was not so good. Something slid . . . then I fell and could not climb."

For a moment her gaze went to the bowl cooling in her lap. As she looked up her voice was firm. "It is a place of cleansing, a place for thought and care. A woman born under the sign 1 Ocelotl, as I was, goes to Tlazolteotl for steadfastness. She wears a crown such as you once gave to Amanda. But not of maguey—hers was of CottonFlower. Like me."

Her face was playful and almost shy.

"You?" I said.

"Ichcaxochitl," Amanda said. *CottonFlower*. She might at least have told me.

"You did not know my full name, did you Ixpetz. . . ."

On the third day I was able to get up and walk about a bit. All morning Amanda was helping her mother prepare a feast for a mystery guest the following night.

But what an uproar had been coming from the corrals since yesterday. Finally I wobbled out to see.

What had sounded the day before like the cattle of Peleus being savaged by a sea wolf was in fact only slightly less dramatic—our cows being bred to the black bull from Chimalhuacan. This normally took place in the far paddock but with the pumas about and the jaguar attack some time back, mother had brought the bull nearer the house. Two days in bed and already life had passed me by.

Abuelo intercepted me between the library and the kitchen. "Are you sure you're strong enough to be up? I should have dried you off properly myself."

"I'm feeling much better, Abuelito."

He didn't say anything for a minute. Normally he would have had his arm around my shoulders by now. "Maybe you should stay inside, Juanita. We've been seeing a lot of snakes in the yard since the fire."

Snakes. Was there to be a plague of snakes now? All this time Amanda and I should have been reading Exodus! Standing next to Abuelo, with the portal so excruciatingly near, I had visions of our captivity here being drawn out by spiders next, then scorpions. Vicious termites, butterflies . . .

"Angelina, would you mind coming to read something for me? There are some pages in bad repair. With all the smoke in the air and the dust, my eyes . . ."

I saw, finally, that he'd come out expressly to keep me from the corral, yet his green eyes were indeed red and bleary, as though he'd been the one ill. Titanic on the day of the fire, he had seemed subdued since.

Cancionero general. A waterlogged and mouldered copy of an anthology of lyrics. It looked three centuries old, but proved to be scarcely half that. The selection truly *was* hard to read, but as much for its beauty as for the damage to its pages. Verses by Jorge Manrique. In time, I would come to know this, his most famous poem, as if it were my own—the one, when the day came, it was a mercy not to have to write.

> *Recuerde el alma dormida,*
> *avive el seso e despierte*
> *contemplando*
> *cómo se passa la vida,*
> *cómo se viene la muerte*
> *tan callando . . .*

It was this poem Grandfather asked me to read now at the little table under the library window. After the fourth stanza he held up his hand. "There. That was the part I had been wanting to hear again." We sat quietly a moment afterwards. "I must have told you. Manrique's father, the Count of Paredes, was an Iberian hero. The second Cid, they called him, so great was his glory. Founder of the Order of Santiago, our highest military order. And fighting at his side was his son, our great poet." As Abuelo added this, his chest was big with emotion. He rested a trembling hand on my arm as was his habit, while for a moment his eyes wandered into the empty space above the courtyard. "Then the father would die, then the son—both defending Queen Isabela."

"But Abuelo, we live in America."

"One does not cease to be a loyal subject of the Crown. Not by mere accident of geography. Without *los Manrique*, truly there would be no Spain today."

I asked Grandfather to tell me about tomorrow night's dinner guest. I knew he was a military officer. Yes, of the rank of lance-captain. Isabel had met him while chaperoning Josefa and María at the ball in Amecameca. A *ball?* Yes, Juanita, two nights ago.

At the courtyard's centre stood the well, a small turret of mortared field-stone. On the east side of it, a big armspan away, lay the firepit, bounded by squared blocks of the same origin and shape as the flagstones but thicker. Within that ring the flags had been pulled up; outside it, lengths of log lay in a gnarled circlet girdling the pit. Stripped of their bark, they were otherwise indistinguishable from those around a real explorer's campfire. And this was exactly how Abuelo had made it feel for us, from the very first night of our arrival from our old home in Nepantla.

On a clear evening, if we went there straight after dinner, from behind the hills to the west a good deal of light would still be coming up, the stories flowing as the light ebbed, infused, in that fading, with a loneliness. It would be just the two of us now. My sisters had lost interest. Amanda was not allowed.

In that silence I would sometimes think about our first night in Panoayan, the only time Amanda had ever been there with us. María and Josefa were swinging at cobwebs with brooms. Xochitl was in the kitchen. It was full dark. Abuelo emerged from his room with a lantern and, tucked under his arm, a rectangular board. I caught sight of something else in his left hand. It was the first fire-bow I had seen.

"*You* know what this is, Amanda," he said, "do you not?"

She nodded shyly.

"Can you show me the Fire-Bow?" he asked her, swinging the lantern behind his back. What was this about? The thing was right there in his left hand.

But Amanda had not misunderstood him. She pointed up at the sky, and though it was a mass of stars, I was fairly sure she was pointing out Orion.

"Not those two?" Abuelo asked, pointing towards the constellation of Gemini. She shook her head. There spread across his face an immense smile of satisfaction. He turned to me excitedly. "As I thought, Angelina. There has been a confusion. Many have written that the Fire-Bow for the Mexica was in *los astillejos,* which we know today as Castor and Pollux. But the confusion was ours, since none other than Nebrija translates *los astillejos*

directly from the Latin to mean not Gemini but Orion. And can you not
see it there, clearly, a fire-bow in Orion's belt and sword?"

He held up the little bow and drill as if to impose them on the stars.

Still smiling with pleasure he offered her the bow. "You know how," he
said without a doubt in the world. He produced from a pocket in his vest
a bit of paper in a tight fan-fold between his thumb and forefinger. As if
it were a delicacy to eat he offered it to me, which eased the sting I'd felt
at being passed over for the main honour. He explained that, in days
gone by, papers folded just so had served as the ceremonial tinder. "And
to drill this first fire, *señoritas,* was once the very greatest of occasions."

And so we bent to the task as he guided us in how to work, very cer-
emoniously, together. By then my sisters had left off their sweeping and
come to join us at the fire and together we prevailed upon Abuelo to let
us sleep around the firepit, just this one night. The stories began. His
first, as I recall, he left unfinished. And for this I blame my sisters' wide
eyes and gasps of horror. For, pointing confidently at Orion now, Abuelo
invited us to see the sky as he believed the first people here had—sitting
perhaps on this very spot—as a chest cavity, a great carcass of night, the
shell of its darkness cracked open, and at its heart the fire-bow drilling
the first sparks of light and—

And that was all. He'd decided we were too young to hear the rest.

I was speechless the next day to hear Xochitl tell me Amanda wouldn't
be coming to the firepit again. She would say no more. I simply could not
imagine it was Abuelo, who had singled Amanda out for the honours
just the night before. I ran to him to protest. He looked very grim. I
believe he was hearing of it for the first time himself. He would say only
that it hadn't been his idea. So it must have been Isabel—who didn't
answer me at all. But why should she care?

The truth was that she didn't. Keeping Amanda from the firepit,
keeping Amanda from being hurt, was not her concern.

WALKING FISH

 tilted my face to the morning sky. Up from the pale thread that limned the peaks there fanned overhead a gradient of soft hues, and in its velvets and peacock plumes glinted brilliants of ruby and crystal, glimmers of ice blue and apple green . . . But I had no time to waste on sunrises. I ran to meet Amanda in the kitchen.

And then we did go. No earthly power could hold us, nor unearthly frog plagues, nor blood-spate, nor vicious cattle lice. We passed the first two streams that boiled and battered down the mountain. A little farther along and just before the third, the string of boulders where we crossed the river was wet and slippery with muddy brown water roaring and seething in places over the rocks. A day or two earlier we couldn't have crossed. At the trout pool we had a twinge of disappointment, but also what I took to be our first good omen. The water was too muddy to renew our acquaintance with the trout, but we did see an otter trundling off up the bank, and sideways in its mouth a big fish bobbing like a trout moustache. Amanda ran ahead of me up the long bridge of Ixayac's nose, each steep step a grimace in the muscles of her calves.

The face we saw in the features of the place—the nose and forehead, the eye-hollows and pine-topped brows—only emerged when we were far enough along the bridge to have left the surrounding trees behind. I finally caught up to her at the *umbral*. After three days in bed I felt faint, eyeing the handholds to the first bench.

"I'll follow you . . . up . . . in a minute."

"We go together," she said, puffing but pacing still in her eagerness to go on. She waited with me a moment, then picked up both our satchels. She slung them over her back, their straps crossed like bandoleers, and climbed ahead of me to the top. . . .

Back at last.

The sky was not so cloudless as on our first day up. In arroyos and valleys all the way along the east side of the lake, mist hung in wisps and shrouds like a row of tars in winding sheets tipped for committal to the deep. Through cloud rifts, quicksilver beads fell in showers. White birds, brilliant in the sun, sailed against storm clouds of blue-black and charcoal. Yet for all the beauty of the scene, we didn't sit, didn't bounce our heels against the ledge, didn't scan the valley for more than a minute. The anticipation of exploring, which we had once thought to prolong for a day, had become an agony.

The bench was as deep as our courtyard was across . . . maybe thirty *varas*, I thought, gauging one against the length of my arm. Amanda pronounced its depth to be twelve *matl*,† making its width thirty on each side. Popocatepetl smouldered sullenly across from us—*next* to us—way up yet just to the right. Straight overhead, from the snow line, thin plumes of waterfalls stepped like cloud ladders down the face of Iztaccihuatl. One chute would stop and disappear, to be relieved by another a little over and farther down—until the last plunged into a cleft of rock ten times our height above us, to re-emerge as a small, calm stream from the thicket directly at our feet.

The only way in was to wade up, ducking under the bushes overarching the stream. The water had been ice not an hour ago, yet the shock we expected did not come. It was not at all cold. We waded swiftly in to our knees and then, to get under the thicket, frog-walked over large smooth stones.

We might so easily have been disappointed. After ten days of frantic anticipation, what place could live up to such feverish visions?

Ixayac could.

So many first impressions we never discussed. The splash and sparkle of water, the shelter and hush, as if from the rasp and rush of breaths—indrawn, checked, endlessly prolonged. Blackberry bushes in bloom, and among them a hummingbird's soft throstling. Tiny frogs creaked, shy yet urgent. From the upper bench down, a fine spray of mist drifted, fog from a cauldron of rainbows. The faintest echo whispered from the rock wall behind the waterfall—did she murmur something, a word . . . did I? We straightened, searched each other's eyes in disbelief. A minute ago we had been high on the open flank of two great mountains, yet now we crouched, enclosed, in a nest of calm. Ixayac *was* the heart of the earth. It throbbed. Soft as a bird in the palm of god.

Amanda's almond eyes welled for an instant but then she smiled like a maniac, and hugged me hard. I felt the strength in her.

Up on the right was the old *temazcal*. A few grey stones had tumbled from its sides. We set to work restacking them. The largest were too

†'armspans'—units of measure close to the Spanish *braza* or fathom

heavy to lift alone. When we were done the walls came to our shoulders. We plastered the chinks with reddish mud and laid pine boughs across. I streaked her cheek and wheeled away with no hope of outrunning her. By the time she had thoroughly smeared my hair and dragged me into the pool, the sun was barely two palm-widths above the horizon. As soon as Amanda noticed, still wet we started packing up. It was hard to leave.

Just before taking the handholds back down we stopped at the edge and gazed out, like emperors come to a balcony to gratify the fawning multitudes. The mists had burned clear. After the heavy rains, the lake's expanses of blues and greens were hedged at each river mouth with frail blooms of mud. Yet in the pale blue around the city, its floating gardens still gleamed an emerald green. The air was clearer than ever, and I was sure I could see the cathedral tower, and even the scaffolding of the corrupt construction works that so scandalized Abuelo and never seemed to cease.

And there, the falcon again—two! One hovered, while the other folded into a dive on a flight of rock doves wobbling along like paper ash on the warm afternoon air. The dive scattered them—a blow struck through smoke—sending them to ground. The two falcons swept overhead screaming, talons empty, caught a draft above us and—wings motionless—went soaring up the face.

The stream at our feet tumbled over the precipice, then reappeared briefly where it glided into the stand of pine well below. The river Panoaya emerged from the far side of the woods and began a long muddy arc, bending past the maguey and our reading spot and out into the valley beyond. At this height the maguey field was a scatter of pineapple tops across a chopping block, the vanes of the windmills spinning like the wheels of small sleepy toys. We were looking toward the hacienda, yet though we had a sweeping view to the south and west and north, our view of the house itself was blocked by a little rise. It dawned on us what this meant: even here on the upper bench no one could see us from the hacienda, even had they ten Galilean telescopes.

It meant Ixayac was ours.

Next morning, we lit the lamps then made a tremendous commotion grinding corn and mixing paste for the day's tortillas. Performing with incomparable industry, we pretended not to notice Xochitl limping sleepily in from the pantry where the hammocks were slung. At the end of the counter she stood with her arms crossed until we acknowledged her.

She took her time assembling our lunch, an especially large one. Then instead of letting us bolt off, she wanted to talk. Placing her hands over Amanda's satchel, Xochitl made us both sit across the narrow table from her. She asked if we had stuck close together, as she had warned us to do. She asked about the trout pool. She asked about the *temazcal*. We answered proudly that we had replaced the stones and made a roof with fresh pine boughs. We told her how we had sealed the walls with mud.

So had we remembered to bring materials to make a fire today in the bath? "Mother, I packed them last *night*." I'd rarely seen Amanda impatient. Palms flat on the table she leaned as if to get up.

"Look at you two," Xochitl chided, "panting to go. Like you had drunk a potion of jimsonweed." Had we even seen the *axolotl?*

"The what?"

"Walking fish," Amanda said. It had legs like a dog but also fins.

This was like guessing at proverbs again in the mule cart from Nepantla. A *salamander*. Xochitl looked doubtful. There were many kinds; this was a special one that breathed water but also air.

"Xochita, they *all* do that."

If she was going to be such a sceptic, I could be difficult too.

"They are not all *sacred*. And," she added, less sharply, "they are not all gold."

Was it just loneliness, or that she would have liked to come with us? With her hip, clearly it was impossible. Even to get across the river meant leaping from rock to rock. It felt cruel even to consider offering.

"Normally, Ixpetz, they are in lakes, not streams," Xochitl continued. "Ocelotl brought them there."

"Why did he, Mother?"

The walking fish was a double, but a double of water and sky.

"It is a favourite of the god Xolotl. . . . But no, you are impatient to go."

"Xochita!"

Her smile showed in all the triangles of her face except her lips, pressed together in a firm, straight line.

"We'll look for them, Mother," Amanda said. "How do they look?"

"Big."

"How big—as a dog?" Amanda asked, excited.

"As your forearm, sometimes, but also hard to see. They hide well in a marsh. But up there you will find them before long."

They could be of many different colours. Pure white with red eyes, or black and white like our Spanish clowns, by which I took her to mean a harlequin,[12] or blue or grey-green. Or gold. Ocelotl had brought them up to our special place, to the Heart of the Earth, but only the golden ones. For among the *axolotl* of this colour some went on to become spotted, like the jaguar himself. Then, a very few of these transformed yet again. They lost their fins and walked out on the land like *lizards*. I searched Xochitl's face for the slightest sign she was teasing us and could find none.

But all colours, she added, had the one quality sacred to Xolotl. God of twins and strange births.

"Twins?"

"Ssh, Ixpetz—what quality, Mother?"

I hadn't been shushed by Amanda much and was sure I wouldn't grow to like it. But what Xochitl told us next made me forget my annoyance. She wasn't joking now.

"It is timid, but has a magic even Ocelotl lacks, a power even the jaguar cannot match."

"Xochi, *please*."

"Axolotl has the power to remake itself. If I cut off its tail, it makes another. Or a leg, or a claw. I have seen this myself. Ocelotl believed even a heart or a head, if the stars were right, but this I am not sure I believe. . . ."

We lifted the pine boughs from the roof of the *temazcal* and laid them aside, thinking to replace them once the fire burned down—if we could ever get it lit. But after striking flint to fire-stone about four hundred times the tinder finally caught. We fed it dried branches and ringed the fire with large smooth stones. Tomorrow we'd leave nothing to chance—bringing not just *pirita* and flint but steel, and a lens for the sun and even a fire-bow. We were half-frantic with so many things to do at once—light a fire, explore, search for the axolotl . . . and I had a surprise of my own for Amanda, but it had to wait till after our bath.

What first? We scouted the perimeter of the pool in case axolotls had been everywhere under our noses yesterday. We found only frogs.

Then to make sure more treasures were not just waiting out there for us—yet other pools teeming with axolotls, schools of them basking like otters on the banks—we set off, each of us, to explore our own side of the bench. I quickly gave this up. If there was treasure on my side, it was buried deep under any one of a hundred stunted pines, which, aside from a huge wasp's nest on a branch overhanging the blackberry bushes, was all I found. No other pools, no golden salamanders.

On the far side Amanda staggered out of the trees, the belly of her *huipil* bursting with pine cones.

"For the fire," she called, pointing to the *temazcal* with her chin.

"Like *copalli!*" I called back, delighted, and rushed to help her.

We tossed the cones beside the fire, which had begun to burn down, then hardly breaking stride we went up to the hot spring. We had thought we might jump in for a minute on our way up to the second bench, but so hot was the steaming water that it was taking us forever to ease in. I was sweating like mad and sticky all over, though standing only ankle deep, the hem of my dress in my hands, ready to pull it over my head. And yet I couldn't force myself any deeper. Amanda, naked beside me, was not sweating half so much but she couldn't get in either.

"*Ya!—estoy harta*. Let's go up and see. We can do this later."

"We shouldn't be running everywhere, Ixpetz."

"What do we *do*, then."

All of a sudden I felt drained.

"We sweat," she said. With her *huipil* and skirt in one hand, she led me down to the *temazcal*. We replaced the pine boughs and threw in the pine cones one by one like incense. We squatted naked on the dirt, soon slicked to mud with sweat. Standing now and then, heads bent beneath the boughs, we smoothed the sweat down our own thighs and belly, and across each other's back as if smoothing out a dress for ironing. We made mud masks and with them still on made forays into the hot spring, eventually immersing ourselves almost to our hips. Any higher and the heat seemed so thick we couldn't breathe with it. Each time we returned to the *temazcal* we brought water cupped in our palms and threw it on the hot stones. The steam started up at us in searing waves. Tomorrow we must bring a bowl up for this, and something to drink from.

We tried the spring one last time, but unable to bear it a minute more we waded on half-scalded legs into the pool below the icy waterfall. At the shallow end, where the hot spring ran in, the water was warmest, but step by step we pushed a little deeper, colder, farther up. How very similar then were the sensations of ice and fire.

At the deep end of the pool, beside the little waterfall, was a black slate ledge warmed by the sun. We lay on it to dry off, our chins propped on the edge, and peered into the water. We could just reach the surface with our fingertips. In the lee of a heap of rocks the water eddied softly, disturbed only by the trickles running from our hair. We babbled mindlessly about this or that, almost as though talking to ourselves, while keeping a weather eye out for axolotls.

"Sacred to Xolotl," said Amanda, digging an elbow into my ribs.

"Prized by Ocelotl," I muttered back.

Soon we were setting each other *trebalenguas*.[†]

†tongue-twisters

"The salamanders Xochitl says sacred to Xolotl, and brought to Ixayac from Xochimilco by the wizard Ocelotl, are they striped, spotted or speckled?"

"Are they walking fish or water dogs?" Amanda shot back in Nahuatl. "Or are they otter?"

"Ixpetz now asks NibbleTooth if the axolotls—speckled, striped or sometimes spotted, salamanders sacred to Xochitl—were sent by sorcery to Ixayac from Xochimilco by the wizard Ocelotl—"

"You said sacred to Xochitl—sacred to *Xolotl*."

"Alright but say it *faster* now, NibbleTooth. Like this . . ." Here was something I could do with a quickness even Amanda could not match.

Eventually the surface of the water grew still, and a pair of explorers very much like we two looked up at us from under high cowls of stiff, dark hair. But what struck me then, aside from their exotic head-dress, was not how like us they were, but how like each other—the one's eyes larger and rounder, the other's chin a little squarer. Only natural that I knew Amanda's face better than my own—I saw mine only when hazard brought me before a mirror. It was a station I rarely took up willingly since I had always found Isabel's features there, in a sense, before my own. Now, as we stared down, the strange thing was that Amanda could look so much like me, yet not at all like Isabel. Here was another gift from Amanda for me to treasure—

"Wait," I said, leaping up. *My surprise*. I had almost forgotten.

A specialty of our region has become all but indispensable to the

women of Mexico. It is a cream made from a butter of avocado and
wild honey, widely thought to stay the ravages of time, or at least those
of our sun and the high mountain air. We of course cared for nothing
of this yet—but oh the glorious feel and fragrance on the skin. Seeing
what I'd brought, Amanda's almond eyes grew round as owls'.

Giggling we smeared it over each other, an aromatic lard. Scarcely
had I finished Amanda but we were batting away the first wasps. In no
time at all, we stood aswirl in them.

"Spin," I yelled, spinning like a top to keep them from landing. We
ran up to our thighs into the water but still they buzzed around. One
landed now on her.

The only thing left to do was plunge headlong into the coldest water
we had ever felt. And yet we waited: the game began. . . .

From that day forward, after the *temazcal*, after the masks and the
hip-deep dip in the hot spring, we would bring out the honey cream
and slather each other as fast as we could. Then as the wasps swirled
we held still, held still, there at the edge by the most supremely icy
spot, beneath a waterfall not half an hour old, so recently was it snow.
Nothing but a peltful of wasps could ever have persuaded us to
jump—and there we stood until we imagined—or did it?—it did it
did it did, the first one began to sting

    and

      we

        leapt!

          and came up gasping shock and squealing laughter.

Afterwards, exhausted, we would lie splayed out on our backs beside
the big pool. Now was the time for listening to the water plunge, for
watching the clouds over at the tip of Popocatepetl smouldering there
across from us. Eventually, when we could bring ourselves to stir again
we would peer down, on hands and knees, to the bottom of the pool
and point out to each other with our noses the locations of crayfish
and frogs. And in a certain light with the surface of the pool slightly
wavering, I could not have distinguished her reflection from my own.

But that day we still had a mystery to solve. From the lower bench
we had seen the last of the high cataracts laddering down from the
snow line to vanish into a crevice a good way up the bare, dry wall that
formed the forehead of Ixayac. And yet there was this stream here
beside us.

The holds for hands and feet were not at all easy to make out, and the rocks, continuously wet, were slimy and treacherous. But the climb proved worth the risk. The upper bench was as wide as the first but less deep, the bare rock wall vertical, soaring hundreds of *varas* above us.

But what we were ecstatic to discover was a single jet of water, waist high, bursting from the dry stone in a long rooster tail.

"Let's stand in there!" Amanda cried, dragging me in. We tried to hold out against the force of water but anywhere near the opening was impossible. The horizontal surge had scalloped out a shallow teardrop from the smooth bedrock. There in the pool where the jet fell to our shins we could just hold on, clutching desperately at each other's arms for fear of being swept down to the lower bench. The water—a liquid snow—sent an ache like a deep bruise through our knees and shins. When we could take no more we staggered out to come and sit sideways at the ledge, stretching our legs out on warm stone worn smooth as a hide.

I came to see that the skin cream of our region did have magical properties, in the delicate spell of stopped time. For the next year we ran past the trout pool to Ixayac, and never told a soul. Perhaps we kept the secret for Xochitl, who could not go up and had told only us. It was a time of searching—it was only a game—for rituals and visions and secret ceremonies.

I have been instructed to meditate upon all the crimes of my life, to overlook none, no matter how seemingly small, and truly who can tell which sins are great, which insignificant? I return to this time and find they are not few.

Yet there is so much here I find difficult to regret. It was a year of pleasures so intense I ached with them, and do still some nights. We woke so fresh each dawn, ready to use our hearts again, ready to make them run. In this manner the circuit of our childhood quietly crossed its equinox, and into a season of lengthening shadows, where, if anything, the air was brighter, clearer. I feel that year still as a memory in my legs, my knees, my thighs, for we ran everywhere—we ran in delight, we ran to joy, and it turned and waited. For one more year. Childhood, the purest part of it, was drawing to a close.

For the Greeks, whose language I have still not learned, the word for this particular excellence I think is not *aretē* but *átē*, which some call 'ruin.' Once, though, it meant divine infatuation. Sophocles must have preferred this sense, for it was he who said mortal life can have no true greatness or excellence without the special infatuation that is *átē*.[13]

But while we were at Ixayac, the heart of the earth beat only for us, and time seemed to stop.

A los triunfos de Egipto
con dulces ecos
concurren festivos
la Tierra y el Cielo,
pues están obligados
ambos a hacerlo;
y acuden alegres
a tanto festejo,
el golpe del agua
y el silbo del viento,
el son de las hojas
y el ruido del eco.

Coplas

Ya fuese vanidad, ya Providencia,
el Filadelfo invicto, Tolomeo,
tradujo por Setenta y Dos varones
la Ley Sagrada en el idioma Griego.
    Quiso Dios que debiese a su cuidado
la pureza del Viejo Testamento
la Iglesia, y que enmendase por sus libros
lo que en su original vició el Hebreo.
Mas ¿por qué (¡oh Cielos!), por qué a un Rey Pagano
concedió Dios tan alto privilegio,
como hacerlo custodio soberano
de la profundidad de sus secretos?

. . . .

JUANA INÉS
DE LA CRUZ

B. Limonsneros, trans.

The triumphs of Egypt
in dulcet strains
the Earth and Heavens
in concert hymn,
since neither can
refrain;
while upon such festivity
joyously attend
the purling of streams
and whistle of the wind,
the rustle of leaves
and the echo's lament.

    Coplas

Be it vanity or Providence,
the indomitable Ptolemy Philadelphus[14]
assigned seventy-two sages to the translation
of the Holy Scriptures into Greek.
    God so ordained that to his care
our Church should owe the Old Testament's purity,
and that by his hand be corrected
wherein the Hebrew original erred.
But why (O Heaven!), why to a Pagan King
did God grant so exalted a privilege
as to make him sovereign Guardian
of His deepest mysteries?
. . . .

THE GREAT
GEOMETER

After the decline of Athens and before the rise of Constantinople there was the city Alexander founded on the ruins of ancient Egypt, at the mouth of the Nile. In Alexandria's harbour stood the island of Pharos, its lighthouse a wonder to all the ancient world. Fifty fathoms high, and in its curved mirror the whole world stood reflected, as in the panoptic eye of God. A promontory shaped like an hourglass lay between Pharos and Alexandria, and behind the city spread a lake, Mareotis.

City of the suicides Cleopatra and Marc Antony, site of Alexander's tomb, built by his viceroys the Ptolemies. From Ethiopia and Upper Egypt, Persia and Palestine, Rome and Athens the settlers came. The Ptolemies constructed a museum and gave orders that every ship entering port surrender its books so that copies could be made, and so to collect a knowledge that came and went on the winds. Books from everywhere—not just in Greek but in Persian, Hebrew, the holy languages of the Indies, and in the hieroglyphics.

At the firepit I exclaimed over the great works inspired by the liberal patronage of the Ptolemies. Troubled by my first doubts as to the vastness of our holdings, I asked Abuelo how was it he'd never brought out books on Alexandria before. And might not the generous collections of Mexico City have a similarly inspirational effect here? Which was my way of asking when he had last been to Mexico for new books.

Since, he ventured in reply, Alexandria was my current area of scholarly interest—with, evidently, a sub-specialization in the romances of Cleopatra—did I perhaps recall reading that the Serapeum had housed also the Nile-gauge, sacred controller of floods? Geometry too was a gauge. The Alexandrians became great geometers precisely because the flooding forced them to revise their land surveys so often.

"You see, they *practised*." He let the word hang a moment in the air. "So, *señorita*, perhaps we might soon be seeing a revival of your own studies in geometry. . . ."

On Grandfather's book tray the next afternoon was just such a work. All of them, in fact, had to do with geometry, as if he'd simply lifted an entire section onto the tray. The topmost volume was the most appetizing, with quite beautiful engravings. It was in Latin, which he of course read and I still could not without guessing at every second word. Finding me still there frowning over the figures at suppertime, Abuelo said he was happy to see me working at my mathematics again. He said this gently, not reproachfully at all. I studied his face closely for the irony I expected there and found none. What he had chided me for on one day he seemed to have forgotten the next. That is what came to my attention at the time. But how painful to wonder if he had been hoping I would ask his help. I'd been neglecting so much more than mathematics and Latin. This would come to me in time.

Alexandria's was a revival that would have made even Alexander's strict tutor proud. There was Euclid, and Heron, master of the triangle, who invented a water wheel driven by *steam* alone. Apollonius of Perga—the Great Geometer they called him. Even Archimedes had come to Alexandria as a boy, had absorbed its passions as he walked beside the Nile and visited the lighthouse at Pharos. For did he not invent a screw for raising and lowering water levels, did he not install a great curved mirror in the lighthouse of Syracuse to set fire to the Roman fleet, did he not die trying to keep a Centurion from carrying off the very diagrams now before me? Well, if he died to preserve them, surely it would not kill me to study them carefully, even in Latin and Greek. For this was precisely what the natural philosophers of our century were doing. Ours was a revival of the Alexandrian revival, a rebirth raised to the second power. Galileo, of course, but others too in Italy and France, divining and reformulating the forgotten geometric techniques of the ancients, as laid out in the *Conics* and the legendary *Plane Loci*, a lost work that had raised endless speculations for the past thousand years. I worked with great speed. If I was to be of any help there was no time to lose.

The Nile may have made the Alexandrians great geometers, but it was into the conic sections that their greatest passion was channelled. The cone in itself was intriguing enough: in outline a triangle, in surface curved like a sphere. But where transected by a plane, precisely there at its edge, like a broadsword's swipe through a gorgon's neck, the joining spawns the most marvellous hybrid brood: parables made of mind and number, planes *and* solids both, the straight and the curved, intersecting there at order's edge in the cut that does not stop, time itself turned to stone. . . . At last, *there it was*. For through the conic sections and with

Alexandria's help I had finally seen it: Geometry as the swordhand of Perseus raising the Gorgon's head aloft.

As I read and worked, the sum of books in the library of Alexandria was mounting towards seven hundred thousand. A staggering number, and more flowing in every day. There came to me late, well into the night, an image of the Nile itself as that river of knowledge, and the beginnings of a verse.

> *Soothe, sinuous Nile,*
> *your liquid swells . . .*

I saw knowledge in a river, libraries in the sea—one blue sea as the library of the Nile, and all the rivers of the world that verse there, collected, catalogued, held. I saw a city in an hourglass, the eye of God in a lighthouse . . . and it came to me that the bright geometric figures, these and the arcane equations that represented them, were themselves so like hieroglyphs. For if hieroglyphs were symbols drawn from nature, might not Nature herself be distilled in formulas just such as these?

Long after I put out the lamp, behind my closed lids danced traces of light—triangles and parallelograms, spheres and cones, shapes called tetrahedron, dodecahedron . . . secret formulae, $r = a\theta$, $A = \pi r^2$ . . .

Early in our explorations at Ixayac we had been forced to concede that the axolotls were gone from the pool or we would have seen one, no matter how cunning its camouflage. But we had found enchantments enough as the days and months passed. In the shallows scuttled crayfish, and tiny snails. Little frogs that heaved and leaned at each croak as if crooning to a duet partner. And as in a gathering of the very highest aerial society, we decided, red-trimmed butterflies danced minuets devised by dryads, while blue dragonflies shuffled and snapped and skimmed over the water. One day we carried two small turtles up from the river to keep them all company. The turtles grew as the snails disappeared, but there were a few tadpoles left that we decided were very much like salamanders.

There was a kind of solemnity in our nakedness now as we bathed or swam or lay on the dark slate by the waterfall to dry off. Amanda no longer lay splayed to the sun but kept her ankles joined and her arms crossed over the slight swelling of her breasts.

"Have mine changed?" I'd asked anxiously a few days before. I didn't think so at all, whereas her nipples stuck up like raw little chessmen.

"They *have*, I think," she not-quite insisted. "A little. . . ."

Lunch was almost always on the upper bench, next to the teardrop pool. It was cooler with the mist and more comfortable to sit, where the stone was worn smooth. And when we did grow too warm we made dashes through the icy jet of water bursting from the dry rock face. The game had been Amanda's invention, as the game with the honey cream had been mine. But today she didn't want to play. She said she wasn't feeling well, though she'd been eating like a goat. Yesterday she'd had a nose bleed that wouldn't stop for half an hour. Still, we did not lack for things to do—the falcons from last year were back. We had been watching them for hours each day. Their nest was in a niche above the upper bench, three or four times our height up the face. Soon there came a batch of chicks. We could hear them— even over the crash of water the clamour was riotous whenever one of the parents would swoop back with lunch. A dove, a grouse, a crow, occasionally a water bird. Once, we thought, a kingfisher. What a sight it would have been to see a falcon take a kingfisher as it swiftly skimmed the river.

At first one of the parents would perch at the lip of the rock niche and tear its catch apart for the other, which brooded almost constantly over the nest. We were sure this must be the female, even if falcons didn't seem much like chickens. From the rock she would gather with a pre-cise delicacy gobbets of rent flesh or guts and feed them down into the nest. After a few weeks we could see the chicks, their beaks at least, reach up to take the meat. We thought there were three, and once they were bigger we could see we'd been right. How curious to discover they were entirely white, as though tarred and dipped in fluffy clumps of cotton. Which lent them the most tender, confused expression. They looked like lambs—we had to laugh. But what savage lambs these must grow to be.

By now both adults were constantly bringing these lambs their meat. More than once over the course of our own lunch we'd see each of the parents swing by the niche with a crumpled bird and simply drop it whole into the nest, then fly off again. Within a few more weeks the young presented a reasonable likeness of their parents. Their faces grew fierce and barred, and but for some cottony tufts on their heads, they were real falcons. They took turns now leaping up to the lip of the niche and spreading their wings in great shows of falcon daring and vainglory. . . .

Amanda and I were almost eleven. María was sixteen, Josefa fourteen. Isabel was spending more time with them now, evenings of sewing and embroidery. Twice a week she took them into town for *la manzana,* with their personal military escort riding along beside them on his dappled gelding. As for this guest of ours, Diego Ruíz had been reaching the hacienda a little earlier each time, often now before Isabel was back from the fields. The lance-captain would let his dog run out with him from the garrison for exercise, a heavy-headed mastiff. If we happened to come in not through the kitchen but through the main portal, the dog's yellow eyes did not stray from us, though the thing never stirred from its master's side unless released.

One evening I went the short way into town with the others. It was the day before Isabel was to take my sisters on a journey to Chalco. Delighted to be getting the hacienda all to ourselves, I agreed to go in and see this legendary *manzana.* But only if Amanda could come. Even Abuelo decided to join us.

Our mother drove, with my sisters next to her, foundering in their farthingales. Amanda and I rode in the cart-bed on a heap of fresh straw and the blankets we would need for the chilly ride home. She wore a white *huipil,* and a green sash and skirt, its hem delicately embroidered, and a heavy cotton *rebozo.* She looked beautiful, a shy queen riding in the bed of our rugged cart. Diego rode his pied grey horse just at Isabel's left shoulder; Grandfather rode behind to keep us company, though such was our rising excitement (or mine) he could hardly get a word in.

For once I would have to agree with my sisters. The *manzana* of Amecameca was the most extraordinary sight, though I'm not sure María or Josefa saw it quite the way I did. We arrived just before sunset.

The little *zócalo* was already crowded. In the arcades about the perimeter all the shops were still open, their lanterns lit. Amazingly, this was a nightly affair, the atmosphere less of excitement than of expectancy. At the plaza's heart pulsed a fountain among the fig trees, beneath whose green eaves spread an array of *tianguis* offering *elotes* and tortillas, tacos and *atole.* The crowns of the trees were filling with *urracas* come to the fountain to drink, then squabble and gossip and roost for the night. The fountain basin formed a hexagon, and around it were benches, two to a side. Distributed across these—posed like rock formations or mineral accretions—were the village elders, among whom we had arrived in time to find Abuelo a seat. Finding an open seat was not the problem. Getting him to it was. "Don Pedro, ¡qué milagro! Don Pedro, tanto gusto en veros." At first the men, then the women too, came to pay their respects as he settled in, these seamed and grey-headed ancients in black. They crowded in till he sat as beneath a small, stooped porch of goyles and caryatids.

It started out as a trickle, but soon what must be the region's every last unattached male—anyone able to walk unassisted—had joined all the others in circling the plaza's outer perimeter. Gradually fleshing out a ring just within the bachelor's circle came an almost equal number of their female counterparts. And behind each virgin walked the family, proud and vigilant. In our group María and Josefa went first, holding hands, then Isabel and her lance-captain, then Amanda and I a good long way behind them.

The outer ring, los machos,[†] advanced right to left, cross-grain to the setting sun. The inner circle of las hembras circled left to right, or viewed from the top—north, east, south, west. It was as if each ring were a cog, but then what was the mechanism? At first I was reminded of the great Ptolemaic[15] machineries of heavenly congress. Or no, a press, perhaps, for extracting cider[†] . . . And then it came to me. Here was just such a machine as Pascal had invented only a short time ago, the automatic arithmetical machine whose fame was spreading like a wildfire all across Europe, and even to us. Ha! Now I was truly beginning to enjoy myself, for it was clear that our own Iberian genius had long predated the new Gallic invention. In short, our manzana must certainly be a very ancient arithmetical machine for the calculation and apportionment of dowries.

Not just that. Here was a living breathing demonstration of double conic sections just such as I had seen diagrammed by the Alexandrians and emerging now from the swirl like an hourglass—yes, the double conic was just like an hourglass, why hadn't I seen it? Two cones joined at their apex as though mirrored but in fact traced by the sightlines—fore and then aft—of any individual on the outer circle as he obsessively follows the progress of a special someone on the inner . . . follows her from the tangent of her appearance to that of her agonizing, if temporary, vanishing.

[†]machos, hembras: males, females

[†]manzana—block (as in city block) but also, 'apple.'

And I had seen enough of our lance-captain's dowering to guess at the basic motives and parameters. We may call these Focus, Locus, Vertex, Directrix. F is the dowry—the focus. The directrix (D) is an obtuse, oblique or generally tangential pursuit of F by making a beeline to the means, that is, to the woman in view. The vertex (V), then, will be the true measure of the woman's charms; and the locus (L) will equal the distance between the truth (V) of said charms and any statement praising them in the pursuit of F.

On the elliptical side of the field lies any understatement. But by far the more common of course will be the hyperbolic. Our lance-captain's strategy usually consisted in paying the same compliments to all the females of our house. This, I now realized, executed a cunning double or even triple arc—hyperbolic toward us, and folded within that, a subtle ellipticism toward my mother. In my view, his praises of her beauty, if only from a poetic perspective, had for all his gusto fallen well short of their object. But then what of the parabolic? I wasn't quite certain— surely even the great geometers did not work everything out at once.

To give rhetorical precision to all this romance, one may say that the elliptical comment, parting from the plane of the vertex at an angle shallower than the generator (the angle of first or last glance), will always be too soon, or too late. The hyperbolic comment, on the other hand, cuts the plane of the vertex along the axis at a sharper angle than does either the generator or the elliptic. The maximal amount that can be communicated by the seeker along the outer circle (where it intersects the directrix) will depend upon how close after tangency the woman is sighted, as well as upon distance, relative velocity, her hearing's acuity and, above all, the man's readiness of wit as conveyed by his speed of composition and clarity of elocution. This is speaking in the raw quantitative sense. Qualitatively of course, one word, one glance might suffice.

Though this particular wording may not have come to me then, the images did with very great precision as we went round and round the *manzana* of Amecameca. Eventually I found myself coming to an appreciation of *roulette*, another invention of this devilishly clever Pascal and of which I had only read vague descriptions. I now wondered if that cunning French monk was not a parodist as well, one who had closely studied the Iberian dowry machine in action in Spain, and had thus been led from mere mechanics to certain conclusions about the marriage of geometry, chance and finance in affairs of the heart.

By this time I found myself stopped inside the ladies' circle, with Amanda tugging at my sleeve and the fortunes of so many lovers whirling in the *camera combinatoria* of my head, beginning to open out into an Archimedean spiral . . .

"You look drunk," she whispered. "We'd better sit down."

Our mother took Josefa and María off to Chalco in the morning. We could stay up at Ixayac as long as we liked. After failing to spear a fish in six tries each we generally agreed to return our spear to its hiding place and move on. But today something was holding me there.

The trout *were*, as Xochitl had said. Just not *there*. But maybe they were not there *twice*. If the new geometers were right, light was bent by its entry into a medium of different density, water being obviously denser than air. . . . And if *I* was right and the vent at the pool bottom was hot, then we had water at two different temperatures and densities. But though Aristotle argued that light followed the shortest route between two points, a refracted trajectory was obviously longer than a straight one. So either he was wrong about the geometry or wrong about the properties of light, or there was something I'd missed. . . . Had he actually meant shorter in *distance?* Couldn't he have really meant shorter in *time?* If the light travelled at different rates—it might be like a traveller destined to arrive at a certain hour no matter what route he took. And though I knew I hadn't quite unravelled it, I was irresistibly drawn to this riddle of something like Destiny in light. . . .

"Ixpetz, come *on.*"

For the second time in less than a day here was Amanda tugging at my arm. My shoulder ached, my whole arm in fact. I must have thrown the spear twenty times and not given her a turn at all. But two throws back I was sure I had nicked one.

So, progress on refraction; and tonight we would just see about light and time. I had in mind some tests with candles and as many mirrors as I could connect in a line. . . .

By noon Amanda and I were already on the upper bench, sitting on the dry stone on the south side of the teardrop pool. The view to the west was clear. We could see to the lake's north shore and to the villages beyond. The parent falcons had returned, but rather than bringing food they had been roosting quietly atop one of the pines rising from the lower bench. Aside from the crash of water, which we hardly heard anymore, it was quiet. A cool spray drifted around and between us as we picked at the great mass of tamales *con rajas* we had brought all this way up for lunch.

Amanda wasn't a bit hungry. What was *wrong?* We were very close to quarrelling. She hadn't wanted to swim in the lower pool for two days now. Or take a *temazcal.*

I was reading the *Pinakes* by Callimachus. So I'd brought her the *Argonautica,* a book by his student. But I could see she wasn't really reading. It couldn't be that she was bored—not now, with the falcons. We had everything we needed here. And what could be more fascinating than Jason and the Argonauts? And yet I felt it. High in my stomach a nettled sensation.

Alexandria was making it next to impossible to keep Greece and Egypt safely apart—the forms and the riddles, the now and then, the parallel lines of our mornings and my afternoons—to keep them from converging. It had even crept into the books I was picking for us to read. Callimachus and Apollonius, though they wrote in Greek, were librarians of Alexandria. I so wanted to tell Amanda of this white hunger that had awoken in my heart, this thing like hope, pushing to be born in me, to join in the great work of deciphering the emblems of universal knowledge, tracing its forms, charting its equations, its infinitesimal changes. In Alexandria the signs had been so hopeful, a revival that was like a foretelling of our own: Galileo, Descartes, Pascal, Bernouilli, Torricelli. Even now, this very day perhaps, Magister Kircher in Rome was adding new wonders to a universal museum not unlike Alexandria's, and so resurrecting the dream of the Ptolemies. The great work was happening right now and yet an ocean away, in the studios of the artists and physicists of Italy, the mathematicians and philosophers of France. How could I even begin to tell Amanda of this, and yet how could I not?

Very casually I started in with Alexandria's librarians, the poets Callimachus and Apollonius, the grammarian Aristarchus. Already Amanda was wrinkling her nose. Grammar was her least favourite subject.

"Seven hundred thousand *volumes,*" I put in hastily. Could it even be imagined, such a sum? What was our library here, next to that? With so many books coming in, another library was set up in the temple of Serapis. This new repository, they named the Serapiana—*the daughter library.* I asked Amanda if she did not find this lovely. She made no comment. Scholars began streaming in from all over the world to Alexandria, so the Academy of Athens founded a daughter Academy there too, under a librarian named Theon. Not a poet, this one, but a powerful mathematician, who taught astronomy and divination.

"Magic, Amanda. He must have been a wizard, like Pythagoras, like Ocelotl—"

She suggested we go down.

Was she even listening? Because this was the best part—this Theon had a *daughter*, Hypatia. He believed she could become a perfect being—a *girl*, NibbleTooth. Barely eight and she was already helping her father study an eclipse of the sun. I knew I'd caught Amanda's interest, yet she was adamant about not staying. I felt a flush of anger but tried to calm myself by thinking thoughts that, if not altogether wise themselves, were about wisdom.

And then as she started to her feet there erupted a din of screeching falcons such as we had never heard. On the lip of the niche two fledglings were jostling to spread their wings and wildly crying out as if their wingtips were raw nerves in agony. An even greater commotion came echoing back from the uppermost branches of the pine opposite—swaying under the weight of two—but no *three* screeching falcons. A second of the fledglings vaulted now from the niche and came crashing awkwardly into the boughs. Only by clutching desperately at the branch with its talons did it keep from toppling backwards to the ground. The third, still back at the niche, flapped and lunged without letting go until at last overwhelmed by the sheer pitch of urgency of the other four beckoning with shrieks. No sooner had it leapt off the ledge but the parents launched themselves, soon followed by one, then two, then all three.

Amanda and I had come to a crouch, breathless, stunned and all but deafened as they wobbled then swooped screaming back and forth over the bench.

It was dusk when we came down.

In the morning I took the lead and kept it all the way up, with her straggling behind. We worked our way along the river towards the bracelet of stones where we crossed over. A flock of white pelicans was wheeling and diving at the trout pool ahead. From a trot I broke into a run. Each pelican following the next, they dove and rose again, dripping like the paddles of a waterwheel. Gaining height they merged a moment against the snowfields, then broke into the blue just in time to fold again and plunge to the water like spatulas after their handles.

I spotted an otter where it stood on the pool's far bank, one forepaw raised delicately, muzzle uplifted to sniff the air. I could not have said whether in contempt of their proficiency—for not one pelican in five ever needed to break formation to actually swallow a fish—or in resentment of these interlopers fouling his larder on their way from the lake back to the sea.

By early afternoon we were close to quarrelling once more.

With Amanda refusing yet again to swim or take a *temazcal*, we'd spent the whole morning on the upper bench at flying lessons. She sat, distracted, hardly watching at all as the adults hovered above the fledglings, dipping and turning at the merest tremble of those beautiful wings. Wings the very shape of loveliness and power, tips tapering to an archer's bow, to a single pinion of grace. I watched them now as if to save my life. I watched them with falcon's eyes. As the adults led, all five soon dove and swooped and swept in widening relays and volleys. Wild shrieks like the clash of steel. What were they feeling? Was it joy? If so, how wild the heart to give such voice to joy. Shrieks and shrieking echoes—one after the other—terror, terror to wild exuberance, fierce exultation, to a joy like rage. Their echoes crashed against the face, careened off the water. Tears started from my eyes. I blinked the chill into my lashes. I was the one exalted, exulting in these echoes.

And what had been that terror if not the fear they might never fly at all?

By mid-afternoon Amanda wanted to start down.

We still had at least an *hour*. How could we leave even a minute early, with so much for us here? Two benches, two pools—*five falcons*. With her face so closed off from me, it felt as if all the secret shapes and silent tides of the world were trying to divide us. I began to tell her more about Hypatia, whose father had been teaching her about mathematics and stars, divinations in the flights of birds. But there were things even he did not know, so he let her go off to study in Athens, at the Academy, under the direction of Plutarch himself. . . .

Amanda had collected her things in her satchel yet stood hesitating at the ledge where we climbed back down to the lower bench. I stood close behind her, looking out into the valley. Imagine that journey, Amanda. See, that was the Aegean down there—the near shore was Egypt, the city on the island was Athens. And see that canoe just entering the *chi-nampas?*—the galley taking her away from home. We had each other, Amanda, but Hypatia was *alone*. She missed her father terribly, but she was following her destiny. And did Amanda not think I missed Grandfather sometimes up here? Did she think I'd never felt bad about always being here, with her?

Still she wouldn't look at me, as if convinced everything I said was only another trick to delay her. Which was true, but it wasn't because of the falcons and it wasn't just so we could stay late. It was because I was afraid. Could it be we no longer loved the same things—or no longer loved what we shared? This was my punishment for wanting to keep Egypt for myself, concealing it from her.

When she started down without another word I wasn't even angry. I only followed her to the next bench, talking all the while, talking as we gathered up our things, and as we walked down the little stream and under the overarching bushes. I slipped ahead of her to slow her down.

"You know, Amanda, Hypatia became a teacher so famous that men came to her from everywhere, and so beautiful half of them grew sick with love of her. But she was a healer like Ocelotl. Like your mother." Since I could not stop her I was walking backwards, talking quickly, unsure of the remaining distance to the ledge. "She cured one of these men with a therapy of *music*, a medicine of harmony—do you see? And to another of these lovesick men she showed her soiled undergarments—"

Amanda stopped. Suddenly, mystifyingly, I had her full, angry attention. Her eyes narrowed.

"Why would she do that, Juana?"

Were things so bad between us? She seemed suspicious of everything I said or did.

"Tell me why you said that," she demanded.

"I said it because she did it, that's why! To show him his idea of beauty was not where true beauty lies."

I stood facing her, my heels at the ledge, the whole Valley of Mexico—Athens and Alexandria—falling away behind me. I was desperate to talk to her and could not find a single thing she wanted to listen to. And now the tears did come.

Amanda looked at me for a long moment. Her eyes shimmered. But when she still said nothing I turned, embarrassed, to start down.

"Wait, Ixpetz," she said. I felt her fingertips on my shoulder. "The other song. For the girl. Mother is teaching me. . . ."

I turned back, watched her pause an instant to collect herself. On a ledge overlooking the city on a lake she sang me the song for the newborn girl. And still I did not understand yet why.

> My beloved daughter, my little girl, you have wearied
>   yourself, you have fatigued yourself.
> Our lord, Tloque Nahuaque, has sent you here.
> You have come to a place of hardship, a place of affliction,
>   a place of tribulation.
> A place that is cold, a place that is windy.
> Listen now:
> From your body, from the middle of your body, I remove,
>   I cut the umbilical cord.
> Your father, your mother, Yohualtecutli, Yohualticitl, have
>   ordered, have ordained
> that you shall be the heart of the house.
> You shall go nowhere,
> you shall not be a wanderer.
> You shall be the covering of ashes that banks the fire,
> you shall be the three stones on which the cooking pot
>   rests.
> Here our lord buries you, inters you,
> and you shall become worn, you shall become weary.
> You are to prepare drink, you are to grind corn,
> you are to toil, you are to sweat, beside the ashes, beside
>   the hearth.[16]

When she had finished she told me how the midwife takes the girl's umbilical cord and buries it in the earth next to the hearth. The girl does not take the cord with her to the fields of battle. A girl goes nowhere.

"No Amanda—it's what my mother says too but it won't happen to us. Look at Hypatia." Canoes flashed in the sun on the lake and by the landings where we had always discerned vestals going to their altars. "See, she's already reached the dock. Our city is right there. We've *seen* it—it's too late to keep us here. Somewhere down there is the greatest library of the New World, as hers was of the Old. Our Academy will be the Royal University and—"

"*No*, Ixpetz. It's not that."

She hadn't told me about the song to talk to me about our destinies. Or our umbilical cords. There was something else. Well then *what?*

Le había llegado su luna . . . Amanda's cycles had begun.

"But. Let me *see*," I said stupidly.

She shook her head, and in her shyness I saw suddenly that *this* was why—all this time. She hadn't been bored with us or me at all, or with Ixayac.

She confided that Xochitl had known it was coming even before it happened.

"If *I* didn't know, how . . ."

"Mother wouldn't say," Amanda shrugged. "You know what she's like. But she had the cloth ready for me."

What cloth?—and why hadn't I known? Why couldn't I see? I wanted to ask again—but no. Tomorrow.

Once again Amanda was the faster one, I thought, as we walked ever more quickly back down to the hacienda. So far ahead I might never catch up. I was the only one left. The only one at the hacienda not quite—still and ever almost—a woman.

As we came through the kitchen door, I asked Xochitl, wasn't ten terribly early?

"I'm almost eleven," Amanda said.

Xochitl didn't pretend not to understand what I meant. "Early, yes. Only by a year or two."

"Will my time be soon?"

"Maybe, maybe not. Your sister Josefa was twelve."

"Xochita, how do you know these things?"

"This sorcery, Ixpetz, is called doing laundry."

"What about María, then?"

Xochitl shook her head. "I should not have told you Josefa's secret."

"Xochita, please. Don't make all the secrets here from *me*."

Her eyes widened slightly at this—she looked not so much startled as stung. "There is no reasoning with you when you are like this."

"Like what?"

"*Moyollo yitzaya.*"

Your heart turns white with hunger.

I told her I didn't need another proverb, I wanted an answer.
"Three months."
"*Ago?*" María was *sixteen*. I might be five years away?
It was unthinkable.

And in those days there appeared in Alexandria a female philosopher, a
pagan named Hypatia, and she was devoted at all times to magic, astro-
labes and instruments of music, and she beguiled many people through
Satanic wiles. And the governor of the city honoured her exceedingly; for
she had beguiled him through her magic. And he ceased attending
church as had been his custom. . . .

BISHOP JOHN OF NISKIU, *Chronicles*

hat night I read until tears of rage streamed from my
eyes. I had hardly slept in days and yet as I read now,
it felt more like dreaming.

Heresy. This new thing was in some way that still
escaped me the collision of Egypt and Rome, and
Alexandria was where they met. I thought I understood
that in Rome treason had become heresy, but now in Alexandria heresy was
being made treason. Of all places, *Alexandria,* a crossroads for all the faiths
of the ancient world, a city much like Mexico. Heresy—it made no *sense,* for
what could Xochitl's parable of the trout have meant but that all faiths, all
visions of god, were only the masks of what cannot be known?

I could not understand this hateful book, much less how it was making me feel. But perhaps I had begun, in some small way, to blame
Ixayac. There, too, everything was changing, everything verged on trans-
formation. Coming upon us so swiftly, it had overtaken even Amanda.
It shimmered all about us, and the magic of stopped time no longer felt
so sovereign. Late that night there came to me the idea of making some
ritual to mark the changes. I knew a lot about rites and initiations into
secret ceremonies but I didn't *know* any, or they wouldn't be secret after
all. I did know that the Eleusinian mysteries had five levels. Purification
was the first, knowledge was only the second. Next came the riddles of a
third level, then a fourth, where there was nothing more to know except
through silence. And that was all I knew.

Well, then Amanda and I would have to make up our own ritual. Surely
that was better anyway. It should be like a coronation, a rising into loveliness through holy fire, a secret theatre of sacred gestures. In the hours
before dawn the magic lantern of my mind swirled and smoked with the

possibilities—rites of the Maenads and Corybantes, ox blood and *hippo-manes*. I would bring the *Metamorphoses* and mark all the transformations—but no, that would be the whole book. We'd read just the stories of Thetis and Proteus who changed bodies as naturally as the flooding Nile redrew the shapes of the fields. Indeed this was the message of the Egyptian Hermes: that the flow of god's truth plunged all around us in a swift flood, and that to bind its meanings into a single form was to dam that flood and incur the most terrible violence. Such a torrent must be touched only in tangents—riddles, enigmas, proverbs and chants. Secret initiations.

We didn't have seven hundred thousand volumes to choose from, or the painted books of Ocelotl, but I had Exodus and Proverbs. In Proverbs I found lovely lines.

Doth not wisdom cry? and understanding put forth her voice? She standeth at the top of high places, by the way in the places of the paths . . .

. . . hear the instruction of thy father, and forsake not the law of thy mother: For they shall be an ornament of grace unto thy head. . . .

Surely in vain the net is spread in the sight of any bird.

With just such incantations as these might Amanda and I deflect the tides of events into channels of our design, just as we had done all around our house the day of the forest fire. At first light, I marked the passages with green strips of ribbon to show Amanda. I went to meet her, and there coursed through me a tremendous flood of energy. As we reached the far end of the cornfield a half-dozen deer leapt the fence just ahead of us. I chased them a little way up the path shaking a fist in mock threat, then turned and waited for Amanda. I began talking about our ritual, and tried not to take her silence for disapproval. It wasn't so unusual for her to be quiet. But how very awkward talking was while in the lead—on narrow paths, head turned to trail a kite-tail of ceaseless patter, glancing back every so often to gauge the effect only to lurch over some tree root risen up to trip me.

Today she truly looked tired. Had she slept? I asked. No, not very much.

We were sitting quietly on the flat rock beside the little waterfall. "Aren't you going to swim?" she said after a while.

"Not if you're not," I said. She shook her head just perceptibly. "Did Xochita tell you, you shouldn't when . . . ?"

"No, she said it would be all right to."

"Well, if you don't want to that's fine."

She looked down a moment and smoothed her skirt over her knees.

Then she glanced up slyly and asked if I still wanted to see the cloth. For a moment I thought she meant the one she was wearing, so I tried not to look disappointed when she brought three out of her satchel instead. They were pretty much as I might have imagined, but three?—four, counting the one she wore.

"Mother said today there'd be a lot."

We decided to climb to the upper bench to check on the falcons. She had always been swift, always graceful, but had rarely seemed delicate—and clumsy, never. As we probed next to the waterfall for our handholds and footholds, I heard from below me a sandal scuff as her foot slipped. When she reached the top after me, her right knee was scraped.

We set down our satchels and took up station at the lower end of the teardrop pool. The sky was a pale, clear blue. The first wisps of cloud gathered at the lip of the volcano. The falcons, all five of them, far, far above us, gyred at their leashes like slow-swung lures. From time to time the faintest cry reached our ears.

We picked a little at our lunches. For the second day in a row I'd lost my appetite, not from annoyance this time but from excitement, though I tried not to let on. Since getting the idea for a secret ritual I could hardly contain myself—within me I could all but feel the ingredients stirring, churning, as in the mortars of the Moorish alchemists.

"And Nibble Tooth you can make a dance for us and I'll try hard to learn it. I know—we'll throw the corn grains to read our destinies. What else . . . no need of holy water—we have that here. We'll take an extra long *temazcal*, then hold ourselves in the hot spring longer, deeper, than we ever have. We can even cook some eggs in the spring for luck. What do you think of that?" *Still no answer.* "Then we dip ourselves three times under water, like people do against the evil eye." I realized that I knew so many of these things from lists of practices banned by the Inquisition. What else had they banned? *Chickens*—the drawing of spirits with hens. The African *curanderos* only ever used a black hen, which they would then rub hard on the victim's body. If the bird didn't die right there from the influx of spirits, its throat had to be slit. So maybe a chicken. "We don't really have any caiman's teeth, either, or stag's eyes. But we can check under the falcon's nest for bird bones and claws—come on! Or . . . all right. Later if you like."

She just sat there, her legs folded under her, looking out over the valley, not joining in at all. I so wanted to offer her the perfect gesture.

"What should we *do*, NibbleTooth? This is the place of women's secrets, isn't it, for the women of your family? *This is the Heart of the Earth.* We'll be doing it for Xochita too—I'll bet she told you she would have liked to bring you here herself. Didn't she."

"Yes."

She had picked up a pine cone, was studying it intently as she turned it in her hands.

"We'll bring chocolate, and tobacco, and flowers. What else?"

She shrugged.

"Should we stay the night? Should we bring *peyotl*?" I was not entirely sure what *peyotl* was—she glanced away from me now—but one needed rare ingredients for secret potions. She was always picking herbs for Xochita, so why shouldn't she do it for us? "That's it—jimsonweed!"

Staring vacantly down at the lake she had begun plucking bits from the pine cone. After a moment she said, "Mother's teaching me, already."

"Teaching you what?"

"The ceremony."

The ceremony. The real one.

My frustration chased my temper through bright spirals behind my eyes. I waited until I could trust myself to speak. "No, Amanda, we need something of our *own*. Or do you just want to sit around up here all day doing nothing all the time? No wonder it's become boring."

"It's boring for you?" she asked, startled.

"We hardly read anymore. We don't swim." I knew I was being unfair now. "You're not even interested in the falcons. You just sit around staring off into the sky."

"That's not true."

"So we'll get jimsonweed, no? We could go down right now, try to find some." I started to wrap our tamales back up. "What does it look like?"

"I can't say."

"You don't know or you won't say?"

"I can't."

"So you do know."

"I can't Ixpetz. I promised."

I was getting sick of Amanda's secret knowledge. Had I not been telling her all about Alexandria? Did she care nothing for finding a destiny all our own?

The fledglings had come back to the niche. The adults were nowhere in sight. A chill mist of tiny prisms drifted round us. Without our swim the sun was especially hot.

"I'll learn your dance. I'll work hard to learn it quickly. And I'm writing a poem to teach you. I've already started. Listen . . ."

I recited what I had written. She gave no sign of having heard my little verse, not nearly so impressive as the one for the newborn girl.

"Of course, it's not finished yet. . . ."

Her eyes had settled on the city on the lake. Something in her face then looked defeated and helpless, unbearably sad. I thought I was the one who was sad. At work in Alexandria now was something that I could not quite grasp and yet that could not be stopped. The Christians had begun destroying the temples of Mithra and then the synagogues. By the command of a Bishop named Theophilus the temple of Dionysus was pulled down, and after it the Serapeum in Memphis—though he dared not touch the temple of Isis there. When the other peoples of Egypt still did not rise against him, he sacked the temple of Serapis and the daughter library in Alexandria and took control of the Nile-gauge. And when he died, the new Patriarch, Saint Cyril, the nephew of Theophilus, carried on his uncle's heart-sickening work. *Saint* Cyril? These barbarians were *Christians*. Theophilus meant *beloved of god*, but how could that be? What sort of god was this?

Flying back with a teal in its talons, one of the adults hovered now and tumbled the body into the nest. The young falcons set to quarrelling over their meal with the most terrible screeches. For some reason their squabbling made me furious. I was on my feet, casting about for a stone to throw at the nest. There were only a few pine cones.

"Ixpetz, you can tell me what's wrong."

Amanda sat there watching me, her hands still, shards of pine cone patterned on her skirt. There was such a chord of resignation in her throat, it was almost as if she'd been afraid too, was asking even now to hear anything save what I needed to tell her. But I was no longer sure what that was—what was it I was afraid to say? Or was I more afraid there was nothing left to say?

Hypatia's private classes were banned now by Cyril the Patriarch, and only her Academy lectures on mathematics were to be tolerated— no more classes at the homes of leading citizens. And then something happened that I could not bear. The details were few, and horrible. I could tell her in the hateful words of John of Niskiu. No, for us, I had to find words of my own. . . .

Hypatia began to take long rides south along the Nile by chariot, making short forays into the desert. South of Alexandria were the Natron lakes, whose salt waters had since the most ancient times been used for embalming. In the desert lived five thousand warlike hermits, assembled now by Cyril and roused to a fury against Hypatia. One day as she had almost regained the safety of the city, the monks of the salt marshes pulled her down from her chariot and carried her to a church called Caesarion.

The Nitrian monks stripped her, tore off her philosopher's robes, then battered her to death with heavy pottery jars. To her chariot they hitched the naked body and dragged it through the streets to a place called Cinaron. There the monks took the one who had been Hypatia and scraped the flesh from her bones with oyster shells and pottery shards.

These were the details.

That day at Ixayac, I had just these few incidents to offer, and endless questions. For all their horror, they danced and japed about like tantalizing clues to a riddle whose answer I felt must seem one day, as in all the best riddles, obvious once found. Why had Hypatia in a time of such danger been out alone, driving her chariot through the salt marshes of Wadi n' Natrun? How could it be that the warlike men of God were led by an illiterate named Peter the Reader, that the manner of her death was in Alexandria the penalty for witchcraft—inflicted now on superstition's great opponent . . . ?

Hypatia's murder was the end of Alexandria as a great centre of learning as the students and scholars and mathematicians and librarians began to drift apart and leave for other places. And as the Dark Ages began, the pages of seven hundred thousand books heated Caliph Omar's baths for six months. Six months of heat and light for a thousand years of darkness. What sort of equation was this?

And yet, despite my confusion, from the expression in Amanda's eyes I was convinced she *had* understood—everything, even why I was telling her. And seeing this I was so sure the silence, this new, dark shape between us, would just dissolve and we could talk about everything, and my fears for us—

"We should go down now."

She'd said it not unkindly, but infuriatingly all the same.

I led all the way, not once looking back. Down the ridge of Ixayac's nose, through the woods, past the trout pool and across the river. I skirted the maguey plot and then, instead of cutting through the cornfields for home, I waved her on and turned for the far paddock. Baggy grey clouds hid El Popo's tip, and through them rose a plume of brownish smoke and steam. The sky was otherwise clear, the deep blue of late afternoon. Hummingbirds and bees wavered and mumbled over sprays of wild-flowers. The pastures were a furnace, moist as the *temazcal*, the air a bel-lows—the cows' heavy calls, the cicadas' eddy and pulse, a bright grist of sound milled in its intervals and ratios. . . . To walk in that air was to eat, to feel it fill my mouth with moist earth, life.

I walked to the fence of the far paddock where we had watched the black bull among the cows. The bull on whose sharp horns Amanda had hung for me a cornflower crown. Just a year ago, but so much was now different. My twin had had the change that would make her a woman. My own time floated near like an intimation. I felt my breaths shorten, a diffuse, liquid sensation in my knees and in the soles of my feet. It was like standing barefoot in warm shallow mud.

HALLS OF JADE

here was a mild earthquake just before dawn. I found the kitchen door open and Amanda already outside, her black hair plaited with blue ribbons. She wore her best *huipil*. In the dim light her knees and shins were dark against the whiteness of her cotton skirt. She had cleaned and oiled the leather of her *huaraches*. I glanced down at my own, the sandal straps dusty and spattered.

"Where have you been?" Now she was eager to go—would I ever truly know her? Maybe she had understood after all what I'd been trying to tell her, or maybe Xochitl had said it would be all right. "It's *late* already."

It *was* late, but I had been up for an hour packing my satchel with magnets, pyrite, flint, a fire-bow just in case, the *Metamorphoses*, the Bible, a block of oily black chocolate, a knife to cut it with, our lunch, then, on top, cornflowers, *cempasuches* and agave spikes.

We spoke very little, having decided to run almost all the way up to give ourselves more time. She took the lead easily. I was carrying the heavier satchel but I didn't mind at all and didn't once ask her help. Though I was not quite out of breath, my knees felt weak as we reached the lower bench. We made our way up the stream then clambered up to the *temazcal*.

"Let's go see the falcons first," Amanda said.

We usually went there last but I did want the day to be different. Still, I wouldn't leave until we had started the fire so that the coals would be ready when we came down. I laid fresh pine boughs to one side as a covering for the roof. Then I refilled the clay jar we used to splash water over the stones and drink from. We'd just reached the upper bench when the falcons launched themselves out into the valley in single file, up and up, far above a long vee of ducks arrowing towards the lake in the distance below them. Today was to be a hunting lesson.

I was anxious to come down and get started. I laid the bundle of *cempasuche* flowers at the threshold of the *temazcal*, so as to have to step over them going in and coming out. But Amanda wanted to swim first, though that too we usually did afterwards. I saw how the cloth was attached as she undressed. It was of the same dark, tightly woven cotton we used for *rebozos*, folded half a dozen times and tied front and back to a sash around her waist. She undid the sash. She looked at me anxiously, as though I might laugh or even be repelled. But as she stood, otherwise naked, half turned from me—her breasts like little barrels, small spigots at the tips—my breath caught in my throat.

"You look like a warrior, now, NibbleTooth."

At that her head dipped, a little nod of modesty, as in surprise, as if to check: *Was it true . . . ?* And I remembered how just last year we used to stand on the slate rock above the pool and stick our bellies out like the women with child who had once come here to await their time. Now she could *have* a child. For a moment we were both serious, a little shy. But she grew more animated as we smeared ourselves with the honey-avocado cream. Almost immediately the wasps began to circle and her quickness made a spectacular game of it as she dodged and whirled, squealing madly, away from them. I had already leapt into the pool.

"Amanda, hurry!"

She faltered then and had to launch herself in a long running leap into the pool to keep from being badly stung. As we stood in the sun to dry off, I noticed our two turtles sunning themselves too, as they often did, on a small rock next to the waterfall.

"Do you do your dance first or should I do my poem?"

Her eyes wavered and I had the distinct impression she'd forgotten about the dance she was to prepare.

"Your poem."

It still wasn't finished but I gave what I had so far, the refrain, two verses. When she said nothing, I asked her to teach me her dance. She improvised the most dispirited little shuffle, hardly better than I could have come up with myself, and I knew I was right. She had forgotten all about it.

We'd put this off long enough.

"The *temazcal*," I said, and stalked off ahead of her. Brusquely I laid the pine boughs overtop, grabbed my satchel, stepped over the flowers at the threshold and squatted in the heat. A full minute later she ducked in after me. She really didn't seem to care about this at all. Well, I did care, and I knew how we had to do this, and with great seriousness. The heat was intense. Taking the knife from the satchel I reached up and pried little beads of dried sap from the branches, then threw them into the fire for incense. From beyond the walls the little waterfall plashed and a smoky light fell through the doorway. Once I had tipped all the water from the clay jar onto the stones, the air was too hot to breathe through our noses. As we squatted there, heads bowed, our breaths came in little gasps through our lips. Runnels of sweat puddled under us. Through the pine smoke and steam and the sweat blinking into my eyes it was hard to say how much blood was under her but it didn't seem like much.

"Listen carefully. What we do next is daub ourselves in blood. You do me, I do you. We draw signs. On me: sun, hourglass, quarter moon, pyramid. On you: lighthouse, quarter moon, jaguar, cotton flower. All right?" She nodded without looking up. "Then, when we're ready to come out, we each dip a finger into the mud and place it in our mouth." There was a formula I had heard somewhere that came to me now. *Dare Terram Deo.* Render the earth unto god. "That's it, we say this first, *then* we put our fingers with the mud into our mouths." This was the Heart of the Earth after all.

"Repeat it."

"*Dare Terram Deo.*"

That was better. She'd said it just right. Once outside, we would stand by the pool while I read from Proverbs. After that we'd dry off on the slate rock and weave crowns of cornflowers and agave. We'd put them on and it would be like rising through a plane of loveliness, *ornaments of grace* upon our heads. Then, solemnly, we'd take each other by the hand and plunge into the pool—head first, for once. "Okay?"

"Okay."

"Then we eat the chocolate. *Yollotl, eztli,* right?" *Heart and blood.*

"Yes," she said. "Heart and blood."

And last of all, when we were ready to go down we'd leave the lunch we'd brought as an offering. Was she ready?

A stillness settled around us.

She was facing the door. I edged next to her, facing the back of the hut, and turned slightly towards her, my right shoulder to hers. The coals glowed red in the shadows. I dipped my finger into the puddle under her. She started nervously when I touched her back with my fingertip. It left only a dirty little track, with hardly any blood at all. I dipped again and scooped but with all four fingers now. Again, sweat, a little mud, the faintest hint of blood.

"Is that *all?*" I said.

"There was more yesterday."

"But this is the most important *part.*" Blood was for the mixing of the secret salts and balms, blood was the essential agent, blood was for bind-ing the spirits and resins. *Blood.* Wasn't that obvious?

"I—I'm sorry."

It must have been the way we were squatting, facing past each other, my shoulder to her side, but I had the idea it might be like milking a cow. You didn't just wait for the milk to fall, after all. So I put my fingers there. She flinched, then held still and quiet. There wasn't anything really to squeeze but I did a kind of kneading with my fingers, as we did with the cornmeal, or when squeezing water through the muslin for the curd. I raised my fingers to my face to see better. Just plain dirt on the knuckles, and on the tips was nothing like paint at all, only the thinnest smears of rust. I shook my head, disgusted, furious.

"What should we do?" she asked, her eyes wide.

"We need blood."

I picked up the knife where it lay next to the green rabbit satchel.

Slowly, gravely, Amanda offered her arm.

I looked into her eyes.

"Not you," I said, mollified. "We need something to collect it in." And then I remembered. "Wait here, I'll be back."

The turtles were still there sunning themselves on the far side of the pool. I snatched one up and sprinted back to the *temazcal,* ducking in out of breath and suddenly dizzy. For a moment I kneeled, bent double, my elbows in the mud. When the dizzy spell passed I looked up at Amanda still huddling where I'd left her. I settled back on my heels, the knife still in my left hand, the turtle waggling his legs in the other.

"Why do you want to hurt it?"

"I don't, but we *need* to now."

"But *why* do we need to?"

"If you'd warned me there'd be so little blood we could have brought a jar of it—collected some from you yesterday, if there was as much as you said."

"But why our turtle?"

Why was she making such a fuss? We could get another. There were dozens down by the river. How many chickens had I seen her plucking with Xochitl? How many lambs had we seen Isabel slice through the throats of? And we had *eaten* them. This was just for blood. "Where else are we going to get blood *and* a shell?"

"Why do you want to use his shell?"

"Are you so stupid or just pretending? Like a dish, like a mortar for alchemical elements, like a palette for paints. *Now* do you see?"

She stood suddenly, knocking the boughs away as she straightened up. The sudden light was bright. Her face was a hard mask with thin tracks through the grit beneath her eyes.

I squatted there, exasperated and a little embarrassed now.

"Aren't we just like them?" she said.

"The turtles?"

"The priests."

"What priests?"

"From the desert."

"*What* des—"

What desert.

She was asking me a question.

To this simple question, there must be an answer.

I could say they were not priests but monks. After all, I was very learned. All the correct words came to mind. Desert monks. Hermit, eremite, anchorite. How should I answer?

I set the knife down, carefully. And the turtle.

"We're *not* like them."

It bumped over my toes on its way out of the hut and began working its way through the tangle of *cempasuche* stalks strewn across the threshold. "We're not, NibbleTooth. *You're* not."

She said nothing.

"Do you think I am? After everything I've told you? I wanted to do this for *us*. Something just for us and Ixayac. Weren't we doing this together?" Her eyes skimmed mountains we had looked at hundreds of times. "You're the one who talks about real rituals. I wanted this to be *real* for you. As real as Xochita's."

She was at least looking at me now.

"You have your mother, Amanda."

"Well you have your grandfather."

Abuelito . . . Yes, I had my grandfather. I remembered his face the day of the storm as he handed me Hesiod, the day he sat quietly waiting for me to ask for help with my geometry. And it felt then as if I hadn't seen him, truly talked to him in years.

"Why don't you go down to Xochitl now."

I wasn't angry. I felt the words coming from a long way away, from a desolate place. All my confusion and resentment and hurt and envy were a heaviness pulling, sagging down in me, at my guts and lungs and heart.

"Go on. I'll stay for a while. No. I want to. Be by myself, for a little while. Don't worry. Two palms," I said, and smiled weakly. It felt as if my lips were sliding off my face. And the truth was, she looked as I felt. Stricken. My twin. Her face pale as my white heart.

I slipped my shift back over my head while she dressed, then went with her to the edge of the bench and the holds. We stood a minute looking out over the city on the lake.

As I watched from above she started silently down, then hesitated at the bottom. She looked up. "Ixpetz. I'm so sorry." She said it too quietly to hear, but I could tell from her lips, from her chin, its edges crumpled like a leaf.

When I was sure she'd really gone I slipped the satchel strap over my shoulder and made my way to the upper bench. My limbs were so weak with trembling I was afraid I might slip. I sat for a while in the mist beside the water jet. I spread the contents of my satchel out. The cornflowers and agave strips for crowns. The *Metamorphoses*, green ribbons sprouting out of Proverbs.

I watched the falcons returning after another hunt. This marvel of falcon flight, such slender, trembling wings were these, to marshal the wildest legions of the air, to plummet as each wing folds itself as neatly as a letter. I listened to their voices, for what they might tell, but they had nothing to say that I could ever decipher. Through what mysteries had Egypt made the falcon the god of silence? Who was this child of Isis, and what mysteries did its silence hold, this speaker of such wild speech? Did the truth dwell in the pauses between its cries, as with the trout in the pool? Or between these echoes reverberating now—like blows from a shield—off rock and water. And what was the exultation in that throat and those wings but the talent of flight that resolves itself like a target in the archer's eye?

I wanted to run, to call after Amanda, but to say what?—that they cry after the knowledge of it, with the sudden wild joy of it, this talent in their wings. To know at last what those great bows are shaped for. *In vain the nets are spread for them*, before their sight, in those clear eyes. To have found the talent that will not betray them, never to surrender it again, and know to what high places they are bound.

I had wanted visions, I had wanted us to pant on jimsonweed like water dogs, like walking fish—for us to lie gasping on the bank, and wake as tigers—I had wanted to see into everything, all the mysteries and silences. But now something had slid, something had smashed. We hadn't stopped the Nile together, but we had stopped the running. I believe I already sensed this but refused to see the import of what I'd done. I spent the next month, then the next years explaining it away, why the year of running had stopped. And each time I did this, it felt a little worse. I had scratched the jade.

ll the way down from Ixayac, I thought of Abuelo, how badly I needed to hear his voice, to feel his big knobbly hand on my shoulder, his forehead against mine. Just to talk, as we used to, and to ask him to help me to understand friendship, and how and if and why it must end; to help me know my talent and my destiny, for I had come to know that they were not separate, these riddles and my life. While my life was rich and I had discovered a lot, if only I knew more, looked harder, opened my eyes still wider, I might yet see the wonder of secret meanings woven into everything, every word and gesture. This was Pandora, this was the universal gift.

I came in through the main portal. At the end of the passageway into the courtyard my steps faltered, stopped. The black mastiff crouched before the library door. His baleful yellow eyes fastened onto mine as I stepped over him. I could feel his breath on my ankles as I stopped short of the doorway and leaned in to call to Abuelo. Seeing the dog should have served as warning. I was caught completely off guard.

Standing behind Grandfather's chair and stooped indulgently to read what Abuelo was writing at his desk was lance-captain Diego Ruiz Lozano. Casually he turned—both of them turned—at my call. His face was utterly bare of the slightest guilt or gloating. Abuelo's face, though, fell, as he read the hurt and shock in mine.

Who was this popinjay in uniform, that he should stand in that library as if born to it, when I had only stopped at its threshold like a church beggar. I had read half the books *in* there. Abuelo opened his mouth to speak. Stepping back I turned, trod upon the mastiff's paw—a yelp, a bark of fury, Diego roaring at the dog—Abuelo calling *Angel, wait*—

My satchel thudded to the ground. I ran through the courtyard, past the well, the firepit, to my room, stopped at the door—turned back and ran furiously up the watchtower steps. And then I had nowhere left to run. I was trapped. Trapped by these mountains, this tower, trapped by this place. I turned away. My eyes went past the threads of smoke rising over the red roofs of the town, past the vegetable plots to the west—dust hanging like a shower of gold in the sun—past the orchards to the north—and finding peace in none of it. I collapsed sobbing fury in the shadow of the wall.

A few minutes or an hour passed, and hearing him labouring wheezily up the steps I dried my cheeks on my sleeve. Quietly he set the green rabbit satchel next to me on the yoke of the cannon carriage and leaned awkwardly between one wheel and the barrel to catch his breath.

"Angelina, I am sorry about this," he began. "A painful moment. For both of us...." He seemed at a loss, and to see him struggle to apologize, I felt worse than ever. Because *I* should be the one.

"Abuelo, no—how could I blame you for wanting company?—but *Diego*." He held up a hand to stop me. Maybe he would have said, then, exactly why the moment was particularly painful for him: for what Diego had been watching him sign was a promissory note for a hundred pesos. But I didn't let Abuelo finish. It was all tumbling out of me now in a rush. Not directly about Ixayac but about turtles and trout, about the falcons and how it felt to watch and hear them call. At first he was mystified, then stood, his hands hanging down helplessly, as I mumbled and rambled on about Amanda and friendship, about my selfishness and all my fury at the riddles I could never quite solve.

Did he see? But no, how could anybody understand any of it. Or me. Or my fears that I might do something truly terrible one day. His frown uncreased at this and he opened wide his arms. He patted my back as I cried against his belly for a while, blotching his shirt and the lacings of his doublet. Even then I did not think of what had happened at Ixayac as anything more than a horrible failure.

"How odd," Abuelo said, "that you should be speaking to me of falcons." He pulled me up to sit on the warm cannon barrel next to him.

"Did you know that in Andalusía hunting hawks were a kind of universal madness when I was your age? It was . . . either 1599 or 1600 . . . *y esas malditas escopetas*[†] had not yet ruined the hunting. In the streets of the towns anyone of substance had a hawk on his wrist—or hers. The Moors were the greatest masters, in hawking as in so many matters. Yes exactly, Angelina, in mathematics, too. Once on the banks of the Guadalquivir I held a gyrfalcon on my wrist. *Y te lo juro, Angel*, the power in that bird's talons could have crushed my arm. It came into my mind then that I had only to remove its leather hood to have it carry me—as if unfurling a sail—off across the Gulf, right over Cadiz, and home to Tangiers. For this was a falcon of *Africa*. What a moment that was. Of

[†]'these damnable fowling pieces'— shotguns

course a gyrfalcon was not for children, or even commoners. In many countries it was then an offence for anyone less than a king to own one. And if a child might possess nothing more than a kestrel, what bird, do you think, was exclusive to an emperor?

"An eagle?"

"An eagle—*exacto*. Or a vulture, though I know of no emperor who kept a vulture. But for hunting there is nothing like a falcon. Marco Polo's friend the Emperor of Cathay never went on a hunt with fewer than *ten thousand falconers*. What do you think of that?" he said, giving my knee a jocular tap. "Eh? Well yes, as you say . . . I've always thought ten thousand a lot myself. But you know, Pope Leo[†] was just as mad for falcons, as was only natural for one of his noble ancestry. And during his time, it is said, bishops all across Christendom wrote countless letters of admonishment: nuns were not to disrupt Mass—or come to confession either—with their falcons and bells. Letters uniformly ignored, for the ladies knew perfectly well that no mere bishop would stand against the Pope on this subject. Nun-falconers, Angelina. Imagine that!"

†Leo X, second son of Lorenzo de Medici

His arm around my shoulders, we sat silently for a moment watching the sun slump behind the hills, scanning the sky with the eyes of hawks. "And yours, Juanita, what kind were they, these five?" I didn't know what kind. I supposed there were a lot?

"A lot?—all *kinds*. Lanners, gyrfalcons, peregrines. And merlins—very game for their size. I have heard of them attacking even herons. There was a book . . . *Dios mio*, I'd almost forgotten. *El libro de la caza*. . . . The favourite book of all my boyhood after that day on the riverbank. Don Pedro López de Ayala wrote it out in a Lisbon prison after the fiasco at Aljubarrota. His and King Frederick's were the two greatest master-pieces ever drafted on the art of the falconers."

He glanced at me to see if the topic of books might still be a painful one, then rose stiffly to his feet, putting a hand to the small of his back. "And how is it, I ask myself, that I have neither of them now? Then you could have found for me an engraving, shown me these falcons of yours. You know, Angel, you were right after all. It is high time I made a little trip to Mexico City."

My stomach dropped. No, no, he assured me, he'd been meaning to go for some time, but I couldn't persuade myself that he was not going just for me. I felt the gentle yoke of his arm across my shoulders. . . . *Not now*. To be apart from him was the last thing I wanted. Not even at the thought of him pulling into the courtyard with a whole wagonload of books. This grand notion only came briefly to me the next morning anyway, as I watched the wagon my grandfather drove disappearing up the road. For the first in all the times I had watched him leave, he was not on horseback.

What I was thinking now was *war*. Now—with Abuelo away. If a preening varlet in *charreteras*[†]—who I felt sure had hardly finished a book in his life—could just stroll into our library, now was very much the time. Grandfather would not be here to see me at my worst and be ashamed for me. Once I hit upon my strategy, I steeled myself to act very badly indeed.

[†] epaulettes

Our perennial dinner guest was not remotely like my father, had none of the qualities I might envy him on my father's part. Neither vital nor mysterious, not noble, nor in any discernible way intelligent. So it had not been long before I was back reading at the table. Isabel gave no sign of minding. It was not that she had grown so very flexible in her ideas of etiquette, however; it was that he was no longer quite a guest. He sat on my right, while on my left Abuelo would sit hunched at what I thought of as the head of the table. Very occasionally my grandfather might speak with Diego on some military question, rumours of a disturbance or unrest at one end of the territory or other. The lance-captain replied sparingly, as though invested with a chaste secret, or with what struck not just me but Abuelo too, I suspected, as an affectation of modesty.

Once Abuelo left for Mexico hostilities got underway. At supper Josefa fairly glistened in Diego's company, as she had ever since their return from Chalco—she and María both, like porcelain, though I had not yet found out why, eyes glazed, they so brightly basked in our guest's *proximidad varonil*,[†] in the radiant kiln of his smile. At least his teeth were straight. And he did have a thick head of wavy hair, almost black. The beard was of a rich oily black like a Moor's. I knew little of men's grooming, but those sweeping moustaches had always seemed not so much fashionable as the very locus of his vanity. Then there was the dashing uniform my sisters made so much of. Did no one notice him spilling food on it? Compared to the designs of Jacobi Topf, what a paltry thing that uniform was—all cloth, clusters and buttons. Less like a fighting soldier's armour than a court juggler's motley. As different as a pauldron was from an epaulette. And he may very well have danced

[†] proximate virility

splendidly, as Josefa insisted, but I'd have liked Amanda's opinion before conceding even that.

Tonight for *el plato principal* was a fiery *manchamanteles*.[†] Stew green chillies for a full two days. Mix with roasted sesame seeds. Grind in mortar. Fry with chicken, sliced banana, apple, sweet potato.

Season as necessary.

Not for the first time I watched our parlour warrior displaying now the most sweetly piquant delicacy of constitution: sinuses and pores that fairly gushed at the slightest spiciness—making, to be sure, the stores accumulating there in the pilose pantry of his upper lip all the more savoury, despite all the hapless daubing and wiping of his overmatched napkin.

Isabel had known I was up to something from the instant I took up my station—without a book—next to Diego. And as I started in, those huge black eyes fixed me with such a look, as I addressed our military attachment with the first words I had ever spoken to him other than in answer to a direct question. What did he think of our little library? Surely in his travels he had seen much finer. Did he find anything in there he liked yesterday, had he flipped perhaps through a book or two? What were his own favourites and beloved authors? Novels of adventure, I guessed, as was only natural for a gentleman of action, but surely too the epics of chivalry, the exploits of the great knights, must fairly course through his veins—El Cid, Orlando. Why, he must be able to recite whole reams by heart as easily as breathing. On a day, that is, when his nostrils were less burdened. His martial intelligence could no doubt call upon vast stores of verses with which to inspire his men before a campaign. Like this one, wasn't it fine?

> When to gather in the taxes went forth the Campeador,
> Many rich goods he garnered, but he only kept the best.
> Therefore this accusation against him was addressed.
> And now two mighty coffers full of pure gold hath he.
> Why he lost the King's favor a man may lightly see.
> He has left his halls and houses, his meadow and his field,
> And the chests he cannot bring you lest he should stand revealed.[17]

How did the next stanza go again, don Diego? No, but surely the simple soldier was only being modest. Even Cortés's captains had time for literature, and they actually fought real battles, faced constant, cruel, relentless death. And hadn't the odds against them been tremendous? To take the battlefield today must be so disappointing, against a foe so reduced—diseased, defenceless, starved. . . .

Exasperated to see me acting up at supper, Josefa came into my room afterwards with the marvellous news. Our mother was *pregnant* again. We would have a new brother or sister. They had known for ages already.

The next night, seeing that Isabel had said nothing so far, I felt my own valour fairly soaring, and with it my volubility. How could I fail—I fought on the side of right. As Saint Teresa herself had once said, God moves even in cooking pots. And from there to our table through the transubstantiations of spinach purée, *pollas Portuguesas*, rice tortes, *clemole de Oaxaca*, *turco de maíz* . . .

After heaping my plate with food, I had not so much as touched the cutlery, so busy was I with chattering at our guest while maintaining a commanding view of the terrain. I sat in a superb position to inventory the contents of his moustaches, accumulating as he ate. Even had this last observation not come to me quite so vividly, I would not have been tempted to touch my food. The hungers of my body were as nothing compared to those of my mind. And yet I cannot say my thoughts ran yet to victory: rather, to the image of my dying unflinchingly in the attempt. Unlike my sisters, I had never seen our mother pregnant; but over these past few days and particularly since last night I'd divined something at once frightening and thrilling in her eyes. Something hooded and veiled, yet serene—the brooding of some great magic. But no, I told myself, this was only the mystery of life growing within her, and an everyday sort of magic that was.

Over the next few hours I found myself casting about for words more adequate to express the new sensations those eyes provoked. Naturally she was still annihilatingly beautiful, her eyes lustrous and black, enormous. But now there was something in the relentlessness of her focus, something pitiless. I saw a lioness stalking belly to ground, painfully, her milk pooling angrily in the dust . . . but no, hysteria would not do. Composing lines in my head as I watched her, caricature was what I reached for—some disarming conceit on architecture. Instead, what came crowding in were more like verses of incantation, propitiatory—a counterspell.

Her tresses chestnut freshets;
her front a banner's vellum
scroll
on capitals of temple columns;
her brows an ogee archer's unstrung
bows;
the aquaductile nose:
to rule and compass a triumph of compliance—
a rose bulb on a seraph's wings declining;
    while panther jaws (tabby's chin)
gape like Night's own portals
at her smile's pure radiance.
But those two black moons in their orbits,
scattering sable shards and glints—
are they obsidian
or flint?[18]

In such desperate fashion did I screw up my courage, and so it went for the next few nights as I waged my crusade against the Infidel.

Through it all Diego nodded, sweated, stanched his nostrils, smiled and took more roast chicken, nodded bemusedly as my contempt grew. Just as I thought. Here was nothing but an opportunist, thick as pudding, and plodding and utterly without pride. It went on until even I began to pity him. With Grandfather there, I could not have done it. On the eve of Abuelo's return, Isabel put an end to it.

"All right, Inés."

"All right what, Mother?"

"You *know* what." I did know to heed the warning in that tone. "But you'll have the courtesy to ask him first."

Ask Grandfather's permission, to enter *our* library?—it was the merest formality. It was over. It had been so easy. At first I was surprised that she hadn't intervened, if only to spare our guest. I had beaten him. But by now I knew my great ally had been neither valour nor righteousness but splendid timing. I had nature on my side, and Isabel had weightier concerns.

Within hours I would see by how much I had underestimated him. In my sisters' eyes now he would be nobler than ever. They would gaze upon him with something less like hunger than tenderness. As for our mother, from that night forward she stopped asking him to leave her bed before dawn. Before I dismissed it, the idea came that she'd been sending him back to the garrison, just perhaps, to spare not Abuelo's feelings but my own.

As far as I could tell, Diego never slept in town again.

Here, then, was a better strategist and actor, a mercenary more disciplined, than I had given him credit for. Never letting himself be angered, remaining to all appearances confused, too vain and dim to be anything but despised and dismissed by me.

I had worried only about my keys to the library, rather than his to our gates. I had talked loosely of war, but what I had won was only a skirmish.

What's more, I was to discover that he'd fooled not just our mother and my sisters, not just me, but somehow Abuelo, too. For in a manoeuvre worthy of *los contratistas milaneses,*[†] he'd persuaded my grandfather to accept a loan. Though I would not know it for some time yet, this had been the very business they were concluding when I first stumbled upon them in the library. I never found out precisely how he managed it. Would it have been a gesture of restitution for leaving—or rather not leaving—Abuelo's daughter with child without marrying her? Whatever the stratagem, he must, with the most superb delicacy, have left the merest suggestion in the air. . . .

So it was not, no, the poetry of El Cid that coursed through his veins but the icy blood of the Sforzas. Here was the best investment a hundred pesos ever returned. A payout on the arithmetical dowry machine like a win at roulette.

When Grandfather returned home he took the news of our great good fortune with admirable calm. I'd been looking out for him from the watchtower for hours. At a dead run I cut across the bean fields to meet him halfway up the track from the main road. He had brought the wagon back empty. Abuelo reined in the horses right there in the road and retrieved a single book from his *carpeta.*

"Here it is, Angel. *El libro de la caza de las aves.* . . . Now we shall find out about those falcons of yours."

But did he think I had run to him only for this?

Looking anxiously into my face he went on. "I mentioned it was written in prison, did I not?" Now he seemed to think my expression one of disappointment. Hastily I accepted the book he'd been holding

[†] the condottieri of Milan; 'contractors,' soldiers of fortune

out to me. "But did I remember to tell you that our author was also a kinsman of *los Manriques?* Queen Isabela's noblest defenders—the poet and his father? the founder of the Order of Santiago? You've not forgotten. . . ."

The beautiful verses in the mouldering book he had asked me to read for him last year. No I hadn't forgotten. And I was not disappointed; no, I was grateful for his safe return, but puzzled, and yet could find no way to frame the question without seeming to complain. All that way for one book? Why take the wagon, then?

Naturally we had a special dinner to celebrate Abuelo's homecoming. There was a beet and apple cordial to drink, and red wine for Diego and my grandfather. Even María had a little glass. As we sipped and dabbled at a *sopa de ajo*, our mother smiled and chatted easily with my sisters and Diego, while equally I avoided glancing at the moistening tip of his nose. There was such an air of occasion I was half expecting her to announce her condition to all, although it was ridiculous: this was not at all the way to break such news to one's own father. And yet it seemed suddenly mean and unfair that Grandfather should be the last to know. . . .

In fact, I had been the last to know. He had been the first she'd told. It had prompted his trip. Abuelo had gone to talk to Uncle Juan about my one day soon coming to Mexico.

After Amanda had cleared the soup bowls, Isabel encouraged Abuelo to tell us of his journey, which he did with surprising economy. Returned from such excursions in the past, he had treated us to accounts of hairraising encounters with highwaymen and wild beasts never before seen outside of Africa, and to rousing denunciations of the grasping churchmen from whom we leased the hacienda. Tonight he mumbled only that it had gone well. Taking in his weariness, Mother asked gently for simpler news, of Aunt María and her husband; and as Isabel waited for a reply the black eyes I had lately been composing apotropaic verses upon glanced an instant into mine. Just then Amanda came in with less than her usual grace as she strained under the weight of a great china platter almost her armspan wide.

I had managed to avoid *her* eyes for days now. I hadn't played—had hardly spoken with her since the disaster at Ixayac. If I had looked at her now I might have seen *she* was the one who thought she'd done something wrong up there, that she had let me down somehow, or hurt me.

Nor did I see that she had followed my lead and stopped eating too, just as I had while Abuelo was away, as evidence of my seriousness. It was a gesture Amanda had read instantly and answered in kind, in the language she understood better than anyone . . . and so much better than I, who took so long to read her reply.

And how like Amanda to speak as she spoke to me now.

Under a sprinkling of black olives and pine nuts, raisins and *chile chipotles* were two enormous trout, grilled whole and entirely filling the platter. One trout lay on its side, the other on its belly—they must have weighed five *libras*† each. They could only have come from one place, one way. And indeed the platter had been placed before me and turned to show the wound in each trout's side, where the spear had gone through.

†1 'libra' = 1 lb.

How could I avoid her eyes now? I couldn't, but for an instant I still tried, dreading what I might find there—triumph, vindication, scorn? Instead I found what looked like exhaustion, like Abuelo, as if she had carried that platter all the way from Mexico. And then she was gone.

The morning after my grandfather's return I was up early, and it was back to the watchtower I went now. Not to watch the sunrise, as Amanda and I had used to, but to keep an eye on Abuelo's room for the first signs of stirring. It took *hours* for him to wash up for breakfast then shuffle back after it from the dining room. By then I was freezing even under the heavy wool blankets I had dragged off my bed.

†lozenge, troche

Beside the well a *pastilla*† of ice sealed the full bucket over, as if with wax. A light frost glittered on the slate flagstones. Grandfather rocked his way over them unsteadily, cautiously, as if his soles hurt. Heedless, I raced down the steps and across the courtyard after him.

I caught up as he reached the library door. He looked surprised to see me—was he teasing or had he really forgotten? Then I noticed that despite the cold, the cloak he wore was not his heaviest but the formal one. And from the gentle smile spreading across that big face I felt sure he'd remembered all along.

"*Si la damisela sonriente* would do me the honour. . . ." He moved aside, and with a little bow invited me in ahead of him.

I stepped across that threshold for the first time. I couldn't help glancing down—half afraid that whatever force had prevented me all this while might even now reach out to trip me up.

And then I was inside.

He did not follow right away. Feeling him watching, I walked in a fashion I hoped sedate straight down the narrow aisle I had probed ten thousand times with my eyes. Right to the end, to the huge, broad desk where it sat edged in sunlight beneath the window. Beyond the bars I could see the mountaintops, but I had to stand on tiptoe now to see the roofs of the sheds above the window ledge.

According to my calculations—and depending on the thickness of the books, their arrangement and the height of the shelves, which after all ran almost to the ceiling—there just had to be space for three, perhaps four thousand volumes. I was sure I had read part or all of almost fifteen hundred books. So as I turned now from that first aisle—the only one I had seen all the way to the end of, no matter how I'd craned and stretched and crouched—I was nearly strangling in the anticipation of making *two or three thousand* new friends. Whom might I find at this next turn, what great teacher stood ready to meet me in the very next aisle?

It was the coolness in the room that struck me, as if the books still stored the night's chill within their covers. Then I noticed the smells, all familiar, and in a familiar combination, but until now never anything but faint. Leather, most of all, and glue, the mustiness of mildew and dust, tobacco from the pouch on the desk, the wool of Abuelo's cloak . . . together it was these that had smelled to me once like fresh dough rising in an oven.

I went down the next row. I ran a finger through the dust thick on the shelves—and along leather spines and over stamped titles, tapping hello to old friends. Though I could discern no particular system or order, a surprising number in these first rows were familiar.

All together, it was a lot of books. And yet as I crept along the aisles there could be no doubt: I had over-estimated. Gaps of varying sizes separated clusters of books. Not a single shelf was tightly filled. Towards the back on the north side, closest to the kitchen, some of the upper shelves were bare or with just a book or two at each end of a row. The idea of a theatrical set came to mind. Had there been more books once, perhaps while we were still in Nepantla? Or was it possible that in the years since, during each trip to Mexico, he had been taking more books away than he'd brought new ones back? Lost in thought I began to close the circuit of the room, coming back along the west wall, on whose outer side I had sat, so many times, beneath the arcades at the little table under the window. How curious the sensation to be standing at that window now, not peering furtively in but gazing out, at the Hammock of the Sacred Nap slung between the columns. As my eyes wandered out into the sunlit courtyard beyond, I tried not to think too much about what I might be feeling.

In the far corner was an armchair whose existence I should have guessed at before this. The little chess set, on this side of it, I had seen many times through the window.

I had read almost all of the books. I hadn't three hundred left.

After a moment I became aware of Abuelo at his desk sitting over an open book and was glad he hadn't been watching my face. I came up the aisle behind him and a little to one side. I was struck for the first time by his frailty. He was not much taller than Isabel now. From the front, his face was full and round, though no longer so brown, a little yellowed even. The bristling mane, once red-brown, was almost pure white, with just traces of cinnamon. In profile, his head if anything looked heavier— the heavy jowls and loose folds swung under his chin like a bull's. At the dinner table his dewlap hung like a small bib as he frowned over the slippery quarry on his plate. But from the back, his neck was frail as a stalk holding up the great head of a sunflower.

He turned in his chair and smiled as I drew near. "Welcome, Angelina," he said, holding out his hand, "I hope we have not left it too long. . . ."

I took his trembling hand between mine—resting my left in his palm, supporting both with my right as if to cradle a sprain. It was only as I opened my mouth to reply that I caught sight of something on the ceiling.

The construction was the same as elsewhere in the house: pitch-blackened oak rafters the width of my hand and spaced a little less than a *vara* apart. Perpendicular to these and cutting the room into three were two massive transverse beams propped on rough-hewn pillars as thick as my waist. Over the desk the rafters formed panels, a triptych, and spanning it—crudely painted, though skillfully drafted—there floated a host of angels. Mouth agape, head tipped back on the hinge of my jaw I just stood there staring as Abuelo proudly pointed out to me the angelic choirs, fashioned from jewels as man was from clay.

"Just as the genii are," he added, his eyes glowing, "from a fire of gemstones. Or so say the Moors." Craning up as he was, the loose dewlap drew almost taut, like the bib of a pelican bolting a fish.

There hovered the archangels Gabriel, the messenger, and Uriel, God's fire. Cherubs, seraphs—there in all their celestial orders, the thrones and principalities, the virtues and powers—all the angels in their seven choirs. Here, just beyond my outstretched arm, was a thing I'd never dreamed of: My grandfather loved angels, the sight, the very thought of them.

I was willing to admit there was much I didn't know about him, but his love of angels had been here all along—so close, just out of sight. How fine it was to see him excited again, to be there with him—*in*, not just looking in—standing together beneath the nine celestial orders. Silently I thanked each one for their heavenly intervention in conveying me here at last.

What he told me next was if anything a greater surprise. My mother had drawn these for him, when she was almost exactly my age.

"When she had finished it for me," he said, "she never came in again. Our classes of reading were over." Not long after, she stopped sketching too.

For the next few days I was in the library at first light, anxious that no one intercept me, anxious, perhaps, not to see the image of Amanda standing at my bedside, her brown eyes brimming with accusation.

First I lit the lamp above his desk, then lit a lantern and went along ranks still in darkness shifting books, shifting shadows, from shelf to shelf. Piled on the left of the desk were the four titles he was working through. Jumbled over the other side were, he said with a shrug of excuse, the dozen or so he hadn't gotten to reshelving. But reshelve them where? If there was a system, he'd been quite at a loss to explain it, and so he consented to a minor tidying up—I wouldn't disturb him, would do whatever I could before he was even awake.

But as the work proceeded, he began grumbling at the sudden descent of a celestial order fanning now in ever-wider spirals from his desk. By way of reassurance I decided to recite the entire index of everything I'd reshelved so far—where I'd put each volume and why—as he sat dazed beneath the angels, his chair backed against the wall. After a minute of this he raised his hands. "If I need something—"

"Anything at all, Abuelito. I'll fetch it right away."

I collected all the books I had left to read and put them alone on three bare shelves at the far end of the room. One hundred seventy-four in all.

I would have to make them last. And no more skipping chapters—I would read everything, cover to cover, and go back over all the ones I had left unfinished.

In my eagerness to share our library I found myself, during Abuelo's naps, dipping into the books he was reading too. I had the idea of teasing him, by sketching things—objects, people, towns—mentioned in the first few pages beyond his bookmarks, where I then inserted the sketches for him to find. Into a work on the hydrology and drainage works in Mexico City, I slipped the picture of an aqueduct and a good likeness of Abuelo at the top standing next to me, each of us holding a mattock. In another book, an account of Magellan's explorations, I hid a simple map of Tierra del Fuego: at the tip, mountains and fog, and Abuelo and I dressed as tars, waving banners and holding up oars. And then there was a report by an early friar in America, and in that one was a drawing of the horse—rendered as a two-headed deer—that the Mexica spies had drawn for Moctezuma. I turned ahead a page or two and slipped my own rendering in for Abuelo to admire.

Much of the morning my grandfather would spend softly dozing in the armchair, or nodding over his desk . . . under his neck the folds and fine creases filling like a small bellows finely ribbed with whalebone. When after a week Abuelo still hadn't said anything, I began to wonder if he was reading at all.

Then one morning as I sat quietly in the armchair in the corner, a book in my lap, my elbows straight out in order to reach the armrests, a great roar burst from the general direction of the desk.

"Now she reads my *books!*"

I giggled nervously, no longer quite sure of my joke. "Juana Inés, come here—*¡ahorita mismo!*" Not Angelina, not even Angel. . . . As I edged toward him he turned—chin tucked, neck ruffed like an ancient grouse in display.

I thought he might really be furious.

Finally I saw the smile in his eyes. "You shelve my books, only *you* know where. Now you read them, what's next for me . . . examinations?"

Indispensable at last.

And so the rest of our mornings together passed. Eventually I returned to Reverend Kircher's Egyptian Oedipus and only with regret came to the end. For a long while I sat with the book in my lap. With a fingertip I traced the colophon: it presented an engraving of Harpocrates, the Greek

Horus, holding a finger to his lips. Was he saying, I wondered, that there were mysteries that went beyond speech, or else secrets that should not be spoken?

As for our afternoons they passed once again as they'd used to, *Abuelito* snoring away in the hammock while I worked at the table outside. Waking usually with a snort, he would clamber down from the hammock with little grunts and sighs, and we would sit talking things over until dinner. We spoke of the arts of falconry and armoury, of knights and wars and crusades. We consulted on the case of poor King Frederick II . . . it was very sad. A man utterly obsessed. Such was his passion for falconry he once abandoned a battle—during a *Crusade*, a siege of Jerusalem, no less; he simply left the field to go hawking. Abuelo thought probably he had captured some great falconer or other among the Saracens and was determined to learn his secrets before fate, Allah or God could cheat Frederick of his prize. How could one fail to feel a certain empathy, even kinship, for such an unfortunate? And as we talked of the Holy Land, Abuelo remembered the Pharaohs, who had been such keen hawkers they were often embalmed with their best falcons. . . . Egypt again, whether I looked for it or not. If all roads led to Rome, they led there through Egypt.

From the little table I looked through the window into our library. This was just the beginning of the great store Abuelo and I would one day have. *Here* would be my place of visions—*mi claustro,*† my magician's cave. Not Ixayac. Here I would build up a collection worthy of the *studiolo* of a princess. So much more than the cell on the hill in far off Nepantla, this felt like the place I had been born to, and wrenched from.[19] In here, I would find the missing part of me.

I hardly saw Amanda in that time, aside from at supper, and I had no answer for the platter of trout. From inside the library, when I thought of Ixayac, I thought only of the maddening riddles I could not solve and all the changes Amanda never wanted to hear of. But being here in the library was a change, too, wasn't it? A wonderful one. In the teachings of Thrice-Great Hermes, it said the acolyte's frustrations were to grow to such a violent pitch that he became *as a stranger to the world*—as surely mine had, but if things had gone slightly awry up at Ixayac, maybe it was for trying to say something that shouldn't be said. Maybe certain riddles were solved alone. Which is why I didn't really want to talk to Amanda right now. Or no, I told myself next, I had simply tried to fly too soon,

†in Spanish either 'cloister' or 'womb'

before I'd understood the simpler lessons all around me. Could it be said any better than Hypatia herself had?

Life is an unfoldment, and the further we travel the more truth we can comprehend. To understand the things that are at our door is the best preparation for understanding those that lie beyond.

When I had found wisdom in instruction, when I had solved the equations and deciphered the hermetic messages written in the heavens in living gemfire, when I had found at last my talent—then I would be ready to fly, too.

Or no . . . in searching for a magic ceremony I'd let myself forget the distinction Paracelsus made between magician and *magus*, for the true magus concerns himself not with the supernatural but with natural forces as yet unseen or misapprehended. Here was the work of discovery going on all over Europe, the great work I could be part of.

And yet this was also much like the great life and work Hypatia had led. Neither then nor later could I ever quite let go of the riddles in her death, in its savagery, in her nakedness and defilement.

nce, we had sat under the stars, we two, through every phase of the moon: the snowfields above the court-yard glimmering in starlight or moonlight, or tower-ing blind in the darkness of new moons; and there Abuelito would spin out stories of the wilderness and of discovery, lost empires and lost knowledge, cities of gold and white cities of the sun. From the fire, sparks started up like fire-flies—and one night there were real fireflies—as we prodded the embers with our traveller's sticks. In that enchantment of lights hovering and blinking all about us, Abuelo told me he had seen our volcano answer one night with its own crimson shower the swarms of shooting stars falling all that August night, firefly-green, through the sky.

With the years, such flights of poetry from him had grown rarer, the evenings shorter, the silences longer. During the past year I had hardly spent any time by the fire. There were hardly any new stories, which wouldn't have been quite so bad if so much repetition had kept polish-ing the old ones. Instead, I heard him speaking now in a tired sort of blur, often trailing off. . . . Not only would he forget the details, he'd for-get he'd been talking at all. Many nights he stayed out there alone. But sometimes Josefa or María, or even our mother, would go out to sit with him for a little. Afterwards, he would go back to the library. When I got up in the night I could sometimes see the lantern casting its light from above his armchair deep in the corner.

But now the firepit was once again the indispensable end to our day in the library. And it was almost as before. After one of these new evenings together, when the fire had finally burned down, I lurched exhausted to my feet. I hugged him and kissed his dry white hair.

"Good-night, Abuelo."

"It was a good day, was it not?" he said softly, looking up at me. And I remembered. The many times, when I was just a young child, that he had carried me from the firepit and tucked me into bed. If I woke, he would kiss my hair, and ask if it was not just the finest of days. To which I would murmur in answer as I answered now.

"*Sí, Abuelito.* We had a wonderful time. . . ."

I could help him with his stories now since I knew most of them. More confident of finishing them, perhaps, he made more of an effort. And at last I began to sense that to keep the blur in his right eye and the blankness in his cheek from tripping up his tongue, the effort it cost him was not small.

He spoke of such things as the comet that hung like a sword over the hills of Rome for months after Caesar's death. Caesar had ruined the republic with his presumption. I was hoping to hear a word or two about Cleopatra next, but Abuelito wasn't finished with Julius Caesar just yet. "Pontifex Maximus, he appointed himself, Angelina. Infallible high priest, bridge to God! The comet, they called the Soul of Caesar, called it certain proof of his divinity. And a very neat trick it is to establish one's divinity by dying—do you not think? Dictator for Life, indeed."

Other stories, some I'd heard often, he no longer liked to tell. However much I asked about the Mexico of our day—the Royal University, its library, the city's drainage schemes and countless construction scandals— it had become for him an emblem of fallen greatness, of all the chances we, perhaps he, had lost.

But the Mexico of the Triple Alliance he would always happily talk about. Texcoco, Tenochtitlan, Tlacopan. The valley of the three capitals, three kings. Some things I could add to the telling. I knew that unlike the Athenian alliance at the time of Melos, Mexico's never dissolved. It held firm to the final hour. And I knew that Tenochtitlan was the greatest in power, as Texcoco was in learning. In Europe of that time, the only city to compare it with was Florence. Texcoco of the greatest poets, astronomers, historians. Texcoco of the archives, the painted books, the annals. For me, Texcoco was Athens, then Alexandria, and in the end, Florence.

Tenochtitlan was always Rome.

The last time Abuelo spoke of this was the last time we ever talked of the past. Both eyes were alive again that night with an emerald fire. He had just been telling me of his intention, as a young man, to explore to the very tip of *la tierra del fuego,* just to see for himself that the land did not simply trail away into smoke. Now he spoke with a passion I had not seen in so very long, and this night, three stories were new. Three. An unhoped-for bounty.

We had been in the library after dinner and were late lighting the fire. It was an hour or two before moonrise. On a night so clear, the skies above our mountains cannot be called dark at all. The darkness is in the land. Its dark rises up and through that sky of lights in finest tendrils … like shoots through the brilliant muslin of a bedding cloth. We walked out of the library together, out from under the arcades, and to move beneath that sky, to arrange the tinder and kindling then strike these tiny kindred sparks under the eyes of such multitudes, we were touched by a shyness … as perhaps of newlyweds before a vast and joyous wedding party. Or so it seems, looking back.

As Abuelo drilled sparks into the tinder I blew softly, then, as little pink and tangerine flames licked up, blew myself dizzy. It was like coaxing a flower into bloom. Once it took, I backed up, my bottom seeking out the smooth hollow I liked to sit in. Finding it I sat, facing east toward our mountains. Less trusting of his bottom, Abuelo reached out a tentative hand and settled stiffly into his place.

The first of Grandfather's three tales was about Nezahualcoyotl. FastingCoyote. Emperor of Texcoco and the greatest poet and philosopher of all the Mexica.

Abuelo turned and fixed me with his light green eyes. "This FastingCoyote founded a Council of Music—not just musicians but painters, astronomers, physicians. Poets and historians. This, at the exact moment the Medicis were founding their Academy. Can you imagine if they had known of the other's existence? Here was such a ruler as even Lorenzo the Magnificent would have been honoured to know. Such a synod that would have been!"

There came a time in the Triple Alliance when a particularly brutal general was to take the throne. To block his ascension, FastingCoyote offered to subject his people, the city of Texcoco, to the rule of Tenochtitlan. Forever. "This is the calibre of man we are dealing with, Angelina. A generation before the Conquest, FastingCoyote will give proof of his vision yet again. The leadership of the Mexica is now in the hands of one man, Moctezuma the First. FastingCoyote goes forth from Texcoco to warn him, as the poet's son will one day go to repeat his warning to Moctezuma the Second as Cortés approaches. Do you see, Angel? Disaster was near."

Sparks shot up like molten beads as Grandfather poked at the flames. I had never really seen the boyishness in him. The soft pelican pouch at his neck seemed almost to pout as his chin nodded and wagged at the fire. His thoughts turned to a temple that FastingCoyote had raised, a temple to the Unknown God. My grandfather praised the king's delicate poetry, regretted how many of his writings had been lost when the archives of Texcoco were burned by the friars. Abuelo recited a beautiful fragment in Castilian for me, and I decided to try to put it in Nahuatl again for him. I would ask for Xochitl's help with the translation and tomorrow night recite it. It did not occur to me that she knew it in the original.

> I, Nezahualcoyotl, ask this:
> Is it true one really lives on the earth?
> Not forever on earth,
> only a little while here.
> Though it be jade it falls apart,
> though it be gold it wears away,
> though it be quetzal plumage it is torn asunder.
> Not forever on earth,
> only a little while here.[20]

Abuelo grew quiet for a while. A three-quarter moon rose and shimmered through the plume of Popocatepetl. A few tongues of flame sputtered up. Once clear of the volcano, the moon bathed the courtyard in a creamy radiance. It softened the edges of everything, smoothed the lines and creases away as even our cream of avocado and honey could not do.

As Abuelo tried to tip the unburnt end of a log into the embers, I watched the big-knuckled hands grip and waggle his traveller's staff. From earliest memory my eyes had been drawn to those sausage fingers, and in that soft, milky light I thought of the blankness just below the elephant's eyes where its trunk seems grafted on. The thought seemed to come from such a long way back. . . .

After a while he began to talk of the last great sorcerer, who had no doubt sat at many campfires on this very spot. Now I learned that he had not lived all his life in the mountains. Just before the Conquest, Ocelotl had gone to live in Texcoco and study at the archives, for it was a time of restlessness. Then, great temples of sail were sighted off the coast. Moctezuma II, disturbed by the portents, summoned the seers and historians. But he imprisoned them. Their pronouncements displeased him. Next he summoned the sages and the sorcerers, and Ocelotl first among them.

"We do not know, Angelina, the precise words Ocelotl chose. But from what I have been able to learn of his character, I believe they ran to something like this: 'Lord Speaker, I can dispel certain mysteries for you. The auguries have become ever more evasive and strange because those who brought them were afraid and had no taste for prison. Whatever is coming is rooted in the past, and I have come from Texcoco just as others have in the past to say this: The Speaker has not listened. The levies have become excessive. Tenochtitlan is feared and detested far and wide. And this, for generations. Whatever advantage the Mexica might have gained from fear, we have lost to hatred, for a sufficient hatred overcomes much fear and caution.' And so Ocelotl spoke to an emperor. You know how Moctezuma thanked him for his troubles?"

"He threw him into prison!"

"*Eso, hijita.* As Ocelotl must have expected." Abuelo's smile was less rueful than wry. It was good to share such things. "And as far as I can tell, he was not released until some time after Moctezuma was himself Cortés's prisoner. . . ."

The moon had swung high into the south. The light fell slant on the rock faces and the snowfields, faintly purple now, like the milk in a bowl of *moras.*[†] The sloping cone of the volcano above Grandfather rose pale and featureless, like a tall Bedouin, I thought, in his flowing headdress, or a jinni, its face in shadows of amethyst.

The fire had burned down. Sleepy now, I looked up at the sky as I listened, the constellations just visible in the starry profusion. The Great Bear, Gemini . . . the Fire-Bow that Amanda had known how to find for Abuelo in Orion.

Grandfather's third tale too was about Ocelotl. It had to do with the Inquisition and Ocelotl's new friend the Bishop. We spoke of Ocelotl often here—Abuelo and Xochitl both. There was nothing strange in this. As she would say, *Truly his mist has not scattered.* And yet as Abuelo began, something was bothering me.

"The races of Man come and go, Angelina. This I understand. And I have seen enough of the rest of Europe to know no other nation would have done better than Las Casas, Sahagún—and Antonio Vieyra, today. . . ."

No, what bothered me was this: We never all of us spoke together— of Ocelotl or anything else.

"And Lord knows, Angel, an honest man expects no thanks, even from a Bishop. But God, O God, how we lied to them. . . ."

And then I asked, as if it were nothing, a question I had not asked for years.

"Abuelito, what happened between you and Xochita?"

Now that I had startled myself by asking it, I expected him to be angry. He was staring into the ember glow. Drafts played in shadows over the coals. The tip of his traveller's staff lay among them, smoking, motionless.

"Some things are better left unsaid, Juanita. It does not mean we were not friends."

After another moment or two he looked up and turned stiffly to face me. He did not look angry at all. "But it is good you ask about this. I have need of your help."

"With what Abuelo?—anything."

"Her."

"*Xochi?*"

"And Amanda, yes. Your mother is pregnant. . . . You knew."

"Josefa said."

"From now on, it will be harder for Amanda and her mother."

"*De acuerdo, Abuelito.* We'll watch over them *together.*"

At that, his frown eased. He scratched at the ruff under his chin.

"Yes we will. Now do you want to hear about our Ocelotl and his Bishop or not? Good. Well, you remember I once told you Ocelotl had a twin. . . ."

When I awoke, he had one arm still under me and was bending to pull back the sheets. He had not carried me to bed for years and I wouldn't have thought he still could. Moonlight flooded into the room through the doorway. Moonlight spilled under the eaves and in through the window. Pure white now . . . the tint of amethyst was gone, as if a trick of light from the fire. In that milky light his face was rinsed clear and clean of lines, as if the blankness had spread from his sausage finger to an eye, a cheek, finally to fill the room, the moon . . .

My arms were still around his neck. So close above me, the eyes in that big fine head were like opals, black yet clear, like smoke through lantern glass. Reluctantly I let go of him, regretted it. Over my forehead a big hand hovered ever so lightly now as if cupped to shield a candle. He smoothed my hair and kissed it.

His mouth was firm, resolute, an old lion's. The smile was only in his voice.

"Has it not been the finest of days, Angelina?"
Ah, sí, Abuelito. The very finest.
We had the most wonderful time.

I

Recuerde el alma dormida,
avive el seso e despierte
contemplando
cómo se passa la vida,
cómo se viene la muerte
tan callando;
  cuán presto se va el plazer,
cómo, después de acordado,
da dolor;
cómo, a nuestro parescer,
cualquiere tiempo passado
fue mejor.

II

Pues si vemos lo presente
cómo en un punto s'es ido
e acabado,
si juzgamos sabiamente,
daremos lo non venido
por passado.
  Non se engañe nadi, no,
pensando que ha de durar
lo que espera
más que duró lo que vio,
pues que todo ha de passar
por tal manera.

I

Recall the soul from its sleep
kindle the slumb'ring brain and wake
to contemplate
how life passes by,
how death arrives
so quietly . . .
  How soon pleasure leaves—
how its memory
returns as pain;
how, it seems,
any past time
was better.

II

When we see the present,
how in a heartbeat it is finished
and gone,
if we judge wisely
we shall wonder if what is past
has ever come.
  Let no one be deceived, no,
to think what is hoped for
shall last,
any more than what we've seen go,
since all things must pass
so.

III

Nuestras vidas son los ríos
que van a dar en la mar,
qu'es el morir;
allí van los señoríos
derechos a se acabar
e consumir;
   allí los ríos caudales,
allí los otros medianos
e más chicos,
allegados, son iguales
los que viven por sus manos
e los ricos. . . .

IV

Dexo las invocaciones
de los famosos poetas
y oradores;
non curo de sus ficciones,
que traen yerbas secretas
sus sabores.
   Aquél sólo m'encomiendo,
Aquél sólo invoco yo
 de verdad,
que en este mundo viviendo,
el mundo non conoció
 su deidad . . .

III

Our lives are rivers
running to the sea
that is death;
there run all our dominions
straight to their end,
to be consumed;
   there, the mightiest streams,
there, the lesser
and small,
all lie together now, equals,
those who live by their hands,
those who command. . . .

IV

Here I let fall the invocations
of the famous poets
and orators;
I am not healed by their fictions,
though they bring secret herbs
strange flavours.
   To this alone do I commend me,
This alone do I invoke,
truly,
that in a world of living,
this world knew not
its deity . . .

JORGE
MANRIQUE

B. Limosneros, trans.

EARTH
TEARER

Amanda was the one who brushed the damp earth from my knees and walked me back from the plot in the shady spot where she and I used to read. It was Amanda who sat close beside me at the table in the kitchen as Xochitl did her best to console me without ever quite speaking of him. It was Amanda who, for weeks, waited just inside my room each morning for me to rise, and waited near the library for me to come out again, just to walk me back to my room. Every day she brought each meal there. Was there anything else I needed, was there anything special Xochitl could make for me? Anxious, almost anguished, she wore an expression I saw often during that time but would not recognise, because she was the mirror I did not want to look into.

Diego moved in. My sisters went to live with my aunt in Chalco. I did not think to wonder if they'd asked to go. Yet even with Diego around, there came a time when I could no longer spend all my days alone in the library.

I had been sitting at the desk, a book open before me, staring out the window at the mountains, just as I had sometimes surprised him doing. When caught, he gave such a sheepish little smile. And at last, there it was in my mind, that little smile.

Abuelito, I'll put your books away now. And clear off your desk . . . ? If that will be all right.

The ones jumbled on the right were easier; these he had read. But four, he had not finished. It took a moment to touch them, a little longer to shelve. The last one dropped. Cursing my clumsy hands I bent to pick it up where it lay face down in the aisle, awkwardly folded. A little roof unevenly pitched. A small hawk covering a kill. It was like finding him all over again, turning that book face up. On the stone floor underneath lay a scrap of paper, a crude map. Mountains, sea, two stick figures dressed as tars with oars and banners. A girl and an old man with a sunflower face, waving grandly from Tierra del Fuego.

When I came out that day Amanda was there. It was early evening, the air already cool, the sun behind the hills. Her eyes looked searchingly into mine, her eyes big and full, colt's eyes of softest brown. She came to a decision, drew a little bundle wrapped in sacking from the folds of her *rebozo*.

She had made a doll. Body of hemp, arms of braided wool bound tight with cotton thread. Corncob head, cut cross-wise to make a round sun face. Cornsilk hair, faintly red. I was without a thought in my head but could not stop staring at the doll.

Numbly I asked what this was. She was afraid I did not like it. She said I could take him with me now, wherever I went. I could feel my face working as I tried to find the words. I should have hugged her, held her and never let go.

Just then, Isabel came in from the fields.

She looked so tired and dusty, and so pregnant, a giant egg lumped under her dress, a camel's hump come uncinched and slipped round to her stomach. Huge—hatted booted skirted—she grimaced, wrenching her chin back and forth as she tugged at a knot in the cord of her riding cloak. Hands high, chin high, head cocked to one side, a dangerous exasperation in her black eyes. Seeing us malingering at the library door she barked at Amanda to go help her mother.

Amanda's face went wooden. As she turned for the kitchen I clutched at her arm. Isabel brushed past. I remember shouting back, something about Isabel's touching concern for Xochita all of a sudden. For an instant her gait faltered, but her physical distress must have been such that she could not turn back. I led Amanda into the kitchen by the hand, showed the doll to Xochitl, railed against all my mother's injustices. After a few minutes of this, Xochitl broke in brusquely to tell me not to make such a stew of my chameleons, by which I took her to mean that I made too much of my travails, dressing them up in colours not their own. Even Xochita, now.

Once the baby was born we started seeing a great deal of Diego, and of Diego's black mastiff. No matter how far up the river we walked or how deep into the woods, the dog found us. It clambered over us excitedly— panting, lolling, trembling—insolent snout, yellow eyes dead, corrupt, breath foul like an animal rotting in the brush. Though the mastiff smirched and pawed and slavered over both of us it took special interest in Amanda. This was the breed so efficient against the Mexicans during the Conquest—to this in peacetime come the war dogs and warmongers. It could smell a difference between us.

I had never felt a hatred so intense for any living thing, and fury and disgust. It was not a difference of race it smelled, but that Amanda was a woman and I was not. Yet it was not only that it found difference where I wanted there to be none. And it was not that I was shocked. We had lived on ranches all our lives. These things were natural with animals. And this was not natural at all. It followed us with its nose, it followed us as Diego's eyes followed us at home—all of us, my sisters, Amanda, me, even Xochitl. And lo, after a while, on his big pied gelding, handsome Diego would come riding along to liberate us and let himself be gazed upon . . . the glossy hair kinked in the manner we call *chino* and drawn tight into a short pigtail of briars . . . the wide, full lips such as any woman might wish for herself, the thick gleaming brows, the fine pale forehead under the splendid sombrero, the eyes deep-set, a turbulent dark brown, and yet in their darkness a little dull. Dullish knots twisting in smooth white pine.

It was Amanda they watched. Each time he caught up with his dog he waited a little longer before calling him away: Bad dog. But once he had, the thing came instantly, and we knew it had not wandered off. It had been sent, like a message. How I detested that animal. Amanda was afraid of it, I was not. And I was not afraid of its master either. Such a striking figure he cut—of the soldier clown, preening varlet in battle dress. Was there nowhere an uprising to put down, did he never go anymore in to the garrison?

He sat at the head of the table, the man of the household now, to whom all its appurtenances and comforts fell. I was not afraid, but then, it was not me he looked upon as property. Protecting her or hating the sight of him in that chair—what played the larger role in what I did next? It occurs to me that I may have hated him for something I had discovered in myself.

What I thought then was that if I had beaten him once, I could again. In one night. I was forgetting for an instant how limited the first victory had been, as I prepared a little parable and concealed it in a snare. Speaking to the dining room in general, I said they would never guess who Amanda and I had seen out in the woods. Diego's head shot up. He glanced down the table at Isabel. I said, though I lied, that Amanda and I had met the woodcutters, the ones from the forest fire last year, and had taken our lunch with them in the woods. A younger one had started to tell a story, but was hushed by an elder. I had, naturally, no idea why.

How frustrating that had been. Something about a bridegroom's promise to the Devil, and a wedding night that ended with an impalement on a cedar tree.

The nursing blanket halfway down her shoulder, Isabel had been staring into the baby's little fox eyes as it grasped and sucked at its blue-veined egg, but now she looked up.

In truth, this legend was so well known to everyone in our valley that any large tree might be called a *wedding tree*. Diego, of course, was not from our valley. I had come prepared to do more of the work myself, but he proved all too eager to display his local knowledge now. And displayed, thereby, a good deal more. Isabel warned him that I already knew his story but he pressed on, oblivious or unable to help himself. Yes, a landowner, he said, granted enormous riches by Satan, in exchange for one small promise. I did not ask what it was, making his eagerness to tell me all the more plain. But Isabel was already watching him closely.

The promise was, he went on, that when the landowner should one day take a woman to marry, Satan was to . . . *precede* the man on their wedding night. *To speed the plough, so to speak.*

Saying this, he gave me a wide, slow smile. Such a promise—who could blame the poor bridegroom for not wanting to follow such an act . . . ?

Speed the plough.

This was more than I could have hoped for, this was providential, pure gift. When his voice had quite trailed off to the stoniest silence around the table, I thanked him for the story and—fair turnabout—coldly offered the one I had prepared for him and for which he had so admirably prepared the ground. An old story. Also about a woodcutter. A man named Erysichthon, who had cut down a grove of oaks sacred to Cybele.

For this sacrilege she visited upon him a hunger, such a hunger as was in that country called the Wolf, and in other places the Ox. A hunger so great and so foul as to make him eat anything, any sort of filth. And so he did, until he had devoured all the bounty of his lands and bartered all his wealth and property for the filthiest stuff, since his desperation was obvious to all who had trade with him. And when he had lost everything to the Wolf, he reached out for his own daughter, who had a great and precious gift—to change her bodily form, like Thetis who had shifted through so many shapes and yet failed to prevent her own rape. In his sickness the man saw Fortune smiling upon him now, for thanks to this gift of hers he could offer his daughter—ever fresh and ever new—to every man for miles around.

At some point Amanda had come in to clear the plates. She was standing awkwardly by the table, hesitating over the half-eaten meals. Something in the scene kept her from interrupting to ask if we had finished. I asked Diego if it was not indeed a sad tale thus far. And here was its ending: Such was this hunger that the accursed man, panting and slavering like the diseased dog he had become . . . devoured him*self*.

Oh and there was, I remembered, just this last detail. The man's name meant *earth tearer*. So what had his crime really been—did the lance-captain have an opinion? Was it in cutting down something sacred? Or in trying to speed the plough where he shouldn't?

As I finished, I was looking at Amanda. I had meant only to glance meaningfully in her direction, but I could not look at my mother and could not trust myself to look any longer into Diego's eyes. Amanda blushed furiously. All three of us now were looking at her. . . .

The most perfect silence settled over the table, for what felt like an hour. I could hardly breathe. I simply could not believe it had gone better than I had dared dream. I was first to find my voice. Nodding curtly toward his plate I asked if he had quite finished. Amanda would like to clear.

Isabel whisked me out of the room. I could not help thinking she was taking me to the killing floor, which I remembered vividly as the scene of my last great correction. Instead she announced I would be going away just as my sisters had, but to live with her sister in Mexico. *Mexico*—just like that. I told myself I should have humiliated our gallant defender weeks ago.

But in fact everything had already been arranged by my grandfather. Isabel had only been waiting for the moment.

The next morning, dishevelled from a long cold night garrisoned on the rocking chair outside my mother's door, Diego cast about calling for his mastiff, calling to it as he walked stiffly to the portal, calling awhile outside, coming back in and climbing the watchtower to bellow from up there like an unmilked cow. Isabel took over his chair and sat rocking while she nursed. How calmly she sat, and at an hour when she had always been out in the fields.

I went into the kitchen. Although Amanda had been mortified to have everyone at the table looking at her the night before, this morning she was all smiles to show me she understood I had been protecting her.

I was bursting to tell her our news, about how hereinafter our lives in Mexico would be like a storybook—but, smiling excitedly into my eyes, she said *she* had a surprise. She led me out through the corn and as we walked she stayed close, lightly touching my arm, brushing my shoulder, and finally took my hand. With the mastiff already outside, I expected it to find us any moment now, here in the tall corn. We threaded our way through the field. As we reached the fence I started again to tell her about what had happened after dinner and how I had been expecting the worst thrashing of my life. Yet now we had the most glorious news, she and I. Rather than asking what it was, she was pointing out a bucket leaking drops of water where it swung from a cedar branch just beyond the fence. I was trying to tell her we had *permission*, we were going to my aunt's in Mexico City at last, maybe even tomorrow—

Who was?

We were.

My first lesson on the world as storybook was long overdue, and yet so slow I still was. The pace of my classes was picking up: two questions she shot back in quick succession, the first, unthinking and innocent, the second, to cover her hurt and embarrassed pride.

Is your mother giving me away?

Am I going as your maid?

A minute ago she had been all smiles, now this bitterest sarcasm, this patient anger one has for a stupid child. Where had all this come from? What on earth had gotten into her? I'll never be your maid, Ixpetz. But Amanda you're *not*. I'll never go there. Why, Amanda, why *not*? Our people only go to that city for one thing—what thing?—and always have. Who says? My mother says. What *thing*?

To die.

I could find nothing to say to this.

So no matter what, I'm better off here, to let him have me, just like Mother when your—

Whole worlds flashed then in her eyes—fury, sadness. Then shame. I could not ever remember her ashamed. What could Amanda ever have to be ashamed of?

What, Amanda—when my *what?* Come back! Finish what you said—come back! She ran up the path through the trees, her white soles lifting like the tails of deer.

I was left standing there. I was left to read her language of signs.

I lowered the pail. Over each other and up the sides, two turtles clambered on a thick wet cloth. Surely not the same two as up at Ixayac. But they were the same size. . . .

A little water still sloshed in the bottom but their backs were already dry. I started back towards the house, the bucket banging away at my calf. I went in through the main portal thinking to get the turtles water from the well.

Xochitl stood just inside the kitchen door, wiping her hands with a kitchen rag. Her dark face seemed oddly youthful through the doorway. The sun lay like purest silver in her hair. Across the courtyard, Diego had the fieldhands lined up like a platoon for inspection. The scene that ensued caused an uproar that ended in Diego storming off for a day or two. The dog was still missing. Diego had roused himself to a towering fury and, until Isabel stopped him, had been bent on extracting a confession from one—any—of the bewildered men.

It was not until after supper that night, a delicious meat sauce of chilli and black chocolate, which Xochitl had served us herself, that I went, feeling strangely light, to have my talk with her. Chocolate had once been a sacred thing, and Xochitl had never cooked with it for us. It was a sign of great favour, though I did not know the reason for it tonight. And the turtles were surely a sign of Amanda's forgiveness for before. Now I would find out what Xochita had been telling her and clear up this misunderstanding about Mexico. I would reassure them both. I would promise to protect Amanda just as I had at dinner the night before. I felt proud. I had kept a promise to Abuelo, who had asked for my help. I was at peace. And I had even solved another riddle, from a previous evening of stunning insights into elliptical and hyperbolic statements during the *manzana* in Amecameca. Neither elliptical nor hyperbolic, the parabolic is not so much a truth as a parallel, such as when the attentions paid to a girl are of the sort only meant for a woman. Part parable, part parody.

Everything was falling into place, as I knew it must. I felt in my bones the time had come for us to find our destinies. . . .

"I said *no*, Ixpetz. That is final."

The kitchen was a shambles of unwashed dishes. Xochitl sat close beside me at the table, which was dusted at one end with corn flour. Insects tapped blindly at the lantern glass. The pantry door was closed, the door into the yard was open. A sallow panel of lamplight fell on the beaten earth pale with starlight. A breeze agitated the blades of the corn leaves . . . an army of spearmen on a night march.

I was so astonished. A flat no, the third. The words clear, the tone unmistakable. I had tried everything. But how could that be? When it really mattered I had always been able to persuade her. She wouldn't even let me go in to talk to Amanda.

"It is not just you she does not want to see. She is angrier at me."

"You?"

"For knowing this day would come."

"But *why* does it have to come, Xochita?"

Whenever I had cried before, cried hard, whether out of shame or heartache or rage, Xochita had always comforted me. Even now I could see she wanted to, but it was as if she couldn't raise her arms. When the scene ran through my mind again later that night it seemed that all the triangles of her face had been pulled out and down, as if a baby were pulling at her cheeks.

"It was not easy at first, Ixpetz, to take you to my breast. . . ."

She averted her face, looked into the empty dining room. Her hands on the table widened slightly—to take her weight as she rose or to keep themselves from slipping into her lap, I couldn't tell.

Helpfully, I asked if it hurt very much to nurse, if nursing me had been as bad as Isabel said. But this only seemed to make things worse. I put an arm about her shoulders, the other hand to her dark forearm, left small, pale prints as I patted her. I asked her not to feel badly. I knew why she could not entrust Amanda to me, because of something I had done.

"No, Ixpetz. It is something I have done. . . ."

She seemed unsure how to begin, was worried about what Abuelo might have been willing or unwilling to tell me. There was something that happened long ago. . . . But I knew all *about* it, the fall from the horse when she was almost ready to have Amanda. And to have turned her hair white almost overnight it must have been unendurably painful. *Of course* she couldn't work in the fields anymore with her hip . . . and though I was anxious to help, I could not help mentioning that surely she did not miss life in the fields so much, any more than I believed she regretted so very much coming to nurse me. And though my mother was sometimes harsh, I thought things would be better now, and Xochitl did not really think a life of fieldwork was for Amanda. Xochitl stopped me with something puzzling.

"But I did not work in the fields, Ixpetz."

She had first met my grandfather in her village. He had ridden up there more than once, interested to learn more about Ocelotl. She asked me something still more puzzling, if I had ever once seen any of her people on a horse. "Spaniards ride horses. We do not."

Then I saw it with perfect clarity. My mind recoiled from the thought. *It was Abuelo's horse.* He would never have forgiven himself—*of course. . . .* Though this was something that happened even to the finest horsemen.

"I always walked back down to the village alone." She could not look at me. "But we were late. The horse was going fast. The light . . ." So clearly then I saw her riding behind him, at dusk, her arms at his waist trying to hold on—with her so pregnant, as Isabel had just been—reaching around that great egg between them to cling to his coat—just as the horse stepped into a *toza* burrow.

Now she was talking about her village, her high standing among the villagers as the *curandero's* daughter, the blood of Ocelotl. Whose mist had not scattered. She had been a healer herself already, and almost a midwife—it was proper that she had never married. Old for a bride, they said, but young for a midwife. The joke had been gentle, and in it their approval. A fish of gold they called her, with pride.

"*Quen tehito. . . .* Can you understand, Ixpetz?"

"Regarded by the people."

"They said this of Pedro. I mean your grandfather." I had never heard her use his name, but who else could she mean? I felt a rush of pride.

"They say it also of your mother. The land is in her heart, the earth."

This, I did not want to hear. Heart of clay, more like it.

"They respect you, Xochita. I could always tell."

Slowly she shook her head. "They do not say fish of gold now, Ixpetz. *Tla alaui, tlapetzcaui in tlalticpac. Quen uel ximimatia in teteocuitlamichi.*"

Things slip, things slide in this world. Fish of gold, what happened to you?

"Did you know Abuelo asked for my help, Xochita?—to look after you and Amanda."

Again a moment of surprise, that I should feel better for trying to comfort her and yet that in trying to comfort, I should seem so to wound her.

Now, I thought, surely now with her face so tender. If I just asked her once more. Why else had she been telling me all this if not to convey her fears for Amanda, and how delicate a thing was destiny? But Amanda and I would be together, we would care for each other.

"For the last time, Ixpetz—No! Will you never open your eyes? Amanda will *never go to that place*."

The words hung in the air as I fled—out through the dining room and into the courtyard and up the watchtower steps. She had never spoken to me like that. It stayed in my mind all that night.

I sensed it in Xochitl's voice if not her words. The more I thought about it, the more clearly I saw it in her face. She had scratched the jade, had torn the quetzal feather. *Xochita*. Who was wise and strong and good. Whose ancestor was Ocelotl. Even she could do something terrible.

And if she could, I could.

In the quiet of my room the tears came as a relief. So much had happened in the past two days. There was so much about the world I had never found in books. I saw Isabel's face, not gloating, but as if to say she had been telling me this all along.

There began, at about this time, two dreams that have recurred many times. Two nightmares, or perhaps they are one in two parts. A black dog at the killing floor skinned and bloated and swinging from a pole, and Amanda at Ixayac, naked beside the plunge pool. As she slathered our magic cream of honey and avocado all over, her eyes never left mine, never left them as the wasps began to land, never left them until she was furred in gold and they began to sting and sting all over her face, her breasts and thighs that purpled and swelled, her eyes that ran gold. . . .

By morning I was sure I knew what Xochita was telling me. *I had scratched the jade, too.* I had been afraid of this myself, the words had even come into my mind, though I had not truly understood what this could mean. Now it was clear. It *was* why she would not let Amanda go with me. Because Amanda had told her what had happened at Ixayac.

And if Amanda could not come to Mexico with me . . . ?

For eleven-year-olds, things need not be complicated. All reduced to this: What was my perfect gesture to be? How would I answer hers?— all her perfect gifts to me. Isabel was sending me away. Just as she had sent my sisters away. It was to protect them from their willingness, I saw that now. How I wanted to go, but Amanda could not come. How I wanted to stay with her but I could not stay. I did not want to go without her but she could not come. I can't stay, I can't leave.

I had only wanted to solve the riddle.

It was a game. Find the magic recipe to stop time, turn back the Nile, find a destiny in light. I was eleven now—so what would my perfect gesture be? All my great gifts were as nothing if they could not save Amanda now. Solve the riddle, dissolve the conundrum, resolve the dilemma. *Absolve my failure*. For until now it had only been a game with a marvellous prize. Solve the riddle and learn your destiny.

It was dawning on me that this was no game for children, and that failure had a price.

What is our punishment for failures such as these? And is it for failing to solve the mysteries or for shredding the fabric that veils them? What is a golden age, how does its end begin? What does it mean to lose a friend? The best part of myself.

There came into my mind images of that day up at Ixayac, of squatting in the smoke and the steam, of symbols and magic signs traced in mud, of black hens and turtle shells. Amanda never understood what I wanted. But she trusted me. And I saw then Sister Paula's face the day my grandfather came to take me home from school. Abuelo promised me I had not polluted the other girls. That I was not infected. That this hunger to know—*everything*—was not a disease. But now I knew differently, and he was no longer here.

We had climbed to the Heart of the Earth, we had walked in halls of jade. If I had not done something terrible at Ixayac, even had I not hurt her then, I could not deny I was hurting her now. What difference did it make whether I had scratched the jade or had done something that only *felt* like that? She is not safe with me, she is not safe if I go. What will my perfect gesture be?

And then I knew. I could not solve it. I knew I would fail, I knew I would leave.

During the next two days I could hardly bear to be near her. Each time came the shock of a horrified recognition: *this is your life*, I thought, over and over. *This will be your life*. There is a prize, there is a price. Solve the riddle, to save and keep her. I saw Amanda's face each day more drawn and gaunt.

The prize is to learn my destiny and join the great revival in Europe, a new golden age. The price is to end the race of gold, and stop the running to Ixayac.

The price is an age of iron when children are born already old.

The price was Amanda.

JUANA INÉS
DE LA CRUZ

B. Limosneros, trans.

      Pure waters of the Nile
recede, recede
and deny
thy tribute to the Sea,
for such bountiful
cargo she can only envy.
Cease, cease, roll on not one more mile,
For no greater joy awaits thee
than here . . . nigh.
        Recede, recede . . .

      Soothe, sinuous, Nile,
thy liquid swells;
hold, hold fast,
to gaze in rapture
on what thy beauty brings to us,
from earth, from Heaven's Rose and Star,
whose lifeblood thou art . . .

four years later, after my ride through the Sunday streets with Magda and María, I wanted to go home. The price had been too high, though I would not quite see how high until I had made the journey.

Uncle Juan had offered to send me by carriage, a different carriage, but understood when I declined. With a porter close behind us with my little *lío*,† he walked me himself all the way from the house. The bundle contained only a change of travelling clothes, but slung over my shoulder I carried for luck the green rabbit satchel Amanda had made for me, and in it some keepsakes. As we approached the canal there was just room to go two abreast alongside the file of wagons advancing still more slowly than we were.

†bundle, muddle

"You were wise to want to walk, Juanita."

The wharf on the canal was a pandemonium. Landing here four years earlier from Panoayan, I'd thought it like an anthill. The anthill had been kicked over now. With *la Virgen de Guadalupe*'s festival in just two days' time, the waterway was as choked with canoes as the street and landing were with heavy carts. Jostling to land, the dugouts were backed all the way down the canal like a string of stewards serving at a cardinal's table. In one canoe, bunches of bananas each as big as a man. In the next, their feathers dusty from the trip, a half-dozen black *guajalotes* squabbling like curates with scarlet wattles and smoke-blue heads. Every third canoe all but overflowed with fresh-cut flowers and—out of season in our valley—roses rushed in relays of express post horses up from the south. I'd have no trouble finding passage to the eastern shore. An unbroken file of empty dugouts was heading there.

Something stirred in the air like a scent, faintly exhilarating. What I had taken for shouts of confusion I now heard as a kind of workmanly raillery. Near me a tall African took an armload of flowers from a snowy-haired Indian, who had the wildly bowed legs of some ancient cavalryman. I caught a snatch of something in a decent Nahuatl. The African was asking him if he hadn't maybe kept a few for a sweetheart. The old man laughed outright, then—glancing toward us—stopped. It occurred to me that all these men might in fact work for Uncle Juan.

"The northern canal, Juana, will be even worse, and the basilica itself—*olvídalo.* Ten times as many as at the poetry tourney on Saturday."

"A hundred thousand people?"

"You should go. I would take you," he said, still taking in the scene. "What your aunt and Magda did . . . it would never happen again."

"I have to go back, Uncle."

He glanced down at me. "I just wanted you to hear it."

"I know. . . . Thank you."

He went to find a boatman to take me. As he walked down I noticed a pink bald patch the size of my palm on the crown of his head. He found a boat in less than a minute. I met him halfway down. It was difficult to hear, to talk. To say good-bye to him.

"Say hello to your mother. Tell her it's been too long."

Afraid I might cry I said nothing in answer. The boatman shoved off with a paddle blade. Uncle Juan called out. "If you do decide on just a short visit, consider being back for the audience with the Viceroy. Royalty can be a bit particular about their invitations. . . ." He began this with a shrug, but hearing him raise his voice awkwardly to bridge the distance gave me an inkling of what was at stake for him. First prize. Our first prize. I had forgotten it entirely. Before I could make an answer we were too far off with so much noise on the dock. I met his eyes, held them and nodded. He nodded back. The boatman manoeuvred us into a throng of dugouts bumping hollowly and angling towards open water.

With the mountains dead ahead I did have a little cry—the surfeit of an emotion I couldn't identify quite. Sorrow, regret . . . and something like relief. Foot traffic on the eastern causeway went at a crawl. Halfway along, a herd of cattle was broken into smaller clusters by pilgrims struggling to get past. Seven smaller herds, perhaps fifty cows in each, with five or six horsemen strung among them like sea serpents rearing above a flood. After a while I reached into my *lío* for a little lunch of dried figs tied up in a handkerchief. When I turned back to offer the boatman some, he smiled and shook his head. Sweat stood out on his brow; he was paddling smoothly but hard. Each stroke sent little whirlpools spinning away behind us.

I slept now, warmed by the sun, no screaming rising from the streets, no processions, no candles. No carriages, no forges, no hell. And dreamed of Ixayac.

The wharf behind us had been the picture of my own confusion, and yet I had left it strangely heartened. The feeling, or the word for it, had been not quite *relief* but *reprieve*. So much like the day of my arrival when Aunt María had met me at the landing, it was as if I were simply turning back and none of the intervening four years had happened. The dirty village on the lakeshore did not lack for mule teams. It took an extra hour to find an honest-looking young driver with a team of oxen.

On the morning of the second day, we entered the highest valley. Soon I knew that we could not be more than an hour away. In no time we had turned off the main road onto the track running up to the hacienda. I clutched tight in my lap to the satchel of keepsakes I had brought against the accusation that I had not written in all this time. How hollowly it rang in my mind to say that I had not looked back, or tried not to, because I was afraid I could not otherwise find the courage to stay away. I had not wanted to look back but had brought the things I had loved with me, because I could not bring the people. And I had never blamed Amanda for not coming out to say good-bye to me.

I knew that things could not be as they had once been but I understood now that Xochitl had been right, that the capital was no place for a daughter of hers. I knew something now about servants and Indians, and about all she and Amanda had kept from me and how much they had given by withholding it. And I wanted to tell her that I saw at last the enormous difference between having a fate and pursuing a destiny, and that if there was ever a problem for us to have tried hard to solve, it was not how I might find mine but how she might escape hers. We were fifteen now. Things could not be the same, but maybe in a few years, when we were older, we might find our own way in the world, together.

But above all that day, there was something I needed to say to Amanda about what had happened at Ixayac. I saw how much I had wronged her. And since then I had understood even something of why—though I must not let this sound like an excuse. It had taken years, but I had resolved the one mystery that I had allowed to drive us apart. How these things had consumed and bewildered me. That the Alexandrian renaissance died that day in the body of its most illustrious expositor, a rebirth ripped from the womb in a church called Caesarion. . . . That the heavy vessels used by the monks of the Natron lakes were certainly Canopic jars filled with embalming fluid, to make the dead last a thousand years. That the pottery shards and oyster shells the desert monks had used to scrape the flesh from Hypatia's bones would surely have formed the conic sections called parabola. That the commentaries on the *Conics* of Apollonius, the highest glory of the Alexandrian revival, were written by none other than Hypatia and her father.

A mystery called Cinaron, a riddle call Caesarion, a puzzle of broken pottery. But out of so many riddles, in all the years of my exile, there was one whose edges had never lost their sharpness. And this one I had solved. *Ostrakis aneilon*. Oyster shells . . . and also the roofing tiles on whose fragments the name of the one to be banished was inscribed. Hypatia had been ostracized, for ten centuries. But for this solution there was to be no prize.

Oyster shells, pottery tiles, parabola. . . . One other conic section is the turtle shell.

In the whiteness of my hunger I had sacked the Sarapeum, destroyed the Serapiana, violated all that was chaste in a time that has gone. Hypatia's role had not been mine to play at all. This part was for another. The best part of myself.

As the ox cart came to a stop behind the house, it was this I was remembering, and Ixayac. I had seen something of the world, and knew now that heresy was not just about books; neither were treason and betrayal only things of distant countries and pasts. And I had more yet to learn about the Inquisition, and from Magda. Even now I wonder what I might have found to say. I was not to get the chance, for not even Hypatia's banishment was truly mine to play. But I think I had already sensed this. A *campesino* I did not recognize was making his way toward us. I pointed out to the driver the water troughs for the oxen and promised to bring him water to drink from the house. My hand trembling a little, I gave him an extra centavo for the journey. I called to the farmhand to put 'good' corn into the feedbags. Good corn. I must have sounded even more foolish to him than I did to myself. He plainly had no idea who I was. Standing here talking nonsense—trembling hands—was this how I was to face Amanda?

I forced myself to think instead of Xochitl. How I had *missed* her. I rapped shyly, then a little louder. The kitchen door had never been locked. A young Indian woman opened now. She stood before me in the doorway, nursing an infant under her *rebozo*. "*¿Sí, señorita? A sus órdenes,*" she added in a good Castilian. Perhaps seeing my distress, she stepped back and beckoned me in. "*Pásele.*"

A pale, curly-haired boy of four or five was playing with wooden soldiers on the kitchen floor. Struggling for calm I went into the pantry. A single hammock was slung in the corner, where a cross-draft between the windows made sleeping more comfortable. I felt my blood turn to rust— a ball of iron in the pit of my stomach. "Where is Xochitl?" I could not even have formed Amanda's name. The young woman's eyes widened. She clutched the infant more tightly to her.

"Who?" she asked, and stepped between me and the boy. He reached up to where her hand fumbled to find his, this boy who was my half-brother. I rushed from the kitchen into the courtyard looking for Isabel, for anyone.

In the middle of the courtyard, where the firepit had once been, I stopped. Like a sentry, yet somehow broken now, a man sat in the rocking chair by Isabel's door, where he had often sat, our dinner guest waiting for her to come in from the fields. Lance-captain Diego Ruiz Lozano was much changed, much aged. The head of hair once so thick with curls lay lank. Lacklustre now the black beard, and from the upper lip hung limp tatters of black rag. A blanket covered his legs, his knees thinned as if by palsy.

"No, Juana, they have not been here for some time. . . . You've grown."

To be hearing this from his lips, how I rejoiced that the years had been so unkind, that the wellsprings of his life, its roots, had proved so shallow—that four years should sap them dry.

"How long?"

"We never did get to say good-bye."

"How *long*, Diego?"

"You look more like your mother than ever. . . ."

I said nothing. After a moment he looked away.

"She found a place for them on the far side of the pass. She went to a lot of trouble. Isabel should never have let Amanda have so much *money*. She should never have let them leave with it. I warned her, I warned them. . . ."

They never arrived. He had sent troops everywhere looking for them—to Nepantla, to Xochitl's old village, every village on the far slope

of the volcanoes. The roads were dangerous. He blamed the fifty pesos.
A ridiculous sum to give a child, to give any Indian.

I turned away from the blue ruins of those eyes—walked unsteadily
down the arcade, could not bring myself to enter the darkened library.
Taking up the satchel I'd left by the kitchen door I walked into the
fields, through the dry corn, out towards the river. The shady spot
where we used to read lay in a strip of trees between the maguey and
the corn. At the foot of a cedar, a giant among the pines, stood a small
granite cross. There I sank softly to the ground, sat mindless, empty,
emptiness itself.

Then into the vessel of that abhorrent emptiness rushed such a violent swarm of faces, voices, memories . . .

It had never occurred to me that she would not be here, that this life
I had left was not simply waiting upon my return. For four years I had
fought not to look back at these mountains and think of Amanda here,
looking from Ixayac down over the city. I looked up to them now, the
mist thinning . . . the cone of El Popo cut by a wedge of cloud,
WhiteLady stretched out below him . . . chin, breast, knees. What was
the use of straining to see the secret shapes hidden in the world if I could
not see into myself?

On a patch of grass by the water troughs, the cart had been pulled up,
the oxen unhitched. They had drunk their fill and were milling away at
feedbags of the good corn I had called for. The young driver had slept his
siesta under the cart and was stirring now. I watched him stretch, the languor of having no cargo to load or unload.

I spread my keepsakes out before me among the pine cones and
rust-coloured needles. I had been right not to look back. It solved
nothing. Worse, I'd had this truth right before me for years. Into my
lap I took the *Cancionero general*. It fell open to the very page, so often
had I read it.

> Let no one be deceived, no,
> to think what is hoped for
> shall last,
> any more than what we've seen go. . . .

In the shade of that tree, there came to me the idea that the thread of
my life had been broken. Perhaps it was the sheer hazard of holding the

battered copy of *El cancionero general.* Or something to do with pottery
shards. Whatever remained of my childhood had ended during a ride in
a beautiful carriage through the streets of Mexico; but though I might
blame the Holy Office, it was a childhood that had no right to outlast
Amanda's, just as I felt no right to grieve its loss. And that city was no
place for a child. With these few things before me I would make a new
start, not by looking back but by carrying my life forward with me. The
poet must never look back.

I turned at the sound of the ox cart as it lumbered slowly past the
house, felt something stirring within me to watch it leave. . . .

One last time in Panoayan I ran—I ran *from* Panoayan, as I had never
run in four years in the city. I went with all my strength after the cart—
a broken book in my left hand, my satchel flailing and flapping in my
right. As I ran up the track between the orchards and the fields and as
the rich bloom of damsons filled my mind I would have let myself see no
similarities between the past and what I was doing now, no precedents or
patterns at all, not even in the explorer's compulsion to abandon the
known world, to discover the new. Yes, I had quit Ixayac for a library I
had barely glimpsed, and yes I had abandoned Panoayan for a city I had
only seen from afar and as if in a dream. But I had *seen* Mexico City now.
The receptions, the poetry jousts, the prizes. I had met the Viceroy and
was to have an audience and meet his blond wife. So of course I knew
that world, and ran toward it. There I would make a new thread and spin
out my dream of a different destiny.

Too breathless to laugh at the young driver's confusion, I clambered
up on aching legs to the cart seat. Such a whirl of seasons lay ahead of
me, such episodes, such deep tones and bright hues, like the brilliant
shadows of a magic lantern cast blindingly from a lonely darkness.
Behind me lay the mountains, a painted pane of glass, a child's pyramid
of ice gouting smoke and beet-juice fire.

Ahead, three commoners, three young poets, arriving at the most
brilliant palace in a new world. The audience with a vice-king, the fas-
cinations of a vice-queen—the most exotic creature I had ever seen, a
princess in a dream.

Glass.

Afterwards, staying up all that first night with Carlos, reliving every
detail. Pouring out my heart to him, all our hurts to each other, telling
him things of Nepantla and Panoayan. Discovering our shared passion

for the great work in train in Europe, so far away . . . his growing doubts about becoming a Jesuit.

The bastard country girl installed at the palace as the Vice-Queen's handmaiden. The thousand wagging tongues, the slights, the propositions, the rumours, the envy. The spectacle of a public examination by forty scholars of the Royal University to determine if the prodigy of my learning were divinely inspired, as in the case of the Angelic Doctor,[†] or inspired by an angel of an altogether different order. Red devils on glass.

†Aquinas

A night of masquerade. By now I was the practised one, the initiate of masques. And in our disguises Carlos and I stopping at every *pulquería* in the city. The harlots, the humble broken faces crudely painted . . . Watching the dawn together from a rooftop after a night of gazing for the first time through a fine telescope Carlos had built himself. Hearing his vow of undying friendship when I so needed a friend; the unspoken offer of much more, when I had hurt everyone I had ever loved. It was a night that changed his life far more than mine. His whole existence had been in the city, mine in the country, and now he wanted to know everything about that countryside—because of me, *for* me. But this was precisely what I had left so completely behind. Figures not so easily painted on glass.

These past years I have fancied that my ideas about the changeability of life were progressing—for of course metaphors for poets are very fine. From broken threads to broken books, from everlasting fire to an *hojarasca*, a scattering of leaves. From panes of crudely painted glass to the projections of a camera obscura as detailed and complete as anything a mirror receives. But I have had occasion to wonder if this is really the way to part the veil over one's destiny—to cut the threads of the past only to become tangled up in them, and perhaps stumble on someone else's path.

INTELLIGENCE:
. . . that Woman, who but through sin
entered my dominions,
should then vanquish me,
and, a Slave, crush me beneath her heel. . . .[21]
What mystifying veil does God cast
over a secret so stupendous
as to outsoar my grasp,
yet not quite my awareness?

LUCERO:
Worse, so far from seizing it in your talons
you have it barely sighted,
as by your lights one descries
how distinct are the objects it symbolises:
since Philosophy has, by her various sciences,
assigned it the symbol for Innocence,
and for Liberty made it the most dread
hieroglyph in Egypt—while for Victory
no less, in other nations. Oh memory!
How it afflicts my Intelligence to divine
liberty, victory, and innocence,
in one glyph signified.
    Conjecture, what do you make of this?

CONJECTURE:
Much and nothing.

ENVY:
Whereas I, as is meet, quite outdo myself
in impugning its qualities. And thus to its undoing
let us hasten.

LUCERO:
This I do intend.
But so as to build its ruin on a solid foundation,
show me, Intelligence, another scene,
and let us see what new quarry your prowess takes in.
. . . .

JUANA INÉS
DE LA CRUZ,

THE SCEPTRE OF
SAINT JOSEPH

B. Limosneros, trans.

Sea Cow

If Beulah at dinner, over our Chateaubriand, had just expressed a few of the things she was to write in her journal afterwards, maybe matters could have taken a different turn. On that night and others. I do remember her saying something she has omitted from her account. Something she said at the car, on our way to the motel.

It was a clear winter evening, the sky heavy with stars. I had never seen her before in a dress. Over it she was wearing just a light coat, and shivered slightly as she spoke. "I bet people like you . . ."

"People like me," I said, agreeably, as I bent to unlock her door.

". . . see all that dark," her voice came softly now with her head craned back, "see all that *night* as just absence of light."

Here at least was a topic more congenial to the occasion of Valentine's. Yet I found I had no answer.

She had, I'll admit, a sharp eye for the conflicts and contradictions my accidental career had led me into. Early success took me in directions I couldn't have expected, wouldn't have chosen or wanted. Mark Twain had been one of my best sources for a wry look at James Fenimore Cooper. But though on Cooper's failings as a writer Twain was devastating, his critique of Cooper as historian ultimately revealed more of Twain's biases than Cooper's. So I found myself quickly backing away from that aspect of my study about which I'd been in earnest—Cooper as liar—and while opportunity still knocked got serious instead about what had been pure knavery on my part: literature as negative way to truth. I had Mark Twain to thank for what came next.

People in distressing numbers assumed that I valued and even enjoyed the good yarn, the tall tale, the whopper. I can't begin to count the number of keynote addresses I firmly declined to give at conventions of oral historians and storytellers. A personal low point was my invitation to be a race marshal at the Calaveras County Fair. At first I felt affronted, then simply annoyed—no doubt these people imagine the forensic psychiatrist chooses his field out of affection for homicidal mania. Or the virologist because he likes a good, brisk pandemic.

Over the years such *ressentiments* passed.

And she was perceptive about my special dislike of a certain brand of fiction. Eliot was quite right that Joyce had spoiled poetry for ladies. If only he had done half so much for fiction's kitsches of the past. The stagy accents, the 'lexical curiositie shoppes'—though I don't recall putting it quite so colourfully—and more distasteful still, all the nodding and winking and the chest-thumping pieties over lying with one's facts straight. Her citing Shakespeare as a practitioner of historical fiction, or as an argument for truth in anachronism, changes nothing. The gentle folk who really cannot wait for the mini-series will still insist on taking such fictions as History lite.

All this pales, however, beside my horror of magical realism. The whimsies of Imagination's triumph over rolled steel, all the fabulist tigers in the pantry, the retreat into private worlds—Truth slowly reduced to rose-garden psychosis. Even the colossal fabulations of a Melville at least are a massed force in the field, whereas, yes, rooting out the lie in Latin America means bringing the battle house to house. That much she recorded accurately.

All of the foregoing to say that I am a scholar, or was. So, where possible, I prefer to approach certain aspects of Beulah's story as one would an accident reconstruction. Scientifically, methodically. Tarmac conditions and weather bulletins, witness statements and pathology reports, flight plans and scatter grids—these are my materials—her journals, the fragments. I can only assemble them for you, put them in some order. Somewhere in the wreckage lies a black box. . . .

Mirrors do not always conceal the horror beneath.[22]

19 Mar 93 [Calgary]
SeaCow rises through thermoclines of hot and cold. Sails steams drifts, a continent through dark waters. A vast, blubbery seaslug sub—Leviathan—flabbiest float in the mayday mayday parade, the manatee idylls in the shallows, oil-slick eddy coiling in her wake. . . .

Wake slow from dream, reluctant, nauseated, nauseous—light filters weak, thin, through green polyshades drawn tight against sun. Glance down over bulbous form swelling in-gloom, roll out, rolypoly igloo. Press dimply knees for purchase, push to stand. Pull nightie down, waddle to bathroom. How soaringmorningglorious it would be to soak it off in a vast scalding bath. Look with disgust at the tiny tub. But how graceful we seem in a tank, how frolicsome there the dugong/sport.

And on waterbeds.

Run the shower, cold, colder—feel the invigorating shock—*colder*.

Lufa sere and stern behind broad neck, under meaty arms, across pen-dulous breasts, abrading tips. Do not flinch. Single out navel and soft netherfolds of interthigh for special care. Tender hinterland. Scour for clues and errors. Under the cold flood everything burns. Rub softened scabs off fingers, study all pink wounds for signs of life. What's happened to your hands? he asked, refilling a goblet.

Turn off shower, step out. Feel queasy belch escape lips, watch dark-some blur slouch across the glass. Through a swipe across the misted surface stares back his eentsy *debauchée*—*su libertina bailarina*—blood-shot eyes, pigpink cuts. See the blotchy body scrubbed a mottled pink in broadclawd strokes—cruel Miss Strawberry in the kindergarten play. Pinchpinchpinch—*there* and *there*—a pound there, another here.

From the bedroom's half-dark a counter digital owlblinks baleful orange. Hit playback, start to strip the wine-stained sheets.

Hello? Beulah? Honey, it's me. I promised not to call so much, I know. I've been good, haven't I? It's just—I want to take you out for lunch. Something simple. Jonas is out of town, I feel like a little company. *Say it Grace—you can't bear to be alone.* Just a simple meal. I promise. Call me back if you'd like to come. I'll just let you call *me,* this time. Please call. . . .

Such a feast we shall lay you, your Royal Thymus—sweetbreads of hearts and spleen, our gall's ripest harvest . . . spiced with humorous asides phlegmatic nods enchanting philtres to decant our bile. Rotted pots of ripened flesh laid bare / fresh-gummed parsley for our halitosis / flowers for our hair. And so we'll sit and sit—blades whetted, blood-wed to bone-handles daintily clutched, flint hearts on plates / a waxen sheen on each sallow face. My sapper's dissent just one wafer-thin mem-brane from blowing full migraine—a radioactive bloodspot in the yoke of your sunny subjugation.

God bless the family meal—blud-simple gut-thick. Gutappetit mine heirs! Grand unifying theory of the nuclear family / blood thicker than deuterium. Gut-blocked plague vector that is this family flea circus.

Say grace—give thanks for your surfeit and my lack. Let's raise a toast—goblets clenched by knucklebone stems—hoistem high! two high hearts furiously beating. Callow the youth, craven the elder—reso-nant glugs from copious cups of resin and mead. God bless this meal— the tithes that bind the lies that blind. Thanksgiving for our harvest.

God bless this meal that gobbles us, his daily bread—gullet-stuffing delectable well-fed. Gobbets we—all abob in his giant crop. Lord lord it over us with a riding crop.

Art thou meekly meetly swallowing whole?

God blast this meal.

MUMMY

BEULAH, HONEY, IT'S YOUR MOTHER. Insistent visitant mother of all migraines pounding pouting at the door. Beulah? Beulah please. A little louder why not so everyone can hear. The trouble with letting mummies in is you never know who you're opening up to—mummy *capaz* or mummy *capo*. Can't know till she comes unravelled.

Beulah I know you're in there—please don't make me stand out here disturbing the neighbours.

Crack the door to the chain end—Why didn't she phone? Hello darling. She didn't *phone* first—that was the agreement—no she didn't, because I wouldn't have answered, wasn't that so, wasn't that true? It drove her mad it really did, what if there were an emergency—but Mummy there always *is*—god forfend her fable should end.

Okay she was sorry, she should have, but there was a good reason. Was I going to keep my dear old mother standing out there forever in the hall? *Open up*—yes time to get this over with. *What* good reason— and what the hell is that for? A little TV—television silly they invented it in the fifties, I'd heard of it? Here.

No.

Take it for company. *I'd rather die.* It isn't my birthday. She knew that, who would know better than she? Give your mother a kiss—were those cold sores again honey you never had them as a kid. Christmas either— *why is she here?*

She just knew this would be upsetting for me . . . but we were going to have to put our crucifixion dinner on hold. For just this Easter. She promised. Promise #1, here we go.

My fath—Jonas was taking her on a cruise—to the Levant!

Oh mummy le vaunted Levaunt. Turkey Syria Palestine Israel— mummy's own unchosen people—book a day trip a faery passage a Joppa-hop to Tarshish. Meanwhile I could just find myself a substitute family—*on TV.* Why didn't she do this twenty years ago? When it might have done us some good, she could have remarried a TV.

Here, let's just put it there, move the coffee table—My, what a lovely view of the park from here but this apartment—sorry hon but what a dump so dark. All these books everywhere, it looked like a riot in a library. At least let her throw out these plants—her dear daughter, the brownest thumb in history—how was it going, my thesis my . . . book?

Swimmingly.

They'd always known I would do something extraordinary—something dread strange uncanny she meant—but look at overworked me—my colour was good but those eyes I couldn't be sleeping well. Here, take a few of her sleeping pills—the doctor's wife, my somnambulant dispensary. I had to get more rest. Really honey. Tender motherlook nurture-hand raised to cheek, caressy. Beulah, honey, if you could see what I see . . .

If she could only see what I feel.

White-blond hair almost natural but for the blondrusted peroxidated superannuated tips, and thin! that Grace was grace itself so thin her name was destiny. Haunches stairmastered, flanks tanned, ultrasuede-jacketed—no dowdy dowager she—nay aging Gracefully, sloely, courtesy of gin. Matron's veins natron-thinned, inner weather bombayed and balmy. Just the faintest whiff of camphor and balsam but such an exquisite corpse had the bride of doctor Frankincest—his addled and bridled bride all stitched, faintly riddled with a fine-welterwork of tummy tucks liposucks and lifts. Why for doctor daddy cardiology was such a waste, with all this cosmetic surgery spruce up so close to the back forty.

If she could only feel what I see. . . .

Never mind all that now, dear. She was here to spend the afternoon together it'd be our Easter. Let's have lunch come now don't pull that face. So many good restaurants near here. Come now young lady, even scholars had to eat occasionally didn't they? *No lunch.* All right all right you win Beulah as always. How about a walk? She was not leaving here without spending quality time. Fresh air, come, please? pretty please, contact with the outside world, that couldn't be such a bad thing could it for a writer? Reality—life . . . ?

A walk then. Down to the Bow banks our unmusical procession—buzz of grasswhips, moan of mowers—past boxy little houses, window washers in kerchiefs. Smileygreetings between strangers—howdy neighbour, incredible weather, init? Blame it on El Niño again, blame it on The Child. Nay we see naught sinister in March's green grasses and trees full-leaft.

Come on, Beulah, let's run for it!—bolts over to the river across four lanes of traffic big horsey laugh leaving all in her wake. Such good fun so tenniscourt nimble so full of sport is nimbussed blond-haloed Grace. She looks back at me from the far side of the street, smile fading face paling. She's still scared of what I might do.

Sky a psychopathic blue, the riverpath a Grimm freakshow of bikers skaters weaving—you call this in-line?—stay on your *side*. Blank-faced joggers on endorphin drips scuttling to fix. Skateboarders—flailing grunge-herons on asphalt dream quests. With each heathen faceplant, another tattooed communicant kisses Stonehenge.

Lonely as immigrants we the few walkers. In the park now we are the foreigners—among the strange-tongued families lolling around barbeque spits. How can kids so beautiful look so sad? Toddlers chasing goslings—insideous sinus hiss of geese. Starlings an oily weave of colours like cheap plastic wallets. Two black squirrels—bushy-tailed golems, their clockworks overwound.

Rodent frenzy, manic horror in the grass.

Come on—just two more blocks—let's do some serious window shopping. Right, quality time it was her dime her loonie her dying afternoon.

Kensington—urban planning's village idiot—slackjawed, adrool, oxymoronic. Toyshops loveshops health food humidors lumped under awnings in promiscuous congress. Let us stroll now you and I, scrawl doubt across the neon sky like a pornqueen bowdlerized in a stable. Let us wrinkle lordly turned-up noses at glo-bowlization's rich smorgasbord: gimmicked Greek restaurants, a Vietnamese sweatshop back of each gleaming Acropolis.

Let's go in. What *here*? A *walk* she said. She promised me. Promise #2. It was okay they had a salad bar. How did she know that—she phoned ahead didn't she? So did we have a reservation already, something cosy for two? At last she unveils: ever our mistress of fun and diversions, Mummy capo, ever the camp doctor's collaborator. O arbiter of tabled entreaties, architect of the imaginal line—black underground pipeline siphoning off the rank swamps of our family romance. Eat what your stepfather oh so logistical has provisioned—four place settings, four players on an edible altar. Doctor daddy's two square metres of European soil under a chessboard tablecloth—checked aggression, advantage to white. Spanish Conquest of the New World same channel at six each night—*provecho*, take profit from your meal—*provecho* eat if you know what's good for you eat if you love your mother eat. . . .

Mother and child walk on, lost in their reveries, stop down the block before a little prairie church between the parking lots. Oh look honey, they haven't torn this one down yet. Chapel of Abundant Living. Looks like some kind of cult now.

I had only to say the word and she'd cancel their cruise just one word we'd all spend Easter together. And miss le Levaunt! And spoil such a nice coincidence? Wouldn't hear of it, vouldn't vant that at all. Don't cancel for me no please take an extra week or century. Bye-bye, mum, gotta run. Say so long. No don't cry mummy too graceful for tears too old for new tricks. Thank U4 dTV, thanks for the day, thanks for the memorex. No really, gotta go now. LuvU2.

Where were you then mum?—swamp-hid twenty years cowering in the delta sunkdrunk in the family muck. Eat, child, what I have prepared for you. Garbage in, garbage out.

I will not eat in your house.

The local-colour cruises, disasters of the month in four-colour separation / racial harmony by Benetton. The rhinestone volunteerism on the sadsad soup-lines one day a month. The heartfelt human interest stories, all the seize-the-day literature all the bittersweet inspiration—when I hear the word *lifestyle* I think handgun, I think hangin, reach for my lasso. FUCK your penny-epiphanies isn't life a marvel, turn the page.

Never met a pagan I couldn't make my best friend at the stake.

Come, mum, let's step into the chapel a while instead, where it's cool, like the one you used to take me to. No need for reservations here. No it's not a synagogue but you're not a jew anymore, and yes confession is not protestant but it was a church once, what do you want? Let's not protest let's both CONFESS. Who goes first—my turn?

I do love you.

How's that for a shocker—does that make me a fool? Isn't that Christian of me after all we've been through? I love you still, sweet stitched bag of skin. Unto stillness itself, unto the stilling of days. . . .

I shouldn't have left you back there alone in the street.

I am so tired. Tiredimetiredimetired. So very tired. Of fighting. Fighting you. Even him. I'm almost ready to take your offer. Denial. Forgetting, suspend belief, make disbelieve. Who says it's a cult—garbage in, garbage out. Deprogrammer's logic.

I only wanted you to make it go away. I wanted you to make me good. I want still to be good. I want

To be still . . . to be good.

How you tried. To make everything nicelypressed sweet-smelling tastyclean mannerly. Not just for yourself. For us all. For me. How I wish I could hate you even now. Making what's to come so much easier. Cleaner. Clearer.

You are the one mountain I cannot lift cannot clear away. I thought to move mountains lift them in my mind. I'm so tired inside my head I just want to rest. So empty now.

Here, I'll rest awhile, here, I wait for you. On the church step like a child . . . feel your cool palm on my cheek, your fingers smooth my hair. I see now that you are tired too. Not much longer, we're almost there. We're in the homestretch now.

11th day of July, 1667
Ixtapalapa, New Spain

My dearest Juana,

By now you know I have given up trying to persuade you and have left Mexico City. And if they have not told you already, you should also know I lied. I did not leave the Jesuit college willingly. I was expelled.

Seven and a half years ago voices—angelic voices, I thought—began flooding my mind, imploring me to study with the Jesuits, to enter into their service and care. But over the past few years another voice has come to haunt my sleep. It has returned almost every night. Indistinct yet imperious it leaves me no peace. Eventually the college had to find out that I'd taken to wandering the streets of Puebla, after everyone was asleep. It was not what they thought, what they tried to get me to confess, but it would have been too humiliating to try to explain. I said nothing in my own defence.

If I say now that I left because of you, Juana, it is not to lay blame. . . .

But enough of this.

As you well know, the Viceroy's cousins are returning to Europe, speaking of nothing but you. You were a splendid success at their farewell party. They showed me the verses you composed for the occasion. You have done better work.

Tuesday, I came upon them in Mexicaltzingo just as they were having the last of their trunks hauled across the river. The girl is slightly more intelligent than her brother and the rest of their playmates. She remembered me as a friend of yours and has invited me to travel with them. How lucky to have had some of your fame rub off. I will grant it has been fascinating to journey with the lesser nobility. How many times have I made the trek between Mexico and Puebla and never once had an entire Indian village turn out to entertain me with dances and song.

It would have been uncivil and a little stupid to travel just ahead of them all the way to the coast. With my luck we would have ended up making the crossing to Havana, or even Cadiz, on the same small ship.

We in our position cannot afford the luxury of making enemies among the ruling classes, can we.

There. Go ahead and laugh. Here I am, travelling to Spain with the

THIS NEW EDEN [23]

Carlos writes to Juana at the Viceregal Palace. More than three years have passed since they met, at a poetry joust.

very class of Spaniard that is driving me from Mexico. Yet I know you can understand how much less painful it will be for me to watch these parasites sucking their own country dry. Well you know my feelings; and now you know my plan, which is to leave this strangling, benighted continent. I say it again, Juana. There is nothing here for us.

Enough for now. It has been a long, full day.

Your faithful servant, Carlos.

16th day of July, 1667
Puebla de los Angeles, New Spain

Dear Juana Inés,

I have reached Puebla. My noble companions will be staying on a few days as guests of the Bishop. A Dominican, he has been known to me by reputation for some time now. The Jesuits here are convinced that without their intervention he is sure to become Archbishop one day. In the meantime, where you and I would do very well on two hundred pesos a year, he will have to make do with his Episcopal stipend of sixty thousand, raised from the blood of our soil.

I have been anxious to find myself free of the Viceroy's cousins. I tell you I could not have suffered their company a minute more. Nor, I would venture, could they mine.

The Indian dancing I wrote you about only whets their appetite for more. One day near nightfall we reach a river overflowing its banks. *Gracias a Dios* everyone sees the futility of risking their possessions, not to speak of lives, on that river, at that hour, for a capricious detour to see more dancing. Grudgingly our little raiding party turns back to a *casa de comunidad* about a mile from the river, near the village of San Martín. I had not known such houses existed, but my foreign companions delight in apprising me that almost every Indian village maintains at its own expense a guesthouse to lodge those on Crown business. Very loosely defined, this applies to almost anyone and perfectly to us. By the time the food is served everyone at table is in a foul humour (then, O calamity, too little salt). One of the gentlemen begins roundly abusing the *mesonero*, until, with the greatest reluctance, I have to intervene. Though the royals say nothing, our honeymoon has ended and we all know it.

Most infuriating of all is how, as league by league we draw closer to Spain, their farewell tour through America turns everything to an eversharpening derision. Yet at the same time they somehow manage to treat whatever we pass—farms, villages, orchards, ruined temples—as their own personal inheritance. How these peacocks boast of possessing a thing they claim to despise. It is the sleek who have inherited the earth.

By noon today we covered the remaining three leagues to Puebla. Making the trip to Veracruz alone, so desolate a prospect as I left you in Mexico, now seems truly splendid. Certainly travelling ahead of them will be infinitely better than trailing behind. At each stop I would have found both stores and servants exhausted.

On the other hand, the bandits who along this road run many of the taverns, such as that rat-trap in Chalco, will no longer metamorphose into paragóns of generous civility when I arrive without my nobles. Why is it that at the same inn, the rich are actually charged less and lodged better?

I hasten to add that we did not stay at the inn owned by your aunt's husband but I did walk up the street to see her. A delightful woman, and lovely. Hearing me speak perhaps at too-great length of our friendship, she gave me directions to your mother's hacienda, suggesting I go and make her acquaintance. It is too far to detour now, but I hope one day to make that journey. I imagine she will be beautiful.

Sitting here writing to you, I find my heart lighter than at any time since I decided to leave Mexico City. I think you are still friend enough to be glad of that.

Good-night Juanita. . . .

17th day of July, 1667

  Mi querida,

Remember when we met, and later that month at the palace? Two children in a room full of European aristocrats. There we were, you and I, being awarded first and second place in the *certamen*[†]—teen prodigies, poor, and American-born to boot—with the Royal University's Professor of Poetics a red-faced third.

[†]poetry tournament

My first year at the college in Puebla, your first year at court. Who could have blamed us for turning to each other—then and during each college vacation?

But I hadn't fallen in love with you yet.

I've never spoken of this. The day it happened we were not even in the same city. I was in Puebla, poring over a letter about you from a professor who was there, who saw it all with his own eyes. The Viceroy himself said seeing you that day, besting all those professors in debate, was like watching a galleon fending off a handful of canoes.

Forty professors from the Royal University of the Imperial City of Mexico, the incomparable capital of New Spain—against one teenaged girl!

Whose idea had it been? The Viceroy's?—his wife's? They must have found it all so amusing. Was it done expressly to humiliate America's greatest university? Obviously the stated purpose was a sham: how could anyone hope to tell by examining you whether your learning was innate or acquired, diabolical or divinely inspired? Were you given the opportunity to decline the invitation? I doubt you would have anyway. How did you feel—elated, terrified? Did they tell you there would just be a professor or two? Surely not forty! Were you hoping to please the Vicereine, or to show *them*?

I think I know.

I have many times imagined the scene since then. Ah, to have been there!—noon in the palace's Hall of Realms . . . settling into their seats, the Viceregal couple—sleepy gestures, watchful eyes. . . . To their left, the ladies of the court taking their seats once again, murmuring wickedly behind wavering fans. To the right, the gentlemen still frenziedly wagering.

One girl, beautiful and pale, standing alone at the centre of the hall.

The sages begin to file in, puffed up in the colours of their respective faculties—mathematics, astronomy, music, law, theology, philosophy, poetics . . . I can just see them strutting in, the historians, the humanists, the scripturists, the rhetoricians, the astrologers—peacocks all. And a few parlour wits invited to leaven the proceedings.

Silence falls. A clever preamble by the Viceroy. The university rector receives the instruction to proceed. The first easy questions, dripping condescension. Cautious replies, indulgent applause. The queries longer now, more in earnest. You begin to relax, riposting with precision and wit yet the applause seems fainter now. Through narrowing eyes, the ladies are beginning vaguely to see in this performance a betrayal, the men, cause for disquiet. *Sotto voce* various gamblers curse each hapless professor for a fool as he is toppled by your lance. Yet somehow they envy him his chance at humiliation.

The ranking pundits look increasingly desperate now as their turn approaches. Questions bifurcating and ramifying into such complexities that even their posers seem to lose the thread. Others, you bring to stumble into the very snares they've laid. Spider-like, you reel them in one by one, many ceasing to struggle almost immediately, meekly sitting without even attempting a rebuttal. Those who do . . . manage to sound at once shrill and petty, their objections reduced to cavils.

Now in an attempt to confuse you they put their questions in tandem—history, then theology, then mathematics, then part two of the history question. But like a chess master playing on several boards at once you see their game at a glance, while *they* become distracted by the interruptions.

Finally one greybeard, whose local eminence has been for some minutes crumbling to a highly public rubble, starts to shout you down. The bettors who laid the longest odds rise indignant in your defence. The rector turns to the Viceroy to protest!

Shouting now on all sides.

The Viceroy inclines his head slightly: the Vice-Queen is whispering something in his ear. Suddenly he rises. The room falls quiet again. Smiling he thanks the Royal University for its participation and, suddenly solemn, bows to the red-cheeked girl.

How they must hate you, these wise men. Nothing left to do but paddle their canoes away across a sea of indignity. A rout of unimaginable proportions.

Is that how it was Juana?

And was that the exact moment of my fall?

No.

The precise instant was in the beginning . . . as the learned doctors swaggered in, when you stood alone, head bowed in concentration, unsure of the outcome. I fell in love with you then. In a scene described to me in a letter, from a casual friend.

Juana I've borrowed enough money to get us both passage to Europe. We'll never be free to exercise our talent here. Now that I've really left maybe you'll take me seriously and stop treating me like some impetuous boy.

Come away with me.

I will wait for you in Veracruz until you send me word.

Until you send me word . . . Carlos.

21st day of July, 1667
la hacienda de San Nicolás

   Querida Juana Inés,

I could not quite bring myself to write these past few nights. Emotions too unstable to be wrestled into an envelope and commended to the void, only to be ferried across it by some stranger. By the time this packet of mercury wings its way to you I am sure everything will have slipped and shifted yet again.

It was dawn when I set out from Puebla, exhilarated. . . .

The roads are deserted—the sun rising grandly before me above the fog. But before I have ridden many leagues to the east, a kind of melancholy infiltrates my mood. The road has been climbing for the last couple of hours away from the boggy ground Puebla is anchored to. I dismount and look back over my trail.

The plain below is choked and blue with the smoke of a thousand fires. And looking out over this landscape for perhaps the last time I see a battle scene for one of your Florentines, Da Vinci . . . "War on Eden." A campaign giving no quarter and leaving in its wake an America of drained watercourses and scorched slopes from Quito to Mexico. New Spain indeed. This country will resemble arid Spain soon enough.

My cast of mind sombres to the point where even as I find myself at the first mountain pass, leaving the battlefield at least temporarily behind me, and surrounded by waterfalls and freshets, by the sound of water surging below, all I can permit myself to see pouring forth is the lifeblood of a great leviathan groaning under our assault. Here I spend my first night, cloaked in mist and dreaming of a sea battle sounding all around me. . . .

My aching joints wake me before dawn. My horse, tethered all night in the same mist, is not at all eager to be saddled with me, the mule still less so to be burdened with my affairs.

From here the trail twists its way over an ever-steeper series of grades. Two leagues up for every one down. Killing work for the animals. Negotiating even the lower trails exacts the utmost concentration, as bogs threaten to engulf the unwary at every turn. I have been remembering our talks and believe your grandfather to have been right: I now see for myself that without Moctezuma's help, his gifts of food and of course his unwillingness to attack the Spaniards as they walked their horses along these steep game trails and treacherous marshes, the conquest of America would have died right here.

Then there are these high-country rivers, most of them impossible to ford. What a miracle of water is our New World. I hear the roaring an hour before I reach it. Unthinkable to cross without that bridge. More spume than water, the river tumbles battered from the heights of a glowering volcano as high, I suspect, as our Popocatepetl. On the far side of the narrow bridge, which I must coax the animals across, stands the hacienda de San Nicolás and my first meal in nearly two days. *El terrateniente* receives me courteously, though he is too wary to lodge me at the main house. Only after I have paid an outrageous sum for a chicken, which his Indian cook prepares for me most deliciously, does he say I could have had, for a tenth the cost, one of the delicious fowl that abound in the surrounding woods. *Guajalotes,*[†] of course, but also large woodcocks and something the Indians here call a pheasant . . . he just assumed a city man would prefer chicken.

[†]turkeys

We sit over lunch in a lush garden beneath the blinding whiteness of this volcano, Orizaba, and securely above the inexhaustible source of fresh water it provides. My host is from Andalusía. A simple man of eminently good sense, he confides that this water is more precious to him than all the gold of the Indies. Many of the first *conquistadores* were poor men from his region. In Andalusía and Estramadura it is common knowledge most died paupers. Here, with a few fruit trees a man can feed his entire family, with more than enough left over to barter for necessities. The munificence of one fruit tree, Juana. I'd never really grasped it. With the land so rich, he says, why should there be so many starving on the plantations on the coast?

My belly full at last he offers to show me his Eden. Eden it seems is on everyone's mind. To move through these orchards, through these shoals of blossoms, seems less like walking than swimming through musk. To stop walking for more than an instant is to stand softly plumed in the bright slow wings of butterflies, some as large as my hand. Shuttling by are more kinds of hummingbirds than I ever guessed existed. And weaving among them, honeybees heavy with nectar rumble a short way to the dozens of beehives he has set up among the trees, whose branches droop beneath their burden of flowers. Cherimoyas, other species of anonas, lime and orange, and fruits I've never even seen in the markets. He has me taste something they call *sciochaco:* white fleshed, its flavour like cherry, but with spicy black seeds like peppercorns.

Farther back from the river, he has left wild the surrounding woods that peal and ring with bird calls, and against this carillon, green and blue volleys of parrots screech overhead . . .

Within a few hours he has invited me to stay as long as I like, and repeats the invitation as I am packing up early the next morning. Instead I find myself riding away up a trail through the healing green of a forest I am only truly seeing for the first time. It is as if the waters of the Flood have just receded and granted me, the last man on earth, the terrible privilege of experiencing this world for all humankind. Never have I seen such flowers. Yet they must have been all around me all along. It seems my eyes are become children, and must be taught all over again.

Would they see even now, were it not for our talks of your life in the country? We are city people, on both sides of my family. I would not even be here had you and I not met. One does mathematics perfectly well in a Jesuit college. Only poets need the land.

How I wish we two could share this. Every bird call, the wind across the valley, the rill and rustle of water on every side. In the late afternoon, I watch a jaguar fishing in a rocky stream below me. It looks up, sees us, and I know a moment of fear. But the slope is steep and the fishing good, so we are safe enough. My horse stands stock still and trembles, nonetheless. White-eyed, the mule looks ready to bolt with all my books and papers.

Books and papers. Pointless to imagine I could have stayed on at San Nicolás forever, but that is not what flashed through my mind as my host was inviting me to stay. I thought, *No books . . . there'd be no books here.* We are driven from Eden for the blood on our hands, yet prolong our exile only to plunge them in ink. What makes a man ride alone out of paradise for an insignificant pile of books not yet written? At this moment, Juana, I would give a lot to hear your answer.

I feel this little book growing inside me, an album of verses devoted to this gravid miracle of water . . . dedicated to the verdant destiny of this new continent, our occidental paradise—

The most extraordinary thing! Just as I am writing this, seated comfortably at my little fire—a violent earthquake. The ground heaves under me with power enough to raze a city. I may well arrive in Veracruz to discover it destroyed. Yet the sick terror of a man in the forest quickly passes, as he grasps that there stands over his head only a light canopy of leaves and stars.

It must also be so of flood. Out here the forest dweller only moves to higher ground, while the city man loses all his worldly goods.

The thought occurs just now that perhaps the great myths of cataclysm and flood needed in the end to build cities, in order to make themselves understood.

con cariño, Carlos

1st day of August, 1667
la Nueva Veracruz, New Spain
Juana,

The morning after the earthquake I awake more refreshed and rested than I have felt in months, only to find myself and all my belongings covered in snow. Now at least I know what it will take on this journey to get a good night's sleep. . . .

All day the trail falls steeply into hotter country. After six leagues or so I come upon the *hospedaría de San Campus,* the most abject excuse imaginable for a hostelry. Not a scrap to eat for man nor beast. So many starving dogs and rats skulking about the place you'd have to sleep with your boots on for fear of having them dragged off for food. The innkeeper was another fortune hunter, from Estramadura. One who came for gold but could not settle for water. He goes about the place unkempt and half naked, muttering. A recluse whose penance it has become to serve the passing public. It is my first contact with a breed I will be seeing a lot more of down here, one I should get comfortable among: the failed white man in the tropics.

After another few leagues over flat ground and through a fading light I come on a clean, well-ordered settlement in the sharpest possible contrast to the misery of San Campus. San Lorenzo de los Negros is populated exclusively by runaway slaves. *Cimarrones*—arrows that fly to freedom. Even they call themselves that.

Cimarrón . . . You, Juana, will feel all the pain and yearning in that word.

I decide to stay the night, with some trepidation, but find myself well treated and fed. The Governor at Veracruz allows these people to live here without fear of reprisals, as long as they supply the port with the surplus of their well-tended fields. But whatever dignity this should have permitted them has been stripped from these unfortunates by the one condition haunting their existence here: they must refuse to shelter—worse, must return to their owners—any new runaways who reach San Lorenzo.

The next day, I arrive with no little excitement at the outskirts of Veracruz, but find here little more than an outpost in sandblown squalor. Sand everywhere. Rotting houses half buried in it. Laughable city walls. Here some contractor has brazenly defrauded the Crown, for you could breach these pitiful defences without even getting off your horse. No point whatever in closing the city gates to pirates.

As I already knew, the sailing season for Europe is still months off, but the ship I was hoping to take to Havana, where the waiting is said to be much more comfortable, sailed without me. No room, said the Captain. Unless of course one is in a party of rich Spaniards getting an early start on their triumphal return from the Indies.

Incredibly there are no inns in the New Veracruz. And the Old, where Cortés first set foot on the shores of America, is just a collection of fishing huts. Standing on this infernal shore watching the only ship in port sail to Havana without me, I understand perfectly Cortés's decision to burn his ships to keep his men from deserting.

No other ships for a *month*. I simply have to get on the next one. In this season many fall prey to the fevers. The airs hereabouts, when still, are positively foetid. Or they blow a northerly gale, driving sand deep into every crack and crevice. Just a few weeks ago, Juana, I imagined us taking long walks at the seashore. However, the sea here is not the sparkling blue of our lakes but rather a sullen grey-green. Salt marshes and estuaries everywhere indent this coastline, and the crocodiles, which even on land can be swifter than a man, litter their banks exactly—and treacherously—like logs after a storm. No such thing as a carefree day at the sea, with sharks to one side and crocodiles to the other.

They are mad for dog meat apparently.

The contents of my purse have dwindled alarmingly. I've taken up hunting in order to pay for a cook (a recent widow with six children), who will work in exchange for the lion's share of whatever fresh meat I can bring in. You will probably laugh at the idea of me as a hunter, yet the turkeys stand thick on the ground and make easy targets.

On several of my jungle forays I have come across the overgrown ruins of one ancient temple site or another, but the mosquitoes here are so ferocious I am never able to stop long. Would it surprise you to learn that the part of America most proximate to Spain is infested with parasites? And not just of the two-legged sort. The jungle (and to a lesser extent the town) crawls with gnats, wood lice and mites. Nightly the remorseless hunter repairs to his lair only to find himself the mottled prey of more resourceful foragers—ticks and leeches grazing implacably on the flesh at my neck, wrists and ankles. Leeches enough for all the physicians of Europe. Certainly there should be no ill humours left in me. So after a week of this (and of eating turkey every day) I am ready to beg the fishermen in Old Veracruz for fishing lessons. At least there'd be just the sharks and the crocodiles.

your most faithful servant, Carlos

14th day of August, 1667
Juana,

I begin this having waited a fortnight to write you, hoping my mood would brighten. Yet how could it, when with each passing day I learn more about the workings of this place? The Inquisition's censors infest the port, crawling all over incoming book shipments in search of works by Las Casas, Erasmus, Descartes, anything on the new sciences. But since the royal seal was issued two years ago, they search also for anything touching on Indian cults and superstitions. Even Cortés's letters to his king may no longer be read here in America. A century and a half after the Conquest—what is it that the Crown fears so much more now than then? Or is it that Madrid now fears everything and everyone from Cuzco to Versailles? Truly I despair of ever seeing my own work in print if I remain on this continent. And yet even if publishing in Spain is not quite impossible, in order to be read in Mexico my texts will have to get past the censors in Seville, then here, only to find my fellow colonists preferring European writers.

For their part, the port authorities care nothing for books. Instead their tariffs and regulations are expressly framed to strike down anything that might impede the Crown as it deflowers this land and squanders our patrimony. Forbidding us to export finished timber, the Spaniards burn down leagues of forest for their cattle to overgraze. Then they tell the American he can do what he will with the meat but not only is he required to export his cow hides for the manufacture of Spanish shoes, the Crown forces us to repurchase those shoes by forbidding us to make our own. For over a century now the *gachupines* have run like wild horses through the verdant pastures of our America while we the Creoles, who are born here, lurch about under hobbles and trammels—formally denied key posts, and informally, the most lucrative opportunities.

This I have witnessed first-hand since my boyhood. In Spain my father tutored royalty, but born here his children are treated as foreigners in our own land. America is in every way richer, more abundant, more enterprising than Iberia and yet in what does the true scope of our enterprise here consist? This trading system benefits those who already have capital, and benefits most those nations that have already accumulated the most. It bleeds us dry while enriching the few stooges here who do the bidding of the merchants surrounding the court in Madrid. Meanwhile the Royal Treasury has been all but bankrupted by the importation of manufactured goods from northern Europe in exchange for—what else?—gold and silver, the only Spanish products that the northerners do not already produce more efficiently.

Spain has become Europe's laughingstock. And what does this make us? Surely our America deserves better. Castile has been given stewardship over a New World—a second chance for Spain and for Man—only to exhaust and despoil it so much more quickly than the Old. More damage has been done to our America in a hundred years than to Europe in five thousand. I am told it is worse out in the islands. Wherever the land was once the richest and most densely populated, the Indians are now completely gone and the land is worked to death by half-starved negroes. The yield steadily falls, but at the same time the acreage is expanding so rapidly that the price of sugar keeps slipping, such that the merchants are always looking for new ways to use sugar and so maintain its price. They will be building our city walls with it next.

This past fortnight I have found myself retracing the journey that brought me here, the route of the Conquest in reverse. And in a sense for me it has been a conquest reversed. I cannot claim to have liberated the lands I have crossed; instead they have conquered me. I have you to thank for this, for teaching me to see through your grandfather's eyes. The Conquest has entered into our past, but that other America is not dead. She lies as if in a fever dream while these foreign parasites feast on her prostrate body. This is my homeland. How can I bring myself to leave her? I may not go to Europe, after all—there is so much work to be done here. I know this now.

Made desperate by the infernal hunting and my wasting purse, I decided to give up the house and, with great reluctance, threw myself upon the mercies of a local monastery. The Jesuits were clearly out of the question for me. The Augustinians nearly destitute. After two days with the Dominicans (nearly as hard up as the Augustinians) a friar meekly asked if I had ever visited the lovely Franciscan monastery not a league south of town. . . .

I am only now getting the chance to finish, having arrived just this afternoon, but you can write me here if you care to. I will be staying on here as long as they will have me. They have invited me to collaborate with them, but more on that later.

Enough for now. It has been a long day . . .

Carlos.

17th day of September, 1667
Convento de Nuestra Señora de Dolores
Veracruz, New Spain

Juana,

I am sure you have been on tenterhooks to know about my new home. Some years back a rich patron donated a tract of fertile property to these Franciscans, which they have cleared and cultivate judiciously. The land reliably yields three crops yearly if properly rotated. The monastery itself is spacious, surrounded by trees, and constructed to take advantage of breezes from the sea.

My first impressions—of a place more concerned with cultivating the earth than the mind—were quite mistaken. Rather than giving way to luxury, the comfortable conditions here permit these men to carry on the admirable work of their great Franciscan father, Fray Bernardino de Sahagún. He has, I can confidently state, invented a new science of Man. It undertakes to map systematically the constellations of these American societies, the patterns of their superstitions and attendant practices. Without him and a few others (I am convinced your grandfather was one of them in spirit), the Conquest would have extinguished this alien sky, which may yet be blotted out by smoke from the Inquisition's fires. Sahagún's writings were twice confiscated as tending to mar the glorious portrait being painted of the Conquest back in Spain. Yet the Franciscans only chart these systems the better to guide the Indians to the safe harbour of our Catholic Faith, by the light of *their own innate reason* and not by the torchlight of fear.

Brother Manuel Cuadros, the most learned man here in the things of the New World, has himself only just arrived from the Indian college at Tlatelolco, where he claims to have learned more theology from his students than ever he taught them. He believes the native Americans to be natural Christians, and cites as an example Our Lady of Guadalupe's chapel on the Cerrito de Tepeyac, the same hill where the Mexican goddess Tonantzin was once worshipped. Tonantzin, *Our Mother.* Tepeyac, from the Mexican—*stone that crushes the serpent.*

Meanwhile, how often do we ourselves portray the Mother of Christ as a new Eve protecting her Child, crushing the Serpent beneath her heel? And did you yourself not tell me you have heard Guadalupe pronounced as Coatlalocpeuh?—*she who has dominion over serpents.*

My Franciscan friends now regard the fast-growing veneration of Guadalupe throughout New Spain as an illustration of how the natives can be led naturally to the worship of Christ. But our fellow Creole, Fray Cuadros, has made me see much more: Guadalupe shall be the mother of our liberation. As he puts it, the Spanish have made orphans and bastards of us all, *criollos, indios* and *mestizos* alike. Guadalupe is fast becoming—though we might be only beginning to grasp it—the Mother Protectoress of all America's peoples. The mother of our sorrows. And this is why Fray Cuadros and a few others fear the Church will try to discredit her: precisely because it is now widely held that Guadalupe *is* the new Eve, who has come to protect this new Eden. Imagine my excitement, after the journey I have just made, to take part in such work.

Interesting times here, and dangerous.

And you. Tell me you have finally quit the palace and I will be there to fetch you in a week, I will set a new record reaching you.

Juanita, good-night.

25th day of October, 1667
Convento de Nuestra Señora de Dolores
la Nueva Veracruz

Dearest Juana Inés,

At last a letter! What a pleasure it is to read whatever flows from your agile quill, even if you disclose nothing of your life these days. If it is tact, do not worry, I no longer delude myself. Still, I cannot stop dreaming that you will one day tire of the palace and join us here. Brother Cuadros has complimented me on my knowledge of Indian customs, which I have been quick to explain are but scraps picked up from you. He has heard a great deal about you, of course, and has confided he hopes one day to meet you. If you were to come, I know you and I would find a way . . .

I am dismayed you find our project here so objectionable. Yes, it is dangerous, but in these benighted times what ideas are not? You are right to remind me the Church's greatest fear here in the New World is still that the ancient beliefs will be rekindled to ignite a revolt. The Indians still vastly outnumber us, after all. But the Church has no cause for suspicion: What these Franciscans are attempting is to restore the ancient bridge between our Mother Church and the native Christianity of America. Brother Cuadros assures me that among the Indians the conquered accept it as their duty to worship the stronger gods of their conquerors alongside their own. And what better evidence of God's strength and will, for both victors and vanquished, than the bloody miracle of a conquest against all human odds?

Clearly the policy of forced conversion, as prosecuted through our extermination of their gods and priests, has been a failure. Fray Cuadros has convinced me the Indians convert willingly once it is demonstrated that our Catholic faith is indeed universal and encompasses their own.

Rightly you warn against manipulating symbols to release forces we cannot possibly understand. But did not the early fathers of our Church run a similar risk at Ephesus, grafting the veneration of Mary onto the cult of Diana? And yes, the common people are bound to invent a lot of superstitious nonsense. Meanwhile others try to make the New World a repository for the unsolved mysteries of the Old—El Dorado, Atlantis, the Amazons . . .

And some of this nonsense is not so innocuous. Like the Beast of the Apocalypse etched in the terrain around Mexico City—the lake of Chalco its head and neck, its wings the rivers of Texcoco and Papalotla, four lakes formed from its spittle. Fie!

But you know how I despise this sort of thing. The Dominicans see devils everywhere as it is. Rightly do you remind me of the resemblances between our portrayals of Guadalupe and the woman of the Apocalypse, *a woman clothed with the sun, with the moon under her feet, and on her head a crown of twelve stars* . . . But this only shows how deeply these soul-sick and weary times of ours crave an Apocalypse. And in this the Indians are more like us than in any other thing. How our age yearns for the Kingdom of God to be restored in this New Eden.

And how the Spaniards fear and resent this American virgin who begins to escape their control! Guadalupe is the mother we orphans of America desperately pine for. Is it possible your objections to our project are of a more personal nature? The Viceroy's cousins told me that the aristocrats have taken to calling you Our Mexican Athena...

I leave you, then, with a question.

Carlos.

PROFESSOR CHRIS RELKOFF stood next to the rental. I had a hand on the steering wheel, the other on the key in the ignition. He bent forward just far enough to make eye contact. I'd never asked myself till then if my old colleague and I were even friends. Yet that Friday afternoon in the faculty parking lot, with the news drifting across campus like the stink of sewage, there he stood—stooped, diffident—forehead creased with concern, offering me keys to a family cabin near Cochrane. As a retreat. He also offered their second vehicle, an old Jeep beater.

FRIENDS

"Thanks," I said, taking the keys to the cabin, "but I'll feel a little less your ward by hanging on to my rental."

"Sorry to hear about you and Madeleine."

"Yeah."

"The cabin's a special place for Mariko and me."

"Great of you to let me stay there."

"Long as you like."

We went over the directions again. I started the car. He stood back, hands jammed into the pockets of a worn pair of walking shorts. A checked grey woollen shirt under a red hunting vest rounded out his professorial ensemble, along with the grey wool socks and leather sandals. He appeared to be leading up to something. "Don, did you ever . . ." his weight shifted slightly from one foot to both, "with Mariko?"

"Since I'll be sleeping out there in your bed."

"Something like that."

He leaned down suddenly and braced two big raw hands on the unretracted slice of glass above the door frame. An impulse toward intimacy gone awry, lightly skewed toward menace. Rather than stare straight down into my face now he looked off into the distance beckoning from just over the roof of the Ford.

"No, Chris, I can't say that I have. Thought's crossed my mind, though," I added, slipping it into gear. "About a thousand times." I backed the car out of the stall. "Since you ask, how about you and Madeleine?"

A slight reddening of the craggy Slavic mien. "Once."

"Mariko know?"

"Madeleine told her right after."

"Just once. Not so bad then."

"Years ago. They worked things out."

Who were he and I to do any less?

"Guess with the cabin then, we're even. Huh Chris."

A new plateau in our friendship. Funny, his timing, though it made a kind of sense. As much as anything did.

I saw her only a few more times that year, 1993, mostly off campus. By then it was clear that I had quite abysmally failed to get through to her about her methods and their dangers. Folk etymologies, metaphorical free association, a madness for synthesis unchecked by the slightest analytical scruple. In her raptures of research she was the professional sceptic's worst nightmare, the empiricist's anti-Christ in miniature. It had been my responsibility to counsel her against all this—more aggressively. Or no, not more aggressively, but earlier.

She did register for graduate studies in comparative literature in the fall of 1993, as I had urged her to do. As far as I can determine, she never showed up. But before she quit school and then vanished into Mexico a year later, she took what remained of her waning interest in the twentieth century and transferred it to me. Pretty much exclusively.

I had only wanted a quiet life lived in scepticism, infidelity and doubt. But as she had intended, my simple life started to take its own sharp turns. She was building a bear pit to my size, baiting me with morsels I was sure to find choice, daring me to step inside. But even when I realized this, I still hadn't the slightest inkling I might one day follow her to Mexico. My flight would reach Mexico City, via London, from the northeast. Months earlier Beulah's flight had come in from the northwest. . . .

[10 Dec 94]

ON BEHALF OF OUR CAPTAIN and cabin crew, thank you for flying Delta. Delta for change. Miss, don't forget your tourist card, we'll be landing soon.

Focus the nozzle feel coolness jet over this, my friendly face in these our open skies. I am your companion your sister your Canadian neighbour, I am just like you. Peace, sleep, hope, delta for destiny. A new beginning, a return to the aleph, the whole universe a tiny ball an atomwide inside my mind. Infinitesimal perfect point I see you.

    fixed.

        unmoving

            axial.

                whole.

Look. Aztec country, Aztlan, ancestral home of the Chichimeca . . . this cold barbarian desert . . . jut and thrust of burnt-sugar breakers and ashen washes, lapping a smoke-blue shore.

Horizon spectrum-shifts from smoke blue to dirty purple to brown. Begins the city, endless adobe ruins tonsuring the hillcrowns. Below, the imperial city of Mexico . . . twenty minutes, now thirty of jet commute and still no downtown . . . the scale of staggering sprawl, all the world's most ancient shanty towns—ringing Cairo, Babylon, Troy, Tollan—all bulldozed stunned ajumble. No light, pavement, water, plan—a million hovels fed on pure proximity to empire.

Ladies and gentlemen we are coming in to land. . . .

Turn.

Level.

Down.

Airport taxi. *¿Á dónde, señorita?* To a hotel. See his rearview sneer. We have many hotels in Mexico. Cheap, near the centre, you choose I don't care.

Keep the change—no you can't come upstairs.

He's brought me to a brothel, Welcome my international friend! Funhouse of the most antic guild—hark to midday whorehumping through the guilty walls to left and right. So this is *la siesta*, Mexico City style. *Olé.* Overhead TV ever-tuned to the Playboy channel no subtitles no subtleties for bilingual lubricities in stereo.

5 P.M. Take a plankwalk through the teeming streets. Return room key to the evening deskclerk, startle-eyed, concerned. Do you know where you are *señorita?* This is not a hotel for you. Moanrush of air through the doors / traffic blare. Walk left or right?—what difference will it make in 2294?

Walk down the road past idling rushhour cars, bumper to bumper, through backstreets choked with the parked, double parked—their purgatorial pretense of motion / a life-sentence to commute. *¿Taxi jovencita?*

I walk these streets people calling out to each other, to me. *I know I must be here—people stop and talk to me.*[24] How sweetly strange to hear to speak my fathertongue after so many silent aeons in the Dominion of Forgetting. Our White Eden of Pretend.

How strange a thing it is to speak aloud sing along shout take words out of the ear into the mouth. To share them out, like bread.

How different here—you must speak and speak and speak, be by your own tongue remade. No selfserve no takeout no safeway to supermarket. Eat in. Speak and be served. *Háblame, dime, diga señorita. Para servirle, a sus órdenes, mi amor.* At your service, my love . . . how unlike servitude they make it seem. What a joy to speak like this—sweet tongue I remember you. I want to speak to talk to everyone. I will know you all, all 100 million souls—headcount of America before Cortés.

Walk to the corner, a juice vendor, her emporium one mangled shopping cart. Tiny leatherfaced indian, four feet tall, tired her eyes but warm. *Juguito, mi hija?* A little juice, my daughter? Her juice bar just a longhandled hand-press nailed to a plank. Three sallowgreen oranges left in the cart. Half-price if I sell these I can go home, I live far from here. Thank you, young Miss, you are kind, if you come tomorrow I will give you two for one.

Deft draw and slice / swift hemispheric pivot of the world-is-herorange / pressclank and hissquish / wristed discard of pip and pith / filtered and flourished martini pour.

These sad sallow-cheeked oranges burst with bright sweet *juice.*

Her eyes see my eyes' surprise. Impassive plank wipe of dignified hygiene, white rag returned to bleach. Delicious. Solemn nod at this my tribute. Another, *por favor . . . si será tan amable.*

Are you here for the day of Our Mother, Guadalupe?

Yes *señora,* my quiet answer.

Then go with god tomorrow, *mi hijita.*

*Y*es, she promised her protection—the protection of a monarch—yet what could I possibly need protecting from here? For surely there could be nothing left to fear as the favourite, the indispensable handmaiden to the Vice-Queen of the Imperial Court of New Spain. . . .

Every winter, elegant ambassadors from the capitals of Europe set sail, ears ringing with tales of New Spain—Mexico City! streets paved with silver, its poorest beggar better fed than the King of France.

The story is well-known: Cortés's men weeping at first glimpse of the city that now lies beneath these stones. These same men on the eve of the Conquest then toured as Moctezuma's guests the wondrous place they were about to sack. And though they had already seen many marvels in many lands, still more men wept to see the central market. For its variety and colour, its cleanliness and order, for the sheer generosity of a soft continent offering herself at their feet.

Today it cheers me to imagine those hard-handed conquerors sobbing like little children; for now, at the height of the shipping season from the Philippines, weekly mule trains from Acapulco totter into market under fragrant loads of pepper and clove from the Isles of Spice. Bolts of silk, crates of porcelain and bright lacquerwork from Cathay. From the south, the last delicate figurines of gold from Chile and silver from Perú. Then by December the first shipping sails in from the East. From Africa, ivory and diamonds, slaves and hides, Arabian incense, balsam and carpets. From Europe, wines and knives, fabrics and olive oil . . . All these distant wonders come now to contend with the local wares: here blankets, turquoise and walnuts, there cotton tapestries and quilted jackets, cloaks woven of iridescent quetzal plumes, jars of Yucatan honey—scented of orange, papaya, mango—bubbling black chocolate, blazing bushels of flowers, broad baskets of spiced and roasted grasshoppers . . .

Scarcely can humankind have known such an intermingling of colours and flavours, scents and textures—and sounds. Today as I wander one last time lost and as though drunk through the winding alleys of plunder, the air fairly ripples with the soft murmur of Indian voices, the cries of hawkers, squawking parrots and caged songbirds, a donkey's bray, an aristocrat's mocking laugh, the tocsin of an anvil . . .

Within weeks of crossing over from Spain some of our courtiers, accomplished veterans of the amatory combats of Europe, can be heard in public declaring—with a sincerity astonishing in professional flatterers, astonishing even to themselves—that nowhere are there women so beautiful as those of Mexico; and overheard in private lamenting that never again will they enjoy the same surfeit of sensation, never again the same intensity of desire as here, in America. They have known such hungers.

Here at court the new envoys marvel indulgently that the fashions of Mexico should lag so little behind those of Paris, even down to the cork-soled slippers with the half-moon buckles that were all the rage less than a year ago, and marvel that the necklines should dip deeper than in Madrid, that the lace should be so fine. But while our gallants flatter the Europeans with their evenings, their nights they consecrate to the negresses, the mulattas, and particularly to the *zambas*†—cinnamon-skinned, the most exotic of all. Through the shops and avenues they glide like dark swans, trailing scents of Nubian civet and Syrian spikenard, swans collared in jade and lapis, braceletted with garnets from Ormuz, rubies from Ceylon and Sicilian coral. Dark swans alighting from mahogany carriages they themselves have bought—along with their freedom—through the wicked application of their special virtues.

And so it is that here at the palace the emissaries of the Old World to the New consider it part miracle, part scandal, when the rare priest dies attestably a virgin.

So beautiful herself, and as exotic, with her pure white hair, her blue eyes of an Orient cat, the new Vice-Queen too is fascinated by these creatures. She acknowledges the most exquisite as we pass them in the street, on a whim summons one of the most elegantly attired to the palace for an audience. The Vice-Queen clears the reception hall.

She wonders—her curiosity does not seem entirely idle—if a titled courtesan might make her way here, as a certain down-at-heels Duchess has been able to do in Madrid. They talk, while I put in not so much as a word. Practical matters of prices and services, of domestic arrangements and security, now medicines . . . Leonor's smiling blue eyes never leave mine long—my face is hot, my head spins to hear the questions she matter-of-factly asks.

†'zamba': woman of mixed Indian and African blood.

"Oh there is money enough," she yawns when the woman has been shown out, "but there are as yet too few gentlemen in your lovely Mexico with whom to consort not-too-dishonourably."

I do not know which to find more breathtaking, the questions or the cool calculus in her findings. But at fifteen I come too quickly to two conclusions of my own: that a palace exists precisely to be a place like no other on earth, and that I exist to live in one.

In the beginning everything fascinates her. And in her company, for the first time in so many years I am free to move through the streets. The Vice-Queen, twenty maids- and ladies-in-waiting, and her guard of cavalry and pikesmen. Our progress raises a furore wherever we pass, often afoot with the carriages in tow. San Francisco Street for gold, San Agustín for silk. The barrio of San Pablo for pottery, Tacuba for iron and steel. Weekly we stop in at the tobacco merchants of Jesús María and, just across the plaza from the palace, at the elegant shops of the Parian, which its Filipino merchants have so proudly styled after the famed Parian of Manila.

One area I do know, between Mercaderes and Calle Pensadores Mexicanos. The booksellers' district. Here too we go often, at first. Here, I lead.

Usually it is Teresa who guides us, the saucy daughter of a wealthy silver merchant of our city and engaged now to a gentleman of Castile. One day for the Vice-Queen's diversion Teresa takes us to the used clothing market, most of whose articles have been stripped from the dead. The day after, we go to El Baratillo, the market for stolen goods and contraband. At the entrance, the Captain of the Vice-Queen's guard balks. Teresa coaxes, flirts and finally cajoles him in but later, as we approach the zone of las Celestinas, the houses of the courtesans, his objections are not so easily overcome. The accounts of the good man's public dressing-down by our Vice-Queen swiftly make the rounds.

On the way back, we pass a convent where a *sopa boba*[†] is being ladled out before a long file of indigents circling the walls. Leonor stops and ladles soup for two hours, busies us handing out cups, sends kitchen scraps every day for a month.

[†] simpleton's soup

The people laugh to see, one Sunday at the cathedral, a servant fetching a flagon of wine back to her screened box. At her side I laugh, too— at the minor miracle of laughter in a cathedral. But not everyone finds this so delightful. For some, inviting a *zamba* to the palace was already the last straw—a prostitute, her crime punishable by death. The whispers of outraged civic virtue reach us even here now—whispers, Leonor remarks, from the thin lips of those women among the Creole gentry who got there through marrying up, and who give as little satisfaction at court as they are accustomed to giving in lower quarters. And so they have turned— dire and severe—to the Church: *These harlots of Babylon must have their wings clipped, lest Mexico become a modern Gomorrah . . .* &c., &c.

But for our good ladies, I've arrived at a dire prophecy of my own. That these, their pious petitions, clutched in bony hands better clasped in prayer, will be torn from them and scattered by the terrible energy of our times. By this bright whirlwind that leaves us all gasping and dazed. . . .

The Marquise Leonor Carreto. The most extravagant of our Vice-Queens, yet none has been so often seen in the streets, or so widely, even in the humblest barrios. The *vulgo*[†] take her curiosity for care and love her for it, grumble hardly at all at first as she spends enormous fortunes— mock naval battles on the lake; Roman baths and *placeres* on a certain ill-famed island; hunts and hawking on an imperial scale . . .

† commoners

Though each vice-queen renovates, Leonor's wing of the palace is all but entirely remade. Fondly known as the dovecotes, the *camaranchones* under the palace eaves must be expanded for the large number of ladies in her retinue. A hundred women in all, counting the servants of her servants. Her ladies from Madrid are entitled to a strict maximum of three. Those of us added to her company here in Mexico get no more than one—always assuming we can afford so many. The Vice-Queen's patio, the largest of the palace's three, eventually encloses a garden and fish pond in the Asiatic style, a small orchard, arbours of flowering trees, flower-beds, two fountains; yet there remains enough space free at the north end for official receptions and formal balls when the weather is fine. Around the patio, the great halls are renamed after those at the palace in Madrid. Hall of Comedies, Hall of Mirrors, Hall of Realms . . . She names the halls after the Alcázar, but she is determined to lead here in Mexico the court life Queen Mariana only dreamed of having, the life the enlightened are living in Versailles. It is Versailles we must follow now.

The season's fashions have just arrived on a last fast ship before the hurricane season. We are in the garderobe as her dressmaker studies the latest designs. Even on a bright day, little light infiltrates from the salon. Lamps burn at each end of the Vice-Queen's dressing table. She rests her hand on the dressmaker's shoulder as she bends to study the designs. Fuller skirts and tighter corsets are back, which can only bring Leonor's slenderness into even greater evidence. Necklines so wide and so low as to require the fuller figured among us to bow with a certain vigilance. A v-shaped stomacher—the jewelled and embroidered panel is to taper suggestively to the euphemism of a ribbon bow, well below the waist. Sleeves are to be shortened to the elbow. Falling bands and soft tassets are finally and definitively banished. Passable in embroidery, I know less about dresses than any of the others yet am singled out for the honour of dressing her on this special day. She stands in her silk underskirts, as if to exhort the dressmaker to work faster. "We have been at war with France for half a century, and this new peace, I assure you, is written in smoke, yet . . ." She takes the gowned doll from the dressmaker's hands, looks at it more closely, turns it over, as though to check the lady's bare shoulders. "One does not see the wings, Juanita, but though each book and post is examined for codes and Bourbon treachery, these dolls and fashion plates from Paris fairly fly to every capital in Europe. And now here, to me."

"To *us*," she adds, and gives my hand a little squeeze. Once her new dresses are finished, the best of her old ones will be altered for me. The honour is as unprecedented here as it is contemned by the wealthier ladies.

"Beauty, *mi amor*, is the empire that knows no borders."

And Beauty's proper consort is Laughter.

Her first act as Vice-Queen is to solemnly inaugurate the New World chapter of the Academy of Improvisation, modelled on that of Madrid, in which all the writers and court wits contend for prizes and for the favour of a monarch's laughter. But, for our Academy, a startling improvisation: Here in Mexico women shall participate. It is to the Academy that I owe my presence here . . .

We had been summoned to the Hall of Mirrors, for an audience granted the three prize-winners of a poetry joust, and to my uncle, who had underwritten the whole affair. The Viceroy was again much taken with me, though with the Vice-Queen now at his side his interest was more clearly paternal than the first time we had met. But then, that was in a bullring. Uncle Juan had steered the conversation to the precariousness of commercial shipping and supply lines, to which the Viceroy responded by remarking upon the parlous state of the treasury just now, with so many silver ships being taken by privateers. The conversation was tailing off awkwardly, towards the parlous state of the empire itself.

"Excellency, Spain so briefly on her knees," I offered, "still stands taller than all Europe on its feet."

It was a little moment he was grateful for, from a fifteen-year-old. I have since learned few at court express such sentiments anymore. We went on to discuss the bright prospects for peace with the French, after fifty long years. I sensed her studying me, but we had been instructed to avoid looking at her—at either of them—directly, lest she yawn, perhaps, and we inadvertently penetrate with our commoner's eyebeams an aperture of the Royal Person. I still had no idea how contemptible she found such protocols. But though I'd gained her interest, she waited to see how I would fare at the Academy before inviting me to come and serve her at the palace.

At the north end of the west wing, the staircase has been removed to make room for the Vice-Queen's personal study and gallery. From atop the south staircase, then, the weak-kneed visitor is led through an antechamber and a smaller reception hall, spirited through the Vice-Queen's gallery—lest, perhaps, the plebeian gaze deface a painting—and shown into the salon, glittering home of the New World Academy. . . . In each chandelier burn a thousand candles, their lustre glowing in the gilded cornices and on walls panelled in white marble.

If the Academy is in session, it is evening, unless it is well into the night. In which case everyone is drunk. The Viceroy has long since taken to his bed. The Vice-Queen has left her rock-crystal chair and the dais to join the others on cushions on a stone floor softened with deep Moorish carpets. A fire is blazing in a fireplace wide enough, in a pinch, to spit a bullock in. It is a fire which never burns down before dawn, at least while the pages who feed it live.

If the visitor is young, she has smoked tobacco, maybe once, sipped wine once or twice, eaten chocolate much less often than she would have liked. But never all together, not like this. Under the steward's disapproving eye, pages liveried in silver and satin circulate a dozen argent platters heaped high with cigarettes, a dozen gold braziers to light them; while chocolate offers itself in every form imaginable—sculpted or blocked, bitter or spiced, whipped or spiked with brandy . . .

In deference to the Vice-Queen's Austrian tastes, somewhere out of sight someone brightly savages on a clavichord a turbulent organ piece, which Leonor, giggling beside me, says is by the Werkmeister-designate in Lübeck, who has secured his appointment by marrying the old Werkmeister's daughter.

I have done little more than taste each thing to please her. Brandies,

sherries, ports . . . a wine from France that bubbles, hilariously, on caval-
cades of trays that wobble past like upturned balustrades; and indeed
within a few hours, the room entire is upturned and hilariously
unsteady. Even without the fine tobacco smoke too thick now to see
quite through, I might have been drunk on the perfumes alone. Yet I am
far from the most intoxicated in the room. No, holding that distinction
is poor don Alfeo, of a highly distinguished family in Seville.

It is the last round of the night. I have won everything so far. Hiding
my condition is so far beyond me that I'm inspired to take things in the
other direction and, as the incumbent, propose a round on drunkenness
itself. Slurring very deftly, I improvise a ditty on don Alfeo who lies mel-
lifluously snoring now behind a drape.

> PORQUE *tu sangre se sepa,*
> *cuentas a todos, Alfeo,*
> *que eres de Reyes. Yo creo*
> *que eres de muy buena cepa;*
> *y que, pues a cuentos topas*
> *con esos Reyes enfadas,*
> *que, más que Reyes de Espadas,*
> *debieron de ser de Copas.*[†]

Falling in worship to my knees, I then finish with a flourish.

> *Mis amigos, os presento,*[25]
> *Don Alfeo de la Espada,*
> *¡de la capa drape-ada,*
> *de la gloria remojada,*
> *del aguardiente empapada!*[††]

It is, I am told the next morning and to my great horror, not so much
the verse as the besotted delivery that carries the final round. To close the
session, the cleverest of the Vice-King's *sabandijas,*[‡] the dwarf Perico,
cheekily christens me *la Giganta,* and placing a coronet of salad greens on
my head, proclaims me the evening's Mistress of Wit. I am especially
honoured, for Perico was a fixture at the Academy in Madrid. He
becomes my first true friend at the palace. He was once a great favourite
of the Sovereign himself, but with death approaching, King Philip sent

[†] Because your lineage
is so broadly known,
you profess to all, Alfeo,
that through your
veins runs the blood
of kings,
and yes it must be of
purest vintage,
methinks;
for it is said you
outdo the best
of those prickly
potentates, who vexed
by being merely
Kings in Arms,
yearn to be Titans of
the Tankard.

[††] Dear friends, I give
you
Don Alfeo of the
Dagger!—
steeped in glory,
soaked in brandy,
cloaked in drapery.

[‡] *hombres de placer*—
the human menagerie
assembled to divert
the sovereign:
dwarves, jesters, the
misshapen, the insane

his most beloved *sabandijas* to accompany the Viceroy to the New World. Land of prodigies.

"Our promised land," Perico adds with a wry pout. "He thought he was sending us home."

Perico has never used any other name for me, but says it with such warmth and open admiration, even now I wear *la Giganta* as a badge of honour.

New rhythms and new music, cultivated palates and clever tongues. The dangerous new ideas of Europe in free circulation and we, *amazed* by our daring. So many new friends, in my new home. Perico. Carlos, of course, who comes whenever he is back from Puebla. I make a few fast friends among the courtiers too. Fabio I help to devise a betting system for roulette, based on the new theories of probability of my dear friend the monk Pascal. Fabio is decent and light-hearted, nothing troubles him. Fabio I can learn from. He is in love with the Vice-Queen, I know, yet he finds the strength to love her from afar, knowing it is impossible. And among the handmaidens, there is Teresa, who for all her wealth and spirit will only ever be a Creole, as I am, and never accepted by the others.

And yet the Vice-Queen calls me her literary lady-in-waiting. I should call her *Leonor* whenever we are alone. Leonor comes to find me every afternoon down in her library, devouring the contents of each aromatic page like a glutton over a new dish. Hers are the intrusions I never resent. The times spent with her are an extension of my education. Her judgement is flawless, and yet she flatters me by asking my opinion of this or that writer, about the plausibility or structure of a given philosopher's arguments. Our impassioned conversations spill into her bedchamber, where we are more assured of privacy, and where, as we talk, I spend what seems like hours brushing her shimmering hair before a mirror. Sometimes she reaches back over her shoulder and fans my hair across hers, blue-black over palest blond. "Almost the same, don't you think?" Leonor says, laughing sometimes, her blue eyes looking into mine—mine, black and round with disbelief as I see us in the glass. I am not quite so blind as to fail to see, the contrast could not be more complete. Her nakedness is at first a shock to me, but she explains that the body of the Royal Person belongs not to her but to the Realm. All her most intimate acts are open for inspection by physicians and counsellors. In the Queen's case, notaries may be called to stand at the midwife's shoulder as the heir is delivered, to warrant the integrity of succession. It was rumoured that Olivares[†] oversaw even the royal conceptions.

[†]adviser to King Philip IV

"Perhaps this is why so many were botched."

She says this lightly. I tell myself the joke is aimed at the malignancy of Olivares.

A small brazier stands beside the dressing table to keep her warm. We begin with the unguents and pastes, working up from her feet, finishing with a lotion made with almonds. She has heard of a miraculous cream made with avocados in the mountains, wonders how it is I haven't heard of it. Her hair is next. By now her skin has absorbed the creams. I kneel and begin to apply the perfumes and powders with a feather brush. She stands, to assist me, steadies herself with two fingertips on my shoulder or the crown of my head, arches an arm gracefully over her head, then the other, lifts one foot to rest a toe on the chair, then the other. Finally her makeup.

If there are no distractions it takes an hour to finish dressing her for the evening. Leonor says it is important to be discreet: Some of the other handmaidens, with duties less exalted, are from rich and powerful families. There is resentment enough, now that I am so often called to dress her.

Flashing eyes, a Tartar's wide cheekbones and high—a ripe, smiling mouth, and yet her features are strangely delicate. Her figure is full and womanly yet so finely boned she is as small as a girl. Who dominates every room from the moment she wades lightly in, skirts flowing like a river. Playful and teasing, clever and intuitive. Sophisticated, in politics a subtle strategist. The Viceroy never comes to a decision without seeking her advice. Though descended from the House of Austria and married now to a Spanish Marquis, Leonor Carreto was a handmaiden too once, in the service of Queen Mariana. "*Exáctamente como tú, mi alma.*" Exactly as I am. The Marquise says this more than once.

She has decided I must accompany her to Spain when it is time for her to return, so I must learn all about the life there. Mariana was just my age when she came from Vienna to marry her uncle Philip. The palace protocol was odious, is still. The stories are legend. Once, Philip's first wife took a bad fall, and though badly injured, Queen Isabela de Borbón lay in the road for hours while the one man other than the King permitted to touch her person was fetched from the palace. Some time later, a quite dashing Count had the temerity to sweep her up and out to safety during a fire at a theatre. A few days afterwards, he was murdered in the street.

"But then," Leonor says, her eyes glittering, "they say he set the fire. . . ."

She has known the greatest artists and writers of the empire. She met Lope when she was only five, Quevedo at fifteen, Tirso at eighteen. She grew to know Calderón intimately, and met with him frequently after he was made King Philip's chaplain. And while Quevedo was often crowned the Master of Wit in Madrid, she is not at all sure he would have such an easy time of it here in Mexico. Not that my gifts caught her completely by surprise. The greatest improviser the Spanish court has ever seen was from the Indies, too. The poet Atillano could make up the most astounding verses—learned or salacious, or both at once—according to the whimsies of his audience.

And so it is in this that I am keenest to impress her. She can recite the wittiest passages from dozens of comedies, to which, when we are alone, I improvise new speeches and dialogues to divert her from her loneliness.

Finally the court life she and Mariana dreamt of. Mariana, she says, would envy her now.

Leonor confesses to having dreamt of coming to New Spain ever since meeting the great American Ruiz de Alarcón, when she was only nine. We should go one day to his birthplace. Is this Taxco far? She is casually proud of her gift for languages—German, French, two dialects of northern Italy. The Castilian spoken here in the New World enchants her, the pleasant turns of phrase, the warmth and charm of our terms of endearment. *Mi alma, mi espejo, mi conquistador* . . . She delights in finding in my speech some expression or other that had been Alarcón's. I do recall that she had only been nine, but am nonetheless flattered. The seductions of the powerful are seduction to a second power.

Now that the renovations are quite done, Leonor is rarely seen outside the Vice-Queen's wing of the palace but is everywhere within it. For two more years the *hojarasca* whirls harder, as if by the hour. Every day a saint's day, a prince's birthday, a wedding, a confirmation. Rousing displays of horsemanship and jousting with cane lances beneath her balcony. So many occasions to be commemorated with poetry, so many gifts and prizes to be accompanied with a verse. Nights of masquerades, carnival processions, mock battles in the square with flaming arrows, Roman candles. The dances. I have so many dances to learn I am grateful for each single one of the dozen I know. The dignified pavanes, la Chacona, la Capona, and others less decorous—none less so than the Canary and the Folly. But now there are dances to be sung to, and even a few to improvise poetry to. The best by far for poetry is the Rattlesnake. But the revels cannot really be said to be in full swing until the shocking and shockingly popular *bailes bacanales* are announced—the sarabande from India, for one, and an African dance so lascivious it has never been danced at court. Until now.

So much laughter—Beauty's consort too is everywhere. And knows no borders either, it would seem. Leonor has the idea of releasing a crate of snakes into the Hall of Comedies one night during a play. Only with the greatest difficulty do I dissuade her. No?—not even harmless ones?

Parties at the merest pretext or, of late, the rarest: the celebration of a Spanish military triumph. We celebrate, one whole night, the forty-sixth anniversary of the famous surrender of Breda; the women play the Spanish, the men the beaten Netherlanders. Not long after the King's death, there is a party with a secret theme, only later confided to me in greatest secrecy. We fête the loss of Portugal, eight thousand Spanish soldiers lost in eight hours. It is only once Philip dies that I understand how much she has despised him.

But she forgives me my elegy on the King. Because it is beautiful, she says, because I am beautiful, because I am seventeen.

There are some things it is time for me to understand about our late sovereign. His infidelities, his actresses, his obsession with nuns. Even in the Queen's company he made no effort to keep it to himself. The fortunes of a nation rise and fall on the spirit of its queens, and it is the married queen who bears the most terrible burden of all—supreme responsibility without power. So it is the duty of the Queen's ladies to cheer her, minister to her spirits. Mariana arrived at fifteen but each month thereafter aged her a year. Leonor did everything in her power. How terrible to stand by, to watch Mariana's spirit broken.

Our salons of jests and jousts only gain in ferocity, and at first I glory in it. And how it unnerves these men to listen to the verses the cavalier owes to the lady of the Hall—verses of a refined passion—but written by a woman now. Ah, to see their faces. To see hers.

> ... On your most hallowed altars
> no Sheban gums are burnt,
> no human blood is spilt,
> no throat of beast is slit,
>   for even warring desires
> within the human breast
> are a sacrifice unclean,
> a tie to things material,
>   and only when the soul
> is afire with holiness
> does sacrifice grow pure,
> is adoration mute ...
>   I, like the hapless lover
> who, blindly circling and circling,
> on reaching the glowing core ... [26]

Such was the shock, one might have heard a pin drop.

More ferocious, too, the rumours and speculations about this *person* winning almost every night at rhymes; and even the laurels for learned discourses go to almost no one else, unless the topic is mathematics, which I avoid, or is astronomy and Carlos has come. Carlos too is brilliant but a man. Carlos too is poor but has a distinguished name, if not exactly noble. Yes, great things are expected of Carlos. Just not at the palace.

And Carlos at least has a father's name that is his to use.

But this other one, *la Monstrua*—I've heard them whisper it—how can anyone, a girl so young, acquire such learning in the wilds of that demonic countryside? No, there is something too uncanny about it. Nepantla? *Is* there such a town—and what must it be like, if *los nepantlas* are the local word for rabble? This bit of local intelligence comes courtesy of Teresa.

It is just a matter of time. Late one evening a cultured gentleman makes bold to impugn in rhyme an unnamed maiden's paternity—to which, before striding from the room, she rhymes something to this effect: Not being born of an honourable father would indeed be a defect, but only if she'd given him his being, rather than receiving hers *from* him. Whereas the cultivated gentleman's mother was much the more magnanimous (in having him follow such multitudes) so that he might just as freely follow the suit and choose the father who best suits him. . . .

Have I gone too far? But not at all. Leonor is all assurances afterwards. In Madrid, the rough and tumble is more savage by half. I should have heard Quevedo's squibs on Alarcón's hunched back. Truly?—she hadn't mentioned his deformity before? But *no*, Alarcón was not wounded by the cut, any more than my Perico would be. And in administering it, Quevedo had no more dishonoured himself than Velázquez had by frequenting dwarves. No watcher of this curious compendium that is Man must ever close her eyes to this—this is life, life in its entirety. These were geniuses. It may hurt the man, but life nourishes the genius. I, more than anyone, must learn to see this.

The next night she sets the opening topic: the intellectual superiority of the white European born in the New World. In a salon full of gentle-born Castilians she herself takes the affirmative, taking me, Carlos, and the new Jesuit confessor at the palace as her prime examples. Relentless, she chooses for our second topic the effect of African breast milk on the Creole male. Carlos is stewing, has come to talk with me about something. I see him regretting it.

Is it true, she muses, as is held, that the Creole's affection for the source long outlives his infancy? And is this hardy milk, dispensed in such charming vessels and in such abundance, not perhaps the secret source of the greater potency and vigour of his body and mind?—

But Juanita was raised on Indian *breastmilk.*

Teresa.

I see them all watching me. Carlos, Fabio, Perico, the courtiers. Leonor. I have not told her this. Teresa is trying to cause a rift between us.

"The Academy would now hear," Perico leaps onto a chair, "how *la Giganta* answers the charge. Indian milk—*is it true?*" He has said this gently. I know it is in jest, and an opportunity to respond in kind. He'd be the last to care.

I could have spared her. A friend. Is it even true, what I say next? Rumours like this make the rounds about all of us. She is impulsive by nature and not a little giddy at the approach of her wedding. I know in my heart there is no malice in it. I see the ropes of pearl glowing in her hair, her hopes glowing at her cheek. Things will not be the same for her.

Teresilla, you may be a slip of a thing
but you've given your poor Camacho quite a whirl . . .
Those branches on his brow've grown so towering,
he stoops to enter even a vestibule . . . [27]

Carlos comes the next day, under the pretext of taking his leave yet
again, and in truth Puebla de los Angeles has not been graced with his
presence for a while. He gives himself airs, as though he were above the
Academy, but he comes often enough—verily does one wonder if the
seminary is ever *in* session. I know he has come to admonish me, as he
does so often lately. From no one else do I take this, and from him it
has begun to pall. But I am dreading today—could anyone find
recriminations more bitter than those I found for myself during the
night?

I am afraid he might.

In the Vice-Queen's patio I wait for him where we are least likely to
be overheard. Under the trees runs a chain of bowers—flowering
hedges, head high, cut in interlocking els all along the bottom of the garden, from the Hall of Comedies to the palace library. Twice I catch sight
of Carlos wending his way toward me. I have no particular affection for
the new French fashions for men. The tiny jackets as though shrunken
up the rib cage, the beribboned shoes and canes, the petticoat breeches,
the fur muffs. And I am not so finally reconciled to Paris's latest rulings
on what is divine in women's beauty—Heaven knows, they caused trouble enough in Troy. As we women put on our livery, with its *décolleté frôle
aréole*, the latitude of our neckline makes it very hard not feel like pages,
platter, and peaches all trussed up in an expedient parcel.

But any particular style has to be preferable to this new outfit of his.

Carlos has never needed a riding habit to go to Puebla before, a
leisurely ride of thirty leagues. It occurs to me to be grateful: else I might
not be able to face him at all. Bucket-top calfskin boots, netherstocks and
leather breeches, a basque short-skirt with points at the waist, over
which a short sword has been belted. Unfortunate, assuredly . . . calami-
tous is barely adequate. Apocalyptic might do—not Elysian, not
Parisian, but a mix of all the sins of style of all the ages brought to stand
together and be judged. A lace falling band *and* a lace cravat, both frayed
to a hoary fringe, and both plainly second hand. Which only makes

sense—the Plains of Judgement being evidently at the used clothing market, and how much easier to strip the dead where you find them standing. I see fashions from the eras of at least three Spanish kings, a French one, and perhaps a Caesar. Has Perico helped him shop?

By now I am happy Carlos has come. The velvet of his dark green doublet is bare enough in patches to pass for black satin. Across his frail chest a faded orange baldric and over one thin shoulder a heavy buff coat. The ensemble is capped off with an ostrich plume so bedraggled on a wide-brimmed beaver hat so battered I wonder if the ostrich was not captured wearing it during one of its cerebral inquisitions into a dune. As for how the beaver was taken . . . it does not bear thinking about.

He is twenty-two now—and even in a travelling outfit, this is no way to make one's way in the world. The overall effect is like a vision from Isaiah, where the beaver and the buffalo, the ostrich and the goat, the lion and the fatling lie down together. I have not quite lost the last of my nervousness, yet at this range I can no longer ignore his poverty, his unworldliness . . . and am flooded with the strangest emotion, equal parts pity and tenderness. He is so dear. A small frail military adventurer.

I rise to greet him, a little taller in my heels than he in his. He struggles manfully to hold my eyes. We learn here to wield the hourglass, as it were, like a rapier. At times it amuses me to observe the power this simple geometrical figure has over men, this body I have inherited from Isabel. But when I am alone with Carlos, when we are truly free to speak, it is as if we had no bodies at all . . . two spirits entirely free to jouney to any country, to fly anywhere the mind may go. How furious he is when he first hears this from me, and refuses to see in any part of it a compliment. Why?

He stands before me—the eyes made enormous by his thick glasses, bleary from too much reading, and angry, obviously, at the mere sight of me. I notice finally that he has cut his hair. He has left a little hank, a lovelock pulled forward over his shoulder like a chipmunk's tail, bound in a small black ribbon.

This good-bye does not feel like the others. He does not stay long. He has been reading my face, no doubt. But I no longer know how I am feeling. I think to ask him if the sword is a genuine original of the Roman Empire. I think to ask what sort of weather he is expecting on the road to Puebla. . . . I can think of nothing to say at all. I know he is in love with me.

He is in no mood for preliminaries.

"I simply cannot see how you can bear this snakepit another day."

The first harsh words he has spoken to me—no, we have disagreed. It is the tone that is new. How can I, he demands to know, have remained for so long blind to the jeering cruelty of this place—to the racist sneers, this fanatical obsession of theirs with pure blood? Have I not heard them whispering, 'Was her grandfather a *salta atrás*[†]?'

I have told only Carlos anything about him, and have begun to regret it. "And what other place is there," I ask, "for a poet *but* here? Quevedo, Góngora, Calderón. Secretaries, chaplains, chamberlains all."

"Is *she* the one poisoning you?"

This is so like him.

"What point is there for people like us to be envious of someone like Leonor?"

"Lope, Quevedo, Alarcón never had this kind of rival. They never had to be beautiful. I always believed it was *her*, but seeing you last night . . . I'm afraid what may ruin you, Juana, is not her beauty but your own."

He has taken his glasses off and—strange sensation—he seems nearer, as if I were the one having problems with my vision. His face wears the oddest look. As his lips part, I have the panicky feeling he is about to kiss me . . .

"Even as you have ruined Teresa."

Now these letters.

He judges me from afar just as when he was here. Surely he does not imagine a woman could simply go to him—wherever he is now—even if I wanted to. *Why didn't he tell me he was really going away?* Does it have to be love—does friendship mean so little to him? One long perfect night gazing through a telescope together—pouring out our hearts, our souls, into the vessels of the other's eyes—were those hours not marvel enough without bringing Love into it? Was our time together not enough as it was?

And these outlandish projects of his. What business would he have seeing Isabel? Impertinent. Of course she is beautiful. What would he expect? And this great new enthusiasm for the countryside, for what is past. I write Carlos sonnets to tell him I'm sorry—he accuses me of insincerity! Then of disloyalty, even while he writes letters filled with sedition to me, *here*.

And through what strange geometries he pursues me, this future holder of the Chair of Mathematics. Running from the arms of the

[†] 'backslider,' who sets back the cause of racial purity by breeding with one of the inferior castes

Jesuits toward me, then right past me to a monastery. Then from one Indian village to another, where—ledger propped on bended knee—he composes arguments desperate to persuade where they cannot seduce. He asks me to contract to a life of charming escort, intellectual helpmeet, mother to a litter of children poor as church mice and nearsighted like a thin-skinned father whose talent merits rewards reserved for the *gachupines*. A father whose indignation renders him unfit for any lesser employment. He asks me to share a lifetime of slights.

Yet though he offers it to me, he doesn't even see it's not this existence he wants for himself. The respectable lot of a Jesuit scholar is all Carlos really wants. Not me.

And this other fantasy he conjures—my great Examination before the Scholars.

Forty scholars—why does everyone say forty? Even Carlos. Does he so need to see a Catherine against the forty sages of Maxentius, a Christ before the forty learned Pharisees? Can it not just be me?

When the Viceroy calls a halt, his face does not beam with triumph as Carlos imagines it. Replies like mine will do nothing but fire the very rumours the Viceroy wants quelled. He has called for this examination to put an end to the speculations about my learning's origin, which are becoming worrisome. The last thing the palace needs is the Inquisition sniffing about.

Not forty, not sages. A handful learned, none too well prepared. And no one is at all prepared to be answered in verse.

"Now would *la docta doncella*," asks the Professor of Music, "care to share with us her views on the relation of harmony to beauty?"

I begin by proposing that the limits of the senses mean that each, obviously, measures properties in different registers: touch, taste, &c. But not the soul. The soul knows there is but one true proportion. Sirs . . .

Here's an everyday example:

> Place along a line
> a half, a third,
> a quarter, fifth, and sixth—
> fractions geometry uses.
> Convert these into solids
> and proceed to weigh them

Choose an object of some weight
and in like fashion
to the line's divisions,
set out the counterweights.
These may be made to sound in harmony
as in that very common
experiment with the hammer.

Thus Beauty is not only
surpassing loveliness
in each single part
but also proportion kept
by each to every other.
Hence nothing represents
Beauty half so well
as Music . . . [28]

As its import sinks in, he sinks to his seat, his lips working slightly, like gills. In answer to the question in his eyes, I press on . . . *And as you sir, so plainly see, Pythagoras calculated the harmony of the celestial spheres to be a circle of fifths, the music of a silence of such perfection we hear the voice of God in it.*

Sing.

Yet what if, gentlemen, this circle were instead a spiral—picture a figure winding up a cone poised upon its apex, a staircase if you will. Let us imagine a music of not spheres but spirals, whose section is not the circle of fifths but the cutting plane of an ellipse, as in the new studies of planetary motion. . . . A new notation, then, for a new vision of the heavens. A measure not closed, but spiralling like a staircase from the realm of man, up through those of Nature, thence to God. And yet as we climb, so small and so frightful, up that vast winding stair built to such a titan's foot, we find ourselves rising up the scale of that silent concord within which, could we but hear it, the soul finds its rest. . . . [29]

The Viceroy frowns, his mien darkening, and it is on this flattened note that the grand examination ends. But does it occur to none of them that many of my answers were in verses already written? Why doesn't it—because I am so young, or so female, or because one does not, in one's spare time, compose poetry on questions of speculative music?

And since that day, the mill and mongery of rumours grows ever worse. The Viceroy is more to blame than anyone. *After* the fact he is pleased enough with my replies, because the day makes for a good story. He tells the new ambassador from Milan that watching me dealing with my questioners was *like watching a galleon fending off a fleet of canoes.* Greatly pleased with his analogy, he repeats it too often. Too sure of my place, I complain of this to Leonor, of being foisted on the Milanese Ambassador like the Viceroy's favourite talking toy. She answers curtly that my gifts are an asset of the Crown. Velázquez understood this perfectly, without needing anyone to explain it to him.

Wounded, I take it out on the Viceroy, though of course I am not quite fool enough to say any of this aloud. *'Galleon'?—our chocolate-loving Viceroy has become a bit of one himself, comfortably in port, portly now in comfort.* <u>El gran galeón de la Mancerina</u>. *Does the Marquis de Mancera not see the satire in our naming a chocolate platter after him?*

Sweet Carlos, loyal, honest friend . . . the fruits of the victory he recalls to me contain the seeds of the bitterest defeat. There were Pharisees enough to spare, *but no temple this.* Christ in the temple didn't debate with a heart puffed up with vanity, with this insane need of mine to hold up my learning like a fist and shake it in their faces. . . . What Carlos does not understand is the *desengaño*[†] I discovered that day, and which invades me now. The University had been my most cherished hope—hope for a theatre of universal ideas nobly declaimed and defended, hope for a place where I would at last find my teacher. When that afternoon ended, I knew not on this side of the Atlantic, nor perhaps on the other, would I find a teacher to guide me, to trust enough to follow . . . to one day hope to walk beside.

> [†] disenchantment, disillusionment

Faithfully the letters come. To gently shame me, remind me of our talks. Of Panoayan, of my dream of seeing Tuscany, of the Academy of Florence—*Academy,* what a mockery. Botticelli, Da Vinci . . . I have heard them snicker at even Leonardo here, at how he squandered his talent on trifles. *He,* on trifles! Accused by such as these. . . .

But the day I read Carlos's version of the examination, I see the question the Chair of Music should have put to me. And I do not know how I am to answer. *Answer.* I am called but I do not know how. No less then than now. Answer. If I am called, how do I answer? *If* I am called, I do not know *how.* Answer now.

'*Why, señorita—if you are beautiful—is there so little harmony in you?*'
'*And why, Soul, dost thou know so little peace?*'

JUANA INÉS
DE LA CRUZ

B. Limosneros, trans.³⁰

... And though among all Princes,
a custom widely found
offers freedom at Easter
to all those prison-bound:
          within the sweet bonds
of your sacred lights,
where, to be precise,
lies a prison willed,
          (where gold is the chain
that adorns my time and binds it,
and hasps of diamond
the padlocks that secure it,)
          I live, dear Lady
that you, with inhuman pity,
not strip me of those jewels
which so enrich our souls,
          but captive hold me,
that I might freely throw,
for you, my freedom
out the window.
          And to the sonorous harmonies
of my beloved shackles,
while others weep torrentially,
my blessings ring—clear and tranquil:
          May no one keen for me,
seeing me lashed to a stave,
for I would trade being Queen
for being made your slave.

*A*t a turn in the hallway I come upon the three of them, brought up hard against the door of his chamber. The Ambassador of Milan and two of the hand-maidens, in a wing of the palace no woman should visit. He dangles a cluster of black grapes—obscenely plump—above red mouths gaping with the blind hunger of new-hatched birds, bids them suck each grape whole—one passes from mouth to mouth to mouth. A crush of silks, a thigh wedged between two thighs spread wide, a knee lifts . . . Teresa. He turns to kiss Imelda, cups hard her breast, presses the tip clear of the bodice, pinches, a hard dark grape . . . Bites down and splits it, grape juice running down. Chafes it with a fingernail.

Women's hands meet, fingers over wrists as vipers mating twine. He turns his face to me, smiles, as I stand frozen there.

You wanted to see me . . .

Yes, I have come for more.

Leonor is not like the rest. Does she not tell me how much she and I are alike?—and I am not like them. We spend hours together in her gallery, just we two, sitting at different benches, sketching. Hardly a word passes between us over whole afternoons. What need have we for talk, when all around us such brushes speak? Originals by Murillo, Rubens, and one name new to me, of a Greek living in Toledo. Superb copies of Gracian, Botticelli, Titian. She has devoted an entire wall to Velázquez. He brought her to her love of art. They saw each other almost every day near the end. She, the Queen's most trusted lady-in-waiting; he, the King's chamberlain. She loved him like a father, grieves him still. In these half-dozen years since his death, his reputation has not ceased to grow. Madrid talks of no one else. Rubens, they have quite forgotten. Everyone sees his greatness, now.

No one loves art more than she does.

Leonor leads me into her study. I follow willingly. I love this room, try always to see it as for the first time: four unsteady herons stopped mid-stride—precarious stepladders running along shelves that line each wall to vertiginous altitudes; books, maps, illuminated manuscripts . . . the shelves fairly founder beneath their burdens. This is the room I have always dreamt of having. Near the tall windows a whole cabinet of curious animal skulls vacantly ogling. Thrown together in a walnut case, a precious cornelian vase, potash, verdigris, bits of rock and statuary. On brass carriages huge magnifying glasses stand ready for inspections. Leonor dismisses the attendant and herself fetches down folders that bulge with prints and engravings. Two folders for Velázquez alone, virtually everything he has done. Even sketches Leonor has made of some of his sketches from Italy. For the third time this month she brings them out, spreads dozens over the lacquered table, and I do not tire of them. Prints of half the works in the royal collections, even now the greatest in all Europe. In the span of forty-five years Philip IV amassed four thousand paintings. Philip. The great patron of Velázquez.

She says this sardonically, as though to take up my part in an argument, one we had last year, over my elegy for the King.

"Patron? Let me tell you—the King *killed* Velázquez. Went years without paying him for his work. *Four years once*—while they gave Rubens *palaces.*"

I stand looking over her shoulder at the prints. She does not look up. I know better than to argue when she is like this. She is like this often now.

"A servant who painted was all he was. He was not treated as I treat you. At bullfights Philip made him sit with the servants—the greatest painter in the world! I couldn't bear it."

It infuriates her that Philip had paid one of the dwarves—who was it? El Primo, perhaps—a daily ration of nine *reales.*

"Velázquez, *mi amor,* was poorer than most of the misfits he painted."

The drapes are open. She sends me to the windows to pull back the cambric lining. Rain falls in the *zócalo.* A soft grey light falls across the vast walnut table, strewn with papers now like leaves on a pond: prints of the great painter's hunting tableaus, homely scenes in bodegas and kitchens, portraits of the King and of Quevedo. Her fingers stray over a fanciful rendering of Aesop, sketches of gods in the streets of Madrid— Vulcan holding court in a blacksmith's shop. A pale Bacchus, the toast of sunburnt campesinos . . .

She shows me again the work of his last years. The masterpieces.

Las Meninas.

†maids of honour, handmaidens

"Look at little Margarita here. It is no surprise that the Princess comes out so well. He was very fond of her. But *las meninas*† themselves . . .

I knew each of them intimately, and I swear to you he has seen into their souls.

"Not so very long after it was finished a painter arrived from Italy. He had come expressly to see it and left the same day, went straight back to Italy. 'I have just now seen the theology of painting,' he said, and would look at nothing else.[31] *The theology of painting*, Juana."

But the King did love him, I say, hoping to deflect her.

"Yes, he loved him. The man ruined everything he touched. He loved Mariana, too. She cheered him, she bore him children. He thanked God for the consolations she brought. And still his infidelities would not stop. Losing Felipe Próspero broke her heart. How beautiful that child was. Here—here was how Velázquez saw him as a toddler. Was this not a beautiful child? And then for her to lose him, only to give birth to that monster. . . .

"By then Mariana and Philip had been spending most of their evenings with the *sabandijas*. This was the class of diversion they sought. There was an amusing one with flippers they particularly liked. If he'd sent that one home to America with us I would have pitched it overboard myself."

How many times will she tell this? Leonor claims her physician calls it melancholy, but she does this to herself.

Leonor . . . come to the window.

"Philip *should* have felt at home with them—with his incontinence, his haemorrhoids, his nephritis. But her, even the most hardened felt sorry for her. And yet when that baby was born . . . scrofulous, hunched, rickety . . . the joke was, the real father must have been one of the dwarves. Once the jokes started, there was no stopping it.

"And now we have a monstrosity as King."

Leonor, come see the square . . . the rain has stopped.

I have loved her for her love of literature and laughter, for her loyalty to Velázquez, but I cannot help wondering now if the courtiers did not hate Philip, and then Mariana, for preferring *las sabandijas* to them.

She comes to the windows.

Is it not lovely? I ask. Below us a cat laps at a gleaming puddle. All across the vast plaza wraiths and revenants simmer up from the paving. Vendors uncover their stalls again. There is hardly a square to match it anywhere in Spain. Has she not told me so herself? She looks into my eyes, with her palm cups my cheek. "*Mi alma*, once we get back to Madrid," she assures me, "once you have seen *Las Meninas* for yourself, you will feel as I do."

About what, I ask myself—a dead king?

She tells me she needs me, just as the Queen needed her, as the King needed his great painter, needs me more than ever, with everything she loves so far away. She has only me, and this new confessor who is helping her. I should go to him, too.

I do not like the look of him.

"No, he is humble and pious and brilliant."

Perhaps. . . .

"Helping you?"

Leonor speaks of a difficulty between her and the Viceroy.

"A good and capable man," I say.

Too old and fat now to be a husband to her. . . .

I try to change the subject. It is dangerous to be put between them. He too is my patron, a friend.

"Why don't we walk through the square—just for a minute?" Now she is annoyed.

Could we sit in the patio, at least, under the trees? Or next to the library . . . ? No.

It costs her too much effort now to dress and go down before nightfall. She does not want me running off, either. Tell the pages what authors I want and they will bring them up. In the evenings she is more herself but the later the hour, the more reckless she becomes. It is the days that she dreads. Once the night starts she will not let it end. The masquerades, the Academy, the dances and the plays. My plays.

Maybe she thinks I haven't seen her watching him. Does she imagine her husband will never notice? It's dangerous for all *las meninas* but especially for me; the Viceroy sees me as her favourite, but if he could stay awake beyond eight o'clock he would see it is Imelda and Teresa who attend her once I have turned in—when else am I to read, to write these verses and sketches that so divert her? How often has she slipped in at dawn, thinking not to wake me, and found me working? She feigns surprise, each time, that I would lose sleep over her. But in her eyes the tenderness is real, and so I cannot bring myself to ask, to go back to sleeping in the dovecotes with the others.

Whole days we spend in her apartments.

A small private chapel stands between her bedchamber and the Viceroy's. It is the only point of connection between her apartments and his. Adjoining her dining room, the main salon divides into alcoves by

the deployment of tall *biombos*[†] constructed in the Japanese style but   [†]folding screens
elaborately painted with scenes from Mexico's history and streets. Late
mornings before the sun is too strong, we sit on the latticed balcony, the
zócalo before us, a wide plaza filled with life. We watch the secretaries and
functionaries in black with their high starched collars. Priests leaving the
cathedral, next to us. Grandees and their bejewelled trains of slaves coming back from El Parian across the square. Lay women in nun's habits
selling blessed talismans and love potions to halfwits. . . .

Last week strange news reached the palace of a birth in the African
quarter, an infant, stillborn, with the head of a lion. In the past she would
have packed us all off to investigate. No, she is sick of the others. Why
not just the two of us then? Come, she never visits the city anymore. She
used to enjoy that, I remind her. Not the heat, the sun, the sicknesses in
the streets. In her mind she sees the pox scars on their faces . . . the withered limbs. Hunts, then. We could go into the country, I say, but I do not
want that either.

Is this all? The question we ask ourselves. At first we do not notice it,
then we try not to. The homesickness, the furies of tedium, the tedious
furies. She was not always this way. Every day the same. The same conversations, over and over. And what she fears most is the melancholy, the
melancholy is the worst. This could break anyone, she says, this could
break a queen. Truly, I do not doubt it.

Once there were at least four maids and ladies in constant attendance.
Now I am everything to her. Carver, cupbearer, dresser. . . . Her household is running half wild with nothing asked of them until nightfall. I am
the only one she can be with, she says, I am the only one who can lift her
spirits.

Is this all?

Yet is this not precisely how I am to serve? Do I think of abandoning
her as soon as things become difficult? Velázquez stayed until the end.
He watched and he saw, he consoled and he recorded, and it was not easy.

But *how* will this end?

This morning after a masquerade, we wake late, to an unholy clamour
in the plaza. We are in time to watch a man hanged in the *zócalo* for
breaking into a convent and attempting to assault a nun. The Indian
ladies selling fruit in the shade of the gallows do not so much as flinch
when the trapdoor opens. I do not like the look in her eyes. This too is
entertainment.

Just the sort of thing Philip would try, she says, when she sees me watching her. And then, before I can be angry I feel a rush of pity. She is afraid. She sees it herself, what happened to Mariana happening to her.

Barefoot, naked under a muslin chemise she languishes on the balcony and now in the salon until mid-afternoon. I have been dressing her each day for weeks, but in her bedchamber. Her near-nakedness in these semi-public rooms shocks and unsettles me; into her beauty a distracted quality has crept, the thinnest edge of madness. She is chilled, yet her forehead is hot and dry. She pulls back the carpet, draws up her chemise and lies full length on the cold stone floor. Extends her arms fully toward the unlit hearth, as if to lengthen the cold, as if a doll teaching itself to swim. After a moment she turns over onto her back, blinks, as if she has forgotten where she left me, calls me to her. She has come to a decision. There is something she needs very desperately to talk about. Something for us to ... It is dangerous. I must only do this if I wish it. Yes? I sit close over her. The aroma of almonds rises from her, all the creams I have palmed into her skin. Do my own hands still smell of almonds? Yes. My hair spills jet across the ivory of her belly. Such a sweet confusion ... She smiles into my eyes. Almost the same, no? Yes ...

The new ambassador.

What ...?

Until now there has been no one.

Leonor, I don't ... know how.

A hint of this would mean ruin. The Ambassador ... do I—

Of course I know which one. *Does she think I am blind?*

Father Núñez says—what, you've *told* him? Oh yes, everything. *Everything.* Says what—no, I don't care what he says. Tell me ...

I want you to take a message to him. Learn it word for word. I need them to be my words. *To Silvio* ... Tonight, after the play.

Not every day is the same.

Ambassadors—the one foreign power Madrid ever permitted to post an ambassador here was from the Shogunate, before the Great Persecution. Informally the Philippines, Perú and Naples support *enviados*, but the more legitimately they conduct their offices once here, the more suspiciously they are viewed by the Crown. And yet the presence of ambassadors at a court that lacks for nothing else agreeably glorifies the majesty of the Vice-King's person, not to mention New Spain's pretensions to be a kingdom on a footing with Aragón—to the point where every man of honour is a *don* and every *hidalgo* is all but a count, and every foreigner here an ambassador of something or other. But here the marvel is that the one we might with greatest precision call Ambassador is not a foreigner at all, but rather a former Spanish envoy to a foreign power; while the foreigners, not ambassadors except in euphemism, will either be an associate trailing that Spanish envoy here from his last posting, or be of any sort at all, provided he has with some foreign potentate a passing acquaintance—the less meaningful, in fact, the better. Military adventurers, fencing masters, gamblers, idle travellers, collectors of rare objects, arrangers of rare events. Any sort at all. These we call not the Special Envoy of His Serene Highness the Grand Duke of Tuscany but, limply, the Ambassador of Florence. Of things vaguely Florentine. Ambassador of florins.

Yet am I so different? Court poet—what have I let my life become? Was this not the title I once so prized?

How could I not have rebelled at the sight of the other writers and artists here? The worst reduced to the station of jesters, grown parasitic and fat at the King's table—the best, to the role of scold, and still just as much a part of the show. I thought I was above it all, inviolable behind the shield of my learning, invisible behind my masks, invincible on the battlements of my accomplishments. At eighteen the poet of choice for all occasions of state, whenever there is a visiting functionary to praise, a lavish gift to be commemorated. And now, by the time Europe's new ambassadors reach the palace gates, all have heard of me.

New Spain's Vice-Queen needs diversion—it is an urgent matter of state—so I am become her mistress of illusions, her magus, her hunting hawk. She yearns for daring, I write things Lope wouldn't risk. She is my Sovereign: I will be her warrior poet, her armoured suitor, her Giantess, her friend.

I write her sonnets. I carry her messages. Have I come so far not to create a *Las Meninas* but only be one?

Juanita, write us a comedy for Easter, another comedy for the empire. Somewhere in the Spanish dominions, they say, there is a comedy being finished every day. In a good week Lope could finish two himself, in a great month, ten. By the close of this century there will be ten thousand, with the ones I have written for her. Leonor sighs over reminiscences of Madrid, the parties in Vienna, the genius of Lotti's theatrical sets at the country palace—so I design marvels and have them built for her. Once,

I build a camera obscura with my own hands, after designs by Leonardo. For two whole days it fascinates her.

I have sat in the audience among these friends of mine and watched my own plays performed. I have basked in the ebb and flow of their cultivated flattery, and believed it, no, *devoured* it. Seeing my work well received, did I so badly need to think them connoisseurs of art? The empty heads, the empty hearts ... Here we're all actors, with me the most abject of all, trapped in the plots of my own plays, lost in mazes of my own design.

All in the name of *entertainment*.

One by one, each of my lying masks has fallen away. Coquette, raconteuse, innocent. And what then remains of *me*, as finally the legend overwhelms even the charm and only the last mask is left. Freak of nature, monster of learning—*la Monstrua*. For women an object of both envy and disgust, for men, certain men, a trophy.

Carlos, I am not so different from them as you thought. Dear Carlos. The last of the honest suitors. Even were I not now dishonoured, the only ones to pursue me still would be the giant-killers, the dragon-slayers—out to take a unicorn for their mantle. The letters that arrive now almost daily from the coast only make me feel more keenly my solitude. Poor Carlos, condemned to chase after me, just as I am condemned to love one who does not see me, even as I flee one who truly loves me. Poor dear Carlos—a scholar's mind, a mystic's soul ... with the heart of a mathematician and the face of a clerk.

Carlos, what has happened to love?

I thought him desperate, but wasn't I the desperate one? To have remained so long deaf to the flatulent hiss of their clever fakery, to the gnashing and clashing of beaks, the endless disputing over mangled concepts, to the clatter of the finest ideas of the age spilling over the parquet like pearls from their glossy, swinish lips. How long was I to overlook their raucous, wrenching vulgarity?—gorging themselves like vultures on their gossip and murderous jealousies, on their coarse lusts and treacherous intrigues.

The decadence of Mexico imitating Madrid mimicking Paris aping the final degeneracy of the Medicis ...

I carry their messages.

She watched me stuffing myself at a banquet of honeyed compliments and acid retorts—bitter chocolate sipped hot in the sweet night air. Cigarettes heaped on argent trays, gold braziers to light them. Intoxicating coach rides beneath wheeling stars, daring baths on the lake . . . until the worm was firmly embedded in my soul. How I hate these games of theirs now, yet I wriggle caught up in them like a minnow in a net. This puerile rage for cards. Cards, cards at all hours, while the lifeblood of a continent ebbs away through its open veins.[32] I learned too quickly and not *well* enough, won too easily and stayed too long.

Here everything's a game, yes, but not the one I thought I was playing. She spoke so sweetly of my vulnerability, smiled reassurance down at me from the commanding heights of her unattainability. Why did she never explain to me the real rules, the true motives of the game? To keep one married gentleman out of the bed of another's wife. To lead idle nobles, unprotesting, by their privates in the service of their king—with us, the unattached maids-in-waiting, to do the leading. Games to keep a rich girl single just long enough to arrange a marriage, a marriage to someone not yet senior enough to have seen his future wife cavorting like a whore.

What has happened to love?

All around us the cloying scent of too-sweet fruit hangs in the air, as we whirl, beautiful as moths, blinded in this bright storm. Then one is plucked from the vine—for one, the dance stops, the game for her ends in marriage. Among the rest there must be casualties—disease, pregnancy, abortive loves—while for the poorest among us the games never end, except in mad spinsterhood or prostitution. At best, a few years cloistered as a concubine. Then it all begins again, but by then the player's lost her best assets, the adolescent plumpness, the limpidity of her unlined eyes, the undistracted quality of her attention.

Tonight I think of Teresa. What's to happen to her now?

Learned fool I tried to see these *galanteos*—these vile palace games—as some ancient tragic rite, as the dance of male and female satellites around a dying planetary king.[33] Like the seasons, the rules for each dance change: one night the ladies draw by lot their partners for the ball; another night the men compete not for a lady's favour but for the prize of her scorn.

This evening's little diversion called for the gallants to start off the ball in the arms of their second choice. Leaving us all to guess at their first.

But first, Juanita, give us a comedy.

She said I would have her protection. I laughed. I had not meant to wound her. . . . At nineteen, I was not a frightened child. I was not like them but I was not a prude. Was I not born on a farm in a pagan countryside? Have I not seen animals in the fields?—and I have seen things here. In three years at this palace I have seen too much. In a few hours, Silvio will look me full in the face and, with those glittering viper's eyes studying my least reaction, say it was all for a bet, that he and 'a friend' had gone double-or-nothing on whether he could have me in the space of one single night.

Tonight I would trade anything for the peace and silence of my girl-hood in Panoayan, for the stillness of a village and a farm asleep on the dark shoulder of a volcano. I would give anything to see this bright whirl-wind *snuffed*. I feel that mountain inside me now as smoke and solitude and stone.

Tonight I would give up even these things to see it erupt just once in a white cone of *fire*.

Ahh . . .

But instead of getting to play out my small part in a great cosmic agony I watch the next act of my life reduced to low farce—for this audience finds comedy in everything. In death, in the pathetic antics of cripples and lepers, in corruption and betrayal and loss. Anything to mask this fresh wound in their chests.

After the play she came to tell me he was waiting for me in the bowers by the Hall of Comedies. He never deigned to come to the Academy, so she led me to him like a sacrificial lamb. She even picked the place. Knowing of his interest in me, did she come to hate me because the rumours of her relations with Silvio were true, or because they never could be? Decorated soldier, veteran of a dozen duels with married men, Silvio was different, special, *más varonil, más válido. Tell me.* . . .

I am my own executioner.

Leonor Carreto—the most beautiful creature I have ever met. How could I guess that one so beautiful could be so base? The Marquise de Mancera, for all her beauty and attainments, is bored with everything but power. And knowing this at last I feel, looking back, the malice of power in her every moment with me. With a lover's cruelty she insisted I play, learn my part word for word. Make her words my own, as I had offered mine to her. But this, why this? Surely nothing so banal as my purity. Surely something more than a break in the tedium, the voyeur's thrill at seeing an uncommon spirit pawed over, the gambler's at seeing a ruinous wager lost. Learned fool, calculate the probabilities. Was it to convince herself—no, *convince him*—that I would come to be no different than she one day, after a lifetime of petty stratagems and intrigues? Or was it instead to prove one thing? To me above all.

The cut that wounds the mortal, the genius does not feel.

I went like Eve towards the serpent, Ariadne after Theseus, betraying her sex, her blood, her soul . . . only so he could then betray her. I found him at the bottom of the garden, a darker shadow among shadows—tall and powerful through the chest. I had watched him, many times. Disdaining the fashions of the French, he wore his own hair short, shoulder length, drawn at the nape with a simple clip. The beard trimmed close, streaked grey at the cheeks. Over a grey silk doublet he wore a velvet jerkin, black, lightly corsetted, so the adoring eye might contrast the breadth of the chest with the slimness of the hip, roam from the white stockings and hose full along the lithe muscular legs—to the jaunty parting of the jerkin at the jut of the codpiece. The beautiful blue hells of his eyes, impudent . . . the arrogant male, even with her. Did he imagine I might simply succumb without a word?

He stepped towards me into the moonlight, and even as I should have been thinking how deftly staged the moment was, my celebrated self-possession had already begun abandoning me. I heard myself asking how he'd found the play.

"Interesting."

"Surely the representative of Milan," I said, trying to get my footing, "has a more *interesting* response? Do you not find it something more than *interesting* that the play's hero challenges God and defies His order, but then invites punishment for his transgressions?"

"Only as a point of chivalry. But, yes, the old *and* the new. And for once, a noble man's sinfulness is not blamed on some outside force."

"I wouldn't have thought you such a staunch champion of responsibility."

"I believe it weak to blame new evils on old devils. Don't you agree?"

At last I felt myself beginning to relax. "With other causes so proximate, yes."

"Our hero took his fight directly to God, I respect that—and welcomed the return blow as an act of *nobleza*. He has committed a misconduct in his host's house, after all. But I see this subject has begun to bore."

"No, no it's just—this isn't the face you show in there."

"'This painted semblance you so admire / sets up false syllogisms of colour . . .'" he quoted, bowing slightly.

"You know it?"

"I know all your work, Juana."

"I never see you at my plays . . ."

"Good of you to notice."

When had I become such a blunderer?

"You mustn't take it personally, child, I'm just not one for sharing. Anything. But let's not waste your time on the trivial. As the whole world now knows, you're no mere poetess but a formidable philosopher. Perhaps you would help me? With a little syllogism."

"If I can."

"Excellent. Let's see . . . if it is true that to delight in evil creates a horror of solitude . . ." He glanced down at me. "Are you with me."

"Oh yes."

"And if to flee solitude is to pursue the complete and perfect joining that is *love* . . . then this would mean that to flee solitude is both to love and to delight in evil."[34]

For an instant I hesitated. And then, instead of remarking that his syllogism consisted of verb phrases rather than common nouns, instead of subjecting him to a lecture on syllogistic figures, moods and distributions, instead of reducing the ramparts of his premises to wet straw and his propositions to so much hot air, I stood like a witless quail before the gamekeeper and found myself admiring the meagre kernels he was tossing to the ground. Already I should have guessed the whole thing was rehearsed, every word, under Leonor's direction. But I had let myself find something fatally compelling in an idea, as she knew I would. So instead of running—or standing to *fight*, I stuck my empty head through his little loop of string. . . .

"And therefore, *signor*, to delight in evil . . . is to love."

"Good girl, I knew you'd see."

"Oh I see more. I see how this makes a certain breed of man a kind of victim—at least in his own eyes—*forced* to commit evil in the pursuit of love."

"And don't forget," Silvio nodded appreciatively, "this breed of man is at the same time forced to love even in the pursuit of evil . . . especially in the pursuit of evil. Meanwhile—"

"Meanwhile the Ambassador of Milan was about to say that I must then surely see how committing evil, even as it deepens his horror of solitude, also deepens his capacity for love. Therefore," I went on, so eager to play the game, so keen to feel the braid around my throat tightening, "to love replenishes the well from which evil springs."

"*Brava, regazza!* An observation altogether worthy of the hero of our play—"

"Yet you've also no doubt considered, *signor,* that to desire solitude sufficiently—*heroically* let's say—is to make love, for that man, both unnecessary and impossible, while removing all limits to his delight in evil."

"Delightful! Utterly delightful. You, *joven,*[†] are everything they said you were and more."   [†] young one, little one

"And you, *Señor Embajador,* are nothing they said you were."

Who was he really?

"Come child. We've begun so well. You don't want to join all these other clerks of love—insisting I find a fixed address."

I stood there in the moonlight listening to him hammering away at love. At retrograde, reactionary love that shuts the door on change, at baseless, insubstantial love—a pious vow like peace on earth or universal brotherhood. How love imposes closure, a passivity—not to choose but to be *chosen.* Love as an end to creativity, to questing, to living . . .

And though there was not a single premise I could not have dismantled, there was something in the whole, in the relentless energy of the assault, an echo of something faceless yet familiar, that I had glimpsed before.

"Still, if we must have hypocrisy," he said, his delight evident by now, "I much prefer the hypocrisy of women to that of men, don't you? I mean that for a woman, just as for a man, to delight in evil and to love both act upon the greater horror of solitude as cause and effect. But a woman . . . a woman transforms this horror into a positive, an *active* quality. She nurtures it, and it, her. Even while she is loving and sinning, this horror—the fear of loss and emptiness, this fear of becoming an empty vessel—is never far from her soul. And so, with the new anti-Christ of tonight's play, women share a special *genius* for evil, do you not think so? And a special sensitivity to the solitude it implies. Thus do they love and sin more intensely than a man, and it is this that nurtures him in his pursuit of them—even as he himself indeed becomes more . . . womanly."

So we played on under a watchful sky. The smile, the candour calculated to disarm. Into every woman's life walks at least one like him, the consummate player who knows all the steps of the dance, the feints, the pretended disinterest. How to make a show of hating hypocrisy, how to make himself an ally of the worm in her soul. And then, for all his mastery and virtuosity, to win completely, absolutely, he has to break the rules. The same rules that have served him so well.

Silvio broke the rules, but only after he had ground me down, outplayed me at a game I played with all my heart but only half my mind, a game I'd never seriously imagined losing. I never imagined how.

Hot with wine, the tumult of the evening—with years of *games*—my blood ignited. I had had enough of moonlight. I put my fingers to his lips, the lips of Leonor's lover. I had had enough of talk. I put my fingers to his heart, show me where it hurts, show me how. I placed his fingertips beneath my breast. Say it here, yes, and here, yes, and yes and here. God, my Lord God, how I wanted this, with a want and a craving that crept and called in me like madness. At that moment I would have permitted him anything, had he only asked and not taken. At that moment I would have gone with *joy* . . . He could have swept me up and brought me to his bed through the whole crowded ballroom.

He could have told me I was his second choice.

Silvio that I could err and place my love
in one as vile as you has made me see
how heavy a weight sin's evil is to bear,
how harsh desire's vehemence can be.

Sometimes I think my memory deceives:
how could it be that I in truth did care
for one embodying traits I most despise,
whose every word of love conceals a snare?

Dearly I wish whenever my eyes behold you
that I could deny a love so badly flawed;
yet, with a moment's thought, I realize

there is no cure save bruiting it abroad.
For crimes of love admit no expiation
save to confess and face humiliation.

JUANA INÉS
DE LA CRUZ

Alan Trueblood, trans.

UNDERWORLD

11 Dec [19]94

Mexico City

BULL ROAR OF A GREAT BOULEVARD. Over the meridian squats a replicant Arc de Triomphe—new world Champs Elysees, swift metallic flocks, Elysian van of horns trumpeting triumph. Maniacal rosebowl parade fun / knelled through the stone archway. *Arco Triunfal* that heralds my allegorical arrival / portalled portent, gather your omens where ye may.

Fifteen unmarked lanes each side—a shoaling river of cars it takes ten minutes to ford. Never cross on WALK crossing at the corner is for suicidal sitting ducks, never stop looking left and right J-Run don't walk in the middle of the block. Run headswivelling incessant—run graceless run. Thrill of danger in my guts—let's call this fun, more than I've had in years.

Headswimming chestpained bends on the far shore. The air's most travestied region—two kilometres above the sea. I walkandwalk ears ringing, spots of darkness skating in my eyes like waterbugs. Copper tongued—*my mouth is full of blood* but no it's this air this—tasty, odorous, colour of ash—gas.

Sharp right at the next corner into the quake zone. Low rent housing in the middle of the business core ten years after the Big One—five minutes' walk to work at the stock exchange buy now! Upscale vagrant lots of rubble—foundered tumblewalls, concrete wracked and insubstantial. Catch glimpses of colour, laundrystrung or hampered, ladies hauling water in oilcans.

See stone-soled children play rubblefield football, while infant archaeologists—solemn, slow—sort crushed rock and cokebottle potsherds.

Olfactory gusto—*¿Te gusta, a ti?*—to smell is to taste is to swim in an excremental infusion a million molecules of dogbaby-shit-per-cubic-metre-tea, but flowers too and frying onions tobacco soap—a funksea.

Ssst—oye, bonita. What are you drawing there in your notebook? Why don't you draw my picture, *chiquita*, I love you. Whistle past the graveyard / hum the hymn hyaenal / hear the packhunters gathering for a fresh meatkill. Me. Sharp left to a main street.

Broken sidewalks / sclerotic, narrowed arterium of vendors warey with watch straps extension cords blender blades sport socks. Adidas bags for the unathletic—pauper Samsonite. Cheap blasters blare brazen pirate music—cassettes adollar apiece—prepare to be boarded! Newsstands papervendors self-possessed resellers of obsolete textbooks—this collapsing rubble of perished technology.

Overhead a featureless sky bounded by the sootstained enthusiasms of fifties office blocks. Bauhaus bowwow byebye. Into the Centro Histórico Centre of History, the spiral's eye. Colonial construction, arched architecture of darkness and light, igneous and granite geometrics. The ground is porous, illfounded. Massive block-long buildings list to left and right, angling like bombed battleships sunk at shallow anchor.

Sidewalks like cheesecloth—worn and holed—knee-deep trashsinks—cripple machines. Beggarmakers. A million people a day stepping around holes in their lives. Or inside.

I can't bear to see the cathedral. Not today.

O happy day I stumble onto the *Palacio de Bellas Artes*—Palace of the Beautiful Arts—whither the ugly ones?—but this place is a dream of white marble domes and columns and muscled friezes and awestruck I mount the broad steps. Surely they will bar me entry to this mosque of loveliness. Inside, unshod, sandals in my hands I walk the cool parquet. Soaring murals of pain and blood, insane greed and longings betrayed. And at the margins, pale glimpses of my bookfed ignorance of this land writ large, ten metres high. Walls a soulswept panorama, floors cryptcold—above, a skull-lifting cupola a cranial vault / brain pan trepanned by a chromatic stainglass EXPLOSION. Vertigo, a slumping on the stairs.

Señorita, you're not unwell? Skinny guard skinny moustache gentle eyes rustygun. No I'm not unwell. Sometimes the beauty is too much, no? Yes, *señor*, sometimes the beauty is too much. *Gracias*—a thousand graces, I'm all right now.

Outside across the street a fifty-storey office tower, the only one around. Tower of Babel of Rubble-in-waiting, detumescence forestalled. Earthquaked it will swing like a pendulum like a lightbuoy a lightning rod for calamity.

Down into the metro, embowelled earth / refuge from the thunderbolt sky, this copper air.

BIENVENIDOS AL METRO DE MEXICO—WELCOME /

WILKOMMEN / BIENVENUS / NAHUATL SUN SALUTA-
TION—100 STATIONS / 200 KILOMETRES OF TRACK /
FIVE MILLION PEOPLE MOVED DAILY HALF A MILLION
KILOMETRES—to the moon and back through the shortcut guts of
the underworld. To the dead lands. Troglodyte sons of the dog, fetching
the bones of a lost race of men. No Eloi beyond this point, abandon all
hope, ye the well-heeled who enter here.

Waiting, waiting, the platform a dammed flood of passengers massing—a streaming anthill, a hive. Xenophobic flutter in my guts flushed
like quail. Rising pressure a high distant whine a rising wind—heralding
an ochre rubbertired train . . . dopplered deceleration. People dis- and
embarking, turbulent collidings.

But even whirled and battered, half-drowned, I am schooled in this
people's incomprehensible restraint, their regret, absence of malice: these
trains affront an outraged, deepheld courtesy.

Packed cars, stockyard buzzer, swish of doors. Basset-eyed gentleman
of the primordial school—broad-knotted polyester tie, frayed collars
and cuffs, impeccably clean—half-stands to offer me his seat. I smile in
declining, strange cheek-tweaking musculation this. Salmon in sardine
cans, the diffident press of bodies—hairspray, aftershave, mesquite, soap.
Censered return to the olfactory sea.

The ochre-train's vulcan whine rises and coils whiplike over its
groaning burden. This human cargo, this packtrain of burrowing burritos spurred by the *neo-gachupines*. These tender-hearted llamas on the
Andean brink of despair. *Inframundo en llamas.* Landlocked sub-
mariners—what's the weather like up there? Pressganged landsmen
who inwardly cringe at each sonar ping, at the sinister wash of ventilation props.

At each stop they spill debotched from this subterranean bottle-
plant—hopes replenished, lungs decarbonated, goals recalibrated—
consumptive discards returned. Recycled refills, these, bobbing up, rising to the light, redeposited at the famished gates of a pearling sky. And
such a school of entrepreneurship they rise from!—neo-con worldbank
wetdream—a million MBAs in humility. Ambulant vendors elbowing
apologetic through the cattlecote with their sharecropper's haul.
Pitchmen's singsong patter more dove-croon than hawking—selling
scissors, slide rules, palm calculators / palmed contraband, psalmed
bookmarks / keychain thermometers—what's body temperature?

Refugee-army knives, penlights / biographies of Mexican Nobel laure-ates / Aztec herbologies / tricks with rope and lariats / tiny brass pad-locks against the crime wave.

Then, sweet moment of stillness—write it . . . quiet, a solemn con-centration, the passing of a precious gift: suckling a newborn, a young Indian mother teaches her daughter—cleanfrocked glossyhaired—her alphabet, from a scrap of stock quotations.

And these, the deracinate holders of common property, how have they trespassed against thee, O great Captains of Calvinist Industry?

I ride for hours, train after train, scanning light-panels advertising the same: cosmetology, astrology, typewriter repair, keypunch dexterities. Parchment illustrators, programmers in Pascal and other dead hierat-ics—join a fraternity, wear a uniform—cloak, cowl and lifeguard whis-tle—preserve undead knowledge through the dark age to come.

I try to turn away from glaze-eyed children selling gum—*chicles . . . chicles!*—from these, the glued and leaded IQs of a lost generation. Train after train, through this tatterdemalion pandemonium, we are god's freak retinue limping through the holes in our lives. Jesters poets minstrels / the blind and pocked and crippled, playing ballads, early Beatles / protest, folk/ranchero, a cappella salsa. Guitar/banjo, clay flutes and fingerdrums . . .

And oh the neap tide of voices rising and falling, a peso a song. Sing along. Quaver and plaint, sharp discord and flat melodrone. An intoning, a litany, a rosary, an incantation—all the heartbreak, the lovesick invoca-tions. Now and then an angel's voice to wake us from our subcutaneous sleep. And somehow for each and all, even the most tone-deaf, we find a coin. A tiny disk of embossed foil to pass along.

Shellshocked smiles—*would you smile at me if you knew my mind?*

Songs for bread. Belts cinched, one man's family eats a little less this night that another's—ranged round a guitar case—may feast on yes-terday's unsold bakery. In train after train salarymen in vast transit and pilgrim families and teens shyly break out their little lunches, make self-conscious offers to total strangers. Like me.

How can I eat with you?

But how I want to. *I want to.* Why does this wound me so sweetly, make me want to weep? I glance around me to ape the right reply. How should I behave? How do I act, I am a child among you, O Mexico—old soul, *México hondo.*

To the barefoot, grimycheeked urchins—eyes like dazed fawns—I learn to give money only when changing trains. Some try to follow but they are too small in the crowds, too light, leaflike in this forest so heavy-limbed.

Were you there? Somewhere in the crowd—hiding your omnipresence, did I talk too loud? Did you sell me chicklets—thine, those glazy leaden eyes? This little compass, did its needle swing to you? I found you not. Was't from you I bought this tiny penlight to light my way each night?

Or maybe that was you sharing food—a thin day of fishing. The loaves ran out.

No, I didn't find you—but O the five million souls shunting through the underground. Shot star trailing its disastrous train in *hideous combustion down* / through the earth's honeycombed heart—abuzz awhirr adrone. Underground railroad, mine eyes have seen the glories of thy *via negativa*. Fly us to the moon and back through swisscheese skies of green. Ratheride down here with you than in a host of Elohim. In limousines.

By this upflung tide of songs, am I not washed clean? Sing me sweetly to my rest this night / I wish I may I wish I might / in these lost bones, keep and hold you for to-night . . . lost human race.

We who falterfall to kingdomcome in second place.

I ride and ride for hours until the shiny coins and worn-kid bills are spent, paperthin vellum treasured notes swapped for lenten songs.

I know this stop, I know this name, have known it all along—*Bellas Artes Underground*.

Night, a light rain falling.

7th day of August, Anno Domini 1668[†]
TODAY I, FATHER ANTONIO NÚÑEZ DE MIRANDA, take my share of satisfaction in a great good: to have preserved our New Spain and the Viceroy's household from the mortal peril of a great temptation. Today I convinced Juana Inés Ramírez de Santillana to take the veil. Divine Providence ordained that I be in attendance at the cathedral wherein, an hour after Prime, I found her in a state of great agitation, which in turn exerted a powerful effect on me, for here was a girl of extraordinary beauty and distinction whom I had met (though not often: she confessed also to having avoided me), and of whom I had of course heard much discussion, at the Viceregal Palace.

At first I stood outside the chapel, unsure of how to proceed as she, thinking herself alone, collapsed before the altar and gave vent to a storm of wracking sobs. Her skin, already pale, was ashen, the more so in contrast to her black hair. Her large eyes, black in the dim candlelight, were wide, filled with tears and what seemed, from where I stood, like horror. At last I entered. As I drew close she looked up and at length recognized me as the confessor of her patrons. The girl and I began to speak. Though the details of our conversation remain in confidence, I can record that she expressed herself with astonishing precision for one in her state of unconcealed disarray, and with a remarkable maturity in one so young. I had the overwhelming sense that here was one whom God had marked for a special destiny, and resolved thereat, though I am not by nature impulsive, to offer her my protection, in this way to serve as His instrument.

The child spoke of an evil that followed her everywhere, saw visions of a black beast that stalked her, dogging her every step. Though she retained a rigid control of her faculties she was also clearly in anguish. She declared she would leave this world sooner than face it again. Finally I overcame her reticence to make a confession. As I listened with unrest to the distressing tale that ensued, I knew that she must be persuaded to enter a convent, a sanctuary from the temptations and predations of the world. The Carmelite convent of San José is known for its austerity and, moved by the ease with which she acceded, I have agreed to her own suggestion that her penance there be especially harsh. . . .

TAKING THE VEIL

In a chapel of the cathedral, the Viceroy's confessor has recognized one of the Vice-Queen's handmaidens, the celebrated Juana Ramírez, weeping. Later, alone in his cell, he finds cause for both jubilation and mortification.

[†]photostat copy, likely source: archives of the Seminary of the Archdiocese, Zacatecas, Mexico

The errors you have made with this girl. Read them again for yourself. Unforgivable mistakes for a man of your experience. After all you are not a young Theology professor anymore, fresh from the provinces—no, not fresh at all—yet on the eve of her profession, of her seclusion, you arranged all the candles on the altar yourself with the trembling hands of a young groom. . . .

She is far more beautiful than any nun should be, and her physical beauty pales before her qualities of spirit—such clarity of mind, breadth of learning, the incomparable wealth of her talent. With such jewels as these does one stud the mitre of St. Peter. But did you really think, Fool, that it would be so easy, that the Dark One would not fight you for her every step of the way? How pleased you were with yourself, thinking to have brought her soul safely into harbour. And now you will both have to pay.

If you are to be this child's spiritual guide, you will have to begin again. Start with what you have in common. Recommence with the awareness of your own emptiness, of your essential worthlessness except in the service of a higher power. Make common cause in your war against the flesh, the enemy you and she now share. And, books . . . you must begin all over again with her—make them *your* ally not hers. You have both lived your lives in libraries, but where you find heretics, she finds friends, comfort, bread. Her shield of learning?—*vanity*, futility is what it is, a paper army interposed between her and God. You know her, *you know her soul.*

So how then could you have been so wrong? How could you have so misjudged the fantastic power of her concentration, her mind? You thought, separating her from her books, to put her soul on the path of Virtue. Instead you have sent it careering, spiralling down to this, to vice. Did she not warn you?—of how, deprived once of her books a few short days by doctor's order, she had quickly felt the terrible energies of her mind breaking free of their ballast. But you were so anxious to dismiss this as silly self-indulgence, excess of poetic temperament.

How can you recognize her as exceptional one minute then in the next treat her as you have all the rest? She *begged* you to impose any penance but that one—solitude without books—one voice, her own, its echo turning round and round in ever-tightening spirals. . . . Thinking, thus, to humour her like some child, you permitted her one—but just one. Kircher's *Oedipus Aegyptiacus.*[35] You suggested others, but sinking a little deeper into your fatherly good humour you allowed your child to prevail. What harm could it cause.

She is not *your* child—you *deserve* to lose her. Seeking to dilute the power of her books, instead you concentrate all into one. You should have *seen* the signs, you must have. These dreams, first this black beast of hers and then the Sacred Heart. You told yourself nuns have these dreams all the time. Christ comes to the sleeping woman's bed, extracts her heart from her wide-open chest—excruciating pain then overwhelming joy. Three days later He returns and holding His own large, still-beating heart in His hands—those beautiful hands covered with His precious blood—he inserts the Sacred Heart. It fills her entire corpus with pulsating warmth as she weeps with the ecstasy of total communion, the absolute joining of body and soul. At last wedded to him, a true Bride of Christ.

In the morning they come and beg you to tell them it was not Lucifer.

Lucifer masquerading as Christ. You warn them against allowing their passion for Him to become too . . . literal, too material. You give them a special penance, the renunciation for a few days of any sustenance. They leave gratefully, smiling.

But she is not like them—is that so hard for you to remember?

You did nothing. You heard the reports. The endless hand-washing, the fasting, mortifications increasingly severe. But *you,* you persuaded yourself they were only in just proportion to the enormity of her sins and her gifts. But her soul is not yours. Her soul is not a mathematical equation. For her, you must master new subtleties: not every battle is a frontal assault. You will not have her become an *extática,* not while her soul is in your custody. All this is your fault. And now this letter. What an unmitigated disaster.

    Padre Antonio Núñez de Miranda,
    Collegio de San Pedro y Pablo,
    Pax Xpti,[†]   [†]Peace in Christ

    Father, it is with extreme regret that I must write you about a novice whom I know you have taken it upon yourself to protect and counsel, Juana Inés Ramírez de Asbaje. After careful consideration and much prayer and consultation, I have decided that for the girl's own welfare it is necessary that we ask her to leave the convent of San José.

    As Your Reverence well knows, ours is an austere order, in keeping with the vision of our founder, Saint Teresa; and the girl's harsh penitence was not at first out of keeping with it. Hours of fervent prayer, days of fasting with only lemon water as sustenance are not uncommon with us. Neither is a certain amount of self-discipline. However, the ardour with which she has surrendered herself to these mortifications has become alarming. I must confess that to witness one so lovely become in so short a time unkempt, her hairshirt caked with the blood of scourgings . . . the icy baths, the hours spent praying on split knees, her gauntness . . . These are painful evidence of a disordered zeal. Nuns in cells adjoining hers claim she has not slept in a month. Sounds of weeping are heard issuing from her cell in the dead of night.

When these same sisters came to me about the chanting and the invocations, I felt compelled to investigate. For some weeks we clung to the hope that her fervour was for the Blessed Virgin. But the girl admits to spending entire nights poring over a tome by, I believe, a learned member of your own most esteemed and revered order. Reminded that ours does not tolerate the reading of books of any kind in private, she claims perhaps falsely that you, Your Reverence, allowed her to bring it in with her. It is this pagan—it pains me to use the word—Egyptomania that was the final straw in our decision.

By day she carries herself haughtily as though she were still at the palace, but her nights are haunted (though of this, she still admits nothing). And although she freely confesses to having broken our rules by reading, she refuses to concede that her conduct has in itself been in any way impious, or even wrong. As you must already know, it is useless to engage her in debate: no matter the extremity of her suffering and disorder, her mind burns bright and clear as the Pole star. If it were not for this, I could perhaps accept—many of the nuns here are often confused. She is not. And were it not for my deep respect and admiration for you, Father Núñez, and for all you have accomplished with the sisters of Mexico, I could not have stayed my hand this long.

She warned us that if we took this book from her she might very well go mad, and it is as if she has. I could cite other examples, but suffice it to say that the rigours of our Order have plainly unseated her too-sensitive nature. Her pain is patent, her need is real. But, however great her need, it is unacceptable that this girl, extraordinary though she is, raves of 'Naustic unions' and venerates an Egyptian goddess within the walls of our cloister!

I must ask that you prepare to receive her at your earliest possible opportunity. Once again, please allow me to express my deepest regret that she has not been able to find here with us the rest and solace she so badly needs.

Your obedient servant,
Madre Felipa de Navas
Convent of San José of the Discalced Carmelites.

No, the Reverend Mother will have none of her novices cooking up Naustical unions in their cells. She would not know a Gnostic union from a nauseous onion. And, yes, the woman is ignorant, but *you* are the fool. Your tactics are hardly less crude than hers, and far less subtle than the Enemy's. You could bully the woman into acknowledging Kircher's orthodoxy in the eyes of the Holy Office and that Isis is a blessed prefiguration of the Virgin. But you would only be compounding your own errors, the errors of which these journals must be the unflinching testament.

The austerity you imposed on this girl is really the one you covet for yourself. Grown fat on so many easy successes are you now to meet with your greatest failure *just when it matters most?* To lose the greatest mind on the continent to pagan madness?—a woman hand-delivered to you by Providence?

No. A thousand times, no . . .

Perhaps as a spiritual director you *have* no true vocation. But you have a *will.* To bring the great ship of her soul into port may have become your career's crucial campaign, its greatest challenge and danger, its turning point. You must put this right. You *will* right this ship . . .

But more gently, more patiently. A soul like crystal, lucent and brittle, must be polished. Polished, not broken. Ground down like a lens.

Let her return to the palace. Her life there is more untenable than ever. When she comes to you again, as she must—who else is there for her now?—sooner or later you two will talk of San Jerónimo, a convent known for its loose discipline and worldly pursuits. . . . And if marriage is truly reprehensible to her, or indeed no longer practicable, then a convent is the last respectable option. Bring her to see it as the only path from the palace that does not lead to perdition, to the ignominy of a *beaterío,*[†] or the infamy of a *recogimiento,*[††] a place of reclusion so complete that the windows themselves are to be mortared in.

Arrange a visit, if necessary. If our young poet thinks the convent of San José severe, give her a glimpse of life without sunlight.

[†]shelter for indigent widows, reformed prostitutes and retired actresses

[††]women's prison for delinquents, thieves, murderesses, adulteresses, street prostitutes . . .

JUANA INÉS
DE LA CRUZ,

THE SCEPTRE OF
SAINT JOSEPH

B. Limosneros, trans.

(Enter INTELLIGENCE, SCIENCE, ENVY, CONJECTURE, LUCERO.)

LUCERO:
Beauteous Intelligence, my bride
who, from the first joyous instant
I knew myself in that most blest of Realms,
have been to me, not less than Envy, companion
through good fortune and ill, so constant
so fine, so loyal, so loving
as not once to have strayed from my side
through that most terrible of times
when, deserted by Grace and by Beauty—
they unto the Almighty Seat cravenly cleaving—
only you, in your constancy, me never leaving,
into the Abyss in my company descended;
perhaps that within me should rage such a torment
as to blaze hotter yet by the light of your eyes . . .

CONJECTURE:
Let that be for Conjecture to decide,
since your daughter am I, and your Science's;
through me alone shall you divine the consequences.

ENVY:
And through me, those of feeling, since I am Envy,
your daughter too, asp that writhes
through the embers of your breast
and from the ravel of your bowels unwinds;
for, once your Science perverse
conceived on her its monstrous stillbirth,
your favourite I became, of all the vices,
that you deploy by so many exercises,
panting ceaselessly after
war unrelenting waged on Heaven. . . .

19th day of October, 1667
Monasterio de Nuestra Señora de Dolores

Juana Inés,

Another letter from you on the heels of the last, and after so much silence. Your words come to relieve me in my torment. Each night I sit down to write you and fill the page with such trash. It seems I have nothing to write that I can bear to have you read. Then your letter arrives and my head teems with things to say.

Truly am I honoured by this sonnet on Guadalupe. You said you would write it for me one day and you have. These lines I love:

> La compuesta de flores Maravilla,
> divina Protectora Americana,
> que a ser se pasa Rosa Mexicana,
> aparaciendo Rosa de Castilla;
> la que en vez del dragón—de quien humilla
> cerviz rebelde en Patmos—huella ufana,
> hasta aquí Inteligencia soberana,
> de su pura grandeza pura silla . . . [†]

But do not think you have thrown me off the trail: I know how easily this kind of elegance comes to you.

You ask if I am truly interested in the Indians' salvation, if I am not perhaps more concerned with my 'Americanist project,' as you refer to it. The world's myths, as you say, are treasures of the imagination, not to be plundered for worldly advantage. Is this what you suspect we are doing? But even if it were true, could one not answer that the gains go far beyond politics, to the healing of the American soul? Then, you ask if the Franciscans are not more devoted to taming Eve than to venerating Guadalupe. Point taken.

And you are right of course—to 'have powers over the serpent' does not necessarily mean she must use them to destroy it.

But proceed more carefully now. You intimate that the Church has modelled the Blessed Virgin on the Egyptian Isis even while stripping her of her godhood. Then you argue persuasively—and dangerously—

[†] Marvel wrought of flowers, America's divine Protectoress, who becomes the Rose of Mexico in summoning Roses from Castile; she who brings down from on high not the dragon— whose neck she bowed in Patmos— but sovereign Intelligence, and glorious sign of its greatness and purest Majesty . . .

that the Church has struggled as much to prevent her regaining the divine plane as it has Lucifer.

As a friend I repeat the question: Are you not afraid of them making you our Queen of Wisdom? I do not think the fear an idle one.

It is becoming imperative that we develop a code so as to express these thoughts more safely. Indeed like a dragon in its death throes, the Inquisition is these days at its most dangerous, flailing out in all directions . . . at perversions, heresies and false gods. At women falsely claimed to be saints, and at female poets who make Mary into Sophia, a seductress of Christ, but cloak her in the costume of a Greek wood nymph. . . . Be very careful, Juanita, with this rash plan of yours to finish your *Divine Narcissus* after all. Be more careful still to whom you show it.

un abrazo, Carlos

12th day of November, 1667
Monasterio de Nuestra Señora de Dolores
Juana,

I wish you the happiest of birthdays. To think that I have known you almost four full years. To think you were barely fifteen. . . . And is it really possible I shall soon be twenty-three? My senescence may even now be revealing itself to you in the gaps in my reasoning and the infirmity of my hand.

Still not one word of the palace. Each day you become more mysterious. I cannot shake this stubborn hope of mine that you have left that den of fops. But no, as you have said, where would you go? I readily admit that for one with neither means nor connections, life in Mexico is quite difficult enough, even for a man. You could of course come here, without prejudice or conditions. A woman's reputation is not a thing to be surrendered lightly—not even as the price of her independence—but can yours truly survive their palace so much longer than my jungle? I take you at your word: you have written how much you envy me the collegial atmosphere and the freedom of this place, the soberness of this work—my mind flashes to you on your way here and my heart races for an instant. But no, enough. We have each chosen our place, and this one, for all its satisfactions, is not palatial.

If you will say nothing of your present life, let me tell you of mine. The monastery has been astir with a discovery that lends credence to the

rumours that brought Fray Cuadros here in the first place. In the jungle
a full day southwest of here we've discovered a village, Pital, at the edge
of a ruined city. Although their ways and manner of dress are unfamiliar
to Brother Cuadros, the villagers do speak a dialect of the Mexican language and have moreover made themselves the custodians of a large
codex, an ancient Mexican book that they venerate in one of the old
temples.

We are expecting a native interpreter to arrive any day from the
Indian College in Tlatelolco, but the difficulty here, as Brother Cuadros
explains it, is not strictly one of language. These painted-books, which
we misleadingly call histories, are only the pictorial notation, not unlike
a musical score, for a performance. It is not enough to read the glyphs;
they are just the cues. The performers once carried within them the
script, and when they needed to, redrafted it. I am learning that history
was for the ancient Mexicans a dramatic art. Nor do they seem to insist
there be one sole version: it falls to each people to continually create and
recreate its own. (To us, the Creoles, who find ourselves orphaned by history, how could this fail to bring inspiration?) While for the European,
the age of myth ends and history begins with the birth of Christ, for the
Mexican, the frontier between myth and history is fluid and the influence reciprocal. Time is both linear and cyclical, and so history is also
prophecy and pattern, but nevertheless admitting of a series of variations
on central themes.

You have perhaps learned all this at your wet nurse's knee; but for me
it remains most difficult to grasp that the Mexicans not only use the
past to interpret the present, as we do, but the present to reinterpret the
past. Am I right, then, in concluding that they see Time's effects flowing not just forward but also backward? How strange to contemplate, as
if to reverse the river of causes, make it flow uphill, see the sun setting
in the east.

They keep their codex in the temple of their war god, at the western
edge of this ruined city. The book rests on a stone altar the length of a
man. Cut into the altar is a series of channels draining to a stone basin
embellished with a relief of skulls and flowers. In the shadows, overgrown with moss, is a statue with a woman's face, one side fleshed, the
other side peeled back to reveal a death's head. As for the codex, it is well
cared for, and the villagers are protective of it. We now believe their
ancestors were not just left with the book but also with the story.

Someone in this village still carries that story within him ... Though we have been allowed only cursory readings, Fray Cuadros is sure it comes from Cholula and deals at least peripherally with the Conquest. Most intriguingly, images of Cortés's interpreter Malintzin appear on almost every page.

Sleep well,
Carlos

8th day of December, 1667
Pital

Juana,

I am sorry to take so long to reply. Your letter took longer to reach me here.

Today Pital is just a fishing village on a lake, one of many linked in a network of canals and streams. The beaches are black, laced by the runnels of freshwater springs—some steaming, others deliciously cool. The shore lies shrouded in jungle and studded with curious hillocks; but on closer inspection one sees these arranged along straight broad avenues starting out from the shore. Only those building mounds immediately surrounding the village have been kept clear of the encroaching jungle.

Your letter might have taken longer still, had not Brother Cuadros's interpreter brought it in from the monastery on his way down from the capital. We thought he had come too late, but it turns out he is just in time. Just as we were preparing to return to the monastery last week, a village youth came to offer his help with the codex.

Although Fray Cuadros seems perfectly fluent to me, this new science, as practised by the Franciscans, requires that the Indian testimonies be recorded with rigorous precision. Which means, in this case, two interpreters—one whose mother tongue is Castilian, the other a native speaker of Nahuatl. The two must constantly check each other's assumptions and understandings, which are in turn tested against the testimonies of others.

This former student of his is most impressive. Brother Cuadros tells me Juan de Alva Ixtlilxochitl has become their foremost translator of the Bible into the Mexican language. Their secret project is to prepare together a version of the Song of Songs for the day when the Church deems it safe to translate. Incredibly enough, Juan's direct ancestor was

Nezahualcoyotl himself, the legendary poet-emperor. I indulge in the hope that this might finally be incitement enough to bring you here—this *is* your grandfather's work we are at. As for myself, I feel at last that my life might be close to acquiring a more weighty purpose. Surely at twenty-three it cannot be too late for me? I am like a man from the mountains first finding the sea.

And yet for all the combined skill and vast knowledge of our interpreters, the work proceeds haltingly. We suspect the boy either knows more than he lets on, or has not been completely initiated. "Did someone send you?" we ask but get no reply. At least we now have full access to the codex.

Juan de Alva and Fray Cuadros now concur: The book travelled here with a party of Mexican priests fleeing after the sack of their capital. Our codex begins where, after the kidnapping and subsequent death of Moctezuma, Cortés's army—routed and driven from the capital—returns battered and bloody to Cholula, a city swirling with rumours. Everyone, including the Spaniards, is desperate to understand what has just happened. Then, as now, so much depends on the translation. The conquest of our New Eden hanging in the balance . . .

The picture script shows us the wife of a Cholulan general, who goes to meet Cortés's beautiful interpreter in the market—the Spaniards have not eaten for three days. Each woman angles for information. The interpreter Malintzin apparently wins the contest, since at some point her new friend, thoroughly captivated, first warns then begs her not to go back to the compound where the Spaniards are housed. An ambush is planned. Malintzin is able to spin out their talk for long enough to piece together all the details of the attack. She then returns to the compound on the pretext of salvaging her personal affairs and forewarns the Spaniards.

This codex, then, contains the gossip she left with the general's wife, an account of Moctezuma's last days as a captive in the very heart of his own empire.

As I sit here among the ruins and conjure up the scene of these two women gossiping amiably in a marketplace, yet with such deadly implications, I think of Scheherazade. And of you, the palace's most enchanting songbird singing for her life.

ever yours, Carlos

2nd day of January, 1668
Pital

Dear Juana Inés,

I wish you a prosperous new year. I truly hope you celebrated it surrounded by friends, as I have.

Cuadros is kind and learned and generous, and our Juan de Alva looks
every bit the Indian prince in face and bearing yet conducts himself in all
humility. He is without a doubt the most handsome man I have seen. A
mestizo, and therefore more an exile in America than even we are, he
works ceaselessly, speaking with the natives, learning details of their
dialect, patiently listening, gaining their trust. He and Cuadros are
teaching me some of the Mexican language. So you and I shall be able to
converse a little in the language of your childhood when I get back to
Mexico. . . .

For my part I have been unwell, too feverish to concentrate long. At
the fever's highest pitch, their healer came to sit with me. He examined
me closely for evidence of bites, then, presumably to join me in my delirium, ingested quantities of a dried toadstool in order to complete his
diagnosis. I give Brother Cuadros great credit for permitting his visit. It
appears my condition was precarious and Cuadros had seen native
healers work wonders with fevers similarly severe. My recovery has been
equally wondrous. I am being treated for a loss of soul.

Cuadros smiles and tells me the diagnosis is only natural, since the
native Americans have three souls to the Christians' one.

With the worst over now, I divide my time between short, shaky walks
around the village and visits to the healer, where I strip naked to be swept
clean of noxious spirits by egret's wings. I then drink a bitter broth and,
perspiring rivers, sleep a peaceful siesta beneath leaves the size of parasols.

My walks have been fascinating. More than once have I heard the
Indians' capacity for work praised in the same measure as their short
lifespan is lamented. But then, I had never seen an Indian settlement not
in service to the Crown. While I do see great industry, I see also many
old white heads. . . .

What strikes me most forcibly is what I can only call a genius for
fashioning fine tools and materials from this wild place. Cylindrical fish
traps of woven reeds, three-pronged spears tipped with horn and bone.
All manner of baskets and platters and ladles. Polished and painted
gourds. Spinning drills for piercing jewellery, and a sort of *tarabilla:* by

pulling at handles mounted on a drum one drives an axle that in turn twists fibres of hennequen and agave into ropes fabulously strong. The principle of the wheel, Juana, they seem to have mastered quite nicely on their own.

On the twentieth, we helped the people of Pital mark the winter solstice. Even in the ruins, they preserve the ancient knowledge of the heavens. How this gladdens my astronomer's heart! Four days later we celebrated Christmas Mass. I should not have been surprised that these villagers have at least a rudimentary knowledge of the sacraments. Christians have after all passed through here from time to time. But Juanita, to see a native American so willingly taking the host into his mouth . . .

I know you are not a little disdainful of this theory of ours bringing Saint Thomas to the New World. Much more troubling to me is your observation that our theory risks making the spiritual glories of the Americas mere mimicry, and the Indians incapable of getting the details straight. But consider for a moment the Mexican conception of the Eucharist. For the centrepiece of their most holy festival, their priests grind seeds and grains into maize flour, then, stirring in quantities of blood, make out of this dough a man-sized figure. After which, at the close of a month of processions an arrow is shot through the figure's chest by an archer whom they equate with the Feathered Serpent, Quetzalcoatl. Each member of the community then receives with great awe and weeping a portion of the body and, having swallowed its flesh, cries out—*Teocualo!* God is eaten.

God is eaten, is this the savage hunger of a cannibal or the hunger of the human spirit for communion with its god? They even possess an equivalent to our Holy Wafer, in the form of little idols of dough, which they call 'food of our soul.' Who could help but recall the Gospel of John?

Whosoever eateth my flesh, and drinketh my blood, hath eternal life. . . .

The great glory of the Mexican spirit is to have perceived as well as any Christian theologian the deepest intent of Christ's ultimate sacrifice. We ourselves might well have worshipped exactly as they did, had Christ not revealed to us He wished otherwise. Indeed, the Mexicans understood this alternative perfectly, for it was from the Feathered Serpent that they had chosen to turn away, their god-prince who forbade the sacrifice of men and yet sacrificed himself.

You knew, perhaps, that the Mexicans baptized their infants as we do, and that they practised confession leading to absolution. That their earthly paradise was lost when a woman ate of a forbidden fruit. Heresy, the Inquisition will call it, but how can it be heresy when we have so miserably failed to communicate a deeper understanding of our Faith? Monasteries and convents, the symbol of the Cross, and a young man-god who willingly sacrifices himself while promising to return—so much our peoples already shared! So much in fact that the Dominicans have convinced themselves Satan, no less, must have visited America to propagate a perversion of the Gospels. Who, indeed, could blame them?—to cross an ocean and find a faith in many ways more similar to ours than that of the Jews or the Moors.[36]

No, Juana, it is undeniable. An overwhelming series of correspondences exists between the Old World and the New—if, as you have often argued, Egypt shaped our beliefs as much as did Greece, perhaps we should really be looking much further back than Saint Thomas. Lucian writes of grain ships of two thousand tons' displacement leaving your beloved Alexandria. If the Egyptians could sail around Africa, and the Phoenicians dispatch fifty ships to colonize its west coast, then why not here?

Such similarities in weaving, pottery and metal work. Both architectures developing spiral staircases, sculptured doorways and lintels—pyramids and hieroglyphs. The same insignia of kingship—sceptres, canopies, palanquins, the conch shell as royal trumpet . . . [37]

I walk through the ruins of this city that encompasses the village and see glimpses of these things. A long colonnade . . . pillars weeping lichen and lime. Fragments of fresco under moss, itself bright as paint—a face in profile, a bundle of reeds, daubs of hectic red, cobalt. Pale lintels carved with stone flowers and leaves. Sprouting from the midst of these, living rose-pink polyps, sprays of orchids and other leaves green and alive.

I have come to see this city laid out around me as a text, a living palimpsest slowly being rewritten by older scribes of Time and Vegetation—and deciphered at hazard now as I turn, wander, glancing this way and that, as if to follow the waver of a finger down a page. . . .

So now I turn your question back to you: If not through the visit of an Old World apostle how to explain such bewildering similarities in the New? We have been talking here about little else lately. Fray Cuadros can go on relentlessly reciting the lists he's compiled. Still more wondrous to me than these twinned inventions of the world are those of the spirit. In both the Mexican and Egyptian skies, a hero is birthed from the waters of darkness, beset by dragons, forges a hazardous passage through the heavens, is devoured at dusk in the Western lands of death . . . *then is resurrected.*

For the villagers here, as for the ancient Mexicans, the world has already been created and annihilated four times. And the Fifth Sun, which passes over us today, will also die, and will be the last. At the end of every fifty-two-year cycle, their universe hovers between a final, eternal destruction and a temporary renewal.

When Hernán Cortés first stepped ashore in America on Good Friday, four vast myth systems came into collision. Like four great ships rafted grindingly together in a turbulent sea, with mankind in the water, struggling not to be crushed, not to be drowned, fighting to clamber aboard any one of them and gain the shores of a new world. Good Friday, 1519, marking the death of the Son of God, was also the first day of One Reed, the year of Quetzalcoatl's death, and also the year of his promised return. Good Friday that year fell on the first day of the Mexican new century.

In Cortés the first Mexicans saw Quetzalcoatl. In this Feathered Serpent, who forbade human sacrifice and yet sacrificed himself, the first Spaniards saw a parody of Christ, and Cuadros now sees Saint Thomas. Your Athanasius Kircher finds, in Christ, Osiris resurrected. *You* have seen Narcissus. In Quetzalcoatl, the god led unwittingly to incest and his own destruction, who would fail to see Oedipus?

While in you . . . in you, Mexico sees the Phoenix.

29th day of January, 1668
Pital

Juana,

There is so much more to this settlement than we realized. Last week I think I mentioned that a string of islands reaches almost to the shore. During a walk through the village I thought to take a certain route to meet them at the beach, drawn as I was by a curious configuration of rock there. At the edge of a clearing behind the village stand two thin jagged spires and between them a gap of perhaps three armspans. The spires are not more than two storeys high, and glisten with minerals deposited by countless small springs leaking from the rock. The formation itself is not man-made, but the hollowed-out trunk that spans that gap

undoubtedly is, for through a string of perforations in the wood trickles a
fine mist of spring water. When I made inquiries as to its purpose I was
told at first that the mist kept the clearing cool, which indeed it does. And
in reason of this coolness, I thought, many women and children work there
at the water's edge, on the fresh green grass, at looms and *metates*.

But what we have at last been shown is how this archipelago once was
linked by bridges. Whatever its present purpose, I think this veil of mist
was originally intended to conceal that first bridge from the casual
onlooker. The islands constitute what I believe to have been a string of
fine craters, high-sided along the periphery yet flat and open through the
centres, which apparently still house many fine buildings. Even when
fully populated, this city on a string of jagged emeralds would have been
not just invisible from most angles of approach but virtually impreg-
nable. And yet there is every evidence that already by the time of the
Conquest, the city was abandoned save for a coterie of priests. . . .

Juan de Alva has persuaded our hosts to take us by canoe tomorrow
to the islands. It turns out that the women and children of the village live
there, in comparative safety, while the men defend the approaches. But
then why, I bade Juan ask, do we see women and children in the clearing
on the shore? *There are no villages without women,* the answer.

From the beginning this place has been an illusion maintained for our
benefit. And at last we are being allowed to peer through the mist.
Tomorrow night I will write with a full report.

Carlos

24th day of February, 1668
Pital

Juana,

Thank you for writing after all this time. I will take your anger as a
sign our work has at last piqued your interest.

Yes, there was darkness in the Mexican past. But Fray Cuadros and I
have seen on these islands the warmth and light and joy that were its
counterpoint. Juan de Alva is seeing it too—perhaps, like us, for the first
time. Last night he spoke to us with enormous passion of the work of
reform that his kinsman the poet-emperor Nezahualcoyotl began.[38] The
poet's son continued it, as did Juan de Alva's grandfather, until his work
and his life were ended by the Inquisition. It is hard, even here, not to
speak of this in whispers. Talk of reformation is as dangerous for

Catholics and Creoles now as it ever was for the Mexicans.

Our work of transcription is nearly done. You are right of course—our theories may, in the end, accomplish no more than making the Indians imitators of not the Christians but the Egyptians. But then so are we, it seems. Which would make our similarities to the native Americans almost inevitable, I suppose, as those between more or less faithful copies of one original. But there is so much more at stake here than originality, as the followers of Sepulveda tirelessly press the argument that these Indians no more have souls than do apes, and may therefore be uprooted and enslaved without conscience or compunction.

And yes I deserve to be reminded that it was sometimes the blood of slaughtered children the Mexicans used to bind their sacred dough. Tell me, is this why you seem so determined to turn your back on these stories of your childhood?

And no I had not stopped to consider that in one obvious respect the Mexican rite is the opposite of ours: for us, the wafer and the wine become the flesh and blood of God. For them, human flesh and blood become the divine ambrosia and soma.[39] They are more literal-minded in this than even we. But was it not the unfinished work of Nezahualcoyotl to sing of an unseen god whose hungers were less material?

These Indians are not, I know, the same people as the Mexica of the past. During these peaceful weeks here, perhaps I *have* been too willing to overlook the daily hardships and horrors of that past. Cuadros has reluctantly recited for me the gruesome calendar of passion plays—tearing the still beating heart from a victim's chest . . . decapitation . . . searing off the living victim's skin in a brazier of coals . . . riddling the victim with volleys of arrows . . . flaying and wearing his or her skin over one's own . . .

But is it not always to the stupefying scale of the carnage that the discussion inevitably turns, as it now has with even you and me? The thousands of victims scaling steep temple steps to be stretched out over the spine of a sacrificial stone. The endless, mind-dulling repetition, the stones grown slick under foot, the gut-lifting stench . . . With all the emotion of a peasant husking corn, a priest plucks a palpitating heart from a man's chest and sends the still conscious carcass flopping down the pyramid steps.

This picture you paint is not false. And Juan de Alva admits that where once the sacred flesh was to be eaten only sparingly by the reverent few, the capital's markets soon fairly bulged with meat for sale to any merchant hoping at the banquet table to impress a client with that most prized of dishes, the Precious Eagle Fruit. No one denies that by 1519 the Mexican empire had become a terrible engine of death. But Brother Cuadros insists the numbers we learn as schoolchildren are grossly exaggerated. One hundred and thirty thousand skulls found in one heap— who could have counted them? Where were they supposed to have been found, where are they now? What's more, this wild story of eighty-five thousand victims sacrificed on one temple top in the span of a single day—no fewer than sixty per minute? It is all but physically impossible.

And I ask you this: How do we weigh their hunger for mass sacrifice against our thirst for massacre?[40]

Our sky, like theirs, is dominated by eternity, but the eternities these two skies conceal are mirrored opposites—ours a brief death and an eternal life, theirs a brief life and an eternal death. For these strange and wondrous people of our America, the world, the cosmos entire, is a flowery temple dedicated to death, with the sacrificial stone its central altar and the temple itself poised at the edge of an abyss. Four suns, all destroyed. The close of every cycle a time of terror and omen and reproach—when a tenuous New Fire must somehow be struck in the open chest of Night.

I wonder, did you already know they call this wrenching-free of the heart 'husking the corn'? That to give birth is to 'take a prisoner,' and to die in childbirth is to be made a sacrifice?

Juana, if you can just permit yourself to suspend for a moment your admirable sympathy for the sacrificed, you will admit that to offer up to your god the thing you hold dearest—your life, your very heart—is at least a faint echo of Christ's sacrifice to the world. True, the victims are made to drink the 'obsidian wine' to calm their fear, but most go on to die without resisting.[41] After questioning Juan de Alva and Fray Cuadros closely I believe for the Mexican the greatest privilege was this, the warrior's death, precisely because of the sublime opportunity it represents: to choose his fate, and so take upon his own flesh the impress of the World's death. It was the hearts of men that sped the Sun, it was the Precious Eagle Fruit that fed even Time, and none fed as well or as long as the warrior's heart, of the captive who chose to die well for his captor.

I confess it leaves me sick at heart to contemplate the bloody strangeness of this history, the awful poetry of our Eden. Yet how extraordinary it must have felt, to be desperately needed by one's gods.

And I have been giving thought to what you seem to be suggesting: Christ, Osiris, Quetzalcoatl, Oedipus, Narcissus—all tricked or betrayed and brought low by love. All loved by goddesses, nymphs, priestesses. Woman as deceiver, as nemesis and whore—or the woman of sorrows, who has failed to protect. . . .

Indeed the Mexican war god BlueHummingbird of the South triggers his first war by arranging for the daughter of a neighbouring king to be married to a Mexican. The father arrives at the wedding ceremony to see a Mexican priest standing in the bride's place wearing her flayed skin. At the end of another fifty-two-year cycle, the BlueHummingbird beheads his own sister to spur the Mexicans to wage war for the promised land. Another woman of discord, another century of violence. After the office of Emperor, the second highest in the Mexican hierarchy is that of the Snake Woman, so called after the goddess Cihuacoatl, who leaves a sacrificial blade in the cradle of every newborn. It is to the man who occupies her office that the greatest number of blood sacrifices is made.

More Snake Women—Coatlicue, Serpent Skirt, wearing an obsidian blade swaddled like a child on her back, and a necklace of skulls. Chicomecoatl, Seven Snake, crying out in the road at night, some say for a lost child, others, for human hearts and blood.

The Mexicans did everything possible to exaggerate her monstrosity and, killing her, unleashed their wars.

Here in Pital, in the broken temple of their war god, the blood trail is still fresh, the pug marks still distinct. Is that it, is this the book you would have us resist opening? That in these signs—not so ancient, not quite buried—lies the contour of the Apocalypse, the key to its violence, its symbolic notation, its codex. . . .

2nd day of March, 1668
Pital

Juana Inés,

Until your last letter I had been thinking about going on to Yucatan. Fray Cuadros is leaving soon for Veracruz. From there, he and a few others will launch their peaceful conquest of the Maya, among whom there have been heard legends of a bearded god called Votan and of an underground treasure of books guarded by his priestess. I believe in Cuadros at least and wish them Godspeed.

Today Juan de Alva has asked me if I thought I could stay and live here. But for all the peace and beauty we have found, so unexpectedly, I cannot reconcile myself. Cuadros has the gift for living among an alien people; I do not. I have for too long felt an alien in my own land. For his own reasons, Juan cannot stay either, and bound together in our separate exiles, the Creole and the half-caste, we have I think become true friends.

Now that we have finished the translation and finished asking all our foolish questions, the elders of the village have come forward and offered, as a parting gift, to perform the codex for us tonight. Is it truly a parting gift, I wonder, or as a seal on our promise to leave? Brother Cuadros is worried we will be called on to share this food of visions they call *peyotl*.

I sit here alone at the top of a ruined temple in the midst of a jungle calling out to itself. The monkeys are roaring like lions. In the forest it is already night. It speaks to me, day and night, this hot forest, but in tongues I do not know. Birds that croak like goats, the buzz and clatter of insects shaped to inconceivable ends. The soughing of branches in the wind off the lake, and back in the trees a rich belling, like bottles half full of water dropped into a pool. . . .

Over the lake a half-moon rises pocked and golden. A buttery light sits on the skin like a second skin. Young girls go about the clearing lighting torches. Musicians arrive with their instruments. Slit drums, little gourds on sticks, flutes of clay and reed, notched thigh bones. A man brings a kind of *vihuela* or guitar with a pumpkin belly. A few dancers gather, bringing animal masks, shell tunics, colour whisks of iridescent feathers.

From the black forest at my back, moths the colour of vellum float past towards the clearing, eyes glinting ruby. . . . I sit brooding on the implications of the drama about to play itself out below me.

So accustomed are we to seeing Cortés as protagonist that this new codex cannot help but startle; for revealed therein as neither god nor apostle, he drives the plot merely through his insatiable appetite for the abstractions of power and gold. Meanwhile, Moctezuma, captive in his own palace, brooding on his fate, retreats to the seclusion of the fabled Black Room, its stinking walls smeared in blood. Is he the blood-spattered devil rumoured by the Mexicans themselves to gorge daily on his favourite dish, the tender flesh of newborns? Is he a monster of vicious passions with four hundred concubines, among them his insatiable sister? Or is he the chaste and mystic philosopher-king described by the Spaniards who knew him, and who after all would have had every motive to vilify?

Moctezuma knows that choosing the warrior's death at the hands of his captor means submitting unflinchingly to its ironies and humiliations. Their chief instrument is Cortés's ignorant and slow-witted country chaplain, Father Olmedo, more mercenary than priest, who has the effrontery to lecture, to try to *convert Moctezuma II*—the most learned man in the New World, its equivalent of Saint Augustine. The emperor whose title is the Speaker. Yet now, who else is there to talk to, who else will enter the Black Room, who else can help sort through the haunting intersections of their hopes and faiths?

The Mexicans are a chosen people, with a duty to convert by force the peoples of this earth—force them to worship and to nourish the Sun, keep it moving through the heavens, serve the god of war who takes and holds all other gods prisoner. Moctezuma is not merely responsible for his people, his empire. No, he has custody of the very universe, the frail Fifth Sun. Has any mortal known such a crushing destiny? In his place what man, Christian or pagan, would not have succumbed to doubt, to guilt? For by now the brief rise of the Mexica must seem, to the prisoner Moctezuma, more and more like a time of cataclysm, famine and death, perpetual war. And sin—the Mexicans understand sin, know the stench of rotting roots, of a sacred tree overwatered.... Fifty thousand sacrifices a year, ten to purchase each hour of sun.

You and I, Juana, have spoken often of destiny. Mine, I thought, was a simple one, until I met you. Their destiny has led them here, and his, to this: to suffer until his death the insolence of a dullard and the mocking eyes of this woman who sees everything but whose own outline is constantly shifting. If he is elusive, she is multi-form. One name could never suffice. She is forever sloughing skins, mistress of tongues, master of language, oracle. La Malinche interprets for him, who speaks for the people. But, a prisoner now, without her he cannot speak *to* the people. And so for a brief time one person—a woman—occupies the two highest offices of Tlatoani and Cihuacoatl, Snake Woman and Speaker. Small wonder the Indians revere the woman they claim to revile.

This woman controls the information. Without her he cannot act. But she serves Cortés, and her words have the power to humiliate and deceive. She knows just how to goad him, to accent the ironies, to underscore the chaplain's plodding insolence, just as once she knew how to temper and smooth the rash words Cortés first spoke to him. But the emperor knows that, more even than words, she interprets actions. This is why he needs her now, and she understands. La Malinche understands how to exploit the confusions that surround her. She knows too how to exploit the growing confusion in Moctezuma's mind.

She is everywhere, the great mother whore in the arms of all his adversaries. She tempts him with her beauty, offers to become his lover as she has with Cuauhtemoc, FallingEagle, the commander designated to replace him. But she also knows at times Moctezuma still thinks of Cortés, his captor, as his father and so must not lie with her. Mother of mercy, she holds the power to comfort and forgive. She holds the key to his redemption and to the encrypted destiny of the world. Woman of discord, she grows to fill his mind.

I cannot help reading our transcription of the codex with a sense of what might have been if not for her. And for me, had I not met you. . . .

In a marketplace, two women sit gossiping, suspended in time, on the eve of one battle and the morrow of another, reducing all battles and all outcomes to this one moment. One woman tells the other of an emperor she has known, how just before his death she held up to him his own fallen image, how she became his eyes, his ears, his voice. His nemesis.

Leaning back against a warm stone in the midst of a nervous, bustling market, this woman who is all women and none complacently pats her belly that ripens with Cortés's son, with the fruit of a new and hybrid race on a continent that she, the new Eve, has given a new destiny.

This jungle all about me lies littered with the shattered symbols of our New World, yet I think of nothing but you. And I am not alone. The Viceroy's cousins offered me a parting gift also. It is one I had thought to keep to myself but now share with you: that secretly they have begun calling you the Pythoness of Delphi.

Whenever I have asked you to join me, you have always said no, but in this last letter you say you cannot, you say it is too late. What has happened? Something is wrong, I know it. I will be in Mexico in two weeks. Please, hold on. Too late for what?

Carlos

JUANA INÉS
DE LA CRUZ

Alan Trueblood, trans.

refrain

Black is the Bride,
the Sun scorches her face.

verses

     Red clouds swirling dark
make the Bride think she's black,
yet there's no shadow in her,
of pure sunlight no lack.
The crucible of the Sun
leaves her purity intact.
     Black is the Bride,
the Sun scorches her face.
     Placing next to the Bride's
the Sun's spotless light
makes the creature look dark
since God is purest bright.
Yet, basking in the Sun,
she grows fairer in men's sight.
     Black is the Bride,
the Sun scorches her face.
     Bathed in sunlight,
the Bride burns with his rays,
growing in fairness
as she draws near his blaze;
spotless, without flaw,
in his unceasing gaze . . .

*Villancico: 'peasant'
songs especially
cherished by the
poor, particularly
in New Spain. A
cycle of lyrics or
simple carols to be
sung on a religious
holiday; these, at
the Feast of the
Immaculate
Conception in
Puebla, Mexico.*

GUADALUPE

In Mexico, each
December 12th, as
many as two mil-
lion pilgrims—the
devout, whether
Christians or of a
different faith—
come, many on
their knees, to file
through
Guadalupe's
Basilica. Near one
exit is a hall
crowded to a height
of several metres
with rustic,
postcard-sized
illustrations above
simple testimonials
to Guadalupe's
intercession over
four centuries . . .

[12 Dec 1994, Hotel Xanadu]

GOOD MORNING GUADALUPE, it's your big day today, how are you?
We are so calm after this night of firecrackers, siren-night of writing
shooting stars through my mind and through this pleasure dome in
stereo. All the stately joys of home, my Hotel Xanadu. Lifted now its
latex siege of Paradise's milk machines rolled back its fell artillery /
decamped the Trojan whores. Their honey-dew melodies plucked on
dulcimer / before the Tartar hordes. . . .

Up at dayglo dawn by Dupont friends my compliments, tanks for the
chemistries. Down at nine to seize the day, notebook in one cramped
hand. Down through mildly maidly ribaldries, Hoover wheeze, crusted
sheets . . . slow day in the ancient trade. At the reception Deskclerk
Beetlebrows fingers breathmints, condoms in a candy dish. Bordello eyes
boring into mine—sleazesmirk: sleep well, *señorita?*

See him browbeaten now at my reply. Not at the Basilica today, infidel?

Ah, Guadalupe—nervous fingers start from the delving dish—Some
protector, she is—seven people died up there last year. Don't tell me
you're going there.

Al banco primero, I turn to go—why talk to him.

The bank!—yes even better, he answers smiling now. The pickpockets
on the hill will thank you. The banks are closed today—but you all use
machines don't you. Careful they don't kidnap you in the little room.
What, you haven't heard the stories? Come back—*amiga, ven un ratito,
que te lo diga.* Sometimes these guys kill you but then one married a *victi-
ma* just last week in jail. Better pray to Guadalupe you get one of these,
cabrones banditos románticos. I'll pray too.

Thanks for the bulletin. Enter the streets. Banco ProMex on the
corner. Jangle of nerves but it's not the romantic bandits, it's you,
Mother Protectress of Mexico. I could stay away, not go—like the
cathedral yesterday—fly eight long hours from Canada, just to ride the
metro again.

But the corner brings more succour than bargained for—know this
traveller: the ATMs, their uniformity, are your friends. We too have our
rites, universal truths—polling booth verities. Insert card here, strip
down, strike coded blow for global shopocracy. Out on the sidewalk

sandalled pilgrims pause, hats-doffed, as the supplicant withdraws absolved / from greed's confessional.

I swell by a single insignificance the tide of pilgrims lining up to ride battered breadbox buses to her Basilica. Brown hills shorn like sheep, or bristling with TV-towers. All, save the slate Basilica on Tepeyac, her sainted montecule. Guadalupe it's years I've dreamed of you.

The traffic tangle slows, checks, bogs, on this pilgrim flood swelled on tributary lust. Bus after bus stuck fast in amber. We get down to walk, we are a hundred thousand here. On foot we follow a shattered causeway over the dustbed of an ancient lake. An Aztec avenue of skulls straight as a die / straight as an assembly line kilometres long. Cookiecuttered babycrania one thousand two thousand three carved in stone, I try to count these low reliefs alone isn't anyone keeping score?

More, ever deeper without relent—last metro stop: Talpa. Thousands stream out jostle to cross this *burning plain* to meet the mother of their maker, Virgin Bride. Muttered prayers parched on lips slaked on hopes fed on highway dust from across all Mexico. Most walk others crawl on bludgeoned knees. Some now fall to join this bloody joinery of unhinged martyrdom. A brother and sister hand in hand, unspeakable torment in their unlined faces gory knees, smoky eyes defiant. Please get up please stand take my hand.

There an old man, his running sores—is this leprosy?—is that plague over there *Welcome to the Decameron*—bring me your disease I shall make it holy.

From up North / from the icecrystal palaces borealis we never get a view like this. *I will never forget this.*

Stop! Hey you can't stop here to rest *to write?*—are you a journalist what are you doing?

I am afraid.

Between two grandsons a shrunken waif on a litter—*abuelita, abuelita* it's not much farther it's very near now we will get you there don't fear we have carried you this far we would carry you a million miles to her she's just ahead.

Guadalupe.

It won't be long. We are half a million now. Guadalupe, mother of our sorrows mother of our pain. Heal me. I am afraid.

So too cloaked in terrors these shitscared men in riot gear. SWAT bottlefly blue. Alien visors, plexiglass shields / black billyclubs clutched to wield. Last gasp gasmasks-to-don for fear of extinction / for block after block they stand shoulder to shoulder as past we walk this alien avenue of skulls. How many skulls how many of us now is anyone keeping score isn't anyone keeping count / when does the indigent insurrection start? Cue the newsreel. Move along.

What are you writing there?—I said *move along.*

At the gates waits my deliverance from terror, my comic disbelief: BANCOMEXICO LES DA LA BIENVENIDA A LOS PELERI-NOS GUADALUPINOS.†

†BancoMexico wel-
comes Guadalupe's
pilgrims

Red, white and green, a huge banner. This is better much better this devil I know. *Gracias* BancoMexico, a thousand graces.

Inside the compound a fine cold drizzle falls purgatorial. Aztec dancers circle just inside the gates, solstice impending. Logdrums boom—echoes snuffed, fleshchoked in the dusthued mass. Clay pipes . . . a sinister fluteshrill gaiety—symphonic panther caged in too few notes. On the ground, prone, a small stiff girl. They lift her from the pavement pass her round lift her to the sky I lose sight of her in the sun's harsh emergency. Movealong humid humansea of faith—two hundred thousand eyes overflowing. Mine . . . River of salt that wells us to the old Basilica above the new—

Old Basilica. Terminus of a million hearts. We move through by the thousands by the hour, through the great doors. Some deep place in us knows already this strange mobwalk evolved for paying respects / homages to monumental art and kingly death. Where have I learned this shunting, metronomic shuffle, keeping time marking time dancing to time's forward ripple—instant of momentum arrested, then, again, dancesteps for the leg-ironed . . . shift, rock, glide. Hypnotic puppetry of unhinged hips and knees coaxed, tugged—expertly jigged.

We are a million now.

Floor smooth as a stone watercourse. River of whisper, hoarse glide of soles. Voices funnel up through my chest—sternum-tuned, resonant—up through the nave—

A cough a whisper, a baby—its brief cry . . .

Slate. Stone.

Smoked light slants through a vaulted hush.

Incense, intense resins of pine . . . this is *copal* burning. . . .

Wet hair, sweat—plump fatty flowerscent—what are those *señora*? Her eyes a mass of seams narrow an instant—*Nardo*, tuber rose . . . have you come from far to see her, *joven?* Yes very far, a distant galaxy. Her answering glance of shared piety, linked faith.

And we do share a faith—*Old México,* this truly *exists,* still, for now, this motherland of contingency—eggshell earth, famished sky, time recycled, spinning down to die. Time as cannibal dish, simmering, shrewd—apocalypse as not time but *place.* Guadalupe our public defender, all rise as the celestial court enters. Dusky maid / mistress of roses, mothershimmer of immanence. . . .

Then, unasked, unhoped, the brief miracle of a quiet mind. . . .

Moment of mercy, grace. Blind reprieve.

Peace. Stay.

I sway forward without thought, without eyes.

Stay with me.

Slow feeling returns, old sweet pain of penshaft to callused finger— writer hold out your crooked hands.

It begins again—*this,* this I must write as I'm carried past—a children's exhibit a *crèche* of handmade paper faxpaper crêpe-paper garlands festoon an oval placard, petal-trimmed. It hangs at the neck of a *papier maché* effigy in white and black: *Sor Juana Offers Her Love to Guadalupe.*

Sor Juana offers . . .

Hello old friend.

But the shunting tide again carries us apart—I'll come for you wait for me. Just a little longer I promise. A day or two when I'm stronger. Thighspierced fasted and clean. I've come for you. I can be strong for you. Soon.

On we the million drift, and above the shuffling mass Indian headdresses bob like quail crests. On through the hall of happy endings—*exvotos,* tales with childlike pictures—tableaus of propitiation embroider the walls with little testaments and thanks to our mother intercessor stormshelter / opener of the way.

And Juanita standing guard at the hall of happy endings—tell me it's an omen. *Tell me.*

12 December 1872: Thank you Guadalupe for saving our brother during a mine explosion . . .

12 December 1914: Thank you Mother for healing our daughter who was burned by kerosene . . .

12 December 1971 . . . for saving our tractor from a grave engine fire . . .

12 December 1771 . . . his wife and all the farm animals thank you for saving her husband from a deadly fever . . .

12 December 1763 . . . from bandit rapists on the highway to Puebla . . .

12 December 1930 . . . for helping our father escape from prison. . . . 1982 . . . for the cure of syphilis. . . . 1940 . . . from a sinking ship. . . . 1961 . . . breast tumours so large she could not feed her newborn son. . . . 1827 a firing squad. . . . 1931 trainwreck. . . . 1786 the tempation of incest. . . . 1867 a mine cave-in. . . . 1894 for the rescue of our daughter from four months of *desequilibrio mental*. . . . 1794 gored by a bull. . . . 1852 attacked by a maddened female burro. . . . 1987 a chemical spill. . . . surgery small-pox cholera plague. . . .

River of time river of mercy river of milk and honey / flow on sweet secret Nile / carry us home on the breath of god. I am hurt, I am heart-sick, and broken.

carry me

I am weary I am yours please / I hunger I thirst—carry me—I love I want I burn

sweet time, wrap me in your arms I can't go on.

Carry me.

At the exit across from the new Basilica, a Mass. We are two million now. A song surges up from the thronged amphitheatre, song for a hundred thousand corded throats, one monstrous organ, one slow hymn piped gasping belling through a hundred thousand souls. Calling so lightly to god.

But this music, this alien grace, I know this melody. *Blowin' in the Wind. Can this be happening?* How strange now, this sixties poetsong here and now and always. What is the language, what lyric are they singing to this Dylantune, what Mass can this be?

How can I write this?

I cannot go in there I cannot go down cannot go on I am too filled with you. In my eyes I heard you, in my ears I saw.

From what Beulah termed the 'fuckmuck' of twentieth-century psychoanalysis, an undeniably unsavoury industry has sprung, resorting to theories of psychosis, narcissism, lesbianism, masochism and even penis-envy in order to account for Sor Juana's prodigious hungers and accomplishments. Beulah, for complex reasons of her own, dubbed these new inquisitors 'Scarabs.'

PSYCHIC MASOCHIST

" . . . all human beings—to differing degrees—become addicts of 'psychic masochism. . . .'"

EDMUNDO BERGLER†

ACCORDING TO FREDO ARIAS DE LA CANAL (a disciple of Bergler, and another of Sor Juana's posthumous psychoanalysts), poets wish to be 'poisoned and devoured by the serpent,' and in turn wish to poison and devour it. The psychic mechanism is as follows:[42]

> 1) 'I wish to be killed by the maternal breast.'
> 2) The daemon's reproach: 'You wish to be killed by your mother's breast.'
> 3) Defence of the 'I': 'On the contrary, I wish to kill my mother's breast.'
> 4) The daemon's reproach: 'You have been aggressive towards your mother's image.'
> 5) The 'I''s acceptance: 'Yes, I have been aggressive towards my mother's image for which I feel guilt and a desire to be punished.'

For Arias, the punishment consists in a desire to have the penis devoured, the penis which is the projection of the maternal breast. The symbol of the devouring penis is the asp. In sex, the vagina is the projection of the mouth, and the penis the projection of the maternal breast, and the semen a projection of milk. The whole represents an inversion and a form of revenge: the serpent (penis) poisons and devours and in turn is poisoned and devoured (by the vagina).

The source of aggression towards the mother is hunger: 'You are starving me.' Even when he is fed, the poet's anger remains: 'Even when

†From "The Superego" by Edmundo Bergler, as quoted in *Intento de un psicoanálisis de Inés Juana y otros ensayos Sorjuanistas*, by Fredo Arias de la Canal. Arias de la Canal, during his attempt to psychoanalyze Sor Juana, describes Bergler thus: " . . . the most brilliant mind of the twentieth century. A man who has given humanity the opportunity to know itself. It would be a tragedy that that humanity should come to destroy itself for not having understood this man . . ."

you feed me you are poisoning me.' The poet says: 'I will feed myself by fashioning objects of oral beauty . . . milk and honey.'

And Arias continues:

In order to go more deeply into her [Sor Juana's] repressed curiosity or libidinized ignorance, one will have to take into account her mad hunger to know, to expound, and to put her learning on exhibition. And thus, in this so simple manner will we be able to induce and prove that this woman at her most tender age acquired what Bergler called psychic masochism; that is, that her fear of death, impotence and rejection she converted to unconscious pleasures. . . . [43]

Just as the Middle Ages wracked its mind inventing instruments of torture to apply to criminals, the seventeenth century underwent fevered contortions discovering ever more subtle and dolorous means to torment and mortify one's own body. Medieval man prosecutes, punishes and avenges crime in his neighbour; Baroque man hunts, finds, and wreaks vengeance for crime in himself. But in the convents of the 17th century, the masochistic modalities of asceticism have rightly celebrated their most cruel and delirious triumph.... [44]

    LUDWIG PFANDL, *Sor Juana Inés de la Cruz, Mexico's Tenth Muse*

DELIRIOUS
TRIUMPH

BEULAH SURELY SAW THE IRONY: In 1684 Sor Juana's friend Carlos Sigüenza received a commission to write a history of the aristocratic convent of the Immaculate Conception, a few blocks from Sor Juana's own. Long excerpts of Carlos's chronicle come down to us through one Ludwig Pfandl: German historian, the first of Sor Juana's psychoanalysts, and for Beulah, the dark prince of Scarabs.

Beneath the delirious triumphs detected by Pfandl lurks the old theme of convent as harem, and of the male ecclesiastics who visited them as sultan-stallions. A certain vein in Medieval literature fairly courses with the lubricities of nuns, monks and priests, of which Boccaccio provides among the more pleasing examples. The convent or monastery as house of corruption continues as a literary device beyond the Renaissance, finding perhaps its most influential expression in de Sade, whose treatment is stripped of the past's light smirking and tainted in the more sanguinary hues with which his name has become synonymous. Nor were dark tales of misconduct confined to the European side of the Atlantic. From their respective journeys across seventeenth-century America, an Englishman, Gage, and an Italian, Carreri, bring us snapshots (the latter's at least untainted by Gage's Protestant bias) of moral laxness and not infrequent scandals in many of Mexico City's convents. Gage writes:

> It is ordinary for the Fryers† to visit their devoted nuns, and to spend whole days with them, hearing their music, feeding on their sweet-meats. And for this purpose they have many chambers which they call

†friars

Loquitorios, to talk in, with wooden bars between the nuns and them, and in these chambers are tables for the Fryers to dine at; and while they dine the nuns recreate them with their voices.[45]

More reliable witnesses confirm that the nuns received their visitors without veils, in open defiance, as it were, of the prohibitions of numerous bishops. Not even the chastening rule of separation by a grille could be strictly enforced. . . .

Heady indeed the atmosphere in a nunnery housing up to five hundred cloistered women: as many as a hundred and fifty brides of Christ, along with, as their servants and slaves, three to four hundred more mulattas, *indias*, and *mestizas* . . . for the most part poor and vulnerable. In most of New Spain's convents, a communal religious life was rather the exception. The cells of the wealthiest nuns were two-storey apartments with inner staircases connecting the kitchens, bath-tubs, water closets and servants' niches to the extensive sitting, dining and sleeping rooms above. The ratio of servants to nuns was as high as five to one. To round out the household, there often figured either girls from the convent school or else a class of women intriguingly designated as 'favourites.'

And so even today, images of the cloister-as-devil's-playground linger, due at least in part to our own idle misconceptions. What do they do in there? we wonder. Idle hands . . . In actuality Mexico's convents were a veritable font of good works, nourishing much of the continent's educational infrastructure, alimenting ceaseless missions of charity, and, perhaps most significantly, preserving islands of decent entertainment amid the bullfights and the charnel houses.

Girls under the nuns' tutelage performed uplifting plays and concerts for the public, while into the convents' locutories streamed a sparkling file of aristocrats and rich burghers to hear music, recitations of poetry and elevating conversation. So although the occasional misadventure was not unforeseeable, it was far from being the norm. In fact it might be fairly said that without the civilizing influence of its convents, Mexico City would have appeared less a polished colonial jewel than a coarse and fractious Wild West boomtown, for a boomtown it was.

Convents were also hives of industry, teeming with stalwarts producing handicrafts and wines for the communal purse and cultivating orchards for the confection of conserves and sweetmeats, both for sale and for the liberal delectation of convent visitors. Only natural then that such worldly occupations should give rise periodically to financial and political intrigues. Cases of nuns charged with plotting—even carrying out—the murder of a fellow sister, or less frequently a prioress are not unknown, in the annals of the Church.

The darker current of convent life that Pfandl presents undoubtedly existed, a potent decoction of sexual repression and spiritual hunger. To this day something inexpressibly poignant—a palpable, honey-sweet longing—clings to the term *bride of Christ*. But, even here, there exist alternative renderings. Judith C. Brown's *Immodest Acts: the Life of a Lesbian Nun in 17th-Century Tuscany* is a model of just proportion that glosses over neither the baroque contradictions in the spirituality of one Sister Benedetta, nor the persecutions she was brought to suffer. Brown is a paragon of scholarly restraint in her handling of scenes such as one in which an abbess reads out a sermon while her repentant charges lay on the whip.

In Pfandl, on the other hand, we find both the tone of dubious regret and the whiff of pious sadism we might recognize from the five o'clock newscast. In Pfandl's seventeenth-century convents, even a lenient one such as that chronicled by Carlos Sigüenza, the inmates hunger for miracles. What's more (and lest this seem too strong, Pfandl soon cites Sigüenza's findings at length), many holy sisters *thirst for blood:* 'to see it, to smell it and dearer still to spill it in a bloody holocaust from one's own body.'[46] Pfandl adduces such circumstantial evidence to construct a picture of Sor Juana 'in the grasp of a dark sexual delirium and tortured by obsessive visions of self-castration.'[47]

Again, the convent of the Immaculate Conception was considered lax. Juana, an ultra-sensitive girl then still in her teens, could not therefore have failed to be terrified by what she discovered in the cloister of San José—renowned, among all of New Spain's twenty-two convents, for its austerity. Indeed, in such a setting who might not be terrified, also, by what one finds within oneself?

Pfandl (citing Carlos Sigüenza) documents five individual cases of what our dabbler in psychoanalysis characterizes as a 'cult of cruelty':[48]

...a nun of the royal convent, the Reverend Mother Isabel de San José († 1642), by her ascetic mortifications provoked chills of horror and admiration. Mother Isabel paid one of her own servants to whip her; money and gifts were administered in proportion to the efficacy of the lashing administered to the nun. Further, every Friday noon she arrived in the convent refectory, where her fellow sisters were gathered to eat, removed her veil, stripped to the waist and while whipping herself confessed, between cries and laments, to the little sins and imperfections of her religious life. ...

Mother Ana de Cristo († 1652), a fanatical auto-flagellator, devised for herself a special instrument of martyrdom. She wore against her skin, day and night, two crosses, one against her back, the other against her chest, crosses covered on one side with sharp barbs of iron. ...

Mother Antonia de Santa Clara († 1659) petitioned that her face be branded with the following dictum: *Esclava del Santísimo Sacramento* (Slave of the Most Holy Sacrament). Her petition denied, the nun took a knife and carved the inscription in her left forearm. ...

Mother Francisca de San Lorenzo († 1663) favoured the lash. The walls and floor of her cell were reddened and spattered with blood. Nevertheless, her most fully pleasurable agony, or fully agonized pleasure, derived from being whipped by several women (selected from among the huskiest servants) at once. ... Fasting, she would present herself at lunch, eyes blindfolded ... over her mouth a set of clamps. ...

Mother Tomasina de San Francisco († 1675) bound her arms and legs and half her body with rough cords and iron chains; moreover against her back and chest she wore metal grates ... in her shoes she placed pebbles, and in special cases of penitential rapture she scattered sharp tacks in among the stones ... but the unhappiest and most saintly sacrifice ... was an invisible cross of singular weight. Her mother lived in the cloister with her, and the nun (who as a girl must have suffered unspeakable humiliations and mistreatment) endured day after day as the mother satisfied in their cell a sadistic relish for whipping the long-suffering daughter. ... [49]

PAST MIDNIGHT NEWS SPREADS through the streets stranger to stranger to me: *gracias a Guadalupe*, there were no deaths on Tepeyac hill today. And maybe in all of Mexico or the whole wide world the flood is dammed—at death's stadium, the turnstyles jammed—for one spin from sun to sun, a fasting Death's Ramadan. Near dawn I sit night table to knees and though again I can't sleep, for the first time in a very long time the engine in my head is fed, on something other than me. Difference engine, engine of siege that severs me—I will find it other food—it sleeps, it leaves me peace. By the intercession of her grace, heal me.

On the way home this afternoon from her Basilica, bus after bus in mind-numbing succession passes. We walk and walk, quit turning back to look at the sound of the next bus overstuffed. Elderly the walkers mostly, and amputees not nimble enough to bus jockey. Amputee veterans of the factory wars, human bulwark against the domino effect of equality. One skates past me on a trolley—double-amputation at the groin—a jester's nod and wink, simian knuckle-push—he sails off on his plinth, heroic bust to Fortitude. And I am ashamed now to write this.

At last a metro stop. Out of the furious sunset we lurch and pitch and clop down the granite steps past row after row of holographic portraits of Our Mother. Their manila backing stamped SHELLTOX INSEC-TICIDE, frame after frame the same—what does this mean, does it mean *anything?*

Get off at Metro Hidalgo: breach again to breathe the copper air almost dark except for the west's glower and sulk, while across the street a stage starts up—an animated film lurching to life. On a platform of battered plywood boxes a troupe acts out a holographic diorama of the Guadalupe legend, here known universally, like the nativity.

Humble Indian Juan Diego thrice visited by a vision of the Virgin in native form and dress on Tepeyac hill, ancient shrine to the Aztec mother goddess. Three times Juan Diego goes to the Bishop—episcopal sophisticate incarnadine—but only on the third is Juan believed when he spills out onto the palace floor a clutch of roses blooming out of season. And in the robe that carried them, an after-image—miraculous transfer—of the dusky Virgin.

GRACE

Last scene plays out, winds down, the actors young and striking strike the set. Full-lipt kohl-eyed Juan Diego comes up to me—with every step more handsome toothsome—says *Buenas* . . . Guadalupe watches.

You're not from here.

No from far away.

Do you know the story of the play?

Yes I know it.

Well?

Why do you perform it here?

Where?

Here, the *quemadero*.

Ah, you mean, *where the onlookers clung to the branches of the trees like human pine cones.*

You know.

Yes we know. We know our history.

Then why.

The government—*el PRI*—pays for us to perform it here. We are graduate students but this is how we live. . . .

I start to walk, he says how well do *you* know our history? Do you know that that cinema on the corner sits exactly on the burning ground? Why not go in and ask them how they can go there and watch Sylvester Stallone and Cantinflas?

What would they answer?

Some will say if you don't learn when to laugh this place will kill you. You are from the North. Is it true Stallone is only four feet tall?

Do they laugh as much at him as Cantinflas?

You are joking, my friend, but they do, yes. Go in and see for yourself. Many of the people in there laughing also know where the *quemadero* was. They will tell you nothing happens for nothing. Coincidence does not exist here. *Mira*, a few of us are meeting at the Opera Bar. If you come I promise *not* to show you where they tell the tourists Pancho Villa rode in on his horse and shot a hole in the ceiling. The atmosphere is good.

I have to go.

It's not what you think. That is my wife standing over there.

Guadalupe?

Smiles his beautiful young man's smile as Mother of America comes forward, shakes hands hard like a man. More serious, older, a little less beautiful than he.

All right if you can't come, walk with us for a moment.

Estoy cansadísima.

I understand your weariness, you've come from Tepeyac.

It shows?

It won't take long, this will interest you.

We walk over to a little plaza joined to the cinema. Plastic tarps strung overhead, bindertwined to parking signs and pounded stakes in the asphalt roadbed. Through the cough and sough of hurricane lamps slinging shadows over vendors' stands we walk. Soft drinks bob in galvanized tubs, with ice chipped from blocks slid from the beds of cattle trucks. Bonecages of meat. Meat racked hooked diced shaven cleavercleft. Fatsizzle onionhiss -

Why—?

To show you.

Show me what? *show me food show me blood show me what—*

Were you here for the Day of the Dead? Just last month. No? You must see that sometime.

What do you want me . . . ?

This is the exact place they set up the stakes and scaffolds, right here, where we're standing.

They know—?

Oh they know. Look at them.

I don't *see.*

They are eating, with . . . joy. They are eating their own deaths. . . .

Ah so you *do* see don't you—wait, don't go.

On and on I walk alone lapping the park always swinging back to here blackhole of truth and slowly I do begin to see, by the coughed light of hurricane lamps and stars poking through the awningsky. There the slow burble of aluminum vats, *atole* and hot chocolate, there electric blenders clear fruit-clogged throats, wicker baskets of tamales—little cornhusk bundles swaddled, tucked like quail in beds of rushes. Cornmeal gorditas stuffed with zucchini flowers, resolved on the griddle like tea leaves, low-tide skiffs—in gypsy patterns that whisper beckon—*Oye, hay flor de calabaza,* delicious, try one—

And he spoke true: this is the word for how they eat.

Joy.

Sweet corn—*elotes* with mayonnaise, *¡ven prueba, amiga!* green mangoes diced on sticks like ginger flowers like pineapple *grenadas*—tart grenades bursting on the palate's steppes. *Ven, señorita,* try this too—mine are just as good as theirs and different—no you don't pay, not this day, you have come for her from far away. *Oye*—here, try sweet papaya with chilli and lime. *Mi vida*—try these *tamales con rajas*—very hot. No you don't pay, my boss is off in Acapulco. *Oye, flaquita,*[†] from California?—all you *chicanas* are so thin—eat! Don't listen to him, *corazón*—look, these tacos with *piña mi hija* are to die for—how many, only six? let's make it eight, they're small anyway—*taquititos!*—how much they charge you for the tamales?—*nada?* that is only as it should be on this day.

† skinny

Mexico sweet bed of rushes I remember you—once as a girl I walked these streets. Childbride of the jack of hearts, do you remember me, that girl?

And how could I not trust how could I not eat with you who ask me are we not all dying, *señorita,* are we not alike in this? Who is not alone? Let me feed you. Together let us eat our deaths. What counts more than this, this one meal this night? *¿Quién sabe lo que nos trae la mañanita? ¿Quién sabe, de veras?*

All the gentle courtesy—how can people speak this way, even here or especially in the quake zone, world's largest landmine—time's chalked endzone.

Twenty million people / seventy thousand taxis licensed to kill / twenty thousand factories big and small vomiting a chemical mind-sucking in/solvent-sea. How can it be that still you speak this way? *mi amiga mi hija, mi vida, mi corazón*—my friend my daughter my life my heart. Is this how to speak to one another in the jaws of hell—teach me, how you do this how you live, teach me this poverty.

Let me stand beside you when the trumpets bark

Hide me in the flowerscreen bower of your gentle smile, archaic courtesy

Yes I will sit down and eat. With you.

April 12th, 1995.

ERIC HEFFNER, LL.B., LEFT HIS OFFICE EARLY and drove out to see me. He was coming to collect my cheque, a courtesy call both to save me the trouble of coming into the city and because a certain journalist was keeping her dogged eye on his office. He was not particularly good at cloak-and-dagger. I think she found me in the first place by following him.

It can be mildly deflating to see your lawyer in weekend clothes. Orioles cap, corduroy shirt bulging over a thin brown belt. Jeans, hiking boots. All of which brought a certain youthfulness to a freckled face lengthened appreciably by the receding hairline. He had something about him of the summer camp director. In fall.

"What if, just for argument's sake," he said, "and I stress, speaking hypothetically—you could keep your job?"

I sat silent for a moment. Awkwardly he leaned back in a willow chair across from me on the couch, a driftwood coffee table between us. His features were hard to make out at first against the bright white drapes shutting out the afternoon sun. The possibility that things might simply carry on as before had never occurred to me. I'd only just got used to the idea that I might be facing a stay in prison. Now this vague, unreasonable sense of having been cheated of my dessert. I was being rehabilitated?

"Not so fast. What I'm trying to tell you is if, and I mean *if* the police decided not to file, everything else'd be up for grabs. That is, if you aren't determined to fuck things up thoroughly and completely."

"You're saying they're not already."

"Thoroughly, but incompletely."

"That's good, then."

"If the girl doesn't die." Watching his face soften slightly I sensed my lawyer and I were arriving at a new plateau in our relationship. "I'm sorry, Don. It's rough and I've been pretty hard on you."

"Drink, Counsellor?"

"What do you have?"

"Scotch. Ice."

"How about some ice water."

ROUGHING
IT

He accepted the glass without comment and leaned toward me without pausing to drink, glass in both hands, elbows propped on out-turned knees. "I need to know what you want, Professor. The less the police do, the more it falls to the university to handle it internally. This would be a nightmare for them. I'd see to that and they know it."

Did I want to keep my job.

No. I wanted an unending series of ever more distinguished situations offered to me over the years at a manageable but rapid rate. A stately, considered ascension towards eminence emeritus. No, I did not want just to keep my job.

"Anyone following the news of course will want to see you get yours—there's tremendous pressure to fire you. But such purgatorial agonies they'll suffer! Meetings and more meetings. Committees struck, policies parsed, ethicists consulted. Cagy and conflicting legal opinions tendered . . ."

This kind of proceeding had become a graveyard for careers, and not just for the accused. Perhaps I'd heard. Schools all over the continent had been badly chewed up, from presidents on down. This would just be another case where proof would prove perversely hard to come by and a wrongful dismissal suit just a misstep away.

He paused to swirl the cubes in his glass, glanced down undeterred as a bit of water splashed over his fingers. A man warming to his topic.

"And for them, it gets worse. Here the *potential* plaintiff is in a coma. Nobody's got the faintest idea yet whether she would even want to pursue the matter."

I had an idea, hundreds of pages of her ideas.

"It might be days, weeks before this shakes out—and what are they to do with you in the meantime?"

"Their options?"

"Stick it out and see what happens or negotiate a severance package. My guess is, if you're ready to fall on your sword here and resign, they'll fall all over themselves in gratitude. Could be very substantial. That college trust fund for your daughter would no longer be a worry. Something funny?"

Funny? Oh yes, little gags fairly multiplied before my eyes, looping lightly like nooses through the quiet air. Beulah paying for my daughter's education . . .

"No. Go on." I tried yet again to dismiss the notion that she had foreseen all this. Orchestrated it, made a very public theatre of my life.

"In exchange for seeing you gone," he said, "the family could be persuaded to raise no objection to the size of the settlement."

"Yes, I imagine they could."

"Of course all parties'd eagerly agree to complete non-disclosure. As it is, I think I can arrange an interim deal right now. Indefinite leave, full pay. Non-disclosure till the police go one way or the other." He paused to glance around the room.

"You know, you should consider getting out of town when the police are done with you. By the looks of things here you could use a break."

What my friend Chris Relkoff called 'the cabin' was in reality a five-bedroom ranch house built by his father, who'd paid for an early retirement by selling pastureland to the south and east as acreages for wealthy executives moving out from Calgary. As Chris tells it, his father was already wealthy when oil was discovered in the north pastures. A run of good luck that ended in a violent, early death.

Chalet construction. A snug loft in the apex converted into an office with a fold-out couch, low pine bookshelves and an antique, oiled-mahogany writing desk. The living room where we now sat and the loft above us faced southwest through a towering wall of windows all but overwhelmed by a sweeping vista of the Rocky Mountains. Stone fireplace, walls of bright varnished log, cast-iron woodstoves, fully renovated kitchen, mod cons. A palace of rusticity.

I'd been here a few days. Papers—mine, hers—sorted into several ragged stacks on the floor. Bulky manila evelopes half-covered in colourful Mexican stamps stiff with glue, like military braid. A quantity of unwashed dishes, socks lying where they fell, a rumpled blanket on the couch. I was catching up on what felt like years of sleep, nodding off wherever it overtook me. Another blanket on the willow chair that Eric Heffner was sitting on, as his eyes scanned the scene. Crumbling pellets scattered in the dampness around the dog dishes at the door. Jewel would be out chasing rabbits somewhere. The usual bachelor clutter. Nothing worse than you might expect, under the circumstances. A certain, dim airlessness maybe at the moment, with the curtains drawn tight. On a bright day with snow still up on the mountains it could be blinding inside. Sometimes I opened up towards evening.

He had the names of a couple of good divorce lawyers. If ever I felt the need.

"Do you have somewhere you could go?" he asked. If this kept up, Eric (Rusty) Heffner and I were at risk of winding up bosom buddies.

I told him Madeleine and I'd been planning a trip to Britain, a celebration of sorts. "Next month when classes were done. Her parents have family over there—star turn with the new baby. I was going to leave her in Kent. Do a week's research in London."

"You could still go." He set his glass down, got to his feet. "Just let me know what you want." He paused at the door to adjust his Orioles cap against the glare. "We've got a couple days at least till I get a read on which way the investigation's headed."

I trailed him into the bright sunshine and out to where his old Volvo was parked behind my rental. Right foot resting on the floorboard, fingers lightly grasping the door frame, he glanced past me toward the house. I followed his gaze back to the low porch running the length of the southwest wall. It rests on pilings driven into the brow: from there the tableland tilts steeply down to the river. On the far bank begin the foothills. Tipped back beneath the window ledge was the twin of the willow chair he'd been sitting on inside. Another blanket crumpled heavily beside it. Nearly dry, evidently, after last night's storm. A plate or two left for the dog to lick clean. An ashtray half-filled with grey rainwater.

I was left with the distinct impression my lawyer thought me a likely source of further trouble. His concern for housekeeping I was just then finding profoundly irritating. No doubt he had some anxious little helpmeet to handle his.

"Take care," he said. "Call you soon."

13 Dec [19]94
[Mexico City]

IF I MAKE A PRAYER FOR YOU this night, will you come . . . ?

Dusky maid in the flower dress, let me kiss your apocalyptic lips. The crown I've made you wear, is it heavy, is it you? I'm sorry, but I need you to—walk again barefoot on a sickle moon, firewalk the four hundred malevolent stars.

Blessed Queen of Sciences, how may we call you?[50] Which of our immaculate conceptions wounds you least? Guadalupe / Coatlalocpeuh, she who has dominion over serpents or Quetzalpetlatl, who loves FeatherSerpent as brother, or Coatlicue who takes him as an emerald on her tongue?

By which of your exploits do we remember you? Who takes the secret name of Ra. Who challenges BlueHummingbird to nourish his children on milk not blood. Mother of the child god, who seeds herself with the clay of the Nile and the life that is in her mouth. Androgyne who swallows horns and engenders dilemma, whom some call Phanes, others LadyLord 2. Sacred harlot—Aphrodite, Xochiquetzal—who couples the sexes in mutual love. FlintButterfly, who severs them at the ankle and unleashes history on us and us on history.

Are you Toci, Mother of All, or Toci, Woman of Discord . . . Mistress of Tongues, who leads us to our destiny. Can you be both and neither, none and all?

Please . . . ? Do we ask too much of you?

Which of your gifts do we need more, treasure most—best measures us? Attending us in childbed—reliever of birthpangs, Nephthys, Artemis, Citlalacue. Protecting us at the night's crossroads haunted by the demons of women lost in childbirth, taken prisoner—O Proserpine who shields us from malice, O Chicomecoatl, who cries out our anguish for the child lost there.

You who wander sacred groves, cause roses to blossom in winter, who raise the New Eden—unwalled city, forest without scar. Regent Nemesis, who escorts her son the sun in his transit, and his sister the moon. Who makes each give way in turn—dawn to dusk to dawn and so to forever's end. Cybele of the axe, Ceres, harvest mother, or she who shucks the corn, harvester of hearts. Mother of the sweet corn, the tender corn, on your back you carry the flint knife swaddled, from its scabbard you draw the blade of paradox and leave it in each tender corncrib.

Who are you—are you all of these? Queen of the Night Sun, the Fifth Sun, the last—liminal swamp mother intercessor, mother of sorrows, of the fled the orphaned the failed—rushweaver, barkbuilder, boarhunter, houndslayer, wearer of the necklace of skulls. Cihuacoatl, secret silent commander of the armies of the Speaker—sister of the daysky, queen of the night, sister of the dark twin, mother of the light.

Monster, mystery, betrayer—diseased alien whore of the gorgon hair—vagina dentata, mother cunt-tooth—who are all things to all—one thing to them, another for me—*feed me now*. Feed me the life in your mouth, strain the bitter fruitsap between your filed teeth, let it drain and trickle into me. Incubate the flint rough like a cob in my wound. Teach me not to fear you, to spin out my life on a cornsilk thread, to eat their disease, to eat my death—with joy—and vomit *life*. I hunger I thirst I burn. I am alone here now, filled with you, in a place far from home.

If I make this prayer will you come?

Teach me, touch me. Help me touch *her*—see her through my fingertips, taste the lips she spoke with. Give me ears to hear her silences, breath to quicken them again. Anything to bring her back to me—even for an hour—let me take her captive, anything not to fail her she is slipping away. . . . I can't hold her, can't follow her. Not in there, not to the end. Sor Juana Inés de la Cruz.

Please by all the names in all the tongues in all the voices you are called let me start again, make a new beginning to this old end. Show me a new alphabet—how to piece together the name of love from *letters spelling everlasting ruin*—these are her letters, her words. Can't I give them back their tongue? She swallowed fire!—can I not lift her a single instant from these ashes in my hands? This is the palingenesis this is the ultimate magic, to lift the Rose from its ashes.

And if we can't love this Love without need show me at least how to love without hope

stay love

stay hopelessly in love. *Show me* how to love to live with living ruin long enough to finish this for her.

Then only then give me peace. Rest. Dust.

Sombra . . . Polvo . . . Nada

DREAMING.

    Dreaming, she dreamed her self.

    Dreaming she dreamed herself at the heart of a great roiling in an all devouring blackness in the eye of a vortex drawing her down, down to the bottom of a turbulent, lightless ocean. The turbulence was all around her and within her and was her. And she thought, *I am this dream, and this dream spins out of me. I am this Creation* dreaming itself spiralling down through a cyclone in the all consuming darkness . . . *and I am alone.* In the word was the beginning of her pain. The pain of her loneliness spun a whirling fever threading through her mind as she dreamed herself, arms split wide and bent, spinning like a flat disk, while with each dizzying turn she dreamed another thing which did not yet exist.

    And though the tangle of pain had not yet unravelled, at the end of the first night she dreamed herself come to rest in the clay at the bottom of the primordial waters. And she slept. . . .

She dreamed she woke. She dreamed herself awakened to her hunger. To her hunger for the clay. Her hunger for the clay wound around the pain in her heart and though her gnawing hunger grew with each deep sweet swallow of mud, she forgot for a time that her pain was her solitude.

    Her hunger for the clay was devouring her. She hungered for the smell of the earth that upheld her. She hungered for the feel of its smooth oily texture filling her mouth, opening a passage down her throat. For the gnash of grit against her teeth, for the taste of warm clay filling her mind. But these things did not yet exist, and the pain grew.

    She would never get enough. Though she ate mountains of clay, oceans of clay, worlds of mud, still she doubted. For if she did not really exist but only dreamed, there would be no end to her hunger. She could never get enough, never. Her doubt coupled with her pain, her hunger strengthened and nourished it. Until she began to hope, to *wish* she did not exist.

    And so in her belly in the belly of a dream, the pain grew. Beyond fear, grew beyond doubt. Her pain became her certainty, and while at last she believed she existed, she wished she could die.

    But death did not yet exist.

ISIS

When at last her pain had grown until she could bear it no longer, feeling within her a vast rift splitting—a sear, a vent in the husk of the void—she vomited up the sun. Vomiting she tore light from the veil of darkness, *she drew flame from the scabbard of night* and the silent waters were filled with light. . . .

She gazed at what she had made, *at the sun*, her firstborn. She thought, *I am not alone. I exist, for I have made another.* And there, at the end of the second night of dreaming, she slept.

She dreamed she woke. She woke to her terror that the sun would be gone. But opening her dream-encrusted eyes she found him still there with her. From then on she would know him before sight by the warmth on her face. And while still great, her pain was diminished.

But it was not over.

She vomited up the sky, and felt release. She sundered bright sky from dark, day sky from night. She vomited the moon and all the glittering stars. She vomited up the earth, and felt relief. She vomited the horizons, east and west then north and south. She vomited oceans. She vomited mountains. She vomited the great river and at its headwaters the great lake. She vomited up the shapes of all the things under the sun. And when at the end of the third night she had brought forth all that was within her, had turned herself inside out, her heart, her belly, when her very self had spun down the silk of her entrails and flung them out across the sky, she slept.

She dreamed she woke. She woke to feel the sun warm on her upturned face, to feel its rays enter her battered frame. She opened her eyes to the light of the first new day, to the storm broken, to the waters receded . . . the wide world glistening in every direction below and around. She opened her eyes to a fine rainbow mist clinging to each hidden valley, the sight of her sun blazing in a fine blue sky. She had not expected the colours . . . blue sky, red earth, gold sun . . . and in the mists danced the promise of still more colours to come. The smell of the warm red clay baking moist in the sun surged through her body like a current of joy. . . .

But soon this gave way to first sorrow, for when she looked about her she saw in her creation no life. There were the gravid shapes of grain and fruit, the fragile lines of plant and web, the forms of animals and birds, but they did not live. In the beautiful new world all around her not one thing moved.

Just then she felt a desperate hope—perhaps somewhere? Somewhere in this bright creation there would be, *must* be life.

She would find it.

She rose into the air on the wings of a vulture, wings spread half as wide as the world, a great vulture with the tail and tongue of a serpent, with the sun for her left eye, the moon for her right. She soared over a world still glinting wet beneath the sun. All day long she flew south along the great river, her brilliant eyes, her serpent's tongue, questing for the merest trace of life.

When the earth was finally firm enough to walk upon she veered west and landed on the western shore of the great lake. Her wings could no longer bear the weight of her first grief and remorse. Though she had been unable bear the birth pangs an instant longer, she should have, should have waited. Time itself had not yet ripened.

They say then that even as the world lay deaf to the roar of her grieving, to the sound of her weeping, *death was in her mouth*. Half-mad with her anguish she began destroying the brittle things she had made. The air boomed with the clatter of clay that shattered and ground in the terrible beak of the vulture. But there was no one to hear. *Death was in her mouth* as she swallowed the bodies of her children, the images of her dream . . . as she wrenched even the eyes from her head and devoured the moon and sun.

And filled with a great weariness, at the end of the fourth night, she slept. . . .

At first her sleep was so deep, so dense and so dark that her dream could not enter. But at last a slow frail bubble rose in a tremble to the troubled surface of her mind. She dreamed she woke. Flooded with the light of her hope, buoyed on its currents, she rose once again, clutching the crushed forms in the hellish, coiling bowels of her belly. Her great wings banked on the south wind, she flew north and then east to a point near the beginning, where she landed on a high cliff above a breathless sea.

She braced herself. It began again. She vomited up the sky. She divided bright sky from dark, earth from heaven. At the eastern horizon she vomited the dawn. And the sun rose with the new joy of its motion! Bathing the world with an ochre lustre, the sun was beautiful in its movements. As she brought forth each new thing, she imparted to the glistening lumps of clay not just shape now but colour. First black, white and red, and then all the colours of the rainbow mists that hung about her. Then all the myriad combinations of these. Then scent, now texture, with some rough and some smooth. When she had waited patiently for the things of the world to harden and dry into the shapes she had made for them, she held each thing up before her face and gave it a name.

And the world shook at the naming of the names.

They say then *life was in her mouth,* for when she had named every separate thing, she lifted some and holding them close to her lips she gave them breath.

And the sky smiled at the warmth of their breathing.

When this was done, she raised up some of the panting creatures and gave them voice, and to a very few of these she then gave song . . . to the birds of the air, to the whales of the sea, to the people of the land. The air trembled gently to the quavering of their songs, and *the world heard them.*

At last she raised the people, to whom she had given form and colour and name, given voice and songs and life itself, and pressing each to her forehead *gave them dreams.* The dreams unstopped the silence in their souls and poured forth words. She spoke their lives to them, but it was their dreams that gave her heartspeech back to her.

They were alive. At the sight of their living and speaking and dreaming she wept, and they wept with her. Her second joy was greater for containing her first . . . and for containing her first sorrows. Tenderly, she bade them look around at the wonders she had made, and in a voice like the rolling of rock said:

All these things are ours, yours and mine, and we are each other's.

And when with the milk of her breasts she had fed them, hesitant, they began to speak to her:

Every thing has its shape and colour and name. Every living thing has breath. Some have voice, some song. Thou hast given us dreams. But Thou hast no shape and no name. How shall we call Thee?

And she answered:

> *You will know me in a thousand shapes and names and dreams.*
> *You will know me as Maat, the mother of heaven,*
> *As Nut or Neith or Hequet in the primordial waters,*
> *As Nekhbet in the city of the dead,*

> as sovereign of the abyss, the opener of the way,
> As Seshet or Hathor in the power of the flood,
> in the fire of the desert, or the fires of the blood,
> As Nephthys, protector through childbirth and pain.
> And as Isis, you will know me in the wisdom of your words,
> in the beauty of your work, and in the terrible joy of your dreaming.

And because Isis meant *the sound of weeping*, in the tongue she had given them, they asked if hers were tears of sorrow or of joy. She smiled her first smile. Then a few looked about the tear-streaked world and understood.

And at the end of the fifth night of dreaming, she slept.

She dreamed she woke. She dreamed she woke to the sound of voices.

Some of the people had come to her from the desert, as she knew one day they must, just as there must be two kinds of dreaming. Their faces were troubled. They said:

There is Another in the desert. He has many followers and His words are strange. He has a secret name. At first we could not understand Him, but He learned our tongue, and He said to us:

> I am the One. To you, I am Ra.
> One name is all you will need.

But we answered:

What of her? She who is great in magic, whose spells have spun the fabric of the world, who gave us form and breath, who gave us song and the dreams from which all words come?

And He said:

> Forget her name. Forget all the names she has taught you.
> One word is all you will ever need to remember.

And we said:

But is she not like a vulture in effecting Thy protection? And is she not like an uraeus serpent established on Thy brow? Does she not make Thee rise like the sun every morning, as she does us?

But He said:

Forget her name. You will learn from me to forget.
In your fear of me you will forget all the names.
All the names she has taught you
    for the things of the earth.

And we said:

But she breathes life! Her songs are life, and in her mouth are the words to revive even hearts gone still. She has entered into the heart of the great mysteries. She bore the sun! *She is the daughter of her son and the mother of her father.*

Then He said:

I am the father.
She is not my mother.
You will learn to fear me.
Enough. Go—insects!

He spat upon us, and His laughter was like unto thunder. We *were* afraid and fled him.

Crossing the great river, she found him in the eastern desert. There, she said:

You have terrified the people.
Do you ask protection from the Eye of the Serpent?

He answered:

Children into beetle life
Beetle life-maker am I
Children's children's beetle bodies
Grabbed My Cock I
Fucked My fist
In strength I
Fist-fucked in gentleness.

At first she could not understand him. She said:

You've split the secrets from the mysteries.
You have assembled an army of slaves.
Do you need protection from the power of the serpent?

And he said:

> Heart made soft by fist-love I
> Drained salt water
> Through My cunt-fist
> Back into Me I
> Fucked My shadow
> Rained seedwater
> Spewing into My open mouth and the
> Mouth of My anus.

To this she said:

> You've made your name a secret.
> You threatened the people.
> You spat upon my children.
> Do you beg protection from the potency of the serpent?

But he said

> God bird house
> Phoenix recurring sun
> Universe water bowl
> Spittle from My lips
> Shit-fucking Khepri the
> Dung-beetle at dawn
> Dung-beetle rolling the shitball sun.
> Walking out of My mouth
> And the mouth of My anus
> Beetle sky-lady
> Beetle mummy fucker
> Beetle cunt river
> Beetle sage pig
> Children's children's beetle bodies
> Walking out of My anus.

He tried to hide in the strangeness of his tongue, but she had learned its secrets. He said:

> I am the firstborn of My fist.
> Fist-born, I am the Sun!

He laughed. He spat into the dust at her feet, and walked westward toward the river. Toward the city of the people. Some say she was frightened for her firstborn. Some say she knew her first anger, and said as he walked toward the western horizon, *You are not my son.*

She bent and mixed the spittle of his mouth with the dust at her feet. She added to this the muddy slime from the great lake's deepest crevices. Great of magic, she fashioned from this clay a serpent. Great of magic, she rolled in her hands a magnificent dragon which, coiling and rearing its hooded head, could reach through the clouds to the heavens.

Stooping, she swallowed the serpent whole. She opened a way through her throat and with the life that was in her mouth she vomited the holy serpent onto the grass along the riverbank. Holding the head of the dragon to her lips, she breathed its name. *Apophis.* She released it to slither through tall grass, towards the path where the oarsmen of Ra rowed His Sun Bark westward through the heavens.

When at noon the Sun Bark with Ra standing in the prow passed above the holy serpent, it reared up and bit him at the eye of his phallus. The terrible fangs drove venom coursing through Ra's loins like a spring flood through the great river. Never since the birth of the world had the sky heard such agony.

The oarsmen, chained to their oars, could only call out in panic:

What has happened? What deadly thing has risen against Thee?

But for a time Ra could not answer. The bones of his jaws chattered and the limbs of his body shook like branches in a typhoon. Spittle fell from his drooping lips. Moisture poured from his face. All the fluids of his body began to desert him at once. There arose a great stench all around him. At last he found his tongue and cried out:

> *I know who has done this!*
> *Call her. Who wields the sceptre of the serpent.*
> *who wears the vulture headdress*
> *who holds the cross of life in one hand*
> *and the feather of truth in the other.*
> *Call her. Who is great in magic,*
> *in plague destroying spells.*
> *Call her!*

Grown old, made feeble, skin slack about his bones, he cried out pain beyond words. For the first time she felt pity, and though her eyes were dry she said to him:

I'm here. What is it you called me to say?

And he said:

Is it really you? My Eyes are clouded.
I am not even able to see My sky.
The light of the world has been taken from Me.
The light of the world has abandoned My Eyes.
I ask protection from the Eye of the Serpent.

But she answered:

You've threatened my firstborn.
Tell me your secret name.

Lips quivering, voice unsteady he said:

I am who bound the mountains together in chains.
I am who acted as The-Bull-of-His-Mother
    and brought sensual pleasure to the flood.
I am who sits on the Throne of the Two Horizons
    in the broad Bark of the Sun.
I am who opening His eyes makes light
    and closing them brings darkness.
I am who creates the hours
    from which the days come into being.
I am who made living fire.
I am Khepri the Scarab at dawn, Ra at noon, Atum at dusk.
I need your protection from the tongue of the Serpent.

But she said:

I'm not interested in your boasting.
Your secret name is not among these.
Tell me the name.

The venom of the holy serpent writhed toward his heart. His agonies grew and sharpened without let. He felt his soul swimming in a fiery lake, he felt his heart shuddering as in a moonless desert, he felt his old body stripped naked to a wintry wind. Hard mountains crumbled at the sound of his wailing. He cried:

> But who knows My secret name
>> shall have power eternal over Me!
> I beg your protection from the potency of the serpent.

He felt the Eye of the Serpent lick at his heart. He felt the cedar between his legs wither like a leaf. He stared into the face of his everlasting death, his immortal corruption, and he pleaded:

> Promise Me you will use the name
>> only to protect the potency of your son.
> Tell it to no other but your firstborn
>> and swear him to silence.

And she answered:

> The breath of the serpent
>> will restore you to life everlasting.
> Now tell me the name.

And he said:

> Please! Protect him, yes. But ask him to veil the secret
>> in the silence of his heart.

But she said only:

> The name.

And at last, as he felt the rotting wings of death beating above his face, he bid her enter his heart and learn the secret name of Ra. And she called out to his followers:

The name of the great god has been taken from him.
The secret of his Eye has passed into me.
I will restore him to life everlasting.

She made a poultice from clay, mixing into it a paste of crushed seeds and leaves. She applied it to his withered member. She sang the song of life into his dying heart. She said:

The venom dies, he lives.
Ra lives, the poison dies.
Long may he live through the power of the Eye.

And opening wide her jaws she drew the Eye of the Serpent from his body. Then, curled up in the warm belly of the sixth night of dreaming, she slept. . . .

Sappho   BOOK THREE

Some say nine muses—but count again
Behold the tenth: Sappho of Lesbos

PLATO

CONTENTS

CONTENTS

. . . And now,
know ye that my late-night
inquiries into Nature have cast light
on the most arcane secrets
of Natural magic,
and that through my sciences might I
feign even the moon
in the perspectives of a mirror,
or in the condensations
of terrestrial vapours;
or project spectral bodies,
by dazzling the eyes.
And failing this,
trick the mind to switch
allegorical creatures
into visible objects. . . .

JUANA INÉS
DE LA CRUZ,

MARTYR OF THE
SACRAMENT

B. Limosneros, trans.

PLUS ULTRA![1]

Year: 1680. Twelve years in a convent, Sister Juana Inés de la Cruz now enters her most productive period, writing carols and graceful love lyrics, but also virtuosities in form hailed today as precursors of the modern experiments of poets such as Mallarmé. Many of her plays, meanwhile, have become too complex for the stage, or at least to be played by nuns and novices. And perhaps too dangerous.

[†]*probably Sor María de la Agreda, abbess, spiritual advisor to Philip IV*

"And yet you have made an application to purchase your cell. How is it I am only just learning of this?"

"Perhaps, Father Núñez, you might ask the Mother Prioress, since she's held my application for two years."

"She may have wanted you to reflect upon the kind of cell you are buying yourself."

"Meaning?"

"Is it a convent cell you want, Sor Juana—or the prison cells you so exalt in verse?"

"Whatever is the matter now?"

"The life in here corrupts you with its ease."

"*Ease?* Am I softened by the barbs of envy and intolerance and vicious gossip that beset me within these walls? The Prioress now schemes to correct even my handwriting—'too masculine,' she calls it."

"Mother Andrea claims you called her a *silly woman,* to her face."

"Your superior dealt with this, Father."

"How he spoiled and pampered you. A little more each year."

"You say this now that don Payo's gone."

"*Don Payo, don Payo.* A country nun on a first-name basis with a Prince of the Church. And yes, Juana, he *is.* Gone to meet his cousin, our new Viceroy. To tell him all about you, I have no doubt. How fashionable it has become for every rake in Madrid to have a nun confidante. What am I saying?— for one's personal mystic."[†]

"I think I can forego the raptures of discussing mysticism with viceroys, if that's your concern."

"Once here in Mexico, don Payo's cousin can be offered the most famous nun in Christendom to comfort him during his trials among us here in the wilderness. He will not fail to find her irresistible. She will prove a marvel of comprehension who knows, as if by miracle, our new viceroy's every intellectual interest and spiritual need, can quote at length from all his favourite poets."

"I suspect don Payo has done much the same for you."

"And with your future here secured, don Payo sails for the Alcázar— *that nest of nuns*—with a trunk full of your plays and poems and treatises. Souvenirs of his travels, is that it?"

"He asked for a few trifles, yes."

"Verses for a few friends."

"Not forgetting his family, Your Reverence. After seven years in the New World who would want to go back to one's family empty-handed?"

"Ah you mean his *other* cousin."

"Yes, Father, the King's Prime Minister."

"And do you really believe he can protect you from there?"

"Protect me."

"Did you think your don Payo would not show it to me before he left?"

"Show you wh—ah, I see you'll be telling me."

"That abomination! *Martyr of the Sacrament.*"

"How could I think he'd dare not to? He was only our Archbishop and Viceroy after all. But I assume your abomination of my play does not quite extend to Saint Hermenegild himself?"

"So now we have martyred you here—"

"Father, you persist in reducing everything I write to self-portraiture."

"Because it is—or no, you do not make portraits anymore, your plays contain whole embassies. The Greeks, the Visigoths, Saint Hermenegild, civil war, faith, magic, apostasy, Isabela of Castile, Columbus—"

"All that, Father. In one play? You're certain."

"You think we are in one of your little comedies?"

"Just once, before you save my soul for all eternity, how I would love to see you laugh."

"You may not enjoy the moment as much as you imagine."

"In truth I cannot imagine it at all."

"You think yourself back at the palace, perhaps. But as I remember it, you were not always laughing then."

"Just once, to see you come here without a grievance."

"Could your intent *be* more manifest? You salute not just the Queen and Queen Mother but the entire administration—you have a character addressing them from within the play itself!"

"So you've come to correct my art."

"Is there to be no end to your worldly intriguing? You are a nun, a bride of Christ, buried alive, dead to the world—"

"This, from an officer of the Company of Jesus."

"But such a clever nun—a jesting, writing nun. A nun magician. How you dazzle us with your theatrical sorcery—or do you call it science that so holds us in its thrall? Soldiers, souls and spectators all suspended between New Spain and Old, you take us back a thousand years to the Spain of the Visigoths—and not content with this, back *another* thousand to the ancient Spain of Geryon! Two continents, two centuries, three or four millennia all on one rather crowded stage. Why, Sor Juana, you are a veritable *sorceress* of space and time."

"The doctors of the Church, as you know perfectly well, Father, have defined magic as nothing more than the power to uncover natural marvels. That's all the magic I care to know about. The magic of Columbus was merely that of human genius."

"Of which you have an abundance, should Madrid still be needing any—"

"Human genius, even in abundance, is but a pale reflection of the mind of God."

"And since the natural marvel of the New World always existed, its discovery was the triumph of that genius over our own pious ignorance. You remind a bankrupt Queen of how much Spain has owed to the bold spirit of discovery,[2] a spirit just such as yours. Not enough for you merely to play the magician, the alchemist, no you are all the silver of the Indies, all the wonders of America rolled into one. Let us all bow down now to this prodigy of piety—the writing nun who makes rhymes on the rebel martyr Hermenegild. *You try to drive a wedge between Church and Crown.*"

"And who was it, just now, lamenting the influence of nuns at the palace in Madrid?"

"You have Columbus's marines shout *Ne Plus Ultra, Ne Plus Ultra,* Here ends the Universe! only to hear their echoes rebounding from the unseen shore—but no, *from the future.* Where we sit and smile down at them from the new certainties of this very clever future. How you use Time to mock at us, the ignorance of our simple faith."

"I find nothing simple about your faith, Father."

"So limited, so straitening, so narrow for one so bold—"

"Nor was I the one who made Hermenegild a saint."

"No, Juana, Pope Urban did. And thus you cunningly remind us of his unfortunate protégé Galileo Galilei—another sainted rebel in a prison cell. You would have us confuse this Galilei's impudence with the daring that once so enriched Spain and expanded its dominions! You think your hieroglyphs cannot be deciphered. You think to send don Payo with the key. To supply him with the pretext for an audience with the Queen."

"As always, Father, your learning is a wonder."

"As always, Sor Juana, you offer up a false surrender. It might shock you to know how much help I have had. There are many of us watching, more closely every year. How slyly you allude to a navigational technique you could only have read in Columbus's journals—also on the Index, as it happens. As Censor for the Holy Office, I might ask who has brought them to you. I could insist, we could make inquiries. . . . And yet you do not stop even at this. You simply cannot resist, even when you cannot hope to benefit—is all this rebellion truly in the name of liberty? Or is your own ambition even more vainglorious than the Florentine's?"

"And who, Father, cannot resist?—banning a navigator's journals when there can be no imaginable harm in reading them. Banning even the letters of Cortés to his King—under Royal Seal, but only here in America. Who, if not you, requested the seal here? And who spends his days extirpating books I could read freely as a child?"

"And look where they have led you. You might as well have written *eppur si muove.*† And so you mock at the science of the Jesuits, just as Galileo did, our Columbus of the skies! Is that your ambition, Sor Juana—to be the Columbus of a new Heaven?"

"You seem to think I have imagined a Spain—*at the time of Herakles*—teeming with Jesuit scientists."

"I think there is no end to where your imagination may lead you."

"It does *not* lead me to confuse the Earth's flatness with its centrality or its motility. Even before Galileo's death—"

"Of course, of course, the Church permits discussion of the Earth's motion. As a *hypothesis.*"

"To want more was unnecessary. Signor Galilei's mistake was—"

"But not his worst, Sor Juana, not his worst. Yes, our scientists in Rome opposed him and are now divided—"

"Since you simply will not let this go, tell me what *was* worse, for the soldiers of a geocentrist Pope—"

"So dangerously you tread with me."

"Which was the greater heresy for the Jesuits, Galileo's heliocentrism or his insubordination?"

"Many in the Company of Jesus thought Pope Urban too lenient, yes, just as your play makes Hermenegild's father, the heretic king, too lenient."

"Now it is your imagination that misleads you."

"One has only to scratch a little at the surface to find the vein of heresy in you."

†'nevertheless it moves'—words attributed to Galileo at the close of his trial

"No, Father, I wrote only of Hermenegild. As you say, of a thousand years ago."

"Precisely so you could cast us in the role of your heretic bishop, the Arian from whose hand the martyr Hermenegild refuses the wafer and the wine. How guilefully you show our Queen how time turns traitors into martyrs, Arians into heretics, boldness into riches, water into wine. No, do not bother. Save your rebuttal for the proper time. But take this as a token from a father who has been too lenient for far too long. You think to split us from the Church by meddling in a question upon which the whole Church is divided. Yet it is not the Jesuits, but quite another target you are striking at. And Galilei's example contains many lessons, Juana. One such is this: Not even a Pope can save us from ourselves. The vain and insubordinate—"

"Revolve around themselves . . . ?"

"I see, everything amuses you now. All is fit material for your laughter. In the figure of Columbus's marines you make clowns of the faithful and the fearful. This art of yours makes fear so comical. And makes *you* bolder every year. But then, I see you are right after all. I did come to correct your art. Indeed consider this, while there is still time. That today a single work of Galileo Galilei remains on the Index. It is not a work of science but of *art*—a play, Sor Juana, a dialogue. Three good Christians—and how strange that you should use the same device— debating planetary motion. Your fellow playwright makes one of them a simpleton of faith. For comic effect. And into whose mouth Galilei puts an idea cherished by a pontiff who has spoiled and coddled our vain and insubordinate natural magician, and now is mocked for his pains. What is the simpleton made to say? That a God who has the power to create the universe—"

"Would also have the power to make its laws and regulations, its causes and effects, appear to us quite other than they truly are."

"I *knew* it."

"An idea more promising perhaps than Galileo realized."

"You just could not help showing me you have read even this most infamous of tracts. Or keep from showing us how clever you are—more clever even than the Florentine. You have seen all his errors. You will play the same game but play it rather better, you too will write a play but conceal your game from all of us, even as you announce it to be an allegory and so defy us to divine it. And see how this *promising* new idea turns God himself into a great magician, revealer of natural marvels—and you, into a goddess in her theatre, a veritable fountainhead of inspiration!"

"Truly Father it is you and your collaborators who are inspired—to fit an ocean's worth of inspirations into the shallow basin of one woman's mind, a lowly country nun, as you say. No wonder they all flock to work with you."

"When they should flock to you? It is worse with you than even *I* could have believed. It is as bad as they say. So anxious to show off your clever-ness at any risk. How much better to have pretended never to have read it—instead you *quote* from it. *To me*—an officer of the Inquisition. And even here you direct the conversation to exactly where it should not go."

"And that would be?"

"Towards water, Sor Juana. Water. Your new theology, your new sacrament. Which, yes, may very well martyr you. . . ."

Many things have changed since my years with Núñez, if not so many as I'd thought. The room itself I have had redone. Its three tall narrow windows still of course face west, but the grate that divided the room—and us in our cloister from the worldly—I have had torn out. The bars had run north-south, putting all three windows on the visitors' side, and in the late afternoons Father Núñez had had an unfortunate way of placing himself between me and the light—hitching a shoulder or sway-ing at the grate—to let the dying sun strike my eyes. So now, a light grille bisects the room from the eastern wall to the middle window, and thus runs not north-south but more or less parallel with the afternoon light. The exact angle varying slightly with the seasons. The new arrangement gives me one window, my visitors another, and the third we share, sitting together at the grille.

Since he was last here, the room seems less grim in other ways too. From the high, raftered ceiling depends a silver chandelier on the visitor's side, a gift from one of our convent's many patrons; behind an arras on the convent side is the pantry and staging area from which our guests' crystal glasses and silver cups and platters may be replenished; down the west wall runs a row of wide, cushioned benches. Two clavichords—for duets, but also so that the cantor[†] and I may work together efficiently at our commissions. Armchairs of ox hide stretched over oak, carpets to cover the cold stone floors . . . Flemish tapestries and a selection of maps and paintings relieve the impassive thickness of the walls. Polished cases and

[†]cathedral musical director

cabinets lining the south wall, on both sides of the grille. Books, of course, but also the many curiosities and conversation pieces brought by visitors from the Philippines, Cathay, Europe, Perú, the missions of California and Nuevo México. . . .

So, all in all, the arrangement of the room since the time of Father Núñez feels much less like a prison, even now. The old grate's bars were spaced barely far enough apart to permit the passage of a book, whereas our grille is carved in rosewood, beautifully, to resemble an arbour of wide-spread boughs, full-leafed and bent with pear and grape and apple. Among the branches are gaps a child or slender woman could wriggle through. I might manage it myself, for another year or two, but it is a comfort to think I could break that grille down if I needed to.

In places the enlacement of the boughs permits the most extraordinary intimacy, when there are two, especially in late afternoon. Each of us with a chair pulled sidelong, each murmuring through as we sit as if at an assignation in a private garden of warm redwood and rose . . . light plays in the turns of brights and darks, and as the space behind each recedes into glades of shadow and cool, we might almost forget where we are. And who.

There are rarely, now, only two.

My parlour is famed for many things, but the one I have most invested in is its gaiety. This afternoon I have several friends, all arriving separately, all appearing almost at once by different avenues, come to see how I am bearing up after this morning's sermon. A company of six fallen faces that it falls to me now to cheer. Five I have known for years. Carlos longest of all, and then our convent chaplain, but there is also the cantor, Diego de Ribera, and with him the Dean of the Cathedral. My friend Gutiérrez of the Inquisition has also come. And, for a while, Father Xavier Palavicino himself, my defender, glummest of all.

Much more significant is the list of who is not with us. Father Arellano comes only on Fridays, only for confessions, and avoids this locutory like a contagion. The Bishops of Oaxaca and Michoacan, meanwhile, have not been seen here for some months. The Bishop of Puebla was until recently a fixture here. The Archbishop, well, the Archbishop would rather wade into a lake of fire than set foot in any convent, let alone this one. Indeed such a misstep might very well hasten his eventual visit to that shore. And Father Núñez has not been here for ten years.

Haltingly Father Palavicino has begun to tell us how after his sermon this morning—right here in the street just beyond these walls—he was accosted by a self-proclaimed friend of the Inquisition. "He would not give his name." Palavicino lowers his voice and all but glances over his shoulder. "He ranted of sacrilege and my blasphemies. In front of twenty witnesses he called the sermon *heretical* —"

If only my champion had been less brave this morning. The change in him since then is distressing. And if the long face and hushed tone were not annoying enough, he stops talking each time he hears a sound from beyond the door. Laughter in the locutory down the hall . . . the scrape of a watering can in the garden . . . footsteps.

Just then, under a sifting of road dust, a small new personage drops by on his way to the palace to present his credentials. While the dusting in his heavy moustache and brows suggests he might be the Viceroy's new baker, the fellow instead claims to be Baron Anthonio Crisafi of Sicily. In the quiet that follows the round of introductions, he says he cannot stay long. He points out what should have been casually obvious, that he has not been to the palace to present his credentials—it would be awkward if the breach of protocol were found out. And yet he shows no sign of being about to rush off. Recent days have made me perhaps too suspicious. On the evidence, he is so newly arrived he can have no idea of my current situation, and yet I wonder. There are no more innocent visits. And then he says, "That is an extraordinarily good copy of the Velázquez."

The remark could seem natural enough. It would be easy to see why the painting has caught his eye. Across the north wall, the sun brands a narrow wedge—its tip cuts across the canvas to light up the geographer's globe. A smile, especially lustrous now, candles his simpleton's face like a child showing off a favourite toy, as by the crook of a geographic finger he bestows guileless favour on a lucky continent. The geographer's bangs are cut along the jagged hemisphere of a badly fired bowl; under the shiny tuber nose the moustache sprawls, a black caterpillar, feebly rampant. The lace collar is the white of greying snow. . . .

"You're aware, sir, that his model for *The Geographer* was a lunatic?"

"Yes, Sor Juana, the fellow was a favourite of the King. His name escapes me just now."

"Philip."

"The Fourth," Carlos adds gruffly.

Ribera almost smiles. The dean looks up mildly from a book he's been thumbing through.

There, that's a bit better.

After a few more minutes of this I see the Baron is thinking to make an exit and to save his message for a time when we can be alone. But just how much time do I have? Being alone may be less of a problem soon enough, but at the moment this locutory is watched. Today he has come to introduce himself, but unexplained visits in the future can only invite unwelcome speculation.

I need to know who has sent him—the Countess? or even someone from my time at the palace?

Rising, the Sicilian expresses the hope he might soon return to visit America's Tenth Muse. I am so widely called that now, and for almost a decade, it should come as no surprise that he knows this, given everything else he knows. Palavicino leaves immediately after him, and as soon as he is out of earshot Gutiérrez confirms that Palavicino's accuser did indeed come by the Holy Office.

And at last it comes to me that one other person might have briefed the good Ambassador, who has perhaps just arrived, but perhaps not—or then again, has been met somewhere on the road from Veracruz. But then his interceptor would have to have known the Ambassador was coming, which suggests a network of informants, and someone persuasive enough to bend the man to his purpose.

Someone like Núñez.

"As ever, Juana, you test my loyalties—to you, to the Company, to the Holy Office—even as you mock me for my conflicts. And how you repay me, who paid for your lessons in theology! For years, they have come to me, saying, Father Núñez, if the Jesuits can give her theology but not self-discipline, discipline comes in other forms. You think you cannot be forced to name the one who brought Galileo's dialogue to you, or the explorer Columbus's journals, or Cortés's letters. As usual you think only of yourself. You do not care whom you endanger. But now to your greatest error, as you are so short of time. Yes, you very cleverly detect divisions in the Church—of policy, even of doctrine—and think to exploit them. *Divide et impera,* perhaps. But on the very point you attack, the Church is not divided at all. No, at this, you are very much working alone."

"So you say. But at what, may I ask?"

"The sacraments, Juana. Your play."

"An entertainment."

"Oh yes, and so you entertain us with three theologians on your stage, quarrelling amusingly of course as theologians do."

"*Two*, Father. You keep saying three."

"Thank you, two, the third is a mere adept of the new science, an honest broker, a Galilean who puts himself at the service of the fractious two. How could I have mistaken him for the priest of a new natural philosophy? Honest, neutral, wise, cheerful. Admirably equipped to resolve the eternal vexations of theology—the sacraments, the Passion, the *finezas*, Gethsemane, the Supper. Nothing is enough for you—you must best us all at everything, even theology. Augustine, Aquinas. Me."

"Nothing I do, Father Núñez, is *enough* for you. Nothing pleases you anymore. You've become so unjust. Do I not give the Thomist the upper hand by giving him your—"

"That is not why you give him my restatement of Saint Thomas to speak. You do it to better me, my position."

"Was it so futile to hope America's foremost authority on the Eucharist would be flattered? But of course, to be so praised, Your Humility must be mortified."

"Always this cleverness, always your insolence. Now, let me spare you the inconvenience of having to formulate your subtle and undeniably original theology in terms we the unimaginative, the fearful, the simple may understand. Working together—something *you* would not understand—we have done this work to spare you the effort. Be grateful. You should marshal your energies. Nothing clever to add yet? No, of course, it is late, and you are short of time.

"Your play returns us to the hours before the Passion, to the vexatious question of Christ's greatest proof of love for Man. Is his greatest *fineza* in giving us his undying presence in the bread and the wine, as Thomas maintains? Or, after poor simple Augustine, does it consist in dying to the world, for the world? Even as a *bride of Christ* is vowed to do. You give us the Angelic Doctor, you give us Augustine, but still you make no mention of the other great *fineza*. You do not mention the bathing of the disciples' feet. Why is that?—no, rest, I will tell you. Because later, when we your bedazzled audience *thirst* for it, you will offer us your answer."

"Truly, Father, you find too much in it—"

"A new sacrament, a new Host—one far finer, as surely the common people will see. Because it is free. Better than bread, which we have taken as a symbol of scarcity."

"Even I thirst to hear it now."

"But you know already."

"Please."

"Water, Sor Juana. The humblest thing, the purest, everywhere free. In tears and springs and seas. Such poetry you make for us simpletons, with the simplest of things. And it has been with us *since the beginning*. We admit you are clever. You have your Hermenegild clearly, ringingly, repudiate this Arian heresy of a Christ co-eternal, co-equal with the Father, uncreated. No, indeed, you have him created by God and fashioned from nothing short of God's Free Will. So far, so much to the good—or is it. Oh yes, your case will be hard to nail down. Much like water itself. But now, with this new Eucharist of yours, you have Christ Our Lord transubstantiated in water, a kind of infusion, like tea, I suppose, a kind of witch's broth. Christ in the sacrament, the sacrament in water, water everywhere in nature, nature as Christ everywhere present—no, no, not co-eternal with God, but now *omnipresent, co-extensive*. God's love everywhere embedded within the beauty of creation.

"All nature as our temple—forest springs, rivers, rain. But no, not quite a temple, more like a ... bath. A pagan bath. And all the naiads and nymphs and dryads restored to cavort again. And free, all free.

"And so you return the world to us, return us whence we had been cast out, to the garden. You make the world into an Eden of floods. Water everywhere, all is holiness—nature, existence itself is the sacrament now. What need has one for bread in Eden? What need have we for priests at sea? No—not priests but navigators, scientists—natural magicians. And they must be bold, boldness itself, to make daring from humility, from a simple washing of the feet. If we are truly to know God, we must entrust ourselves to the sea, to go beyond the humble limits of our ignorance.

"And who shall make the new theology, whom shall we make priestess of this new Queen of the Waters? Who shall interpret for us the mysteries of this new Sophia rising from the Galilean sea, this goddess in nature everywhere, who presents herself as beauty to all our senses.

Queen of the Baths—in this pagan *orgy* of sensation, where to know god is to swim in god and all her sensations. *Was this your experience at the palace . . . ?"*

Was I wrong, was it madness, to think I could do without him? Was I to live in fear of him like everyone else here—my whole life? How could I work, with him coming every week to rob me of my strength, harvest it?—to milk me, his rubber tree, his adder.

Better to make of him an enemy than to let such a one near me as a friend—and arm him myself.

"You think this one of your little comedies," Father Núñez said.

Jokes, I made in answer. For the jester and only he—not statesman, knight or prince—may sometimes mock the Emperor. Núñez is impressive, I thought, and yes, there were many other clever ones working on my case but however much they might insist, they were not infallible. For in his exhaustive catalogue of my play's pernicious contents and sins of rebellion, Núñez had all but missed the obvious. Hercules. Ten years ago I listened to my Atlas sitting across from me, piling the weight of the world and heaven on my back, because I was not free to answer him.[3] And so as not to be quite suffocated, not altogether crushed, I found myself composing, to myself, another little comedy, while he talked, while he talked. . . .

Something like this.

How the world pins poor Hercules, stoops the braided shoulders, bows that thewy nape, bends the water bearer beneath his earthen urn— ay, what persecutions of gravity! *Herakles, pobre de tí*—made passive pillar, pole and axis—mortal champion reduced to Muse. While at your antipodes, lesser men sail in fitful affray west, eyes straining ever west to the world's abysmal end. Yea, would that it had an end for one who knows it round, *knows it moves*—and still, and yet, who is forced to stand, fixed point on which all the watery world spins. Ah to see that end in the stony face of Atlas coming back across the straits with apples in his cheeks, flushed with worldly success.

Ay Herakles, pobre de ti, I thought, sitting across from him. To be sentenced to the bond service of a lesser king.[4] For one act of madness. But what greater madness than to choose to bend to this man's yoke? To toil twelve years, and watch my Atlas perform the labours of Hercules.

In those twelve years since finding me weeping in the cathedral, since he began to hone his sermons and circulars on me, his grindstone and paragon—what successes his service to high Heaven has brought him here on Earth. Rector of the Jesuit College of St. Peter and St. Paul, he shapes not only the New World's young Jesuits, but Jesuit policy throughout the Spanish possessions. Prefect of the Brotherhood of Mary, he dispenses his ethical and practical guidance to a dozen of the most senior officers of both Church and State. Among these Brothers of Mary have been four vice-kings, all of whom Núñez has served also as confessor. And Father Núñez confesses others—the archbishops of Mexico.

Bridle the head and the body will follow.

For twelve years bridled but not blinkered I had watched him while he preached submission and humility, while he quoted Augustine to me, that with great gifts comes a greater responsibility—to endure, to be exemplary, to be strong. To suffer to lead from the rear.

While the work of Titans goes on in Europe.

Until, ten years ago, I told myself no more Hercules. No more pillars, no more *ne plus ultra*. Be their legend no longer, serve instead the daughters of the sea. Let them think me their theological Muse but quietly I will be my own—my own fountain, oracle and deeps.

¡Sí, plus ultra hay!

Or so I hear myself whispering as I sat across from him that day and said nothing.

Instead I plotted to reveal myself in increments, divert them in obliques, advance the sturdy fishing fleet by infinitesimal degrees until they found themselves far far beyond the pillars of Hercules. If Núñez is suddenly so interested in the geography of the oceans, I thought, let him read the welcome I will write for our new Viceroy and Vicereine: their Excellencies the Marquis of the Lake and the Countess of Walls. . . .

Déjame ver . . . how shall I title it? Something, like . . . Allegorical Neptune.

Sí, plus ultra, mas ultrajes, hay. More comedies.

It was another November. Not long after my birthday. 1680.

... This other canvas paints in bellicose
hues the Triton[5] goddess,[†]
once-engendered, twice-conceived,
never-born inventor
of arms and sciences;
but here in lucid rivalry
with the deity[††] who adores the tireless
Ocean—the Sun's foaming tomb—
whose greenblack lips' myriad kiss
spurs the dawn to greater glories,
and who, with spray and sea-spume,
Minerva's regent salt-limned foot
shods in silver buskins;
yet Minerva outrivals even Ocean,[6]
and even the Great Mother, unscathed withal,
though girt in strands of seas that seethe,
no less pacific for all their teeming
than she who decks the branches of the olive tree
with signs of peace and the fruit which—if but lightly pressed—
yields the precious oil the bookworm worships
as the Apollo of night;
and yet if too hard pressed, hotly she burns to meet
with Athenian aegis and brutal armada
the watery warships
of the Trident ...

JUANA INÉS
DE LA CRUZ,

"Allegorical
Neptune"

B. Limosneros, trans.

[†]Minerva / Athena

[††]Neptune

November 1680. The new Vice-King and his wife made their entry through two triumphal arches,[7] theatre sets of plaster columns and effigies, painted canvases and inscriptions, all explicated in a quote-studded companion booklet running to perhaps sixty pages of verse and prose. The arch for the cathedral was designed by Sor Juana, the other arch, in the Plaza de Santo Domingo, by don Carlos Sigüenza. His eschewed the usual mythological treatment for that of historical fact. He contrasted the peaceful governance of pre-Conquest America with the bloodiness of European power. Indeed arches should not be called triumphal since "... never was an arch erected for anyone who had not robbed five thousand enemies of their lives ..." His arch was not a success. Sor Juana's, meanwhile, depicted the Viceregal couple as a beauteously proportioned Neptune[8] and Amphitrite, naked on sea shells à la Botticelli, and elsewhere as Neptune and Minerva contending in wisdom for the guardianship of Athens. ...

onight, at last, he comes. February 24th, 1681. The anniversary of my profession. Of course he would come tonight.

Always the theatre of his disappearances, home to Zacatecas, to keep me waiting on the indulgence of a visit so that I may know the Reverend Father Núñez is displeased. Every Thursday night since November my locutory has lain in darkness, as a sign of deference. The other three chime with music and laughter, while the one reserved for my exclusive use—the most notorious parlour in Christendom, as he is so fond of calling it—lies dark. But Father Núñez is not a man to be placated.

New Spain's most relentless mind—bright like a blade. *Tragalibros,*[†] they call him for his learning. Living Memory of the Company they christen him for his complete recall of all he reads and hears. There is another title that chills me. The Jesuits' Living Library.

Living Library? I have one more exact—*Living Tomb of Tomes.* He makes hecatombs on the books I read as a girl and loved. For now comes the honour he has coveted more than all the others: the Holy Office has made this humble son of a silver miner Chief Censor. At the Inquisition there is only Dorantes to rival him.

Scratch the surface just a little, Núñez says, to read the vein of heresy in me—and how he rasps and scours, *mi escofina escolastica,*[†] to mine that vein before the others reach it. He has built his reputation on me, plundered for his oratory the spiritual journals he has ordered me to keep. But why, why does he still come? He has no more need of me. He is done playing the Father to me. Except in his absences.

Everyone fears him now—even our Viceroy admits to his own fear openly. At the Jesuit college the novices are reduced to whispers as their rector approaches—Sssh, *el Tragalibros,* hide your books and pamphlets. Sssh, Sor Juana's confessor . . .

In those three words, I have my answer. For my fame, still am I mined; my gilt adds lustre to his hoard. But how theatrically he defuses the charge, going about in that ridiculous cassock of his, torn and threadbare, teeming with vermin. Bleeding himself like some ecclesiastical barber—his scalpel, the flail. No, *mi escofina,* humble you are not.

[†] bookswallower

[†] my scholastic rasp

Why may I not be proud, why should this be a sin? To feel pride in the exercise of God-granted gifts. Am I born in a field, was I raised among weeds? Was I cradled on a crag, am I some wild beast?[9] Or am I a woman descended directly from Adam, with the rational soul that ennobles us all, that reflects as in the mirror in the lighthouse—the panopticon of Pharos—the greatest glory of God. . . .

Mind.

Why should it have been impossible to explain this to him *of all people,* to explain myself? Why have I tried and tried? Out of gratitude—because he was a father to me once, because he has loved my soul. But that was such a very long time ago. Can my simple arithmetic be so faulty, truly can it be that in the dozen years since that first day in the cathedral, he has come to me here *five hundred times?* Half a thousand times to scour my heart. Until I can no more.

And so I have sent for him. Tonight he will know I have had enough.

He comes at dusk when he comes at all, afternoons no longer. I have begun to suspect the sight is failing in those eyes the grey of cooling lead. All the long years, all the late nights of reading and banning by the mortal light of one candle. . . . Or is it that the bonfires have been so very bright?

Tonight we will sit in the locutory without so much as a single lamp. He will not surrender the slightest advantage to me. He will not give me the satisfaction of seeing it: *The book censor will one day be blind.* At dusk he comes like an owl, like Nyctimene,[10] to steal the oil from my lamps. And so it is in this dusk that I sit and brace myself, to face that face, to meet the exorbitant eyes, to see the rage under lids heavy with humility, the dry tongue, the lipless lips . . .

Courage do not fail me now.

"You asked for me."

"It's good you've come."

"We shall see."

"Very well, Father, we shall. I am hearing from every quarter that you are unhappy. Is it something I've written?"

"You are writing so much these days. It must be hard for you to guess."

"It must be hard for you to choose, with so much for you to censure, and so *many.* . . . I see it is official."

"You mean the nun."

"So we are finally saved from her *Mystical City of God*. And yet there are so many left for the Holy Office to extirpate. They pop up everywhere these days, these cities of God. Why do you suppose that is, Father?"

"Manuscripts may be suppressed for many reasons, Sor Juana, and not solely by the Holy Office . . ."

"What are you getting at?"

"The proposals you and Carlos sent over created a great stir in Madrid."

"You know even this."

"Very bold, very inventive. Refinements to the pendulum. A musical clock—admirable. Your idea, I understand. Other notions for marine chronometers—such stunning breakthroughs for navigation, strategic advantages to the Crown . . . if they could be made to work, if the proper studies could be funded, tests of your designs. A pity to have destroyed them."

"*What?*"

"Your Queen buys bread on credit, Juana. Perhaps you think the Crown's bankruptcy a figure of speech. There is no money for studies. Yet if those designs were to end up with the Portuguese, or the English, or worse yet the Netherlanders . . . So you see, you divide not just the Jesuit scientists, Juana—you and now Carlos—but the Queen's scientific soothsayers also. About half were in favour of saving them, no doubt with thoughts of brokering a quiet sale. Yes, I am surprised your don Payo did not think to tell you. As are you, I see. But Carlos must have made copies, yes?"

"Even from Madrid, don Payo reports to you."

"To *us*, Sor Juana, he writes to us. Always this exaggeration of my influence. In some quarters, I think, your imagination hinders you. You imagine you know him, but do you know His Grace left Mexico in such a hurry so as not to miss the *auto* in Madrid? No, I thought not. By all accounts—and I have read several—it put those of our poor Mexico to shame. Thirty-four burned in effigy, nineteen more in the flesh, twelve burned alive. *Twelve*. And two women, this time. . . . You *do* know he sat with the Queen Mother. No, not even that? In the royal box, with that dwarf of hers your Leonor prated on so about. What was her name? It was so long ago."

"Had I told you a century ago, you'd still know."

"Yes. 'Lucillo.' *I* imagine them that day discussing your *Martyr of the Sacrament* together, at breaks. Now. You have called me here, you have come this far. Am I expected to offer my help?"

"Help, Your Reverence?"

"You stall but do not refuse it outright. Well then. How shall I oblige you—by asking how you and our new Vice-Queen are getting on? Something of a poet, this one, though I am a poor judge. And she is a Manrique! Countess of Paredes, no less. How perfect for you both."

"The knighthood of the Manriques was not always such an amusement, Father. Your saintly Loyola did not jeer at the Order of Santiago, nor did he refuse it. At least I don't recall your ever saying so. Need I remind you?—when the Marquis and the Countess first announced their intention to visit me here, did I not plead for *two days* to be allowed to remain secluded in my cell?"

"But the Mother Prioress denied you—"

"At your insistence—why *was* that?"

"And how assiduously you have been attending them, Sor Juana, to have missed confession so often lately—and how many of our Thursdays together?"

"Two, Father. Only two."

"Countess of Walls! Marquis of the Lake! How Fate makes Life convenient to your poetry—how your poetry bends you towards your fate. Allegorical Neptune! *Water,* again."

"The arch was a cathedral commission, the Chapter approved it—unanimously, as you well know."

"And do you call her María Luisa yet? Have you explained to this new one about your *past?* How it was with the other one? *Queen of the Baths.*"

"Always these imaginings of *yours,* Reverence, about the baths at El Péñon."

"Have you explained to her your new aqueous theology?"

"Is it impious on my part that duty has blossomed into loving friendship for her, whereas Your Reverence guides the immortal soul of her husband, though you harbour no feelings for him whatever? And once again you confess Viceroy and Vicereine both."

"It is not a question of feelings."

"This too has changed with you, Father. It was not always so."

"I suppose you profess some admirable depth of feeling for the Archbishop-*elect.*"

"Why do you say it like that?"

"Only to say your manoeuvring with the Bishop of Puebla carries risks. But no, forget I mentioned it. He is after all another protégé of don Fray Payo."

"Is there a problem with the Bishop's election? What do the *Jesuits* know of it?"

"As for whom I confess, it will be the new Archbishop's privilege to confess the Vice-Queen, if he wishes it. But as you say, the Viceroy will likely remain with me. Or do you call him Neptune now?"

"How unlike you, Father, to misspeak. *Do the Jesuits have another candidate?*"

"Was it the comet, Sor Juana?"

"Was what the comet—the comet is gone."

"Yes, precisely. Two days ago. And here we are. Like sorcery."

"No magic I possess tells me on which nights Your Reverence will deign to appear. And on that subject might we not try the everyday magic of a lantern, Father? It is getting rather dark."

"But you *have* been busy reassuring the Vice-Queen."

"She spoke to you of this."

"We have conversations, much as you and I—"

"Told you in *confession*."

"Conversations."

"Intended to terrify her—'God's Wrath.'"

"And how did you reassure her, Juana? With Galilei's rubbish about comets hiding behind the moon? Did you show it to her in your telescope, show her the moon's face—*poxed like a whore's?* Did that reassure? Nothing divine about it, nothing heavenly in the heavens!"

"That, Father, you will *never* hear me say."

"Tell me—I never understood it, why they hide behind the moon. . . . Great elliptical orbits, was it not, out among the heavenly spheres? How helpful the Chair of Mathematics and Astrology could have been in comforting your new friend. A shame you and Carlos are not getting along."

"We will sort it out. As we always do."

"I am glad to hear it. Because the spectacle of New Spain's two brightest children squabbling is less than inspiring. You of course are entitled, you are only thirty-two, but Carlos is old enough to know better. *How like you to turn on an old friend.*"

"But such venom, Your Reverence. Is it really over me? or still over your slip about the election. The Archbishop-*elect* will be intrigued."

"Your poor Carlos, how confused he must be. Privately, you share his view that the comet is a natural event, yet write a sonnet glorifying his adversary's position. A position Carlos has risked much to denounce as superstition, and is being attacked for it even now. These natural philosophical debates are filled with such—"

"Vitriol, Father?—spleen? Yes how ill-humoured these natural magicians, and in comparison how benign the gentle quibbles of theology must seem."

"I have noticed how amusing you can be precisely—"

"So Your Reverence may catch his breath."

"No, Sor Juana. Precisely when you are in moral difficulties. You seem to be distancing yourself from don Carlos lately, who is, unlike you, hopeless at diplomacy. His *arco* caused the Viceroy precisely as much annoyance as yours gave delight."

"He was lucky not to be arrested."

"Perhaps this makes Carlos a hindrance to you now, or perhaps you feel justified after he insulted you. What was it he called you afterwards? *Una limosnera de leyendas!*"

"*Mendiga de fabulas.*"

"Fable beggar, yes, thank you. A sharp quill, your friend has. It might have been better to keep him as a friend."

"Why do the Jesuits not reinstate him?"

"You seek to ease your conscience, Juana, by taking up his cause. But I will tell you. We prefer to have don Carlos looking in. He does more to restrain himself this way. The Company would be too small for one such as he, whereas you, for all your attempts at caution and secrecy, your deepest impulses are—"

"After all the petitions he has made, it is pure cruelty."

"You want us to solve your problems for you. How many petitions of marriage has he made to you? Have you no loyalty? *Are you proud of what you have done to your friend*—by siding with his adversary?"

"I . . . no."

"Was it *wrong?*"

"I said I was not proud of it."

"Yet your conscience does not trouble you. It has been weeks and I have heard not one word of this in confession."

"You have often been away. Zacatecas, I imagine."

"That is why this convent has a chaplain. For the times when your spiritual director must be absent. But you have not confessed this to him, either."

"You sound certain."

"False confession, Sor Juana, is a most serious matter. I know also why you have sent for me."

"Do you."

"You have been planning this for weeks."

"And if you know—*how* do you?"

"For weeks and yet you have delayed, and delay even now. I will help you one last time. *Tell me what you are writing.*"

"If you think you know, Father, why do *you* delay—why not just be forthright?"

"That a nun, *a woman in my charge,* is now called Tenth Muse from Cadiz to Lima to Manila is already utterly repugnant to me! Had I known you would waste your convent life on verses I would have married you off!"

"You think me a dog or a slave to dispose of."

"But with this latest, you make it impossible for me to defend you, Juana."

"Defend me! You think I do not hear of them—the reproaches you make against me to anyone who'll listen? You call my conduct a scandal, you make the substance of my confessions a public matter. Defend me— there's not a man in New Spain to stand up to you. Even the Marquis himself—Regent of half the world—*fears* you. The last viceroy still writes from Spain to ask your guidance. Now I ask you, Your Reverence, to tell me what I have done to so infuriate you this time."

"In which role have you conspired to make me look the greater fool, as your confessor or New Spain's Censor?—in the plays or in the verses? *Tenth Muse.* Can you not grasp how obscene that epithet is for any Catholic, let alone one of *my* nuns?"

"Even the Holy Virgin has been called the Tenth Muse lately—would you censor her too?"

"Do not push me too far."

"Is that prospect so fantastic—when your Office has just banned the *Mystical City,* a set of parables on the Virgin's life?"

"Not parables, Sor Juana, prophecies. For some nuns it is not enough that María should be the Mother of God. No, they must make her into something *more.*"

"But this still isn't it, is it Father. They have been calling me Muse for some time. This is not quite what makes you so . . . *passionate.*"

"A bride of Christ under my direction composing love poetry—"

"Yes?"

"On *Sappho*."

"At last."

"What could possibly *be* more of a—"

"Humiliation?"

"A disgrace! *I am your spiritual director,* charged with the safe conduct of a nun's soul to her Husband's embrace. I should know every single detail of your life, every thought, every dream. The contents of your soul should be spread wide for me to inspect. And now—yet again!—you've defiled the sacrament of confession by your lies of omission."

"*I* defile it, Father? And what of the sacramental seal? And if my privacy means nothing to you, how long am I to conceal from María Luisa the contempt in which you hold hers?"

"'María Luisa.' Only your Countess could make you think to get away with this. *Sappho.* Who could even have *imagined* this outrage—poetry to a Lesbian *puta!*"

"You forget yourself, Father, you forget where you are, you forget who is the true Master of this house—and make it abundantly clear you have no idea what you are talking about."

"But I *will* know. You will bring these . . . *things* to me and we will read them together, then burn—together—each and every one, down to the last scrap, the last strip of paper!"

"No, Father, *we* will not."

"Now you defile your vow of *obedience* and revel in it!"

"No, Father, I do *not*. But saintliness is not a thing you command. No being of free will—I, last of all—can be brought to God by coercion. If it could be commanded, my soul would have already ascended to Heaven a hundred times. Tell me, does my correction fall to Your Reverence by reason of obligation or charity? I too have my obligations. If it be charity then proceed gently. I am not of so servile a nature as to bend to such mercies, as you well know—"

"I see we reach the part you have been rehearsing."

"Any sacrifices I make are undertaken to mortify my spirit and not to avoid censure, no matter how public. From you—such has always been my love and veneration—I could bear anything, any amount of injustice, *in private*. But these public humiliations, these extravagant . . . exaggerations unjustly tar this convent's good name."

"What little remains of it."

"Everyone in the capital listens to your words and trembles at their stern import as though you were a prophet of old, as though they were dictated by the Holy Ghost—"

"Go carefully."

"How many times have I found *your* words and your commandments *exceedingly* repugnant yet held my peace? But after so many years my breast overflows with the injustice. *I have done nothing wrong*—nothing criminal, nothing sinful. If sin there be it is only pride—our shared affliction, Father. I am *not* humbled as might be other daughters on whom your instruction would be so much better lavished. Your opinions in these minor matters are just that, and unwelcome. *They are not Holy Writ.* If you cannot find it in your heart to favour me, and to counsel me calmly or even harshly, but in in the privacy of confession—a sacrament *you* defile whenever it suits you—then I beg you think of me no more. Release me from your hand and grant me no more favours, for I am doomed to disappoint you."

"Think, now, what you ask."

"God has fashioned many keys to Heaven—which contains as many rooms as there are different natures. Do you not think my salvation might be effected through the guidance of another? Is the dispensation of God's mercy limited to just one man, no matter how wise or righteous?"

"And just whom did you have in mind?"

"Father Arellano."

"That ecstatic?"

"Your disciple."

"Your *worst* possible choice! Someone who will indulge you, who will let you make him a fool."

"You claim that's exactly what I've made of you. Choice, Father. Choice is what you are always exhorting me to. Arellano understands passion, he understands faith, and penance best of all."

"You have said nothing of reason."

"Reason, I understand."

"Too well. Or, just possibly, not quite well enough. . . . Reason carefully then, child. You have called me here for this. Your Countess has given you the nerve. But calculate well. This thing is not easily undone. . . ."

"That much I know. After so many years."

"Do you wish a short time to reconsider?"

"Father I ask only that you commend me to God, which I know in your charity you will do with all fervour."

"So be it then. I commend you. To your God."

SAPPHO
OF LESBOS,[II]

"Sapphic
Fragment"

Guy Davenport, trans.

*Early in the 20th
century, a portion
of Sappho's work,
long thought lost,
was rediscovered in
Egypt, where her
poems had been
recycled, torn into
vertical strips and
used as the papyri
in which bodies
were wrapped and
mummified.*

[   ] slick with slime [   ]
[   ] Polyanaktidas to satiety [   ]
[   ] shoots forward [   ]
Playing such music upon these strings
Wearing a phallus of leather [   ]
Such a thing as this [   ] enviously
[   ] twirls quivering masterfully
[   ] and has for odor
[   ] hollow [   ]
[   ]
[   ] mysteries, orgies
[   ] leaving
[   ] an oracle
[   ] comes [   ]
[   ]
[com]panions
[mys]teries
[   ]
[   ]
[   ] sister
So [   ]
[   ] wishes [   ]
Displays again Polyanaktidas [   ]
This randy madness I joyfully proclaim.

CUE THE NEWSREEL to the mid-1980s. Here flowers the good life, in Calgary. Here it springs eternal, from the genteel wildernesses steeping in the compost box. There it is—just back of the barbecue pit. Lately I've had some trouble keeping track of it. . . .

THE GOOD LIFE

If in this country Toronto plays the spinster aunt to Vancouver's kohl-eyed flower child ageing sad, then Calgary is the good life's tow-headed majorette. A Toronto whose plumbing still works. Let's see, that would make Montréal the bitter divorcée . . . *mais non, ça suffit.* Certainly the future belongs to Calgary. The next big score's just three first downs away. A whole new ball game out there, a world of enterprise. High tech jobs, plans for a new convention centre and casino, big event hospitality. Volunteer armies raised by racketeers.

We have green spaces and rising real estate. We have country stores in the inner city. We ski to reading weekends in mountain cabins, breed pure dogs, grow organic gardens . . .

It was a good life. But all during those years, when people would exclaim over my wife's beauty I felt a kind of puzzlement. Alluring, yes, seductive, most days. But *beautiful* . . . the word sometimes came from a man lip's as a rebuke, from a woman's as something abject, a sigh of capitulation. And over those same years, even as our shaggy pride of university dons slouched soft-bellied about the backyard barbecue pit, slipping into the clichés of our lechery and hockey scores like a well-worn pair of mules, our wives—in the kitchen, the bedroom, the gym—were becoming each day more tawny, more trim, more lion-eyed. Particularly mine.

So that now, in the '90s, our wives emerge for us as creatures of not just flesh and blood but bone—at their cheeks, their jaws, their clavicles. And just when we in our stifled desperation see they could be our mantle, the laurel staff of our high office, they are no longer ours to wield.

They run their own consulting firms, and four miles every morning. They wear their hair shorter than ours. Their shoulders are more cleanly defined, their wrists more richly veined. Our hands are soft and white and smooth, theirs are the hands of carpenters from handling hoes and rakes.

They are elemental in the garden, we are pallid in the shade.

Beneath straw hats they glow with the rude health of an honest tan. Hats, they wear beautifully—men's hats, and with an authority perplexingly denied us. Stylish in berets, bowlers and fedoras; cosmopolitan in leather pillboxes and felted fezzes; striking in sandals strapped up the calf—embroidered vests, gladiators' skirts on gladiators' thighs—they are a tribe, fierce and golden.

What are we? A troupe . . . a troop? Surely not a pride. Pride's too proud a word.

She's teaching herself piano, so one day she can teach our Catherine.

So simple to be superwomen, so hard to be just men.

Kept from saying farewell
sweet love, my only life,
by unremitting tears,
by unrelenting time,
    these strokes must speak for me,
amidst my echoing sighs,
sad penstrokes never yet
more justly coloured black.
    Their speech perforce is blurred
by tears that well and drop,
for water quickly drowns
words conceived in flame.
    Eyes forestall the voice,
foreseeing, as they do,
each word I plan to speak
and saying it themselves.
    Heed the eloquent silence
of sorrow's speech and catch
words that breathe through sighs,
conceits that shine through tears . . .

JUANA INÉS
DE LA CRUZ

Alan Trueblood, trans.

*Year: 1688. The
Viceroy and his
wife, the Countess
of Paredes, have
remained in
Mexico two years
beyond their second
term of service. At
last María Luisa
can postpone their
departure no longer.*

HYPERMNESTRA *28th day of August, 1688,*
Mexico City

la excma. señora doña María Luisa Manrique de Lara y Gonzaga
Condesa de Paredes, Marquesa de la Laguna,
Madrid

Queridísima María Luisa,

 *thought to fast from news of you.*[12] Yet it is not a fast if the hunger is not chosen. Better said, then, when you set out for Madrid, I had thought to starve. I confess this Lenten faithlessness now, as one so deliriously fed since your letter arrived. You vowed you would not forget; yet so weak is my capacity for faith, at times I could not quite believe. And even summoning belief, still I could not *hope*—so very much lies beyond our control.

The year has been a bitter one. Your leaving, and then within a month my mother's death. (But could it be you have not received my last two letters . . . ?) I did not even know of her illness.

Carlos went, thinking I suppose to represent me, though even had I wanted to, I could not have kept him here. Panoayan, it seemed, was always on the way to anywhere Carlos was going. It is hard for me to see them as friends, and yet he had known her twenty years. For nearly as long as I had not seen her.

This time he found Bishop Santa Cruz there, who had come all the way from Puebla and had stayed to celebrate her Mass—for me, but especially for my nephew, Fray Miguel now, who is devoted to him. Greatly do I doubt the honour would have meant much to her—she had little use for churchmen, or for her grandson Miguel, I gather—but it meant a great deal to me, and I was happy for the town. I doubt the church in Amecameca had seen a bishop in quite some time.

How coldly this all rings in the air as I say it aloud. As you know, Isabel and I were not reconciled.

In his visits here since, Bishop Santa Cruz has skirted the issue with great delicacy, as is his way. He has been such a friend, and with you gone

I am more than ever in his care. Still, I was stunned to learn he had been there at the end, been the one to administer her rites. Something in the scene unsettles me. Strain enough to imagine that she had confessed— yet what?

But how can I answer your first letter with such chill gloom?

You have *written*, you are safely returned, your son thrives, and your dear Tomás's prospects for advancement look more shining all the time. You even mention you have looked a little into publishing our collection, and from the way you write of it I will follow your lead and not let my hopes rise too high. As you say, securing the support of the Church there when I do not have it here will be difficult. But since you ask me for a title, perhaps I may still hope a little?

To that small bright thought I venture to add others, and kindle myself a small new fire here in the hearth. I share its little glow now with you: the Bishop, you see, has brought not just support but help and company. A secretary, who should be taking this down even now. *No 'Tonia, that's what a fair copy is for. Take down everything. We decide what to cross out afterwards—and you, we do not cross out—*

Would I, the Bishop asks, have any use for a young woman, with lit- tle fortune but with a good orthography, a decent Latin he himself has seen to, a passable style in Castilian, a rough familiarity with Italian and Portuguese—and who, if that were not enough, plays the clavichord beautifully? I have since learned she has a fair and improving knowledge of Nahuatl, too, and she is in return teaching me phrases of an Angolan dialect taught her by her mother. What's more, in the privacy of our cell Antonia has been sharpening my fluency in curses, which she spouts with more flair—should she dislodge a book or drop a plate—than a seafaring apostate.

She is also lovely, with a brambly thrum and tangle of tresses such as I have never seen.

My Most Excellent Lady Countess, I take great pleasure in present- ing Antonia Mora, ~~my godsend and salvation~~—*did you just cross that out?*—until recently resident in Puebla and now an oblate here in San Jerónimo. Officially her dowry was paid by me, though Bishop Santa Cruz arranged for everything. She lodges here and half her time may be spent working at this table. Henceforth, you shall never have cause to complain of the brevity of my letters. In fact I promise amply to repay (if not in quality then in lines) each line you find the time to write.

The Mother Prioress raised few objections to the Bishop's arrangements. Four thousand pesos is not an inconsiderable sum for a dowry, even were Antonia a nun. The Bishop shifts the credit to me, arguing that I bring the convent treasury many times that amount in donations and commissions. But I have been doing that for years. No, if Mother Andrea is more tractable now, it is for the same reason that she acquiesces in the Bishop's wishes: That nothing short of seeing every nun in Mexico barefoot[13] will placate Archbishop Aguiar. In the past few years the Prioress has discovered that in the Archbishop's eyes whatever good we do is little, whatever ill incalculable. I cannot help but laugh remembering that first day he came from the backcountry after his surprise election, the hasty plans you and I laid to win him over with an evening at the palace. Not knowing of his hatred of theatre you made him our comedy's guest of honour; not knowing of his hatred of worldliness in nuns, I dared to write it. Win the Archbishop over—what a fiasco. And remember how we laughed (what else could we do?) over his contortions to avoid you at official functions—so dire, so very grim, the reports of your beauty! How wonderfully you mimed the sudden swerves, the myopic glaring—it was as if I saw him there myself.

Strange to think that I have never once laid eyes on him, on whom so much now depends.

The Bishop of Puebla, meanwhile, has proved in almost every respect the Archbishop's opposite. And while the Archbishop of Mexico has never been to San Jerónimo or any other convent in his city, the Bishop of Puebla rarely misses a chance to call. He comes to the capital so often lately it's said Mexico has two archbishops. Though there is little he may do to soften the Archbishop's anger, there is much he may do behind the scenes, as he does now. And so at long last it seems there is help for me.

As an oblate Antonia is bound to the rule of our convent by every vow but that of enclosure. In the way of the Indian cooks and the servants of the wealthiest sisters here, Antonia, our sole oblate, is freer than we sisters are, if only in this one regard. So trivial it must seem to them, this liberty, and yet so enormous to me. She insists on doing everything within her power, from the cooking here in our rooms down to the most repellent of chores. She persuaded me finally to divest myself of my one servant, who had become pregnant—which started up all the speculations again about just what sort of errands Sor Juana sends one on. She swore the conception was immaculate, and while I did not doubt that it seemed so to her, I sent her nevertheless to my sister Josefa, who will treat her kindly.

A secretary is of course a source of vanity, mortifying in a nun—and in employing five secretaries simultaneously, truly the Learned Aquinas must have been an Angelic Doctor not to succumb; so it would be ungracious of me to reproach my friend the Bishop for not having arranged something like this years ago. In his own defence he might simply answer that there are not five Antonias in all the New World. In addition to taking dictation and writing out fair copies, Antonia arranges for their delivery, wears a penitential groove into the flagstones between my bookshelves and the convent library, treads out still other channels from the porter's gate to the city's printers and booksellers.

And yet she persists in vexing me with complaints that she would prefer to stay here, when a walk in the streets is for me a dream slow to fade. She might not go out at all, could I not bribe her with a few classes in poetry. In exchange for which she pretends to enjoy helping me with two new duties I have been given. Nominally similar, one I dislike as much as the other I enjoy. Leading religious instruction in Nahuatl for the servants is the first, but the second is preparing classes purely of my own devising for a dozen of our more promising novices. With respect to the former, I well know how their thoughts bend our Faith to flow in courses more natural to them, and who am I of all people to say they should not bend? It makes me feel like a Jesuit. But as for our academy, bending our thoughts is precisely the object of our academic devotions, even as one bends both in penance and in pleasure.

Once again it is the Bishop's intercession I have to thank—and Mother Andrea's newly tractable mood, but even here Santa Cruz presents her with an argument worthy, in its cunning, of a certain Florentine counsellor to princes.[14] 'My dear Mother Andrea, while so many of our leading citizens come to consult the myriad wise and learned nuns throughout the capital, and come to be edified by still other sisters skilled in music and poetry, San Jerónimo—in competing for patrons—depends more than do all the city's other convents on so very few of its gifted sisters. . . .'

Sly enough on the face of it. It also quietly reminds her we must work doubly hard to repay his favours here, with the new convent of Santa Monica taking up so much of his time in Puebla. And lying beneath this reminder is one not so gentle. For while Father Núñez is vain about his humility, Bishop Santa Cruz is supremely serene in his considerable vanity—unless the compliment of his favour is returned with too little gratitude.

In evidence I give you a recent sample of the gossip that the sisters bring by my cell in any unoccupied instant. If there is one treat of which we are insatiate it is news of our sister convents, and this particular story even I cannot resist, since it concerns not only ours and the new convent of Santa Monica, but a young woman from near Tepeaca, about a half day's travel from Puebla. (Antonia's eyes have gone wide—she is from near Tepeaca herself, a town with which I have associations of my own.)

The young woman of our story, having one sister already professed at the convent of San Jerónimo in Puebla, had been trying for twelve years to take the veil. Living in an outbuilding on the family hacienda, mortifying her flesh, praying in her solitude, fasting and having visions. The people of the town had taken to calling her the Hermit—with scorn by some, no doubt.[15] But among the *campesinos* of the haciendas were those who revered her as a *beata*.[†] A vocation that the Holy Office has been making more than perilous. So this and a terrible loneliness, I suspect, gave her excellent reason to seek the protection of the veil. Bishop Santa Cruz had initially found sufficient cause to take her. She was of a good family that after the death of the father fell into straitened circumstances. Despite her emaciation she must have been pretty, for it is common knowledge that Santa Cruz favours pretty nuns. For obvious reasons, I have never quite found a way to ask him if this is true, or why it should be so. Does he imagine a plain woman needs no protection, or is there no pleasure in a secret possession unless others, knowing, would covet it? In any event he was disposed to take all seven remaining sisters into the college that was about to become the convent of Santa Monica.

What, then, could possibly have happened that even months later she had still not been granted entry? She was further away from it in fact— as far away as could be imagined. The scene I'm about to present is still almost unimaginable to me . . . Santa Cruz has just celebrated Mass. A half-starved girl throws herself at his feet, begging admission to his newest convent, as she has done every day for weeks. And indeed, though she has done nothing differently today, he loses his temper, shouts at her to stop harassing him, and thrusts her angrily away. The cathedral of our second greatest city was filled that day with worshippers. He still wears the chasuble, the dalmatic, the stole. Stunned, anguished, in a weakened state, as the girl makes her way from the cathedral she stumbles and falls heavily down the steps.

This from a man usually in such complete possession of himself. A man I like and respect.

Here is what I believe led to this. When first learning of the Bishop's plans for his family, the brother of the poor hermitess protested. He had just taken over the family hacienda, was about to lose all his sisters at once, and was now faced with not just losing their aid and company but somehow finding the means to pay seven dowries. (For once I am able to put Carlos's laments about his university stipend to some use: each dowry equalled some fifteen years' salary; the seven together would be enough to pay 105 professors of Mathematics and Astronomy for one year.)

And yet this was only the material component of the objection, and the lesser, I suspect. For here is the rough crux of our story: *the punctilious pride of these men.* Apparently the girls' college had been, before Santa Cruz took it over, a house of reclusion for prostitutes. Complicating the matter further, the Bishop had the idea of naming it the College of Saint Mary of Egypt, after the prostitute who had signed on to the sea voyage from Alexandria to the Holy Land. How does the *Lives* put it?—not for the pilgrimage *'but in the hope that life on board ship would afford her new and abundant opportunities of gratifying an insatiable lust.'*

The brother balked at the blemish such a name (even of one who on that voyage became a saint!) would leave upon his own. The fortunes of seven women turned on this—and for one woman in particular, the hopes of a dozen years. For his part, Bishop Santa Cruz, incensed at the slight to his honour (or to his tastes in nomenclature), had refused to so much as speak to her again (and refused also to pay her elder sister's convent dowry, allegedly breaking his solemn promise). Matters would have rested there, if the Bishop's own spiritual director hadn't intervened after the scandal at the cathedral. Santa Cruz was finally persuaded to reconsider, and the Provincial of the Dominican Order went himself into the country to collect her.

Having ears to hear, Mother Andrea needs no help to grasp that the only thing worse than the Archbishop's enmity is compounding it with the Bishop's. Thus, in the matter of our new classes for novices, it now pleases Andrea no less than it does me that in our refectory once a week I am training a whole *generation* of my own replacements.

How I would love for you to be our honoured guest and, should you so incline, guest lecturer too at our academy—this week especially. I had thought to do a close study of the *Ars Amatoria* as a farewell to Ovid, but then, with Antonia's anxious assent, took a more prudent tack. And yet if I tell you we will be studying *Heroides 15*, perhaps you will not think me quite so much the coward.

(Wait, I've thought of a way to have you present, or rather bring our echoes to you, as you shall presently see. . . .)

And as for our collection of verses, I promise to think about a name suitable to an introductory volume. All year I have felt myself slowly sinking beneath the weight of a thousand unasked tasks and cares; as a consequence, the titles that have come to mind are quite ghastly. My ideas run to such as the Danaïdes: the fifty granddaughters of Poseidon and the Nile condemned unfairly by the judges of the dead to haul water in sieves for having murdered (but in self-defence!) the fifty sons of Aegyptus. From which tender reflections spring such inspiring titles as *Hypermnestra's Sieve, Lernaean Lake* . . . I had almost settled on *Amymone's Spring,* as it is a source that never runs dry even during the cruellest droughts on the driest of plains. But since the water springs from holes in the stone where the trident's tines went in, just before Amymone's ravishment by Poseidon . . . Well, you will see the problem instantly.

If a nun absolutely must be pagan, she should at least be chaste.

All my love, and to your two men my warmest embraces.

día 28 de agosto, Anno Domini 1688
del convento de San Jerónimo,
de la Ciudad Imperial de México,
Nueva España

SCENE I: *After Nones, hour of siesta. A convent refectory, between the convent kitchens and the temple. The refectory is thirty varas long by nine wide, its ceiling ten varas high; just beneath the ceiling are windows, a clerestory of three at equal intervals along the north and south walls; high up on the chapel side, a screened lattice behind which appear, from time to time, figures in vague outline. Behind a closed double door, the kitchens, from which now come the sounds of pots and dishes being washed. From the kitchens to the rostrum, two long oak tables run in parallel, the full length of the room, to where two women sit. One in a rough brown shift, the other in the Hieronymite habit: white tunic (silk) with full, tapering sleeves, black scapular, white coif, parchment escutcheon high at the breast, black cincture at the waist, rosary extending to the knees. . . .*

ACADEMY

[*Antonia holding a book*] Juana, tell me you haven't.

I have.

But *why?*

You thought *Heroides* 15 rash.[†] So I prepared something else.

†'Heroines'

But the *Ars Amatoria?*—a banned book!

You're sure.

No, but I've been reading it, haven't I?—a book like this *must* be.

Mightn't you be thinking of Ovid's own banishment? Which I suspect was more about the conduct of Ovid's relations with the emperor than about the *Arts of Love.* You don't imagine Roman emperors were so easy to shock.

But why teach it *now?*

You mean why here. The *Amores* I would teach as the first pedestal of courtly poetry—with which a nun, if she is to entertain the courtly in her locutory—

But this—[*lifting the book*]

Whereas the *Ars Amatoria,* I would teach as a manual of self-defence.

But—

But I will not be teaching it, after all—ever eager as I am to please you, 'Tonia. Which leaves us with the *Heroides,* since they'll be here in ten minutes.

You never planned to do the other at all.

Antonia!

It was so I wouldn't argue anymore about doing the 15. But Juana, the *Archbishop*—

Would hate the existence of these classes more than any particular thing we might teach in them.

But he hates *us*—our songs—our *voices.*

Plays and music have had a place in the cloister for centuries. It will take more than one archbishop, however lunatic, to change that.

You, he hates most of all.

Why I've never met the man. Which is fortunate—for we might have to warrant his grievance if he actually knew me.

It's not a thing to smile about—why aren't you *afraid* of him?

Whatever would make you think that?

You shouldn't *provoke* him.

Come Antonia, you've been telling me all week how hard they're working. San Jerónimo's best young minds. This is the Hieronymite convent of the learned widow Santa Paula, after all. Think of this as our Holy Land—and Paula herself, not the Vicaress, back of the lattice smiling down at us.

[*faint knock*]

There—listen to them giggling—their *voices.* Female scholars. A miracle!

But the Prioress—

Will know soon enough. We're keeping them waiting, 'Tonia. Our little academy of beauty . . . Are they early?

You know why.

Then we give them extra algebra first, since they're so keen.

Not for algebra.

At least we may hope therewith to lull the Vicaress into that deep algebraic rumination best expressed in counting sheep. After that, a bit of astronomy. Half the girls like *that*, at least. Then the Ovid for anyone still upright. There now, *mi amor*. It really is all right to smile. You've marked the sections? And not just the pirates and the Amazons, I trust. . . .

[*Enter twelve young women between the ages of fifteen and twenty, in the robes of postulants.*]

SCENE II: *An hour later. Throughout, the refectory door has been open. The afternoon light through the orchard leaves plays indistinct shadows over the floor beside the rostrum.*

The nun, still attractive for her age, walks to the door, stands a moment looking out. Along the refectory wall runs a long narrow walkway over-arched by orchard boughs; through the trees, glimpses of extensive garden plots, tinajas†, shady colonnades. She turns back to the somnolent classroom and, glancing up at the lattice above the rostrum, gently pulls the door closed behind her. She speaks . . .

†fountain basins / water tanks

. . . All right, enough astronomy for today—none of you is listening anyway. And why would that be, I wonder? Are you all with Tomasina here?—who seems to think the telescope was invented so the novices of San Jerónimo might miss nothing of what goes on in the rooms across the street. And again all I get is laughter for an answer! Enough, then?—or shall we turn to Ovid?

Yes!

Please, Juana.

María, Belilla . . . Anyone else interested?

Sor Juana, you know we are.

You're teasing us.

Why bother with these old stories?

¡Cállate! Tomasina. Juana, don't listen.

Be a bit kinder, Belilla. She's started us off with an excellent question, even if asked a few weeks late. So. Why read Ovid's old stories . . . ? Quickly now, not much time left.

They tell the exploits of heroes?

And heroines too, *verdad* Isabel? Anyone else?

They show a pagan world—the world of sin before Christ.

Yes, Ana, and something of the world's sins since, don't you think?

But why teach women at all?

Sor Juana, don't encourage her.

Ask Tomasina why she even comes then—*why* Tomasina? Tell us.

Didn't Saint Paul say *mulieres in ecclesia taceant?*

Why Tomasina, how nice to see our lessons in Latin bearing fruit! That women should be silent in Church is not necessarily bad. Men also might profit from a little more silence before their God, don't you agree? Even a saint may say too much—

Sor Juana!

Don't you think Saint Paul would smile to see his *dictum* used by a girl who hates homework? Ah, dear girl, a smile from you is heavenly reward indeed. Isabel, what if I told you Ana had a cold last week? Old news, you'd say—

Sor Juana, I wouldn't!

No dear, you wouldn't be so rude, but you'd be thinking it—or some of you. What makes some old news last a thousand years?—mere stories outlasting an empire, as Ovid's have outlived the empire that exiled him. Maybe you'll consider this during our work today. Antonia tells me you've given *Heroides* 15 your close attention. . . . You've read his *Metamorphoses*: what's the most obvious difference here?

They're in the form of letters?

Good, on this we're quite agreed, but to whom?

To their . . . lovers?

Yes Isabel, some might say that. And number 15 is purportedly written by? Come now, quickly—

Sappho.

Ah, a little hush stills the room. At last we've everyone's attention. Sappho . . . apparently the learned woman isn't such a novelty after all, Tomasina. But what do we really know about Sappho? Antonia?

That she was a teacher of women.

So they say. Good, what else—Belilla?

That she was a—

She was called the *Tenth Muse.*

Belilla thanks you, Antonia. And how many Muses were there supposed to be?

[*in unison*]

Nine!!!

How lovely!—our own chorus.

But Sor Juana, they call *you* that.

Really Isabel? [*mock coquette*] Then it seems they'll call anyone that these days. But Ovid puts her in a whole regiment of heroines—alongside . . . anyone?

Ariadne?—

Phaedra—

Helen!-

Stop, please—

Hypermnestra!—

Medea!—

Stop, *señoritas,* no need for all of them!—thank you. Now, what is Ovid up to? Heroines, he calls them—his gallery of adulteresses, parricides, Amazons. And how does a flesh and blood woman end up in such a collection? The Greeks called Sappho the Poetess in the same way they honoured Homer as the Poet. Yet Ovid has her heaving great sighs over a boatman named?

Phaon—

A *boy.*

Why yes, Belilla.

Young enough to be her son.

Ah the ups and downs of motherhood—ask Procne, ask Iocaste. Ask the sisters Ariadne and Phaedra—indeed, half Ovid's heroines have taken a rather disastrous fall. How curious, and how precarious for Sappho. Ovid puts her on a cliff ledge, spurned, her wondrous poetic voice stopped, mimicked now by a plangent echo. Antonia, will you read for us? You know the place.

> I come upon the forest that offered us many times
> the bed we lay upon, and whose abundant boughs covered us in darkness.
> But I do not find the master, the forest's lord, and mine. The place
> is only impoverished earth; his presence was the grace that endowed it.
> I recognized the grass, pressed down, of the familiar hollow
> our bodies made in the blades on the green remembered bank.
> I lay down and touched the place, the part in which you lay.
> The earth that once delighted me was thirsty and drank in my tears.
> Even the branches have cast off their leaves; they seem to mourn;
> the birds are quiet; none make their dear lament.
> Only the nightingale, only Philomel, whose terrible grief took vengeance
> most terrible against her husband, laments for Itys . . .

Once again—Philomel?

Procne's sister.

And what happened to Procne? Hurry now.

Her husband cut out her tongue and locked her away and said she was dead so he could marry Philomel.

Such a mouthful!—thank you, Antonia. And his son, Itys?

The sisters killed him. To take revenge.

And then?

Secretly they chopped him into pieces and fed Tereus his own son's flesh.

Tantalizing tale. I commend you all. You've learned Ovid's old stories well. Even Tomasina is despite herself nearly a classical sage. So . . . Ovid, whatever is he up to? In the passage you just heard, what associations is he creating for his Sappho? Is she Philomela or Procne, or both? Ovid's Sappho is driven to the brink by the love of Phaon, a common boatman—her forest lord and master is little more than a boy, as Belilla has pointed out. Ovid has the greatest lyric poet of antiquity call this young sailor her 'genius,' her voice—and who can doubt this is how Ovid sees himself? So now who has cut out *Sappho's* tongue, so to speak.

Phaon?

Ovid?

Sor Juana, why is he so cruel to her?

Yes and yes, and I've asked myself this, too, María. And yet there are touches of sympathy that puzzle me. Earlier he has her shrieking in grief, at times invoking her love for her pirate brother, but also the love of a mother for a murdered son. Let's come back to your question in a minute—may we, dear? 'Tonia, just a few more lines.

> The nightingale sings of Itys, her abandonment is Sappho's song:
> Only that; all else is as silent as the dead of night.
> There is a shining spring there, its water clearer than any glass . . .

Is there not something very strange happening here? Who is the abandoned nightingale singing for Itys?

Philomel.

But Philomel killed Itys.

As you say, Isabel. And how touching it is, how tender—to hear the lament of the murderer 'abandoned' by her victim's demise. And if Philomel sings for Itys and Sappho sings Philomel's song, for whom does *she* sing?

Phaon?

Ándele, Belilla.

And so does Ovid's Sappho grieve for a lover or a son—or are we to suspect he is both? And has he abandoned Sappho or instead been devoured by her? So many precipitous conclusions Ovid leads us to. But wait, how thoughtless of us—we've left Sappho at the edge of a cliff! Where again?

Cape Leucas.

And why was it called the white rock of Leucas?

Because it was white?

[*laughter*]

But why not, Isabel? We won't let these Spites make fun of you—in my dreams those cliffs *are* white. But there's more, too. Who was Leucothea?

The White Goddess.

Excellent. And what happened to her? Anyone . . . ?

She threw herself into the sea.

Goodness, why?

She was . . .

You can say it, María. It's ancient history now.

Violated. By her sons.

And there is yet another unfortunate who threw herself from the white cliffs of Leucas—yes, 'Tonia?

Queen Artemise.

Who was . . . ?

Commander of the Persian armies.

A military fiasco, I imagine.[16]

No.

Not love again.

She'd fallen in love with her own son.

Not so unlike the Sphynx's priestess—

Like Iocaste!

Iocaste *exactly*, María. And the mother of Oedipus. Now, Menander tells us that at the top of that white rock stood also a temple dedicated to Apollo Leukatas, and that each year—or in time of plague—a criminal was hurled down to ward off evil, an outcast hurled into the sea to purge the unclean. Some might call it a whitewash. A detail survives: to the scapegoat's shoulders, wings were strapped.

Like Icarus.

Quite possibly, María, on a hot and sunny day. . . . Curiously enough, Apollo's cliffside shrine was also once thought to offer relief from the pangs of love. Aphrodite herself came to visit it, driven to grief over the young Adonis—and what happened to him?

He was gored.

Yes, to death, by Apollo, in the guise of . . . ?

A boar!

Why *María*—it seems you too are becoming a scholar. And yet I remember someone coming to my cell just last week, lamenting with a great shedding of tears how hopeless she was. Now she's positively beaming. Not so hopeless after all, it seems. And now to the rest of us it should be clear the Hellenes' use of irony didn't begin with Ovid or even Homer. What final irony did the Greeks reserve for the goddess of love? Antonia?

She threw herself into the sea.

Yet another leap from the cliffs of Leucas into the foaming surf. Aphrodite—of sea spume born, into spume returned.

But what does it all *mean*?

What indeed, Belilla. Is this the meting of poetic justice, do you think, or the judging of poets? Wait, though, not all the evidence has been weighed. As always, there's another version: It's said that on the way to the island of Leucas, Aphrodite, though grief-stricken, nevertheless managed to fall for a new lover—dextrous girl. Now, guess what *his* name was. No one . . . ? Antonia.

Phaon.

The same Phaon?

Depends whom you ask, Belilla. 'Tonia, give us the story, please.

They met on a boat.

Do tell, a shipboard romance.

Phaon was the boatman, but very old. Out of pity Aphrodite changed him into a beautiful boy.

Out of pity, you say. What then?

She fell in love.

Ay pobrecita, to tumble head over heels for one's own creation.

So Ovid is saying Aphrodite's really *Sappho?*

Well, Belilla, it's a theory at least.

What else could it mean?

That Sappho's Aphrodite?

Please, Juana.

All right, what's your question—whether it's plausible that a poet might fall in love with her own creation? Or, maybe you're asking if when any of us falls in love it is with our own creation.

Be serious!

Bueno, Belilla, me esfuerzo. 'Phaon'—tell me what that means and I'll give you a serious reply. Guesses? Anyone . . . ?

Is it like 'Phaedra' . . . ?

Or 'Phaëthon'?

And just when I was congratulating myself for not being able to teach you Greek—yes, Antonia, a little like Phaedra and yes Belilla, like Phaëthon. 'Bright,' like the moon, and bright like the sun. So were the lovers Sappho and Phaon, or Aphrodite and Phoebus Apollo, or perhaps earliest of all, the rise and fall of the moon and the sun?

You *promised.*

Here it is then, my most serious answer, Belilla. Not a little violence has begun with a myth deliberately passed off as a substitute for history. In which case we might wonder if perhaps posterity's war on Sappho begins here, with her myth. But we might also ask ourselves if there is not an equal violence waiting to be unleashed if we mistake what history brings us for the more complex truths myth helps animate— as the sap does the tree. To those who would ignore this, the living forest of myth becomes invisible even as the tree of truth desiccates and hardens. And in the heat of battle we might even succumb, ourselves, to fashioning spears and arrow shafts from its boughs. In Sappho's case the battle is brought by those who would confuse Sappho with . . . ?

Her poetry?

Yes, María. We could study for a lifetime the tales the name Sappho has been tarred with, but I would not add another feather's weight to the speculations clinging to her life.

So Ovid just made it all up.

But Belilla, why should we expect art to be so simple—so much simpler than our own lives? Yours or mine, much less Ovid's. As a man condemned to exile maybe Ovid was more concerned with preparing his own leap into legend. So perhaps it's wisest to leave the myth of Sappho where Ovid leaves it: poised on a great rock standing like a portal, a white veil between this world and the next, an angry sea reverberating up the sheer cliffs of Leucas like the steel of Damascus dashed upon shields . . . Here we stop for today.

Maybe he made Sappho up too.

We'll take up some of these threads again next time.

But what about Sappho? Her *poems*—her voice, her *loves.*

Next week, the letter of Paris—who none too wisely preferred Aphrodite to Athena, beauty to wisdom—

And your poems to Sappho, Sor Juana—what about those?

[*Antonia, furious*] How could you possibly know about that Belilla? Are you listening at our door? Do you have any idea how much danger—?

What about you, Antonia? You're like a pet! A fat, spoiled house cat. Not six months here and you walk around like Juana's your property! 'Sor Juana says this. Sor Juana's writing that. . . .'

Juana, I've never said a word! [*near tears*] Not one word.

Everyone? Would you let me have a word with Belilla alone? See you all next week. Antonia, you too please . . . ?

[11th day of September 1688]

CASTALIA

la excma. señora María Luisa Manrique de Lara y Gonzaga
Condesa de Paredes, Marquesa de la Laguna,
Madrid, España

Lysis,

second letter—so quickly. (I have your letters of the 1st and now the 13th of July.) As Antonia placed the envelope in my hands I knew it couldn't be the answer to my last to you, which will be weeks reaching you—crossing uncounted mountain passes, one Atlantic and all the vicissitudes of storm and tide and fog and faulty charts that this implies. And then besides, two sets of censors, one on each side—as if from Veracruz to Cadiz they faced across a functionary's desk, to make the sea of faith for censors but a pond.

And yet even knowing all of this, when I saw how slender your letter I could not help feeling some careless phrase of mine had angered you. In this frame of mind (askew) I read and read once more the opening line.

Send me a title, Juanita. Our daughter needs a name.

How have you managed it so quickly? Licences from the Holy Office, thirty letters of support from theologians. Thirty!—have you so much as unpacked your travelling cases?

You say the printers have *started*? A title then, a title . . . to do with the Muses? but no, one hears far too much talk of Muses over here. Wait.

There is a spring on Mount Parnassus, sacred once to Ares. It lies a little north and east of Delphi. But that was Ares' day, and then there was a nymph and then it was Apollo's time to shine. Castalia. (Pagan, *and* chaste, Castalia.) To escape Apollo's attentions she plunged from a cliff to a spring far below, a small spring at the bottom of a deep rock basin. Here in the tale, the spring transforms into a source of inspiration, to both Apollo and the Muses, who were for this reason called (if rarely) the Castalides. All this is quite fine, and the idea of our Castalia as the Muses' muse quite gratifying, but what amuses me not a little is a glimpse of Apollo's 'inspiration' as his quarry launches herself from the heights and dissolves into a shower of silver.

So, yes, 'Castalia,' but what? *Fuente de Castalia? Manantial Castálida? Salto de las Castálides?*—*Chubasco, Aguacero, Chaparrón, Diluvio*—*Haz Castálida?* I am at a loss. May I surrender the decision to your most exquisite discretion? *Hazme este favorcote?*

Of a sudden, nervousness consumes me. Nymph. What *sort* of nymph—naiad, dryad, nereid, hamadryad—which? This is not some backwater we are publishing in, this is *Madrid.* Some wag is sure to suggest our collection's namesake was instead a rash Oread[†] who sank to the bottom like a stone. Or like a certain ill-considered tome . . .

Ah what a pendulum of anxieties I am become. Anxious first not to get my hopes too high that it might be published, next, feeling just as fearful that it *will* be. Fearful of there, dreadful of here—the very image of Castalia as she leaps. So for our title, we could not have chosen better. But as for the other . . . I know I have not answered you. You have hinted that the printers, who are holding the first signature till you hear from me, would have room in it to print my *Letras a Safo.*[†] How it thrills me to know you have not forgotten them. If I say 'not yet,' will I break your heart?

†*Lyrics on Sappho*

I lack the courage still. I am afraid to break this truce. Núñez has kept to his word, and for these last seven years I have not heard a word of his against me. You will lose patience with me for being cowardly. And yet in these quiet if not peaceful years I have been able to work, much bad, some good—but some of that work we are publishing now. If honesty forces me to concede it is not yet my great work, modesty does not stop me thinking that in *First Dream,* at least, I have given something of my measure. There is not a poem quite like it in our language.[17] (You have said precisely that of *Las letras a Safo,* I know.)

But if the Inquisition here can ban Montalbán's albeit terrible play (seen throughout Spain without pleasure perhaps, but also without censure) for the blasphemy of having a character *pray God hasten the course of the sun,* then the holy officers would not hesitate to ban our Castalia for a dalliance with Sappho. And even in the unlikely event that their decision be overturned someday by the Holy Office in Madrid, it could take years. I do not know whom it would bring more pleasure to see our collection seized and held till then—Father Núñez or Fray Dorantes. Both consulted on the Montalbán case. For Núñez, any brief pleasure he took would surely have been in banning a play by the author of *The Nun-Ensign*—an old favourite of mine. Dorantes was, meanwhile, the more vociferous in his ruling and would take pleasure now in seeing Núñez chastened for his past association with me or for any lack of zeal in condemning our collection as soon as it appears.

Already, then, it takes all the courage I can summon to have you publish, along with so many love poems, *Martyr of the Sacrament* and *The Divine Narcissus*, knowing as I do how angrily Núñez views these. Sappho's hour for the stage is not yet nigh. Infinitely worse than the frustration of holding back this one suite a little while longer is the pain of imagining the whole collection seized.

Can you forgive me, then, if I send you another rarity in its place?— to fill the signature, and if you approve it and accept it as a portrait, might you let it open the collection . . . ?

The other night well past Matins, after reading your letter for the dozenth time, the verses I enclose came all in the most marvellous flood. I pray you read them as token of my love and gratitude, a tribute in seventeen quatrains. Sálazar has written something using this structure of dactyls, but I have strengthened it and even bettered it, I think, after a practice poem or two. Even after these, if someone had offered as a wager that a poem of sixty-eight lines each beginning in a dactyl† could come out any better than the beating of a beggar's drum to the thin jingling of his purse, I would not have taken it—would fain have taken the purse.

† one stressed syllable followed by two unstressed: rárity, líberty, álgebra, cínnamon

> Tránsito a los jardines de Venus,
> órgano es de marfil, en canora
> música, tu garganta, que en dulces
> éxtasis aun al viento aprisiona.
>   Pámpanos de cristal y de nieve,
> cándidos tus dos brazos, provocan
> Tántalos, los deseos ayunos:
> míseros, sienten frutas y ondas . . .

Though I had tried to give it something of the tabor and pipe, yet does one hear in this tribute to you the fife and drum . . . there is a stirring on the plains of Troy, for it seems a fighter of great moment has joined the fight; only it is not Achilles but Helen who moves among us. Or one as beautiful.

You are a Manrique. It is your way to face the field and if there must be a fight to force it, choose the day, the place, the arms. Only wait a little longer, wait a little more. They are strong and many, and you are so very far.

And farther still with the hurricane season descending full upon us. The wait for your answer will be an agony.

With all my thanks, with all my heart.

día 11 de septiembre, Anno Domini 1688
del convento de San Jerónimo,
de la Ciudad Imperial de México,
Nueva España

If we consider that distinguished female writers, poets, researchers, and thinkers in general, exalt the megalomania of their female colleagues in order that they might develop a dynamic to compete with the masculine version of the human being, for which version they express a latent, and occasionally manifest, hatred; if we consider these facts, I say, we will associate bisexuality with every thinker's oral neurosis, and anti-masculine aggressivity with a symptom of hysteria, understanding that the defence of feminine aggressivity is only a reaction against an unconscious infantile adaptation to a passivity that is unbearable to a homosexual being, that is, to a being who acts like a man while being a woman . . .

Let us take the example of the Mexican poetess, Sor Juana Inés de la Cruz. . . .

FREDO ARIAS
DE LA CANAL

"Freudians on
the Muse"

*Attempt at
a Psychoanalysis
of Juana Inés*

B. Limosneros, trans.

PUBLIC
LIBRARY

"Hello?"

"Ms. Limosneros?"

"Lee-mos-NEHR-os."

"Sorry. Uh, good news. We've just received two books for you on inter-library loan."

"Octavio Paz?"

"And another in Spanish. Something about psychoanalysis of a 'Juana Inés.'"

"I'll be right down."

"No real hurry. We can hold them for you if you'd prefer to come in during the week."

"I said I'll be right there. . . ."

Or so someone reading Beulah's research notes might imagine the call. Though her diary entry tells a slightly different story, her notes here mark the end of an eternity of waiting for Octavio Paz's book to come. Arriving with it was a book she would come to loathe: Fredo Arias de la Canal's *Intento de psicoanálisis de Juana Inés.* . . . From the title alone, Beulah must have had an inkling: the unctuous familiarity of calling the subject by her given names, as if to say, our Juana Inés, or his, to do with as he pleased. And of course Beulah's antipathy towards psychoanalysts will already be clear.

Sunday at the public library. A first foray into new territory—smaller, and less anonymous than the university's MacKimmie Library. People unaccustomed to her appearance and less harried than the university crowd would be turning to look at her. At a desk to one side of the check-out counters, a man, perhaps the same clerk as on the phone, placed two forms before her.

"Why has everything taken so long?"

"Excuse me?"

"Why has it been so long?"

"The books can come from anywhere in North America. Sometimes they have to be put on recall."

"But it shouldn't take *this* long."

"Miss, if you would like the books, please fill out the forms. If not, we'll send the books back. Which will it be?"

Prepared to stomach any humiliation, she filled out the forms.

"You understand they're due back in three weeks unless a patron of the original library recalls them sooner?"

"I read your forms, didn't I?"

"Do you understand this?" he asked, placing a restraining hand on the books.

"Yes."

It would have been all she could do not to snatch them out of his thin-fingered hands. In other circumstances she might have stopped to savour the heft and solidity of Octavio Paz's *Sor Juana;* she might have inspected more closely Arias's cheap glue-bound edition and discarded it right there.

[25 Apr. 1993]

... tumult of sunlight and wind. False spring. Four days a warm chinook wind arcs down over the mountains. Sky a swift hovering without wings, warm mother's breath too-close, exultant. Citizens shuffle outside obedient, muddled—stand in the wind, turn, walk this way and that, rise up on hind legs blink stupidly at the sun.

Walk down along river. One rodent-thought crackling through a thousand edgy brains—they stroll like regular prairiedog titans beside a stream deceived by false hopes of spring. SeaCow too walks down to the river flesh jiggling with each sodden step. Stands an instant above the water shot through with sunlight / disembodied clean. Ice-bound banks. Liquid rill of cool mint-green. The path bends through a stand of birch leafless and stark / fractures of shadows darkshards and light. A rutted mound of slush slumps across the path, tilts to the river's unsteady brink. Black plane of ice—a skew a crash to knees near toppling down the otterslide—hand outthrust—pudgy outrigger mulched in slimy leaves / thaw of mud and dogshit. This hatred of dogs. Massive heaving lurching to her feet—wipe it clean *wipe it clean.* Scrapes the stinking mess off with a stick. Looks down.

Wedged below—ajostle in ice blocks, green rushing water—a young doe's battered carcass. Modest feet tucked to a bloated belly, forelegs frail as insect wings. Neckflesh chafed bare, a marblepink finish / high gloss and raw. Draw queasy lungfuls of air, quell it quench this urgent thirst / to slip to the water's edge lay hot cheeks against the cool cool marble—someone might see someone might see. One last linger and glance at the bloated carcass . . . SeaCow moves on.

Ahead the Eau Claire mall-called-Market / this riverside regatta this redsea on rollers—bikes skateboards babystrollers. But parting them now, lofty, stately, slow-haloed in sunlight a golden couple. SeaCow stands an instant watching him, stupidly happy to be near. A bearded god beside his swollen-bellied lioness turning—smiling at some goddish jest he's made—to kiss the grey-streaked beard. Her belly an egg's perfect curve, breasts majestic full to suckle unborn heroes.

He leans so close, mastered by love. See her at last so blond beautiful so perfect with him—*look at them* together—don't look away—it was just a crush anyway—feel the heartswell eggshell ache of shattering ribcage. Swift flensed eyeflayed SeaCow turns away yet across a flaming gulf a mind's-eye-wide still sees, sees the lioness reach down / draw from between perfect lion thighs the baby hero. Lifts him the child by the feet— high Tantalus! severs the fateful cord with gleaming feline teeth. Licks her son's bloody stump with a roughtongue flick. Amniotic sap she sucks from the stout little lungs / holds him up laughing steaming lustily in the sun . . . lifts slick lips to kiss the bearded god-sire rough on the mouth.

O perfect trinity! O circle self-sufficient—bonded tight the family thermonuclear. At last, she, the-profane-watcher-who-contaminates-and-defiles, blinds her sightless eyes, retakes the sodden body returns to a mind stripped to one Truth: To everything she must submit. And so submits. And so endures. Everything.

No more make believe.

To me he seems like a god
that man facing you
who leans to be near
as you speak softly and laugh

in a sweet echo
that stings my breasts
and jolts the heart in my ribs
if I dare the shock of a glance

I cannot speak
my tongue cracks, thin fire
spreads beneath my skin
my eyes are dead to light

my aching ears roar through their labyrinths
chill sweat slides down my sides
I convulse, greener than grass,
my mind slips

neither living nor dead
I cry from the narrow between
but endure, must suffer
everything . . .

SAPPHO OF
LESBOS[19]

SANTA CRUZ

here is a house from whose top floor, and looking south, one may see the last of the arches of the aqueduct where it spills into the basin of the Salto de Agua. The house is large, one of only two on that block, and without adornments of tilework or cornices or coats of arms to call attention to itself. The two gates leading to its courtyard are backed with heavy canvasses, to deny the passerby so much as a glance of the interior. Carriages come and go frequently, but at night.

The servants' entrance is deeply recessed, down a passageway tunnelled with an ivy oddly untamed for a house so well kept. A tall, strongly built woman in her mid-twenties, dressed in the plain brown *sayuela* of a convent or hospital domestic, has walked swiftly yet indirectly to the house: east, past the convent of San José of the Discalced Carmelites, then several blocks south, weaving gradually west among the corrals and outbuildings of the city stockyards and stables. Once, she briefly halts and reaches between the rails of a corral to feed two crab-apples to a colt that comes to the fence at first sight of her. She hurries on along the canal of the Merced, crossing west over a bridge three blocks south of San Jerónimo, wending north and now west again to enter this passageway. A door opens at the first knock. She is taller by half a head than the elderly porter, and seems taller still by reason of a wild mane of waist-length hair tamed at the nape with several turns of orange ribbon.

She is shown upstairs. He is standing a step back from the window, the drapes drawn back just sufficiently to see the pure water of the aqueduct fall in a long clear muscle, a fold of silk. In contrast the room is dark. Turning, he beckons her to the plain wooden chair and seats himself comfortably upon the purple velvet divan facing it. The plush is of a shade very close to the piping and cincture of his Lenten cassock. She sits without moving, looking slightly past his face, as unhurriedly he studies her. His hair is a pale brown, the forehead high and broad, the crown of the head slightly flattened. His features are fine, the long slender brows slightly knit, as with a hint of temper. The eyes are large and dark. The nose is strong, the cheekbones wide. The jaws taper to a frail point of chin beneath a small-lipped mouth. Above it, a charcoal line of moustache. The pinkish icing of a burn scar shows just above the high collar. Only after several moments does he speak.

The voice is a sweet tenor.

"Convent life seems to agree with you. Who would have thought? In other ways too, I feel you coming along nicely. Your handwriting is more like hers all the time. And your style—she has been working with you to improve it, hasn't she. . . ."

She does not respond.

"Let's not begin awkwardly. Has she or has she not?"

"Yes."

"It is only right that someone with so many correspondents, and of such calibre, should have a secretary. Someone discreet for her messages, someone for delicate purchases, books. . . . What was the purpose of your outing today?"

"To come here."

"No, what did you *tell* her? Come. Tell me."

"Something I needed to do for my family."

"Not untrue. Clever. And she asked you no more about it. . . ."

"No."

"Excellent. Trust and consideration. I would say she has begun to like you. Would you say she has begun to like you?"

"*Don't.*"

"Does she *trust* you?"

"I don't know."

"Of course she does. May I see the list of books she has had you purchase this month? It was not in your last letter."

"I forgot."

"But you have it now."

"I haven't made it up yet."

"Now you see? this is the problem. The handwriting is good, the style is more literate all the time, but the reports themselves have become . . . disappointing. They lack detail. They are not concrete. Detail is exactly what I ask of you."

"I can't do this."

"But you can. You have more than proved yourself capable with many others."

"That isn't—"

"You can't do this *anymore*."

"No."

"You can't do this to her. Is that it?"

"Yes."

"To her *anymore*. . . . Answer me."

"Yes."

"Those things which you have, nonetheless, done until now."

"Yes."

"You are too hard on yourself. I have no doubt that you still can. It is the only reason you are here now, in Mexico, after all. Where your duties in this regard are, overall, less onerous than in Puebla . . . ? *Are they?*"

"Yes."

"It is good that you display loyalty. To earn her trust you must have this quality. Do display it. Just not here. For me, to me, but do not display it *with* me."

"Manuel, I—"

"You do not help your cause by calling me that. We have an agreement, and that part of it is finished. We do still have an agreement? Unless your feelings for your dear sisters have changed. Have things changed?"

"How *could* they have? *¿En este mundo de la chingada, las cosas—cómo van a cambiar?*"

"I am prepared to endure a little petulance, because I value your sincerity. A useful quality. Perhaps not much frightens you, after the life you have led. Though you must admit it was more frightening before we met. But *they* do frighten. I think they *are* frightened. I have explained to them that they may not be able to stay in Puebla much longer. They are doing very well in school, though they may falter a bit now. I have brought their letters, as I agreed to. You may read everything here before you leave. I think you will find them enjoyable. Even the little one traces out her letters quite charmingly. And can sing out her whole alphabet, too. If you could see them, there is such a bloom on their innocence just now. . . . So. Our agreement stands, nothing has changed."

"Nothing."

"Details. *Not* evidence. I am not documenting a case. It is the state of her soul I would gauge, its dispositions, its readiness. You understand, these are only for me. I am not the Inquisition. They have their own sources there, and if anyone can protect her from those, it will not be you but me. You do see this."

"Yes."

"Excellency."

"Yes, Your Grace."

"No, dear child, this we reserve for the Archbishop. Excellency is quite enough. Will you say it now?"

"Excellency."

"There. In this arrangement, I too make sacrifices. And penance. You have not been easy to replace in Puebla. You see, it is not just your information I miss. Your absence has been painful to me in every respect. As painful as was your presence, come to think of it, though of course differently. But now I am convinced, once again, that we still have it, this understanding of ours, and so I am resigned to my sacrifices. In my own life I have found happiness fleeting. But you, I think, are happy there. Are you happy there? Otherwise . . . ?"

"*Otherwise?*"

"Yes?"

"Yes, Excellency, I am happy there. Otherwise."

"Then I can be happy for you. Do be happy, dear child. Be happy as long as you can. The letters are in the top left-hand drawer. Face the window if you like. You have earned a little privacy . . . there is so little where you are. *Left.* There. Go on. I will watch from over here. . . ."

JUANA INÉS
DE LA CRUZ

Alan Trueblood, trans.

Silly, you men, so very adept
at wrongly faulting womankind,
not seeing you're alone to blame
for faults you plant in woman's mind.

　After you've won by urgent plea
the right to tarnish her good name,
you still expect her to behave—
you, that coaxed her into shame.

　You batter her resistance down
and then, all righteousness, proclaim
that feminine frivolity,
not your persistence, is to blame.

　When it comes to bravely posturing,
your witlessness must take the prize:
you're the child that makes a bogeyman,
and then recoils in fear and cries.

　Presumptuous beyond belief,
you'd have the woman you pursue
be Thais when you're courting her,
Lucretia once she falls to you.

　For plain default of common sense,
could any action be so queer
as oneself to cloud the mirror,
then complain that it's not clear?

　Whether you're favoured or disdained,
nothing can leave you satisfied.
You whimper if you're turned away,
you sneer if you've been gratified . . .

[6th day of January, 1689]

CASSANDRA

la excma. doña María Luisa Manrique
Condesa de Paredes, Marquesa de la Laguna,
Madrid, España

Dearest María Luisa,

 weet friend, beautiful Thetis of the Seas, you seek to fashion me a peerless armour at the glowing forge of your cares. How I love that you would protect me still. First, to let you know we are alone. Antonia has gone out on an errand. Please know that we will always have these moments, these letters written in my hand. But the simple fact of being alone does not leave me free to speak. And things we said here in this cell, just we two, I am not free to write, when the mails may be opened at any time by the Holy Office or the Crown. I know you know this—I want you to hear me say it. Still other things may be written to be read obliquely, as one reads fables written by a friend who has read and loved the same stories, as have you and I. And then there are lines that may only be spoken in the theatre you and I make here, that no longer resonate in the world outside, as with an instrument whose sounding board is split. If together we could not create such a place where the instrument could be heard again, what use would writing be, what use theatre?

Last, let there also be things I may say in these letters that I could never say with you here with me, sitting so near. We must always make a place for these, as I will before I stop tonight.

But if I am to keep my promise to write often, I will need help. To burden you with tedious plaints in the too brief hours we had alone together in this cell would have been too graceless even for me. Even now I hesitate, but hope you will give me leave. . . .

You write to warn me that these seven years of quiet I celebrate as a truce are in truth a siege. So I tell you now that Father Núñez has indeed caught wind of our plans and has begun to rail against our Castalia before she even reaches here. It is as if he believed Sappho's lyrics were in it—but how can that be, if the source of his information is the Holy Office there? Surely he knows they would have mentioned any verses on Sappho had they been there. And if he has some other source so early—who?

And yet, sweet Lysis, even with these fresh worries, what I most suffer from has little to do with Núñez or Archbishop Aguiar. Not a siege but a blockade—and I am that grain ship, that silver galleon straining at its hawsers to run the line, anxious, chafing to put to sea before I sink beneath the worthy new duties they heap on me almost daily. These will keep me from any work I might call mine more surely than any Church injunction can.

The daily Masses, the Friday chapter of faults, the public acts of contrition that bring the envious among my sisters so much satisfaction . . . yes, these weary me a little more. But there is yet much more than these. The prayers of the Divine Office I barely mention—these you yourself have grumbled about often enough in my stead. The very thought of being woken mid-night for the prayers of Matins (with those of Compline still on our lips), you find hideous; but I sleep little anyway. Often as not I am reading or writing when the chimes call us, and these at least I do not mind. Have we not always found them among the loveliest bells of the capital?

I have been elected convent accountant for the third straight term. Few convents in the city have ever earned six percent per annum. Of course we must first have money to invest, so by far the task most prodigal of my time lies in hosting the convent's many patrons. To do this effectively, though, means rehearsing our *niñas* and novices in skits and our choir in musical entertainments. Then there is the writing of these—if something better suited really cannot be found. And because I have not been clever enough to conceal my familiarity with Nahuatl, I am become a sort of Solomon of disputes among the three hundred servants here, though far from all *speak* Nahuatl. Worse, because one set of apartments or another is always being renovated to accommodate still more servants, I very often find myself Superintendent of Works:[20] most of the workers are also native Mexicans, whose overseers are seemingly selected for their inability to let them work in peace.

Other charges I take in turn with three or four other sisters. Besides the classes I wrote you of, four of us see to courses in reading, music, dance and arithmetic for thirty young girls. Then there come occasional turns in the infirmary, the cellars, the archives, the library—this last, as you can imagine, I do not resent so much.

Having now quite exhausted myself (and surely you) I pass over a few other, minor tasks, to close with the sermons and arguments I am consulted on by various monks, priests, bishops and inquisitors, never forgetting the carols, lyrics and plays I am asked to write for the churches and cathedrals—these I do on my own time, though the commissions go chiefly to the convent coffers.

Perhaps you will understand after all this complaint why I can almost not bear the thought of doing without Antonia now that I have found her. I was thoughtless not to explain all this to you first in a letter in my own hand. (Even as sensing your hurt has made me see, if belatedly, how the similarity of her hand to mine only made things worse, and troubles you still.)

You have always been anxious about my friends. Gently you remind me that Hypermnestra's husband, the sharp-eyed Lynceus, by showing kindness at first, killed more Danaïdes in the end than did all his forty-nine brothers combined. But I depend on so many people for so many things; I would be consumed with anxiety if I felt I could trust only the friends I did not need. This would be no way to inspire alliances anyway, but this you know better than I. A spirit of mistrust entrains its own surprises.

The Inquisitor Gutiérrez I admit to needing as much as liking, though I liked him instantly . . . he of the bland looks and feigned bemusement that clothe a sharp mind in an almost childlike frankness. Scarce a fortnight over from Spain, he first ambled into my locutory to register his disappointment that so many otherwise serious individuals in this city were making fools of themselves with ridiculously exaggerated praise of a certain nun in a certain convent. He stayed three hours.

On his next visit we worked through some of the briefs he was preparing; I took a no doubt wicked pleasure in suggesting corrections he might make to a certain priest's newest manual of devotion for nuns. Later, when one detailed argument in particular was singled out for commendation, Gutiérrez openly acknowledged my help—at the *Holy Office*, before a roomful of his colleagues! Everyone was talking about it. Can one even imagine it, the impertinence of the thing? The Jesuits and the Dominicans disliked him about equally for it, with the result that—we laugh about this—he's now seen as something of an honest broker. One wry Augustinian to keep the Dominicans and the Jesuits from each other's throats.

My prickly friend Carlos, for his part, made a terrible start with you—*con ese asunto del arco.*[†] Certainly you of all people owe him nothing, not even the gift of your comprehension, having stayed your husband's hand and kept my slightly seditious friend out of irons. You scarcely knew me then, yet heard my petition—which said so much for your openness of mind and heart. But if Carlos had made a better beginning I know you'd have seen under all that awful pride and irritability a beautiful mind and such a generous spirit. Yes I do take his employment with the Archbishop as a betrayal, but of our principles, not of me. In the matter of serving His Grace, Carlos has little choice. The University's stipend is a mean provocation—among his relations he has a dozen mouths to feed—and you've seen for yourself how profitlessly he conducts himself at the palace. Almost any extra income he gets is at the Archbishop's sufferance: his chaplaincy at the hospital, his commission to write the history of the convent of the Immaculate Conception (and you cannot begin to know how galling his newfound 'expertise' in convent life can be), and now this post of Almoner.

It is only fitting that your questions turn to Antonia's origins, for the defence of our good name is our best guarantee, however imperfect, of honourable conduct. What's more, it is entirely in keeping with your own nobility of spirit that you have been able to forget the towering elevations separating your origins from mine. You will be angry even to hear me mention this again; but that I have never forgotten it is entirely in keeping with the natural laws of perception. From the depths of the lowest valleys, one cannot forget the majestic altitudes of the summit; whereas at the summit one is struck by the grandeur of what one sees, not where one stands.

I was born a natural daughter of the Church. My father was an adventurer barely of the hidalgo class whose name I do not even have the right to take. Antonia's origins are not much different from mine, and if she has been so very much less fortunate, it serves to show me, as nothing ever has, how things might have gone with me. She too was born in the countryside. East of Puebla, not far from San Lorenzo de los Negros. Her father was a military physician who retired to the country to sire a score of daughters on the mulattas and negresses in his employment there. His less common passion, though, was educating them, and thereby proving

†'that business of the arch'—the triumphal arch of 1680

to his satisfaction a theory of his that women, even of mixed race, may become *gente de razón*,[†] if thoughtfully trained. I cannot decide if this lets me like him a little more, or a very great deal less. And yet I profit by his results.

†creatures of reason

Dearest Lysis, I know you will not let yourself be repelled when I tell you she was once forced to sell her body as a courtesan. In the better houses the men would ask for the educated one, the tall one—for White Chocolate, as though to order a hot beverage from a palace steward. But it is clear that in the beginning she was not in such fine houses.

There is the frailest line of scar—by glass, or sharpest steel—that runs from the corner of her left eye all down her pale cheek to the corner of her smile. Yet it has neither disfigured her face, nor maimed her spirit. She has been willing to tell me much more, but I do not want to know—while unspeakable, it is not quite beyond my capacity to imagine it. I have seen them in the streets. For years I heard their screams at night. We hear them even here.

Knowing that the situation of those dearest to her is precarious, I have begged Bishop Santa Cruz, who has done this much, to do whatever else he can. She has become a friend to me. You cannot know my loneliness when you left, my thoughts during this cold year. Until I met you I was content to stay in here, within the walls of this cell, with these friends who are my books my only company. But since you left how I hunger to see the streets again, to walk in them *just one hour.* . . .

I have forfeited that liberty, but at least I have Antonia—a warm salt breeze, salt in speech, strong as the sea. She is tireless in my service, sleeps almost as little as I, though rather better, and though she is not yet twenty-two to my forty, fusses over me like an anxious mother hollow-eyed with worry and nights of care. (And as you are always chiding me for not making copies of the verses I give away as gifts, here is someone now for that work, too.) Know that in her you have the strongest ally, for she is always trying to warn me against one prideful folly or other. She has been my Penthesileia—no, like the Angolan warrior princesses of her grandmother's ancestors, such strength, to see her in the orchards and the gardens they say . . . the quiet rage in her that must find its release somewhere.

If I have never seen her there, it is because I do not go. . . . For you see, dear friend, the flowers in the orchards, the smell of the earth, the hard rain that lays bright bracelets of coin on each blade of grass, all these things bring too near the absence of another time. And of a kind of poetry now lost to me.

As the years go rushing, rushing by, in things absent I feel a presence as of stone—your absence as of a stone in my breast; your distance the darkness behind it, and all that holds it in are these letters from you: the presence of your absence. Absence—yours, others'—is become a presence ever before me, an ever constant pressure, the mass of a stone I am afraid to roll back. Always for me lately, this absence, this dance. This too is a kind of siege.

I have been afraid to speak to you of all this, *amada dueña de mi alma*, for fear I will not know how to stop, or when I must.

There was the day you first came to this convent. . . .

Sweet Lysis, I too regret, bitterly, every hour together we could not have. With this letter I enclose a few verses that, hesitant yet, reach for your hand. . . .

I send you all my love and anxiously await word.

*día 6 de enero del año 1689
de este convento de San Jerónimo,
de la Ciudad de México,
Nueva España*

[2nd day of April 1689]   HELEN

Her Excellency, Lady María Luisa Manrique de Lara y Gonzaga
Condesa de Paredes, Marquesa de la Laguna,
Madrid

Mi querida Lysis,

ur daughter has safely arrived. Castalia has reached the New World. I have our collection under my hand now as I write, as I have written for thirty years, so many countless hours, with serried rows of books in friendly ranks, standing watch close at my back.

Something else I have never said to you, I say it now. That a man I loved more than the sun, my kinsman, loved your kinsman with all his great heart. How beautiful it would have been, and how strange, to have known so very long ago that today—under the aegis and seal of the House of Paredes—I would reach up to shelve my own first book only to discover that it fits between his two best loved authors. Between these two books I still have of his, between Homer and Manrique I stand: Juana Inés de la Cruz, Sor.

I exist.

This book. Our first. I open it. I cradle her, this child of ours, run my ticklish nose down her bumpy spine, snuffle out her newborn's scents. I hold up a world in my palm. A life entire.

I laugh a little through the springs in my eyes at the saucy title you have found. *Castalian Flood.* Run, ye mockers and sinners and poetasters, run for the arks!

Such a feeling of dangerous peace creeps over me, Juana Inés de la Cruz, Sor. Between Manrique and Homer, between peace and fight. One book—isn't one enough? Why do we have to struggle so much not to be crushed? Surely now all the fighting could stop. And yet I know it does not.

For a long time after my girlhood ended it was hard to love the *Iliad* as before. Even now I prefer the *Odyssey,* and there are parts of his *Iliad* I dislike still. For a while after leaving Panoayan I disliked it all, every chapter. As a young woman at the palace, what I saw in those chapters was the endless waste and horror of all that is most beautiful in men. The finest flowers of an age cut and trailed through gore and dust. This epic of deflowering men. And then just when it all becomes too much, a Homer transformed writes a kind of miracle for us, an interlude, as though by a different pen, as though the Homer of the *Odyssey* drops by for a turn. The working of Achilles' shield at Vulcan's forge.

On that shield, as Thetis of the silvery feet stands tiptoe at his shoulder, anxious yet marvelling, the smith Hephaistos works the heavens and beneath them two cities. In one, a civil peace: festivals and marriages, through the streets wind bridal processions by torchlight; women crowd doorways to watch the maidens pass. A marketplace wrought in silver, sober heralds and arbitrators sit in open court . . . sage elders in session on benches of stone slow-worn to gloss.

The other, a city under siege. Outside its walls not one but two contending armies ring the ramparts in glittering bronze. Beyond, Hephaistos works soft fields triple-ploughed . . . teams of oxen till in the sun, to each teamster a man brings sweet wine in gold flagons. Under a silver tree a feast is spread. Women scatter white barley for the workers to eat. Beside a fire a brass ox lies jointed and trimmed. Copper reeds sway in a silver stream, sheepflocks gleam. A player with his lyre refreshes the harvesters, as with light dance steps—for their fardels were light—they keep time. . . . And enclosing all, the deep gyres of the Ocean River running at the shield's outermost edge.

Why has Homer given us this shield, this paradox of an object of war, yet a refuge from it? Is his an act of defiance, or does he merely tease out the moment, an idyll before the bloody climax? Whatever his purpose, it is an interlude of all that is beautiful and fine, all that is worth living, striving for, all that made that war terrible and cursed. All this was lost, the Poet suggests, over Helen. We should despise her, even when the Trojans themselves cannot. This daughter of Zeus and Leda, Delusion and Nemesis, hatched from an egg to a beauty unbearable to men. But which Helen? For there were two. . . .

The poet Stesichoros was struck blind and his sight restored only once he had admitted that Helen was never in Troy, that she had instead been spirited to Egypt by Hermes and replaced with an illusion fashioned by Hera from a swath of cloud. It is an illusion so real as to trigger a war, a myth so real to us now it may as well have happened. A myth wrapped in an illusion cradled in the hull of a dream.

Among those who have been to Ithaca and know its coast are some who believe that Odysseus never made it home. That the coast described at his landing was not Ithaca at all, but Leucas, Isle of Whiteness, Isle of Dreams. And that his return, therefore—or the *Odyssey* entire—was a journey in a dream, real as a city on a shield.

The last of Helen's husbands was Achilles. According to one who claims to have visited the White Isle himself, Achilles and Helen were married after their deaths and lived together there. And so we wonder if the shield was to protect Achilles from Hector or Helen. And which Helen was this and which was war and which one love? Two cities on a shield, two Helens, each looking out to sea. One over the plains before Troy, one over the shores of Egypt. Helen of Sparta, Helen of Troy. One the illusion of a possession, one the dream of a release, both of an impossible beauty.

Since my childhood I've known, as one knows an old dream, how the fires and floods and storms conspire with the illusions of the years to keep us from Ithaca.

Sweet Lysis, let our daughter be the siege raised, let this book be our shield, let these pages be our dream of release from all cares of consequence, all delusions of possession, all the torments of absence. Let us make of this book—this shield, this dream we have shared—the place where we come from so far to meet, I from the west and you from the east. To our island of dreams, our dream of an impossible beauty, and in it, together, we walk the white shore.

Juana. . . .

día 2 de abril del año 1689
de este convento de San Jerónimo,
de la Ciudad Imperial de México

CHRISTINA   [29th day of June, 1689]

María Luisa Manrique de Lara y Gonzaga
Condesa de Paredes, Marquesa de la Laguna,
Madrid, España

Lysis ...

o the incomparable Christina of Sweden is gone. As your letter arrived, the first rumours had only just begun. It is true, then; she was interred at Saint Peter's Basilica. The Pope forgave her every excess after all. In abdication, poverty, obloquy, even in death, she commanded a queen's respects.

For another moment after finishing your letter I could not quite believe—in the sense that one could hardly ever believe she really was alive, so very alive was her legend. Here at the convent, as it had been at the palace, the talk was often of Christina, just as she was fascinated by convent life. (For Christina, it was the married woman who was truly a slave; nuns were only prisoners, and even the queen was not free. . . .) They are probably talking of her now in half a dozen cells around this patio. All the rumours that she would come, was coming, was in Seville, then in Cadiz itself, waiting for a proper embarkation. For an entire fleet, more likely. From my earliest days here—and perhaps it never quite stopped—I had the notion she would come to stay a while with us at San Jerónimo, with her menagerie of parrots and apes, with her equipage of fourteen thousand books, and we might sit together and while away the days. I would tell her of our academy, of Antonia and Tomasina, María and Belilla, and she would tell me of hers, of Bernini and Corelli and Scarlatti. And we would talk of Descartes and astronomy, of languages and the fighting spirit of queens, of horsemanship and marksmanship, of a life of the mind and men's breeches.

When they asked her about this—her loves and her pistols and her breeches—do you know how she answered them? *The soul has no sex.*

You write me gently of her death, but it is I who should be consoling you. You had much higher hopes than I that we might one day win her patronage for a nun in the wilds of America. It was a cruel twist that the emissary of your friend the Grand Duchess of Aveyro was due to leave for Rome the following day. How much less cruel for me to have read of it across this time and distance, than for you—when not a week earlier, you had placed our collection in the messenger's hands. And with it a manuscript copy of *Las letras a Safo*. How could our Castalia fail, you wrote that day in such high spirits, how could *Sappho's* lyrics fail to enchant Christina of Sweden? By the time I read those words, she was two months dead, and only now the news is confirmed. How cruelly time and distance work at the edges of irony: one edge they blunt, its opposite whet.

Her influence was enormous, you write trailing off. . . . Between the lines I read what you do not quite say: If Sappho's lyrics had *been* in *Castalian Flood*, Christina might already have read it and taken up our cause.

The collection has gone through two print runs in two months. You write that we should be thinking about another collection—surely there is something to be done about Núñez. What is it, *really*, that fuels this grievance of ours, you ask, that it blazes up from embers banked long ago? Can he not somehow be persuaded to tolerate *Las letras a Safo* in our next collection, when that bright day comes? By which I take you to be asking if there is anything you can say to overcome my fears. In answering the first, perhaps each of us will find our answers to the second.

While you were here, your protection sufficed, but the House of Paredes is back in Spain now. My relations with the Viceroy are cordial but not warm. The Count is decent enough, but it does not help to know he is part of the faction that has brought such grief to your husband's brother. As for the Countess de Galve, if it did not so inflame the Archbishop to hear of her visits here, she would not come at all any longer.

Do you know what she has just done? She put on *Amor es más laberinto*, knowing full well from what happened to us that he would not come to any play, least of all this one. All this may bring her a childish satisfaction, but I do not see what good it can do her or me, and though I cling to my love of comedy more grimly each year, it is not exactly why I stayed up from Matins to Lauds for two months writing it.[21]

The Archbishop persists in his refusal to serve as her spiritual director, even as he did with you. Unlike you, she takes it personally, though he would gladly do as little for any woman. Since His Grace will not minister to her, the Viceroy stays with Núñez as well. Father Núñez is happy to oblige. You kept him as your director because in your life you had found so few with the nerve to challenge you—better the adversary one sees, you said, as befits a Manrique. But it was you who convinced me to find another director precisely because I did have much to fear. Now you wonder if I have not become 'more timid in my rebellion than I was in my submission.'

The question is a fair one. As I say, in the answer to your first, perhaps we'll find our answers to the second and now this third.

Twenty-one years ago the Reverend Father Antonio Núñez led me to see the service of Christ as Loyola himself first had, as a mission of chivalry. The verses of Juan de la Cruz speak of the soul's longing to be ravished by Him, a prospect Núñez can just countenance. But that in the verses of Juana *Inés* de la Cruz a nun should speak to Christ as to a courtly lover . . . no, this Núñez cannot bear. (Even if there'd been a hundred Teresas, such raptures would still for Núñez be intolerable in a nun.) How he must have suffered until he had me in his power. For so soon as I was safely locked away, gone the chivalry, gone the cavalry. The virtues of the footsoldier are entirely other. Obedience, forbearance, humility, suffering.

For all that, things had not acquired the bitterness you have yourself witnessed between Núñez and me until near the end of what was already a dark time. In 1674, the Marquise Leonor Carreto died suddenly in Tepeaca, on her way home to Spain. The incoming Viceroy lasted four days before he too expired. I had narrowly escaped death myself—having lain at its door for nearly a month through an attack of typhoid. It was during my illness that the Holy Office sentenced a Franciscan—Carlos's dear friend—to burn at the stake for his activities among the Maya in Yucatan. Father Núñez had not yet reached his position of eminence at the Holy Office and has always claimed he was not intimately involved. Until the end. For he was one of two Jesuits assigned to bring the condemned to contrition. The harshness in my relations with Father Núñez dates from that day.

Much of the rest you know, but for a detail or two. Almost immediately after Bishop Santa Cruz's election was overturned (almost certainly with the connivance of the Jesuits), Santa Cruz took an interest in a text by an Irish Jesuit whom I had known in my locutory. Father Godinez had been highly critical of the Jesuits here as spiritual directors, the gist of his criticism being that they too often clipped the wings of their penitents for fear that our mystical flights might soar too perilously high, commending us to penitence rather than love, to obedience rather than communion.[22] The Society of Jesus refused to publish it.

Highly irregular, then, for Bishop Santa Cruz to have his Dominican secretary edit and publish a Jesuit text that the Jesuit Order had disapproved. It seemed obvious that Godinez was speaking of Núñez in particular. Many at the time thought I had been the one to bring the text to the Bishop's attention. But while Núñez is himself a veritable apostle of self-mortification, I know that he believes such extremes and rigours are not for women, for we fall easily prey to the ultimate wickedness of ecstasy. It is his view (and having endured six months among Teresa's Discalced Carmelites, I have never been much inclined to protest) that excesses of physical mortification are in women the shortest path to the demonic loves of Loudun.[23] That it is so very different with men, I leave for others to decide.

But to compensate for the relative moderation of our physical trials, Núñez would substitute a cruelty of the heart. I give you your former spiritual director, and a sampling from his latest circular to us. . . .

I very much desire, for the *alivio* and *decoro* of your convent and the estimation of your persons, that you avail yourselves of all good tokens and qualities, from the infinitesimal firsts to the supreme and ultimate . . . and, finally, that you gather unto yourselves all the good works and talents that you can.

And why, you might ask? To use them for ostentation and proofs of your efforts? Not in the least: that you might keep them protected and ready to hand, and only take them out and use them when and as the convent may have need of them. . . . That you raise and fatten and spoil the plump flesh of your talents and commitments, but in order to slit their throats and bleed them with the knife of Mortification, on the altars of Charity, in the temple of Obedience. This is sacrificing to God your thanks; the other, is offering your talents to the idol of Vanity.[24]

You will perhaps recall the sentiments.

And so it frequently amuses me to note how many of the churchmen under his direction have become just such *extáticos*. His Paternity don Pedro de Arellano, now my nominal director, was a Núñez disciple. During his time with Father Núñez, don Pedro acquired a most holy fear of sin, most notably his own—as he found himself stabbing the patron of an inn after a twenty-four-hour gambling binge. Domingo Pérez de Barcia, another Núñez acolyte and more ecstatic still, had to be replaced recently as the head of the Archbishop's new women's prison: the cat, I gather, had been set among the very pigeons of ecstasy. And we have the Archbishop himself, who now takes to his bed in murderous rages a few days each month. Even though Núñez is the only one who can so far control him, he controls a depreciating asset, for everyone here watches with malign anticipation for the day when the most unpopular Archbishop in living memory reaches that apoplexy of wrath from which there can be no recovery.

But now, in the span of a few months, Father Núñez has dedicated to Bishop Santa Cruz first a rehash of a text he wrote years ago on the reforms of the Council of Trent,[25] and then recently some new text—I am still trying to get the details, but I hear it is another tome on penitence. So Núñez has begun courting my most powerful ally within the Church. It seems he was only waiting for you to leave.

Finally I have admitted it, you will say. What more evidence do I need that this is no truce? But at least he does not defame me, and his courtship does not succeed. I will not let it. (One cannot walk two blocks in Mexico without tripping over a theologian. Bishop Santa Cruz has only one of me—indeed is the only one in the Church who can now claim to *have* me in his collection. He has known me for fifteen years, and yet however often I tell him the *via mística* is simply not in my temperament, Santa Cruz has never given up hope that he will one day find the mystic in me. The risks of (my) ecstasy he is prepared to run, for the nun's transports are the oil that lights the altars of the Church, the blood of renewal, the blood of Christ himself. So you see, Núñez detests the very thing the Bishop has never given up hope of finding in me. But finding it, what then? I suspect that Santa Cruz, the great resolver of Biblical contradictions, has this idea that he will one day shape my holy ravings, or play John to my Teresa. Or perhaps it is the reverse. . . .)

It occurs to me tonight that since the first rumours of Christina's death, I've been half dreading Núñez would come to bring me the news himself. The Nun-Empress, he used to call her, with that sarcasm, that Philistine tone and that memory he wields like a scalpel, with which I know he has made you suffer, too. 'Beware of her, Juana. Christina of Sweden did more to silence Descartes than we ever could.'[26]

Silence Descartes? If Núñez ever does come to gloat I will offer him this—from among those letters of hers she had published, here is her note to a Descartes who had recently expounded his ideas on the infinite amplitude of the Universe.

> Monsieur . . .
> If we conceive the world in that vast extension you give it, it is impossible that man conserve himself therein in this honourable rank, on the contrary. . . . He will very likely judge that these stars have inhabitants, or even that the earths surrounding them are all filled with creatures more intelligent and better than he; certainly, he will lose the opinion that this infinite extent of the world is made for him or can serve him in any way.[27]

Who can doubt that Christina, who had negotiated the Peace of Westphalia and knew the hearts of men and the tides of politics no doubt better than he, imposed upon Descartes a quiet moment or two of reflection then?

There it is. Now you know the circumstances that fuel the fires of our old grievance. Núñez has taken up too much of our time this night. It is late, soon it will be day. Antonia is asleep.

I want to tell you a secret. As you know I am widely envied the location of my cell, for its sunny mornings, its views of the mountains. You are among the few from the outside world to have seen those views. But there is quite another reason I would not trade this cell. Behind a tapestry, there is a small door opening into a stairway. A century ago many of our cells had such doors, as one may see from the architect's designs (to be Superintendent of Works has its compensations). But not long after the convent was finished, the stairways were ordered walled over, for the nuns had begun to congregate on the roofs at the slightest pretext, at street festivals, religious processions—there is no end of things to watch in the streets once one begins to take an interest.

A convent has many secrets, and this is among our best kept. I am not the only one to have restored my cell to the original design. There are three of us, as far as I can tell. We know who we are. We do not go up by day for fear of being seen, even though the archbishop who ordered the stairwells sealed has been dead half a century.

But very late at night, when I cannot sleep, or a scream in the street or in a cell has woken me, such things in a telescope I have seen. . . . Some nights it is only the stars that bring relief. The stars were always distant, the stars do not change. Looking up at the night sky—unchanged since in the childhood of our race we first traced their constellations—have you ever felt your spirit mounting to those heights up through your eyes?

The Twins, the Fire-Bow, the Great and the Little Bear, Cassiopeia . . . And is it not with a child's eyes that we trace again in letters of wonder this starry alphabet, and through those eyes feel our own childhood reaching back down to us?

When it is very clear and the magic lantern of the night glows brightly, when the horizons stand traced in stars like figures cut from black and laid on lantern glass, I swear to you, even when it is cold, I smell fresh-picked corn baking in the sun as I once did in Nepantla. That, for me, is what these moments on the roof have come to mean.

Eight years I have waited for the Archbishop's permission to buy this cell and I wait anxiously still. For in these rooms, so long as they are not mine, even this secret doorway can be taken from me.

And now, as I say good-night, I promise you before this ink is dry to slip up to the roof and think upon the infinite expanses of the universe, the limits on the hearts of men, the closeness I feel to you despite the distances that separate us . . . and to look into the east to you, for you.

Love . . .

día 29 de junio, Anno Domini 1689
del convento de San Jerónimo,
de la Ciudad Imperial de México,
Nueva España

Post Scriptum. Mid-morning: remembering last night's stars, I have yet one more favour to ask. I should tell you right out, it is less for me than for Carlos. All his studies and observations, his proofs and calculations—

it breaks my heart a little these past few years to see him so freely sharing all this with visiting scholars (while rounding on the local ones like a wounded stag). He has understood that he can never publish most of his work, and so tries to advance the work of those who perhaps one day can. For six months now he has been attempting to obtain a copy of *Philosophiae Naturalis Principia Mathematica*, a new work of natural philosophy. Technically speaking it is not banned, but since this Newton is a Lutheran and apparently goes further than Copernicus, Galileo and Descartes combined—indeed pulls together and builds upon their studies—most booksellers here sensibly assume his text will soon be on the next Index and want nothing to do with it. Apparently the holy officers at the port in Veracruz are of the same view and have confiscated at least one copy that we know of. If, however, as happened earlier this year, a nobleman from Madrid happened to be travelling to the Indies with a parcel under seal of the House of Paredes, it would not likely be opened. I hasten to repeat that he would be committing no infraction. Technically.

JUANA INÉS
DE LA CRUZ

Alan Trueblood, trans.

I, like the innocent child,
who, lured by the flashing steel,
rashly runs a finger
along the knife blade's edge;
    who, despite the cut he suffers,
is ignorant of the source
and protests giving it up
more than he minds the pain;
    I, like adoring Clytie,[28]
gaze fixed on golden Apollo,
who would teach him how to shine—
teach the father of brightness!
    I, like air filling a vacuum,
like fire feeding on matter,
like rocks plummeting earthward,
like the will set on a goal—
    in short, as all things in Nature,
moved by a will to endure
are drawn together by love
in closely knit embrace . . .
    But, Phyllis, why go on?
For yourself alone I love you.
Considering your merits,
what more is there to say?
    That you're a woman far away
is no hindrance to my love:
for the soul, as you well know,
distance and sex don't count. . . .

*G*he locutory stands in readiness. By a bookshelf I sit radiating an admirable, a mighty calm. Gutiérrez has just left. I need not remind myself that in the past he has brought reliable information from the Holy Office: rumours of cases, advance word of rulings, gossip of the Inquisition's inner tensions and debates—monthly casualty reports from the war between the Jesuits and the Dominicans. Today, as one of two consultants on the case, Gutiérrez brought news of a licensing application—routinely approved, yet whose implications for me cannot be routine.

Father Antonio Núñez de Miranda is to be granted licence to publish *The Penitent Communicant*. It is written, Gutiérrez assured me, in a prose as rigorous and subtle as it is dead. Following Thomist doctrine, Father Núñez holds that the act of transmuting His flesh and blood into the wafer and wine is Christ's most sublime expression of love for Man. Not a half-dozen theologians in all the Catholic commonwealth can match Núñez's learning on the Eucharist. And it is his secret conceit, as a good Creole, that to further deepen our apprehension of this supreme mystery, no one is better placed than the (sufficiently disciplined) theologian raised among the ruins of cannibal Mexico. According to Gutiérrez, who has dubbed it *The Shriven Communicant*, the work's underlying message is that anyone who finds grounds for an ecstatic communion, in so holy a mystery, had better think again.

But while I was speaking of this with Gutiérrez, my mind could not be deflected from a detail I found sobering enough to meditate upon. *The Penitent Communicant* is dedicated to don Manuel Fernández de Santa Cruz, Bishop of Puebla. The Bishop is my friend, the Bishop is not here yet, the Bishop was to be here an hour ago. Suddenly it is not beyond imagining that the Bishop has come all the way from Puebla to look over Núñez's manuscript, not to see me.

Antonia sits fidgeting at the desk, having filled the inkwells and twice restocked the paper and quills. At the middle window, the little table is set for two, one to each side of the grille. While I radiate calm, the afternoon sun streams brightly through crystal wine glasses, blithely over bowls for whipped chocolate, blindingly across the matching sideplates—pleasant peasant patterns of pheasants and ferns on the blue-on-white ceramics of Puebla. No, *calm*. On the visitors' side rests a platter of the *dulces encubiertos* for which San Jerónimo is extolled by our sweet-toothed patrons. Candied figs and limes from the orchard, candied squash and peppers from the garden. Behind the arras in the back, the giggling has stopped, which almost certainly means that today's *escuchas*,[†] Ana and Tomasina, have abandoned their listening posts to search the street for signs of our eminent guest. It has been some time since the Bishop's last visit from Puebla. The times are anxious— Antonia, ever incapable of hiding her feelings, looks more worried than I would admit to feeling.

[†]'listeners' assigned to each locutory to report eventual improprieties to the Vicaress

Carlos has been home from his latest expedition for several days now, but chooses this precise moment to pay a visit. Thinking it is the Bishop in the passageway I rise to stand fetchingly by the grille. As Carlos comes through the doorway I would like to be angry—and try to look it, but in truth it is good to see him. He has been away through most of the winter and all of spring.

A bachelor dressing without a woman's touch, Carlos has today achieved somehow a shadow of mournful elegance in a black cape too heavy for April, a small, reasonably white collar and a high black tunic laced firmly at the neck.

"Have you run out of people to see, Carlos?"

"This is lavish even for you," he says, glancing over our preparations. "Are you so pleased to have me back?"

"I am, exceedingly."

He takes the Bishop's seat. I stand a moment longer trying not to look exceedingly pleased, staring down at the broad pale forehead, the hairline seeming a little higher than six months ago, *con mas canas*. He is almost handsome, the cheekbones finely formed, over cheeks a little too hollow just now.

"So this isn't all for me."

"You don't eat sweets, or still didn't the last time you graced us with a visit."

"I've been a little unwell."

"The malaria . . . ? 'Tonia, will you bring our friend a cordial?"

"Probably."

"Lime, beet, tamarind?"

"Lime . . ."

Antonia, who is fond of him, hurries over with a glass. *"Gusto en verlo, don Carlos."*

"Hola, Antonia. Gracias."

"Something more substantial, Carlitos—a soup, a stew?"

"I'd be glad to make you something, don Carlos."

"The cordial is fine, 'Tonia. I'm fine. And yes, it is nice to see you too. But *you*—I leave for a few months and come back to this. What deviltry have you played on Núñez now, after so many years? *?En qué avíspero te has metido ya?*[†]"

"Aside from publishing without seeking his approval?"

"You couldn't have sent one copy to Núñez?" He shrugs, a maddening little hitch of one shoulder. "Not even as a courtesy?"

"You mean, Carlos, as an invitation to meddle. But you're right—had I realized there'd be advance copies turning up everywhere . . ."

"He's the one turning up everywhere. The university, the *Audiencia,* the Brotherhood. Criticizing your spiritual director—"

"Before Dorantes can blame it on him instead."

"Was that Gutiérrez I just saw leaving? Tell me the Inquisition isn't involved."

"He had been hoping to see Bishop Santa Cruz."

"Ah, a war council."

"What have you heard?"

"Something about a sermon. Given by Núñez, I take it."

"He preached an old sermon by Antonio Vieyra, so he could—with suitable humility—knock it down again in private at the rectory afterwards."

"So, for a few select churchmen," says Carlos, "you knocked his straw man down, what—more *elegantly* than he?"

"Something along those lines, yes."

"Have things been so dull?"

"If he's so bent on talking about me, let him have a sturdier quintain to tilt at."

"I thought you'd cured it, this mania of yours for taunting him."

"Unlike you, I do not have the option of running off for months at a time. And if you know so much about my affairs before even showing your face here, it just goes to show how little privacy I *have.* Nor do I have the option of being ignored."

"Thank you."

[†] 'What hornet's nest have you stirred up now?'

"You know that is not what I meant."

"And now the Bishop is coming all the way from Puebla. . . . I should tell you, then. I've invited an interesting young Frenchman for you to meet."

"When?"

"In a minute or two."

"*Estás en tu casa.*"

"Don't be annoyed. Most of these types are rather less than they seem to be, but I'm convinced this one is rather more. He's spent half his young life at Versailles. He has brought me a letter from the King, in fact."

"Not theirs."

"Louis XIV."

"You're serious."

"Perfectly."

"We could be at war again with France any day now—how has he been allowed to come?"

"Well for one, he appears to be a near relation of every monarch in Europe. I haven't really the head for this sort of thing, but he seems to be the grandson of Henri IV and Catherine de Medici—"

"Marie. Catherine was her mother."

"He is also the nephew of Isabel de Francia—and therefore first cousin to María Teresa by his aunt Isabel, making Philip IV—"

"His uncle by marriage. But this would also make Louis XIII his blood uncle, which in turn makes Louis XIV his first cousin . . ."

"By blood *and* by marriage. Yes, Juana. Moreover, on his father's side are Stuarts. So I may be about to introduce you to the future King of England. Or France, or—"

"Spain. Permission to come, then . . ."

"Would not have presented an insurmountable difficulty. What I have not worked out yet, is *why* he's come."

"Other than to deliver your letter."

"He says he is in America to round out his education, is quite wide-eyed at the prospect."

"What better education than Mexico for a future King of Spain?"

"He claims to have no interest in politics."

"Then what does he claim claims his interest?"

"Generally speaking, literature . . ."

"And specifically?"

"You."

"Me."

"He wants to translate you. To France. All of France, I gather."

"So now you want *me* to help you find out what he's really up to."

"They have a way of revealing themselves to you."

"Because naturally he couldn't have come so far for a thing so trivial as his stated purpose."

"That's not—"

"Juana, don Carlos—*disculpen* but there's a French gentleman here. Tomasina swears he's as beautiful as an angel."

"Yes, that will be him," Carlos smiles.

Antonia used the word beautiful. And so he is, with the beauty of sculpture—features pale yet warm like finest Carrara marble, lips full with just the faintest hint of rose, ice-blue eyes shading to lilac ... older than the face, more knowing. His hands are pale, blue-veined, with long, finely-wrought fingers, broad palms. An angel's hands, and clasped with no apparent effort in one is the strap of an impressively heavy looking satchel.

"Sor Juana Inés de la Cruz, *je te présente René Henri de Borbón. Vicomte d'Anjou.*" Adds Carlos, in accents vaguely Italianate, "special envoy of King Louis XIV *de Francia.* The Viscount has just arrived from Paris after a few weeks in Seville. We spent a marvellous afternoon yesterday discussing the latest astronomical discoveries—a wonderfully educated young man."

"I apologize for the intrusion, Sor Juana," begins the young nobleman, "but it's really out of clemency to your learned friend don Carlos, whom I've been hounding for five days straight to be given the opportunity of at last meeting you. An honour all Europe may now envy me." He adds, with a little flourish and a low bow, "My compliments."

"And my compliments on your Castilian." I indulge myself in another moment of looking him over. There is nothing quite like French men's fashions on Frenchmen. The hair is beyond doubt his, but his habiliments are those of the latest fashion doll. It seems the ostrich-plumed hat is no longer. The petticoat breeches are of course an incalculable loss. The collarless, fitted coat is almost knee-length now, this one in lilac-coloured silk, and embroidered at the cuffs and buttonholes, with violet sash and waistband. An ensemble worn with perfect assurance and without the slightest irony. And so the French man sallies forth dressed *for* it but not *in* it. I sense Carlos following my appraisal and avoid his look. With Carlos drab is good, drab is wise—it is in the flourish that disaster lurks.

"You are kind, my lady. The languages of France and Spain were spoken in our household in almost equal measure, but I confess that the Castilian tongue always gave greater joy. . . ."

"Carlos tells me you were able to take great pleasure, too, in walking about Seville."

"A good deal, yes. It holds up much better than does Madrid these days." Brightening, he adds, "But even in Madrid—everywhere I've looked, in fact—the booksellers are out of your *Inundación Castálida.* Three Spanish editions sold out in five months—and here the first shipment gone, I'm told, in three days!"

"Carlos and I were just talking about my local channels of distribution. Have you been able to get a copy yet, *Vicomte?*"

"Don Carlos was good enough to give me his."

"How kind of him."

"I *had* read them, Juanita, or most, in manuscript. . . ."

"How I envy you that privilege, *señor.*"

"Or the unenviable duty. Our Carlos has so many."

"I'll get another copy eventually, Juana."

"Now it is his patience that we are to envy—"

"*Pardonnez-moi,* Sor Juana, but was not Castalia the Sibyl granted eternal life by Apollo in exchange for her favours?"

"That was Deiphobe."

"It is a shame that a Sibyl so aptly named," says Carlos, "could not see into her own future. You see, sir, she forgot to ask for eternal youth."

"Carlos will tell us next that to wrinkle eternally comes as just punishment for refusing the advances of Apollo. Now if our friend has said enough on Deiphobe, I can tell you, *Monsieur,* that the Castalia you ask about was a nymph—I am hoping a water nymph. . . ."

"You must think me entirely lacking in culture."

"But not at all. You were exactly right about the connection with Apollo."

"If I might exculpate myself a little. My thoughts have been with the Sibyls since yesterday. At the house of don Carlos, we were speaking with a Brother . . . ?"

"Bellmont," Carlos says gloomily.

"Bellmont, yes—where I heard him refer to you as the Sum of the Ten Sibyls. People all over the city speak of nothing but Sor Juana—"

"Come, *Vicomte*, we have so many more interesting topics before us. Tell us about your King."

"But you must call me René Henri—please do me the courtesy of informality, my lady. Now where to begin? Aunt Ana taught Louis a passable Castilian, which, after his marriage to my cousin, *la Infanta*, he spoke often with her. Even after her death he takes a great interest in Spanish affairs—"

"An interest some find worrisome." Carlos is about to continue when Tomasina and Ana burst shoulder to shoulder into the locutory—barely suppressing giggles—each bearing a freshly heaped tray, but with eyes only for our beautiful guest.

"I've heard rumours he has remarried."

There seems an excellent chance that Tomasina will step on Ana's robe and one or the other of my *escuchas*—or both and the trays—will crash through the grille into the Viscount's pretty lap.

"We have heard those same rumours, Sor Juana," continues the young noble, plainly accustomed to such attentions from novices. "The happy date is not something he disposes to announce. She is well beneath his station. His lover of many years, even before the death of her husband, the poet Scanlon. Not that this has, for me, the least importance. What matters rather more is—"

"That the King and his new wife have a shared love of poetry?"

Carlos is being particularly obstructive today, given that the guest is his. The Viscount seems not to have noticed. Perhaps the wit at Versailles was too quick for our young émigré.

"Tell us what matters, René Henri."

"Gladly my lady. Louis' great interest in the lessons taught us by Spain have led him to emulate her in proclaiming our own golden age. And what better model for a palace life than that of our uncle Philip's *Palacio del Buen Retiro*? A great patron of learning, Louis has empowered me to offer don Carlos a singular commission. *Royal Cosmographer!*"

"A gallant offer."

"He's serious, I assure you, sir. Your income would be handsome. Your skills as an astronomer are well known to him—to all of Europe, after your besting of the famous Father Kino."

"Skills not much esteemed here, sir, I assure you. Notably by our local poets."

"So often the case, don Carlos, with prophets in their own land. And Sor Juana, we've convents too in France . . ."

"Yes, some quite near the palace, I've heard."

"If my king had the faintest hope you might be persuaded—"

"*Nonsense!* She can no more leave than I. We're Mexicans, our place is here."

"Yes of course," the Viscount looks slightly bewildered. "I intended—"

"No offence given, René Henri, it's an old debate," I say soothingly. "After all, you will have noticed with what equanimity Carlos ponders his own departure, if not yet mine. Tell me, is it true they've taken to calling your cousin the Sun King?"

"Perhaps because he throws about so much gold," Carlos mutters.

"Spoken like a true astronomer, Carlos."

"Indeed they have, my lady. It is a title which doesn't displease him."

"Might the title fit so well, *Vicomte*, because his new home is a palace of light?"

"*Ah le Palais de Versailles! Mais c'est une merveille!* Which is not to say Mexico—Mexico City outgleams even Paris. But Versailles! Apollo's palace of the dawn *a du luire ainsi a l'aube du temps!*"

"I hear he's lavished almost as much on the palace," says Carlos, "as on the artists he stables there."

"Louis does seem at times to love his artists more than their art. He's spoiled Boileau beyond redemption and *Racine*—*mais* what a *pauvre type* I am! Sor Juana I've brought for you from France—" says our young visitor, reaching into the leather pouch at his feet, "Don Carlos wrote . . . that no gift could be more precious to you than books. You've read Molière I'm sure. And Corneille? Yes? I must be making a terrible impression— blathering away like an idiot."

"Not at all, René Henri. The candid is one of my favourite modes. You wear it well."

"I had only wanted to say that to gaze on Racine today, once the brightest light of all, is to make one fear our brief golden age is already in its sunset years. The horizon contains none with his talent now. Ah, what a colossus he was!—clawing his way up out of the ooze *des origines des plus obscures* to command centre stage in Paris and defend it against all comers. A sensation at twenty-eight—younger even than Corneille.

When as a boy I first met him, you should have seen the man. But, already at thirty-eight—"

"Not quite your age, Juana."

"Carlos's sympathies remain with Deiphobe."

"But no! Were it not for your air of gravity and—"

"Ah, my *gravity*," I say, unable to resist, "another little reminder of time's swift transits and steep descents. Carlos will be grateful to you."

"Forgive me, my lady—" he stammers. I feel myself blushing now at the pleasure of seeing him blush, as he struggles gamely on. "I express myself poorly. It's just that if you could see Racine now—hero of my youth—a genius, now grown docile enough to accept the King's commission to write nothing but the Royal Historiography."

"I suddenly see my existence there as Royal Cosmographer."

"Have you forgotten, Carlos? You've already refused our guest's offer. Or does it suit you to do so twice in the same hour?"

"Don Carlos may be right, Sor Juana. When I see you both here working at the height of your powers . . . He might well find the spectre too haunting."

"If you'll permit me, René Henri, perhaps I might restore some small part of the regard you once held for your Racine. For although it doubtless helps to have served perhaps all Europe's last great king, it will not have escaped an artist of Racine's stature that the burden of service grows heavier these days to the precise extent that the king himself loses the gravity of substance. Though they command realms and empires larger by far than any of the old principalities, how our kings today envy the humblest Asiatic princes the strut of their unthinking despotism, their thoughtless hold on power. How much less need have these little satraps for painters and plays and soaring panegyrics, whereas even the Sun King grows desperate for any art magnifying the faint lustre of his divine right . . . rather than simply reflecting it as the Moon cannot help reflecting the Sun."

The Viscount, flushed, struggles in the grip of some beautiful emotion. He seems about to stand. "Clearly, my disappointment has made me ungenerous, my lady. I *am* grateful to you—I think you've come very close to the mark. For it has always seemed to me his collapse began with the failure of his *Phèdre*. By far Racine's greatest work, and not one that much glorifies kings. I've summoned up the nerve to bring you a translation I've made into Castilian, for Mexico's author of *Love is a Greater*

Labyrinth. What a masterpiece," he says, passing the book through the grille. "They had it in for him. The most famous, the most gifted, the most brilliant—he was too . . ."

"Superlative?"

"Antonia, will you get Carlos a refresher of the cordial? Perhaps not the lime . . . something sweeter. And another for the Viscount."

"But yes, exactly, don Carlos. Superlative. Just half a glass. Thank you, Alexandra. Is it futile to hope my proposed translations of your Iberian classics might help" —he asks this as though it could be anything but futile—"bring a fresh blush of dawn to our French letters? Beginning, as Carlos and I discussed yesterday, with a few of the lesser known poems of his own illustrious progenitor, the great Góngora. And, if this does not come as both premature and presumptuous, some of your own, Sor Juana?"

"Certainly of the obscure variety," I say pleasantly, "you'll find many more of mine to choose from than among Góngora's."

"What an oaf you must think me!" Again the beautiful blush. "*Justement,* the whole point I was about to make is that the one luminous quadrant in the French literary firmament is the irrepressible vitality of our women of letters, clearly one thing we share with New Spain. I've brought you a sampling of my favourites. Louise Labé. You'll find in her a kindred spirit. Perhaps you'll give this little volume," he says, producing it with a flourish, "a small place in a collection fabled throughout Europe. How often have I pictured you, America's Phoenix, in her nest spiced and feathered with books. . . ."

"Candied *jalapeños, señor?*"

"Why yes, thank you, I have been wondering what these were. Candied, are they. Your servant here—"

"Antonia's an oblate here at San Jerónimo and a friend."

"*Je vous prie pardon, chère demoiselle. . . .*"

"Oh, I'm sure she's already forgotten it, René Henri. You'll no doubt find women's memories as short here as they are in France."

"I was about to say she probably saved me from another indiscretion, but perhaps that would have been too much to hope for. It's just that meeting you in person, it's just so . . ."

"Fabulous?"

"Antonia . . . save a pepper or two for Carlos."

"Peppers, you say?" the Viscount asks, having just bitten into one.

"Let me—oh, oh yes, so they are. Perhaps some of that cordial, Alexandra?

"Antonia."

"Eh?"

"Antonia.

"Of course. *Antonia.*"

"The lime, *señor?*"

"Yes, yes, Antonia, any kind at all."

"You were telling us," Carlos puts in before he can take a drink, "about France's women of letters."

"Yes—Labé, *bien entendu,* but we have more than just *femmes poètes.*"

"Though what could be more exalted than lady poets, *verdad?*"

"More beet cordial, don Carlos?" Antonia asks, eyes merry.

"There is Christina of Sweden—who was of course not one of us but wrote French like a Frenchwoman. There are those among our women of letters who have been in mourning for months—but perhaps I should be extending my condolences. The world's two most learned women— you two must have corresponded."

"No."

"Truly what a pity, for you both. She maintained quite a lively correspondence with France. Including with Anne Lefèvre Dacier, daughter of the distinguished classicist, and a formidable poet and scholar herself. But among our contemporaries is one still more notorious. Madeleine de Scudéry is making a new kind of literature, very novel. Poor Boileau waxes apoplectic on the new genre. Women's writing, he calls it—love letters, naked passions . . ." The Viscount launches into an enthusiastic defence. "What Boileau will not see is France's women writers offering the delicate folds of their inner landscape as an intimate response to the swell and thrust of the great massed forces of History as written since Herodotus—"

"The Viscount," Carlos observes, "fairly peppers his speech with vivid metaphor." Although the tone is still dry Carlos seems somewhat anxious about the turn in the conversation.

"So wide is her renown," the Viscount presses on as though he hasn't heard, "so broad her popularity and so great the respect for her erudition, all France has begun calling her Sappho—as I believe you yourself, Sor Juana, are called the Tenth Muse here . . . how curious! Her first book of letters takes Sappho for its heroine—"

"After Ovid."

"Precisely, yes . . . Antonia." He has glanced at her more than once, and who could blame him, but does so now with a more complex interest. "And though the style has evolved, this, the tenth book of her great inner epic," he says, extracting another volume, "makes Sappho her protagonist once again. She's very subversive."

"Sappho?" asks Antonia sweetly.

"No—well yes, but de Scudéry I meant. If Louis read her more carefully he might be less enamoured. Though excessive at times, my regal cousin is fundamentally conventional."

"Subversive in what sense, René Henri?"

"She makes Sappho the daughter—the offspring *plutôt*, of Scam-androgine, an androgynous entity. To her discerning readers it's very clear that all creators—all humanity really, not just artists—*sont au fond bisexués.*"

"*Monsieur*," Carlos sputters, "*estamos en un convento!*"

"You're entirely correct, *señor*—as a nun, such ideas must be repugnant to Sor Juana. But surely," adds the young aristocrat, eyeing me appraisingly, "to the scholar and the poet, they cannot be so entirely offensive."

Such an amusing child. Does he expect with such a pallid challenge to get me to raise my colours for him?

"Carlos has spent enough time at convents to know they are less an island of virtue than an isthmus. The heart, *Monsieur*, is the same, no matter how tightly bound the breast. No word or idea is in itself offensive to me. It's a question of intent."

"If I have expressed my intent poorly . . ."

"If you have, you must feel free to express it more precisely. Please, go on." And how my strange young visitor does go on. I had been willing to help Carlos discover what the Viscount was up to, and whether the offer from Versailles should be considered sincere. For if it is, Carlos is in no position to be dismissing it so lightly. But I have begun to sense where this is leading—let him at least get there quickly.

"De Scudéry's Sappho inverts the conventional picture. De Scudéry has Phaon propose marriage—Phaon is—but of course you know. Sappho accepts his suit but not his proposal. She will instead co-habit with him, but only if he consents to follow her and live among the Amazons. Instead of being ruined, the androgyne's daughter dictates the terms, and continues to write every day! She will not submit to what she charmingly calls the *long slavery of marriage. . . .*"

"Now there, *Vicomte,* is a subject fit to discourse upon at length. Carlos will bring you another day, perhaps . . . ?"

"I do hope we may, for I know you will not fail to be fascinated by what Mlle de Scudéry is attempting, with an artistry capable of transforming even the basest passions—the insatiate inversions *du saphisme*—into pure elegance. The signs are all there for those willing to probe a little—Louis would never stand for open talk of *l'amour lesbien*—"

"*Señor!*" barks Carlos.

"Sor Juana, do you not think this might be the singular gift of women's art? To ennoble yearning, and imbue with a kind of grace the grotesque impulses of our inner life . . . ?"

"You seem to insist, Viscount, on the grotesque and the debased," says Carlos heatedly. He can at such moments be very dear. "Clearly this is neither the province of women's art nor the special province of art itself."

"Yet is Sor Juana herself not at this very moment making a poetical study of Sappho . . . ?"

Carlos goes pale, Antonia positively flinches.

"Does everyone on both sides of the Atlantic," I ask looking at each in turn, "think they know what I am now working on?"

"Juanita, I'm sorry. It just slipped out—in the spirit of yesterday's free exchange of ideas."

"Such a rarity, Carlos, the free and equal exchange. Your generosity gets the better of you at times. And *Vicomte,* you should bear in mind that as a confidant Carlos is something of an amphora—straight necked, wondrous capacity, but susceptible to gushing forth suddenly on all sides."

"Please don't blame don Carlos. I know I shouldn't have been the one—but might we not speak of this? I was so hoping to bring us around to it. It is precisely this work I hope most to translate."

"You do, *Vicomte,* seem rather to insist. An insistence that leaves your intent looking decidedly unnatural. And were I ever to devote a work to Sappho, I would avoid the grotesque and the debased altogether. Of this you may be sure. If you insist so on the names of de Scudéry and Labé, Sappho and Christina—is it to intimate that one might find in France, or is it Versailles itself, *toda una comunidad Sáfica?* Am I then to take this Sapphic community to be a refuge, or just one more exotic birdhouse for the palace grounds? And is there some point to this? Does one hope to incite me to some brazen action or blushing declaration?"

It is as I thought. The mask of shyness, the blundering and blushing are gone. The Vicomte d'Anjou sits smiling through the grille, world-wearily amused. Is there more, I wonder? What lies beneath this next mask?

"Perhaps, *Monsieur*, a man of your beauty believes he may speak with no particular purpose at all. Just what sort of translation is it you hope to make to France—of my poetry, my person, or do you merely hope to make a diverting report of me? Or perhaps you serve your King not as his procurer but as his proxy, making your mission the inversion of what you say it is: to translate France rather to *me*, by way of the salacious flirtations of a bored king who has proclaimed himself nothing less than the state itself. This is the Sun King's notion of a golden age?—to interrogate a bride of Christ on her sensual inclinations? Or is this what passes for wit at Versailles . . ."

Were it not for the anger that a jaded smile from one so beautiful and so young strikes up in me, I would be the weary one. Once I thought I would suffocate without the diversions of this locutory. Now I am suffocated by them. Was Carlos right after all? Have things really been too quiet?

Tomasina rushes into the room, "—excuse me, Sor Juana—the Bishop's carriage. It's *here*."

chorus

To the new Temple
come all and find
how its stones are made Bread
and its Bread made of Stone.
Ay, ay, ay, ay!

verses

If there in the Desert
He refused to transform
stones into bread for
His sustenance,
    Here, for our own,
He saw fit to conceal
the foundation, which is Christ,
in the Bread of His Substance.
    Now on this, His new altar,
to us He reveals,
that He is of His Temple
the cornerstone,
    and since he would sustain
us with a delicacy,
the sweetness he feeds us
is a Honey of Stone.

JUANA INÉS
DE LA CRUZ,

"Carols for Saint
Bernard: the
House of Bread"

B. Limosneros, trans.

LYSISTRATA

Lysis,

I t is a giddy time. One notices we have been cele-brating the king's wedding to the new queen for over a year now, though we hadn't quite intended it. A sort of accident. With the first queen's sudden passing and the haste to secure another upon which to sire an heir, the dates we've been getting to cele-brate were all long past; and since we have never known when the next occasion was coming, except to hear we've missed out, we have never really taken the banners down. First we improvised a Festival of the Seeking of the New Queen's Hand (last May there—here, in July), fol-lowed by her marriage by proxy in Neuburg, then her departure on that leisurely seven-month tour *de soltera* through Europe (this, the most exhausting part—we fêted the iron nerves with which, each fresh day, the virgin queen combatted her impatience to join her mate). And now this year there has been her arrival on Spanish soil in the spring (here, last week), then this week the Spanish wedding, the royal entry into the capital . . .

The new Viceroy had been desperate to set the tone for his adminis-tration, and in those festivities has found it, while the Vicereine has found it is not a party until she has broken something—a heart, a treaty, a treasury. Together the two set off the first volley of scandalous balls and lavish banquets. And never have we seen so many weddings, or so few new entries into the convents. At the price of a dowry one may offer up one's daughter to the Son of God any day, but these past months are as close as any burgher here will ever get to marrying a daughter to or for or with the King of Spain.

And so it almost seems we find ourselves transported back to the Mexico City of my early years, for through the streets and late into the night flood upwards of seven thousand coaches drawn by silver-shod horses—coachmen in gold lace, their hatbands struck with pearls— wedding bells and serenades, bullfights and bawdy festivals, wild rumours of fertility rites held at the outskirts of the capital . . . but then we at San Jerónimo are at the outskirts here and have seen little of this for all our vigilance.

A giddy time and a desperate one, for it is not only the Viceroy and the Creoles who would make their mark. The Church initially joined in with special Masses and midnight orisons, but lately the theme from the pulpits is more often the hoary one of Sodom and Gomorrah. Perhaps it is only the lost dowries that has them vexed, but I believe our year may be ending—

On your side of the Atlantic everyone, you say, is clamouring for a second collection. Five Spanish editions now of our Castalia's flood—your printer weeps Castalian cataracts of gratitude each time he hears your name or mine, or talk of a second collection. Your friends in Mantua are ready to translate our Castalia to Italy, your friends in Vienna, to Germany, and a fresh new friend of mine asks nothing more than to bring her to Versailles.

I glean from your teasing that you've had nearly enough of my timidity. Since *Las letras a Safo* are an open secret and since Núñez rails against them anyway, why not publish and at least silence the speculation? What is it that so exercises Núñez, you ask, in *not* finding Sappho's verses in our collection? Does he read in their omission not respect for him but weakness? Cowardice ... though you are too kind to say this. I know how it must look to a Manrique. Please, María Luisa, please do not give up on me. I need to believe too that Sappho's time may come soon, even as Castalia's has.

Yes, these verses are an open secret, more open than you perhaps realize, given that Núñez now roves from pillar to pillory pronouncing darkly against this new and unprecedented wickedness. Here in Mexico— where so much may be spoken, and spoken almost freely if not open sedition or undisguised heresy—to publish is quite another proposition. In this respect we are not like Spain, and so it has been difficult to make this difference clear. What is written is not just better evidence for the Inquisition, the written is Writ: it occupies another realm of existence entirely.[29] Picture Cortés reading his *Requerimiento* in Latin over the heads of the Indians he is about to attack. There, you have it. Things since then are not so much changed.

But I also need to help you to see that in another respect things are already not as they were when you were here. I ask you to read me now obliquely, in the way we have spoken of before. Think of Aeschylus and the art of lyric tragedy, in which an entire story may be told though almost none of it happens onstage. So . . .

The Inquisition has asked Carlos to furnish a complete list of the reading materials in his possession. In Spain I know this is rarely done any longer but the Holy Office here is its own beast and master. Carlos blames me. Which is only fair, since any blame I can remotely connect him to, I do. He has decided the demand for a book inventory is linked somehow to Núñez's campaign against me and what he, Núñez, insists on calling *The Sapphic Hymns*. Very sanguine is dear Carlos about my publishing difficulties, as he reminds me of how many of his own manuscripts go unprinted. So while he understands my frustration, and yours, as no one else does (he will tell you he understands most things as no one else does), every risk I take makes his caution seem, well . . . cautious. Caution beseems the woman, and as a complement to her modesty can never be excessive; whereas in a man it is, in anything but the quantities required for his barest survival, a disgrace.

So yes, you are right to ask. I have withheld my favours for eight years now, and what has it brought me? What I offer these Churchmen I am now scarcely in a position to withhold. Núñez has me almost completely encircled. I can no longer sit by and watch him undermining me.

I *know* you are right. And so since April I have been pressing a number of counterattacks, but obliquely—as Aristophanes resorted to comedy so as to beard the tyrant Cleon. How else are we to answer the tyrants, how else to raise their siege? Here is how the campaign stands.

Picture, María Luisa, a stage set by Aristophanes, from *The Wasps* or *Lysistrata*. A whole little Troy town on a mountaintop—Mount Eryx, or the Hill of Ares, or better yet the sanctuary of the Erectheum on the Acropolis. Yes, the very thing. A great hive then, with dozens of locutories, open in profile to the auditorium. A play of comic comings and strange goings on. Let us set it during a siege, but in a castle with honeycomb walls and the soldiers of both sides—paper wasps in red, honey drones in gold and lilac—all slipping in and slipping out for the honey of the harlots of the hive . . . all the while the harried queen crouches off to one side laying eggs in moments of privacy as fantastic as brief. Her cell too is open to the gallery.

Enter in stunning array the thirty theologians of Castalia's preface to a fanfare of ram's horn trumpets, a stately pavane across the boards and then another blast to rival Jericho as once again they exeunt by thirty different exits.

Enter two platoons of holy officers carrying torches, Jesuits and Dominicans jostling. Our defenders of the ramparts against the Saracens, Jews and Lutherans, and yet for these keepers of the wall, no glorious fanfare of shofars.[†] The Theological Thirty have made them look quaint—keepers of a mighty fortress over a mere mill race. So far, these stalwarts will not quit the stage, though they stand near the exits and get in the way.

[†]Hebrew war trumpets of ram's horn

Enter Núñez declaiming, as he moves from cell to cell to cell, three lines of Castalia's poetry, over and over, the three having remotely to do with Sappho.

Enter Dorantes reminding the audience that Sor Juana was trained in theology by none other than Núñez.

Enter Bishop Santa Cruz, bent on rescuing all pretty nuns from perfidy.

Enter the Creole delegation paddling out of rhythm, a longboat at their waists, its figurehead a carven effigy of Guadalupe. And yet who is it they ask to intervene with the Vice-King to stay their charges of sedition? Not Guadalupe, certainly. How curious they seem: they hate the Viceroy's administration and yet, were someone to make him a king, like puppies would they follow the humblest of his clerks.

Enter Carlos carrying the Archbishop's magical hat—the mathematician and natural philosopher as archepiscopal mendicant bartering alms for miracle cures. And this one once called *me* a fable beggar.

Enter an officer wearing the coat of arms of which Archbishop Aguiar never stops boasting, of a family so ancient they trace their name back to the Centurions. The venerably outfitted officer tows a trundle of books to the booksellers. See him wheedle and threaten until they surrender all their comedies, which he exchanges for his copies of *Consolations for the Poor.*

Enter other officers fanning out to close down the *palenques* and *cosos.*[†]

[†]cockpits and bullrings

Enter the Vicomte d'Anjou who may be the next King of England or Spain, or even of France, or he may be here to translate me, or he may be here to spy on us.

Close Act I with the Archbishop walled in by stacks of comedies by Quevedo and groping myopically for an exit. . . .

How I weary of these silly wars and the siege they lay upon our thoughts.[30] Even as Lysistrata and the lusty women's assembly so wearied of it all they were willing to withhold their favours (O supreme sacrifice!) until their husbands made peace. A sacrifice, Aristophanes tells us, made all the more stark by a war scarcity of Milesian comforters to help them bide their loneliest hours.[31] So you see, these comic women of Aristophanes were serious. As are we.

Tonight my thoughts turn to the end of war, to the weddings and the banquets that seal the peace—and to the difference between the false peace and the true, the siege and the truce. Thoughts that form the basis of *este entracto* and the parabasis for Act II. Picture next, dear Lysis, a stage set for a series of banquet scenes. As for some other antic comedy by Aristophanes, but to be read remembering the art of Aeschylus. Prudence calls for us to practise this art of lyric comedy for the next letter or two....

The first banquet scene here was three months past, after the Maundy Thursday sermon at the Metropolitan Cathedral, to mark the feast in the olive grove of Gethsemane. Taking its inspiration from Christ's washing of the disciples' feet, the sermon's theme is humility. Naturally, then, Núñez would see himself as the obvious one to give it. Except his choice of sermon was not obvious—first, it was published by a man detested by the Inquisition, and second, it was not at all humble. I was not the only one to find the whole business dubious. My locutory soon filled with Churchmen who came to hear what I might make of it. What's more, one of the late arrivals had come directly from the college rectory where Núñez rebutted in private the very oration he had just given in public. Caught up in the mixed emotions of the moment—their outrage and perplexity, my merriment—I upstaged his rebuttal with a full demolition. Since then, I have had misgivings I cannot dispel. Not for fear of reprisals so much as over my own motives. The Last Supper. Of all the beautiful banquets in the stories of all the world, surely this is the loveliest, the most terrible. Two courses: a *plato fuerte* of the bread and the wine; and a *postre* of a delicate, an ineffable sweetness ... Christ's humble washing of the feet. Then, as a final toast of Grace, there comes the Mandate to His companions: *A new commandment I give unto you, That ye love one another; as I have loved you....* And on the morrow of the Passion and on all the morrows ever after He leaves us to ask and ask and ask: But *how* has He loved us? That night He showed us, so beautifully, how we may be made humble by love.

Act II, Scene Two. A few days after the sermon, the sisters of Saint Bernard sent to ask that I write a cycle of lyrics for the dedication of their new temple just two blocks up our street. For weeks I cast about for a fitting subject. Here was a fit challenge, for me especially, something simple for Bernard, advocate of a holy ignorance. Hearing that Núñez was to celebrate the penultimate Mass and with my blood still up, I chose my topic and wove into the lyrics an entire sermon to rival the one I could predict Núñez would give. On the Eucharist. There is no mystery more sublime than this; none finds my heart more surely than the mystery of this sacrifice. If Father Núñez so detests water, I thought, then he shall have his sacrament of bread. But this was not a commission from the Churchmen, not a favour to an ally in the Holy Office, this was the highest honour, a call from my own sisters. A call and a sublime sacrifice that plucked at my heart as I began to write. And though the reasons for my choice had been so vile, it was conceived as is a life, and from that passionate mire grew a small simple miracle for the simple people of the neighbourhood who would come to fill their new temple. This temple of Christ as the womb of Mary, this flesh of her Son as the Host rising in her womb, this temple of Christ as a house of bread.

Here is a mystery to feed the hungry, here, in three voices, a mystery the simple people need no theologian to understand.

> 1.–You who hunger,
> come and find
> Corn grains and Wheat Spikes, Flour for Bread.
> 2.–All you who thirst,
> Love has provided
> Green Grapes and Ruddy, Must for Wine.
> 3.–They will not find them!
> 2.–They will!
> 3.–Not these shall they find—
> but Flesh and Blood!—
> not Bread and Wine . . .

The house of bread is the temple, the temple is Word and world. The bread of Christ springs from her nature, the wine is her harvest, the love of Nature springs from her beauty, as beauty itself springs from love, and love from the greatest Beauty of all.

This cycle too was to have been a banquet. The dedications in the temple begin next week. Núñez has read my lyrics and in them found what I had woven there. A sermon by a woman, expressly forbidden now by the Council of Trent. The issue is clear. To press matters too far here would be foolhardy. It is almost certain that my lyrics will not be sung.

I have not so much as objected. Who, after all, is to blame? But it is only just beginning to come home to me, how this coming week may feel. I can see the new temple from my window. I will hear the music from here.

Act II, Scene Three. With all this, the prospect of peace seems more beautiful than ever to me. And more like a dream. We turn to *Lysistrata* for comic relief. As is fitting for a comedy, it ends with a picnic, but spread in the solemn sanctuary of the Acropolis; for as a dream of peace, *Lysistrata* is a serious comedy. After drenching the men's chorus with pitchers of water, reversing thus the unfair judgement against the Danaïdes, the women's chorus sits down to eat with the men. A picnic of peace that serves as preamble to a wedding feast.

Act II, Scene Four. Two camps and their aides are sitting down to dine, out in the open air—next to our academy, let us say, at the refectory. The long table is laid in the passageway beneath the boughs of our pomegranate trees, as was laid for us and the ladies of your court half a dozen times here in the convent courtyard—where our talks and our dreams ran to topics thought impious by many. You will remember the ones I am thinking of. Plato's *Symposium* was another such night, another such dream. Under lamps bright with finest oil, the two sides face one another, raise toasts and make gentle, generous jokes, and pass the vegetables and gravy boats. The guests Plato has assembled are to make speeches in praise of love. As the others discourse, Aristophanes sits silent until Socrates enjoins him to speak—a matter of duty for one who has devoted his life to Dionysus and Aphrodite. To this challenge and this banquet we owe a lovely legend of the sexes. You see, at first there were three: male, female and hermaphrodite. And here, as I recall, the story takes a turn, for it is from this third sex that we are descended, says Aristophanes, as can be plainly seen in our lurching about half our lives in search of our lost half.

No one could doubt, after such a wistful rendering, that the great comedian liked to be taken seriously. One might almost pardon Aristophanes his role, not long after, in the trial and conviction of Socrates. How strange that Socrates' great disciple Plato, so mistrustful of the theatre as it was, should befriend Aristophanes. Plato once wrote of the soul of Aristophanes as the Temple of the Graces. Then again, Plato was given to such compliments. . . .

But surely we must infer that they were friends—perhaps it was some secret shared love of contradictions, for such a bundle of them was this Aristophanes! Mocking the gods yet not denying their existence, mocking old-fashioned Aeschylus yet accepting his greatness. Mocking the art of lyric tragedy that died with him, even as the comedy of Dionysus would die with Aristophanes.

The old theatres had been of wood. Pericles, in his wealth and his love of glory, remade them of stone, to outlast the age. Yet stone is for Apollo; the art of Dionysus is not made to last. In his art lies something Pericles has not grasped: that in its decay, the temple and the theatre, the city itself, possess a greatness that the original could not capture. For now in the mossy lineaments of each ruined façade, in the tumbled furniture of rotted dados and cleft pediments, scrawl the worm-scripts of chance and circumstance, whispering of a different plan. The ruin invites us to reimagine it, reseed it, it needs *us* to complete it, as the perfect original never does. The art of Dionysus does not outlast its age. It laughs it off the stage.

Act II, Scene Five. Lysis, there are things we may no longer write to be spoken aloud, for it would mean we must first rebuild the theatres, which Apollo would never permit. Even so long ago, Aeschylus knew his art was dying. I believe he must have, for in this art the chorus writes the artist. The lyric tragedy is a drama not so much of *héroes y heroïdes* but of the great race that bore them. Homer may begin in the tenth year of the siege, aware that the audience knows the first nine fully as well as he. Centuries later, Aeschylus begins the greatest play cycle ever written and laces the *Agamemnon* with the briefest of reminders. King Agamemnon has lured his daughter Iphigenia to Aulis, to marry swift-footed Achilles, or so the father tells her as he leads her to another altar. Ending her life there, the King procures not fair weather for the crops but fair winds for his armada. Returning victorious from Troy with Paris's sister in tow as his concubine, Agamemnon is met by his Queen, Helen's sister. Clytaemnestra has waited twenty years to avenge the murder of their child. And who is to say whether this second hatchling, Clytaemnestra, is not the other city on the shield of Hephaistos? The city of the wedding procession and slow judgements.

But Athens is changing quickly and by the time the trilogy is complete, the lyric tragedy of Aeschylus is dead. Dead without an epitaph. The

Eumenides is a great play but of another kind, heralding a new age built on the passing of the old. In the trial of Orestes, the people of Athens are not chorus but jury. The trial offers a final contest between the young defender Apollo and the ancient Furies of the prosecution, but in the end it is the guile of the judge Athena, her wiles of Reason and Persuasion, that win the Furies' parting blessing on Athens and its harvests.

> Let there blow no wind that wrecks the trees.
> I pronounce words of grace.
> Nor blaze of heat blind the blossoms of grown plants, nor
> cross the circles of its right
> place. Let no barren deadly sickness creep and kill.
> Flocks fatten. Earth be kind
> to them, with double fold of fruit
> in time appointed to its yielding. Secret child
> of earth, her hidden wealth, bestow
> blessing and surprise of gods . . . [32]

The audience for the *Eumenides* no longer truly knows and feels who the Furies were—or rather of what they were born, these daughters of Night. The new Athens has lost its fear of the dark. And so, unmarked, lyric tragedy slips into the night even as the Furies must. The play opens before the temple of the Pythoness at Delphi and closes before the Erechtheum in the sanctuary of the Acropolis. The comedy *Lysistrata* ends in the same sanctuary and on these four lines of praise, with all kneeling before the shrine of Victory.

> Athena, hail, thou Zeus-born Maid!
> Who war and death in Greece hast stayed:
> Hail, fount from whom all blessings fall;
> All hail, all hail, Protectress of us all![33]

The greatness of the comedian Aristophanes is to see his art as that epitaph, to know that the death of an order, even one day Apollo's, must be sung drunkenly, by an old reveller of Dionysus. And for all that, Aristophanes could not bear to see the new move beyond the old. The greatness of Aeschylus was to see that a new order just might, if it is built upon the old, but he could not bring himself to write its epitaph as a ruin. In the *Oresteia* he has given us the greatest play cycle made. In the ancient Furies' blessing on a young Athens, he has shown the way. But he could not take that path himself, he could not end the *Eumenides* in comedy. He was too great to ruin it.

Who am I, with one book, to stand in judgement of Aristophanes, much less of Aeschylus who wrote seventy tragedies, with the seven to come down to us each greater than our greatest? What work is left to us who follow giants such as he? Perhaps a few small steps are left. What indeed would be the last great work of a golden age but both the proof and chronicle of its dying? A lyric end to the cycle, a tragedy written by a comedian, to be played in a burning theatre. Now the paradox: that its end be written by one not great, whose worst fear is not ruining the work but no longer knowing what greatness is.

For our next collection, María Luisa, here would be a purpose and a dedication, no? And yet once written we could not publish—it would not be heard, its place does not exist, except we rebuild the old theatres of wood. No, we live in an age of stone that calls for guile and persuasion, and it is not the righteous Furies we must cajole but Apollo, choleric now in his middle years.

Act II, Scene Six. And here is the final scene of our lyric comedy tonight. I ask that you read this one, too, obliquely, and by its conclusion I may have convinced you it is not yet time for Sappho to take the stage. There is another banquet I am thinking of. It was in 1611 or '12, at any rate not long after Galileo Galilei was made a member of the Lyncean Academy. The banquet was in Florence, at the palace of the Grand-Duke of Tuscany. Galileo Galilei was there, as was a Florentine cardinal. After the meal, before the dessert, a debate was staged, much as in the *Symposium*. That night the contest was between Galileo and a professor of the Natural Philosophy of Aristotle. Plato would have been delighted, no doubt, particularly by the outcome. The question addressed floating bodies: why some float in water, like ice itself, and why others sink. Galileo took up the question eagerly against the Aristotelian. The contest was not close. Those companions not among the judges were invited to take sides to make the affair more interesting. Taking what was clearly the winning side, Lord Cardinal Barberini expressed eloquent support of Galileo. Galileo had skill and knowledge, the Cardinal had skill and subtlety; both debated with passion. The two easily carried the evening. Afterwards His Grace the Most Reverend Lord Cardinal, one day to be elected Pope Urban VIII, was reported to have prayed God preserve Galileo and grant him a long life, for such minds were for the enduring benefit of Man.

The book I asked if you would get for us a few months back, that you say you now have and are only waiting on a messenger to bring it across … you know the one, on the floating and sinking of all sorts of bodies. It might be best not to send it for a while. The climate, just now, is not good for ice.

I cannot tell when we will be able to write in the old way again, or publish Sappho's lines, but for the next letter or two let us make little songs of prayer for fair weather, and sing blessings over the land.

Love,

día 22 de junio, Anno Domini 1690
de este convento de San Jerónimo,
de la Ciudad de México,
Nueva España

. . . . Regarding the advice you proffer,
I'll take it as part of the bargain
and do myself violence, although
no violence can make me a Tarquin.

      Hereabouts there's no spring of Salmacis,[34]
whose crystalline waters, I'm told,
possessed some magic or other
from which masculine powers flowed.

      Such things are not my concern;
with one thought I came to this spot:
to be rid of those who'd inquire
whether I am a woman or not.

      In Latin it's just of the married
that uxor, or woman, is said.
A virgin has no sex at all—
or indeed she has both, being unwed.

      So the man who looks upon me
as a woman, shows want of respect,
since one embracing my state
is foreclosed to the other sex.

      Of one thing I'm sure: that my body
disinclined to this man or that,
serves only to house the soul—
you might call it neuter or abstract.

      And leaving this question aside
as more fit for others to probe—
since it's wrong to apply my mind
to things I shouldn't know—

      rest assured, my generous stranger,
you've not left lustrous Lima behind
when your homesick heart can emote in
a style so Peruvianly refined . . .

JUANA INÉS
DE LA CRUZ

Alan Trueblood, trans.

*Replying to a
Peruvian gentleman
who sent a poetic
gift of clay vessels
and the advice that
she become a man.*

IVORY TOWER

BEULAH'S PROFOUNDEST PASSIONS were otherworldly, mine are not. It makes me somewhat vulnerable to attack. But if I'm to take on the role she offers—her goat god, whatever—if I'm to play Beulah's comic foil effectively, we need a closer look at her godlike professor on the make, this mighty hero she happened to see strolling by the river with his mate. An unpleasant way to learn about my wife's pregnancy, I admit. There are other such scenes Beulah was not privy to, however hard she might have tried to imagine them. It falls to me, then, as a penitent form of amusement, to bridge certain gaps. But how? She had attended my classes, observed details, heard things. How might it please her to see my currency debased? Not content to make her attacks personal, clearly she intended to mix business with pleasure, and make them professional as well.

So though it be jarring, unseemly, even a touch obscene, it's well past time we had a peek under the scholar's gown, if you will, at his much shrunken divinity. . . .

To begin.

Comedy ends in marriage.

Mrs. Madeleine Gregory is a successful child psychologist. She once liked to say it was what attracted her to her eventual husband. She works in early developmental education and has never practised clinical psychology. This has not prevented her from dispensing free analysis, though in his case only. Psycho-babble infuriates him. His basic problem, he has been recently told, is compensatory guilt and shame: too much success too fast. That is, for someone of his back-ground. Yes, their backgrounds: heiress of a construction baron weds princeling of the trailer courts.

She'd come to him through an introductory English course, his fifth year of teaching. His classes were still popular back then. She sat near the back of the lecture hall. By the time her turn came she knew per-fectly well what she was in for. This academic year's co-ed number six.

Firm knock at his office door. Mistaking it for a graduate student's, he calls out to come in. The confused freshman's knock is tentative, half-hoping to be inaudible. The willing co-ed's trails off lingeringly.

These last he likes to meet at the threshold. Overall, his office has become a fine place to meet young people.

He has been running over in his mind the stirring conclusion to today's class, the final one of his course. Art, love and healing. It amuses him to think of this as the scholarly equivalent of a song by someone, say, like Marvin Gaye. He likes to save it for the final day, a kind of lazy trolling, and will continue to do this until near the end of his career. But already he is choosier than in the early years, more sporting, likelier to throw the little ones back . . .

. . . *The schism between thinking and feeling runs as a mildly psychotic thread through the warp of Western civilization. So rare and strange it is for us to feel intense emotion attaching to an <u>idea</u> that we tend to experience it as rapture, riot, epiphany. Like love itself, perhaps—do we not visualize our beloved and our union with him as a kind of blinding and rapturous <u>idée fixe</u>? Aristotle believed it the province of art to heal this split, this rawest of wounds. To create moments that fuse the most intense passion with the most profound ideas . . .*

He paused to send a mystic glance down at all the pretty maids in the front row, and thought of his own art as more akin to the snake charmer's. To weave a spell of complicity out of the cold stuff of distance and diffidence and respect. To charm intimacy from the chaste cobra of discretion and *pudeur* . . .

And looking out into this lecture theatre today, I feel sure of seeing many discriminating and generous practitioners of the loving arts . . .

She catches him leaning backwards in his chair, his feet up on the desk. As the office door swings open he swings his feet down and hunches forward, clasps grave, modest fingers over his *mons* of scholarly briefs and folios. He notes she is a few years older than the others, about halfway to his own age. She has never sat in the front row. She takes a seat now, uninvited. Not the one for students—the straight fiddleback across the desk—but instead the stuffed armchair in the corner, reserved for sober reading and one or two esteemed colleagues.

"Word's out on you."

"Word?"

What comes next she says with a deliberation oddly softened by a note of Western twang. Madeleine never lets her smiling eyes leave his.

"The word, Doctor Gregory, is that you're a pussy hound."

Hearing something like this today, he would have hit the ground running for the exits. But ten years ago, well, that was a simpler time.

Even five. The idiom, not much used in his circles, still charms—
though perhaps it doesn't just yet, in that precise instant, as she watches
him duck behind the fig leaf of a frowning rectitude.

"Maybe you prefer 'womanizer,'" she adds amiably.

Opportunity here, certainly, but exactly how much dignity is it
going to cost?

"Skirt chaser?"

"There's synecdoche in its favour, certainly. . . ." he concedes. He
allows himself a last, speculative stroke of the philosopher's beard
before yielding himself up entirely to her ice-breaker. "Or, is that
metonymy, do you think?"

"Cunt-struck."

"The hero laid low. Good, but too . . ."

"Too Beowulf," she suggests.

"I see what you mean."

"Sex addict, then."

"Exculpatory," he cautions, "boastful."

"Philanderer."

"This is better—aura of a Greek curse. Classical. But, for my
money your . . . 'pussy hound' is as nice as any. A certain waggish
inevitability. Dog meets cat." Suppressing what must be a smile she
raises a coral-tipped index finger to her small, upturned nose. "Which
would seem," he adds gravely, "to bring us round to you. You're one of
my undergrads."

"You know who I am."

Perfectly true. Also true: her grades are fine and it is end of term.
Not a compromise in sight, he thinks, but then his apprenticeship is
only just beginning. The woman lighting up a corner of his office is
evidently from the hardy faction of campus perennials given to wearing absurdly little clothing at the slightest upturn in weather. Though
April now and sunny, it is hardly mild. Yet bared for his delectation
are two finely muscled shoulders, slender arms and—converging
enchantingly towards an abbreviated jean skirt—hard, tanned thighs
suggestive of immoderate amounts of spring skiing. Better yet, bare-
back riding. Yes, much better.

Her soft blond hair—frost-tipped then to a pinnacle of Nordic
authenticity—is parted to fall aslant one blue-grey eye. He has schooled
himself to take any veiling of the eyes or mouth as favourable indices.

"You're some kind of undergrad Argonaut," he offers, "a cartographer of erotic odysseys, perhaps. As I myself am on occasion."

"I work as a nurse."

"Yes, precisely."

"I'm not an English major."

"Perfect score so far . . . Madeleine?"

"Educational psychology. I want to work with children." No objections, at least none of the slightest concern to him.

"And you just happen to be free this evening. . . ."

Certain gaps in the story, especially as they concern me, I insist on being free to fill in any way I please. It is still my fucking life, after all.

My fight for an open marriage would turn out to be a non-event. Madeleine raised not the slightest objection. I doubt I'm the first man unable to enjoy to the full the fruits of such an arrangement. Nothing more deflating of the myth of animal priapism than your wife offering to let you bring your little friends for a sleepover. While more than one candidate was game enough, the breakfast theatre of post-coital détente—Madeleine's serenity, my furtive satiation, the girl's triumphal arrival on the shores of sexual sophistication—turned out to be more than I could face. At least after the first few times.

Nor, in the end, did I care to meet let alone share even one more of the post-apocalyptic primitives that Madeleine had begun to take as antidotes to me. Another African drummer, another dancer. Fluid orientations—moral, postural and sexual—suited Madeleine's purpose best. Which was to smoke me out.

The open marriage experiment lasted less than a year. In the nine years since, our marriage has flourished on a strict regimen of secrecy and discreet cunning. To the principled ones I say Madeleine and I have an understanding. To the bold I hint at a breakdown in marital communication. The crazies, I tell as little as possible. But to none would I admit to having an active sex life with my wife.

Beulah was the last. Omega. No more covert dinners in fashionable clothes my wife had lovingly picked out for me. No more weekends in charming trysting places Madeleine would never visit. I had the impression I'd begun to repeat myself with these girls, and anyway the arrival of our first child would have complicated things further.

During the sexual abstinence that descends briefly on new parents I thought of Beulah often, and of the change I was now committed to. October, 1993. It had been finished between us by then for over two months. Since a meltdown in Banff that summer.

Fitful nights. Madeleine's exhaustion. Catherine's hungry cries and breathless silences. Confusing dreams. Flashes of the birthing, sex with Beulah—am I making that connection just now, or did it already occur to me more subtly then?

In lovemaking as in other things, there is something four-square about Madeleine. A rootedness, straight up from the pit of her. An acute and refreshing contrast to my own inner parentheticals and obliquities. She managed—will manage still I hope, with someone— to be startlingly forthright about her need yet light-hearted about her pleasure. Part of a Swedish inheritance on her mother's side that three generations in Canada have done nothing to erase. There was nothing—no role, no pose, no prop—that Madeleine would hesitate to try. My sex genie ever prompting me, *Tonight, Donald, who do you want us to be?*

In writing of this I can only affect a certain light-heartedness myself, as marginally preferable to involuntary self-parody.

Madeleine used to take a perverse joy in dragging me, thrilled but protestant, to a love boutique in a strip mall near our home, to shop sex like a fishwife. Tips, discounts, free samples, demonstrations. To duel at close range in unbuttoned candours and naked curiosities— canny and veteran testimonials—with the proprietress, a heavy-lidded dominatrix with a predilection for snakeskin, who'd taken to meeting us at the door with a childlike eagerness.

I am given to worldly pleasures. As I say, it makes me an easy target. I am tempted to gloss over what follows, mask it at least in a cod-piece of delicacy, but is this not to be the parody of a rapture? Better the parody intended than the one unseen. Describe the scene, describe the scene . . .

Typical Friday night at the mall. Family car parked in the sputtering glow of red neon. Window displays in the rich, red satin of casket linings and Halloween capes. To the proprietress Madeleine spins out a 'longtime fantasy of ours' that was still news to her bookish mate. While he stands in the next aisle, numb with fascination and thumbing something rubbery, she specifies dimensions, declensions, proclivities. When the kit is complete she will take it home to try out on him, sharing out shock-resistant attachments and modelling slotted lingeries without the slightest reserve or trace of nervous over-acting.

As the specifications become ever more fantastic he makes his way towards the back of the store, past snap-on clamps, collapsing o-rings. He goes deeper, ever deeper . . . through a bristling of upstart prongs, the pucker of leather pursings, only to fetch up against a back wall of trusses, teetering towards the geriatric . . .

My wife is a gifted sexual comedienne, with a sharp eye for the farcical, implausible indignities that collaborating on the sex act calls for. All the swellings, gropings and clapping conjunctions—the creakings, jigglings and abject dribblings were just part of the game, the whole far-fetched package. She thought it was what I wanted. What we all wanted.

I did, Madeleine, it is.

I loved sex with my wife. I would never have given it up for anyone.

Catherine's arrival only added a deeper dimension. Madeleine put off weaning her for weeks. The pleasure of nursing was intense. Her eyes would roll mock-incredulous at the criminal ecstasies and tortures of being so barbarically suckled. She loved to be penetrated while she nursed. My function was to remain still, acting as a lightning rod to draw her pleasure down to a more decent seat.

Are you laughing somewhere still, Madeleine?

PAZ   MAYBE QUITTING SCHOOL wasn't so terribly difficult for Beulah.
She would have missed the Library's borrowing privileges but she didn't
cultivate friendships. I can't think of a single friend I might have seen
her with or heard her mention. Most people found her mind and
manner intimidating. She loved music, it turns out, but discussing the
latest pop stars or sitcoms would have provoked feelings of not just
awkwardness but something like rage. I believe she saw herself as from
another time. She pushed people away, perhaps for fear they would
come to see her as she saw herself. Certainly she would not miss the
overtly curious and overly sympathetic stares she occasionally received
from people she'd shared a class with and who now had their own cautious graduate projects well in hand.

The only person in her life she admitted to caring about was her
half-brother, Gavin, who'd put several hundred miles between himself
and their parents by enrolling at Simon Fraser University in
Vancouver. Well-heeled parents happy to keep their studious children's bank accounts topped up and considering the resulting tranquillity of their own lives more than worth the investment. At least,
this seemed to be Beulah's point of view.

Did she tell them she'd quit school? Far from certain. For several
months, she said nothing about having seen me out walking with my
wife, about four months pregnant at the time. It was a discovery to
which Beulah attached a more than casual importance.

There were many things she proved capable of concealing. Not that
she seemed ordinary, but I wasn't the only one who failed to notice, to
really *see*. Your first impressions were not of her beauty, but rather its
mutability. Vitally to wanly luminous from one day to the next. Icy to
darkly erotic just as quickly. . . . Fine features, skin easily bruised. A
full-lipped mouth with a determined set, as though in rebuff to its
own sensuality. The changeability was mostly in her eyes I suppose,
ranging from hazel to grey, flecked with green and gold. *Ojos de miel*, a
Spanish term. It all depended on her inner weather.

There was a susceptibility to cold sores . . . and yes she'd lost some
weight. But when a man of forty discovers that his exquisite twenty-
year-old lover is developing the body of a small runway model he can

be forgiven, perhaps, for being just a bit slow to investigate. Or perhaps not.

Either way, if I'm to pursue a little while longer this fiction of the redemptive value of truth, I must be prepared to submit myself to a full accounting, even if the testimony may at times seem harsh. How in god's name could I not see what was happening to her? First, *no one* guessed, not for a long time. Second, we were already seeing one another less often. By the time she left school we'd decided it was mostly about sex, anyway. And leading up to that time, I had a strong suspicion that her threatening to drop out was calculated to manipulate me—*calculation,* not anguish, not affliction, not the approaches of madness. Why didn't I *do anything?* some of the same crowd will ask. Others would reply that I'd already done quite enough.

I gave her the wrong advice. I refused to help. Rather I offered her only the help I wanted her to have, not what she needed. I failed her as a lover and teacher. I was a fool. There. A few hard truths I'm determined not to turn away from. For the record.

But repeatedly I *did* try to discuss her project, then later tried more than once to persuade her to return to the university, but the whole subject became too hot to handle. She was convinced I'd fobbed her off on lesser scholars.

Time, now, to move on to other topics.

In the past half-century much has been made of Sor Juana's 'emotional instability,' and more recently of her sexual orientation, or orientations. In an earlier chapter we bore witness to—in all its clinical rigour—Ludwig Pfandl's interest in the penitential practices of nuns; yet this interest forms but the backdrop to his main theatre of operations: Sor Juana. Unabashed by a quite perfect lack of psychiatric training, Pfandl unleashes upon Sor Juana a torrent of diagnostic speculation as he proceeds to dine out on her accomplishments.

But a book written by Nobel laureate Octavio Paz,[35] coming into Beulah's hands when it did, armed her to defend Sor Juana against the interrogations of her twentieth-century inquisitors. The book was the magisterial *Sor Juana, Or the Traps of Faith.* In it, in response to Pfandl's conclusions about Sor Juana's final capitulation, Octavio Paz comments:

Pfandl writes with astounding assurance that the 'enigma is resolved': she was the victim of psychosomatic disturbance. A neurotic constitution, menopause . . . her case was aggravated by asthenia and thinness of physique. . . . The clinical portrait is completed with her immoderate tendency to brood, her masculinity, her narcissism . . . her masochistic tendencies.

We may at least be thankful that in lavishing his attentions on a patient three hundred years dead, he had commensurately less time to inflict his interests on the living. At times Beulah must have felt oppressed by the sheer momentum of Pfandl's diagnostic élan; whereas in Paz she found a feather-light touch and subtle, poignant glimpses of *her* Juana:

Solitary amid the flurry of San Jerónimo, wilful and independent; one day inspired and the next spiritless; frequently afflicted by imaginary ills that were nonetheless as tormenting as physical illness—her true, her only, companions were the ghosts in her books.

Beulah marvelled at how easily Paz moved through the world of ideas, turning effortlessly from science to philosophy to history to poetry and, finally, to love:

Love is a passion, a longing that forces us outside ourselves in search of the desired one and then back to search within ourselves for the trace of the beloved, or to contemplate the beloved's ghost in silence. Sor Juana's poetry reproduces this dialectic movement with extraordinary authenticity.

And though on occasion Paz too had recourse to Freud, through Paz's eyes Beulah saw confirmed Sor Juana's palpable eroticism.

In terms of psychic economy—to use Freud's expression—Sor Juana's malady was not poverty but riches: a powerful but unused libido. That profusion, and its lack of object, are evident in the frequency with which images of female and male bodies appear in her poems, almost always converted into phantasmal apparitions. Sor Juana lived among erotic shadows.

Perhaps it was at that moment, during that very passage, that Beulah first began to wonder about Octavio Paz the man, the lover. Did she see him then at the breakfast table, hair ruffled, sharing a single cup of coffee and a cigarette with a sleepy-eyed fellow Olympian? Or did she spare him the acid emulsion of *her* eroticism?

> Sor Juana has a keen awareness of the 'thus far and no farther.' That awareness is both existential and aesthetic. Existentially, love borders on melancholy, that is, on absence, solitude and self-reflection. Sor Juana constantly questions herself and the images of her solitary musings: love is knowledge. And the art made with that knowledge is neither excess nor verbal extravagance but rigor, restraint.

Reading this, one wonders whether Beulah didn't feel even slightly chastened by Sor Juana's rigorous example.

We must nevertheless concede that in startling contrast to her intellectual rigour and polished manners Sor Juana's writing offers rich servings of guilty brooding and self-absorption to analysts like Pfandl hungry to find autobiography in a poet's verses. In fairness, this contrast verging on total disjuncture would likely have jolted and dazed even those who knew her best. But in Paz, Beulah finds a powerful response:

> As for brooding: it is not a cause of melancholy, as Pfandl seems to believe, but an effect. . . . The close connection between melancholy and narcissism has been pointed out any number of times. The differences, nevertheless, are so profound as to suggest they may be opposing tendencies. The melancholic is not in love with himself but with someone who is absent; this is why Freud associated melancholy with mourning. The melancholic believes, furthermore, that he is responsible for the absence of the beloved, hence the unrelenting accusations he directs against himself. The narcissist in love with himself and his unattainable (but not absent) image, suffers from an incapacity to love another being. He cannot objectify his desire.

Octavio Paz goes on to articulate what Beulah had already sensed: that Pfandl's own 'sympathetic' obsession—*Sor Juana, c'est moi*—leads him to neglect virtually all the social and historical determinants of her actions.

Through several hundred pages he [Pfandl] turns again and again to Sor Juana's psychic and physiological conflicts, from infantile penis envy to the disorders of menopause, but he overlooks one circumstance that was no less determining than psychology or physiology: the masculine character of the culture and world in which Sor Juana lived. How, in a civilization of men and for men, could a woman gain access to learning without becoming masculinized?

If indeed, as Paz suggests, melancholy and narcissism are polar opposites, then between them may lie a wide, wild world of sexual attitudes. Was Sor Juana a lesbian? Was she bisexual?

Her writings refract and redouble facets of her sexual persona. Donning poetic masks by turns ironic, allusive and sincere, the author variously portrays the 'I' of her verses as essentially male in her rationality, as virgin and therefore sexless, as a woman transformed into a man by Isis (the etymology of Isis in turn being *doubly man*), as a disembodied soul in amorous rapture, as double-sexed, as hermaphrodite, androgynous. . . . A cascade of possibilities that overwhelms the flimsy edifice of Pfandl's simplistic sexual schematics. Again Paz:

> One cannot read Pfandl's lengthy description without being struck by the rashness of the claims and the brashness of the conclusions. Of course Sor Juana was bisexual, but what does that say? All but a handful of humanity is bisexual. Furthermore, any somatic masculinity in her case is pure fantasy: look at her portraits. Neither is it psychological: read what she wrote. . . . I further argue that what is surprising in her poetry is precisely the keen awareness of her femininity, which can range from coquetry to melancholy or take the form of a defiant challenge to men. Thus it would be more exact to speak of erotic ambiguity . . .

Here is an instance of a woman using complexity as disguise and concealment—not the drawing of a single veil but a dance of seven, deployed to leave the Pfandls pfumbling through the halls of scholarship like guilty schoolboys. In doing so, she goes even further, conceivably, than many gender theorists of our day: rather than sexuality as a continuum on which the individual is situated somewhere between poles of male and female, each individual—godlike, monstrous—*is* the continuum, a riotous spectrum of sexual colours and emotional shadings, male and female becoming, instead of opposites, contiguous points huddled along a vast and turbulent arc from godhood to monstrosity and back again. . . .

Now, a certain breed of searcher leaves no question unanswered. To the occasionally near-comic spectacle of Pfandl contorting himself to fit answers to his own questions (and not infrequently, the reverse), Octavio Paz often stands in elegant contrast:

> . . . just when we think we can grasp it [the figure of Sor Juana], it eludes us, like the ghosts in her poems . . . the nun Juana is Isis, lady of letters, and also the pytheness who makes predictions in her cave (her cell), pregnant not with child but with metaphors and tropes . . .
>
> As we have seen, the examination of Sor Juana's erotic tendencies is inconclusive and ends with a question. In accord with the classic definition of melancholic temperament, its two extremes were depression and mania . . .

Certain questions Paz refrains from trying to answer, finding perhaps more truth in the indeterminate. Beulah is not so scrupulous; in fact she takes Paz's delicacy not as a model to emulate but as an invitation to drag his inquiry several steps beyond the limits of good taste.

And still the fact remains that Sor Juana's most impassioned and erotic poems have other women for their object. To lesbianism, Paz proposes an alternative reading: passionate but Platonic love; whereas in Pfandl's account, Beulah finds Sor Juana's fall describing a long-charted trajectory: from the inversions of Sapphism to a libidinal leap into the mythic abyss of mania, depression and paranoia. It would seem that under Pfandl's tender ministrations his patient, once merely neurotic, has begun showing signs of a budding psychosis.

The sympathetic reader will perhaps see how, desperate to refute Pfandl's diagnosis, hating herself for feeling its temptations, Beulah would find it increasingly difficult to resist a martyrology. Equally difficult to resist seeing clerics and psychoanalysts alike—Sor Juana's male superiors and the psychotherapists of Beulah's adolescence—as representatives of that same orthodoxy, of the same alienated, analytical turn of mind.

So I can only suppose Beulah copied with something approaching jubilation this passage buried in the endnotes of Paz's book.

What is truly eccentric in Pfandl's interpretation is the energy it expends on Sor Juana's supposed instability while failing to devote a single line to the mental problems of the three prelates who censured her. Fernández de Santa Cruz's now-sugary, now-sadistic letters to the nuns of Puebla are filled with disquieting expressions that combine the fragrance of incense with the stench of the sewer. In Núñez de Miranda's notes, his self-contempt over his eternal defeat in his battle with pride knows no bounds: 'I am a sack of corruption, stinking and abominable, and what is worse is that, knowing this, I am not humble.' On one occasion, when removing lice from another priest's cassock, he said, 'See this, my brother, our harvest: lice, corruption, and stench—yet we are filled with vanity.' As for Aguiar y Seijas, I need not recall his obsessions and manias, his hatred of women and his pathological charity. . . . To my mind, the fact that Juana Inés was able to resist so long, that only at the end of the siege did she abdicate and follow her critics in these inhuman mortifications, is glorious proof of her spiritual fortitude.

Nevertheless, one is forced to ask: does Beulah really differ so significantly from the object of her fury? Which researcher, Pfandl or Beulah, does the truth greater violence in the name of sympathy?

But I digress into abstractions just as we are recalled to the concrete by a modern artefact of the Baroque, a throwback: Beulah's budding infatuation with Octavio Paz.

Perhaps it will not seem so surprising, after all, that Beulah should have begun writing him or that this should parallel certain . . . disappointments in her personal and scholarly life. Clearly it started with the hope that at last in him she had found someone to share her vision, grasp the mystic enterprise that was becoming her life.[36]

April 1 [1993]
Dear Señor Paz,
I thought I'd take advantage of the date (do you celebrate April Fool's in Mexico?) to amuse you with a little request. You see I've finally obtained a copy of your biography of Juana. It's fantastic—not in the sense of fantasy, not that you need someone like me to tell you. . . .

April 2

~~Querido~~

Estimado Señor Paz,

I have been attempting a study—of course on a much much lesser scale than yours—of Sor Juana. Your book has given me the courage to think I could finish mine, crouching on your shoulders. . . .

April 10

Estimado Señor Paz

Estimado Mars y Pan

Esteemed Marzipan,

. . . Reading your book the second time through I'm filled with its completeness. I couldn't hope to add a word to it—but my study deals with an area that will probably be of no interest to you. Or maybe everything is of interest to you. . . .

April 10

Estimado Abuelo,

How could I hope to add anything to what you've written? My mind is like a sail, a puff of wind I turn to see where it comes from it's GONE. Head full of cotton—wads of filthy cotton / slackflaccid sails they can't hold enough long enough can't make the connections I know are there. You could. But you've done so much already. You could help me. . . . I don't want to fail her—I won't let her down I am SO IGNORANT. I am barbaric. The classics must be like comic books to you how many languages do you read? I have no where else to turn. Except to you, but when I read my scratchings through your eyes . . . I hope you're kind. You must be kind I know your kind, *Abuelo*—show me the signs teach me the symbols tell me the stories let me sit at your knee. Show me how. Show me . . .

[April]

She's a scrap of fresh meat flesh torn at by hungry dogs. Pack hunters—anal-ists shiteating insect princes swarming over her, mantises—preyer books in hand. ~~Catechistic cataclystical converters—thug clericanalists psychopriest houndmasters~~

RAGE. The rage in Spain rains mainly on the maids.

My name is Beulah Limosneros. I've read your book. Three times. It is a very great book. I'm writing a book too. About hunger. Hunger is sex hunger is love hunger is rage it's revolting. This little civilization our trivializing drivelization is making promises it can't keep. And we know it, deep down we all know it we've known it for three hundred years. She knew—she was the first. The first! Their contradictions are the jagged ends you cut out of a can. They want us to swallow it whole, their botulistic can of wormy contradictions—

Hunger is love but they build a wall around it. It's behind the wall they say but the wall's too high to see over too smooth to climb. How do I know it's behind the wall I can't FEEL it PLEASE—We promise! it's there we told you—have faith—but how do I get over it? You can't get over it have faith it's inside you where there is no light no air no one no hope—have faith. We promise. Have faith.

Get over it

Late spring, 1690. Writing daring theatre and poetry is far from the most dangerous of Sor Juana's occupations as she finds herself increasingly embroiled in theological questions, disputed by the Princes of the Church with quiet savagery. The mind of Sor Juana Inés de la Cruz, even half-engaged, is a prodigious resource. Her letters and arguments are coveted and examined by bishops, confessors and inquisitors alike.

. . . His Excellency may well have thought, seeing me draw towards a conclusion, that I had forgotten the very point on which I have been commanded to write: What is, in my view, the greatest expression, the greatest *fineza*, of Divine Love. . . .

As Christ our Redeemer preached his miraculous doctrine, and having performed so many miracles and marvels in so many places, he reached at last his native country, in which he should have been owed greater affections, and yet directly he arrived, instead of singing his praises, his neighbours and compatriots began to censure him and list his supposed faults. . . . With the result that Christ, who had wanted to work miracles for his native land, and to award them all manner of benefices, saw then in their bad faith and dark mutterings how they would receive Christ's favours, and so He withheld them: so as not to give them occasion to do ill. . . .

And regarding Judas, upon whom He showered many particular favours not given to the others, in the hour of his betrayal Christ lamented not that Judas had hanged himself, but rather the damage such favours had done him. . . . By which He seemed to regret having favoured Judas with the benefice of creation, saying that it were better he had never been born. . . . And from which we may conclude that the greatest expression of his Love would be to withhold His favours. Ah me, my Lord and God, how blindly and clumsily we lurch about not seeing the negative favours You give us! . . .

ABYSS

aturally enough my thoughts keep returning to this one afternoon, and each fresh return yields some small new detail. What I do not ever recall is the slightest premonition. Just before the Bishop of Puebla arrives I am forced to spend another hour in the locutory when every free moment has become so precious—only to discover that Carlos's latest guest has come for a flirtation. Once I might have been amused, or flattered that he had been sent to me across an ocean by Louis XIV, in the sort of gesture the French King so likes the world to expect from him. But those times are past; I am no longer a girl at the palace.

I see the beautiful young face of the King's emissary, recall deciding to bring points of colour to those smooth, pale cheeks. . . . I ask if a man of his beauty believes he may blunder along with no particular purpose at all. If the rest of the distaff world stands before the blunderbuss and counts itself disarmed. Is it the Sun King himself, I wonder, who eagerly awaits this blundering's translation, ear cocked to the report? I suggest that my young friend press on, as earnestness may yet win the day. But why not raise his aim—and set his sights not on mere flirtation, but on a conquest less abstracted—

Always at this point Tomasina returns from her watch at the archive windows and rushes into the room.

"The Bishop's carriage, it's *here*—parked beside the canal," she adds, as if this in some way added to the drama. Then there comes that moment after an arrival is announced when conversation falters. Carlos gets up grudgingly from the Bishop's chair and pulls another to the grille from the far side of the room. Antonia hastens over with the chess table. As she places it within easy reach behind me she bends to my ear and asks to be excused. She does not look particularly well. I look over at Tomasina and Ana, both standing attentively now at the arras, ready to fetch the slightest thing from the staging area behind them. Finally both my *escuchas* are actually listening—just when the very authority in whose name they are to eavesdrop will already be present.

"'Tonia, look at those two standing there, between ecstasy and panic. Will you try to stay a moment—"

"Ah, chess," says the Viscount, "I'll wager you play like Greco himself."

"Stay, Toñita—just till he's settled in?"

"Did the great Greco not die near here?"

"Not at my hands, *Vicomte. Gracias, 'Tonia.* As a child, *Monsieur,* I'd always intended to learn. And then I ran out of time. But the Bishop sometimes consents to a lesson when he has business here."

"One of the better players in New Spain, I understand."

"What a curious thing for you to know."

"I've been hoping to meet him."

"Have you? Of course you have . . ."

As Bishop Santa Cruz enters, the change in the Viscount is quite complete. It is clear that he has some business to transact. I find myself half-admiring the young man's duplicity even as I am resenting being used as a stalking horse. Bishop Santa Cruz is also, for an instant, quite transformed. At first I think it is recognition, or surprise, but it is not quite either. He is our most handsome churchman. Indeed many of the sisters here, and I can only imagine how many in Puebla, confess at our weekly chapter of faults that when Satan visits at night, he is as likely to take the guise of Bishop Santa Cruz as to masquerade as Our Husband. Santa Cruz's features are boyish, which in a man of fifty can be appealing. Fine brows carrying the suggestion of a frown in perpetual warning to triflers, the chin slightly too delicate for the width of his jaw. The teeth are good and big, indeed better fitted to a slightly wider mouth. . . . I had always thought his most striking feature his eyes, large, a deep liquid brown, accentuated by pale hair almost blond. More than pleasing enough, but the Enemy appears to me rather differently. A little taller, a little younger, more . . . statuesque.

The Viscount on the other hand—though he is now beyond any doubt a viper—is angelically beautiful, with his gold locks and lilac eyes and hands of marble. The features and the hands, though, are not a cherub's but the warrior Michael's. Square chin, wide mouth, pale, full lips, a nose prominent yet fine at the bridge. For an instant they face each other: A younger man, beautifully masculine, an older man, boyishly handsome. And in that instant, the Bishop's face is almost unrecognizable. It is the clearest moment in what remains of the afternoon. What appears, what seems almost to rise up—as the Viscount's beauty strikes it like the slap of a glove—is the figure of an enormous vanity. And though Bishop Santa Cruz and I are old friends, I shudder to think of that poor girl in Puebla looking into his face as she begged to be permitted to enter Santa Monica.

For a moment I fear some real violence must pass between them, but it is only the usual cut and thrust. An insult here about the Bishop's lineage, another there about the Viscount's immoral king and country, vague hints of war and excommunication . . .

"Obviously a spy," says the Bishop, as the Viscount's footsteps die out. Santa Cruz fixes his dark eyes on Carlos.

"Don Carlos, you spend so little time in Puebla anymore. You must still have many friends there."

"A few. Who tell me your work on Genesis is nearly complete."

"That's so, yes."

"Two thousand pages, Lord Bishop. Monumental."

"A book like any other, don Carlos. To be read a page at a time. But you, *señor*, almost daily I hear of you winning some new distinction for the Chair of Mathematics and—is it Astronomy or Astrology? I never remember."

"Astrology."

"We are told you are predicting an eclipse of the sun for next August."

"The margin of error is still considerable."

"Yes, isn't it," he says, holding Carlos's eyes an extra heartbeat. The Bishop's gaze shifts to Antonia. "I bring good report of your sisters at the convent school. The youngest takes after you, I think. Very clever with her languages. What was her name . . . ? *Antonia?*"

"Francisca."

"Will you play something for us, Antonia? I haven't heard you at the clavichord for—how long has it been?"

I ask Santa Cruz if she could play something brief, she is not altogether well. To which, after listening a moment, he answers that brief will be best if she finishes the way she has begun. Antonia plays well, and yet her playing just now is not quite soothing. She is unhappy, no doubt, that I have kept her.

"I notice you have something of a Puebla reunion on your hands, Juana."

"So I have."

"The time may not be far off for those carols we have been scheming about."

"For Saint Catherine?—you're in earnest?"

He has not quite promised but the commission is clearly mine now to lose.

"It would be good to hear Puebla talk of Puebla again. There was a time when our little Puebla de los Angeles stood up very nicely against the brilliance of the capital. We have our splendid volcano, though Mexico does have two. . . . While Mexico has its cathedral, we have ours, lovelier and almost as large. We have the Jesuit Seminary, Mexico has the great Colegio de San Pedro y San Pablo. But while we have a children's choir, Mexico has Sálazar. And since don Carlos left us, Mexico now has the two of you."

It is the second allusion to Carlos's unhappy departure from the seminary more than twenty years ago.

Santa Cruz shakes his head ruefully. "And now during Holy Week to have the great college's rector Antonio Núñez, giving a sermon by none other than the immortal Vieyra. Your four-time winner of the Seal of the Holy Crusade delivers a homily from the Prince of the Catholic Orators!"

After the false modesty regarding Puebla, the mock heroic tone of the tout nicely inserts the skewer: a delirious prestige attaches locally to the Seal, our highest prize for eloquent sermonizing, but even in Núñez's case, it is quite eclipsed by the informal title of Prince of Orators, which was devised for Vieyra alone and by which he is known throughout the Catholic dominions.

"Don Carlos, I suppose you were here for Sor Juana's analysis after the sermon?"

"Regrettably, his Lordship the Viceroy wanted some prominences surveyed on the coast, for gun emplacements."

"So there were at least two of us to miss the great moment of Sor Juana's rebuttal."

"The moment was not particularly great, don Manuel."

"As ever, she is too modest." Santa Cruz's eyes have not left Carlos.

"I hadn't noticed."

"Your holy crusader and our Catholic prince both out-manned, out-gunned by a simple nun—they should have seen the emplacements ranged against them and put out to sea. A pity, don Carlos, that you were not there. You at least could have given me a competent summary. So I've come to sort it out for myself. Our Mistress of the poetic *fineza* corrects—"

"Questions, don Manuel, merely questions."

"Of course. *Questions* New Spain's most original thinker on the Eucharist."

Carlos glances at me, a look of warning that finds me torn between cheer and dread. He knows what the Bishop's patronage means to me, now especially. He knows how long I have wanted this commission. But Santa Cruz has been provoking him since—well, since he stopped provoking the Viscount. Is it something Carlos has done, something he has said—everyone here hears everything, or thinks they do—is it to do with his services to the Archbishop?

Carlos is not one to hold his fire for long. I fill my return glance with the fervid hope that Carlos follow the Viscount out.

"I should be going," Carlos says, getting arthritically to his feet, "*Su Ilustrísima* the Lord Bishop has important matters to discuss. And I have some records to check at the Archbishop's palace. From the time of Bishop *Zumárraga*." His eyes glitter as he looks my way. It has come out with a strange emphasis but now he is bending to add, conspiratorially, his smile including Santa Cruz, "You can tell Antonia it's not the music."

As the slight, stooped form disappears through the doorway I sketch ambitious plans for his next visit, to shower him with proofs of my gratitude. The remark about Zumárraga, Mexico's first bishop, is not so very odd, I tell myself. Carlos is always nosing about in some archive or other for the chronicles he is asked to write. And the jest about Antonia's playing defused the whole situation wonderfully.

All in all he has handled the Bishop with unwonted forbearance and grace. Yet what I distinctly recall feeling as he leaves is annoyance. Annoyed that so many of the people upon whom I most depend seem to dislike each other. Annoyed, as always, at Carlos for half a dozen things. Annoyed, too, at my own weariness, the sense of wasted time, that I will be up until dawn now finishing the convent accounts. And at Antonia for the mournful music she has chosen, when she knows so many pleasant lays; at her ingratitude towards the Bishop who has brought her here, and just perhaps towards me. Annoyed at the Bishop—for his shabby treatment of Carlos. And at myself again, for giving voice to my great pique with such a little peep.

"You were cruel to him."

"I thought his temper might get the better of him."

"And what would his temper tell us that it hasn't already?"

"It may only be prudence, given his friendship with the Franciscan they burned. But it bothers me that he always manages to be away when something happens. Like this sermon. And his silence on the Eucharist. Fifteen years ago he talked of nothing else, and has abandoned the field to Núñez ever since."

"But you've said it yourself. Prudence."

"It is not *why* he goes that I wonder about, but *how* he always knows far enough in advance to arrange things so tidily. It is not *why* he has been silent for fifteen years, but *how* Núñez from that time became so knowledgeable on the old cults. Are we all to retreat from theological questions the moment Antonio Núñez shows an interest—are you to hand over all the beautiful verses you have written on the *finezas?*"

The compliment is sincere. If I persist, this will become unpleasant.

With Carlos gone I am determined to be done with this quickly. It is as he has said—the Bishop does have matters to discuss.

"You do know, don Manuel, that Father Núñez has dedicated this new work to you."

"A sobering look at Communion."

"Are you here for the manuscript?"

"I have it." His hand starts towards the tray. He checks the impulse, then takes up a candied fig with a kind of languor. "But I don't have to come from Puebla for that. I am more interested in his motives than in his book, more still in his motives for the sermon."

"A straw man. Vieyra has written—what is it, thirteen orations on the Eucharist, many of them sublime. Núñez attacks perhaps the weakest. Why not strength on strength? There would have been a contest to watch."

"This Portuguese, Vieyra, is an old favourite of yours, is he not?"

"He and Camões have removed any doubt their language can soar as high as our own."

Santa Cruz asks my opinion on the local edition of Vieyra's work on Heraclitus. "I admire it. Though I haven't read their translation—but some sense of the grace of his style could not fail to come through. No one in our tongue is writing a prose to match his."

The Bishop smiles before biting delicately into a walnut square. "Certainly not the plodder your Royal University found for the translation. But I am told the editions in Madrid—the '76 and '78—were awful translations also."

"I haven't read them."

"But you've seen them."

Not having seen either, I answer instead that any speaker of Castilian should really read Vieyra in the Portuguese, the quality being so high, the languages so close. I promise to send Santa Cruz home with my copy. He promises to bring me the Castilian editions next time.

He pauses to dust sugar from the purple cassock. "Perhaps we should be translating him in Puebla." His eyes shine with mischief. "You would be interested?"

"For Vieyra, I would need time. Without it I would only make a fool of myself."

"Time might be something I can arrange. Now to Núñez. You had begun to say why that sermon suited his purposes. Our discussions in Puebla have run along those same lines, though going somewhat further. . . ."

By 'our' discussions I take him to mean the Dominicans, whose stronghold is Puebla and whose warlord is the Lord Bishop Santa Cruz. They still find something not quite clear about Father Núñez's motives. It is a game with them to analyze the adversary's positions endlessly. I brace myself. Núñez, the rector of our Jesuit college, invites to his chambers not just Jesuits but Dominicans, a Franciscan and three officers of the Inquisition. And yet he does this to attack a fellow Jesuit. Why? Yes, Vieyra is influential, but he uses that influence not for the Company but to persuade King John to suppress the Inquisition throughout Portugal. Stunning enough in itself, Vieyra next has His Holiness himself declare him to be henceforth beyond the jurisdiction of the Holy Office.

The Jesuit Vieyra has become the greatest living threat to the Inquisition just as the Jesuits are infiltrating it; the Holy Office, through its rigour and universal reach, stands as the main obstacle to Jesuit designs on global power. In America but also in the Orient, the soldiers of Christ have only to adapt certain points of Catholic doctrine slightly to make it palatable to local rulers, certain other *minor* points in the Philippines to counter the incursions of the Moor.

The Jesuits, unchecked, will destroy the Church.

Santa Cruz makes no effort now to conceal his passion. I rarely see him so unguarded. The heavily bejewelled fingers delicately prowl the platter. Walnut, date, fig. *Suspiros* and *aleluyas*. A bite from each. The platter's losses mount up on the Bishop's side plate of Puebla porcelain. I try very hard to share his passion. Manila, Macao. Mexico, Lisbon. Rome, Madrid. Even Versailles. I am about to be asked to play my small part in a mighty conflagration reaching into the heart of every continent. His Holiness setting forth from the Papal Palaces to join the other great champions in the field—the King of Portugal, Emperor of Cathay, Shogun, Inquisitor General of the Spanish Inquisition, Cardinal Inquisitor in Rome, General of the Company of Jesus . . . And somewhere in all this lies the fate of the Jews, and the mystical advent of Vieyra's mysterious Fifth Empire. Only the Lutherans are not invited. But then they were the ones who ruined things in Japan.

Were I a writer of romances, were I a general or a prince, were I half so brave as the nun-ensign, I would surely fly to the fight. I would not fail to seek my place in the universal theological struggle. But I am pledged never again to set foot beyond these walls, a nun who may not freely walk across this room.

With Father Núñez, my chief interest in speaking on theology was that he did not want me to, whereas Santa Cruz has always tried to draw me into these questions more deeply. It would be an insult to our friendship to show a lack of interest now, especially with him in this humour, so pleased that I have let myself become—*fool*—involved. And in his unwonted candour I have a measure of his frustration. For even as Vieyra beards the Inquisition and holds His Holiness in the palm of his hand and Bishop Bossuet guides Louis XIV over the narrow path between insubordination to the Pope and excommunication, Santa Cruz, a bishop at thirty-five, is still a bishop and has been for seventeen years.

Antonia is playing more brightly now, a sonata that sounds like Scarlatti, but even if it isn't, I am almost sure the Bishop once mentioned a dislike for Scarlatti. Tomasina and Ana watch attentively, so sober and discreet.

Suddenly Santa Cruz has my full attention.

" . . . one of just several signals that Father Núñez is distancing himself from Archbishop Aguiar." What has he just said? "Quietly the Inquisition commits all its resources to overturning Vieyra's exemption to its jurisdiction, and he is losing ground. The Jesuits do not like working in the open, yet Vieyra does precisely this. Just as the Archbishop does now in his defence. As a show of support for Vieyra, the Archbishop asks Núñez to deliver this sermon."

"So although Núñez will not refuse a direct order," I murmur, "his refutation of the sermon afterwards serves notice that if the Company of Jesus must choose between Vieyra and the Inquisition, Vieyra loses."

To which the Bishop responds, fully including me now, that we have it on unimpeachable authority that Archbishop Aguiar and the Portuguese Vieyra have never so much as *met*.

"And yes," the Bishop continues, "if Núñez is forced to choose between influencing real events in Mexico and accommodating an archbishop's fantasies of eminence, His Grace the Lord Archbishop also loses...."

It is vital that I make sense of this day if I am to find the source of the misunderstanding with Santa Cruz. And yet each time I think this hour through, so much remains unclear. Clarity is a thing to prize, clarity of mind I prize most highly. And yet at about the time of Carlos's departure things become considerably less clear. I am clear about my annoyance, I am clear about the sensation of unreality. And now I am clear about one other thing: this annoyance I know. I know it exactly. It is that which precedes waking at three in the morning at one's work table as one is being shaken by the shoulder and called to choir. The dream need not be particularly good, but is preferable to opening one's eyes.

As Santa Cruz asks me to reprise my arguments in this crisis over a sermon, the sensation is of being asked to explain a complicated joke, which, moreover, was never amusing.

Forty years ago, with great flights of oratory already behind him, and decades more ahead, Antonio Vieyra wrote a flawed sermon that, worse, boasted even as it was exposing its own flaws. He is blind now, ill. Eighty-two. He has left Portugal to return to the country he has loved for half a century. Brazil. Sworn enemy of an Inquisition that has real reason to fear him—five defiant years in its prisons and under attack again for the past decade, and also now by the landowners who hate him; outspoken defender of the Jews and New Christians; tireless protector of the enslaved Africans and the Indians; master of twenty languages and American dialects.

Antonio Vieyra is a flawed man, and a great one. The New World has not had such a holy instrument of Christ's true conscience since Bartolomé de Las Casas. And the writing is the least of his greatness. It is one thing for me to be impulsively foolish, quite another to be rehearsed in it. How have I come to this place? How do I find myself on the wrong side, with the buzzards circling a great, embattled, eighty-year-old man? I too am flawed, I too am not humble. And I have not fought all my life for others as he has, accepted prison and torture. For others. Yes, I have made other choices.

And now I remember something I should have remembered then, from a time that is gone. . . . My grandfather speaking of Sahagún and Las Casas, with that fierce pride of his that was itself like firelight. These two, he said, and Vieyra, were the proudest sons of the Iberian Peninsula. For all the horrors perpetrated by us since Ferdinand and Isabela, not another race in Europe would have produced three such men. He spoke to me of this at the firepit, the last night we spoke of anything.

Bishop Santa Cruz assumes an expression of absorption. And as I prepare to begin, I would be anywhere but here, saying anything but this, thinking any thoughts but these. Weakly I ask why he even needs my arguments.

"Whatever Núñez is up to, Juana, if he plays the jack again, as Jesuits do, quietly behind the scenes, we answer with a queen."

Amused, he asks Antonia to bring the chess set over. I could easily reach it myself but I suppose he wants her to stop playing so we may concentrate. She looks like she might have been crying. It's so selfish of me to have forgotten she is ill. As we are shifting the candy tray to make room for the little chess table I touch Antonia lightly on the shoulder and tell her she should go. Santa Cruz has the idea she should take notes for me to help with the dictation later. Instead of asking why write any of this down, though the answer is obvious, I am saying she is not well and agreeing to write it out for him myself. And there I have promised it, with not so much as a demur. There is no turning back. But instead of letting her go he asks her to stay anyway. Antonia has a temper and coldly now insists that no, she really would like to stay, as though he's instead given her permission to leave. The scar in her cheek stands out pale against her colouring.

"Excellent, Antonia. If you are quite up to it." Indulgently, the Bishop includes her in the conversation. "A few details, so that you may be useful later. In the service of your mistress, what counts are the details. *Fineza*, Antonia, in its theological sense refers to the subtleties of love at work throughout Creation. Such is the love of Christ, masked, reserved, discreet, and above all, Antonia, *watchful*. . . ."

Conceding the advantage, Santa Cruz accepts Black. White takes his pawn, Black takes mine. And then I am beginning in this language I am not far from despising, the language of canonical lawyers playing at theology, "First, don Manuel, the Jesuit Vieyra boasts that he will contest the findings of not just Augustine, but Aquinas and Chrysostom too, then improve upon their positions, finding a *fineza* no one can match. Augustine holds that Christ's greatest sacrifice for Man was to give His life for us. Vieyra responds that since Christ loved Man more than life itself, the greater sacrifice was to absent himself from Man. But to this, we must answer that Christ is not absent at all but is present in the wafer and the wine."

Bishop Santa Cruz nods in satisfaction. He has been over this point carefully with me, has corrected me quite gently, as a friend. But I am not at all satisfied. It is not just the language—for the sake of this argument I go against everything I most intimately feel. "Present not only in the Eucharist but also in His Word."

I take another pawn, Santa Cruz takes mine. "Next, the Reverend Vieyra treats the Host as a remedy—a substitute for His presence rather than *being* that living presence. A confusion as fundamental as between metaphor and analogy. . . ."

"*¡Vale!*" approves Santa Cruz, "Augustine vindicated."

In his enthusiasm he reaches out to sample a sweetmeat, falters, then gives in, but this time with deliberation. "I know you are loyal Augustinians here at San Jerónimo, but will you only intercede," he wonders, "for one saint and not the other two?"

Black takes my pawn with a knight. I take Black's knight with mine. "In claiming to refute Saint Thomas," I say, "Vieyra illogically argues from genus to species; in attacking Chrysostom, he confuses cause with the expression of its effect. . . ."

I carry on in this fashion until I feel I have refuted myself, and Antonio Vieyra only incidentally. Santa Cruz takes my knight. "But surely," the Bishop suggests, "complete victory lacks one final step. Proposing a *fineza* greater than Vieyra's."

I answer that what makes this whole matter vain is that among so many sublime demonstrations of love we insist on deciding which one is best. We are like children picking blackberries. With our jars filled to overflowing with a harvest of such sweetness, we set to squabbling over who has picked the most. For Chrysostom it lies in the washing of the feet, even the feet of Judas. For Aquinas in the wafer and the wine, for Augustine in the Passion. We should give thanks to all who have discovered such richness in the Mysteries, then find what sweetness we can in our own little jar of blackberries.

"What Vieyra has found," I add, "is undoubtedly rich and lovely. So if

I seem now to repeat Vieyra's mistake it is only to say he should not speak of besting the *finezas* of three maximal Doctors of the Church when a simple nun might find one, if not better then at least not worse than his. . . ."

White queen, with a glance of triumph, takes his rook. Black pawn, with a glance of amusement, takes my queen.

"Look at it this way, Juana," he says, queen in hand. "Vieyra's faring no better here today."

"And here," I continue, more cautiously, "I direct my attack not at Vieyra's logic but instead at his imagination. But since in all matters theological, errors of the imagination are infinitely more dangerous than errors of logic, you must promise, don Manuel, to correct instantly the slightest unorthodoxy in my position—anything that, by sheer inadvertence or feebleness of mind, might exercise the Inquisition. Errors in art, after all, are rightly answered by mockery and contempt"—he must have known my reluctance was not feigned—"but errors in theology must be answered before the Holy Office, and for all eternity."

"Of course, of course." His frown is one of impatience.

Clinging to the slim purchase of that promise—*his promise*—I press on. Black queen takes my castle.

"Christ's greatest finesse, Vieyra claims, was that He loved humanity without wishing that we return His love. Unless it be for the good that loving Him does *us*. Here Vieyra's greatest fault lies not in confusing wishing with needing—though this he does peerlessly—but in reducing love's rich dominions to a single impoverished colony. . . ."

I wonder if it is really possible that Santa Cruz has not seen his own queen in danger. In taking mine he has left his unprotected. The sense of unreality only deepens. I have never beaten him. I feel my annoyance and self-disgust dissolve to a slow-rising elation. White knight takes black queen.

For just a few hours it's as though I am waking not from but to a dream, to find myself a citizen of Plato's submerged Atlantis . . . speaking the language of Atlantis, flooded by Atlantean cares and intrigues in a parlour at the bottom of the sea. Antonia's pallor, the Bishop's languor—the slight displacement between his gestures and his words—all seemingly the natural consequence of our submersion . . . occasional echoes of speech rising to the surface of my recollection in tremulous bubbles.

"Surely if Our Father's house has so many rooms," I am proposing now, "it is because there are so many ways to love and as many dispositions. What shall we call loving for the good that being in love will do you? Let's call this *amor egoista*. Loving for the good your love will do your beloved? Call it *amor magnánima*. For the benefits accruing to you from the return—the requital of your love? Call that love mercantile. Loving for loving's sake, with no *desire* that it be returned? Vieyra's *amor fino*— selfless love. And truly, this *is* beautiful, but in this he only follows Saint Bernard. Loving without desire is perhaps a feat the greatest among us may manage. Whereas loving for loving's sake, but without any *need* that it be returned—this we may truly call a divine or sovereign love, for such a love lies beyond us. . . . God alone is not completed by His love's return. His love is already complete. Divine Love is for Him alone."

White rook mates black king. The Bishop has lost his first game to me, gracefully. His face is curiously open, with a nakedness that in a simpleton we take for Good.

"The queen sacrifice was particularly nice."

"You taught it to me once." I no longer feel particularly triumphant. Against a more experienced opponent he would have seen it for what it was.

"I thought your mind elsewhere. . . . But as Vieyra and Father Núñez before me have discovered, humility is a most democratic virtue whose benefits apply equally to all. The mortification you bestow upon me in my defeat is a favour."

With my loctutory crowded after the sermon a fortnight earlier, this was as far as I had gone. These were the arguments Santa Cruz had come to hear for himself. But now he has said, with the most disarming simplicity, this curious thing: '*my defeat is a favour.*' What I say in reply is spontaneous precisely where my other foolishness has been rehearsed, for here is an idea that touches a genuine chord in me. If I could just say one true thing today, one thing I *feel*. . . .

"But in Christ, don Manuel . . . in Christ we feel this mortifying Love drawn and tempered to a fine and lacerating edge. Of such a gift we have already a thousand times proven ourselves unworthy. So to chasten us for our unworthiness of His *finezas* is also a fine thing, for He chastens whom he loves. But God's greatest *fineza* is a still more negative favour— to release us from his hand, to spare us his *finezas*, to grant us no favour at all."

The Bishop—startled from his languor—asks for an explanation.

Of errors in judgement and character I was already a hundred times guilty, but my single sin that day was speaking aloud thoughts that should have remained silent. For if the Word made flesh is God's greatest gift, then returning that gift to God—in the soul's gift of silence—is our most sacred offering, the highest of which we are capable. Our holiest prayers are those addressed in His secret Name, as the Hebrews taught so long ago. Our most sacred offering is a silence beyond naming . . .

And yet I do not keep silent.

"As I have said, don Manuel, God is not completed by our requital of His love. But by making us incomplete, he gives us the chance to choose completion. By leaving us free, he makes it the highest expression of our free will to *choose love.* How beautiful this is. But when He asks that we respond to the boundless favour of His love by loving as He loves us, the most faithfully we are able to reciprocate is by loving Him especially for the favours He does *not* bestow upon us. His greatest gifts we shall surely crucify. Withholding them, God spares us the opportunity to commit the most diabolical evils. So you see God's greatest benefaction, his subtlest finesse, contains in its belly another: the gift of not having to revoke our freedom.

"And what is its highest expression? The freedom to choose love, as we have seen. But *which* love—to love, yes, but *how?* Loving, not without need, not without desire—these are both beyond most—but loving *without hope.* This we may call loving heroically. This, even the worst of us at the best of times can do. . . . To love without the slightest hope of being worthy of our love's Object, or of His love's return. And to exercise our free will as if with hope, as if we were in fact capable of good, of love, of being loved, in the terrifying absence of His Grace. . . ."

I sit here in Atlantis replaying that dreamlike hour in a mind filled with a silent roaring. Is this deafness—a roaring we can no longer distinguish from sound? Swelling to drown out all other sounds and then receding, the mind no longer able to hold to the featureless din. Caught up in the moment, I go further in ten minutes with my friend the Lord Bishop Santa Cruz than in twenty years of confession.

ZEALOT

ANY FOOL KNOWS there are things a man does not tell his lovers. Still other things an adulterer conceals from his wife. Conversely, the disclosure of certain confidences may prove a tactical asset. Any fool knows this too. The trouble, at times, is knowing which is which.

Towards the end of our brief intimacy I submitted to the tedium of a puerile game Beulah imposed on me. It was literally a game of truth or dare. I now see that on this particular day, and others, I gave up more than I got in return. I tell the story now as I told it to Beulah then, with the same innocence. . . .

I have an aversion to religion.

My grandmother lived in Manitoba, a zealous member of the local Pentecostal congregation, a church of charismatic preaching, of speaking in tongues. Still, zealot is too strong a word.

She was a nurse. She saved my life when I was six. My parents had brought me twenty hours by train across the Prairies. In three more hours I went from charging through her sprinkler to kneeling at death's door. She nursed me day and night, the pneumonia soon so tangled in my lungs that the sole life sign was the slightest fogging on a spoon placed against my lips.

She had watery blue eyes, and favoured paisleys. She baked rhubarb pies like an angel. She smelled like lavender, liked to laugh. She detested drink, abhorred Sunday sports and commerce, and knew Catholics to be idolators. Her bunions, forcing an end to a forty-year nursing career, utterly deformed the soft slippers she was by then reduced to wearing, even to Church, where she played the organ. Really played, a genuine holy roller. I can see the tiny grey and russet curls that wriggled free of the severe bun she wore. A heathenish coiling at her nape and temples as she banged out those same gospel hymns for me on the piano at home. Any day of the week, not just Sunday. She loved the music.

Zealot is too strong a word.

I owed her a life. I wanted to make it for her a life truly saved: *Grandma, I felt the baby Jesus enter my heart last night,* I whispered, and believed. She cried, and as she wiped her eyes, my own searched for something neutral to settle on: the kidney-shaped hollows on either side of the bridge of her nose, which over the years her glasses had scalloped out.

My conversion was as fleeting as it was shallow. When we came back the following summer I had to tell her I couldn't believe anymore. I waited until the last day, but I was taught to tell the truth.

So taught, I'm obliged to state that there was no miracle cure. No breakthrough in nursing science saw me through either, but rather a hodgepodge of folk remedies that may or may not have abetted a child's natural resiliency. This was the Prairies in the early sixties. For pneumonia, burning hot mustard plasters applied every hour around the clock, the nostrum of preference in southern Manitoba. My father claimed she'd drawn the phlegm from my chest through a tube down my throat, drawn it from my nostrils with her lips. I didn't know whether to believe him.

Maybe she hadn't really saved my life after all. Maybe, for a while, she had only watched over it.

ADVENT

O n the island of Mexico, from the old barrio of Nacatitlan, a street goes north through the new streets intersecting it, running west and east straight down to the lake. Here, where the shacks and shanties and huts are low, one may see the white volcanoes to the east, the southmost gouting steam above the other, white and still. A whiteness washed faint copper in the smoke of scores of small fires set in the western hills.

North of the barrio of Nacatitlan, the street is called Calle de las Rejas where it approaches the porter's gate of the convent of San Jerónimo, and from there past the slaughterhouses and butcher shops to the monastery of San Agustín, the richest in all Mexico. Here, in the days after the first Sunday of Advent and leading up to the festival of Our Lady of Guadalupe and in the fortnight beyond this to the Nativity, the beggars gather in great numbers at the monastery gates. The street passes them by and proceeds along the west face of the convent of San Bernardo to arrive at the *zócalo*, a vast plaza bounded on the south by the edifices of the city administration and on the east by the long façade of the Viceregal Palace. On the north stands the massive yoke of the Metropolitan Cathedral, its second tower at last nearing completion. It is the hour approaching sunset in this season of festivals and the end of rains. As though upon a living coat of arms, the central plaza of the Imperial City of Mexico lies embossed and embroidered and crisscrossed and braided with tens of thousands of people, afoot, on muleback and horseback, and in litters and carriages.

Over at the Cathedral and unconstrained by the solemnity within, celebrants have hemmed its walls about with exuberant bouquets the violet of Advent—irises, jacarandas, violets, hyacinths. Along the blank west wall the bouquets lie tumbled at its base like the sprays of violet breakers, while standing lost and awash among the flowers, here at the customary place, wait a few score unemployed carpenters and masons still hoping to be collected for the late, last work of the busiest season.

Three blocks farther north, the street reaches a smaller plaza at whose southeast corner agents stream in and out of the Customs House, its west windows reflecting a sky orange with the approaching sunset.

Hemmed too in violet bouquets stands the small rose-coloured temple of Santo Domingo, on the north edge of the plaza itself. Across Calle Puente de la Aduana to the east stands the edifice of an austere authority: two tall storeys, a stone coat of arms, a cloth banner above the tall front gates at the southwest corner. There the sky blazes red-orange in the glass; farther along, the light slanting over the plaza leaves some windows in shadow on the upper floor. In one of these, six north of the gates, a lamp burns.

A second is lit as the first arrivals enter. Their carriages come in not through the front but by the rear gates, backed in black canvas to discourage petitioners and relatives and to frustrate the few inevitable daredevils. From the courtyard, where carriages wait in deep evening shadow an attendant leads each new arrival down a long black corridor lighted by rough torches. There are many doors; all are shut. Among the cracked and battered doors one is new: torchlight gleams dully in its heavy bosses and rivets.

Second-last to arrive is one who walks this corridor for the first time. He is young. He carries in one hand an Italian tricorne hat. His hair is blond; he wears it fashionably long, in ringlets. The tall robed attendant walks swiftly ahead. The young man tries not to fall behind, while trying not to try to keep up either. Tall himself, long-limbed, he is nevertheless hampered by the high-heeled shoes, canary yellow to match his long velvet *justaucorps* and yellow satin suit. He curses himself for a fool, first for accepting a last minute invitation to leave the comforts of the palace, no matter from whom, then for getting into a carriage without knowing its destination. He knows it now. The shudder he has so far managed to suppress gathers at the base of his spine and skull. He reminds himself that he comes to give what amounts to a literary assessment, which he intends to render concisely and then just as quickly leave.

Led now through a small patio behind the front gates he sends a last wistful glance out and climbs a tall staircase, its railing wrought of flat iron, unturned, unadorned. At the second door on the left, the attendant leading him knocks and returns swiftly the way he came. The most important guest is yet to arrive.

The door opens. Inside are five men. Straight ahead, behind a desktop as deep as it is broad, its clutter of dossiers pushed to one side, sits a burly man of about fifty in a white tunic and scapular. His beard is full and heavy, thick, starting high on his cheekbones, almost at his eyes. The heaviness of the beard and brows make the alert eyes, deep in their well of wrinkles, seem small. The heavy black curtains to his left are closed. Before them a secretary sits attentively at an *escribanía*. Another Dominican sits on a plain chair midway between a divan and the door. Over his scapular he wears a black mantle, the hood drawn back. He glances up briefly from a dossier on his lap as the man in yellow makes his entrance. A red-bearded friar sits at the edge of the divan. His habit is black, the hood especially large, of a soft material. The Augustinian's smile seems friendly.

To the right of the desk the drapes are parted a little, letting in the day's last light. Through the smoke in the air over the city, high thin clouds trail plumes of crimson. Just beyond this armspan of sky is an unoccupied chair, thickly upholstered, walnut arms inlaid with ivory and nacre. Beside this a low table, and upon it a small platter of sweetmeats. Across the room a Spanish gentleman paces to pass off his unease for impatience. He gives a familiar nod as the young man enters, crossing over to him. Without rising from behind the desk, the Master Examiner beckons to the empty chair next to the Spanish gentleman's. For several moments no one speaks. Sounds are heard in the hallway. All come to their feet, the young man reluctantly, as a man comes in, removing his travelling cloak on his way to the chair by the window. The servant hurries from the door to take the cloak and broad-brimmed hat.

In this season, the cassock the man wears is black, its piping, like its cincture, purple. The hair is a light brown, his eyes large and dark. The other men sit once he is seated. The young aristocrat is briefly chagrined that he has not been shown the same courtesy.

"Refreshments, Excellency?" the Master Examiner asks. "Water? Nothing at all . . . ?" The secretary leaves the room. The servant follows. "We'll begin, then. Your time in the capital is short—at least for now. Our foreign visitor, you know. And don Francisco here, as the Viceroy's representative, comes as a neutral observer."

The Spanish gentleman sits with his elbows on the armrests, fingertips resting lightly on the gloves in his lap. He inclines his head towards the man by the window. The Master Examiner continues, "In the unfortunate event that His Grace the Archbishop were no longer able to carry out his functions, the Viceroy would share our need to have as much warning as possible—"

The Viceroy's man raises a hand in a gesture of caution. "But I am also here to prevent any unpleasantness attaching to the Viceroy—that is, if his spiritual director *or* the Viceregal Cosmographer were ever indicted. Our particular interest would be any evidence connecting don Carlos with the Creole seditionists, which is of course a secular matter. Your co-operation will be noted. And of course, appreciated."

"Naturally. As will yours be by us, if your own investigations link these new pamphleteers to the ones publishing slanders against the Archbishop."

"And writing that filth on his walls."

"As on the Viceroy's, yes."

"I should not be at all surprised," says the Spanish gentleman, "to discover that they use the same printer."

"Yes, don Francisco, they might." The Master Examiner turns back to the Bishop. "Our new *Calificador*, you have met."

The red-bearded man shifts in his seat. "Lord Bishop."

"And Prosecutor Ulloa here is with us so as to be familiar with these proceedings from the outset. Ulloa?"

"Even in complicated cases, Excellency, some of our best evidence is gathered through simple tactics," says the Prosecutor. "The simplest have stood the test of time. Apply pressure, watch for cracks. How and where depends upon the case, with which I am just now acquainting myself. . . ."

Master Examiner Dorantes glances at the red-bearded man.

The Calificador smiles affably. "Perhaps, Prosecutor Ulloa, I might begin. Having learned of the so-called *Athenagoric Letter* from an old associate in Puebla, I felt it my duty to obtain a copy of the printer's proof and show it to His Grace the Archbishop. To whose quarters I was accompanied by Master Examiner Dorantes, two weeks ago today. November 22nd. Understandably His Grace, who had taken to his bed, takes this attack on the Jesuit Vieyra as one upon himself. He has been nothing if not loyal—"

"To a man vehemently suspected of heresy," puts in the Prosecutor, "whom our Office in Portugal has once condemned and now has under examination again."

"I next expressed to His Grace," the Calificador continues mildly, "my bitter regret at not having heard of the nun's letter of attack earlier, given his recently announced intention to deliver a more recent sermon by this same Jesuit Vieyra. For then I might have spared His Grace this added . . . awkwardness. Once he had regained mastery of his emotions—and my visit was not without its harrowing moments—I did point out how things might have been much worse."

"And did His Grace the Archbishop wonder how they might?"

"He did, Lord Bishop." The Calificador smiles. "To which I answered, first, that the attack was published, taking it out of the realm of vague rumour and into one where we may prosecute. Second, that the *Letter* was signed, saving us valuable time. And third, that if the Archbishop would care to consider the matter philosophically, the prologue by this Sor Philothea—who has thus done our Office a great favour in arranging for publication—significantly rebukes its author for her worldly pride and vanity, thereby mitigating what would otherwise be a most grievous insult to the veneration in which His Grace is everywhere held."

Not quite pleased with the tone, Master Examiner Dorantes takes over the recitation himself. "The purpose of the visit was to put the full weight of this Office at His Grace's disposal. Unfortunately Father Núñez has allowed himself to be absent during this moment of distress."

"If you'll permit me, Fray Dorantes? At this point we were able to confirm that His Grace had been unaware of Father Núñez's own criticisms of the Jesuit Vieyra directly after the sermon. The Archbishop was so incredulous that it was fortunate I had witnessed Núñez's refutation myself in his chambers, and could confirm it personally."

During the interruption the Master Examiner sits quietly contemplating a point near the centre of his desktop, a scratch in the varnish, an ink spot. He lets another moment pass before concluding his report to the Bishop.

"Our discussion turned to certain speculations, lent substance by the timing of his absence, about Antonio Núñez's possible duplicity in this *Athenagoric Letter*. That it seemed close to using Núñez's own arguments from the rectory that day. This did little to quiet the Archbishop's unrest. The idea of cancelling his own participation in Gaudete Sunday and the Nativity was entirely the Archbishop's idea. I did caution that his absence on two such holy occasions would only draw further public attention to the affair and fuel the most unhealthy speculations. At this point, speaking more to himself than to us, he raised the possibility of going 'home' to Michoacan for the entire season."

In the chair beside the window the Bishop sits unmoving, his expression neutral, the large, dark eyes extraordinarily alive.

"There we have the Archbishop's reaction. Meanwhile the affairs of this Office do not rest, in any season. We have a disinterested party ready to make a formal denunciation of the text as heretical, when the moment to increase the pressure arrives. A series of anonymous leaflets has already been written, taking the denunciation further. Our printers are standing by. As to the *Letter*'s author, the Viscount here has been good enough to accept our invitation."

"Anything to oblige the Holy Office."

"The Lord Bishop mentioned to us your business here, and that you are so recently arrived. What you may speak to are her current resources in Europe. We have our own assessments. But we will add yours to the file."

"Yes, do feel entirely free. In return I shall be grateful for any intelligence you may be able to provide, and especially for material assistance with travel permits. As you may know," he turns to the Bishop, who seems to be looking not quite at him, "I am charged by my King with the mission of bringing one or, ideally, both of them—a matched pair, as it were—back to Versailles. If forced to choose, his preference is for her but he understands that her vows make this is a matter of some delicacy. So I must ask you one last time, Lord Bishop, is there no way of securing the necessary permission to have her taken?"

Raising his left hand to the curtain, the Bishop inspects something farther up Puente de la Aduana street. To the beating of drums and coronet fanfares, students of the Jesuit College of San Pedro y San Pablo are advancing on the Plaza of Santo Domingo; it is the *procesión burlesco* that by custom marks the six-week break in instruction. During his boyhood in Spain, the Bishop himself participated in several, though perhaps not quite matching the notorious Mexican exuberance. As in Spain, such displays offer useful glimpses of issues of concern to a diocese. In the street now the theme is a common one, the world upside down. Men costumed as women, women as males, others as fanciful animals, feet waving in the air and heads dragging along the ground. Still others as infants holding up placards marked *Senility*, or dressed as prostitutes waving *Chastity*. . . . But what has caught the Bishop's interest is at the head of the procession. A giant on stilts garbed in a purple chasuble, over it, a prisoner's *sambenito*, and on this Archbishop Aguiar's coat of arms. A horn sprouts on each side of the mitre. Costumed bulls and fighting cocks caper just out of reach as the Archbishop whirls and staggers and lays all about him with his wood sabre. . . .

The Bishop continues to gaze out the window. In the plaza the lamps of the workshops burn bright. Apothecary, printer and engraver, candlemaker, carpenter, farrier . . . the last straggle of communicants after Vespers.

Imperturbably watching the young aristocrat's colour mount, the Master Examiner eventually answers. "The nun, Viscount, is a problem of our own creation. We do not need France to solve it for us."

"It is of course as you wish," the Viscount says with elaborate casualness, "but if I may not have her and therefore may not have both, I must absolutely have him. His Majesty is remarkably uninterested in failure, even mine."

"Your King should thank us."

"He may thank you, but he will not thank me. He had his hopes set on her."

"It would be irresponsible of us to turn such a pox loose within his borders."

"A pox against which even an ocean, I notice, has not so far imposed a perfect quarantine."

"Do not trouble yourself unduly. The reach of our Office is long. As for the other one, you do understand that should he be called before the Tribunal, we can reach him even in Versailles."

"My mission is to get him there, not guarantee his piety."

"I remind the Master Examiner," interjects the Viceroy's representative, "that we have as yet heard no evidence of misconduct—ecclesiastic or civil. We are speaking of a distinguished natural philosopher—"

"Not an occupation that this Office inclines to take as an endorsement."

"The most distinguished in all the Spanish dominions."

"That he finds so few colleagues *in* the Spanish dominions we take as cause for rejoicing."

"Rather take it as a reminder, Doctor Dorantes—that I am here because his maps and studies have rendered valuable service to the Viceroy and to our King."

"Reminding me," says the Viscount, "of my services to mine. So, gentlemen, if I might continue, I should be going soon." The Viscount rises as though to announce a considerable grandiloquence. "As I was leaving Spain it was vividly impressed upon me that the support of the Countess of Paredes is unshakeable. On the other hand her husband's family's fortunes are, as you know, at the moment somewhat vulnerable.

Her husband's brother, the Duke de Medinaceli, is more likely to be recalled to Madrid on charges of treason than to be reinstated as the King's Prime Minister.

"Less favourable to your purposes, however, were the rumours of a mission to solicit the support of Christina of Sweden whose influence in Rome went to the highest level, as you know. I neither expect nor care to be privy to the finer details of your affairs here, but I assume it is more than hazard that none other than Christina apparently intervened with the Pope to secure for this Jesuit, Vieyra, his first pardon from the Inquisition. A papal exoneration of all past *and future charges* of heresy? My dear friends, it seems quite fantastic to me. The mind fairly boggles at the sums to be made trafficking in such blanket pardons." The Viscount continues with an amused frown, "No—as I say, the finer details are not for me. . . . But had the Pope been similarly persuaded to offer such a pardon to your nun, I suspect you would have gladly surrendered her to my King after all, as I shall be so ruefully telling him.

"But there is Providence for you," he shrugs. "As to the first collection—this *Inundación Castálida*—it has proved wildly popular among ladies of the finer sort. That said, neither the collection nor her name is as yet well known to the other courts of Europe. Were the ties that bind the thrones of Spain and France not so very close, she would not yet be known in Versailles either. But I can also assure you, and I travel as widely as I read, there are not three poets in all of Europe today writing at this level. In ten years or even five, your nun may not need a Christina to be heard in Rome. There, Master Examiner, you have my assessment."

"One that gives no further cause to expect interference from Europe, which fits with our own assessment. Thank you, Viscount. So we have, in the matter of the *Letter*, the means to apply pressure to a number of points at once, as Prosecutor Ulloa has put it. Our anvil, let us say. Similarly, there are a number of potential hammers, one being a line of inquiry we have maintained for many years. . . . I apologize, Ulloa, for waiting until this morning to turn this other file over to you. But you will have read enough by now to understand why."

Glancing over at the two outsiders, the Master Examiner continues, his tone neutral. "Whenever a widely respected servant of Holy Mother Church has used her auspices to win widespread trust and high esteem, there are repercussions when that individual is condemned to the stake. Upsets are to be expected, divisions within the Church itself, even within our Office. The trial of the Franciscan Fray Manuel de Cuadros fifteen years ago is an incident that I am sure the Lord Bishop well remembers. The charges were of a varied character. Some minor, most not. Eventually Brother Cuadros was persuaded to make a full confession and, as often happens, confessed to particulars unknown till then to us. Particulars to be found, Prosecutor Ulloa, in the dossier you now hold. I was at the time only an assistant to one of the examiners on the case, and so had little direct contact with the man. Antonio Núñez, on the other hand, whose task it was to secure his full repentance, spent a great deal of time with him. We were able to secure a number of manuscripts—translations and the like—enough of them to make his sentence inescapable. But certain other papers vanished. Heretical monographs on Indian practices. Blasphemous comparisons of their demonic rites to our most holy sacraments, or rather of these to . . . cannibalism. The examining magistrates were confident of seizing them in a raid that was to be carried out the next day. But by then they had disappeared. Fray Cuadros, a stubborn man, could not be induced to give testimony confirming our suspicions, but all the signs at the time pointed towards Carlos Sigüenza, who was prudently absent during the trial. We had drawn up plans to move against him, but after the Franciscan was burned, feelings in the Church and within this Office were, as I say, divided. The Archbishop of the time, being also our Viceroy, urged us to wait until we had more conclusive information. To date, it has not surfaced.

"The difficulty is that no one has seen these manuscripts for fifteen years. Were they destroyed? And if they still exist, where are they? Sigüenza is not stupid. It is doubtful that he would try to conceal them either at his house or the university—"

"Doctor Dorantes," says the Viceroy's emissary, chin lifted, cheeks faintly colouring, "what strikes me as *doubtful* is a line of inquiry that by your own admission has turned up nothing in fifteen years. Until credible evidence is produced, the palace shall suppose that both don Carlos and the Reverend Father Núñez continue to give faithful service. The Viceroy's administration will not be undermined, as the Archbishop's clearly has, by baseless suspicions."

"Of course, don Francisco, of course. We are aware Sigüenza is a friend of yours"—the Master Examiner raises a weary hand—"*and* that this can of course have no bearing on your deliberations. But your concerns are temporal. We take a longer view. Fifteen years is but a heartbeat."

"Unfortunately, *messieurs*, like don Francisco here, I do not have an eternity either. And if you have been hearing the same reports I have about an unfortunate and ill-considered alliance between great Spain and a certain insignificant enemy of France, time is scarce indeed. I would really rather not have to make arrangements to smuggle a subject of the Spanish Crown out of Spanish territory in time of war. Unless you have further need of me this evening, I will leave you to get on with things. For my part, I leave reassured that you do not have enough to be arresting him any time soon."

The Viceroy's representative rises to follow the Viscount out. "In the morning I make my report to the Viceroy. Keep us apprised."

When the two have left, the Calificador runs his fingers through the red tangle at his throat. "Did he say keep us surprised?" he asks, of no one in particular.

"Coming late to this case," Prosecutor Ulloa frowns over the open folder, "I do not yet see why the foreigner has been brought here tonight. How do we know this *Francés*," Ulloa says with distaste, "will not run and tell Sigüenza everything he has just heard?"

"If only he would."

The Prosecutor considers this.

"You see, Prosecutor Ulloa, the good don Francisco and the Viscount," explains the Calificador, "are part of the pressure."

Dorantes looks up from pondering the scratch on his desk. "Were the foreigner to do just as you suggest, Ulloa, although it is almost too much to hope for, Sigüenza might, in a panic to destroy the evidence, lead those watching him directly to the documents. What we can be sure of is that he will not leave New Spain until they are destroyed, since he cannot doubt that we may reach him even in France. So as long as he is here, there is still a chance. All the better if he has both reason and opportunity to leave. But where are those manuscripts? The most likely thing is that they are not in the city."

"Still," says the Calificador, glancing about him, "what if these papers *were* here? A question interesting to contemplate, no? One place would be a convent. Almost impossible to enter without giving warning. Too many corridors, too many escape routes, too much time. San Jerónimo, for example, is just such a warren. The difficulty with manuscripts, from our point of view, and His Excellency will appreciate the irony, is that they are so much more easily destroyed than books. We have only to arrive at someone's door, and if a fire is burning in the hearth, loose leaves are up a chimney in seconds. With books, even after half an hour, one might retrieve enough evidence to condemn half a dozen men. Writer, printer, smuggler, buyer, seller, accomplices . . ."

"But has the publication of this letter," Ulloa asks, "not put her on her guard?"

"It's hard to say with her. She has so very many interests—her poetry and her little fables, her locutory and her library. It is touching. And the few things that do not intimately concern her . . . hardly exist at all. His Excellency knows her better than I, but I would say she knows nothing of the world—has she ever lived in it, I wonder?"

The Bishop looks at him, his eyes glowing darkly.

"What the Calificador is taking so very long to say, Lord Bishop, is that she has no reason to connect the letter's publication to our interest in the missing manuscripts."

"Forgive me, Master Examiner," says Ulloa, "but we do have sources at San Jerónimo. Before taking the risk of alerting her, would it not have been wise to at least try to reassure ourselves she does not have the manuscripts right now? Could a way not have been found?"

"A way has been found," says Dorantes.

"I have been wondering . . ." This time the red-bearded magistrate does not look at the Bishop, who has turned his attention back to the plaza, but addresses himself to Master Examiner Dorantes, "just how reliable we consider this 'way' to be."

With a scowl at his confrere Dorantes says soothingly to the Bishop, "With a little more experience, the new Calificador may come to understand that even when the end result is assured, there are no certainties in the moment. The nun or the Frenchman may lead us to the manuscripts. The manuscripts will give us Sigüenza or even give us Núñez. Núñez will give us what we need against her—he can hardly hide behind the sacramental Seal now. Or in the matter of this letter, the Archbishop—that is, should he be well enough to continue—moves against her on his own. Or, finally, we press this question of heretical quietism in her *finezas negativas* and clean up at least one mess the Jesuits have made.[37] *Dejada, alumbrada, gnóstica* . . . she has given us options."

"Excuse me," the Calificador offers, "but have we not missed a step? How are these manuscripts to give us Núñez? Is he not more likely to be taken in the event that he has failed to burn her journals?"

"There are other proceedings, Calificador. Many others, which you have no present need to know about." Dorantes runs the heel of a small pale hand wearily across one brow. He leans forward, weight on his elbows, and places his interlaced palms on the desk. "You may go now, Calificador."

When he has left, Ulloa asks, "As to the sequence, does the Lord Bishop have a preference?"

"Who falls first?" The Bishop turns from the plaza. "No. I do not much care."

"We take our exemplum in patience, then, from His Excellency. Anything before we adjourn?"

"Master Examiner, Lord Bishop . . ."

"Yes, Ulloa."

"While I, for one, am satisfied that the case holds promise, one final worry occurs to me. Bringing don Francisco here was prudent—he now knows himself to be the prime suspect if don Carlos is warned. But are we prepared to have the foreigner go to her with what he has heard?"

"It is as you yourself have said, Ulloa. Pressure at as many points as possible. He would be doing us a favour. But he has not the slightest chance of getting her out if we do not wish it."

"And we do not wish it?"

"We do not wish it."

The Bishop seems about to rise. The others tense to rise with him. For the past half hour he has seemed unaware of the tray of sweetmeats on the table beside him. His hand sways idly now over them, stops, settles on a choice. A slice of candied squash. Raising it to his lips, he stops. The heavy rings glow in the lantern light. It is full dark outside.

"Not knowing quite what he expects to get," the Bishop says softly, "the Viscount may indeed go to her, as he has once already. At first he will find himself enjoying again this power he has over her, which lies precisely in her not knowing that he has it, and this knowledge that she does not really see him. But since he cannot get in, and since he cannot get her out, he will see that this is all there is for him.

"I do not think he will go again."

Something has been troubling me, a care
so subtle, so fleeting, it appears,
that for all that I know of the feeling
I scarcely know how to feel it for me.
    It is love, but a love
that, failing to be blind,
only has eyes to inflict
a more vivid punishment.
    For it is not the terminus a quo
that afflicts these eyes:
but their terminus being the Good,
so much pain in the distance lies.
    If this feeling that I harbour
is not wrong—but what love is owed,
why do they chastise one
who pays on love's account?
    Ah, such *finezas*, so rare, so subtle are
the caresses I have known.
For the love we hold for God
is one without a counterpart.
    Neither can such a love,
ever meet with oblivion,
since contraries are not
to be conceived upon pure Good.
    But too well do I recall
having loved in a time now past
with a quality beyond madness,
exceeding the worst extreme;
    yet since this love was a bastard,
of oppositions wed,
swiftly was it undone,
by the flaws with which it was cast.
    But now, ah me, so
purely is this new love enkindled,
that reason and virtue
are further fires to feed it.
    Anyone hearing this will ask,
why then do I suffer?
Here an anxious heart responds:
for this very cause, and no other.

What human frailty is this,
when the most chaste and naked spirit
may not be embraced
except in mortal dress?
    So great is the longing
we have to feel loved,
that however hopeless it becomes
we are helpless to resist.
    Though it adds nothing to my love
that it be requited,
though I try to deny it—
O how I crave this.
    If it is a crime, I avow it,
if a sin, now it is confessed,
but however desperate my attempts,
I cannot bring myself to repent.
    Who sees into my secret heart
will bear witness
that the thorns I now endure
are my own harvest.
    And that I am the executioner
of my own desires, fallen
among my longings,
entombed in my own breast.
    I die—who will believe this?—at the hands
of what I most adore,
and the motive of my death is
a love I cannot bear.
    Thus, nourishing my life
on this sad bane, I find
the death on which I live
is the life I am dying for.
    But courage, heart,
however exquisite the torments
through whatever fortunes heaven sends,
this love, I swear never to recant.

JUANA INÉS
DE LA CRUZ

"Divine Love"

B. Limosneros, trans.

DEIPHOBE   *[27th day of November, 1690]*

la excma. María Luisa Manrique de Lara y Gonzaga
Condesa de Paredes, Marquesa de la Laguna,
Madrid, España

Queridísima María Luisa,

or weeks I have no news of you. And now your letter opens saying you will not be able to write for some time. Were this not agony enough—there is the why. I beg you, write even two lines the first instant you can, just to say your Tomás is recovering. How galling for you to hear his physicians changing their diagnosis like so many weathercocks. And how very selfish I have been to burden you—can I have forgotten you might have cares of your own?

I continue to believe Tomás's recent difficulties with our new Queen are temporary. If she so far continues to overlook his qualities, we may be certain it is the work of that same claque that has orchestrated his brother's removal as the King's Prime Minister. It saddens me to be so far away and so ignorant of matters there that I can now offer such thin comfort and no advice at all except, believe all will be well even as you act all the more resolutely to make it so.

Let me at least try to allay fears I myself have raised so unkindly, with regard to the recent activities of the Inquisition here. The time for reading obliquely, as one reads Aeschylus, has passed. As soon as Carlos duly supplied them with a book inventory, the whole business faded away. The Inquisitor Dorantes was only sending a message to our distinguished Chair of Mathematics and Astrology. No, not just a message, a reminder. For it is ten years ago now that Dorantes censored a set of observations Carlos had published on the phases of the moon. (Twenty years ago Dorantes even censored Núñez—for 'an excess of enthusiasm over the immaculacy of the Virgin Mother's conception.' Truly, one hesitates to imagine what this could have meant . . .)

I am sorry to have alarmed you unnecessarily. You once said you thought my fear of the Inquisition exaggerated. These days, anyone in the capital will tell you that the Holy Office's power is on the decline. That if you are circumspect and curry favour with the authorities, do not rise too fast among your neighbours or speak out too frankly among strangers, do not think the wrong thoughts or read the wrong books, that if you miss no opportunity to express your enthusiasm for the Faith, you have nothing to fear from the Inquisition.

At any rate, if the Holy Office had launched a proceeding against Carlos I would have heard—first the whispers of the well-informed, then a great murmuring among the ignorant. And soon after that he would be a guest of the Tribunal.

There has been nothing of this. So I hope to have laid your doubts (and most of all your loving fears) to rest, if by this somewhat gloomy avenue.

Things have been otherwise calm. Right now, all the talk at the cathedral is of the Archbishop's sermon for the Vigil of our Lord's Nativity, or perhaps it was for Gaudete Sunday, I'm not sure which. The point being that he seems to have decided not to give it. I will send Antonia out this morning to find out what she can. The affair has occasioned as much mirth as curiosity among the clerics here, since it has become an open secret that the Archbishop, who never misses an opportunity to trade on his intellectual connections in Europe, has become all but incapable of delivering much less writing a sermon, such is his near-constant state of upset.

As I wrote you recently, the Bishop of Puebla has followed through on his promise to secure for me the one commission from the Church that I have truly coveted in recent years. A suite of carols on Saint Catherine of Alexandria, to be sung in the cathedral in Puebla. In a few more weeks I hope to have finished, but I may say with a small shudder of poet's superstition that they are on their way to being my best work since *First Dream*.

I am not quite over my bitterness. I have written you about my lyrics for Saint Bernard, that Núñez had his way in the end and that they were not sung. This has brought more hurt than anything in the years since you left. And yet because in all these months you have not mentioned it, I cannot help suspecting you've not received that letter either. No matter, it's over now. I brought much of it upon myself. Such squabbles over theology are no place to speak one's heart. I do not much care for loose talk of God.

You asked last year about my grievance with Father Núñez. I gave you what it is built on, the circumstances, but what lies at its heart, what lies on its altar is simple beauty itself. Though Núñez might fulminate against this or that formulation of mine, and insists on seeing attacks against him any time I encroach upon his holy exclusivities and prerogatives, in the end it is about this. His positions on the Holy Mysteries lack for neither learning nor subtlety. What they lack is beauty. He sees it, and it enrages him that this should enter into it at all. But from the simplest peasant to the most exalted sovereign of the world, we are swayed by beauty, we turn in its orbit. Womanish thoughts! Paganist poetry! he fumes, yet sees the evidence all around him. Even he. For it is said that at the Jesuit college Father Núñez has built with his own hands an altar to the Virgin that only he is permitted to tend. They say that the altar of Rector Núñez is very beautiful, that its beauty is of an Asiatic extravagance. When I remember this altar, my thoughts wander to a day in the distant past when things grew so bitter between us that I asked he be replaced as my director. It was your husband's uncle, don Payo, who tried to mend things between us. In refusing my request, he let slip a small detail I would never have guessed at, but without which I would find the altar incomprehensible. That as a novice, the boy Antonio Núñez wrote beautifully, of a beauty reminiscent of Saint Jerome's. As a result his noviciate with the Jesuits was made especially hard; his punishments were of a cruelty almost fantastic, until he had stripped the least marks of grace from his thoughts and writings. Is it for this, I wonder, that I could never quite bring myself to hate him? Oneness, Goodness, Truth. The transcendental attributes of God. But there is a fourth. It is in Her; it is in Her Son. Our souls sway to a fourth transcendental.[38] Beauty. The poets overrunning theology! he cries, but I am only following Saint Jerome, the Ciceronian. And Núñez, better than anyone, knows this.

Obedience, forbearance, humility, resistance to suffering. This is what he answers with. In Núñez's Church of the Holy Infantry, to have a gift is indeed a great burden—the burden of annihilating it. No favours, no special gifts or sacrifices. To be an ordinary infantryman is more than burden enough.

I understand our sacraments as well as he, if differently, and while I find them of a majesty and depth that goes beyond our comprehension, they do not console me. I am not fed, I am not filled, by this bread.

He has made himself our authority on the Eucharist, but if others could only read the monographs Carlos will never publish on the ancient

Mexican sacraments. The Reverend Father has made himself our authority on communion, and takes the *finezas* of Christ to be his exclusive province. He treats the *fineza* like a demonstration, a proof, an axiom of love. Yet the *finesses* are an expression from which we *infer* love. They derive from our gift for inference. Love is not a truth that insists. We infer, Christ does not insist. And so Núñez's positions are never beautiful—they insist, they prove and reprove. And against the love of beauty and the beauty of love he knows he cannot win.

A love of Christ that is passionate, yet pure and disembodied—we both claim to believe in it. I believe that to develop the capacity for such a love here on earth, here in the flesh, would only make our love for Christ all the deeper and truer. Núñez cannot believe that any such love may exist among us, and reviles my need to feel it. I believe in this Love with every fibre of my being, yet from Him I do not feel it and so can find no way to return it.

What I feel is His absence. It is why I once sought for him in the beauty of the world. This at least I can feel. My mind infers it, but so does my heart. This is an absence at least bearable to me—and in the hours when it is not, I look to the mountains in the east, I look to the stars, and feel my love returning, flooding me. . . . I know you will understand but I add this in the event this letter is intercepted: If I could be less than utterly convinced of His existence, how much more bearable would my Lover's absence be.

Núñez hates this. Every tone and syllable. Because he more than anyone understands this failing in me, comes closest to sharing it. Passionate yet disembodied love. Before Christ, it fails him—it lacks passion; before Her, this love shames him—it does not feel disembodied enough.

Remembering that altar of his, I know that what he despises in my writing on sacred subjects is the well of sensual beauty I draw it from. Father Núñez has extinguished his gift. Only to find it reborn in me, rising to oppose him.

I am the books, I am the beauty, I am the gift.

And so my thoughts return often to that day with the Bishop when I went too far and yet, even sick with self-disgust, I continued to abuse the gift of speech from the heart in my lyrics for the humble Saint Bernard. I have heard Bishop Santa Cruz was in a rage when he learned they were cancelled, for it is precisely this heart speaking its secrets to God that for fifteen years Santa Cruz has pressed me to reveal to him. In banning them, Father Núñez has dashed any hopes of an alliance with the Bishop. So one less worry, a boon it is hard to feel I deserve.

Santa Cruz calls this failure to feel the presence of Christ entirely normal. Spiritual aridity is the term, and it is a step on the *via mística*. What he mildly disapproves are the traces of worldliness still clinging to my sacred verses. Worldliness, the Bishop does not want either; what he wants is rapture.

My, but how melancholy this letter has become. If this was to be my attempt to set your mind at rest, it is hard to pronounce it a success. I pause for now and will start tomorrow afresh. My thoughts are with you, the thoughts and prayers of the entire convent are with Tomás. Sweet Lysis, I pray that a note from you of happy news is but a league or two off from here, and that I shall be able to start again on a note of joy and thanksgiving. And if that note has not yet been written by the time you receive this one, give not another moment's thought to writing until Tomás is well. Unless, dearest María Luisa, you should just need to talk. . . .

There. I hear Antonia on the stairs. She has news. And more energy at times than either of us knows what to do with. It is like trying to curb wild horses. More soon.

Love,

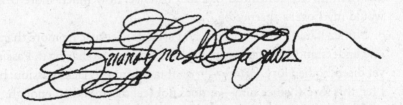

día 27 de noviembre del año 1690
del convento de San Jerónimo,
de la Ciudad Imperial de México,
Nueva España

Extract from Sister Philothea of the Cross (I)

My Lady,

I have seen the letter in which you challenge the *finezas* of Christ predicated by the Reverend Father Antonio Vieyra in his Maundy Thursday sermon. So subtle is his reasoning that the most erudite have seen in it his singular talent outsoaring itself like a second Eagle of the Apocalypse, following the path laid out earlier by the Most Illustrious César Meneses. . . . In my view, though, whoever reads your treatment cannot deny that your quill was cut to a finer point than both men's, so that they might rejoice to find themselves outdone by a woman who does her sex honour.

I, at least, have admired the liveliness of concept, deftness of proof and energetic clarity that you have brought so convincingly to bear, this last being wisdom's inseparable companion. For this reason the first utterance of the Divine Wisdom was *light*, since without illumination comes no word of wisdom. Even the words of Christ when he spoke of the highest mysteries, but under the veil of parable, did not evoke much wonder; and only when he chose to speak with clarity was his universal knowledge acclaimed. Such clarity is one of the many favours my lady owes to God; for clarity is to be had neither by effort nor persistence: it is a gift instilled in the soul.

So that you might see yourself in letters more clearly traced, I have had your letter printed; and also that you might take better stock of the treasures God has invested in your soul, and be made thereafter more appreciative, more aware: for gratitude and understanding are twins born of the same childbed. And if as your letter claims, the more one receives from God the more one owes in return, few creatures find their accounts more in arrears than yours, for few have been bequeathed such talents, or have incurred thereby such a debt to Him. So if you have made good use of them thus far (which I must believe of anyone who professes religion), hereinafter may you use them better.

My judgement is not so harsh a censor as to condemn verses—by virtue of which you have seen yourself so widely celebrated—a skill Saint Teresa, Saint Gregory of Nazianzus and other saints have sanctified with examples of sacred verse; but I would wish that you follow them not just in metre but also in the selection of your subjects.

Nor do I subscribe to the vulgar prohibition of those who assail the practice of letters in women, since so many have devoted themselves to literary study, not a few even winning praise from Saint Jerome. . . .

Letters that engender arrogance, God does not want in a woman; but the Apostle does not condemn those that do not lead woman from a state of submission. It has been widely noted that study and knowledge have made of you a willing subject, and have served to hone your skills in the finer points of obedience; indeed, while other female religious sacrifice their free will to obedience, you make a captive of your intelligence, the most arduous and pleasing holocaust that may be offered up for slaughter on the altars of Religion. . . .

I see her pale face in the doorway. This news, I do not think I shall like.

But her news is not of the Archbishop at all, and for just an instant I mistake the two booklets she holds for the most recent issue of our city's *Chronicle of Notable Events*. She is trying to explain, so breathlessly as to have likely run the whole way. . . .

"I was at the Hindu's, the one with the turban—"

"Hindus—"

"'Two copies for you and your mistress,' he says. 'My compliments.' They all have them—*all the booksellers,* dozens of copies—next to *Inundación Castálida*. People are already buying them as if they were *yours*—"

"One *is* mine, I gather. Come, I'll take the one you haven't quite crushed yet. . . ."

"Juana, who is Philothea? *E igua puta*—how did she get your letter?"

THE ATHENAGORIC LETTER
by the Reverend Mother
JUANA INÉS DE LA CRUZ
a nun professed to the veil and choir
of the very religious
Convent of San Jerónimo of the City of Mexico, capital of New Spain.
Printed and dedicated to her by
SISTER PHILOTHEA DE LA CRUZ
her most studious and devoted follower
of the Convent of the Holy Trinity of Puebla de los Angeles.
Licensed in the City of Angels, Diego Fernández de Leon, Printer. In the year 1690.
Available in Puebla at the libreria Diego Fernández de Leon,
under the Portal de las Flores

This is not possible. Printed by Sor Philothea, costs assumed by Philothea. Using the Bishop's regular printer. Licence signed by Santa Cruz, dedication by Philothea. The preface addressed to *me*:

Sor Philothea is the Lord Bishop Manuel Fernández de Santa Cruz y Sahagún. If Antonia wants a harder question it's this: What is the use of a disguise that lasts not five seconds? What is he doing—what has he *done?*

I have seen the letter?—seen it, of course you have! I sent it, you *asked.* Why not 'received' it?

But no, it was not Philothea who asked. Santa Cruz asked.

"The Bishop did this? But Juana, it was *private.* He said—you said . . ." she adds helplessly.

He said, I said. He said little, I on the other hand said rather a lot. No, but *this,* this is beyond belief. *Like a second Eagle of the Apocalypse . . . her quill cut finer . . . Deftness of proof, energetic clarity . . . Even Christ when he spoke of the highest mysteries, but under the veil of parable, did not provoke so much wonder. . . .* He cannot think this is helping anyone—to be compared to Christ. *Favourably?* He cannot think this helps *me.*

"Who is the Eagle of the Apocalypse, Juana?—¡caray!"

"'Tonia, if you're angry now, look at the third paragraph, where he complains about your handwriting."

So that you might see yourself in letters more clearly traced, I have had your letter printed . . .

"What? Oh." She almost manages a smile. "And now *ese hijo de la mierda* expects you to be grateful?—what he wants is everyone to see how clever he is!"

Pacing in and out of the room reeling off questions and curses, reading out loud, whirling about at each turn, tresses swinging out like rope ends, Antonia is becoming quite magnificent in her fury. I would not like Santa Cruz's chances if he were here. It is almost as if she truly hated him. But whatever her past grievances with Santa Cruz I have my own to nurse just now. And yes, talk of the Apocalypse I also could have done without.

"Now if you'd like to try something truly difficult, 'Tonia, try reading, talking, cursing, asking and answering your own questions and the next hundred of *mine.*"

No, furious was easier—her face looks awful. Seeing it, I have the sickening sense of one who has been dreading something so long she has forgotten what it was.

"Toñita, would you give me some time to think this through? Then we'll get to work, *mi amor. ¿De acuerdo?*"

She goes into the study, greenish eyes glowing, rattles purposefully about at the workbench, getting ready to take dictation. I have no idea what 'work' means, but it felt good to say.

This beggars belief. How can he be so stupid—can he not see what he's done? We've done this together a dozen times. A private letter has every advantage, advantages a published one lacks. Power: in possession. Control: in choosing who gets access. Elusiveness: the letter is a ghost. The target hears snippets, conflicting versions, is never sure to have heard it all, to have seen the whole shape of the plot. Fighting it, Núñez feels himself flailing about, sees the hapless spectacle of ridicule he makes. But all the advantages are as dust: it's the *liabilities* that count. The letter in private circulation is a rumour—published, it is evidence. And here the target is the Chief Censor of the Holy Inquisition! Publication plays right into his hands.

We have made him a gift of his revenge, and made taking it his duty.

But Santa Cruz has never been stupid. He knows the game better than anyone. He taught it to me. This is not a blunder. Is this to be some sort of lesson in the finer points of obedience? Then there has been some misunderstanding, I have given him no *cause*. He talks of gratitude—but how have I been ungrateful? *And if as your letter claims, the more one receives from God the more one owes in return, few creatures find their accounts more in arrears than yours, for few have been bequeathed such talents* . . . He paraphrases Saint Augustine. He mocks me with my own past . . . *Indeed let the rich galleon of your genius sail freely, but on the high seas of the divine perfections* . . . This is my examination by the scholars at the palace! But twenty years ago? I have never spoken to Santa Cruz about this. He was still in Spain—or is this about my Columbus and the *Martyr of the Sacrament?* He mocks me through my works. Mentions the mastery of Saint Joseph to tar another of my plays—or my carols, sung in Santa Cruz's own cathedral this year—then deliberately confuses Joseph with Moses as a pretext for maligning the learning of Egypt. Calls it barbarous, and slyly denigrates my passion for Alexandria. . . . *movements of the stars and heavens* . . . *disorder of the passions* . . . Can this be about my carols on Saint Catherine? Yet if he was unhappy why give me the commission?

No, this is not a lesson, this is a *provocation*. Catherine, Athena—he mocks me through my past, my work, my sex—*our* sex. Sor Philothea. *Athenagoric, worthy of Athena*, she titles it. Such wisdom, such energetic clarity. Such honours to our sex.

But these are just provocations, dear Philothea, these are not so far from threats. *Nor do I subscribe to the vulgar prohibition of those who assail the practice of letters in women . . . Letters that engender arrogance, God does not want in a woman. . . . lead a woman from a state of submission. . . .*

A friend would not do this.

It is night. Pleading illness I have asked to be excused from the prayers of Compline. Everyone knows why. I insist Antonia go.

Publishing the letter, Santa Cruz deliberately exposes me. He publishes it in full. Even where I close stressing once again that this is for his eyes only. In a private letter, such a closing is what it seems to be. Published, it makes me look like an intriguer. The transparency of the pseudonym is now an asset—plainly Santa Cruz was making no effort at subterfuge. Philothea was merely to keep any worldly indignity from fastening upon the princes of the Church.

And so the full weight of their opprobrium attaches . . . to me.

By the time Antonia returns I am in a fury.

Santa Cruz and I have been friends for seventeen years. I simply cannot believe he came that day intending to do this. Then what has happened since? Something in the letter itself. He is obviously angry about the negative *finezas*. He cannot think I meant him—that the greatest *fineza* is receiving no favour at all. Does he think I am asking to be free of his favour, my obligations to him? Free of him? Could he not see that for once I was speaking my heart? Is he so unaccustomed to my sincerity in questions of theology that he could mistake it, think I was playing him for a fool? When I write of those who are 'blind and envious' in my letter—does Santa Cruz not see in the humble Núñez, almost blind, a more likely target than himself? It is incredible. Can Santa Cruz be that dim, that proud, feel that unsure of my sentiments for him?

But then maybe this can yet be undone! A misunderstanding after all?

No. Yes. Quite incredible. No, not believable at all.

Morning. Through the east and south windows a brilliant morning light streams past me and over the floor on either side of the writing desk here in the corner. It is as if I am hiding from it now, this energetic clarity. For almost a full day I have explained nothing, and for the past twelve hours have refused to see the obvious. The obvious is quite terrible.

Our target was never Núñez. The target was Francisco Aguiar y Seijas. Archbishop of New Spain.

I have been answering the wrong questions. Yes, yes, it's clear why the pseudonym, even such a transparent one—but why a woman, why a *nun?* I had thought the irony directed at me. It is not. Archbishop Aguiar will see himself fairly surrounded now by nun theologians, Sor Juana and her followers. An attack of the Amazons, led by Athena herself. And everyone will see that he must see this. And he will know himself mocked for his hatred and his fear of us.

Sor Philothea is a fiction, a figment, a demon. Sor Juana is real. Mine is the only name that is real.

In my own letter so worthy of Athena I name neither Núñez nor Antonio Vieyra, nor even Santa Cruz. It is a letter, requested by a superior, on a certain sermon delivered by a certain predicator. I sign it only because anonymous documents send a dangerous signal to the Inquisition. But Sor Philothea in her preface—to *me*—names not just Vieyra but Vieyra's own teacher, his mentor: Meneses. Just to say my quill is cut finer than even his. Why?

Or might it just possibly be that Menenses is to Vieyra as Vieyra is to the Archbishop.

Philothea, seeing no one named, sees her opportunity: she makes it seem as if my letter strikes at the Archbishop himself. The last vestige of an unstated connection to Father Núñez is quite forgotten. There is only the Archbishop now. How is the reader to think otherwise? I would believe it myself. Then, admonishing me, Philothea sidesteps his wrath.

Sor Philothea is the matador, Sor Juana is the cape.

Seventeen years. Santa Cruz has been a *friend*—to me, my nephew, my family. He gave my mother her *last rites,* took her confession, celebrated her funeral Mass. Have I been such a terrible friend?

This makes no sense. He sounds more and more like Núñez. He writes of the haughty elations of our sex, exhorts me to obedience, to sacrifice my will, to hold my mind captive.

I have done this thing out of obedience, put my mind at his service, done everything he asked. Then he turns on me that old shibboleth of Saint Paul, that a woman should not teach—yet even Saint Bernard admitted women might profit from study. I should really write more theology, Philothea says, even as she admonishes me in the preface to the theology I have just written. My lyrics to Saint Bernard *were a sermon*—and though such a thing is forbidden by the Council of Trent,

Santa Cruz was furious when Núñez forbade the singing of them on those grounds.

I have not answered it: what has happened since then?

I should read occasionally in the book of the Lord Jesus Christ? How cruel, how cruel is my sister Philothea. I should write more on sacred subjects, she chides, when I have written how many religious plays and sacred *loas*—even as I was writing for Santa Cruz a suite on Saint Catherine.

Now I am turning in circles. For even if Santa Cruz's target was always the Archbishop—why *publish?* The question is the same. A private letter directed at the Archbishop has almost every advantage. Unless the Archbishop is so close to madness—does Santa Cruz imagine His Grace might collapse before he takes action against me? Does Santa Cruz even care?

I see the face of my friend. Yet knowing what he has done I do not trust my memory of his face that day.... The eyes shine. A face like an adolescent's but slightly bloated by the intervening years. The boyish smile that stretches the sparse moustache across a row of teeth perfectly formed yet overlarge for the narrow mouth. The thin lips, the impish chin, the muscular jaws, all this might have rendered the face squirrel-like, were it not for the incongruous languor of the Bishop's voice and gestures. No. I would have it be incongruous but it is not. I have seen it many times before—his hand hovering over the confections of our convent, and it always seemed dear and comical, the way he attempts to resist his sweet tooth. Fairly torments himself before giving in. He thinks it is not noticeable. We think our notice is not noticeable....

There is a moment, something from that afternoon ... But am I recalling it or planting it now, in the light of what has happened? The Bishop has just entered, the Viscount rises to greet him. Something comes into the Bishop's face. Even as it strikes me that the Viscount's beauty, for all his youth, is masculine, it crosses my mind that with the stickle of moustache shaved, and with it the little ridgeback of bristles that runs to the chin, Bishop Santa Cruz in a cowl could quite easily pass for one of us. Sor Philothea ...

No, this memory I do not trust at all. But neither am I quite certain that somehow I did not see too much that day, as well as too little, and showed too much of what I saw....

No, no and no. I do not accept this. All this for some *thought* of mine he might have guessed at? Ridiculous. This is just not good enough. Whatever happens next, I want to *know* why a friend has done this to me. And I want to know why *now*. That was *Easter*. It is almost Christmas. Why wait seven months? Easter, Christmas . . .

The Archbishop's cancelled sermon, his trip to Michoacan. It can't be about this.

"Antonia! Get Gutiérrez for me, please. Quickly? If you hurry you can be back by Vespers."

I will not be going down for Vespers either. Let them think I am afraid. Let them think I am scheming. Let them think what they will.

Why *now*?

If Gutiérrez had not been an officer of the Inquisition the turnkeeper would have challenged him, arriving after Vespers unannounced. Antonia shows him into the locutory. She lights a lamp over on his side of the grate and hurries down the corridor, through the porter's gate and back in, fusses with the lamp on ours. . . .

One does not expect cheer from a visit by an Inquisitor but in the three years I have known him, this is often exactly what I have been given. A funny gnomish face, the sparse little beard, as though the entire scraggle were attached to his lower lip. I have liked him from the first, having from the first an intimation of our secret bond. He has precisely as great a vocation to be an Inquisitor as I to be a nun. He has his ideas on faith and Faith and how to serve them, but that he should find himself in his present profession still seems wildly improbable to him.

He has come quickly. Everyone has seen the letter by now. A sheen glistens on his freckled forehead. With just two lamps lit I am reminded of Núñez's visits.

Has Gutiérrez heard anything?

"His Grace is 'home' in Michoacan. He hadn't made a formal announcement but the topic of the sermon he was to have given was no great secret either."

"You're not telling me, Gutiérrez. Is it bad—is it as I thought?"

"Another sermon by Antonio Vieyra, yes. He must have decided to deliver this one himself, Núñez's having gone over so well."

"He had no idea what Núñez did at the college rectory after. . . ."

"I think we can suppose not. But His Grace of course has many . . . distractions."

"Is he really so unstable? Could Santa Cruz believe this might unhinge him?"

"Who is to say it hasn't? They might be able to tell us in Michoacan tonight."

"Can you find out?"

"We'll know soon enough, I suspect. But yes, I might find something out. This letter, Sor Juana. Very neatly done. It was also an enormous risk."

"You do understand, this was to be about Núñez. It is Philothea's letter that makes it seem otherwise."

"Yes, now that you have pointed it out. Publishing it is incomprehensible, as you say. In fact, I can see him finding the phantom letter, as you put it, even more maddening. But Antonio Vieyra . . . His Grace has been nothing if not loyal."

"If one were to exempt everyone in Europe the Archbishop imagines he knows, one could not discuss anyone *but* phantoms. And you do see that not having heard about Núñez will have skewed his perception from the outset—"

"Clearly, clearly. And His Grace has been nothing if not a bit embarrassing. To hear him trading on his contacts—"

"He seems never to have grasped the basic point that one already expects an archbishop to have them. Like someone who cannot stop auditioning—"

"For the job he already has, yes. But I hardly think Vieyra qualifies as one of His Grace's many phantoms."

"How so?"

The watery blue eyes blink owlishly. He seems almost to be about to tell a joke, then frowns, lightly clears his throat. "Juana. I assume you have your own copy of Vieyra's sermons." I do. He asks to see them. Summoning the patience to indulge him his bit of theatre, I turn to send Antonia up, and find her already at the doorway. . . .

She comes back with a single volume. Gutiérrez asks if I don't have both. I explain that as far as I know the Portuguese edition collects the complete sermons in a single volume. My heart is sinking. There is something unpleasantly familiar in this turn of conversation.

"I'm sorry. I was referring to the Spanish editions. Could you have her bring them down?"

"I don't have them."

He thinks about this for a moment. "But surely you've seen them."

"Any reader of Castilian should really make the effort and read Vieyra in the Portuguese." *As I was saying to someone else a few months ago.* "What is it, Gutiérrez?"

His eyes are of a childlike roundness. "I'll let you see for yourself." He gets up to go. "I'm sorry to drag this out but there are a few things I want to look into before it gets too late. I'll be back first thing tomorrow."

Antonia sleeps downstairs tonight. She has been quiet since Gutiérrez's visit, as have I. After clearing away the dishes of a light *cena*, she stokes the fire and goes downstairs. Though it is dark, I find myself as often as not looking out one window or other. One to the south, from the library, another east from the bedroom, two looking east from the *sala*. I am awake when the chimes call us to Matins. It is not fully light. When Antonia does not meet me at the bottom of the stairs I go into her room, thinking she has slept through but she has gone on ahead.

In the past I have not spent much time dwelling on Archbishop Aguiar. There are unseen prospects and faces that it is as well not to contemplate too often, lest they begin to set themselves like hooks in the imagination. As has happened, apparently, in the mind of the Archbishop himself.

But now the stories of his near madness run endlessly through my mind. His famous bed of vermin . . . the bedding he has not allowed to be changed since his installation at his palace. His fear of poisoning. His refusal to eat food cooked by a woman's hand or to eat the meat of any female animal. His furious hatred of a woman's traces—our bodies, our perfumes, our voices, our singing. His loathing for cats. There was the time he had the flagstones of his palace replaced on the rumour a woman had walked across them while he was away at the Cathedral. The story of how his mother gave him up as an infant to be raised by the Church at the death of his father. The countless, laughable pretexts to boast of the antiquity of his family. And, of course, there is his vast acquaintance.

But now it seems I am the one who may have let her mind be overrun with fictions. It seems he has become *my* phantom, and with this letter I am now made his. A figment, a demon, and yet unlike the others, this demon is real, has a name, has a place, has taken a woman's voice and form. And now this Sor Juana incites others to follow her example, such as Sor Philothea.

But this is idle brooding. I have a more active brooding to do. These past few years the Archbishop has acted as if I did not exist, for reasons not unlike mine no doubt: for the horrible aspect the fact of my existence presents. God, O God, after the insult of this letter, after the discovery of this intrigue of an attack on Vieyra, and on top of this, the mockery these direct toward him . . . he will loathe and detest and abominate my very name.

The night has not been a pleasant one. Gutiérrez returns, but not first thing. It is mid-morning, windy. The sky is white, the light carries tints of faintest orange.

"Fires," shrugs Gutiérrez. "An infestation of some kind in the crops. *Mira.* Nothing yet about the Archbishop's state of mind. I do know Núñez has left for Zacatecas and will not be back before the new year. The Spanish editions," he says, handing them through the grille. "The '76 and the '78. See for yourself."

"Yes?"

"The first page," he says, watching me intently.

The first page. 1676 . . .

"Go on, now the other."

1678 . . . Both Spanish editions of the sermons of Antonio Vieyra . . . *'are dedicated by the author with respect and affection to don Francisco de Aguiar y Seijas* . . . Then, Bishop of Michoacan, now His Illustrious Grace the Lord Archbishop of New Spain.

Gutiérrez and I sit in silence for a while. I hold the books, closed, on my lap.

The connection is real. But it is not a connection it is a *friendship,* and the friendship is deep. Once one contemplates the thing seriously, they do not altogether lack for things in common. The younger Jesuit who seeks a bishopric in New Spain writes to the greatest Jesuit in the New World. Now the one is Jesuit Inspector General for Brazil, the other Archbishop of Mexico. Both hated by the local authorities, though for very different reasons. But because a man is widely disliked it does not mean he has no friends. It may even be that His Grace is loved. By one man, a great man. Of an age to be his father. . . .

"I am informed," says Gutiérrez, "that they have been close correspondents for almost twenty years." He scratches the red tuft under his chin but for once the effect is not comical. "His Grace's secretary is in deep shock, and will be spending the Christmas season in Michoacan condoling with the Archbishop. Sor Juana, I cannot for the life of me tell you why, but the how is clear enough. Bishop Santa Cruz saw you did not know."

"The whole afternoon remains gallingly unclear but I do remember we had a nice long digression. What did I think of the Spanish translation? I said one should really read him in the Portuguese. And then he used almost your exact words. 'But the Spanish editions, you *have* seen them.'"

"To make absolutely certain."

"And then he tested me. To see if I'd correct him, if I knew of their correspondence. Santa Cruz let it slip that the Archbishop had never so much as met Vieyra. It must have been then. The haziness could really, I think, make me scream. He claimed he had just learned of it. . . . He had it on unimpeachable authority," I add, my face beginning to flush. It sounds like an excuse.

"It might even be true," Gutiérrez says graciously.

"I'm sure it is."

"I reread it last night. My copy." He shakes his head. "Unpublished it could have been so effective. But this, this is about something else entirely. I've been thinking about it all night. I'm at a loss. I'll keep checking around. But I don't want to stay too long."

"It was good of you to come. Don't make that face. Truly, I'm in your debt."

Gutiérrez gets up to go, checks himself, turns back. His freckled hands come to rest on the back of the chair.

"Just a thought . . . This business of haziness, vagueness. It would be better if you did not talk about this too much."

"What do you mean?"

"You're familiar with the guidelines for assessing mystical visions. Well, the principle is the same. The main criterion of distinction between a God-gifted vision and an intervention by the Enemy is exactly this. Clarity. Heaven forbid, but you may eventually be called to give testimony about this day. No shadows, no diabolical vagueness, only clear recollections. . . . Whatever you say, say it with your usual clarity."

I shouldn't keep him but suddenly do not want to see him leave.

"Gutiérrez . . . which sermon was the Archbishop to give?"

"*Heraclitus Defended*," he says, a smile swimming into the watery blue of his eyes. "The printers at Santo Domingo have a thousand copies they are not so sure they will be paid for. I can get you as many as you like. The price, I'm sure will be reasonable."

Philothea's letter is neither a mistake nor a misunderstanding, neither lesson nor pique. These are not just provocations and threats, this is a betrayal—not even in the heat of anger but deliberate, premeditated for years, or months, or at least weeks. If the Archbishop's connection to Vieyra is a deep and abiding friendship, then without question Núñez would have known. And even he, even acting under Jesuit orders, would not have exposed himself and his career to Archbishop Aguiar's rage without seeking assurances. The rebuttal of a Jesuit by a Jesuit, a gesture made moreover in a Jesuit college rectory, marked the boundaries of their support for Vieyra and for the Archbishop himself. Of what Santa Cruz had led me to see, that much had been true. But the gesture sent *two* signals. The audience for the first one being the Holy Office itself and the Dominicans within it—but the second embedded within the first had a separate audience. The message was personal, from Antonio Núñez to Santa Cruz. Far more than offering his services as he had in the past, Núñez was indicating his readiness to switch allegiances from the present Archbishop to his clear successor—perhaps even to work, as Aguiar's confessor, to hasten the man's collapse. Responding to the signal or to the risk taken in sending it, Santa Cruz had come to Mexico to hear Núñez's proposition.

Arduous and pleasing holocaust for slaughter on the altars of Religion. This may as well be from Núñez's latest circular. Philothea speaks like Núñez far too often for it to be hazard. There can be no more escaping it. She is speaking *for* him, from him, of him. The Apostle Paul on women's learning . . . Augustine on gifts and responsibility, the whipping of Saint Jerome—beauty, obedience, the *galleon* . . .

It has happened. The thing I have worked so many years to prevent. Núñez has won Santa Cruz over. As Philothea has in so many ways been telling me. And if it happens to be true that Vieyra and the Archbishop have never met, Núñez will have known of this too. Santa Cruz's unimpeachable authority in my locutory that day was Núñez himself.

Núñez and Santa Cruz have found a common enemy.

I will be clear, I must. Núñez and Santa Cruz. I should be flattered they have laid down arms, lain down together, the ox and the dog. The beast has two heads now. I will stop being such a fool. I will stop asking and asking why.

Why?

Why ask me for theology—why are sacred verses no longer enough? Why praise sacred verses, *if* they are not enough? . . . *not so harsh a censor as to condemn verses . . . a skill Saint Teresa and Saint Gregory of Nazianzus have sanctified. . . .* As examples of skill in verse, why use these? Why Teresa— whose skill as a poet was secondary—and not John of the Cross whose mastery was sublime? And if it is because she is a woman why mention Nazianzus at all? A vulgar poetaster, a dog in the manger who gave the order to burn . . .

It cannot be. All of this cannot be about the *Letras a Safo*—just because I did not leap at the chance to have Santa Cruz read my lyrics? For this, I was ungrateful?—and all this is just a bout of pique? But his face showed none of this. I see him getting up to leave that day. . . . He asks if I do not have something for him to read during the long carriage ride back to Puebla. "Something other than our Father Núñez's *Shriven Communicant.*" I offer to send Antonia for the Vieyra sermons in Portuguese. He smiles, asking if he might not read instead some of these lyrics for Sappho he has been hearing about. Antonia pales, as I remember Carlos had earlier with the Viscount. I say the verses are not quite ready yet to be read. He accepts readily enough, saying something about the perfectionism of poets, and that he looks forward to reading the transcription of my negative *finezas* very soon.

He didn't even try. Who could be that petty? No. Not even Santa Cruz could be so vain. He had what he came for, the promise of my written arguments. Or was it that he resented having to hear of her lyrics from someone else? Someone more vulgar, someone who does censor verse, who does speak of them to everyone. Someone like Núñez. . . . Are *Las letras a Safo* Núñez's price? His prize. No. No. It can't be this.

The night is cold. Tired of pacing from window to window to desk to bed, I move into the sitting room. Antonia comes out of the library, where one has more room for pacing, and lights a fire in the hearth. She goes out and leaves me to my thoughts.

Gutiérrez is right. The haziness is not amusing, and 'dreamlike' is not comical. It is dangerous, for many reasons.

This is certainly a betrayal, but there is something else here, something more. I can't help thinking the preface that introduces it is only secondarily about my letter, or how Santa Cruz feels about it, or me, or even about telling the Inquisition why he publishes a tract so dubious.

No, here too is a gesture. To show the world what he has done, and tell me what he may yet do.

In one stroke Sor Philothea publishes the nun who bests both the Archbishop's idol and Núñez, his captain. Pronouncing herself a follower of this nun, Philothea shows His Grace how his horror of Woman is become an object of general merriment even as Philothea slays the dragon herself. In binding all this up in the skullduggery after the sermon, Philothea flushes Núñez from cover, who has been working at cross-purposes behind the scenes. In this she drives a wedge between Núñez and the Archbishop, or rather burns Núñez's bridges and his ships, for in now speaking for Núñez she signals to all a switch in his allegiances without having to name the beneficiary. Any criticisms Philothea makes of the traits that the nun displays in her letters—want of humility, excess of worldliness, ingratitude, insubordination—apply equally to Núñez's conduct towards the Archbishop. Indeed should that final apoplectic crisis come now, let it be on the heads of Núñez and the nun.

The next move is of course mine. Which the Holy Office, now called publicly to attention, will be watching. Philothea does not even fear to raise the head of Cerberus.

One move. The breathtaking beauty of it. All question of causes and effects aside—and speaking only of the beauty of the game, for beauty's sake—how often can even a consummate player, even one such as Santa Cruz, expect to be offered such a move?

When?

But can I not let this go? Surely it doesn't matter now, to know when my friend of seventeen years decided to do this. Or whether he came from Puebla to Mexico with at least some of this in mind. Perhaps he had sensed his opening in Núñez's latest overtures, a chance to humble me and capture Núñez in one move. Or maybe it was only in my locutory that he began to contemplate the possibilities. Coming to collect my letter and Núñez's manuscript as one does minor pieces; then Núñez's proposition, a slightly more important piece. Discovering next that a fiction planted by Santa Cruz himself had taken root in my mind: that I was unaware that the Archbishop's friendship with Vieyra was neither pretence nor another delusion. Sensing, in this, the most tempting hint of an ironic symmetry: my scorn of Núñez's manuscript dedication to a knowing bishop, my ignorance of Vieyra's to the Archbishop, a man he'd never met.

And now Santa Cruz has Núñez, too. It seems to be what Núñez wanted. Well then, they have each other. But Santa Cruz's fury over Saint Bernard would not have been feigned—he was afraid Núñez and I, in our resumption of hostilities, would spoil things before it was time and rearrange the pieces on the board. What ecstasies of anticipation Santa Cruz must have suffered!

Now I have at least an answer. All the answer I will likely ever have. And it is a mercy to see something clearly, if even just this one instant, during our chess lesson that day, something suggested to him by the game itself. . . . This is the moment. The most spectacular gambit of all.

Bishop Santa Cruz has sacrificed his queen.

The gambit he himself taught me, an extension of our lessons, brought now into the world for all to see. We are not to take this as a betrayal but as a sacrifice. It is one thing to do it on a board. How many can execute it in the flesh?

I see the hour. The late afternoon light angles through the window bars, strikes a painting on the north wall, filters through the boughs and leaves of the rosewood grille. Tomasina and Ana moving back and forth, refilling bowls of chocolate, replacing half-empty trays of sweets and fruit. The light falling across the board, the chess pieces clustered in one corner. Black has just retired, its king mated. I have never beaten him. Santa Cruz is being gracious, but clearly had I been a more experienced player he would not have mistaken my queen sacrifice for inattention.

"I thought your mind was elsewhere," he said simply. "But . . . humility is a most democratic virtue, whose benefits apply equally to all. The mortification in my defeat I take as a favour."

It is the sort of thing I expect him to say with irony. But his dark eyes are liquid and full. Neither anger nor hurt, not mortification. Almost . . . gratitude. But for what? Of course—I have released him from the scrupling of his conscience, whatever that might be. But no, it is not that. His boyishness has never been more manifest than in that instant. He is leaning back . . . crumbs of sugary crust lie in the purple folds of his cassock, sugar crystals in his small moustache. I had never thought of him as anything but relaxed, but all the tensions in his face I see now are gone.

In his eyes, all the affection and goodness of a child after the most severe punishment, and yet deserved. A guilt not purged but absolved.

And then the moment passes without my quite seeing it. Seizing

upon this idea of defeat as a favour, to ease his embarrassment at being
beaten by a novice, I launch into my own earnest effusions on the negative expressions of God's love, the withholding of his favours, which we
shall surely abuse and for which we show the foulest ingratitude. And
permitting Santa Cruz to glimpse it—just the possibility of answering
my insufficient gratitude for his many favours with a salutary correction,
a negative *fineza* so sublime . . .

Is it possible that the affair turns on the fortunes of a moment? A
stroke of hazard: the conjunction of a game and a chance remark. Is it
possible that one without the other might not have been enough?

Six months later the opening presents itself. The Archbishop lets it
quietly be known that he will follow the Maundy Thursday with a
Vieyra sermon of his own. In this, Santa Cruz must indeed have seen the
hand of Providence, a blessing, a sign of *favour* for his strategy, the negative *fineza* of his sacrifice. For the great players, there are days when one
plays with such a brilliance. It is as if the game is guided by another
hand. . . .

Then the game is up. It was just a game: the consummate player lives to
play his queen again. For I am more in need of his favours than ever. Now
he will teach me a deeper gratitude. Favours I will not take so lightly.
Favours I shall crave desperately. My very life is in his hands. My teacher
teaching me still the ways of the game.

A lifetime of shoring up defences. A bishop blocks a priest, a vice-queen
holds an archbishop in check. Then she leaves, the bishop wants promotion, it all collapses. No one expects an accounting, no one demands to
hear your excuses. Just a game you lose, then disappear.

But it is not a situation that lacks for humour. One has only to work
at it a bit. One may of course win a battle and lose the war. I find myself
entering a new stage, exploring a more extreme hypothesis. That I, Juana
Inés de la Cruz, Sor, can win every battle and still lose everything.

For the game is not up at all. And he is a fool if he thinks he can control the Holy Office. He only thinks he knows where this may lead, and
my redeemer may soon have to look to himself. No one controls them
once they begin. It is why even kings do everything they can to give
them no reason to start. Even the Sun King. Insubordination to popes
is one thing, but Bishop Bossuet keeps him from offending against the
Sacred Canons.

On Friday, the first leaflet appears. It is the Feast Day of the Immaculate Conception, the eighth of December, 1690. Yes, Gutiérrez, let us be clear. The moment is chosen to heighten the outrage. The leaflet rants, the leaflet raves. It is signed 'the Soldier.' Not long after, a second leaflet by the Soldier. It refers to a certain nun's *Sapphic Hymns.* Núñez. The phrase was first his, a deliberate distortion of the title, but he has been speaking against them for years. These things take on a life of their own. Their life now is blasphemy.

The leaflet inveighs against the only verse I recall having published that refers, alludes to or in any way hints of Sappho. *Sáfico,* I shall tell them, is a dactyl.

Elación, arrogance in a woman, disobedience, ingratitude.

Now the hay cart starts to run downhill. Next come the sermons of attack. My friends scrambling to plan a defence. Better, I say, to give no answer at all. Let it lie, let it rest. So far there have just been threats. By the Feast of the Epiphany, the furore may have died down; the people will have had Christmas. It is the people the Holy Office will not see troubled. But I fear there is no stopping it.

It is the work of convents to pray for the well-being of the community that supports us. For the surrounding neighbourhoods, to take their sin and suffering upon ourselves. But now Mother Andrea calls for special prayers to be said for the convent of San Jerónimo itself, for deliverance from the threat that hangs over us, the shadow that has fallen across our good name. My fellow sisters file past the door of my cell with looks askance. They seem to find me somewhat unlucky these days. But what do they *want* from me?—to waste my life gossiping mindlessly at the convent grate? Is this so becoming of a nun? The whole convent savours seeing me stumble—*ah maybe her life is not charmed, after all, her intelligence not quite divine. Seems like she was over-reaching . . . perhaps she would have seen this coming if she'd lifted her head out of her books for once. So it took the Bishop of Puebla to put her in her place. At last! She wouldn't dare defy him now. She needs his protection more than ever. . . .*

I've done everything they ask! Entertain the Viceroy?—I do it weakly, meekly, weekly. *She's too worldly.* I remain in seclusion. *She's too good for us, standoffish, selfish*—I hold classes, direct plays, direct the convent's finances —*she's trying to take over. Just like the Spaniards—she prefers them, you know. Like Malinche did, Cortés's whore*—so I write Mexica *tocotines,* reams of popular verses in dialect. Now I'm pandering to the rabble. *Her mother's half-Indian they say.*

Yes, write verses, says Philothea. But write on theology. And here is a taste of how it is for women theologians, how it is when the Muse takes up the quill. Can Santa Cruz not see what Núñez has known all along?—if I take up theology they'll have me a heretic by the end of the week.

Theology was the last thing Núñez wanted. It is why he burned my journals fifteen years ago. It is how I finally escaped his command that I write for him. If Santa Cruz speaks for Núñez now, how can he ask this of me? How can they even want the same thing? What is it? *What do they want from me?*

They implicate me in order to attack each other. They reconcile in order to see me punished.

Without a doubt the Archbishop wants me destroyed. The Holy Office is now at least curious, and Santa Cruz cannot be sure he can stop it. Núñez, on the other hand, has given me fair warning. He said I would destroy myself. Is this is what they want?—to see me destroy myself?

How? What would permit them to orchestrate it? What little manoeuvres and adjustments? Something I will write, something rash, ill-conceived? Something I'm writing now. Is the Saint Catherine commission a trap? Or is it something I have already written? What would hurt the most, humiliate best, give the most satisfaction, what would be their most negative finesse? Something I might refuse to give up, too intimate, too painful to let them paw over. And in refusing to hand it over, to repudiate it—and in the writing itself—all will see how the arrogant nun has brought this upon herself.

To prove their correction is just, what might I be asked to surrender? . . . as the ships of the alliance fill the horizon. An armada of men schooled in the affairs of the world, who send a message, who bring a lesson. To teach us our abecedario, to bring us our primers. Egypt taught us our first letters, but Athens is our first school. Lesson number one. No one stands apart. There is no neutral ground. Lesson number two. Give way to the greater force, that takes itself for a force of nature—the volcano, the quake, the flood. Lesson number three. Loyalty and justice are only questions among equals. The rest must choose. Slavery and criminal cowardice on the left. Or annihilation on the right.

Left. Or right. Decide. But we are children who know not our left from our right. Where is Athena, wise Athena now? Does she hover still over Athens, as the Dove broods upon the abyss? They come to set the dice upon us, and the dogs. Whom shall I call to defend us? Perhaps Antonio Vieyra, who saw the needs of others as no impediment to his pursuit of greatness. . . . Is this the irony they want me to see at the end?

EXTRACT FROM SISTER PHILOTHEA OF THE CROSS (II)

Trusting to this analysis, I do not intend that you curb your genius by renouncing books; only that you elevate it by reading from time to time in the book of Jesus Christ. . . .

Was there ever a more learned people than Egypt's? With them began the first letters of the world and the marvels of their hieroglyphs. Such was the wisdom of Joseph that the Holy Scriptures call him a past master of Egyptian learning. Nonetheless, the Holy Ghost plainly states the Egyptian people are barbarians: for at best their learning penetrated to the movements of the stars and heavens, but did nothing to rein in the disorder of the passions. Their science aimed to perfect Man's political life without enlightening his journey toward the eternal. . . .

Study not ultimately consecrated to the Crucified Christ and Redeemer is wicked folly, sheer vanity. Human letters are mere slaves that may occasionally be used to serve the Divine. . . .

Angels scourged Saint Jerome for reading Cicero and for having preferred, as if a bondslave and not someone free, the seductiveness of eloquence to the solidity of Holy Scripture; yet this Saintly Doctor of the Church did at last come to make exemplary use of secular learning and letters. . . .

What a pity that so great a mind as yours has stooped to a base acquaintance with the world without desiring to know what goes on in Heaven; but sullying itself on the earth, let it not descend yet further, to discover what goes on in Hell. And, if that mind should ever crave for sweet and tender demonstrations of love, let it direct its apprehension to the hill of Calvary, where, observing the *finezas* of the Redeemer and the ungratefulness of the redeemed, your intellect should find a limitless scope to examine the excesses of infinite love and to derive, not without tears, fine formulas of atonement at the very summits of ingratitude. Or, at other times, indeed let the rich galleon of your genius sail freely, but on the high seas of the divine perfections. I do not doubt that it would go with you as it did with Apelles who found, while painting the portrait of Campaspe, that for every brushstroke he applied to the canvas, love sent an arrow into his heart, thus leaving, in the end, a portrait painted to perfection and a painter's heart mortally wounded with the love of his subject. . . .

I am quite certain that if, with your great powers of understanding, you formed and depicted a concept of the divine perfections (to the limits permitted within the shadows of faith), you would find your soul illustrated with such brilliance, your will in an embrace of fire, your heart sweetly wounded by the love of its God, so that this Lord, who in the sphere of nature has so abundantly showered you with positive favours, does not feel obliged to rain purely negative ones down upon you in the supernatural. . . .

This is desired for my lady by one who, since kissing her hand so many years ago, lives still enamoured of her soul, a love which neither time nor distance has any power to cool, for a spiritual love admits not of change, nor grows save in purity. . . .

From the Convent of the Holy Trinity of Puebla de los Angeles, on this the 25th day of November, 1690.

Your devoted servant kisses your hands.

Philothea de la Cruz

DUMPING
DONALD

❧

[31 Aug. 1993]
ROW ACROSS THE MOUNTAIN LAKE, tubby Pocahontas in the lead,
Hiawatha steering. Just like golden olden times happy times with
Gavin, brother dear. Soaring sky's stillness mountains' pendant mass—
pure abstracted fact. Unapologetic. Mute. Ice and granite's crystal
union—white a brilliant blinding smooth. Monolithic skirts a scaly
cuprous green. Iron neckline plummeting unmoved / in still collision
with a lake of doctored blue.

Glacial like his eyes.

Far shore a goat trail spun through spare tenacious pines, one thin
scar fierce along the rockface sheer and pale. This way he says, Hiawatha
lord of nature takes the lead, a wheezy Pocahontas trailing. A thousand
feet above the lake a crow's nest chiselled from palest stone. Lichen's cool
flickering across a stony screen.

Log railing, picnic table clefted in the rock. DO NOT LEAN
AGAINST RAILING—Parks Canada. Safe intercourse with shaggy
nature shake a paw, roll over. Play dead. In the fabled distance another
golf course.

How'd you know about this place, Beulah?

How Hiawatha? Family camping trips—me Gavin Mummy Jonas,
the immigrant way familial bliss.

Lean against the railing cinematic vertigo . . . Disneyed drop a thousand feet. Feel the loft and draw of empty space. Far below . . . sandpaper
riverbanks emery riverbeds . . . the coiling pause and glint of polished
jade. A lone hawk drifting with the stream . . . Confluent tongues of jade
and turquoise. The lilt of stone . . .

Why bring me here, Donald? asks Pocahontas. Hiawatha's answer
mock surprise his eyes reflecting bright a turquoise mask of ancient blue.
But you brought me here first Beulah, didn't you?

Why today.

It's your birthday 'case you'd forgotten. Donald what if someone from
the conference—No it doesn't start for four more days. But if someone
comes up early? Who's gonna see us way up here? Such a joker such a
comic, Why aren't you worried they'll see? I know why I'll tell you
why—you've brought me here to end it. What on earth would make

you think—*why didn't you tell me she was pregnant Donald* when were you going to get around to that? It's been months—HOW LONG were you going to keep lying to me? How long have I been waiting to hear one *word* of truth from you?

Ah the tricky joker's pause mid-flight / crestfallen peacock, turquoise eyes bedimmed.

How did you—What the fuck do you care how? You didn't tell me she was so beautiful, Donald—Beulah *you're* beautiful—STOP LIAR get *back,* You didn't tell me you'd started fucking her again. Liar do you / did you ever stop? Why go to so much trouble Don? Why not end it with a phone call leave a message—letting me down easy is that it—one last time a blaze of mountain glory a savage little sympathy fuck for me to cling to? Is all this getting too messy for you too unscholarly Doctor Gregory?—cutting your losses—so what's plan B?

Far down the valley storms sift the hills   a pall of incense ash.

You're so fucking pathetic—she's beautiful and you're in love with me. And you don't even *know* it WHAT'S THE MATTER WITH YOU—

Truth or dare Donald. Beulah get down from there! Truth or dare fact or fiction I can make it easy for you Donald easy as falling off a log. One small step for manKind—one giant step for Woman. Come Hiawatha, come on up. I can make you a poet, right here.

All right Beulah that's enough get down come on.

To earn your muse you've got to suffer a little isn't that right Doctor Gregory isn't that what you want from me—gonna myth me Donald, isn't that it, just a little abyss? Why so pale bright eyes? The falling never kills but O the sudden stopping!—now, just a bit more railing from the railing and I can hand you back your complicated conscience. Guilty little clockworks all wound up. Just look at you now. You protestant boys find guilt such WILD MEAT. Beulah please come down!—you want to own a muse Donald? earn her! she's a high maintenance high altitude date Show her some guilt doctor—and if she wants you to really see her she's got to disappear. She can change your life right here—priest to shaman—small-town-boy-made-good to wolfman in one easy step— Oh Grey Owl, you should see your eyes right now.

Don't *move* Donald careful one step more you join the human race— you know? just one second not to wonder if a feeling's real before the trap howls shut again. Please Beulah don't *please,* you're just a—Just a what a baby *girl?* Don't waste—Waste what Hiawatha, or you mean don't make a mess. Things too white trashy for little Donny?—don't blame me, blame your mummy she's the one not me the homewrecker, blame her dissect HER for the little sister you've never seen—the oil-town trailer courts / the terrycloth beertables—your daddy's boozy breath forlorn. Through dry-well oilman lips not one apology ever crossed never truly kissed—blame them not me, white trash nomad boy made good—Then turn your back on everything one more time, on them on me make us all pay. See everyone? not one grease spot on his phony pedigree / hide behind your Ph.D.—O doctor of philanthropy—

Now. One more little backturn for you, one more little two-step for me—PLEASE Beulah don't *do* this. What Donald—resurrect your cock crowing thrice rejected humanity? LOOK! look around you look at this white Eden.[39] All this can be yours the whole frozen panorama— come up come out little hermit crab hiding in another's shell, look down at the shore WAY DOWN stick your neck out—that's it set your eye stalks aswivel—stand on this precipice peel back your carapace—all this bliss I offer all this I can do for you Donald.

Easy as falling off a log. Watch me—

As Beulah's version of that day may demonstrate, I've never been especially brave. Particularly when it comes to heights, a faintness of heart that, inevitably, became in my late teens a source of humiliation. Oil was the family trade: grandfathers on both sides, my father, one uncle. Not magnates but derrick men, wresting a living in the cruellest extremes of weather from bloodthirsty machinery a hundred feet in the air. The success of a man's working career could be gauged not by fame or publication but by the number of fingers he retired with. An unforgiving trade demanding a physical courage and tough- ness I lack, though I do like to think I've inherited some of the family discipline.

So I found it just a little troubling—and, yes, intoxicating—on that narrow mountain ledge to discover I would have been willing to climb onto an unsteady railing a thousand feet above a rocky lakeshore. For someone else.

I think I might have, had there been time. But there wasn't, and Beulah knew that. For several moments she held me, helpless, cap- tive, able to hear but barely speak, making me listen in a way I'd never

listened before, with wonder and terror and—why not admit it—awe.
She didn't jump of course. I say this not to suggest she was incapable
of it. Just then, she was capable of anything—and for an instant, with
the mountains as our witness, I believe we both were. No, I say 'of
course' because her story would probably have died there with her.
This, she was not yet ready for. I had absolutely no idea what was
going on behind those beautiful eyes. But if I had, would I have submitted then to following her into the maze of her journals? I doubt it.
I just don't know. And even though she knew me better than I knew
her— in some ways better than I knew myself—she couldn't have
been certain either. Not yet. What she showed me up there on that
ledge was the part of me that *could* be made to follow. I still had no
idea what else that part of me might be capable of.

On the night I retrieved—a year and a half later—the box of
papers Beulah set out for me to find on her desk, I would begin asking
myself, *what did she want from me.* I'd always supposed it was my help
she was after. But that morning on the ledge it was clear she was after
a little more.

As she worked and wrote, to what extent was she aware of baiting
me—writing scenes, planning chapters, anticipating and manipulating
my reactions? Deliberately leaving gaps or taking positions I'd feel
driven to react to—toying with me. Did it amuse her to picture me
plodding through material I was so ill-prepared to deal with, on so
many levels?—to cast me as the villain in jack boots. Rule-maker,
violator, appropriator. Charges, she had to know, I will never be
allowed to answer—given the times we live in, and a domain totally
lacking in due process. Except here in these pages, before the Universal
Court of Ideas.

But why do this? Was she just looking for a spectator—just setting
the scene for this staggeringly baroque passion play? Or maybe she
saw me as the one to be sacrificed, while she—and the local news
audience—sits eating and drinking behind a flowery screen, settling in
to watch the spectacle I'm now making, the contemptible monster hiding from the cameras' righteous glare—retreating to Cochrane,
England, Mexico, anywhere. All, of course, for my own good. So righteous these young girls, to rescue us. Because we are living a lie. And
the lie is not theirs.

But that day in Banff it was still too soon to guess at any of this.

Now she can't answer. Beulah went back to Calgary. And a day later, shaken in ways I worked at not thinking about, so did I. I skipped the conference I'd worked for weeks to help organize, and back at home felt like a child feigning illness, Madeleine hovering over me. Maybe I should have felt a little more than that.

On that ledge was one of the last times I would ever see her. Though I did continue to receive the odd report of a sighting. And, after the initial shock, a few days of disorientation, a few weeks of sexual withdrawal, I came to suppose it might really be over. And finally to think it was for the best.

After all, I was a few short days from becoming a father. A shot at redemption. My chance to start over.

DEAREST SAPPHO,

In this stone cell trapped in your myth's incandescent calculus—unable to deflect its path much longer I peer into the gathering firestorm bunching and billowing black before me like a veil of obsidian.

Before I too am brought to complete the circle of betrayal, one last time together, sweet daughter of Lesbos.

I who will soon betray you first found your verses' last remnants clinging to the forms of the Egyptian dead. Lines steeped in myrrh . . . the incensed body, embalmed, embarking calmly at last for its eternity's far shores. Seven hundred lines—torn pages greyed to wasp paper, whisper against the cured flesh inaudibly . . . with such delicacy. Seven hundred verses are all that survive. Listen to them carefully, listen longingly, hear them lovingly.

Once they simply called you the Poetess. Everyone knew. As him they called the Poet. Two millennia—though torn from their shoots the flowers you coaxed into bloom wear yet their scents, keep their hues. Out from dim Chaos, out from the inchoate roaring of the undifferentiated throng, one voice, one lyric, rings clearly—

And it is the voice of a woman.

I who will betray you this night, and have already begun by beginning this, try one last song of restitution for what is lost, for a sole incomparable echo whispering down through the last passionate ear's frail spirals.

While a girl, as you lay on that sea-girt isle, bright Lesbos, did you ever dream yourself stalked by a beast of flame? There, see it tracking you to Alexandria's great library, burning . . . and thence to Rome, from Rome to Constantinople, now leaping, now low and unsteady, ravaging you. Your sins were multiple, inflammatory. You the spirit unaccountable, first and final fusion of flame and desert sand—figure of clear liquid glass!

Poet of rapture, architect of ecstasy, love's empiricist.

You were the mistress of flowers, nectared hyacinth at your belly. You mocked war, and the warmakers, you circumnavigated the world, undefended by navies, making beauty its circumference, putting love at its centre.

How you sang for bright Eros! As the Wonder Worker of Nazianzus crouched in the haven of Herod—in aromatic smoke masked, the fires hot on his face—did the song he cast upon the fire burn for him brightly?

> Percussion, salt and honey,
> A quivering in the thighs;
> He shakes me all over again,
> Eros who cannot be thrown,
> Who stalks on all fours
> Like a beast.

Sifting the ashes of your songs, I have found, unconsumed, a verse for all the Gregorys ...

> When dead you will lie forever forgotten
> For you have no claim to the Pierian roses.
> Dim here, you will move more dimly in Hell,
> Flitting among the undistinguished dead ...

And even as I sift, hands blackened, slandered in cinders, I try not to think. I sort through the ghostly gray ash like a mendicant. I try not to think of a world all but devoured by flame.

Yet even in my despair I find other fragments, too bright for even mortal fire to extinguish ...

> down from the blue sky
> came Eros
> shedding his clothes
> his shirt of Phoenician red [ ]

Surviving still, verses in slender strips all the shades of the firebird's shimmering plumage.

> [ ] robes the colour of peaches [ ]
> purple coats and silver jars
> And things made of ivory.

All yellow gold and like a daughter [   ]
Just when dawn in her golden sandals [   ]

five red oxen [   ]
the rose red moon [   ]
they wore red yarn to bind their hair.

Leave your siege of her violet softness [   ]
Violet breasted daughter of Kronos [   ]

Remember what has been, the rose-and-violet crowns
I wove into your hair when we stood so close
    together heart against heart

To temper the red desire
That burned my heart.

The black earth's finest sight [   ]

Black dreams of such virulence [   ]

Out of the ashes I pluck the remnants of flowers and the firebird's
aromatic herbs—charred vegetation, incense and balsam—

Peach-flower crowns, crowns of flowers
    and dill [   ]

Roses, tangled parsley, and the honey-headed
    clover [   ]

A coronet of celery

A leaf melody plays among mellow apple trees [   ]

[   ] fields thick and rich with flowers [   ]

[   ] see the lotus under heavy dew on the banks of
    the Acheron [   ]

The mountain hyacinth trod underfoot by shepherds,
its flower purple on the ground [   ]

Once upon a time, the story goes, Leda found
a hyacinthine egg [   ]

Out from the still glowing embers I tease abstractions like taffy, spin
them out fine like threads of glass . . .

whittled perplexities . . . round truth . . . misery the size of terror
. . . peace become havoc . . . my longing hovers on wings around your
loveliness . . . that island-born holiness of Kypros

How at its height the bonfire—sap pockets exploding—must have
incandesced with your adjectives!

. . . quick with astonishment . . . arrogant of heart

tall in our certainty
famous in every ear
young beyond Acheron

Now lost, after so much labour and death . . . Asleep against the
breasts of a friend . . . Half asleep with love . . .

deep in the cushions on that softest bed
where, free in desire

. . . voluptuous . . . softer than a fine dress . . . more melodious than
the harp . . . more harmonious than lyres . . . bold as friends before
each other . . . our knees weaker than water . . .

Flaring hotter still, that lyric conflagration stoked on food and drink
and spices and vessels—

. . . to every god his ambrosia . . . bowls of cassia, cups of olibanum
and myrrh . . . magic liquors . . . poured from a leather bottle . . .

Pour nectar in the golden cups . . . golden goblets with knucklebone
stems . . . mix it deftly with dancing and mortal wine . . .
And around your graceful neck, the oils of spices . . .

For unspeakable losses then, make restitution, O destitute flame,
retrace now in ashes the scorched path of conquest, of hecatomb and
holocaust. Charred geographies from Lesbos to Heliopolis—

That famous place
with its strange towns . . .

and from Sardis . . . Mytilena . . . embroidered, Persian . . . crying
Asia!
A sacred grove . . . a ford at the river . . .

Not just in its geographies lies the world bereft: hangs blistered the
very air. Once there existed—

steep air . . . charmed air . . .

The wind is glad
and sweet in its moving . . .
the wind a crystal crash in the apples . . .

. . . the west wind blows upon me . . . sliding across the air on wings
spread wide . . .
High winds . . . storm wind . . . heavy weather . . . gales . . .

And make restitution for the birds that flew there—by Sappho made
rare—by fire made dust . . .

sparrows reined and bitted,
a quick blur aquiver . . .

With quickened heart they hovered
fluttered, and lit with folding wings
the doves . . .

Swallow, swallow
Pandion's daughter
of wind and sky
why me, why me?

In the fire's blackened track, anatomies of love stunted and twisted,
fire-hardened sentiment where once there existed—

Graces with wrists like the wild rose . . .

wild hearts . . . wandering hearts . . . hilarious hearts . . . tethered
hearts . . .

a fury that rages in the breast . . .
for a lost desire that shakes the mind
as wind in the mountain forests
roars through trees

. . . the bittersweet . . . disgrace, rising . . .

. . . love . . . strong / grievous / sharp . . . bounden

Make restitution, O self-righteous arson, for the human tongue,
blasted, for the *eyes, scarred and blinded,* for the *ears that roar in their
labyrinths,* for the minds parched and blunted.
Once there were similes *bold as friends, haughtier than horses.* Once *sleep
sifted down like dust* and *night poured over eyelids like liquor.*
Now against the lids' blind scrim only the shadows of questions
smoulder on.

. . . the fetching way she walks—*who was she?*—and I yearn / and I
hunt—*for whom and for what?*—I loved you, Atthis, and long ago—*was
she worthy?*—I talked; she talked / and all in a dream—*what was that? what
were you saying?*—if only they had woven me such luck—*what then would
you have wished for dear Sappho?*—downward my tears—*what has moved
you?*—I gave you a white goat—*was its coat thick and soft?*—gaze with candour—*what love now shines in your face?*—I am willing . . .

I am willing but what have they left us?—seven hundred lines.

Restitution is a fable, a complacent vindication—more and less and other than what was lost. The traitor's sop, the liar's seal, its violent impress in a wax of silence—another vain translation. So what then is left after the onslaught, what is left to us? The thin consolations of farewells. Ritual.

Farewell to the fire-split wonders of the human hand's artifice.

carved toys incredibly strange

and things made of ivory ...

keen flutes, and tight drums ... crowns of leaves ... golden houses ... a bright abstruse chair ... holy altars ... mules hitched to high-wheeled carts

Farewell to the humanity, into the infernal, cast unscripted—

the dusty messenger, winded runner silver with sweat ... dancing grandmothers who shout the marriage song ... bachelors who lead the chariot horses and charioteers like gods who sing commands ...

To the gods themselves made vivid in your lambent eyes

Hera, strange in a dream
ghost or visitation but in a shape all grace ...

Andromeda, Zeus, the dark lord Aida ...

Hermes who enters my dreams ...

Apollo of the harp, archer of archers ...

Eros, child of Gea and Ouranos, taking off his clothes ...

Aphrodita crowned with golden leaves ...
the gods' stunning daughter breathless Aphrodita

At last, to the girls, lit by the torch you carried—

. . . a black-eyed girl from Theba . . . a girl in a country frock . . . a girl picking a flower just opened . . . a wild girl with charm . . . a bride with beautiful feet . . . a shy little girl . . .

she who comes in flowers . . . my lazy girl, on this soft cushion . . . with your blouse off, in your soft arms . . . to the girls of Lesbos . . . chaste and holy daughters, daughters of God, Priam's daughters . . . my constant girls . . . the pure and chaste . . .

This beauty of girls . . .

What are songs of restitution next to this? What have I accomplished? I've only betrayed the beauty of a girl. Inspiration's hacked limbs reassembled falter, it is just the life that lacks, that matters. You were never to be another's Muse. In these lines I have only made Athena foolish, made Aphrodite love like a judge, like the Sun.

Sweet daughter of Lesbos, small islands must know the times. And it is time, though Time is not quite why. The work is false.

Wisdom does not love. Love is not wise. This breach, this split, I cannot repair it. There are too many now for the sacrifices. Mercies are small, and not enough to go around.

But I, who hold the corners of these pages now to a single candle's flame, do not put it out when its work is done. Let it flicker on, and tomorrow night another, and each night when the Sun is gone, let there burn a smaller, mortal light, beyond repair but not recall. Let the ash remain that is falling now. That I might not easily forget, the fire that once trembled in your eyes and in your lines.

Phoenix BOOK FOUR

The sun is calling me . . .

CODEX
CHIMALPOPOCA

In Cnossus did Daedalus build a dancing floor for fair-haired Ariadne.

ILIAD

CONTENTS

CONTENTS

IN THAT TIME, before the march of days had begun, at that time, before Quetzalcoatl had brought the calendar to men, there in the thirteenth level of heaven did Ometeotl, the Lord and Lady of Duality, lie. Inseparable and indivisible, embracing.

And Lord/Lady Two[1] *was* the heart of heaven.

Beneath the Place of Duality in all directions stretched a lightless ocean, flat and empty, flatness and emptiness in each direction stretching, without light and without air, where no thing moved or trembled or flowered or sang.

Came a time when the heart of heaven embracing grew warm. From the thirteenth to the eleventh level, the first to descend was Itzpapalotl, ObsidianKnifeButterfly, mother of the flint blade of sacrifice from which all the things of this world are descended, even the sun. Then into the ninth level of heaven spilled forth both the dark and the precious twin, already twining and coiling, joined at the ankle.

Then were they dragons—hurricane and blackness, Wind and Night. Then were they dragons, darkness and night sun. Through time without beginning over the blank face of the world they roiled and tumbled until Itzpapalotl feared that one or the other would be killed.

And so it was, so it happened, that Tezcatlipoca lost the foot shared with its dragon-twin Quetzalcoatl.[2] Forced to choose, Itzpapalotl favoured the twin more precious—in favour of the precious twin she severed, and the dark twin was freed of the laws that had bound the two. There where its foot should have been, there at the flowering stump sliced clean by the mother of the blade, sprouted the smoking mirror of prophecy.

In that time and at that time and in that lightless sea, SmokingMirror and FeatherSerpent found EarthToad floating, still and wondrous and terrible—at every joint eyes, and jaws slavering blood.

Then were they dragons filling the sky. Even as EarthToad thrashed and roared and trembled the celestial twins came together to raise her up and, twining about her middle, rent and rifted her with a great tearing. Wide, from the sea to the seventh level of heaven they split her, and from

THEN WERE
THEY
DRAGONS

her created the world. From her upper half they formed the sky, from her lower the earth. From her hair the trees and grass and flowers. From her tear-filled eyes the springs and fountains. From her hideous drooling mouth the great rivers. From her shoulders and hips the mountains.

Pouring forth from her body came all the fruits of man. And her blood soaked the earth.

But though they had created the world from her and for her, still did she weep unconsoled. Her cries for blood filled the night, and everywhere was night.

Then did she bring the sky crashing back down upon the earth, crushing all that lay newly made upon it, unleashing the celestial waters to flood the land again.

Again were they dragons, boring four roads to the centre of the earth demon's body, Tezcatlipoca entering her through the mouth, Quetzalcoatl through the hole in her belly; and where they met at the crossroads, where they met at her heart, again did they split her, did they wrench her apart.

To prop up the sky, to protect the earth beneath it, then were FeatherSerpent and SmokingMirror mighty trees, extremely tall, extremely high, very tall and high—Green Willow and the Tree of Mirrors, the pillars of heaven.

FeatherSerpent and SmokingMirror were playful, and they played to the death.

Four times on the sacred ball court on a smoking mountain on the ninth level of the underworld did the twins struggle to create the sun. Four times was it created, four times destroyed.

Came the sun 4 Tiger, the sun of night and earth, weak and pale in the sky. Tezcatlipoca invaded its body and ruled over it for thirteen bundles of time, until FeatherSerpent came to cast SmokingMirror out and into the gleaming night sea.

In that time were all the giants of the earth consumed by jaguars, and the sun and all beneath it destroyed.

Time itself had an end.

Came the sun 4 Wind. For thirteen bundles of time above the sacred ball court rode the sun like a child on the back of the feathered dragon, until SmokingMirror attacked. Then was the sun destroyed, then were the children of the earth swept away by a great hurricane. Not one survived.

Time itself ended, and the night returned.

Came the sun 4 Rain. And during that time in the swamps and filthy hollows of the earth lived the people, until a terrible rain of fire came from the sky to destroy them. Only the birds survived. Then did time have an end.

And darkness fell.

One last time over the sacred ball court did the dragon twins play together to the death. One last time did they drive the sun through the underworld's narrow portal.

For they were great in adultery.

Came the sun 4 Water. But a great flood swept the people of the earth aside, and those few who survived became frogs. Only the frogs survived, until time itself ended in darkness.

No longer were they dragons, coiling entwined across the night sky. No more did the dragon twins come together over the sacred ball court.

Came the time of the sun 4 Movement, the fifth sun, the last. But though FeatherSerpent called out to her in all the voices of the wind, still SmokingMirror did not come. Some say out of bitter envy or anger, some out of shame or fear. But who can say why? From the beginning no law bound her, not even fate, not even time.

Yet even without her must the fifth sun be born. For it must be the last.

Then did FeatherSerpent summon his kinsmen to gather about him in the city of the gods.[3] First came Ehecatl, the wind, with his shell trumpet, his wind jewels. Then the Lord of the Dawning resplendent. Then came the lesser kinsmen, also with their attendants. Then slowly, with the greatest reluctance, came Xolotl limping in the body of a small dog, reddish and lamed. And behind Xolotl came Nanautzin, the scabby one, covered with reeking sores, horrible to look upon.

Together did they come to stand at the heart of the city beneath the malevolent, blinking, four hundred stars. All around them in the night could they feel her presence, near and far. All around them to the four directions did Quetzalcoatl one last time call, but still she would not come.

And so they asked themselves how they should light the world and warm it.

Against the night they lit a great fire and stoked it with whatever they had brought.

And everything the Lord of the Dawning offered was precious; always the most precious were his offerings. When the scabby one offered maguey thorns anointed with his blood, the Lord of the Dawning offered thorns of red coral. Instead of pellets of hay, he offered pellets of gold; to the flame he offered good copal, not the scabs of stinking sores.

And so when they had burned all they had brought and nothing remained but themselves, rightly did they honour the Lord of the Dawning, rightly did they offer him the honour of lighting the world. Four times did they offer, and the fourth time he accepted.

High as a mountain did the holy fire burn, and it threw a trail of embers across the night sky. Approaching, the Lord of the Dawning felt the heat. Great was the heat and he faltered. Again did he turn to face the fire. Again did he prepare to cast himself into it. And again with the terrible heat of the fire in his face did he turn away. Four times did he try and four times did his courage fail him.

So at last, when the scabby one stepped forward, no one laughed, no one contested the honour. For all were greatly afraid.

Drawing near, closing his eyes against the brightness and heat Nanautzin rushed forward and with a great leap cast himself into the flame. Then did he burn, a great burning. And his skin burned and crackled and hissed like green willow wood, and the sounds of his burning filled the night.

For four days did the sun burn red beneath the horizon. For four days did the blood of the sun stain the sky, and still the heart of the day could not rise from the body of night. Seeing this, understanding this, yet lacking still the courage of Nanautzin, they chose Ehecatl quickly to sacrifice them.

One after another the chests of his kinsmen and their attendants did Ehecatl open, and the sky was filled with blood.

Came a time when only Xolotl remained, yet his heart was not resolute. Swollen with tears were his eyes. He wailed. He clung to life, to the life of his body. He fled into the East, into the eastern swamps and there hid himself in the body of a salamander. And there did Ehecatl find him and seize him. As Ehecatl at last plucked the precious fruit from the chest of Xolotl, as he lifted the still beating heart to the sky, so did the fifth sun at last break free of the body of night; but weakly did it rise, to hang low over the eastern horizon. Lacking the strength to rise higher the sun wobbled and shook, blood red in the sky. It wavered and swayed but could not rise.

Then out of the East came a great wind roaring, the voice of Ehecatl himself roaring, offering up his breath. For four days raged the hurricane, four days across the face of the sun. And only as the winds grew quiet, as Ehecatl lay spent and quiet as death, only then did the sun 4 Movement rise in the sky, splendid and pure.

And so the sun rose, flanked by the souls of his kinsmen. Then did the sun's rays light the world, shooting like darts into every cave and crevice and hollow. Like an eagle the sun rises shining! fed on the eagle's precious fruit! Hungry in the morning is the ascending eagle. Thirsty is the sun at noon, just before battle is joined. Know that only fed on the precious fruit whose meat is life, whose sap is blood, will the sun 4 Movement gain the strength to break free each day from the body of night.[4]

Know this.

Yet know also a time will come when even the eagle fruit will not suffice, when four hundred times four hundred hearts no longer suffice, when the fickle one grows weary of this game as she did all the others, when SmokingMirror snatches the fifth sun from the sky.

At that time, in the time of 4 Movement, a great calamity is to come out of the East, when the heart of the earth is wracked by a great quaking, when the jade and turquoise palaces come crashing back to earth, when the smoking mountain bursts into flame, when the noon sky grows black and the four hundred eyes of night prey upon the land, when the march of the days falters, when the vessel of the earth lies shattered.

In the time of 4 Movement the shattered earth will die into timeless night, into night without end. No other time will there be.

In the time, in the year 4 Movement.

Ascendent Raptor—speak,

victor yet vanquished by my constancy,

what has your arrogance won

from its siege against my steadfast peace?

For though your lance's barb

be sharp to pierce

the hardest heart,

what point has the most violent cast—if,

finding its mark,

sweet reason clings yet to the target?

   You hold great sway, Lord,

but though your dominion

obtains against our inclination,

it masters not our liberty.

And thus to this I trust as my ransom

from the madness of your audacity:

for while my freedom

is held captive, under siege,

my discretion might be yielded,

but never my consent.

   My soul is cleft

confusedly in twain.

Half—a thrall to passion,

the other—reason's slave.

Civil war, inflamed, importunate

afflicts this breast:

each strives to overwhelm his counterpart;

but amidst such mutinous counterstorms,

both helmsmen must perish,

neither, return to port.

   From the field, Love,

never once did I win the palm of your favour,

but now, with you lodged within,

denying you the trophy of my soul calls for all my valour.

So then let that very resistance

drive out Love's heartless garrison!

—for when you, Tyrant,

invade the soul, without constraint,

you take as spoil the castle,

yet lose your hold over its chatelaine.

   Invincible reason now has wrought

rebel arms to oppose your vicious rages;

even as the breast cedes scant terrain

for so bloody a conflagration.

And so, Love, you launch in vain

your insane onslaught:

since it will be said—to see me fall

yet not surrender—

that you managed to kill

but failed to conquer.

JUANA INÉS
DE LA CRUZ

"In defence of
reason, prey to
Love"

B. Limosneros, trans.

CRAFT FAIR

IT WAS JANUARY 1, 1993; time to hang the new calendar. It seemed we had forgotten to have kids. But Madeleine wasn't laughing. Children. Seriously. I might have known. She was a child psychologist. Childless, she was like the horticultural consultant with a brown thumb.

And I did know . . . right from the beginning. I had been stalling her for almost ten years. To the ticking of clocks I couldn't hear. She would soon be thirty-four. Madeleine and I fought rarely, and with all the attendant awkwardness. Not for us the rebarbative tonics of invective and mutual recrimination; never the Latin meltdown nor the Gauls' blighting derision. Ours was the careful and reasoned recitation not of the wrongs themselves, but of our *experience* of grievance. Not 'you hurt me' but 'I felt hurt when . . .' Textbook co-therapy.

We sorted it out like adults. *She intended to get pregnant—end of story.* Perhaps it was already too late? I ventured. (Not a successful counter.) *Birth control, if there was to be any, was now my responsibility.* The cost of raising a child would be hers. *Fine—she'd already missed her period.*

Game. Set. Match.

As her belly swelled I found various ways to console myself. There was a wading pool in the park on the way home from work and soon I would be spending quality time there among the young mothers and the about-to-drop, wading through the tenor riot of children out of school. . . . In the grassy shade of poplars, young women with infants slung on a hip, new mothers, melon-breasted, giving rapturous suck . . . adrift, becalmed in their animal selves, sated, paunched . . . bodies broken in the most primitive ways. My daydreams came as a sort of benediction. But I digress.

There was also the indulgence of the black Saab ragtop I'd been wanting. I started stopping in at dealerships. I took the odd test drive.

And Beulah.

Often it began with a call left on my office answering machine. Never at the house. By mid-March she had stopped coming to class, at least to mine. This wasn't high school; there were no gold stars for attendance. Neither was there cause for alarm. Based on the coursework already done she would at least pass. And if she deigned to take the finals, her Honours status would not be in jeopardy. After the last few rounds of cuts, virtually every department in the humanities or pure sciences was starved for top-drawer grad students. I'd already talked to Comparative Literature. She'd be accepted on reputation alone.

With the school year ended, her call caught me killing time at the office, filing papers, running over my plans for the summer. May 7, 1993. It was still four months from that day near Banff when she took me to the edge.

Did I have plans for tomorrow? I'll admit to being pleased she remembered my birthday. A day which Madeleine had chosen to spend away, visiting a colleague in San Francisco.

I remember that birthday for a number of reasons. As perhaps the first day I neglected to tell Beulah about the pregnancy, for one.

Saturday, May 8. Beulah's diaries contain no entry for this date— odd, given the religious discipline of her diary maintenance. The trouble with coil-bound notebooks is that one can't always tell if pages have been torn out. In hindsight I'm convinced they must have been, given the day's significance, at least for me. In a perfect world she could tell it herself. I cannot write it for her, tell it as she would, and if I do write it, I do not do it for myself. No. Here, at this intersection of our shared story and my tardive reading of her brief life's work, it first began to dawn on me: the enormous, shaming, vertical chasm that yawned between her experience of life and my own. While I was making thinly clever cuts at art and fashion, she was processing the 'tottery pottery' before us so much more deeply. . . . No, let me say this plainly. Of a day I had made shit, she had somehow made art. I saw this when I came to her chapters on craft, saw their origin and knew I had been there too . . . at a craft fair.

An act of penance, then, as sincere this time as it is small. How would she want to see me tell it? How does the defendant answer to the charges?

He pulls up in front of her apartment, its little ground-floor balcony set back in a shock of untended honeysuckle. He resists the urge to hit the horn. The Saab convertible is a sober testament to European-engineered elegance, stately in its understatement, and this is not a young bachelor's spree.

If she is impressed she does not show it much.

"Very menopausal." She buckles in, looking straight ahead. His sphinx in a bucket seat. Leather overnight bag, quilted cotton jacket. Long-sleeved black T-shirt, black jeans, white sneakers. Her glossy hair is drawn back in a long braid, reddish in the bright sun.

He pulls away briskly from the curb. Madeleine called less than an hour ago from San Francisco to wish him a happy fortieth. When the phone rang he was in the bathroom conducting a critical survey of his hairline. He has taken to cutting the ponytail shorter—more or less regulation length for the Cartel hit man, Hollywood style. But before it thins down to a sort of white-coolie look he may have to crop it off entirely. Madeleine was calling also to tell him she was extending her trip by a few days. By all means, stay. Call it recklessness, call it young love, but now he doesn't really care who sees them. He will make several mistakes this day. His first at being forty. Call it a kind of innocence.

His mood is buoyant, and why not? The plan is to indulge him with a night's debauch in Pincher Creek, and to indulge her with a stop en route at a craft fair. In a town called Okotoks. Over the past few months she has acquired a taste for prairie anthropology—not, mercifully, wagon-wheels and arrowheads, but small-town flea markets, antique shops, country fairs.

They drive with the top down through new-planted fields, past silos like fifties rocket ships, through the sweetish reek of hog farms. Over the blast of air at seventy miles an hour they talk little. This suits them both. He has learned the hard way how quickly these girls can abuse his confidences. Anyway, she has always disdained small talk. From the first days in her first class with him, she kept to the essentials. When eventually she did open up—no more than a handful of times—it came as a shockwave. Passion, probing insights, sharp turns of mind that poured forth in a stunning rush. Here was the author of those amazing papers, all but invisible, inaudible, at other times.

He hasn't seen this version of Beulah for some months now. A shame but, he supposes, unavoidable in the circumstances. Their future is nowhere, their past officially meaningless. The present? Well, the present is much like today, a hunt for scalps and souvenirs.

Okotoks, he seems to remember, is about an hour south. On the freeway in a Swedish sport sedan, the trip turns out to be thirty-five minutes to what is fast becoming a bedroom community of Calgary,

for people driving cars much like his. As he pulls into the parking lot
by the school's gymnasium he sees a real chance of running into someone he knows.

Beulah and he never touch in public, making their intimacies the
more intense when they come. And there's always the age difference.
Scant cover, but in a pinch he will introduce her as a student. It would
have helped had she been less beautiful. But then, on the drive down,
glancing at her profile . . . implacably his eyes seek out the indispensable *flaw*. In this case a slight recessiveness of the chin. Making a little
double-chin a near inevitability in forty years. Or even less. It helps
him to imagine it lightly whiskered. Her nose, in profile, is just prominent enough to mark her ethnicity. Of course it would be wrong, he
chides himself, to ever think of this as a flaw. Rather it is just the sort
of flaw to put a face on the cover of a fashion magazine.

With Beulah, the pleasure has now palled somewhat, certainly, but it
is still more intense at its best, at its worst, than anything in memory.
The truth is, it never occurs to him to end things that day. But that
she might think otherwise is a natural mistake: he does have something on his mind, something awkward to tell her. Awkward, yes, but
it also never occurs to him to keep Madeleine's pregnancy a secret.
Honesty is the bedrock on which all his adulteries are founded.

He turns off the ignition, crisply pulls up the handbrake. He leads
the way up the walk. Welcome to the Okotoks Art Trading Post. On
an upturned washtub in the foyer some poor sodbuster in chaps and
hushpuppies declaims cowboy poetry. In the gym, a savage hunt for
relics. Silver-haired ratepayers in elbow-patched tweeds mingle with
clod-booted landsmen. Tell me again why we're here? he asks. She calls
it a kitsch hunt. On a dais paces a tanned master of ceremonies with a
microphone headset, a selling wrinkle picked up from the shopping
channel. The MC is making protean use of the word *wonderful*. Don't
miss the wonderful artists' panel discussion in Room 101 at noon.
Snacks welcome. Bring your purchases in for signing. Come meet the
artists, be among the elect. They're just like you and me. This is
Renaissance art's logical conclusion: craft superstars. Michelangelos of
needlepoint and duck decoys.

He lets her go on ahead, feels a dark flowering of lust as he watches
her merge into the crowd. He moves off on his own, tends it, this
cruel petulance of pleasure postponed.

Meanwhile he gathers in his own harvest of tribute, registers the flicker of a tall woman's glance that sifts the evidence, deciphers the sex code: white male, six feet, blue eyes, light-brown hair, close-cropped beard, touches of grey. Bare feet in leather sandals, blue T-shirt, cream linen suit. Hit man on holiday, shopping for handicrafts. It is a lot to take in.

Enjoying himself he wades into the pop-art bazaar. Prairie chapels made of Popsicle sticks. Elk fashioned from clothespins, pipe-cleaner antlers. Salt-dough poodles. Brooches and pendants out of something called Fimo. Pot holders, oven mitts, WELCOME mats. From corncobs, a cat's scratching post. And some abomination based on an aboriginal dreamcatcher—a kind of jute-hoop medicine wheel with bits of cut-glass ruby suspended in the centre, satin tassels from the lower rim.

In a perfect world he might have found his mother's pencil landscapes here.

The roving eye is drawn to the intense action at a table of Sante Fe-style silver and turquoise. All are women in their mid-forties, well-kept, hungry-eyed. New-faded jeans and jean shirts, little feet in gleaming cowboy boots.

Farther on, further out, the Lace Lady models her wearable art, a selection of shoes, handbags and hats, aprons and dresses, all garlanded in lace and dried flowers. She wears a velvet choker trimmed with lace, tiny dried roses at that whitest of throats. Elbow-length gloves and granny boots festooned with flowers and lace, scented with potpourri. A flesh and blood altar to Prairie Victorian.

Some time later he glimpses Beulah on the far side of the gym and wends his way towards her to the strains of whale song and pan pipes. She stands before a display of what appear to be crystals—a big egg sac, ruptured to reveal amethysts in their raw and perfect potency. He follows her at a little distance and off to one side, keeping a screen of shoppers between them. A few tables farther along she stops beside a sandwich board bearing the Spanish word for *snail shell* or *conch*, but these are unlike any shell he has seen. Through the crowd he draws a little nearer, steps gingerly to avoid having his sandalled feet crushed by pointy boots. Perplexed she picks a shell up and cradles it in her palm, flinches slightly as the aged vendor reaches for her wrist; the old man hesitates then raises one to his ear, shakes the thing gently. To show her. With an expression of something like fascination she holds a cupped hand to her ear.

He can see the objects clearly now: ovoid, walnut-sized, earth-coloured. They might be some kind of mineral accretion or a seed pod, but are more likely fired and lightly glazed clay. As she lifts her eyes finally to meet his, the old man blinks. Quickly she replaces the thing and moves on.

He catches up to her between the soapstone walruses and a rack of Indian braves in copper intaglio.

"Let's get some air."

"A few minutes."

"How about I buy everything from here to the exit," he says, "and we sort through it later."

"It's your birthday, not mine."

"How about Hiawatha here? Maybe the guy's got a Pocahontas, too. Let's ask." He turns towards the metal smith without taking his eyes from her face. "Sir?"

"Don't." A flash of anger as she turns away.

"Not that way—the cafeteria, out there."

He needs to eat, he knows this edge, of a hypoglycaemic cruelty. They go out the gym fire-door to the tent pavilion: Cowboy Cafeteria, three self-serve food counters on cut-down chuckwagons. In the ceaseless prairie wind the white canvas awnings sag and bulge. In them he sees the burst bellows of a piper's cheeks—and where *is* the piper? The Tourettic hoppery of a Celtic revival is all this event lacks.

They take a table. Across the aisle teen punks drink Diet Pepsis while their parents shop. A reminder, if he still needs one, of how near the city this is. Two girls about sixteen. One tonsured, the other's mohawk teased into violet and lime spikes. Across from him, one thigh scissored over the other, elbows on the table, Beulah twists to look out over the prairie. Away from the burgers and chili dogs, the Tom Thumb donuts, the nachos and the cheese-flavoured vinyls, away from the bearded epicure who gnaws at a cinnamon roll. In a sawdust mumble the sage starts to share with her the oceanic depths of his fashion intuitions: Such an astonishing assortment of piercings, he observes, crummily. We are perhaps to interpret all this as a resurgence of the Dionysian. Notice the Swiss precision of the tiny silver barbells through each nostril; the outermost rim of the punk's ear pierced at short intervals for a brace of overlapping rings. The tandem disks of farm machinery, or a blade array—for a surgical appliance, wouldn't she agree? Notice the metal standards—like so many prospector's flags planted at each tip and prominence—brow, lip, tongue. The body's final reclamation for the machine age. Slowly we are become recyclable. The more delicate the formation the better: septum, nipples, navel, glans, labia. "*Chic* kebabs," he lisps and looks at her keenly—surely this she cannot fail to appreciate . . .

They've shared this savage jocularity a dozen times in the past. Or rather he's shared it with her, in the manner of two world-weary business rivals met in some street, chatting, at the intersection of his abstract humanism, her theoretical misanthropy. . . . He exclaims over the inquisitorial joining of metal and parted flesh. He thinks he knows how to bait her, but perhaps he has been too complacent.

From the corner of her eye she is studying him not quite clinically.

Still no answer? Still she would have him play both their parts. It is a relief to oblige. This is the safest kind of talk left. With a nod towards the suburban pincushions in black leathers he asks: "Did you ever, I mean were you ever tempted to—" He was going to say, *to pierce something.*

"You do that a lot," she says.

"What?"

"That." She nods. "Rubbing your hands. The silent movie villain."

It was an old tic Madeleine had helped him break. He finds this oddly embarrassing, he finds this faintly annoying.

"No—of course, you'd never draw attention, you want to be invisible." He has no idea what he is talking about, yet he is not so far mistaken. She wants to be invisible, to everyone else. And in all the essentials, she is, to him. One word too many, one careless comment and everyone will see. Except him.

"You didn't answer."

"But you just ask away, Donald."

"On my birthday."

"Fuck your birthday."

"You called *me*. If you don't think you can get through this . . ."

She tilts her plastic cup, pokes at her lime wedge with a straw. "So. Back to town? Your call."

She looks into his face, then away. She has folded her straw into a tiny white accordion. "Not yet."

His voice softens. "Help me out a little, will ya?"

She thinks about this. "Try again."

"You never want to talk about school. . . . *You* pick, then."

"*Pick?*" She looks up at him in disbelief.

He looks out into the schoolyard, except for the trampled grasses indistinguishable from the prairie just beyond the fence.

"Why only Mexico? Why not myths from here?"

"We're finished with all this, Professor. Remember?"

"That crack about Hiawatha—"

"Pocahontas forgives all."

"Local Cree figures like Berdache and Wiokachuch fit the research you've shown me. So why not, Beulah? The Aztecs, you use *them*."

Her lips twist into a wincing smile. "Who hasn't?" Two fingertips of her left hand slip to a small sore at the corner of her mouth.

He leans back in his chair, ankles crossed under the table, hands resting comfortably in his pockets. She looks away again, fixes her eyes on the farm machinery. She asks him if they can go now.

"Better Beulah, do better."

"So guide me, O Grey Owl."

"Can you answer me or not?"

She hesitates, still not looking at him, shakes her head slightly, as though in answer to an unspoken question of her own. Begins. At the time he understands only a fraction of what he hears. . . . We all start with certain global rights, to the fruits of the tree, she seems to be saying. But some forfeit their rights to some of the fruit, for what they have done. Locally. And those rights must be earned back, if at all, with heart and blood.

"Listen, Beulah. This may all sound very biblical to you, but somebody out there—and this, I can guarantee—will hear Wagner, a whole New-Age fascist Ur-symphony. Racial memory, folk kitsch, sentimentalizing the past—it's irrational, it's dangerous, and it never goes away. Like plutonium."

"Two. Three. Eight."

She says this in a voice so low he can barely hear. And in that murmur there is a tightness he does not hear at all. But he has her attention now, her fullest attention. And she has his. For an instant he stares into the green eyes across the table. Large, intent, a thread of gold around pupils contracted to a point. Flecks of jasper and rust . . .

Geology. So many of his father's lessons he will apply today. But right now he must work hard to interpret what she is saying, this striking oracle of his. She takes the lime from the glass. There is no juice left to squeeze out, though she twists. He notices the little nicks and scrapes, some half-healed . . . second knuckle of each index finger. He concentrates. No not Plutonium, Don, a teeny tiny bacterium, a benevolent microbe, our symbiant friend—like intestinal flora. Is it all just going too fast Professor?—call it a metaphor. Call what?—myths, Doctor, myths. Without them we are not nourished we are not fed. They are a bacterium, a global super-organism.[5] *Clostridium dificile*— our difficult cloistering, a cluster that darkly blooms in us, like lymphoma. Tiny muscular corpuscular they swim in our blood, they squat in our guts, they help us digest. Too much and they eat *us*, too little and they starve us to death.

"Yes I see." Someday he will come to think of this as the day he saw too little, remembers too well.

"Then they become our disease and we become—"

"I have my answer, Beulah."

These eyes so bright, this stunning intensity, this face a mask of twisted smile. Does she have any idea how it looks, this mask of herself? He sits straight now, his back not quite touching the chair. What an amazing creature, *what a waste*. He has offered his help but she has rejected it over and over. He steels himself not to lean back, away, not to flinch.

For once, she is not the first to worry about what others will see. Has she forgotten where they are?

"How's our chat so far Donald? How's it for you—did I pick right?"

When the cup snaps in her hands, spilling ice over the table, he feels something rising up in him.

"*Enough.*"

Three tables away a pair of brown eyes meets his and he knows that this one knows him. He does not remember her but she knows exactly what's happening.

"You wanted to go, let's go. Get up."

And he too knows what is happening. He knows that after too

many years of this, each one gets a little crazier, and he knows the
pattern is in him, not them. He is on his feet. He feels his own rage
rising to answer hers—he is not her father and on this day of days *I
am not as afraid of a scene as you think.*

Something has reminded him of his childhood, long rides, empty
highways, a small town off by itself. "Come on. Get up. We'll be like
two strangers on a bus." He knows he is the one not making sense
now, and it feels very good. It is the best feeling of all. "Telling everything, if that's what you want. Spilling their guts . . ."

And for the first time, though she has always guessed it was there,
she is seeing it in his face. Sincerity. . . . At last. It is something real.
"Where, Donald?" She is ready to go with him.

Get her in the car is all he can think. Get her in the car and tell
her. Doesn't matter where. He savours the look that will come into
her face.

She stands, her eyes searching his. "How much time do we have?"

They are in the car. They are on the highway. She is quiet now. But
instead of seeing in this a confirmation that this has all been to provoke him, he is perplexed, he is troubled. His chest is still lightly heaving, his face still flushed. He understands he is afraid of her, for the
violence he knows she can bring out of him.

The air is cool. He tries to give himself over to the spell of the land.
They are heading south, flanked by deep green fields. Puffs of cloud
scud east, and under them the straight road ahead seems to warp to
the west.

Later, droplets on the windshield. One, then another striking his
face. He fumbles for the wiper switch, he is still unfamiliar with the
car. She is shuddering with the cold, the wind. He has not noticed
this.

He pulls sharply over to the shoulder, a scrabble of gravel. When
the convertible top is latched they sit, rain pattering on the canvas,
cars rocketing past. Tell her. Now and then a tractor trailer, the heavy
blast and tug. The car rocks faintly in its wake. He knows the moment
is now. Tell her. But she is the first to speak. Something about this
angers him.

"Like you said." She waits. "Strangers on a bus." He does not answer.
He has decided to make her suffer. Let him be judged by his acts.

He pulls back onto the highway.

"Have I ever asked for . . . anything?" Her voice is quiet. Perhaps she thinks he cannot see her fingers twisting in her lap. Perhaps she thinks he would not care.

He shrugs. "We talk."

She looks at him a long time. He drives several more miles.

More, they ask, more, then more than there is to give. He has nothing left. Tell her. "Okay, Beulah. How do we do this?"

"You want games. You want rules."

"I hate games."

He is surprised by his vehemence.

"And they're all you know." She waits, but he will not bite. "One day soon, Donald, maybe somebody will find a game you love."

"Are we doing this or not?" Tell her everything this time.

"Truth or dare."

"Whatever, Beulah. Ask." *Everything you never wanted to hear.*

"First the dare."

"For Christ's sake." It comes to this. Childishness to embarrass him. His position, the difference in their ages.

"Show me how much you mean it, show me you care. *How much.* You want this as much as I do. You should see your face. Truth or dare."

"Christ . . ."

"Okay tell you what, Don—I go first. *Truth* . . . or I go back to school for you. How's that?"

"At this exact moment, Beulah, I could not give a shit what you do."

"Better, Donald. Much. A baseline for our polygraph. Now you."

"It's always something like this. Some crazy shit or other."

"Nothing to dare?—this is sad, old man, sad very sad."

She sits sideways in her seat. "Leave your wife."

"Leave it the hell alone."

"*So protective. So noble.*"

"I've told you before—"

"Fine, protect her. Do. *Truth*—tell her about me."

"Fuck this."

He wants to help her out, she wants to pull him down.

"You're the specialist, Professor Gregory— how come you're so bad at this? Okay something easier, let's see, Truth . . . or you come to Mexico with me. Call it a sabbatical."

He knows she means it. She has risked asking him to come with her. And now she sits, brave child, awaiting the lash of his contempt, shaming him. Fucking childishness.

"Tons of hot springs in Mexico, Don."

She refers to a small water fetish of his. He imagines the two of them locked together in a death struggle in some tropical hotel room . . . this is just about the furthest thing from his fantasy. Tell her.

"You're just begging me to hurt you," he says. Still the fading hope they could just let it drop.

"I don't want *her* life, Donald. I just want into yours. Once."

He takes his eyes from the road to look directly at her. "But that's not all of it."

"I want you to look at yourself."

"You want to save me. Because I'm living a terrible lie." He keeps his eyes on her, as the car hurtles through the rain at ninety miles an hour. She is unconcerned that in the next instant they may die. He reads this clearly in her eyes. This is not a death she fears. He looks back to the road.

Always near the end, these scenes. The tawdry, the plangent, the operatic, the sophomoric—they are relentless, they are legion, these young women. Just once he would like one of them to do this with grace. Stoke contempt to a cold burn, this is his trick. Use it again. The antidote to this thing that clanks and scrapes up inside his skull like an iron grate.

"Something nobody knows about you. Something you've never told a soul. Told . . . her."

It is in the way she says this, something in the reverence she pays his wife. He has an image of the pain about to enter that beautiful young face. *She is just a girl.* But is it pity he feels now or something more familiar, something sickening. They are not good for each other. She is not good for him. She wants him to hurt her.

"Is it over, Donald? Isn't that what you've been waiting to tell me?"

"*No.* But . . ."

"Soon?"

"How can I know a thing like that?"

He is not so angry, now. He knows that in her way she is doing this for him.

"No, Beulah, not yet."

She sees he is very close to telling her. "You ask me what I want. See *me*. Not *this*." Her small, long-fingered hands give a little flick as though sweeping crumbs from her lap. "Just once."

What he says next is not what he meant to say.

"The first time she left my father I was a year old." The edgy little gesture he makes—little toy soldier saluting—to keep her from speaking feels comical, such an urge he gives himself to laugh at times.

"I'm supposed to believe this."

Her voice is small and hollow. She has given up hoping for this. He glances over at her.

He sees how much she wants to believe.

"She ran, for almost ten years. The first time, he found us the same day. At the side of the road."

"And you've never told Madeleine."

"You and I've talked about this, Beulah. About why there's no point to all this *talk*—because it's meaningless. You've said as much yourself. I thought we agreed. You have the present, she gets the future."

"And your past nobody gets."

"The past is irrelevant. And it is endless. It is Raymond Carver country. Believe me, I've lived it and there's nothing left to add but more kitsch and clichés. And one leads to the next and then I would be telling Madeleine as I am telling you now that my mother died in an institution and it would become a refrain for us, for her and me, for me and you. It is endless and it is meaningless. It is not what I am. It can never . . . *define* me." He grates this out. This surprises him, how difficult.

And precisely because they do not have much time left and because it is all meaningless he sings her the whole folk aria, the old ancestral blood song, the white trash anthem. The poached deer and trailer courts, the violence and squalor, the UI fiddles and odometer swindles. The runaways. How his mother would stop at the roadside with the boy and her suitcases and sit down to sketch . . . trees sometimes, mountains mostly. Ordinary pencil, lined notepads. And it was usually there, in a ditch with her sketchbook on her knees, but sometimes in a motel somewhere, that they would find her. Usually with the boy, but a few times she ran on her own. Mostly his father found her. The Mounties, if she got far enough. The last time, she seemed to know they were coming for her, as though this time she herself might have phoned. She had packed him a little bag and fixed herself up. She helped him with his shoes though he was almost nine. She told him his father would be there soon.

But the father was already there, waiting in a hotel bar just down the street. Until the thing was done. See the stone cold eyes over a row of boilermakers and tomato juice.

She slicked down the boy's hair and kissed his forehead. They sat waiting on the bed, side by side. When still no one had come, she got him up to wash his hands in the sink. She seemed to be listening for them to pull up front but they were slow in coming. She kept washing his hands, kept washing them. Until he was crying and scared, until they were raw, until they bled. When the men finally came she almost ran to the door, to open for them. To these men who would find a place for her. And there, it would come as a relief to be who she was and what. And for a few years he took long bus rides to see her there, who she was and what.

He and this girl head south on the highway. So much noisier, he notices, in a convertible, even with the top up. The wipers' weary chug and caw, the rain's spatter on sodden canvas, the tires' slick hiss, a scouring roar through pools here and there collected in the road. Pop songs low on the radio, too low to bother turning off. He switches on the headlights, to feel the glow seep from the dash.

She sits facing him now, knees drawn up under her chin, her back against the door. He wonders if it is locked, wonders if he wants it to be. Though he has not asked, she tells him about her last trip to Mexico. When she was thirteen. Her stepfather taking her there alone. Feeding her obsession for gaining news of a father widely believed dead. The casual mention of a small community from Galicia, resettled now near Mexico City. Old neighbours, one or two childhood friends who would have old stories of him. She knew the price, what the trip would cost her.

She has hinted at this before, and at something with her brother. The only person in her family she speaks of tenderly. Before today he has passed over these veiled mentions, taking them as something fashionable, confessed by girls these days to make them appear embattled, dramatic. He has passed over this because his awakened contempt would have made it so much more difficult to continue with her. He is surprised now to be telling himself that it doesn't really matter, how much of this is true. After what he's just told her and not told her, he can still say this. And at the same time he is scanning a highway sign—luminescent green in the headlights and glittering in the late afternoon rain. Pincher Creek, already. The story is true for her in some way, and like most everything else, untrue in others.

As he takes the road for the Crowsnest Pass she looks back. "Pincher Creek. You wanted to stay the night . . ." He tells her now that he was born here.

In a few minutes they will swing north and angle back and up towards Calgary through the Kananaskis Valley, over a new highway that threads along the empty east slope of the Rockies. Next fuel stop: 144 k. / 90 mi.

When he was a child, this drive was an adventure, a string of doglegs up little secondary roads, the 517 and the 940. Thirty years later, it is a late Saturday afternoon in early May and it feels like an adventure again. So many weekend getaways since then, but this feels . . . the intimacy is of quite another kind, an adventure more danger- ous. This is a fresh topic, interesting to him.

Steady rain, approaching dark. Mountains veiled in cloud, the wet- ted grain, matte density of rock. The greens of trees richer in the mist. The new blacktop engulfs the headlights, casts light back in concen- trated arcs and bursts of gold.

He is only half aware of taking her somewhere she has never been with him. Home. Not hers but his. When they get back to the city it is almost midnight. He shuts the headlights off half a block from home and coasts the remaining distance in the dark. This is the night that made everything possible that should not be.

They stand naked before one another, and for an instant, just the briefest of instants, maybe he does see her. In his wife's bedroom, next to their bed. Queen for a day. Who could it hurt.

 What followed was a night that should never have happened. A night that became two full days behind drawn blinds. This I can't quite for- give. I think she came to feel this also, that there must be a reckoning, for things I should never—she should never have let herself do, to a woman she had never met. For putting on clothing not hers, for touching things. Items in our night table I cannot bring myself to list. Thinking of this now I feel a kind of panic—disbelief, the briefest flicker of voiceless denial, as the precious vessel slips from the child's fingers and shatters at his feet—

I did this.

At some point late on the first night she said as though in answer, though I hadn't said a word, "I believe you, about your mother. A lie, here, would be too ugly."

And in that one line I sensed everything she thought me capable of.

But I had *not* told her everything, so she was not wrong about this. Put yourself for a moment in my place. Perhaps you do not want to. I understand you. Try, just for a moment. The moment when you understand she was right all along, that you have been wanting to end it, that ending it is more important now than ever. Something new and dangerous is happening. You've done things, anything to poison it, but it will not die on its own. End it.

But that moment comes and just as quickly goes, and you tell yourself: Next time, I'll tell her next time.

Next time to tell the truth will be that much harder.

The next few times you see her, you wonder why you are going out of your way to be cruel. *Tell her, yes, but after we've fucked. . . .*

Cruel in ways you've never had to be with the others. You think of it now as your summer of cruelty. But was that cruelty an exaction for what you have told her about yourself, or for what each succeeding failure to break it off teaches you? About yourself, your weakness, your cowardice. *Your* rage, not hers.

Banff, you'll take her up there for her birthday. Revenge for Madeleine's selfish pregnancy is just a pretext now. August, just a few weeks more. Ten or twelve more weeks, of cruelty in between. You'll do it there.

And then in Banff, because it's easier, for you, you let her break it off for you. Just like all the other young women, and not like them at all. You will watch but pretend not to see her sever you like a limb, the authentic pain of a last phantom attachment to the world. Or, her last but one. There's still her brother Gavin.

DIET JOURNAL   Date: *31 Aug. 1994*

> MOOD: low to normal
> WEIGHT: 47.1 kilos
> BREAKFAST: hot lemon water, cayenne, olive oil, 3/4 Kit Kat,
>   5 grapefruit seeds
> LUNCH: tea, 2 1/4 Kit Kat, 1 cinnamon Danish
> SUPPER: 1 sausage roll, 1 cheese Danish, tonic and vinegar, tea, Kit Kat
> SNACK: 3 bran muffins with cream cheese, 1 box of Triscuits, bran cereal,
>   olives, cinnamon toast (4) with brown sugar, sardines, Cheezies,
>   beef jerky
> LAXATIVES: 102, plus 13 at 2 A.M.
> REMARKS: Not too bad a day. Snacked till 1:30 A.M. Laxatives ineffective.
>   Had to get it all back up. Slept. Many dreams. Try again with exercise
>   in A.M.

In the first, the world outside, the surf of the sea, spirals inward: the shell is the house of echoes. In the second, the interior life, the ideas and angelic intelligences, open out into the firmament in glowing and radiant configurations ... Two emblems and a double movement that unfolds or draws back into itself. The echo spirals into the shell until it becomes silence; or, trumpeted forth. . . . it becomes fame and the distortions of fame, gossip and slander. Or it ascends to become a hymn: music is a kind of starry sky that we hear but do not see . . . The reflection rises and reassembles in the mysterious order of the constellations, silent music we see but do not hear.

OCTAVIO PAZ

PALACE
OF THE
INTESTINES

IF I CAN FIND LITTLE TO EXCERPT from Beulah's diaries for most of 1994, there are two reasons. The first: that virtually nothing happens, in the way of events or human contact. The second, and related to the first: that much of what she has written verges on incoherence. Monkeys at typewriters. I take no pleasure in saying this. It is not until she leaves for Mexico toward the end of that year that I can pick up the trail again. And by then, what her Sor Juana had been through had left her also much changed.

Beulah's labyrinth research had given me fresh horizons to explore, but by the time I read in her journals where the work was taking her, it was too late to intervene. It is also true that by then I wouldn't have tried—but as she was writing them in '94 I could have helped, or gotten her help. Maybe the best that can be said was that we had once crossed paths in the corridors, and for the briefest time we might have helped one another.

For more than two years she'd laboured to draw nearer her quarry, to feel what she felt, know what she knew, to think her thoughts. Two years of struggling over an incline so slight as to render any upward progress imperceptible, then, just ahead a sudden vista *like a door opening onto the sea*. In the work of Octavio Paz, Beulah detects an echo, a reflection of a formulation that carries her forward through her own research like a mantra: *swallow the world*. . . .

The following would be, incredibly enough, high ground for Beulah, from which she could look back over her struggles, her furies and frustrations, her sacrifices.

[7 Sept. 1994]
It's HERE—in Paz, everything I've been looking for. *Thank you O Paz!—poetic dialectic: sky = visual hymn; hymn = audible sky.* Juana in her cell—her books instruments collected—she reads and listens . . . inward ear tuned to an audible sky. Echoes incast, winding ever more tightly down to silence. She writes, whispers verses, her eyes scan the outcast sky for hymns. Reads like no one has ever read swallows the boundaries splitting her from a sky of promises . . . writes in ink an echo distillate, turns inside out, lungs ovaries diaphragm, fallopian tuba—the instrument of our fallibility our fall—dispersed, immersed, dissolved a squid in ink projected. Swallow and integrate or be digested. Dissolute. Assimilate. Double-headed dialectic that civilizes as it kills. Dog Head thrown back howling at a sky of mirrors—high hyena whine, o hymnal hyenae—you'll never get enough never know enough never love be loved enough—then Ox Head rips you deep down low / spills coral entrails across a marble floor of echoes. . . .

From time to time I find myself rereading passages such as these. One must after all try to imagine Beulah happy. But as on previous occasions, the happy moment was brief, a sense of triumph even at the turning point of defeat. The ground was never solid beneath her, struggling as she did to each sand dune's crest only to stare out over countless others, over endless ranks of barren breakers, stacked monuments to the wind.

I cannot help seeing Beulah hunched over her notebook, scabbed knuckles whitening around a pencil stub, blinds drawn against the day, the room's strew and scatter of books, junk food wrappers and encrusted plates more squalid in the gloom. . . .

If youth is not wasted on the young, surely ambition is.[6] She had been determined to run every lead to ground, every allusion, every reference, every myth along the way. Yet even if from the outset she'd recognized the objective for what it was—the virtual sum of human knowledge—still this might have been insufficient to discourage her. At any rate, Beulah finds her method of approach bringing her time and again to the brink of an abyss of complexity beyond her human grasp.

In a chapter devoted to *First Dream* Octavio Paz initiates Beulah in the vast literature on the 'voyage of the soul' and medieval dream theory . . . Paz on Sor Juana's greatest work:

> In *First Dream* she relates that, while her body slept, her soul ascended to the upper sphere; there her soul had a vision so intense, so vast, so luminous and dazzling, that she was blinded; once recovered, she longed to ascend again, now, step by step, but she could not; as she was wondering what other path she might take, the sun rose and her body awakened. The poem is the account of a spiritual vision that ends in a nonvision. . . .

Enchanted by the image of souls in transit while we sleep, for the first time in months Beulah finds herself not just cannibalizing texts for quotes and selective truths, but actually reading again. Inspired, she plunges headlong into the literature Paz cites: Athanasius Kircher's *Iter exstaticum*, Artemidorus' *Onirocriticon*, Cicero's *The Dream of Scipio*, Macrobius' *Commentary on the Dream of Scipio* . . .

But after a two-week binge of consuming texts she lifts her head, synapses crackling, fluorescing with points of light—and feels no closer than before. A sharp swing in mood, a return to a familiar pattern. Her notes here revert to near incoherence and to her sedentary fetishes— 'the rank red-gummed rotting smile / the stink of failure clinging to my clothes like fear—animals and children smell it on me. . . .'

What moves her at this precise point to copy the following quotation?—an exercise of sympathetic magic, a conjuring. Or maybe it is just to write down something coherent.

> *First Dream* is the first example of an attitude—the solitary soul confronting the universe. . . . The solitary confrontation is a religious theme, like that of the voyage of the soul, but religious in a negative way: it denies revelation. More precisely, it is the revelation of the fact that we are alone and that the world of the supernatural has dissipated. In one way or another, all modern poets have lived, relived, and re-created the double negation of *First Dream:* the silence of space, and the vision of the nonvision. The great and until now unrecognized originality of Sor Juana's poem resides in this fact. And this is the basis for its unique place in the history of modern poetry. . . . [7]

Hardly, it seems, has Beulah taken Paz as spirit guide than he teaches that Sor Juana, unlike all the dream voyagers who had ever gone before her, travelled without a guide. Maybe this is why Beulah is now so quick to discard Paz, her esteemed guide and teacher— again, the familiar pattern: blame the teacher, not the method. Hoping to limit the avenues of approach by following him, she has instead discovered them hugely multiplied. She has badly underesti-mated the breadth of Paz's erudition but, more, she has once again failed to grasp the fundamental lesson: the labyrinth that is one mind. And so, repenting her ill-invested hopes she finds herself alone again. Perhaps it is in that solitude that she came closest to joining her Sor Juana.

At any rate, it seems strange that she should think herself at another dead end just as she is led from medieval dream theory to the sprawl-ing corpus of labyrinth scholarship; and that in the very midst of a tangled bower, our maze-runner stumbles at wits' end into a vast library devoted to . . . labyrinths. Despite her own childhood intima-tions, Beulah was not at all prepared for the reach of the maze phe-nomena across the ages and around the globe, from Neolithic Scandinavia to Tierra del Fuego to the hedge mazes of twentieth-century Nova Scotia.

This business of labyrinths must seem to the modern reader quaint and antic, his most recent acquaintance stemming perhaps from child-hood trips through the fun-house mazes of seedy carnivals. And hedge mazes—*really*. Even those of us craving the exotic, the mildly dangerous, would find ourselves hard-pressed to conjure anything more threatening here than some geriatric Priapus hobbling through a set of well-trimmed alleys with a silver tea service in one hand and a set of bloodied pruning shears in the other.

If the reader's patience had not already been sufficiently taxed, one might sample the catalogue Beulah was about to acquaint herself with: mazes *in malo* and *in bono*; mazes with centres and without; mazes concealing grail or monstrosity; mazes in two, three or four dimen-sions; the maze as pleasure dome, bower of lust; mazes of the mind and mazes of the body—palaces of the intestines[†]—inner pathways of ear, brain, bowels. . . .

Yet all of this would amount to no more than an arrangement of markers charting the maze as *idea*.

[†] *ékal tirâni*, the palace of the intestines evoked on the ancient Babylonian clay tablets describing divination by animal entrails

In 1967, at Montréal's World Exposition, more than one and a half
million people lined up for hours on end at the *Labyrinthes* Pavilion for
one thing: an authentic *experience* of the maze. For this is precisely
what is lacking today, not the view from above but the view from
within. Not the thin, tepid wash—the littered flood of meaningless
information, but the avatar it displaced: the deep, blue dive into an
infinite complexity. What most eludes our grasp today is not the maze
as idea, but as experience. Or so my own research has suggested.
What the fair-goers in Montréal are on the verge of discovering is that
each maze-runner is the architect of his own labyrinth, each forking in
the path is marked by his doubts, each passageway excavated by his
questions, each blind alley walled in by his ignorance and errors and
pretensions. From metaphors to myths and on to dreams, thence to
voyages of the soul and labyrinths, what we lack today is the experience of blundering through a maddening series of detours into the
tangled heart of a mystery that conceals what we most fear—that
there a monster waits, and that it wears our face.

TEOCUALO THE FOLLOWING ODDITY seems addressed to me, though Beulah never sent it. Maybe it was intended to echo a certain strain in the Baroque, recalling the salty side of Donne or the Coy Mistress of Marvell or any number of romps by John Wilmot, Earl of Rochester— "The Disabled Debauchee," to name one. I do not know how it was to be taken. I offer it here not as one of Beulah's amusements but as an exhibit in my defence.

Some background on the text. According to her notes, in pre-Hispanic Mexico there was a rite, since compared to that of the Christian Eucharist, that involved moulding an effigy of God out of amaranth or cornmeal moistened with blood, then proceeding to eat it with the cry: *Teocualo! God is eaten.* What I still cannot decide for myself is when she wrote this—it was lying among other papers traceable to early 1994, which is to say, before she left Calgary. I can't even begin to imagine the strangeness she would have felt to have written this, only to experience the actual rite first-hand a few months later on a mountainside in Mexico.

I would be your maker—please let me be.
There are other wonders a wheel can
     wreak.
Let me show you, you shall see
There's more to this than pounding meat.

'Top a wheel I'd throw you—
yet like clay, not kindling,
not a breaking nor a grinding down
but a building up—from the ground.

I would spin you hard and long,
shape you on a potter's wheel
—milled and turned, a meal
not of earth, but harvest corn.

To start:
these stiffening carp—
your bony feet,
hamstring strung,

tarsal-finned,
arch, pedestrian.

Afoot! the nascent effigy:
tickle-ankled, razor shinned—
the fluted drumstick of
your fatted calves,
kidskin 'cased, racked
and pinioned to the knee
where it hollows—
a dollop's scalloped gap,
a nice cream scoop
of delicacy.

Soft-gloss't horse-meat
of your thighs: all but hairless—
unbranched cedars—
their striate checks
and bulges I'd
approximate

with celery sticks
(and Velveeta).

Next a platter nudge—
swift-trick, artfully turned:
about face, fella!
. . . to (dis)simulate
your low-slung base,
your bottom—globed
with musk melon
or else, cantaloupe.

Still to assay, still untried:
the tough, reluctant nut between . . .
to probe and crack and crease
by a deft tongue's
delving auguries.

Then just athwart the tailbone's ridge,
that sacral scar mimicked
with an edgy bit
of star-fruit
topping—
heralding the unclasped bracelet
of your plaited
vertebrae.

Rising, still rising,
by cupped-palms sculpted,
just above that lightless
nethermoon (melon-saddled),
there squat the addled cod-cheeks
of your frowning, stub-winged
saddlebags—O flightless
groundling Pegasus
of corn!

Ay, but that crab-back,
Tin Man—now there's the rub!:
savage concave, vexed . . .
blackfired and hardened
on cynicism and sun,

brazen of despair,
embrittled on distemper.

Pivotal point, fatal curve—
invert it, crack and peel it back!
So, plattered on that convex carapace
together yet, might we dine—
I thine, thou mine—
as kings, as gods
as matched and
blissful equine
arthropods

browsing spines and thistles,
crowns-of-thorn,
men-o-war—
we two: paired now,
fitted,
slow enstabled,
embayed, ensilted . . .
not delta-hilted
but spitted, gorged, and
lordly gored.

After that shelly back,
your doughy head's
a little simpler,
if by a hair and not
a ton;
stubborn topknot,
prickly scalp,
I've thought of cloaking it
in kelp.
For the features
of that dimpled face—
a knead, a
knuckle, a
pinch, a poke—
gouge the eyes,
thumb the nose,
cleave the chin,
fork the tongue.

That shepherd crook of larynx,
(by macaroni elbows, aped)
into your wishbone's flaring
V-neck, tucks, so
as not to rudely flop,
into the pulmonary
cranb'rry
sauce.

Gizzard, crop,
sweetbread mysteries
moulded, folded, rucked
like pennies in
a cake;
subsurface currants, plotted
in the vaunt and swagger
of that swelling plover's
chest—
O Tin Man, lovelorn,
forlorn cockerel, crowing,
dying
to save face.

So now into that fowl barrenland—
breast of partridge, breast of quail—
I would place a transplant
heart of amaranth meal . . .
dampened, formed,
blood-wetted through
a catheter of
thorn.
Thus emboldened, over
your blood-sped cadaver
heartened, spurred,
my tongue would trace
and serpent-track
a slippery path—
a zig-zag,
snail-silver,
tongue-lashed race.

To and fro, would I course pell-mell—
chocolate nipple—macaroon yon—
over the belly's pursing velt,
leaping in long
marsupial bounds
'long the grassy pout
of your abdomen.

I'd there pause, against
this salt-lick graze,
and on it place
the leech and linger
of my calf lips
—groined, insatiate—
and rash my chin on
that bearded nest's
asperities.

Seaweed beach, desert strand,
shovel-tongue, tremblehand . . .
I'd score and scour and palp and,
from this turbid littoral,
coax and glean
the raw—so raw!—materials
for the sandcastles of
our ecstasy.

On!,
my sickle fingers'
curlew swerve
o'er amaranth sand,
and in the hand
the brief-cupped, meaty curve
of thickening blood
in its silken gut;

Heft!
the swallow's
plum-swelled,
dewlap
nest;

Pluck!
the dew-harp's
gristled
fret;

Flush!
the nightingale
of flesh
to sing
its bloodrush
melodies;

Mark!
the long-
billed carnivore:
through sweet-stemmed
reed-brakes mapling sap,
a heron stalks
the shoaling corn
—eyeblink bolt
falcon stoop—
epiglottal juke—
and crane
to shuck
the throated
husk.

And now the heron—
minnow necked
in a pelican
maw—
begins
to hump
and thrust
its prim
bobbed
camel walk . . .
homing cross
the blood-dimmed
dusk of
lust.

Drumbeat galley,
gullet of oar-song,
draw and scull and
featherstroke home
from the weary wars—
Row! row for
the foaming
shore!

Thrum the drumhead
gourd—Hum that anthem
Sound that triton horn—
Thumb and Cock
the apoplectic
mushroom cap—
Uncork the vial
of tantric storm—
To the sinner—succour!
the sot, liquor
the fasted, sup—

Ship!
the last
long gleaming
oar in its salted lock
of gushing
spawning
salmon
roe—

now Dock!—
with a Venus suck,
a sparrow swallow,
veined and bitted,
smooth as spittle,
lithe as licking—
TEOCUALO
Don is eaten.

ZOMBIE

WE RETURN BRIEFLY to my own little life. The first day of 1995 offered the usual bleary hours of unwelcome reflections. Maybe it wasn't the career of high academic adventure I'd once dreamed of, but I felt I was learning at last how to settle into my future, into what it might no longer hold. The dramatic mists of my own early promise had begun to thin, revealing the berms and hummocks of a more regular professional landscape. To thin? The verb, I believe, is dissipate.

Even so, the lamp of ambition smouldered bravely on like a censer, flickering with some recent successes. A new line of publications well-received, nomination to the committee organizing an important cycle of conferences slated for Calgary—'the Learneds' were the scholarly equivalent of the Olympic Games but with more bloodshed. There was an invitation to guest lecture at a good school in Britain. Madeleine and I were talking about a European vacation with stops in the U.K. for meetings. As we are about to see, I was working in what was for me a new area. One, in fact, that Beulah had put me on to. One more thing I have to thank her for.

But the charges of academic theft, one does not give thanks for. The official penalties pale next to the unofficial. The tainted party is, academically speaking, a pariah. Once the stain sets, it's almost impossible to remove. The stain has set.

So yes, perhaps a motive for serious countermeasures—but not this degree of violence. Shattered glass everywhere, blood smeared on the walls, sprayed across a ceiling, a bed. Sane, educated people do not do this. It is counterproductive.

And for anyone prepared to consider that I might care, I believe there are moral issues.

If I had to guess when she decided to drag me personally into her apocalypse I would have to trace it to the weekend of the craft fair, the weekend of my fortieth birthday in May of 1993. But over the course of our last summer together, I handed her the tools to do the job more professionally. If our weekend adventure had begun rancorously it was only because I'd insisted, where I usually made no effort at all. I had taken a genuine interest in an aspect of her work. Yes, the first ideas were hers. This is not theft. This kind of cross-pollination happens all the time between students and their advisors. I've already conceded that my work had gone somewhat stale. If I had a vocation it was Scepticism. Postmodernism had been a career accident—a fact of which she tirelessly delighted in reminding me. But in the spring I'd said something off-handed about the Baroque, to which she'd replied that the Postmodern was just the Baroque with its heart torn out. How had she put it? "Bled—bones cracked, marrow sucked. Your Postmodern is a zombie."

The remark got me thinking. About using the Baroque as a way of getting at the Postmodern. This too, I admit, was her idea first— though I'd always had the impression that for her it was more about getting at me. I believe subsequent events justify me in this completely. Or incompletely.

But this is not theft either. She had no interest in the Postmodern, which was part of her charm, while I had none in the Baroque, per se, had in fact to overcome a certain squeamishness. I had conquered a similar antipathy towards things Latin American, initially by telling myself that the great master of the maze, Borges, was really one of us, his mother being English. It was a start. Surely I could do as much for the Baroque, by means similarly primitive if necessary. So when shortly after my birthday weekend she slipped through my office mail slot a copy of a Baroque play, I read it with attention. *Love is a Greater Labyrinth*. Partway through it I saw a connection, saw in the idea of a labyrinth something I could use. It was a fresh avenue by which to go beyond the usual: of pointing up to what degree the postmodernist repudiation of authority relied on quotations of their own godlike authorities; of pointing out that deconstruction was a construct like others, that Foucault was dead—indeed had always been—and that his texts and intentions were the flotsam of power discourses to the same extent any other author's were. This was where I had begun with *The Liar Paradox*.

But what I glimpsed in this conjunction of the Baroque and the labyrinth was a way of looking at the new that was itself very old. I had a hunch that the very antiquity of mazes would show up pomo as old hat. But I found more as the maze research progressed. I am only speaking now of what I had glimpsed. It was embryonic; some were good leads, others not. If this were about me and not about how I was once perceived, I might try to give some idea of where the trail has finally led.

In the Baroque and the Postmodern we had two periods obsessed
with end-times: one bent on fulfilling the conditions for Apocalypse,
the other in proclaiming itself the End of History. Two periods
obsessed with games and their rules—but for the Baroque it is the
game of Life and Death, while for the Postmodern the real game is to
spot the trick in the magic, and thereby dispel it. (Which is to say, if
the trick makes the illusion, spotting the trick makes the illusion unreal.)
Construction, deconstruction. Basically, Derrida turning Descartes on
his head. But the next step is an odd one, if we substitute 'the construct of Reality' for 'illusion.' Having spotted the tricks in our construction of Reality, the Postmodernist goes on to treat the very
notion of the real as if it were a magic. Performed by a charlatan.

What could produce such a fantastic leap? Maybe a few interrelated
things: a long habit of safety; a complacent illusion of magic as mere
parlour trick; the presumption that while illusions may be dangerous,
dispelling them is play.

For the Postmodern, the game is not true, not therefore real, and
neither are its consequences—what matters is getting to the end.
Which is where the Baroque comes in. For the Postmodern, mind is
error, truth in the eye of the beholder, and beauty irrelevant. The
untrue is unreal. For the Baroque, Truth is given, beauty is in the
mind of the beholder, and in the eye is error. The Untrue is fatal.

The thinkers of our period taunt power from a position of privilege
and the habit of safety; those of the Baroque serve absolute power
from a position of ambivalence—of, say, fear and longing and contempt. Ergo mazes. The Postmodern's experience of the maze could
be said to be from above, the Baroque's from below and within. But
there were mazes of other kinds too. The terrain was extraordinarily
rich.

These were all architectural metaphors of knowledge and experience. I had been publishing on the subject since Beulah was twelve.
She knew my work, as only now I have come to know hers. How can
they say the development wasn't mine? How does someone with no
track record make me a pariah among my colleagues?

The answer is not complicated: By being prepared to go far enough.

I might instead have hoped she would be delighted by my renewed
interest—though I only mentioned it to her after she was technically
no longer my student. It had barely crossed my mind to point out that

she had not listened to me and now her project was going nowhere, or rather everywhere at once; whereas I had picked up a small corner of it and turned it to account, by working with method and discipline. But this was our summer of cruelty. I have admitted my conduct toward her in other respects was unsavoury. Still, I thought of this as something entirely separate. I thanked her for her input, gave her regular updates over the summer. All part of a healthy model of cross-fertilization. If it is fair to say I had come to a dead end in my work, it is also fair to thank Beulah for providing me with a way out of it, a kind of rebirth. Any sane person sees we are speaking metaphorically. What Beulah saw, or heard, rather, was a call to rip a hole in the bright shiny fuselage that was my life. My Lie.

A little less than two years later, I would be buying a last-minute ticket for one, one-way to London.

THE POET'S
LABOURS

like a pain that advances and opens a pathway
between viscera that yield and bones that resist
like a file that files the nerves that bind us to life

OCTAVIO PAZ

B. Limosneros, trans.

yes, but also like a sudden joy
like a door opening onto the sea
like peering into the abyss, like reaching the summit

like a river of diamonds
 and like the blue cascade that tumbles
  in a landslide of statues
    and whitest of temples

like the bird that rises and the lightning that descends
oh beating of wings, oh beak that rends and splits
      at last the fruit

you, my cry spouting plumes of fire
wound, resonant and vast
 like the wrenching of planet from the body of a star

oh invisible fall on a floor of echoes
on a sky of mirrors that reflect you
 and destroy you
  and make you
    innumerable
     infinite
      and anonymous

wo long months had I been given to consider my situation. Sor Philothea's preface to the letter so worthy of Athena was dated November 25, 1690. The first leaflet denouncing it appeared on December 8th, the Feast of the Immaculate Conception. The leaflet was signed simply *the Soldier*, who fairly wrung his spleen dry. And though he used phrases I was sure he had heard from Núñez, truly was the good soldier all but deranged—raving, emotional, unable to follow a train of argument, and I could not help wondering if the author was not His Grace the Archbishop himself.

On the third Sunday of Advent, a new series of leaflets appeared, all signed *the Soldier*. Polished, learned, theological. Sane. Now there were two soldiers. This one's denunciations branched out, amplifying on the hints Sor Philothea had obligingly given the Holy Office. The negative *finezas* were clearly and foully heretical. As for Sor Juana, the list of her heresies was long, and would grow. *Illuminist. Gnostic. Arian.*

The inventory was unnerving enough. Surely we had to do something, my many friends urged—write a response, mount a defence. But so far the Inquisition's involvement was unofficial. It would be undignified for them to display the least sign of haste, in moving against a mere woman especially. The people themselves must be seen to clamour for protection, yet the *vulgo* had thus far been quiet—no, not quiet but Decembers offered much else to talk of.

January was a quieter month. Though the days were lengthening, the nights were longer.

The day after Epiphany another run of leaflets flared up, these ones signed. Manuel Serrano, Franciso Ildefonso—two non-entities from Puebla, along with five other complete obscurities. *My seven slanderers, my impugners, my persecutors.*[8]

On the second Sunday in January the sermons of attack began all over the city. There was no stopping it now, and no stopping my friends, who had taken to meeting without me, since I would do nothing to help myself. They had to have Father Xavier Palavicino. Palavicino was ambitious, brave, eloquent, and a great admirer of the much slandered nun. Here in the temple, before the month was out, my attackers would have our answer.

Most Sundays, the only threats to the calm of a solemn Mass are the neighbourhood delinquents who have made a sort of ball court of the plaza. The double doors giving onto the ball court, while thick, are in such poor repair as to let bright brawling day sift in through the rifts and splits in the thick oak panelling. On a crisp Sunday morning in January there may be two dozen children outside, and it can sound as if there are twice that number. As Xavier Palavicino waded ever more perilously into his discourse, I found myself praying for another hundred young scufflers to drop by for a game outside.

Father Palavicino chose his moment carefully if not his words. The date being the feast day of the learned widow Santa Paula. Our convent chapel had received distinguished visitors before, but rarely in such numbers. Front row, centre, kneeling on cushions, were the Viceroy and Vicereine, the Count and Countess de la Granja. On her right the Archbishop's Vicar-General. On the Viceroy's left a nobleman from the highest ranks of the Spanish aristocracy, exiled to Manila and sufficiently forgiven since then to make his way back as far as Mexico. Beside him the fallen angel of Versailles, le Vicomte d'Anjou. Three rows back is a Creole suspected of sedition on whose behalf I had once interceded with María Luisa, to secure his early release from prison. Though he perhaps meant well, his presence was not a comfort.

Standing as it does on the compound's north side, our chapel is notable for its cool, and can be quite icy on winter mornings. Notable also for its tranquillity—when not a ball court—a place where I have spent many quiet hours. This January morning our chapel offered neither calm nor quiet. Never, I would wager, had the Holy Office been so well represented here. Consultors and familiars, assessors and censors, prosecutors and examiners, one by one they filtered in, in all the sulphurous pomp of their offices. Even the Holy Tribunal's accountant put in an appearance, who rarely partakes of anything more carnal than the inventories of iron tools and personal effects. Even our Reverend Father Antonio Núñez de Miranda himself was there. Slowly, from where we sat behind the chancel lattice, the whispers among the sisters of St. Jerome rose in fits and gasps—at the entrance of each new official—to a pitch of strangled panic; until finally the Prioress was forced to rise, and striding before us at the grillwork—quenching light as she advanced, shedding it in spokes—furiously gestured for silence as our guest began to speak.

And as he commenced, the quills of half a dozen secretaries seated at little writing desks in the aisles scratched like dogs at a kitchen door.

To the nave of our chapel now I saw drawn every rift and resentment, Dominicans to port, Jesuits to starboard—patterned like filings scattered on a parchment—no, arraigned along the axis of a needle pointing to a nun hidden in the upper choir. Who diverts herself with conceits such as these.

It would be saying too much to claim that Father Palavicino's discourse was in my defence, as indeed he did, say too much. He began by predicating a more conservative position than mine on Christ's *fineza major*, His greatest expression of love for Man. But even though taking a position somewhat distanced from my own, Palavicino did not contest the propriety of a woman, a nun, *taking* a position, and this would have been all the defence I could have asked. For then he did a brave thing, given his auditors, whose attendance he may not have predicted but by now was well aware of. Xavier Palavicino looked the Chief Inquisitors squarely in the eye, and opened with a quote from Jonah: '*Now the Lord had prepared a great fish to swallow up Jonah.*' *And now this bride of Christ, our Minerva of America, has been summoned as a great fish to bear us up her prophecies, and to cause many a holy doctor to shake the dust from his books and sharpen his wits.*

With Father Núñez, half-blind, somewhere below us in the chapel, Palavicino defended me against the blind depredations of the Soldier, this Soldier of Castile. Palavicino praised my intelligence, the deep learning implicit in my position, my grace in stating it. He was only echoing, in this, the published judgement of a bishop-nun but if I was not mistaken, much dust would indeed be shaken, many quills sharpened. What kind of black mirth would the fishers of souls make on this one day? Why did he not come to me first? Still am I treated like a child in theological matters, *un menor de edad*—speak when consulted, theologian's muse. They do not need a woman to tell them how to act—to think, perhaps—but action requires courage. Yes, gentlemen, but thinking requires *thought*.

Still, who was I to criticize anyone for this?

Minerva, pagan goddess . . . Letter Worthy of Athena, her prophecies . . . a great fish—this last he said knowing I was writing carols for the cathedral on Saint Peter, fisherman. The allusion no doubt struck him as clever.

Oh yes, and glaring down at the Inquisition's saintly officers, Father Palavicino likened my persecution to the persecutions of Christ.

My defender qualified me as an innocent lamb, spoke of a *wound in my side* from the Soldier's cruel lance. What on earth or in heaven's name had made him think to say this?—another helpful friend comparing me with *Christ*. Was he completely mad?

With defenders such as these . . .

Worse, it was not even me they defended—woman, prophetess, leviathan—nor any living creature at all. It was a principle they made of me. Some new category. They were like men born to the desert: rain they had seen, small springs, salt lakes, storm-born freshets foaming into sand—yet coming over the last dune at the world's end, what they saw was mere water no longer but the *gates of Atlantis*.

Irony or iron consequence? For I had been the one to play this category game for them, lead the merry chase through monster, muse, paragon, virgin—the female in me being thus incompleted uncoupled unachieved, the dam of our perfidy not yet burst in me—they presumed to praise me as all but a man in *validez y valor*.

In my locutory afterwards the mood was somewhat glum. Each of my visitors had been at the sermon, but as the parlours were not opened Sundays until three, all made the trip back by their own separate paths, presumably to see how I was bearing up. Ribera was sitting in an ox-hide chair at the grille nearest the clavichord. Dean de la Sierra had not taken a seat at all, but stood rummaging in the bookshelf against the east wall. Carlos sat next to Ribera but not quite at the grille, as if he too were less than keen for a good frank talk. First to arrive, our convent chaplain sat quietly on a bench by the window closest to the door while I tried to cheer things up. I was becoming not a little resentful, not only of my lack of success but that it should fall to me, in the circumstances, to do such a lot of cheering.

Palavicino arrived last, and had a choice of the bench beside the chaplain or the armchair next to Gutiérrez, who had not been here for weeks yet appeared now. Slumping down beside the chaplain, Palavicino told of being accosted outside the chapel by a raving madman who had denounced the sermon in my defence as heretical. As Palavicino pronounced the word it took every mite of self-possesion not to glance at the Inquisitor Gutiérrez, who was staring at the chandelier.

Just then, a small new personage dropped by on his way to the palace to present his credentials. Baron Anthonio Crisafi gave the general impression of being the Sicilian envoy of the Spanish viceregal adminis-tration of southern Italy. I had not known we needed one of these. There was something funny and flighty about his eyes, which seemed never quite to meet mine. Although in better days I would have found his pres-ence in every way comical he quickly proved much better informed than could be expected of a recent arrival, and moreover was taking pains to make clear that his information extended to me. He had arrived know-ing that on my locutory wall was a copy of Velázquez's *The Geographer*—more improbably still, he knew that the painter's model was a lunatic at the court of Philip IV.

Glancing about him, the Baron took the empty armchair and as he sat, pulled it closer to the grille. He was all but telling me he came from Spain with a message from María Luisa. And yet I did not trust him. I had been having some trouble lately telling my friends from my adversaries.

Trying to marshal my wits I launched into a little peroration on the painter's true model for *The Geographer*: Democritus, the laughing philoso-pher—a man so ruled by candour, the people of his own village thought him insane. I had the distinct impression the Sicilian knew this, too, per-fectly well. *Who has sent him? If it is María Luisa why has she sent him knowing this?* Lest the frantic workings of my mind show in my face, I rose and made my way to the back of the room to pace back and forth, I hoped theatri-cally—the nun beneath the globe beneath the lunatic on the wall—as I cobbled together a few ideas from bits of Justinian,[†] and from Mondragón's treatise on the virtues of insanity and the holy truths of the mad.

[†] Byzantine emperor and lawgiver

"Indeed, *mis señores,* we the sane, who never cease to thirst for con-quest—to rule, found cities and cultivate our own holdings—can only look with envy on the estate of the one we call mad. *El loco* pays neither tax nor tribute, suffers neither vassalage nor servitude. Small wonder kings seek his candid councils, and the slyest of the sane feign holy madness. . . ."

This won a few wistful nods from the *cuerdos*[†] among my interlocutors.

[†] the sane

"In the ears of the king, gentlemen, such sooths are bittersweet, but in the eyes of Democritus are so filled with gall he puts them out to maintain his philosophy of cheer. . . ."

The Sicilian may have known all about the gravity of my situation and all about the painting—nevertheless he looked slightly dazed by the shift in tone. Foreigners—even the Spaniards themselves—were never quite prepared for the intensity of this game the way we play it, we the children of Spain and Mexico. The blood in the lace, the sword in the cape, the red in the tooth as we smile. I was thinking to draw the 'Ambassador' out, but in truth there was something I could no longer quite trust in such jests. It was a loss of dexterity I found unsettling.

"What say you, Baron—does not the lunatic's smile as he contemplates the world make elegant comment on the philosophy of cheer?"

"*La Casa del Nuncio*," the Baron blurted, "—in *Toledo*, Sor Juana, is not to be missed."

What was this? What was he trying to tell me? "Has the Ambassador visited many of Spain's *casas de locos* during his travels?" I asked. "They are a great favourite, I understand, of foreign visitors."

"Yes, Sor Juana, that is true."

"And do foreign noblemen come expressly to such houses, as in Lope's day, to shop for a suitable fool to return home with?"

"They do."

"And you've seen them at palaces other than Madrid's?"

"In fact, yes."

I left off pacing, making my way somewhat absent-mindedly to my seat by the grille. Of course the House of the Messenger was a madhouse famous throughout Europe, fools and gold being Spain's last remaining exports. But it was the way he stressed its location . . . I racked my brain for the rather-too-much I knew of Toledo—eighteen Church councils, capital of the Visigoths, of Saint Hermenegild and the Arian heresy—the royal seat of Alfonso, Emperor of the Two Faiths . . . of El Cid, El Greco, La Mancha and Quixote, the ancestral castle of the falconer López de Ayala . . .

Seeing me at a complete loss the Baron bent to extract a small packet from his satchel. "I had planned to present this once we knew each other better. But I think this is the moment after all." He took the book from a soft wrap of oiled leather. "I have heard that you read Italian."

"From whom, Baron, may I ask?"

"Perhaps the most original and most daring poetry written in this century. On *our* peninsula, at least."

The Scelta. Campanella's *Scelta* was written in an Inquisition prison cell after a plot to expel the Spanish from Calabria.

Thanking him, I rose quickly and placed the book on the shelf farthest from the grille. Would there be a message tucked in its pages? From

María Luisa, perhaps? But no, this was the worst sort of book to conceal a message in. The message had to be the book itself—but what?

There was so much to consider, I was relieved to see him rising to go. When he had taken leave of us, the chaplain took the opportunity to see him to the street.

"Someone has sent him from Madrid," offered Ribera.

"Or even Sicily," added Carlos dryly.

"Or else Rome," said Gutiérrez. He had not asked about the book. The tone was casual.

In the silence after 'Rome' was let fall, Palavicino sat stewing. De la Sierra had been standing by the bookcase nearest the exit for half an hour, and I had begun to wonder if he would be back. As Dean of the Cathedral and the Archbishop's Vicar-General, his presence here before today had already been barely tenable. Father Xavier Palavicino was the next to find an excuse to leave, a plea for forgiveness in his eyes, a man with much on his mind. Well, no matter, it was good of him to come.

Who were these men in my locutory? Which were foes, which friends? And which had the capacity to do me greater harm—maleficence, accident or foolish acts in my defence? It was dawning on me that a fate might be decided by questions such as these, and by such men, as much as by my own actions. I could not quite decide whether to feel fury first or make straight for terror.

I had had enough of company. It was time to clear the room.

Reverting to my disquisition on lunacy and cheer, I reminded them it was always like this. Each time a new Viceroy arrived. You make too much of it, dear friends. Remember? The threats, the manoeuvres, the betrayals . . . it goes on for years. You've just forgotten. Things looked so much darker ten years ago, and yet for these ten years, have I not seen my freedoms multiply? I am not free to travel, but yet the world freely comes to me. Half the gentry of Europe files through this locutory; half the books we here are not free to buy, they bring over as gifts. The thoughts I am still not free to write openly, I have only to ply in parables and allegories; while whatever I am too cautious to publish gets published for me. Even the learned Inquisitors bring their proofs and arguments now for my candid opinions, too freely given.

Gutiérrez, slightly flushed, edged for the door.

Come again, Gutiérrez, come again soon.

The dean chose that moment to give me the news that my commission for the Feast of Saint Peter had been cancelled. And this with barely an apology, though I knew the final decision on this was at least technically his. What Dean de la Sierra wished to impress upon me instead was that the Archbishop did not even bother to consult him before announcing it.

I answered that, as the Dean himself had admitted, *while approving my lyrics,* the common people needed a voice for their hardships and grievances, which were proving especially painful this year. Returning his book to the shelf, he was good enough to concede this again, before slipping out. Once he had, Ribera told me Agustín Dorantes had dropped by yesterday with an offer to help him rewrite my lyrics on Saint Peter. Dorantes was a passable rhymer and before my time had been the man most often favoured with such commissions.

Agustín Dorantes was also Master Examiner of the Inquisition. The man most likely to preside over a process against Palavicino's sermon.

Many came to the chapel that day, but Dorantes was not among them. Many explanations were possible but the most likely was this: he was already involved. It would not do for the Chief Magistrate to be present where and while evidence was being gathered. There could be little doubt the Holy Office's involvement was now official. But the case could not yet have been Palavicino's—

No. Though there might be a file opened against him soon, the Holy Office did not move so quickly. The case was not Palavicino's, the case was mine.

But Núñez, Father Núñez *had* come. Could that mean he was not involved? How very curious the sensation, seeing him in the chapel. He had not changed so much these past ten years, not so much as I might have thought. It was clear the young monk walking with him was less assistant than guide, but other than in the decline of his sight, he seemed no more ancient than he always had. Ten years earlier, almost to the day, we had spoken of Hermenegild in prison—Núñez had never been so threatening.

Choose, he said, a convent or a prison cell. I answered then with Herakles. How should I answer now?

Why neither, Father. There are as many thralls among the free as there are follies among the sane. Just so many mad slaves to honour, romance, lust, necessity. But not you nor any other shall ever make a prison of my mind. Irons are not all iron, yet they hobble. Bars are not all wrought, yet ring and girdle. Stays are not all of whalebone, but detain us only if we let them.

How like empty bravado this sounded, ten years on.

"You think this one of your little comedies, Sor Juana, but this sacrament of water may well matryr you," Father Núñez had said, exactly ten years ago. "Just how far are you willing to go, Juana? As far as Galileo?— or *plus ultra*, as far as Bruno."

It was late in the locutory. All but two of my guests had left. The *escuchas* were washing up behind the arras, speaking in whispers. Ribera had been working at something quietly on the clavichord. He rose to leave, promising to return soon. He had an idea for a new musical project for us but had to go straightaway to consult someone. Only Carlos remained, leaning quietly against the wall, over by the window. He had secured a commission to write a chronicle of our Viceroy's great naval victory in Santo Domingo. We were sure the actual news of it must arrive any day. Carlos was trying to persuade me to write a dedicatory poem to open the chronicle. A show of loyalty to the Crown should be a welcome opportunity, for both of us. Things had never been easy between the new viceroyals and me, with her especially. They arrived with the presumption that I would serve them as enthusiastically as I had served past viceroys and vicereines, and rather more blindly.

"What can it hurt now?" Carlos asked, coming to sit across from me.

I had been thinking there was at least one other message in the *Scelta*: the perils of a person of the cloth meddling in worldly matters. But after today's events I had begun to wonder if doing nothing was a luxury I had.

"So tell me please about his great naval triumph. Is it fair to say the French in Santo Domingo—and *where* else?—would have been rather heavily outnumbered?

"Tortuga. And yes, heavily."

"You have a title?"

"*Trophy of Spanish Justice in the Punishment of French Perfidy.*"

"Stirring. We might actually win."

"Yes."

"I can't bear her."

"The Vice-Queen."

"I assume her husband did little more than relay Madrid's orders to the fleet?"

"Correct."

Another commission. The very thought. . . . Such a lassitude I felt. Even the carols to Saint Catherine, which I had wanted so badly, I was barely a week from finishing and yet could not. I could only dread what use Bishop Santa Cruz might yet put them to.

Antonia had made her way finally through the *portería* and along the corridor to join Carlos on the visitors' side. Quietly, listening to every word, she went about the room collecting dishes and depositing them where we on our side could reach them. I envied her the freedom in this humble task, a freedom she would say meant nothing to her, who wanted only to be on the other side, with me.

"Was I so very arrogant, Carlos, or too weak? Should I have forced the issue ten years ago, while don Payo was still Archbishop? Would I be better off now?"

"Or incomparably worse."

"Truly, things did look so much darker then. Don Payo gone, then news of the *auto* in Madrid, then the comet. . . ."

"A nice test of your scientific principles."

My principles. In all this time I had never apologized to him about the comet . . . the poem in praise of his adversary. Each time I had wanted to, I felt as if it were really Núñez wringing it from me. It would feel no less so now.

"Listening to the Sicilian today, as we talked about *nuncios* and madhouses—and then that remark about Toledo, I was thinking that for some games one may know too much."

"Too much . . ."

"Too much to solve it, to bear not finding the answer, or finding one. Too many answers to bear."

"Such as?"

"Things, facts . . . That the onset of the Thirty Years War was remembered for the three comets of that year. That while all Europe watched them through his telescope Galileo was too ill to get up and look at them. That his troubles with the Jesuits began with the one event he did not see, with the facts he did not observe."

"Yours sound like facts in search of a hypothesis."

"That at the death of Caesar, who had declared himself emperor, a comet hung over Rome for six months—and who is to say the Archbishop does not owe some facet of his election to the effect of a comet?"

"I ask you again, are you so sure it would be better if Bishop Santa Cruz were Archbishop now?"

He was right, of course. Such a curious instrument was this chronoscope that is memory. One had only to look through it a second time to see the whole world inverted. And yet a third glance did not right things.

Núñez, who was surely my enemy now—could it be that day he had still been acting as a friend? Ten years ago it looked like madness to stay with him. Was I to think now it had been madness to dismiss him? Better or worse, then, to have refused every commission . . . and watched every special privilege I have won in here evaporate. Watched the thousand leaden chores and communal tasks here close over my head like the sea . . . accountant, peacemaker, Superintendant of Works and Masonry, paymaster, catechist. Explaining the sermons, chiding the novices, leading the choir.

And now I sat here envying Antonia's freedom to pick up dishes.

Curious inversions these.

Next to the window, Antonia's gatherings accumulated on the little table that spanned the grille. Glasses and decanters, flasks and cups, a city of glass in the setting sun—smudged glass towers and crystal minarets, inverted cones and earthen domes . . . a city of the sun on its own plateau, rising up against a plain of roses crossed in shadows.

Answer the question, decide.

I got up to help Antonia with the dishes. Carlos bade us good-night.

As we finished, the last light fell across the rose bushes outside the window. The little courtyard lay in shadow. The Prioress came to stand at her balcony, looked down a moment at the locutory, then faded into her apartments to light the lamps. I set the Ambassador's gift on a chair by the doorway. I would send Antonia to him tomorrow, ask that he return at his earliest convenience. It had come to me, what I had been trying to remember since the Sicilian left.

After the rebellion in Calabria, Campanella feigned madness to save his life.

JUANA INÉS
DE LA CRUZ

B. Limosneros, trans.

For an hour, sad thought,
let us pretend
I am happy
though I know I am not:
  since they say what afflicts us
has its conceiving in the mind,
to imagine ourselves blest
is to be a bit less wretched.

  Oh that my mind this once,
should serve to bring me peace,
that it not always run
counter to my ease.

  The whole world holds convictions
of such divergent kinds
that what one deems black,
another proves white.

  What entrances some
enrages others;
and what this one finds irksome
adds to that one's comfort.

  He who is sorrowing says
the happy man is heartless;
and he who is joyful smiles,
to see the sufferer in his toils.

†Democritus,
Heraclitus

  Those two thinkers of Greece†
long pondered the matter:
for what brought the first to laugh,
to the second brought grief.

 Famous has their opposition
been these twenty centuries,
yet without a resolution
that can so much as be divined;

  to their two banners even now,
the world entire is drawn,
with the colours that we follow
determined by our disposition.

  Democritus claiming that our one
worthy answer to the world is laughter;
Heraclitus that the world's misfortunes
are cause for lamentation . . .

Sunday January 28th. The bells of three o'clock, two hours more to Lauds.

On the Friday night after Xavier Palavicino's sermon, I did finally sleep. Antonia woke me at daybreak or I would have slept through prayers. During these, the coldest nights of winter, when we woke to frost on the flagstones and ice on the *tinacos,* she would often sleep on a cot by the fire in the library. At midnight I sent her in to sleep in my bed, preferring to read the Sicilian's gift with my back against the chimney. I doubted she would sleep much either, but she liked it there.

It had not been easy to be with her these past two months. She took the letter, the pamphlets, the sermon, hard—raged at him—quite refused to see that Santa Cruz had done anything at all for her sisters, and she was very close to rage with me for doing too little to defend myself. It was true, I'd done little but brood. Yes, brooding I was doing rather a lot of.

In the hours since the sermon I had been going over the entire day, the Sicilian's visit, the gift . . .

After writing his *City of the Sun,* after the uprising in Calabria, Campanella lived twenty-seven years in the Inquisition's prisons, feigning madness to stay the proceedings against him. But reading his *Scelta* I wondered what kind of madness this could have been, and what kind of prison, that he could write such poetry there. How did his madshows seem? Were they ever the same, or different each time: did he laugh, did he cry, did he tear his hair, bring himself to grief? I wondered if he ever, for an instant, lost his mind, I wondered if he ever, for a moment, forgot his lines. I wondered, if I were to feign madness, what kind I might try. There were so many kinds.

There was the lunacy of the court buffoon; there were the rages and fears of His Grace the Archbishop, his hatred of us, of all things that give pleasure; there was the sad and yet laughable madness in his choice of Heraclitus for the Gaudete Sunday sermon. Gaudete, 'rejoicing.' Heraclitus, 'the weeping philosopher.' Which is to say, if one may not laugh on this of all days, then one must weep ever. Or brood.

In June they had cancelled my lyrics for the sisters of Saint Bernard, in December my lyrics on the Nativity. Now those for Saint Peter, fisherman. How was the poet to feel about this, what was she to say? It was not so very far from madness—but whose? That of Democritus who finds comedy where there is confusion, and puts out his eyes to preserve his vision? That of the geographer, the dizzy simpleton bestowing his simple blessings on the globe as it spins by too fast?—or perhaps it is his head that spins too fast.

It felt like illness, it tasted like bile. Was the geographer seasick, did he need to rest awhile? Perhaps the geographer was only lost. No, it felt like falling. It truly did. A sickness not of floating bodies but of falling ones. Which only made sense after all. The sane objection to the world as globe was always that at bottom one must fall off. And yet even the mad geographer couldn't have it both ways, he had to decide: round or flat, floating or falling, convent cell or prison cell—

Or madhouse. For the sensation now was very much like falling—up. This madness of mine, this madness of the mind that spins too fast, that finds comedy where there is none, yes, but also threads of mystery everywhere and signs, always signs and holy messages. Where there were none. As here, in the coincidence of Democritus and Heraclitus, about whom I myself have written . . . in my first volume for María Luisa. Two holy messengers—I found myself swinging from one to the other now like a kind of pendulum for marking time: the philosopher who laughs, the one who cries. Two holy authors: Vieyra and Campanella. Two thought mad but not: Campanella and Democritus. Two gifts: a painting and a book. Two Vieyra sermons.

Too many twos, one too many coincidences . . . but wait. Madness is not the message, for the messenger is *not* mad.

The messenger is not mad . . .

"Antonia!"

Just as I'd thought—she was in the doorway almost at once, pausing there, hollow-eyed, to slip her nightshirt on. "Bring me Vieyra's sermons, please? Down at the end. I *know* you know where. Red leather. Next shelf up—left. There."

She padded back, greenish eyes curious, my pale Angolan warrior princess in a torn nightshirt.

"Put something on your feet—here take my slippers—how can you walk around like that? As soon as it is light, I want you to go to the palace and try to find the Sicilian. First thing on a Sunday morning it should not be too hard, if he is in fact staying there. Ask him to come at his earliest convenience—but bring him back with you if you can."

"I could wake the turnkeeper right now."

"No, we may need the favour later. Go down and get dressed—it's cold enough for *snow*. By the time you're ready I'll have a note for you to take to him. . . ."

I laid my hand on the cover of soft red leather. . . . Vieyra's sermon was a famous one. Less for its content than for its origins: Christina of Sweden's drawing room in Rome. Vieyra had just arrived from Portugal to seek the Pope's protection from the Inquisition. He'd had the general idea for his oratory already, but during a visit to her apartments improvised the exposition with such stunning success Christina asked that very day that he become her spiritual director. Which he declined. Vieyra served one man alone, the King of Portugal.

Here it was . . . 'The Tears of Heraclitus Defended in Rome against the Laughter of Democritus.'

> Democritus laughed, because the affairs of Man seemed to spring from ignorance; whereas Heraclitus wept, because these same affairs seemed miseries. Heraclitus therefore had greater reason to weep than did Democritus to laugh, for in this world there exists such a host of miseries that owe nothing to ignorance, and yet no ignorance that is not a misery . . .

What ignorance was a misery, an ignorance of *mine?* These emblems were not threads fallen together at random. These were the makings of a message—*and I knew what it was*. The message Baron Crisafi had brought me in the gift of Campanella's *Scelta:* the Archbishop was not mad.

In the two hours Antonia was away at the palace I had the idea of launching a counterattack.

None of the libels in the other pamphlets mattered, but those penned by the second Soldier, those we had to answer. For in them the Holy Office was sounding out its own arguments. But even more urgent now was to repair the horrible, gaping breach Palavicino had opened in my defences. This nightmare of the Soldier's cruel lance in my side, as in the side of an innocent lamb, as in the side of Christ. . . .

Just then, seeing Antonia come swiftly up the steps, cheeks flushed, a strident scarlet ribbon in her hair, it came to me how we might do it. The wound in the side, there was no wiping away the image—but if we changed the soldier, the wound, the side . . . the lance. The shepherdess Camilla. Virgil's own Amazon, I had her right in front of me. It could not be be more perfect. It must be Camilla's lance, through another side altogether. . . .

The Tyrrenian giant Ornithus advances through a wood. He is a colossus dwarfing his little war pony and bearing savage arms never before seen. Espying Camilla in a clearing he turns and bears down on the one he has been searching out. Her flock scattered, she stands firm, watching him come—draped over his shoulders is a hide ripped from a bullock, his helm the gaping jaws of a giant wolf. A rough-hewn prod, thick as an oak bole, is clasped just behind the iron goad by a massive hand of granite. Ornithus springs from his war pony—three swift strides swallow up the meadow. Smoothly, quietly, swift as Achilles, she runs him through the chest with her lance. . . .

And then the insult as he falls.

'And did you think, my friend, to come into these woods hunting game? The day has arrived for your vaunting to find its reply in a woman's arms. To the after-world, hie!—and when you get there tell the shades of your fathers that the one who sent you, and how swiftly, was a woman!'

I looked into her greenish eyes. She read mine. "Work . . ." Antonia said, her smile engagingly grim.

Yes, *work.* Something for us both to do. We would answer Sor Philothea with a letter of our own, published in this case under a pseudonym—Sor Seraphina de Cristo. Christ's finest angel. And even as it poked a little angelical fun at our devoted follower and friend, and this for missing the point of a certain recent letter of ours, missing even whom it was meant to address, we would make it clear that dim Philothea had been involved in it all from the start, indeed had commanded that the sword be made, only to grasp it from the wrong end.

Then we would see what the world thought of clever Philothea. In this affair there was mud enough to cast about.

For our purposes today, Antonia, think of irony as having not two surfaces but three, its blade a triangle[9] in cross-section—inserted, the wound it inflicts takes a good deal longer to heal.

Baron Anthonio Crisafi arrived by three, having cancelled one appointment and rescheduled another for that evening. He cut a dignified figure, in a fitted velvet doublet of an almond brown, a high collar, and across his chest a heavy emerald-studded chain. A matching jewelled band girdled his brown velvet hat, and a heavy calf-length cape with a satin lining hung by fastening cords about his shoulders. I could not help noticing as he sat close by the grille that one eye was slightly skewed in its orbit.

"The Countess of Paredes sends expressions of her love and concern. . . . They are in Seville, at the home of her brother-in-law. The Medinaceli Palace has every imaginable comfort. As you may know, her husband, the Marquis . . ."

The Sicilian could tell me no more than that Tomás was still unwell. Baron Crisafi had only been there two days, and did not see him. Preparing to leave just as my manuscript arrived, the Baron stayed on an extra few hours at María Luisa's request and sent his affairs ahead to Cadiz by carriage.

"The Countess asks me to tell you that your second volume is ready for the printer in Seville. All that lacks are the endorsements and licences. She is holding the text you asked for, in hopes of 'a climate more favourable for ice.' Did I get that correctly?"

"Yes, thank you, Baron."

"She also emphatically agrees with the idea of publishing in Spain your letter on the Vieyra affair—of having it approved there before it can be formally condemned here in Mexico. She already has letters of enthusiastic support from nine poets, but the theological endorsements are not coming so quickly. She wishes you to know that in every free moment she is working to that end—and I can assure you she is working with great passion and energy. So far she has three. . . ."

"She had thirty for *Castalian Flood*."

"So she said, yes. Vieyra is an enormous figure in Seville—not much less revered than he is in Portugal. But during King John's suppression of the Holy Office in Portugal, many Inquisitors took refuge in Seville. Few theologians want anything to do with the matter as long as the Inquisition is pursuing him. What the Countess wanted you to know was this: while soliciting approvals she has learned that certain distinguished officers of the Church in Seville *already know something* about the Vieyra controversy here in Mexico."

My guess had been correct. The Archbishop's correspondent had hinted, the merest hint of a hint, that His Grace was perhaps not quite so unstable as was thought here. "Baron Crisafi, I do not know how to thank you. Perhaps one day I may be in a position to render you some small service."

"I am afraid, Sor Juana, there is more. This was the Countess's message *before* your package arrived. What I am about to tell you now, she had not wanted to worry you with, at first. You see, it appears the Archbishop's correspondent in Seville has also read a good deal about *you*." The Baron leaned forward, lowering his voice. He did his best to meet my eyes. The emerald chain about his neck swung free, sparkling in the light, sending splinters of green across the chocolate doublet.

"The Archbishop has never given the slightest sign he knows I *exist*."

"But Sor Juana, that is exactly right, that is precisely how the correspondent put it. On bad days, His Grace the Lord Archbishop pretends you live in someone else's archdiocese."

"Does he indeed, sir. Why, this happens also to me. But then I take it His Grace has his good days as well. Truly does one wonder what such days might be like."

"I will tell you. On a good day, apparently, he almost manages to forget you are alive."

Baron Crisafi looked genuinely pained to have said something so unpleasant. He assured me the Countess had reread my note accompanying Philothea's publication of my arguments three times before finally deciding this was information I simply had to have now. "The Archbishop's correspondent," the Baron continued, "spoke of an antipathy dating back to the year 1683. The Countess said you would remember. And I am afraid that's all I know, Sor Juana. I should be getting back," he said, straightening in his seat. "This is not a day to be away from the palace—especially for foreigners."

"I'm sorry, I don't see what you mean."

"My quarters are just down the hall from the French Viscount's. He mentioned you have met. Yes? Well it appears the Viscount d'Anjou has made an unannounced departure."

"The stewards have checked the silverware by now, I hope."

"In a manner of speaking, yes, Sor Juana. You see, a treasury official was found murdered last night. His wife says he left home late yesterday afternoon in great excitement to be meeting a very distinguished foreign visitor, but could not say more."

"You are going to tell me this official is privy to information about the silver fleets."

"It appears a shipment left for the coast recently."

"The Viceroy will be happy to see you are still among us."

"I am hoping he has not sent out a search party. It might be hard to convince his men I was on my way back to the palace."

After thanking him, urging him to come again and expressing the very keen regret that he had not arrived in Mexico much sooner—last year, just for instance—I rose to let him go.

Two entire days the Baron had spent with María Luisa—*just weeks ago*. I wanted to ask him about each minute, I wanted to ask him how she was, how she moved, if she smiled.

I could keep Baron Crisafi no longer.

I hoped he might come back, and gave a little wave as I stood at the grille, which was as close as I might come to seeing him out.

The fourth of October, 1683, was among the greatest days of my life, but also of the Archbishop's.[10] At the time I did not give much thought to this, but without a doubt he *chose* that day, knowing perfectly well. . . .

The city had been awaiting the new Archbishop's entry from Michoacan for weeks. The speculations were endless as to the reasons for the delay. His selection had been mysterious enough, for Bishop Santa Cruz's election had already been announced. But now all the talk was of my *Trials of a Noble House*, an entire festival authored exclusively by me. María Luisa and I had been rehearsing the actors for weeks here in the courtyard outside the locutory. A professional theatre company within the walls of a convent—truly a testament to María Luisa's influence, as actresses are known to be prostitutes and actors thought to be men.

The Archbishop chose Monday, October 4th. On short notice the cathedral chapter threw together an uninspired triumphal arch to celebrate his entry. A solemn Mass of reception was celebrated in the cathedral. A stirring *Te Deum* was sung. It had all been quite nice, no doubt.

My festival ran for hours, an entire evening of festivities, well past midnight, and dances until dawn. A *loa* to begin, *sainetes* after each act, and another play within a play to conclude. Usually these are all written by different authors; all were written by Juana Inés de la Cruz, Sor. Monday, October the fourth, 1683.

Trials of a Noble House. He would have died rather than come, I would have given ten years of my life to be there. Perhaps, in some way, I had.

Gutiérrez did not come until Thursday morning. From Sunday to Thursday it snowed. I could not remember five consecutive days of snow down in the valley. As he entered the locutory the enormous capuchon of the Augustinian habit was drawn up, obscuring his face. It was the cold, I knew, but I could not help thinking he did not want to be seen entering. The hem of his habit was sugared in snow, even the long black cincture that hung at ankle-height was white-tipped, like a tail. He shrugged back the hood. His face was ruddy with the chill. I remembered that his mother was Flemish and, as I recalled, a Lutheran.

He was sorry to have been so long. It was a busy time at the Holy Office. He said this as only Gutiérrez could, the tone light. I apologized for my pique in the locutory last week. He answered that I was holding up better than most.

Today the novices were hopeless, dropping things in the back, hands trembling as they set down cups of hot spiced chocolate for us. Again I told myself it was the cold. And again there were no platters of convent delicacies for our guest. The kitchen says no, Tomasina whispered, wide-eyed. They won't say why.

I asked Gutiérrez if he thought Xavier Palavicino was doing someone else's bidding. My defender was of course a learned fool, bent on showing us how much he knew. But did he not perhaps know too much? How many people knew of the carols for Saint Catherine—was it not conceivable that Palavicino was acting in concert with Bishop Santa Cruz?

"Well if he is," Gutiérrez ventured, "he should look to himself." He looked down gratefully at the cup of chocolate warming his hands, bent his head to sip.

"But then," I added, though not quite believing it, "perhaps everyone's forgotten the sermon already—with the vanished Viscount and the murdered treasury agent to gossip about."

He looked up at me sharply. "Hardly. Since one of the last places either was seen was here in the chapel on Friday."

"The treasury man was *here?*"

"As was a convicted seditionist called Samuel, also a foreigner, I believe. And who, like the Viscount, has also disappeared. It *would* have been a convenient place to exchange messages."

"But were they seen together?"

"People have seen all manner of things—including horns on the Frenchman and a halo on the poor fellow from the treasury." Gutiérrez scratched speculatively at the scruff of his beard. "Such rumours are sometimes of some use to us, but I would not want to be the secular authorities trying to find out what actually happened."

It had been two months, and I had never congratulated him on his promotion. Examining Magistrate. Something of a change from correcting and censoring texts. Was it more awkward for him to come here? No, not so far. Lowering my voice I asked if he had ever heard of any arrangements to intercept my mail. He looked startled that I would ask such a thing of him so baldly. Before answering he glanced over at Antonia and the novices.

"No, but I'll look into it," he said quietly. "You know I can't tell you what I learn. . . ."

"Of course not."

"But you would feel better if I knew."

"Much."

"You've been careful."

"About doctrine, yes, careful enough. About certain personages, I'm not so sure. If Núñez, for example, has intercepted certain letters and shown them to Santa Cruz . . ."

"I see. As I said, I can't tell you what I learn. But I can let you know *when* I know—if and when."

"*Gracias*, Gutiérrez. Don't take too many risks. San Jerónimo can hardly be considered neutral ground at the Holy Office these days."

"No, Sor Juana," he said, "but then it never was."

He set down his empty cup, and added after a moment that if I could think of anything to do to help myself, I should do it. It came out a little coldly, but he was anxious to be going. There was some checking he needed to do. For me but also for himself, I saw. He did not credit the poisoning story. The Archbishop had been crying poison for ten years. But to the possibility that I had raised—that the Archbishop's madness might be a device of some kind—this, Gutiérrez was giving some sober thought. It was not often I saw that insouciance falter. I could only imagine how many of his own actions he was re-examining in this light. And he confessed now that one thing had been bothering him for weeks: the rift one might have expected between Núñez and the

Archbishop over the Vieyra affair . . . there was as yet no sign that it had opened.

He promised to return soon. The last time he promised this he was gone six weeks.

If I could think of anything to do to help myself . . .

Yes, and if Bishop Santa Cruz was still thinking of swooping in as my Redeemer, he should swoop very soon.

Antonia, who had doubtless heard every word Gutiérrez said, insisted we finish our Seraphina letter and send it to Santa Cruz. I did not have the heart to tell her the letter was ridiculous.

Satirical verses are like wolves: once loosed they close straight on the weakest, fattest offering. Whoever the second soldier proved to be, the first still stood every chance of having been His Grace. If in my letter on the Vieyra sermon I had struck the Archbishop a glancing blow, the Seraphina letter was making straight for His Grace's throat. . . .

Worse, I was no longer at all sure who the second Soldier was. It had startled me to hear Palavicino protesting that he was not the Soldier. Not once had it occurred to me that people could suppose it was anyone but Núñez. The thing was so obvious—Sapphic hymns—the phrase was his; the charges of heresy, especially that of Arian, were precisely those Nunez had threatened me with. It had to be him. Or someone wishing to sound like him. . . .

But who could have managed this? Master Examiner Dorantes could.

Dorantes did not come to Palavicino's sermon, did not want to seem to be involved, though this had not stopped him offering to help Cantor de Ribera—what, rewrite, *repair?*—my lyrics on Saint Peter.

Why had no rift appeared between Núñez and the Archbishop? Could the second Soldier have been Dorantes, doing Santa Cruz's bidding? But then what if Núñez had never been involved? Just listen to me—such contortions to believe Núñez was not the one. Why could I not bring myself to think the worst of him? Why after all these years, after everything that had come between us, had I not rid myself of my affection for him? *Father Antonio Núñez de Miranda was not my father.*

I had been walking in the snow.

When Gutiérrez left, I set out for the kitchen to see Sor Vanessa and Concepción, who were among my few friends within these walls. That there were no platters of *delicias* today for my guests was a painful turn, and yet I found myself stopped outside, standing in the lightly falling snow. I looked back.

I'd come out along the high temple wall, the cool stone slots we confess through partly snowed in. Parting from the wall, tracks wound through the orchard and ended with me, here in the midst of the winter growing season. After a moment I added to them, wending through the branchless lances of papaya trees, green goads in massy cluster at the tips —a line of maces groaning beneath the extra weight of moistened snow. I ducked in among the pomegranates and apples, ruddy-cheeked amidst the little hods and barrows of snowy leaves . . . in through branches broken where not bowed or bent to their stays like Bedouin tents. A finch startled ahead of me and, catapulting into the air, freed the softly nodding bough—such glory for that tiny weight, such masses to dislodge . . . launched not up but down.

There was such a stillness out here now, and for a moment, I was not sure how long . . . it had come inside. A cool, a quiet in my mind. Thoughts falling to rest, not memories quite, but everywhere falling, the presence of what was past piling up in drifts. . . . The quiet in the orchards after snow in Panoayan.

As I came in through the refectory it seemed I had quite forgotten my grievances. I did not come to visit the mistresses of the kitchens often enough. Vanessa, descended from the aristocracy of Navarre, small-boned, elegant. Concepción, an Indian servant old enough to be her mother, round and bent. And yet they were very much a couple, a partnership in here. It was like another country, indeed one in which Spanish was rarely used, since it would have returned to Sor Vanessa the very advantage she had chosen to surrender. What speaking they needed to do, Vanessa did in the Nahuatl she had learned, and Concepción in her few set phrases and words for food in Basque.

I had once had the idea of learning Basque, which Vanessa warned me from the outset I would not have time to learn. And so the joke among us was that I would tease Vanessa about her Nahuatl, which was good now, while Vanessa sadly warned how far Concepción was ahead of me in Basque. And then I would ask when she was going to take the time to teach me. Now they were mortified to see me come in through the kitchen doorway. I saw it was not their doing—that the Prioress had ordered that there be no more special courtesies for my guests—and so my coming could have been a painful moment that just now I would have given anything to avoid. It was too late to turn back. My wet feet saved us.

Concepción scolded me in Nahuatl, dragged me over by the fire and pulled my shoes and stockings off as though they were a child's. She had hardly towelled my feet dry before Vanessa thrust into my hands an aromatic cup of chocolate spiked with some kind of *aguardiente*. They would not let me leave until my stockings had dried, and in truth they dried too quickly. As I sat before the fire Concepción came by to stir the pot from time to time, and Vanessa brought morsels of this or that on which I was asked a grave opinion. Concepción told her to make me try everything. I was too thin, too thin. I listened to them softly chaffering over sauces and spices. I stared into the fire . . . along the walls . . . at the clusters of clay *ollas* and copper pots, strings of peppers and of garlic, baskets of red and white onion, all strung from the rafters. More than once my eyes had sought out the open doorway to the pantry at the back . . .

As I was leaving I asked Vanessa when she was going to take the time to teach me Basque.

"You do not have the time to learn," she said.

If it came out a little awkwardly, it was only that her face had fallen, to hear what she had said. I smiled and shook my head.

On my way out through the refectory I glanced at the rostrum. It was a shame to let drop all Antonia's work on Camilla. She had done a fine translation of Virgil, another of Catullus. I would ask her to give us a class on Camilla at our academy on Monday.

At first I was afraid it was the typhoid again. Even before the symptoms, the sense of something gone wrong. Then hot and cold, fever and chills, bouts of drowsiness between the headaches, a vise about my skull, forehead and back.

I was a fortnight in bed. In that time Antonia had gone down to meet little delegations of well-wishers, a bookseller, a theatre-manager come with an actor or two, and tears and flowers. And gossip. A day or two later, a few impresarios from the bullrings and cockpits, with bottles of good wine and still better gossip. *There* was a visit I was sorry to have missed. Write one sonnet on a bullfighter, make fast friends for life. We shared a bond, I realized. The Archbishop's hatred. The news was no longer a matter only for the clerics—the Archbishop's persecutions of me, his bans on my carols for the people. Next the Creole seditionists would be bringing me chocolate.

The Viscount and Samuel and the treasury man had all come to our chapel—perhaps had even chosen it as a meeting point. What drew them *here*? Rebellion was in the air, and our convent was fast becoming a symbol, if not of insurrection then I did not know what. It was not just my locutory now—all the parlours were brewing rumours and gossip. The French were coming, the Viscount was leading them through our defences! It was not completely implausible. Eight years earlier the pirates had held Veracruz for six weeks, then sailed off with fifteen hundred Spaniards to be made slaves. Still, one might doubt that all were virgin girls. . . .

Then Antonia brought up from the locutory a story I made her repeat twice. That Father Xavier Palavicino had been in Veracruz at the time, having boasted of going among the dead and the dying, giving last rites even before the French had returned to their longboats. I teased Antonia for wondering if Palavicino were somehow in league with the Viscount. Xavier Palavicino, pirate curate. But if not, what did this mean?—nothing at all, except to the simple people of Mexico, which was not nothing. It did not matter if it was true, it could seem true enough to them. Was this why so many came now? My well-wishers could not really have thought I was involved—and in what exactly? Was I thought to be the new pirate queen? I had a not unpleasant moment imagining myself at the side of the Viscount as pirate king but put it down to the fever. . . .

Comedy where there is none. Palavicino among the pirates—it was absurd yet somehow chilling that events so incongruous should so conspire. What *had* brought them all to the chapel that day? *There was no connection.*

The connections are in the weave of the net. The fish in it are not cause but <u>consequence</u> *of the weave. The fish do not weave it, nor are the fish woven into it. The fish are only caught up in it. Change the weave, change the fish. A different weave catches different fish. The word is* coincidencia.

I am not the fish, I am the net.

February 12th. There were to be no more classes at the academy, and the other teachers would take up my classes of music and dance. The

Prioress had chosen this moment to announce it, while I was in bed. She thought me weak. We would see. Rebellion was in the air.

I got up and dressed, still tottery. Mother Andrea was expecting me. Yes, she had told the kitchen no more special favours. These had been for friends of the convent. She was no longer sure that I knew any. She was unusually sure of herself—as I recalled it, Palavicino had been her idea, not mine. She could not hold my eyes.

I told her I did not care about the food, but the classes, these would continue.

Yes, the classes, she said. They had not been her idea in the first place; as *she* recalled, they were the idea of Bishop Santa Cruz—who was also, it appeared, not such a friend of this convent. And cancelling them had not been her idea, either. They were suspended by order . . . she held up the letter by a corner. I might read it myself, if I wished. And if I wished, I could take it up with him, His Grace, the Lord Archbishop of Mexico.

That afternoon I sent for Gutiérrez, where had he been? It had been two weeks already. *I am stronger, I am not weak.* A little dewy at the temples, a little clammy under the tunic—but far from the only one, in this place. I was better, much, or would be if the headaches would ease.

February 15, 1691. Gutiérrez came. I went down alone to meet him. No news on the letters, but he had been wondering, what if Núñez had not burned all my spiritual journals? Just a thought, but what if the journals—not the letters—had been what he used to so change Bishop Santa Cruz's stance toward me? How did Gutiérrez know about these? But I had told him, had I forgotten? In making his inquiries this week he had discovered there were men at the Holy Office who had not forgotten Núñez's talk of my journals so many years ago. *Who*—Dorantes? It was no sooner said than regretted. Gutiérrez risked enough by coming here. I apologized. I had not been well.

Yes, he could see that for himself. He insulted me wryly enough and the moment of awkwardness passed. He had other news.

Palavicino still persisted in his mad intention to publish the sermon. He had found a printer, and most of the necessary signatures. One was the Viceroy's. Gutiérrez was surprised, but I explained that the Viceroy had been grateful for my poem on his great naval victory in Tortuga. He was only too happy to license the excellent sermon written in my defence. He had been trying to do me a favour.

February 24, 1691. The twenty-second anniversary of my profession. The day I entered here I was not quite twenty. . . .

The second time I left the palace I went out the main gates—not by the servant's quarters, the way of shame—straight into the main square, with Perico alone to see me off. He led me out through the Hall of Mirrors, as if to remind me I had nothing to be ashamed of. Of course not, Perico. On the way to the door I saw her passing through mirror after mirror: a young woman fighting for her composure, at her hip gliding just above the mirror frames the tousled head of a dwarf.

Mostly it had been a relief, not having to face her after that day. Her nakedness in too many mirrors, too many rooms, the nakedness in her face. I had not had to look into a mirror for twenty-two years.

I caught glimpses of course. Drawing water from a well . . . a face in the lamplight on the baths we drew. And there were nights I missed her, that passion, that pride and rage. Was she still here, had she gone away?

And I missed Antonia, the way she had been when she first came. For though we looked nothing alike, she had been about that age, had something of those traits, that pride, that rage.

A breeze from the sea . . .

Look at her today. It seemed the cloister did this to all of us. This anxiousness, this anger. This frustration and bitterness. She was not happy here any longer. I should have let her go. Where, where would my Antonia go?

We were at the table in the sitting room. Beyond her left shoulder a fire burned low in the corner. We had not spoken much all day. She'd prepared a beautiful meal for the anniversary of my profession. Vanessa and Concepción had sent up a lovely stew, chicken and *chayote*, peppers and squash. There was no hope of finishing all this food. Antonia was eating quietly, not looking up. Her hair was draped back over her broad shoulders in long black coils and streamers. Sometimes on festive occasions when it was just we two, we wore dresses. But tonight she still wore the rough brown *sayuela*, and I a damp white tunic of cotton . . . too thin, too thin.

Losing our classes was a bitter thing. Explaining it to the novices more bitter still. These past few days I had so wanted to bring the other Antonia back to stay. I wanted to tell her we would get them back, our classes. I wanted to say, I know you are not happy, Antonia.

Let us pretend, a little while, make believe for a week or two, that we are. . . .

"I have been thinking, 'Tonia, that you and I should write a play together." The window over the table was closed against the cold. Her form moved through the warps in the crystal panes as she cleared the dishes from the table. She did not yet look at me, but paused—about to lift a bowl of grated jícama and beet. "We have all the elements we need for a marvellous comedy—like *los empeños* that the Archbishop would so have hated, if he'd given himself half a chance." Her eyes, hazel in the light, met mine. She straightened. She was allowing herself to hope I might be serious. "I am serious. You and I. A play of mistaken identities—like *Amor es más laberinto*, which you know as well as I, having copied out all those drafts for me." I could see her excitement now—to be *doing* something.

"But how can I . . ." she asked. She shifted the bowl in her right hand to rest on the plates in her left, and nervously tucked a strand of hair behind her ear.

"Don't worry—we'll take another play as a model. There's one by Tirso that might be just perfect. With a maid named Serafina, I recall, and a secretary named Antonio. Tirso has all the tricks. You'll get the hang of it." I saw the light going out of her eyes. She thought I was making fun of her. Could she think me so cruel after what had happened with our classes—with Camilla? I pressed harder. Truly—I actually wanted us to write it. A play of masquerades, cloaked figures, assignations in the shadows of a garden. Couples reflecting other couples reflecting each other. Servants mistaken for their masters, and vice versa. Two hooded soldiers, each passing for the other. Archbishops feigning madness, bishops veiled as nuns. A Sicilian count we take for an enemy but who represents a friend. A French viscount introduced by a friend but whom we discover to be a seducer on a king's behalf—but who then reveals himself to be a pirate king bent on treasure and conquest. Seizing the moment in the capture of the silver fleet, the Creole seditionists rise up, proclaim the pirate viscount king! and thereby achieve their dream of making the viceroyalty a kingdom. We have all the elements—we could write it together in a week or two. . . .

And yet with every word it had gotten worse. Dishes still cradled against her side, she stood, head bowed, hair veiling her face. Her shoulders heaved—she set down the dishes violently. The bowl of salad tipped onto its side. "You wouldn't defend yourself from him!" Her hands shot up—the long blunt fingers splayed, tendons standing out in the strong wrists. "Someone had to."

The gesture was of imprecation or pleading, but it was only when I said his name that she would look up at me.

"Who—*Santa Cruz* . . . ? "Tonia, what is it? Why are you crying?" I got up and rounded the table to her side. I took her hands, folded the angry fingers up against her palms. "Toñita, look at me. Tell me . . ." I smoothed back her hair, with a fingertip touched the fine scar at her cheek, the damp tip of her nose, raised her chin. Her eyes brimmed.

"I sent it."

"Sent what? What did you send?" But already I knew . . . I was remembering her in the locutory—turning from the clavichord the day of his last visit as the thought had flickered through my mind that she'd been crying.

"The Seraphina letter, to Santa Cruz."

Our letter—did she have any idea what she'd done? There was much more she tried to tell me. No, Antonia, not now. I had never asked to know about her and the Bishop. I already knew where she had come from. Of course there was more, Antonia, there was always more. I did not need to hear it. I had chosen to trust her—*chosen*. I would not live my life racked with suspicions. Their gossip, their stories, their envies, I did not hear them. I did not listen. No, Antonia, I am too angry to hear it tonight—it was cruel but I would not give her the relief of confessing it. I do not care right now to hear what he has done to you—do you have any idea what you've done to *me*? If you hate him so, if he has done so little for you that you should find yourself trapped in here with me, then write your own letters—don't send him *ours*—or go to Puebla yourself and tell him how you feel, for you are not nearly so trapped in here as I.

No, Antonia. I will ask you when I am ready. Not before. Just now, I do not have time to help you with your conscience.

Now there really was work to do. Now let Santa Cruz have my answer. And in it let the Inquisition know I would not go without a struggle. Let them take their time, make their preparations, polish their arguments, for they would have such a fight.

And tell the shades of your fathers the one who sent you was a woman.

JUANA INÉS
DE LA CRUZ,
1 MARCH 1691

*abridged and adapted
from the translation of
Margaret Sayers Peden*[II]

†published only
posthumously, five
years after Sor Juana's
death

REPLY TO SISTER PHILOTHEA†

My most illustrious señora, dear lady:

It has not been my will, my poor health, or my justifiable apprehension that for so many days delayed my response. How could I write, considering that at my very first step my clumsy pen encountered two obstructions in its path? The first (and, for me, the most uncompromising) is to know how to reply to your most learned, most prudent, most holy, and most loving letter. . . . The second obstruction is to know how to express my appreciation for a favour as unexpected as extreme, for having my scribblings printed, a gift so immeasurable as to surpass my most ambitious aspiration, my most fervent desire, which even as a person of reason never entered my thoughts. . . .

This is not pretended modesty, lady, but the simplest truth issuing from the depths of my heart, that when the letter which with propriety you called *Atenagórica* reached my hands, in print, I burst into tears of confusion (withal, that tears do not come easily to me). . . .

I cast about for some manner by which I might flee the difficulty of a reply, and was sorely tempted to take refuge in silence. But as silence is a negative thing, though it explains a great deal through the very stress of not explaining, we must assign some meaning to it that we may understand what the silence is intended to say, for if not, silence will say nothing . . .

And thus, based on the suppostion that I speak under the safe-conduct of your favour, and with the assurance of your benignity and with the knowledge that like a second Ahasuerus you have offered to me to kiss the top of the golden sceptre of your affection as a sign conceding to me your benevolent licence to speak and offer judgements in your most exalted presence, I say to you that I have taken to heart your most holy admonition that I apply myself to the study of the Sacred Books . . . I confess that many times this fear has plucked my pen from my hand . . . which obstacle did not impinge upon profane matters, for a heresy against art is not punished by the Holy Office but by the judicious with derision, and by critics with censure. . . . I wish no quarrel with the Holy Office, for I am ignorant, and I tremble that I may express some proposition that will cause offense or twist the true meaning of some scripture. . . .

I have prayed that He dim the light of my reason, leaving only that which is needed to keep His Law, for there are those who would say that all else is unwanted in a woman . . . I deemed convent life the least unsuitable and the most honourable I could elect if I were to ensure my salvation. I believed I was fleeing from myself, but—wretch that I am!—I brought with me my worst enemy, my inclination, which I do not know whether to consider a gift or a punishment from Heaven. . . . it seeming necessary to me, in order to scale those heights, to climb the steps of the human sciences and arts for how could one undertake the study of the Queen of the Sciences if first one had not come to know her servants? How without Geometry, could one measure the Holy Arc of the Covenant and the Holy City of Jerusalem, whose mysterious measures are foursquare in all their dimensions, as well as the miraculous proportions of all their parts? . . . And without being an expert in Music, how could one understand the exquisite precision of the musical proportions that grace so many Scriptures, particularly those in which Abraham beseeches God in defence of the Cities, asking whether He would spare the place, were there but fifty just men therein; and then Abraham reduced that number to five less than fifty, forty-five, which is a ninth, and is as Mi to Re; then to forty, which is a tone, and is as Re to Mi; from forty to thirty, which is a diatessaron, the interval of the perfect fourth; from thirty to twenty, which is a perfect fifth, and from twenty to ten, which is the octave, the diapason. . . .

In this practice one may recognize the strength of my inclination. . . . What have I not gone through to hold out against this? Strange sort of martyrdom, in which I was both the martyr and my own executioner.

Often on the crest of temples are placed as adornment figures of the winds and of fame, and to defend them from the birds, they are covered with iron barbs . . . the figure thus elevated cannot avoid becoming the target of those barbs; there on high is found the animosity of the air, on high, the ferocity of the elements, on high is unleashed the anger of the thunderbolt, on high stands the target for slings and arrows. Let the head that is a treasure-house of wisdom expect no crowning other than thorns. . . . Seeing so many varieties of crown, I was uncertain what kind Christ's was. I think it must have been obsidional, which (as you, my Lady, know) was the most honoured and was so called from *obsidio*, which means siege. . . . The feat of Christ was to make the Prince of Darkness lift his siege, which had the whole world encircled. . . .

I confess that I am far removed from wisdom's confines and that I have wished to pursue it, though *a longe*. But the sole result has been to draw me closer to the flames of persecution, the crucible of torture, and this has even gone so far as a formal request that study be forbidden me . . . [12]

[And yet] I find a most wise Queen of Saba, so learned that she dares to challenge with hard questions the wisdom of the greatest of all wise men, without being reprimanded for doing so . . . I see many illustrious women; some blessed with the gift of prophecy, like Abigail; others of persuasion, like Esther; others with pity, like Rahab . . .

If I again turn to the Gentiles, the first I encounter are the Sibyls, those women chosen by God to prophesy the principal mysteries of our Faith, and with learned and elegant verses that surpass admiration . . . I see the daughter of the divine Tiresias, more learned than her father. An Hypatia, who taught astrology, and read many years in Alexandria . . . I find the Egyptian Catherine, studying and influencing the wisdom of all the wise men of Egypt . . .

Then if I turn my eyes to the oft-chastized faculty of making verses —which is in me so natural that I must discipline myself that even this letter not be written in that form—I might cite those lines, *All I wished to express took the form of verse*. And seeing that so many condemn and criticize this ability, I have conscientiously sought to find what harm may be in it, and I have not found it, but, rather, I see verse acclaimed in the mouths of the Sibyls, sanctified in the pens of the Prophets, especially King David. . . . The greater part of the Holy Books are in metre, as in the Book of Moses; and those of Job . . . are in heroic verse. Solomon wrote the Canticle of Canticles in verse; and Jeremiah his *Lamentations*. . . .

And if the evil is attributed to the fact that a woman employs them . . . what then is the evil in my being a woman? I confess openly my own baseness and meanness, but I judge that no couplet of mine has been deemed indecent. Furthermore, I have never written of my own will, but under the pleas and injunctions of others . . . That letter, lady, which you so greatly honoured . . . I believe that had I foreseen the blessed destiny to which it was fated—for like a second Moses I had set it adrift, naked, on the waters of the Nile of silence, where you, a princess, found and cherished it—I believe, I reiterate, that had I known, the very hands of which it was born would have drowned it . . . for as fate cast it before your doors, so exposed, so orphaned, that it fell to you even to give it a name, I must lament that among other deformities it also bears the blemish of haste . . . If I ever write again, I shall as ever direct my scribblings towards the haven of your most holy feet and the certainty of your most holy correction, for I have no other jewel with which to pay you . . .

CARACOL

y spring, the fears of winter had faded, yet the atmosphere had scarcely changed—the winds might change from excitement to anxiety to giddy folly, but unrest and shifting alliances had become our constants. It felt as if we might wake any day to a new state where stones would rise up and floating bodies fall. One had only to glance away for the kettle to come to a boil.[13]

She should not have sent our Seraphina letter, but it had taken Antonia to rouse me if even a little from my latest bout of melancholic humours. In fanning sparks Antonia had struck, I found the flame flickered up and fed itself a while—the letter ran to over fifty pages, which I had only just sent off when Carlos at last published his panegyric on the Spanish naval victory over French perfidy and piracy—a testament writ on water to Spanish valour and overwhelming numerical superiority. To thank me for my verses of dedication the Viceroy came in person. Our relations were entering, it seemed, an unusually cordial phase, even as mine with his wife had decidedly cooled. The Count de Galve left his guard to take up positions in the street and came in without attendants, a small man under a small hat on a massive periwig, which only made him seem all the younger, more forlorn. Not without humour, he praised the lines inspired by our weather, and was interested to hear me confirm that the cloud serpent of the verse took its source from Mixcoatl, FeatherSerpent's father.

> . . . *Así preñada nube, congojada*
> *de la carga pesada,*
> *de térreas condensada exhalaciones,*
> *sudando en densas lluvias la agonía*
> *—víbora de vapores espantosa,*
> *cuyo silbo es el trueno*
> *que al cielo descompone la armonía—*[14]

The rain had not stopped since the naval battle, nor indeed at any time during the dry season. It been raining for ten months. And in the Viceroy's face the strain showed. He'd acquired the habit of gnawing at the inside of his cheek, and by his winces I gathered it had become cankerous. The flooding in the outlying neighbourhoods was grave enough that Carlos had agreed to lend a hand designing new diversion schemes, though he knew the risk as well as anyone, a risk he had made clear to the Viceroy. Floods in our valley and the failures to control them had been ruining careers for as long as anyone here could remember. Corruption scandals, bankruptcies, colossal earthworks of shifting blame and dirt. Each viceroy at his inauguration was beseeched in verse, implored in speeches to please deliver us, as each year the lake shrank a little and yet the floods grew worse—the waters sluicing swiftly down denuded stretches of mountainside. This year was already the worst since '29, and the wet season had scarcely started.

Then a new danger. During the dredging operations, the men working under Carlos had discovered in the foul ooze at the bottom of the canals thousands upon thousands of small clay dolls in European dress, men and women in various postures of torment—pierced by lances, cleft at throat and chest. Though there was no saying how or when these effigies had found their way into the canals, Carlos had promptly warned the Viceroy that an Indian uprising might be imminent, thus dredging up the oldest fears of our colony.

The blight had continued its spread through the wheat. Bread prices had doubled for loaves halved in size. If the same were ever to happen with corn . . . But the growers did not even want to sell at the official price, which the officials had been rightly afraid to let rise. And yet that he, the Viceroy, was blamed for the onset of the rains seemed the height of injustice, was it not? A king's wedding was an occasion to be celebrated! Even the Church raised no objection for a year. And yes, Excellency, the Countess's parties were said to be stunning. The longer the Count de Galve stayed in the locutory, the more it seemed we sat together as two people who no longer knew who our friends were.

I had never stopped writing carols for the humble—on the Nativity and the love of a child, on fishermen and the miracles of abundance, on temples of bread. But for a year, almost none of these had been sung or published. All that had been heard from me were praises of a childless king's potency and the beauty of an unseen queen. It was Antonia, on her errands in the city, who first detected that my verses on the Viceroy's dash and competence were nowhere warmly received, unless by His Excellency. No matter that Carlos had devoted an entire book to

Spanish naval prowess—he at least was not making cruel pagan rhymes on rain and thunderclouds.

Not long after the Viceroy's last visit to San Jerónimo, the Cantor de Ribera brought two pieces of news from the Cathedral. The surprising: that he'd persuaded the cathedral dean to allow my carols on Saint Peter to be sung after all, to the music Ribera and I had written. The theme of Peter the fisherman had proved irresistible this year. I managed not to ask Ribera if Master Examiner Dorantes, who had volunteered to rewrite my carols, had lost the knack. The second piece of news was a simple delight. We'd often spoken of a manuscript I had started during my years at the palace and subsequently lost. *Caracol.* Now he'd finally convinced the dean that in these anxious days the cathedral needed something rare and unusual, an eight-day cycle devoted to sacred music. I would set down my ideas for *Caracol* again and together Ribera and I would develop the companion lyrics and musical illustrations. I had written so many verses on music that it might simply be a matter of adapting the existing ones. There would not be much money but enough for three. Three? Yes, he had persuaded Sálazar, no less, to join us.

Certain to be Ribera's successor, Sálazar was already the finest composer in the empire and in his better moments the only one able to approach the great Italians, Monteverdi and Scarlatti. Where Ribera was at his best with a simple melody, Sálazar was a master of the polyphonic. My friend was the first to admit that by Sálazar he was quite outstripped.

As Ribera sat across from me I remembered that when he and I had first met some fifteen years earlier, I'd composed in his honour a sonnet painting him as a swan, sacred bird of Apollo and Orpheus. In truth he did resemble a bird, which had almost made the sonnet come off, but the bird one thought of with Ribera was another. He was lanky and tall, grey-headed for as long as I had known him and beardless, though never quite clean shaven. His neck was thin; and as with long thin necks, his Adam's apple protruded and bobbed, but more like a peach pit than an apple on a bough. Though the nose was too short to be thought beaked, and was from that point of view disappointing, his heronness lay—and bounced and dipped—in the long black brows, glossy and sweeping. Still, while one might compose all manner of sonnets on the singing of swans, herons were a stiffer challenge.

His eyes searched mine, his brows signalling antically. Did I share in his excitement?

If his idea had been to cheer me, it was a magnificent success. I felt a rush of warmth and was happy not to have to worry for once about seeming ungrateful.

June 29th. The children have a game here in the capital, one I arrived too late to play myself but of which I had often made good use in class. In this game the city itself was the music and each church and temple, each cloister and monastery, was a saintly instrument on a musical map, each ringing at a certain pitch. The lowest of these was the bell of San José— *Ut,* our C. San Bernardo, three blocks north, got *Re. Mi, Mi, Mi,* was for our most elegant, Jesús María, whose bell was said of pure gold. The cracked brass bell of Santo Domingo got the semitone, *Fa. Sol* went to the convent of Santa Teresa. And the highest of these was our own, *La.* The low note on the overlapping hexachord gave us an *Ut* in F, and so on. Depending on whose bell first struck the hour, the map gave a different melody of pitches and chords—time running through the city as Re, Mi, Sol, Fa—or Ut, Fa, Sol, La, Mi, etcetera, children leaping up when their note was struck, a good deal of laughter . . .

At first I heard the ringing, then Ribera's music from the cathedral. As the bells died out I could almost hear the words. The rain had nearly stopped, the sky almost cleared. I leaned far out the window over Calle de las Rejas, startling my neighbours across the way. Saint Peter Fisherman . . . did I hear my verses, or only imagine them?

> . . . *Pescador de ganado,*
> *o ya Pastor de peces,*
> *la red maneja a veces*
> *y a veces el cayado,*
> *cuyo silbo obedece lo crïado* . . . [15]

After the music had faded away, I stayed by the window, my eyes roaming the bases of the hills beneath the low cloud. I had been hesitating to do *Caracol.* If anything, recognizing how badly I wanted to do it made me more hesitant. What I resolved to do instead was write a second birthday poem for the Vice-Queen. The one written on her birthday, when she'd come unannounced with her entire retinue, I had composed not merely in haste but in anger. Not with her for once but with one of the handmaidens, who had begun gossiping about the affairs in the palace dovecotes with the express purpose of making a slighting allusion to stories of my own nights on the upper floors. I had written the poem on the spot, while they listened and watched, lacing it with ironies, one or two dangerous. A line referred to the Countess's sequel as 'mondongas.' Little used, it was a word she could be counted on not to know, yet someone would eventually point out that it could mean ladies-in-waiting but had once meant prostitutes.[16]

It was during my time in the dovecotes that I had lost the manuscript of *Caracol. Speculative harmonics.* The beauty of the world as a music cascading from the mind of God. I had not been that far along. I could have started again, and yet I let the idea go, something so beautiful. For the first time in all these years I wondered if I had perhaps believed that I'd tarnished it in the puffery and the vaunting of my examination at the palace. Or that in the dovecotes I had perhaps tarnished myself.

Why, Señorita, if you are beautiful, is there so little harmony in you?

And why, Soul, dost thou know so little peace?

I saw what taking up *Caracol* again could be for me, and wondered how much of this Ribera had seen. Not a commission, but a second chance. A chance to say good-bye to the girl who had been seen out through the Hall of Mirrors.

To set the proper tone for *Caracol,* our eight day cycle required an opening note of cheer. I well remembered how dark and cold the cathedral felt when it rained. Something striking, new astonishments, fresh hopes. For it seemed to me that what we found most dispiriting just now was this sense that everything was being stripped from us, by Spanish incompetence, by French predation, by blights of pirates and weevils, by the waters themselves that gnawed away at our island.

And yet there was so much here that we might yet accomplish. What Ribera and I would offer them was the example of a musical clock, another project I had left unfinished years ago.

Ladies and gentlemen, *compañeros, compatriotas* . . .

It is often said these days that the age of discovery has ended. And yet Europe has never seemed farther away. But the age of discovery never truly ends, for it is always starting somewhere else: and it is time for us here to make discoveries for ourselves.

No empire has had more to gain or lose than ours in the question of longitude, for on this depends Spain's claim to all the lands lying beyond a certain meridian line imaginatively traced north-south on the sea in 1493. The trouble being that in the two centuries since, we have still found no method for tracing such a line out of sight of land. So while we have long been fond subjects of the Spanish kings, we here in Mexico may yet wake up one morning to find ourselves Portuguese. . . .

No country in Europe began with a greater advantage than did our Spain of the Two Faiths, for our learned Moors once had access to the writings of the mighty Persians—the astronomers of Baghdad, venerable Al-Tusi and Abu'l-Wafa, and the geometers of Kabul, Mansur and Al-Biruni.[17] How circuitous are the tracts of history: It seems one has only to digest the problem, in 1493, to discover one has just expelled the solution, in 1492.

Perhaps this is why it was our Spanish kings Philip II and III who first envisioned a great prize to the solver of the problem—six thousand ducats outright, and two thousand a year for life! And still, we in Mexico await the solution as anxiously as ever. What city suffers more grievously than our own the losses in mercantile shipping on the world's two greatest oceans? or the pillage of our silver in the Caribbean? or depends more upon a healthy Spanish treasury to fund its own defence?

The *Académie Royale des Sciences* of our great Bourbon adversary has lately made some little progress—if it can be called that, for the most recent calculations have reduced the map of France in the west by a full degree of longitude; such that the mighty Sun King complains of losing more land to his geographers than to his enemies. And so, inspired by these great pirates of land, the geographers, it is indeed the piratical nations of England and France that are pursuing the solution to longitude at sea most doggedly—to catch our laggard age up with the Persian tenth century, and catch up with our silver fleets.

If anything has saved us thus far, it is that the pirates do not know where they are. . . .

You will say we do not know where they are either, but surely our best hope lies in finding out where *we* are before they do. Waking up Portuguese is not the worst to be imagined: we might find ourselves, not far hence, the westernmost city of France. Which could be even worse than it sounds. For if we do not know where we are, or in whose empire, or even whose language we should be speaking, *it is because we do not know what time it is.*

To which problem we humbly propose a solution: the Mexican musical clock.

The sailors tell us that could they but tell the time with accuracy, they could greatly increase the precision of their navigations. We begin, then, with the science of the publican, who raps on his casks to check their volumes. And as we have just heard with our own ears, different volumes of water can be calculated to make the vessels they fill sound out the hexachord. As the curtain rises here in the atrium, the musical clock we see before us is composed of six water vessels shaped like funnels, each of increasing volume, each designed to tip into the next larger as the water level rises to a given height. And so unto the largest. To the height of the water corresponds a volume, and to the volume a tone when the vessel is struck lightly with a baton.

Aboard the ship, the water is made to flow at a constant rate from a reservoir filled each day by sailors at a water pump. Every six seconds Vessel I tips into II—and if struck at any instant it sounds with one of six notes. As the water level rises the note drops. Vessel II is a basin whose tone every ten seconds drops by a note and tips itself once a minute into Vessel III. The sum of the first two vessels gives the timekeeper his seconds. Vessel III drops by a whole note each minute and spills itself every six minutes into vessel IV, whose tone changes by a note every ten. The sum of III and IV gives the timekeeper his minutes. Vessel V changes by a whole note each hour and tips every six. Vessel VI varies by a whole note every six hours. The sum of V and VI gives the timekeeper his hours.

The timekeeper does not need to check the time continuously. Rather, when the navigator calls *Time!* he takes up his baton and lightly taps each vessel, smallest to largest, yielding the precise time by way of a sequence of six notes. When the navigator is seated at his table, the timekeeper sings them out or pipes them back to him. Ut—Sol—Mi—Re—Fa—La!

Converting these back to the corresponding values (6—2—4—5—3—1), the navigator proceeds to multiply each by the appropriate unit: 6 units of 1 second, plus 2 units of 10 seconds (equalling 26 seconds); 4 units of 1 minute, plus 5 units of 10 minutes (equalling 54 minutes); 3 units of 1 hour, plus 1 unit of four hours (equalling 7 hours). Time: 7 hours 54 minutes 26 seconds.

Which translates, depending on one's habits, to the hour of breakfast, between Prime and Terce.

In theory, then, we have the musical clock, and the practical demonstration that music is our most perfect and pragmatic idea of Time. . . .

It was evening, after Vespers. The storm outside was worsening. At dinner, beneath closed shutters, the candle flames dipped and quivered to each big gust of wind. After the meal we moved into the library. Antonia was taking dictation for *Caracol* as I paced about the room to various tempos, here and there a pause to pick up instruments and curios, pull musical texts down from shelves. Over five months since she sent our letter to Bishop Santa Cruz, and in that time I'd refused to let her unburden herself to me. She had tried—had gotten as far as saying our Seraphina letter was to blame for everything. Ah, the vainglory of writers. But that night during the wildness of the storm, there was no stopping her. The weather explained everything now if we wished. Perhaps I could blame my cruelty too on this.

I had already guessed at half of it, or not quite the half. I understood that it had to do with her sisters, but her hatred of him had less to do with the ones he had not helped than the ones he had, the little ones in the convent school of Santa Monica. She and Santa Cruz as lovers would have seemed common—but he had never touched her, she had only watched him disciplining himself, and afterwards tended his back. Here, too, there was more, but I deflected her by asking where she had gone to meet him. A house near the Salto de Agua, at the end of the aqueduct. It was a relief to her to describe it, though I had not asked as a kindness. And since that night, the room has come into my mind many times—always clear but with slight variations. Santa Cruz wearing the black cassock of Lent, or a violet mozetta. On a desk by the window there are cigarettes or flowers, chocolate or wine. Oddly the one constant is a detail she did not give. The view from the window of the Salto de Agua, where the water of the aqueduct falls in folds, like clear silk. . . .

But when I asked Antonia if he had read out my letters there, I saw how close I had come to breaking her heart. She had never shown him a single letter—nor ever discussed a single one. The truth was he never asked, and if he had she didn't know what she would have done. *What then?* Reports—but I had to please believe that not a word she told him had been true. Reports . . . She had to tell him something, but lied about everything. He said all he cared about was the state of my soul. This sounded like Santa Cruz. He asked if I still kept a spiritual journal for myself, he asked once if I had any manuscripts not my own. He said he didn't care about doctrine or secret books. He said it wasn't for the Inquisition, that they had someone else watching—someone in here— and that only he could protect me from them. Unless she thought she could. So if I was reading X she told him Y, if I was writing one thing she told the son of a wayward bitch another. But most often what he asked for had been details, personal things. Where I brushed my hair at night, brush or comb, left hand or right, if she had ever seen me disciplining myself . . . and so she lied, had been lying for three years and the bastard knew—she was sure of it. This was part of the game, that he made her lie—once he asked which she thought might place me in greater danger, a lie or the truth. And she was terrified—she didn't know, it was true how could she know that? And then he came that day for my arguments, the day I beat him at chess. My pages for him were the one letter she almost didn't post—but if she hadn't, what then? She didn't know how to protect me. He was the only one who could. I had to see, I had to believe her . . .

The truth was that I did, and yet I was not sure she would ever let herself believe *me*. So I told her things, about myself, my past. I spoke to her simply and quietly, as though she were a child, for she was quite childlike by then. About my own years in Mexico as a young girl, about how frightened I had been. I spoke to her of how happy I had been to know her, and have her here with me. That it had been too long since I had seen her laughing, the mischief in her. Yes, I'd known there was more, flashes of darkness and trouble. But she had been like a secret book I had never wanted to leaf through, a sort of miracle that she had made such a difficult journey to me intact. Well not quite intact. She smiled then. And I told her that I had always known there was more between her and Santa Cruz, that it had been a point of pride that if I treated her with love and friendship I needed never worry about any of that, and I had been right after all. That even friends have secrets, that friends could risk hurting each other.

And so we lay on my bed and I stroked her cheek and kissed her hair, as the sky paled in the windows in the east. We missed the prayers of Lauds and again at Prime, even knowing not a few of my sisters would be saying that it was for sins such as these that it did not stop raining anymore.

She told me how frightened she had been for me. She had never seen me as I was after the letter from Philothea. Not writing—not even to María

Luisa, hardly reading, melancholy, sarcastic—who? not me . . . yes, you. How she hated him, how she had wanted to die when she came into my room and saw the fragments of the *Letras a Safo* in the ashes on my desk.

I had thought of Seraphina as our first work together, but she had felt those verses had been ours. She and María Luisa were the only ones ever to have read them. Though it had been six months, it was still painful to talk of them so I asked what she thought—what we might do for her sisters.

There was no place safer for her sisters than where they were, in the convent of Santa Monica, nowhere he could not reach them if he chose to. And nowhere he could not reach her. He had threatened once to take her away from me and put her back where he had found her. But she thought Santa Cruz was finished with her now. She had not been summoned to the house by the Salto de Agua for over a year.

But has he finished with you, Juana? she said, after a little while. Is it love? she asked. Could it be he is in love with you?

I asked her if she knew what the Mexicans say about someone who takes a gift back, for she has been a gift to me. What do they say of persons such as these?

Oppa icuitl quiqua.

They eat their excrement twice.

Caracol . . .

> *Dulce deidad del viento, armoniosa*
> *suspensión del sentido deseada,*
> *donde gustosamente aprisionada*
> *se mira al atención más bulliciosa.*
> *Y luego:*
> *pues a más que ciencia el arte has reducido,*
> *haciendo suspensión de toda un alma*
> *el que sólo era objeto de un sentido . . .* [18]

We take up again the case of the spiral shell, cut now with a very fine saw not cross-wise but at a parabolic angle. The section yields not the orbit of a circle but an ellipse. And if, as we have just argued, the celestial harmony were conceived not as Pythagoras did, as a circle of fifths, but as a spiral, a winding stair, ever widening in its compass, then we should soon see each turn on the stair offering a mutation on the scale with respect to the position just beneath it. As a symbol then we may say the winding stair is Grace and detect, in the very properties of the spiral, its structure and agency. For as we have seen in the properties of the speaking trumpet and caracol, the spirals of the ellipsoids propagate sound, lending it strength and amplitude.

On this voyage, Mind is the guide, Grace is the strength we are given to rise.

Music is the Mind of God brought into Time, spiralling down through the Creation. The spiral shell is the voice from the depths of the sea, that silence from which the echo springs, the instrument through which we speak to the sky. Here in Mexico the Lord of the Wind wore a conical hat and here in this city his temples were round, with no sharp angles to stand against the wind. He was called Ehecatl. Here, the wind was the breath of heaven; the storm, the music of the sky—the thunder his drum, the wind his strings, the rain and the snow and hail on the ground were his water sticks. And the caracol was his wind-jewel . . .

And so we find in the caracol the hidden emblem of our soul, the secret shape of Grace, the echo of a celestial correspondence; even as we hear in ourselves, if we listen, a distant echo of God.

July 5th. The composer Sálazar came, alone. Would Cantor De Ribera be joining us later? First one musician was missing, then the other. The world of course revolved around musicians, but if we were serious about setting the *Caracol* to music we really should meet all together, very soon.

Ribera was ill. Truly?—please say it was not serious. No, a cold was all. The cantor was only a little hoarse. Sálazar was smiling now and I found myself glad he had come, even though we could get little work done. Cantor De Ribera was always hoarse, the irony being that a musician whose title derived from chant and song should have such a raucous voice. This was his speaking voice; his singing was a truly pitiful thing to hear. But with perfect pitch. He was particularly hoarse when excited—which, when speaking on musical subjects, was often. He was good, Ribera, and a good musician, and knew Sálazar to be a great one.

There had always been something stiff in Sálazar's demeanour toward me—perhaps it was only the younger artist thoroughly sick of hearing about the older one. He was making a special effort to be cordial today. To both of us the Heron Ribera was especially dear. And yet I had the distinct impression Sálazar was considering a withdrawal from our *Caracol*. Though we had talked but a few times, he and I had known each other much longer than he realized. Almost thirty years ago he had come to the palace as a boy of six to play the violin for the court. He had spent a horrible day waiting to be called upon, had sat for hours with his violin in an adjoining room. Finally a page was sent for him, only to return saying the child seemed too frightened to play. As the youngest member of the court I was dispatched, one child to another, to coax him out. I found him sitting on the floor in a corner, lonely and over-awed, and angrily hurt now that someone had finally condescended to talk to him—though what could there be for *us* to discuss. And so we had a talk about being a prodigy.

Today I considered asking him if he had any memory of this, but did not want to spoil it with worries, mine or his, that I was trying to influence him to stay with our project.

Sálazar had just been saying, with some delicacy, that the cathedral had never seemed a promising venue for *Caracol*, but neither he nor Ribera had expected the Palace's patronage to be in doubt. Until yesterday. The Viceroy began by expressing his untiring admiration for Sor Juana . . . but the year had been difficult. Sálazar was explaining this to me as though perhaps I had just arrived from Perú. Very difficult for the Viceroy. Yes, I saw that. Hastening to reaffirm his favour for me and friendly feelings, the Count de Galve joked that the past year of our association had been dogged by ill-luck. The Vice-Queen, never a friend, had been pleased to begin a list and sent a servant for writing materials so that it might be taken down. Others chimed in from among the courtiers on the couches and cushions around the dais. Much drink had been consumed. Sálazar was at pains to attribute our setback to the hazard of the moment. The hour was late. They were in the Hall of Realms. The fire had been allowed to burn low, dry firewood being at a premium. Firelight flickered dimly over the maps and charts on the walls, long shadows cast up from the busts on the mantle. The tone at first was rueful, then mock-dreadful and dire, as when one eggs on the teller of a ghost encounter. Blight, flooding, pirates, rumours of insurrection, the Viscount's disappearance, the French, the French, the threat to the silver fleets, the dolls in the canals. . . . Before long the Count de Galve, his thin face already anxious and careworn, was visibly frightened. It had been clear from the first he was not a strong man, but he had once wanted to be.

It was don Carlos who'd partly succeeded in changing the subject. Carlos? Partly . . . He pointed out that recent days were *not* the worst in memory. The year 1611 had still to be given the edge. Many of course had heard about the earthquake, the most devastating in over a century.

A few had heard of the eclipse. The hall grew quiet. The empire's greatest scholar since Juan de Mariana was in his element. When Carlos had finished his relation, no one noticed for several minutes that even the musicians had stopped playing and were raptly listening. It might have amused him to speak up for me in the very place where I had once been the most at ease and he the most miserable. But I refused to suspect him. And I knew perfectly well what he had been thinking—to strike a final, fatal blow against superstition everywhere, in all its guises. It was such a terrible way to come to my defence, only Carlos could have tried it.

I tried to put a brave face on this for Sálazar. 1521, 1611, 1691 . . . note the pattern of declinations in the intervals of calamity, I said. Sálazar put in something about mutations and musical intervals, I answered in downward spirals and rates of fall. Sálazar gave more details. I knew others.

In 1608 one of the most gifted Princes of our Church reached Mexico. Fray García, the new Archbishop, was learned, eloquent, dedicated, a lover of music and bullfights, a man at ease in the world—and to whom, on the evidence of his having risen so quickly to his station, it seemed almost nothing untoward had ever happened. On the day his Viceroy met him at the outskirts of the city, the carriage they were sharing overturned suddenly on a flat, well-travelled road. Later, at the Dominican monastery, the dais of welcome collapsed, hurling Fray García again to the ground, and with him the others on the platform, crushing an Indian beneath it. On another day the mules drawing the Archbishop's carriage stampeded, for no discernible reason. Fray García acted on an impulse to leap to safety, but caught his foot in the carriage step. The fall was heavy, but he was still considered lucky not to have been killed. At the news of his appointment to succeed the outgoing Viceroy, Fray García laid plans for the most elaborate of triumphal entries parading the trappings of both offices. The Archbishop's pallium alone required twenty-two men to hold aloft. As a further extravagance, he declared that a grand program of bullfights be held every Friday for a year to celebrate this rare convergence of the two offices. The next Friday was Good Friday. There were murmurs. There was a nun who took it upon herself to warn the Archbishop-Viceroy personally. Inés de la Cruz was a musician whose convent he visited regularly, but despite her admonition the Good Friday bullfight went ahead. The very next Friday, a strong tremor rocked the plaza just before the spectacle commenced, and this time the event was postponed. As the *corrida* began on the third Friday, a quake destroyed the grandstand and several of the buildings nearest it. From just above Fray García's balcony a section of stone masonry broke free and killed a dozen spectators below, missing him by the narrowest span. Soon after, as he entered the Plaza del Volador at the approaches to the Viceregal Palace, one of the Indian fliers performing there for his benefit lost hold of his tether and plunged from a great height, crushed to the ground at the Archbishop-Viceroy's very feet. That same month, June, a total eclipse of the sun. In August, the quake of 1611, and forty aftershocks of nearly equal violence. Forty exactly. At Christmas, an eruption of El Popo, the city choked in ash, flash floods that same afternoon. His mood sombered, his injuries, never fully healed after the leap from the carriage, worsened. Turning to Sor Inés de la Cruz for consolation, he was told only to prepare for death, which preparations he put into effect on February 12th.

Vexed by all the superstitious chatter, Carlos had only thought to turn to account a parlour game played by the foolish and anxious and bored—I did not judge, I had been one—and I knew beyond a doubt that at some point the game had entirely ceased being an entertainment. In the art of Aeschylus there are stories in which what happens to the individuals tells the fate of a people. But though the fate of the Archbishop-Viceroy in 1611 involved many others, and though many died and suffered throughout the valley, our Viceroy took all this to be about one person, himself. It was not hard to picture him, his darkling thoughts returning to the year of ostentation in honour of the king's wedding, the exaltation of his offices as the King's representative, the balls and debauches, the Church's dire warnings.

And if Carlos had told his tale to such stunning effect at the palace, I thought it only a matter of time till the recital reached the Archbishop. Twenty or thirty courtiers, as many servants—in a week the news would be spreading from every church and brothel in the capital. Like the Viceroy, His Grace would find lessons to draw from it.

They came a few days later. Two lackeys in the Archbishop's livery. Safety in numbers, it would seem. By the Archbishop's dispensation they entered into the cloister, entered this cell without knocking. But so swiftly does word fly through the alleys and corridors that we were already waiting for them. This is a women's place—no man enters here without this warning.

Wordlessly one of the lackeys handed me the order, under the Archbishop's seal. Silently, mercifully, they turned and left. After a moment to compose myself I followed them to the door to make sure they'd gone. My sisters in the cells across the way stood gaping in their doorways.

> . . . the petition dated January 4th, 1679, received by the Secretary of the Archdiocese on November 20th, 1681, for the purchase of one cell. Pursuant, a complete inventory of its contents is required, for the purposes of determining if said cell in its dimensions and appointments is adequate and appropriate to the purchaser's requirements.
>
> > By order and disposition of His Illustrious Grace,
> > Lord Archbishop don Francisco Aguiar y Seijas,
> > signed this, the sixth day of July, 1691

The game was obvious enough, if subtle for a man of the Archbishop's temperament. The inventory would reveal the cell to be too full and therefore inadequate to its purpose . . . until an as yet undetermined number of items had been auctioned to raise funds for the Archbishop's ferocious campaigns of charity. The people's need was insatiable in these trying times. Who would deny it, who would refuse? Even if she could.

I wondered if he would next send Carlos, his Chief Almoner, who knew the contents of these rooms as well as any man. Almost thirteen years I had been waiting to buy this cell. All these years without a response, and yet the request had been neither forgotten nor lost. Was the Archbishop's secretary so very competent, or were they aided by a memory in which nothing is forgotten or lost?

I had begun to wonder if there had ever been a rift between Núñez and His Grace.

But the cell, Your Grace, is it too full or instead too small . . . ? For I have so far found no room for a botanical garden, or pleasaunces such as those of Versailles. A full astronomical observatory would be a splendid addition, and a bestiary, too. If not so large as that kept by the great Khans, then something more modest, such as Moctezuma's own. . . .

The soul of Teresa of Avila is a palace, one of the most beautiful that has ever been. That we may understand a little, she presents it as a palace of passageways reaching inward, an enchaining of seven chambers or abodes. In the innermost, on a priceless rock-crystal throne, waits her Beloved.

My soul waits at the top of ten steps, behind a lacquered folding screen in the Japanese style, in a long narrow room that houses my *studiolo* and library. Here is where the Inspector will wish to begin his list; it is this room that contains the most priceless of marvels; in this chamber my Beloved rests.

But before entering, the gentlemen may wish to get their bearings, to fix this particular arrangement in their minds. At the top of the stairs, there, to the left, is one of three doors connecting this room to the other two. Just inside the doorway is a second folding screen, also in the Japanese style but decorated with scenes from Mexico's past and streets.

Nine *varas* in width by ten in length, the upper storey is six *varas* high. Three rooms: on the east side, a sitting room with dining table, a bedroom with a desk; the third room runs the full length of the west side and occupies a third of the total width. The geometry will not be difficult, though the accounting may so prove. While there are writing desks in every room, here by the window is the largest. The window has been altered, is large and low; as the Inspector sees for himself, the view across the rooftops is to the south. Note the step-ladders, the shelves built to line the walls from floor to ceiling—the workmanship is excellent. Note carefully the openings cut to the exact contour of the window, the fireplace and doorways; see the hooks set in the dim top shelves from which to hang a lantern while one searches. The four transverse display cases stand at two-*vara* intervals, each successive case from the south window a little wider than the last to catch the light. Take note that all must be dismantled if they are to leave this room. Yes the cot and the reading chair by the fireplace, these come out easily.

That space beside the stairs, there behind the low shelf? No, not a hidden stairwell, I assure you, just a chimney shaft.

If we think of the library as a window looking out from an enchanted palace, then the prince's *studiolo* is the world brought in to stock the cave of the magician, the workshop of the alchemist.

Its elements are to be deployed with care, in sections and harmonious intervals. The *studiolo* is a theatre of the soul, the mind is its orchestra; its sweetest solos are played on its finest instrument, *admiratio*. We may imagine this instrument of wonder as a slender violinist seated, a little nervously, among the reeds and flutes and clarions. In the ideal arrangement featured here, in which the library and *studiolo* flow one into the other, the two chief sections—perhaps think of these as the strings and the winds—consist of instruments of spirit and sense, the upper and lower choirs. And yet this business of upper and lower is really a convenience, for the instruments are free to move about, and really owe it to themselves to do this. So it happens that we so often find *logica* down in the kitchens, where the knives come out.

But you will want to get under way. First, the musical and audible instruments, since this is a sort of auditorium. No, I do not play them all unfortunately, but quite a few. Clay flute, clavichord, *vihuela*, violin . . . There you see an echo chest, here two automatons that dance and sing. Try them if you like, they are very lifelike. One pendulum, which, courtesy of Signor Galilei, we can use to regulate the tempo by lengthening and shortening the string. One musarithmetic box such as in the famed *studiolo* of the Reverend Kircher at the Jesuit College in Rome. Oh yes, the Jesuits have these too. Bigger. One music box, one speaking trumpet, one conch shell trumpet, yes, a *caracol*. I was just coming to that.

If you don't mind, I really must sit down, I really must stop a moment. You would not consider coming back another day? Surely the Inspector must see this will take a little while. What you are asking is the inventory of my soul.

Friday afternoon, a cold grey rain. It was the turn of those of us who confess with Father Arellano. The Mother Prioress preferred that the most senior of the black-veiled nuns not go to our own chaplain, who had influence enough here among us. I had been called and could not delay long—our patio being the closest to the chapel. Reluctantly I made my way along the arcades to stay out of the weather, down the short passageway, past the chapel entrance and out into the rain. The orchards were ahead, a drab of yellowing leaves, the gardens to my left, mostly mud and a sprig or two of green. Sister María Bernardina was kneeling on a stone slab, soaked to the skin, confessing through a small slot in the thick chapel wall. She finished as I drew near, blinked water out of her eyes. More drops tumbled from her brows. She almost smiled. The *craticula* is the width of the mouth, such that on neither side of the wall may we see each other with both eyes, leaving one feeling not unlike the Cyclops confiding in Odysseus. I was not even sure I knew any longer what Father Arellano looked like, to those with sight in both eyes. For ten years he had been my nominal director, entitled to meet with me more comfortably in the locutory whenever he wished. He never wished.

I am too beautiful, he had once explained. Nice that he still thought so, for a Cyclopean attaining a certain age—though were it intended as a gallantry, and it was not, it would have meant somewhat more were he indeed able to see me.

It was cold, it was raining, there was pain in my knees, I was prepared to be brief and Arellano rarely spoke beyond prescribing a light penance. But today he did speak; through the patter of the rain and a channel in the masonry the depth of a forearm, I only heard him with difficulty.

. . . failing you . . . I cannot much longer . . . protect you. When had I ever asked such a thing of him? He meant to protect himself . . . The rain, the stone was cold now. *A time to study the writings of John of the Cross . . .* But I *knew* his work—he was the poet I most revered. *Another spiritual director. Father Núñez . . .* Father Núñez what?—he could not mean . . . protect *me*? This could have been amusing, from someone else, in another circumstance, in sunlight. But from Arellano it was not. For Arellano found nothing amusing in the monstrous face of sin—at least since he had looked down fifteen years ago to find his dagger separating a fellow gambler's ribs.

I had wanted to listen to the pain in my knees, but changed my mind when Father Arellano admitted he'd approached Núñez without my leave. . . .

Father Arellano, you must not worry yourself overly about failing me. My previous spiritual director did so utterly, was quite unable to answer questions such as these, or not satisfactorily—can you hear me all right, can you hear me clearly? It is awkward to speak to one's spiritual director in this way rather than in the comfort of the locutory, but at least His Paternity don Arellano is dry? For while I treasure John's poetry, in his commentaries there are concerns. . . .

John writes of even the adepts in spiritual matters as being like children in their knowledge and feelings, in their speech and dealings with Him. In the first night of the soul, ours is the love of a child, for this is the easiest love, our love of the infant Christ and our sadness for his destiny. In answer to that love, He sends the sweetest milk flowing through our prayers and meditations. But through this night He will wean us toward a more adult love, so that in the last watch of the first night, the soul is more like a young lover slipping out of a darkened house, the house of the senses, to be with her Beloved. *Beloved of my life, I run to you.* Delectable moments, stolen, brief, promises of a still greater richness and fullness to come.

As in the Canticles.

Yet as the first night draws to a close the love has become difficult and painful: we are to be deprived again, but of joys now of the spirit, weaned again. And the first trial of the second night is this frustration, for one is a lover and not a child anymore. But why must it always be thus? If in His house there are many rooms, why must love abide in each indifferently? And the love He returns, is it the same for everyone, or is it a love of each of us? Surely he would not love as if we were other than we are, surely he loves us knowing *who* we are. Does this love take no colouring from its vessel—is it ever and forever the same?—while the face of the ocean, the wide eyes of a lake change with every tick of the sun, every shred of mist, every lake-bottom and sea-floor lift, every alteration of the deep—silt, sand, rock, mud—every angle of its run and pitch?

What is more constant and yet more various? What is more constant in its variations than water? If not love?

Silence from beyond the wall.

I should have known by now. I was not, in fact, a child. I did not need his advice, I did not need direction. And so I started out, as so often happens with me, clever . . . as a child hoping if she were only clever enough she might keep him. . . . And then I end up kneeling in the rain, pouring out my heart to a slot in the wall—scent of stone and must, rain in my mouth, taste of salt—to a man who once found me beautiful and cannot bear to see me now, who probably cannot hear me, who has perhaps already gone.

The books, I could see, were different. The books might be dangerous. But these other things of mine, would they take all this from me? What harm have they done anyone when only I may see them?

Please do not take these away. These are only instruments of beauty and wonder, these are only innocent things.

> 1 astrolabe, 1 helioscope, 1 telescope, 1 set of compasses
> 1 microscope built to designs by Reverend Athanasius Kircher; an assortment of fine steel scalpels, 1 of obsidian, suitable for the most delicate dissections and slide preparation
> 1 magic lantern, 1 camera lucida built to designs by Leonardo
> 1 magic square (& alchemical equipment & materials)
> 1 collection of glass paperweights, 1 of seashells collected from the seven seas

7 magnifying glasses of different strengths and sizes
1 toadstone; 1 fish skeleton embedded in limestone; 8 gallstones of divers
and disputed origin; 4 *perlas barruecas*; 1 horn of an Atlantic unicorn . . .
1 chronoscope . . .

No more brooding on how little I had accomplished these past ten
years, or the past twenty-two—a few verses to take pride in, the glimmerings of an idea or two. I would not ask how much time I had. I would
not lament that it was not enough. I lamented now only wasted time.
Work harder, work faster now.

I finished the last remaining lyrics on Saint Catherine in a day and
sent them to Puebla, city of Angels, to Santa Cruz. If he had any intention yet to play my Redeemer . . . Let that be up to him. It could not
hurt now.

One morning a little before noon a young nun came to say a man had
come for me. The way she had said this put a small spur to my fears. Her
expression was kindly and solemn, almost pained.

"From the Inquisition?"

"No, no, Sor Juana, a composer."

One composer. Which one was it now? One or the other, they could
wait if they would not come together for me just once. I finished the page
I was reading at the window, and an extra three, slowly, for good measure, then went down. Sálazar. Looking angry and wounded in his pride.
My gaze went out to the little courtyard, past the rose bushes to the long
yellow grass, less like lawn than sedge. The rain was making the ground
frail, everywhere returning the island to the marshland it was. Gardening
had branched into masonry: the gardener's every step these past months
laying tiles of sky in the earth.

Sálazar stood waiting some way from the clavichord and well back
from the grille, hands down at his sides. He was tall, a man fully grown,
but it was the expression of the six-year-old he wore—a proud artist
kept waiting like a page. As I studied his face what softened my anger
was that his own seemed quite dwarfed by his hurt. I almost apologized,
for I was just then remembering him as he was the second time we spoke
together. A tall boy of seven, Antonio de Sálazar was by then known by
all to be a prodigy. He had come to the Palace again, to play the clavichord this time, not the violin—and to play no one's music but his own.

He had not been made to wait. He recognized me among the many who came afterwards to congratulate him. Later we had a moment to talk. He led me to the same vestibule and thanked me for my kindness on his previous visit. I had been like a princess to him—he flushed then. "But how stupid, perhaps you are one."

"No Antonio, I am from here, just like you. And do you remember the advice I gave you?"

"I do, and won't forget it."

"And will you tell me?"

"Take time from my music, to make friends and keep them. Save a little of myself, for myself."

"Anything else?"

"A genius can be hurt like anyone else."

Now I was forty-three, he was still ten years younger, and the one who had given him the advice was now the one who had wounded his pride. He had forgotten the princess in the palace, or did not see her in a middle-aged nun. Or rather a middle-aged nun in her. That was understandable. But I wanted to ask if he remembered what she had said, so many years ago. Her advice. And if it had been of any use to him.

Instead I thanked him for coming, made no excuses for the delay, and was the cantor perhaps coming later?

Fury stood in his eyes then—no, Sor Juana, he was not coming later, and he, Sálazar, did not like to be kept waiting. He had a lot of work to do—many new commissions—now more than ever. This *Caracol* had never been his idea but the Cantor de Ribera's, and another thing he did not appreciate was being asked by the Vice-Queen to look through my poetry to her for musical insults. At last night's ball the Countess had drawn him aside to tell him at length of her conviction that she had been slighted during her last visit to this locutory. She'd had the distinct impression that in my verses on that day I had called her handmaidens whores. Which made a musical composition I had penned on the occasion of her birthday at the very least suspicious, and who better than Antonio de Sálazar to ferret out the insults most certainly buried there. And precisely what, he wondered, was he to do?—pretend he could find none the least bit suspicious, only to have someone else do it for him and make him look either a fool, or very much like the man who has played the Countess for one? Half his commissions *came* from her, and if I was determined to throw away what was left of my career—which I seemed to be, however little *that* might be—he had no such intentions for his. He would not lie to her, for Ribera maybe, but not for me. And so as he was saying, he had more work than he had ever wanted and a burden of responsibility he wasn't even sure he could cope with, so this was not at all the right time for a collaboration.

I was glad I had not asked him about that day we first met, for though he stood as a man speaking of a great career to one who had not quite had one—he looked so terribly hurt. He was that boy, about to cry, and I was no longer sure what was happening.

Well, Maestro Sálazar should do as he saw fit. Who knew indeed what the future would bring? For the present, Cantor de Ribera and I would be fine. We could finish what we started.

Sálazar's eyes went cold, the boy quite gone, but he had already shown me his hurt. I had not been the one to inflict it after all, but he was nothing averse to passing it along.

"No, Sor Juana. I am afraid that will not be possible. That is what I have been kept waiting so long to tell you. Cantor de Ribera died this morning. Two hours ago."

The rain had stopped. Sálazar had gone. I sat at the clavichord working out some notions Ribera had once had for *Caracol*. From the courtyard, quiet now, I heard water running in the gutters, droplets falling into puddles from the rose bushes, without blossom in this season. Those leaves that remained had gone yellow.

Did you ever wonder where the princess went, Antonio? Don't you ever wonder where they go?

I think Sálazar had remembered after all. The advice. I was happy he had taken the time to know Ribera, to love and keep him. Ribera was proud of that love, of the younger man's gift, not at all like a rival.

> *Suspende, cantor Cisne, el dulce acento:*
> *mira, por ti, al Señor que Delfos mira,*
> *en zampoña trocar la dulce lira . . .* [19]

I had had a thought for Cantor de Ribera that morning, two hours before. To have been there. Though in a convent one grows used to friends dying elsewhere. I could not quite picture him then, or quite hear. On other days, yes. The hoarseness in his voice, as he announced he had secured for us this last commission. The long neck, the big Adam's apple, the long black brows darting up, dipping down. I wished I had tried that sonnet on a heron, so many years ago. My problem had not been entirely poetic. In praise of a cantor, a song heralding his voice as a heron's could not help but be suspected of irony.

It could not be good to be a heron and called a swan. In truth if the swan was the emblem of Apollo and Orpheus, it was as likely for the graceful curve of its neck. For Apollo and Orpheus were lyrists, first of all. An injustice to herons . . . the swan's neck was graceful, the heron's just long. And yet I wondered if the heron's song was any more raucous than the swan's . . . save its last.

Who could live a life anticipating how every act, every step, every gesture, good or bad, might be remembered one day? Every line said or written in earnest or anger or jest. Who could live this way?

After our father Saint Jerome, maximal Doctor of Holy Mother Catholic Church, we may see Beauty in terms of the three transcendental attributes of God: Oneness, Goodness, Truth. Beauty is the transcendental perfection of God in time. Beauty is God's plenitude, an overflowing—vast yet in nothing superfluous—pouring down in a cascade of music through the orders of Creation, through the stars and heavens, through the whole sublunary world—human, animal, vegetal, mineral—down to the smallest of atoms. Since the Fall, so is it also with our human senses: each being an instrument crafted to resonate differently. In full possession of our senses we are like unto a prism breaking beauty into its spectra and gamuts and separate registers—red, blue, gold—mi, fa, sol—sight, hearing, touch—that scatter in tints and tones and hints and hues, in flocks, in flights, in schools, through water, into air, over ground.

But to return us whence we have fallen is a long climb and arduous. And in assembling our provisions for this ascent, it is not enough to lay the evidence of the senses side by side. These instruments of mind must be fused, in the sense that Lope tells us the painting of Rubens is a poetry for the eye. Imagine poetry, then, as painting for the ear. It is the mind that slowly teaches us to weave together these separate elements into a score, and in this sense we rightly call Theology the Queen of the Sciences, for it is she who enters the final chamber, the abode of the Beloved.

Even as to the lover every aspect of the Beloved is beauty . . . the turns and pauses of His mind, the fragrance of His skin, the warmth of His breath as if the radiance of a perfect fire . . . but here one must not go on too far. In recollecting these, the Queen in her actions is like a lover straining to learn every small and separate thing of her Beloved. These are the notes, and she strives to show us how to compose them in their very fullest arrangement, to fuse them in perfect union, making full use of each and every instrument.

Mind is the shepherd, Mind is the falconer, Mind is the net that recalls and collects, Mind is the guide that shall one day bring them all home to rest. Our mind is an instrument of collection, and a collection of instruments. *Logica, inventio, divinatio,* and the finest of all is *admiratio,* for it is this gift of marvelling at the world that brings us most closely on its own to our condition before the Fall.

But it is the soul in Grace that plays them. The soul is in the grace of the orchestra, the Soul is the orchestra of Grace. And its Music is Love.

Entreme donde no supe
y quedeme no sabiendo
toda ciencia trascendiendo . . . †

DARK DAYS

nnumbered times had the capital been warned, a dark day was to come. Make ready. It would be for all to see, a terrible majesty written in the sky.

It was Carlos's plan to prepare everyone this time. With the mood in the city now, could one even imagine it, the pandemonium?—to which I wondered why the authorities feared our panic so much more than our fury.

With the Archbishop's blessing, Carlos had spent the past weeks going to the churches to explain what was to come. Forecasts of doom and darkness from the pulpit were hardly a departure. The predicators were agreeable, pleased at last to have a date and that date so near. And even an approximate hour. Sermons were polished and studded with quotations from the books of Revelations and Amos, dark references to the breaking of the seals, and to Nineveh. The forecasts propagated from the churches and spiralled out through the plazas, amplified by doomsayers in the streets and echoed in the marketplaces. The people were frightened, the people were prepared. They had no sense that the source of this foreknowledge was in any way different from prophecy. All had the date now and an hour and the hour was drawing nigh. August 23rd, 1691.

There were small flaws in the plan, but chief among them: no one is ever quite prepared for a total eclipse of the sun.

Carlos had only just purchased a new telescope and with a generosity typical of him gave the old one to Antonia. He explained to her, and again with diagrams, how the parabolic mirror had greatly enhanced the quality of the sightings since Galileo's day. He came to San Jerónimo several times to instruct us in its features, and the day before the eclipse spent all afternoon with me reviewing patiently, despite his growing agitation, the geometric formulas I would be using in *Caracol*. Before leaving that evening he fitted several layers of dark brown glass over the telescopic eyepiece and stressed that they must not be removed until the sun's eclipse had reached its totality. The plan was that Antonia

†I entered I knew not
   where
and thus and there
   remained:
all sciences trans-
   cended . . .
—John of the Cross

should set up the telescope in the very centre of the patio, for there were numerous events to watch for in every quadrant of the sky. I did not think the chances particularly good. It had been raining for a year.

Thursday dawned cloudless. On this of all mornings, a clear blue sky was itself an uncanny sign, but particularly for those who still doubted. The sun shone over the city on the lake and the lake within the city, scintillating in ten thousand places, in the sloughs of the streets and in garden puddles and cattle troughs. Just before nine o'clock in the morning, two before the hour fixed by the prediction, the street dogs disappeared from the alleys of the barrios. Not long after, five thousand Indians along the canals stepped from their traces—to be restrained by neither shouts of threat nor curses, by whip nor iron goad—and according to the witness of their overseers, melted away like wraiths. At nine o'clock on August 23rd the sun died.

The imperial capital of Mexico, city of the centre of the earth, was cast onto an otherworldly plane of night as the Sixth Seal was opened, and the *Sun became black as sackcloth of hair and the Moon became as blood.* Swiftly, with the bellringers standing by, the bells of the city began their tolling from fifty belfries and campaniles. Many who had lived through the comet of 1680 said this was far worse, the fear, the wretchedness, the loneliness in the violent milling darkness, as the streets filled and the light failed. To four hundred thousand people came the moments of greatest terror they had known.

Moving as though blind, stumbling falling through the dark, the people of the city made for the sound of the bells. Beneath the belfries lay shelter. In the movement of the bells lay life and hope of Life. The churches were lit by thousands of candles, the churches were Light. The plazas before the churches were thronged with the bereft, crying out for succour, calling out for comfort.

Before the sermons ended—indeed before they had quite begun— the light was already returning to the world, though the people did not seem directly to notice it.

By noon, processions of ascetics groaned their way through the streets, like carts heavy burdened, from the churches and temples past the convents and monasteries, and echoed within the walls by smaller processions moving round the patios like larger wheels of penance and within them cogs.

It was to have been a moment of triumph for human learning and science. We had been prepared, to prevent panic. There were small flaws in the plan. Yet the Grand Plan had emerged triumphant.

When he came to San Jerónimo afterwards, shortly past noon, Carlos and I quarrelled bitterly, but it would never have occurred to me I might not see him again. This is not to say I had no sense of approaching danger. It was never far if we were not careful, and I at least was not—how pleased he was that the plan had proven useful. The Church had not been caught off guard.

There is a peasant science of prediction that has not yet been fathomed, one that links eclipses to earthquakes. When the first quake came three days later we half expected it—the half who did not dread it. The quake itself was not violent. Anyone raised here had experienced worse. More unusual were the aftershocks, their intensity, undiminished from first to last over the course of a week, but most of all their number: I had not thought to count, but it came to be said there were forty, forty exactly.

It seemed that a people in distress was versed in an older learning, its holy texts in the scripts of stillbirths and deformities, in the flights of birds, in the spill of fresh vitals in the dust. . . . Known to this ancient wisdom is that eclipses exert malignant influences—stillbirths and live births of disharmonious proportions, deformities of ominous shape and configuration—infants with limbs shaped like stars, the heads of animals. It was a Mexica word that was used. *Coatepoztles.* Serpent's children, born without souls. In Europe these were the *monstra* catalogued by the magus Paracelsus.[20] *Inaminatis, lemures, umbragines, gnomi, gigantes, silvestres, vulcanales*—in the locutories we began to hear talk of these, though the source of this learning here in Mexico was not clear to me. Portents of end-time and disasters yet to unfold, creatures conceived in illicit couplings, born *ex negativo*—apart from Creation, from a life out of Time, away from God's eyes. The common people had become learned in Paracelsus, but then, he had learned this from them.

It was not long before there appeared an anonymous leaflet plastered to walls in the plazas and public markets, near the prayer niches and places of worship—and all around San Jerónimo. Were women *monstra*, the text began, were they too without souls—like the stillborn and malformed they brought into the world? The author had assuredly read Paracelsus. The leaflet might simply be the latest in the series of attacks on me, a warning or some kind of crude slur. But it might be something else, for in just this manner did the Inquisition sow its seeds to determine what fears might find congenial soil. In Spain the fear of witchcraft had never taken, whereas in France that horror and its harvest seemed inexhaustible. Here in the New World, elements within the Church still viewed the Indian rites and customs as a parody of our Faith propagated by the Enemy, Corrupter of Worlds. Despite this, the knowledge of the midwives and healers, their skill with plants and medicines, usually seemed, to the common people, more wondrous than malignant. But the climate was much changed, and the new leaflet could be seen as an attempt to gauge it. The author had taken up this theme and twisted it, for though the *monstra* were from Paracelsus, the idea of Woman as *monstra* was not. How was one to oppose this, unless with Paracelsus himself? Woman was part of the Creation. God was the first world, Man the middle; but Woman was the last, her matrix the smallest world. The baleful influences in her womb were not from congress with the Devil but from conjunctions of planetary influences called the Ascendents—to which Woman was naturally more susceptible, for we carried a planet within us. Paracelsus did not believe in witches, considered women too soft-headed for heresy and believed the greatest calamity that could befall us was chastity, which, if persistent, predisposed Woman to a deep and dangerous melancholy. So while a certain nun was torn between her predispositions and a diabolical temptation to defend her sex, this seemed precisely the trap. What new pamphlets and sermons of defence and counterattack might this not spur? Who would be the next hurt?

September, 1691. Gutiérrez paid a visit unannounced. I had seen little of him since late spring, when he had been unable to discover if the Inquisition was monitoring my mail. As for the authenticity of the Archbishop's madness, it was an open question at the Holy Office, with adherents on both sides even today. Gutiérrez no longer had an opinion. He did not know anything about the leaflet and knew little about Paracelsus. The truth was, Gutiérrez seemed to know less all the time.

As if reading my thoughts he excused himself for not having come sooner but there had been little to report, till now: on June 4th of this year, Doctor Alonso Alberto de Velasco, priest of the Tabernacle, member of the Brotherhood of Mary, advisor to the Holy Office of the Inquisition, had made a formal denunciation of the sermon of one Xavier Palavicino, pronounced in the convent of San Jerónimo at the feast of Santa Paula. In response, Prosecutor Ulloa had written to the Tribunal, attesting that he had received the denunciation of the sermon and naming two Inquisitors to examine its propositions for pernicious error. The Inquisitors were said to be Mier and Armesto, thorough, capable men.

I did not want to seem ungrateful, but June 4th, this was almost *three months past.* Gutiérrez shrugged. He had only found out about it a week ago. Or two. The thing to note was that the prosecutor made his decision to launch an investigation less than a week after receiving the denunciation. By the standards of the Holy Office, this was particularly fast; this seemed very much like haste. Antonia looked at me strangely after he left. How could I take this so calmly?

But in October Gutiérrez brought better news. A printer's proof had been submitted in an application for a publishing licence from the Holy Office in Puebla. It was the same printer that had published the Letter Worthy of Athena and Sor Philothea's preface last year. Diego Fernández de Leon. A pause for effect. Bishop Santa Cruz's own printer. Yes, go on. The licensing application was for the printing of my carols on Saint Catherine of Alexandria.

It appeared Santa Cruz was to let them be sung after all. After Gutiérrez had gone, I turned to see Antonia's face younger by years.

Is it love, Antonia had asked that night. Surely if Santa Cruz is in love with you, she said, there is a chance. But how much better my chances seemed today if he didn't, if none of this was personal at all. And now this, after everything else. *Was* it love? How was one to know with such a man—who was to say what certain men were like in the secrecy of their rooms? The things he had asked of her. This was lovemaking for him—with a young woman so beautiful, so carnal—only that she watch during his mortifications?

But perhaps this was precisely the point, that he had always resisted such sublime temptations. Asking nothing more than to have Antonia making reports to no worldly purpose—not even caring if they were true, perhaps even knowing they weren't. How I brushed my hair? Did I use a mirror? No, for him the game had been to picture it, *to watch her watching me, and suffering for it.* Watching me just as she had watched him.

Lord God, did I discipline myself? harshly, strictly?—did he imagine he and I were alike?

Is this love?

How exquisite his pleasure, then, to imagine me after his betrayal, thinking about what he had done, seeing the sublimity of his games-manship as I first glimpsed the negative benefit of his sacrifice. For the point of the game had become that I should watch *him* now, moving beneath the veil of Philothea's letter. Yet how could he be sure I would?—the consummate player would want me to give him proof of my contemplation of him, by finding the solution to a problem, a puzzle, a riddle.

. . . And, if that mind should ever crave for sweet and tender demonstrations of love, let it direct its apprehension to the hill of Calvary, where, observing the finezas of the Redeemer and the ungratefulness of the redeemed, your intellect should find a limitless scope to examine the excesses of infinite love and to derive, not without tears, fine formulas of atonement at the very summits of ingratitude . . . What sweet and tender demonstrations he had concealed for me . . . *I do not doubt that it would go with you as it did with Apelles who found, while painting the portrait of Campaspe, that for every brushstroke he applied to the canvas, love sent an arrow into his heart; thus leaving, in the end, a portrait painted to perfection and a painter's heart mortally wounded with the love of his subject.* Apelles, a painter. Campaspe, the lover of Alexander. Obvious—he, the all-conquering Santa Cruz, was Alexander, the beloved was Christ, and I was to learn to be Apelles, wounded by the beauty of Christ.

But with Santa Cruz *nothing* is obvious. I had been careless. A painter too is a watcher—Santa Cruz was telling me *he* was Apelles. Was I the beloved, then? But that would make Christ our conqueror, Alexander, and the two of them competing in their love for me. This made little sense—or I could conceivably be Santa Cruz's conqueror but surely not Christ's. What *was* it, what was I missing? *This, this, this.* The beloved, the Lover, was love itself: the love of Apelles, discreet, deep, a love that does not insist, a love that is only inferred. Sublime in its finesse, the discreet, Christlike, suffering love of Santa Cruz.

For me.

. . . This is desired for my lady by one who, since kissing her hand so many years ago, lives still enamoured of her soul, a love which neither time nor distance has any power to cool, for a spiritual love admits not of change, nor grows save in purity . . .

For how long had he wanted me to see him as Philothea, to love as he loved, as Christ loved? Philothea was powerless to resist such a love, and yet Santa Cruz had so valiantly resisted the enormous temptation to declare it. If I could only see that. But Philothea's love *had* changed. Precisely because I had not grasped, seen, contemplated his sublime restraint—and since that love was not purely spiritual, it could not forever resist the arrows of my heartless, blind ingratitude.

And yet how could he be sure that I had not seen his love from the beginning—that I was not returning it just as discreetly, as two astronomers contemplating each other from afar? What did he *see*—what incontrovertible proof that his restraint was a matter of total indifference to me? Truly, could it have been that day with the Viscount? In that one instant of a monstrous, wounded vanity . . . of the boyish man faced with the masculine beauty of a youth. He had never before seen me look at a man *as* a man. I could not have denied I felt desire then. And in truth it did not so much as occur to me to conceal it—from whom?

Yes Santa Cruz was powerful, and wounded in the power of his pride, but the secret heart of his vanity lay in the immense power he exercised over his own temptation, restraining it, withholding the immense liberality of his affections. But since I had proven incapable of seeing this, now let me see instead a more negative benefit. This was the message he had been returning to me in the preface to my own letter.

And yet even if I had now seen it, finally solved it, how to let him know after all this time—how was I to answer, to steer a path between false sentiment and utter surrender?

At San Jerónimo the stories that held the greatest sway over the mind of the convent were those of the *beatas*, not witches but false saints and holy women held in the Inquisition's secret prisons, soon to be secretly tried and burned at certain convents across the city. The rumours were repeated in the work rooms, the gardens and orchards, at the water basins and in the refectory. Rumours became near certainty, confirmed in letters from sisters and cousins and friends in other convents, in other cities. The number of letters multiplied. Eighteen convents in the capital alone, three thousand nuns—all writing and reading letters, all circulating the same stories in endless permutations. The letters flew like flights of startled doves.

There came an item of news from this time that I could not help believing. It had come in a letter from our sister convent in Puebla. Bishop Santa Cruz had asked *la mística*, Sor María de San José, to put to paper for him an account of her spiritual journey. It was a singular sign of favour for a countrywoman from Tepeaca he had once all but kicked headlong down the cathedral steps.

Eleven months had passed since the publication of my Letter Worthy of Athena, eight months since my reply to Sor Philothea, three since I had sent Santa Cruz the *villancicos* he had commissioned on Saint Catherine. Four weeks remained until they were to be sung on her feast day at the cathedral in Puebla. I had begun to let myself believe that he had no further wish to bring out the *mística* in me, had found his Teresa. Perhaps, as Antonia had hoped, he was truly finished with me.

Friendship was impossible now—truly he was capable of anything. But if I had caused him pain, I could acknowledge it, if I could find a way. Who would not try to keep an old love from turning to fresh hatred? What would I not give to be forgiven certain things, to have back the friendships I have lost, to take back the hurt I have caused to the people who have loved me?

Esteemed Philothea,

The love upon which you close your letter, on the kiss of the hand, I received as no less than the sweet wounding that you hoped and wished I might one day have the joy of enduring. I am enduring it now. I have meditated long hours on the heart's truth of your letter of loving correction, and have finally realized what should have been as clear as it was true and constant from the outset: that the kiss of Christ's hand has for some time been the very emblem of the illuminative path, active in learning, passive in love—love of a kind not quite unknown even in times since Alexander. And known perhaps even down to this day of ours.

You and I have often spoken of the learned Reverend Athanasius Kircher. Was it not his disciple who entered, through the intermediary of a mutual friend not unlike the discreet Philothea, into a correspondence with Galileo under the pseudonym of Apelles? 'Masked Apelles,' 'Apelles behind the painting.' This masked Apelles, the Jesuit Scheiner, was the very figure of vigour in learning and discretion in love, for who could doubt that love motivated his earliest overtures to Galileo on sunspots? It was, after all, Galileo's early publications of his findings in the heavens that had inspired Scheiner to purchase his first telescope. And yet for years Galileo did not know with whom he was dealing: for masked Apelles had begged that their shared friend, their Philothea, not disclose his identity. In truth, then, Apelles had corresponded with Galileo long before the first quill was put to paper.

Apelles and Alexander both looked with love upon Campaspe, even as masked Apelles and Galileo looked up with love upon their Beloved in the heavens. For truly did both men love God above any other. But where Galileo saw only the Beloved, Scheiner saw also their shared love. This is the kiss of Christ's hand, this is the love He would have us bear one other. For twenty years the masked Apelles persisted in his love, even through all the bitterness that had come between them and, restraining his passionate pride, published his own great work, in it conceding that indeed his figures now confirmed that the sun inclined on its axis, precisely as Galileo had argued, and that Venus indeed revolved around the Sun. These were the words, but had Galileo taken the time to ponder the gesture, in it he would have seen Apelles inclining towards Galileo. How could one with the eyes of Galileo be so blind, we wonder; how could the son of a great musician be deaf to the discord he himself had created?

And yet we could almost believe that he was not quite insensible, or regretted, or repented, for here is what Galileo wrote to their shared friend the magistrate Welser, their Philothea, who was no doubt wounded for them both that the correspondence had turned out so badly:

> Nevertheless I shall not abandon the task in despair.[21] Indeed, I hope that this . . . will turn out to be of admirable service, in tuning for me some reed in this great discordant organ of our philosophy—an instrument on which I think I see many organists wearing themselves out trying vainly to get the whole thing into perfect harmony . . .

Might Galileo have been sending a message, this one of regret, to Apelles through Philothea? Even if that was not the message Galileo intended, we may still hope the passage contains one, and the message is this: Know thyself. This is the highest wisdom bequeathed to us by the ancients, a wisdom that should have been well known to Alexander, for Aristotle surely once communicated it to him. And it was also known to Reverend Kircher, who had taken it directly from Hermes Trismegistus and without doubt communicated it to Scheiner, his disciple. Know thyself. Is this not the highest wisdom imparted by any teacher to his acolyte?

Galileo had failed to know himself, to see himself through the eyes of others, see the other in himself. In refuting the Jesuits, the followers of Aristotle, he had forgotten himself.

What happens to friendships, how do we forget the immensity of what we share, our love of love itself; how do we fall out of sympathy and into discord once we have corresponded? Why does our playing become so bitter to us?

Still more tragic is the hidden sympathy never detected. How much better to have proceeded as did Catherine of Alexandria, sensing how much she shared with the pagan scholars who debated her, finding the basis of their sympathies in shared ideas, our shared debt, and a shared capacity to correspond in a great love.

Galileo forgot himself, forgot his debt to Aristotle, and acted brutally, like a pagan conquering other pagans. There is no room for doubt that Galileo's difficulties with the Inquisition's magistrates grew from his lack of civility, nor that the growing enmity of the Jesuit scientists stemmed from the seed of a neglected regard. And still did the masked Apelles try one last time to communicate a secret correspondence, *sub rosa*, under the title of Scheiner's work of twenty years: *Rosa Ursina*. Dedicated to the Duke of Orsino, an Alexander of our time, the symbol common to the two Apelles is the rose of Alexandria: the very emblem of a passionate restraint, a silent, unspoken love—love of God, of the heavens, of love itself. The masked Apelles had demonstrated such patience and discretion, such *finezas*. How bitter, then, the disappointment of his love.

After long contemplation I have decided that the similarities between our times cannot be cause for surprise, once we have understood that these were loves of the spirit. For as the discreet Philothea has herself written, spiritual love does not admit of change.

With this, and from the convent of San Jerónimo, I return the kiss of Christ's hand.

Your devoted servant,

If music can be seen as our most perfect idea of Time, then perhaps History too is a musical science. The mutation to a higher key felt inevitable when it came: soon the talk in our letters and the locutories was of not just one *beata* but several, then not just *beatas* any longer but nuns, adulterous nuns. And there were other campaigns and speculations more to be dreaded. Any day it might begin, with leaflets condemning a sin that in Mexico had never before been spoken of: sodomy between nuns, parties of sodomy among us. It had all happened in Venice, as everyone knew, where the convents had become brothels and their parlours nests of spiders, and was not Mexico the Venice of America? I had begun to wonder if my own learning was a help to me now. But . . . had not the people been saying that the cause of these calamities was instead the eclipse? This was only asking to be told that fornication had brought on the eclipse.

Carlos and I had not spoken in the three months since, though he still came to the locutory for Antonia, for their classes of mathematics and science, and history. She left sheepishly to go to him, while I tried to let her know I did not mind, without ever quite saying why. I did not want her to misunderstand, lest I hurt her too. Her friendship with Carlos was real, and growing, the gallant preoccupation of the older gentleman with a beautiful young woman at a delicate age. For her part . . . no, those thoughts were for the privacy of her heart.

And yet for all this, when he came for her, I knew he came for me; what had come between us that day had never really been about the eclipse. In all the turmoil of the day's events, the last thing either of us was thinking about was a quarrel. Antonia and I did not even know when we would see Carlos next or in what state we might find him, but he came that afternoon. He found us in the locutory with Gárate, the convent chaplain. Chaplain also of the Metropolitan Cathedral, Gárate had been there at the appointed hour, and had just been telling us of the Archbishop's immense satisfaction with the turn of events—had an archdiocese ever served more effectively in an hour of sudden calamity? There had been a great cleansing in the capital. Many a lax Christian saw his faith forever renewed, many a secret Jew saw his faith in the law of Moses shattered and forever forsaken. And then there was the rate at which alms had been pouring in all day, to the cathedral, to our own temple, no doubt to every church and cloister in the city. Gárate had heard about the Archbishop's requisition of an inventory of my cell, and wondered now if His Grace might feel less need to resort to auctions to raise funds for his charities. I was determined not to entertain false hopes, but found my mind racing, nonetheless, to the other consequences that the Church's great success might have, for me particularly.

Gárate rose to salute the man of the hour with a ceremonious bow. Carlos shook his head. "I only thank God for having put me in the way of a conjunction of events so rare and about which so few observations are dispassionately recorded." Never had I seen Carlos look happier. I held my tongue. This was the fulfilment of a dream, his no less than Galileo's—of science in the service of the Church.

Carlos was too excited to sit, but rather stepped stiffly about the locutory closely inspecting things on the walls he'd seen many times before and today was clearly not seeing at all—almost a bust of himself, stiff-necked, stiff-jointed all over, heaped in glory. There was something in the long face, in the long, broad-bridged nose and the huge dark eyes, that reminded one of a terrifyingly intelligent fawn, grown ancient—bending arthritically now to examine a map as the chaplain continued to sing his praises, marvelling at the precision of his art.

"*Science*, sir," Carlos corrected, still facing away from us, hands clasped at his back. "Merely the rigorous application of a method." Half turning toward the chaplain, he added, "And we still missed the prediction by two hours."

Here he remembered his old telescope and asked Antonia if the moment had been worth all the preparation. In no time they were leaning close to the grille, Antonia by half a head the taller, conferring volubly and leaving me with Gárate sitting at the window, listening more to them than to our chaplain discussing the weather, which, yes, was holding. It was the first fair afternoon in months. The sun was all benevolence, the sky a radiant blue. Across the room, Antonia was asking Carlos how it could be that the moon had fit so perfectly over the sun.

"Do you hear, Juana? Such a natural philosopher we have here in our Antonia!" At this angle, few gaps showed in the grille. His face ducked into view as I sat back to see him more clearly. He turned back to her. "And yet what you so accurately observed, Antonia, is merely a stupendous coincidence."

Again I bit back a reply. If the phrase 'stupendous coincidence' had any meaning whatever, it was surely an invitation to probe more deeply, instead of an irrelevance—which I knew Carlos had not meant—for, with so many bodies in such a busy heaven continually swinging in front of one another from some perspective or other, an eclipse did not exist without a point of view. And what was a perspective separate from our experience of it?

Just then Gárate ventured how helpful it might be if, after such a universal display of penitence, the rains were now to cease and the city were given a reprieve. I could hold my peace no longer. "Tell me, Carlos, how does glossing over the stupendous improbability that produces a total eclipse allow us to properly account for its most significant effect—the power it exercises upon our minds and upon our times? Were there ever odds more properly called *astronomical*, that the angular distance for the sun and moon—their apparent diameters—should prove identical, two bodies so vastly unequal in size and in their distance from us? Doubtless you can fill in the trigonometry for yourself, but pull the little moon in closer by a few thousand leagues and suddenly the eclipses that have for dozens of centuries moved admirals and histories and kings fade to a pallid glow in the darkness; nudge the little moon out another twenty thousand and in a flash—no totality at all, but rather a small dark smudge against the glare, a bit of soot on lantern glass. Instead, what we are given—in this coronet of ice in the heavens—is the overwhelming impression of *Design* and *Intent*. But whose design and what intent?"

At the gap in the grille the smile faded, succeeded by the bemusement of someone who has bent to inspect the contents of a cage and found something unexpected. But if the chaplain had not taken it upon himself to defend him, our quarrel still might have ended there.

Surely Sor Juana must admit don Carlos had performed a great service. And who could say what might have happened if he hadn't. Initial reports were of two children killed by runaway wagons, a few drownings in the canals, but though the distress had been worse than anything in memory, the Church had been *prepared*, had withstood the flood, brought the faithful safely into fold and harbour.

Carlos said nothing. How convenient to let others answer for him, how delicious to have the Church itself uphold the righteousness of one's scientific principles and not have to speak to how they are used.

"Is this also your view, Carlos? Your vision of the new science? To terrify people in churches even as the Jesuit Kircher used to do with his magic lantern—projecting devils into the air! And what of the science of history to which don Carlos has dedicated his many monographs? Are the fatal events of this day too insignificant to merit the historian's notice?"

"Juana, don Carlos, I . . ." Antonia began, bewildered.

"It's all right, Antonia." Carlos came to stand where he could speak to me without raising his voice. "An eclipse is many things, Juana. But surely it is also a rare opportunity to test hyphotheses of the sun's composition, to refine estimates of its mass and, yes, distance, and to theorize on the properties of light." His tone was grave, dignified, as he then asked if I might care to discuss my own observations of the event. I could still have stopped. I had only to be evasive.

Instead I told him the truth, that I had not looked through his telescope at all.

At this, Carlos turned his enormous sad eyes on Antonia. "You see, it is just as we feared, Antonia. No, it is worse. Not only does the artist challenge our empirical observations with poetic cavils—she makes this poetry on what she has not even bothered to *see*. It is forever this way with Sor Juana. As with mathematics in the past, as with virtually everything else, she has lost all interest in science now . . ."

What happens between even true friends, why do we not take more care—indeed insist on being careless with our most dear? Are we hoping to prove our friendship indestructible? That morning as if by a miracle the sky had cleared long enough for him to take detailed sightings with a fine new telescope, one of the finest in the world. And I begrudged him this. For weeks Carlos had toiled long hours selflessly and all but pointlessly over the infernal dredging projects at the canals; the disappointments in his life were not few. Then, one day of glory, a day when for once the deepest of his passions had no need to be hidden, from me or from the Church, when his faith could be served by the depth of his learning and his love for astronomy openly declared. How could I have let this happen—how many times have I turned it over in my mind? Even after I had accused him of letting himself be used by the Church, the argument did not quite tilt out of control. Only when he heard me telling him what I could so easily have kept to myself, that I had not so much as looked through the telescope, only then did the last of his restraint fall away. And yet we could have stopped there, avoided the worst, had I not let myself be goaded—and shamed, on a day of such appalling events—into feeling a petty stab of jealousy, of Antonia.

I asked Chaplain Gárate to leave, and then Antonia.

How dared he say I had lost interest in science—in everything!—in front of them? Did he have any idea how many people Gárate might tell, to what uses they might put such information?

Carlos's face was pale as always, but the eyes behind the spectacles were enormous and angry: this was a formidable fawn. How dared *I* impugn his feelings for this city, this country—and truly, he wondered, was my first concern the people's plight or my own? And was this compassionate concern of mine quite historical—or was it for how a day of triumph for the Church might diminish my precious liberty? And was the heart of my interest truly Mexico, or only in those parts of it that affected *me*? As always, with me—everywhere a conspiracy.

Conspiracy. How interesting to hear don Carlos sound more like a Jesuit with each passing year. On the subject of conspiracies, what could he tell me about the Archbishop's demand for an inventory of my cell? Ah, so don Carlos was truly claiming to have no knowledge of this—perhaps one does not see everything in a telescope after all. But such concern in his face now, and would that be for me or the fate of his own manuscripts? Equally curious that *in* some of these manuscripts were recorded the Mexica testimonies of comets and eclipses, yet among us here and now such things were only superstitions entirely devoid of interest.

Indeed yes, *superstition*—this childish notion of a destiny inscribed in the sky between a comet and an eclipse. Sor Juana's distresses had all the seriousness of astrology, a weak excuse for persistent melancholy—

He could speak to *me* of astrology? Not only did our Chair of Mathematics and Astrology consent to teach the skills of a science he detested, but he then complained of being *underpaid* for them.

A thirty-year-old quarrel is itself a natural wonder. This was the only man in the New World who could ask when I had last done work the equal of my talent, and chide me now for my loss of interest in the passions we had once shared. But for years it had been clear to me if not to him that we could never practise here a true and free natural philosophy. Most of Carlos's colleagues in Spain had forsworn the practice of science altogether. But he had persisted for the love of it, though we could only follow distant developments, confirm conclusions made in freer places, and in places not so much freer. He and I had quarrelled more than once over Galileo, whose fate, Carlos insisted, owed to an excess of pride, chief among his many character flaws. Over Descartes we argued less harshly, over the change in him—unflinching in the *Discourse,* conciliatory two decades later in the *Meditations.* For Carlos this softening was a sign of maturity, a judgement that he pronounced with all the dignity of someone whose best work would always be unpublished.

In a quarrel of decades, each thing said echoes with the hundred said before. So when he said 'melancholy' I heard his laments that in me the masculine virtues—intelligence, analysis, curiosity, independence, scepticism—were forever undermined by the feminine vices—moodiness, willfulness, faithlessness, inconstancy, duplicity. Particularly the last three, which for him were the true reasons I had not married him. But hearing these in turn cut me so deeply not because he was saying 'marriage' but because I was hearing 'betrayal.' Of a friend, of an ideal, of a love, of a gift. These past years the few moments of sweetness Carlos and I had found were when discussing our various ideas for inventions. Musical clocks and maps, wind harps and steam clocks. When I thought of all these whimsical creations, it seemed we had begun to find a poetry together for what could not be done here, could never be published, for the great synthesis that would always float just beyond our grasp. And so perhaps the heaviest blow to our friendship had come only recently, in a book by a Lutheran with a good biblical name, but then, they loved their Bibles. Isaac. We still had not read it, but had read formulas and arguments copied into letters from Carlos's correspondents in Europe. From what I could see, this Newton had accomplished it—fused the Archimedean infinitesimals with the Cartesian translation of geometry into algebra, next integrating these into the Galilean equations on falling bodies, all to solve the riddle of Hermes Trismegistus: universal attraction at a distance, expressed now in the language of mathematics. Just such an enterprise had been my great dream as a child. Carlos and I had been outstripped. We would never catch up, and now to follow even the rest of Europe meant to be left ever further behind. This was something I had never been able to endure. To hear him say I had lost interest in mathematics was to hear him say I had betrayed a gift. What he could never understand was that I had not betrayed it but had failed that gift terribly, and so, abandoned it.

And then just the day before the eclipse, had I not swallowed my pride and finally asked him to verify the formulas I'd used in *Caracol?*

He had been generous as usual, and gentle. No simple business, this, he said, frowning over my calculations for cross-sections cut by various spirals winding through cones of differing amplitude. It was a good afternoon in the locutory, a good journey without moving, with the rain falling in the courtyard past the window bars. I noticed his threadbare clothes, the skinny legs and patched hose, the little chest and shoulders under the great faded cloak. The conversation had turned from the conic sections to the Cartesian vortices, to Christina of Sweden and back to her famous tutor. There had been much gentle talk and laughter. How grey his hair was becoming. How thin I was, like a girl again. How pleased he was that we had at last built a model of my musical clock. And so for once I gave no utterance to my faithlessness, my doubts that the essential Catholic doctrines, which Carlos so tranquilly expected to confirm through his new telescope, could ever be construed as having foreseen not just a sun-centred heaven, but a cosmos of infinite extension crowded with an infinitude of suns like ours, and spiralling through these, the turbulent music of the starry vortices. Infinite worlds, infinite presents and pasts and futures, coincident—all things number, the number infinite.

It was one thing to know this about our Faith, another to make him admit this. But having hurt Carlos on his happiest day and so grandly placed History on the winding staircase reaching up to God, was I not then bound by conscience to turn the instruments of that science upon myself? As opposed to viewing an eclipse through a tube, the challenge of a historical science lies not in the rarity of observations but in not being engulfed by them.

And it was true my faith was not so great, my science not quite like his. But I was not so inconstant, Carlos. I had not lost interest in everything, had not betrayed the loves of years, or not so completely. I watched the eclipse, it came to our convent too. . . .

We had made our preparations at San Jerónimo. While there could be no contesting that this was a Sign from God, Mother Andrea did permit it to be said at our weekly chapter of faults that eclipses did not always portend disaster. As far as I could establish, the chief danger was blindness, and while prayer at such moments was only right and natural, I asked the sisters to please pray in the manner usually pleasing to God— eyes closed. For there was every reason to believe staring at the sun would be as harmful then as on any other day. I had spent some days rereading the old accounts of eclipses. It was hard to winnow the truth from the exaggerations: there was the suddenness, the total darkness; there were descriptions of birds falling from the sky. I arranged for lamps to be primed in the convent patios and in the infirmary in case of need. Our preparations seemed sensible.

There were small flaws in the plan.

The sisters around our little patio had been standing just inside their doorways, casting dark looks at Antonia and the telescope, and over at me, who had surely put her up to it. I was standing just inside, like the others, waiting for a sign. At the first indication I intended to light the lantern from the breakfast fire we had left lit in the kitchen.

I knew what an eclipse was, yet I felt the nervousness, too. There was nothing wrong with the sky. So calm, so blue, the sun sovereign, un-assailable. The darkness came upon us. I was prepared for the sudden-ness—it had to be like a thundercloud drifting across the sun. I knew the cause yet the temptation to look up was all but impossible to resist. It was for this that blindness was such a danger in the old accounts. But the darkness itself, I was not prepared for at all. The moon's edge was at first invisible against the sun's glare, fast diminishing. There *was* no cause, no moon, no cloud—and through this no-cloud passed no light at all. Something unseen was wrong with the sun—then a scythe moved against the fields of light.

The sisters came through their doorways and fell to their knees as one, and from them as one a groan of prayer went up. The onset was so sudden, the reactions as if rehearsed—the sisters of our patio streaming into the open—half-moon faces turned toward heaven—a practised play set swiftly into motion. I had forgotten to light the lamp. I too found myself in the courtyard, calling out that they should please close their eyes. Though I could scarcely see by then, I felt they must be looking up, even as I was. At the sound of my voice Antonia bent to the eyepiece. A chill fell upon us with the darkness, as if we had stepped into an icy room, the room that was the world. The screaming started with the chill—I could not distinctly hear the screaming in our own courtyard though it was all around, but felt I heard it in the *gran patio* and blankly started forward, to be away from where I was. Howling dogs in the streets and plazas—if they had run off, it was toward us.

Full dark came upon me as I was crossing toward the orchard thinking, not-thinking, to take the quicker path. I had a rueful thought for the lantern, then another to think of the little good it would do unlit. My steps faltered, a dizziness coming over me, as I had sometimes felt in an earthquake. It was not so much to see the stars at that hour, or even their breathless number, but seeing them *coming out* before my very eyes. An eclipse does not need a telescope, Carlos. The eclipse within a tube is one thing, and the eclipse without, another. The spectacle above is only the stage: the drama is below and spreading through the theatre. Rapidly.

The chill was of draft, of premonition, of the devil and death. The warmth still lay on my left shoulder as if I had turned away from a fire, as if the sun had just gone out. I stopped just at the trees. It was too dark to go forward. The sensation was of blindness, the impression of total dark, yet it was not—no, the eye saw and what it *saw* was darkness. Then a stirring, darkly, in the branches. Hundreds upon hundreds of grackles were roosting in the trees. At dusk the clatter they raise is ungodly. But here was utter silence, and in that instant I felt it, sheerest terror—the still panic of a groundling hunted from the sky. I had the thought that they were blind, countless chattering birds silent now, helpless, too frightened to cry out in their blindness.

Design. Intent. Terrible flaws in the Plan.

I looked into the branches, stood staring but did not understand it, like a child, all science transcended.

With time, the senses seeped back through their prism. Venus and Jupiter glowing red as blood. The howling of the dogs, subsiding. The braying of a donkey. Crickets nearby, it seemed all around. The crow of tentative cocks in the *gran patio*—was it dawn, midnight, dusk? Nine o'clock in the morning—midnight dark, but for the frail pink of a sunset in every quadrant of the sky. Chaplets of rose, shimmering coral rings in the puddles in the mud. Then a pearl light on the walls of a convent I had come to understand I hated and in equal measures loved. Nuns crying, whispering, though I saw none about. My eyes clearing. Vanessa and Concepción standing outside the kitchen, a flicker from the fire behind them, Concepción's arm over Vanessa's shoulders.

Bells tolling in the churches, a summons, a sounding, a song. San Jerónimo, San José, Santo Domingo, Jesús María—Sol-Fa-Fa-Re-Fa-Sol-La—Sol-Sol-Sol-Fa-Sol-Fa-Re-La—Sol-Mi-Sol-Mi-Sol-Re-

La—a babble like baby talk, more and more bells joining now throughout the capital, its map crumpled and convulsed. Dancing across the city now, not Time but the echoes of its stop.

As if a dreamer has forgotten to breathe and woken up.

> . . . *De paz y de piedad*
> *era la ciencia perfecta,*
> *en profunda soledad*
> *entendida vía recta*
> *era cosa tan secreta*
> *que me quedé balbuciendo*
> *toda ciencia trascendiendo* . . . [22]

I too had written verses on the night, the finest I had ever made, had thought her a friend, had found the glory of the day sky blinding. I thought in that moment of John of the Cross, our great poet of the night, of his love for her beauty, of the verses that had inspired mine.

Yet first was there Night, then Terror, only then did Science and Beauty and Holiness come.

The Jesuits who stop over in Mexico, coming home from Cathay, tell us that in the Middle Kingdom eclipses are suns seized in the jaws of vast dragons. In the tenth century, Al-Biruni and Abu'l-Wafa used the happy event of an eclipse to chart the slight difference in longitude between the cities of Baghdad and Kath. Fifteen centuries earlier, the Medes and the Lydians listened to the wisdom in their hearts—that there are few wars we are not better off without, and any war we can stop we must—and a peace was sealed in that place with a double wedding.

And yet the courses of wisdom are less easy than eclipses to predict. Only fifty years later, when calm Thucydides tells us eclipses and earthquakes were more frequently reported, the most cautious of the Athenian admirals neglected his own counsel after an eclipse of the moon. Nicias had been against the fated expedition to Sicily all along, had quickly called for reinforcements, had now decided on a withdrawal from Syracuse. But the sailors were fearful of putting out to sea, and the soothsayers were foretelling calamity for any sailing within the four weeks of the eclipse. The fate of Athens hung on this delay. The result was the annihilation of the world's greatest navy—those who made it to shore numbered forty thousand, hunted from Syracuse, herded like deer by the tens of thousands and brought down.

... of all the Hellenic actions which are on record, this was the greatest—the most glorious to the victors, the most ruinous to the vanquished; for they were utterly and at all points defeated, and their sufferings were prodigious. Fleet and army perished from the face of the earth; nothing was saved, and of the many who went forth few returned. Thus ended the Sicilian expedition.

The heart of Thucydides just this once moved with his pen.

> *Este saber no sabiendo*
> *es de tan alto poder*
> *que los sabios arguyendo*
> *jamás le pueden vencer*
> *que no llega su saber*
> *a no entender entendiendo*
> *toda ciencia trascendiendo.*[23]

Dearest friend, I should have listened, I did not mean to hurt you. It is you I should have written to. You built the first telescope I looked through; my stories of the land first coaxed you to leave the highways between the cities. This land that has become your life, that you love as I once did. Our love is a difficult one. But if we love each other is it not because we love the same stars, the same land? Please let us be friends, let us stay friends forever, let us not always fight. This was what I should have said.

The account of an eclipse, without us, is like a play without actors, a story half told. I did not betray the loves of years or our principles today but only failed them a little. I will try not to be ashamed of losing my head, of standing as a child who did not know the night; and you must not be shamed by astrology, whose proper study and wisdom should be, perhaps, coincidence itself—to see that we look through the telescope from both ends, taking note that the views do not quite match, and taking wisdom where we find it, where they overlap. The courses of the planets, bird flights, stars—if we read these for clues to our destinies, is it not because first they are written in the heart?

This was all I had wanted to say to my friend, as Christina had once written to hers about the hearts of men, and wars and ending them. One does not remake the world from first principles, but neither do we truly see it by observing each thing separately, as if from nowhere. We are not nowhere, we are in Mexico. We are not separate, we are here together for an hour. And though each eclipse might be tracked through infinite pasts and into infinite futures, this one hour will only happen this way once. In everything we feel and see and know lies this more ancient wisdom. The dying of the Sun, in all its terrible beauty and glory, comes only once, for us.

How doth the city sit solitary, that was full of people! how is she become as a widow! she that was great among the nations, and princess among the provinces, how is she become tributary . . .

n the weeks after the eclipse the rains returned to the city, hard, unrelenting, while against the mountains broke thunder and black storms it was said one could not breathe through, save with a hand cupped against the face—rain plunging not in drops but unbroken sheets as from upended cauldrons, and much hail that laid waste the fields, flattened grain and the tall corn, stripped orchards and the long plots of beans, scattered flocks, killing many lambs outright and even calves in the upper pastures. Flash floods such as had never been seen rolled down the bare mountainsides, and from the volcanoes as down the sides of a field tent, gathering mud and rock over slopes stripped of trees, sweeping the soil itself now from whole fields, flooding the watercourses with high walls of water. Behind these, slurries of mud, tree trunks and boulders rasped out the arroyos. Bridges, roads, whole farms were carried off, churches and monasteries broken apart and sloughed into the pleasant draws they had overlooked. How fragile a building of stone, once the foundations are made to shift. So it was that in the next weeks and months, the provisions that might have come from the surrounding hills to the valley flooded and blighted and infested with weevils did not come, or came so meagrely as to nourish old grievances and ever kindle the rumours of hoarding, through autumn and into the first months of 1692.

Increasingly did the valley of Anahuac depend on cities farther afield. Pack trains and heavy wagons heaved and plodded over muddy tracks and mountain passes from Puebla and Oaxaca, Queretaro and Guadalajara. Many mules and burros and draft horses died. Beasts of burden grew scarce, with ever more needed to haul ever smaller cargoes over roads steadily nearing disintegration. Even within sight of the city the wagonmasters and muleteers were unsure of delivering their cargoes. The roads approaching the causeways now were fields of mud where thousands of Indians toiled. In heavy rain the men deepened the ditches, dug drainage channels in the sloughs that were once fields, sectioned small tree trunks and laid these cross-wise in the roadstead, and over this laid gallet and gravel from the lakeshore.

Sections of the new causeways built in the last century subsided, weakened by the constant rain. Covered ever more deeply in mud, they clogged with the slower traffic even as the shipments dwindled in size. As the pack trains and wagons queued to cross, cargoes of vegetables mouldered in the damp. Ripe fruit rotted. Disputes arose. The shippers and wagoners demanded compensation. Fewer were willing to risk the journey. Contracts were rewritten to make the delivery point the lakeshore not the city. Whence the cargoes had to be transhipped, onto beasts of burden supplied by the city administration. Food, coal and firewood were reloaded in smaller bundles into lighter carriages, into enormous corn baskets to be ferried across the causeways by Indians on foot and into any available canoes.

The Indians were no longer needed to dredge the city's canals. Now they laboured from first light to dark building dikes. The lakeshore encroached; the canals overflowed their channels and spilled through the streets, a few passable now by canoe. The Merced canal along the west wall of San Jerónimo had overflowed, and could be distinguished from the streets on each bank by deeper tones of red and black. Black with the usual filth and sewage, red with the mud of foundered adobe houses and blood from the slaughterhouses where the livestock sickened from the damp and hunger and rotting feed. At the first sign of infirmity they were slaughtered, eventually in the corrals themselves.

Then the bakers and *tortilleros* began to close—one day no wheat, the next no corn, on other days grain but no fuel.

By March there was hardship enough for all. The greatest markets in the world were humbled. The grain was wet in the garners. The lack of bread was hard for everyone, but the want of corn—for tortillas, gorditas, tamales, *pozole*—was especially cruel for the poorest, for the mothers, for those of an age to be warriors, for those old enough to remember. This had once been a people of the corn. The new corn was a child in its crib, the young corn a warrior, the hard corn a blade of sacrifice, and this sacrifice the shucking of a heart.

The mud dikes, while not easy to maintain, were at least not as hard to build as they might have been, for as the houses of the poorest foundered, the adobe slumped into the streets. The rivers in the road beds and alleys ran with little sticks of poor furniture, bits of cloth and rag, baskets.

Many died.

By April, what was once the best growing season was drawing to an end. It had been raining for almost two years. In the convents the cellars lay under water to the ceilings, the kitchens ankle-deep, the provisions piled now on the floors of sitting rooms and in bedrooms on the upper storey. We subsisted nervously, guiltily, on stores of rich conserves, jams and sweets, on the rare piece of fruit coaxed from the orchards. The young children in the convent school no longer chose blue for the sky but shades of grey, blue-black, purple and brown. Books on the shelves mouldered and mildewed, the pages warped and swelled, the boards bent, the bindings split, packing the volumes more tightly, making them harder now to take down, often not to be returned to the same shelf.

Books, letters . . . were we never to attempt poetry on human afflic-tion, how much space would be left vacant on our shelves. The Old Testament reduced to a few spare passages read in the pleasant gleanings of an hour, Sophocles and Aeschylus to be dispensed with entirely. Thucydides and Herodotus thinned to a recitation of places and dates. Much of Hesiod—and all that was fine in *Works and Days*.

On the sufferings of animals we make no literature; except we give it a purpose, their agony bears within it nothing of the redemptive. It is not tragic, it is obscene. But on a human suffering, neither may we make free to spout just any sort of poetry. It is one matter to take from Music a per-fected idea of Time, and to make thereby of History a musical science, but it would be better to say why this should be so—though we cried out for answers, we might still find consolation in detecting some machinery of redemption, the mechanism of a purpose, though these remain ever fugitive, ever mysterious.

This. That a people, to the extent that it is a people or becomes one through just measures of joy and pain, might be considered possessed of a soul. A simple soul, instilled with an ancient learning, instructed in a Music old and simple and terrible, in the beauties of eclipses and the earth itself rending, in the detonations of lightning and of mountains that erupt.

And so perhaps needing to find some purpose, we might speak of a nation entering a night of trial. Of this dark night we are told by its poet that if the child-soul of a people is to be instructed it must first be weaned of the pleasures of the senses and all delectable things. Though the soul is being fed manna, the tongue does not taste it. For the flavour is delicate after the flesh-pots. In their hunger and their want the people of our valley dreamed of different things, some of meat, some of mangoes, pomegranates, some of good fresh bread.

In a person or likewise in a city, one cannot properly speak of constant panic—panic either subsides or else ends in destruction, self-destruction or madness. To see a beggar on a street corner or in a market, a starveling in rags muttering in singsong and telling stories to himself, it is lunacy we first think of. During those days, in the ceaseless repetition and mutation of our rumours we had become in this sense one lunatic; they were as if the rumours and singsong of one mind. There was anguish and hunger, moments of panic, and the rumours were our delirium.

The blight worsened. The *chahuixtle* spread like locusts, though people from the city were not sure how these creatures moved—if they crawled or flew. It was said that a farmer would look over a fine field at sunset and wake to its devastation, that the infestation travelled now as a swift horse galloping. A deeper fear was disease, that the sicknesses that had attended upon the Conquest, and so greatly abetted it, would be returned now as our harvest. Cholera, and typhus, and the most feared, for its hideousness, was the small pox. Disease did come—not from the country but from the barrios nearest the slaughterhouses to the north of San Jerónimo, and the feedlots to the south. The cattle especially were frail, and their handlers and slaughterers seemed most afflicted by these new fevers and died quickly. Many prayers at our convent were said for the dead.

And still the rains. Even in our prosperity, we could not get dry in the cells and workrooms of the convent. Leaks in ceilings, along window ledges, water standing on the ground, mildew high on the walls. Even in the shelter of the colonnades clothing never dried on the lines. If it were raining during confession, one might be wet from one Friday to the next.

The waters rose until long spans of the causeway decks went under. It had been hard to imagine, was hard still to believe. The causeways were a mighty thing, the city's pride, leagues long, and straight and high. So wide as to let six carriages pass abreast. The water was wider. Those few who imagined they might find a haven on the sea of mud that had been the mainland waded out over the long causeways with what belongings they could shoulder. Then the raised borders went under and the water on the decks stood waist deep, and no one sure of the way. It was said that among the last waders were some who had stepped off the edge. Heavy-laden they sank without time to call out.

Strange the sensation to see the city cut off—the causeways vanished were a fearful sight, and maddening to the eyes, as of a figure hastily painted over on a canvas—there, yet not. Though in a convent one could not see this. To see nothing for oneself, this was also maddening to the eyes.

The city was made an island once more. Four hundred thousand souls sustained now by a few hundred canoes, their passage from shore to shore growing longer, slower, by the day. A few barges had been completed but the work had begun too late. For weeks now the water had depth enough for deep draft ships, yet these had only plied our lake once, caravels built by the marines of Cortés to lay siege against the capital. As in that time, the hunger grew terrible. The poorest ate insects and grass, fodder and rotting hay. The street dogs disappeared once more—into cooking pots, when there was fuel for the cooking. And now the soul of the people took instruction in irony, for it was noted that the residents of this city had always eaten insects and dogs. Other people noted differences: there were caravels then, and only canoes now; the mission of the Spanish, who were not loved here, had been to starve the city, whereas the work of the Indian boatmen now was to keep starvation from us.

From the want and the deprivation, the breasts of the negresses and Indian wet nurses dried up. And among the mothers better fed, yet who had let their own milk go, there was sorrow as the infants were weaned on sops of bread. Sorrow, too, among the wet nurses who had no sops for their own.

In a city all but inundated, there was some thirst and more fear of thirst. Many wells were already fouled by the water standing on the ground. And each time the earth shifted with even minor tremors, a clay water main broke in one barrio or another, and could not be repaired or even dug down to through the water on the surface. To drink that red-black water, poisoned with blood and mire and the offal of diseased cattle, was as yet unthinkable, even if there were enough dry fuel to boil it. But there was still the aqueduct, which brought good water from the springs of Chapultepec. For some, indeed for ever more people, the walk to the Salto de Agua was long, the wait longer, the return a long torment. Our anxiety in the convent grew, for should our water main break, our vows did not give us leave to go out to fetch the water ourselves.

And so when there came a quake not violent yet not so mild, and reports arrived of cracks in the arches of the aqueduct, there was terror. And the murmurs that the water would no longer come were difficult to quell. But there was still rainwater where there were barrels to catch it, and there were many cooking pots free for this, since there was little to cook. Our small patio sprouted a garden of such pots—of enamel, clay and iron—and though we could not hear it, one could imagine a music of water drops as they fell throughout the valley at different pitches into divers vessels filled to various levels. Such distractions were welcome and brought relief but not much, for the hours between prayers seemed ever longer. And all our prayers were special prayers, for the Salto de Agua, for a family, a barrio, a house. Many hundreds died.

The question arose, how much can a people bear? In the mouldering books many stirring answers offered themselves but the simplest was that it depended on the people itself. Some seemed outwardly strong but soon lost the strength of their purpose, the heart of their convictions. The fortitude of the *conquistadores* could not be contested, and even now the Spanish *tercios* were feared throughout Europe, yet the French had begun to say of our empire that while its limbs were immensely strong, its heart and head were infinitely weak.

Other nations were born for trials. Israel was one. Such were Israel's sufferings that John draws upon the prophets Jonah, Job and Jeremiah, and David, royal poet of the *Psalms*, to speak to us of the night of the soul. The people of this valley of Anahuac were another born to trials, for this was a land of plenty in which the heart of the earth trembled, flash floods struck from a cloudless sky, mountains groaned and burst into flame. The last of the valley's peoples was the Mexica of the Triple Alliance. They too thought of themselves as chosen for a special destiny. And even to such a people come times when it is asked to endure more. The days of sea and fire ending in the year of the caravels on the lake was one such time; also the year 1611; and now. Our valley was filled with a babbling, of waters, of fables, of demons, of the confusions of the soul in darkness.

For a time it had seemed that in our suffering we had become one, that the fates of the peoples of the valley were not separate. But how much can one people take before it breaks apart and its soul falls into discord, before it bursts, and its heart.

On April 7th of the year 1692 the sermon at Easter Mass was given by Father Antonio Escaray. Two years had passed since a pleasant day in a locutory when those assembled had discussed the Maundy Thursday sermon. Father Escaray had been among us. It might have been two centuries.

With the Viceroy, Vicereine, and all the magistrates of the Royal *Audiencia* in attendance, Father Escaray decried the scandal of the scarcities. He hinted openly, baldly, at the rumours of hoarding and price speculation among the Viceroy's favourites. Rumours as true as they were persistent, and in their persistence lay their proof. *Vox populi, vox Dei.* Father Escaray's too was sacrilegious abuse of the solemnity of the pulpit for profane ends; yet he was applauded—roundly, deafeningly, in the Metropolitan Cathedral during the most solemn of Masses.

In the days following, people talked openly of uprisings in the provinces, and revolts on the plantations led by the runaway slaves based in San Lorenzo de los Negros. And yet such stories, if they were not invented here, would have had to come to us by canoe. The boatmen, who fed us and nourished us and had little time for gossip, themselves came to be feared and resented, for upon them we were as dependent as children. And had anyone forgotten the dolls in the canals, and the pagan rites still practised in the mountains? Whispers came now against the Indians of the countryside who were surely hoarding their crops, which was a cruel injustice since any crops they tended were not theirs.

The Indians did not lack for grievances. Remembered from the days when there was food were the wealthy Spaniards and Creoles who had helped themselves to whatever tempted them in the markets without a thought to paying for it. Now there were the fourteen-hour days of hard labour without rest; now the half-*real* of pay that bought almost nothing when prices were low, not even tortilla to replenish a man's strength; now the cold and sickness, the infections and fouled water, the drownings and foundered houses; now the breasts that would not draw, and much death among the new corn.

But we did not know what was said in those houses and in the streets unless the people there came to tell us. In the convent there was helplessness, that we could do so little, see or know so little for ourselves, and frustration that even so recently as Teresa's time, the sisters might go among the people and be of some use. The Franciscans were busy in these days among the Indians who had been brought in from the villages in work gangs. But the people of the nearest barrios did come, to the chapel, and to all the locutories; this was work all of us could do for the

people who could not read, and for the women who came after the worst
of all losses. Some came for answers, answers I no longer had; some
came to know how others had suffered, that others had lived through
such trials. There were books and verses for this. Most of all the work
was to sit with them . . . Filipinos and Africans, Creoles and Spaniards.
But for the Indians who turned to us, the poorest of the poor, I felt I
could do a little more, listen to their stories of how they had come to live
in the city, remember little songs to sing with them. The same scriptures
brought comfort, though never enough. Perhaps the Indians appreciated
especially the Lamentations. In Nahuatl, the voice of Jeremiah could
seem familiar, not unlike verses they had heard as children.

> . . . because the children and the sucklings swoon in the streets of the city.
> They say to their mothers, Where is the corn and the wine?

In our valley, the burial songs had been not so very different from the
songs for births. I was surprised to remember so many of the words. But
I did not know enough of them, and there were few elders. Our capital
was made up of many peoples, yet none quite whole any longer. And
though many of the instruments lacked, and the music in its movements
was perhaps no longer vast, many simpler melodies remained, beautiful
in their own right. For only when the last of a people is gone, in its language, its way in joy and suffering, can the music be properly said to have
gone out. Then may we take up a fragment, a bit of pottery or a shell and
hold it to our ear.

It became hard to remember the purpose; then, to hear the music;
soon, to imagine these could exist.

Though Father Escaray was a Franciscan, the Viceroy and Vicereine
had begun frequenting the Franciscan monastery, a place of refuge in a
time of need perhaps not far off. From their choice it was clear they
feared the poor more even than the wealthy Creoles, for it was the
Franciscans who were closest to the people, and could best protect them
from the people. Six men were said to have died in knife fights in the *pulquerías* in just the first week of June. On Friday, June 6th, an uproar broke
out at the public granaries on the rumour that they now stood completely empty. A restless mass surged about the granary doors, thrusting
a pregnant Indian woman up against the nervous troops. They clubbed
her to the ground. She miscarried there on the stones. A way was cleared;

a delegation of fifty Indian women and twenty men bore her up to the Archbishop's palace where the women were turned back, were always turned back. And again from the gates of the Viceroy's palace they were turned away. There were several hundred by now in the square—men and women. At nightfall they dispersed in knots and clusters of twenty or more, toward the taverns and *pulquerías*. Shouting and fights were heard through the night.

On Saturday nothing happened, though the *pulquerías* were said to be thronged with insurrectionists, with people drinking and hatching plots outside in the streets. Here at San Jerónimo, Concepción came with a dozen of the older servants, most of whom I had given religious instruction in Nahuatl. They were wounded by the stories: Yes, there had been many drunk at the granary yesterday—but not half were of the people— and none from among the women who had attempted to get justice for the brutality of the guards. The drunkenness was a slander, for as I surely knew, *pulque* was once a sacred drink. Not the actions of drunkards—but of women, and had it not always been thus in the face of injustice? Had not Our Mother one day challenged the war god to nourish the people on milk not blood? And maybe Madre Juana had heard of the time . . .

The title they used for me was one of respect but it felt uncomfortably formal now, for they were very much at ease, visibly proud of what the women had done. I suspected that some of the convent's servants, Concepción in particular, had been among them. I thought of telling them a nickname I had once had as a girl. But to persuade them to use it would have required a long story, and they had so many of their own and some of these were new to me. How the women of this valley, in their defiance, had always given the people their new destiny.[24] There was Coyolxauqui, the war god's sister, who opposed him, and whom he slew to inaugurate war. Even Malinalli, who had translated for Cortés, was only avenging upon her own people the injustice of being sold by them into slavery—was that not true? And so we passed the afternoon quietly in my sitting room, nodding as each began a story the others knew, Antonia trying to make them comfortable with cold tea, these women unused to being served.

On the morning of Sunday, June 8th, a large assembly of women had waited for the Viceroy after Mass and had insulted him openly in Santo Domingo square. A mob was milling in the central plaza. It was said they were a drunken rabble and Indians. It was also said that the Viceroy had come to the balcony to speak to the people and been felled by a paving stone. But though we did not know it, the Viceroy had already slipped away to the Franciscan monastery, disguising himself in the robes of a monk. In the late afternoon, as a mob numbering in the tens of thousands pushed toward the palace gates, another woman, an Indian, was bludgeoned to the ground. The crowd was chanting *México para los Méxicanos,* and for one more hour, it seemed, we were a people in our suffering.

The woman, near death or now dead, was taken up by the crowd—many women—and brought down the street to the Archbishop's palace, as had happened before, where they were again turned back without a chance to be heard. At dusk a paving stone was thrown up at the Vice-Queen's balcony, then another. Abandoned by the Viceroy, an outmanned palace guard assembled before the gates to face the mob, which turned briefly to looting the stylish shops of El Parian. The guards charged the looters. The mob charged back with stones. As the guards retreated a few opened fire, taking a hail of paving stones in answer. Two soldiers were knocked down—the mob fell upon them.

Others tore apart the market stalls for torches. The *ayuntamiento* was first. Then the palace. Through the barred gates, fire was set to the doors, then to the window shutters; then firebrands were thrown up at the balconies. The latticework of the Vice-Queen's balcony caught.

With flames already raging through the administration offices, Carlos led a party of students inside to retrieve the city's collection of Indian documents and histories.

Then, at the height of the revolt, the cathedral doors swung open. A priest flanked by a guard of altar boys emerged bearing the tabernacle of the Holy Sacrament. Seeing it raised on high, the crowd—blood-lust in their eyes, paving stones still clutched in split-nailed hands—fell to their knees while the procession traced the slow perimeter of the square. The young priest spoke for a few moments to the crowd in Nahuatl and Castilian. There the uprising ended for the day. When the rioters had left, many dead lay untended in the square.

Distressing to me in a way I could not grasp was the idea of the balcony itself, burning. True, I had spent many hours there, but few happy. Was it the image of the paving stones breaking through the lattice, or the rosewood in flames—what was this, grief?

That night we stood in the courtyards, near the locutories, took turns there, exchanged word. The rumour came at dawn that Puebla had been destroyed, that Malinche itself had opened and engulfed Puebla in fire—Iztaccihuatl too had woken, a thing that had not happened in all the histories of the valley. It was not credible, and yet hard to disbelieve. In the half-light, a fine grey ash was falling, the hills obscured by cloud.

All day, the story persisted. Surely the ash was from the Smoking Mountain and the fires in the plaza. And even if Puebla had been destroyed—how would we have heard so quickly? But our role seemed simply to echo the others, as throughout that day the people of the barrio stopped to tell what they had heard and to hear what others had said before rushing out again. By nightfall the effect of the rumours reaching in through the walls had become uncanny, as when by candlelight one first hears a hidden choir in a darkened church, voices sourceless in the air, hidden behind a wall or a curtain or a lattice. . . .

And yet we were that choir, we were that chorus, a chorus that was blind.

In the night, Monday, the arrests began. It was a night for the settling of grievances, parties of armed men in the streets. This, one could see from any window. There was no cause to believe the Inquisition would choose this night to make its arrests, for the Inquisition was accountable to no one and needed no pretexts. And yet it was hard to disbelieve, hard not to look for faces in each clot of men coming down the street. Hard not to run to the window at each shot fired, each flicker against the ceiling, each shout. I could not stay in my cell any longer.

Don't let them come for me, don't let them find me in here, behind so many walls. Let them take me in the open, not from my bed, let them take me from among the others.

Chaplain de Gárate sent word he would lead special prayers in the chapel, deserted except for us in the upper choir. Not a Mass, no vestments, a few candles on the altar. I did not know what he should read— he sent for me, he could not think. I could not either, I could not let myself. What should he read? *The Lamentations of Jeremiah*, I thought. But these would bring neither calm nor comfort.

Is this the city that men call the perfection of beauty, the joy of the whole earth . . . ? Thy prophets have seen vain and foolish things for thee . . . false burdens and causes of banishment . . .

It was while we were filing out of the upper choir afterwards, crowding at the top to take the winding stair. A sister just going down turned back to another, above her, and said something. It was in her tone, or rather that there was no tone at all. "Unless we are already dead . . ."

It was perhaps this, as much as anything.

I joined in all the prayers that night. No longer could I hold myself as one apart. I moved in all the processions, out in the open—women on their knees, ash falling, blackening us, our foreheads and faces, the makeup of actors, court clowns. Steam from a torch, mud and cloth, sharp stone, a knee gashed. Frightened novices, a young nun. Nothing separate, none of us separate now—all the fragments collected, one.

At the end of the night, with the sky gone grey, we went in to the prayers of Lauds. When we emerged at first light I thought to look one last time, truly look, to see for myself. To lay to rest the stories, the destruction of Puebla, the old volcanoes burning. La Malinche, Iztaccihuatl. To know, perhaps, that none of this night had been true, that we had been in no danger at all. I moved the shelf from the wall and lifted back the tapestry, reached in and felt for the latch. Stiff with disuse the hinges shrieked—I stopped, listened for Antonia, who might only be pretending to sleep. On the rooftop in the early light of morning I looked into the east, out over the grey lake to the volcanoes, the sky behind them blue-black. If I could just see, with my polished eyes. Iztaccihuatl lay dormant, as always, as she had since my earliest memory. A pale grey plume rose from the cone of El Popo. And yet for all the violence in that cauldron I saw such a majesty—how little touched by events, how still.

If I could but see to the camber of its hills, to the roots of its ravines, to the boughs of smoke holding up the sky. With polished eyes. Yet how changed the world below that horizon, the grey flooded fields, the vales of mud, the flood wrack floating all about the city as the *chinampas* had once done. Oh my city, white city of the sun, the lake in among your buildings now, the long mooring cables of your causeways gone. City of Empires, Venice of America.

White Sunflower. How solitary now.

I looked down over the dikes in the streets, the beggars crowding as ever at the gates of San Agustín. Beyond that, up Calle de las Rejas, to the charred timbers and scorched stones of the municipal building tumbled into the square. To the palace blackened to the parapets, the corner closest to the cathedral gone, carrion birds above the plaza. And to the sun, a sickly slug of tin.

There were verses I knew of consolation, that had given and brought it. And there were lamentations, and I sought them out, this time for myself.

Woe to the bloody city! and from the eyes of Ezechiel fled desire. . . .
And the Lord came as an enemy, and devoured her palaces. . . .
And David stretched out his hands in his affliction, and cried. . . .
And the flesh and the skin of Jeremiah were made old, and his bones broken,
    and his liver was poured upon the earth. . . .

But it seemed then the prophets of old spoke for their own people, and not to me. I thought of the heron Ribera, and many things besides. But the closest I could come to giving voice to that anguish was this. It was as if Music itself had died.

THE FURIES

This is my prayer: Civil War
Fattening on men's ruin shall
not thunder in our city. Let
not the dry dust that drinks
the black blood of citizens
through passion for revenge
and bloodshed for bloodshed
be given our state to prey upon.
Let them render grace for grace . . . [25]

On Tuesday came the first executions. It began slowly; for we had learned that during the rioting someone had put a torch to the public gallows. Four Indians given death for insurrection. Three lived to be executed; the fourth killed himself. At each corner of the central plaza a pair of hands was stuck on pikes. Concepción came to ask, for the others were asking her, why their hands. On Wednesday, the Viceroy moved into the residence of the Marquis of the Valley, the title and the palace Cortés had been awarded. Six more Indians executed, one *mestizo*. It did not rain. On Thursday, a man from Madrid. No one had expected this. Insurrection from a Creole perhaps, but not from a Spaniard.

If even ten thousand had risen up in the plaza on Sunday, there was work to last a thousand days. It was hard to find a limit to what to believe, hard not to be drawn into imagining what was to come. Without the anchor of the Church, it did not seem impossible that the Viceroyalty might be swept away and all trace of Europe with it. What was to become of us—were we a people?

Work began on a new gallows. By Friday came the news that the Viceroy had ordered the hanging of twenty-nine negroes in the *zócalo*. The men had not been involved in the riot, but on Tuesday had lost control of a herd of pigs they were driving from one of the barrios to the slaughter-houses. The pigs had stampeded just beneath the Viceroy's barred and shuttered window at the palace of Cortés. The Viceroy ordered his troops into the streets, his nerve being insufficient to bring him to the windows.

It was said he was hanging the herders now to silence the jeers and restore the dignity of his office. The charge was to be sedition.

I did not believe the rumour, but the stampede and the hangings had happened—after the unnatural events leading to Fray García's death, the sudden vacancy of the posts of Archbishop and Viceroy. In 1611. Such confusions were not surprising. We had acquired a hunger for strange events, portents of end-time and what must come next. Only the previous week there had been the story of the Viceroy coming to his balcony and being struck down by a paving stone. This too had happened, but to Moctezuma, in 1521.

In truth these were echoes of older stories. The fear of sedition, the war on the enemy within, these were as old as the valley itself, as the stories of the dragon twins. I thought I heard in their resurgence now a kind of rhyming.

The people of our valley were once a people of poetry. Their leader was the Speaker. Those who had not learned the people's tongue were mutes, and so the enemies to be feared came from within, for how could the Mexica be overthrown by a people lacking even speech? When the translator Malinche found her way to Cortés, the enemy was no longer mute.

In the week of the riot in our plaza there had been an uprising also in Tlaxcala. Here, it was remembered, uneasily, that for many years prior to the Conquest the Mexica had permitted Tlaxcala its freedom so as to keep a ready supply of war captives within the frontiers of the empire. When the moment came, the Tlaxcalans had fought beside Cortés. The enemy within.

These stories had not been easy to keep from my mind; within them I heard still other echoes of an older tongue. The volcanoes WhiteLady and La Malinche had not come to life, but the women of the valley had. And though Puebla had not been destroyed as we had heard, there had been a kind of rebellion, and there too the enemy within had spoken. For when the Viceroy sent men to commandeer Puebla's grain stores, it was the Bishop of Puebla who barred the way. In Puebla, Santa Cruz was the supreme authority and for weeks before the crisis had been buying grain at high prices and selling at a loss, precisely to pre-empt all talk of hoarding and speculation. Facing down the Viceroy's troops he vowed, before an anxious crowd at the granaries, that the grain of Puebla would not be taken before his vestments were soaked to the last drop of his own blood. I did not doubt his readiness. To sacrifice his martyr's blood before a multitude would have been such an ecstasy. A few days after the riot, the Viceroy addressed to the Bishop of Puebla a public letter of apology.

How it must have haunted the king's representative, that moment when ten thousand Mexicans of every race and class fell to their knees as if with one mind at the sight of the Sacrament. A moment the Count de Galve did not see, having slipped away in the dress of a monk. One cannot know what goes through a mind at such times. Perhaps he had most feared being dragged to a balcony and stoned.

In the week after the uprising, a crude sketch was affixed to the gates of the deserted palace and beneath the drawing a caption. *For Rent: Coop for Local Cocks and Spanish Hens.* This piece of sedition was authored neither by Indians nor by rabble but by the Creoles—even here their wounded pride showed, for at the palace in fact there were never many local cocks but not a few local hens. I knew this, for I had been one. Everywhere throughout the capital, the Count de Galve was the butt of jokes portraying him as a dandy, a coward, a cuckold. Without the Archbishop he could not govern. His Grace moved vigorously to guarantee public order by threatening hoarders and speculators with anathemas and excommunication, but in truth there had been little to hoard. Within a month and in the Church's hands, the worst of our fears passed, just as they had after the eclipse. If recently the incidence of irregular births had truly risen throughout the parishes, the obvious cause was the months of privation endured by pregnant women, not the work of the Enemy within the womb. But the Church was quick to respond to our hunger for strange events. Neither was the insurgency of the women in the plaza forgotten. From the pulpits came warnings against insubordination, exhortations to obedience, of daughters to their fathers, women to their husbands, sisters to their older brothers, servants to their masters.

For a time, the star of Dean de la Sierra burned brightly. It had been his inspiration to send the young priest and altar boys into the midst of the rioting. Now he sent word through Chaplain de Gárate to ask that I write the carols again this year for the Feast of Saint Peter. He was sorry it was no longer prudent to come himself. I might have tried writing a cycle to placate the Furies, to pronounce words of grace. But this was not what was wanted. I wrote them quickly, hymns to Saint Peter. Father of light, man of the sea, master of the air. New Caesar, great lover of Christ.

Much was said in this time, much was false. Little was said of the Inquisition. I had no reason to expect them. And yet there were days I could not quite face the idea of being in the locutory if they came. I preferred to be where I was happiest, among my books and collections, and my thoughts. Perhaps I still imagined these to be a form of rebellion. I looked through the shelves, shaking my head at the deterioration there, taking inventory of the damage. The Italians were in a bad state, above them in the ceiling a hairline crack we had not seen. Many volumes waterlogged, the *Commedia* falling to pieces. *Purgatorio*, the journey up that mountain, unreadable. Sitting by the window, I thought of Dante, his part in the fratricidal fighting of his youth. Civil war . . . his betrayal by the Neri, his banishment from Florence on pain of death by fire. It was not long before I remembered that Galileo had once given two mathematical lectures to the Academy of Florence on the configuration of Dante's Inferno. I was not certain, but I thought the figure had been a spiral. That evening in the library I came to see the Inferno, too, as a sort of instrument. Devised for the amplification of suffering.

In August a letter. This handwriting I knew so well. A letter from a friend on a day when it was needed. I felt my spirits rise as I turned it in my hands. If we were already dead, it was at least a place where letters were delivered . . . if slowly, for as I opened it I could see the date: April 22nd. There was no saying whether it came directly from the mails, or from some other source. No one had seen the deliverer. Of the three nuns assigned to the porter's gate that day, it was the third who brought the letter up but she had found it already there at the beginning of her turn. With all that was happening, anyone could have accepted a letter without noticing. It would have been better to leave it at that, for eventually the idea came to me that if someone had delivered it on that day in particular, it was because he had been instructed to.

22nd day of April, 1692
Seville

My dearest Juanita,

I shall permit myself to forego the histrionics with you. You were a friend, he was a friend to you. Tomás is dead.

The first great benefit of widowhood is asperity, the second, that it allows me to retire from court life. Even after all we have endured these past two years I cannot quite say it killed him, but Tomás never fully recovered from his early difficulties with the new Queen. Yet I pity her—the King cannot conceive a child. She has said she knows she is intact but is no longer sure she is quite a virgin. These things are never a secret at court. The watch on his efforts has been like watching a three-legged calf lurching about in a barn. He can scarcely walk or hold his head up. You can imagine the jokes this has tended to, but it is too sad now even for the courtiers. The mirth is quite wrung out of them. And so it is in sober tones that the latest makes the rounds, that the King has begun to consult certain nuns in Oviedo known to be possessed by demons. One has informed him that his impotence was induced when he was fifteen by a potion of dead men's privates mixed into a cup of chocolate by Queen Mariana. One could weep. Because the King and Queen Mother are involved, the Holy Office pretends to consider a distinction offered by the King's confessor: that is, between Satanic divination of the future and now these of the past.[26] In the end someone will likely burn for this, the King's confessor, or a nun.

We have had news of troubles in Mexico and of floods. If I do not quite bring myself to hope all is well with you, I may at least send my hopes that you are safe. The Council of the Indies has received complaints against the Viceroy and chances are he shall be recalled. If he has not been thus far, it is only that there are few men left here to send into a bad situation, and bad news arrives from all over the Empire. And now to have the French sniffing at its carcass, after all the battles my family has fought. I should let myself off too easily to say 'had I only been a man.' I have seen good men fail here, men like Tomás, and men more capable. Tomás was also a little unlucky, prone to gaffes; some of my advice he listened to, but it was not uniformly good. You have made much of my family's greatness but it is unclear to me what we have accomplished since the Manriques took the field to fight for Isabela. We have had two great centuries, but what does the Order of Santiago stand for now?

Yet even as our hopes have failed all around us, there has at least been the glory of our art. This century has been of a brilliance only France even dreams of matching. They have the playwrights but not the poets, Italy more sculptors but fewer painters—it would take all Europe, or as you have shown me, it would take the court of the old Medicis. Yet for all this time we have been failing. As a girl I saw Velázquez knighted, but by then his heart was already broken. I do not understand it. I wish I could have you here, to help make sense of it for me.

And now I must tell you I am withdrawing too from my efforts at publishing. I retire with unfinished business. *Las letras a Safo.* They meant so much to us. You said the time was not right then and it is not right here now, but there was a moment, I thought, when all seemed possible. Yet with Tomás ill these past two years, I could not have managed more. Your *Second Volume* I will have shipped in three separate sailings and, God willing, at least one shipment shall soon be reaching you. Although this is a stronger collection even than the first, the endorsements did not come easily. There were moments I feared we would not get the Holy Office's licence at all. I must warn you there were only eight theologians willing to lend their names to this, even though your letter on the Vieyra sermon is well thought of privately. Someone has even written from Majorca or somewhere for permission to publish it separately. But officially I am told the Spanish Inquisition stands with Mexico's, even though its judgements often seem unnecessarily harsh to us in Spain. If the Holy Office here is quiet just now, it is not resolve that lacks but prey. In these times no one is eager to offend, still less for a sermon written over fifty years ago. The great Antonio Vieyra has left many scars in his battles.

So, there are not many endorsements, but the quality of the people is high, as is their praise. It is a considered opinion among the leading figures here that you have, in this one volume, matched the greatest poem of our century's greatest poet, the prose of our peninsula's greatest stylist, and the theology of the greatest predicator of the age. I know you, and I know you will take this praise hard, and the encomium as irony. Phoenix of America, Pythoness of Delphi, Sum of the Ten Sibyls. I ask that you take it simply for what it is, and perhaps also for the truth.

You have said that little lasts, but we Manriques believe in the few things that might. So I prefer to think of my own efforts as having had a small hand in that rare thing. It is as close as I have come.

You will think I have abandoned you, but if money can be of any help to you now, know you have it, or a word or a letter.

I prefer to do my grieving here alone. But in the fullness of time I expect to enter a convent. Then you and I shall be sisters together.

There are things I shall miss. I shall miss my Tomás. I shall miss your letters of times past, of weddings and great banquets, and War's end. You.

With love,
María Luisa.

JUANA INÉS
DE LA CRUZ,

"Herb-Doctors"

B. Limosneros, trans.

What star was in the ascendent,
holding sway over heavenly bodies,
to have thus inclined you to me
and made duress seem free will?
What kind of sorcerer's brew
did the Indians confect—
the herb-doctors of my country—
to make my scrawls cast this spell?

 here came the illusion that after the flooding and the revolt the world outside might be again as it had been. The lake returned the city to us, street by street, though as lake bottom. It would be for us to make them streets again. The dikes came down. Some were used to rebuild houses, though this work went slowly—for so long as there had been such habitations of adobe, they had been built by work parties, but many neighbours were lost or had walked back into the country when the causeways rose up. Trading houses went under and did not rise up. Shippers, feedlots, shops. This time there could be no help from Europe. The Viceroy could be replaced, but it seemed certain the empire and the illusions it rested upon were never to be restored. He himself may have sensed this, for the killings stopped. Ten thousand executions would not have been enough. The Church alone was stronger than before. Never had the Church here seemed so powerful, the world of princes so weak.

There was much praise for Archbishop Aguiar. He had been decisive, though his decision to turn the women from his gates, twice, did much to spur the riot. The Archbishop was strong, because he was not the luckless Fray García, because he had been the voice of Wrath all along, because he had not fallen. The Archbishop was strong because the Viceroy was weak, strong because we needed him to be, strong because from that day forward he would be unopposed. Everywhere the Church's power, incarnate in the person of Archbishop Agiuar y Seijas, was in the ascendent. His coffers were full. His men had much success in the book-stores exchanging *Consolations of the Poor* for the texts of comedies. But I have misjudged many things, among them the Archbishop's magical hat, which in those days was said to be working great wonders for the sick. This was not superstition. Again I had been too hard on Carlos. The object of the hat was not to cure, the object was to bring consolation to the suffering. And in this, it had been more successful than all my learning.

History I had always sensed as a wind that moved just beyond these walls, to be brought inside only through the portal of books. But repeatedly these past two years, History had come to me and I had not known how to answer. History was all around us, trying the gates, rattling the bars, tapping at the shutters. And when the world did finally enter here—the responsibility, yes, I felt, but I found no use in my great gift. In the face of so much suffering, I had lost the purpose. My city had been tearing itself apart. How had I answered? *Caracol* unfinished, a few carols. With the Empire collapsing all about him and the Vandals at Hippo's gates, Augustine *had* written—kept writing, to restore the faith of the world in the world. *City of God*, the *Confessions*. John's *Canticles* written between sessions of torture . . . Campanella in prison, feigning madness to write the *Scelta*.

On the worst night, I had thought only of myself, feared only for myself, yet could not think for myself. No purpose, I had had no vision. A vision of nothing at all. In our valley we were once a people of poetry, and to its Speaker there had come a judgement more to be feared than the enemy, a presence more troubling than the poetry within: its end. The revelation of an emptiness, the end of a music.

September brought its own questions and judgements. There arrived the first of three shipments of the *Second Volume* of the collected works of Juana Inés de la Cruz, a nun professed under vows at the convent of San Jerónimo. Whatever its reception in Europe, the reappearance here of the letter on the Vieyra sermon was as gall, the theologians' endorsements bright *banderillas* to goad the bull. A bull that loathed bullfights. The letter had been retitled. "Crisis of a Sermon." More impudence. The dangerous proposition of God's negative *finezas* had not been withdrawn, and the criticisms of Vieyra's positions on Christ's greatest expressions of love for Man had not been softened by so much as a word. A priest had already been condemned for defending that criticism and the nun's right to offer it, though still the sentence had been neither published nor executed. I had been among the few privileged with knowledge of this.

Towards the end of September, a visit from the Holy Office. A requisition, signed ·by Master Examiner Dorantes, for an inventory of all books, monographs and manuscripts in my possession. To the Inquisition familiar who had brought the requisition I answered that the Archbishop already had such a list. But I was forgetting myself, for they knew that.

Not long after we had submitted our new inventory the Holy Office requested another, and warned that omissions from both lists could only be considered deliberate, if an unlisted book were subsequently traced back to me. This we had anticipated. Antonia had kept duplicates of all our lists. Then came another missive: certain manuscripts already known to be in my possession were missing from both lists. Yes? If Master Examiner Dorantes would describe them in detail—titles, author, contents—we would be sure to conduct a thorough search. There were two small victories in this, and against the Inquisition this was no small thing: the first, to have it even partly confirmed that not so very much was known about these manuscripts; the second, that the Holy Office did not immediately pursue the matter, meaning Dorantes was far from sure I in fact had them. So if I thought the victories small, it was in knowing the much that he could yet do to reassure himself.

My *Second Volume* had arrived in time to be added to the inventory. There had been three thousand four hundred twenty-seven books. Then, twenty-eight. It had been childish to count them, for it was only the list that was required, not the count, but it had been the ambition of my girlhood to have four thousand. At this rate I would have them collected in five more years. This, though the titles were not always easy to obtain, or to hold on to. I had arrived in Mexico thirty years ago with two hundred favourite volumes and fifty pesos, and it was then, in my uncle's house, when I let slip something of my ambitions, that I had first been told of the book collector Pérez de Soto.

Now, as the days and weeks passed, I felt myself coming to a better understanding of his case. Born in Cholula, son of a mason. Cathedral architect, astrologer. A practical man, a man of numbers and plans, but with imagination, as I have, and with many friends at the cathedral, as I had. A man knowing himself largely innocent, holding out reasonable hopes for his release. The collection of Pérez de Soto totalled sixteen hundred sixty-eight books, all but eighteen returned to his widow, from which it was plain that the evidence against him had been slight. He had gone before the Tribunal, given a full and frank accounting of his activities, stoutly declared himself innocent. Though of charges unknown to him. And then, without even bothering to question him, the Tribunal sent him back to his cell: that he might make a full and complete recollection of his trespasses. A bad shock to a man who had braced for an interrogation. He was given time to recollect. He was given weeks. He was given months.

He was killed trying to murder the mulatto cellmate they had just that day given him for company. It happened in total darkness, when the lanterns in the hall were put out after the supper. I have been told there are no windows there.

Toward the end of November a possibility came to mind, stayed for some time: Pérez de Soto was already mad. Because, long before he was arrested, the rumours had half broken him. And then, as arrest became imminent, every conversation ended as he entered a room, a tavern, a workshop. The other half was broken when the rumours stopped.

There were always other possibilities . . . the solitude of his confinement, the Tribunal's indifference to his testimony, the impossibility of a full recollection, his confessions to an escalating series of false crimes— if only so he might be lightly convicted of charges he could at least know the basis of. All were possible, any of them sufficient if Time in the Inquisition's prisons was as I imagined it.

This was how it might have happened with him, but Pérez de Soto's was a different life. He did not live in an echo chest; neither was he called to worship eight times a day, there to face his neighbours. For my part, I did not go to taverns, though I had once, in disguise, during my time at the palace. One did not go far disguised as a nun. Our cases were not the same. And though each case was special in its own way, mine must be conducted carefully. This had been explained. There would be time. I thought it best nonetheless not to walk into so many rooms without knowing who was in them. This would have been a harder thing for Pérez de Soto to manage. Few friends came for me now, so another difference. Gutiérrez and Santa Cruz, to name two, but since I was not sure they had ever been friends I did not think their staying away counted. Carlos I no longer saw, though this I could blame on myself. He still occasionally came to give a class for Antonia, and once when he learned of the book inventory. Since he had not asked specifically to see me, I told her to go back down and tell him not to worry, his manuscripts were safe for now. Scientific treatises, tables of celestial observations, studies of the old Mexican calendars . . . Antonia and I had worked long hours, late nights, had recopied them, hidden the originals in the convent archives, disguised as account books and registries, sent copies in separate packets under assumed names to distant friends. The next time, I told myself, he could go to his friend the Archbishop's office for secretarial services.

I came down for prayers, less often for walks. In the orchards, one or two trees had to be cut down, their roots pulled up, the gardens restarted.

It was work Antonia was keen to do. Vanessa and Concepción worked long hours beside her.

Briefly there was the illusion that the world outside was returning to normal. It was painful, but now is gone. Inside we had fewer illusions. It is the work of convents to take on the sufferings and prayers of the neighbourhoods, but we had been marked by this, had taken many sufferings and written them into our backs and onto our knees and the convent was a darker place for it. By December there were nightly processions around *el gran patio*. Mother Andrea had tried to maintain rules against excesses of mortification but the rules had given way. The factions now were against their reinstatement—had the floods not abated, the riots and executions ceased? The flails had always been of braided hemp, to be knotted at the ends if a sister wished, but never to be pierced with tacks. Ever more of the sisters came to the refectory and choir wearing barbed crosses, iron gags and branks. The younger sisters had had no experience of this. Many were frightened, a smaller number were lit from within. I had seen it before. It is a sort of enthusiasm. And unless we are fortunate, it is the start of what no earthly force can stop, once it has begun.

When it might still have made a difference I had undermined Andrea in a dozen ways. I had so resented the slightest infringements on my liberty. How easily I had given up even the duties I had loved, the academy, the music classes for the youngest children.

If a convent could be said to be possessed of a soul, San Jerónimo's had changed. Could we have withstood together the tide of events outside? I did not help them try. This had been a good place, precisely what I thought it would be. I had not been deceived. But it was a convent. Instead of blaming it for my own failings, I should have been grateful for the excuse.

In the refectory, at our Friday chapter of faults, I went to the rostrum before a hundred and fifty of my sisters and pledged what I had always refused, never again to miss our communal prayers, for the rest of my life.

1693. Early in January a novice came to say don Carlos de Sigüenza y Góngora was waiting in the locutory. *Please,* will you come? Antonia asked. But he and I had reached a place where there was too much to say. I had no wish to see him—for it was seeing him that always softened me. I had heard the story of his quarrel with the Archbishop, had at first thought it exaggerated, but though it had happened weeks ago,

Antonia assured me the marks were still hideous and pitiful. During a discussion, Carlos, never one to tolerate another's inattention, had asked if His Grace could please make an effort to concentrate, since he was being spoken to. The Archbishop rose in a rage, walked across the room and struck Carlos full in the face with his cane, smashing his glasses, cutting him deeply. The cheekbone, crushed, had set badly. The scar healed jagged, livid, the full width of his eye, an eye he must have come very near to losing. Of course an astronomer has two.

I had generally found it difficult to hate anyone I had never seen, but though I had felt many things for the Archbishop—pity, fear, disgust, contempt—hatred I managed the day Antonia described the injury.

This in no way lessened Carlos's capacity for infuriating me. At the end of his last visit, he had managed to give Antonia a few parting words of advice to pass along. That though the Archbishop's ways were strange, Carlos was sure there was still a way forward—if I could just let a few months pass without some fresh provocation. A way *forward?* Only he could say something like this with his face disfigured by that man. I had no wish to repeat the experience of the day of the eclipse. We had counted on each other for so much. How we had wearied ourselves, our friendship, with these quarrels. The best it seemed we could manage was not to speak them.

In a few moments Antonia was back.

"He's asked for you."

"Has he."

"He is leaving today—*para la Florida.*"

"Another dramatic exit."

"He wants to say good-bye, he says it might be a *year* this time. Please go to him. You know it's you he comes for."

The regrets would start before he had even left the room. Today it would be his scarred face, the sight of him in his travelling clothes again. The ancient buff coat, the spyglass tucked into a baldric, the belt with pouches dangling—a notebook, magnifying lens, powder horn. A small military adventurer. *Don't go again. Don't leave me behind.* Then I would remember the times I had said good-bye to him like this before, once at the palace . . . the many injustices I had done him over the years. I had punished him in so many silent ways for becoming a traveller, but not like my father; for becoming a scholar of our past, but not like my grandfather—and especially for never letting heartbreak stop him. Yet he was sufficiently like them that I resented him each time he left. And how I'd resented his friendship with my mother, that he had insinuated himself into my past.

No, I would not go down to him.

Anger served Antonia best—better certainly than melancholy and regret served me. She was only mildly angry when I first refused to go down to him, somewhat less mildly when I refused a second time even knowing he had come to say good-bye. But her anger was as much with Carlos as with me by the time she returned with his manuscripts.

"How can he leave these things with you?"

Still at the top of the stairs, she stood as though unwilling to enter without a satisfactory answer. She held the bundle hanging at her side as one would hold a brick. But I did not know which manuscripts she held. And when I did know, I knew also that for once I had made the right decision, not to see him. This time the argument would have been inescapable—bitter, and still more bitterly regretted—the damage irreparable, for I would have voiced then what I had never said: that though he cherished the memory of Fray Cuadros and the memories of their times together in the jungle, he would abandon even these and suffer a thousand deaths himself before he would blame the fate of Manuel de Cuadros—or mine—*on a single defect of Our Faith.*

Antonia spread the papers out on the table beneath the library window. Precisely the sort of documents Examiner Gutiérrez had once been fishing for, the very ones perhaps: a translation of the Song of Solomon into Nahuatl, which had been expressly forbidden; land titles Carlos had rushed into a burning building to retrieve, belonging to his friend the translator Ixtlilxochitl; my letters to Carlos in Veracruz, several verging on heresy; three letters of his, unsent, to me. And at the bottom of the pile, the most dangerous. The recitation of a painted book they had discovered there: Moctezuma's last days as Cortés's captive, and the outlines of a theological discussion between the Speaker and Cortés's ignorant chaplain. But I suspected Manuel de Cuadros was the author of this text. It was the sort of work he had gone to the stake to protect.

My greatest fear in that time had been that Carlos might be implicated. His friend Cuadros I scarcely knew, had met just the once, a few months before the trial. And by then, Carlos said, he was not himself. Perhaps Fray Cuadros, too, I understood better now than I once had. Thirty-four years he had spent among the Indians, first as a student then a teacher of their languages, then as an instructor at the Indian College of Santa Cruz, then finally as the leader of an ill-fated mission to the Mayan highlands. Carlos said Cuadros was never the same after the Church ordered burned a lost cache of ancient Mayan books and artefacts he'd been instrumental in unearthing. A year later there came the Franciscan's turn. At first light, they stripped the balding heretic naked, smeared him with honey and daubed his body with feathers. All day in the punishing sun he perched—a heaving mass of wasps and flies and stinging ants—wavering barefoot on the thorny palm of a *nopal*. The pyre was lit at sunset.

And now Carlos had made me responsible for the fate of his friend's manuscripts. Was this to be punishment for all my injustices, to suggest that I too had had even a small role in what had happened to Cuadros— in that my stories of the countryside had set Carlos on his path? But the question was not how or even quite why, but why now?—when it was these very legends that had been so much on my mind. But in the end Antonia had the better question.

What are we to *do*?

Lysis,
I cannot simply send this without a word, so if circumstances dictate that I answer your letter only now, months late, I am sorry.

I am sorry.

I had thought not to write again, to let your last letter be our final one, to have answered it only with the verses I wrote the night it arrived. There was nothing then to add—it was so wrong of me to think I could guess at the feelings of one who has lost a husband, and yet for those few hours while I was writing for you, I thought . . .

I am sorry also about the pseudonym, and that you will have received this package that you will not want, signed with a stranger's name and delivered by a stranger's hand. It is only that I do not know whom else to entrust it to. I have bound these manuscripts under a separate seal for your protection, though you must please feel entirely free to open them, or to destroy them, seal unbroken—the choice and the responsibility will be as unwelcome to you as they have been to me.

For my part, I will not do the holy officers' work for them, or Time's. What I fear most is not their power to silence us, but to erase. Here, they have the power to erase whole centuries; before long they will have erased ours, as already they have blotted the boldest pens of Spain.

The climate here is not favourable to ice, and will not be for a very long time.

But though there are troubles here and fears, at least are we spared the sadness at court in Madrid, spared what you have seen, the sight of our king—spared the news that arrives from the other corners of the Empire.

Yet here in Mexico too, the French circle nearby, as though we were already dead.

Or, perhaps we are, perhaps we have long been—and this, our golden century, was merely the soul of an age making ready to depart. Who can say that this is not all that a golden age ever was? . . . a sort of afterlife, a golden shade hovering above the carcass of empire. We are left here, we are left behind, to watch a greatness that has dimmed. Had the heart of the Velázquez you knew as a girl been smaller or harder than it was, he would not have been the one for that work. Athens and Alexandria, Florence and Madrid. Mexico. Versailles. When finally the French breach our fortifications here to tell us we are dead, we will explain it to them—that what they scent on the air is not their glory, but the fresher vigour of their own decomposition.

Lysis, I will never see Athens. But we have many ruins here, built into living monuments of shops and churches, city gates and bridges. Our stones here are used again, as was the custom once in Alexandria. So it is also with our stories. Those of our valley are ever with me now, their murmurings in the night are little serpent's tongues licking at my ears.

Lately the convent's servants have reminded me of a lesson I had once learned and since forgotten. Here, there are not so many Helens. The women of our valley are more like Iphigenia, when they are not like Clytaemnestra, the other hatchling, the other city on the shield.

One last tale, then, though it ends with no wedding, though it brings little peace.

Malinche. Tell me about her, Antonia asks, to draw me out, as we sit copying together at a table, like two children over spelling lessons. Her bell-clear voice, my reluctant, mumbled answers, the scrabbling of quills, their clattering in the inkpot. Conversation of the ordinary sort has become almost unbearable to me. I feel my jaws, the string beneath my tongue, grow each day more stiff and strained, like curing meat. Another day, another turn on the vise, another turn on the cleat. Antonia says I've become cruel so as to have no one weeping over me. Perhaps it will be for my cruelty, in the end, that I am remembered here.

For the woman called so many names in life, history has reserved just one. Malinche. All call her that now. Born a princess near Veracruz, named after the sister BlueHummingbird slew to propel the Mexica toward their destiny, sold at the death of her father into slavery to the Maya. Malinalli, Malintzin, Marina. . . . Her beauty spares her the numbing drudgery of the fields; her gift for languages lifts her from the foetid anonymity of the brothels. Precisely these gifts of hers make her the perfect gift for the foreigner, Cortés, when he arrives. More than just a consort, she speaks for him, tempers FeatherSerpent's vengeance, interprets his actions. Do the Mayas have an idea of what they have just loosed against the Mexica?

On the night Moctezuma is felled by a paving stone, Cortés and his men are attacked and driven from the capital. They flee to Cholula. There in the marketplace, Malinalli meets the wife of a commander. Each seeks information, each attempts to beguile the other. Malinalli tells a story of the Emperor. In turn the commander's wife says there will be an attack on the foreigners—Malinalli should save herself. The Mexica reinforcements are due at any moment.

Two women sit in a marketplace on the eve of a battle, two others over their orthography at a kitchen table recopying the story, two more over one letter a thousand leagues and a thousand years apart, and in it, a fable. Malinalli's mastery of tongues brings to life the strangest friendship in all the world, and the shortest. She conjures two interlocutors— without her, they would not even have known how to find each other interesting. Only she knows what Moctezuma and Cortés are really saying to each other.

Love or hate? Antonia asks. What . . . ? You haven't been listening, she so gently chides. She wants to know why Malinalli returns to the Black Room even after the chaplain begins to stay away. Perhaps she is troubled that her lover has abandoned Moctezuma just as he begins to fascinate. Cruelty or kindness, love or hate. Is she drunk on love? seduced by power? bent on revenge—has she gone to gloat? She is there for what they share. He'd thought himself untouchable, she'd thought herself loved. She cradles Moctezuma's head to her breast, comforts an emperor who's mistaken himself for a god, been seduced by an imposter and cast aside. Both now feel the burden of their choices. He, the Fifth Sun's divine priest, she, the woman of discord, come to lead the Mexica to their destiny. How Moctezuma aches to submit to it, to what is ordained . . . if only she will help him determine what it is. This she consents to try, for in Moctezuma's fate she has a foretaste of her own. He, the scapegoat for a god, she, the stand-in for a bride.

Loving and hating now are as immaterial as words. Oracle, she has just seen how quickly interest wanes once the other is possessed, sees this in the straining instant she conceives the son who will be called Martín Cortés—the first of two so-named, for names too are made redundant once the conquest has been made. When Cortés returns to Spain to marry, he will name his second firstborn, too, Martín. The tyrannies of a woman's flesh—forced to love the sons of men we've grown to hate. Traitor to the powerful, liberator to the weak, she who speaks and speaks has been by her own tongue betrayed. Speak oracle, speak. What speech can redeem the Sibyl now but silence? Now that the conquest has been made.

Dear Lysis, dear friend, I sense in these legends a script so configured as to be read by me . . . or completed. And yet it is as if a cloud had settled over my mind, my eyes. If I could but *see*, *know* if it is already written, or whether I might yet change it.

I pray that a tender God keep you close to his breast, until the day we are made sisters again.

Your loving servant,
don Juan Sáenz del Cauri[27]

JUANA INÉS
DE LA CRUZ,

LOVE IS A
GREATER
LABYRINTH

B. Limosneros, trans.

THESEUS:

Beautiful Phaedra, whom I adore,
—as you are well aware,
from the first instant
I saw you, I surrendered
my soul entire, so completely
and without reserve
that even a lover's anxieties
were not truly mine, nor could I so much as
lay claim to my own distress,
since none can be credited with
what is owed to someone else;
and all that is mine being yours, in truth,
it would also have been an impropriety
to offer you my affections—
thus consigning to you a property
already your own; hence
how vainglorious of me
to have put myself at your service,
given that the greatest *fineza*,
reduced to its purest expression,
was to be incapable of any other gesture.

    You know, also, that Ariadne,
whether out of pity or nobility,
took it upon herself to liberate me
with such heroic *finezas*,
such generous actions,
and cunning devices
that had I a soul to give, or a heart,
scant payment would it have been
to offer it to her . . .

SOME DAYS I CAN'T STOMACH one more forkful of crow; others I just can't get my fill. Let the transcripts show it. Bring on the angry clown. Unclap his bracelets, ungag him.

I miss my daughter.

Not a deep longing, naturally, given my handicap, a discernible shallowness of emotional response. Madeleine advises me it's termed *poverty of affect.* This species of penury isn't nearly as uncommon as we let on. But this evening, out here at the cabin as the ranch lights blink on below me one by one, I miss the view from the nursery, where I would often sit at dusk, winter especially, until Catherine could fall asleep. A panorama less dramatic than these Rockies certainly, but with home's little consolations, hidden possibilities . . . swing set, garden gnome, rabbit hutch. Most nights Catherine's terrified of the dark. If in a child there can be anything at all unusual in this, it's that the terrors came into the world with her, on dark wings. It has been with her from the first howling night. And from the beginning, for this one thing, she needed me more than her mother. Does still, I know. I make a better scarecrow.

I came to fatherhood resentfully, it's true. For months the pregnancy swelled between us like the accidental seed of Madeleine's ever ramifying competence and self-mastery. Prenatal classes were pure calamity. The movies were appalling horror shows—bloody, crudely shot, amateurishly played. Projected for us with admonitory grimaces by our instructor, as we all lay paired and splayed on mats around her. I struggled vainly to find in these screenings something other than a squeamish, squirming affront, sex education run amok—cuddling up with granny for a porn flick on the couch.

I found pretexts for missing classes. I was breathtakingly unprepared for what I was about to undergo.

Forty years ago our fathers mimed the incidental character of their role in conception by passing out cigars in waiting rooms. We, their sons, enact a comparable futility today by playing at birth coach in the delivery room. So goes the theory. Then there are moments that thrust themselves upon you, that overrule your every objection, overcome your reservations, overrun your fortifications. Flood you with the here and now.

SCARECROW

Bind you tight to *ever always   must*. This is how it must be, has always been, will ever be.

You are lifted on a tide, overwhelmed by simplicities elemental as buoyancy. On blood, on gore, on a carnal squalor and reek you are lifted—a speck of flotsam—lifted high like untold millions before and after, and in one single inexhaustible plunge, you are driven headlong down and smashed upon a dark shore. Gowns the green of new leaves, blue-greys and reds of blood and living meat. Polychrome reflections smear in the convexities of chromium steel. Mangled battle cries— harsh and clanging—lost heraldries more ancient than speech or mind. By the power of seas moon-pulled, wind-driven, you are broken down. Overthrown. And raised up whole again.

White light, white masks, white sheets. Superhuman intensities burn in our eyes like life like light like need. Donald, look at me. Donald can you see? Tell me what you see. Can you see her yet? Is she breathing? Is it alright? Donald talk to me. Are you crying? Let me see. Let me see you. Look at me. She is *ours*. She is between you and me. Let me see your face, don't turn away.

A miracle, unbidden. Then elation, post-catastrophe. The hurricane met and weathered. Aftermath. A giddy relief on wobbly knees carries you clear of the wrecked carnival ride, and the exhilaration leaves you undone. If only for an hour.

Few men, through millennia, had been admitted to this wilderness. Now we're reserved a front-row seat beneath the arc lamps, just when the savage run of nature is elsewhere all but done. I'm no poet, cer- tainly, but no words can capture a thing so raw. I am left fumbling with clichés. Madonna and child. Madeleine and child. Catherine Rose. Mop-head dolls. Catherine Rose. Hummingbird mobiles. Catherine Rose. Clichés.

Pietà.

I could have loved my wife again. We had a chance.

She loved *me*. It took a lot of things to make her stop, finally. The worst was watching me retreat from this new beachhead, back again to the arid safety of my own sea of tranquillity: stale and dead and drained. My airless desert of inner space. I called it making sense of things, getting my bearings, regaining perspective.

But in that delivery room, dazed and chastened, I swore on my daughter's eyes, on Catherine's eyes, no more infidelities. I will always be father to this child. I will do what it takes. I will keep her out of harm's way. Something in me needed to promise Madeleine I would keep our child safe, though I know I can't, have begun to fail. A whole lifetime of failing lies still ahead of me.

How will I protect her from here?

For the record: I did keep that first chastened oath. Though when news of the scandal broke, Madeleine wouldn't let herself believe it. In body, at least, I was faithful. Though not in dreams, not in memories.

A view I miss is from the nursery. Catherine Rose.

This Mexican idea of time fills me with anguish tonight. With a terrible clarity I see my past, our present, Catherine's future moving along different loops of the same fatal arc. Just enough variety in the details to obscure the pattern and—mercifully, most days—the path ahead. So supremely sure of having buried my own childhood, the sludge of its toxic waste, I see this thing, now—seeping up out of my past, staining her future . . .

Calgary Star, Friday, March 25th, 1995

QUIET FLEES THE DON

by Tarah Tinsell

... the daughter of one of this country's finest heart surgeons still lies in intensive care at the Foothills Hospital. Yesterday crime reporter Vijay Seth covered the growing mystery surrounding the case.

And now surfacing in this affair is the name of a certain mainstay of our academic community, once voted in these pages one of Calgary's ten sexiest men—one of those university dons widely available for in-depth consultations with certain of his students at any hour of the day or night.

Yes ladies, many of us alumnae know this man, having studied directly under him. Think ponytail, think twinkling blue eyes, think close-trimmed beard à la George Michael ...

More on Monday.

In other society news, which avant-garde playwright with the initials B.B. showed up three sheets to the wind to speak at the Mayor's charity fundraiser? ...

LATELY, ABOUT ALL I CARE TO TAKE of the outside world is walk- JEWEL
ing the dog. Each time I come up to stay, Relkoff lends me Jewel, a
Blue Heeler pup. For company, he says, though I'm generally assured
of company of another sort, were I to want it. To keep from trespass-
ing, my media entourage has to stop at the property line, out of sight
below the evergreens. Jewel and I like to walk the other way, over
through the cottonwoods. She's crouching outside the screen door
now, her whole body trembling with play. Pausing, in the tirelessness
that's in her breed, to coax me out. One end of the stick is clasped
lightly in her jaws to remind me she plays fetch perfectly, dropping the
stick daintily each time at my feet. I have always liked dogs, had talked
about getting one much like this for our Catherine when she was old
enough to care for it. I may even have told this to Beulah.

I stand in the living room, at the bottom of the stairs leading up to
the loft. On each side of the main window all the louvers are open
though the main drapes are closed. The weather is good. You might
swear it was summer but our hopes for May have changed. Spring
comes earlier, stays longer, cedes more reluctantly. Summer rarely puts
down roots before late July.

Today the fields to the east have a verdancy that is almost painful
to see.

On the property's northwest corner a stand of fir has been left as a
windbreak. Just south of the house a fringe of leafless trees follows a
creek bed. A small arbour of willow, apple, and European birch stands
at the foot of what was once a substantial garden, now overgrown with
wildflowers.

From somewhere out in the yard comes the three-toned ratcheting
of magpies . . . *ric-kric-rick*. A little breeze sways through the cottonwoods, temptingly. Scents of apple blossoms, and sap like bitter wax.
From branches bent low with overstuffed catkins, chutes of fluff billow
on the wind. Not drifting like snow but pinwheeling weightless in the
sun, like blizzards in gift-shop paperweights.

Jewel's eager yelps dart at me through the flyscreen like the creaking
of little springs.

Not just now, Jewel. A little later. Soon. I have a little work left to do.

By this point I had ample evidence that Beulah had been studying me so much more closely than I, her. She knew my tastes and my preferences, my work and my weaknesses, knew much more of my family life than I had ever intended, and things about my past unknown even to my wife. In notes, letters, poems, and in the work itself, I'd seen ample evidence she was baiting me, transmuting certain elements of our shared experiences, knowing I could not help but find touches of myself, of us, in those pages. This is what feeling people do. At first I assumed this was the main challenge, as she saw it—did she really think it would be so difficult for me to *feel?*

But at some point I could no longer ignore the possibility that the work had a whole other component—plotting, real-world actions. Leading up to the final night there was a lot of this other component. Heroic gestures, deft devices—witness the academic charges, the early press involvement. But *after* that night? What outcomes could she possibly anticipate, which of my decisions and responses? And what was bothering me more?—how she had counted on me once, or the ways in which she'd been counting on me since. Troubling to contemplate, it made the work into almost the opposite of what it had seemed: not to lose myself in the fiction but to find the fiction in me. In my life, my Lie, the game was to compare my tribulations, always of course in miniature, to those of a great figure, and to find within myself the qualities of a Hawkeye, a Faust, a great conqueror—not, as it were, to identify with Napoleon but the little Corsican with myself. Yes, this felt more like her, the dare, the trap: and agreeing to go along with it, well, this was just asking to be made quixotic, a figure of fun, a Don of the Woeful Figure. It was all but asking to be locked up.

Transcript
Action #: 9504—56893
Judicial District of Calgary
Proceedings
5 April 1995

I've heard quite enough. Dr. Gregory, I've given you
considerable leeway. In connection with this matter, you have
already compromised--and may well have forfeited--a presti-
gious and I'm sure altogether satisfying line of work. Your
sexual and professional conduct have been held up to public
scrutiny and even ridicule in the national media. You must
be under a good deal of stress.

Nevertheless your testimony here today has been evasive
and uncooperative in the extreme. I will be forwarding the
transcript to the Solicitor-General's office with instructions
that it be examined for evidence of perjury.

At the Discovery last week, your attorney was to have
brought in this young woman's journals, which you do not deny
having in your possession. Why they're *in* your possession is
unclear to me. What's more, it has come to my attention that
these same journals were the subject of a warrant to search
your home a few weeks ago.

I find this disturbing. What should have become clear to
you by now, Dr. Gregory, is how much trouble you are in. You
have just given dubious testimony, under oath, in a Civil
proceeding; and I understand there may be criminal charges
pending the outcome of a police investigation that you may
very well be obstructing. Under normal circumstances I would
not hesitate to find you in contempt on the basis of what I
have heard today.

Instead, because of conduct that in the absence of anything
like a reasonable explanation I can only find bizarre, I'm
going to suggest to your counsel that you undergo a
psychiatric examination--with a view to reassessing your
defence strategy--and another for himself should he continue
to work for you in the present circumstances.

I am giving you three days to bring this material forward.
Three days to think about your rapidly deteriorating legal
position.

No human being of good faith could look into the faces
of this agonized family and not feel compassion. If your
comportment here today was an attempt to protect someone,
perhaps the girl herself, or to protect your own tattered
reputation in this community, I suggest that you instead
attempt to think about avoiding prosecution. Or about
preparing yourself for it, if, when you next come before
this court, your attitude has not changed. . . .

DON JUAN

SUNRISE OVER THE PLAINS. The lights of Calgary in the distance. I need to pause for this, a celestial pageant that lifts me, however briefly, up from this place. I would not trade the mornings up here for any in the world. Is it only dust, high-altitude ice crystals? What lends the sunrises this quality that I find so stirring? Strokes of colour fanning out, a childlike reach—*how high is the sky?*

Shades as beautiful as their own names. Vermilion. Fuchsia. Carnelian. Crimson.

Rearing up before me a scallop shell of cloud—lambent hollows, inky fingers—high-spanned, arcing east to west, splitting like a fruit's dark skin to reveal a fissured meat of light. Clumsy feet snagged in darkness, I turn to face west, where pressed hard against the western dark the sky distils its colour down from wine to Concord blue to greenish-black above the mountain battlements. Back in the east, a swirling forge of copper, brass—a seething diamondback of coals.

A day is made, but the human eye in its earthbound infancy perceives this red, primal rite as a crisis—of scale, orientation—a breech-birth of interstellar gases propelled *up*, projected onto still higher clouds of jet. And yet, from far below I can't shake the impression of looking *down*, as if over a molten plain . . . liquid floes of lavender spill over it, fading like a blush.

Day.

Things were not always so cozy between me and Eric Heffner, LL.B. A day or two after the family filed suit to have Beulah's papers returned, the *tonus* between client and lawyer was slightly charged. He had a musty smelling office on Kensington Road. Bad shag. A lot of pro bono work. The sort of place where one is grateful not to meet the other clients.

"Counsellor."

"Sit down—and why didn't you tell me about her papers? We were almost in the clear."

"Wasn't germane."

"Germane. I'm sure you've got some reason to think hanging onto this girl's personal effects is a noble act. No, no, I don't wanna know.

But I can guarantee you're the only one who's gonna see it that way. *I* see this civil suit bearing down on us like a fucking train. *Germane.* I mean, the press is already eating you alive, the headline writers are going wild. *Quiet Flees the Don*—this Don Juan thing is killing us."

"She knew."

"How's that?"

"Don Juan—she knew."

"She planned all this."

"I'm saying she saw it would go this way."

"Smart, pretty, psycho—and now psychic, too. You can pick 'em."

"You've never met anyone like this."

"I don't know, I'm a lawyer, I meet interesting people. But okay you're a university don—name's Don, the press loves puns—let's say it's not beyond the realm of imagining. Now about these *papers* of hers."

"I wasn't expecting you to understand."

"Oh. Well I can't profess to understand her but I did get a look at this oracle of yours—"

"You *saw* her—why . . . ?"

"It's my job, I'm good at it. Good means thorough. You wanna know what I saw in that hospital?—a child, a beautiful child. Or what's left of one—and that's how everyone in the courtroom from judge to gallery will look at it. I take it at least you haven't been to see her."

"No."

"So far it's the one smart thing you've done."

"I go to the lobby sometimes. I talk to a nurse there."

"*You what?* Fuck. What does it take to get through to you—stay the hell *away*. If the family gets even a whiff of this—we're talking about a top-drawer surgeon, here. Yeah well I don't care what you see, Professor, the public sees a Great Healer. You seem to have no idea how deep you're in. Forget the criminal charges for a sec. Start with this civil case—*they can wipe you out.*

"And then these other little items. Breach of a fiduciary duty— from the Old Court of Equity, pretty creative stuff their counsel's dig- ging up. And expensive. For them, for you. They're angry, I get the message. I was surprised the judge found sufficient grounds to enter- tain an action in negligence. I don't think she would've normally, but she smells a rat here and wants us to know it. If you haven't stopped to think about your wife and child in all this—baby's new trust fund, the house, the fat termination settlement I just worked my ass off to get you, your entire estate—I invite you to start. . . .

"So I have your attention. Good. Their guy tells me the family will agree not to press the civil thing. All you have to do is just return the girl's property—"

"Good of them."

"It *is* good. If I were their lawyer I'd wanna go after you anyway. Every time we go in there I promise you it gets worse—what's the deal with these papers? They're an irritant, we've got bigger worries. Give them back."

"Aren't you the least bit curious?"

"About?—and no."

"Why they're so keen to get their hands on her diaries, for example."

"I could give a shit—and why are you so keen that they shouldn't have them? What is it you don't want them to see? Call me out of touch, call me behind the curve, but I thought we had put this whole idea of academic theft to bed—this entire business of *who maybe stole what from who*. We've been over this, yes? Because if we haven't laid it to rest, it speaks to motive. Have we, Doctor?"

"Yes."

"Good. Because I was beginning to wonder if I could believe you. This is not a good feeling for your lawyer to have. And it is precisely the feeling I did not want a judge to get. Which is why each unneces-sary court appearance is so *regrettable*. But okay, say I'm really trying to understand now, I'm the least bit curious, I'm keen to know. Let's say you're protecting her. Why in Christ's name would you be ready to throw everything away on that, after what she's done to *you*?"

"What if I'm protecting myself?"

"Protecting yourself is exactly what you are not doing."

"Protecting my sources then."

"You think this is some kind of joke? It's not a game, you're not a journalist and this is not a stand on principle—if I've missed some-thing, clue me in. You're walking around in some kind of fog here. I'm not your therapist, I'm your lawyer and it's my job now to wake you up. We're not talking about saving your job, like before. You're about to be crucified—did you know they've found at least one student willing to come forward and talk about a past relationship with you?"

"There are pleasures I've never refused myself."

"No, they're going to say it's professional privilege you've *abused*. If this witness decides to say you promised her better marks—"

"Something I'd never do."

"No?"

"And Beulah wouldn't have needed it."

"Fine, great, good for her. But the damage'll be done anyway. Listen to me. I took you on as a favour to Relkoff. And because I thought we could make things interesting, maybe win. Seems like open season in this country on you professor types lately. This civil thing, obstruction, perjury, okay—but the next stop is contempt. Not a damn thing I can do about contempt—bam, automatic."

"So I've noticed."

"You do drugs together?"

"What?"

"Sexual stimulants maybe?"

"This would be your idea of a joke now."

"No, literally, did you. I'm talking about the tox report, about the strangest recipe for a drug cocktail I've ever laid eyes on. If there's the slightest hint you two have a history of this kind of activity . . . She's half your age—it'll be way worse than the sex. Christ if the judge gets to hating you right off the bat, it'd be almost better if you'd killed this girl. Sorry, just making a point."

"And that is . . ."

"That unless you turn over those papers, I'd just be taking your money. I don't mind losing, but I *hate* losing bad. Half these charges the cops threatened you with are chickenshit and they know it—breaking and entering—*theft under!* for Christ's sake. So if everything happened that night the way you told me . . ."

"I told you the truth."

"But you don't know the whole truth yourself, do you? Or there's something you're not telling me about. Doctor Gregory, is there anything more I have to know? Abortions. Miscarriages—missed periods. Answer me carefully, now. Anything?"

"No."

"I hope not. 'Cause then there's definitely no grounds for a charge of attempted murder. And we say the drugs were her idea of an anaesthetic, and we call the wounds self-inflicted . . . though painkillers or not, a pretty determined girl, your friend. Counselling to commit—

hard charge to prove. So unless they're going to find a whole raft of letters from you telling her, say . . . life is hard and ugly, her thesis is fucked, her career dreams are dead . . . You know."

"No I don't think they will."

"Think . . . ?"

"No I have never written anything to her. Not a letter, not a note, not a card."

"Good. A bit cold but good. We're halfway home. And we're pretty much out of motives, aren't we, Professor. But I want to warn you—people here remember murder charges. This isn't Houston or Detroit. They remember the guy even if the charges are dropped. If you hope to keep living in this area code, all this'd better be the truth. And pray she makes it."

ARIADNE:

What is this, unjust Heaven?

What is this which passes through me,

that I know how to suffer

yet not to define?

Such agony—

so halting her speech, who knows how to feel!

No sooner, tyrannical Love,

of your arrows did I learn

that she but whets their edge

who struggles against them—

than I saw that you know

how to do more damage than wound.

I cannot feel, no, that which pierces

my mannish heart,

nor, of the winged harpoon

that vibrates in your vile quiver, sense

the golden

point that gilds my blood's carmine.

Nor that your deceits could ever

persuade my haughtiness

that to conquer consists

in giving in to surrender:

that, vanquished,

one might live and never envy happiness.

But when I do feel, yes, it is while

to this charming Athenian

I give the keys to the kingdom

of my free will,

and then see

that I die for one who dies not for me . . .

JUANA INÉS
DE LA CRUZ,

LOVE IS A
GREATER
LABYRINTH

B. Limosneros, trans.

HERESIARCHS

had not paid sufficient attention. My mind had not been clear. There were messages in the days, months. Years. It was in the dates. The visits, the rulings. The judgements. One could see the orchestration, the patience, the planning. I had missed so much, been careless. Days of sun, days of cloud—I must pay more attention now. Every minute of every hour.

January 26th, 1693. Word came that Examiner Gutiérrez of the Holy Office was in the locutory. He was leaving for Manila. His work was finished here. A bright clear day, warm for January. During his last few visits, not suspecting him had become impossible. And now his work here was finished?—I had *been* his work. I had forbidden him ever to come again—leaving, he'd vowed that should he ever return, the visit would be official. I had not seen him for fourteen months.

Was it official now?

In September of 1691 he had brought word of the denunciation of Palavicino's sermon and the names of two Inquisitors assigned to investigate. That October he came with the news the carols on Saint Catherine were to be licensed and published—but *when* in September, *when* in October? November 12, 1691, he arrived with the identities of two of the three examining magistrates appointed to try the case. November 12th, my birthday. I apologized that the convent had so little to offer visitors now. A few sliced apples, a green mango Antonia diced and sprinkled with chillies. Gutiérrez thought us lucky to have our own food supply in these trying times. The magistrates were Master Examiner Agustín Dorantes and Examiner Nicolás Macías, two Dominicans. To maintain the appearance of objectivity, there were to be no Jesuits, Gutiérrez said. In this case the proprieties were paramount. I had misunderstood. Why should the Jesuits be thought partial to Palavicino?

"Not partial, Sor Juana, *hostile*." He paused to finish the unripe mango before turning with satisfaction to what remained of the apple, soft and withered and worm-eaten. He did not seem to mind a little calamity. "And this seems no longer about Palavicino."

He glanced down to produce his latest piece of intelligence from the folds of his black robe.

... I, the undersigned, Prosecutor of the Holy Office of the Inquisition, do therefore reiterate that said sermon merits harsh punishment, and so do ask and plead that an edict be drawn up for the recall of all extant copies and that its condemnation be published in the convent of San Jerónimo, with an additional order that any and all desist from all discourses praising the fame or person of the nun in question ... [28]

Strange that a script so crabbed, so hard to read or even in that instant to see, should prove so hard to clear from the mind.

"But this reads like a sentencing...."

"Unusual, no?—for Prosecutor Ulloa to have already written it out ... since the judges have not yet made their rulings."

"But Gutiérrez, something here is not right. Why would a prosecutor—even if he's written it—*file* his sentencing request, if there is such concern for the proprieties?"

In times of old, the smile might have seemed less forced, the answer less hasty. These were not times of old. "It appears the Prosecutor is overly eager."

What had Gutiérrez let slip?—either they did not care so much about appearances as he had suggested, or the sentence had not been forwarded to the eventual judges at all, and if it had not been, then it was not part of the official record. Which meant Gutiérrez had not retrieved it from the files but had been shown it by the Prosecutor, who either trusted Gutiérrez or was feeding him information. It was Gutiérrez now who seemed overly eager.

"Do you remember, Gutiérrez, the first time you asked about the spiritual journals I had once written for Núñez, so long ago? I see that you do. I asked how you knew. The Holy Office was aware of them, you said. A reasonable answer. But it was not your first. Tell me the first answer that came to you."

"I said you must have told me about them once yourself."

"But I never did that, did I."

What came into his pale blue eyes then I would not have expected, not anger, or triumph, or guilt or even shame. Relief, it was relief. That came as a comfort to me.

I would not have been surprised if my dear friend had simply never returned, but it had turned out otherwise. The date of his last visit was not difficult to remember. It was two weeks later, the Feast of Saint Catherine. November 25th, 1691.

Rain fell each day that month—the waters gaining on the streets, puddles joining to form ponds. Painful for as many years as I was willing to recall, Novembers reached their lowest ebb at my birthday on November 12th, their high point near the end. November 25th. It seemed heartless in a time of such hardship and distress to wish for even an hour of happiness. But once one gave in, gave oneself over to it, the thing might prove irresistible. Not for a day, just for an hour. This was all I hoped for the celebrants that day in a city thirty leagues to the east. After I had long since given up hope, it seemed my carols were to be sung after all.

I had never seen Puebla but knew its cathedral was thought beautiful, up a short flight of steep steps from a shady central plaza much smaller and more intimate than our own. The cathedral choir was considered excellent; I had met the choirmaster. And so I could not help myself—the joy I felt to close my eyes and imagine the people filing in, to hear the music Ribera and I had written rising through the vault, the voices in the choir . . . to see the girls from the schools coming to hear verses on the learning of a girl, reading them afterwards in the libretto on the way home, reciting her story in the convent schools all across Puebla.

Three centuries after the Crucifixion, when the *Acts of Pilate* were drawn up to promote hatred of Christians, a girl of eighteen went before a Roman emperor, to denounce him, and to refute his paganism with arguments. In Catherine of Alexandria there was much to love, and to fascinate. Her courage, her audacity—a Christian, a young girl, going before Maximinus, persecutor and mutilator of Christians; then, her victory over the forty pagan sages the emperor sent to refute her. . . . Or some said fifty. With a saint so well loved the story ever ramifies—finally to a second emperor whose cruelties were instead attempts to seduce her and force a marriage. Since then she had been reverenced for her patience, her fortitude, and above all for the restraint of her passions. Many believed she had achieved as her reward a mystical marriage with Christ, some said first consummated on Mount Sinai.

Burnings and marytrdom, a serpent and a sacred ring, a bladed wheel, a beheading, a headless trunk flowing milk . . . Catherine had proved irresistible. Among the girls of the valley of Anahuac, the first saint we love is most often Teresa, for her strength and humour, for the palace of her soul, for her writings in a language and from a time so close to our own. Teresa was my second love. Among all the saints my first was Catherine . . .

We went in to church from Panoayan scarcely six times a year, and one extra time at Pentecost when Father was there. Each of us had a favourite occasion. In the spring came the feast of the Annunciation—this, for Grandfather, Good Friday for our mother, and Easter for my sisters. In December came Christmas and Gaudete. And in November, the Feast of Saint Catherine, for me. First the slow torture of the ride in to Amecameca, then taking a turn around the *manzana* before Mass . . . the special gaiety of the girls that day, and in the church itself, for Catherine was the patroness of cloisters for maidens and female scholars, and of young women at risk in the world. She was known to be one of the fourteen most helpful saints, and that a girl's learning could be thought useful struck a blow against a certain faction at the hacienda. Always, then, this day of the learned saint opened with excitement—vindication, too, should I happen to catch the eye of the lay sisters and of one in particular. A Sister Paula.

But by the time the homily was delivered—and to give a poor one on this day was an embarrassment priests worked long hours to avoid—a sadness would have tempered our elation. Martyrdom, of course, was sad, with a drop of gall, for martyrdom was mixed with a special draft of injustice; just so with Catherine's beheading, a vindictive insult, an outrage of her mind. The scourging had been hard too, but the sweetest of balms then came in the vision of the angels lofting her up to Sinai. The turning point in the homily was the shattering of the wheel. Yet a mystery lay within the marvel, and a cruel one—that the miracle had not saved her at all, and that there should follow upon it such insult and desecration.

In the Church afterward, we were given time to spend at her altar, a little statue of white marble not much bigger than a doll, quite overhung by the bushels of roses hemming her in—roses of Alexandria, or so they were for me. During the cart ride home it was not Catherine's martyrdom I worried over, but the fate of those she had persuaded by her learned arguments. Those scholars who had admitted their defeat to the emperor had been burned, but it was even worse somehow with the empress and the general Porphyry, who had gone to her terrible dungeon to convince her to renounce her faith and save herself by embracing the worship of idols. And by Catherine's great learning, the empress and Porphyry had been saved from idolatry, to live as Christians for barely an hour, before they too were martyred by the idolators.

In those years it had been difficult to keep separate in my mind the idols of Egypt from the little statue in Amecameca and the dolls of Panoayan. For many years afterwards I thought the path of learning the more dangerous, the path of mysticism the more burdensome. Until the years came when I wondered if it might not be the other way around. It was Teresa who reminded us—through her acts, her books and her trials—that the paths were not separate at all, nor were these incompatible with friendship. I was twenty before I understood that the intellective vision was not an operation of reason but an inner lecture, a reading of the Presence within, and so the highest form of mystical vision. In the pages of our great mystics I had been offered a vision not of the senses but beyond them, a glimpse behind the mask. I had never lost trust in visions but in myself as a vessel for them and for that Presence. These were the doubts of a girl who had taken too long to resolve them. I had left the palace, only to grasp, with such a scalding of irony, that I had been on the illuminative path for some time: *active in learning, passive in love.* But by then I was in a convent. San José of the Discalced Carmelites, the order Teresa had suffered so much to found. What had happened, what had gone wrong? Where had the spirit of her humour gone?—of a woman who spoke to God in loving friendship, who, complaining of her trials, heard Him answer, 'But Teresa, this is how I treat my friends.'

'Yes, my dear Lord, and it is why you have so few.'

The great gift of the saints is not sanctity but to take from us even the humblest instruments of our everyday humanity—a bowl, a scrap of cloth, a gesture, a doll—and return it to us immensely enriched. Teresa was one who could immeasurably enrich even the most precious of gifts. Illumination, friendship, laughter. The paths did not separate unless we let them. I had tried to make this a matter of faith since then.

All these odds and ends I remembered the day I learned the carols were not sung.

That afternoon, a man in the Archbishop's livery was waiting in the locutory. It appeared I still had a place in the Archbishop's calendar. It had been almost five months since two of his men came, requisitioning the inventory. Unlike the others, this one met my eyes. Good news, he said kindly. The inventory had been reviewed and the cell purchase approved. No, Sor Juana needn't get up, he would set the papers right here. For me to look at when I was ready. I had only to file a full statement of savings and assets, to be used for purposes of collateral in case of default. It was not for him to say if the cell's price was excessive, but who could say the funds raised were not needed, how much charity was excessive in these times, who could be sure of not one day needing His Grace's goodness and forgiveness? His Grace's secretary would expect a response by the 31st of December or the application would be voided.

Gutiérrez came that same afternoon. The omen did not seem a good one at the time, but not everything was a sign. The sky was lightly overcast, the air very cold. Though it had not rained yet, there was still time. He was sitting by the window, the enormous black hood pulled back from his face. He no longer felt the need to come hooded to see me. No more games of *capa y espada*, no further pretense of having smuggled copies out in the black folds of his habit. His face was serious, composed, the pale blue eyes mirthless. Resting on his knees was a small scrip of Inquisition documents.

"You know you cannot come here anymore," I said before he could speak.

"Yes."

"Good. You may begin now."

"After the Philothea affair, you asked if things had become awkward for me yet. Lately I have been trying to tell you that they have become so. You have been slow to suspect."

"You do not know that."

"I am the third examiner, Sor Juana. Dorantes, Macías and I. I am to judge Palavicino, and will be forced to follow this through. I am here to tell you now that my verdict will be the same as that of Dorantes. We can both see where this is going now, and no, I cannot come here any longer. If I have to come again, it will be because I will have been given no choice. I can go now if you like. But because this visit is still *ex-officio*, I have come . . . let us not say as a friend, but prepared to tell you everything I know or can anticipate, knowing what I know, hearing what I hear. And in return, if you have anything for me, any information, a manuscript, any statement to offer, I believe this will be your last chance to choose your ground. Once it becomes official, you can only choose how to respond. The offer I am about to make expires at the end of this year."

Before continuing, Gutiérrez retrieved two folio pages from his scrip and passed them through the grille. He sat back, giving me time to read. Dated that day, November 25th, 1691.

At the instigation of his Lordship the General Inquisitor, I, Agustín Dorantes, Master Examiner of the Holy Office of the Inquisition, having studied with particular attention the attached sermon, find the author to have been making a vain show of theology ... making plausible dangerous subtleties and futile novelties ... *such as making even speculative provision of a three-dimensional wafer the length and volume of a man in order to restore to Christ the use of His senses in the host. ...*

The sermon's author then makes an allusion to Our Lord Jesus Christ on the cross, whom the author claims was already transformed into a lamb, and whom a soldier then wounded in the side with a lance, an allusion being made to a Sor Juana Inés de la Cruz ... by way of using the Latin name Agnes ('Inés' deriving, as all know, from Agnes and meaning 'lamb') ... with the more fundamental intention being clearly to praise said nun, thereby abrogating in spirit the reforms of the Holy Council of Trent, and thus contravening Regulation 16 of the Expurgatorio of the Holy Tribunal of the Inquisition.

In respect of which I declare to the Lord General Inquisitor that it appears on this point intolerable, despicable and deeply troubling that, to indulge and gratify the ingenuity of a *woman meddling in theology (this so-called scripturist)* and applauding her subtleties, the author should make of the pulpit an arena for a settling of profane accounts, using for satire a mystery of our faith as grave as the Eucharist, and publicly citing a woman he refers to as 'Maestra,' moreover referring to her later as 'Minerva' in citing a passage of hers that contains a certain form of indecency, if not in her lack of authority, at least in materially traducing the seriousness of the pulpit and of the Holy Scriptures; and that he should cite her among a list of saints and fathers and doctors of the Church such as Augustine, Chrysostom and the Angelic Doctor, all having distinguished themselves in treating of the question of Christ's greatest *fineza* of love. ...

Gutiérrez waited until I had looked up from the page. "Henceforth, Sor Juana, anything concrete I say will be regarding Palavicino's case, whereas anything regarding a hypothetical case against you will be precisely this, hypothetical. I have persuaded Dorantes to let me bring you an offer. I would like you to consider it seriously. A statement from you, ideally an expression of contrition and conformity, but in fact discussing anything you like—any manuscripts that might still come to light, or your negative *finezas*, or responses to the leaflets attacking you—even a denunciation of Bishop Santa Cruz, though I would recommend against this. Technically, the statement would be entered into the proceeding against Palavicino, which is ongoing—we have begun to look into his other activities. Your statement, however, may be on any matters likely to come to our notice, *before* they do . . . in the event, for instance, that damning pages of your spiritual *Vida* should be found in the possession of anyone who had failed to report them. As you write your statement of contrition, you might construe such earlier writings as indiscretions of youthful pride, since regretted—an excuse not available to your spiritual director. Any deposition freely given before a notary of the Holy Office will be scrupulously accurate—you can count on this—every word you say, every pause, every expression of your face, every gesture of your hands. There are one or two precedents for this, and advantages. Conversely, an interrogation would leave you considerably less latitude in your replies, less still in the choice of topic. And in your gestures, no choice at all. Similarly, the Holy Office can at any time simply order you to write a new *Vida*—a recapitulation of what you had written for the Jesuit Núñez—with great insistence on its completeness, and to be then scrupulously examined for evidence of evasion, culpable imprecision or falsification."

"When you speak of an interest in my *Vida*, you are speaking hypothetically. . . ."

"It is the only way I may speak—and even this is the most dangerous thing I shall do today. The penalties for discussing an actual proceeding with its subject are extreme."

"But we have had many such conversations."

"If you will examine your memory, Sor Juana, you will note any mention I have ever made of your theological views made no reference to the Holy Office, and any mention of the views or cases of others only ever pertained to the interest these might hold for certain individuals within the Inquisition, never to the actions of the Holy Office itself. Now, you may remember things differently, and I could not hope to match your memory or the mind that contains it, but if, hypothetically, we are ever asked to compare our accounts, I will be consulting not my memory but the field notes signed, dated, and filed with my superiors after each of our meetings over the years. It is not personal, Sor Juana. Most of us do it, even when we are not encouraged to. It is the path of success at the Holy Office. Generally we fear each other more than we do outsiders. Please do not reject out of hand this olive branch. I went to some trouble to convince Dorantes. It will be offered to you only once. . . ."

No. I could not give a statement—it would not be the end but a way to begin. The Inquisition needed no help with the end. I could not afford to trust him.

"How clumsy of you, Gutiérrez. This should have been left to someone else. This can't have been your idea. Are they trying to humiliate you? You've been the third examiner for some time now—the time to tell me was when you first knew."

This won me a change of tactics, all pretense abandoned now. And it came as a relief, it came as a consolation. Was it too late to tell Sor Juana that her mulatta had been meeting for almost four years with Bishop Santa Cruz? That she had come to me as his spy? Yes, Gutiérrez, you should have told me that last *year*. Did I really believe she had stopped? *Liar.* And was it too late now for him to tell me she had been delivering my letters to the Holy Office for inspection before posting them? *Liar!* And was it too late to mention that once a month for the past four years the Holy Office had held meetings on the circle of those closest to me?

Then, though I had not asked and would rather not have had it enter my mind, he described many of these evenings in the Master Examiner's office across from the rose-coloured church. Who had attended. Santa Cruz many times. The French Viscount twice. And so Gutiérrez took pleasure next in anticipating for my benefit the conduct of a plenary session of the Holy Office, nine days hence, when the Dorantes verdict would be read, along with the other examiners' rulings. Yes, including his own. Prosecutor Ulloa would then be allowed to read the sentence he had already written a month before the verdicts were handed down, not being able to help himself. To which, on December 4th, he intended to add a further request: that Palavicino be excommunicated, banned from receiving the sacraments anywhere in the archdiocese, defrocked and banished from New Spain. He might be permitted to go to Quito or Manila—but never again to Spain. Palavicino's sermon would be recalled—the entire print run to be accounted for and burned in the plaza before the chapel doors of San Jerónimo. This was the best that

Xavier Palavicino could hope for.

On the other hand, the matter lay largely in his hands, for the way ahead was straightforward, if narrowing. Should he refuse to abjure, all available methods of persuasion would be brought to bear. In any event, before he departed he would be forced to give information on his other associates and activities, after which, the path of his salvation was clear: The appellant should state his guilt with expressions of sincere humiliation, declare himself convicted, beg in all earnestness for pardon in appealing to the judges for special leniency, express his sincere and vehement desire to purge his sin and offence, beseech the saints to intercede in his behalf. . . .

Gutiérrez asked next if it was also too late to tell me my carols would not be sung in Puebla that day, in the cathedral, or anywhere near it, or on any other day. This, I had guessed without his help. It was foreseeable. So why did this hurt so?

Whatever Santa Cruz's true purpose in publishing my carols, the result of not allowing them to be sung was foreseeable also, that those verses touching upon Catherine's audacity, her defiance of imperial authority, her pride and learning—all published in my name—could not but further madden all those shocked by my Letter Worthy of Athena. Even the printer was the same, if anyone needed reminding. A year of pressure, a year of leaflets and quiet warnings from every imaginable quarter had done no good at all. She would not be stopped. Catherine, Athena. Alexandria, Athens. The names might change and the places, but not Sor Juana's impudence, her willful pride and disobedience. And this time there was no preface of kind admonishment from a loving friend. Here *was* a difference, not in my attitude before God but in the Bishop's toward me. A shift Santa Cruz could not have signalled more clearly than by barring my carols from his cathedral.

"Sor Juana is pensive. She will want time to think. The Holy Office's time is limitless, but its charity is not. The offer, as I say, expires on December 31st."

Two visits on November 25th, two deadlines of year's end—not everything was a sign, but neither was everything a coincidence. For if it were I would have to call coincidence the next piece of information Gutiérrez brought: the date of the judgement filed by Master Examiner Dorantes, and which I had just read. November 25th, 1691. Yes, Gutiérrez, today, the Feast of Saint Catherine. I was quite aware. No, he was afraid it was not quite that, or not just—but rather one year to the day from the publication of the Letter Worthy of Athena by Bishop Santa Cruz in Puebla. *This I had not seen.*

Santa Cruz had been planning to forbid the singing of my carols for a year, had awarded the commission purely to cancel it, and Dorantes by dating his ruling on that anniversary was telling all, telling me, the Holy Office had been part of this all along. The Palavicino case at the Inquisition and the publication of my letter had one sole object. The interests of the Master Examiner of the Holy Office and the Bishop of Puebla had one sole object. The same hypothetical object, one point of convergence: one Juana Inés de la Cruz. One hypothetical nun. Not everything was a coincidence. These were signs. And the visit from the Archbishop's man on the same day was another—but of what? Santa Cruz wanted my annihilation and my adoration, Núñez my subordination, Archbishop Aguiar my public humiliation, preferring this even to my private destruction. And their wishes were not the only ones in play. Núñez was accountable to the Archbishop, but also to the Jesuit Provincial, his Inspector General. Dorantes to the Dominican Provincial, perhaps to Santa Cruz, and both Núñez and Dorantes to the General Inquisitor. Yet now I was to believe that they had laid down arms and were working together—fist in glove—in a miraculous convergence of hostile and competing interests. All joined now in a sort of fraternity, along with a dozen scurrilous and anonymous pamphleteers, and Velasco of the Brotherhood of Mary, the denouncer of the sermon. And at least one Augustinian. Most of them detested each other—what could possibly bring all of them together? I did not believe it. I would not. Why would they want me to believe this? I could not bear to.

"Tell me Gutiérrez, if the Inquisition has so much time at its disposal, why do you look like someone with so little? Is the Inquisition's time, perhaps, measured by the rise and fall of its functionaries? If I have been the path of your success, then perhaps I may yet serve your failure just as liberally. . . ."

Showing now in his cold blue eyes was the frustration of having so nearly succeeded. For if he was out of time, I was clearly weak—after all, I had not yet asked him to leave. He had to know how close I had been to giving in, giving him something, giving him anything.

"You look more and more the desperate rat, my good friend. Do you face penalties at the Holy Office for your insufficiencies?"

The convent had seen a lot of rats as the waters rose. I'd been thinking of their morality, but I could not help seeing how Gutiérrez might take the remark as a reference to his appearance—how near both the sublime and the tragic cleave to the childish. From the first, Gutiérrez had been funny to look at even when he didn't intend it—scratching under his chin, accentuating his chinlessness, as he had just been doing. The next few minutes were quite out of character but then I did not really know what his true character was. He became vulgar, spoke of heresy as an illness, one that did not end with death—just as banishing Palavicino unbroken would not so much be to expel an ordure but pass along an infection. And as for the Inquisition's use of time, I might profitably study its employment now with Palavicino. The Holy Office was disinclined to move against him until its inquiries were completed, and would only do so if Sor Juana attempted to warn him, though she should feel free. As the only person outside the Holy Office who knew, let her choose—let her give him the truth or leave him with the illusion. So I would feel the blow twice, twice watch him fall, be in no doubt where the responsibility lay. Twice.

But if Sor Juana wanted to know why she should expect the Inquisition's patience in *her* case—did she want to hear? Then he would tell her.

There was always a certain anxiety with heresiarchs.

Since by definition they were adjudged to have the power to corrupt princes, the cases had to be handled delicately. Such investigations were likely to cost a prince or two along the way. Executions of that kind poisoned relations at court for decades. The case of the Florentine was taken up early enough, yet so leniently as to merely aggravate the problem. There had loomed a real danger of having to open proceedings against not only a Medici Grand Duke but the Archbishop of Siena, and some feared for a time for a certain Jesuit scientist named Scheiner. By which Gutiérrez was telling me Santa Cruz had shown to him—and who knew to how many others, and given them pleasure and laughter and much jollity—my letter on Apelles. . . .

But Sor Juana was not paying attention.

Further, and as he had been saying, the corruption of the heresiarch did not necessarily end at death. One could only guess how long the Lutherans would use the Galileo matter to discredit not only the Holy Office but Catholics everywhere—making a martyr out of a monster of vanity, crying Injustice, publishing their *Areopagiticae*, invoking the just tribunals of old. In the Vieyra case, whereas, the problem was caught too late. How the Jesuits ever allowed an insubordinate—and an ecstatic into the bargain, with these visions of a Fifth Empire—to confess the King of Portugal was a mystery and a scandal. But it had happened, and now Mexico was embroiled in the sequels to a sermon written on the other side of the Atlantic *how* long ago? One heresiarch, it seemed, begat another and then who knew how many others over time? At least in her case the potential for a problem was caught early—

Meaning. Hypothetically speaking? Yes, Gutiérrez, yes. The Holy Office had been receiving reports on a certain case for . . . years. From whom—how *many* years. If he would not give me a name—a year then, *when*, 1675, 1670? Oh, earlier. At the *palace*? Oh, no, before.

Before.

Consider the year 1663. But perhaps he had already gone beyond his brief. To sum up, then. Time, the Inquisition had a great deal of, a very powerful advantage. With the heresiarch, not an advantage to be surrendered too easily. Care should be exercised. This one had quite ruined one priest, with two more likely to follow, had corrupted royalty—just how many viceroys now, and vicereines?—had seduced one prince of the Church and set two more at each other's throats. It had come to poisonings. Spying with France.

To take on such a case without a measure of reluctance was a thing only the very ambitious or the foolhardy would do. Master Examiner Dorantes did not seem to be one of the latter. He was determined that the Holy Office in Mexico make its own mistakes and not repeat those of the Inquisition in Lisbon or Rome. But no one was so sure of his theology as to oppose her in print. Everyone had seen what she had done to the Prince of Catholic Orators. Proceed slowly, indirectly for as long as possible, and only with force as a last resort. Until her mind was broken. Hypothetically. It would not happen straight away. It would take time. It was the safest path. She shouldn't take it personally. He was sorry to have upset her, but she had asked. Still, she was entitled to her doubts. He admitted he had often lied to her, and was perhaps no longer credible. She would want to draw her own conclusions.

Sor Juana should study, next, the Inquisition's way of proceeding against the *beatas*, which there was every chance now she would be able to do at close range. The rumours long abroad were correct, a trial was pending, and a sentencing: a woman had been in the Inquisition's prisons for some years now. The campaign against false sanctity was to receive more resources. There had been two secret trials in just the past few years. When? February of 1688. March of last year. I had heard nothing of this—why were we hearing about these now?

A glint of amusement. This was why they were called secret trials.

But this next one was to be different, special. There were other locations yet San Jerónimo was felt to be promising ... spacious, the orchards, the *gran patio*, the home of Sor Juana. No, a date had not been set, and would not be before the Archbishop's new *beaterio* was completed. A place for unattached women of fervent faith to have their visions under a watchful eye, under lock and key. And so the trial should prove useful to His Grace in his drive to fill the new places with women of quality. Until then, Sor Juana was free to write. Indeed, please. Statements freely given, as many as she pleased. Speaking of which, did Sor Juana perhaps remember Sor María de San José, Bishop Santa Cruz's hermitess? Certain irregularities had emerged in the relation of her *Vida*. Years of visitations from the Enemy, who came to her in the form of a naked mulatto—came still, apparently. Quite prodigious. It was not at all clear to the Lord Bishop Santa Cruz that she hadn't sought these visions actively. Clearly the quality of recruits was everyone's problem.

Now if Sor Juana had nothing further for him, he should be going ...

Not everything was a sign, not every sign was of a conspiracy, not every conjunction was in the stars, not every influence heavenly, not every irony was a coincidence, not every coincidence a sign.

That poor girl—struggling to be allowed to live as a holy woman in a cave, prepared to sacrifice everything to be with her Beloved, dreaming of nothing more than admission to a cloister, denied it—again and again, while for twenty years I had dreamed of escape. Had they decided to connect our fates in some way, to make examples of us? But examples of what—we were so unlike. One of us saw the Enemy as a naked mulatto and rebelled against his touch, the other had first seen him as Lucero, shining, Prince of Scholars, divided against the light within himself. And as his demon assistants read him the verses I dreamed of one day writing on the Nativity, he saw prefigured there the story of his fall.

But who in the depths of the night had not heard his mockery? Would she and I have heard him so differently? Truly, how different were we? One who dreamed of nothing but knowing the touch of His graces, the other to touch the grace of His mind. A hermit's cave, hers, a magician's, mine. Both born in the countryside on a hacienda, both families fallen, indebted, impoverished. For her the danger was a charge of false sanctity, for me, heresy. *Via mística, via intelectual.* Write freely, write a *Vida*, as had been commanded of Teresa. For how many months had even Teresa's *Interior Castle* been torn apart line by line by her enemies at the Holy Office? The paths were separate only if we let them be. It was Teresa who had shown us this. We walk the same path, María de San José. I must warn her. Could I write?—no, send word to her through her sister at San Jerónimo in Puebla. But I could only guess what terrors she was enduring now. I might only terrify her more—in a time like this, in this frame of mind—in hers, in mine—I might only make her see in me another demon trying to deflect her from the path. Had I not heard what Gutiérrez said about warning Palavicino? They would move against her if I tried, *because* I had tried. This was the trap—the special trap for me. Two fates in my hands, and yet neither, for one was already condemned, the other I could do nothing but harm. *Stay away from her.*

The rains had continued through November of 1691 and into the following month. Before December ended I had furnished the Archbishop's secretary with the inventory and a statement of means. The other deadline, the other statement, I had allowed to pass. I would not be taking any commissions from the Inquisition that year. The first days of the new year went by anxiously. But as January wore on, I saw I had been foolish to fear the Inquisition would come for me so soon, for Gutiérrez had promised it would not be like this—that there would be time, a great deal of time. And I could neither believe nor discount what he had said. On January 26th, 1692, came the first anniversary of Palavicino's sermon at the Feast of Santa Paula. As promised, for two months he had kept his freedom, precisely because I had made no move to alert him. Or so I was to believe, that it was I who let him have his life, another day, another hour, though it was not my right. Tried, convicted and condemned, all in secrecy, he would be permitted the illusion of a normal life while his activities and alliances were more deeply probed into. Giving his sermons, having his dreams, making plans.

On February 1st the Archbishop's contractors completed his new *beaterio*, on time despite the weather. This was fact. The *beaterio* was built and consecrated. This could not be denied. People had seen it, entered there for the inauguration. The date was February 24th . . . the anniversary of my profession. The timing was a reminder from the enemy that everything was orchestrated; every thought had been given to my discomfort. They were trying to involve her too in my fate, her fate in mine, in my mind. Six weeks later, on April 7th, Father Escaray went to the Cathedral to denounce the price-fixing by the Viceroy's intimates, and the hoarding of grain. Escaray had been to my locutory two days before. Fact. Coincidence—no *not* coincidence, he had come to seek my advice. There was nothing wrong with my mind. And then in the last months leading up to the riots we forgot our own concerns for a time, for this was a moment when the fate of a people was being decided.

Not all was true, not all was false. But these had become facts and observations in another science, conceived not to lessen uncertainty but to increase it, not to remake a world from first principles but to tear one down, in time. Its instruments of spirit were not *admiratio, inventio, divinatio, contemplatio,* but doubt and isolation, bitterness and suspicion, dread. Its instruments of sense were not astrolabe, compass, vacuum flask or pendulum, its instruments—that is, the work of the senses in this science—but no, these did not bear thinking about, these should be avoided by the imagination. But if I had let him, Gutiérrez would have agreed to describe them for me, in time. And with instruments such as these, with this new science, somewhere they were building a new cell for me.

This was the game of the Enemy. These were the paces through which Gutiérrez had been instructed to lead me all these years. One part truth, one part lie, the third made up of what was missing—not seen, not said, not imagined or expected, not properly read. A kind of triangle, and this third side, this edge of the blade, was by far the most terrible. Events conspired—events were now arranged—to make each day, each hour rich in possibilities, abundant with hypotheses, each single moment inexhaustible. And now it was very important to have missed nothing, if I was to face him again—not to give him hope, a sign. For the date of his coming again, this was no accident, no more than the last time had been, and not a coincidence. January 26th, 1693, the Feast of Santa Paula, the second anniversary of the sermon—so either the visit was official now, or his departure was a lie. Before going down I sat fidgeting at the studio window, the sun bright, looking across at the farrier's, the cartwright's, trying not to notice Antonia watching me collect myself.

Perhaps it was only the conjunction of two things I had not thought of together since my childhood, though I had had many occasions to contemplate each separately over the years. Events of the past few months had brought them together again. The carols for Saint Catherine, the Letter Worthy of Athena. With his two commissions, Santa Cruz had meant to link them from the start—Alexandria and heresy. Could this truly have been his game all along, was it humanly possible, such cunning? But how could he know . . . who among the living knew so much about my past? Núñez, Carlos, Antonia—my nephew? Who knew that much even in my family. No one. Everyone together, then? No, they were *not* all together.

I had been careless. There were messages. And now Gutiérrez was in the locutory. Why had he come—was it official? What had I missed? I could not get Palavicino out of my mind. January 26th, 1693 . . . Palavicino was fine, still unaware his sentence had been written. Time yet for one more dream, another plan, for a life to which he had already died, a life he would still be in love with. I told myself it was not bad to imagine him in love with his life, that this one thing was not a lie, and that they would not move against him until they felt close to having what they wanted from me, or until they had it already. One difficulty had been in keeping a firm grasp on what this was, if there was any limit to this, if it would ever end. How. Another difficulty in all these months was in keeping myself from wondering without let or cease, if I was already dead to mine. But I should not think so much about this—if I was not to give them a sign of weakness, submission, collapse. Palavicino, María de San José, the *beata* in chains, Catherine of Alexandria—reminders all, all together, not coincidence but signs, of what I had refused for as long as I could bear to recall. The charge and care of another's life, of any life save mine. A convent was the safest place, a place with walls, safer for both sides, and yet I could not protect them all, or myself, not even from inside.

And now I would go down to him. He was leaving for Manila. New Spain was finished. His work was finished. On the 27th day of January of this year, Antonio Gutiérrez, still with the Inquisition or not, left for the Philippines, or did not. They came the next morning. The sun was shining.

I LET MYSELF BELIEVE my friends at the Calgary Police Service might not lay charges. And so far there'd been none. At that moment getting out of town looked very good. The lawyer was right. The trip Madeleine and I'd been planning together, I could take alone. Plenty of money in the bank. I'd move up my flight. I drove in to Calgary to clean out my desk towards evening, when the office staff and tenured faculty would be home. My decision was made.

By way of career transitions I gave brief consideration to a speaking tour trading on my quarter-hour of infamy, my assorted lectures to offer a moveable feast of provincial scandal, from the wilds of ante-diluvian Alberta to Iowa, East Anglia, Lille, Tübingen . . . "The Liar Paradox, an Epilogue," "The Postmodern Minotaur (a Victimology)," "The Timeless Topos of Tupping Tutees . . ."

Scholar, get thee to a nunnery.

As a longer-term prospect, pariah scholar was a role I might inscribe with a certain fugitive cachet. There were pariah states: I could apply to represent them at scholarly conferences in unfriendly places. The main drawback being the prospect of meeting old colleagues—the few who've heard nothing; the many who've heard a little, or wrong; the sophisticates who chat warmly as if nothing has changed, before catching someone's eye and slipping away. And the handful to be avoided at all costs— who quietly extend their support, even friendship. Moments of stunned commiseration, a forehead pressed to yours, a hand gripping your shoulder. Buck up now, this too shall pass. One or two would have friends running little English schools in Korea or Dubai. Did I need somewhere to get my legs under me?

A sunset smouldered somewhere behind the university Art Parkade as I finished packing up my office. Into a battered leather briefcase bought cheap years back in Colombia—what had the pre-Colombian briefcase looked like? can't recall—I packed a few papers I'd been working on, and anything of a remotely personal nature. *Of a remotely personal nature.* Even friends might think this an apt character sketch, a career epitaph. I stepped out into the hallway.

I've made my share of mistakes, remotely personal. One of them was now clicking down the hall toward me. Briefcase bulging open I stood witlessly patting my pockets for the office keys. Looking anywhere but at the approaching Department Head.

When I'd arrived two hours ago the entire floor seemed deserted. Computer screens snuffed in the secretarial station, dark grey doors closed all along the hallway. From the pavement below, the lonely scuff and whallop of a skateboard. Above my head the ashcan clank of a ventilation fan out of true.

She would come to stand slightly too close, smelling of strawberries. My options were unpromising. Dart back into the office. Or turn to contemplate the fiery sunset and let her walk by. More desperate still the imposture of staring—lost in monkish contemplation—at the floor's piebald marbling.

Red and white knotted scarf. Navy blue power suit, the skirt two brazen extra inches above the knee. Small, neat figure, good legs. Pale brown hair, straight, shoulder-length. Anita Stanwyck was bright, tough, wary. About my age, she'd fought the wars. Not fatally beautiful, she'd stayed sexy even when this had been impolitic for a woman in her position. Which was no position from which to be judging me now: She liked men, and liked them young. She'd risked some strife of her own to tear her pleasures through the iron gates of campus life.

Our department was superbly run, our funding fiercely defended, the cuts ably distributed. She had made it her mission to shield us from the ministerial wrangling—chiefly concerned with keeping the vanguard of dissent busy filling out efficiency reports—and to cope with the savaging of our course offerings. A task I knew she detested. My early departure was creating a few new administrative headaches. Final exams to invigilate and grade. Understandable that she would insist on taking over the marking herself. Any mistakes in allocating grades now would be a disaster compounded.

She stopped in front of me, face serious. Her eyes were a striking blue, bright with an author-photo sort of alacrity that people often mistook for glaring. I'd thought it myself more than once.

"Hello, Anita."

"Need a hand?"

"Carrying my books home?"

Something stirred in her eyes, something unexpected.

"The rest of this junk," I said, quickly nodding at the taped boxes, "I'll send for later. You don't need the office right now do you?"

"Too many empty already."

"With me gone, you might not have to empty another next year." A thought: *Who was next in line?*

"Your friend, Relkoff."

"Works out, then." Now my landlord and I were even.

"You know it gives me no pleasure."

"No, Anita, I don't believe that it does."

"Still going to London?"

"Probably."

"Call when you're back and settled."

"Right."

Absolutely time to go.

"Don?"

This is where the sad, sorry character should just keep walking.

"You did some fine work for us here over the years. For what it's worth."

JUANA INÉS
DE LA CRUZ,

THE SCEPTRE OF
SAINT JOSEPH

B. Limosneros, trans.

IDOLATRY:
            So long as rage endures,
never, Faith, shall you accomplish your designs
whereby—though dispossessing me (for all my loving cares)
of a Crown I had worn peaceably for an aeon—
you imposed your tyrant dominion
upon my Imperial Realm
and installed a Christian Rule
to which ends violent arms have hacked clear your path;
and though Natural Law,
which with me was somewhat
violent in these lands,
has knelt down before your ensign;
and though virtually all my peoples
to the force of your persuasion
have been made thralls
and embraced your Dogmas;
for all that (I repeat)
you had no need for such force
as to tear up so heartlessly
the most deeply rooted of my customs!
And so, though you see me submitted,
be it never so far as to quell my resistance
to all who would demolish the Altars whereupon
the sacrificial victims
are human.

FAITH:
Just who is this, who opposes
our intentions,
and with such sacrilegious boldness?!

IDOLATRY:
For all your outrages against me,
I am still one who knows how to defend
her ancient codes;
I am, that is, Allegorical Idea,
abstract Reason,
which virtually all of this kingdom
still collectively embraces . . .

. . . viviendo en tanto pavor,
y esperando como espero,
muérome porque no muero . . . [29]

 ll one day and then a second, the cell was stripped. Eight men, three in the Archbishop's livery. I wondered what the other five did when not doing this, I wondered where they lived. Not stripped. Some furniture was left, many pots and plates. Two beds. Upstairs a table. The glass cases, especially, had to be taken down, the bookshelves broken out. I begged them to leave the folding screens. Instructions left no room for doubt.

The table under the window, then . . . the tapestry at the top of the stairs.

This also they took down, but showed no interest in the door behind it. Instructions did not extend beyond these rooms, to the locutory downstairs, or views from the roof. I expected Antonia to be hurt, but she gave no sign of having seen it there. I had not known anyone could be so discreet.

The sisters of our small patio were considerate, standing pale in their doorways. Though we take a vow of poverty, we are each attached to our cells. We come to think of this place as our home, of each thing as our own. Our belonging. The cell itself is mine now: the men brought a bill of sale.

One of the men in livery I knew, the one with the kind eyes. He had come before, to bring news that the sale had been approved. I had wondered then, how a kind man could succeed in the Archbishop's service. But I had made this mistake before. When he came into my cell now with the others, he did not look up from his work. I watched him carrying out boxes and bundles, delicate instruments rolled into rugs. And watching, I was given to wonder whose eyes had been averted these many years. The Archbishop's coat of arms . . . I had seen it frequently. A family among Spain's most ancient. An ancestor had been a knight attached to the court of Julius Caesar, had met the Apostle James on the Spanish shore. A story if true, incomplete. Hearing it, I had once asked how an apostle of Jesus might feel, to be met by a Roman officer after Judea.

On a maroon ground, within a silver border, the Archbishop's shield encloses five seashells set against a cross.

The smallest things, at times. Of these do they build a new cell for me.

Antonia took their coming so bitterly, imagining this to have been some fault of hers. As well to say she brought the floods. Shhh, Antonia. Emptiness has many positive qualities. A caracol makes no sound at all, until it has been emptied out. And then you can hear the sea. Shhhh. There, can you hear? The difficulty can be in persuading the animal who lives inside to leave.

Tonia, hush . . . John of the Cross was asked, repeatedly, severely, Since God is Light, how can the approaches to God be dark? Even in a soul purged of its attachments and impurities.

The poet's answer was ingenious. Listen.

Imagine a room with nothing in it. Two windows, facing each other, the Light of God streaming through, one window to the other. One never sees the light, only what it strikes. As a hand lifted between the windows is lit, or as motes of dust whirl as if sparks in a wind. Do you see? It is why a cell must be stripped.

We obstruct the light.

In all these months, in the refectory, the workrooms, the choir, the *sala de devociones*, the one rumour that had not ceased was of the *beata*, the trial. It was a prospect some of us dreaded, but not all. I knew when the sisters were telling it by the way they looked over at me. There was little doubt why our convent had been chosen.

I had been supplied with details the others did not have. That she was half-Indian, that she had been a midwife, arrested years ago. Gutiérrez claimed never to have seen her, but said that he had walked many times past her cell; that its door had been more recently replaced, its newer braces and rivets glowing softly in the torchlight of the halls; that the trial was to take place at night. He did not say why, but the possibilities were obvious. It made for better theatre. Gutiérrez was a liar.

I had been weak then. I had asked him if he truly did not know who she was, if she existed at all—or if the *beata* . . . if I were she.

Then in a letter from our sister convent in Puebla, word of Sor María de San José, that Bishop Santa Cruz had read her *Vida*, the spiritual journal he had commanded her to write, and turned it over to the Inquisition. But this I already knew, and here also had I been given knowledge the others did not have. She was to be examined by the General Inquisitor himself.

Were the visions frequent, were they actively sought or passively received? Did they follow the path of previous mystics? Did the visions uphold or break with doctrine? Were they frenetic or calm? Were the recollections hazy or clear . . . did they bring a sense of peace? Did they lead to God or toward the Enemy?

This was how *beatas* were to be examined. Now Sor María would have to find her own way to answer. I had asked myself what Santa Cruz had ever wanted from her, wanted from us. I wondered if it was merely to raise her up and make me fall. Or to make the writer a mystic, the mystic a writer. To reverse our fortunes. But it was clear now, what Santa Cruz wanted. He simply wanted what we do not. He had never wanted Núñez to join him, but by turns favoured and thwarted him to divide him from the Archbishop. He had not cared if the Archbishop were mad, only to drive him mad with the possibility that everything he touched was poisoned. And then to teach this to me.

They say Sor María is half-Indian, but that is what they always say if one learns Nahuatl. I could write to her, too late, but now at least there was little danger. Send a message in Nahuatl through a servant. María de San José, our paths are not separate. Here is a man who takes back what he has given, who eats his excrement twice. Here is a man who does not care about the outcome, only that there should be conflict. Here is a man for whom the game does not matter, only that he should set two sides upon one another—that in playing him they play against themselves, that to everyone he brings pain and trials. You know this, as I do. You have entrusted to him your secrets too. But the traitor is a gossip—*in necoc yaotl, ca chiquimoli*.[30] This expression we have in your valley and mine. We have known him here, we have known him all along.

Necoc yaotl. Enemy of Both Sides.

Once I had been afraid of the dark.

First as a child, then as a girl, in Mexico. Now though the nights of trial were filled with doubt, my fear of the dark returning, I ceased trying to sleep except during the day, between the hours of prayer. I wanted to be awake, on my feet, when the Enemy came. I ceased going down to the workrooms, the refectory—though I did try to eat. They wanted me weak. But there is something else I have feared. I have feared it all my life.

This void . . . this lightness, without books or ballast, without work or measures for my mind, this mind turning round, emptily, hungrily, upon itself. Now in darkness. It was clearly explained, why they would not leave a lamp or a lantern. If the Church requires something of Sor Juana for which she has need of light, then she will be brought a candle.

For one who does not sleep the nights are long. Longer yet in darkness. But the cell is not always empty now. The emptiness comes and goes. When it comes, it is, but when it has gone, I am sometimes grateful for the company. The demons come in many forms. To some they come as a naked mulatto. This is to be preferred. Sometimes they come as revenants of the dead.

I had a visitor, in the locutory—I did not take visitors. She said she was my cousin. Magda. Magda was dead. But then what harm in seeing her? This was cunning. Had Magda said that?

The locutory was dusty. Mould and rust at the base of the window bars. Mildew had crept down from the ceilings, the finish on the grille scored with it and dull. The clavichords, the things on the walls, in the shelves, they should have been taken with the things in the cell. I would no longer be attached to these. These were not to die for. They could come for them when they liked.

A sour smell, as of fermentation, hung above the stench of the canals.

The woman was not Magda, but she had Magda's eyes. An onyx cross. Cunning. A long white dress, silks and silver. She dressed like Aunt María had, if without the veil. Ravaged face, blossoms about her nose and cheeks from drink. Almost hairless. Dead, Magda might come to look like this. And if she were not dead, a veil would have been wise. But the eyes, these were alive, not terribly so for eyes but for inanimate objects. Like Magda. Small, hard, polished. Like beans, lychee pips. They were alive with their hatred of me.

"Hello, Juana."

Magda died not long after her mother had, Uncle Juan many years before that. María had sold off all his enterprises but one. She kept the *pulque* concession, the most profitable. At her death, Magda inherited. She married soon after, and followed her husband into the north. Zacatecas . . . ? No, it was Queretaro. When he left her, she died there by her own hand.

Magda had been exhumed by the Inquisition, and sent to me.

"The Archbishop has asked me to come."

"A recent one?"

"I'd heard you were like this."

"And I you."

She did not quite understand but never could, and hated me now a little more for it. A spiritual hatred, it seems, is not unchanging, but grows beyond the grave. Like hair they say. I looked over her sparse pate. She was not long dead, maybe.

"Why send you?"

"I asked to come."

"To see for yourself."

"More or less."

"To bring a message."

"More than one."

"How does he look? Describe him."

"You know His Grace does not consent to see us."

"You spoke to a secretary."

"I bring an offer, a last chance."

"To save myself."

"Not you, Juana. She will be condemned. The sentence will be death. She will burn here."

"Will you come?"

"Are you prepared to have a woman *die* for your pride?"

"Who."

"Don't pretend. It's weak."

"Tell me her name."

"They did not give me leave to speak of that."

"Just a last chance."

"Her last chance."

"To have her die not here."

"Or not at all. Perpetual imprisonment. The trial and the sentence to be carried out elsewhere."

"She cannot hold out much longer. The difference is small."

"You don't believe that."

"You know not the first thing about it—"

"Yes, how small of me."

"And now I am to believe they would modify her sentence. Or is this merely to spare myself the trial?"

"Think of your convent, at least."

"The conditions."

"No contact with the court. Here or in Madrid. No letters to or from. No visits, except as directed by the Church."

"There is more."

"A general confession of your sins, a renewal of your vows, a return to the state of novice."

"A stay of all proceedings against me."

"The Secretary did not mention that."

"Was there anything else."

"Two things. A reminder, and also a message. If you want it. I have it here."

"From."

"From you, Juana. From you. . . ."

The seal had been broken.

"Did you know, Cousin, your father took care of delicate business for my father?"

"Why are you telling me this?"

"No harm can come of it now."

"You mean, no good."

"Yes, I mean no good."

"Then why, Magda, listen to you?"

"Because you want to know—always, everything, or to think you do. You agreed to see me today, didn't you?" Into her eyes came a look of triumph. The letter would come at a price. Knowing the contents, she already believed I would pay it. "But first you shall hear everything else I have always known. About you, Juana. And for this, there is no charge. Did you know that our grandfather—*our* grandfather—introduced my father to yours? Or that my father was engaged to your mother when *your* father met her? He had heard so much about the beautiful daughter. Uncle Pedro wanted to see for himself. So you got her looks, and I got the other's."

"You have them still."

"Tell me, Juana, when was the last time you saw your*self*? But no, let's not quarrel yet, not when there's so much left to tell. . . . Did it never once enter your head you were named after my father? There, you see? It was only when Aunt Isabel had *you* that he gave up. I was almost four when he married my mother."

"You owe your legitimacy to me, then—take it as payment for the dresses."

"And always so clever about your fifty pesos. Such a bargain hunter. My father paid *thousands,* ran around to wherever you'd been, paying off your debts like a *secretary.* But I am forgetting the reminder now . . . from Bishop Santa Cruz: When he went to give your mother her last rites, they had a long talk about you, about their many hopes for you."

"I suppose you'll be taking the canal back."

"He said you would see. . . ."

"Swimming again, I imagine—you should have insisted on a boat."

"Did she never tell you about the other fifty pesos?"

"When you get back, do give my regards to Sáenz de Mañozca."

"Did Isabel ever tell you it was the name that broke her heart—?"

"And my respects to Torquemada—tell them the one who sent you was a bastard, too."

"Amanda—the cook's daughter. You remember her—"

"Get *out.*"

"But you don't know why yet, Juana, *why* it broke her heart. You will want to know this, Cousin. . . ."

Gutiérrez had promised me I would be brought to remember things, bear witness against others, as others would against me. Gutiérrez was a liar, Gutiérrez was a Judas, Gutiérrez was my friend—surely it was shame that had made him leave the Inquisition, book passage for Manila.

Magda did not leave the locutory for some time. And if I did not either, it was because there were things I needed so badly to know. She was right about this, right about me, and would not leave until I had heard them. She had made no move yet to hand me the letter. I added a condition, before giving her what she wanted, a single piece of information. Hearing it, she nodded in satisfaction, as though it had only confirmed something she had already known.

If I felt shame, then, I told myself it was because of the condition. I told Magda I wanted to know the *beata's* name if I co-operated. More childishness. They could give me any name they liked. Magda did not answer directly, though I could see she wanted me to believe she knew who the woman was. But I knew they would bend to my will. I would have a name, eventually, for the holy officers who had sent Magda knew it would be worse once I had one. It was only afterwards that it seemed like haggling over the *beata's* name to get what I wanted.

As the hours passed, my mind returned to what I had told Magda—because I could not bear to see that letter in her hand, and the seal broken. I told myself they had already known about Carlos, about his last visit, about the manuscripts, of course they had. I had suspected him for days, since he last came. No, I had suspected him for months—Gutiérrez had said there were testimonies and reports on me dating back thirty years, even before I moved from my uncle's house to the Palace. Why tell me this unless the identity of my betrayer would be a devastation? *Carlos.* Magda was dead. Even if I had thought of her, even if it were true my own cousin had informed against me, this would come as no great surprise, at best would make me furious yet not hurt me. I could not possibly think less of Magda. And Magda was dead. What would be the object?

After Carlos had left for Florida, of course I began to wonder why he had truly come. To say good-bye, or was it to test my defences, my readiness to express contrition? But I was forgetting: he had come to show me a way forward with the Archbishop. Yes His Grace and I had so much in common, much common ground. Our interest in the philosophies of Heraclitus, our regard for Antonio Vieyra—like a father to one who has never known one. And, of course, our friendship with Carlos. What did I know about friendship—who had my friends been? The seed of doubt sown by Bishop Santa Cruz had long since put forth its flowers. Carlos always knew when to leave, always managed to be away when unpleasant things befell his friends. Had he so much as tried to warn me the day of the chess game? He had merely left, excused himself. He was going to the archives to study the papers of Bishop Zumárraga.

Zumárraga—why even mention him if not to make reference to stories I had heard from my grandfather the night he died? Stories I had told only Isabel after, because I could not help myself. Mentioning Zumárraga the day of the chess game only reminded me Carlos had gone behind my back to be her friend, who in turn had betrayed to him my confidences. Isabel I knew I could never count on, or turn to—but Carlos was only telling me that everyone here informs on everyone. A little earlier would have helped, dear friend, but I had it, now. Thank you, Carlos.

Carlos was exactly the one to have been sent to strip my cell—he was the Archbishop's almoner, after all—yet Carlos was always leaving, just as he had been away when Fray de Cuadros went to the burning ground.

And now the Holy Office knew without a doubt that I had his manuscripts. It was clear that Carlos had brought them to incriminate me and save himself.

Magda too had come to show me a way forward with the Archbishop. And surely here was the meaning in the message she had brought from Santa Cruz, that he had taken my mother's last confession, had taken from her my confidences and my secrets—everyone betrays everyone, everyone informs on everyone. This was a lesson Santa Cruz had been giving for some time, the same lesson someone had been preparing for me since 1663. It was not too late to believe it could have been Magda: it was too late to believe it could not have been Carlos.

They have turned me against a friend.

Who is the Enemy of Both Sides, if not I. . . .

Emptiness. It is the sound of such a vastness.

It brings other sounds with it, other voices. Sometimes, hearing them, one would leave, go anywhere, distant times, places. The holy officers can arrange this, change verdicts and sentences, book passage to Manila, send fools into exile, spare the *beata*. They can bring Magda back from Purgatory, where mortal sins are purged not with the Light of Love but by dark fire. They can bring me to fail another friend, to fail the living or the dead. Magda came many times. I did not like her visits. I did not know why I always saw her. I was not to have visitors. The Enemy comes in many forms now, living and dead. They come as payment for too many questions and doubts, for the petitions for special knowledge, for this hunger so displeasing to God.

Does the vision bring peace, is it actively sought or passively received, does it lead toward God or the Enemy . . .

Sometimes they come in visions, but sometimes take no form at all. As when Antonia comes to sit in the dark with me. Remember our lessons, Antonia, remember irony? Close your eyes. A blade with three sides, in profile, diminishing to a point in an infinite regression of triangles—inserted, the wound it inflicts takes an eternity to heal.

Philothea, Bishop of Puebla. Theophilus, Bishop of Alexandria.

Philothea, Loving God. Theophilus, Beloved of God.

This is the knowledge the Enemy offers me.

Theophilus, Christian tyrant. Hypatia of Alexandria, pagan maiden.

Maximinus, pagan tyrant. Catherine of Alexandria, Christian maiden.

And note, Antonia, how a fine-drawn wire wound round the blade forms a spiral. With a wire fine enough, one may turn around the three-sided blade endlessly. Like this . . . the minions of Theophilus pull Hypatia down from a chariot, scrape the flesh from her bones with oyster shells. The henchmen of Maxentius behead Catherine spun upon a wheel. The followers of Hypatia turn upon themselves. . . .

But I knew now why Magda came. She had given me the hint I needed. To desire vision, to hunger for knowledge excessively, this was to admit the Enemy. This was why Magda had been sent to me, with messages and reminders. *For the Enemy has no power over the soul except through the operations of its faculties, and especially through the medium of knowledge that lodges in the memory. If, then, the memory annihilates itself with respect to the faculties, the Enemy is powerless.*

They had sent Magda to keep me from annihilating my memory.

Turtle shells . . .

I did not want to remember. Not here, not now, not like this.

We had gone out through the tall corn behind the hacienda, a herd of deer going over the fence ahead of us. . . . She had a surprise for me, hanging from the branch of a cedar, something in a bucket leaking water. She wanted me to take the bucket down. Her eyes glowed with excitement. Wide, almond eyes. I also had a surprise. The night before, there had been an incident at dinner, an old story I had led Diego into telling, about a bridegroom impaled on a wedding tree, and something about a wolf. . . . In the telling, it had become clear that he had been using his dog to track us into the woods. After, my mother had said nothing to him in our defence but had spirited me out of the room instead. I would be going to live with my aunt.

Reaching up for the leaky bucket that morning I said we were going away to Mexico. Her face stiffened—she asked if she was to go as my maid. She ran away from me then, too fast for me to follow. In the bucket that morning were two turtles . . . we had had such turtles at a special place of ours, high on the mountain. I walked back alone to the hacienda, water trickling onto the dust beside me and across my feet. I came through the passageway leading from the portals and saw Diego in his dress uniform in the middle of the courtyard. Before him, he had lined up the *campesinos* as though for inspection. But it was my mother, rocking calmly, he looked at as he drew his sword. Impassive, she watched him pacing up and down the file, screaming questions in pidgin Spanish at the bewildered men— *Who did who did it, point him point him, save you, not save him, I won't kill . . .* I could not tell what he was asking. They could not have understood. He questioned the next man, holding the sabre beneath his chin. Wild with frustration he turned to the man next in line and waved the sword-point back and forth close beneath the *campesino's* eyes. He twisted the flashing blade a hair's breadth above the bare chest of a third, as though to drill a hole. They were too terrified to answer. Wilder yet, he stepped to the next. As he raised his sword in both hands, something relaxed in him.

Isabel's voice was not loud, yet rang clearly over the ranting man's, rang through the run of blood in my ears.

"Diego, *enough.*"

She had not moved, had not so much as sat forward, but the rocking had stopped. The baby let the nipple slip from between his lips to look up at the source of that voice.

"You do know innocence, don't you, Diego? You do *see . . .*"

Or perhaps she truly did mean innocents.

The tone, calm, agreeable, lent the words an edge of menace and contempt. Slowly Diego lowered the sword.

"Back to work," she said, without taking her eyes from his. The workers vanished. Eventually he looked away, as I knew he must. Beaten, he turned and went out, the sword arm hanging loosely at his side. In a moment or two we heard his horse gallop by.

I set the bucket down and went, legs wooden, to Xochitl, to discover what had been happening. While we had been out, a man had rushed in from the fields to spread the news. Out in the maguey field a *campesino* had found Diego's mastiff at the killing floor, suspended by its hind legs from a cross-beam supporting the roof thatch. A heavy bludgeon lay by its head. It had been clubbed to death. Gutted. Skinned and dressed. The hide was staked out, to be made into saddle bags one day, a scabbard, a woman's boots.

I had been three months in the convent of San José when I sent for my uncle. It was mid-winter, then as now, 1669. At San José, visits were rarely permitted, except in cases of greatest urgency. I had written out a message, a letter I could trust no one else to deliver. And I knew without a doubt that it was that letter Madga now held in her lap. I had written it to my mother, a call for help. Only Juan could deliver it, because he would have to read it to her, because above all Diego could not be the one for this. Would she please come for me, would she let me come home? I had nowhere left to go. San José was a house of anguish and agony, a place of blood and instruments of torment, a place without light, without books, or laughter or wonder. She had been right all along, she had been right about me.

And now I saw my cousin's eyes shining with the knowledge of those lines, with her knowledge of me and the memories of her hatred. How many years had Magda known—the years since Aunt María's death, or for all the years since Juan's? All the years I had been in here, at San Jerónimo, waiting for my mother's answer.

I had guessed the essentials. Magda gave the details as she handed my letter back after twenty-four years. And for this also there would be no charge. But by then she had my information, and I had from her the real reason she had brought the Bishop's message with the letter. A simpler reason. To remind me that I had once refused his dispensation to leave the cloister, to be with my mother as she was dying.

"So, Cousin, you have your letter back. I would have returned it anyway, even without your information. I loved him. He loved her. And now you know why my father would have been such a willing messenger. Do you want to know the rest? Are you ready to hear? Don't just nod— tell me you are."

"Yes."

"Aunt Isabel told my mother she had already guessed about your father and the Indian. But what broke your mother's heart was a name. Did you realize she had been planning to call you just Inés? But hearing that other name, she named you after my father instead. This part he told me when you were leaving for the palace. And for the past many years I have known the rest. *Amanda*. Would an Indian choose such a name on her own? No, Amanda was your father's choice. Amanda, loving, conceived in love. So then, Cousin, whose choice were you—and what were you conceived in? I know your mother wondered.

"You and the cook's daughter were sisters, Juana. And your father was a Jew. And you are welcome. For the dresses. . . ."

The night of trials contains a good deal of pain, we cling so to things. Our illusions of sense, our instruments of mind, our memories, we would cling to these even when they hurt us. We forget we are another's instrument. Our grasp must be prised open, our fingers parted. All affections and attachments and faculties must be burned away, like a log in a fire, like grime and rust encrusted to base metal. And the soul is to be its crucible.

It is said the sensations are as of one lying beyond the walls of a familiar city—one's own, perhaps, forbidden to enter, forced to keep watch, tracing lovingly from afar the shadows of the parapets, the chapels and towers. Or the longing is as of a lioness who goes forth in the night to seek her cubs, who have been taken from her. It is said she cannot long endure this state, and must soon recover what she has lost or die. On other nights it is like being released by a hunter to be hunted again.

And again.

Again.

Again.

And in the deepest dark in the last watch of that night, there is a crossroads.

JUANA INÉS
DE LA CRUZ

Alan Trueblood, trans.

Fate, was my crime of such enormity
that, to chastise me or torment me more,
beyond that torture which the mind foresees,
you whisper you have yet more harm in store?

  Pursuing me with such severity,
you make your heartlessness only too plain:
when you bestowed this gift of mind on me,
you only sought to aggravate my pain.

  Bringing me applause, you stirred up envy's ire.
Raising me up, you knew how hard I'd fall.
No doubt it was your treachery saddled me
  with troubles far beyond misfortune's call,

that, seeing the store you gave me of your blessings,
no one would guess the cost of each and all.

8th day of February, 1693

Carlos,

ne letter, the most difficult, the last. Then I can get on with what there is left to do. I send this through your friends at the monastery in Veracruz, and hope they will find some way to make this reach you—I must risk it. If it's intercepted by my holy censors here we are lost, but if I do not try to warn you, Carlos, and you are taken, I am the one lost.

I have told them, about the manuscripts—not all, and the papers are safe yet—but that you brought them here, that we had quarrelled months ago, that I turned you away. How fortunate my coldness to you just this once has proven. I told them I did not know what the packet held, but that I thought they were scientific treatises.

So upon your return you must not be manoeuvred into thinking they know more than they do—and while you are away you must contrive an accident, with witnesses, so you may say the manuscripts were destroyed or lost. I have thought and thought and thought through everything I have told them, and this is the one thing that poses great danger.

You are asking yourself how I could have done this. Or it may be that from me it comes as no surprise. They came so soon after you left. . . .

The almoners brought a bill of sale—as if to say I had purchased these things from myself, only to donate them again. It was as if they were *taking them from me twice.*

Only now as it all sloughs away like scalded skin do I realize how deeply, bitterly angry I've been, and how unjustly. Not coming to you when you came to say good-bye now leaves me sick with remorse. I know you didn't betray me. Life is not so simple, so symmetrical. The friends of my enemies are not my enemies, any more than your friendship with me makes the Archbishop my friend. Might it be that day he broke your cheekbone with his cane, you were defending me? But what I have also come recently to learn is that neither does being the enemy of my enemy make that someone my friend.

And now, what I have come so late to see is that if you've left your most precious possessions with me it's because from this fool's errand to Florida you never expected to return. What made you think you would be the first to die?[31] Too proud to refuse the commission which may end your life, too sentimental to accept the one which might have saved it. Who is to say you might not have made a life at Versailles? You just can't leave her, can you, this New Eden of yours? After all these years, this is how you still see her. The ever faithful suitor you see her as she was, not as she's aged. Faithful generous suitor, you share whatever you've learned of her with every passing scholar—a lifetime of discoveries reduced to footnotes in the books of lesser writers.

I have recopied carefully each of these letters of yours from Veracruz invested with so much tenderness, and blush at how much less was returned in mine to you. So critical was I of your Americanist project— why invest your life, risk a career on a pursuit so unpromising? To find political virtues in the Mexicas' tyranny, to make FeatherSerpent out to be the twin of Christ—doubting Thomas, the most sceptical of all the saints. Christ had a brother, Carlos, but his name was Satanael.

Yet you were unworried by consequences, and unwilling to believe me indifferent. How could I be? you asked. These were the stories of my own childhood. Do you have any idea how it felt for me to watch you take possession of those stories, one by one, when I'd let them go?

And now I hold the last remaining account of Moctezuma's last days even as my own conqueror approaches. All my strength it takes now to look forward without blinking. Carlos, I have sent a plea that Father Núñez return as my confessor. I will not even try to explain. Through Arellano, he has demanded a sign that I at last see the enormity of my transgressions. A sign. I see nothing but signs. I have written for him the one he seeks. Mine, I do not seek.

You think you'll be the first to die. You may be right. For see how death eludes one who desires it—even death, when in demand, will rise in price. The Archbishop's auction raised a good part of the ransom, but not all, for they knew I had something left to sell. . . .

How can I ever make you see how I could have thought—for half the span of an hour—that you had brought these things to implicate me? *Who has sent him? Does even Carlos know? Who has brought us here, to this pass? How can he do this—after all that has happened, to Fray de Cuadros, to us?* I could not understand it—to remind us of what might have been? Of what cannot be brought back, what we failed to prevent?

You who knew me—surely you could see how dangerous their stories were. The Mexica. The most rigorous and unsparing, unblinking, glaring straight into the sun . . . people devouring their idols, a people swallowed by the sun. And now Fray de Cuadros is dead. Carlos, I am not indifferent. Carlos, I have not forgotten. Stark, the invitation: Who will feed the sun. How dangerous all the little love stories we tell ourselves of god. The conqueror approaches, see his footprints in the rock . . . ? After each slow step a dust of dreams trails up. The Emperor of Dreams awaits his destiny, awake. He tries to flee, to hide himself within a cave, but the earth will not harbour him. He returns in shame. Desperately he consults the sorcerers, the oracles, the ancient texts—the ones not burned by his own father's order. Through dream-plagued days and sleepless nights, prodigies, portents, ill omens drift like smoke through the capital. All who dream of the end of the world, all must come before him. The capital is made to pay a tribute of dreams. The *Massacre of the Dreamers* is what one day they will call it. So many dreams . . . Moctezuma sifts them, immersed in one vast dreaming.

Tell me your story.

"I saw a strange bird with feathers like ashes. Its head was a mirror. I looked into it and saw the sky full of stars at midday. I looked again upon a plain full of armed men surging forward on the backs of deer. . . ."

Tell me your story.

"Last night I saw a smoking star dripping fire, like an ear of corn bleeding fire. The night sky was filled with blood and smoke. . . ."

Tell me your story.

"The temple on the great pyramid burst into flames. Lightning struck it from a clear blue sky. Even now it's burning. We keep throwing water on it, great quantities of water, we cannot put it out. We cannot put it out. . . ."

Tell me your story.

"Everyone in our precinct heard her again last night. Weeping for her lost children. Weeping for the city. . . ."

Tell me your story.

"On the lake I saw a waterspout as high as a mountain and through it saw the gods descending. . . ."

Tell me your story.

"Last night the streets were filled with two-headed dwarves and hunchbacks asking for the king. . . ."

Tell me your dreams—who will feed the sun?

Destiny approaches him who knows the histories. The histories he knows himself condemned to repeat, for this history is prophecy.

Tell me your dreams.

The jails are full of sorcerers. But all those brave enough to tell their dreams, the Emperor of Revery has had put to death. The flood of dreams that left the prisons awash in dreamers now runs dry, and more terrible to him than all the dreams is the moment of their ceasing.

"This Christ of yours," he'll one day soon now ask the startled chaplain, "he died to save his father? He gave his heart to feed the sun?" The beautiful interpreter smiles and shakes her head.

Tell me your story. Tell me your story of the end.

Dreamers given death, sorcerers grown still, seers lost from sight, jailed prophets, shrouded, silent . . . slowly silence falls.

Drums booming, flutes piping . . . the last sounds from the outside world to reach his ears. Soon even the dreams of the Emperor, the last to dream in all the world, fall silent.

Soon enough, soon with great relief he elects the warrior's death. Death at his captor's hands. The nobility of the captor vouchsafes the nobility of his dying.

Who will feed the sun? the captive asks, but gets no answer.

I am sorry, Carlos. Can you ever find it in your heart to understand.

Your friend,

Juana Inés Ramírez de Asbaje, *la peor de todas* . . . [32]

Delicious prison!

whose irons,

seeming torments,

ornament an existence

that makes pearls of fallen tears,

a jewel box of a prison cell.

  Such consolation I find in Thee,

seeing myself stripped of everything,

not least of all, my burdens,

and thus lightened left more apt

to dare to launch intrepid

flight from earth unto the Heavens.

  By events, the royal purple

is made the morrow's garish sackcloth;

the hand that gripped, imperious,

the sceptre in its fist,

in fetters offers direst demonstrations

of how tenuous the glories of this suffering earth.

  Yesterday was I obeyed

everywhere the Guadalquivir bathes

fertile Andalusía,

the greater part of Spain;

JUANA INÉS
DE LA CRUZ,

MARTYR OF
THE SACRAMENT

B. Limosneros, trans.

today beneath a brutal Bailiff's

boot am I held prostrate:

Yea, there exists in human realms no sure estate . . .

. . . . Such reflexions my brooding

brings, and yet, these spur on no fresh tortures:

since whatever is lost has been for Thee

it causes me no sorrow:

but rather joy

that for Thee all shall now be forfeit!

  Thou alone hast given

what from me Thou hast taken.

Be praised ever,

for Thou wouldst that I possess

every benefice, so that for Thee

I could relinquish these.

  The sole heresy I still embrace,

is to cherish e'er this one true faith.

Yet, in this, in no way is it tarnished—

since in its own crucible it is purified.

Time to lay aside the noble Gothic laurel,

for to have kept one's faith is to have conquered all . . .

. . . y abatime tanto, tanto,
que fui tan alto, tan alto,
que le di a la casa alcance . . . 33

n the evening, I went to find Xochitl, still hoping to convince her to let Amanda come to Mexico. In the kitchen the door to the fields stood ajar. Moths whirled at the lantern glass, throwing shadows over the packed dirt of the yard. I remember that it was a clear night, the moonlight a burnish on the blades of corn. We sat at the small table, the evening's unwashed dishes piled behind us on the blue-tiled counter. Xochitl had said no for the second time, and for the second time I had asked why. Instead of answering she began to tell me of her youth, as a girl respected by her people, a fish of gold. But I had heard this. Though young, she had been a healer, was soon to be a midwife, as Amanda would be one day. I had grown impatient, for this was precisely what she had never wanted to teach me. Xochitl talked then of first meeting my grandfather, when he came to her village on the far slope of the volcano. Soon after, something had slid, and she was no longer honoured. *Tla alaui, tlapetzcaui in tlalticpac.* Fish of gold, what happened to you?

She had been returning late to the village. It was after dusk. She was pregnant. The horse, going fast, had stepped into a *toza* burrow. I saw so clearly then how my grandfather would have blamed himself for the accident, though it was something that might befall even the finest horsemen. It was only afterwards that she came to Nepantla to nurse me. Xochitl had been trying to tell me the one story I had always dreamed true, yet I was hardly listening at all, and afraid, just perhaps, to hear that she and my grandfather had done something improper. I had always thought of her as his age, her hair had been white even before his.

Something had slid, but she did not mean her fall from the horse. Something had broken but she did not mean her hip. This something had broken months before. Two Spaniards, not one. Pedro Manuel de Asbaje, Pedro Ramírez de Santillana. Two don Pedros, a father and a grandfather. Two superb horsemen, two horses . . . The horse was not my grandfather's. The horse Xochitl had fallen from was my father's. Pedro Manuel de Asbaje. *Aca icuitlaxcoltzin quitlatalmachica.* Who arranged his intestines artistically.

I had heard this as a child, on a cart ride from Nepantla to Panoayan, and had vowed to resolve it for myself one day. And so I had. And now another from that time—I believed Magda: Xochitl had been trying to tell me Amanda was my father's daughter.

Even as Magda said it, smiling through the grille, I knew it to be true. Because she knew how it would hurt me to know this, now. Amanda was my sister.

Four years after I had left for Mexico I made the long return journey by ox cart only to discover Amanda and Xochitl had been sent to another hacienda. They never arrived. It was from Diego's lips I had had to hear this, and that he had sent men searching for them everywhere.

Isabel had only been waiting for me to leave. She had sent them away without so much as sending me word. I had been thinking precisely this when I saw her, riding fast along the maguey field, past the killing floor, slowing towards the house. In a moment or two, from where I sat among the trees, I saw her go in. She would have been waiting for me to come back to the house; but as the wagon staggered on, I ran to catch it, vowing never again to look back to Panoayan.

I broke that promise to myself. I looked back once, from the convent of San José, my new home among the Carmelites. And when my mother did not answer my call for help, I believed she was paying me in kind for having returned to Panoayan only to leave without speaking to her. I had never forgiven Isabel for never replying, for not coming for me. We never spoke again. Not a word ever again passed between us, not a message; never had I a kind thought for her, never did I permit myself a fond memory.

And I also believed Magda about Uncle Juan. He had promised to deliver it himself, the next day. He always kept his word. Some weeks later he was called to Acapulco on business. In the wide bay before the city, his body was found by a fisherman. Juan had not gone to Panoayan, had hesitated. He was still in love with her.

My mother never received the letter.

February 6th near dawn a light rain stopped. Father Arellano came not long after Prime. One by one the other black veils around our small patio went down to confess at the slots. Terce had come and gone. All that morning I waited for my turn to be called. María Bernadina was the last to come back from the *craticulas*. His Paternity would see me in the locutory. I wondered if he had conquered his fear of beauty, or had been told there was less to fear. He had not agreed to see me there for years. As I entered he turned his chair to face the window bars, his shoulder to the grille.

We sat shoulder to shoulder looking into the garden, out over the rose bushes. It might have been pleasant, a visit from among the living. We might have talked about the passing of the years. I looked more closely at him. His body had run to fat, his jaw to jowls. His hair was still black at the crown, had greyed at the temples, whitened around the ears. I had forgotten that it was not just the thickness of the walls—Father Arellano, when in the presence of sin, mumbled.

"*Este* . . . as of today, Sor Juana, you must no longer consider me your director."

He was very sorry, but it went hard for the confessors of heretics. He said this glancing sidelong, his voice high for one of his bulk. He did not think he could face it. This I could believe, if he could not even face me; just as I could believe him a man who had just recently made his first visit to the offices of the Inquisition.

Was it true Sor Juana sought the protection of the Prefect of the Brotherhood of Mary? Yes? Then His Reverence had sent him, Father Arellano, to say that she would have to agree instantly, that day, to meet his conditions, meet them all, meet them fully, lest she soon come in for a more rounded discipline.

By what token was I to believe he came from Núñez?

Prefect Núñez had expected this. His terms were these, which Father Arellano would now try to present verbatim, that there be no misunderstanding. Having heard them Sor Juana could judge of their source for herself.

First, Sor Juana was to cease all visits to the convent archives, all study of any kind. She was herewith forbidden to read even among the saints and learned doctors of the Church. The time for Augustine was past. For the moment, as a kindness, she was to be permitted one text. Father Arellano placed it on the table that spanned the grille. If she cared to, let Sor Juana read her John of the Cross as often as she could bear. Not the verses. These she was never to read again. But *The Ascent of Mount Carmel*. This was the only mountain left for Sor Juana Inés de la Cruz to climb. All else was vanity. One candle per week would be permitted for this purpose, if she was prepared to meet the other conditions.

Which ... ?

Sor Juana was to cease all writing, except at the express command of her director. And this next point the Prefect had enjoined Father Arellano to make with some clarity: Sor Juana was never again to write poetry.

Not in any form, no devotional verses, no carols for the Church. This condition was not negotiable, and was never to be rescinded under any circumstances, for the rest of her days. God did not need her poetry here, and in Heaven are enough who sing.

Sor Juana would first draft a preliminary statement of guilt, in preparation for a full examination of her conscience, of all the unnumbered crimes and vilest sins of her worldly life, from the beginning. . . . Father Arellano was sorry. These had been the Prefect's exact words. Nothing had been forgotten. Nothing is ever forgotten under the eyes of God. Gaps, omissions were no longer to be tolerated. With even this simple condition the Prefect doubted very much she could comply, after so many years of evasions, for *the thing that hath been is that which shall be . . . and there is no new thing under the sun.* It was the Prefect's view that she could not change, would not. And even if Sor Juana might delude herself for a while, he was not given to delusions. Too much of the Prefect's time had been wasted on her already—his time, and that of so many others working on her case. So much waste and vanity and vexation of the spirit.

No doubt Sor Juana would want some time to make her calculations.

Vexation of the spirit. . . .

It was with Magda I had first seen the Palaces of the Inquisition, the banner above the front gates, two girls flirting with the sentries . . . the rose-coloured church on the plaza, the workshops, the forges. It was with Magda and María that I had first learned of the great *auto* of 1649, retraced the route to the burning ground, heard described the uncanny likenesses of the effigies. It was in Magda's voice I heard whispered the names of the Grand Inquisitor and his nephew Sáenz de Mañozca, and those of the family Carvajal, Ana and her brother Luís. Magda had even learned the brother's poetry. *And from myself, without You, who would deliver me, And to You, without You, my Lord, who would carry me?* . . . Magda, too, was a scholar. A chronicler of family and the familiar. And it was on that day that I had first heard of the book collector Pérez de Soto, who had also too little respected the Holy Office. She talked then of a smaller *auto*, more suitable to the edification of children, the *auto* of 1656 ... the year Pérez de Soto was arrested.

Magda had made it clear from the first that she was prepared to bear witness against her own father's parents. Nor was I sure it was untrue that they had been secret Jews. If they were convicted of Judaizing, their remains would be exhumed and burned, *sambenitos* hung in their parish church, in Mexico, and in their birthplace in Spain. I did not know if even Magda could give evidence against a father she had loved, though he was beyond hurting now; but she would not hesitate against mine. Others would believe. Was this truly why he had left us, as Magda said, to escape the *auto* of 1656?

No, I would not let myself believe it, because she would know how I wanted to—which from Magda would make it false. What else did the scholar Magda know, what had she told, to whom? What lies could I refute? What truths . . . ?

1663. This was the year, according to Gutiérrez, of the first testimony against me. For Magda, her first visit here would have been a kind of anniversary. Thirty years ... perhaps to the day. *There are many working on your case, Juana. You would be surprised to know just how many.* . . . Núñez had said this to me a dozen years ago. Núñez too would have known about those first files—had he been warning me even then about Magda?

But though she might be an asset to Dorantes and to Santa Cruz, as her files had been to Gutiérrez, Núñez had never needed Magda. Father Núñez had other assets. And so in the night after the first candle burned down I saw Núñez come to stand vaunting over me, brandishing his war tools, felt the rasp of his mockeries, heard him boasting of his advantages, of the perfection of his memory. It would be as with the second inventory of Dorantes—I would need to remember all I had told him, every confidence in a dozen years of confession—even *how* I had told him, and everything I had not, beginning twenty-five years ago. I could face the Inquisition or else Núñez; I could face the Dominicans or my own conscience. This was the challenge in the message, which he had always believed me too cowardly to accept. At least before the Holy Office I could protest my innocence. *Vexation . . . no new thing under the sun . . . remember thy Creator in the days of thy youth.* Three times Núñez had recalled Ecclesiastes, and in doing so, warned me of where we might make a beginning. . . .

On the day of the service, the old men of the town had come out. The priest from Chimalhuacan read gently from the Gospel of John; then Brother Anton from Texcoco came forward and recited beautifully from Ecclesiastes. My grandfather would have liked it. It made me think of Hesiod. Uncle Juan had not come. I had not met him yet, and had not imagined they had been friends. Across the hole in the ground stood Magda, behind her my aunts and other cousins, my sisters beside my mother. I had been furious to have been asked to choose the place, had refused to—*choose?* I choose that he still be here with us. Amanda cried quietly beside me, her arm about my shoulders. Xochitl sighed once, and stroked my hair. There came my turn to read, from an old book with a broken spine. Kneeling in the fresh-turned earth I read the first four stanzas without crying or so much as pausing, it seemed, to breathe. But when I did pause, I did not go on.

By that evening the last of the guests had left. My aunts were not guests, as my mother pointed out, but had grown up in this house. They were to have my sisters' room, which had once been their own. Josefa and María were to be in my room with me. It was just for one night.

Late that night I was still in the library, asleep in the corner armchair where he had used to sleep. I thought it a dream, at first. I saw my mother standing before me. The lantern guttered, its oil run down. Her veil was drawn back. I thought it strange she had not changed, though the dress was beautiful. She had bent slightly, then seeing me awake, seemed to hesitate.

"I wanted to be sure it wasn't him." She smiled faintly, embarrassed. It might have occurred to me, she had bent to pick me up.

"I thought you never came in here."

She straightened, the swelling of her belly formidable, pronounced.

"Who do you think put him to bed all these years?"

It was the kind of hidden knowledge that I had always known lay all about me, and had always sensed about to rush in at me from some unexpected quarter. "Your eyes are clear, Inés, for seeing far. But up close you're as blind as the rest of us."

I looked away, to the floor, the cold hearth, the desk in the shadows behind her, unshelved books in a jumble on the near side. On the other, stacked neatly, the four books he had been reading, on them a thick envelope. *A mi hijita Isabel.* My eyes had lit dully upon it that morning, but it had lain there for the week since. Embarrassed, I slipped past her and went quickly to the desk.

"This was for you."

It did not occur to me to offer to read it for her. She started down the aisle toward me, casting shadows over the ceiling ahead of her. I could not see her face against the flicker of lamplight. She would be angry that I had forgotten. It would seem typical of me. "I don't know when Abuelo put it there. It wasn't there . . . that night."

She came to stand very near, very tall, waiting perhaps on a better explanation. Her fingers touched the envelope but did not quite grasp it. I did not know what she was feeling, but craning up with her so near I saw it was not anger.

"Did you really paint those angels for him . . . ?"

Startled, she looked up into the shadows of the cross-beams, which divided the composition into three, the figures crudely painted but finely drawn. Cherubs, seraphim—the thrones and principalities, the seven choirs . . .

She stood a long moment, remembering. "Your grandfather loved angels, like a child. I was a child myself. I thought it was . . . nice."

Unable to stop, I asked why she had given up drawing. Her eyes left the ceiling, glanced over the desk covered in books, at the map above it of the southern oceans. She looked at me finally, in their hollows her eyes large in the unsteady light. She drew in a long breath. "Inés . . . no matter how clever you are, no matter how—"

"A library is no place for a woman—you've told me."

"That's not what I was going to say."

It was only partly because of what she said then, that I told her about the last night with him . . . to give her something more of him than a letter. And so we sat up late, and I told her the stories he had told, how animated he had been, how his eyes had seemed like emeralds once again. How I had woken up as he put me to bed. I told her because of the angels, and because he loved her. I told her because I needed to tell her, more than anyone. When I had said that the library was no place for a woman, she had started to replace her veil, but then gently placed her hands on my shoulders.

"No matter how clever you are, *hija*, no matter how hard you work or you try, you can never bring them back."

Núñez would not care why my father had left. Núñez would not ask me about the *auto* of 1656. He would demand to know why I had left her— left refusing to speak to her, twice. He would ask why things were not better between us, even after this night. He would ask how in a rage, just three months later, I could accuse her of driving my father away and ask if she had ever loved anyone.

Quen uel ximimatia in teteocuitlamichi. Things slip, things slide in this world. Fish of gold, what happened to you?

I sent for Arellano on February 23rd when Núñez had still not come. I had given a statement of my guilt, agreed to the terms, and I had requested—no, I had been hoping that he might come for the 24th of February, for the twenty-fourth anniversary of my profession, that we might begin my noviciate together, my year of trial. Why had he not come?

Father Arellano was sorry, but he did not decide for Prefect Núñez, nor did Sor Juana. He would come when it was time, when there were signs that she had truly understood what she had been given to read, had truly *heard* this time. I reminded Arellano that he and I had spoken of Juan de la Cruz in confession not so very long ago. His Paternity might remember the rain. Did he have some new direction for me now?

"Sor Juana, that is the day I was referring to, when I communicated to you a final warning from Prefect Núñez . . . that while there was yet time, you should study the writings of John of the Cross for a path to God that still included a little poetry." Even so recently as then, the Prefect had indicated he was prepared to confront the Archbishop and defend Sor Juana's practice of poetry on purely devotional topics. "But the Prefect's warning went unheeded, and that time is now past."

Unheeded? No, Father, I had not heard. Would it have made any difference, you ask? How, Father, could either of us know that? And *why* had I not heard?—because His Paternity had been unable to bring himself to meet with me in the locutory. So why, I wondered, did he come now? Was it not true he had been forced to, as a punishment? And how could Father Arellano make accurate report of me, if he could not look at me, if he did not examine me? Why would anyone send a messenger to give messages I could not hear, or who warns me that I might next come in for a discipline 'more rounded' when Father Núñez had in fact said *circular*? Was that not true—yes? Why, then, should anyone rely on such a messenger?

As he rose, he glanced at me without wishing to, his eyes round and dark. They looked as mine might. He had not slept, looked more frightened than I, or I hoped he did. It was as I had guessed, that he was being sent for his negligence. And if they so chose, his penalty could be the same as mine. And it could be death. He had confessed a heretic for almost a dozen years without raising the alarm. To defend himself he would have had to admit what I had guessed all along. That he had been unable to bring himself to *listen*, had been too frightened to.

I sat for a time when Arellano had gone, and looked out into the garden. What could it *mean*—that I had tried on my own to take the very course of action Núñez had urged upon me through Arellano that day, two years ago? What was it they thought I had not heard, had not yet grasped? I understood that the poet I had loved, whose echoes in my own poetry Núñez had most despised, whose voice was never far from my mind, was to be turned against me. For the one book I was to be permitted, now, was of the night of trials, not the poems. I understood also that this was to be done to demonstrate that everything could be turned against me, to make an enemy of a friend, to remind me of how much Juan de la Cruz had endured not for his poetry but for his faith.

Núñez would say that God had guided his hand in this choice of book, but then why had I not heard his messenger—had I been guided not to hear the warning? If He has guided the hand of Núñez to triumph, has mine been guided to fail? Was I to be returned to the beginning only to be shown that the night of trials never ends, but only opens into deeper trial? I had looked down that path, into a darkness that Juan had made beautiful. I had drawn from the springs of his sources to bring comfort to others, to bring some sense to their suffering, but I could not make that path my own.

If only Núñez had come, we could have talked together. With him I would have spoken my heart, I would have tried again, in a manner more sincere than with Arellano. Father, why have you offered this path now, you who warned me from it, the path of the ecstatic, you who said it would lead me to destroy myself? Why send Arellano to me, when for twelve years he and I have been as strangers? It would be better to have left me to myself, to turn on myself, than to send such as these to me, who are afraid even to look upon rose bushes without startling.

But Núñez had not come. And to this last question at least I knew the answer. We had been sent to punish each other, Arellano to me, for his concupiscence and fear of sin, and I to Arellano, to mortify my pride.

The next day, for my twenty-fourth anniversary, I put on again the rough *sayuela* of the novice, much as Antonia wore, and cropped my hair. I chose the evening, after Compline, so as to have some hours before being seen. My vanity cost me much of the week's candle.

I was afraid Antonia would try to stop me. She was stronger, angry. I explained that it had been shorn thus twice before—surely harder on those who would have to look upon it than it was for me. I could not stop her cutting her own in turn. I was not strong enough. I had loved her hair.

We helped each other, in the end. The places farthest back were hardest to reach.

I sent Antonia with an apology to Father Arellano. He did not come for weeks. It amused Núñez to send him on April 13th, the Feast of Saint Hermenegild.

I could see Arellano dreaded coming now. I had won that much from them.

Would Father Núñez be coming soon?

If and when Sor Juana had given positive signs of her will and disposition, the Prefect would come to examine them himself.

But had I given no indication considered positive?

The cutting of the hair was positive.

What other sign had I failed to give? Arellano was sorry, but as Sor Juana herself had said, he was only a messenger. No, Sor Juana's apology was unnecessary. Her criticism had been correct. The Prefect had indeed said 'circular,' and said now that there was perhaps time yet to choose between a cell and a closet, to follow a circular path or one still more tortuous—neither should she imagine such pleasant quarters as had held John or Hermenegild. *Ne Plus Ultra.* Here the Prefect had instructed Father Arellano to ask Sor Juana if she understood. Yes. To repeat it. Yes, I had understood. No, to say it.

Ne Plus Ultra.

Perhaps this talk of signs had been misleading. Sor Juana, as a natural philosopher, a master of navigation and circular paths, would prefer to think in terms of treatises, observations. Evidence. In the absence of which, the Prefect continued to believe that a path without poetry and philosophy would be far too narrow for one such as she. Now if the message had been communicated adequately, the messenger should be going.

Circular paths . . . closet or cell. In the last century Teresa had written to Philip II about Juan's abduction to Toledo and his imprisonment by the unreformed Carmelites, his former Order. She said she would have preferred to see him fallen into the hands of the Moors, who had more pity. Had he not effected a daring escape in the night, he would almost certainly have died there.

He was kept in a cupboard. It was not high enough for him stand upright in. Juan was not tall. In the refectory he was made to eat sardine scraps from the floor. There where he knelt, the monks went round him flaying his bared shoulder blades with leather thongs. The circular discipline.

In purgatory God purges the soul with fire. In this life, with love. The same love with which he purges the angels of ignorance. The monks of Carmel crippled Juan's shoulders for life.

The ignorance went in roughly where the wings would have been.

Some paths were narrow. How straitened a path could I be made to follow, how narrow were the straits I could be made to pass? Núñez was taunting me. He mocks my work, he mocks me through my works. How silent the machinery that turns the tides. How now at the antipodes? Great Herakles, now that we have you here, explain it to us. Now that you have decided. We have time. How did one such as you come to take up *Ne Plus Ultra* for your banner? You who stole the milk from Hera's own breast, milked a goddess like a cow, who dammed the Nile, freed Prometheus, raised the pillars of Calpe and Abyla.

Even of such gifts your shining Bridegroom, rich beyond imagining, has no need it seems. Look around this cell, Sor Juana. Tell us what you see. For twenty-four years you have worn the habit of a clown, the King's fool in the ermine, with sceptre and crown. The Queen's handmaiden posing in her gowns. Or would you rebel even now—pull pillars, sky and pedestal all crashing to the ground?

Look once through the chronoscopic lens: Hera's Glory, Theologian's Muse.

Now Herakles, look again, two dozen years along: Hera's lunatic, God's clown.

How differently the poetry of prison rings now. And these echoes from the future, in these cells, how unlike themselves they sound. But that should not surprise us, after all, for so it is with echoes that what one mostly hears is the end.

Twice more that month I sent to ask when he would come. Always Arellano instead. The second time the memorized message carried a suggestion. If Sor Juana was in a hurry, if Sor Juana insisted on knowing when, she should practise her sciences of prophecy, by which the nuns in Madrid had so ably served the Crown. Thus did he summon to my mind Sor María de la Agreda, spiritual advisor to Philip IV, and the book of her prophecies banned across Christendom, recalled and burned. Thus did he recall to my mind the Inquisition's power to erase, which I feared more even than their power to silence me.

How it must have amused him on the Feast of Saint Hermenegild to remind me of my *Martyr of the Sacrament*, and its verses on natural magic. For by now I must have seen: that it was the holy officers who mastered the arts of illusion and the sciences of uncertainty.

The more that is stripped away, the less that remains to be taken.

I began to use the stairway again, late at night, while Antonia pretended to sleep. One did not need a telescope for stars in such multitudes.

The weeks passed quietly. Father Núñez was a subtle man. Four months since Magda's visit, four months since I had first sent for him. Time and quiet in which to brood on each message, to solve the riddles each concealed—to wonder if they had ever been there, if Núñez had taught this game to Santa Cruz or learned it from him. Time and quiet in which to ponder the completeness of my acquiescence, the emptiness of my rebellion, the contents of his messages, the terms of my defeat, to let these grow to cover me like a second skin, to all but heal and then be torn again from me. Four months without poetry, four months with one book. Four months in which to wait for the most terrible riddle to be answered, of the *beata's* identity, the secret dread that Magda's visit had awoken.

What did he still want from me? Evidence of what—that I had found the path on my own? But the path is another's, this path is not my own. I lacked the faith to follow wheresoever it led, I lacked faith in the administrators of the circular discipline.

Late one night, the light of the candle almost spent, I thought I found in the pages of the one book permitted me an answer. *When the understanding lay in darkness, the will in dryness, the memory in emptiness, the affections in bitterness, and the feelings and the faculties lay stripped. When, all senses*

consumed, the soul lay as helpless as a prisoner bound hand and foot, able neither
to move nor to see nor to receive any consolation from earth or from Heaven.

And had been thus bound for years.

Then, and then only, would Father Núñez come to examine what he
had wrought.

On May 18th the Archbishop published an edict against the insuffer-
able disorder of women's friendships in the convents, in particular
among women of different quality, between nuns and servants, between
the sisters and their favourites. Penalties for those who persisted could
vary, banishment, lashes, excommunication. In some quarters the edict
would be met with satisfaction, in others taken up to revive the rumours
of sodomy. Unless I preferred not to heed it, I could take it as a warning,
that Antonia would be the next to suffer for my sins.

The more that is stripped away, the less we may offer in surrender.
What was left to offer them that was not Antonia. I was not sure how
much I had still left. But if I could do nothing else—I could perhaps
force the moment.

Arellano came quickly, as one who had been readied for the call.

So it was true. How long had Sor Juana's eyes been banded like this?

Father Arellano would please convey any messages, before he became
distracted. Of course, yes, it was no longer his business to inquire. The
Prefect had asked—would Father Arellano please raise his voice?—*The
Prefect asked* if in these twelve years in which Sor Juana had had her perfect freedom, she had accomplished what she had set out to do. Her
poet had his *Canticles,* her Velázquez his great canvasses. Had it been
worthwhile, that so many others, the lowly, should have suffered so and
might suffer yet more? Had she worked enough magic, had she had
enough of fame?—for who knew what new triumphs her countess
would bring her to, what bold lyrics she would next publish. Truly, having achieved so much or so little, could Sor Juana be content now to give
service as an ordinary nun?

Had Father Arellano brought no other word? No, that was all. Then to
His Paternity's own question: First, he should notice that my secretary
had served to guide me here, and note that if anything were to happen to
her, I would lose my way entirely and never find the path. Second, the
question was not how long but how much longer, for the next time Father
Arellano came, he would find my writing hand splinted and bound, not
just my eyes. And if on that occasion he could still not announce Father

Núñez's arrival, then he would return to find them put out, as evidence of my sincerity. Father Núñez would of course want evidence. Now if His Paternity would try very hard to remember the gist ...? That there were orbits within circles, and circles without orbits, and if I was to walk a circular path, perhaps I was also to take this as a sign that in the circular manner of things, Father Núñez sought in me a Christian Herakles. I had shorn my hair, I would bind my hands, as I had my eyes. And next I would offer up to the Prefect of the Brotherhood of Mary the final *evidence* that he and Mexico lacked—so that we might together take sightings of these fresh new orbits by the light of our mutual darkness.

There is a false peace, when for a time it seems the Enemy sleeps while we wake, wakes while we sleep. One day this peace must be cast out, back into the darkness whence it springs, and as it leaves there comes a spirit of dizziness in its wake.

Solve the riddle. How he had tormented me with his knowledge—my childhood love of riddles—to set my mind riddles whose answers were in the book, so that I would be forced to read it only as he wished me to. The circular discipline. *When the mouth was pierced with sorrows, the vitals were consumed with hopelessness, the heart lay gasping, like a fish on hot coals, and the eyes blinded as those of an owl in the sun of noon*—and when I had read the poet I had loved, read him not with my eyes but through those of Núñez—then would he have me believe he was to come.

But I would not be deceived. No, what would more surely bring him was the threat to put them out, his eyes. The poetic solution.

Little fool.

Antonia tried to help. Cook, talk, draw a bath. Yes, she could draw me a basin of cold water to wash in, leave it on the table, go to bed herself, leave me in peace, not come up again until she was called. I said again, perhaps she should not live with me. Her only answer was to bring me a vase of flowers. Iris, marigold, rose. She set them on the window ledge. If I did not want them, shove them off. Her anger was better for both of us.

He had not come. Núñez was not a poet.

For two days now, Antonia had respected my wishes, left me to myself, the upper floor to me. Two days to contemplate where pride had brought me, the prideful threat by which I had trapped myself, the narrow road out. Two nights to turn about from room to room, up to the roof and back to this.

Perhaps Sor Juana would prefer a closet.

Bed. Table. One fresh candle. Materials for writing—what? another plea that would not be believed—one upon which he might look favourably? Table, vase, basin, light silvering on the surface, breaking through my fingers. Whose hair was this, whose black eyes, who was this novice? Núñez had heard the hollowness in the threat, the weakness within it, and had not bothered to answer. At the table I picked up a pen, dipped it, idly trailed a thread of black across a page. How was I to do this, with a quill tip?

Once I had used the years to mark his absences, and exulted. Since February I had marked the months, then the weeks. Now the days. Soon I would be counting off the hours. They could wait decades.

Late in the night I rose, moved into the next room, simply to listen to my steps moving through the empty studio, then soft on each stair to the roof. I went cautiously to the ledge to sit above Calle de las Rejas, looked down past the windows of my cell to the *portería* grate, a single lantern flickering. Warm night. Stars. Lean into the light to see down, lean out to see up.

The chapel bell tolled once, quietly. In the distance others sounded. A noise from below—*una india* arriving to set up her stall beneath the lantern at the grate, an infant sleeping in the sling of her *rebozo*. Fresh *tamales* and *atole* for the worshippers at Lauds.

What more could I be instructed in dispensing with? I did not need their books, if there could be only one—I did not need this book, which Núñez had poisoned now. In my mind I had the verses. Juan's and many others, many hundreds. But what of the rest?

How many stars did one require? I thought over how many I might remember, more or less, over how I should recall them, as they had been on some other night or as they were tonight? If I could fix them in my mind, tonight, hold them fast, glowing still in the simple sketches they traced in the sky, as if a finger a thousand years ago had traced them behind my eyes. Perhaps it was the constellations one remembered, not the stars. After all these years I still could not connect them, knew so few of the names by which they had been called by other peoples in other places and times. Fire-Bow, *Los Astillejos*, Orion. Taurus, Gemini. How many constellations would suffice? I wondered how I would remember Night itself. Like this, or as I had once feared it as a child? And this new night, as final and complete as the living may see, there was no way to know if it was more to be feared.

Poetic nonsense.

And having taken out his eyes, could I at last be free of his voice in my mind?

I had thought to force the moment—but had left myself no way out. They who could wait decades had only to wait now a little while, a week, a month, to see if I would follow through. If I could, nothing in their files had changed—I was only where I had been—but if I could not, they would have the measure of my weakness, would know that I am beaten. Would know that I know it.

I wondered what it was that led me to this. Was it only pride, or weakness? No, there was something more.

It was in his messages, his taunts . . . *prediction, natural magic, divination.* He had something more in store, something better, someone else, after Magda—*I had to know.* What—charges they could bring against Antonia? But she had done *nothing.* Or the trial, it was to be any day now, was it the *beata*—was that it, that the charge against her was to be divination? But I could not see how that was to make for a more devastating discovery. What had I missed? Were these to be the charges against *me?* Divination, sorcery? There was the hex on Sister Paula, the *sorcerer who passed* through the classroom in Nepantla, but it was only an expression—this was childishness. What else would Magda testify to? Or had they found someone *else* . . . ?

Another possibility had slipped into my mind, into the quiet, with a dread unlike anything I had ever felt. The one final truth the holy officers were only waiting for the moment to reveal. One last discovery. That in the Inquisition's secret prisons, in a cell whose occupant had been held for years, only to be used one day as an instrument against me, as Magda had been . . . a holy woman from the country, a healer, half-Indian, a midwife . . . that the secret within the secret trial, was that the *beata* was Amanda.

And within this vertiginous spirit there dwell such intolerable blasphemies that even in desolation it were better not to pray. Far better to kiss the dust with one's mouth . . . for the remembrance of past evils, the ignobility of past actions, reveals such vileness as to make the soul believe God its Enemy, and itself the enemy of God. . . .

How long they have instructed me in uncertainty, how long I have been fed on doubt. When was the first lie told that brought me here, now? Days, months, weeks, thirty years, three thousand. I cannot wait longer. It must be tonight, while I have the strength to pray for strength.

I thought the answer hidden in those pages—that to know what would bring him, I had only to read with care, closely, deeply enough. But I have not solved it, because the answers were never *in* the book. The solution is the book itself. This is not about evidence or messages or instructions. It is not a question of my willingness to change or submit. It is not that he disbelieves I could be made to follow the path, but that he is afraid I could, for a time. For if it goes so hard on the confessors of heretics, how much harder on the director of the heresiarch. There is a safer path. It is as Gutiérrez said. A convergence of interests. The paths are not separate. Núñez will come when I have destroyed myself in search of answers to the false questions he has planted. This too is a kind of divination, circular discipline, a natural magic. The book serves as both method and sentence. It is his instrument. This book is killing me.

And when the work is done, the magic course is run, together will they come to pick over what is left, strip off whatever yet has worth, put away the rest. In a cupboard, or a closet.

I do not know what else to do, what else to pray for. I have lost faith that he will come at all. He may leave this work to others. How am I to pray for answers when I know no question I can trust?

No, there is one. One question . . . for all the answers I will never get. Who is the *beata*? One name I would give anything to know, one face I would give everything to see.

To know, to see. Can I give my eyes to see?

No one sees more clearly than blind Núñez how much I fear this place he has led me to. My mind. An empty room, a night with nothing in it. How much strength need I pray for, to lift a feather? Twice. To let the madness out.

Christian Herakles, set me free.

I will not rise from this table until I have chosen, will not leave this room until it is decided, till I have done it, or discovered I cannot and know that I am beaten.

Table. Basin. Vase.

How small has the world become. Brown. Turquoise. Red. How plain the palette. For twenty-four years I have sat at these windows overlooking the spectacle of other lives passing by. The neighbours across the way whose routines I know so well—I have never heard their voices. Never spoken with the old widow lodging in the lower rooms, helped her with her packages, exchanged greetings with the wheelwright. And I will never see more of their lives than I have seen until tonight. The chapel bell chimes the hour. Two past midnight, three to dawn. How brief, how few the hours ahead . . . how long, how many, those behind.

Convent, palace, prison. The worlds in these. Firepit, pantry, library. Prolix memory. Cornfield, river, killing floor. Prolix memory, what did she want from me, for me? Her lamb. *Your eyes are good, Inés, for seeing far. But up close, you are as blind as the rest of us.* Isabel. How must it have felt for you to hear me call you that? To watch me—driven by this hunger—turning away from you, turning to Xochitl for the things she could teach? And to be deserted by my father, only to see your own father turn to me for the one thing you could not offer him?

Window, night, cloud. Three, the chapel bell. Ink, paper, quills. Take one up. Feel free. Remember . . . ? Delicate scratch of quill over parchment. The quill's cool, lacquered shaft . . . unvarnished tabletop, worn to the roughness of petals. Again, more softly with ink, its pitch on the page a little lower. From the canals an ever fainter croaking. Stench of black water. Scent of flowers faded in a vase. Faint, sharp sizzling of candlewick . . . bare footsoles on stone slab, rough wool on skin. I sit here unmoving, a ghost haunting its body, and yet how far these senses are from extinction, keen to every fading sound and texture. Taste. Smell. Sight. Study the quill tip, its bead of ink. Not yet?

Horses. A coach crashes blindly through the streets toward some unspoken assignation.

Once I thought I had a gift, a special gift, a greatness within me. *Why.* Why give me a mind that devours my heart, enslaves me to my pride? Words—why this curse of easy eloquence? I choke on it. It has choked this cell on its wages. Books, instruments, curiosities—loyalty for trinkets. I have lent my voice to every passing cause until it no longer recognizes me. When did I agree to barter greatness for fame? Show me the contract—where have I signed it? Show me my name.

Show me my name.

Is it for this that my work has not served? Why must so many others suffer for me, so pointlessly? How do you see me—do you see me? Will you not lift, Bright Lover, your shining face to me? Beloved of my life, so happy and so new, I run to you—lover of my life, in the darkness of the night, so high and so wide . . . I do not find you. Where have you run? Why is there so much pain in this love you offer us? Why must we be broken to love, and crushed—why may we not love as lovers—with a love that is our own, even one willful and rich and turbulent? Surely there is One with a heart to answer such a love. What woman ever brought a lover to love—or having lost him won it back, by waiting on her knees? Why can I not suffer this, to lie with my face in the dirt of the yard?

Four. See, you have me counting now the hours. Below, hear the *tamalera*, palms slapping flatly at the *masa*. Inspect the tip, closely, bead of ink, small globe of night. How little left to surrender. How much.

Five. For the third night running I hear the piping. Is it a festival? A day of feast on the calendar of some unfamiliar subject tribe? For three *madrugadas* running he pipes against the dawn. Three notes rising and falling, shrill—shattering insanely against the empty stones. He must be in the street just below. I lean to see. The turquoise basin slips from the table edge. I leave the shards where they lie. There is not much time. You gave me a sky to conquer—a night I now cower beneath. Why give me these gifts, then not allow me to use them? Why shower them upon me only to let me forsake them, turn them against me, upon me, abandon me to my self, my Enemy? Court freak, *mujer de placer, menina*. You bring me to the brink of this black prospect only to turn your face from me—didn't I sacrifice, didn't I try, who is the sower of discord, who is the enemy of both sides if not I?

Or am I not . . . me?

If I must be another, then let me be another's—if I may not be mine, make me yours, not theirs. Manipulate me magnificently, make me round and roll me in your palm, dance me and sing me divinely, let me make you laugh.

Let me make you laugh.

Hera's lunatic, God's clown. Christian Herakles, who cannot lift a feather to let the madness out.

You mock my eyes. To make them see what I have not been—and yet see nothing of what you have in store for me. He mocks these eyes. Take up the quill. Prepare to sign for him with Night. Two beads, each a small globe. Shoulder them, now, whole worlds. Take them up. Feel how light, the lightness one feather brings. What shall I write . . . how. Guide my hand. A sign.

Silence. The piping has stopped. Still no word. Still I must wait. As I thought . . . you remain hidden. More silence.

False dawn . . . dawn. Rest . . . false peace. The first light coppers the cathedral spire. Hear the map of bells.

Lauds.
Where does the piper sleep?

So I had lost, and soon enough he would know. This path, this ecstasy was not mine. I could not make myself one even to defy him. The *ecstatics* have an answer, and I only questions. No face in the darkness, no sudden illumination. I do not know who the *beata* is, or even if she exists. But whatever comes I have found an answer of sorts, a kind of negative answer lit as by a small ray of darkness. The *beata* is not Amanda.

My faith in this is unshakeable, because I choose to make it so. It is a kind of certainty.

Whatever else I may be brought to doubt or fear it will not be this. Whatever else they still wanted from me, whatever the action, whatever the surrender, if they had Amanda, and knew whom they held, they had only to show me her face and I would have done anything they asked. Until the moment she is brought before my eyes, with this love shall I be purged of this fear of the face hidden from me.

It is perhaps with such a love that the angels are purged of ignorance.
Núñez will never come.

I, Juana Inés de la Cruz, the most worthless and ungrateful of all the creatures fashioned by your Omnipotence, and the most obscure of those created by your Love, appear before your divine and sacred Majesty, in the sole manner and form permitted by right of your Mercy and infinite Clemency; and prostrate with all the reverence of my soul before the most august Trinity, I do hereby affirm:

That in the proceeding before the Tribunal of your Justice, against my grave, enormous and unequalled sins, of which I acknowledge myself convicted by all the witnesses of Heaven and Earth and by all that is alleged by the Criminal Prosecutor of my own conscience, which sentences me to eternal death, and even this will be treating of me with leniency—that I were not sentenced to infinite Hells for my unnumbered crimes and sins; and whereas of all this do I find myself convicted, and recognize that I merit neither pardon nor so much as to be heard, in spite of all, knowing your infinite Love and immense Mercy, and while I am still alive to this life and before they have closed off from me all avenues of appeal . . . I beseech you to admit this plea in the name of that intense and incomprehensible act of love by which you suffered so terrible a death . . .

. . . You well know that for many years now I have lived in religion without Religion, even as a pagan would; as a first step in the purgation of these faults, in faint proportion to my derelictions and yet in token of my desire to assume again those very obligations that I have so poorly met, it is my wish to take up once again the Habit and submit myself to the postulant's year of trial under the examination of your Minister and the father of my soul, acting as your Prosecutor and testing the will and liberty by which I am disposed to these trials; and as concerns my dowry, I offer the alms I have begged of the Community of the Blessed; and if there should be any shortfall, I count on the intercession of my Mother and yours, the most holy Virgin, and of her husband and my father, the glorious Saint Joseph, who will (as I commend myself to their pity) undertake to pay said dowry, candles and gratuity.

Wherefore, I implore Your Sacramental Majesty to grant all the Saints and Angels your permission, licence and leave to readmit me to the good graces of the Celestial Community; and this being granted—as

Plea, in forensic form, entered before the Divine Tribunal, in entreaty for forgiveness of her sins.[34]

I might hope of their pity—that I might be given again the sacred habit of our father Saint Jerome, upon whom I count as my advocate and intercessor, not merely that I be received into his saintly Order, but also that in the company of my mother Saint Paula he entreat you to grant me the perseverance and increased virtue that I have always asked of you . . . All of which I shall receive by the good and charity of your infinite *misericordia*, provided in the appropriate degree. And for all these do I beg mercy, &c.

What is destined for Zeus but endless rule?
Ask not, neither set thy heart on knowing.[35]

After Vespers, Father Arellano brought a message. The Prefect was coming. Coming? Tomorrow. *At dusk.* Possibly, yes, Sor Juana.

Arellano was sweating still from the streets, though it was cool inside. Was there more? His lips had begun to move before the words tumbled out— his relief to be finished this penance, evident.

"Prefect Núñez will determine for himself the sincerity of Sor Juana's dispositions, whether, having been given the tip of his golden sceptre to kiss, she could truly settle now for such humble burdens—to lead the choir, instruct the servants, keep the books. *Superintendent of Works.* Or whether she still seeks to serve her prince by a more wandering path, farther afield. Blind poet, prophetess, seer . . ."

But why now? Sor Juana could ask the Prefect herself, tomorrow. And now he, Arellano, would leave her to her doubts.

What sign had I given, what sign had he read—none. But after some hours I saw. That for four months I had misunderstood completely all the taunts—it was not these I was to draw his lessons from. All the messages were *one*, made of the events of my life, of what I have known, one message that explains everything. Explains *everything*—why, all this time, he had even *pretended* to want to shield me. For I am not the one he comes to keep from the rack. I had not seen. . . .

Why come after so many months? Because I am exhausted. But why tomorrow, why not two more days' wait, three more days' exhaustion? He could come without warning—why the annunciation?—and if he *is* coming, why the message, why a message so much like the last? Because I have missed something. Try again, Juana Inés, try harder.

Superintendent of Works. He is telling me he has intercepted my letters to María Luisa. But something more. *Blind poet.* How this amuses him, the wandering . . . farther afield. *Service. A prince in the field*—the poet

Homer. This is about my grandfather—something I am to be made to remember. This. He saves the most painful for last.

"Even in America, Angelina, even here we serve the Sovereign of the Two Worlds. . . ." It was the last night we were together.

Even now the fund of Núñez's derision is not spent. This blind man who hails my new career as blind poet, mocks my threat, applauds my decision—there being so few poets who know how to write for our kind—who afflicts me now with the one confidence I would give so much not to have disclosed to him. But oh how I do grow weary of reading my past through this man's eyes, seeing only what and whom and how he wishes.

It is in the darkness after the last prayers, Father, that the visions come most clearly. I see you now in the only way you may now see me. I close my eyes, I open them. And you are the same. Antonio Núñez de Miranda, Master of the Collections, the Sources—now the Visits. My Turnkey. And was it not you who arranged my uncle's permission to visit the convent of San José? This I had forgotten. And were you not the one who'd guided me there? But first through a *recogimiento*—a place of recollection, for prostitutes—with every window bricked shut. Do you remember it Father as I do, or do I remember it now, as you? Antonio Núñez de Miranda, Controller of the Book, that I might have *one*, approved by you, thereby concentrating its effects, as a point of sun beneath a lens—all brilliance at one point of focus, half-light all around it—a map of light and shadows spread before you, knowing it to be unfolding within me. So that you might study it for fresh points of ambush, for the cardinal points of your Direction . . . How studiously you read—and *I was the book* whose pages you would cancel and correct. And as it was with books, do you attempt this now with my own memory?— you are the lens, I am the map, and my own life the light that scores and scorches the path. Antonio Núñez, Master of the Recollections, keeper of the keys to the palace of my memory. Who maps the rooms, the halls, registers their contents perfectly, then slides the bolt and bricks the windows shut.

Who is this Jesuit, who does not live among us but is never far, who speaks to me through silence and absences, who still asks *whom* I would serve—and where and how? Head or heart, heart or soul, soul or flesh. What vast wrongs have I done, that Fate has sent him to me—*and what has this man done* that he should appoint himself my judge? I who have wrought paeans on naval victories over foes poorly armed and over-whelmingly outnumbered, raised arches of triumph to the failing, worked hollow magic with theatre sets, drafted scripts to make gods of the king's representatives and make kings of God's. Thus have I served—two popes, two kings, three queens, four viceroys, three vicereines, two archbishops—count the counts and countesses, all the dukes and mar-quises. All for them, all the couplets for gifts.

Yet not everything do I repent. I have composed things for people I have loved, for the hurt made carols, and for the hungry. Even as he once suggested. And I have never been ashamed of my elegy for the king, though they laughed even then. Planet King. And since those days I have wished the son of the Planet King a happy birthday many times. Invalid, incoherent, impotent—Carlos the Bewitched, descended from Juana the Mad. He is thirty-two now. Sovereign of the Two Worlds. It has been hard for him, and I am sorry for that, but I am glad the Monster survived.

So there are certain things it were better not to deride, certain friends it were better not to attack. It is unnecessary, when he has won; it mis-judges its effects.

Or might Antonio Núñez de Miranda be nostalgic? Does there per-haps remain one piece of information he had always wanted to have—to see his inventory of windows and doors completed before the palace is pulled down? No. A man with such a memory does not feel nostalgia.

He does not know he has *won*.

Tomorrow he brings one final brutal revelation to finish me, warns me to expect it, transmits the subject to amplify his effects—ever my mag-nifying lens.

I am come to make war on you, Juana Inés, against the Evil in you, against the Enemy, for the dominion of your soul. And because you are a house divided in all that you do, I am confident of defeating you.

He comes to tear the palace down himself.

But it seems even the Prefect errs. He had only to wait. The time to come here is when the admission of my cowardice is before us both. Then, how much more easily do the palace walls crumble. Misjudgement, tactical error . . . what is this that I am feeling? Is this hope? There is time yet to find some advantage—what *is* it about that last night with Abuelo, what has Núñez discovered since, that he would threaten me with it now? How much did I tell him then, *in what words*, about this night I have not mentioned since, scarce returned to in my mind for a quarter of a century? He would remember as if it were yesterday. What is it, Father Núñez, that you would have me remember, what fresh horror do you bring—or is it hope?

Princes, golden sceptres, blind poets, wanderers . . .

I think I remember . . . fireflies. The night was cold. We had stayed up late by the fire, leaning close, pausing now and again to poke at the coals. He had rarely spoken about the war, this war half again as a long as the siege of Troy. *No wonder the Poet had gone blind, he said, straining to see the end.* My grandfather's war had begun in a year marked by three comets, hanging over the horizon even as the Soul of Caesar once had over Rome. Summers of fire, autumns of plague, winters of hunger. A war to announce the coming of the end. He had always dreamed of travelling; he travelled then. Westphalia, Prague, White Mountain. He left in '24, happy to have missed Magdeburg. And yet he was proud to have fought for the young king.

The stars were fading to the last constellations. . . . I was leaning toward the fire, my elbows resting on a book in my lap that I had hurried into the library to retrieve. Abuelo had been speaking of the chivalry of Spinola at the raising of the siege at Breda, and regretted never having served any such prince in the field. *Iliad.* . . . I had found it quickly, on his desk, to read for him the speech of Zeus's mortal son to Glaucus. It was to be years before I could read the *Iliad* again.

> . . . He leads his people. As ye see a mountain lion fare,
> Long kept from prey, in forcing which his high mind makes him dare
> Assault upon the whole full fold, though guarded never so
> With well-arm'd men and eager dogs—away he will not go
> But venture on and either snatch a prey or be a prey . . .

Alone and hurt my grandfather walked home from the front, through half-empty villages to his own on the bank of the Guadalquivir, but everyone was gone. His family, the friends he had known. He followed the river to where it ran into the sea, then kept walking, to land's end, to the pillars of Calpe and Abyla. And as he talked over his plans for explorations here, in America, his eyes glowed green as emeralds, as they had not in many years. And so it was that he began to speak of the end of the Mexica and the last sorcerer, Ocelotl.

"As I have followed his trail, Angelina, it has sometimes seemed to me that there went the last honest man. . . ."

Kings and princes . . . service and counsels . . . honest men . . . Ocelotl, Vieyra . . . Vieyra defending the Jews . . . condemnation, to wander to the end of the world. The Wandering Jew—

Magda. Magda will testify Abuelo was a secret Jew.

No—Núñez does not need to do this—why? to show me the full measure of my cowardice? Would you tear the palace down, Father, or rally its defences? He cannot think even me such a coward, to recall this of all nights to my mind and then expect me not to fight. If I know you, Father, your motives are not these. If these are your motives, I do not know you.

Could it be he has concealed a *code* within Arellano's messages, woven from all that Núñez knows of me? He does not ask me outright so as not to give me the opportunity to lie; rather I can only break his code if I have the very information he needs to know if I possess. He has trapped *himself*—four months of getting no answer from me, four months without the reassurance he seeks. It is not merely a question of what Núñez knows, thinks he knows or pretends to, but of what he *doesn't* know, thinks I *may* know, *fears* I do. There is more here, more than a threat, there is weakness, and not merely mine. Wandering, world's end, prince, sceptre . . .

In the legend, an old Jew taunts Christ at the foot of Golgotha. Why does the mighty King of the Jews drag a humble cross up so slowly? *I go on*, Christ answers, *and long shall ye wait for my return.* For his jeer the old Jew is condemned to wander without rest until the day of Judgement. And yet the story mentions no war—no golden sceptre.

Núñez has sent messages through Arellano *because it is dangerous to come himself.* For if there is danger, the messages Arellano carries must not appear to be in code but instead seem what they have seemed even to me—mortifications of my soul. What sort of code is this—with a clue that seems to be about my letter but is not. His is a code with a missing key—it must be, for if any message or even all of them together were to carry all the necessary elements, Núñez could never be sure it would not be decoded by someone else, someone other than . . . me—I alone hold the key. No, I am the lock. Núñez has inserted his code into my memory.

There is another children's story Núñez would recall. One that contains every element of Arellano's messages. *Wandering, war, world's end, prophecy, divination, service, a chosen race, a king's favour. Escape. Resistance. The time of sea and fire.*

The Conquest. One night holds the key.

The moon was rising, late, high above the mountains. . . . He had asked for my help, to look out for Amanda and Xochitl. Yes, we would watch over them together.

"You remember I once told you that Ocelotl had a twin. And that together, from here in these mountains, they launched an uprising against us—do you know it started right around here? Maybe from a campfire exactly here, on a night just such as this. . . ."

Though the fire had burned down to red embers the night was no longer dark. The snowfields glowed faintly violet.

"Ocelotl's second summons to the capital had gone quite as disastrously as the other—first with Lord Moctezuma, now with the Lord Bishop Inquisitor Zumárraga. So it goes for one who would serve the Sovereigns of Two Worlds, eh Angelina? At least this time things had begun better. This new lord had offered him his friendship and protection. But then after a few months came the request that should have sent Ocelotl running. Before long he was arrested on the charge of divination. He found himself in prison again, this one too the nightmare of a race. . . ."

Tracking the sorcerer Martín Ocelotl through a countryside Grandfather had travelled so far to call his own, this was the last great passion of his life. Ocelotl might have been the one man to have escaped both from Moctezuma's prisons and from those of the Inquisition—twice, and Abuelo's fascination with those escapes was perhaps more personal than I had ever realized. In the months before the Conquest, Ocelotl had gone to the archives of the Triple Alliance, in the city of Texcoco, for it was a time of strange events such as had been related in the old histories. Ocelotl was next summoned to Tenochtitlan to give advice to the Speaker, and was imprisoned there with the other seers and sages. Abuelo was never able to determine how Ocelotl escaped, but some said he had been released by none other than Cortés. The sorcerer returned for a time to Texcoco and worked with the Franciscans there who were recording the things of the past while there remained time. The archives had been put to the torch shortly after the fall of the city on the lake, and FastingCoyote's temple to the Unknown God razed. The memory of an entire race survived now only in the minds of a few elders.

Ocelotl's reputation among the Franciscan brothers led to his invitation to meet Bishop Zumárraga, which led in turn to their friendship and to his second imprisonment. It was the patterns of likeness and contrast that had fascinated my grandfather, on that night and other nights. Texcoco of the Unknown God, Tenochtitlan of two thousand gods. The warnings from Texcoco to Tenochtitlan, of one emperor to another, father to father, then son to son. FastingCoyote to Moctezuma I, FastingPrince to Moctezuma II—then the three warnings and the three escapes of Ocelotl. Twins, doubles ...

"The same and yet not the same," Abuelo shrugged. "Almost the reverse, *verdad*? It reminds me of a company of knights I once watched riding along the banks of the Guadalquivir. So many ensigns and banners, differently patterned, and yet all part of a deeper emblem of—what would you say, Angel? Honour ...?"

"*Sí Abuelito*, and truth—and *valour*."

"*Eso*. Honour, truth and valour. But in the histories here, though I have tried I can never quite name the deeper emblem. Do you know they stopped for the night in our village, those knights? Of course, even in my boyhood they no longer wore much armour. It was only a hunting party, and yet how proudly and how high the pages had borne the old standards and ensigns—but I have never told you of the great knight companies of the Mexica! Truly, have I? The Eagle Knights and—"

"The *Jaguars*."

"Ah, so I have. Companies as great as our Order of Santiago, reduced now to two men. And they had one last battle to fight, those two, under the old banners."

The uprising began not long after Ocelotl had quit the capital, having escaped his fate a second time. "The jailers claimed he had help, but it was what their kind always said." Ocelotl and his twin Mixcoatl—even knowing it to be hopeless, with so few men of fighting age left—invoked the ancient prophecies and launched a series of attacks leading toward the capital.

"The Indians Martín Jaguar and his brother Andrés CloudSerpent were arrested and convicted by the Holy Office of falsely claiming to be gods, or the doubles of false gods. The Inquisition could not even decide on the charges! As in the ancient prophecies, CloudSerpent went to the burning ground but, that morning, Martín Jaguar's cell had been found empty—ha, for a third time. Ocelotl had vanished in the night."

Why has Núñez used one children's tale to refer to another—why not refer to the second directly? What is the deeper pattern he would have me read? So long as his code is not broken, even if I myself were, I could give no other answer even under torture, and he would be in no more danger than before. But with each fresh message, each new hint, he brings me closer to guessing what he would have me reveal unwittingly, and the danger to him increases.

It is a code that points to one thing to point to a second to a third to what the messages never quite say . . . from Persia to the courts of Europe, to the Jews of Africa and Asia, to Golgotha and Mount Carmel, the hills of the Holy Land . . . but the land that he never directly mentions is this one, these hills, this continent, these old palaces, this New Eden.

Scrolls . . . the burning of the painted books, Sahagún, the Franciscans, an honest man.

Not nostalgia, not cruelty—there is one last window in the palace of my memory Father Núñez needs to look through, into a room whose contents he very much needs to inventory. Though I do not yet know what it is, the basis of Núñez's code and the source of his fear are the manuscripts Carlos has left with me. And if he comes now, it is because after four months he is becoming desperate—and if he is desperate he cannot afford to come to me empty-handed. There *is* hope here, but I cannot delude myself. Even he does not have the power to offer me my freedom. He cannot raise the siege himself—at best he offers a trade, an exchange of prisoners. The manuscript and my silence for . . . and now I see. In the darkness after the last prayers one sees most clearly, as on a blinding page.

Somewhere on the south bank of the Guadalquivir is a village, and in it the parish has its church. Within that church, the sacred canons stipulate that a yellow <u>sambenito</u> *be hoisted into the vault, such that the light that filters past it through the high windows and over the parishioners casts shame in hues of sulphur. And thereafter shall begin proceedings against all those related to the family Ramírez de Santillana by blood or association, who, if convicted of following the law of Moses shall be condemned, and if dead, burned in effigy. . . .*

He trades with this. But I do not yet see how—no one controls the

Inquisition—and if his offer is to suppress the evidence, how? if Magda began giving testimony in 1663? I did not even know Núñez until . . . 1666. Three years. Who gathered that testimony? Dorantes is my age. He would have been a boy. Gutiérrez was in Spain, also a boy. Santa Cruz, also in Spain.

It could have been anyone, it could have been Núñez.

But he does not control the *files*. Gutiérrez has seen them—but seen exactly what? And yet even if Núñez has somehow held back parts of Magda's testimony, and comes here to offer them in trade, there is still Magda now. . . .

She did not come from the Archbishop. That was a transparent lie. Even she did not pretend he'd agreed to see her. Magda does not care about Faith. Magda's love is the Inquisition. Núñez does not control the files, he does not control the Inquisition, Núñez controls Magda. Magda the scholar. A father to a fatherless child. He is good at that, a man of books. There is a chance. . . .

No, there *was* a chance, there *would* have been hope, had I the manuscript he needs. But I have recopied them. There is nothing there that Núñez should particularly fear, nothing with which I could trade. But *think*—he cannot not know this either—because of course there are other manuscripts. It only makes sense that Carlos would not bring them all to me.

It is not yet dawn—I have a few hours at least. What is in the manuscript that Núñez fears enough to come now with the danger to him greater than ever? Even to guess the general contents might be enough to convince him I have what he seeks, to induce him to speak of it more openly. . . .

Prisons, ~~gallows,~~ pyres. Archives, libraries, burnings. Books: *The Ascent*, the *Confessions*, Ecclesiastes, Esther, the Scrolls. ~~Kings: Ahasuerus, Hermenegild, Moctezuma II, Philip II, Carlos II.~~ Poets, scribes, chroniclers: ~~Homer, Augustine, FastingCoyote, Manrique, John of the Cross,~~ Manuel de Cuadros. Noble servants: ~~Mordecai, Sarpedon, Glaucus, Spinola, Velázquez, Ocelotl,~~ Manuel de Cuadros.

~~Doubles, descendants of gods: Sarpedon, Jesus, Moctezuma, Ocelotl, Mixcoatl.~~ Presumed heretics: ~~Hermenegild, Bruno, Galileo,~~ Manuel de Cuadros. Sentenced, imprisoned: ~~Mordecai, Jesus, John of the Cross, Moctezuma, Ocelotl,~~ Manuel de Cuadros. ~~Escaped: Mordecai, John of the Cross, Ocelotl.~~

Did not escape: ~~Hermenegild, Mixcoatl, Moctezuma~~ . . . Manuel de Cuadros.

Judges, Inquisitors: ~~the Vizier Haman, the Bishop Inquisitor Zumárraga~~, Father Antonio Núñez, Jesuit. . . .

It is only a theory, the slimmest of possibilities. What if the missing manuscripts were not an assortment but a collection, with a theme, the raw materials for a book . . . a book of conversations, say, between prisoners and their captors: Ocelotl with Moctezuma, Moctezuma with Cortés, Ocelotl with his Inquisitors . . .

Fray Manuel de Cuadros with Father Antonio Núñez.

On the day Cuadros died, Núñez came here well after Vespers. The day had been clear. Then a fine rain had begun to fall. The pyre was slow to catch fire. He arrived well past his appointed hour. He came in like a basilisk—stooped, heavy lidded, the small head, the jutting chin—ordered everyone to leave, spoke as a superior even to the Dean of the Cathedral. Always so grimly deliberate, so controlled . . . that day the sight of him—exalted, enervated, the light of Truth burning in his eyes. I could smell the *leña*, and something else. He told me he'd just come from the Plaza de San Diego. I would never again smell smoke without thinking of Padre Antonio Núñez de Miranda on this day, or see him without smelling smoke. I recall the rasp of deep feeling in Núñez's voice. At the last possible instant, Cuadros gave some sign. They took his confession. They gave him absolution. His confessors embraced him. Such a great shedding of tears up there on the scaffold. In the emotion of the moment even the executioner embraced him and apologized for some slight—then strangled him, quickly, leaving the Adversary no time to snatch the lamb back from the fold. A great shout from the crowd . . . the *leña* was lit.

I rose to leave the locutory—where was I going? He had told me now—what more was there to be said? I asked if he had come to confess with me, I asked if he had been the one to give the executioner the signal. It came out before I could stop myself. Yet had I stayed—to hear what, I did not know—how he *felt?*—he would hate me today, I am sure of it, with an all-consuming hatred.

But now I wonder what he might have come to say.

How often before that day had Núñez gone to see Cuadros in his cell?—how many subtle attempts had he made to bring his charge to contrition? Might Fray de Cuadros have made a record of some kind and had it smuggled out? He would have needed help but had many friends in the Church. His trial was a bitter controversy for years, even after he was taken to the stake. It was why his contrition was such cause for relief. It would be this record that Dorantes has been after for so long—he would like to add a chapter, or two, possibly, to the collection: the conversations of Master Examiner Dorantes with Antonio Núñez, certainly. And, if the hunting was very good, with me.

An hour to Lauds. So frail a shield it seems to protect Abuelo now, and so many ways—even if I have guessed correctly—in which this becomes more dangerous. For if I convince Núñez I have what he seeks, or know its location, and he falls first into their hands, they will have it out of him, with all the conviction of a man under torture, and then will come for me.

Abuelo, I would repay your gift of fifty pesos now, and Uncle Juan's. I have been mistaken about so many things; I could be wrong about this.

But of one small thing I am certain now. There were fireflies. Or no, only one. . . . I was almost asleep. It had been circling lazily about us. Abuelo noticed it after a while. Lifting the tip of his traveller's staff from the flames, with a smile he traced its green track with an ember. . . .

Why these stories, why that night? Why did I find the *Iliad* so quickly, on his desk, and the Manrique poem beneath it the next morning, among the few books he was reading at the time? Why two books he had read so often, why the two he had perhaps most loved? And on top of these, in the morning, though not that night, an envelope. *A mi hijita Isabel.* Did you hear death coming, Abuelo, while I slept? Through the courtyard . . . did you know her step?

And I am certain he had started to tell me these stories for a reason that night. But then the last of his stories had ended—of Bishop Zumárraga and the sorcerer—and he had not told me. Perhaps he had raised details in the telling that he had not fully considered beforehand. Allegations of theft against the Indian servants in the Bishop's household, the betrayal of a friend, questions of honesty and forthrightness. One twin escaping his fate while the other did not. Or if it had not been about Amanda, I cannot help but wonder if that night at the fire he had been trying—knowing I was soon to leave for Mexico—to warn me of the dangers ahead, in my appetite for secret knowledge, in my childish passion for visions and natural magic, and to speak to me of a threat he had felt hanging over our family for his entire life, and which, just perhaps, he sensed hovering also over my uncle's house.

Or else, as I listened to the rumble of his voice, and watched his big hands grappling with the traveller's staff as he poked at the night's last embers, I had only fallen asleep. So many possibilities come to me, in things said and only now remembered. Perhaps he told me as I slept.

Dawn. The bells of Lauds. I may have hours, or only minutes. It could be anything: a record of their conversations, a list of certain monographs Núñez might have failed to report to the Inquisition—or Cuadros's monographs themselves if they have somehow since gone missing. The most dangerous would be something on the Eucharist that Dorantes might link to a sermon or paper Núñez has delivered. The best I can do is lead him to think that I may know but, also, may not, and in this way he will be hampered in his questioning lest he reveal more to me than he learns.

Yet if it is divination Núñez would have me practise, then what I divine is a weakness in his position, an uncertainty in his design. It rings hollow, like a boast. The strong do not boast or threaten, or prepare the ground with books or messages, and if it is the science of uncertainty Núñez would still practise upon me, perhaps the alchemist has too long handled the mercury and quicksilver poisons the messenger. One sees its tremors in Father Arellano. So is it also with the Superintendent of Works. Having intercepted one letter, Núñez would have me believe he has seen them all, when it is clear from the message itself that he has not.

Miscalculation, impatience—weakness, this smell I know. This natural science as they practise it begins to seem inexact, its illusions not yet perfected, for in Núñez, they have given me an adversary of flesh and blood, however formidable. It were better to leave me to myself, turning in upon myself, my worst enemy. They think to deprive me of my collection, but return to me my memory. Now Núñez comes too soon—yet already they have left me too long in the darkness. In the hour after the last prayer, in the last watch of the night, there is a crossroads. And at that crossroads something waits. It is a jaguar.

I fear it, but if Núñez in his blindness thinks I fear it more than he does, I am no longer convinced of this.

Threats, weakness, boasts . . . to their science of uncertainty, I answer with a faith built on disbelief. All interests do not converge in me, not everyone betrays everything, not all the sources can be controlled or collected, time exists—if not for the Holy Office then for its officers. Gutiérrez is a liar: Gutiérrez ran out of time. And I discount on principle everything a liar says. Neither will I believe Carlos knew of Bishop Zumárraga by way of a betrayed confidence, but instead came to his own knowledge of the story, and thinking I might know it, used it to warn me. And whatever Santa Cruz may have learned of my early life, he did not hear it at my mother's side. She did not like churchmen, she would not have liked that one. She would have told him nothing, even at the last. And as for fear, it is human to fear the worst, but our strongest reason for expecting the worst imaginable is fear itself. I will fear the worst but without proof I will not *believe*—howsoever Núñez might imply that the other prisoner in the code is the less fortunate twin. Of this unbelief I make a fortress until it be proved otherwise.

Divination of the past leads in unintended directions. It were better not to deride certain things, stir certain memories. Even Magda I am indebted to, as one held long under water is grateful to find the bottom of the swamp. *Thus far and no farther—Ne Plus Ultra.*

Whatever may come, whatever stratagems and half-truths may yet be revealed, our position is better than it was three days ago. An exchange of prisoners is better than an abject surrender. I have been fed on lies and am fat with ignorance. I am not sure I have understood. I cannot know what to expect today, cannot divine all the possible alliances.

But if the game be to pursue the secret Jew, then I invoke the great King Alfonso!—and stand with the Emperor of the Two Faiths.[36]

And if the game be to teach me more of chess, I invoke the great tacticians Ruy López and López de Ayala—and together we shall serve the Lord Instructor of the World. For though there are stronger players, even the Inca Atahualpa honed his game in prison—and let them remember who once inspired Santa Cruz in the sacrifice of queens.

And if it be a hunt of those who would wander in the open without cringing or cover, then I invoke the great falconers, Frederick II and again López de Ayala and an unnamed Moor on the banks of the Guadalquivir —and together we shall fly the colours of the Lord of the Two Horizons. For who does not fear threat from above?

And if it be simply to give honest service, I invoke the last sorcerer, Ocelotl, and don Pedro Ramírez de Santillana, my grandfather. And together shall we serve the Sovereign of the Two Worlds. This is whom I would have served, and would still. Heart *and* head, soul *and* heart, body and soul. On the banks of the river Guadalquivir we ride under the banners of the Eagle and the Jaguar, under the Ensign of the Trout and on our shields the Salamander. On the south bank there is a village where we shall stop the night, and a little parish church where a yellow *sambenito* shall *not* be hoisted into the light. For there are colours we will never consent to put on, and a chapter in our family chronicle I will not live to read.

If Núñez comes here to threaten this, or to lie, with no credible assurances that he can return that spite to her jar, then he will discover for himself that it is not the all-powerful who grips the helm of Necessity, but the unforgetting Furies. My memory is my own, hereinafter. He will not take this palace again. And not all the windows are bricked shut. I remember those grey eyes—colour of cooling lead, yet not quite cool, the horror and the elation in them. I remember his strange speech, curious un-Christian admissions, the smell of his cassock. I smell it still, and I have begun to wonder if Núñez does not also. I remember other things, on other days, and still other rumours that I have heard, and can attest to. And I too will be believed. There is a weakness in his position. It smells of smoke. And he should hope that I find it before long.

For if he miscalculates again and Magda gets her chapter, then so too does Dorantes—at least one to add to the collection of Manuel de Cuadros. Even if it means giving him two. And they will have their rebellion and their fight, though against the Holy Office we cannot win . . .

> . . . . O friend, if keeping back
> Would keep back age from us, and death, and that we might not
>   wrack
> In this life's humane sea at all, but that deferring now
> We shund death ever—nor would I half this vain valour show,
> Nor glorify a folly so, to wish thee to advance:
> But . . . there are infinite fates of other sort in death. . . .
> Which (neither to be fled nor scap't) a man must sink beneath—
> Come, try we if this sort be ours and either render thus
> Glory to others or make them resign the like to us.[37]

"*I*" prayed that you might come."

"Your prayers did not bring me. I was sent."

"You're looking well."

"I am not looking well—I am told neither are you."

"Might we not light a candle before it is quite dark?"

"*No more of your evasions.*"

"Surely a little light—"

"Even with your life in the balance you cannot help yourself. Insolent wretch—I see perfectly well like this. I see *you* better—throne room of the Nun-Empress. I could not bear the sight of this place then—this auction house, these *toys*. Candlelight will not improve it now."

"Does nothing remain of your feelings for me?"

"As much as remains of my youth."

"And has age so hardened you?"

"Age does a lot of things. As you are now discovering. And in you I discover my worst mistakes. I should have left you with the Carmelites."

"I would be dead today."

"At San José you would be buried, but not lost—dead, but not for all Eternity. Yet what is even this, next to Sor Juana's boundless knowledge, immortal Fame? I do not hear you. Perhaps you would like me to believe you have changed. That you now believe worse things exist than death."

"This I believe."

"Than obscurity."

"Yes."

"Than *ignorance?*"

"I only sought to make of my mind a vessel worthy—"

"This is why you begged that I come?—to sing me this old song, to justify yourself? None of this matters now, Sor Juana. None of it, not to anyone. Not your poetry, not your experiments, not your precious studies. Except as each and all attest to your total indifference to the life of a bride of Christ."

"Indifferent?—never."

"Your conduct betrays you. You have reproduced within these walls the earthly world you vowed to forsake, surrounded yourself with—"

"Gifts. Most from friends of the Church—I've given them away."

"No, you let him take them. Hardly the same. But things can be reacquired. As you say, they cost you nothing."

"No, Father. I only said they were gifts."

"They assured me your suffering was genuine, but they do not know your theatrical talents as I do. You feign illness, distraction—"

"What do you know of this?"

"Do you think you are not watched in here, Sor Juana, do you think you are not *seen*? And now you feign contrition. Anything to persist in your defiance—"

"Father Núñez, could it be you have not heard my statement read?"

"So vast the sins, so meagre the details. Yes. The statement, *the plea*. Nothing has changed."

"No, Your Reverence, you're wrong. This winter . . ."

"This winter."

"The 24th of February . . ."

"A *Jubilee?*—you dare mention that to *me*. A general confession? The fasting, the trials, the meditations—it was too much once, why go through this with you again? All the sins of your life?—twenty-five years of *new* abominations. It would take *weeks*."

"I am ready."

"You think you are but I am not. Neither of us is young anymore. I have not been well. No. Find someone else."

"There is no one else. You must see that. Who knows me as you do? I need your clarity—"

"Seduction—more flattery. It's always the same game with you. But even you, Sor Juana, cannot seduce them all. If you could, I would not be here. The Vice-Queen despises you. The Viceroy has let himself be convinced your sympathies lie with the seditionists, if you are not yourself one of them. Those Creoles who do not hate you for your service to him are made anxious by the spectacle of your rebellion before the Church. Even your don Carlos is away a lot these days, I notice."

"He too was sent. He too performs services for a higher power. Another mission to map bad-weather harbours. A prudent undertaking, in such uncertain weather. He has always travelled among the people, Father, as have you . . . wandered quite far afield."

"I am told you would not say good-bye to this dear friend you are somewhat late in defending. Have you ever said good-bye *to anyone?* So quiet now. No clever reply?"

"Truly, Father, why have you come? Have I given no sign that those who have sent you seek—no proof, no *evidence?* You once said there were many working on my case, to interpret my hieroglyphs. Is there not some writing of mine that might now satisfy them? Please, Father? A letter, a *manuscript* I might surrender?"

"Your cell has been voided."

"Some ill-considered offence against the sacraments—my House of Bread, my writings on the sacrament of water?"

"Your cell has been voided."

"Yes."

"No. You are playing for time. If only the weather would improve, the earthquakes would stop, if only, if if if. So many hypotheses. But in a time of so much strangeness, Sor Juana Inés de la Cruz is one prodigy too many. I once heard you boast this city was yours. It is not yours now—you are detested by the pious no less than by *los nepantlas.* And it has scarcely started. The things the rabble already says: Malinche, Malinchista—how painful, given where you are from. Yes, the sacrament of water, the house of bread—soon it will be the humble people of the barrios who denounce you, those for whom you have written such heart-felt carols. If only you could convince them that the time of calamity is truly over, it was all happenstance—hazard and not God's wrath, but that is impossible. They are not natural philosophers, they do not reason as you do."

"I have read their histories. Some have survived, some we may still interpret, Father. Do you not think it possible that some new wonder might surface to surprise us all?"

"What do you *mean*—would you win my confidence with this double-talk? The only tales of wonder the people of your city have an appetite for now, Sor Juana, are told by my condisciple, Martínez— and that appetite is insatiable, and these are people of every class. On a Thursday afternoon he could fill the cathedral itself. Six editions of his sermons, stories largely about the Devil. *There* is a publishing success for you. How is it that you, Juana, who are so quick to make poetry on our theology, have written so little of Satan? I have always wondered. On this point you were always so evasive, even for you. Do you ever give him a moment's thought? Is he still a scholar, your Lucero—yes, there is a clever character, sly. You might make him comical now. Such comical stories Martínez tells of Satan thanking false priests, bishops with concubines, the mighty making false confessions. You have seen how quickly they turned even on the mother prioress whose case has become so notorious these past days. Condemned to eternal perdition for a single omission of a carnal sin during her girlhood. How the people applaud this, Martínez tells me. And how they would turn on you, if they knew the depths of viciousness your false confessions conceal. *Queen of the Baths.* That balcony where you and your Marquise spent so many jaded afternoons, Juana Inés, it is gone. It is ashes. The people of *your* city have burned her wing to the ground."

"Have you come to hear me beg? This time will be different. My word must still be worth something. If I promised those who sent you my discretion . . . ? My submission."

"You used me, you use me now."

"I needed you."

"My influence. You used it to abuse the generosity of a Church that gave you a home when you had nowhere else to go. *Take your word*—do you even know what the truth is anymore?"

"I need you. It is the truth."

"But you do not say why—"

"But I have tried."

"Why *else.* Tell me. The plain truth, from one whose word I am to take. Tell me why I am the one, why Arellano will not do—why *else.*"

"Your influence . . . with the Holy Office."

"Yes, better. So let us speak calmly and plainly, one last time. As we used to. Father to daughter. Your friend Palavicino has destroyed himself defending you. He thought to make his mark. He has made it. The man has no idea. And now he has made an application to enter the Holy Office as an *examiner,* when he is about to be examined *before* it. Ulloa has already written out his sentence. Lashes, banishment . . . In a few days the Tribunal will issue a proclamation, naming him in the sentence and you among the charges, to be posted and read in every church in the New World. And throughout Spain I take it. You may take this as a compliment. Any proceedings against you here, I have not been made privy to. But then, that is the procedure. And Dorantes will miss no opportunity to use procedure to embarrass me. As for any remaining influence I might have with the Holy Office, I have it very much in spite of you. How long did you think it would be before I had the preface of your latest volume read out to me? 'Phoenix of America . . . Glory of the New Eden, Glory of her Sex.' Did you think that if every poet and scholar in Spain wrote a letter in praise of you that it could protect you for *five minutes* here? Do you think that your countess, the King, Queen, Pope—all eight Urbans—all the civilized world banded together could stay the Archbishop's hand on the day he decides to move against you *here*? This is the New World, Juana Inés. Our New World. *Do you*?"

"No . . ."

"That day is not far distant, I assure you. You are a nun of the convent of Saint Jerome of the Imperial City of Mexico. Our authority over you is absolute, inescapable, implacable, eternal. Or is it truly possible you still fail to understand this? Do you imagine the Archbishop needs the Inquisition to deal with a miserable country nun, be he so moved? The Inquisition, Sor Juana—you would be begging for it within a week. Do you doubt it?—*do you doubt it.*"

"*No.* No I do not doubt it."

"So this time will be different."

"Yes."

"And what of this 'destiny' of yours—have you now abandoned it? *You thought you had a calling.* So now, yet another change of heart? I do not hear you, Juana Inés."

"I thought . . ."

"A calling to what? Do you even know—did you ever? If you are to have me believe you have abandoned it, should we not know what it was? To *greatness*, perhaps? But no that was my error. If you thought that. . . . And another of my mistakes to tell you my hopes. I was wrong. There is none in you. And now you want me back."

"All my life—"

"If those are tears I hear, I want none of them. The time for us to cry together is long past."

"Father, since I was a girl, you have asked a choice of me. Palace or convent, convent cell or prison cell. All my life I have fought you. I *choose* this now."

"Choice? I asked you to *serve*. Choice was always your idea. I have never cared how."

"But Saint Ignatius . . ."

"I asked you to search your conscience, I asked you to reflect upon the sins and crimes of your past, even as you now beg me to do with you, just as you refused me then. I only mentioned Loyola when I could not rid you of that antiquated nonsense. *To serve a prince in the field*, wasn't that the phrase—that was *your* design. Not mine. I have never much cared how you served. Was that not your *calling*, or have you forgotten it? To serve one who asks more of himself than he commands . . . ?"

"Father—"

"I—Sor Juana, I am not the one!—this is not *poetry*, now. He has been with you all along. Your Prince has stood so near by and watched you. *With such pain.* You say nothing. Could it really be you had not seen it? If you will not answer plainly even now, there is no point. . . ."

"Father, don't leave. Please. Not yet."

"It is too late for this. I am old."

"Can it be too late if He wishes it?"

"My faith in you . . . in us, is spent."

"I would do anything to restore it."

"Nothing you could ever say. Actions, Sor Juana. Actions."

"Anything I can give. . . ."

"No, give it to your Husband, not to me. For me no one thing can be enough. I am rather smaller of spirit, rather lacking in Charity. Somewhere within myself I would have to find at least a faint ember to rekindle, a spark of faith. And even then I would come only if my Provincial ordered it. Nevertheless . . . there is a certain pagan manuscript. If finally you see how inconsistent all such matters are with your profession, a nun's vocation, if this manuscript were to make a miraculous and silent reappearance, your secret could remain between us, and you might begin to gain my trust."

"But—"

"Do you try now to back out?—it is you who have been hinting at this."

"Your Reverence . . ."

"What I *will* take your word for, is that by then you will have destroyed all the outstanding copies. Then, were I to hold that manuscript in my hands, it might be possible for us to make a beginning."

"Father—"

"That is, *if* I am ordered to come again. . . . In the meanwhile, your friend the Bishop of Puebla has told you what you must do. Take his friendly advice. Sor Juana, you are already forty-five. On insignificant trifles you have spent more than *twenty-five years*. Contemplate the mysteries of our Faith. Nothing else matters now. The cleverness, the comedies, the double-talk, the lies of omission. These go, these end here. The inventory and record of all your crimes and sins must be *complete*. No evasions."

"But Your Reverence, I don't—"

"Gaps will not be tolerated—do you *hear* me?"

"Of course, Father."

"Are you prepared to surrender that manuscript, *today?*—do not even pretend not to know which."

"Yes, Father. Father?"

"What is it."

"I *have* heard you, and there is something I have told no one else. It should not wait."

"Go ahead, Juana Inés."

"About this manuscript you have called *The Sapphic Hymns. . . .*"

JUANA INÉS
DE LA CRUZ

Alan Trueblood, trans.

Verde embeleso de la vida humana,
loca Esperanza, frenesí dorado,
sueño de los despiertos intrincado,
como de sueños, de tesoros vana;
  alma del mundo, senectud lozana,
decrépito verdor imaginado;
el hoy de los dichosos esperado
y de los desdichados el mañana:
  sigan tu sombra en busca de tu día
los que, con verdes vidrios por anteojos,
todo lo ven pintado a su deseo;
  que yo, más cuerda en la fortuna mía,
tengo en entrambas manos ambos ojos
y solamente lo que toco veo.

Green allurement of our human life,
mad Hope, wild frenzy gold-encrusted,
sleep of the waking full of twists and turns
for neither dreams nor treasures to be trusted;
  soul of the world, new burgeoning of the old,
fantasy of blighted greenery,
day awaited by the happy few,
morrow which the hapless long to see:
  let those pursue your shadow's beckoning
who put green lenses in their spectacles
and see the world in colours that appeal.
  Myself, I'll act more wisely toward the world:
I'll place my eyes right at my fingertips
and only see what my two hands can feel.

The craft of the forger is weaker far than Necessity.[38]

Date unknown, year 1693 . . .

. . . charges that in clandestine distribution from America even unto
Europe, and in conspiration with Lady María Luisa Manrique de Lara,
Countess of Paredes, with the Creoles Carlos de Sigüenza y Góngora
and Antonio Núñez de Miranda, Jesuit Prefect of the Brotherhood of
Mary, and with the aid of the mulatta Antonia Mora, the nun has traf-
ficked in heretical tracts, monographs and forbidden translations, including those of the Franciscan Manuel de Cuadros, already consigned to
eternal damnation on related charges.

    Ask the nun's response.

The heresiarch will state a response for the record.

A: Before the Lord Judges I freely confirm that manuscripts were copied
and sent, but there was no traffic, no profit, no distribution ring. Further,
the orthodoxy and character of the manuscripts are still to be determined
here before this very Tribunal—but if even a single one were deemed
heretical, I do not doubt, Lord Judges, that all the parties named here
would willingly—

Tell the nun again to address herself only to the Lord Prosecutor.

A: I have only addressed myself to whom addresses me as an expression
of respect.

Should the Tribunal require expressions of the heresiarch's respect, we
will extract them.

Reverend Lord Judges, our Office begs the Tribunal's indulgence: that it
abide the heresiarch's impudence a little longer. The next days' testimony will
show her to be descended on both sides from a long line of false Christians;
to be infected with Judaic and pagan abomination from her earliest years; to

be weaned on necromancy and superstition. A sworn statement will be presented, and attested to tomorrow before the Tribunal, to the effect that her own wet nurse was a sorceress descended from an Indian insurrectionist condemned by the Holy Office long years ago.

Proceed.

úñez was not wrong. I could not help myself. Rebellion. It was this—the falsity of my courage, the weakness in my defiance—that I wondered if he had wanted me to see on the day he came, to see this as a danger to us both.

For his part he had not been so foolish as to threaten me with Magda before knowing how badly I could hurt him in return. I had so few advantages—that he was forced to be careful of not revealing more than he learned, and his fear of being spied upon in the locutory. How much easier for him to question me in a prison cell. My one hope had lain in drawing him out, letting him lead me to where he feared to go. Instead he had only to scratch at the surface, rasp a little at the vein of defiance in me, and within five minutes we were already at manuscripts. I would not have Sappho to divert him a second time. His next such visit would be his last, and my next gesture of rebellion the thing most certain to lead us both back to those chambers.

But no longer would I permit myself to doubt he would come at least once more. It were better that he not delay too long, *but I shall tarry, Father, until you return.* Neither would I let myself wonder when, or about his motives. Even about the web of his alliances, I would try not to care. Like this, I could only destroy myself, tilting at every shadow.

Not an hour after Núñez left and already late in the evening, I was allowed to take delivery of a letter from Lord Bishop Angel Maldonado, informing me of his visit, though Father Núñez had told him he was wasting his time. But since Maldonado had not been dissuaded, and since the journey was not just long but dangerous, I wondered yet, would he come just for this, does he come as a friend, why would he have written of me to Núñez to begin with? It was painful to be reduced to this. It was Maldonado who had my carols on Saint Catherine of Alexandria sung at his cathedral when Santa Cruz had refused them.

The morning after the letter, the Archbishop's secretary came in person to explain about my new cell.

"It is on the northwest corner of the *gran patio*, where Sor—where the postulant Juana will be more comfortable with the other novices, though they are somewhat . . . younger." I forced myself to take an interest, at last to be seeing him, a sleek and officious man with a long nose, over which he was studying me for some reaction.

There would be a great deal more noise, voices, cries in the night, the nightly turbulence of the processions. The secretary might see the new arrangement as a hideous coming down in the world, but my concerns had nothing to do with either noise or privilege—I would be one step closer to the convent prison cell, a barred door opening from a cellar onto the southwest corner of that courtyard. I pointed out to him that I had a cell, for which he himself had signed the bill of sale. Ah yes. A careful review, however, of the contents since removed had shown the current cell to be too large for my future needs. They continued to play at their games of irony. And I to fly to the lure, at each slow swing, though I had had weeks to see this coming.

The new cell they had found for me proved to be half as large, and there was no stairway to the roof. *Superintendent of Works* . . . I had persuaded myself to believe Núñez had intercepted only one—but in that one letter, I had mentioned the hidden stairway.

. . . next, the Reverend Lord Judges are asked to consider how the heresiarch has made her nest in corruption, and with corruption feathered it. Over the course of decades and in flagrant violation of her own vow of poverty, she had, by the performance and peddling of various favours, amassed a collection of curios, instruments and books lately confiscated and valued at thirty thousand pesos. Most recently she has attempted to suborn Bishop Angel Maldonado of Oaxaca for the purposes of gaining illicit foreknowledge of the present proceedings against her. Previous to this, she had induced another Prince of the Church, since stripped of his charges and titles, to publish under his licence an insolent suite of verses on the holy virgin Catherine of Alexandria, therewith subverting the veneration of a saint of the Church in order to draw the thinnest of masks over the true intent, being to praise and exalt a pagan sorceress, also of Alexandria, and a mortal enemy of our Holy Roman and Apostolic Church. In another letter to the former Bishop, the heresiarch praises this Hypatia's learning overtly and belligerently. And it is a perversity no doubt fulfilling the heresiarch's perverse designs that even as a pagan once corrupted the Prefect Orestes, so also has this paganist of our day corrupted the Prefect of the Brotherhood of Mary, not least in the trafficking of documents. Leading to the question of how long the heresiarch's own collection might take to burn.

A: Lord Prosecutor—

Instruct the nun to wait to be addressed.

The heresiarch will wait to be addressed, or will be gagged until her responses are called for. All of the foresaid, Reverend Lord Judges, being of a piece with other writings by the heresiarch sympathetic to various heretics and schismatics from the early Church. Which returns us to the heretical proposition of the *finezas negativas* of God, this also published under the Bishop of Puebla's licence, and the charge which the heresiarch still guilefully avoids addressing. . . .
    Get the nun's response.

The heresiarch will make a response.

A: Lord Prosecutor, any confusion of Catherine of Alexandria with Hypatia does not originate with me but has persisted for some centuries, and for good reason if, as seems the case, the pagans in their treatment of Catherine took inspiration from the Patriarch's work with Hypatia. As to corruption, the destruction of the synagogues across Egypt coincided with the takeover, by Christians, of the Jewish monopoly on the grain trade between Alexandria and Constantinople. Corruption comes in many forms. As to the burning of my own collection, it is a technical question, but one traditionally within the competence of this Church to answer. Certainly the destruction of the Serapiana was a test and precedent available to Caliph Omar as he made ready to burn the main library. But let us say, if indeed the Lord Prosecutor requires my response, less than six months.

Instruct the nun to answer specifically to the *finezas negativas*. . . . The Tribunal awaits its answer.

A: The Lord Prosecutor has not yet conveyed to me the Tribunal's instructions.

The heresiarch will answer to the *finezas negativas*. . . .

The day's warmth had not yet ebbed from the column at my shoulder as I stood, unnoticed, at the door of our new home, looking down over a courtyard lively with activity. On the *gran patio* I would not have expected laughter of the sort I so craved to hear, to share, based in neither fear nor anger—not these torments of irony.

It was as the Archbishop's secretary had said. The sisters for the most part were younger, many wealthy, with one foot still planted firmly in the world, the wealthiest with their favourites, then the novices, the slaves and servants, the young girls from the convent school.

Lying as it did on the far side of the chapel and refectory, the work-shops and orchards, the *gran patio* was another world though I had once imagined I knew it well enough. Like the others, I came for the torch-light processions; and after quakes I had often come to supervise the masons. While the colonnades around the first and second storeys had been preserved, to anyone acquainted with the original plans, the place was a bewilderment. Each according to her means and whimsy, various residents had made modifications, all being expansions of one sort or other—a third storey kiosk on pillars in a vaguely Turkish style, or ground-floor additions shambling a third of the way into the plaza. Flat roofs with crenellations, peaked roofs of thatch or of canvas, all more than likely propped on untreated uprights. Walls were of adobe brick or simply mud over wattle, some painted, a few limed, most left bared to the elements. Then another extension is built to abut on a wall that may or may not survive the next tremor . . . leaving more or less at hazard, blind alleys, light shafts and hidden recesses, and balconies giving onto blank walls. In appearance it was as I imagined a bazaar of Persia, or a market town at the edge of a desert. Our Santa Paula's first convents in the Holy Land might have looked thus.

Late afternoon was becoming a favourite time, for though the blood-sport of the processions was to begin again in a few hours, there was no sign of this yet. The nights were as written in sand. By the first light of each fresh morning, *el gran patio* was itself again. In the looseness of this order lay a resiliency one had to live here to notice. The fuss and fluster of chickens darting under foot, the call of songbirds from their cages . . . throughout the day, servants gossiping at the fountain, hanging laundry, fine articles of silk, others of cotton, and among them, ranged indifferently, hairshirts torn and darkened. Schoolgirls strolled in pairs, novices and lay favourites sat on the stone benches in the passageways.

Our new neighbours had grown used to us. At the outset there was bound to be resentment. Though small, it was still a corner cell with two storeys, and views to the north and west. More, my presence threatened to mean more scrutiny from the other patio and beyond. But when Antonia and I arrived, barefoot and tonsured, all our belongings in our two hands, perhaps the resentment grew a little less.

I wondered if it was not another dangerous fantasy but I let myself imagine Antonia and I might grow to like our new home . . . though so far she was having the more difficult time, to find her place. The nun's return to the noviciate for her Jubilee is provided for in the statutes; a good deal rarer is the secretary to a novice forbidden to write.

After Núñez had come and quickly gone again, there came a change. The Church began to authorize the visits of friends to the locutory once again. For the longer walk, one of several minutes, I was grateful though it was an occasion for more gossip, as I now had to walk past the entire convent.

San Jerónimo had not had a bishop's visit in over two years. His Excellency Angel Maldonado kept his promise, and I let myself believe he did indeed make the long journey from Oaxaca for me. Save for the bright blue eyes and the purple cassock, he might have been taken for a native of this country, his cheekbones high, his nose prominent, fine-bladed at the bridge. He seemed surprised that I was aware of the *beata* trials—but he knew María de San José well and though he disliked Santa Cruz, he did not believe there was any immediate threat to her. He did not mention any rumours concerning our convent as the site of the next trial, and it was a relief not to have to discuss it. What he had made the six-day journey to tell me was that the Holy Office was mere days away from publishing charges against Father Xavier Palavicino, whom I must know well, given that he had risked so much to defend my letter on God's negative *finezas*. Very gently he asked if even Sor Juana Inés de la Cruz did not have a few small sins she could freely confess for her Jubilee?

Bishop Maldonado was a decent man. It would have served nothing to point out that Oaxaca was very far away from the affairs of Mexico, that Father Núñez had been withholding his intercession for months, that I hardly knew Palavicino at all—and to tell the Bishop he was bringing me news of charges I had known of for almost two years, this would have been callous while leaving me to appear all the more intransigent. There was little he could do to help me here, but I preferred to think I might still have a good friend in Oaxaca, who before he left did his best to impress upon me the precariousness of my situation—certainly I must accept Father Núñez's offer of protection, at least from the Archbishop. The progression of events was in the bishop's view methodical, and his main concern was with what or who should logically follow now that the Palavicino affair was coming to a head. We parted on my promise to give our discussion my most urgent consideration.

> . . . that for three generations the family Ramírez de Santillana, of the province of Andalusía, has here in the New World intermarried with other families of false converts for the purposes of perpetuating secret worship of the laws of Moses. And that of this third generation, the nun calling herself Juana Inés de la Cruz has not ceased in her open defiance of our Holy Roman and Apostolic Church even while exploiting the trust owing to her position within it in order to publish various pseudo-theological tracts purporting to defend the Sacred Canons but which covertly undermine them. And that the nun has been recently so emboldened as to go beyond even this, publishing a tract (and within this, the proposition of God's *finezas negativas*) vehemently suspected of heretical Quietism and the Illuminist heresy that so persistently springs from the ranks of her cohort: new Christians, false converts, false Christians, crypto-Judaizers.

> Ask the nun's response.

The heresiarch will make a response for the record.

A: To the first charge: it is false, inspired by pure malice. Charges of this sort shame Holy Mother Church. To the second: if the Lord Prosecutor adduces particulars I will answer to each. To the third as to the first: false. This is not my cohort. But I remind the Lord Prosecutor that from it have come not only saints Ignatius de Loyola and Teresa de Ávila but Juan de

la Cruz—a year under torture, three times his writings denounced before
the Inquisition. The torture was the shame of his century, the denunciations, of ours. The latest being so recently as 1668, even during the proceedings leading to his beatification. I repeat, those who make such
denunciations before the Holy Office abuse it even as they shame our
Church.

Instruct the nun that not Juan de la Cruz nor any saint or beatific person
is here charged; that she has not properly answered the third charge; that
she desist from presuming to make pronouncements imputing shame—
to this Church above all; that it is not her place; that this is not her place.

I could not bear to ask it—to be brought by such as these to ask: Was it
possible that my grandfather had been a secret Jew? Could a truth and
fear so vast have hovered, sensed yet unseen, over all our years together—
could we have shared so much, yet not that truth, that pride, that fear?
However much I searched my memory, I scarcely recalled his mentioning the Jews at all, even while he had talked so often of the other great
peoples, those of Cathay and Egypt, the Persians and the Moors, the
Spanish and the Mexica.

But if ever there was a fact, a truth, a pride he found painful above all
others, it was that the Spain he so loved had once had a special gift, an
example to all Europe. The gift was tolerance, and the Moors had given
it. Under the Almohads, in their capital on the Guadalquivir, the city of
Córdoba alone fathered, in the span of eight years, two universal geniuses: a Moor who would go on to write the great commentaries on the
Greeks, and a Jew writing treatises on medicine and philosophy in
Arabic. In Córdoba, the Jews had embraced Arabic, writing only their
poetry in Hebrew, *the secret language of the heart.* The phrase had been my
grandfather's. And among the early Christian kings, some had been
inspired to lead by the Almohad example. But the inspiration did not
last; the gift withered on the vine, and the expulsion of the Jews began,
under Isabela. A great queen, Abuelo said, and a great error. Here was
the true Spanish heritage that the Conquest had betrayed, the great
hybrid that Christian Spain had failed to coax into flower. And yet, for
all this, Maimonides was the sole Jewish writer I ever heard mentioned
by name, his *Guide for the Perplexed* the only text, and this only in passing: a work of paradoxes on the unknowability of God, denounced as

heretical by the Jews themselves—or rather, Abuelo added with that sad smile, by the still perplexed.

And that was all. But was it, truly?

Why did he come to America? the prosecutors would not fail ask, after their false witness had given her testimony. They would say it was to hide himself in the wilds of a demonic country, as a place conducive to the practise of his secret rites. *No.* He had served his king, he was tired of war, a commoner who loved books and Spain equally, and who dreamed now of exploring. But what first brought him to Xochitl's village? What was the source of his lifelong fascination with the escapes of the sorcerer Ocelotl, or with the verses of the poet-emperor of Texcoco who had built a temple there to the Unknown God? I had only to remember some of the books in Abuelo's collection to glimpse the paths he had travelled. I had only to think on this to see that it was a collection of just such works that I myself had greatly added to. I asked myself now if it was not just possible that he had come in search of that secret flower that the Conquest had failed to produce but had not quite succeeded in destroying, and to which the greatness of Spain could once have been grafted, or by which revived. What name could one give to such a search, of which Abuelo might have been only half aware, and yet which I had, just perhaps, half-heard woven through all our talks and into the silences of his life? Of our life together, which they would now try to make a lie.

And I had only to consider these researches seriously for a moment to realize that Abuelo would surely have *written.* If only notes—knowing that these had to remain strictly hidden, perhaps to be destroyed at his death. And if he had truly heard Death's step in the courtyard that night, he might have been burning his life's work at the firepit as I slept. My fear took on a new guise: that his writings were not destroyed but concealed—at the hacienda, its hiding place a secret my mother had taken to the grave—or in some hidden recess behind the bookshelf at Uncle Juan's, near me all those years. And that the Prosecutor would next bring forward these papers to ask if I had seen them—claim to find it incredible that I had not, had not in fact *based my own heresies upon them*—before demanding that I repudiate them, that I watch them burned before my eyes.

How better to explain this rage like the pique of a child whenever I heard them—and I had only to close my eyes in this darkness to hear the holy doctors judging the beliefs of the country of my birth as superstition and heresy. Or whenever I felt them turning to derision the loves and passions of my childhood—the riddles and puzzles, the hidden forms and secret knowledge.

There were answers I would never have, fears and doubts I could no longer let myself entertain, but what was true beyond any doubt was that the hidden connections I had sought in stories and in the world all around me were real: the flesh and blood people in my life, the stories I was not to be told. No need even to close my eyes to see him, a man in his prime, a fine horseman riding into Xochitl's village, and now see her as she must have been then, before the accident. His daughter's age, with Amanda's grace, for that grace had first been hers. A young woman wise beyond her years, except perhaps foolish in love, even as one of his own daughters had been once. And how those two must have talked, for Xochitl had stories quite the match for his, of jaguars and walking fish, trout that were not there and the masks of god. Eventually a thing had broken that had made their friendship impossible—and yet after all the injustices of the Conquest, he must surely have seen this as but a feather in the scale. Perhaps it was precisely this, the scale of the incommensurate, that left him unable to resolve things in his mind. Like a problem with zero in algebra. Impossible, yet impossible to abandon altogether. Over the past few months it had occurred to me that she'd chosen to come to live with us as an act of contrition—to serve the daughter of her friend by nursing the daughter of her lover. But though Xochitl had lost her place in her village, she would not have agreed to come to Nepantla if she had not loved and trusted my grandfather. There was something between them she did not wish to twist—they never spoke again, and lived together until he died. Friends for life.

The untold stories, the unspoken correspondences between the legends, were real, as real as mountains, and strong. And it had become troubling to think on the ways in which their hidden influences and sympathies had not ceased. Is it possible to walk a path all our lives and not know—even refuse it, to think we have turned our back on it—even as we think we are following another, making each choice at every crossroads for reasons we do not see, and which might as well be the opposite of what we think they are? When every choice seems a turning away. And might one not end thereby in hating choice itself . . . ?

And so who was to say that one mention of Maimonides was all I had learned from him of the Jews, whose god they seek everywhere to know by his secret name. But if that god were my grandfather's, how painful that I should only hear of this from his accusers. Had he ever tried to tell me? How much of this might my mother have known, if I had known how to ask? I had wondered if he was trying to protect me, but perhaps he only hoped I might be fearless. It had worked for one of his daughters.

Without so much as rising from the rocking chair where she sat nursing the baby, my mother had stopped Diego with a word and a look, and sent him slinking off with a question. *You do know innocence?* She looked at me then, another question in those black eyes, but I had as yet no idea what had happened. And I remember Xochitl, hair glowing softly in the light, her face strangely youthful, I thought, as she watched my mother. She was standing in the courtyard, a few steps beyond the kitchen door. At her bare feet, a rag lay forgotten. Mother's eyes met Xochitl's, whose face had split into a grin of almost painful width. The two looked at each other for a long moment as though each daring the other to laugh first. Just then the baby coughed and cried, fists like tiny angry planets making small arcs in the air. My mother frowned down at the balled hands, the bald head grimacing, and with a little shush gave him her breast. Xochitl bent stiffly to pick up the rag.

Eleven years they had lived together, raised daughters together. Between those two women lay an entire world that I could scarcely begin to guess at. The moment had passed, but it had happened. I no longer doubt there had been others, though this must have been one of the last. In a few days I would be in Mexico. In a few weeks, Amanda and Xochitl would leave for a destination they would not reach. But that night Xochitl served us dinner herself, for the only time that I can recall. I was relieved, this once, that Amanda had remained in the pantry, for it had been just that morning that she'd asked if she was to go to Mexico as my maid. When I saw Xochitl coming in with our plates I jumped up to help, but she answered in Nahuatl, "No, let this be my privilege."

The main course was a *mole*, a meat dish in a sauce of chilli and chocolate. While this was now common in the recipes of Puebla, *xocolatl* had once been a sacred aliment and Xochitl had never cooked with it or, if she did, had never served it to us. Instead of making a solemn event of it though, Xochitl was relaxed and smiling as she limped about. It seemed now that around my mother she had always been conscious of her hip, standing very straight when she spoke with her, often waiting to move until she had left the room, out of pride, I'd assumed. But I wonder tonight if it wasn't, instead, consideration.

As Xochitl leaned down to clear my plate, I murmured in Nahuatl, "Delicious, Xochita, but that *was* lamb, wasn't it?" I was half-joking, but she had a way of squinting that could make me laugh even when the joke was mine.

"*Tepescuintle*," she said, then hobbled off towards the kitchen, leaving all the day's tensions draining from me in laughter—gales, *carcajadas*. At the far end of the long table, Mother had looked up from nursing Dieguito, her long brows raised. *Escuintle,* she knew. A Mexican word Abuelo had often used for a naughty child. So I explained, feeling the humour of the moment fading, that it was short for *tepescuintle*. She had only been mildly curious and I regretted starting, for not only was she unlikely to find it funny, I might end up getting Xochitl into trouble. And I felt confused, as well, for only now was I giving serious thought to who had actually killed the dog. Seeing Xochitl, smiling, hobbling around the table, I knew it had not been her after all.

Tepescuintle, I began, cringing inwardly, was a small, voiceless dog the Mexicans used to fatten . . . to eat. And even as I said this, I recalled that just the night before, when I had told the story of the bridegroom impaled on the wedding tree, my mother had not been amused in the least. She didn't laugh now. But to my surprise, the hint of a smile played over her lips.

"But you *like* animals," I said.

"There was always something not right with that one."

"Is he gone for good?"

"I would say the dog is."

"And you'd just let Diego come crawling back." From long habit I shot this back before I'd really heard her. I saw her joke too late.

The baby began to fuss again, as if needing those great black eyes as much as milk. When they met his little fox eyes, his fists eased again and loosed stubby petals fingering the air. She crooned to him a lullaby in a singing voice it shocked me to hear.

But by then I had decided to be furious that she should find this a thing to joke about after what Diego had done. How could she keep a man around that I knew she did not love? Had she loved my father, at least? Love was not everything, she said. No, not for her, obviously. I would understand when I was older. Truly I hoped not—

"*He* was older—*he* didn't understand, did he, why love was not everything. Wasn't that why he spent so much time away?"

"Maybe he knew he couldn't stay."

Was she saying he had avoided us?—why, so we could get used to it?

"I'm sorry if this hurts you—you're too young to be hearing this, but we've run out of time, you and I. . . ."

"Hearing what."

"Yes, Inés, he avoided me, as you put it. But the one he avoided most of all was you."

It was a mother's instinct, to repeat the child's words to convey an adult thought. I knew even then she had not been trying to hurt me, but having heard her echoing the very phrase I had used to conjure the ghost—of my father avoiding me, staying away from me, who waited only long enough to get to know me to stay away completely—the words went like a knife through my chest. She tried to go on, but I'd heard much more than I'd wanted to. Before leaving the room—so I would not cry in front of her—I asked as calmly and coldly as I could manage if she even knew what love was. If she had ever loved anyone.

The night before I was to leave for Mexico, she came to find me again in the library where I was choosing books among the shelves for the dozenth time, adding just one or two more to the already-too-many making the trunk all but immoveable. Perhaps that had been the idea after all. I had a few hours left, just time enough to finish the argument. I was sorry it had to be there. She had come to give me the fifty pesos. Her face was guarded. I saw with some satisfaction that I had hurt her.

I felt more than saw her expression soften. Perhaps it had been finding me standing in the shadows amidst the ranks of books. "This is the countryside, Inés, not Madrid or Mexico. A woman does not always get her first choice. I love his son, now."

"Why a man at all?" I wished I hadn't asked. I had her thoughts already about a woman's place in the world, and her judgement on my ambitions for Mexico.

"Your father did not care for cities. . . ." If by this she was trying to say he'd feel as she did about my plans, I did not want to hear it. In fact, I never wanted to hear her mention him again. "He was like you, Inés. He always had somewhere else to be. I had been planning to move to the city with your aunt. After your sister María was born I went back there a few times to visit. You might like it. I did, more than I expected. But your grandfather had already rented the hacienda in Nepantla for me. Most fathers would have disowned their daughter. You only saw me helping him, but first he helped me. He showed me a way to make a life for myself here, and for his granddaughters. Whether your father returned or not. And in Nepantla I would be easy to find. About what I said . . ."

If she would just let it lie, just let me leave like this, not make it any more painful than it was.

"You weren't wrong about everything. . . . So maybe it was true, he didn't want you to love him too much. But there was another reason." I told myself I wasn't even listening.

"I hadn't thought of it this way until the other night, but he might also have stayed away so he wouldn't love us quite so much."

"I should go to bed." It was too late for this, too late to see the past other than as it was.

"Yes. Tomorrow will be a long day."

When I did not move, she went ahead of me. I thought she had gone, when I heard her call to me. She stood framed in the doorway, behind her a few stars. Among them beamed a planet white and still. I could not see her face.

"As for the other . . . I was distracted with the baby. I thought you two were too young. But you could have come to me. I would never have let any of my father's granddaughters be hurt." With that, she was gone.

She did not come out the next morning to the wagon, though for once she had not gone out to work. She had stayed in her room, but had left the door open. Amanda had gone out into the fields very early, and did not come back to say good-bye. Xochitl held me briefly, but we did not speak.

My father's granddaughters. My mother had been thinking, then, of Abuelo's other bequest of fifty pesos, as much a message from Abuelo to Xochitl as a gift for Amanda. It would be four years before I learned of its existence, another twenty before I learned from Magda that Abuelo had borrowed the hundred pesos from Diego. But I had remembered my mother's words clearly, for it had been an odd way of putting things. It was the one concession I had ever heard her make to the game of twins Amanda and I had used to play. It had struck me as generous even then, and had only deepened my confusion, generosity not being a quality I had associated with her. Generous. I did not know her at all.

Friends, enemies, it seemed to make little difference now. Bishop Maldonado's gentle remonstration on the subject of confession felt not so very different from being asked by Núñez if I had ever said good-bye to anyone I had loved. It felt some days like being asked if I have ever loved at all.

Other friends came to the locutory, and after a few such visits I no longer doubted their sincerity, but neither were the choices that my friends urged upon me easily distinguishable from those of my adversaries. On the question of winning the protection of Núñez by my confession, my friends were divided by how full and how sincere it should be. They fell between two extremes—of a partial confession as a tactic of expediency, or a sincere expression of contrition.

But surely those who urged sincerity saw how this might well entangle me more deeply in questions of heresy, and could the camp of expediency not see that my confessor was attentive and experienced, not easily deceived? Even this was not the true dilemma, because it admitted of a third possibility: choosing to face the Holy Office. And in its implications that third avenue left me more dependent on Núñez than ever. For if commanded to recant the negative *finezas* I could not choose to, even knowing the consequences. Why could I not, because I was right and they were wrong? I might be a heretic, but not in this.

Before all the Holy Community of Saints and Angels and the Celestial Tribunal I still ask—and ask again even after all that has come—what is a heretic? Giordano Bruno's case was clear. He had simply pursued the mysteries so far as to become a stranger to the world. Galileo Galilei was no stranger to the world—and attacked nothing in the world so righteously as unquestioned authority, and the Jesuits. The manner of Hypatia's death was Alexandria's penalty for sorcery, but one might as well ask if Hypatia was just as truly the heretic, not for charting the flights of ravens and the courses of Sirius as her father had taught her, but for challenging barbarism and hypocrisy.

But if she *was* a witch, let us begin by asking if a witch is truly superstitious, for Hypatia was known to say that to teach superstitions as truths is a most terrible thing. *The child mind accepts and believes them, and only through great pain and perhaps tragedy can he be in later years relieved of them.* Or is a witch, I wonder, philosophic? *All formal dogmatic religions are fallacious and must never be accepted by self-respecting persons as final.*

But if she was a heretic, it is as well to call Galileo a witch—his witchcraft was his method, his heresy defiance; her heresy was her eminence, her witchcraft, memory. Again of this Holy Company I ask: Is it heresy to recall an older faith? A wisdom before the Light, a fall before the Fall, a woman of more ancient tears, a sun, a son, before the Son? Is it heresy in an age of iron to remember one of gold?

What, then, does the Lord Prosecutor's idea of heresy amount to but a fear of choice itself, and a superstition rooted in the fear of that which is older than itself?

On this night the Prosecutor made no attempt to interrupt. I was allowed to speak at length, for the secretaries to record. A witness was brought to challenge certain of my assertions, but I was allowed to question the witness in turn, though this was unusual. And yet each session had in its own way become more frightening than the last; and as I was shown courteously from that room and back into the darkness, I could no longer ignore that these fantasies were not harmless, though at first they had kept my fear from overwhelming me entirely. In the first days after Núñez left, little scenes such as these ran swift and incessantly behind my eyes—with Gutiérrez's depiction of those chambers all I had to go on. Unusually high, windowless, stone floors, stone columns of eight sides. With time I had flooded the chamber with light, colour, turned stone to marble, iron to brass. But imagining the room differently did not make it any less likely I would one day be taken there.

Thus was I about to send myself to the stake still upholding my negative *finezas*, in defence of free will, I who have always hated making choices. This was not the calculation of longitude at sea. There were no prizes for making discoveries such as these—or that the *ostrakis aneilon* used in Hypatia's death were likely to have been the tiles of ostracism, that the infallibility of Caesar Pontifex was modelled on the Egyptian cult of the living God Serapis, that doubt itself has become heretical and that the punishments of Hypatia and Galileo were less for witchcraft or heresy than for a new kind of treason. One from within. And with each passing night it was becoming harder to imagine standing my ground before the holy officers, because through Magda they might know things even about my own life that I did not. Even as I dreaded how these would be revealed to me, when, in what tones of irony and triumph, it became more urgent to anticipate what might be coming. Truly frightening was the eagerness with which my mind returned to that room, to confront the false witnesses, who were now almost always Magda, examining me. And in the midst of my rousing defence of heretics, it was Magda the scholar who had drawn the link from oyster shells to turtle shells—and I had stood revealed then as a hypocrite, as she forced me to admit it: I had always seen that Amanda had my father's eyes, that she had been his choice, and that what I had most envied of Amanda was not her secret knowledge, nor merely her grace, nor even her gift with a gesture. It was her heart. I am not a child anymore—certainly I could bear this coming from one such as Magda, but only for so long as I can cling to my faith that they will not bring Amanda before me in chains.

After I had slept a little, I saw how far things had gone. They had made of me an officer of the prosecution.

It is my friends who have shown me this. For if it had become a new torment to answer to those who clearly wished me well, surely this means I had given my adversaries too much credit, for intuition, for special knowledge of me, for the genius of a cruel empathy. Much of what they know of me holds true for all—and what I fear, everyone must. There is a curious remark Núñez has made more than once. *Gaps will not be tolerated*—and well do I know that the fear of these can be intolerable. I have already sensed it in Núñez's vaunting of the perfection of his memory. *Nothing is ever lost beneath the eyes of God*—before the eyes of God, perhaps, but beneath them, much is lost upon us. The weakness I have smelled was fear—but hardly mine and his alone. For it is precisely what the holy officers do not know and cannot see that is a torment, for them as it has been for me. I detect it in the careful reports Gutiérrez had filed of our every meeting, against some future treachery among his compeers. This same fear abides in the inventories of Dorantes, in the careful comparison of the first with the second. It lies in the method of their interrogations, scribes trained to record in teams so as to miss nothing—they have made a special lexicon for the language that goes beyond speech, a shorthand to mark the crack of bone, the sinew's snap, the long vowels without consonants or stop. And if I permit myself a memory of my tour with Magda to the workshops of Santo Domingo, I see it even in the instruments their smiths and forgers make—the branks and gags and pears—for the plugging of gaps.

These sealers of windows, these cloisterers, with their mortar and shutters and locks, they too fear all that escapes them. They cannot rest until they have seized it, known all, had this allness tallied, until they have entered into their logs all the testimonies. Until the record is complete and buried in the archives. Just as I had once made myself trace the constellations, to make a friend of Night, they are as children afraid of the dark, who cannot bear to see the sky until they have made an inventory of all the stars. How many stars does Núñez remember, I wonder, when he closes his blind eyes at night? How many more than I can—and is the difference enough for him? In this, I have come to understand him, and through him, them. It was not empathy or cunning, on my part or theirs. It is this fear we share. Through it, I had become one of them.

And so as if by a long ride in the desert was I returned to the dilemma of my confession and perhaps, I thought, to the beginnings of a solution. A confession not full, for there can be no such thing, but of a fullness that yet gave the enemy no comfort, no rest, no peace—for whose conscience did not trouble him in the night, whose mind did not contain an inventory of secret doubts? Who is to say what Núñez feared most, a missing manuscript or darkness, or what he dreaded—if there was a dread we shared—more than the images conjured in the scent of smoke.

Gaps will not be tolerated, yet are everywhere. It would be for me to forge a confession of these, and let the holy armourers see what I had glimpsed, through long trials in the night, that mail is lighter and just perhaps stronger than plate.

But this was the solution to a false dilemma. The true one is a question of not armour but armaments. And in the wait to face the Holy Office, I have come to see the mind itself as a sword. The more one knows and the more keenly one remembers and sees what one has missed, the more sharply cuts the edge. It is whetted on knowledge, it lies between you and your adversary. We either take the haft or are taken by the blade. But even the rapier's hilt is a parabola; and some nights, how heavy its handle lies in the hand. I have not found any higher purpose for my gifts but if such a mind as mine has any purpose at all, surely it is not to wound me—needlessly conjuring images such as Abuelo's papers burning before my eyes. Lately, these come no longer as taunts nor even innocent fears I must learn to avoid but flails I have summoned willingly to hurt myself. Nor am I the only one wounded thus. I have only to look at the change in Antonia these past months, who is so eager to learn from me, who has already learned too much. My cheeks flush as I remember what I have taught her about self-pity and three-sided blades. But I will try to lay shame aside with their other instruments and not make of this too a gift to my adversaries. And this also have my friends taught me.

Yes, there is some knowledge of me in the punishments and torments the holy officers inflict, but how much, and how much of this is from me? What brought Galileo Galilei to his knees? It was not that they had found someone more clever—a Jacobi Topf, some anti-Galileo of the Soul—nor that Galileo was old, or ill, or almost blind. It was not even quite the pain and the fear imposed on an old man's mind, but the special shape he alone could give these. More likely, Rome and Florence supply the same crude materials as are furnished here. Time. Doubt. Fear. With these, we forge the instruments ourselves, from our own faculties, and yes, the soul is to be the crucible.

It is not that a fated few bear within them some secret flaw—neither is this to be found in a single trait or faculty. It is not that we contain the seeds of our own fall, but that the shape of that fall—forced upon us— takes its imprint from us, our whole selves. Not only our conscience but our reason, memory, heart. Our imagination. And also our defiance, freely willed and chosen. So many olive branches Galileo was offered. What is a heretic, even one who recants, and why could he not take the olive branch? Why could he not curb his strength in strength, and not wait to have it broken? And what was it that brought a book collector and astrologer to attack the mulatto with whom he shared his cell, to try to murder him with his bare hands in total darkness? What had he seen, what had been summoned for his sight, if not the most appalling vision of himself?

But, then, I could not be sure if these were fantasies at all . . . or rather prophecies a mind in that dark had driven me to fulfil.

JUANA INÉS
DE LA CRUZ

B. Limosneros, trans.

When Pedro, as a man of the sea,
finds himself denying
Freshets, Springs and Streams—
all run down to the sea,
they laughingly
and Pedro to weep.

verses
The Freshet does not forget
its beginnings in the spring,
the font of all its being;
since from the silvery rills
of its laughter springs forth
the most pleasing of confessions
to the Source:
but if Pedro denies all this
with ungrateful evasions,
Freshets, Springs and Streams—
all run down to the sea,
they laughingly
and Pedro to weep.

 The Spring laughs on
as it crashes from the summits—
in an oblivion without sorrows—
recollecting on the lowlands
the Flashing Eyes, the Lucid Matter
of its earliest existence:
but if Pedro denies all this,
though with a mortal shudder,
Freshets, Springs and Streams—
all run down to the sea,
they laughingly
and Pedro to weep.

 The mightiest stream, unswervingly,
with impetuous fire
surrenders unreservedly
to the sea, meeting there
its Final Destiny,
finding there its quietus:
but if Pedro denies even this,
turning his eyes from such glimmerings,
Freshets, Springs and Streams—
all run down to the sea,
they laughingly
and Pedro to weep.

EPIMETHEUS

The heresiarch will cease her denials and respond fully to the third charge, concerning the so-called negative *finezas* of God, and then recant them.

A: Lord Proscecutor. God is a superabundance surpassing every category, even that of divinity, flooding the three transcendental qualities of Oneness, Goodness, Truth, overflowing these as Beauty, cascading in a Music down through the Creation in Time. We have called this Mystery, we have called this Night. And well we might, for its darkness is not dark nor absence of light but the mystery of an immense plenitude over-whelming our small faculties, as the brilliance of noon floods the pupil of an owl.

So when I say that the restraint of such a superabundance may come to us as a favour and mercy, language itself is found wanting. To my persecutors I say the negative is in the eye of the beholder . . . as when we close our eyes on a scene brightly lit and find projected against our lids the brightest things dark, the darkest light. To my slanderers I say that if there is darkness, it lies not in God but in the overturning of our categories. The negative lies in the reversal, but the negation lies in us.

Is the negative bad, the positive good? This is heretical Manichaeism that the pamphleteers beneath the mask of their pieties are near to practising. Good Evil, God Devil, Light Dark. This is the very heresy that first seduced Augustine until such time as he had seen the teacher Faustus with his own eyes, heard him for the first time. A negative favour is still a favour, God's restraint is not a negation but a finesse, the finesse is not evil for being indirect, and this very hostility to the nega-tive, the oblique, and the hidden is itself a kind of childishness, super-stition abetted by language. Yes, Good; No, Bad. Even Odd, Straight Bent. The thinking of infants, who do not know night from day, their left hand from their right. Are these any less superstitious than the beliefs of the country of my childhood, whose practices are called dia-bolic, their sacred images idolatrous? It has been claimed by those whose offices are holy that I have held myself to be above faith as a thing no better than ignorance, paganism, superstitious visions, as beneath contempt. It is simply not true, it is not simply true—for I have felt contempt for none of these things. As a child I was taught that the face of God was unknowable, and its masks only mirrors in which the peoples of the world might find themselves.

And so to my attackers, my slanderers, my persecutors among the pamphleteers I say that even if it were my authority alone that Xavier Palavicino had cited, my authority is not mine alone, as the figure of the pupil of the owl is not mine but John's, as the ray of darkness that strikes the eye is from Saint Dionysus—these are my authorities. John, Jerome and Augustine, Dionysus and Hermes Trismegistus, FastingCoyote and Maimonides . . . poets of the flood of superabundant Mystery.

> . . . *Sé ser tan caudalosas sus corrientes,*
> *que infiernos, cielos riegan, y las gentes,*
> *aunque es de noche . . .* 39

hether I could recant. The one question left, for me. The rest I leave for others.

Truly, who can say what secret springs and silent vectors have carried us to any given moment, and what hidden currents had brought me to speak of the negative *finezas* on a moment's impulse that for two years I had found myself unable to repent by choice, and left me unable to imagine anything I would not say—no matter the danger—to evade the judgements of the holy officers upon them? What is it now that I still cling to, through great pain and perhaps tragedy, like a child to a fable? Is it to the fable of trout, there and not there, at the bottom of a pool, or to a certain wise way Xochitl had of making me laugh? Or I wonder if it is to the gesture of two trout speared, together on a platter, or to some notion of justice written in an anagram.

Or only the weight of my grandfather's hand I've felt on mine, all these years, each time I took up a pen to write.

But surely I who have gone to such lengths, who once took such elaborate steps not to look back, cannot now find it so difficult to turn my back on that past, again. Not after I have been given so many fresh reasons to remember old regrets.

Recant or refuse. This choice is not false, not a fantasy, though dangerous, nor is it complicated. Once the question is put and the decision commanded, any third option—silence, indecision—is merely an illusion, to be dispelled by a torture that is not at all a figment. And then the question is put again. I who have lost so many, to come so far, for all I claimed to care for—is it all to end here in a battle that cannot be won? Recant or refuse, a simple dilemma but the true one. I know this in my heart. What is it I cling to?

It is only a gesture.

I may never hear the exact charges I am convicted of, but heresy is not always punishable by death—the unrepentant are. A statement of error: brief, no longer than a sentence. If I cannot resolve this, compose it—now, in my mind—the choice will be made and the sentence written for me. The outcome is not in doubt. And if I am to find a way forward, I can only hope I find it in choosing to look back. For if it is to some fable of truth itself that I still cling, or to a sentence spelling ruin in a child's anagram, if I am to rewrite it, there is one journey to be made again, to a place where the paths begin and to a moment where they intersect.

On the landing above the canal Uncle Juan said good-bye and sent his respects to my mother. I did not trust myself to answer. He apologized for María and Magda, asked when I would be returning. I did not know how long it would be. The boatman pushed off. We were soon out of the canals and out on the lake. Flotsam and deadheads bobbed at the surface. Most of the streams and rivers feeding the lake had been in flood. The sun was briefly out, and hot, thinning the mists that lay in the valleys. I had hardly slept the night before, and through drowsy lids thought I saw a seal ahead of the canoe. Then two, which could not of course be seals. Two . . . three . . . six . . . The canoe surged powerfully under me with each paddle stroke. The sun was warm. Into my mind swam the sea calves of Proteus and among them Menelaus, disguised in sealskins on the shore of Egypt. Homecomings . . . how long had he been away from Sparta, and Odysseus from Ithaca? Little shards of sun glinted on the water.

It was mid-morning of the second day as we entered the highest valley. The lower slopes were shrouded in a drab mist—shifting, softening landmarks. The young ox driver grew more animated, asked a hundred questions. He had never been so close to the mountains. As we turned off the main road onto the track running up to the hacienda I looked back, though I knew there were no other turn-offs to mistake ours for. And yet while the landscape had seemed changed, it began to seem as though the changes its tenants had made had somehow never taken. There were no workers in the orchards. Close beside the road the plots of tomato and squash had been ploughed under and no one worked there.

We rolled over the brook and past the sentry box. The black cedar shingles on the house faintly glowed with pale green moss. Around back, the cart pulled to a stop. The mist had begun to clear. The cone of Popocatépetl floated above the earth upon a plane of white billows stretching south. In the calm air a white plume of steam went up as if pouring through an inverted funnel, an upturned hourglass of cloud. Fresh snow gleamed in the sun like fields of white obsidian. I got down, stiff, hesitant. . . .

Up on those slopes is a place with a waterfall, and a rooster tail of water bursting from a dry rock face. But for all its beauty it is not Ixayac I would give the most to visit again for an hour, nor even our library, but a shady spot at the base of a giant cedar among the pines. On the banks of the river Panoya, between the cornfield and the plot of maguey. In hindsight it is not always from the highest point that one sees farthest. From here one sees the orchards and the green rows of vegetables, the house itself with its watchtower and chapel, the corrals and the mountains, the windmills, and in the mind's eye at least, the trout pool and the waterfalls of Ixayac.

And here, next to the granite cross, was a place in which to have solved some of the mysteries that had always surrounded me. And who is to say that my destiny—a butterfly pursued as by a toddler—would not have altered its course? Solving one of these at eleven I might have refused to leave my real and true half-sister in Panoayan and, like my mother, never left for Mexico in spite of all my plans. Solving it at fifteen, when I returned to find Amanda gone, I might have set out to pursue her through the wilds of the New World as the nun-ensign would surely have done.

But for clues, it is to the objects spread before me in the shade of that tree I look now, more carefully than at fifteen when in my distraction I felt more than saw them. Corncob doll. Bird's nest lined with a blue-green down. Cornflower crown, pressed between the leaves of an old book. The beginnings of my first collection. They were never mementoes, nor did that collection, so much grown, ever serve me in this way. It is closer to the truth to say that I had carried them back home from Mexico as keepsakes, or as evidence against an accusation, though I cannot say what charge I most feared—of having forsaken the past, perhaps, or of emptiness itself. I had *not* forgotten, but had carried them away precisely so I would not have to remember.

Here it is tempting to see so many lines converging and patterns laid. A wedding tree and a turtle pail, a shady spot in which to sit with Amanda, and to read from Ecclesiastes and the poet Manrique, on the day I first met Magda.

Of Necessity, the imagination of the ancient Greeks fashioned a net, of Fate, a thread. Then what is Destiny?—of the many riddles I'd set myself as a child, this was one of the earliest. And to this, I did arrive at a solution of sorts. If fate is a thread, necessity a net, then a destiny must be found in the weave, in the gaps between. So it seems I have not come so very far since then. It would be better to remember this from now on. Had I done so earlier, it might have come to me why I found Gutiérrez sympathetic from the start—though the rodent chin was but the faintest hint, for in fact my grandfather's chin was quite prominent. But each had a habit when amused of scratching at the beard below it, and Abuelo's had once, very long ago, been more red than grey. And if any of what Magda has said is true, there were other things too that might have occurred to me, about my own family, the secrecy in which my uncle's parents lived, my grandfather's friendship with them; and to ask what my mother and María knew about the secret poetry of his heart, and the language it was written in.

So if anything was to prove fateful, it was my resolution, leaving Panoayan, never again to look back, at the age of fifteen.

So many fine reasons I had found for this in the works of the famous poets and philosophers. *Life is an ever-living fire kindling in measures, being extinguished in measures.* Heraclitus. Nothing lasts, says the poet Manrique, and all our lives flow to the sea that is death, such that we may wonder if the past ever was. But it was the story of the poet Orpheus that exerted the decisive influence, for it was precisely by looking back that he had lost the one thing most precious to him.

Here. If there is an answer, still some way out, it is here.

The convent chaplain's visit this morning brings it back, my doubts, how frail my defences and all my resolutions seem. He had gone to the cathedral for me, to learn what he could about the new developments Bishop Maldonado had warned of. A warning now confirmed. It continues to be harder with friends, harder to pretend. After Vespers Antonia comes into my room and asks me to go for a walk with her. It is so hot, she says casually. It *is* hot, the heat of mid-summer, and before May is fully out. I am about to suggest it would be cooler in here, but relent and get up from the table at the window.

Down in the courtyard the heat radiates from every stone and column. Down here, at least, one does not smell the canals: a light breeze agitates the smoke of a dozen fires. It is too hot to eat inside. Tables of different heights and sizes have been laid under the trees around the fountain. As we cut across the patio Antonia shifts to that side as though to guard me. I am not sure she even notices. Most of the women have finished eating, the servants moving among them clearing, the young girls chasing each other about, playing at hopscotch, skipping. Strumming a *vihuela* quietly by the water is a girl I recognize. She could not have been more than five or six at the time but was soon good at her scales. Wearing the habit of a postulant now. Our path takes us quite near.

"Sor Juana."

Others glance up. Nuns, novices. Not all the looks are hostile. Some sympathetic, a smile or two.

"Sor Juana."

"Sor Juana."

"*Dando un paseo, Sor Juana. . . .*"

"*¡Qué calor de infierno! eh Sor Juana?*"

I say to Antonia they should not be calling me that. I am a novice now.

"Of course you are."

I see she is taking me to another part of the convent, through a long arched passageway that leads from the patio. At the end of it the orchards and gardens stand off to one side. A breeze blows here, gains strength as we advance. All down the passageway, along the ledges, clay vessels of water stand; from the ceiling hang water bags for cooling. Simple convection—cool orchard air rushing through to replace the hot, rising from the patio. It is as if, just ahead, someone has opened a door onto the sea.

An arch of soft light before us, more light behind, in the passageway it is all but dark. I pause a moment, to stand in the breeze, lift the rough woollen cowl from my neck. "These things are itchy in the heat. I'd forgotten."

Wordlessly Antonia turns to take the lid from a large clay jar sweating on the ledge, lifts back the cowl from my head, sprinkles cool water over my scalp. In three months the hair has come back slowly, straight, black, like bristles.

"I feel like a porcupine."

"You look like one."

"You're one to talk. Take yours off."

Swiftly she stoops to lift the hem of her shift, stops at her thighs. A few years ago, the faint light of the patio well behind us, she would not have stopped at a threat. I reach up to remove her headpiece. She inclines her head. I free her hair.

It is like a roper's workshop, little finger-length drills and twists of cord. On tiptoe now, I reach up slowly to take down a smaller water jar and in one motion pour it over her head. She gasps. I feel her strong hands at my wrists, watch coils and rills spin from her hair to fall against the light.

"Where are you taking me, 'Tonia?"

"It's a surprise."

"So was that."

"So we're even."

"I'm not very good with surprises today."

It is not too dark to see the change in her expression. "Of course—I'm sorry."

"No . . . it's just this heat."

"I'm taking you to Vanessa and Concepción for supper."

I know it is not the whole surprise, and that it has to do with the chaplain's news, but I had been afraid she was taking me to the locutories. It is not a question of trust. The dread is never far.

"Show me your herb garden while you dry off." I need a moment, and the detour I know will please her. It is where she grows the herbs and essences she puts in our baths. "If we go to those two like this, who knows what pranks we'll put them up to."

We skirt the edge of the orchard along the infirmary wall, faint grey, texture of muslin. The branches nearest us are heavy with blossoms. Something is always in bloom. Now it is the pomegranates. After the herb garden we take the long way around, drawing out the hour, before the quarrel we each know is coming starts up again. Plots of beans and squash, *jícama* and *chayote*, past the trellises. I do not know how to say good-bye. But for weeks I have been trying to persuade her to leave. I have some money put by for her and for my nieces, an attachment on the convent accounts. It is not an inconsiderable amount. I have shown her the location of the codicil in the archives, and though she did not want to listen, made her promise at least to inform my nieces of its existence, in the event I should be taken.

We turn at the water tank below the windmill on the roof, blades spinning, water knifing from a clay pipe angled just over the surface, the tank nearly filled.

She must see that it is more difficult for me that they can still threaten her here. Can I not see, she's asked in return, how cruel it is to say this when I know she is not leaving? No what was cruel was the delusion we could be happy here. There is nothing here for her—there is nothing for her anywhere *else*. But that is no reason—it *is*, but I'm not listening. We could start again in secret. No, she has her own vocation to follow now. Then name a better place for a woman to write poetry than here—certainly not the house she came from.

But we do not continue. The evening is warm, the first stars are out, and Venus and a sliver of moon. Bats flit through the branches, their cries a glimmer of sound less heard than imagined. And so I walk in the quiet with my not quite sister, not quite daughter, barefoot in the soft, deep earth, sandals in one hand. Left again at the chapel wall, past the refectory, toward the kitchens. Vanessa's slim form in the doorway. Concepción's round bulk appearing behind her.

It has been thirty years since my carriage ride with Magda, thirty-eight since the hex in the classroom of Sister Paula, thirty-nine since my father left us. I have resented, hated, then feared the Holy Office of the Inquisition for almost a lifetime, even it seems before I knew what it was, and even now I suspect I may yet find new reasons why. But it seems that there are times when to look back is to see more clearly ahead, for precisely there, where Magda and I neared the end of our first and final journey together, I see another about to begin. A cortège, duly consecrated at the rose-coloured church, sets out from the Plaza de Santo Domingo. In all, four outriders, a wagon and a carriage whose coat of arms bears a rough wooden cross that matches the banner above the iron gates through which the convoy departs. In the wagon, otherwise empty for the outward passage, are implements for digging. In one of the trunks lashed to the carriage roof is a quantity of *sambenitos*. Inside the carriage will be at least one senior official of the Inquisition. I cannot prevent myself imagining it to be Dorantes, though I have never seen him. But Magda I see clearly enough. And over the past few days and nights, her journey is like a waking dream.

The holy officers with their shovels and *sambenitos* will not be embarking from Mexico in canoes as I did. But departing from the village on the far shore, where the deadheads lie high on the strand—dry now amidst the flood wrack—the path is the same. There is only one way for carriages and carts to take. At this time of year they should have no trouble fording the river at Mexicaltzingo, to arrive in Chalco by nightfall. Even setting out well before dawn, the cortège will not enter the highest valley before mid-morning. When they turn off the main road, they will be heading east, the mountains towering high above, seeming almost to lean down over the path. Beyond the oaks along it lie orchard rows. Apples and mangoes, peaches, pomegranates. By mid-day the first rays of the sun reach this side of the hacienda, with its square watchtower on the north. And in the watchtower a little bronze cannon. If the day is clear, the sun strikes a stained-glass rosette set high in the chapel face, and in the rosette the image of the angel Uriel framed in gold. It was my grandfather's idea that should the little cannon fail, the hacienda should be defended by a higher, purer fire.

My grandfather's first child was born here at the hacienda, and here she was baptized, Isabel. So it is here that the first of the *sambenitos* is to be raised, up behind the glass, to take the light. And as with the firstborn, so it shall be done with my aunts, and finally a *sambenito* will be hung in the church in Chimalhuacan where I had my baptism. But there is other work to do here first, once the outriders have unloaded the digging implements.

Recant or refuse. Choose well, choose carefully. The letters are the same, but the sentence now is changed. Recant, and protect the place while betraying its spirit. Refuse, and preserve an idea of justice but see its site desecrated. It is not a dilemma to be solved by a simple defiance. I have come back for a clue, a way to relinquish a fable of truth that once lived here, or that I brought back with me at fifteen. Perhaps I am to find it in a story I ignored then, for I had not let the Poet himself have his say.

When the enchantress Circe sent Homer's Odysseus into the underworld to know his fate—if he would ever make his way back to Ithaca—she gave precise instructions. Beyond the stream of Oceanus, which forms the outermost limits of the living world, they would find a level shore. Enter Hades' house by the groves of Persephone. *To call the one you* seek, the blind seer of Thebes, you must sacrifice a black ram there at the entrance and fill bowls for the bloodthirsty shades who assuredly will come. Odysseus was to stand just within the gates, the ram's head facing into the Underworld. But as the beast's throat was slit, he was to cast his eyes back, to Oceanus. *Don't look back* is not the injunction of poets, but against one poet by the Judges of the Dead.

After the meal under the trees outside the refectory, as Antonia and I are making ready to leave, comes the moment for the surprise I have been expecting. With a nod at Vanessa, Concepción disappears inside, to return a moment later with it held out solemnly before her: a candle easily the thickness of her wrist and the length of her forearm. To cover my emotion I ask what such a thing could be for, a sure occasion for the sort of ribaldry Concepción tries to shock us with. But the two of them are as solemn as children with a handmade gift—and this gift they have made for me themselves.

"Madre Juana is permitted a candle a week," Concepción offers. Clearly they have heard something of the chaplain's news. Knowing them to be my friends, perhaps he has told them, to make me see sense. They are trying to keep me from giving up.

Vanessa too has rehearsed an offering. "Maybe now, Juana, you'll take the time to learn Basque."

"How far is Concepción ahead of me?"

"Leagues."

"For Madre Juana we can make one bigger next week."

"No this will be big enough. I don't think Basque so difficult."

I am eager to be away. We say our good-nights. There is no mistaking Antonia's elation. I am regretting not having pursued our quarrel in the orchard, now to have to dash her hopes. She carries the candle for me like a spear or a standard clutched in her fist, a gesture of defiance to a patio almost deserted; the women are preparing for Compline.

"You could carry that more discreetly."

She begins to ask how it would look to be caught with it underneath . . . then sees that I am serious. I tell her that nothing has changed, that what I said was for Vanessa. For Vanessa, she says, but not for her.

"No 'Tonia, you don't understand."

She detests hearing this from me. By the time we reach the cell we are each close to saying things we would regret, and are fortunate to be called by the bells to prayer. She argues now with a kind of desperation, perhaps senses that tonight will be her last chance. What can I still find to say to help her now, how will I explain? It is not so much giving her reasons to leave, but to convince her that she leaves for the right reasons. Once, I had been more persuasive.

The vigil after prayer is less bloodthirsty than it can be. It is too hot for the extremities of piety. Our argument is not long in starting up when we return—I am barely halfway up the steps. It is Antonia who has found a new tack. She agrees to leave—but only if I will. An opening that permits her to take up all the past weeks' arguments in reverse and turn my own against me. We should be at it most of the night. And so, although she has been accusing me of being cruel to drive her away, it is only tonight that I explain what Bishop Maldonado was anxious to make clear, that my hatred of the Holy Office risks blinding me to the more immediate and perhaps greater danger: an ecclesiastical tribunal, its rules of evidence and procedures entirely at the discretion of the convening bishop, or in this case, archbishop. Unlike the Holy Office, the Archbishop has little in the way of contacts or reputation to cultivate across Europe, so the Inquisitors here are pleased to allow His Grace to take the lead, and will limit themselves initially to deposing evidence. Only after what remains of my own reputation has been destroyed will the Inquisition instigate its own proceedings. It is the tribunal's composition that Archbishop Aguiar summoned Bishop Maldonado from Oaxaca to discuss. His Grace wants one judge of the *Audiencia*, to represent the Crown, and wants Church representation at the level of bishop and provincial, particularly since His Grace hopes evidence will be heard that implicates a bishop. Maldonado's cold relations with the Bishop of Puebla make him a leading candidate but as my friend hastened to add, they have also given him leeway to decline.

The tribunal will be constituted to investigate errors of doctrine, insubordination, alleged violations of the nun's vows and the holy sacraments, but also—and most worrisome to my friend Maldonado— accusations of secular and political abuses committed within the walls of a holy sanctuary. What sort of abuses? I wondered. In such times as these, he said, hints of sedition are heard with the same hostility as is the mere suggestion that the Crown has ever been susceptible to private influence. Surely a rarity, I put in, the tribunal constituted to hear, in the same proceeding, not just charges of sedition but also the peddling of influence. A point Bishop Maldonado willingly conceded, to make his own: The Crown, too, will be pleased to let the Archbishop proceed. Evidence, grievances, denunciations of every possible stripe will be entertained—and what will emerge, as much as any particular crime or sin, is a portrait.

And so, I tell Antonia, whatever my success against the other charges, breaking my vow of enclosure is the one I would find impossible to contest.

"Only if you're caught—we could just disappear."

"I can disappear in here, 'Tonia."

"No, Juana. You only think that."

I answer that the threat of an ecclesiastical trial is what Núñez holds in reserve. He too is fond of surprises. So I have become cruel, it seems.

Maldonado insists Núñez is my only chance. For while Núñez cannot claim to control the Inquisition, he holds sway over the Archbishop. It cannot be stopped once begun. A general confession is the one way to keep it from starting. Bishop Maldonado seems to know nothing about the manuscripts of Manuel de Cuadros.

Mail is lighter than plate, but stronger only if it can be made more supple. There are so many unknowns. Does Núñez control Magda, or only think he does, or pretend to, and what if Dorantes in the meanwhile finds the very manuscript I only pretend to have, or hope to? And what if I cannot manoeuvre Núñez into betraying what it contains before he detects that I do not have it? And what of Panoayan? For unless I learn to play at his game more deftly than I so far have, and unless Fortune takes a friendlier hand, the ways of the false dilemma and the true lead to the same terminus, and the shades and judges of the dead will have their bowls of blood. Down the path of confession it is Núñez who waits at the pyre to extract my contrition. Down the path of defiance it is Dorantes, with Núñez lashed beside me. The paths are not separate. For one way or the other Magda would have her chapter—and while I may succeed in destroying Núñez, it is a resolution—even should my courage not fail me—not a *solution*, not an escape. At the end, Manuel de Cuadros did not escape his fate, and far braver than I, could not even cling to his defiance, but changed his mind before the brushwood even fully caught fire. If I am to go there, at least let me have found one resolution I can keep.

For himself, Núñez *has* a solution—more dangerous than if I had collapsed, yet a path with at least one acceptable outcome. For once I have submitted myself to his power and protection, if it seems I have evidence that may be used against him, it is within the setting of an ecclesiastical trial that he can have the Archbishop negotiate immunities with an Inquisitor General pleased to let His Grace take the lead. And then Núñez will have solved, once and for all, the problem of the missing manuscripts.

I have shared no more of this than I thought strictly necessary to persuade Antonia. But it is myself I have thought to spare most of all, for it can be more disturbing to see her frightened than to face some things myself . . . she has been my Camilla. She was upset, pale, but on the whole I thought she had taken it well. On even this subject I can be persuasive after all. But well after Matins, when I think she has surely fallen asleep, she comes upstairs in her nightdress to see the new candle. I am caught, sitting at the table by the bed. The flame flutters lightly next to the window open to the west. For the breeze I have left the door open on the upstairs colonnade over the patio.

We talk quietly for a moment or two. She seems tired. There is not much fight left in those hazel eyes. But as she turns to go she looks at my hands and asks if I am starting a new collection. Her face is drawn, the faint white scar from eye to mouth more noticeable. She does not wait to hear my answer.

Good-night, Antonia.

Through the room moves the scent of flowers from the trees by the fountain and the smell of horses from the corrals to the south. I look out over the Merced canal, low now, a solitary canoe slipping under the Monzón bridge, rippling the quarter moon. The dry season is ending. With a little rain, but not too much—one hesitates to ask—and cooler days, the smell rising from the canal will not be so bad. There is a young family on the upper floor of the old house across the street. I think they have just moved here too. I will have to ask one of the sisters on this side. The flower market below is interesting to watch. Funerals, festivals, young lovers. The time, long or short, will pass quickly enough.

With the idle hands that are a source of such anxiety here and new hope to Antonia, I have fashioned from common garden clay a puzzle much as I made once as a girl. The puzzle offers a test of dexterity. The object is to roll a small clay ball, against its natural inclination to fall, up the spiral. A simple spiral tower in miniature, modelled on a diagram of such a puzzle from the territory of Persia. I believe, somewhere in that land I shall not see, one may make a pilgrimage to climb the spiral ramps of temples following this design. Nothing is easier to build, nothing is harder to climb. I climb it now.

Such rousing contortions—such hip sways, such elbow fluxions and wrist rolls. Then as now, just such were mine, that day in the shady spot by the granite cross in Panoayan, as I gave myself over to the puzzles that cannot be solved—or if they can, not with hand and eye but heart and soul. Where I tried so hard not to choose by choosing . . . everything.

Then, failing, I had thought to put all such childish notions out of my mind. Now it seems incredible that I thought it all behind me. The riddles and puzzles, the alphabets and anagrams, the forms hidden in the land, the house divided against itself, the wars of the past. The lost ages of Man. And I would not have liked to think—no, not at all—that the destiny I had always looked forward to could be woven merely of these, of such emblems and patterns and habits of mind. Just behind me.

Refuse or recant, erasure or silence. Consider well, choose carefully. Perhaps one begins to answer by wondering if it's been a mistake to think such puzzles only childish things and by asking if the Persians were so very different, and if their spiral temples were only for children.

Down by the river Panoya, windmill blades turn sleepily like pinwheels on a breeze. The shadow of a cedar branch nods over the arm of a granite cross. The sun's warmth lays a soft sash across my back. Over at the water troughs, the driver stirs, wakes from his nap under the ox cart. A cluster of fresh-picked wildflowers leans against the cross beside me. Beyond it, I notice a clump of weeds, freshly pulled up. The long mound of earth is pocked, subsided in places like bread left out in the rain, like an old hut covered in sod. A green rabbit satchel lies at my knees, its contents spread out among the cones and dried needles before me.

I take up an old book. With a forefinger I bend the corner of a page. It arches like a cat stretching after a nap, trembles in the slight breeze and tugs at me, a sail eager to be launched. At the outer edge of the maguey field a movement catches my eye, my mother's chestnut mare spinning out trains of dust behind her.

I no longer believe it is fate that brings us to meet here, or not fate in the way I had once understood it, but it is a moment of decision. For Amanda and me it may already have been too late: the nun-ensign did not always triumph. And in spite of everything that went wrong between us, everything we needed to know had been there all along. Amanda and

I were *cuates, cuates* were enough.[40] Nor is it any longer so clear that the destiny I chased was so unlike the fate I did too little to help her escape.

Perhaps the two things are only the same—one we see in looking ahead, with hope, the other in looking back.

I feel a kind of peace, letting my eyes wend and stumble in the way of bees over a field of wildflowers—bumbling comets trailing pollen—who in their windings weave a fine canopy of yellow muslin against the sun. The weight in my lap is a comfort. The book, mildewed and waterlogged, opens to where it always does. And yet now I read in the shapes arrayed about me that the keepsakes were not precisely evidence, or not only that—not proof that I had not forsaken the past. Not evidence against a charge, but charms in a magic against loss itself.

And for this, for us, it is still not too late. Mother passes quite near, riding hard. Her hair and the horse's long tail run together on the wind gusts, like rain driven through a fountain. The ox cart rattles and groans along the side of the house.

What has changed is not so much the evidence but that I let myself remember it. I have heard her sing to Diego's baby. I know this voice, and that it is not only Xochitl who has sung for me in the night. *My father's granddaughters* . . . I have heard this, too, such an odd way of putting things. I have the fresh flowers at my side, the fresh-picked weeds. It was my mother who chose this spot for him because I could not bear to choose. Even angry and hurt I knew she had chosen perfectly. If there has been a piece of evidence still lacking, it is perhaps knowing a little more of how a woman can need a man, and the need to be fearless to make another proud. And now I have my letter back from Uncle Juan. The swarm of thoughts, the memories that have returned me here, even as they had once driven me down from Ixayac, ease . . . Past the sentry box the spokes falter and at the grassy stream, almost stop. The driver snaps the traces twice down hard on the oxen's backs. The Inquisition cortège waits for it to cross. The wagon staggers on, makes its laggard way over the bridge. No, for this, it is not too late. And for us, that moment is now.

I gather up my things. I get to my feet.

I go into the house . . . to discover some small part of what my mother knew of love.

Brother Francisco Manuel de Cuadros came to the locutory only once, a few months before his arrest. Carlos had given me some warning of what to expect. They had not seen each other for almost five years. He was small even next to Carlos as they came in, Carlos in black, he in his faded brown cassock, ragged with the quantity of its mendings and his poverty. Fine sandy hair, what little hair he had, scorched white at the tips, his skin mottled by the sun. The impression that has lingered was of sand— the hair, the skin, the cassock lightened by the elements. Carlos had been shocked by the change in him. I remember his quiet, the slight tremor in his hands. But perhaps Carlos meant the eyes, a colour one would have said once blue, as of an unclouded sky whitened ahead of a dust storm or fire. Or this is how I remember them now.

He and his fellow Franciscans had been two years among the Maya, earning their trust before being allowed to meet the priests of Votan. "It was an archive," he said quietly. "Thousands and thousands of manuscripts. Like those we know here, but more detailed, more intricate, as if the work of great painters, but these were painting canvasses of text. Speaking figures. . . ." It took two more years to learn the basis of reading them. "It felt like watching not just all of a literature but all of an art burn at once."

His whitened eyes in the mottled face had a staring quality even when averted. The painted books piled in the square in Valladolid had been like a small mountain, a pyramid. He had broken faith with his order and hidden a hundred, for what use was the science of reading them if there were no books to practise it upon. But choosing them had proven worse than watching them burn.

After the Franciscan's death, and when it seemed at last safe for Carlos to make his way back to the city, he and I vowed to each other that should any of those manuscripts ever come into our hands we would defend them with our lives. It was twenty years ago. We were younger. It was an emotional time.

During most of that visit Fray de Cuadros had kept his eyes just slightly down, as if something moved on the floor behind me. I am accustomed to such things in one form or other. They all perhaps learn this at seminary. But I was sure then it was neither in fear nor in distaste, as I like now to think it was not in shame. It seems to me tonight that simply because Manuel de Cuadros expressed contrition as the smoke was rising to his eyes, this does not mean, after all, that he did not keep to some secret decision or pledge. I cannot know what it was, but I like to imagine that for him too there was a place that had inspired it. A place from his youth, or somewhere in the mountains of the south, a waterfall, a village of faces, a text on the wall of a ruin.

But a resolution made in strength and not against himself.

There are two small crosses now at the base of the cedar tree. The cross of granite I have seen, the one of obsidian I have only pictured there. Even five years ago, though I had a bishop's dispensation to go, I did not see why I should, with everything I had loved there gone. The site I chose because she chose it for him. And because it is the place I would choose also for myself. It is a place where with every step you take, you walk in halls of jade.

But the stone—this I chose for her. A stone that is also a glass. It is one of an uncommon beauty, native to our region. We do not always get good-bye.

Among the last of the shades to come to the bowls was Achilles. There, Odysseus began to sing his praises, of his fame among the living and the glorious fashion of his death, but Achilles silenced him, with this: It were better to serve as slave to the poorest of the Living than rule as king among the Dead. *Recant.* And yet, as I turn this puzzle in my hands, I wonder if I have returned to relinquish a notion that I have too long held, or just perhaps, to detect the fable in theirs.

At the margins of the living world there is a secret spring, the origin of all things, and some have called it Oceanus. And Oceanus . . . the ocean river that forms the outermost rim of Achilles' shield, flows in reverse. One does not look back leaving Hell. But being there, one looks back if one ever hopes to emerge.

And among all the living, the one Achilles looked to was Odysseus, for news of his son.

Erasure or silence, defiance or submission. There are puzzles to which the hardest answers last, the earliest endure. At Xochitl's knee I had once learned that Time itself could be looked upon as a spiral. Hold it up, turn it in the hand. Time as a spiral, memory as a cutting plane: the truths it reveals follow from where and how one begins. Roll the ball up the spiral again: the sum of all possible angles is as true as a fable, but the One Truth in the sum is not for the reckoning of Man. Much is lost upon us, a few things remain. Remember these—with pleasure, remember again . . . my mother firing off an arquebus during a jaguar attack in the dead of night . . . the angels in the library. And there was a moment after a dinner, when together we almost laughed.

As it is with magic charms, so is it also with good-byes. Or with refusing even choice itself, so as not to lose the path not taken. But if I have not lost him, and not lost them, it is not because there is something I have not let the holy officers strip from me, or even because the sod remains undisturbed in a shady spot beneath a cedar tree. We do not always get good-bye, but moments such as these. And who is to say if Time itself can take these back from me.

Heraclitus has written that one never enters the same river twice. But the greatest of rivers and the smallest streams share a destiny, however obscure it may remain as they run to the sea. Though their currents be muddy or clear, shallow or deep, though they run swift in the shadow of their *rives*, yet do they bear up, in the trains of their passing, gold and ochre and russet leaves. To spin slowly, dreamily, on their surfaces.

And even as the Nile brings the cargo of her seasons in tribute to the sea, these, all these have come down to me through the intervening years, and down through this night . . . as afterthoughts.

It is almost light, the square of sky pales beyond the window. Beneath it on the table, my collection of two. The newest, the most ancient; the oldest, the first. One I have made with my hands. The other I have brought from the convent archives. A battered book, the husk of its bindings split. I take it into my lap one last time before returning it to its hiding place in the shelves. I close my eyes. . . .

What is a childhood but the end of all past times forgotten, beginning again? And to leave the highlands of childhood for the valleys and currents of one's own time is to lose something akin to prescience, to lose sight of the far ranges at our life's end. Now I cannot see ahead an hour and yet, looking back, how curious to remember, only now, the place where I was born at the hacienda in Nepantla: the gaps in the walls, the breezes blowing through, the stars . . . a hut of pale fieldstone that the people of our region sometimes called the cell. Remember with pleasure, remember it all again, for yourself, remember for them.

More than by the little of the world I knew, my mind has been shaped by books. So it is not so strange that I had come to think of my own life as a book, strongly bound, beautifully made. I had never doubted I would find there my legend and my destiny, and even if its end escaped me until the last page, the last day, I had never doubted it would on that day feel necessary, even familiar, the page already marked. And though I now see at last the briefest glimpses of that text, its language I know well. I learned it as a child. A broken book is still a book. To be mistaken in this is to make of it another kind of destiny, to succumb to the patterns already woven there, even of broken threads. Or, I had thought them broken, but the body offers up its own evidence. For as night ends, I feel that ache even now, so fresh . . . and in my legs, a honey-gold thread of pain.

What is the path that is no path, to an end that is a return? Each time without precedent, to an embrace that is a relinquishment.

What is the collection that cannot be taken, the text that cannot be erased? The silence that cannot be broken.

In the silence in the darkness there is a spiral stair. It leads up and out and into the night, where at a crossroads in the desert, at a secret spring, an unknown god waits, hidden even as the soul is from itself.

And offers us water.

But here I let fall the invocations of the famous poets, the herbs and the potions, the magics, the charms and enchantments, the brilliant feasts and the sable rams. And this last charm with the battered spine, which has been my life, this too do I lay aside. For there is other work, and it will soon be light.

To this alone do I commend me.
This alone do I invoke,
truly,
that in a world of living,
this world knew not
its deity.

IN THE YEAR 1 REED, it is told, the precious twin came down to live among the people of the centre, he who would one day be called Our Dear Prince Topiltzin 1-Reed Quetzalcoatl.

In that time they say the manner of his coming was a thing of great wonder; wondrous and mysterious was his advent. His mother, LadySerpentSkirt, lay dreaming. Dreaming of her king and husband, Mixcoatl, doing battle in the west. And in that dream he sent her an emerald. She woke to find it on her tongue.

Waking she swallowed it.

For four years did Topiltzin grow within her like a promise. For four more did he struggle to come forth. But when at last he had succeeded, when at last he had broken free of her she was already dead.

As though he were her own, another serpent raised him. And though he could not know it yet, she raised him an orphan: for in the night of his mother's dreaming, his father had died in the western desert, betrayed by his brothers. So also was Topiltzin called Son of the Lord of the Dead Lands.

Came the years 2 Flint, 3 House, 4 Rabbit; 5 Reed, 6 Flint, 7 House, 8 Rabbit; 9 Reed.

In the year 9 Reed, Prince Topiltzin asked to know his father. *What did he look like, who did he resemble? What was the manner of his passing? Where is he buried?* But in that time no one could answer him. Then did he set forth into the western deserts, asking on the road for news of the King. So it was that he came to be known in the West as Nacxitl, the Traveller.

Came the years 10 Flint, 11 House, 12 Rabbit; 13 Reed, 1 Flint, 2 House, 3 Rabbit; 4 Reed, 5 Flint, 6 House, 7 Rabbit; 8 Reed, 9 Flint.

In the year 9 Flint in the depths of despair in the heart of the desert he was found by a vulture. Taking pity she showed him how to open the earth and find the bones where the King's brothers had heaped them with sand.

And terrible was the vengeance Our Prince wrought upon his uncles.

Yet returning he discovered himself twice an orphan; returning he discovered the Serpent Woman dead. And so her bones he buried next to his father's in her temple on Serpent Mountain.

Back to the desert, to the land of the vulture did he take his grief and the guilt of his blood sins. And great was his penance. He bled his ears. He pierced his thighs with thorns, and the thorns he used were of jade-stone. For seven years he fasted. Nothing but earth did he eat. Terrible was his sorrow, pitiful his remorse as he cried out to the heart of heaven, to the Place of Duality.

And the heart of heaven heard him.

Nearby, upon the once great city of Tollan the weight of drought and famine had fallen, for great were the sins of its people. And though the priests of Tollan had sacrificed the four times four hundred captives that its warriors had taken, still did the drought continue—the famine spread like a stain unabated, even unto the nobles of the city.

And so in the year 5 House, the nobles sent for him, asking that he rule over them and restore Tollan to its former greatness. But only when the sacrifices of the captives had ceased, when their cooking pots had been overturned and their shinbones buried did Our Prince agree to enter the city.

Came the years 6 Rabbit, 7 Reed; 8 Flint, 9 House, 10 Rabbit, 11 Reed; 12 Flint, 13 House, 1 Rabbit, 2 Reed.

During that time did Tollan grow prosperous once again, and flowers returned to the land of the Toltecs. The fruit of the cacao was everywhere plentiful and the cotton grew already tinted—they had no need to dye it. Easily did Our Prince enter the bowels of the earth and bring forth what many before him had sought: emeralds and jade, gold and silver, amber and turquoise. And truly was he a great artisan, truly did the grandeur of the Toltecs return with him: first, he made the sacred calendar that measures the gaits of the gods in their passage, that charts the stars in their courses; then the painted books, and the precious featherwork and pottery, the fine working of metal and stone. A great builder, in the heart of Tollan did he build his round palace of jade and turquoise, his palace of redshell and whiteshell and bone, his house of penance. And he lived there alone. For though he had brought the Toltecs art and knowledge and plenty, though he was worshipped as one worships a god, yet was he strict in his observances, severe in his fasting, and his penance was harsh.

In the year 3 Flint, Tezcatlipoca descended to earth and sent sorcerers to plague Our Prince in Tollan.

Came the years 4 House, 5 Rabbit, 6 Reed; 7 Flint, 8 House; 9 Rabbit, 10 Reed, 11 Flint.

All the statues the Toltecs had raised in his honour the sorcerers toppled. Our Prince's sacred mirror of augury they stole. In his house of penance they beleaguered him. They mocked him for the meagreness of his offerings to the gods—only the sacrifice of serpents and birds and butterflies would he permit. They mocked the poverty of his fasts.

For nine years did they bait and taunt him, commanding him to return to the harvest of the precious eagle fruit, but Our Dear Prince resisted. Out of love for the Toltecs came his refusal, for the people were precious to him and he to the people.

And the sorcerers grew angrier.

So it happened, so it came to pass that resisting the sorcerers for so long had filled Our Prince with a great weariness. Less and less often did he leave his house of penance to walk among the people. Tired and solitary, he fell ill, he grew feverish. The Toltecs were troubled and uncertain for he appeared greatly aged.

Came the year 12 House. Came the season when the people of Tollan made preparations for the Feast of Toxcatl, for the twenty days of feasting and pleasure, for the time when DrumCoyote came to walk among them, came to lead them in the dance. Then did all the sorcerers gather together with Tezcatlipoca and say: *Let us make pulque. Make him drunk with it. We will make him drink his health.* And they laughed, for they were playful.

For four days did they brew the *octli*, the sacred drink, and in only four days more they had decanted it and blended it with wild honey. In the body of an old woman came Tezcatlipoca to the palace of redshell and whiteshell, to Our Prince's house of beams. In the guise of a healer, SmokingMirror appeared to the palace guards, saying: *I bring strong food and drink to Our Prince that he may recover himself.*

And after he had eaten well of the spicy stew, the strong meat, Our Prince, feeling strength and also a great thirst, said: *Grandmother, what else have you brought, for before you came my flesh felt as though cut to ribbons.*

And the SmokingMirror answered: *I have laboured across a great distance to bring you pulque—taste it, it's strong, it's newly made.* She set it before him saying: *You will find it tempting. It will tempt you like your own fate.*

Only with the tip of his finger did he taste it, but the taste was good. And so she cajoled him to taste it four times, though only with a fingertip; but the fifth time, when she saw him drink deeply, she laughed harshly and said: *This shall be your sacrament, priest.*

Then did she make each of the palace guards drunk with just one taste of the *octli*. Returning to Our Prince where he lay on his mat of gold and feathers she showed him the smoking mirror and in its surface his sister, Quetzalpetlatl, fasting amidst flowers on the slopes of Iztaccihuatl. Among the priests of the Four Year Fast she fasted, and for three years she had tasted nothing but earth.

And she was beautiful.

Seeing her then in his drunkenness did Our Prince Topiltzin 1-Reed Quetzalcoatl send for his sister. PreciousFeatherMat sat beside him, and four times did he bid her taste the sacred *pulque*. And tasting it a fifth time, she too was besotted. No longer were they fasting, no longer forcing thorns through the flesh of their thighs. Never again would they bathe themselves in the Turquoise Waters.

As though in a dream he saw her; through mirror smoke he saw her and tried to approach in the manner of the CloudSerpent, his father, Mixcoatl. The first time his seed fell onto a rock and opened a hole in it. Laughing playfully she seemed to say: *Raise your aim, brother.* Into the hole in the rock she leapt and fled him. And into the Underworld as a bat he swooped down after her. The second time she appeared to him as a two-headed deer. As he drew near her the precious fluid of his body burst into flame. Laughing she leapt into the flames and fled him, and as a crippled dog he limped after her. The third time she stood and fought him. Fiercely she resisted him with her shield hand, and only after a great struggle did he finally possess her.

Through mirror smoke he first saw her; into mirror smoke she vanished, and this time he could not follow. On a mat of precious feathers she left him lying as though dead. . . .

Then over him did the sorcerers bend and hover, mocking and laughing, until Tezcatlipoca said: *Now, let us give him his body.*

Then the sorcerers woke him and made him gaze again into the SmokingMirror. And for the first time Our Prince saw himself horrible to look upon, body withered and crippled and palsied, skin covered with sores and yellowed, all wrinkled and sallow.

And his face was a pitiful thing, like a great stone battered, eyelids inflamed, one eye sprung from its orbit and ruptured.

Unable to look away from the SmokingMirror he cried: *Can this be, truly? Can this be what I resemble? Am I so vile—have I always been?*

But the sorcerers replied, ever playful: *These things, your youth and beauty and virtue, have only fled you. They can be recovered. Have faith.*

Fled where? Where am I to find them?

And the sorcerers answered him: *Toward Tlillan Tlapallan shall you go. A man stands guard there, one already aged. You and he shall take counsel together. And when you return you shall have again been made a child.*[41] *But go now and celebrate with your people.*

And even as they said this the sounds of a great drumming reached his ears. *But how can I go out among them like this? They will be terrified and run from me.*

But the sorcerers said, smiling: *Have we not come to help you?* And for him they made a turquoise mask. Finely wrought it was, and beautiful, with tracings of gold in the forehead, and topped with a crest of quetzal plumes. And red was the mouth and filled with fine, curving serpent's teeth.

Then in the SmokingMirror did he appear truly majestic, truly splendid, and his spirits were lifted, though only for the briefest of times, only for a brief moment did it last. For as he emerged to walk among his people his eyes were met with a scene of devastation.

Withered and blighted were the cacao trees, twisted and bent like mesquite. Blanched of its colours was the cotton. Gone, the precious birds. Filled with smoke lay the streets; heaped with corpses locked fiercely together were the temple precincts where Tezcatlipoca had raised the dancers in the palm of her hand and—sending them into a frenzy— danced them to death.

And when Our Prince had emerged from his round palace of shell and jade to see the ruin of the Toltecs, when he saw the horror loosed upon his people while he had lain gazing into the SmokingMirror, weltering in drunkenness and sin upon his mat of feathers, the spell was lifted; it faded like the memory of a dream.

Then in four hundred pieces did he smash the grinning turquoise mask—

To the sorcerers did he turn to wreak his vengeance—but they had vanished, leaving him to himself.

And the empty city, the dead streets echoed with the song of his lament:

She will nurse me no more,
She, my mother, an ya'!
She of the Serpent Skirt,
Ah, the holy one![42]

He who had produced so many great and beautiful works, who had brought to Tollan flowers and song, wisdom and knowledge, he who could trace each footprint of the gods through the heavens and through time itself, was now undone, now overthrown. Now only shame and misery, remorse and horror did he know.

And so it came to pass that he ordered his pages to construct him a stone casket, and closely did it fit him as he lay in it as though dead. For four days did he lie in his jewelled casket, waiting for death. And all who had fled the city returned at the news of his dying. But it was not yet time.

On the fourth day he arose and commanded his pages: *Bury all these vain treasures I have created—bury them somewhere deep in the earth or send them to the bottom of the Lake of Texcoco.* And they did what he had commanded.

Seeing him preparing his departure, the people cried out in despair: *Our Dear Prince, where are you going?*

The story of his journey into the East, the journey of Our Dear Prince Topiltzin 1-Reed Quetzalcoatl, has since been many times told. How he was attacked by sorcerers on the road. How he and his pages—dwarves with backs hunched and twisted—hid in the bowels of WhiteLady, and for four days and for four more struggled to find their way out again. How at last they emerged in a high mountain pass next to SmokingStone, where the dwarves and the hunchbacks were frozen.

How as Our Prince wept at the foot of a tree and his tears pierced the rock he sat upon, the sorcerers returned and challenged him—*Where are you going?*

How Our Prince answered: *The sun is calling me.*

How the sorcerers would not let him pass until he had surrendered to them all the precious Toltec arts.

How the Traveller wandered on alone.

Alone he arrived at the coast in a place called Coatzalcoalcos and mounting a litter of serpents, a serpent mat, he sailed east, he sailed towards the sun.

There as every child should know he arrived at last in Tlillan Tlapallan, the Red Land and Black, the place of burning, the place of knowledge and death. And there donning his precious feather cape, his wind jewels, his headdress of quetzal plumes did he cast himself into a great fire of his own making. The flames of his burning rose high to the first level of heaven—as a flight of precious birds, scarlet and blue, citron and ochre and vermilion they rose, even as the souls of painted books.

And after four days of burning, from the ashes ascended the heart of Quetzalcoatl, ascended the heart of the morning. Pure and splendid as fine beaten silver did MorningStar rise into the eastern sky. High in the heavens did it rise, into the ninth level of heaven. As Lord of the House of Dawn he rose, he who rises first in the red fields of combat to await the sun.

And every child should know of his promise to return to reclaim his place near the end of the world. And terrible shall be the manner of his coming.

And if he comes in 1 Reed, he strikes at kings.

In 1 Reed was he born, in 1 Reed did he die. And so for fifty-two years, for a bundle of years did he live among the people of the centre.

And this is the story of his coming and of his passing and of his return, in the time, in the year, 1 Reed.

Guided by a silent Clarion
along a path that is no path,
blundered across, stumbled upon,
in search of an end that has no end.

Jerome sat in contemplation of
the Trumpet of the Judgement,
but soon was troubled
to be hearing the very echo
of what he feared most;
and thus, pondering an event
to strike terror in the heart
of the most exalted Seraphim,
advanced a step, without moving,
guided by a silent Clarion.
    He walks toward that City
where his spirit dwells
in ardent Charity—
and though the road is unknown to him,
in truth God is the way—
and, in the manner of a pilgrim, spans
in one long peregrine flight,
the gulf from earth to Heaven
without ever losing his way,
along a path that is no path.

Leaving the track stained red—
holding his blood scant price
to have covered such terrain—
he came to be thought mad
and was subjected to brutal stonings . . .
these, the Holy Doctor answering:
—Since by an easy path
no one to heaven has ever ascended,
let none wonder it should at last have been
blundered across, stumbled upon.
That it comes to me by happy accident
dampens not the ardent
fire that enkindles my soul:
to find the end of my love's quest
in One who has no end.
Thus, eagerly do I go
spilling all of the carmine
that these veins enclose,
till now not a drop is left
in search of an End that has no end.

JUANA INÉS
DE LA CRUZ

B. Limosneros, trans.

Horus

You, Egypt is you, and you are its mask of gold . . .

PAUL VALÉRY

This is the patent age of new inventions,
for saving bodies, and for killing souls.

B. LIMOSNEROS

Contents

CONTENTS

You ARE HERE. You have taken a room near the Warren Street tube station whose stencilled logo, which you meet at every turn, is in the image of a maze. You are alone now: you wanted to get away from her—the idea of her lying there—even for a little while and so on the pretext of conducting research you go to London—where else do former English professors go? You have left your wife and infant child behind. You are here today, you tell yourself, on a study of labyrinths but in fact you are running from or towards the strange and new sensation that you have committed a crime, at least one. After a full day in the British Museum and an evening in its library you return to your room and a stack of books. Wearily you begin Pliny's description of the greatest labyrinth of antiquity—the Egyptian maze, long ago lost—said to be a hundred times larger than the infamous labyrinth of Crete, but it's late so you turn out the lamp and get into bed. . . .

You are standing filled with yearning before the temple of the Sun, the mortuary monument of Amenemhet III, constructed as a labyrinth and now lost beneath the sands of Hewara. It is already past noon, and you have spent an exhausting morning trying one false entrance after another, all ending without issue in some dark subterranean chamber.

The guide now takes you silently to a point you have walked past many times, an entrance disguised to the unwary eye as one of countless crenellations in the base of the edifice. No sooner are you inside than you begin to have doubts. You had not expected the noise—each door is constructed to open with a rumble of thunder; artfully wrought ducts channel air in whistles or moans all along the dim passageways; your footsteps return to your ears with an echo of brass.

But your guide moves forward so you plunge on after her, drawn by fantastic reports of a single complex more splendid than all the pyramids, more costly in labour and resources than the sum of all the architecture of Greece. Here was the project that finally exhausted the empire, a vast structure housing twelve courts and twelve golden palaces, great halls and galleries with tessellated floors and vaulted with marble, laid out on several stories above and below ground, all connected by colonnades and curved passageways and tunnels that wound and advanced and retreated, pathways redolent of spices and rotting flesh.

HARLEQUIN: THE ANNI-VERSARY

You are stunned by the artistry . . . you walk on past murals and mosaics of ivory and precious hardwood, beneath painted ceilings, past ornate porches harbouring statues of marble and stone and brass, carvings of slender kings and perverse creatures part-human and part-crocodile, -hippopotamus and -boar. You recognize jackal-headed Anubis, and a figure of such beauty and power she can only be the Goddess Isis. But as your way winds deeper and down—the dimness illuminated by fresh marvels along paths that snarl and echo with the voices of chaos—you find your pace slowing, each step forward freighted with a growing reluctance. You have been falling farther and farther behind your guide and as you round the next corner she is gone.

Horror rises up through your limbs like an icy sap, through the branching paths of your capilliaries, knotting your bowels, soughing through the chambers of your lungs; your solar plexus resonates with the hammering of a heart, and the winding pathways of your inner ear resound with the long, withdrawing roar of an inland sea. A false floor gives way and you fall into a deeper passage, which you attempt to follow.

Central to the antic experience of the labyrinth is to first believe you stand above it all, with a god's-eye view. Then, like a fading dream, your conviction evaporates.

From around the next corner comes the notion that the little maze-runner, questing—lonely and afraid . . . is you.

It started again with a phone call.

Sometime during the afternoon of Valentine's Day, 1995. I hadn't seen Beulah in almost eighteen months, since our meltdown in Banff. I thought about her only infrequently, briefly, hardly at all.

The weatherman on the drive-home show was in raptures over the arrival of a chinook within the hour. We accept the chinook winds of local winters as a mixed blessing. Temperatures may soar fifty degrees in a few hours, bringing a brief end to long, often bitter spates of cold. Bringing also the full tumult of an ice age lifted: flooded, slush-choked streets, local insanities of intemperate dress, migraines and euphoria—before a hot winter wind that roars in like a train off the Sahara. Other such disturbances of our inner weathers range from mild confusions and irritabilities to mania and sudden rage. On the road home I found myself musing distractedly that the history of war and domestic crimes could be profitably rewritten under chapters like "Wind" and "Moon" and "Tide."

My own little tide was turning, my sea of faith was at the full. If I sensed anything at all amiss, it was the little knot of perplexity I then nursed in the area roughly above a now clouded third eye, and that I attributed to the approaching chinook. The innocent on the eve of disaster make for a touching study.

I arrived home at about six as agreed. Our plan was to tire Catherine out with an hour or so of frenetic fun, then an early supper, breathless bedtime story—and bed. While I played wild animal tamer Madeleine would get a head start on preparations for our own candle-lit dinner.

From our first date, dinners together had been a great success for us. We seemed to be hosting epicurean parties every other month now. To beef up our infrastructure we installed a prep island halfway between fridge and oven. Overhead hung a rack of copper and glass pots, and chromium-steel implements clustered with a dense authority. I could hear her chopping furiously away as I came in. My assignment for the evening was under the table: a little blonde playing mysteriously in a cardboard box with a stuffed grey cat code-named Douglas.

I pause to stress that it is not my intent to wax ironic at Madeleine's expense, Catherine's much less. If irony is due, it's to the man who can live his life in a garden yet be unable to grasp the essential fact of its fragility. This was the best part of my life, of any part—any *time* of my life.

Miracles unremarkable in a neighbour's child . . . the extraordinary names Catherine settled on for pets, real and manufactured. Lucy (goose, stuffed). Percy (fish, tanked). Margaret (rabbit, hutched). Meet Douglas the cat, charmed. The deliberation with which Catherine chose her words and the clarity with which she spoke them startled people, even us at times. She had the face of a old man when she was born. Still had that gypsy face, thin and lined, with down-turned eyes that seemed sad only when she smiled. Bright blue eyes with a cast that in her mother I would describe as watchful. Odd that Madeleine should already have her in pyjamas. I realized I was disappointed. How my life had changed that this should number among my disappointments, not to dress my daughter in pyjamas—fresh-smelling, sturdy terrycloth—the one-piece kind with the padded feet and quick-access snaps along the inseam.

I hoisted Catherine into the Jolly Jumper hanging in the doorway

and watched her catapult herself from the ground. Over and over
again, tirelessly. Catherine Rose Gregory, infant cannonball. Face suffused with the elation of daring, each bow-legged landing the squat of
a tiny European weightlifter—then up again, arms flung wide . . . the
yearning for flight hard-wired into all things alive. Like the nostalgia
for an infancy half-remembered. A moment of grace, unearned. A
hovering, weightless, in the air. A voice whispering, the return to earth.

Poultry is on this evening's menu. The cleaver's sullen *chok*—O the
tragic gulf between flap and fly. I went to the kitchen for a glass of
white, pausing on the return trip at the island of flashing steel for a
kiss, more perfunctory than indicated for the Valentine. Had we spoken yet? Had she answered my hello as I called from the front door? Is
she planning to look at me?

Over the past few months I'd begun to see Madeleine's loveliness
for myself. Where had I been? When did I get back? Her hair was cut
short now, sandy, less blond than when we'd met. Her smooth face had
more hollows these days, endowed with what's loosely called character.
But maybe that was there all along. Like the beauty.

Slate-blue eyes looking up into mine, a pause on the island of steel
. . . watchful.

"How was the day?" I asked, massaging a furrow above my left eyebrow.

"Great." Resumption of chopping. Wooden *chok* on cutting board.
Growing expectation of seeing the cucumber between her fingers
erupt in blood. "We had a call today."

"From?"

"She didn't say."

"Didn't leave a name?"

"You can listen yourself."

"OK." I made no move towards the answering machine.

"Strange though."

"Yes?"

"She wished you a happy anniversary."

I peered through a pearling glass of ice-cold Chardonnay. A narrowing of focus, contraction of light. Clarity. "Sounds like a wrong
number."

I have no clear idea of how my voice sounded.

"You mean since our anniversary's in September."

[10 December 1994]

CALGARY AIRPORT, SNOWSTORM GATHERING. A last flight out. Blizzard breaks blankness on the land of forgetting, on the land of nod a total whiteout. Landing lights snuffed stanched in snowflake seas, in popcorn wreaths of air. Fog on the coast. Vancouver lost beneath, but Gavin is there, Gavin is there.

Weeks of snowbanks and frost—how green this new world where she walks, how green in the fog. Find the four-flat walkup on Green Street. Next door Knight's Funeral Chapel huddled back of hale hedges of holly—haven of rich chlorophyll, drinking her fill from a bench up the street, watching his window for hours till full dark. Will he be glad to see her, will he be home alone, alone as she?

Sweet Gavin. First words at four—spiting a slew of specialists—serenely sucking a thumb, answering with just a nod or a shake. Then says—Can I have ice cream? one day to be rid of them. Dear sweet Gavin, but O how our pet's sucking cheeks must have driven daddy mad. Why should anyone be surprised they'd ended up fucking, little Gavin and big sister?—useless protector. Donald's charming shockthenlust—no don't be ashamed for us Dr. Gregory these things were natural at our house-is-our-palace—it's in the Limosneros line, the royal tradition is dynastic congress, the sport of kings.

The real surprise was it took so long. Years of sweet sibling chastity. Sleeping together, consoling, consoling, but not every night, just *when*, just after. The nights of Mummy's martini migraines. No, admit the real surprise the stunner was the hunger—gone forgotten whereIwonder all those brothersister years of tender comforts? Where? And whither that shyness—his first time after all? with a woman at least and he barely fourteen. That first term at university, Mummydaddy having at it again—hammer n ice-tongs—Gavin coming to the dorm to get some sleep. He said. Two spoons, just like old times. Just not quite. Silvery slippery spoons without drawers—nothing fishy here—only doing what was natural in such a narrow little bed. Who'd've guessed little brother'd grow such a big one.

Remember Gavin? Though she tries and tries she can't forget—jaws that seize them like rabbits at the nape and shake—panic a slippage a

In which Beulah stops over on her way to Mexico, to cut her ties.

sliding beyond their depth / a falling through ice into heat. Jam the young sweet cob down—chew now the gristly stump, rake the smooth back so taut and slender as he fucks her angrytender till the walls tumbledown around the bed / forehead banging against the stead her wattled neck bent back to snap / pale ribbons of serum and sweat streak the sheets / hawkcries from her deathrattling trap / tongues passed from beak to beak like meat.

And she knows now. Knows this hunger is not abstract, a tale to frighten children but pure / sweet / malevolence. A gloating dog presence that follows wherever, that waits slouched in a corner, that raises its black head whenever you turn to leave the room. Gavin leaves near dawn—one parting glance of disgust. She calls out I don't want you to come anymore, knows it's what he wants too / gets up bow-legged, mechanical bullrider—kneels to pray she would never fuck like this again.

One night. Everything changes. As everything must as each thing settles down to dust. Now four years on she wants him to want it again one last time want it with her so she can go for good, burn her bridges / her fleet on the beach—head inland in-country up the creek. She gets up from her bench, walks across the street.

To what owes the honour? says Gavin surprised at the door. The honour's in the offer—of a quick visitation a slick assignation. Not going to ask me in? Please say you're happy to see me, Gavin dear—Christmas, this our last season of cheer. How are they, he wonders. Don't ask, the answer. And don't let me interrupt your pathetic TBdinner—but tomorrow night I'll cook for you a real meal, a real consumptive consummation if you'll let me stay. Of course you can you're my sister. Ah filial duty courtly manners, such a prince of man, the little sun of our benighted clan. And how he's grown straight as waving grain! So tall olive skinned, and brawny—effortless, unbidden, in the royal genes. His upper lip a saddle of softest eider / o how the girlfriends must love a ride on that.

Surprised to find you alone you must have to beat them off with sticks. Studying? What—on Christmas break, birthday of the baby Jesus? Fuck that, let's have some Christmas cheer—a manic, mantic moment distilled in forty ounces of Morgan's demon rum.

Call it a duty-free dance with the faeries.

Duty-free from Calgary? Not that kind of duty, silly. Suspicious now his narrowed eyes. Some enchanted evening—two hours of drinkies hastily gulped. Tell me why you've come, Beulah. *Mexico?* Mexico City, *alone?* But he really means why tonight, why here, why him?

Why?—to chat . chew the fat   break bread, *hermanito.* With you. After all silly it's our anniversary—four long years give or take a week or two. Roseate blush in those olive cheeks, eyes bright, a startled hart in headlights. Never to mention that night our unspoken compact, never to mention the savage little tryst, all our brotherlove hangs on this sibling-ness. Your dream that I'd never mention it / my dream that we'd never have to pretend. You're eighteen, I'm twenty-one. We're not kids any-more, I waited. Rip yourself off some, it'll be unforgettable I promise you. Let's lose our heads together—come be your own man, break with the well-bred, we'll stage our own fuck convention.

Tickle tickle tickle his fly, can't hide that siege engine—here let me give that thing some air.

Please Beulah.

Here, I've brought you a token, a gift a green / silk / scarf, real gold thread in the hem and seam. Wear it like a sash like a pirate you'll look so dashing in that—

At least give your half-sister a little half-kiss of welcome, am I such a hag undine undead dragon queen? That's better. One more—bust loose. Now three—now let me kiss it bigger for you. *Let me.* Such a scholar high-neck collared, but I see your puppy straining dew-nosed at the leash. You loved this once let me set him free. Come Gavin my prince, cough up the little emerald of your virtue. Together let us open our veins on its gem-green gir-dle, renew our blood pact against the common enemy. Won't you give it up for me? Don't put your nobility ahead of my great need.

No? *NO?*

Then let me make you bleed *like you once bled me*—my turn, fair turn-about sweet prince, let me make you suffer for it just a bit.

If it's not raping you want, is it romance? Then stoop with me, my love, amidst these blooms of foxglove and loosestrife, and strive with me this longest of nights, in this green bower, by the glow of the street. There, close the blinds, but not completely. Now let us bewitch us both this hour with potions of digitalis. While on the wall above us the rain pours down the light's frail trellises. I've brought mistletoe—see? kiss me I don't care if it's holly—come sharp-eyed little botanist let me stem that sweet bloom of confusion, let me lay this cool green silk against thy skin, and for breakfast I will serve thee black currants in a stew of brawn and holly berries. Come taste this with me, come taste what I have prepared for thee. See that it is good. Come little battle-hawk make the sea hag a girl again. Come taste all this—the budding splitfig at the crotch of this tree, the furry little foxgrapes at these swollen tips, come taste. Lay down here with me on this bed of foxfur—for, you see, our pelted plot, the leafy periphery of this narrow couch holds toxin enough / to speed the world's wild heart this one long night. So let us make us a solstice, and let our hearts run and rut till the tocsined dawn lifts foxfire from the rotting in our burned-out bed.

Burn. Doubt. Bed.

Fuck yes I'm unhappy you know what I want, you have what I need— and it is not the upright standard of your nobility. Why then and not now, why once and not twice—you *what?* fucked my ass not to hurt my feelings? No Gavin don't worry yourself for me, those aren't tears, really onions are my aromatherapy. Yes well exactly precisely schoolboy, let's dissect me let's see what's wrong with *me*. What about you?—you did me rougher than he ever did.

Come little healer, let us feed our disease.

You don't want me Beulah! you want another chapter for your diary, you want proof, *testimony*—you're already planning to write this up *aren't* you, admit it we're all grist for your crazemill. Do you hate him that much—isn't it because I am *his* son? but I'm not just his—you're my big sister.

I've become just like HIM . . . ?

Have I?

Take it out on little brother, make him pay for the sins of the father? Is it true—is that what this is?—could I do that? What kind of monster feeds the son's heart to the unknowing father? God say it isn't so, make it untrue. I *am* your big sister, Gavin—I will always be. Who has made this thing this monstrous thing? Of me.

They say ruin runs in the family.

What kind of freak was made here—made more and more like him no matter what I do. How have I become so vile *so low?*

Sinking.

Sinking.

Sinking still. Slow the mind REELS—look at him! My little *brother.* No Gavin I can't stay. RIGHT NOW tonight. It's not your fault no don't be sorry, no you're *right* you spoke true, you always do. O Gavin you deserve so much better, every happiness every promise better than this, you still have a chance, a disease less advanced.

I'm sorry for the things I have done. For things I will do. It's just beginning. And it will keep going. On and on until it is stopped.

Yes I'll call you soon, see you in the spring from Mexico—call you soon. Yes, promise.

Gavin . . . ? *I'm so sorry.*

Snow falls heavily all night in the streets. Obliterating steps.

HARLEQUIN:
TABLE

THE SECOND CALL came three days later. February 17th, 1995.

Friday night about eight, Catherine asleep. We'd put a brave face on things since the call on Valentine's Day. We didn't need to talk things over. Madeleine and I were solid, we'd been through all this, been through tough times and come out the other side. Things were almost as before. No reason to cancel our little dinner party. Things were almost as before.

Roast kid in curry. One of the dishes I loved to prepare. Gas oven banked low for the last stage, fresh papadams spattering in oil on the range. Madeleine playing cheerful sous-chef, bright smile, red lipstick, full kiss on the lips, black dress. She stacked the dishes we would need on the antique sideboard, started setting the table for four.

"No tablecloth?" I asked, mildly surprised.

"No. Not tonight."

The furniture we'd bought just after our wedding no longer suited us. The dining room table was by a designer in Milan, a post-industrial statement in steel with which we had once seemed to agree. A blued and riveted whip-steel with an oiled finish the brochure had described as 'salmon,' salmon blues, salmon pinks. Lightly oiled to the eye but dry to the touch. Like the skin of snake, Beulah had said, the one time I brought her here. She called this our Euclidean showhome.

I must have been insane.

Chris and Mariko were due any minute, the couple we somehow ended up seeing the most often. Certainly I hadn't hit it off particularly with any of Madeleine's colleagues. Chris and I had been the last of a hiring binge in the mid-eighties, the end of a golden age of social investment. The youngest turks now on staff, the only ones of our generation to cross the bar, we were well into our forties, married in the same year, destined it would seem to be friends or enemies. He'd cut off his ponytail a couple of years ago, leaving me the last retro-grade. He was adored by his students, though in a different way now. We'd done some whoring around together in the early, formative days at the College of Infidelity. A double date or two. I was looking forward to talking to him about a pleasure in teaching I'd felt reawakening in me.

I glanced out the kitchen window toward the hot tub, saw the plastic cover crumpled off to one side. Odd. Madeleine almost never used it during the day. I walked out onto the deck in my shirtsleeves, the warm chinook blowing around me. I looked up at a sky swept clean, extraordinarily clear. Stars glittered overhead, hung glorious in vast suspension. The stars pause for us, it appears, when we pause to see. The glitter, perhaps, their stilling from the velocities they travel at when we look away. A bright arctic shawl—shaken out, arrested in its fall, it hung over the house, the yard, with a weight. The hard weight of starlight.

I replaced the cover. Maybe the wind blew it off.

I heard the doorbell as I came back in. The porch light was on. They waved through the glass outer door; a couple with their height differential had to be fun. He, the tall, stooped Slav; she, the Japanese imp, mad potter with a wicked tongue and a merciless eye. He seemed to bend more to her each year—elm over a stone fence. Madeleine came up beside me and waved them in.

"She left another message today on the machine," she said.

My eyes asked the question.

"No she didn't leave a name. It seemed to be long distance. Where would she be calling from do you think?" she asked, smiling towards our guests, who'd stooped to take off their boots.

"Madeleine . . ."

"She called to offer her condolences."

February 17, 1995. Three hundred years to the day—to the hour, who knows?—from the death of Father Antonio Núñez de Miranda. Another of the things I didn't know then.

What on earth had I been thinking, bringing Beulah here? This was to be my way of letting her down easy. Was this really what I told myself—while I fucked her on my wife's bed, on the dining room table, in the hot tub, on the deck? For nine months I had been in the grip of a sexual obsession unlike anything I'd ever known—and played with it like a mindless idiot with a wolf. I would have stopped at nothing, let her look everywhere, touch anything, would have broken every trust and did—anything to buy my release.

And what should have loomed in my mind like an icon of superstitious dread, I'd converted into the rueful souvenir of a reckless boyhood stunt. Whew, lucky to get away, narrow escape . . . a difficult student. For the past three days I felt it all stirring up again. Was she still in that ground-floor apartment down by the river? Across from the park? How was she? Not well, apparently.

Remembering her. What we'd done. I couldn't get enough of her. That body, so slender by then, small calves, full buttocks, high round breasts. Long slopes of famished skin. . . . But we were going nowhere, she and I. So I let myself see that beauty, invisible to her. The end nearing, I looked into those eyes.

Bright paradox of the human eye: flexing, clenching with life, yet strangely inorganic—jewel box of a lost fascination . . . like fire, like the sea. Glass eye of a china doll, a radial pattern of facets and flaws— bullet through glass—spokes to a crystalline wheel. If the soul some- where exists, it would not be as butterfly or lotus, it would be mineral. A precious stone, like obsidian. Jade. She taught me this.

Eyes jade green. A gold corona rings the iris, threading through the spokes. Out from the centre, along each spoke an accretion—like coral, like rust . . . a burnt-amber wheel embedded, encrusted in the green of a stream.

One memory twists now in my mind's eye like a blade.

Table of whip-steel. Your knees drawn back for me, heels hard on the table edge. My wife's red silk negligee, too big for you. I stand, enter you, the window of your soul opens to me. A rill, a shimmer, a quiet welling . . . the bed of a stream.

[Mexico City, 16 Dec. 1994]

THERE IS A WORLD outside this room. *It exists.* More real to me more true than I ever could have dreamed. Splendid in its independence from me. Teetering empire of the Fifth Sun, here I will learn to do what remains to do. Find my eyes of wonder. Walk a tightrope through a flame of ice.

And I will find you. What you left behind for us, for me, after three hundred years. I will make you speak to me. I will finish this. And I will make him *see.*

Am I idiot enough to think she is only there inside those walls? She is everywhere. Look! Here. She is on the new two-hundred peso bill! Backed by presidential signatures, legal tendresses of treasurers. Thank them for this, her daily omnipresence.

Juana, I have laid your beautiful face in the hands of beggars. And they have shown me where to turn, where to find you. Let the milkeyed beggars be my guides. Wedded to their hunger, uprooted from their lands, turned away at every city gate. The end approaches. See it in their inturned eyes, this return to the *land*, to the aleph. Let the end then be a return to the beginning, *to see it as for the first time.*[1]

Nepantla. Your little village on the slopes of the smoking stone, Popocatépetl. Miracled birthplace on the volcanic margins of things. I will find you there, Juanita, in the cell where you were born.

Fond farewell to this my flophouse away from home—dingyroom, armoire battered under a hundred hasty paintcoats. Silverframed portrait of the baby jesus ruddycheeked and blond just above the queensize headboard of sin. His Sacred Heart—baled and bloody in its razorwire halo of thorns. In its Galilean necktie, belching aortal fire.

Taxi ride to the world's largest bus terminal. See it just ahead the purling gates of an iron embroidery. Flurry of a tropical dawn—taxis taxis taxis stalled back of trucks offloading pop, chips and Bimbo snacks. Bundled newspapers slung to the curb. Little dense bombs of dread set to whisk us away to a disquieting dislocation.

Ancient porter in rags approaches on enormous bare feet like muddy paddles. Scurvylegged and rickety. Let me carry your bag, *hijita,* you are thin. And you, *abuelo,* are very old. Let me walk beside you then to the gate. All right. Dignified nod at the hundred peso note, handoff at the gate to a uniformed porter with an iron dolly. *¿A dónde va, jovencita?*—your ultimate destination dolly.

Trundle me up to Nepantla, home of Sor Juana. Ahh, this is not so easy, young one.

It's not far—*I have a three-hundred-year-old map in my head, so I know.* Yes but to go direct you must go to another place. Terminal de Autobuses del Oriente. Busstop of the Terminal Orientals.

On the east of the city. Yes it's far. Yes from this terminal here also you can get there. But you must go through Cuernavaca in one of these buses like executive jets. To the city where Cortés built his palace—

After he pulled Tenochtitlán to the ground.

Don't waste time at the counter, buy your ticket on board. Well then amigo let's make this quick. Take me to the one leaving next.

And we are rising now up in our bus like a leerjet—TVs and headsets of success, lacy curtains and courtesy bar. Tissue-paper headrest-covers against the spread of skullpeeling mange. And even with this it is a joy to be out of this megacity of Dis / that has an end after all. A first-class fear escape.

Rising up out of the cupped-palm in the sky that is this Valley of Mexico, up through a vitriolic sunrise, sulphate strata of copper and zinc. Winding up the coral stead of a blueblack asphalt road, bends blasted from a pale puzzled brickrock. Gouged bluffcrests sprout stunted pines, asphyxiate and gnarled. Needle-clump branch-ends like clipped poodles gasping throatslit for breath.

Up and up into a raked light, into the impending rumour of a sky of faintest blue. Rising rising to the light. At the first summit through slantsmoked rays of sunrise, blurred silhouettes of volcanoes six kilometres high cast shadows westward and down through the gloomy lungstew.

And another summit and another, unto the confirmation of a blue empyrean assumption!

Now ahead—like *a sudden door opening onto the sea* a broad plain dappled like a feathercape of greens.[2] Cloudshadows skimming like tugs over a vast busy bay. Orchard grids of hunter green. Watercourses a treelined serpent twine of forest greens coiling through emerald fields of cane.

[Cuernavaca / 17 Dec. 1994]

Take me straight to the Palace of the Marquis of the Vale! Cortés's belvedere above his vale of tears. Hernán Cortés, first lawyer to conquer a universe . . .

His palace of toy Disney turrets stamped pure Castile—no trace no suspect hint of Moorish grace. No arches arcades no fountain garden in a courtyard more armoury than Xanadu. Is this the static architecture of your monolithic dreams? Views of your volcanoes forever lost now in the swirling carbondated mists.

O *marechal* of martial-awe! before I'm done here I will retrace your path of Conquest. But in reverse. Roll up / roll back rescind the sanguinary carpet of your welcome.

From here all the way back to the Yucatán.

On down through the sugar haciendas, third-class tour in a rustred Bluebird schoolbus. Racing over narrow roads through tall green cane. Water glints in the ditches from sprung aqueducts, dripfeeding caneworkers' vegetable plots no bigger than a tablecloth. Children smile and wave at the passing bus every window open to the hot gusts of afternoon.

Running dogs gnashing at the tires.

Señorita, you are bound for the hacienda here in Cocoyóc?—but please you must. There is always a later bus for the mountains. You must see this place more beautiful than Cortés's own hacienda in Temexico. Just follow the aqueduct to its end. You cannot get lost.

Walk down along the white-arched aqueduct sprayed with official slogans. Red white and green of the PRI—ruling Party of Institutionalized Revolution—stamped on the arcadian architecture of yet another lawyer's oxymoron dream. Every foot of this aqueduct built by slaves, this causeway too should be lined with skulls like the Aztec carvers made.

Through the gates and onto the grounds. A walled colony for your security and peace of mind. Flowerflanked red gravel paths among condos lining a fertile crescent fairway. This —I know this now—is a bad *mistake,* but does the pilgrim come so far only to turn her face away? Forward hadji!

White golfcarts beating up and down the pathways ferrying roomservice trays beneath bellcovers like burnished breastplates. Field ambulances back from the battlelines of affluence. Wandering over the fairways pale golfers—dazed wildlife stalked by brown-skinned caddies.

In tow, their aluminum-alloy travois. Mesoamerican wheeled technology still and ever reserved for toys.

Lush flowering trees—jacarandas, *flamboyanes*, African tulip shading unused swimming pools.

And then I am inside the main compound, and this place really is . . . a palace of dreams . . .

In, past the wading pools and arbours and cool arcades. Children's laughshriek voices fade . . . and I walk on in a kind of hush.

I follow the aqueduct. Ferns and giant rhododendrons, swivelheaded, lost. Reader's benches stranded in stands of bougainvillaea fifteen metres high, thick-blossomed veils of shellpink and vermilion.

Massive spidercling of creepers . . . dove-grey walls of adzed fieldstone, mortared.

What is this place? How can this even *be?*

I almost turned away.

Wishing ponds of waterlily and orchid. Figs and lemon trees and oranges—dash and blur of hummingbirds. Faint birdsong and cicadas.

Here, *señorita*, take this. *Ándele*, take it I have another for myself. Oh, you have hurt your hand? I used to weep here too. As a girl, I worked here cleaning cottages. I had other reasons to cry then.

Small brown womanbird, wren-sharp features and curly-hair. Hardbead eyes. Shy sparrowgirl pressed into her skirts. To see this once I have brought my daughter. We live near the border now, in the North. It is a desert. You have not yet been to the waterwheel? Daughter, can we show this young lady what we have seen?

Behind one last wall the terminus of the aqueduct. Massive, reluctant, slowturned . . . a moss-clasped wheel. Black wood split and smoothworn by the ceaseless rush and plash and plunge of
clear
       lithe
               water.
Tissue of muscled light, rent and splaying—knitting, mending as it falls. And you feel . . .
this plunge of beauty
      open a hole in your chest
           and plunging down through this
                your wide-cracked chest you feel
You feel—

this beauty bursting down through your lungs and down to pound—
pound the drumhead of your brightwashed soul. Your breath quakes
with it / you are breathing thunder. And shaking you, singing through
you like a reed it asks how could they not feel this?—not see through the
holes in their chests.

Sun.

　　Stone.

　　　　Shade.

　　　　　　Green.

These things have no need of Conquests. Why wasn't this enough?
An Emperor on his knees offered them a universe. They could have lived
here as gods, as angels in the flesh.

As ordinary men.

Conquistadors you should have been the ones to kneel! Kneel on
blackrot gangrene knees. Kneel on your iron greaves. Ever onward christian soldiers you all died broke—didn't you. Bleeding gold shitting piles
of dysenteric gold[3]—dying poor, dreaming still. Deliverer! goldshackled
dragonslayer—*merchant's dupe*—they made fortunes off you, the bankers'
burros. You traded your own blood for promissory notes.

Conquistador . . . you had only to accept the world to save your soul.
The world as it was offered. But all you saw was *gold*. Coins laid flat on
the clench of your lids.

Your last will and testament, Advocate—your last temptation. So far
from home so afraid to waver. *Liberator*. To weaken was to die overrun
undone, annihilated by this siren-singing continent. Land of monstrous
mystery. Grotesque mockery, Satanic Eden.

But you could have asked for the power to make Eden more beautiful
than new. Where were your eyes of wonder? *Who put out our eyes . . .*

I need to understand. To try.

Was this a place of savagery because they lacked the *names?* The naming that keeps the wilderness at bay. So what about the nameless places
inside? And as we lose the names of things—shapes and colours, taste
and scents does all revert to desert again?—

Perdón, señorita, you are from *el capital?*

What?

Then maybe from Spain?

No.

Canadá?—but your Spanish—I only ask . . I have never been to

Spain, but I do not think they have such places there. El Canadá . . . you must have water like this everywhere. Not everywhere? You see, *niña*, not even in Canada.

Shy sparrowchild straining to grasp this. Lateborn to a grateful mother, godsent on a faded prayer of old rose. No keep the handkerchief, I can embroider another to cry in. You are leaving now. Will you walk with us to the gate?

We walk out along the aqueduct. Steps reversed   hush undone breathless echoes reverting to the world   *human voices wake us . . .*

Your father is a diplomat? you are with the embassies? There are many here for weekends. To get away from the city. I knew many, I cleaned their sheets.

No? Then here, *señorita* . . . I have maybe something else to show you who have come so far . . . See? So many *condominios* each with a swimming pool. So much *water*. You see, Daughter, and no one swimming. Come closer. You too *señorita, si no le molesta*. Let me show you why, I think. No, it hasn't changed—You see the surface of the pools. These scales? They come from the trees. All the pools are the same.

Do you not think these look like human skin?

❧   All night on buses up into the mountains the drone of echoes in their drowning fall . . .

You have come alone, señorita?

So far from home, your family.

Are you not very lonely?

It is not often we meet in a place like this.

But wait, it looks like skin no?

Will you stay the night with us? Our hotel is poor but we have room.

I can't I have to go . . . on.

You think this is why no one uses the pools? I always wanted to ask them.

You have come alone, so far from home?

You know Moctezuma and Cortés both came here for the waters? Not together of course.

You have places like this everywhere in Canada?

You know there are only two statues of Cortés in all of México?

It is not often we meet in such a place.

Our new home is a desert.

You know México City was once in the middle of a mountain lake?
Like burnt skin.
You know the Spanish soldiers wept to see the Aztec capital? Wept through the
gold coins in their eyes.
Your father is a Spanish diplomat?
There are other things I can show you if you like—
Will you stay the night?

Human skin. Eyes of gold. Faces like birds.
Dreams . . .

chorus

Let Heaven's gates be both flung wide,

for Christ to descend, his bride to rise;

to permit one Sacred Majesty

entry, the other to leave,

let the portals of Heaven be drawn aside.

verses

Rose of Alexandria—

a loveliness transplanted

to gardens of eternity,

of winter ever free:

piteously, for you we weep.

  Fragrant waterlily,

flower of the Nile's inundations,

on whose frondy margins

you shine forth triumphant—

mirror of Heaven, its like in purity.

Morning star,

precursor of the sun,

those elevations that its rising gilds,

your own splendour illumines

with a light more tranquil, nearer the divine.

Ever shining moon,

whom palustral mists

have risen up to darken in eclipse,

but whose Faith, unshaken,

discovers even in her waning, plenitude.

Provident Egyptian,

garland ever blossoming,

descended of enlightened branch

and glorious line,

in sum: beautiful, divine Catherine!

These, oh lovely maiden,

are the emblems that living memory

has impressed upon the legend

with your own gentle seal: you who are

rose and water lily,

moon and morning star.

JUANA INÉS
DE LA CRUZ

CODEX: FORGER

Sor Juana's secretary, Antonia Mora, finds herself ordered to write her own journal. But she has done this all along. For the Bishop of Puebla, she made dutiful report. Except, her reports were deliberately falsified. Like a duplicitous accountant, she has always kept two versions of her books.

I COPY HER WORDS like a parrot incapable of grasping their meaning. And now its mindless mimicry has brought the parrot's master to her knees. Don't blame Juana, blame *me, this is my doing.*

This is to be my punishment. How perfectly it fits. How neatly . . . in this too, she spoke true—*it fits me like my shadow.* Isn't this what she once wrote? Now I'm left to fill the void of her voice's silencing. Parrot's imitation of the nightingale—a mockery all the crueller for its sincerity.

I, Antonia Mora, copyist, whore, have read every word you've written these past five years, Juana Inés de la Cruz, every verse, every letter. There is not one of your sonnets I can't recite. How I have slaved to make myself indispensable to you, who raised me up out of the gutter, taught me to think, to give those thoughts form, to write, imitating your flourishes, striving to become your instrument, a projection of your voice, to have you clutch me as tightly as the quill between your fingers.

All I asked was to hear your terms dictated, to catch your thoughts in quivering flight and soar with them an instant aloft. Saint Thomas had five secretaries—I would be the only one you'd ever need!—to be for you a dozen, as you strode across the room spouting verses like a dragon— rhymed arguments yoked to flame.

I pored over your writings, how you formed your letters, each letter a gesture, tracing in their whorls your turns of mind, conforming mine to yours, becoming your forger, a hunched Vulcan to your Venus—*you, Juana, taught me these stories.* This is what you've made me. I am your creation.

At night I would read and reread each day's work aloud to make my voice more like yours, to hear it as I wrote. At night, I dreamed those soaring thoughts were mine, your grace my own.

How many of your correspondents knew—how many?—where your words ended and mine began? Soon only the most delicate of letters did you even bother to reread. How many times did I finish a phrase, a paragraph you'd started, start a letter for you to polish only to have you say: "Go ahead, 'Tonia, finish it. You write more like Sor Juana Inés de la Cruz than I do. . . . You'll be a poet one day, Antonia."

No. Not even you could make it so.

It got so I could see your every thought written in your face—your arching brow for me an entire paragraph, your wry smile a sharp riposte, your pallour a defence, a heartfelt plea. I made myself your paper for-gery—deceiving hundreds but the one I made a fool of was me. Listen to me!—even here I echo you. The vulgar wry-necked chatter of Echo's errant daughter.

Parrot mind in a scarecrow skull—I've ruined everything, understood nothing, not a single thought my own. . . .

Thank God Carlos is back today from Florida, just when everything seems lost, back to help me now, lead me by the hand, explain it all to me like a witless child, show me how to make it all better.

But he's afraid too. I can feel it in his note to her, feel its urgency. Only thinking about him now, so near, do I realize how quickly things wors-ened once he'd left. What could they possibly have offered to get him to Florida—in *his* health? Did the Bishop take a hand in it? Is there any-thing *that monster* doesn't have his filthy paws in?

And all of it beginning with the Bishop of Puebla's sick, secret orders, interrogating me: *At what times of day did Sor Juana write? Was she visited by temptation—did she chasten herself? How rigourously, how often? Does she ask for your help Antonia?*

Do you watch?

And now this new interest in me, in my scribblings, after all these months. Who is really behind it? If it's Núñez, is he testing the sincerity of her petition for him to return, or is he gathering testimony for the Inquisition? As an oblate, my one vow is holy obedience. Obey or they keep my dowry and return me to the streets.

I would never see her again.

And just what is it they want me to explain? They don't need me!—every woman in here is watching Juana's every movement. Do they think she still confides in me? If only I could make it so, but I'm the last one she should risk talking to after everything I've done.

Or is it the Bishop behind all this after all? They say he now has every nun in Puebla scouring her soul for fresh transports to record for his cor-rection. For him to 'decipher and organize'—as though a convent were a grotto of raving oracles. He thinks after betraying her by my stupidity I can be ordered to do it again deliberately.

He knows I'm a liar! He trained me himself. Is it a forger's hand-book he wants to see? It's lies he wants, knowing how I ache to tell the truth. I *have* to lie—but what lies can he use against her? Which truths condemn, which absolve her? Which lies protect and which endanger her?

And do I really believe I can't be made to give information against her if they want it? Santa Cruz would only have to threaten to tell her how long the reporting really went on. . . .

So I keep two handbooks again—one true, one false. One version to deceive and one to protect. One to mislead, one to bear witness. But when the time comes will I know which one is which?

And what if she doesn't want absolution? And what if she doesn't want what's best for her? They all say they want what's best for her. *You're just like the rest, copyist.*

Don't make me speak for her . . . again.

I ASK CARLOS FOR HELP, what does he give me?—he reminds me of our classes, the Mexican painted books. *I don't care about books.* The books of the Red and the Black, of knowing and death. *I want her to speak to me.* The ancient codex is more than a text composed of images. It is like a shorthand notation for a performance that goes beyond speech. *Speech is quite enough for me.* Carlos tells me I mustn't be like the Franciscans—me! That I shouldn't be so hungry to change her that I don't really see. He can only help me if I will be his eyes and ears. If we're to understand a phenomenon, have a controlled effect upon it, then he and I must observe it carefully, describe it faithfully. Faithful to what, to whom? To the one I'm to spy on? To the truth, he says. And just what is that, I'm about to ask, when he waves me off: *he understands.*

Yes he understands but nothing's changed. They're all still asking me to speak for her, still asking me for signs to decipher.

Gestures, times of day, colours, scents, weather, situation . . . but Carlos, how will I know what's significant?

"When in doubt, record. Get it all. The codex must attempt a complete reckoning. Texts can be burned, contexts . . . die harder."

All right I will. Everything. But won't she see me? Won't her knowing what I'm doing change what she lets me see?

"One thing I did learn among the Franciscans, Antonia, is that the observer is always under observation."

She returns from the garden, fingers stained as they had once been with ink. Is she still writing?? Using gardening to cover the traces? Writing secretly in the middle of the night?

Carlos asks if it didn't look like ink because I wanted it to. He says this calls for a hard-eyed observer.

Juana, what kind of observer do you need? What kind of eyes. . . .

If I'm to record everything, then that includes her words.

Can it hurt to try to make her speak to me? Carlos says not, as long as I continue recording everything else faithfully. But he knows me unable to resist this temptation, this craving to hear her speak.

CODEX: TEMPTATION

Carlos receives a letter from Antonia and rushes back from his mapping expedition in Florida. Sor Juana will not see him. She will take no more visitors. Needing as much as Antonia to understand, ever the scientist, Carlos too urges Antonia to take careful notes for them to interpret together.

I've started bringing her books, ones Carlos has chosen for me. I told her I couldn't bear the empty shelves grinning at me like a mouthful of missing teeth. She knows better. What I'm doing is perverse, a test. It's one thing to stop reading when there are no books left.

Carlos is teaching me, again, I tell her. Can I store the books here? How long can Sor Juana Inés de la Cruz contain her appetite for books Carlos thinks even she has not read?

Not all unread: the first one I bring is Tirso de Molina's *El vergonzozo en palacio*. Isn't this the play with the maid called Serafina and the secretary named Antonio? Have you foreseen all this? Her warm eyes, wry smile. Is that the only answer, a smile? How do I record that? A thousand variations on a smile, a million unsaid subtleties. I CAN'T DO THIS!

I'm not up to this.

Snatches of conversation wrung like diamonds from a mop.

If not a lot, you still speak to others—cooks, masons, gardeners— why not to me? Sure a few words, now and then. Thrilling confessions like: "Good-night, Antonia." Your eyes glitter with . . . is that amusement? You know I've started watching you while you sleep. A few nights ago, just after three, you find me slumped against the wall next to your open door, sound asleep, notebook in my lap. Some spy!

Carlos, what does red mean? I rush into the locutory overcome by the sensation of seeing her just now in the orchard, standing on a crate, the red, red juice of ripe plums running, intemperate, between her fingers, down the backs of her hands, staining her slender wrists. Juice welling from the corners of her red lips, plum-red runnels like liquid ruby along the cheeks of her laughing face, head thrown back, jubilant . . . a veiny tracery under the pink shell of her ear and down her nape. Plum-red soaking into the hairshirt's rough brown wool.

Red, Carlos! What does it *mean*?

He answers with some dry thing about Mexicans and Egyptians.

I try again. Have I helped you get here?—maybe this is where you want to be. Did you use me then—would you do it again—manipulate me to deceive your enemies?

Do you know I'm keeping two versions of these handbooks?

Do you know which I'll show to my confessor?

Can the observer change the observed? Does the observer have a right?

Carlos wonders if you wanted me to finish Sor Seraphina, wanted me to send it. To sever your last ties to the Bishop for you. If I've been sick with guilt for nothing. Am I a character in a play, Juana? Is my role to betray you? Would you let me do that to you? Do you want them to think you're some kind of saint? I think at last I will bring her to speak.

"I'm just flesh and blood and breath, Antonia. You, of all of them, should know."

"But how are *they* to?"

"I'm counting on you. . . ."

"For what?"

"To tell them."

Another conversation that never really happened. Words never spoken, never exchanged. At least not her part, this isn't what she said. But I said my lines and saw her eyes fill with pain. What she'd really said was: Yes, Antonia, you've been sick with guilt for nothing.

Should I have recorded this? Conversations that never happened, but they did take place, filled the space behind my eyes while I watched her sitting near me. Is it still a lie?

Does this lie belong more in one version of these notebooks than in the other? Do the observer's feelings count? Do they change the observer's eyes, who forever after observes everything otherwise. . . .

Throwing myself against the blank wall of her silence.

Father Arellano asked to see my handbook today, Juana. What should I do?

There's your vow of obedience. . . .

You want me to show him, then.

An almost imperceptible shrug.

Is she trying to say she doesn't care? I don't believe you!

What do I owe her, how am I responsible? Once yes, but still? For how much longer, how much more? Does she need a hard-eyed observer or a soft-fingered heart? Can I give her both . . . ? What does she want, what does she need from me? Are they the same—can't they ever be?—or always two different things?

Are the people who love her supposed to just respect her silence or interpret it? To fill it in or make her break it? Is understanding it not just another invasion?

Always questions. Ever the answers I make up.

The shades, degrees, gradations of your silences. Silence of the sun spilling across a darkened doorway. Silence behind my eyes, below your belly. Behind sealed lips, what they never say.

At the base of a mountain in the depths of the sea. At the bottom of a flooded mineshaft . . . a silent, soot-spent coal-seam on a cloud-cast night.

You . . . the blaze just one unspoken word could ignite.

I AM SUPPOSED TO RECORD only where she goes, what she does. What about where she no longer goes, things she won't ever do again? Locutory, library, choir . . .

Am I to do these things in her place? Laugh, read, write, sing. Paint her movements through sacred space . . . for now a kind of space has opened up around her. The strict routine of places and times that rules the rest of us parts wide now like the Red Sea as she moves through the courtyards to the orchards, the kitchens, the workshops.

And to a degree I am allowed to move with her in that parted space. Less freely, less visibly, but still. . . .

The others scurrying along on their appointed rounds in ruler-straight flights and crossings, while, path eccentric, she wanders among us like an island of ice, the kind Carlos says number as grains of sand in the northern seas. Cool, self-possessed, immense, visible for leagues.

Even in a courtyard criss-crossed with bell-summoned sisters and novices, she is the one the eye now finds and follows.

Carlos tells me what it is that the Bishop is so avidly mining the convents of Puebla for these days: the biographies of nuns approaching death. Silver or gold, iron or lead?

And what lessons would he have this dying teach? What little treasures is it to yield?

Afternoon, heat abating. She waters plants I've installed before her open door for privacy, as our fellow inmates still stroll by so casually. Knowing this, Carlos has given me a rose of Jericho to add to the screen. This is the one she tends most carefully.

We stand together. A moment's stillness. Suddenly, pigeon wings flap like sheets snapping in the air.

Waking others now. Warbles, frail rumbles . . . a whole brood of bird calls, unfledged, tries the cooling air—its speed, its draft—fading faintly past.

How could I have ever thought to take refuge in this swamp? Juana mutters, bent frowning over the convent's architectural drawings. After each rainy season it seems the lines of pillars and beams yaw farther out of true. . . . Of all her old duties here, the one she's not relinquished, in fact refuses to, is supervising the construction and renovation works by crews of Indian masons. The Indians are preferred, as the least likely to force themselves upon a nun.

I took a vow of enclosure, I heard her say once to the Prioress, I did not promise never again to speak to a man. And so each day for two or three months each year they come to her. The men huddle, cap in hand. Then—the same thing I saw happen in the kitchens—when she begins to speak to them in their native tongue, dark faces beam, excited glances fly among the new men, bowed shoulders draw a little straighter. . . .

Today, with the season's rains abated, an old workman I've never seen before, tiny, bent, face of leather, kneels before her. The same confusion in both their faces as she hastily bids him stand. The foreman barks something out at him. She helps him to his feet.

The first time I've ever seen her uncomfortable among them. . . .

In the kitchens just before New Year, the five of us—Juana, Vanessa, Concepción, Asunción and I—a Creole, a Spaniard, two Indians and a mulatta (I feel just now like I should be telling a salacious joke). . . . High spirits all round, general merriment. We are making one of Vanessa's desserts for a banquet the Vicereine is giving:

> fresh-baked, unleavened wafers
> sliced apple baked between
> upon one half of the plate a bed of burnt-caramel cream, chocolate sauce
>   upon the other
> stewed crabapple garnish
> wafers pierced by taffy cane, a waving, bannered flourish. . . .
> Multiply by number of settings (200), assemble twenty minutes in
>   advance and let stand until serving.

Concepción unthinking licks her thumb and reaches up to wipe a daub of pale flour from Juana's cheek, tanned from the orchards. Her gleaming thumb raised, flour-daub still intact, Concepción hesitates, murmuring: Your skin is dark, like Our Mother, Guadalupe. Then laughs a little and wipes the flour away.

They will say that in the end your skin was like Guadalupe's.

How do I know this? I would bet my life.

Juana and I spend the afternoon with Vanessa, copying out her recipes for an edition to be bound and sold to raise money for the convent.

I weep, to be sitting here at a stained and rough-hewn table in a fragrant kitchen. To see her writing again! To be sitting next to her. As always, copying. . . .

Her handwriting is changing. The bold masculine hand everyone here claimed to find so scandalous is giving way—'masculine' because the lettering was once firm and full, and beautifully-formed; 'scandalous' because beauty of any kind in a nun is an incitation and a temptation. Handwriting.

Who to, an incitation to what poor, pathetic creature . . . ?

As I look over at what she's written her script now seems both more elaborate and more . . . hesitant. Go ahead, write it: feminine.

Isn't it here then I should also mention that, speaking so infrequently, Sor Juana Inés de la Cruz is developing the slightest stutter?

Isn't it here I try to say how this makes me feel?

Stay me with flagons, comfort me with apples: for I am sick of love.[4]

You in the orchards, a wind through the pomegranates, figs and apples. *Ariel*—a crystal crash among the apple boughs. Pale undersides of leaves, wind-canted: the startled modesties of petticoats.

Comfort me with apples.

And am I supposed to copy out too the angry script of lash-strokes across her naked back? Record their obscene utterance? The colour is pink—soon, blue-welted like berries—a flailing alliteration: why not make merry on our way to damnation? The slender lash-lines straight though not parallel. Welted quill-strokes of different lengths and thicknesses—

The way the braided cord hisses through the quilted air.

In a convent, this too is considered manual labour.

Is this the kind of hard-eyed observation that will save her? Then, decipher this.

Cloud-burst, exploding thunder, torrent of rain. Then just as suddenly it stops, sun battering the gleaming stone again like waves against a cliff. Little tendrils of mist rising from the patio's volcanic flagstones.

Nuns in every doorway, staring out, eyes sceptical or filled with rueful wonder. Beneath a startled blue sky Juana crosses the misted yard like
a lonely ghost, to see how the garden has fared. Water cascading from the
roof's carved waterspouts in clattering, prismed arcs. All eyes upon her
as she nears—if she's not careful!—hands balled into little fists, elbows
bent, shoulders slightly hitched she walks briskly through the sheet of
tumbling light—all eyes upon her—our collective gasp—and calmly
disappears, soaked to the skin, through the arched passageway. . . .

Her little joke.

The same dream, again. Write it; the record must be complete.

You, far ahead of me on a high rolling plain, green yet bare of trees.
After following you so far, so long, my legs—now a weary child's—ache
from so much walking. I can't keep pace, can't bear falling farther and farther behind. For a moment I panic, losing sight of you behind a hill.

Cries of racing gulls—is this the sea you've never seen? Where you
turn your face back to me, smile a smile of sweet release that only leaves
me bound still more savagely. . . .

The kitchen's lost Poetics:

Asunción washing up, Concepción putting water in an *olla* to heat for
mint tea. Darkly beautiful, compact, determined, fiercely blushing now,
expression critical, Vanessa stands off to one side of a table spread with
sculpted dishes heaped with colour.

Juana's forty-sixth birthday. Our little surprise party, just the five of
us. Caught off guard, trying to deflect our attention, Juana says to the
room at large that Vanessa's such a genius it would take an eight-day
week, *un octavo dia*, to make another like her. I feel a pricking of unworthy
jealousy. . . .

Chicharrón salad—baked pork rind, fresh basil, picked by Juana's own
hands, vinegar.

Plato fuerte—sauce of ripe Manzanillo mangoes, freshly puréed,
uncooked. Chicken stock, flaked chillies. Sauce served cold. Fresh-
caught whitefish, amaranth seeds floating in a clear, dark sauce round a
mould of bulgar wheat flecked with chilled cucumber. . . .

Dessert—the smell of baking peaches wafting through the low
vaulted room—how I love this room, it seems the only place we can be
happy now. . . .

Another private masterpiece that will never grace the refectory's communal tables.

Near evening, already dusk. You have not returned from the orchards. I run a bath for you: you will be tired. Into the steaming water what scents shall I pour, what essences shall I choose for you to carry into this night's sleep? To cloak you, every mound and furrow, and still at dawn like fallen dew: cassis, angelica root, Italian bergamot, cloves? Marjoram, spearmint, olibanum, rose? Cinnamon . . . I pore over bottled roots and barks and essences like a wizard, a *curandera* over her healing incantations.

Can you be healed of this? Can I heal myself?

The water cools a little, the moment passes. A little later you come in, weary, as I expected. You see the water and smile, beginning to undress. No wait! An eyebrow arches—your dusty face—as if to ask, What's the matter?

It's ice-cold, I lie, putting on more water to heat, making you wait, cruelly.

Gardening, cooking, embroidery . . . Carlos asks me if this sudden interest in women's work—work she would never permit herself in here—is a parody of feminine servility?

I am thinking of this as I watch her silent among the weavers, taking her place at a loom, half-listening as the others weave and spin, telling stories to pass the time. Sitting across from her as she begins to work the loom, hesitantly at first and then more surely, I see her look up at me, dark eyes shining with awe, as a lost skill returns to her forgivingly from a bygone time, as though it were only yesterday she was girl in Panoayan. . . .

Dedicated, rat-sated, battered, ears in tatters—convent cats in their leisure hours stalking wary birds. Juana watching.

The next day the *curandera* returns to her potions, a delicate case, this one, I mutter.

If what the ancient Mexicans believed is true—that a colour, a sound, a scent is as significant to a ceremony as any word—and if to change any one of these recasts the whole, couldn't this extend even to the play's outcome? Dear Lord, let this be so!

If I can't change that outcome with words, why not with scents and flavours? How am I to believe there's no such thing as magic when I have heard you speak of this so often, when I see you now under this spell?

Carlos always says the first step to understanding a thing is observing well . . . a careful description of its properties. The *bruja* unstops her bottles, passing them beneath her nose, one by one, eyes closed: the cream finish of sandalwood. Lavender's true, high notes. The rasp of pepper, deep and feral. Rose: warm and cream, but fine. *Nardo,* rich butterfat; with jasmin—low-pitched and gritty—its perfect complement. Violet: cool and powdery. *Lirio* root: a mushroom's musk—what will it say to the hard-eyed observer to smell that on her skin? Anise mixed with bergamot—a baby's pink fragrance, flesh of velvet creases.

Is this madness? I said I would try anything. Shall I wring my hands over what right I have, again? Am I not entitled to a little hope? Of undoing the hex I've helped put on you?

The cool, sweet convergence of vanilla and cassis, the eggshell whiff of *aldehidos,* the leather waft of *habatonia.* Regal essence of *Acahar.* . . .

From a dream of flowers I wake before dawn, looking to put names to the scented melodies in your bathwater: Temptation, Incantation, Jubilation . . .

Obsession.

Still in bed, arm flung across my eyes, I hear you moving through the darkened rooms.

I follow you everywhere now. You hardly seem to notice, like a wild creature grown used to me. I stand by you tending flowers; I cut a shock of white narcissus blossoms for our table.

You turn to me, your shirt splashed with pollen.

Gold. Carlos has already carefully explained this. The colour of the West as the evening star sinks into the swamp of night. Where souls taken prisoner in childbirth lie in wait.

I kiss your hands. On such and such a day, someone here will soon be saying, her palms tasted of clay. . . .

Weeding, she uproots shoots of basil she planted just last week. She's started forgetting little things.

Tiny, white blossoms in a small, chinese vase, sky-blue. White-porcelain dragon clouds, with wings.

Flowers of such delicacy. Six wide-flung petals, frail rosette upthrust on its calyx like a jewel on a tiny crown.

For the longest time—the flowers seem to last forever in their vase— I can't think what their faint scent reminds me of. High and powdery, like perfumed wax. Chilled cream, honey and paraffin. Marble.

You.

Dawn, fog. Sky the colour of time. This place is filled with ghosts! I *live* with one—no, five hundred. I look out into the time-swept streets and see still others—past or future? Streets filled with mists, miasmas, phantoms. Spectres of vanished instruments and books, and cruel instruments of iron and timber soon, now, to come.

The ghosts of young men playing a ball game against the massive convent walls. And on those grey walls others sketching bright, crude symbols with strange cylindrical brushes. A few words I recognize: *Crisis.* *PAN. México para los Mexicanos . . .*

San Jerónimo: the crumbling ghost of a ball court, an altar, an ancient book.

Tremulous blue light in the rooms across the street.

Mid-afternoon. Sun in a sky of brass. Thousand-throated roar of a bull-ring, five blocks away.

Thread of hairshirt wool stuck in the bed of rough-planed timbers where she sleeps. Strand of hair caught in the scaly bark of a potted tree. Ragged fingernail recovered from the garden soil. Peeled whorls of fingertips, wedged invisible in a pocked column of volcanic rock abrasive like a file. Flesh wedded to a flail.

With these, your textured leavings, I brew your returning's counter-spell.

HARLEQUIN:
CIVIL
DISCOVERY

WE WAITED FOR THE COURTROOM to clear. The scrum would be assembling for us outside. Hostile sound bite on the courthouse steps. Opposing counsel and the aggrieved father were the last to leave save us. Beulah's mother, Grace, hadn't come today. The third time in a week I'd seen Jonas Limosneros and the third thousand-dollar suit. Plastic surgery I could believe—but only with the greatest difficulty that this could be a great cardiovascular surgeon. Thick, wavy hair, lightly oiled. Coal black, with a few crimped strands of white. He was particularly dark-skinned for a Spaniard. The impeccably shaven shadow of a heavy beard. Dark eyes. A very handsome man. A worried man, much relieved. Or so it seemed to me. Theatrical pause before me to check his expensive watch. My chance to find his long-fingered hands artful. No rings. Maybe surgeons weren't allowed, lest they leave them in their work. Our eyes locked. On the way past he took in my rumpled bleariness with a supercilious arch of the brow. Sick fuck.

My lawyer turned his amused blue eyes on me. "There. That went well."

He seemed willing to include our manly exchange of glances in the generally favourable outcome of the day's proceedings. "Now the rest will be just like I said. The main thing was giving the girl's papers back. The clerk now hands them over to the police who, after a brief and muddled flip-through, return them to the family."

"For safekeeping."

"Look, I don't like the father—"

"Stepfather."

"Whatever—any more than you do. The thing was you turning over those papers."

I'd shown up at his office at closing time the night before with a cardboard box under my arm. Chris Relkoff, recommending him, had mentioned precendent-setting pro bono work and eclectic interests. Music and naval history, maybe. Fly-fishing. European jazz. I couldn't help noticing that his assistant, typing slowly away that day in an orange summer dress, was prettier than strictly necessary. I had the notion she'd chosen the colour of the dress to match her boss's thinning hair. Eclectic.

"This mean you're done playing cops and robbers?" he asked, eyeing the box.

"So it would seem."

"Why the change of heart?" He poised his paunchy bulk at the edge of the typist's desk and crossed his arms.

"Think of it as me waiving my exclusive to the story."

"Meaning?"

"I still want a copy."

Shaking his head, he waved me to the photocopier. "Knock yourself out."

On my first day in court it did not take long to understand what I was about to face. I'd left the cabin out in Cochrane two hours early, thinking to avoid the press. A courthouse of limestone and marble. Dun, four-columned porch. A few frieze-bound heroes robed and muscled. Inside, courtroom carpet the rich blue of open sea. A hush. Close enough to what I'd imagined. I was pleased to have come early. The judge now in session delighted me. Cranky lion—aging, preening despot in his den. I thought I matched up well against him.

An hour later, my lion limped out to be replaced by Madame Justice Clements, an animal of a different stripe. Auburn hair, closely pinned in a tight bun. My contemporary. Nuanced, keen, the face of modern righteousness. The eyes of my community, without the blindfold.

You have sinned against the colony. Ridiculous, a puritanical huddle. *You have turned your back on the city.* A palisade, a prairie fort, a pile of sticks. *You have strayed beyond the pale, you are made a thing of scorn.* I return yours richly multiplied. *We speak with your father's voice.* This should be good, he barely used it. *You have made his name a laughing-stock—his clotted clan?* They were one long before me. *The rotten apple doesn't fall so far after all.* From the split and blasted tree. *You're one of us, we knew it all along.* I'm not like you, I'm not like you at all. *Up above us all like some kind of eagle.* Now the chicken's come home to roost. Chicken.

We will see you broken and spiked out in the grass.

What I saw in those first twenty seconds was still not what I'd done but what I *faced.* Prairie opprobrium—knowing, nodding, sage and gloating.

Return her manuscripts? I would have done anything to escape the indignity of their contempt, their round-mouthed satisfaction. Run anywhere. Sold Beulah down the river a hundred times.

I am not that breed of martyr.

But I will answer them in my fashion. A fashion I have learned. Charges are brought, learned counsel is instructed. Show us what you've learned. Address the charges, the faceless mass of their derision.

A higher court is now in session.

Behind the departing heart surgeon and his lawyer the scrolled brass doors swung quietly to, the scent of sandalwood cologne wafting in the aisle. My lawyer put a hand out to restrain me as I made to get up from the table. "Let's talk."

"Don't we have to leave?"

"You in such a hurry to go out and meet your public?" He studied me for a moment. "I know it's a nightmare. But I'm telling you the worst is behind you. Do you sleep at all?"

"Some nights are better."

"Well, sleep tonight. They've dropped the suit as promised. This civil action had me much more worried than anything the cops might have. You've done the right thing here."

I felt an urge to smile. But he was right. It would have been stupid to provoke the judge further. I had other charges of contempt to face.

For days, the way out had been stupidly obvious, though I hadn't seen it. *Make copies.* I was not thinking straight.

"If we avoid mistakes," he assured, "this whole thing goes away, like I told you."

"How?"

"We've got a pretty solid police force. Experienced people are working your case. The more they turn up, the less attractive charging you becomes."

"Why?"

"One, she left the sliding door open that night."

"For me."

"No idea. But no sign of forced entry. Plus, even if they could prove the papers in your possession were at her place that night—"

"The neighbour saw me taking them."

"Taking what? Maybe it was your own box of papers, or a toaster oven. You'd brought it in with you. You see what I mean. Forensics now concurs the wounds were very likely self-inflicted. Meanwhile counselling to commit suicide is exceptionally difficult to prove—impossible here. Then there's her psychiatric history . . ."

"What about leaving the scene?"

"Can't be leaving the scene of a crime if no crime's been proved. Or the scene of a police investigation, since the police weren't on it yet. Arguably there's something under the Good Samaritan laws, like breaking off a resuscitation. But no real proof you'd ever started first aid. She might've dressed those wounds herself, right?"

He was watching me carefully now.

"Of course you might've *forced her* to swallow all that stuff they pumped out of her guts. . . ." When I didn't take the bait he went on. "So you see why they're reluctant. Obstructing a police investigation was probably their best shot. But you've just turned everything over to the judge—all of it, right?"

"Yes."

"Presto, obstruction unblocked. So I guess their main problem, and ours, is waiting out there right now."

"The press."

"Beautiful young girl from a good family, a distinguished immigrant family. Desperate call to a news desk implicating unnamed university professor—oh and some day, Professor, when this is done, maybe you can explain to me why she did that. Thought they had a juicy society scandal, did our journalistic friends. Grad photo of victim now lying near death.

"A picture like that in the paper touches a nerve. It gives the body politic a toothache. The people want an accounting. But how is it possible, they ask, that there's been no crime? The cops are already in a tight spot. Even before they maybe turn up rumours about the father they don't want to follow up on."

"You've heard something."

"Nothing I'd want you to know."

"He's asked the police to drop the investigation."

"No need. That's what I'm telling you—nothing but bloody noses—"

"And bad press."

"There'll be a column or two about lax enforcement, slippery lawyers, liberal laws. But what more can they do? Stir up the local hard-line-on-crime zealots, I guess. Take some tougher angles on crime stories for a while." Eric Heffner shrugged and spread his hands complacently. "Basically, they're out of angles."

"It just blows over."

"On one condition—she recovers. A coma's a precarious thing." He looked apologetic. To this point I'd done everything he'd asked of me, if reluctantly. He rose and started shuffling files into his briefcase. "So, let's go meet our friends in the media." I hadn't moved. He shot a glance in my direction. "I'll do what I can to snub their leash."

"The Foothills Hospital called yesterday."

He eyed me warily. "Why the hell would they call you?"

"Her doctor."

"The girl's? We agreed you were not to *go* there."

"A Dr. Elsa Aspen. Beautiful voice."

"Did we have an agreement or not?"

"I haven't gone since we talked."

"Then how?"

"A nurse was there when they brought her in. Brought Beulah. . . ."

"Go on."

"She mentioned me to Dr. Aspen for some reason."

"What did they want?"

"The doctor's been following things in the papers."

His left hand made a cycling gesture: speed up the reel. "Make this simple for me, will you Professor?" His head jutted forward, mouth slightly open, a frown directed at my lips.

"She thought I might have some familiarity with Beulah's diaries."

"A *shrink?* No!—you *see,* this's exactly the kind of thing—"

"Would I be willing to get together for a few minutes?"

"As your lawyer I am advising you against this."

"In complete privacy."

"Formally advising you."

"A chat."

"Emphatically no."

"Away from the hospital."

"I'm telling you. Listen to me." He shifted as though to block my exit.

"They need my help."

WHAT MORE CAN I FIND TO SAY TO SOMEONE who doesn't want to go on speaking? *Find something!*

What can I bring to bring her back to me? Dreams, memories, news of the world—echoes from the streets.

Check the cellars. Make a list.

A scrap of paper on the floor by a shelf—whatever it says, it's in Nahuatl . . . Carlos has suggested I ask her to read it for me. Another of our pathetic temptations.

So, a scrap of verses in her handwriting. When was it written, hours ago or months?

Her stained fingers. There are a hundred and eighty-nine books and manuscripts hidden in the archives. I wonder for the thousandth time, is she writing again—or still? And in the language of her girlhood? Is there ink concealed beneath the dirt? Is she working in the gardens to conceal it? Again no answers.

Eyes enormous now, luminous, whites stark in their sockets. Glossy ridge of cheekbone, drawn thin, like her clavicles, her sickle-boned hips—skin stretched tight like a canvas before the brush's first shy kiss. Keyed in ivory and bone like a clavichord too delicate to play.

Cheekbone ridge drawing down to tanned hollows. Her jaws' muscular swell. Curved, cracked lips. Hairshirt fustian like a tamarind pod. She looks each day more like an Indian, a gaunt fieldhand.

Strong still, I thought. Only an occasional unsteadiness after climbing stairs.

I told myself.

This morning she has trouble getting out of bed.

Asunción is bringing the poultices. I will spread them out like grape leaves across her cicatrices.

Dreams. I can tell that she really is listening to me whenever I tell her my dreams.

Dreams must seem as real to her as anything in this nightmare.

Through dreams I will reach you then. First telling you mine, then making mine yours. I will reach you, I will fight through to you. I will make you see me, hear me.

Hunger scrimshaws your ivory form. Some long-dead navigator's graven altar—a map, some enchanted isle, its rough topography in bone.[5]

Not a good day. She cannot get up at all. Feverish, she asks to hear me play. Sweating and cursing our weakness, refusing help, Vanessa and I drag the clavichord all the way from the locutory across the convent up to her.

　　From now on I will play every night, as she lies down to sleep. Whether she's listening or not.

　　But she always seems to be listening to something—a voice, a melody?—if almost never to me. . . .

Today much better. Everything back to normal, if that's what this can be called. Only the slightest unsteadiness in her hands.

Núñez is coming! *Next Sunday*—the report reverberates through the convent cells like a shot. As though it's been confirmed—it hasn't been confirmed?! My growing desperation. He will be here *next week*, ten days . . . then it'll be too late, it will have started.

　　To bring Juana news of the world I need to leave this place! . . . just an hour or two each day. Nothing has ever prevented me. Permission of course I need. The Prioress has already awarded me a lot of liberty, but this?

　　Enter the womanly conspiracies of kitchens: Vanessa calls on me to join Asunción for the shopping when old Concepción pulls up lame. A recurrence of gout is blamed. . . .

　　As we approach the market, Asunción turns to me and asks, well what are you waiting for?—just be back in two hours.

　　Free!—that's how it feels, though I know it really isn't. The eyes of men all over me, the oldest game still awaiting me like a dog lolling at the door.

　　That first day I just walk and walk, hardly seeing, just feeling the wind all over me.

Carlos says I must make your America sing to you like a siren. Just as you've made it sing for me. But what does someone like me have to offer you? What clumsy lyrics can I lay at the feet of someone who has brought the world so much beauty?

I offer you every sunny morning since the day we met . . .

Every rain-laved dawning these past five years. Each high-waisted noon, each stooping dusk. Five years of full moons high-risen. Five years of brief-locked eyes and stolen glances quickly broken. Of breathless grazings, staged accidents and soft collidings. Of slow-drawn baths, petals swanning across a tile-bound tub. The plump pad and whisper of languid towellings.

Antonia Mora, you will make a poet one day. No Juana. Not even you can make it so.

At the market I buy a little bracelet for her wrist. Will she accept, will she refuse to wear it? A string of little silver bells and the shells of tiny snails, a talisman to chime and charm and faintly mutter, to fill the silence as she works.

The bracelet was my second choice. I knew she would never wear the brooches I saw the Mayans selling: live scarab beetles, pierced and tethered to a pin by a thin, golden chain. . . .

According to Carlos, in the rituals of the ancient Mexicans the brush of certain words across the vocal chords can be more important than their meaning, and the soft shush of shell anklets more significant than a word—gesture translated into sound, word into thing. Meanings that change, subject to the occasion.

Núñez's approach, murmurs massing like clouds. Ten days, now five. Five years of our lives telescoped down through these five remaining days. I refuse to let her out of my sight for one instant. And even as I feel her drawing away from me, I touch her at every opportunity.

For the first time in two years I sleep in her bed, sleep there each night, holding her. She strokes my hair.

Tell me another Carlos . . . another engine of torture. The cap they call the Cat's Claws. Carlos submits to describe it.

Another morning. Another day gone. A rising tide of panic. And fury— what is left to say? What's left that she'll still listen to from me?

And so the game begins. A game she seems to find touching in a way I can't quite grasp. Each day back from my staged outings to the marketplace, I tell her a series of lies—fables, say, with at least one containing a grain of truth.

The game: guess what I saw today. Heard, said, did, touched, smelled, tasted. Guess which life I lived, bore witness to.

(For you, I mean.) This part goes unsaid.

Close your eyes. . . .

. . . *The wobble of a newborn colt . . .*

A single thread of tobacco smoke rising fine, then fanning into a plume that bulges and checks and eddies as my finger passes through . . .

The starched whisk of a black-pinioned bird past the window, fan tips across stone . . .

Cold stone floor against my back, *pulquería* air a fermented stew, raucous songs, taste of *pulque* wrapped viscous right round the tongue, like a burnt milk's clotted skin. . . .

Holding out my closed hand as if to drop a little coin into hers, I ask, guess Juana, which of these things I've brought back for you.

Three days. I can't think, can't see properly, a kind of film before my eyes. I can't help her, can't help anyone like this! We're running out of time—hundreds of possibilities to try. Find the word that breaks the spell. Makes her look up and see. . . .

Carlos help me! His face haggard, drained of colour. The last few days of waiting are harder on him. At least I get to *see* her. All he can do is come to me, every day now, and wait.

Maybe the problem, Antonia, is that you're looking for a single truth. Juana said something to me once—this should be interesting to you, who play the clavichord so beautifully. Look at the clavichord's harmonics. We approach the truth not head-on but in tangents, he says.

What's that supposed to mean?

Press the keys. The metal tangents strut across the fretted strings, producing not a single note but a chord. The same set of strings, depending on where the tangents strike them, can be made to play several different chords at once. . . .

Tangential truths. Harmonics keyed to chord and discord. Gradually comprehensible to the patient ear. . . .

No. I am running out of time.

Guess, Juana. Guess what happened on the way to the marketplace. What took place, fell beneath time's relentless sway.

The gravel rasp of scissors slicing through a plait of hair.

All the colours called green.

The sensations called pain.

Shark-skin roughness of a young guard's emery cheek, there at the top where a woman's thighs first swell to meet.

Sound of a fist opening, frisk of fingernails across a callused palm.

Smell of poverty and darkness, low-ceilings. A public executioner sitting, leaning over his mother's bed, alcatraz lilies crushed in a pale, muscled fist, rust-red loam beneath his broken nails. The soft plat of white petals striking the stone floor.

Against a hill in the middle distance, a torch flickering forgotten under the noon-day sun.

Guess.

How can you bear to have Father Núñez be your confessor again? To have the same confessor as the Archbishop?

A ghost of a smile crosses your lips—you think it's ironic, don't you. Well I call it sickening! Do you want to have to tell him your innermost thoughts, your dreams, your every project—about Isis? Tonantzin? About . . . but you've just seen I can't quite bring myself to mention Sappho's name. Not after what I've done.

Juana you know he'll go running straight to the Archbishop with everything you say. I'm shouting now: So when Núñez arrives from confessing you, will the Archbishop smell you on him, over the odours of their own so-piously-unwashed bodies?—stench of sulphur and cheese. Will Núñez use the scent of you to stir that madman into a helpless frenzy? Goat eyes rolling back toward his heaven, nostrils quivering with dragon-stench—the groin-thickening odour of Eve—his own scabby back the dragon's scales—

Flail, Jesuit, flail.[6]

Seven to eight, the longest hour of the day, the hour of attending to our special penances and mortifyings. First the evening bath, its fragrant joys for me, if not for her, bound up now in the agonies to follow.

What am I becoming?

She seems to have lost all sense of privacy. Lets me see everything. Is it because she feels all America watching? Lets me draw her bath, dry her back and minutes later watch it lacerated anew. And then cover it with poultices.

It's hard to admit this, harder still to write it, but for all the horror I feel at the spectacle—for all the nightmare rhythms I will later rap out in my sleep to the flail's evensong melodies—for all my UNSPEAK-ABLE DISMAY . . . the sight is now less pitiful to me than seeing the other sisters doing the same thing.

In all the panic and confusion and desperation of these last few days—so strange it feels to being saying it, another little betrayal—but I find the sight now almost calming.

So what kind of monster does this make me?

Her floggings are as severe as any of the others' here, if anything, harder. And harder by the day. The blood just as red, on that frail back. It's not that I'm not afraid for her. I am, I'm terrified. But unlike hers, and more heart-breaking—I don't know why—the light I see in their eyes is rapture, a rapture of the spirit, stoked by each stroke, each barbed cut.

Hers is a kind of cold fury, not rapture, a fire of will or reason that nothing of this world can dominate.

Her soul's rapture I've seen at other times—out in the gardens, and at night under the stars.

Why should I find hope in this?

Hardly sleeping, nocturnal, she sits at the window to await the sunset. And at the door to watch the moon rise smoothly away from the tower above the chapel dome.

And I, hovering a few feet back from her.

The last full day, *do something.* . . .

Morning. Shutters thrown back, warm breeze sifting through the cool rooms.

A dragonfly's high clicking like the snap of twigs, or pebbles against a window.

Sorting through the remaining manuscripts of her poetry hidden in the archives, cloaked now in dust and neglect, searching for anything to trigger any reaction. Reckless now—what's left to lose? I copy a scrap from her *Empeños* to read back to her. A fragment she wrote for the occasion when the Archbishop was first welcomed to Mexico City.

> *The arrival of our joy*
> *Was the joy of his arriving*

I'll try even cruelty. I can justify anything. So I read it out for her. Record it then, the flinch, the rueful twitch of cheek.

So who's her jailer now—them or me?

Noon. Through the trees, the slippery glimmer of fountains shaped like crosses, surface broken by the preening of noisy birds.

I can think of nothing to say. Nothing to do.

Dusk. Along the south wall at the main-floor windows, the level where the envied servants sleep, unannounced visitors slump against the bars . . . a lover's coaxing lean, cajoling fingers trace the black iron that bars him from the sister of his dreams.

Did you never once sleep down on the main floor, Juanita, before I came to live with you?

Guess. Please. I went farther this time. Out into the country for you.

Close your eyes. . . .

Lying on your back, looking at the sky . . . the instant when you wonder if it is the mountain drifting, not the clouds.

The hour spent registering all the fickle changes in the wind—pressure, direction, urgencies, temperatures, constancy.

A warm wind's soft worry as it eddies past the ear.

Smell of moss-cloyed clay, dense, a carpet.

Guess.

Waking from a nap to a faint thrumming, a pressure, the faintest snapping, like fingers calling a distant servant to attention—the hummingbird's reclining hover, shimmer of dawn like oil across green feathers. Head-dipping shift from hover to dart—

Aerial collision of the hummingbird with dragonfly daubed the same shimmering green, turquoise tail, green-chalk patina of its tiny skullcap. . . . Both aerialists stunned by the collision, alighting on adjacent flowers—one red, the other shell-pink.

Guess.

Report of a cannon shot like tight twine fraying along a jagged mountain face, then shredding, gutted, across a swaying treetop reef.

I look at you and see the years we've been together, all the vanished things rendered and surrendered . . . but, now, at least you're listening. Gently . . .

Guess.

The eager clamber of baby crocodiles towards a piece of meat.

One small bird's convulsive chirping, its song a hiccup, a wracking birth contraction. Head's ducking, knees' splayed flexions, pivoting on tiny brittle feet ninety degrees—a quadrant at a chirp. One whit fiercer would surely jerk it headlong from its perch. . . .

The fine, angular distinction between a cricket song and its echo, at dusk before the dewfall, and the cricket's coppery trill from the frog's croak of tin.

I've done everything I can, everything I know, everything to bring you back. To make your America sing back to you. All that's left now, all that remains, is to hear your echo's last receding. . . .

Guess.

In the instant before a clean incision begins to bleed, a pause, like a fallen child reading her mother's eyes for pain.

Guess.

Out of a darkened barn into the light a mosquito's ruby lumbering under the weight of blood drawn from my throat. Like an osprey hooked into a fish too large to raise. I can't let go, can't swim.

Guess.

The wobble of a whetted razor bumping slow across the ridges of the tongue.

The tongue's severed slap against a wetted granite trough.

It's just a game. Guess which, I ask holding out my closed hand to slip the answer in your palm. What have I brought for you, what have I seen? What's true, what's real? Guess for me. Please.

Your eyes welling at last, with too much of everything, hands cupped out before you as though to catch it all, you say to me:

All of it 'Tonia, it's all real, you don't need me to make it real for you. Can you see?

Night. Humid dark like a large beast breathing. Cicada battery ribs the utter black.

Eyes snap wide. You are not beside me. Or sitting at the window or the doors. Body coated in nightsweat, I look for you. The stillness of a gathering rain. I look for you outside—patios, orchards, garden. Faithless I look for you even in the chapel. Running barefoot silently, desperately back to the room to see if you've come back—blank panic—have you run away without me? Left me? It can't be! *Please.* Tilting wildly out the windows into the cloud-blackened streets—west, south—volcano looming invisibly in the blackness to the east, are you going back home? I can't see anything!

First few drops of rain, bloated spatter against the dusty window ledge. Then a movement on the roof across the courtyard as the sky splits—a flash of lightning trailing sparks, lighting you, sweat-drenched, naked, running in the dark away from me. The roof!—your draftsman's drawings memorized, some walled passage or false ending—some secret way. *How long,* how long have you known, been free up there, how often, free of everything, of me? How many nights?

Núñez is coming TOMORROW.

You could have shown me! I'll make you still! One shout, one scream from me could betray you. Another flash—you stand now, gleaming body arched back like a viol, panting mouth to the sky. I bite my tongue—*bite hard down*—till the taste of iron fills my teeth and my face is slick with salted rain.

And suddenly, more certainly than I have ever known any other thing, I know you will never run up on that roof again.

I wake late. Air mocking bright . . . salt parchment stretched across my eyes.

Today is Sunday.

CODEX: RENUN- CIATION

SUNDAY BELLS' INCESSANT TOLLING from across the city. Each hour from the belfry topping the red-tiled dome of Saint Jerome, the chapel bell clangs hollowly from doom's brass throat.

She walks back to the cell, eyes blazing, from seeing Núñez. Once inside she strips to the waist—*in the middle of the day*, I think stupidly. It's the wrong time of day. . . .

I feel it going on and on forever with the whole convent listening, breathlessly . . . how long, how many strokes I can't say.

So in the end the record will be incomplete.

I walk out to the orchards, out to where she would normally be, and begin shearing branches indiscriminately, cropping flowers, plucking leaves.

And now something else is clear to me: I can't stay for this.

The past days' rhythms lie shredded to ribbons all about me. In the deepening dusk I pass by the convent prison—door ajar—just to look, at the cell reserved for me. Prison within a smaller prison, like the blacker shade inside us on the darkest night.

This is where I will end up if I run or if I stay. They expel nuns not slaves. Running away from my rightful owner is petty theft, even if it's theft of me.

Carlos tries to make me see she's not really submitting to Núñez, she's defying him. But how?—*tell me*. See, Núñez would want moderation, control—he's already created enough *extáticos*. Nothing he despises more in all the world. Losing her to this, and losing her in death are what he really fears. These two threats he cannot walk away from, must answer for: death and rapture. Two grim levers. And she knows how to work them.

Is this supposed to comfort me?

Come away with me, Juanita, come out of here! I can't stay a second longer in this place. This stone boat is sinking—*Juana please. I won't go down with it.*

Do I dare ask this? Do you know how it feels to watch these years of ours end? To watch him come to you instead? Can't you see how this makes me feel?

Come, Juanita, Carlos would welcome both of us.

But I already know what you'll say to me, if you'll say anything at all—the same words Carlos tells me you used with him twenty-five years ago:

Would you ask me to exchange the nun's vows against the housewife's: enclosure, poverty and chastity for enclosure, silence and servility?[7] *What kind of bargain is this?*

Carlos comes.

Antonia I was serious about what I said yesterday. I'm not prepared to lose both of you . . . You—we—have done everything we could. Now we've got to get you out of here.

And leave her alone in this place?

You know better than anyone she's been alone in here for a long time now.

But where would I go?

Of course you'd come to live with me.

The Bishop's whore?

You'll come as a houseservant. There'll be food enough for two. Your duties will be light. No please, don't misunderstand me. I'm not a carnal man. My demons are not insistent.

Carlos, I don't need promises—the idea doesn't horrify me, you know. But I'm embarassing you. . . . We could keep things simple then, if you want.

We'll have to think on how to get you out. If you were a nun, it would be harder, but as an oblate . . . perhaps it would be enough to find the money to repay your dowry.

Carlos, I thought maybe you already knew. . . .

Knew?

I'm not here as an oblate. Not really.

I'm not sure I follow. . . .

Two days later, I have him meet me at the market, partly to see if he'll actually be seen walking with me through the streets. Only walking beside him today, away from here, do I understand how lonely I have been.

Carlos wants to buy me. He's asking you to sell me to him.

 I never told him, 'Tonia. You know that, don't you?

 I know. He wants me to come and live with him.

 Toñita, sweet friend, Carlos is right, it's time for you to go now. You should have gone a long time ago. . . .

[Amecameca, Mexico, 17 December 1994]

DARKNESS. My ear bent to her lips.

Daylight. Trying to see, stare down the sun.

Days of there and now / nights of here and then—recanting now incanting then. Cant and descant, these my impure orisons.... And what of dusk and dawn—liminal fall, sudden, tropical. Plunge from then to now, and back again.

Each slow noon slants to past, each midnight sloping back to soon. Too soon.

Scribbler, sort your shards of rubbletime, read and reread the same texts narrowed now to three. Juana's anthology, Octavio Paz, *The Contendings of Horus and Seth*. Dogeared trinity, final mysteries of my posthumous existence. A season, a month or two, a few more weakened weeks—to stall the engines of siege

then rest then peace.

Now down into the there and glare of day.

Sear and gasblast of buses, dueling musics clash and churn the air to white. Powerlines and phonelines sickle-slash this alpen vista crushed beneath a redfisted dawn.

Provincial city sausage-pinched into a gutted valley. Meek streetparks euphemistic and cowed—hardpressed islands huddling in the traffic scream. Lightpoles plastered with dance posters and sunbleached mugshots of politicos in mirror shades. Two chubbycheeked cosmetologists model mother's facial cream distilled from avocado and honey.

Taxi stand in front of the church. Battered white jeep parked off to one side of the cabfile. Aging Pancho Villa slouched against the mangled grille. Who can it be but him? His banter with the passersby, brassy rail and joust with fellow drivers all down the file.

Buenos días.

The hotel told me to look for you.

You are going up the mountain.

They say you're the only one to go right to the pass.

Not the only one, no. But the best. Here let me put that in the back. Ah a *computadora*—then we will keep the computer between us. The doorlatch there is a little rusted—here allow me, *disculpe* I was only going to help you in.

Shall I wait a minute here?—you can see the SmokingStone very well just now, though the other is still in cloud, as it has been for days. But no, I see *señorita* is not here for the scenery.

She's seen this movie before. She's here to see it end.

Esta bien OK then we are off. Hornsquawk—tequila-toss of a wave in riposte—*hijos de la mierda,* they laugh at my truck those idiots in their new four-wheel drives bartered for land. Ten years theirs will be worse junk than this but the gringo will still own the land of their grandfathers. How is this a trade? This is the rape of a child who has been taught no better. *Lo siento señorita, a no ser grosero, pero asi es.* Never mind lawyers, today Cortés is an economist.

Strong dark hands on the wheel burst into flower. Incessant stream of friendly, jetstream of charm—smiles right into my eyes no squints no flinch no doubts—he talks and talks and we have known each other all our lives asking nothing about my hands this mouth.

Ask him.

Does he know where Sor Juana's hacienda is?

In Panoyá—but of course. Is there a museum like Nepantla? Sorry no, nothing like this, everything there is very old, not new at all. Slysmiled irony.

Is it on the way? Not exactly. Will you take me I can pay, just for a look. *¿Cómo no?* no extra charge, you have me for the day.

Off the highway and onto a lane of arching oaks planted as a windbreak—cinematic shuttering of oakboles, stuttered film of sunshot apple trees.

Little bridge over a grassy trickle of a stream. . . . *The well. The wide west-facing porch. A bell tower, a little chapel* . . . I have seen all this in photographs. I have seen this place. Your place. In a hundred dreams. And never once dreaming the mountains were so high, so close.

¿Ya ves? Tranquilo, no, this place of her childhood? *After Nepantla this is a tranquillity unhoped for.* You wish to stop a minute?

After the mountain. What is your name? Raúl. After, Raúl, when I come down. Thank you.

You will let me bring you then. I know the caretakers well. There are things they could explain. . . .

First I will purge my hands of accidents.[8] I will come down to you fasted and lightheaded. It's enough to have seen this place, to know it exists. It is enough for now. . . .

The trip, *señorita*, is about three hours one way. But the time passes quickly you will see. You are well?

Never better.

But no I can see you are tired of questions. It is better that I talk, no extra charge. My wife says it is what I do best—obviously *decencia* requires she say this in front of the children, the neighbours.

There are people who tire of their own voices, of course I understand this—they do not have mine. I have sung mariachi in Reno Nevada. Laboured on cargo boats to Spain and Argentina, sold my watercolours in Santa Fe, Nuevo México. Owned a taxi in El Paso de Tejas, Gringolandia—gringo is a word we use for different reasons, of course, sometimes with affection even. *Americano* we must never use for them— we are *Americanos* too. *¿Sí o no?*

And it's true, his is a beautiful voice a baritone riversong of fathertongue lifting me up on a tide of buttermilk and it is fine a relief to ride beside this strange old handsome man with redbrown eyes in smiley wrinkley naugahyde.

Calling them *Norte Americanos* is better, but México also is in North America. At least the poor geographers still think so. *Estadunidenses es lo peor*—we are the United States of Mexico! But outside of México no one cares about this. There is an expression: *Pobre México, tan cerca de los Estados Unidos—*

Tan lejos de dios.[9]

Ah, then you know this *dicho!* But you are not Mexican, I think. . . . We Mexicans come up in tour buses, sometimes *los chilangos* in cars. And from our countryside, from *los pueblitos,* some come on their knees. Or crawling on all fours. This has been a place of pilgrims for two thousand years.

So now I, Raúl Sada, have come back home to the mountain—a kind of pilgrim too . . . to drive a taxi up to *el paso del gachupín.* You know *gachupín,* I wonder? No I don't think so.

Spurs—what you used to call Spaniards.

So you know our poet, our language, our history—and you are not here for the scenery—or for questions, I know this. But maybe later you will permit me to guess—

Canada.

Canadá? It is like Gringolandia?

Tan lejos de dios.

Just as far from god—as us? you mean, or them—but right now you are wondering if I need to look at the road. *No te preocupes, jovencita,* I could drive this road in my sleep—no but I swear I never do! Paha! Like I told you I am not the only driver to go right to the pass, but most will leave you partway, at the chalet abandoned now—another failed *desarrollo turístico*—and tell you it is not far to walk. But it is. Very far. You have found the right man. I go up even in bad weather. And I am the only one to go up empty. My wife is from a village just the other side of the pass. We live out near Chimalhuacán now. Her family says she does not visit them enough anymore. Because I keep her so busy. What are they supposed to think when she has so handsome a husband? And sometimes there is someone up there who needs a ride to town or to market. Farmers or *alpinistas*—or tourists who find out their *taxista* didn't wait. With me this will never happen! so don't worry I take payment only when we come down—that is, if we make it—pah! you know I am joking by now, yes?

Rocket attacks of laugh, launched from an upper lip pressed onto the lower—swept by the wireshocked handlebars—plosive salvoes of laughter *beware their nervy infections.* Big dark wavy hands shortsleeved red-brown farmer's tan. Silver capped molars, one missing incisor—broken old hound, court jester, but in the dancing eyes—look at me I am old but wise too, careful do not be fooled by the fool!

And I am not fooled, old man.

Which hotel told you about me I must thank them for such a beautiful *cliente*—no no have not one instant of worry, I'm much too old for all that now I have a grandson your age. Three sons and a beautiful wife! But look at me—sixty and not one grey hair. Just white ones and black—pahaa! *puras canas.* Salt and pepper, is this not what you say in English? *Sal y pimienta.* And is that English you are writing in your *cuaderno* and what are you writing now?

Every single word you say.

Pahh!—I thought so you are finding me very picturesque right now, no? Pancho Villa rides again only better looking this time. Everyone says. You are finding my Mexican gallantry irresistible. You can admit this. You are not the first—how could you help it? Even so young and from a cold country you are a woman after all. This is very obvious of course. In the end you will succumb—though it is only a game for me now, a game I have loved. So don't worry I am just talk. And it is dignified that you should take your time but do not bother to resist—it is inevitable. And this *encanto* I have is a great gift, *¿sí o no?* You do not answer but I see you know how to answer without talk. This too is a gift, only not one of mine.

But enough of this for now you still do not look up to the mountains. You are from Canada I understand. But this is not only postcard scenery. Every rock every tree we are passing now contains a story. The old people are glad I am back, they send all the anthropologists to me now. Of course I do not know so much but who is a better talker? I see you have no answer to that.

Probably you know the legend of our two great mountains up there. WhiteLady, Iztaccihuatl, and SmokingStone. Usually it is Popo that is lost in the clouds but it is eight days now we do not see the WhiteLady. You knew they were lovers probably. Yes. But did you know they were from rival tribes? Ah, I see this interests you. A love not meant to be. A wizard's curse and she sleeps for an eternity. Her lover stands over her fuming and smoking and thundering vengeance. In the old times on special dates they would send a pair of lovers up there to be sacrificed.

How many of such stories lost? No more, not as long as I am around. Some countries have gold, some silver or oil, but this pass is the El Dorado of *legends!* This rough road is paved with them—

So let the spirit rise to its new level let it SOAR up into the hills. Lift me unresisting laughing with this laughing man so proud to bring me here, bubbling with talk. Why has he come to me why now?

Racketing over potholes and redclay washboards. Cardboard Guadalupe jigged and swayed from the twisted rearview—smell of hot vinyl, neoprene and pine. Cool air, molared roadgrit.

Lightswells, shadowfalls . . . across a smoking cone spun in candyfloss cloud.

Farmsteads, green pastures, islands of brush. Goats and sheep.

All this land here was once owned by the richest man around. There that clump of pines is where they found him. About a hundred years ago. Impaled on a treetop. Maybe on the big one there but it would have been much smaller back then so maybe that big stump. The forest here is supposed to be protected. It is our patrimony, no? But people need wood, I do not have the answer. A farmer who had prospered through his pact with the devil and had become rich in lands, about to marry the most beautiful girl around. The devil asked only one small thing in exchange— to take the bride on her wedding night. Of course this is easier in theory. When the night came the groom broke his word and took her first. They found the groom the next morning with half the tree stuck through him like a donut. This devil was a symbolist, what do you think?

The woods are full of his children, Coatepoztles, serpent children who tempt woodcutters into deadfalls and crevasses. . . . Ah do not be afraid to fall asleep, *hijita*. I can tell these stories in your sleep as I drive. You will find the air up here restful. You will see. Don't be afraid, child, sleep. . . . There, that's better.

I will watch the road. I will watch out for us.

Wake to the marble clatter of hail! tiny hailpeas leaping off the hood spittlegrilled. Ah, *señorita*, welcome back. We are at the chalet you can just see it through this mess. Let's go in I know a way inside this noise is killing me this is why I never paint this truck. Will you not come inside? this cannot last fifteen minutes maximum but there will be much light-ning leave your bag there is nobody—come let's run together now.

Inside the chalet a scaling up from hiss of rage to pebbleclash to roofroar the hail lancing down through the neardark sparked by flash on flash but no thunder the hail so loud feel it through the floor electric vibrant buzz of hail pounding leaves to pummel—flowers bees juice-extracted. Branches bared and bent to their knees.

Thunder, fading thunder.

Windblasts skittering wrinkles—breaking icy spindrift—across the parking lot. . . .

Quiet. Stormebb echoing behind the eyes.

Ground a slush of grated coconut. Air a riot of scents, cutsap, bro-kenstalks, membranes burst to paste. Pine, cedar, wildflowers grasses— rich black earth! to see is to breathe is to taste this place. *Dare Terram Deo.*

Fill my mouth with this guttered hail mulched with green and petal clips and in the teeth the clack and crunch from slush to swallowsluice. How long since I have eaten how long has it been? I turn he looks at me blinks then smiles and nods.

It is just like carnival ices is it not? maybe I will try some too. Redbrown smiling eyes. Cedar eyes, laughing man, who sent you?

[Cortés Pass]

You do not think it looks like much right now. But there you can see it just the peak of Popo—see the smoke see how near? Do you want to know how high that is in metres and feet? No? Everyone wants to know this, people ask me all the time as though we can see better in numbers than through our eyes.

5,452 metres. 17,887 feet.

Little tibetan tent city of vendors waiting for tourbus Godot. Bedraggled soot-stained canvas flapping in the wind. Ground salted with hail. Sun hot through gaps in cloud.

You will want to walk a little no? Be alone? Maybe visit the monument to Cortés over there—I never go, one day I will blow it up. They name this pass after him even when this is the way the god Quetzalcóatl came as he left us, promising to return. But no they name it after an imposter led by the nose by a traitor—Malinchista, then give that volcano there her name—can you see La Malinche hanging over Puebla just there through the smog?

I will leave the taxi here for you and have an *atole* with my wife's cousin. How long, *mas o menos—no te preocupes*, as long as you like. Just to have an idea so I can be ready for you. No no you pay only when we are back in town. Climb that? You think you can just climb like that, it is already after noon.

No *joven* I cannot take your money now. Do not ruin a beautiful day together I cannot leave you up here like this.

Pahaha—look at you gasping up here like a fish! You are not even above the trees you see it is not so easy or for me either I am getting old for this. Come down now little daughter it is almost dark. If you freeze up here who do you think will have to carry you down? It is a code of mountaineering. You see this is a joke. I see you like such jokes.

Why do you want to climb this *pico de la chingada* anyway—because it is there? If you are serious about El Popo you must first get used to the altitude. It will take a day or two you will need a place to sleep. I can arrange it—you are not planning to sleep in the snow? When the tents are empty at night. Everyone walks back down to San Juan. It is about an hour on the other side. I can talk with my wife's cousin. There are blankets, there is coal. It will be cold but you will be comfortable. Yes yes I know you can pay you are very rich. Come. I cannot go back to town unless I know.

Just think for a minute of the sad silence in the cantina tonight if I am not there. This is bigger than us both. That's better. We understand each other. There is no shame in finding me irresistible. We have already agreed on this.

Laughing man. Cedar man, cedar man with the redbrown eyes and hands, why have you come to me? Are you to be my comic Virgil, are you here to guide and keep me . . . company?

Then why have you come so late?

[18 Dec. 1994]

CROUCHED STAND AT A DISTANCE trunked in trees. Watch the last of the tent people file back down the mountainside. Last to sink down the trail a ponchoed man with a car battery, shouldered. Beyond him the plain already dark, softglow of a city batterylit—Puebla, it must be. Raúl watches me from the jeep over on the turnabout. I enter the tent and only then does he ease away, switching the headlights on.

How strange this world, not Tibet not Canada not quite Mexico. Strange liminal noplace. Threshold, of what. Mystery of highcold and tropical wind. Volcanoes thrown up on a broken plain.

East, a smudge-sashed horizon skirted in dark. Evening starshimmer over Puebla's ochre burn. Roselit cone, canvasframed in the tentdoor, sky of lastgasp light.

Three greywool blankets stacked on a straw mat. Along one tentwall a palmwide shelf, waxspattered and low. Candles, like an altar and woven containers of tortillas, rice, beans. Clay *cántaro* of water. Papers and tobacco. Matches.

Brazier heaped with coal / tequila bottle of gasoline. Advance a trembling match to the brazier, my subway penlight clamped in lightbitted teeth. The gas flares sootedged—scorch and quickfade to a sulkycoal glow.

Windhowl and tentcreak . . . slowflag to silence and stars. Penhand cramped with cold.

Yellowing light too dim to read. Just beyond the door a grey shadow blinks greeneyed into a stab of penlight, dissolves.

Night without sleep.

Dawngrey slopes.

Blink into the smiling black eyes of a child. Day, fullday. Family smiling shyly from the doorway. *Muy buenos dias. ¿Durmió bien, usted?* Yesyes sleptswell—*y ustedes, ¿amenecieron bien? Sí gracias, muy bien*—will your Mercy stay and breakfast with us?

Hasty retreat before they check the altarbaskets.

Please you are welcome to sleep here tonight again. . . .

◈ Another flock of stiff-legged strollers stilting down from the first tour-bus then over to Cortés's sorry monument.

My beaten retreat deeper into the trees. Down the course of a brook threading farther into the snowpatched wood. Back to my little haven out of the wind, through trees fleeced in something like lichen. Beards of Old Testament prophets carved by Michelangelo. *With no more sound than the mice make.*[10]

Left turn at the omensign: *Areas de Trabajo de Control de Plaga,* my aegis my beacon my mission: plague control. A return to this sunsplashed meadow . . . tussocks of grass, daub and violet smear of mountain flower. Slip out of the wind into the bared roots of a pine, gloveclasp of spongy moss, soft needled.

Notebook on one knee . . . somewhere a woodpecker taps taps its hesitant braille. Smoked light, sawshriek of a hawk, or falcon. Scribbler, scratch this note . . . son of Isis, Horus the *Falcon,* but why? if the male is a tercel and the falcon a female?

◈ And each afternoon he finds me. Cedar man, the tinder of his eyes tenderkindled to laughter, inflammable smile. River of baritone, dancing hands, the way he thumbs the shock of moustache smooth. Why have you been sent to me, handsome man with the redbrown eyes and hands?

How do you find me each time—are you some kind of tracker too?

There are not so many footprints out here, your feet are small there is enough snow. You see the coyote there watching us from the trees? I followed him here. You are lucky, it is a good omen. There are not so many left. But it is better not to get so close, some have a sickness. My presence is welcome?—but of course how could it be otherwise. I cannot stay long, this will distress you I know—my clients have given themselves an hour—a hand's breadth in the sky. They tell me this because I have no watch. Pah! My people know what time it is—both in the sky and in the earth there are clocks all around us.

I have convinced my cousin to accept money so you must eat the food they leave. They would never ask money of a pilgrim, they thought you came for a sickness in your family, or some problem of the heart—to San Gregorio del Popo for a *remedio.* You are surprised I see you did not know they call the mountain that. Which Saint Gregory? If you ask them this they will not understand. This San Gregorio is the only one they care about. The volcano is very active now. Did I tell you they sacrificed lovers up there? I am not really so sure this is true.

You know Cortés sent his men up for sulphur for his cannons? Moctezuma sent runners every day for ice. Maybe for margaritas, what do you think? *Los pinches españoles* were always more afraid of life than we ever were of death.

Are you ready for your test after yesterday's lesson? It is good you try to see this place through the Nahuatl tongue of my people. Coyotl?—coyote. But that one is too easy. Atl?—water. Good. Tepetl—stone. Coatl—serpent. Very good. There, butterfly—
Papalotl.

But I did not teach you that one . . . you see down there that cloud that looks like a serpent? Combine the words for cloud and serpent and get Mixcoatl—

Father of Quetzalcoatl.

But you know even this? it is good for me to meet a visitor like you. Ah look our friend coyotl is leaving without his dinner. Our talking has scared the mice. There he goes, Nezahualcoyotl, FastingCoyote. Do you know this poet of the Aztecs? In Mexico there are many great poets, but only two you must know and both of them from very near here. Once you could see both their houses from where we sit.

A breathlessness, under this sky. And still the roaring of the wind in my ears will not quit.

> My love, my liege,
> listen a while to the weary lament
> I entrust to the wind . . .
> to join all the hopes it has taken from me . . .

I am ready, I am willing, I am here. How long—two days or three? All this for what? Another morning of non-event in a rising wind. Another midday of cloud. Mountains—aren't there mountains enough in Canada? Pointless tremontaine ramble, listless wandering. Back to here. To her. Reading rereading her. For what—something I've missed? What hope of finding it now . . . *hope now sacrificed to hopeless love.*

I am fasted and clean. I am lightheaded and calm. And still you do not come to me. But you came up here, Juana, you must have once. Let me find what you found, see this place as you saw.

> See the laughing brook,
> gallant to every flower in the meadow,
> delighting in each, caressing each,
> sharing its affections intimately with all:
> then, let it coursing tell
> how the current of its laughter
> is wrung from my grief . . .

I have stopped the engine in my head. Now day and night all I hear is the howling of the wind. Even here where there is shelter. *I don't hear her music anymore.* I read her constantly now but I have lost it. I keep this journal still but I have stopped the chapters. No matter how I rifle this smashed jukebox for the nightingale's fled melodies—Keats, Rilke, Eliot, Milton, Yeats—

I have lost her music.

Is this the price her tears paid? A roaring in the ears that swallows up the music? Did she sacrifice even this, the music in her mind? Would I—have I already? Is the price of penetrating her silence that the music dies in me? Can I sacrifice even this work of years so close to finishing?

I have come so far. Can I follow her even across this last bridge? Or does it all end now and here? I have reached the heart of Mexico. Hear it?—beat so wildly as I hold it up. Hear it?—pounding in my ears. I have come for the Eye of Egypt, the silence of Horus. To solve the riddle of the Science Queen. I have come for my eyes of wonder.

Where are my eyes?

What do I still have to do—let me lift the veil, hear that silence, see with the power of the Eye Restored!

Or haven't I given enough?

❧ Ours is the eye unrestored, Apollo eye ascendent. . . . Don Juan eye that hungers, that consumes the world—shielded from the Gorgon / turns her into gold.[II]

Eye that hungers, I that thirsts—give it vinegar, put it out it burns.

But if I'm to be made deaf to you now, then I'll hear you with my eyes.

> Hear me then with your eyes only,
> our ears being out of hearing's utmost reach,
> since you cannot hear my croaking tune
> hear without sound, hear groans gone mute.[12]

With eyes made to hear, fingertips to see. Through the lenses of the Science Queen, soothe pain's most silent scream . . . with tongues of flame.

Is Juana's synthesis of the Science Queen a *synaesthetics*—a knitting of the senses for new metaphors? / a fitting of lenses for a new eden. . . .

And how bright there does a green grape blare? There, what hues hew to smooth?

See that softest sadness of blue, cleave / where it trembles cleft and bruised. . . .

Up there. The answers are up there.

Tomorrow I go up. Where I have not let myself look. To where the fire and ice and rose are one. To feel them dance together again in the still throb of this petalled palm, in its livid flame snaking up this arm.

Tomorrow. I find out if I'm strong enough, care enough . . . find what's left to give.

ASCENT

[19 Dec. 1994]

3 A.M. ANOTHER NIGHT, dreams of dreamless sleep. . . .

One day at last not like the others. A day—one day—to break the four-year fast. I take the last breakfast of heroic champions: tortilla card-board, corn in the crop / chewed to kidney paste the brickred beans. Pack the driedrice basket to strew my bright triumphal backpath. Pack up the last three books, the mangled notepads / pencils pens. Powerdown the Powerbook battery light blinking frantic frantic.

Outside I stand planted in the still cold air under the malevolent four hundred stars. Hours yet to red daybreak. Set sail forewarned now four-armed under the ensign of the morning star. Lord/Lady Dawn who does battle with the sun.

Into the gleam of this flagging penlight signs a green semaphore, my coyote-eyed escort. Follow the fasting coyote up. Up onto the near and far of ice and smoking stone. Fasting coyote what do you eat—only Apollonian rodentine plaguevector nectarines, replies the coyote/poet wolfish-grinned. So we'll go together!, share rations, call our mission plague control.

Dead ahead the mountain, a darker shade of night. Disaster's night-shade steeps and stews.

> Pyramidal, funereal, earthborn shadow,
> vain obelisk, skyward thrust . . .

Vain obelisk I will see you scaled and bated. Swordpoint fulcrum of states—liquid earth, glass supercooled, water superheated to steam. Sky that rains fire. And I am that rocking cradle vexed to a quintessence. They send for ice. I will bring down conflagration.

Beware her red hair she eats air like men.

Up and up into breathlessness. Up through mist and the last dwarf trees, hunchbacks bent in drifts.

Up out of the cloud and into blinding day!

This cone a soot-rimmed sear of white. This aspirate light that brands its taper to a gasping throat. *Why was the sight / to such a tender ball as th'eye confined*—LET ME SEE THROUGH EVERY PORE

See through these tricks of light and distance. Shady lightbrakes—
light that stills the eye. Carves and cuts—edges of light.

Light that wedges and splits /
  wisps of It, from blocks of Nought.

2 P.M. . . .

Horizonless distance of rustsmoked sky. How high how high . . .
Windblown ash, swept slopes of slate and rock, faint trail hedged with
cairns.

Black ice and obsidian gleam—plunge to bludgeoned knees. Better I
crawl—my snowy red crayonscrawl of humility.

On humble Humboldt up and on! Gravelpockets of shrub—gentian
this?—a field of tiny cactus purpleflowered—gather a sample for the
Beagle hold it close feel the thorns wake and warm and nettle these
sleepyhead hands. Look see the ice and grit pouched under this talon-
clutch of nails. Peel them back like petals of a rose.

3:35 P.M. . . .

Earthquake in the sky! Grey sway of quaked earth underknee—rumble
of rock, reek of eggshell rot, sulphur mist. TEMBLOR! What next
now—avalanche?

Glimpses of the peak no nearer . . . farther away then? Poor narcolept
doublebent do you still know up from down? know seamonster from
diving belle?

Chestcrack gasp and lunge of lungs. Aspirate rasp, exhalate of ground
glass.

Sit awhile up here and rest. Time . . . a small smooth stone of word,
wedged in the chest.

Uptilt this face to hear the sear the sunbrass blare
Tonguetrace the ripped blue streak of falcon screetch
Answer it!
I hear a cry . . . voice like mine.

Above, the peak . . . adrift in a cloudsped sky. Closer now bends its soar
of near and far.

Dark cloud boiling up from below. Whirl of snow . . . a falling up.
Stormcloud of unknowing climbs from my snowblind feet to muddled

eyes. Whirl of wasp-paper wafers / a roar of iron on the tongue. On, hadji, on through this greyflake storm of ash and snow. Tempest fugit, crawled.

Ahead a tiny redrock alpenhut allcomforts of home / little firehouse in the air is it real is it true? Cactus thornthrob behind one eye . . . realer, this pain than anything now. On, not far my volcano bungalow / my stormshelter squat and snug.

Thresholdstoop to cough and betelspew whorly pink candyfloss on the snowycone snow.
    Pause at the door—ring the brassthroat sun's templed gong
    Ears run blood—eggshell temples thunderhammered to tempura—
    Wash of white, skullcrush fresco of Golgotha . . .
    Shut the door Christ born-in-a-barn
    Can't go up
    I can't go on.

This is all, all I have to give . . . palladial thunderstone foundered, crashed to earth. Sisyphus and stone come to final rest. Phaëton and chariot rubble-parked. Last stop last mansion final abode. Terminus.
    Here I can rest.
        Feel better now?
    Take a deep breath / deeprest.
    It's over. Sleep. Screen to black.

But no, Lady Lazarus wakes! still undead—an hour a minute a year but not too late—so let it find this hadji here! Bring the mountain down to me I'm *ready*—pencilstub sharpened on these filed teeth—bring down the synaesthetic fusion auromantic febrifuge emesis for the gutblocked flea—
    O bring me my eyes of wonder!—synaesthesia to strip off the anaesthetic gasmask of ratio / xenophobic blindfold of Cheops / precious serpent's turquoise mask.
    Come and get me / ready or not here I am / tabula rasa
    Come and get me
        spread out on thy razed-table—stirruped / ready to ride again!
    Ears blasted eyes blinded tongue tied ready for the extreme unction—anoint me with a thrust of transcendent vision—give o give me the green lenses of her Queen of the Sciences

synaesthetic codex

  Mosaic tablets

    Silence's poetics

      hearing of the Eye Restored . . .

        anything

I am waiting. I am here. Kneeling at the altar wedded to this hunger bled and fasted clean.

    Please . . .

      Anything . . .

Do you need to hear it?

So hear: I failed her—eyefailed I've flailed.

Now do I beg?

Nothing . . .

Windroar, no more.

You are alone here.

Foolish child silly idiot—come to the heart of Mexico to find the eye of *Egypt.*

I always knew have known it in four hundred different nightmares. Funny how it feels at last to fail her . . . so finely, so finally. So different from all that failure dreamed. Too weak to rage now . . . to eke for/age . . .

Too tired for shame . . . to weep, *for shame.*

The Science Queen will have to wait. Three more hundred years at least.

The very last thing now left to do, leave a few clues . . . unrepeatable record of failed experiments, cautionary diary of a lost expedition . . . for the sake of forsaken seekers of a future age.

Do not attempt this at home.

Five notepads, a dead laptop. December (?), 2295. Will they read English . . . read anything? Or just break it all up for kindling . . . a little fire . . . one life saved at least. Maybe two.

For another hour. Maybe two.

Say it was worth it, Beulah.

Say good-night.

chorus

Hear me as I sing
of two Gypsies,
the contrasting glories
we find Egypt encompassing!

verses

To her breast, pale Cleopatra
in love fastened the fangs of an asp.
But how superfluous the serpent
there where love had passed.
Ah me, what torment!
Dear God, how piteous!
  But to the heroic Descendant
of an illustrious line,
the greater the Love by which she is wounded,
the more exalted is the death that she desires—
yet who truly dies
whose love has not ended?
  Fearlessly the Egyptian queen
offers up her breast to the venom,
for none feels the body's agonies
whose soul also is tormented
(to suffer less visibly
is not to suffer less).
  Cleopatra's nerve and passion
Catherine emulates, but deepens them,
in an imitation that surpasses

its own original:

just as one who lives for Christ

dies into Life eternal.

   That the Emperor Augustus

might never put her sovereign beauty on parade,

Cleopatra chose suicide, preferring thus

to end her life

than to face its debasement

and the creeping death

of her enslavement.

   Just so, did a heroic Catherine

bare her throat of ivory

to an inferno of blades:

(Hell itself would never break her faith)

and so, in dying, triumphed over

the one who took her life.

   For Cleopatra, infamy or death:

by each, a precious life was threatened;

her choice was death, borne

as the lesser evil

to one who cherishes honour

more than life itself.

   In like fashion

did the greater Egyptian, Catherine,

offer up her lovely limbs to the wheel of knives

and thus to triumph gallantly aspire.

By dying,

to reach Eternity.

JUANA INÉS
DE LA CRUZ

HARLEQUIN: SOUND BITES

MY LAWYER PAUSED ON THE WAY out the courthouse door to give me a free image-consult. "The girl's become a *cause*, Professor. If only the photos they're running were a tad less attractive. You understand, they want blood. Remember: bland, bland, bland. No quotes. Absolutely. You can't believe how stupid and self-serving they can make you sound. And whatever you do, don't say 'no comment.' Say it wouldn't be appropriate to comment at this time. Better yet, say nothing. Got it?" He pulled a black woolen scarf out of his briefcase, shrugged on a grey overcoat. "You might straighten your tie. And *relax*, will you? Take a deep breath. I've seen you on TV—try looking less guilty."

My lawyer, my defender, guarantor of my rights and freedoms, bucking me up.

A string of news vans is parked along the sidewalk. Exhaust tumbling up from the tailpipes of passing cars . . . slish of tires on wet pavement. April weather can be the most disappointing. Bare branches, tiny buds of green candied by the sleet. A sparrow's forlorn twittering echoes in the portico. Overhead, black clouds mass sharply as if painted over glass. Cameramen of competing networks huddle together, smoking. Journalists, wide-scattered, perched on their islands of ambition. We are spotted at last. Television to the front, radio and print on the periphery—they rush up the steps, jostling as they close in.

Icy, the granite stairs. Headline: *Philandering prof splits swollen melon on courthouse steps.*

Malicious whine of motor drives, bursts of light, seethe of flashes recharging. . . .

"Professor Gregory! Professor— why was the civil suit dropped? You cut a deal?"

"No comment."

"Still expecting criminal charges?"

"That would be a question for his lawyer," said mine.

"Doctor." A familiar voice, a sardonic voice. "Have you nothing to say for your*self*?"

"Sorry."

"*Are* you? Can we quote you on that?"

I know this voice.

"That's not what I—"

"Then you're *not* sorry."

"I have nothing to—"

"Come on." A hand tightening on my arm. "Let's go."

"To be sorry for?"

"Nothing to *say*. It wouldn't be appropriate—"

"What's appropriate here? A girl lies dying—"

"Who said she's dying?"

"You're saying the seriousness of her condition is *exaggerated?*"

"Let's *go*." If the steps had been less slippery he might have pulled harder.

"They're being cautious, naturally."

"Because her father is a high-profile surgeon you mean?"

Two steps, a pause. "I said nothing of the sort. It's—"

"That's *enough*." An angry warning in Eric Heffner's voice. "Thank you all. My client has no further comment at this time." We were moving more briskly now.

"Was your client about to say she's not the real victim in this story? Maybe he is . . . ?"

"The CBC hires telepaths now?" I called over my shoulder.

"*Shut up.*"

"You're not to blame then—she wanted to be stopped, wanted attention. That it? Maybe this was all a set up? Don Juan—*victim*. That the real story? Girl bites dog."

"That's enough. You are harassing my client."

"He *is* a victim, then. First of circumstance, now the media. What about the other co-eds, Professor? Who else harassed you?"

"Let us through please."

Questions shouted from all sides in a strident rush as we elbowed our way towards the taxi stand. Electric cords whipped clear of shuffling feet. Faces and microphones thrust across my line of sight.

"We're obstructing *you*? Are *we* obstructing justice too? Wait! Do you deny you've been victimized? Shall we take your silence as confirmation? Is that how you want the story to read?"

The public pillory. She'd foreseen it. Fifteen minutes. I get to be the entertainment. Pathetic sinner. Feed the enormous all consuming maw. The information hole. That which feeds the emptiness. Feel the hole . . . feed the whole. Time to *prepare a face to meet the faces that you greet . . . to murder and create . . . lift and drop a question on your plate . . .*

I stopped at the cab and faced them. "No."

"No what, Doctor? What's your story?"

"No, I am not a victim here."

I turned and reached for the door handle . . . sequined droplets on chrome.

"Dr. Gregory, one more thing: why would a widely published academic be calling vanity presses in Ontario? A respected intellectual— *self-publishing?* Who wants attention, Doctor, who wants to be stopped?"

[20 Dec. 1994]

CEDAR MAN WITH THE BARITONE EYES / *river of dancing hands. Smile . . .*

Pah! I see you have waited for us before climbing to the top but there are better days to go for a walk. You are much stronger than you look—so are we all, *verdad?*—but it takes more than lungs to climb Popo, you need to eat. Don't look so sad *hijita,* at least you left the treeline behind this time. The sickness can strike even the strongest at this height.

Ahh señorita que amable! gracias for the cactus flower there are few women I accept such bouquets from anymore though of course many try.

Meet my wife's baby brother, Gregorio. It is his tent you slept in. Find you?—no magic we looked here because there is no point looking for you out there.

Not how—*why.*

Yes I understood you the first time but we can talk when we are down. No no we cannot go back without you. The code of mountaineers is to take down what you have brought up. You remember. You are perhaps too tired now to smile. We are all tired.

Right now the snow is not yet too deep but in an hour it is maybe too late. 4,460 metres, this hut. Would you want us to be discovered up here next spring in metres or feet? 14,633. You have done well and so have I. Almost three of your miles in the air no? You are very light and Gregorio is strong but it is so very high, and I am old. So we must ask you to help us. The three of us together we can help each other. You have the young lungs, together we can find the legs we three. . . .

No listen please. We are friends now, I see in your eyes you see this. I know many things as I have told you and you would not leave a friend up here—I know you maybe better than you think so do not ask this of me. But wait, before you answer me I will answer you. . . .

Yes, for one minute we should be serious. I came up today for a son everyone loved. For fifteen years. Our last, the youngest. Pablito. He was touched a little, like you. But in the end he could not stay.

I am not here because I need to save someone. But know that each kindness to you is like a smile hello to him. *Entiendes?* A precious flower.

And from Gregorio here, *tambien.* Pablito was his favourite nephew.

Come down with us. We are asking you in my son's name.

Take my hand.

And we begin.

Twilight of thickflake snow shin-deep. Roam and swerve of dogs and goats among the tents. Indios blanketed, sexless bundled wool, old and young alike. Breaths of spume, bent on kindling fires with grasses and dung. What century is this what season what world—below this snow, this cloud, the stonethroes of smog-choked cities. Five million souls east on the plains, twenty-five more in the valley west. . . .

Hijita I see you were not expecting people still here so late. Yes the snow, of course. It is dangerous to go back down to the village now. But most would stay tonight anyway. It is the solstice. You did not know. They have asked that you eat with us. Not much—they respect your fast. Simple food. Mostly of corn—a *pozole*, and a broth of chicken and *chipotle* with lime. Tortilla—did you know we import corn now from Gringolandia?—we who brought the world the civilization of the Corn. It would be enough that you hold a bowl in your lap, to join with us.

It is part of our faith, which is the land, this mountain that flattens churches and villages, even the capital. Mexico City in '85 was like the end of the world I was there. The earth itself died that day. There is much we could teach you about loss. Before you eat they wish you to understand something.

Some say tomorrow is the first day of a new sun. We will make a special ceremony borrowed from what is still known of the old days. They have built an effigy of our San Gregorio del Popo—a volcano from seeds of amaranth and on it put a mitre and *sambenito* as though the mountain itself is jury and judged, saviour and condemned. Then we eat—we cut it up and every one of us gets a part to eat of the mountain of seed that consumes us until the end of time—but each time it dies leaves the richest soil behind.

And when it is done—down to the last seed, we cry—

Teocualo, god is eaten . . . do you say this still?

Yes, child, we say this, you know even this. We believe nothing escapes the cycle of the suns. Not even the mountain, not the gods themselves—and who is around to eat god if not us?

Will you eat with us?

Cedar man with the laughing eyes so strange jesterfriend I know now what you've come to do, why you've come so late.

When the music's fled.

I have lost the music. I've lost, and it's like you say. It is loss you've come to teach. You came for me. I've never had a friend like you. How strange, a friend. Here, now in this noplace. . . .

Yes cedar man I'll eat. For you.

It is pulque they drink. Would you like to taste?—fermented cactus juice a very ancient recipe.

Yes this sacred drink is a must. I can get through this, I try to be calm. Here, *pruébalo, ándale.* Sip of latex over the tongue, ferment of saliva and bile, rolling pincushion of pricks behind these thimblejaws. Old seamed faces smile and nod around the fire. Black glitter of eyes rimmed in cup. All huddle for warmth of shoulder and hip. Tanglehair waif scratches her pet piglet's pink gut / plucks out a snuffled melody of love and contentment.

This old man would like to talk with you. Will you allow me to translate from our tongue?

Susurrus of a soft, clicked sibilance . . . *this is Nahuatl.*

Raúl here says you are from the North, young one, yet I see you feel cold just like us. . . .

They say gringos have walked on the moon what do you say to that?

How far do you think the moon is tonight just behind the snow, white with the moon's snowwhiteness?

I have heard a man could walk up to her in ten thousand days, or if he is lazy, twenty. . . .

Ah here comes the food I hope you will find it savoury.

I can get *through* this—skip the thick redstew *pozole,* take the bowl of peppery broth instead feel its burn untouched in this lap of ice. How nice how nice until it cools. . . .

But then they bring in the tall coneycake, volcano of seed feel the pitch and yaw / chaw and cheer near and nearing—this I have to eat they are watching me. Tanglehair waif shares out the cake on pigscent fingers what difference can it make? Rage of hunger blast of whine through the mind time to eat IT'S TIME—come home Beulah come home for supper—what was their ancient recipe for obsidian wine? you've done everything / tried all but this—

Try then, try. Take the cake open your lips—*swallow the earth that*

vomits life as time runs down to die, chew the seedy mountain of molarshards all
crumble and thrash / tongue bracts of godchaff to a slime of honeyed amaranth /
bolt loss's sup / suck and flush the cosmogonic cud—stomach the stormseed of theo-
machy sweet theodicy diced and iliac / Godflayed flesh threshed / gutted, quelled.
And all shall be well and all shall be well—

No! You WILL eat—for him—you said you would you *can.*

You are tired and sick, you have lost and it's done   let it go give it up
get over it get on with it, do you understand?—*enough.*

When you taste the cake this little girl gives, see her sweetness as what
you eat. There, see? This meal, this night you can, even in front of them.

Especially them. Just eat, and sleep.

❖   I wake from a dream. They are all watching TV. This is why the car
battery, sisyphean haul up and down the mountainside for evenings
televised at ten thousand feet.

Tentwalls spill the blue caravan of icons across a desert screen—
shadowmask fire fed on optic cones and rods. Soft disembodied bundles
here we sit stranded before garlanded ads for retirement beaches, and
operatic soaps—O the creole heartbreak of blond Mexican elites! Then,
this truth stranger than the strangest dream . . . 'we pause for station
identification, this is channel 13—*TV Azteca.*'

Here at last we are arrived at the thirteenth level of heaven.

Aztec TV. Channel 13.

Here beneath the snow in Cortés Pass, Indian mothers—bodies
workbroken and careworn—slump in wonder before nymphs blue-
eyed like Jesus in white bikinis, stunning icons of statuesque per-
fectibility—

These are the griffins. Fabricated from a wishlist of beauty . . .

helium breasted, negress haunched

barbie-legged, waxy-crotched—

labial notch thonged from cunt to hip—

a perfect pelvic V for all things Virtuous.

Twist-tie waists, collagenic lips / butterfly lashes, Nefertiti necks. O
how we worship you. Sphynxes of a monstrous scientific beauty, V for
victory over earthborn nature. Women with wings of wax, scales of gold.
Winged heralds of our mute self-denunciation—*de nuestro auto-*
particular—heretics all, the we of all flesh and superfluity. . . .

And in the smoking mirror blearily we see—see? how they are adored /

adored by the Eye unrestored. See them bask in the love of god, so near us yet so far above, all aglow in its bluish love. Godlove of a billion blue suns that ring the great globe itself, and burn.

Burn like salt.

Who broke the meaning machine—and left us this? this thing this box—decoder / decanter of our obsidian wine. That in its effervescent thrall, up to the altar we all go—stunned and quiescent, mumbling *textos de neutralización* . . . the sacrificial victim's numbing psalmody that strokes our pink gut / plucks out our hearts' melodies while our corpses still live. TV Azteca, Channel 13.

Electronic pillory, virtual confessional that adores the Image profanes the Verb. Get a bigger screen mute the sound!—the better to adore the blue van of vatic visions scrolling down and deeper down through mirror smoke. Channel of home sacrifice, glowing hearth of a heartsick hopelessness. Show host that melts like candyfloss on our tongues.

I've followed my cedar Virgil down to here I've come all this way . . . haven't I? So write it, write it calm, slow it down. Try to get this right. This once, this time. For explorers of a future time.

This is not just the death of fire and air. Or water and earth. *They* call it only entertainment, I call it the death of the fifth element. Not ennui, not absurdity but accidie—Inquisitorial relaxation's soulslack laxity. Call it indifference, inertial victim of the sun.

This is the death of the soul.

Name this!—the dragon Apophis—enemy of both storm and sun. Indifference, Enemy of Both Sides.

FEED US—life love hate anything not this

Together everywhere—even here in this pass we bend before the aura/cling of vastly meaningless event. Oracling of unrequited Godlove rendered down to purest semblance. Welcome to the god channel, vision on a global scale that wakes our hunger for communion.

Once this was the divine ground of archetypal myth . . . this neuron-bombed lot strewn now with spent Cokes and surrendered Nikes—our cathexis confected on Madison Avenue by bluebloods steeped in Classics and Humanities. This . . . vacant scatter of voided universals on the scale of race, the shared needles of a virtual experience—

Rapturous.

And over this, our everlasting Conquest's littered battleground of broken glyphs—cross and eagle, serpent and thorn—transcendent at last, one blue banner waves its parabolic ascendency above the harrowed field. . . .

And higher still a starry sky of burnt out satellites. Beckoning.

Six billion frail hummingbirds hover round an electron bath . . . sugary solution too thin too dissolute to nourish us—endless cycling of little wings—cycling recycling one last lovesong—we the lovestarved, consuming ceaselessly . . . even the BlueHummingbird of the South starves now—for love, for an end.

And hapless, calmed, in this faint blue grasp we are danced to death.

Bear witness. This snowy night, before this blue altar, we are the same. Pressed close for warmth . . . weary shoulders, chilly knees. Here there are no differences. We are together, one, all at last in this. . . . Tonight you are all beautiful to me.

Women broken bodied, living eyes /
   tanglehair waif, pinkgut pig . . .
      cedar man.

Howl of dogs outside, tame to wild.

Scribbler, *you are not here to verify. You are here to kneel, where prayer was once valid.* Lay your stub of pencil down. Close the notebook, the last of books.

[21 Dec. 1994]
LAUGH AND STUMBLE of children's voices between the heaves of dream.

Day, morning it must be, but such a light!—swirl of orange and lavender—here in this mountain pass we are woken into *cloud*. Through the flap of canvas I see the other tents, their snowbent brows / frowning down the dawn. Softest of snowdrifts.

Step thigh-deep into morning!—children running laughing waist-high in this lambent cloud torched by the sun's rising / screened yet in the sway and swirl and bloom—prismed, dry and crystalline—of an icepetal mist. The littlest imps charge up to their chests—launched and caught—fall back cradled, upright still, backed and banked in drifts.

After all you have offered me, let me show your children this . . . all black agleam their widening eyes watch me flap and flail out robes and angel wings, then they see they understand and we are all a choir a host—an angelus tolling out our backstroked script in angel dust.

Now all around us as we sit up / barks then panicked bleat of hounded goats—neck-deep slow-motion chase—slow lunge to ford the flood of white, their prow-throats ploughing out a mole-berm maze, their wake dawnflanked in a crumble of pink.

Another moment of grace, stay of peace.

Vats bubble over low fires gouting char and steam as the tentcity denizens pause to watch their angels fall.

What magic is this?—northwitch craft—
    this tropical snow
        this sunrise without sun
            these falls of weightlessness . . .
Sunshred lasts of cloud . . . rainbow veils slowrent from the pass up towards the still-shroud tops. Slowfade of roseate mist burled and dissipate, up to a white-shouldered day. . . . Glow to gleam to slow flare of light—blinding brilliant the world in snow renewed!—a beyond all etched in clarity.

I stand blinking stunned in this air . . . then feel the river of cedar friendbreath / his tobacco baritone warm my ear.

Good morning, *hijita*. You see La Malinche now over Puebla City of Angels as though we were standing on her slopes? Sixty kilometres, easily! And that cone farther to the east? You see the detail, the folds, ravines, the soot like the velvet on a boy's lip, yes? You are thinking it does not seem so far. This is *el pico de Orizaba* almost at the Gulf of México though we are standing in the centre of our nation. You understand, but maybe even better through numbers this is at least *180 kilometres away* . . . yet as if just beyond the stretch here of my hand. The span of an old man's arm, a hundred and twenty of your miles.

Look long, look carefully. Though you are young we may never—neither of us—have eyes like this again.

Feel the sun hot off the snow, melting everywhere now at a furious pace, can't tear my eyes away, gorged on scans of distance, spans of light. . . .

Up here we have seen this before, this transparency of the air returned to us. I myself once or twice, but the old ones maybe half a dozen times. I wonder if it is not more beautiful than even when Cortés looked on it. Now that we are so close to losing it altogether.

Maybe this beauty of the world—so much, all the time, would be too much for us, what do you think?

Maybe we would all go blind with it. *Maybe we already have, cedar man. Tell all the truth but tell it slant. . . .*

Yes daughter—*todos acegados*, you may be right about the blindness. Come, there is a spot not far from here where we can see the capital, as Cortés first did.

Mexico City 30 k. away through this air's transparency as sharp and clear as a quarry's steamshovelled floor. Street grids under snow like a gallet strand—like the rubble it will be again—raked sandbox of summer dun under a freak of winter, out of season, out of time and tune.

Soft featherfall now, of ash across the newfallen snow.

Here are my eyes of wonder restored to me! Here is the beauty of a world that is lost. The eye restored to beauty is not just awake to loss but *accepts* . . . finds loss itself heartbreaking in its beauty. Welcome it, this heartbreak!—and choose, let's all choose to make the last loss beautiful, together. A little dispensation, oh yes call it a *finesse*.

See it—see it with the Eye Restored! *Love loss*, love its beauty—its contingency.

Without the slightest hope of a return.

Look, child, there at last is WhiteLady, after so many days! Me I have always thought her more beautiful than Popo lying there asleep—see her hip, her breast, her knees? We know all great mountains as gods but everyone comes here for El Popo. She is not quite as high but the WhiteLady is also more than 5,000 metres. High enough for anyone, or should be. But you know?—I never climbed her either, not even as a boy. So many little peaks up there you can't be sure when you are on top . . . I should not be saying all this, next you will be climbing her.

No? but you surprise me now—why not?

Because I can see her from here. *With you,* Raúl.

I am glad, little daughter, because those heights are not for us. We cannot breathe up there. You are right we can see enough of their beauty from here—as much as we can bear, and maybe a little more. Down here there is life for us, yes, and too much work—but friends and loved ones, *¿sí o no?*

Dear sweet friend with the laughing eyes dancing hands. I never had a friend like you, how do I repay all this tenderness? I'll always remember, you. To my last breath's faltering draw.

I'm ready to go down.

This makes me happy to hear—

Take me down, Raúl . . . you are a very handsome man very very irresistible.

Yes I know and you, child, are very delirious. I will take you *a donde-quiera*—but maybe first you will let me take you to a doctor for that infection in your hand. You can leave for the capital first thing in the morning if you like. I will talk to the caretakers at Sor Juana's hacienda and you can stay with them. No—I would ask you to stay with me where I rent a room but with my wife at our home in Chimalhuacán it would not be proper, you understand.

It hurts you that I say this. No it is not because of what you just said. Please we are friends you must not be ashamed you have a fever. Do not be hurt it is only that you are too beautiful for the neighbours not to wonder. No—*Dios!* I see now I have hurt you more with a stupidity—in Mexico beautiful is not a dirty word I do not mean it as an insult now you must try to understand me. Please do not look at me with those big green eyes. To us beauty is a gift. Part of it is very temporary and many people have this. The other part, a few—you, will have always.

Understand that this is for my wife's honour not mine. It is not your fault there were indiscretions in the past. A very long time ago. She is well respected here. With many friends. There is a sadness in her life I can do nothing for . . . except not increase it. And it would hurt our friends and hers to have to wonder about me again. Even for a minute.

Tell me you understand. The caretakers at the hacienda of Sor Juana are good people. They have a daughter who is your age. Quiet people, please stay the night with them. You can leave once you have seen the doctor who is also a good man.

Please I did not mean to hurt you.

I've been climbing the wrong mountain all the time. Am always. Why can't I get it right? Cortesian error mine the same mistake as the stout stoat Cortés—sunblind on gold and transcendence—blind to the enchantment of the fallen world, to the Conquest as clash of geometries—cavalries of the ascending line that crush the helix's infantry.

But the sublime and the transcendent *were never the same*. This is our old mistake. Sublime—sub/liminus—*under* the threshold. Threshhold we can imagine but never live beyond. Not up there in that breathlessness. *Down here*, find the sacred down here—in the high passes yes, but *under* the threshold of impasse.

So take communion—with the earth as host! Tongue with firecleft tongues the wafer'd / earth. Trace the faultless fall of chariots, to ground zero, down.

Make *this* the ceremony of immanence! Eat god—*not the other way round*—our vice is in the versa—in eating the godseed we make the cycle sacred, lend the daysun flight / through our return to earth each night. Here are my eyes of wonder. It was here all along—this wide world under the *night* sun now, so bright so various so new.

This was the greatest magic of Isis—the life that was in her mouth, the magic that returns god to the cycle of the Nile.

So make ready the night sun's ceremony. Prepare the sublime rites of the fall.

On this sorrow's morrow of a busride back to the capital, in this optic of antibiotic calm, Raúl there is something I didn't say to you I'm sorry. Yes cedar man with the laughing eyes dancing hands you hurt my heart—

nada grave nada nuevo without ever wanting to. But you also saved my life
. . . just long enough to show my eyes such *miracles.*
 And now it's too late to tell you. . . .
 You never asked my name, Raúl.
 My name is Beulah.

JUANA INÉS
DE LA CRUZ

chorus

Seraphim, come,
come see a marvel:
that a burial has become
the work of Angels;
and here is the wonder—
that the one they inter
is one of their own!

verses

That ancient Tribunal
of the Supreme Legislator
on stone tablets handed down
a hard law to hardened sinners,
only later exchanging stony frowns
for soft compassion:
proving Time's passage
moves even mountains.
  Eminent is the sepulchre
glorious the shrine
of the incorruptible cadaver,
her mortal remains containing yet
a breath of hope, even as a vessel
retains the savour
of a liquor
it once held.

  Just so does a holy spirit
leave its imprint
upon the lovely Virgin's
martyred corpse;
while the blades that on other forms
inflict dark horrors,
on hers project
only glimmerings and reflections.
  His merest fingertip the burin,
God composed
Ten Commandments
on slabs of stone;
but with a People sunk in vice
(and Moses so zealous they be chastened)
being made of stone did not suffice
to stop them being broken.
  And to this end, it was God's will
that a new tablet be incised—
this, the Law of the Gospels—
in the whiteness of her faultless form.
Vengeance is the Lord's . . .
yet in this holy text
there remains much more
that speaks of tenderness.

Catherine would not have wished
that those vainglorious pyramids
her forbears had raised, however high,
be the final resting place
of her blessed remains,
but rather holy Sinai
whose stony heights
were once, long ago,
the smouldering Throne
of a sacred fire.
Up there, it is not the gravid tonnage
of a mountain pressing down on her
but rather her own sweet weight, as of a lover,
that presses down at the summit.
Rest, then, in peace, there on high,
asking nothing more
than to be so near
a body that is Heaven.

APART FROM ITS LOCATION near the hospital, this struck me as the most thoroughly improbable meeting place. A steak house catering to the insatiate college-age carnivore. It was hard to square the choice with the alphabet soup of letters behind Dr. Elsa Aspen's name. I waited inside the entrance as a congenitally chirpy hostess bobbed up in a tight rugby shirt. The corporation's costume designer had evidently forgotten that rugby players claim to eat their dead.

"I believe a Dr. Aspen is expecting me."

"You bet." She smiled deeply into my eyes, then after the briefest instant lowered hers to scan the reservation book. "No problem—44." Another brilliant smile. "Right this way, sir."

She led me deeper into the narrow-gauge train wreck of lapsed styles so perfectly emblematic of Western low-brow chic. Sallow pools of light from low-slung tiffany lamps lent the room a muddled air of obscurantist mystery. Unplaned planks and high-backed booths evoked the homely cattle car. The salad bar feed trough under the EXIT sign extended a hearty invitation to fill one's boots, as we say, on the way out. Over the whole business hung a 'faint whiff of bear grease.'[13]

Dr. Aspen slid out of the booth and stood to greet me. She was fully my height, almost six feet. Firm handshake. I took up position across from her.

"Thanks for coming," she began, resuming her seat. "The cloak and dagger's for me, mostly. It would have been awkward to bump into her family at the hospital."

"Nice spot."

"I was fairly sure I wouldn't see anyone here I knew."

"No, but *I* might."

"Students. I suppose that's true," she said with what I first took for indifference.

"Yes, I suppose it is." *And so the battle for the high ground begins.* Of course her real work, her true work was not here but *out there,* out in the wards, in the streets, among the multitudes, out on the great plains of Ur-consciousness. . . .

"Actually it's pretty dark in here," she added, sounding concerned now, "and as you can see, not exactly packed on a Saturday afternoon."

"Not exactly, no," I said, forcing a smile. "Let's start over."

"I would have thought after what the media has put you through over the last few days, being spotted here would be the least of your worries."

"It is."

"Drink?" she asked, hoisting hers, nearly empty, as the waiter pulled up.

"Scotch, rocks."

"Would you mind bringing him a scotch and me another vodka grapefruit, tall?" With a wry look she polished off the drink for the waiter to take. "It's supposed to be my day off, after all."

I felt myself relaxing under the spell of that contralto voice. Warm, clear, lying in the ear like liquor under the tongue. I reminded myself that this voice belonged to the Chief of Psychiatry of a major metropolitan hospital. She would be coolly aware of it, her instrument of healing.

"Do you mind if I smoke?" she asked without reaching for the packet. There was one butt in the ashtray already.

"Be my guest."

My companion, as I was about to learn, smoked incessantly with a quiet contemplative air and drank noisily with a great swirling and crunching of ice. With what afterwards seemed a startling willingness, I let her lead me on a long detour of agreeably aimless talk. I was aware that this was her art. But, anything to hear that voice, the rich chalice of her throat welling now with humour and warmth as she put her glass down. "I'm afraid I'm becoming a drunk. My husband says I see too much."

"Men always feel that about their wives," I offered. She smiled gratefully, somehow making me now *her* host. Quite remarkable. A lush, a chainsmoker—a virtuoso. She gave off the impression of a very clear mind and—this phrase, is it from Beulah's notes somewhere?—*a complicit heart.*

We were already on a first-name basis. My trust at this point was implicit. Where was the cross-examination I'd prepared?

It was only after the waiter had set down our third round of drinks, her fourth at least, that I noticed he was having trouble taking his eyes off her. Hearing that she was married had made no impression whatever on me. But I now looked at her more closely.

In this low light her complexion was somehow the voice's complement—that creamy translucence of skin tone favoured by the Dutch
masters. Looking younger, she must nevertheless be at least in her
mid-forties. Hair cut in a coppery pageboy, bangs slightly jagged as
though she'd trimmed them herself. An air not particularly feminine,
yet of an incongruous delicacy for a woman her size—athletically
built, with the proportions of a speedskater. Mrs. Hans Brinker. Her
face was oval, her mouth small, lips a pale rose, slightly pursed, as if in
faint concern rather than disapproval. Light, china-blue eyes.

The Dutch rustics of Vermeer's time would have thought her face
too frail, sickly. What I now saw, thanks to the waiter, was a casual and
undeniable beauty. Is it, I wondered, that I am henceforth to be surrounded, on my happy hunting ground, only by beautiful women? Or
is it that all women shall now be revealed as beautiful to me?

A further revelation was that I stood in serious danger of getting
sloshed. But this glimmer of alarm too quickly faded. "What's your
denomination?" I burbled, warmly. "Reichian, Jungian . . . ?"

She cocked a reproving brow.

I waited.

"The latter. Though as a team, we're pretty ecumenical."

"I'd hoped the former." As the words left my lips I had a brief sense
of delivering a little bundle of emotional junk mail of the kind some
women are all too weary of receiving: Dear Occupant of Beautiful
Lodgings. . . . I felt my face flush. I always let the woman lead.

"Her family has been unhelpful," she said gently. The transition was
sudden without feeling brusque. She could easily have chosen to inten-
sify my discomfort. "In fact the father's been a problem. Or may be. . . ."

"I'm not surprised."

"Dr. Gregory—"

"Don."

"Don, I'm asking you for help."

"Yes."

"You understand I'm taking a risk."

What I understood was how much I was suddenly looking forward to talking about this with someone even slightly sympathetic.
She would know this, of course. There flashed through my mind the
wry notion that Beulah had gone to rather extravagant lengths to get
me into therapy.

"Risk?" I said. "Yes, I imagine you are."

"If a cabinet minister or a CEO has a heart attack within a thousand miles of here, Jonas Limosneros is one of two or three surgeons with a police escort to the nearest helipad. He's also on a first-name basis with every major contributor on the hospital's donor list."

"And this is a problem. . . ."

"A treatment history like hers indicates family issues. Yet the parents have been obstructively vague about the day-to-day of their daughter's life. The mother, I think I understand."

"Champagne brunches start at 10. Seven days a week."

"He has his secretary call me twice a day for updates."

"He wants progress," I suggested.

"What I think he really wants is to send her to a private facility."

"Where the doctors follow orders."

She nodded. "And prescribe a good deal of medication."

"Preferably somewhere distant."

"I have my own little fan club, but if I'm going to stand up to him I need to know what's going on."

"What's going on, I suspect, is the good doctor's scared shitless. It has been my lawyer's pleasure to explain to me that the media machine has made Beulah into Sleeping Beauty. When she wakes she's going to be surrounded by microphones."

"Don, I know you'd rather not . . . and I know you've already gone through a lot to protect her privacy, but I need background here."

"How will you be treating her?"

"Do you have her diaries?"

"How," I repeated.

She sighed. "We'll take a multi-disciplinary approach. Obviously the neurological issues are primary at the moment—"

"So why put a Jungian in charge?" I'd known all along it would have to come to this, but I'd been so enjoying the ride.

"I'm the one who decides the composition of each treatment team."

"And keeps the interesting cases for herself. . . ."

"Our group sees some very difficult cognitive work ahead, yes."

"Oh?" *They had no idea.*

"Anytime someone tries to stage their own vivisection. . . ."

I sat for a moment over my scotch. "Is that what you think?"

"Or C-section, or whatever—I just want to help her, Don. You tell *me*."

"How is she?"

Elsa Aspen's eyes narrowed, then her expression softened. "Coma triggers some pretty concrete connotations. It's actually quite complex and fluid. I wouldn't make too much of it. We prefer the term 'brain trauma.' Scientific shorthand for 'we don't really understand this.' Certainly no two cases are alike."

"And this case?"

"No major physical trauma. A concussion is about all. That's a good sign. Truth is, we can't even be sure what caused this, there are so many possibilities."

"Like?"

"Maybe some combination of contributing factors—endocrine imbalances, ileus, uremia, dehydration. Blood loss, shock. Also some kind of drug cocktail, probably ingested with wine. Trace amounts— the paramedics induced vomiting on the way—phenobarbs, Librium, lithium. Digitalis—what may have been foxglove. Peyote."

"You're not serious."

"And GHB, which is mainly why the police considered foul play."

"GHB . . . ?"

"Date rapists use it. Something fairly new. Even on its own it can cause more or less permanent brain trauma. It's been all over the papers. Any idea where she might have gotten it?"

"You don't think this is . . . permanent."

"Opinions vary. Until a few days ago, all the signs were hopeful. Often there's a surfacing pattern. The first four or five days she progressed steadily to the point of flinching at sudden loud noises. But not much new since."

"What were you looking for?"

"Next they often open their eyes. But then remain in an unresponsive state."

"At first."

"At first, yes. Sometimes forever. Are you going to help us?"

Was I supposed to just cave in now? "Why the diaries?"

"Why? Because these people wake fresh, frail, like newborns. Even before they surface they can be terribly vulnerable. Staff and family have to be coached to speak only in the most hopeful terms. Patients often quote back whole reams of what was being said around them. They find any negatives devastating. The loneliness is appalling.

They're still highly suggestible when they wake. They take sound-
ings. But the chrysalis hardens quickly. Sometimes into catalepsis,
catatonia . . ."

"You need to understand."

"Don't we both? I want her to wake to hopeful signs. I need to
know how to reach her."

Still I hesitated.

"If you've been following this in the press, then you know the family
has her diaries. You're not suggesting I try to persuade them—"

"I need you to get real with me," she said, her voice rich and
reedy—timbre of an English horn. "You've safeguarded her papers this
far—you won't have handed them over without making copies." She
waited for me to deny it. "Show me anything, Don. I never judge." She
looked down at her empty glass. "I'm told it's a gift."

I believed her. I looked into those eyes, I listened to the voice. I let
myself be convinced.

"It's in the car."

Outside we stood in the strip mall parking lot. The air was bright.
The wind lifted the copper bangs away from her face. We stood before
the open trunk like traffickers in stolen radios. I had made a copy of
everything for her in the event she could convince me, everything,
including my notes to that point.

I placed the box in her hands but was slow to release it. "Beulah was
interested in Jung."

"Really," she responded, patiently now. "She had an interest in psy-
chotherapy?"

"No. In insanity."

Dr. Elsa Aspen took up the box's weight. Distracted, she seemed
about to turn away. I held onto the box an instant longer. "Maybe
you'll be able to tell me if she's crazy."

She stared at me across the width of a file box, then around us at
the strip mall. "You know, it seems to me, a little more with each passing day, we're all completely wacko." I let go. Reached up a hand to
shut the trunk lid. "My job, Don, is the ones who can't get themselves
through that day."

During the drive back to the cabin I asked myself for about the
hundredth time. Was she insane? No. I do not think so. But then my
judgement has proved unreliable.

Beulah's, on the other hand, seems impeccable today. She knew I would run from this. I am hand-picked. Plucked from her twisted tree of knowledge. Craziness or insanity? I would very much need to make sense of the difference. She knew why.

So she filled these papers with notes to me like a blood trail. She knew I'd run, even as she was making her last phone call to me. She counted on this. I run from everything. Her salamander, fleeing the insane swamp of family romance, lighting out for the cool temples of reason. I save myself. This is my function. The record survives through me. But I almost didn't go. There are things she could not know.

I was not always quite such a coward.

As a boy I even won a medal for bravery, though my father would not let me collect it. Instead we left town. He would find another job. This was the next story I would have told Beulah, had our game of chicken lasted that long. *Truth or dare. . . .*

My father was a drinker and a brawler. But he loved church music, perhaps still does, alone in his motorhome somewhere in Arizona. In his love of gospel, he took after his mother. Like her, he knew God existed. Only, he hated him for it.

My father's father taught all of his children—boys and girls both—the manly arts. Fishing, hunting, hockey, boxing, a steady escalation of brutalities. Towards the end of the war, with my father still in his early teens, my grandfather drove him from town to town for improvised bouts of backlot bareknuckles. All comers, men and boys, against a sweet-faced kid with a sneaky overhand right and a vicious left hook. Some of those contests must have been desperately, inexpressibly savage. Most of the men, read here 'real' men, were away in France, dying like cattle. My grandfather couldn't go. He'd been disqualified from the service because of a metal plate in his head—an ice-skating accident, the infamous slew-foot incident a hundred times retold to us.

Grandfather did not forgive. There was an iron in the men of that generation, a kind of metal plate in their heads. He never once forgave. That is, until he forgot everything. To forgive, he had to forget.

Once, he caught a man exaggerating, about something not terribly important. A mild criticism of my grandfather. No one remembered anymore what, exactly. But at the time, the man was my grandfather's best friend. For the next forty years that former friend lived on only in infamy, a spectre referred to ever after as 'lyin' Thompson.'

Meanwhile, over that same forty years of his own domestic violence and silent remorse, he could not allow himself to apologize. Never once told anyone he was sorry. It was a word my grandmother never heard him use. She once said she didn't hold it against him.

When she died, he took her effects—and his silences and his sorrows—back to the Ottawa Valley, where he had several distant cousins. For the last ten years of his life he walked from farm to farm. Helping with the harvests, the planting, repairs. Sinking deeper into the purgatorial half-light of Alzheimer's. Each time he came to stay somewhere, he would clear—on a dresser, a night table, an apple crate upturned near a bed—enough space for three mementoes. Grandma's amethyst broach. Her silver hairbrush, with the sort of clip that slips over the hand. Their wedding photo. He continued to do this even when he could no longer recognize the woman in the picture next to him, and then himself.

I saw him around that time. One summer, when I was still an undergrad. My father brought him to see me, the Gregorys' first college boy, to say good-bye.

"I don't remember you," he said, unsteadily, with a lost look. "I'm sorry."

Good-bye then, old man.

My mother had a beautiful singing voice. She had looks. Her marriage prospects should have been better but she was said to have had a head for figures. This was farm code for intelligence and ambition, as much to be concealed as her hand for sketching, code phrase for a suspect creativity. Dirt-poor offspring of an Irish Protestant family scarred by legends of famine and a prairie Depression that raged on in their heads, her only permissible social recreation was singing at weddings. For the first year of their marriage the young couple sang duets together in little churches all over northern Manitoba. Eventually, some of my father's other formative influences took over.

She first started running away from him when she was pregnant with me. It was the fifties. Any self-respecting husband had better know how to keep a firm grip on his property, even if she was half crazy. Into the early sixties he kept finding us and dragging us back. It was usually to an unfamiliar town; her flights served up the little incentive he needed to move on.

He did finally feel the urge to settle down, though, get a double-wide, have his flighty wife institutionalized. It was supposed to be a short stay. A rest cure of the kind then widely available to the hysterical daughters of a Victorian colony. A cure that worked wonders for the colony's sons.

I quit boxing when I turned twelve as my mother died in captivity. The hunting I quit soon after. It was late November, the last time we went out. Hunting season over, not that it made any difference, half-drunk father and sullen son were driving home late after a weekend's unsuccessful hunting, about to take a shortcut across the ice. When I expressed doubts, he boasted it was a lake he'd driven out on a hundred times for ice fishing. Only twice, I countered. And only in mid-winter.

No, it was shallow at this end, ten or twelve feet, would already be frozen hard. The cut across would save an hour. See, two or three fishing shacks out there already. A shack is not a car, I said.

He was right about the depth, wrong about the ice. The precision-welded cars of today would have floated for several moments. In 1967, ten-year-old Mercury station wagons sank in less than a minute. The car heater was broken, so we were wearing our heavy clothes, hunting mitts and overcoats. To mock my anxiousness he'd buckled on his seatbelt, pulled imaginary goggles down over his eyes, then revved the engine before we shot out onto the ice.

We were both good swimmers. The conditions were less than ideal, true. But he might have made a serious try at getting out of the car. He was a big man, by then with a big gut. With the car filling fast, he couldn't find the seatbelt buckle lodged under his paunch and in the folds of his parka. Slipping my head under the chin-deep water I found it for him. I thought he'd follow me to the surface.

I stood on the car hood and my shoulders cleared the water. It wasn't deep. It was stunningly, mind-numbingly cold.

All I had to do was get my feet under me on the roof. From there, half-jump and clamber onto the ice. I wasn't sure how long I would have the strength. Not long. Huge air bubbles were bursting up around me, and as each broke I told myself it was him. But it wasn't.

I filled my lungs with air. The hardest thing was ducking my head back under water so cold it struck your skull like a hammer. I like to imagine that I could see his eyes. I'm not sure. I could, though, see the outline of his head, shaking, no. The window was still up, the door was locked. I don't remember ever seeing him drive with his door locked. No? *No?*

The part of my heritage that I have most wanted to escape is the homicidal rage that rides as a quiet companion to even the most casual family cruelties.

My father loathed quitters. Had tormented me for years by claiming to detect such tendencies in me. I should drive down to the Sun Belt now, look him up in his trailer park and compliment him on his prescience. At that moment, I wanted to kill him.

Was it the drink, the cold? Was it his embarrassment, a long-held despair? I couldn't have cared less. I planted my feet in the mud, gripped the door handle in my right hand and struck the window glass again and again and again with my left elbow. I wanted to feel the satisfaction of breaking something—my elbow, the glass, his face, my lungs.

Once the glass did break he snapped out of it, whatever it was. As I recall, when we got to the surface he was mostly pulling *me* out of the water. An ice-fisherman had seen the whole thing. The motorist who drove us to town called the story in. I was named for some kind of medal, minted in London, England, the papers said. Such medals were to be awarded to a whole group of us by the Lieutenant-Governor. I was a boy hero. The stuff of frontier legend. Reporters came.

He waited upstairs.

He never thanked me. Never mentioned it in fact, or referred to it in any way I could detect. On the other hand he never called me a quitter again.

We moved to British Columbia for a while, just before the ceremony. The medal caught up with us later.

I do not blame him now. Heroism is overdone.

Donald you'd never believe—they've named their Smoking Mountain Saint Gregory and make a volcano effigy of amaranth seed and eat it at the solstice. I wonder has anyone ever bolted the volcano whole?—volcanohole, bolted, that would be me. San Gregorio del Popo they call it. The funniest thing was in the Church where Juana was baptized they had a history of all the Saints Gregory. *Why?*—and which Gregory is the mountain—why so many Gregory popes and saints. Nobody knew, nobody could answer me.

And you, Doctor, which one would you be? If you could, if I could make you. . . .

St. Gregory I: born Rome; elected Pope 3/IX/590; died 12/III/604. During the plague of Rome an angel appeared to him on the rock now called the Castil San Angelo. What did the Angel say that Gregory defends himself as a servant serving God?—*servus servorum Dei!* Thus instituting Gregorian Chant. Was that the first one—a thousand lines of *servus servorum Dei* chanted after school? Was the plague angel satisfied?

St. Gregory II: elected Pope 19/V/715; died 11/II/731. Expelled sect of iconoclasts. Ordered destruction of their fetishes.

St. Gregory III: born Syria; elected 18/III/731; died 28/XI/741. Dubbed the mite of Saint Peter, how strange how odd—mite as pittance or insect? Or was that *mitre?*

Gregory IV: born Rome; elected 20/IX/827; died 11/I/844. Organized armada against Saracens. First of the Pope Gregorys not canonized. How painful, for you all.

Gregory V: born Saxony; elected 3/V/996; died 18/II/999. Forced to flee Rome by anti-pope Juan XVIII. The Gregorian descant picks up speed. Hang on for the ride of your lives.

Gregory VI: elected 5/V/1045; died 20/XII/1046. Took personal command of the Papal army against invaders, all second-comers.

St. Gregory VII: born Tuscany; elected 22/IV/1073; died 25/??/1085. Devised formula *Dictatus Papae.* 'Only Pappy is above judgement.' Yes definitely saint material this one.

Gregory VIII: elected 25/X/1187; died 17/XII/1187. Friend of Barbarossa, helped Christians in Holy Lands oppressed by infidels.

Teeny tiny little sixty-day papacy. May have devised formula 'Carpe Diem.'

Gregory IX: elected 21/III/1227; died 22/VIII/1241. Excommunicated Frederick II. Canonized Saints Francis, Antonio and Domingo. Prepared the 6th crusade. INSTITUTED INQUISITION.

St. Gregory X: elected 27/III/1272; died 10/I/1276. ?? The rest is silence. So saintly, so obscure.

Gregory XI: elected 5/I/1371; died 26/III/1378. Rabid chessplayer. With help of another Saint Catherine, moved Holy See to Rome. The better to wholly See you with my dear.

Gregory XII: elected 19/XII/1406; died 18/X/1417. First Gregory to quit Papacy. Most miserable period of the Holy See (not to mention, of the *nomenclaturum* Gregory).

Gregory XIII: elected 25/V/1572; died 10/IV/1585. Opened seminaries in Vienna, Prague, Japan. Celebrated 11th Jubilee in 1575. Reformed calendar from 4/X/1582 to 15/X/1582. Pope of lost time.

Gregory XIV: elected 8/XII/1590; died 16/X/1591. Incompetent, deceived by counsellors. Excommunicated Enrique IV and quit. Took a professorship.

Gregory XV: elected 14/II/1621; died 8/VII/1623. Took a paternal interest in the missions. Instituted orwellian confraternity of THE PRO-PAGANDA FIDE.

And never forget Gregory of Nazianzus, toasting ants and termites as the architects of labyrinths while ordering Sappho burned. And Gregory of Nyssa who linked Christ to Theseus, Dionysus to Horus, lame god of Isis. 'Nyssa'—Arabic for birthplace of Isis. Another coincidence probably.[14] So synchronistical.[15] So many fished up in one bright shining net of electrum.

Doctor, don't you sometimes wonder if all the Gregorys aren't . . . One?

VERY SOON NOW they—you: my public—will begin asking by what right I've appointed myself editor and taken over Beulah's project.

By the same right she *makes me a character in it.*

And no, not just a character but chorus and audience, accused and executioner. It has not always been an easy thing, seeing myself in the reflections of her journals, but here, in her notes on Old Comedy, I've found something else again. It is not really my area, but such are the forsaken pleasures of scholarship that I've played my part and done some extra research.

Old Comedy: an outlandish form of drama that disappears with Aristophanes after the fall of Athens to Sparta. Often drawing throngs of over fourteen thousand spectators, it was perhaps the oldest and most popular theatre of all. Like its sister, Tragedy, Old Comedy sprang from the threshing floor of the harvest and the fertility rites of Dionysus, a whirl of ritual marriages, bawds and bacchanalian feasts, a threshing ecstasy turning to blood, from blood to raucous laughter—just the kind of transit that would appeal to her. As a form, it depended on ancient religious sanctions to escape censure for its deep obscenity, blasphemies, and seditious political commentary . . .

But mid-lecture, the scholarly paragon pauses, shaken, his index finger still raised to accentuate a telling point. Might she have seen not just the occasional chapter but her entire work as a comedy? Could this be? To have dedicated years of deep passion to a *joke?* One with a particularly savage punchline. Why does the mind, my mind, recoil—is this so difficult to accept? And why does it only get harder to make a joke of it, when this had always been my intention?

Because I was there that night. Because I was there. With her blood on my hands, in these pages. Because I close my eyes and see her every page signed in it.

Everything written is constructed, the scholar reminds himself, recovered now. It's what I've always taught. I hear her voice in the room, taunting, in the semi-darkness around me. Anything written can be deconstructed, unless you'd believe we take our dictation from the muse. But what kind of mind constructs this?

Does she want to show me the mind of God? Is this what she's doing—*rehabilitating god?* A god of old comedies.

Stretch, Donald, whispers the pupil to the teacher. Can't I read the signs?—the deliberately garbled allusions, mock-epic clash of tones, verse and prose in tangled collision, all the mangled midrash of a still more ancient tradition. Is this what I'm supposed to find, Beulah? Even the *pnigos* in the breathless patter of her journals—all constructed for me, her *agon*—her chorus split in two.

So that now to me falls the *parabasis,* the author's jarring attempt to win the audience's approval.

What gives you the right? Who gave *you* permission? What kind of insanity is this to dedicate *years* to a grandiose joke?

I don't want this.

No—no: all this is just your *nihilism.* That's what she's doing—putting me alone in a darkened theatre then offering up her heart's blood to the one person least able to accept it.

Was it less painful this way? For her to grope and struggle towards some doubtful revelation, armed with the absolute certainty that it would not be understood? She was so certain of me, then. Of my limitations. That I would be incapable of glimpsing the slightest trace of grandeur in the ruin she had built.

Why me, I ask now for what must be the thousandth time. Here then is my answer. This is how I am to serve. As the reminder of how little pity and terror is left to this spent millennium of hers—how little comprehension, how little empathy.

She leaves me here to agonize and cogitate in luxury. She leaves me.

She leaves me here to wonder: what is the parody of a parody of an ecstasy?

I am asked to play her one-man chorus, Elizabethan—to sing the part of hoary tradition in my fine castrato's voice. To parody *Murder in the Cathedral* and that great scholar Thomas à Becket. To be revealed as everything he was not, to be made a martyr without a cause, playing at agony, just managing self-pity.

Foil.

Jester.

Fool.

Oh Donald, she wrote for me there in her diaries, *such a wonderful clown you'll make! Just what's it take to make you blink, just how much truth can you take . . . ?*

REFORM SCHOOL

Saint Mary of Egypt Women's College . . . A hard school but holy. So here's the layout and your day's agenda.[16] Every day. Each single day of your lives.

1. Wake towards 4:30. Upon awakening, recall the material to be meditated on: run over each point without giving way to other useless, secret thoughts and shirking. Dress, giving thanks to God for having preserved you during the night from all evil and pray for liberation from all sin. . . .

2. Once dressed, enter into prayer until Prime, preferably behind the chancel lattice, chastely screened, discreetly cancelled. There, read the points of meditation; that is, should they not already come readily to mind.

3. It being the hour, say prayers with the same clear expression, voice and tone of the others in community and with attention—interior and exterior—reverence, modesty and silence, as someone who is speaking to God in the name of Holy Mother Church. As Saint Theresa herself has said: This is the hour to negotiate with Christ and iron out any outstanding matrimonial disputes, by correcting your own numberless faults.

4. Return up to your cell, rest, break fast, read, meditating on some passage from *Contempt for the World.* . . .

5. At eight, attend main Mass, and until nine make devotions. If the community celebrates Mass at another hour, perform instead labours to the accompaniment of saintly discourses read aloud, visit the sick or see to ordinary errands.

6. From nine to eleven (or else eleven to twelve): labour, say the rosary of the Virgin, make devotions and visits to the altars of the Holy Sacrament. Conduct general and particular examination of the conscience.

7. At 12:00, proceed either to the refectory or back to the cell to eat a frugal meal, appetite firmly fixed on the mildness, mortification and presence of God, on the memory of the bitter gall and fasts of Christ and on the poverty of His Mother. *Buen provecho.*† Sorry Father, can we say this in Latin?

†Bon appétit.

8. Lie down some while if such is your custom or need; rest without the slightest exercise or mental care until two o'clock.

9. From two until three, devotions and new visits to the Holy Sacrament.

10. From three to four, manual labour, cell-keeping or the work of special duties and offices.

11. At four, visit an invalid or the Holy Sacrament again, or bless the dormitories, *etc.*

12. From five to six, spiritual readings.

13. From six until seven, pray aloud while conducting an interior examination.

14. Between seven and eight, attend to one's prescribed needs, devotions, exercises or *special mortifications.*

15. From eight until the half-hour, dine and rest a moment in holy conversation.

16. From the half-hour until nine, general and particular examination of the soul and preparation of the items for the dawn prayer.

17. At nine, prepare for bed, thinking of God and the morrow's prayer, and pray to the Guardian Angel to protect and wake you. . . .

HARLEQUIN: FIFTH BUSINESS

I STUDIOUSLY AVOIDED knowing her, but how closely she was studying me. Not just for the pleasure of plotting my humiliation but of calculating how I might be brought, willingly or not, to help her carry it out. Yet somewhere along the way I've stopped believing this is only about revenge—first Beulah's, then mine. Something more, then, something else . . . but what?

And somewhere I decided to help her tell her story by folding mine into hers. But where, when did this sea change come? I try to remember, to find the turning. I can't. I can't find it. I've missed the moment. This, and so many others.

What an odd little life mine has become. Disdaining religiosity yet craving my tiny armageddons— final farewell tilts at foreign travel and languages, honest scholarship, bachelorhood, then at infidelity itself. And, oh yes—ambition. In the end, leaving every last battlefield on the run.

When exactly did I become fifth business? . . . a type to cast in summer stock, the harlequin. How does a man let it happen but not really notice? Become a player just fit to swell a progress, angling for a bedroom scene or two.

But now she offers me a real role, a meaty part with a striking costume: tragicomic jester's mask, split right down the middle. How she must have found her paradoxical harlequin irresistible: humourless yet mocking, craven yet arrogant, cynical yet ambitious. One more critic with an unfinished novel in his desk. Now I presume to finish hers.

Am I to play Salieri to her Mozart, then? To steal her music and pass it off as mine? Salieri publishes his concerto, his great new work, a new direction! Then Mozart recovers, the genius comes back from the dead, and plays for him, plays the unfinished music that should have been. Plays for him. And he sees that he understood so little. Plays for him. And there is more, infinitely more.

Plays for him.

At least Salieri . . . *heard*.

If the mask I'm handed fits so well, why not also wear it well? It's as she predicted, you see, the prophet can no longer tell Providence from Irony. Her satire annihilates me. How can I face her? *I am defaced.*

Let him wear it then, the jester's mask she proffers. Let him put it on. There, at last he thinks he sees: the real difference between tragedy and comedy is not up on the stage.

It's in the audience.

JUANA INÉS
DE LA CRUZ

To be contested by a crowd . . .
  1: Not less than a hundred generations
have held in veneration
the ancient Wonders of the world;
I would not quarrel with the list,
but wish to establish, once and for all,
which of these was greatest.
  2: It is I who will prove the greatest to you!
  3: No wait, you two, for
I am the one to whom
you should listen.
  2: In no way! I was the first
to answer her proposition
and so should have the floor!
  1: If it is to wear yourselves out
that you dispute, how much better
to do so setting forth your arguments. . . .
  3: Let him who would, begin.
  2: Then I will make *my* case:
the walls that Semiramis raised,
I would offer
and suggest,
were such a wonder
of spaciousness

that along the rampart tops ran carriages,

while within the walls were planted

by the city's denizens

the most luxuriant gardens

that have ever existed.

  3: Stop right there—enough of this!

These were not nearly so prodigious

as the Colossus of the Sun,

whose presiding genius was one

Clares Lidio,

and whose formidable stature

was a full seventy cubits,

honestly measured.

  4: My word!

How much more colossal then

were the pyramids of the Egyptians,

so terrible and yet incredible—

one measuring fifteen hundred feet a side—

and many others

not much smaller,

on all sides.

  5: In all my life!

Listen now to me alone

as I tell you of

the Mausoleum that Artemisa

built and ornamented

for her husband's tomb

at the cost of such efforts

as to exhaust herself and her kingdom's coffers.

  6: No need to go on and on—

vastly more extravagant

was the Temple of Diana,

built in Ephesus,

that Erostratos in a fit of madness

reduced to ashes,

thinking such excess magnificent.

  7: Extravagance, yes—

but far greater than this

was the magnificent monument

raised to Jupiter by Phidias

and by which his art was seen

at a glance to have surpassed

not just his wildest dreams

but the subject of his study.

  8: To me it falls to propose

that the most signal of marvels

was the lighthouse at Pharos,

which guided the navies of the world entire

and in whose mirror,

there stood revealed

to human view

all the vast blue realms of Neptune.

9: No. Not one of you has hit upon it;

since of all these wonders, the most exotic

was Catherine of Alexandria:

who was a wall,

proof against all assault;

    a Colossus,

but of a sun more beautiful;

    a Pyramid,

risen in a single flight to heaven;

    a Mausoleum,

and, the more I look at it,

monstrance and also temple

consecrated to the Sacramental Christ;

    a Statue

hewn from living marble,

finely graved, in profile wrought,

and by its finishing touches made a lovely catafalque;

    a Tower,

exalted, eminent,

reaching up and touching Heaven,

and at whose foot the others knelt . . .

    ALL:

This, this is indeed a Wonder

worthy of the title!

This and no other.

Catherine alone.

POSTCARDS FROM THE CLOISTER

[*22 Dec. 1994. Mexico City*]
If I can't find her here, at least let me restore *his* eyes to loss. . . .

Dear Don,
   Donald Donald it's all so clear I can see your house from here, so
safensound—I just spent my first day in her convent. Her *claustro* is a
university now! . . . how could I not think of you . . .
        no.

Don Wanton,
   The weather is here, wish you were beautiful—
   How I wish you weren't.
        fuck.

Donald,
   Excuse the scrawl, I may have to learn to write to you always with this
left hand of darkness. But nevermind that—I have slept in Juana's *bed!* at
the hacienda in Panoayán. I'm friends now with the caretakers there,
friends everyplace, the whole country especially here in this huge Mexico
a city to walk anywhere at all hours of the night and find nothing but
friends now that I have eyes to see . . . spectres of kindness, friendly
shapes circling in the gloom . . .

Dear Dear Donald, suddenly the work is going so splendidly it's clear to
me now, there were so many things I couldn't understand, but *here* . . . her
convent it's not a T-shirt shop mausoleum of maudlinity but a *real* place
where people work—cafeterias a library, carpenters plumbers secretaries—they said it would be closed a month but yesterday the gates
were gaped and again today for Christmas parties. And maybe they're
drunk the same two guards as before they don't care who gets in anymore. Even me.
   I've been afraid to come here after the things I've seen done to her—
you'd call it Claustro-phobia, wouldn't you—but this is a university for
women's studies and *Sor Juana* studies! and four hundred thousand
books Núñez will never get to censor—so let the bookswallower choke,

let them clog shut his gluttonthroat. And her chapel is a *theatre* now—plays to make the Archbishop's worms turn putrid in his grave.

She is everywhere! Everywhere I turn. I am desperately happy here. Have you ever been? Can you understand what it means?

To me.

A wind I let blow unblocked—unstopped unstoppable—through the hole in my chest.

[23 Dec. 1994]
Estimado Profesor,

I come to a convent and find a university. I come for her and get you. You are welcome at every one, but not here—any university but this. You come here to me unbidden unwanted. Once I gave you power over me, now how do I get it back, dispel this spell I've cast? Let these letters conjure you like a voodoo doll that I can finally bury in the palustral ooze. My little salamander doll, *axolotl*—fin-tailed, feathergilled. Salamander do you breathe water or air or fire? Do you walk or crawl, or fly or dive? Where do you really live? What can you still see through those nictitating lids?

But oh I can give you back your eyes your second sight! lost potency of your squandered seed. When it's finally and completely over I'll bind these letters all in a bow—enwrap involve enfold, my little amphibian, and send them all to you. So you see yourself through my eyes *for a spell*. A privilege I promise you. Something special.

Then, you can bury them yourself. Bury you, bury us. In the rosegarden of your Euclidean showhome. Or maybe under the jacuzzi deck where we lay one whole night through, watching the stars spin slowly over us.

Remember us?

I want to be the one to give you back your eyes.

When it's too late.

Gentle Reader . . .

So how then shall I write thee? What will be the tone for the four hundred letters never sent—our lost correspondence. Did you know all but two of Juana's letters are lost? Out of *thousands*. . . . How could this happen? She wrote to everyone, constantly—Europe's leading minds and they to her.

As I have you.

So shall I not play Héloïse to your Abelard? Let us in secrecy wed the epistolary to the apostolic—our scarlet inks swiftsped

on wingbeats of systole and diastole

coursing o'er the earth in the heart's

sparrow chariot

Does it really matter now, Abelard, who is whose vesicle and is there such a vas differenz? Shall we not cut through the chaste?—as a Samurai slices through peasants, to test his edge—but this time we'll bury deep, so very deep, the hatchet's double-blade that it never never comes loose again.

[24 Dec. 1994]

Gentle Reader,

I can admit it now, Donald. Even to you. I have failed. Failed her, so utterly. There that wasn't so hard but can I make myself mail this to you? You told me so, didn't you. All along.

But you didn't tell me how it would *feel*.

All that's left me now is poetry . . . to you. I lied. I didn't come to find her, can no longer hope for that. But what I didn't want, didn't expect to find was you. Here. Of all places, you, in all places. I wasn't ready yet. For this last cruelty.

I have looked for her in books, and museums and now this convent— in the patios, the corridors, the cells. Even in the kitchens. I do not find her. In the fountains, on the roof, in the stars.

I do not find her.

I go into her chapel . . . where she must have prayed and raged . . . a hundred shades of grey this place, so beautiful and dark and cool. And images of her all over, paintings centuries old a hall of mirrors reflecting her back to me in oils everywhere I turn I turn.

I do not find her.

I have lost the melody. The precious voice I always heard so clearly in my ears. As I wrote for her. Why has this been taken?—what does why matter now?

I have come to learn. To find her silence beautiful. Hear her absence with my eyes of wonder.

She stood here—kneeled I know on this X marks the cross of nave and transept. Here on this icy floor where now I lay me down at last before her altar beneath her dome my upturned face—rising up and up from out this open chest a mothgrey shade.

And echoing faint and thin, a little thread of melody . . . one bow, one frayed string . . . that I kindle, kindle, on the blue, curled excelsior of breath.

[26 Dec. 1994]
Gentle Reader,

I've made a new friend at convent camp! she's a friend of Guido-the-guard who found me, flagged—just fit to toe-tag by the chapel altar. She's a medical historian a doctor a Sor Juana scholar and so beautiful! So gentle with a scalpel she asks what did they put on my hand in the mountains—no no in Panoayán—was it a compress of spiderwebs? she thinks maybe it saved my arm—and why isn't gangrene green?

She wouldn't let anyone take me to a hospital. I'm staying at her house—*Christmas almighty*, she won't let me go back to the hotel—*una merry caridad*—and I lie in her bed afloat in a fever sailing on a gull's dream, wanting to believe. And she takes the most careful care of me—on San Jerónimo Street! yes the same as the convent, just down the next block. Across the Merced Canal, long gone now. Quiet calm and shadytreed . . . a house in her family for over a century, except for her now, empty . . .

I know she too is desperately happy.

Her office is downstairs. Her patience her virtue her patients are women from the Claustro mostly. She laughs calls it the convent infirmary. Treating Sor Juanitis has become a medical specialty with me, and laughs at this because she needs to. So badly. I know she is lonely, lonelier even than me, Gentle Reader, lonely maybe as you.

We've talked for two days straight about *everything*. Her name is—no I won't share her, not with you. Call her 'S.'

But don't be hurt I won't tell S about you either. Fair's fair—for you are my voodoo doll my Gregory my volcanic godling of sticky seed, not hers.

[27 Dec. 1994]
Gentle Reader

Last night S and I watched the notorious lesbian film on Sor Juana *Y yo la peor de todas*[†] in her bedroom. S insists I, B, open my mind to what film *could* be. And she is amazed and so kind at the same time I don't

[†] *I, the Worst Woman in the World*

know the documentaries of Studio D—what? how can I not know these Canadian women filmmakers with the NFB? Never heard of them. But how can that be?—not even *The Burning Times*, bewitching witchhunt trilogy? But S still has no idea how ignorant B can be.

We have a copy in our library, B we *must* watch it together soon. I have watched it a dozen times. The witch hunts, the trials. If women working together can take back literature, then why not film as they do? Okay why not I say and we're talking about writing a screenplay—I've started it for her in my head *I think I could start writing again.* I've lost the music but I can still *see* / can read the score of the Limping Kings—Horus Quetzalcóatl Oedipus Achilles—thorns in their paws, nails through their feet.

Maneating savagery for S and B to capture for the first time on film. For Mutual Life of Omega.

She is working on a film project—the story of plague told through the lives of history's great women. She's asked me to work with her she teaches me about film and I talk and talk like never in years . . . about myths and Nietzsche my favourite comedian. *Amor fata!*—love your fate, he cries on his pale lips of a ravished bride. I want to make her love him as I do—how he hates stodgy Plato for making the ideal realer than real, whiter than white. *Are we God's greatest mistake or is God ours?* asks funnyFreddy. Of course we mean Nature not God but the joke is still on us. We are the vacuum Nature abhors. An ice age in the flesh. And O how we spread.

Next B asks S then whom—Hume?—do we blame for making abstractions *unreal*? As if the contendings of image and word / mind and heart—warring twins LadyLord 2—severed at the ankle at birth weren't *real*, just true.

But alright S if the Fifth Sun must end with the apocalypse of the disembodied image victorious—hail, winged victory Nike!—then let our swan song, our last horror flick go beyond film's brute dumbshow to a new hieroglyphics: the codex of our nemesis—just us, S and B—knit ourselves a mail of pure abstractions, filmically.

We'll make the filmglyph for Progress, let's see . . . the razed forest. For Hubris, the golf tee. For Duplicity, the slave ship. A g-string for Victory. Accidia—the parabolic antenna.

And for the most abstract and ethereal Purity, a gaspowered shower.

So much much more than symbols, these are the shapes of abstractions in the flesh.

[28 Dec. 1994]
Gentle Reader,

Better much better today. Strong enough to stand, walk a short way. Ring around the block, down to the convent. Help S a little around the house. She's telling me about all the incarnations the Claustro's taken since the Revolution. When they ransacked Old Mexico's convents and closed them down. One by one.

Her convent as stable. Military hospital. Mechanic's shop. Discotheque.

Once two artists took it over, made a huge studio. Gave themselves Aztec names. Dr. Atl and Nahui Ollin—Doctor Water and the Fifth Sun. Across the street from her convent there's a fashion boutique now, called Vanidades. Next to that in a building as old as the Inquisition is an auto museum sponsored by Nissan. *Auto-da-fé* that restores your faith in Technology, with power steering power brakes, cataclysmic inverters. A friend here taught me if you can't learn to laugh this place will kill you. Quick. I'm trying to learn this.

I already know I will not find her, but here her absence is piled in every stone. So let it be her absence that keeps me company. How will I learn this? this art, extremely well. . . . And how can I explain, even to myself?—the pain of being here in her convent truly helps. Consoling contradiction in defeat that is this place. It's real, there is such a lot of wood here in the buildings, more than I would have thought. . . . It's not all cold stone . . . rafters sweet-oiled and warm. Late afternoons . . . flap of doves in the patio like the snap of wet sheets . . . *certain slants of light* . . . scarred gangster cats sunning themselves, rat hunters coddled by the cafeteria cooks.

How I love to just sit, sun on my shoulders, stare through the heat . . . at the craticulas most especially, how I love this word for the mossy slits the nuns confessed through—to the crackpressed faces of tentfrocked priests. Their sad priapic parody of a smocked maternity.

Today a group of young musicians is practising in the courtyard. Their laughter as one of them tries to teach the others a song on a kind of guitar. They smile at me as I pass. Foreigners come here all the time. From all over the world. Here they have a name for my disease.

Sor Juanitis.

The cooks are trying to make a pet of me. The way you train a bird to come to your hand. A trail of crumbs and sweets and cordials . . .

tamarind, beet, prickly pear. Ladies so simple so bawdy and ribald. Where's the harm? Oh I know but let myself forget for a while.

Next week S has offered to take me to the Museum of Medicine—housed in the old palaces of the Inquisition—is this coincidence or paradox, do you think? One whole wing devoted to pre-Hispanic cures and healing diets. The Inquisition exhibit is in the other wing. In the palace of tortured anatomies.

And there S and I will rediscover the lost Aztec recipe for obsidian wine . . . so many stairs, so steep, so many hearts, so much meat. It would have taken an army just to lift each victim to the top, but instead they walked up on their own. So what was the recipe for their holocaust?—sprinkle of hope / dash of progress / pinch of transcendent glory to take them up the aisle. Bring them to that final deathwed altar.

Obsidian wine to toast the bride.

I want to rest. I'm so tired of doing this alone. S wants me to stay, study here. She'd sponsor my project, I could work in a *tradition*—20th-century habits and mortarboards—and not sprawl and flap and flail reinventing toy prayer wheels on my own. S swears to me my ideas are new and startling and valuable, that I'll find others here like her with their own brilliant new thoughts, that it would be good for me to talk to others.

A world of friends, *true* friends and colleagues.

Then next month we can go to Puebla, to the convent museum of Santa Monica where Bishop Santa Cruz bequeathed his heart to the nuns. S promises me it's true. His heart is on a stick, all dried out, on a silver pedestal—S says it looks like a scouring pad. Rusted out.

I feel like a fool S has me half-believing . . . that I have a second chance, a way out. And I tell her, half-tell, that maybe next semester. After the equinox I must see in Chichén Itzá, with forty thousand others who'll watch the sun trace the shadowglyph of a serpent moving down the steps of a pyramid built for this one day each year . . . after that, when I've seen the glyph of equinox with the *twin tumuli* of my own eyes I could come back and study here.[17] And live with her a while. I could . . . I could try.

How I want to. I don't know who else to tell this to but you. I want to rest, I want to laugh. Be touched and held. Like everyone else. I feel close to ending this work. I've done everything I could for her, given everything I had and failed. Unspeakably.

Then why do I feel that quitting now is a betrayal—of who? Of her? Or someone who never cared about any of it? But if I am betraying *you*, Donald, tell me . . . it should feel better than this.

Shouldn't it?

It's late, very late now. S is asleep . . . with a little snore. Good-night, gentle reader good-night.

HARLEQUIN:
MASCOT

I will become your muse, Donald, and you, my dancing bear. . . .

SO HE IS TO BE MADE a mascot, for the visiting team. A shambling, comic player with his media critic waiting in the wings, parked just outside the gate, down below the trees.

Part of the story would have leaked out in any event. But with one anonymous phone tip, Beulah made certain he would be her old comedy's shining star—her frog-prince Dionysus, her cloud-brained Socrates.

One reporter has not given up on the story. She looks familiar. The road is narrow at the gate. Whenever he drives out, he has to slow, less than a foot between them—Petra something. They're all Petras and Natashas today. She is often on a mobile phone or smoking, the window rolled down.

Was she a student of his, years ago? Shrewd grey eyes. Cropped, curly hair. Angular face . . . attractive, Germanic, her purpose set firm in jaws and chin. The voice, too, he knew. Confident, sardonic, yet with the slightest stridency.

Only one reporter left. But she broke the story; she will see it through. She took a risk and her instincts proved right. She broke it early, before the facts were all in.

The facts are not all in.

THE HARD-BITTEN EX-PROFESSOR lies up in the loft on Chris Relkoff's office couch—a touch of home. He is surveying his castle, his demesne, his paper kingdom laid waste. The harlequin king dons his mask of office, prepares to face the people he shall meet. . . .

Cool, windy day. Mid-afternoon clouds pile up in plum-blue contusions against the peaks. He sees her coming up the drive on foot, his critic, his shadow, his interpreter to the masses. Petra Something. She carries a slim briefcase in one hand, a heavy black tape recorder slung over the other shoulder. Standard issue Smith & Westinghouse. Real jobs, they give you a gun and a badge.

Coming up on foot is a concession. Or he supposes that's how he is to take it. A pilgrimage, on foot—abandoning the high ground of public righteousness for the soggy fens of private right. Welcome to Lourdes, welcome to Compostela.

When she is still thirty yards or so away he sets a fresh scotch down on the desktop. Another little crescent imprinting the oiled mahogany, his script of scimitars. It was a turk's writing desk, after all. Once.

He waits for her beside the door, leaving it just slightly ajar. Though he can't see her any longer, he can hear her crunching up the gravel walk. One second more. He is surprised by how angry. He studies the wood grain in the door. All his cares are supposed to be behind him. Bygone. She shouldn't be coming anymore. Begone. She should be made to go away.

She should be made to go away.

She's set her briefcase down to smooth her hair. As she reaches up to knock he pulls open the door. She looks startled, for an instant almost frightened. Strange. She is the one who's rehearsed her opening scene, he is the one meant to be off-balance, left helpless to improvise.

"Petra Stern, CBC."

"Is that like Rosetta Stone?"

"It's my name."

"Come up to use the bathroom?"

"The ever-charming Donald Gregory."

"I just thought, since you seem to be sleeping in the car. No no—your hair is fine, Petra." Jeans, jean shirt, quilted green vest, new hiking boots. Interesting choices. Was she planning to hound him cross-country?

"I came to talk. May I come in?"

"My world," he says shifting just far enough to let her in, "for you, is an open book."

She squeezes past him into the living room, makes a show of looking around, her composure recovered. "I salute your decorator." She looks at him with a curiosity almost genuine. "Aren't you a bit past living in a frat house? Or are you regressing academically too?"

"Everyone these days takes an interest in my housekeeping."

She shrugs. "You seemed to be asking."

"Mind taking off your shoes?" he asks pleasantly. After a glance at his own scuffed and crusted shoes she begins to unlace her boots. Small feet. *Green socks.* The details. Where does it end? She had been expecting to take off her shoes.

"Grab a seat. Drink?"

"A bit early," she says faintly disapproving.

"Depends when you stopped," he says on the way to the fridge. "By all means, take a good look." He can see her sketching a quick description for her public: *Curtains drawn. A certain dim clutter. Paper airplanes, glasses, blankets. Your average indoor campsite.* He pauses at the kitchen door as she clears a space on the coffee table for the tape recorder, positions the microphone. Strong move, well rehearsed. From the briefcase she takes out a notepad, pens.

When he returns she is sitting in the middle of the couch.

"Cozy?"

"Comfortable."

An annoying feeling comes over him at times, that he's slept with someone but forgotten everything about it. How he was, how she was, if in fact they'd gone through with it.

He's seen her face often over the preceding days. At the bottom of the drive . . . at other times, coming unbidden into his mind. Grey eyes, curly brown hair. Angular bones, not quite horsey. Beauty, it is such a fine line. It was the subject of a lifetime's study. Another lifetime. Someone else's.

Nothing in her face strikes a clear chord of recognition. No, it is her voice. Sharp-edged, brassy. Just right for radio. Somewhere he's heard her laugh once. A short, sharp bark.

"Surprised to see me?" she asks.

"I see you out there almost every day."

"Then you know I'm serious."

"Stern even."

A cold smile hooks the corner of her mouth. She hesitates, feeling her way. "I guess congratulations are in order."

"I hate riddles," he says flatly.

"I had a drink last night with a Detective Curtis. They've decided not to lay charges against you. None, not even a goddam parking ticket. Don't look so relieved. Self-inflicted injuries, they said. Happens all the time, they tell me."

"I can believe it does."

"They're announcing it tomorrow morning."

"You'll drink with Detective Curtis, Petra. Just how am I to take this?"

"I don't want to have to use your bathroom."

"Clever girl."

He eases onto the end of the couch. She holds her ground in the middle. "You know, I just can't quite figure you out."

"How so?" He sips quietly from his scotch.

"Everything in this story is breaking your way. Apart from maybe losing your job—rumours of a huge golden handshake there, too, so excuse me if I don't cry for you—all your problems just seem . . ."

"To slide away."

"And yet here you are. Half-drunk, stewing in your mess, hiding out in the country in the middle of the afternoon. What am I missing?"

"I'm on retreat."

"Full-retreat, yes. All I want to know is why. I've been operating on the theory you're a sleazeball. But a couple of things don't add up."

"Like?"

"Like the 911 call, like the first aid. If you're going to run, run. What the hell were you doing there in the first place? What made you go? Then you show up at the hospital covered in blood just after the police leave. Demand to know how she is. Give your real name, for God's sake."

"Caring guy."

"I talked to the nurse in Admitting. The *guy* was in another world.

But why? Grief, fear, guilt, what? What was it, Dr. Gregory? Somebody runs out of her apartment a minute ahead of the ambulance. A married man, a professional person, eminent even—let's suppose he has his reasons. That same somebody shows up thirty minutes later at a public hospital, shirtless, raving? What was he doing for thirty minutes?"

"Driving around?" he suggests, getting up to freshen the drink. "Looking for parking, perhaps?" He returns to sit in the willow chair facing her where she sits waiting patiently.

"Then there's all these papers. First, why take them, then refuse to give them back—and then fold, but only after keeping them just long enough to draw attention to yourself again. Is there something you want us all to see?"

"I wanted copies."

"So you say."

"So I say."

"You're actually doing some kind of book? I was right the other day."

"Lucky guess, Petra. Or maybe you're just that good."

"Someone at a legitimate press called it in from Toronto. A rumour. Somebody they knew in vanity publishing heard something. A call from a professor in Calgary. It was all I had. I figured it was worth throwing at you."

"So I have a public in Ontario. I'm making it big."

"So tell me. Your book."

"History of Flight."

"As in fugitives?"

"That stack there's Icarus."

"We're both doing similar research, then. Maybe different angles of the same story."

"Right, Petra, we could work together."

"Makes sense. Pool resources."

"Just how drunk do you think I am?"

"I've talked to people you can't talk to now."

"Example?"

"The mother. Grace."

"Pretty, isn't she."

"A high-society drunk," Petra says. "Very, very smart and twice as edgy."

"The father?"

"We didn't exactly talk, no."

"Cold fish."

"Cold as cod."

"*Sick* fish." He offers this in the spirit of co-operation.

"Really?—what have you heard? He had a very ugly feel. Tell you what, you talk to me about him—" Her gaze wavers toward the fireplace. *Don't lose your nerve, Petra Stern.* "—and I tell you what I got from the neighbour lady who saw the guy leaving Beulah's apartment."

"You first."

"Isn't it your turn?"

"Big fish, little fish."

"All right, two for one: the neighbour, plus the Safeway clerk three hours before the call to the news desk."

"I have enough on that in stack three," he says, waving his glass grandly.

Petra Stern is becoming very slightly agitated in spite of her training. Her eyes have been tracing a little circuit from her subject's face to the tape recorder, to the briefcase and back. Her discipline has been good. Now she allows herself a first frank look at the sheaves of papers stacked on the bare hardwood.

"May I?" she asks, getting suddenly to her feet and starting toward the fireplace. No doubt the placement of the stacks is becoming a worry to her.

"Certainly. But don't touch." Hitch in her step, a little segue into pacing in her green socks before the small fire in the hearth. "Please." Taut swells at patch pockets front and back. Tender curves, sub rosa, belie the name of Stern. Stern, Petra, he thinks, swirling the ice in his glass, that must be Indo-Aryan for butt, rock-firm.

"Try this, then," she offers, upping the bid. "I was talking to a very conflicted Grace Limosneros, with so much to lose—"

"So many memberships—"

"Wanting to help more than she maybe knew. She let drop that Beulah thought her real father might be alive." A pause. "You *did* know Jonas Limosneros is only her stepfather."

"Stack two."

"But I do have your interest . . . I can follow up for you. It's what we do. A billion-dollar news machine. We have the resources."

"Though fewer all the time."

"All the more reason."

"Be an interesting angle to your story," he concedes.

"Done. Now you."

"Miss Stone—"

"Stern."

"Name indeed is destiny. Ms Stern, I have the story and you have nothing I need. And as you can see I'm very busy turning it into my story right now. A hot story." Picking up a lighter from the coffee table, he thumbs up a small flame.

"You're bluffing."

"Too many competing drafts. Yours would be one more. So, if you'll excuse me. Unless you'd care for that drink."

"You know, you really do intrigue me," she says. He is supposed to take this as grudging admiration. She leans toward him, a glossy sheen of silk glows briefly at the level of her second button. Tape recorder, quilted vest, hiking boots. Green silk camisole. She has come equipped for anything, all manner of inducements.

"Pray tell."

"Look at you. Drunk, smug smile on your face, you squat in the ruins of your life, with a lighter—like a little boy about burn it all down, his belovèd treehouse."

"And look at you, Petra—rehearsed but ready to improvise. It's been fascinating to watch you work, close up."

"Maybe I've got you all wrong."

"You might."

"You look more guilty than smug."

"Guilt. A hard field to distinguish yourself in." He finishes up his drink. No more.

"So to be distinguished you spend the past half-hour talking like a cheap crime novel?"

"A true-crime story," he says nodding towards the fireplace.

"You find that funny."

"Think of it as parody."

"So you don't really care—about what happened to her. You were just ready to blow anyway. What are you, forty, forty-five—mid-life crisis time? Is that it? Scheduled for your little breakdown?"

"Past due."

"You've used her for everything else. Now as pretext—"

"To talk about me. And what a tonic that is—"

"Really, and who taught you about that?"

"Hysteria, nervous collapse, a good bout of flux. Nothing like it, for clearing the slate—"

"Who says that, Donald—your *mother?* Is that what she thought?"

Broken cloud lays soft shadows over the mountains, without any discernible pattern. A dappling of iron grey, grey-green.

"I suppose," he says finally, "I should be impressed now."

"Just part of the job. If you want a spot on the hottest dance card in town. You have a story, Dr. Gregory? I'll run tape, you tell it your way."

"Maybe you've forgotten, Petra. I've had a little demonstration recently of how you let me tell my story. The interview on the court-house steps is still quite vivid."

"You find the guts to tell it, I won't get in the way." She fidgets a moment with her pen, an expensive ball-point. "Tell you what, you vet the transcript. To hell with it. As of tomorrow the story's dead anyway. Final approval."

"That simple."

"We have the resources to get your story out."

"Not interested."

"You think you've got your little book—people don't read, sure not some ex-professor's vanity publication. You've got a story to tell, tell it to a microphone."

"I do not need *you* to tell *my* story."

"But it's not your damn story anyway, is it Donald? Here's a chance to tell the side we don't push. *You saved her life.* Didn't you?" See the stern face of a hostile community suffused now with sympathy. Petra, thank you. "She would have *bled* to death—right?"

She's become annoying. He has become tired, dead tired. Can't she see. Why doesn't she go away. She should be made to go away.

He looks out the window, never wanting to look at her again. Somewhere to the south, brush is being burned. For miles south, all across the foothills, light breaks through gaps in the clouds. Where it angles through the smoke, it is like the spotlights of some vast ball game. Angling all across the rolling checkerboard fields. *This field on this day shall receive the blessing of light; these shall remain in shadow.*

Soon the gold light will sallow and the scarlet turn to rust.

"You keep thinking I have nothing to offer you in return. But you're wrong. *I took the call,* Donald. I was at the news desk. She spoke to me. *I heard her voice. I heard her plans for you.* What she said, Donald, you need to know. . . ."

"Tell me what she said."

"Your turn, Professor Gregory. You talk, I talk."

Truth or dare.

"How did she . . . ?"

"Sound? I know heartbreak when I hear it."

He considered this. "Petra, the stern romantic. Who'd have guessed?"

"This hasn't a fucking thing to do with romance." Her hands twist at the shaft of her pen. "It's just a chord, breaking. Very soft, very clear."

Prepare to greet the faces that you meet.

Face them.

chorus

1: Of wonders I would sing to you—a miracle.

  2: What, what is it? Tell us all!

1: Stop, wait—that I might speak.

  2: Well, what is it? Quickly, please. I'm dying to hear!

1: Stop, wait—and I'll tell you what I've learned.

verses

As I say,

there was a girl

of tender years,

the age of ten and eight.

Stop, wait—

that I may tell you of her.

  This child

had acquired great knowledge

despite being female

(or so it was alleged,

though little do I see

how this could be believed).

Stop, wait—

that you may discover what I mean.

    Because, it is claimed
by I can't say whom,
that women only ought
to learn to weave and sew.
Stop, wait—
I'll tell you what I know.
    It seems, by virtue of superior reasoning
she could tie sages up in knots;
a slip of a thing, persuading
these great scribes and scholars of whatever she thought!
Stop, wait—
I've told you nothing yet.
    For soon enough they said
she was a saint, no less,
yet in no way did these books she read
detract one bit from her saintliness.
Stop, wait—
the matter is not ended there.
    It is said Lucifer
never sleeps; when he heard
she was not only learned but saintly
he took form as a Mephistopheles—
Stop, wait—
there is much else to learn.

There was something Satan
was desperate to determine:
if there truly was a woman
whose learning surpassed his.
Stop, wait—
that I may tell you something more.
　To this end, how does he proceed?
He goes to tempt an emperor
to bring her by force
to apostasy.
Stop, wait—
There is one more thing yet in store.
　Dear Lord, how brutally
the Emperor sets upon her,
but she lets herself be martyred
so as not to be defeated.
Stop, wait—
but a few words more are needed.
　Ask no more—
to know what one such as Catherine
is made of, and this forever.
I know not. Amen.

JUANA INÉS
DE LA CRUZ

NIGHT OF PAZ

[29 Dec. 1994]

GATES THROWN WIDE—S says the convent's open not just for New Year parties but for the celebrations—*1995!* Magical tricentenary of the passing of Sor Juana Inés de la Cruz. Continuous cycles of conferences concerts plays and special celebrations. Year of mysteries, stunning disclosures—the recovery of Sor Juana's purloined medallion. A rediscovered inventory of all the items in her cell—and rumours of a new *poem* . . . no one will say for sure. . . .

And all the angels dark and light of *SorJuanismo* jetting in and flying back home to Mexico from all over the globe!—Lavrin Luciani Bergmann Alatorre Merrim Luiselli Glantz Bénassy Muriel Buxó . . . the whole honour role.

And Paz. *Octavio Paz comes all the time to the Claustro.*

S knows him or did once—Sweet S waits to tell me till now? He was a close friend of her father before a big falling out.

Paz is coming!!! In two days. A party to ring in the Great Year. First year of the new bundle—to fire the fifty-two-year millennium / talk about acceleration—what the Aztecs couldn't teach us about time.

And conflagration.

Then she says he may not come. His heart, his health. His cats. No one knows. Octavio Paz!—a whole convent aflutter, impaled on pins and needles.

[30 Dec. 1994]

All day yesterday and the past three S spends in the Claustro theatre for rehearsals while I stay away. Our first quarrel.

Oh S I'm so sorry.

S was many many years ago an actress on the stage, and once the childstar of a bad very bad film—*of the silent era*—her laugh and sweet lovely blush, no S you are beautiful and thirty-six is young—*and now for visiting performers I am the Claustro's unofficial—you have an expression in English—welcome wagon?*

The play the fucking play! New Year's Eve! Night of Paz! . . .

Who never wrote. Never once, to me.

S and I fight—for this? No this is the Great Year of the Phoenix of America. All this is supposed to be for *her*.

Really Beulah? you haven't heard of this company? they're supposed to be famous in Canada very avant-garde—*ah, por eso*—musician friends of mine met them at a huge arts centre in the Rocky Mountains. Bumphh, is the name. Is this correct? No, S. Banff. My friends helped arrange this tour. I have to help, you see? But such a strange name for a theatre company, what does Strontium Nanny mean? And how could you not want to meet them they're from *your country* and touring a play on *Sor Juana*? Why B? YBY?

Banff. Am I just supposed to call this coincidence, S, and if that's all it is, why meet them why bother?

And S answers Coincidence?—no, 1995 may be the year Old Mexico discovers *Canada!* Ah yes S and remember sleepy sentimental 1492? when the Genovese befriends the Arawak and 1519 when the Spaniard gets cozy with the Aztec. . . . Oh S, sweet-hearted S don't be hurt / think badly of me. How can I make you understand. I've lost interest in the Land Forgetting Forgot. The White Eden of Pretend.

[31 Dec. 1994]
S finds me in the library. Just opening the latest book by Margo Glantz. A book I've wanted for months. Straight from a full dress rehearsal S has tears in her eyes. *I have to come tonight.* If I won't come for Paz then at least for her. She asks this one favour of me. On New Year's Eve.

Beulah this place has seen everything, every Sor Juana imaginable. Last April it was Sor Juana in Mismaloya—nuns as maximum security convicts in striped pyjamas. . . . I understand you, B, it was hard too for me at first. But the one I saw today is the Sor Juana we have never looked for—and never seen.

She looks nothing like her. Short short hair, white-blond. Tall as a tall man. A dancer—classical training—that much is obvious. *Y una presencia arrolladora* . . . toughness and grace, and so vulnerable at times.

They're all wonderful! so excited to be finally here at the Claustro. I've never seen actors absorb changes so fast. They've written new lines especially for the performance here. And they move so beautifully—relaxation, precision, economy—the director calls it a kind of mantra for them. Strontium Nanny, you still haven't told me.

They're getting nervous about letting us down, B. The acoustics are bad—*y esas malditas puertas de la chingada.* Letting *us* down?—how many times have I complained about those doors—every time they redecorate another office, that's how often. Cracked and split you can see right through them to the plaza outside no wonder the sound—the rector's asked me to say a few words of thanks at the reception after. Thanks? I should be begging forgiveness for those doors.

This too, Beulah, everything that happens tonight is part of your story. You have to be there. Whether or not Paz comes.

She cares. She cares. How can I say no to her?

But how can I come like this S—in jeans with rips?

Ay Beulah, no te preocupes, we'll be the most beautiful women there. For you I have a green dress . . . and tonight a red one for me. You should see the actor who plays don Carlos de Sigüenza. So handsome you'll die.

Treasure this hour of furious hemming, taking in and letting out the gorgeous long-sleeved gown of satin green—Gavin remember me in green?

In at the waist down at hem, cuff and badinage that covers up the bandages—Beulah how can you be so thin and have such breasts? Cause B's a miracle of modern medicine gryphinbride of doctor Frankenstein, stitched and surgically enhanced endowed by Dow but how can I tell this to sweet S? no just shrug and sweetly blush.

Here Beulah try this black shawl—*que preciosa. Eres de una belleza . . .* and S lifts her chin, remembering, from the jewel box lifts an emerald brooch . . . here, *querida,* I always wear it with this dress, it was my mother's. It goes with your eyes.

Oh S of the giant heart, how can you? you hardly know me. You only know my name.

Sweet sensuous S in that dress—red-velvet low slung, stretched taut over a canvas of cinnamon kid. Blue-black hair, high-boned face, fierce as a falcon mask. S your body is so beautiful in that dress. Have you ever been more lovely than this?

Maybe on my wedding night. But that was such a long time . . . she kisses me.

Arm in arm with S propping B on the one-block walk to the Claustro, in heels a size too big / toiletpaper-toed teetering. With every stutterstep—

exhilaration cooling cooling that ebbs out fresh miasmas of disaster. Night of Paz.

Will he come?

Pause at the gate—Beulah you're so pale. Maybe it was too soon—are you strong enough?

For you, S, only for you.

Wait let's not go in just yet. We'll go around to the plaza and sit and rest. Just for a minute. There's still time.

Thank you, S.

We sit in the plaza under a bust of Juana. Patina of brazen indestructibility. Draw strength from this. Though I no longer look for her, no longer hope to see. . . . How practical how brave the little brass soldier.

Children play soccer in the lower court. Past us a clutch of boys—trailing a bigger one pistoning a clattercan of spraypaint. Against the convent walls young brown men shirtless smash a handball—bruising palmslap of Indianrubber, fist thuds of onomatopoeic *goma* pock pock the dusk.

And we sit not speaking as the lanterns are lit. Bats flitting, glancing off soft columns of insects tranced in light. Indigo seeps up from the east. We founder in a lake of ink. Feels like dread as we go in.

Inside the doors at the greeting line's end stands the most stunning woman in All Creation. Auburn movie star in a navy power suit—old money, Swiss-schooled in the most ancient authority—double axe of cash and sex.

Beulah this is la Directora, my boss. Narrowing of the huge brown eyes . . . I'm sorry S but with Paz coming we're completely full. Your friend . . .

S to the rescue whisks me past. Forgive me B, but it was worth it wasn't it to see her face?

Backstage I already have a place for you near the old chancel—Backstage?—*no.*

Really, no? I want you to meet them. No no don't worry then, maybe later. There's another . . . Come, *ven,* this way, up in the upper choir above the nave. Up by the tech booth / electrical confessional. That's right up this little staircase I'm right behind you.

Sway up the spiral dollhouse steps to the landing. Into the light cast up the well quicksteps a guard. *Lo siento, señorita,* this is not for the public up here—

Guido, have you forgotten our friend? Blinks from S to me. *Ayy, buenas noches, Maestra. No la habia visto.* You mean she is the one last week . . . ? But *Maestra* she looks so much better. In his face a kind of wondering. Shy smile, fingertips to his heart in a gesture of pledge. She looks . . . like the painting, no? Not the new one, the one up there, above the stage.

Si Guido, un poco.

Sweet Guido slenderer than a reed ducks into the shadows to retrieve two folding chairs / flashes back before his cartoon uniform has time to follow or sag. Unfolds them at the railing, bids us sit with a low maître d' flourish, schoolboy flush.

Next to the technician's booth two men roost alike as brothers, spectacled barn owls watching us. Baleful the younger, smiling the elder nods at S who whispers to me *the playwright and the director.* Which owl is who who? spiral thread of hilarity unravelling—

The younger is a Mexican living in Canada.

They're not brothers?

No, but I see what you mean. I'll introduce you after.

No need no need.

The elder owl smiles and offers S a pull from a silver hip flask. She puts her hand over his, shakes her head.

Has she been with him?

Do you have enough light, B, do you always write everything?

All of it, get it all down. Brightlit stage near-empty—four chairs, four music stands. Columns rising from the stage, baroque scrollwork of gilt. Scrollframed portraits, gilded scenes of ecclesiasticial grapplings.

but the centrepiece . . . presiding queenly serene above it all, a portrait of her.

Prehispanic soundscape, clay flutes shellhorns and drums. Slow antiphon of cough and countercough in the audience. Scents of mildew, S's faint perfume. Jasmin, dust.

Why don't they start?

We're still hoping Paz will come. They say he no longer has any idea of time.

While all Mexico bends to his magnum agendum.

Shifts of restlessness. Shriek of folding chair on stone. A murmuring. One minute, two, three. Playwright and director huddle now, fiercefaced whispering.

It's him! him! bent dwarfgod shuffles in on the arm of his queen / trailing his Nobel retinue—secretaries editors retainers poetasters poetbodybuilders. Octavio Paz—imagine!, no hard feelings all is forgiven, even the playwright owl is smiling now, let the circus begin. House lights down.

I try I try I try not to look at him who never once wrote to me.

Ah a bilingual play how clever is cleverness left to itself. Spanish and English narrators, amusing Punch and Judy duelling to tell the life of Sor Juana Inés de la Cruz as stand-up comedy for the end of the 20th century—quick fujifilm this somebody, this making of comic history— but wait why not S and me?
PUNCH: The year is 1692. Eclipses—
JUDY: *Cometas*—
PUNCH: Occult sciences and unexplained sightings—
J: *Del cielo, extrañas criaturas chupadoras*—*
PUNCH: Quacks and miracle cures—
J: *Horribles epidemias; una obsesión por lo grotesco y lo deforme*—†
P: Storms and assassinations—
JUDY: *Hambre e insurrección*—‡
P [GRIM]: Oh it's the nineties alright.
Cue titters from the orchestra pit.
P: Today, just this year, the Archbishop of Mexico is attacking Nobel laureate Octavio Paz from the pulpit.
J: *Si el Arzobispo de México quiere atacar a Octavio Paz, debería quedarse en la fila y esperar su turno, como el resto de nosotros.*§

Peal and clap of hysterical laugh—this is more like it, all turn to see how Paz reacts. Does the playwright see how it's his own play he's sapped? The show's let loose in the audience. All now looking at the great man but who wasn't anyhow? Quick get it back, playwright, right your leaky scow now.

Enter the tall dancer. How am I supposed to feel? My first big test— chin up soldier, tighten that gut it's not her, just an actor, that's all. An actor, this is only reality, nothing more, just the last filmreal electric eel, reel it in reel it. In.

*From out of the sky strange sucking creatures

†Horrible epidemics —an obsession with the grotesque and the disfigured—

‡Hunger and insurrection

§If the Archbishop of Mexico want to attack Octavio Paz, he should have to stand in line and wait, like the rest of us

P: In the 17th-century, an archbishop attacks Mexico's greatest living poet for defying Father Núñez—

J: In the 20th, an archbishop attacks Mexico's greatest living poet as the principal obstacle to the campaign for Núñez's canonization.

They want Núñez canonized?—S is this true?

Shhh B shhh.

J: In 17th-century America, even Cortés's dispatches to the king were on the index of banned writings.

P: We like to think publishing is a risky, dirty business today—

Faint laughter severed on a siren wail. From outside a slow risen flood of yelping dog, rumble of trucks gearing down . . . A child's first trumpet class down the block . . . Beautiful stage voices whisked off—

on acoustical

sleighrides

of snowy reception.

Brilliant actors reduced to near pantomime . . . feel a stab of pity for the so-much-better they deserved. Focus sliding like sand out of a glass, like a playwright slumping in his chair, into his socks. Even he is watching Paz—if he walks out now—Octavio Paz can set us free!

S, it's true about those doors.

¡Caray! B tonight is the worst—qué pesadilla—what? now a helicopter? Dios mio I'm going to be sick—how will I face them after this?

Chopchopchopchopchopchop—so playwright, *make this clever in Mexican.*

The director up and pacing now in and out of shadows his chiaroscuro of fiasco. The playwright contorting in his chair and I want to shout down to them Enough!—Actors you have done her honour and your art, you have come so far tried so hard but the times have beaten us all.

Enough.

Will I watch her be silenced again—right here in front of me?—*I want out*—how can I leave S who would never leave me? Just then S touches my arm handsome don Carlos says something to Juana who is pacing too, striding power, then stops—and Octavio Paz leans to hear—

. . . to see time as a spiral is to see history as prophecy . . . as a delicate ecology at the brink of collapse—a double helix of mythic strands recycled and recombined until time itself winds down to die . . .

S grips my wrist and leans to me *we have a play on our hands again*—

look. Feel it feel the stillness in the audience even through the din, see it in Juana's face in her body of a dancer.

The helicopter comes back—is there a riot outside, a student mob gone all Tlateloco?—and as another scene begins the tall blonde enters without her cowl, dressed in suede skirt and blouse of violet silk. Now Father Núñez in sweater and jeans. Are they quitting? The whole cast entering, the playwright agog turns to the director who sees—he sees it and his face is filled with something, they have improvised. They are speaking this strange text in streetclothes as though to save all our lives while the helicopter hovers hovers hovers like a hawk and Núñez smiles at the dogbarks and hornblasts and children celebrating a *tremendous soccer goal*—Paz saw it first but the whole audience knows and I have never felt anything like this—Sor Juana unafraid, a speech that goes—has she made it up? this wasn't the end at all was it, Juana?—while the Spanish narrator echoes her, ever so slowly, to savour it to give me time to get it all down to honour them with this as she honours us—I will write this down for you I will make this mine:

Dawn, fog. Sky the colour of time. This place is filled with ghosts! I live with one—no, five hundred. I look out into the time-swept streets and see still others—past or future? Streets filled with mists, miasmas, phantoms. Spectres of vanished instruments and books, and cruel levers of iron and timber soon, now, to come.

The ghosts of young men playing a ball game against the massive convent walls. And on those grey walls others sketching bright, crude symbols with strange cylindrical brushes. A few words I recognize: Crisis. PAN. México para los Mexicanos . . .

San Jerónimo: the crumbling ghost of a ball court, an altar, an ancient book.
Tremulous blue light in the rooms across the street.

Thank you, sweet actors. For you, I will write this.

Applause a roar of water through the choir drowning out the siren wails and I turn to S, is it always like this are they always so warm generous?—No B, once in a very long while. S's black eyes very full. Your countrymen have honoured us. Her. Will you meet them, B will you thank them in their tongue, speak a few words for me? Come to the reception. Please. This too is part of your story. We'll make la Directora sweat a bit. You two the most beautiful women there and you and I the smartest. Please? We'll sit with the actors.

OK, S, OK but just for a minute. . . .

Actors mill in the corridor outside the patio. Everyone?—meet Beulah, Sor Juana scholar and a countrywoman of yours and dear dear friend of mine. Warm smiles, tired hellos and no one asks where are you from East or West? Suedeskirt Sor Juana friendlysmiles. Her actor eyes searching for a reaction and I want so to tell them tell her how they made us made me feel but don't know how. Not yet not now.

In through the towering doors into *el patio de los gatos,* in past the cold cuts and champagne buckets. Tables ranged all round the arcades—how many faculty work here S?—oh, many, B many. And all rise at the head table as we enter this banquet of Seth my eyes searching out the jewelled casket / procrustean bed not yet revealed to us.

All the scholarly arcadians and their spouses ringing the patio rise to follow the salute head-tabled, but none takes a step, no one speaks, all frozen in attitudes of lost certainty. Instant that lasts sempiternally— Pompeii tableau set in aeons of igneous/lunch. Then the tall tall blonde Sor Juana starts forward strides across the patio—emptiest of all the world's stages—steps to the headtable frieze says hello my name is Denise . . . puts out a hand and we are all released into high relief set free returned to our professorial faculties / who gather round enfold us as we straggle up to be greeted touched shyly in welcome welcome *bienvenidos!*

Soon toast after toast of You have given us back Sor Juana given her back her voice given us a Sor Juana who can weave like a dancer through time and space, who speaks to us in your *idioma* but our idiom, yet remains herself entirely. Thank you, friends from Canadá. We will not forget this soon. We say this with all sincerity.

And they do. As sincerely as each toast we answer—S and B and all the actors with glasses swapped from passing platters—S whispering this is becoming hysterical. Sweet S of the quick black eyes and deepthroat laugh.

Hello my name is Fabiola and this is Tomás. He also is from Canadá. We drove all day from Guadalajara. Are you an actor also we did not see you up there, did we?

Valiant S into the breach of etiquette, no she is a visiting scholar from Canadá, a SorJuanista like us. Fabiola's long ahh, I have been one too, since my first published poem to Sor Juana when I was thirteen. Your *compatriotas* were superb. Two different stories two languages in one single play, I

did not know this could be done. And the doubling of actors—one playing both Father Núñez and that disgusting Silvio—*que maravilla!*

But where is Paz? asks Fabiola the awkward question everasked—and
S laughs he's over in *el gran patio,* do you know his coming to the play was
a mistake? His wife thought it was part of their party for Paz's magazine
Vuelta—do you want to go over?—come let's all go. *Vuelta's* 20th anniversary! I can get us in. *Estoy segura.* I know a friend of Paz's. I have given
him favours.

And we are *in,* through the ivory gates—inserted in someone else's
dream vision—convent patio as Bedouin encampment—tent caravan of
white awnings arcades hung in tapestries, goats slowturned on spits.
Chamber orchestra playing, anemones swaying under a night so clear
even a few stars fall—igniting in fountains, trembling the moon . . .

Her absence in every stone.

Whirl and waiterswarm of white tuxedos brandishing cocktails party
favours canapés. S and B and all the gatecrash actors toasting Paz! toasting Drama! toasting convent life to end the 20th century. The actors
making believe this party is for us. Only the playwright nursing the
drink / the grudge / the sting of being the last to see the moment of
epiphany. In his own play. And now stepping forth in all theatricality! the
goateed actor of Núñez who made us see his humanness—even his,
even me—toasting the greatest night that felt like a century of their
careers that felt like the end of the world, didn't it old friends?—slopping
glass on high, wiping goatee agleam with martini dry very dry—toast!
one more toast—to you, my family—if I'm around for the end of the
world let it feel like *this,* with all of you . . . rousing thespiate cheer from
the company . . . this crazed hilarity effervesces fireflies in this space
where once she moved and dreamed.

Would she approve? who so loved to laugh—are you watching,
Juanita, can you hear the music here? though we are made deaf to you.
. . . See all the cells now? empty and dark. They're classrooms. Your sis-
ters have all gone home. To their rest. To sleep now. . . .

Will you give me leave, Juanita? To let you go. This one night at least?

What is this I see in your face, B? Is this happiness? And S, her arm
across my shoulders, says Though Paz is no saint and all this expense is
obscene when you think of the poor, in Mexico at least a great poet is still
great—as in Sor Juana's day. Paz doesn't have much more time, his

health is failing so badly the President of Mexico has asked to pay all the expenses. Until the very end. It is one of the reasons I can still love this country, still live in this city of shit and autocrats with complicated European names.

Are you ready to meet him? This is your one chance.

Wait S not yet—a toast—a toast to the imperial city of Mexico, long live every unloved emperor dead or alive—*salud!*

And just how many glasses have *you* had?—quit stalling B you know you have to meet him, you can quote me half his poetry. Look, there's so handsome Andreas who played don Carlos already in the receiving line.

Up next to the dais—next to this planter of orchestral anemones plucked by all the little silverfish of Melody—and under the warp of a white pavilion, the great man sits / his own statuary. From out behind this green-eyed Medusa of the all-seeing eye enNobelled that turns all to stone, snakes a line of supplicants, books clutched—white foreknuckled crook that marks the page for The Signing.

After a minute of eternity, up to us sways smiling blue/blur eyed Andreas—I got Paz to sign my book and stole his pen. Want it? See? Seascrawl of signature all over the frontispiece: *Five Decades of Poems by Pablo Neruda.* Do you think Paz noticed, did he *like* Neruda? Do you want to dance?

By the elbow now S takes B for a tutorial stroll through love's academy.

Come B, come meet Paz. I have a friend who can introduce us, I don't think he'd remember me. I was a little girl and he the god of my father. See that tall grey-haired man with the boyish smile? Yes very handsome. Yes he is married too. Maybe you should set your glass down now. He has been a friend to Paz, one of the few writers his wife trusts. He will present us.

I want to say good-bye. To Octavio Paz. Beulah, will you come with me?

Fidgeting S and flinching B—hanging flitches of harem beef in a chorus-line of twenty young women all in pale blue suits tight-skirted like stewardesses—turquoise colour guard of the Air Force of Poesy.

Waiting, waiting to draw near—what's this, S, are they *selling* his books even here? No no, B, *giving* them. The one thing he will sign. Once a woman from California asked him to sign her breasts, she was already lifting her shirt. You have no idea how strange is this life of his. Everyone in the world sending him books, his name in a thousand special dedications from total strangers all across the world. He has a special desk in a special room. His secretary piles up all the books seeking benediction. Once in a while he sits down there and when he can't see out the window sweeps them into an old laundry hamper. For years like this. He must understand Sor Juana in ways no one else can.

And that house of his, full of cats, running wild, knocking down lamps. A fire hazard, as everyone knows but he says let them be. The President wants to give him a new house to die in. Luxuriously.

And suddenly we are near—thank you S for distracting me did you think I wouldn't stay for you? First S whispers a few words to the Oracle, a hello years-old from her father, kiss on the cheek, her hand squeezes the soft round shoulder. Then S's writerfriend with the sad sad eyes of a beautiful hound steps close. Your name is Beulah, yes? You are from Canada? Let me introduce you to my friend. Octavio, this is . . .

And time stands still.

Will things ever be the same *will* they? Will I come away from Sinai blinded thunderstruck speaking in tongues? What can I tell him say how lonely it would have been these years—without him—who never knew I existed? Will I tell him I couldn't have failed without him? Written any of this? No this is nothing for a dying man's conscience.

What will I say in this the only moment left? That none of us has much time and we two just this one instant—he is dying—see it knotted there, his dying in his eyes? The letters neveranswered don't matter. To anyone, not even me.

Thank him, tell him . . . but all sound the whole world over is dying out . . .

All senses reduced to vision, all vision narrowing to this one face edged in black felt. Jowls pulling down the mouth that once spoke so brilliantly—eyes once like precious jades in the photographs yellowed to the lour of mashed peas—*it's so unjust* what is happening to you, this slow wasting—and I am speaking at last but with no idea—jaws working, tongue of burlap flap—am I deaf, am I shouting?—as the light, the greensmoke glow in those ancient eyes gutters lanternyellow down to dim as he looks at me unspeaking. *Is it the poison in my mind that is killing him?* I look up to S who stands on the other side worryfaced and I say God S I am killing Octavio Paz.

Eyes widening, hand to her mouth / instant of pause a peal slips unsnuffed through her fingertips—hard she grabs me by the arm we stagger off simpleton smile smears across my mouth. What is this S, this giddiness this heart tickle/lift—is this happiness? *Carcajadas*—blasts of bellylaugh, hers, ours together. *Ours* . . . So this is laughter.

This place hasn't killed us, S. Not yet.

S—head bent to my breasts—gasp/hitch of little sobs, helpless cling to my shoulders sliding down my arms. *I am killing Octavio Paz, oh B, your face, you should have seen*—

Oh Beulah, I haven't laughed like this in years.

Midnight anti-climax of New Year horns bugling revelry. The band packs up their strings. Paz gets up to leave, a hundred eyes filing after as to a tiny shuffling iron mountain of enormous drawing power. Heavy lean on the arm of his empress, he passes where we sit, falters, turns. Disengages. Shuffles a doddering step toward us, then another. Ten metres over uneven stone. We are all frozen now . . . the anguish—will he stumble will he fall? *is he coming to make me answer for my laughter? Is he coming to answer my letters?*

But no he comes for her not me, little brass soldier—for *her*, for the tall dancer Sor Juana, looking up now at the platinum stars. *She doesn't even notice—oh but she does. Coqueta.* He comes to stand before her, straightens, puts out a hand—*carajo* Beulah I don't believe this, look at them—

Buenas noches, señora, my name . . . is Octavio Paz.

Moment of magic . . . O remember this instant, take this with you to the end.

Breathing again, S whispers, *I'm sure he hasn't introduced himself in thirty years. . . .*

Little bent dwarfgod in a rumpled black suit, shuffling shyly out through the gates of horn.

Good-bye.

Green Eyes.

She loved to dance—did Juana ever dance out here? Under these stars three hundred years younger then—dreaming maybe of her own queen, the Countess María Luisa?—dancing as S and B are, in each other's arms losing track losing count. . . . Is she watching us, smiling down from

Sirius? At S, blackbright eyes, falcon mask, body so beautiful in this dress, my breasts' green satin glide over hers of red velvet.

Couples around us now dancing . . . over the speakers a song a duet— an African man a woman, American. *Seven Seconds* tick past . . . I am humming contented cricket into the shell of her ear. You know this song? S whispers.

Oh yes S I know, this song I have loved. . . . This night, I know every song ever sung.

O if I could just *cease upon the midnight with no pain*. . . .

Juanita, will you let me? With so much left undone, unsaid these three hundred years? Give us this night at least, will you give me leave? Give us this last dance, two hands clasped at her redvelvet hip, mouths filled with jasmine. . . .

Oh S, What can go wrong now? nothing can touch us. Not in your arms. Not in this bliss. Is this joy, rapture—this?

Arms that protect, her eyes pent with a need so long deferred . . . mingled in a diffident grief that will not forget, will not release her, to me. He's gone, S, it's not your fault. Hunger-eyed but so patient in her aching. Oh S I can bring you the sweetest relief, for an hour. I can do this for you. For this, your gift of laughter to me.

Let me clasp this falcon mask between these two cool palms, probe those ebon eyes with mine, coax groans deep from the place where your laughter comes. Let me. Sweet S who rescued me, let me ease the furrows of your brow.

Let me shift them to your panting throat, work the delicate bellows of your ribs.

S, let me stoke you, notch you on my tongue. Like an urgent errand knocked to a bow. Score each bump of gooseflesh with a tongue of arrowsong—scale a shy breast, gather it in, the clustering of a single grape—let me, S—try its resistance between teeth fastidious as the stepping of a deer . . . into wine.

Ruin everything, S, how could we?

O, S, let me feel your small hands on me, submit me . . . to the blind imperium of a single fingertip, chart its long decline on the scroll of one vellum hip. Touch me. Cover me with salt seashell glyphs. Scorch me with Ss—quick brushfire of your lips.

S, O S, who says we're not ready? A year for me, two years for you he's been gone. Was he kind? Was he true was he good to you? No no S, no—we don't need even the best of them—swarming explorers planters of their million teeming little flags, steeping in the green of our need. All that bumping, the lunging, the caliper eyes, the chiselling tongues, mouths caved in marble.

We let them into our guts. Invitation that becomes an invasion—invictus—enough! let's *evict them* now cough them up. Oh S, it's been so long. You don't know how to begin? let me show you.

It begins like this. . . .

Dawn.

Ruin everything—how can we?

Why do I always insist? Oh fuck. Oh fuck. Always this sick sick hunger consumes all that is dearest to me. One night of sweetness is all I asked. One night in this dying century. Of bliss. No. Bliss would be much too much. One night of mercy, that's all, no more than this.

I came here to love her loss, adore it, find her silence beautiful, make it all so lyrical. Now is everything else to be stripped from me too—is this the price of one night's rapture? Why do I never learn why can't I accept—*of course* I must lose everything!—the crystal drift of her music in my ear, now my Eyes of wonder for a day restored . . . my own poetry.

Now S.

I've ruined it, between us, haven't I S?

No no of course not B just a little awkwardness. I never imagined doing that. Let's just give it a day or two. Flatblack coals her eyes, where is her laughter gone? Fled that brightness, musical gleam.

But S what about our film, our tour to the Museum of Medicine, to the Inquisition exhibit? Ah you meant postpone but *said* cancel. No S I know what you meant. You stay here fingering your relics, I'll find another perfect guide with two doctorates and a red velvet dress. Meanwhile I'll go alone instead to Teotihuacan, ruined city old as Rome. The recipe for obsidian wine let me find on my own. Like I was meant to all along.

Recipe—make these filed teeth fastidious.

1 Jan. 1995

The filmscript goes/swell. I have made my resolution. This is to be the screening that starts after the last book is burned. I want this horror show to make us run screaming through the streets. I want to make us gnaw our tongues for pain. *I want to make it feel like hell.*

... It is a fact well known to many here at this symposium and, indeed, a common-place among twentieth-century historiographers of the Spanish Inquisition, that its notorious evils (mass burnings at the stake of witches and other innocents, a plague of sadistic tortures of diabolical cleverness ...) have become, in the public mind, grossly distorted into 'the Black Legend.' Having shrouded itself in secrecy and mystery throughout its history, the Spanish Inquisition must bear its share of the blame.

The unpalatable truth however is that the Spanish Inquisition's only true innovation was the *auto de fe*, the 'act of faith.' A piece of state theatre that has wrongly become synonymous with the burning of heretics at the stake.

In fact, the execution of heretics was already common practice throughout Christendom, not just in Spain. It is to the credit of the Holy Office (that is, after the first 60 years of holocaust up to 1540) that of the 44,000 cases tried in the Spanish Dominions, the ratio of accused sent to the stake fell to below four percent.[18] Of these, at least half burned in effigy, having fled, died in prison, or (among those tried posthumously) had their remains exhumed from hallowed ground and incinerated. Of those burned in the flesh, only a small minority were burned alive; most took the opportunity to repent at the last instant and were garroted before their pyre was lit.

These figures compare very favourably with the rate of executions ordered by secular tribunals of the same period. Further, acquittal rates for heresy rose from zero, under the Medieval Inquisition, to between two and eighteen percent in certain jurisdictions of the Holy Office in Spain. In Valencia, nine percent of cases were suspended outright, while a further forty-four percent were penanced: meaning some combination of fines, banishment, imprisonment, and only rare cases of sentencing to hard labour in the galleys. Another forty percent were reconciled: occasioning more severe penalties. Confiscation of estates, flogging, life in solitary confinement (though often commuted), and, not infrequently, the galleys—but still, never for terms longer than ten years.[19]

True, in the face of wave after wave of denunciations, the mill-wheels of the Holy Office did grind slowly, yet prisoners waiting more than 15 years for trial, while not uncommon, were still very much in a minority.

DE-CANTING
THE BLACK
LEGEND

PEDRO
MARTUROS (ED.),

*INQUISITIVE
MINDS*[20]

And the Black Legend notwithstanding, the secret prisons of the Inquisition were often models of cleanliness and humane treatment, at least in comparison with their secular counterparts.

In its special treatment of witches, often considering these cases to be of mental disorder rather than heresy, the Spanish Inquisition—a few outbreaks of intolerance excepted—was a beacon of enlightenment and forbearance, especially in contrast to the furious and bloodthirsty campaigns of the Parliament of Bordeaux, the Spanish Inquisition's neighbouring secular jurisdiction to the North.

Concerning torture, the figures are undeniable. After the first sixty years of unrestrained excess, fully ninety percent of all prisoners were never tortured, at least physically. And fewer than a third of accused heretics saw threats of torture eventually carried out.

Only three techniques were ever sanctioned: the *garrucha* ('pulley'), the *potro* ('colt'), and the *toca* ('cloth'). Novel methods were actively discouraged, even as innovation flourished in the secular sphere. Church Inquisitors supervised torture but were never to participate: customarily, it was the public executioner who, after stripping the prisoners naked, conducted events.

Even here, in many cases allowances, if not exceptions, were made for heretics over seventy years of age or under ten, especially females. Physicians were often made available, and few prisoners actually died of their injuries. More than a few made a full recovery from their physical symptoms.

Perhaps the Black Legend has persisted and even grown in the face of recent objective and scientific demystifications because for 350 years, thousands died, fled, or suffered imprisonment, torture, banishment, confiscations, desecrations of family burial sites, defamation—and perhaps millions more, intimidation—for acts and thoughts that in our liberal times we would consider not quite criminal.

Continually and conveniently overlooked is the fact that such abuses, regrettable though they may have been, are dwarfed by the subtle omnipresence, creativity, and sheer efficiency of modern methods of social control ... of this century's Inquisitions.

FADE IN:

EXT. 17TH-CENTURY MEXICO CITY--LATE AFTERNOON
View from massive dome of the Jesuit College of Saint Peter
and Saint Paul. Luxurious carriages waiting curbside jam
the street. Footmen stand together. Bantering, calling out
to women passing by. Change of guards taking up positions
around the building. Mood relaxed.

INSIDE THE BUILDING
Chambers of the Brotherhood of Mary: opulent boardroom,
richly appointed. Twelve men--powdered, wigged, dressed in
silks--sit in chairs drawn up along opposite sides of a
long, gleaming table. On it a single glazed pitcher and
twelve crystal water glasses.

Late afternoon light streams over one end of the table. At
the other stands an old man, hunched, bald, nearly blind.
Cassock dirty, threadbare, worn through at knees and
elbows. The voice, though, is clear and firm. New Spain's
twelve most powerful men come here each week to hear it,
and receive their spiritual instructions. The Spanish King's
sovereign representative in the New World, the Viceroy of
New Spain, sits humbly, expression rapt, at the old man's
left.

A young monk distributes to each seated man a little bark-
bound book. Sun Tzu's *The Art of War*, recently translated
by Jesuit scholars in China. Waiting until the last book
has been handed out, the old man, FATHER ANTONIO NÚÑEZ DE
MIRANDA, the Prefect of the Brotherhood of Mary, begins to
read. The lower lip flecks with spittle.

> NÚÑEZ
>
> All warfare is based on deception. Therefore, when
> capable of attacking, feign incapacity; when active in
> moving troops, feign inactivity. When near the enemy,
> make it seem that you are far away; when far away,
> make it seem that you are near. Hold out baits to lure
> the enemy. Strike the enemy when he is in disorder.
> Prepare against the enemy when he is secure at all
> points. Avoid the enemy for the time being when he is
> stronger. If your opponent is of choleric temper, try
> to irritate him. If he is arrogant, try to encourage
> his egotism. . . . These are the keys to victory for a
> strategist. . . . [21]

EXT. QUIET, DESERTED STREETS--NIGHT
INSIDE THE COLLEGE--CANDLELIGHT
Antonio Núñez kneels before the altar he has built to the
Blessed Virgin. It is an altar of *an oriental magnificence.*
His old back is laid bare, a welter of cuts, some nearly
healed, others fresh and suppurating. Taking up an ivory
back-scratcher, ornately carved, Núñez rakes it slowly--
with firm, even pressure--across his back, turning it into
one long, running sore.

The conclusion of a prayer muttered through gritted teeth. . . .

                    NÚÑEZ
    . . . And pardon also, for Sor Juana Inés de la Cruz,
    to whom I am about to do . . . such violence.

INSIDE THE CONVENT LOCUTORY - MORNING
In contrast to the street, the room is dimly lit. Light
filters through a barred window looking onto a small courtyard. Pale walls, stained with mildew. Rough, dark rafters;
five-metre ceiling. Elaborately carved wooden grille cuts
room in two.

A shuffling at the door: the young monk, whispering
instructions, orients Núñez towards the grille, aims him
through the doorway. Núñez enters alone--back straight,
step firm. A nun sits calmly on the other side of the
grate. There is colour in her face and hands from working
in the gardens, a slightly haunted expression in her large
lustrous eyes. SOR JUANA INÉS DE LA CRUZ greets her old
adversary with a grim smile, beckons him to the empty seat
across from her. Only a slight fumbling as he reaches for
the chair betrays his failing sight.

                    JUANA
    Father.

                    NÚÑEZ
                [venomous]
    Sister.

                    JUANA
    It's good you've come.

                    NÚÑEZ
    I have assured them you are only playing for time.

                    JUANA
    I have an offer.

                    NÚÑEZ
    You have called me here to *haggle.*

                         JUANA
An offer.

                         NÚÑEZ
You have something left we *want?*

                         JUANA
They've sent you, have they not . . . ?
     A full and sincere confession, freely given. And the
outward appearance of submission.

                         NÚÑEZ
Submission--you offer us what we already have!

                         JUANA
What you *have* is a spectacle, and a martyrdom in waiting.

                         NÚÑEZ

An apostasy you mean.
     You offer me a bribe--

                         JUANA
A compromise.

                         NÚÑEZ
A *bribe*--to endorse a lying apostasy!

                         JUANA
I understand. You're not accustomed to compromise.

                         NÚÑEZ
Since when are *you,* woman?

                         JUANA
Since the day I first walked through that *gate.* And
each single day since.
                      [pause]
     In return, I ask only that you assure them I am no
threat.

                         NÚÑEZ
God does not compromise! *I* do not compromise.
                   [Núñez stands.]

                         JUANA
I offer my willingness . . . to undergo a genuine change.

                         NÚÑEZ
                 [shaking his head]
Ridiculous—what would you confess to?

                         JUANA
Everything.

                         NÚÑEZ
What will you *confess* to?--lasciviousness and fornication?

                    JUANA
Anything. I have brought down upon myself envyings and
backbitings--

                    NÚÑEZ
Parables! You speak in riddles to be misunderstood!

                    JUANA
'I have provoked wraths and s-strifes and debates'--

                    NÚÑEZ
You take yourself now for the *Redeemer!*

                    JUANA
'T-tumults and confusion'--

                    NÚÑEZ
Do you ask me now to take all this *on faith?*

                    JUANA
        [raises her gaze sharply to meet his]
'Faith'--that, I would never ask, not of you. And blind
faith is the one thing *I* will not submit to. Let us
begin together with this. With what you know to be true.
     Show me why I have failed. Show me why it was
wrong to approach Him through this hunger He himself
instilled in me. Make me see why I must only stand and
wait for Grace. I will help you break me down. I will
help you to remake me in his image.

                    NÚÑEZ
You would challenge God to speak. Through me.

                    JUANA
Through you.

                    NÚÑEZ
You cannot begin to grasp your own arrogance can you.

                    JUANA
Through you.

                    NÚÑEZ
No.

                    JUANA
        [straightening her shoulders, voice flat]
If you refuse a compromise, then a wager: the ante to
be my soul. This renewal of my vows--this *conversion*
will be geniune or I die apostate.
     I leave the judging of its authenticity entirely
to you. In the end, you have only to withhold your
support, inform your superiors and be rid of me, your
conscience clear. *Ningún compromiso.*

                    NÚÑEZ
I do not believe . . .

                    JUANA
              [irritably]
I do not ask *you* to believe. Only that you report to
your superiors what you have heard here.

How to Found Your Own Inquisition

B. Krankeit and O. Pena,

A Manual for the Modern Inquisitor[24]

... In our view, then, the characteristic definitive of Inquisition is not persecution of the heretic, a term at once too narrow conceptually and too vague sociologically, but rather persecution of the *convert* (or false convert).

The defining structural configuration should instead be as follows. First, a society whose axes of spiritual and secular power are unstable, as during the holocaust years of the Spanish Inquisition under the newly ascendant Catholic kings. Second, the introduction of the convert, defined here as the social actor having travelled the greatest distance, both ideologically and socially, in the shortest time. Take the case of the New Christians (*conversos*) of Jewish extraction, who as a result of their conversion gain access to offices and social positions denied to members of alien faiths.

The society initially accommodates the rapidly mobile element, but not without tension from the social strata along the convert's ascent, and as these stresses threaten a social structure already defined as unstable, the Inquisition dynamic is set in motion. (Significantly, in Spain, Inquisitors are drawn from the ranks of aristocratic families jostled by the convert's arrival, while the lay familiars of the Inquisition, of solid working class stock, see themselves promoted in some sense to the stratum that the upwardly-mobile convert vacates.)

The structure now attempts to re-establish equilibrium, first by a conservative retreat into hyper-orthodoxy. The Inquisition, newly armed with codes to which no one had until recently conformed, proceeds to re-examine the convert's assimilation and de-legitimizes it ... in the Spanish context, this transforms New Christian into false Christian. This final operation seems almost deliberately ironic: for attempting to conform, the convert is prosecuted as a heretic (an ideological traitor, in modern terms, and *not*, we must stress, as an alien, or a spy).

This model of a structural dynamic enables us to distinguish, on this basis at least, National Socialism from the Inquisition. The Nazis, albeit informed by the spirit and methodical rigour of the Inquisition, considered the Jews not traitors or heretics but aliens to be first deported, then eliminated. Other links have been traced —in our view more successfully—

to the Stalinist persecution of Bolshevik false converts, culminating in the purge trials of the 1920s and 30s.[22]

A recent study provides an interesting test case for our thesis. Anderson attempts (after Graves, but with rather less documentary support) to recast the myths of Ancient Greece as the by-product of a campaign by patriarchal Hellenic invaders to extirpate the indigenous worship of the Great Mother, and then to prosecute the heroes of their Helladic cousins—who had previously invaded Greece and *converted* to the worship of the Triple-Goddess—for heresy.[23] Thus we would find Sisyphus, Oedipus, Bellerophon, Orpheus, Phaëthon, Icarus, probably Achilles and even perhaps Odysseus languishing in the secret prisons of a Hellenic Inquisition, suffering its humiliations, defamations, and tortures.

The same author goes on to observe that awaiting further inquiry is the possibility of applying this reasoning to the study of appetite disorders. It is argued that women, the most mobile social actors in modern society (indeed among the few who can claim to have made dramatic progress in their agenda) have internalized the Inquisitorial dynamic and so act as auto-Inquisitors prosecuting their own 'false conversion' to the canon of rationalist materialism, partriarchal social structures, Apollonian aesthetics . . .

JUBILEE,
DAY 2:
RAM'S HEAD

THE STREET--MORNING
The young monk, GABRIEL, guides Núñez through the bustling
streets, down Calle de las Rejas. As they pass, conversations stop, smiles fade, a young woman crosses herself. A
few blocks on, a carriage pauses in the street. One of the
men from the boardroom descends and offers them a lift.
Gabriel stops, but Núñez presses on as though he has not
heard. As Núñez and Gabriel near the convent of San
Jerónimo, an old woman kneels to receive a benediction.

Núñez and Gabriel pass without pausing, enter the convent.

INSIDE THE CONVENT LOCUTORY--DAY

                    NÚÑEZ
Sit closer.

                    JUANA
I can hear you perfectly well from here.

                    NÚÑEZ
And you know perfectly well I can barely see. Or is it
something you smell?

*Juana looks out through the bars to the little garden. An
old nun busies herself outside with gardening, stealing
little glances into the room.*

                    JUANA
I smell spearmint and sage.

                    NÚÑEZ
They tell me you always claim to smell smoke when I
enter the room.

                    JUANA
And rosemary.

                    NÚÑEZ
Rosemary helps the memory.[25]

                    JUANA
To remember, but not to forget.

                    NÚÑEZ
Odd that someone as bold as you should so fear the
scent of smoke.

                    JUANA
Only . . .

                          NÚÑEZ
Finish.

                          JUANA
When I smell it on you.

                          NÚÑEZ
Ahh yes, I remember now, this unnatural fascination of
yours for the *quemadero*.

VOICE-OVER: They say the priest you burned that day was jolly
and rolypoly.

                          NÚÑEZ
My superiors have decided to take your *bet*. They would
not be persuaded by my doubts. I warned them: She speaks
in riddles like a prophet, stutters like Moses risen
sputtering from the silent Nile. She is more subtle
than Bruno, I said. They answered that Bruno would
have confessed to anything at the end, had we let him.

V.O.: They say his flesh stuttered and spat like a roasting ham.

                          JUANA
Moses stuttered before Pharoah, not God.

                          NÚÑEZ
Exactly what they told me! Part the waters, they said--
by force if need be, she invites it.
     Blind now to her beauty, you, Father Núñez, will
see her more clearly than any of us could.
     We have her silence already, I protested. But the
silence of the Nile is a pagan silence. We must baptize
her silence, make it Christian, they said. It is we who
decide what her silence shall say.
     I told them, she will confess to a fabricated whole
so as to evade conviction for the real particulars.
     We have experience in such matters, they answered.
No individual can stand against this.

                          JUANA
Guileful, I will catch myself with guile.

                          NÚÑEZ
Prideful, you will catch yourself with *pride*. You are
your own worst enemy. A house divided. They are counting
on this.
     You say nothing now.
     Sit closer.

She drags her chair forward.

                          NÚÑEZ
Closer!

Knees now touch the grate.
Núñez leans forward until his lips brush the latticework.
Voice falls to a whisper.

> NÚÑEZ
>
> You are the dramatist, Sor Juana. If I return to play
> my part, are you up to playing yours? I warn you, God
> will not be tested. If you leap, no host of angels will
> break your fall.
>   [sits back in his chair]
> Begin.

Hands clasped in her lap, forcing herself to look past his
face, she begins.

> JUANA
>
> I have been willful and filled with pride.

> NÚÑEZ
>
> You will do better than this!

> JUANA
>
> I have gloried in my obstinacy.

> NÚÑEZ
>
> You feel contempt for your superiors.

> JUANA
>
> I only thought the value of my learning equal to theirs.

> NÚÑEZ
>
> You think you can outlive us.

> JUANA
>
> The Holy Mother Church is eternal. I am a corrupt bag
> of flesh.

> NÚÑEZ
>
> Yes. Gabriel out there tells me you are fat and sleek
> as a cow. You think you have suffered.

> JUANA
>
> I have fasted.

> NÚÑEZ
>
> You think you can outwit us.

> JUANA
>
> No.

> NÚÑEZ
>
> 'No, no, no?' This is your full and sincere confes-
> sion? For this we are to offer you your Jubilee?

[pause]

Say it.

                    JUANA

Say what?

                    NÚÑEZ

Say it.

                    JUANA

Jubilee.

                    NÚÑEZ

Tell me what it means to you.

                    JUANA

My Jubilee will be a renewal, a restoration. A new
beginning. . . .

                    NÚÑEZ

Do you think I did not hear you savouring the word?
Did you think I would not know that *Jubilee* once meant
a time when the fields lay fallow and all lands reverted
to their former owners?
    You speak in codes. This Jubilee you plan is a
rebellion! Like that of your martyr, Hermenegild.
    Do you doubt that I know you?

                    JUANA

No.

                    NÚÑEZ

Then know beyond doubt that I will transform this
Jubilee you have begged for into a ram's head--to batter
down your defences as at a trumpet blast, trample your
doubts, reduce this wall you have built around yourself
to rubble. . . .
                    [pause]
Do you doubt this?

                    JUANA

It is why I have asked for you.

                    NÚÑEZ

I have waited twenty-five years for you to come to your
senses. I am out of patience.
    And do not succumb to the fatal delusion that
because I have come again, because I have been sent,
that my hands are tied. Know that I have been freed to
stop coming any time I decide. To simply stop. No
explanations asked.
    Tomorrow I will be leaving the city for Zacatecas.
Days or weeks, I cannot be sure. But while I am gone,
by all means, playwright, write your lines well. Because
if I elect to return, you will give me what I want.

V.O.: Behold the Warrior Priest departing on a long tour of
the battlefield. See the narrow hands that curb the mighty,
the heart of rock that feeds despair . . . the basilisk's slow
stone thighs propel it across the lone and level sands; like
unto the King of Men, its majesty scarcely to be borne, away
it slouches towards Bethlehem . . .

FADE OUT

...O Providence most high! Who here contests
that the Law of Grace, through Heaven's influence
found its fulfilment and champion
in Egypt's Catherine?

  Just as in its pure translation of Moses
Egypt kept His commandments inviolate,
the Gospels found in Catherine of Egypt
their minister and advocate.

  All the more so, if the Cross—
despised in Rome and Judea—
among its hieroglyphs, Egypt worshipped
long before, on the breast of Serapis.

  Thus did Catherine inherit
in the very blood of Egypt (though vitiated by its cults)
an ardent zeal for Law and Cross,
and in her veins did God distil perfection from viciousness.

  Her martyrdom was for the Cross, and upon it—
since the opposite diameters of the Wheel enthrone,
at the heart of four right angles,
the Cross as its sovereign figure.

  And on that circle Catherine was crucified,
though she did not die within it:
the circle being the divine hieroglyph of the Infinite—
instead of finding death, she was given Life.

  Rejoice, blessed Egypt, at this blossoming,
of so many regal branches the renewal,
for in this one Rose of Alexandria,
God has granted thee an eternal Spring.[26]

JUBILEE,
DAY 16:
FORMULAS

EXT. THE PLAZA DE SANTO DOMINGO--AFTERNOON
Small, hunchbacked figure exits the Palaces of the
Inquisition, crosses the street. Here Father Núñez needs no
guide. Shuffles across the plaza; little knots of people
part for him. Enters the Church of Santo Domingo--his
favourite in all of Mexico.

INSIDE THE CHURCH
Dark reddish light. Red stained glass, pillars of the same
meaty marble, walls of red igneous rock. To one side, a
coral-coloured altar. Red stone and gold, the Conquistador's
harvest.

Núñez shuffles up the aisle and sits on a bench near the
altar. Face lost in thought. Time passes.

INSIDE THE CONVENT LOCUTORY--EARLY EVENING

> NÚÑEZ
> Name.

> JUANA
> *¿Perdón?*

> NÚÑEZ
> Your *name*.

> JUANA
> Sor--

> NÚÑEZ
> The one your father gave you!

> JUANA
> Juana Inés Ramírez de Asbaje.

> NÚÑEZ
> Were you not born into bastardy--illegitimate?

> JUANA
> *Fui hija natural de la Iglesia.*

> NÚÑEZ
> As I said, a bastard. Did your father not leave you
> suddenly and without warning?

> JUANA
> You know this to be true.

NÚÑEZ
Were you baptized? Have you heard the Christian doctrine
predicated? Have you communicated it to others?

JUANA
[she pales]
Why do you use the formulas of the Inquisition against me?

NÚÑEZ
Did he not flee because he was a secret Judaizer?

JUANA
Is this now about heresy?

NÚÑEZ
We have already bet on your apostasy. Did you think we
could not raise the ante?
    Do you believe in the reality of dreams? Have you
sought visions in the taking of banned plants and
substances?

JUANA
There is no need for this.

NÚÑEZ
Have you attempted to take auguries by means of hags or
false seers, in the readings of palms or stars or in
playing cards--

JUANA
This is nonsense.

NÚÑEZ
Or by means of weasels, or *pinauiztli* beetles?--or by the
throwing of corn grains, or the mixing of blood and ashes.

JUANA
Truly Father, this is unworthy of you.

NÚÑEZ
You seem offended, Sor Juana.
    Have you sought omens in the hooting of owls, the
breaking of mirrors, the paths of black butterflies?
Or in the patterns of the *épatl*'s urinations on the
ground--

JUANA
Will you please desist from these puerilities!?

NÚÑEZ
Such fearlessness, Sor Juana, such haughty defiance!--or
is that indignation?

JUANA
Surely we have more important matters--

                              NÚÑEZ
So eager to do philosophical battle--it is precisely
your intellectual pride that offers the first point of
attack. How quickly you would dispense with all this
pettiness and bring us directly to loftier, infinitely
more dangerous matters. Saint Catherine stretched upon
the wheel! Perhaps your breath quickens at the thought
of torture--

                              JUANA
Might yours, if our positions were reversed?

                              NÚÑEZ
My *position* . . . is awkward. As your former confessor
and as an officer of the Inquisition, I think you can
see my testimony, my involvement in this case--

                              JUANA
Case? I asked you here to help me renew my vows.

                              NÚÑEZ
Every case is different. Think of these sessions as a
dress rehearsal. There will be many such insults to
your pride. Clearly you are unprepared.
     If we are unsuccessful, you and I, at least you
will be well-drilled for the next step.
   [pauses; eyes turning vaguely toward the light]
     But as is natural with you, you are only thinking
of yourself. Think of this: *confiscation of all your
family's properties as a precaution against flight.*

                              JUANA
Yes, property. I have heard the man your Inquisitors
most fear is the Holy Office's accountant.

                              NÚÑEZ
As an accountant yourself, you understand such things.
Then consider this the audit of your soul.
     How good that you can still make jokes about the
Inquisition. Make a joke of what the priest will say in
private the next time someone comes to ask that *una
sobrina* or nephew or grand-niece of yours be baptized.
     But of course you can joke because you believe
there can be no charges.

                              JUANA
What charges?--tell me, Father Núñez.

                              NÚÑEZ
You scheme to win back my protection, yet you should
also understand that I cannot protect you *in there.*
     Let us suppose for a moment--*only a moment*--that I
can be persuaded to disqualify myself from testifying
against you. You should hope for that. Yes, hope for

that. Though *that* would in turn necessarily preclude my
intervening in your behalf.

Yet what I am not sure you grasp completely--your
inexperience in these matters is understandable--is
that the Inquisition, you see, does not need my
testimony.

Testimony never lacks.

                    JUANA
They would solicit false statements? You would be party
to this?

                    NÚÑEZ
Calumnies from the envious, from those who stand to
gain . . . what could be more natural?

But, in fact, the most effective testimony comes
not from those who bear false witness but instead from
those who have seen wonders. All will want to tell the
miracles they have seen, the prodigies of your own
childhood, even when they have seen nothing at all.
Your fellow sisters will fall all over themselves to
testify that verily! they have seen you levitating.

So our Inquisitors will ask you to levitate for
them. . . .

They do what they can to sort the evidence.

                    JUANA
But they're only human, after all.

                    NÚÑEZ
Good, good. I see even on the threshold of tragedy, irony
does not quite desert you. And what a powerful weapon you
shall fashion of it when you face down your accusers!

But you will *never* face your accusers, Juana Inês,
never even know their names. Your judges then: confront
your judges at the trial! Which brings us to the key
point--for you, though not for them, or me. Your innocence. Know this: Your 'innocence' will hold not the
slightest interest.

The sole purpose of your trial or trials . . . shall
be to extract and properly record your confession--

                    JUANA
You are enjoying yourself.

                    NÚÑEZ
Yet if we are already at the trial, it means we have
skipped over your months or years in the Inquisition's
secret prisons. And have passed over the gross familiarity of the contact there. But, there it is, we have
glossed over the truly essential point for long enough:
your humiliation. For you the humiliation will be the
worst.

From the moment of your arrest you will be led by
your vanity and arrogance into a widening gyre of
resistance, rebellion and provocation. From there to
insolence, thence to impudence and on to blasphemy
until, far from forcing a confession from you, they
will not be able to prevent you from favouring them
with your most unorthodox and original ideas, on God's
love, for example.

But then perhaps to prolong your agony they will
instead suspend judgement. And release you until such
time--years may pass--as it pleases them to reopen the
proceedings.

> JUANA

Truly, you are in fine form Father. They said you were
frail.

And we have already gone over this.

> NÚÑEZ

Only to return to where we have been all along, and to
what you have long known: your best chance, your best
bet--

> JUANA

Is here with you.

> NÚÑEZ

So . . . choose.

A long silence . . . that she refuses to break.

> NÚÑEZ

Before I return to this place--*if* I return--I want it
stripped bare. Everything but the *enconchada* of
Guadalupe. The Archbishop should have taken all this
away in the first place.

And take away these chairs.

Next time I will have you on your knees! And next
time you will not come to me fat and powdered and perfumed like you were receiving your aristocrats.

> JUANA

I am wearing no scent.

> NÚÑEZ

Meditate well during my absence. I will have much more
from you than this, or my next time here will be my
last. . . .

At the door, Núñez pauses, turns to Gabriel.

> NÚÑEZ

Is the arrangement of this locutory not somehow different from the others Gabriel?

GABRIEL

Yes, Father.

NÚÑEZ

How, exactly?

GABRIEL

In the others are metal grates. . . . Here, a wooden
lattice separates the sisters from their visitors.

NÚÑEZ

And is this lattice elaborate and ornate, or does memory
deceive?

GABRIEL

Very beautifully made.

NÚÑEZ
[without turning to face her]
Sor Juana, why is this locutory different? Some special
reason?

JUANA

No. No special reason.

NÚÑEZ

No special function? Nothing extraordinary takes place
in here?

JUANA

No.

NÚÑEZ

In the past, perhaps.

JUANA

Not special.

NÚÑEZ
[pause]
Make it like the others, Juana.
    Do you understand me?

JUANA
    Yes, Father, I understand you.

NÚÑEZ

Supervise the work yourself.
    The workmen, they say, will do anything for you.

JUBILEE,
DAY 17:
LODESTONE

EXT. STREETS, DUSK
Guided through the dusk by Gabriel, Núñez makes his way
past a blacksmith's shop. Dim eyes drawn to the light. He
pauses to watch a blacksmith hammer away at a white-hot
iron, each blow casting off a shower of sparks.

INT. UNKNOWN LOCATION--NIGHT
Two young women make love by candlelight, loving, tender. A
bed of soft cushions. . . .

INSIDE THE LOCUTORY--NIGHT
Instead of waiting outside the door, this time the young
monk follows Núñez into the empty room. Sor Juana waits on
her knees. Núñez approaches the newly-installed iron grate,
stops, stands leaning on a cane.

                    NÚÑEZ
Have you checked, Gabriel? Is this grate now like the
others?

                    GABRIEL
Yes.

                    NÚÑEZ
Exactly?

                    GABRIEL
Exactly like the others.

                    NÚÑEZ
                 [to Juana]
Gabriel will see you do not take advantage of my
blindness.
     Gabriel, what do you see?

                    GABRIEL
She is beautiful.

                    NÚÑEZ
Not that--does she move freely?

                    GABRIEL
She seems . . . in pain.

                    NÚÑEZ
You see Juana, your body betrays you, as always.
     And by the time we are finished here, you will have
betrayed everything and everyone you hold dear--because
all that you hold dear has already betrayed you.
     Do you doubt it?

                          JUANA

Yes I doubt it.

                          NÚÑEZ

Do you not feel the least bit betrayed that your friend
Becerra Tanco stopped coming to see you?

                          JUANA

I asked it.

                          NÚÑEZ

He obeyed so readily! Have you heard the rumours that
he, also, may be charged by the Inquisition? No? You
are too isolated in here.
     Does it seem implausible?

                          JUANA

His loyalty to the Indians . . . it has always seemed to
me dangerous.

                          NÚÑEZ

As it has been for others. You understand that your
friend Carlos will be called to testify. And since he will
not be permitted to leave this time--testify, he will.
          [raising a hand to forestall her]
     Before you deny this, you will recall how faint he
has been in your defence. You do not answer--should he
or *should he not* have been more forceful in warning you
that day with Bishop Santa Cruz?!

                          JUANA

Yes.

                          NÚÑEZ

Your life seems to have become a lodestone for conspiracies and betrayals. Does it ever seem that way to you,
Juanita? Carlos, Santa Cruz--your father's, your mother's.
     And Antonia's second notebook--did you really
think we would not know there were *two?*
               [pause]
     Many will be called to testify against you. Some
will go reluctantly, and it will go hard with them.
Still, none of them is innocent. Is this not so?
     Sor Juana has little to say this evening, Gabriel.
Is she unwell?

                          GABRIEL

She seems pale, more pale.

                          NÚÑEZ

We are told by other informants here that you have mortified your flesh.

                          JUANA

With precision and restraint. As you once instructed.

                              NÚÑEZ
You weaken yourself deliberately.

                              JUANA
I am committed to this course.

                              NÚÑEZ
They tell me you have been ill. With fainting fits and
seizures.

                              JUANA
They make too much of it.

                              NÚÑEZ
                    [rising to his feet]
Justifications, evasions--have you anything else to say
before I leave you?

                              JUANA
I have curried favour and used it to obstruct the wishes
and injunctions of my betters. I have discovered deep
within myself an antagonism towards the fathers of this
Church.

                              NÚÑEZ
This is better.
     Against the express wishes of the Church fathers,
you once formed a sort of academy here in the convent.

                              JUANA
Yes.

                              NÚÑEZ
Admit that its purpose was to undermine our exclusivity
in the instruction of its nuns.

                              JUANA
Yes.

                              NÚÑEZ
By teaching against the express and sagacious will of
the Church you have subverted her authority.
     Aside from the incalculable damage you have done
teaching simple nuns mathematics and letters and the
new 'science'--but beyond teaching them disobedience,
you have taught them Sapphism.

                              JUANA
Her poetry, not her practices.

                              NÚÑEZ
You taught Sapphic love. *¡Amor nefano!*

                              JUANA
The love I spoke of was Platonic--

                    NÚÑEZ
More sophistries!

                    JUANA
No.

                    NÚÑEZ
Did you not incite the women in your charge to break
their vows of chastity *with each other?*

                    JUANA
No!

                    NÚÑEZ
We have obtained statements from two of your former
. . . students.

CUT TO: INT. PRISON CELL--NIGHT
Same two women, now in chains, clinging to each other for
solace by lamplight. Jailer enters, leads one towards an
interrogation room. Through the open door a brief glimpse
of an engine of torture.

CUT BACK TO: CONVENT
Juana pacing anxiously at the back of the locutory. Núñez
standing near the grate at the window, his face tilted to
an evening breeze.

                    NÚÑEZ
Let us begin again.
     It appears one of these students is your own
niece . . .
     You still disavow any knowledge of this?

                    JUANA
Is she all right?

                    NÚÑEZ
You disavow their actions?

                    JUANA
I tried to be clear—that none of them should misunder-
stand--

                    NÚÑEZ
But they were less discerning.

                    JUANA
Is Belilla all right?!

                    NÚÑEZ
Less discriminating in their judgements . . .

                    JUANA
Yes . . .

                            NÚÑEZ
Do you know they both claimed inspiration from your
Sapphic Hymns?

                            JUANA
They've never seen a word--

                            NÚÑEZ
Do you understand what you have done? You were their
teacher.

                            JUANA
What they would not learn from me was servility.

                            NÚÑEZ
Our nuns are given the essentials! We have learned what
is dangerous to teach them.
        But you know better. And this bitter fruit is the
result.
        You are a freak of nature--did you think just anyone
could follow you?
        Did you think they could follow you?

                            JUANA
No.

                            NÚÑEZ
Yet you led.

                            JUANA
Yes. . . .

                            NÚÑEZ
You are the most celebrated nun in Christendom, the
most celebrated since Teresa herself. And even *she* did
not have your fame while she lived.
        Your example has the power to do great good, and
even greater harm.
        It would not take much to encourage the Archbishop
to undertake, as the mission of his final years, the
extirpation of teaching in all the convents of New Spain.
Nor would he lack allies in Europe. The example of your
apostasy would be sufficient to make a start. Suppress
or curtail teaching in convents, and the priesthood
will have to take over the everyday instruction of young
girls. If you would turn your back on your sisters,
your niece, would you betray also your entire sex?
        After all the righteous defences you have made of
women's learning?
        Each time a girl reaches for a book, a pious elder
or priest will remind her of poor Sor Juana, apostate.
        By dying unreconciled with the Church, you would make
it impossible for the women who would follow you. . . .

Teotihuacan, Mexico, 1 Jan 1995
I've found a place to rest at the tip of a pyramid in this city of
dragons, old as Rome, Teotihuacan. The roiled road to Old Mexico is
paved in security guards / one old one wakes as I stumble over him—
where are my tiger eyes now? This site is closed, you can't go up there. *No,
no more dead ends! Señorita* do you know how much money this is? I accept
this for my family. But if you cause any damage in this city of my people
I will die of shame, do you understand? Tell me it is for the full moon.

It is for the full moon, *se lo prometo, Abuelo.*

I have your promise then . . . *'tonces, niña, vaya con ciudado*—take care
there are snakes. If you are still around in the morning, child, I will guide
you myself for free.

I can stay! and my world is an oystergleam and the moon is full but
the dragons I see are stone with flower ruffs and roar silently like roaring
twenties socialites in serpent skirts fusing knees, and this comes as a low-
relief to me as I walk the Avenue of the Dead and start to climb the
Moon's Pyramid. And I cling shortwinded to these steep steps with such
elation—here at least I am *admitted*—to climb among the dead elect.

Stairs not just steep but narrowing. Masses despatched near the bottom's wide marches—ever dwindling candidature / fused taper up to the
apex. But way up there only the flowery sacrifice of the fittest—bent
back over a grisly effigy of Darwin on his head. What if the Beagle had
landed here? what of evolution's evolution then?

Up and up this steeped stepness—just a half-dozen more—as the
night pulls back at my shoulders and if I turn it will pull me screaming
into its ribthroated well. At the top the string parts and pitches me face-
first and gasping onto the platform still sunwarm under my palms. At last
I turn to look down and out over this city long lost past longing, half a millennium back already just a rumour of lost greatness to the Aztecs—its
tracings out below me now so unlike the coffeetable books and diagrams.

Avenue of the Dead that runs past the Pyramid of the Sun, yes yes it
is larger, but ending here—ending here, this deadroad, at the *Moon's*
Pyramid. Over there, all along the *Avenida de los Muertos* sprawls an alphabet of children's blocks. Lintels cracked friezes split / chapped frescoes
cob-webbed porticos. A sliver of moon crests the hills—*all agleam!* the

glyph bestiaries, precincts of jaguar temples and dragon and eagle trembling now with creamy light ashimmer as if with heat released as light. Dustdevils of light / helical moonbeams in a bright miasma whispering up from a boneyard of graven stone. . . .

Feel the stillness here . . . feel its hard pull   down at the bone.

Stop. Look.

Feel.

See the full moon draw its clinging sheen clear of the tent-top ridge of hills. The light flares briefly as at the parting of a film of silk.

I could stay

here

forever.

Nothing can reach here, nothing touch me ever just this air so calm. Just this tremulous convection of moonlight not wind, sovereign sway of stillness I breathe shyly in, that fills my mouth . . . taste it run thick like buttermilk down my throat.

Warm stone . . . feel it ebb its heat into me. Pyramid of the Moon. Pyramid / Pyre—find the shape of flame in stone, crayon-traced, stability's hieroglyph, see? Count the sides, count to five. Stablest configuration of lines in three dimensions. Unshakeable. Do you remember, Juana, summing the angles in your head? Do you remember the pyramids you dreamt? we dreamt together.

I lean back on my palms, texture of pumice underneath, and under my heels too—sandals kicked free. Between the stones, here and there small pale blooms, grey in the moonlight.

Gone the city's copper taste—an hour away. Only the smell, the tonguecloak of dust. I tilt my head back to a sky washed of all but the brightest stars, red and white blink of landing lights above, no sound. At the corner of my eye a firefly's phosphorescent wink. Two, three. Out.

Shooting starstreak—swift, serious—to the south. Into the faint glow of Mexico City.

East—strobe of headlights rounding a far bend on a hill.

Pulsefade in my ears . . . fade, fading still, barely audible . . . to the faintest shriek of sharpening steel.

Time passing. My penlight spills its dirty yellow across this glowing page. A dog tests the air, one bark without echo, issue. One roostercrow, dispirited.

Somewhere a rooster slips into the dream of a child, a dog into the dream of a hen.

The sky, a bowl of cream overturned. A landscape battered, chipped, jumbled—spent volcanic cones, moonlit spires of earthcrust—all now slump subside like ice cream melting.

Brief abeyance of the bright solar storm—Nemesis met.

And sleeping at last in me—for a minute or two this melancholy bloodhound questing baying—scenting on a solar wind. Far, how many hours of unplanned flight at a thousand kilometres an hour? faraway the city where I was born. I come to rest in a desert on a pyramid built to the moon. What am I doing here?

Peace, I've begun to make a prayer for you here. When I am done, when I have written it, will you finally come?

And what will make you stay?

[2:34 A.M.]

Ah, love, let us be true to one another . . . [27] What are you doing now, this minute, Professor, do you ever think of me? Remember our last night together . . . did you dream of me watching you sleep, your nose bent, face puckered against the sheet? You said my name, I never told you. When I slipped my hand into yours, you held it there. Skin so smooth.

I never told.

It is beautiful here tonight.

I move with your breath-ing . . .

I breathe with your beau-ty . . . [28]

At this moment, as I shiver through this night of shooting fireflies and boneglow pyramids are you smiling, reading, weeping—making love with her? To someone else? Do you need anybody, ever? Are you like me a little after all? Do you need your lovers at all, what are we to you? Do we keep you from this emptiness even for an hour?

Or does the iceman just need to come.

What would it take to make you break? How much truth can you bear? Bait the dancing bear. . . .

Did I give you anything you really need—comfort? peace? an instant's happiness—furtive, fleeting, guilt-fleeced? Are you smiling now, indulgently, reading me, or have you torn this up—do you hate me more for what I've done to you already or for what may still be done?

Are you playing with your daughter as I write this down? I know you named her Catherine—I wonder if you chose the name. It's your mother's, isn't it—oh you thought I'd forgotten. And why did I think you'd have a son? You know, I've seen her. . . . She is an angel, Donald. Are you reading to her now, is she still too young are you a good teacher a good father to her—will you be? Can you still learn?

[3:50 A.M.]

This chill desert is manmade too. It reminds me of your heart. The valley of Mexico was once a chain of lakes. Now look at these stripped Saharan hills—cracked-rib forest of galleys—O Glory of Rome! Sunken barnacle on the seafloor. And what have these fallen trees built here in México that survives . . . us?

Feel the breeze stir now at this pyramid's peak—feel the cold—as I whirl round and round arms out spinning on this pyramid top. Happy shades of you and me dancing glass figurines on a music box. We are that music—who holds the key who winds us up? Universe of glass supercooled time, viscid, freeze-dried—tremulous turning on a music box winding down to

    pure

        flux

Who winds the clockworks? calls the megaton tune of sky and earth—waltzes mountains weds seafloors to horizons rolls us in his palm makes us round? Do we make the trickster laugh, does he want ice cream, is he bored?—with you me with everybody? And truly does this prankster / thanatical joker really just dance us in his palm as he dances himself to death / alone on time's pyramid—staggersided like a wedding cake / whirling as I am now in his drunken wedding dance / in the empty arms of coldskied eternity teetering—

this flawed palindrome / inconfigurable flux

      volcanic glass that shatters minds at the touch

           that bridge too far / that frame too much

Who will teach me this, Donald? The old man in the poncho sleeping down below? Or do I go alone as Juana went, schooled on paradox and pyramids?

I shudder with cold. Cold claws my hand as I make myself write—and my fingers cry out for rest their talon screech but there will be time soon very soon for the gnaw and clench of surcease—quill as dagger as ignition key under this clenched fist-heel, I scratch my graffiti into the world's enamel coat. . . .

Dawn. I wanted promised poncho man to be down before the first sun-ray broke the ridge / pierced the sky but my cold-drugged knees won't carry me—time to try these stumpy wings? or not quite yet. Pyramid climbs used to be one-way trips, on obsidian wine.

Hail! there All hail—rise to toast the sun!—blue hummingbird whose blood is blinding light! There where it rises beside the Pyramid of the Sun. Manmade rock-heap miming mountain. At its tip I stand, heart in hand—a clutch of precious eaglefruit raised to lure the Ascending Eagle—BlueHummingbird! unhooded now—to the jesses.

The sun warms my face, though I don't want it.

Pyramid of the Moon teach me how to live with loss.

Pyramid of the Sun teach me to die.

Well.

To love it, as you do. Without desire.

On drugged knees I start down, clinging, crawling, face to the pitched steps. But I will walk the deadroad on my feet. This shameroad the FeatherSerpent walked in failure to the burning ground. From here I start down the road to the Red Lands, the Black, land of knowledge and death.

JUBILEE,
DAY 24: THE
BODY OF
A NUN

THE PLAZA OUTSIDE THE CONVENT--MORNING
Flowers clasped in both hands, an old woman comes from the
building opposite Juana's cell. Replaces yesterday's flowers
in the niche altar beneath Juana's window, makes her way
unsteadily back to her door. Pauses in the doorway and,
frowning, watches a ragtag collection of boys playing a ball
game against the convent walls. The game grows raucous. Old
man comes out from a few doors down, chases the boys off. As
he turns, his eyes meet the old woman's, who turns away.

INT. INDEFINITE LOCATION, INDEFINITE ERA--MORNING
Young girls in school uniforms receiving instruction from a
nun. Bright, fresh faces. Intent, innocent.

INSIDE THE CONVENT LOCUTORY—MORNING, BRIGHT SUNSHINE
Before, Juana had been able to approach the window. The new
grate cuts the room lengthwise. Núñez stands now between
her and the light. It costs her an effort to look at him as
the sun spills over his shoulder.

                    NÚÑEZ
Be warned that I will come twice every day until this
is finished. Evening and early morning.
                    [turning to Gabriel]
Stop hovering over me!

                    JUANA
Gabriel is afraid we are killing each other.

                    GABRIEL
Father, her tongue is infected.

                    NÚÑEZ
As I have been saying for years.
                    [squinting in satisfaction]
It hurts you to speak.

                    JUANA
                    [under her breath]
More than you can know.

                    NÚÑEZ
                    [to Gabriel]
I am told she started out before dawn to meet us here.
They say she has licked clean a path of stone from her
cell right up to this locutory.
                    [turns on her with violence]
You will *never* be mistaken for a saint--not under me!

We are now compiling dossiers on three *extáticas*.
Teresa de Jesus, Antonia de Ochoa, Juana de los Reyes.
Three more women passing themselves off as saints--

                    JUANA
I am no saint.

                    NÚÑEZ
The others will get off with a hundred lashes, or two.
    Not you. . . .
                    [conjuring rage]
'The body of a nun should be dead to the world! Dead
to any love but that of a jealous Husband. Christ
shares his bed with *no one*--least of all the pitiful,
narrow cot that is a nun's soul!'[29]

V.O.: Yes, Reverend Father, quote yourself as though it were
Holy Writ.

'. . . And is there any other that a bride of Christ
should love?--Jesus alone, and in what terrifying dis-
proportion to His own love! Not only this, but she must
not allow herself to be loved--against all the natural
inclinations of women! Woman--who so gladly suffers
being loved and celebrated. Unlike her, the true bride
of Christ abominates in equal measure both loving and
being loved.'

                    JUANA
How can I accept this? *Father, show me how.*

                    NÚÑEZ
Accept it? Arrogant wretch! You persist in treating
your soul like some crown of jewels.

*On his feet now, he lifts a face of blind rage to the dark
rafters. Turns back on her furiously.*

                    NÚÑEZ
'Before being vanquished and made a captive, the bride
is first to be stripped of these and clapped in infamous irons, in the dark dungeon of her own flesh, a
vile slave to her appetites.'

*From the folds of his cassock, Núñez draws a leatherbound
book, opens it, presses it flat against the grate.*

                    NÚÑEZ
Castalian Flood--I know who emboldened you to publish
this filth. And I know all about *her* appetites.

                              JUANA

          It's been five years. The Inquisition has made no com-
          plaint--

                              NÚÑEZ

          Because they do not yet know what your words conceal!
          Divine Narcissus. Was Christ's martyred body not beau-
          tiful enough for you? That you should make him
          Narcissus!
                You have sinned more than a thousand whores. He
          does not need *your* love! Do you hear? And He does not
          need that *His* Love be returned.

                              JUANA

          But is it so wrong to fear that this vast difference--
          the self-sufficiency of His Love and the superfluous-
          ness of our own--

                              NÚÑEZ
                    [his face contorting with fury]
          Stop!

                              JUANA

          To feel that this disproportion debases and enslaves
          us--though this defect of the heart is all our own?

                              NÚÑEZ

          How has this piece of heresy *so taken hold of you?!*

          He hurls her collection at the window. As it strikes the
          iron bars it splits. Part falls into the dirt beneath the
          window.

                              NÚÑEZ

          Gabriel. See that no one touches Sor Juana's book. We
          will see how well her work endures.
                    [shakes his head in disgust]
                You have made a mockery of the articles of Our
          Faith. You have violated a sacred trust, the holy
          sacrament of confession, and for twenty-five years har-
          boured these abominations of the imagination and the
          flesh.
                Speak!

                              JUANA

          Yes.

                              NÚÑEZ

          Leave me now. . . .
                If I return we will see about curing this sick
          soul of yours. We will come to the end of your lusts.
          This is the source of these crazy ecstasies.
                And in the meanwhile, take care of that tongue.

INSIDE THE CONVENT CHAPEL--NIGHT
The chapel is empty but for her. Dozens of votive candles
flicker on the altar. Juana stands. Clasps a single candle
in her hands. Faintest starlight through stained glass windows. Camera slowly circles her. . . .

Just audible now the first bars of Arvo Part's *Miserere*
. . . counter-tenor, oboe, counter-tenor, oboe, counter-
tenor, bass clarinet, counter-tenor, oboe counter-tenor bass
clarinet counter-tenor tenor camera accelerating oboe
counter-tenor bass clarinet oboe counter-tenor tenor clarinet
counter-tenor organ tenor camera rising circling circling
counter-tenor organ tenor counter-tenor organ tenor counter-
tenor bass clarinet oboe counter-tenor tenor clarinet
counter-tenor oboe bassoon camera rising—TENOR COUNTER-TENOR
SOPRANO BASS OBOE BASSOON KETTLE DRUM

Rising wheeling wall of sound--light receding--altitude volume rising sheer--altar to nave, stars to heaven--camera
the eye of god--far below a soul is dying a great spirit is
struggling for life very far below--at last a pillar of
sound and lightlessness rising up from the altar to heaven
drives her to her knees. . . .

FADE OUT

INSIDE LOCUTORY--GREY MORNING

                    NÚÑEZ
              [beckoning to her]
     Come closer.

*Juana kneels close to the grate as he stands on the other
side.*

                    NÚÑEZ
     Gabriel, how does she appear to you today.

                    GABRIEL
     Worse. . . .

                    NÚÑEZ
     As I expected. She hardly knows now when she is defying
     me.
                 [to Juana]
          The Prioress says your mortifications have become
     excessive.

                              JUANA
          Precision and rigour . . . rigour and precision.

                              NÚÑEZ
          You think you can escape me as you did the Carmelites.

                              JUANA
          There is no escaping.

                              NÚÑEZ
          Confess your ambitions.

                              JUANA
          Wherever I run my enemy is waiting.

                              NÚÑEZ
          Confess your ambitions.

                              JUANA
          I have no ambitions left.

                              NÚÑEZ
          Confess.

                              JUANA
          My ambitions were grotesque.

          Her lips move slightly, but no sound emerges.

                              NÚÑEZ
          Speak! sinner. Make yourself heard.

                              JUANA
          . . . They watch my every gesture.

                              NÚÑEZ
                         [sneering]
          Yet they do not see you, do they? Do you even exist
          any longer? They see only the brazen idol you have
          built for them. *Only* I *see you now as you really are.*
          Deny it!

                              JUANA
          These past months . . . It's as you said, my example has
          the power to do great evil.
               And it is as I told you. . . . I have brought down
          upon myself and upon the capital a flood of debates and
          envyings, wraths and strifes and backbitings--

                              NÚÑEZ
          Stop these blasphemies!

                              JUANA
          Whisperings and swellings and tumults. These are mine,
          for He has given them to me, the penalties of my
          adulteries--

                    NÚÑEZ
You would drive me away now that we have come this
far?

                    JUANA
Every crime, every sin and fear, each cloud of ignorance, each hurt and cruelty--

                    NÚÑEZ
You would flee into a feigned lunacy!

                    JUANA
These months of calamity are mine. The weevil that
infests the crops is the worm in my soul.

                    NÚÑEZ
It is just as I predicted.

                    JUANA
The blight is the blight on my flesh. The riots and
rebellion begin with me--

                    NÚÑEZ
Preposterous. Have you communicated with the leaders of
the insurrection? Do you even know their names?

                    JUANA
I have incited the Indians to revert to the worship of
their idols--

                    NÚÑEZ
Did you send out secret circulars, preach to them their
pagan doctrines? Give me the specifics.

                    JUANA
I have brought the floods.

                    NÚÑEZ
Vomiting blasphemy!--boasting of an entire continent
punished just for *you*. Tell me how!

                    JUANA
Couldn't it be?

                    NÚÑEZ
It is just as I told them. She will confess responsibility for the whole but claim innocence in the particulars. What are you trying to deflect me from?
    I know you. You still doubt this.

                    JUANA
I am the lock, you are the key.

                    NÚÑEZ
You are nothing but an empty vessel.

JUANA
Emptiness itself.

NÚÑEZ
Look into the pus-hole that is your self! You would
disdain His Grace so as to nurture *this*? Purge yourself
of this sick pride!

You rebel because you fear union with Him. You
fear the tidal power of His Love. You fear annihilation
yet long for it.

[with disgust]

But no, still you withhold your consent, still you
would deny Him. You are utterly and absolutely unworthy
of His Love!

Yet even now he offers it, while you cling to this
abomination that is your *self*.

You claim you cannot feel His Love. But you are
terrified you *will*.

You have spent a lifetime walling in this black
beast of yours. Verses are the scraps you feed it on.

But now you wake in the middle of the blackest
night of all, and discover even the beast of your
nightmares has left you. . . .

Now what remains inside--your tower of empty
speeches.

With difficulty she rises, comes to the grate, standing
before him yet looking past him to the light.

NÚÑEZ
Tell me about your lusts. Tell me about your dreams,
this unspeakable hunger that possesses you.

[more gently]

Juana, do you think you are the first? I have
taken the confessions of hundreds of nuns. Understand
that in this, at least, you are not alone. You are
just like them.

It comes into their sleep as a succubus.

JUANA
[voice faint]
Is there no limit to what He can forgive?

NÚÑEZ
No child, none whatever.

Tell me how it began. Juana, I warn you, this confession must include those events that brought you to
me--to Mother Church.

JUANA
[very pale]
I have confessed this once.

NÚÑEZ

Yes, and had I handled things properly then, you might
not have had to wander lost these past twenty-five
years. It is the work of a Jubilee to till the fallow
field, harrow it, root out all of its pernicious
errors. *Tell me about this black beast.*

JUANA
[lips white, trembling]
I have gloried in the corruption of my flesh. And in
corrupting others. My hunger has whored and defiled
me--

NÚÑEZ

You will give me much more than this!

She raises a hand to the grate to steady herself.

JUANA

I have harboured thoughts--thoughts you know too well,
Father.

NÚÑEZ

Tell me!

*She kneels, clinging now with one hand to the grate, head
and shoulders bent.*

NÚÑEZ

This is not what I need! You will confess again to me
in detail what happened *and how it felt.*

JUANA

I couldn't breathe! It was as something gross and
malignant--swallowing . . . me.

*She slumps to the floor, body jammed against the grate, arm
bent up and back at a sharp angle, fingers still clinging
to the bar.*

GABRIEL

Father Núñez!

NÚÑEZ

What is it Gabriel? What is happening? Fetch some
water, quickly--and bread! Be quick about it.

Núñez, about to stroke her cheek, restrains himself.

NÚÑEZ
[whispering]
You will not escape me, child. You think I cannot
follow, but I will wait for you . . . even on the other
side.

GABRIEL *hurries in with a pitcher.*

> NÚÑEZ
>
> The bread!

> GABRIEL
>
> I sent them for it.

Núñez pours water over his fingers, using them to guide a trickle of water over her cheeks, her forehead, a few drops on her eyelids. With trembling fingers he parts her parched lips, letting the liquid run over his fingers into her mouth . . . She stirs.

> NÚÑEZ
>
> Learn from my errors, Gabriel. I have let her grow too weak--and at this most *critical* moment!

A NOVICE enters from inside the convent.

> NOVICE
>
> Bread, Father. Fresh.

> NÚÑEZ
>
> It will have to do. Give it to me.

Hands trembling, he tears off a piece, still warm, and holds it beneath her nose, presses it to her lips; her eyelids flutter.

> NÚÑEZ
> [whispering]
> I will feed you, Juanita. From my hand you shall eat of this bread. Then you will rest.

The young novice who brought bread stands over Sor Juana, wringing her hands, face unsure. Núñez is trying to feed her through the bars though she is barely conscious. Blindly filling her mouth with bread. Sor Juana revives, coughing up bread.

> NÚÑEZ
>
> I will be back early tomorrow and we will finish what we have started here today. . . .

Gabriel leads him away, the novice helping Sor Juana to a sitting position. At the door, Núñez pauses.

> NÚÑEZ
>
> Gabriel, have them bring back the chairs.

FADE OUT

INSIDE THE CONVENT LOCUTORY--MORNING
A steady rain. From the roof's water spouts, rainwater
falls onto the courtyard's flagstones. At the window, flowers
bend double with their charge of rainwater. Inside . . .
mood of gloomy intimacy.

Juana enters on her knees, makes her way towards the grate.
Shadows in the gaunt hollows of her face. Eyes unfocussed.
Takes no heed of the two men waiting for her. Nor of the
chairs that have been returned to their places.

Gabriel steps back as she reaches the grate.

> GABRIEL

Father, her mouth.

> NÚÑEZ

Tell me.

> GABRIEL

Horrible sores--on her lips, tongue . . .

> NÚÑEZ

You would make yourself mute to escape me, woman?
    You would consume your own tongue?

> JUANA

Does this not--
                [wincing as she looks up]
make me a cannibal, too, Father? Another charge to add
to your list.

> NÚÑEZ

Good. We are back to this. Cleverness. Poetic talk.
    I have lost my appetite for your false confes-
sions. As have the people, for your learning and your
poetry. Your people burn with questions, they thirst
with doubts. So many catastrophes coinciding, befalling
one city. How to explain it? What is the *machinery,* Sor
Juana? You were always one to look for that. Will you
tell them it is coincidence? Surely you can better us
in this. *Queen of the Sciences*--the people have no need
of your beautiful questions. Questions they have enough
of on their own.
    But no answers?--we do not have the luxury. And
our doubts, we are thanked for keeping to ourselves. We
have responsibilities--as do you, who have been granted
so many privileges denied others of your station. And
yet you have taken so many liberties even with these.

V.O.: Then there will yet be ages of the confusion of free
thought, ages of their science and cannibalism. For, having
begun to build their tower of Babel without us, they will end
of course with cannibalism.[30]

                              NÚÑEZ
Get up.

                              GABRIEL
She is feverish, Father. The infection—

                              NÚÑEZ
This science of yours infects more than your tongue.

                              JUANA
Not my science, Father.
     [rising to her knees, a hand at the grate]
     Mine would be different.

                              NÚÑEZ
Your insistence on *feeling* His Love, experiencing it,
this also is a contamination from your science.

                              JUANA
Through the body there are ways of knowing.

                              NÚÑEZ
Our Inquisitors would agree.

                              JUANA
A kind of scepticism.

                              NÚÑEZ
Perhaps, then, they are poets too.

                              JUANA
A kind of eternity. . . .

                              NÚÑEZ
It is doubt that eats at your heart.
     Not only does your Narcissus make the divine a
profanity, *you would make the vile profanities of experience out to be divine.*

                              JUANA
I only looked for the sublime *within* Creation. If we
could but open our minds, we would find the beyond . . .
already here.

                              NÚÑEZ
Yes, tell them there is so much more to know than
Churches, there is so much more to God than priests. No
wafer, no wine, only knowledge--congress, communion
with nature--these are the sacraments now. And they are

free. How the humble people will love this, who toil so
for their daily bread--so sorely taxed--the rents, the
indulgences. How they will love you for this.

     And how, Sor Juana, do you imagine my colleagues
feel on this account? The anachronisms who are my
confreres?

V.O.: Ages will pass, and humanity will proclaim by the lips
of their sages and men of science that there is no crime, and
therefore no sin; there is only hunger . . .

                    NÚÑEZ
By now you probably believe you can multiply the
loaves and fishes, in your house of bread. Do that.
Feed the masses on the manna of miracles. It is a
kindness we also do.

                    JUANA
You would make us hungry enough to eat stones from your
hand.

                    NÚÑEZ
Command, then, that they be made bread.

                    JUANA
We are not nourished. We are not fed.
          [she winces, swallows]
     The bread you feed us is our own flesh.

                    NÚÑEZ
You would teach them to feed themselves, perhaps. No,
you would feed them on *attributes*.
     Yes by all means, gorge them on the delicacies of
your subtlety, fatten them on scepticism. Tell them He
is only a non-count noun--let them be nourished with
that. Salve their hunger and their fear by telling them
He is not substance at all--and not Verb but Adverb—
isn't that your latest heresy?
     Any lunatic can speak for a god, Juana. Ruling
humanity for seventeen centuries is quite another matter.

Using the grate, she pulls herself unsteadily to her feet,
ignoring the chair.

                    JUANA
They will not follow you forever.

                    NÚÑEZ
               [disdainful]
We try to take things a millennium at a time.

                    JUANA
You only protract your defeat for so long that it passes
for victory.

NÚÑEZ

While you would correct His work--resurrect Him, if
ever so briefly.
        End his perfect silence, then!
        Who but the strongest can follow you?

V.O. . . . Freedom, free thought and science, will lead them
into such straits and will bring them face to face with such
marvels and insoluble mysteries, that some of them, the fierce
and rebellious, will destroy themselves; others, rebellious
but weak, will destroy one another, while the rest, weak and
unhappy, will crawl fawning at our feet. . . .

JUANA

Your confreres mistake their contempt for strength.

NÚÑEZ

Your own strength is your weakness.
        And *our* greatest strength, over time, has proved
to be your despair.

JUANA

What the soul hungers for most of all is not transcendent Truth but meaning--a human meaning in the face of
this.

NÚÑEZ

The soul!--what an ungainly, unbelievable, unnecessary
appendage. Your science will soon disprove its existence . . .

V.O.: . . . Bathed in their foolish tears, they will recognize
at last that He who created them rebels must have meant to
mock at them. They will say this in despair, and their utter-
ances will be a blasphemy which will make them more unhappy
still, for man's nature cannot bear blasphemy, and in the end
always avenges it upon himself.

JUANA

You take your disdain as the heaviest burden of all.
        Your Inquisitors use their cruelty and contempt to
make martyrs of themselves.

NÚÑEZ

If you truly believe your way is better, you, who have
been consumed by doubt all your life--if you are who
and what some say, go forth and preach your message to
your fellows. I can arrange easily for your release.
        I offer you much more than your freedom, *I offer
you the world.*
        Conquer them yourself. Give them death-defying
feats. But by all means, cast thyself down, from a
great height, that the angels bear thee up. Pilot your

chariot. Give in to all your fantasies. Your pagan
heroes will surely protect you from us.

No? Do you leave your people to find their own
way?

> JUANA

I will not escape.

> NÚÑEZ

But you could. To your precious María Luisa in Madrid,
or to France. You know we can arrange it. Anywhere you
please. And think what a trophy you would make the
Lutherans.

> JUANA

My place is here.

> NÚÑEZ

You could return in triumph when we are all dead.

> JUANA

I will not live so long.

> NÚÑEZ

Still playing at prophecy.

> JUANA

My place is here.

> NÚÑEZ

Then it shall be decided here. . . .

CUT TO: THE VALLEY OF MEXICO--LATE AFTERNOON, CLEARING
After the rain, water glinting everywhere . . . shallow
lakes, sloughs, canals. Dry hills to the north and west.
The eye rising, moving slowly east. Pine forests mounting
the slopes of the two volcanoes. Snow at the peaks. Clear
blue sky above. Steam and pale smoke billowing from the
southernmost cone. View of another white cone farther off,
the eye is speeding east—over jungles, another white cone
near the coast, a ribbon of beach, glint of sea . . .

JUBILEE,
DAY 34:
REQUERI-
MIENTO

MEXICO CITY--MORNING
Indian crouched in a mud hut, kindling a tiny fire.
Skeletal street dog standing dazed in the sunlight outside
the door.

INSIDE THE CONVENT LOCUTORY--MID-MORNING, BRIGHT SUNSHINE
Juana enters to wait for him. Her lips move soundlessly.
She hardly notices his arrival. She stands at the grate,
again disdaining the chair.

Núñez has begun to shuffle back and forth along the grate,
leaning heavily on his cane. A shaking hand reaching out to
steady himself. He will not sit before she does. Gabriel
has moved to stand just a step or two behind Núñez, afraid
he might fall.

> NÚÑEZ
> How is your cannibal tongue today? Does it hurt you to
> speak? It should hurt you very much now to speak.
> I forbid you these mutilations!

> JUANA
> If you would have me find such pain in pleasure . . .

Pauses to wipe her mouth roughly with the back of her hand.
It comes away streaked with blood.

> JUANA
> . . . why not pleasure in pain?

> NÚÑEZ
> Do you see, Gabriel? Do you see what we are up against
> here?

> JUANA
> There is a Dutch Jew . . . who has said pleasure is
> not evil but inherently good, while pain--

> NÚÑEZ
> Word games, equivocations, digressions--

> JUANA
> Is evil itself.

> NÚÑEZ
> Self-justifications! Take note, Gabriel. All the
> heretic's tricks--

> JUANA
> You, Father, think pain

[coughs then swallows]
is your ally--

NÚÑEZ
Feigned bodily weakness at critical moments--

JUANA
But pain is still more fickle--

NÚÑEZ
Faking even ingenuousness--

JUANA
More *fickle* than pleasure . . . it serves whom it chooses--

NÚÑEZ
Giving herself saintly airs--

*The backs of her hands and wrists are smeared. Though she
still wipes at them, threads of a dark liquid run freely
now down her chin and throat and into the hairshirt's neck,
blackening it.*

JUANA
Your superiors think to baptize my silence. But what
will it say . . . if God takes me from you before you
finish their holy work?
          [turns to face him at the grate]
     You look unwell, Father. You should eat something.

NÚÑEZ
          [he casts about for Gabriel]
Where are you, boy? Come.

JUANA
Empty threats, Father. Bring him his chair, Gabriel.
Sit down!
     You will not leave me now. As you said: we are in
new territory. No more evasions.
     Conquer my doubts.

*Instead of leaving, Núñez sits heavily, begins reciting,
voice betraying an old man's quaver.*

NÚÑEZ
'Representing Charles V, his most Catholic Majesty . . . [31]
     I, his servant, notify and make known to you as
best I can that the living and eternal God, our Lord,
created the heavens and the earth--'

He continues proclamation. Her bitter smile of satisfaction.

JUANA
Cortés's *Requerimiento.* You know it by heart, *por
supuesto.*

NÚÑEZ

'. . . And God gave charge of all these people to one
called St. Peter--*that he should be the head of all the
human race, and should love all men of whatsoever land,
religion, and belief*--'

JUANA

But now let another faculty--reason--serve you who have
served it, too, so well, Father. So obediently.

NÚÑEZ

'And one of his successors, as lord of all spiritual
matters, made a donation of these lands you occupy, to
the Catholic monarchs, Ferdinand and Isabela, so that
they now belong to them--'

JUANA

You who have been its instrument, use reason now to
force this conversion—this confession from my infected
lips—

NÚÑEZ

'. . . other countries have received and obeyed their
majesties willingly and without resistance--'

JUANA

[mocking eyes bright]
Insert a gag between my teeth with the pure force of
your arguments, Father! Claim this pagan territory for
your Church.

*Gabriel hovers over Núñez, peering wonderingly into his
face. The young priest has seen this kind of rapture many
times before, in many faces, but never Núñez. . . .*

JUANA

Become the ram's head you promised me, Father.
     Batter down my defences.

NÚÑEZ

'Understand and obey!
     If you do this you will do well. Their Majesties
and I will receive you with all love and charity.'

JUANA

Is this the best you can do--offer promises, *bribes*?
No! Command understanding, Priest!

NÚÑEZ

'But, if you do not do this and put impediments in the
way, I swear to you that with God's help, I will come
among you powerfully and make war upon you everywhere and
in every way that I can, and I will subject you to the
yoke of obedience to the Church and their Majesties.'

The triumph in her eyes has faded. Her voice betrays exhaustion, disappointment.

                    JUANA

No . . . *Convince* me. Make me *see*.
    Truly, can you not do this for me?

                    NÚÑEZ

'I will take your persons, your women and children, and
will make slaves of them and sell them or dispose of
them as their Highnesses shall command.'

                    JUANA

We are made slaves already.

                    NÚÑEZ

'I will take your possessions and will damage you as
much as I can, as vassals who do not obey or wish to
acknowledge their sovereign, but resist and oppose
him.'

                    JUANA

We are already damaged and bereft. Bring us to give
freely of our assent.

                    NÚÑEZ

'And furthermore, I protest that the damage and death
which you suffer thereby shall be your own doing--And
not the fault of their Majesties, nor mine, nor of the
knights who accompany me.
    Of all I say and require of you, the scribe who
writes this shall be my witness. . . .'

CUT TO: Cortés continuing his proclamation over a bewildered farmer tilling a stony field high up in the pass, the
plains to the east filled with smoke, the hacienda of
Panoayán below.

FADE OUT

BERSERKERS

REMEMBER THIS. Or, if there is still a way, forget.

The iambic creak of jays nesting near Beulah's window. Pale blue walls, grey-green carpet, her bedroom's dark green curtains tightly drawn against the afternoon. The bray and screetch of swing sets in the park across the street. As we rutted on the sea floor of Beulah's darkened apartment I was sometimes afraid, just once or twice, that if she'd asked it in that instant, I would have murdered her. Brutally.

I think I know how this sounds, under the circumstances.

Such an admission conjures some sad escalation from whips to chains to whetted razors. But there were no hooks or attachments, no booted uniforms and scout knots, no ropes or scaling techniques. The topographies were the same as they've been since Eden, since Atlantis.

Everything I should ever have needed in a marriage Madeleine offered me. Throughout those early years, as long as I was passably discreet, Madeleine rarely gave me any need to lie. I was never asked to make excuses about the occasional skipped dinner or weekend conference. She wouldn't be jealous of mere sex.

For Beulah there was nothing 'mere' about sex. Comparisons are invidious; analogies, the last resort of the desperate. But if in love-making Madeleine played the daring spelunker, Beulah was the savage who'd painted the cave.

Madeleine lacked inhibitions, Beulah burned hers like gasoline.

There was a wildness. She would strip herself so bare, always down, deeper into this primitive sea, and take me with her. I had never been there, pared of my hesitations, my crabbed, scuttling fears. I'd known nothing like it, no intensity like this until the night of Catherine's birth, when I swore to Madeleine on my daughter's eyes: No more infidelities.

Tidal, oceanic, but not Birth's violent crash of surf flinging itself up the beach. Rather, the Return. Placid, fatal undertow . . . a first, slow penetration. Short pulse, long ebb. In and down. Back, withdraw . . . again. Subsiding otter-glide, slippery slide over amphibian skin.

Serene, obscene, epicene.

Down through epilimnion and thermocline, down over angled hydroplanes. Bank and dive through the dark. Dive, back, dive. Again.

Here and there the flare and flicker of phosphorescence . . . dragon
fire, distant suns exploding . . . ships' lanterns through salt fog. In and
down. A throb of pressure—ringing anvils, kettle drums locked in
bone. A soft string of mute concussions . . . gleam and fire of batteries
from a shore. Down, retract, return. Ever deeper, brine thickening . . .
a knitting in the protein warp. A faint clutch unclutched . . . a notch,
minutely riven. Deliquescent starbursts in the flesh.

We were dying, knowing at last what it was to be alive. Two minds,
one consciousness, fastened to dying animals. Our death was all
around us yet *outside*. And for that hour we were not alone. Sex and
death—God, I've made enough of a joke of things without dragging
poor Sigmund in. Yeats was bad enough.

But death was not the point. We had just held up our lives—high
up, cupped wildly beating in our hands.

Something I saw two weeks ago in Mexico shook me. It was a mistake to have followed her there. An indigenous sculptural motif as old
as the feathered serpent she so often mentions. At least two thousand
years. Of a youth, emerging face-first from the unhinged maw of a
dragon.

Sometimes with the world about to burst to white, when we had
draped ourselves in the dragon's fresh-flayed hide, our faces a berserk
mask, I could look into those green and amber eyes and somewhere in
them see the face of a girl, staring out at me.

chorus

Seraphim, come!
Come all and find
a Rose that is cut
and yet it lives on;
   that withers not
but revives
to a fierce new bloom,
one stemming from
her own deepest being;
   and so it proved a blessing
to have bent her to the knife.
Harvesters, come!
Come all and find
a Rose that is cut
and yet it lives on.

verses

Against a frail Rose
a thousand north winds contrive:
how hedged in by envy she is
in the brief hour Beauty is given to live!
   Because she is lovely, they envy,
and because she is learned, they ape:
how ancient now is this story
in a world that pays merit with hate.

A thousand panting breaths
give vent to a thousand whirling blades on edge—
that for each fresh distinction score and mark
a great and lonely heart.
   So many deaths
against a single life conspire;
yet none meets with success,
for having sprung from cowardice and rancour;
   so do not read too much into the ignorant,
blind, malignant fate
she suffers on the wheel of blades,
for with this God constructs the chariot of her triumph.
   Although the circling engine
is a cutting courtesan,
it is one whose machinations
serve to restore Catherine's fortunes.
   And to the Rose herself
it is not new, not in the least,
that upon her august splendours
pungent barbs should mount an honour guard
to mark her final glories.

JUANA INÉS
DE LA CRUZ

JUBILEE, DAY 37: HERESY, THE TECHNOLOGY

INT. MODERN DAY--CLIP OF LESBIAN PORN, BY WOMEN, FOR WOMEN
Dom. / sub. Close focus on restraints, engines of pene-
tration--anal, vaginal, fisting . . .

INT. MEXICO CITY--MODERN DAY, MUSEUM OF MEDICINE, DAY
Exhibition in progress, banners strung up at the entrance.
"*Instrumentos Europeos de Tortura y Pena Capital.*" Long
lines waiting to get in. Inside, dim floor lighting, sound-
track music from *The Mission*. A tour guide leads a small
group past various exhibits. Speaking in Spanish, she pauses to model the use of certain items. Translation is unnecessary. Two women, maybe the same two from the previous
scene, trail the rest of the group, handle the objects,
pale, sweating, hands shaking, yet laughing.

CUT TO: The courtyard below, a group of students in jeans
and T-shirts performing a silent play on the theme. From
the radio in the ticket booth horn-blasts of mariachi, the
volume turned up against the music from above. After a long
moment, a man rushes to the second storey balcony. Very
tall, heavy-set, bearded, his face contorted in anguish.
Calls down furiously in Spanish at the ticket seller who
shrugs, turns his music down.

INSIDE THE INQUISITION'S SECRET PRISONS--DAY
Scene of savage brutality. Dominican scribes seated to one
side of the action, recording all. Two women, indeterminate
age. One strapped to the rack, the other on the wheel.
Wheel angled such that the low point of each revolution
passes directly over a flame. Light filters through one
tiny window high up, near the ceiling. Light falls across
high side of the wheel. The wheel spins lazily, the woman
passing through sun then shadow then flame, imparts a stro-
boscopic effect.
    The wheel is spun by public executioner--black hood
thrown back so he can sweat and breathe more freely. He is
busy splitting his time between wheel and rack, making
adjustments. One inquisitor stands by each, interrogating
each subject, pausing frequently to give the torturer
instructions, or to give the scribes time to record every
cry, gesture, word, prayer, every crack of bone and
cartilege. . . .
    Partly concealed behind a latticework set high in the
wall sits a hunched figure.

INSIDE A CONFESSIONAL--LATER SAME DAY
The public executioner kneels, his face troubled. The
hands, clasped in supplication, are meaty. Nails broken and
dirty, under them what looks like red clay. . . .

Taking his confession is Núñez, eyes glowing like
embers in the semi-darkness.

INSIDE THE CONVENT LOCUTORY--LATE AFTERNOON
Panel of sunlight warms the window bars and frame. Lines of
black and red ants runs endlessly up and down the blinding
white plaster, to and from a crack in the wall.

                    NÚÑEZ
  Heresy, the enemy from within. . . . For the rooting
  out of heresies, Europe has developed effective, if
  crude, tools.

                    JUANA
  Such contempt they must have for you, Father, to expect
  you to sell your eternal soul for the price of my
  submission.

                    NÚÑEZ
  My superiors have instructed me to share with you my
  own very genuine repugnance for these methods.

                    JUANA
  Everything is to be permitted in the name of obedience?--even reducing God's highest creation to a dumb
  slavery.
    This is not God's work.

                    NÚÑEZ
  You want me to believe you a coward, Juana, but you
  will bear up well under torture.
    Of course, everyone breaks.

                    JUANA
  Do you think I didn't know that even you have run
  afoul of the Holy Office?

                    NÚÑEZ
So you think you understand me . . . but I do not think
you do, since the pamphlet I was reckless enough to
write has been so thoroughly suppressed.
    It happened just after I first knew you. The same
year I found you sobbing in the cathedral.
    A pamphlet of sixteen pages. I composed it in the
guise of the Blessed Virgin's secretary, writing in her
behalf.
    The secret trial lasted three months. Do you want
to know what I wrote, Juana?

                              JUANA
Yes.

                              NÚÑEZ
It was a plea, that the women and girls of New Spain
refrain from wearing provocative colours during Holy
Week. The pamphlet concluded with a formula of
respect. "Yours, whose feet I kiss." The Virgin here
would kiss their feet as Christ once washed those of
his followers. But the inquisitor saw in my formula a
lascivious intent.
        You will be smiling now. But perhaps when the
smile has died on your lips you will think of the
danger you are in. If this could happen to me. You
will imagine how much and how many of your confessions
I have had to conceal. Try also to imagine how much
these dissimulations have imperiled me. And how hard I
have worked to keep the Holy Office from concluding
your works are a hundred times more scandalous than my
little pamphlet once was.
        And perhaps, at last, you will understand that I
cannot protect you any longer. . . .
        [rises, gropes his way toward the window]
        My great impiety was only to put a few words in
the mouth of the Virgin. But you . . .

                              JUANA
Mute, she is so much less dangerous.

                              NÚÑEZ
    [he begins to nod--then, whirling to face her, cries
                      out fiercely]
Santiago!

                              JUANA
                      [startled]
¿Me darás el Santiago? First Cortés's proclamation, now
his battle cry?

                              NÚÑEZ
They will tear your body down, Juana, block by block,
like an Aztec temple--

                              JUANA
You are the one, Father, whom they have marked for the
first sacrifice.

                              NÚÑEZ
The body you have worked so long to veil within these
walls--

                              JUANA
It will be *your* heart. . . .

NÚÑEZ
And on the same site, and with the same stones--

JUANA
At your life's end you would settle for this?

NÚÑEZ
They will rebuild of you--an altar to Christ.

JUANA
As they have remade you, Father? As they have allowed
themselves to be remade by their own hatreds and fears?
For the serpent, the woman, the Jew?
[pauses]
    Do you think I do not know how they made you suf-
fer as a novice for your creativity? Do you not know
your legend, Father? The pains they took to purge you?
The marks are all over you.
    I know how much you once thirsted to complete the
number, to stand among the elect.

NÚÑEZ
They will show your body to you, Juana.

JUANA
These men you now stand among, Father Núñez, are *these*
the elect?

NÚÑEZ
Then they will return your body to you. They will bring
you back to earth.

JUANA
I know *your* soul, Father. That is why I have loved
you. Fear, respect, hatred—these you have earned. But
my love, I gave freely to what remained of that tormented youth--who once laughed and ran, wrote verses
and plays. Who once knew shame.
    And is that boy not Gabriel today?
    This is why you have chosen him now.

NÚÑEZ
I have taken the confessions of these men. They are not
like us, Juana. They have been coarsened by their work.
They are not holy.

JUANA
I have seen your fear, Antonio Núñez.

NÚÑEZ
There is a kind of complicity, things they are reluctant to do to another man, but with a woman--

JUANA
You have seen terrible things.

                         NÚÑEZ
With a woman, these men's coarse spirits soar to something close to artistry.

                         JUANA
Now, with the end so near, you fear for your own--and
where it might soar to.
        Do you really think you could be allowed to sit at
God's table?--a *henchman* with blood under his nails!
With this your last act?

                         NÚÑEZ
You will be stripped naked.

                         JUANA
They have made you party to monstrosities, Father, the
vilest inhumanities.

                         NÚÑEZ
Juanita, I have seen their dead eyes. You will feel
their coarse hands on your shame.

                         JUANA
Unspeakable crimes.

                         NÚÑEZ
Juana, I cannot protect you, *do you understand me?*

                         JUANA
Your fear is why they sent you.

                         NÚÑEZ
Garras de gato--the skull cat . . . a cap fitted with
iron claws.

                         JUANA
What has been your harvest, Father Núñez? Lice and
ticks and fleas! As you have so often said yourself.

                         NÚÑEZ
Each fresh turn of the screw--drives the claws farther
through the skull and into the brain.

                         JUANA
A harvest of gall.

                         NÚÑEZ
              [the faintest note of pleading]
In this case a very special brain.
        La Pera--the 'pear' comes in two sizes. One for
the woman's place of shame--

                         JUANA
The shame is not ours alone. Is it, Father?

                    NÚÑEZ
A smaller one for the place of filth--

                    JUANA
You have always been a man of books--

                    NÚÑEZ
Wrought-iron, pear-shaped, when inserted--

                    JUANA
A man of reason--

                    NÚÑEZ
Its sharp tines open out--

                    JUANA
A man of learning--

                    NÚÑEZ
Slowly tearing the vitals apart from within.

                    JUANA
Their methods are for you the most terrible defeat--

                    NÚÑEZ
Las mordazas . . . gags, branks, scold's bridles--

                    JUANA
Absolute defeat. Unto eternity . . .

                    NÚÑEZ
An iron mask so tightly fitted as to permit the entry
of air only--

                    JUANA
Your eyes can't conceal from me your desperation,
Father--

                    NÚÑEZ
. . . through one tiny opening--

                    JUANA
So desperate to believe these crimes against our humanity can be justified.

                    NÚÑEZ
Easily blocked with the most playful application of a
fingertip.

                    JUANA
But you lack their *faith.*
    Like me, Father, you are consumed by doubt.
    What if, however improbably, the soul exists--
eternal yet not indestructible.
    And in spite of all, yours still lives?

At death's door, you are astonished to discover
you fear for the death of your soul.

You have discovered that these crude tools debase
their user more certainly--and irretrievably--than the
bodies they are used upon.

You fought against this. You argued that new tools
must be fashioned--that there were already better
methods!

NÚÑEZ

Like *excommunication*.

JUANA

As you've said, the Archbishop has no need of the
Inquisition.

NÚÑEZ

The Inquisition offers you a stage, excommunication
denies you one. And condemns you to your greatest
agony--His *silence*.

JUANA

But they have been caught by their guile. These masters
of introspection who command you.

NÚÑEZ

They insisted the dramatist in you would become their
best asset. We would offer you a rehearsal of your
trial.

JUANA

No, Father, you are the asset--that the dramatist in me
would see that your fear for me and your shame are
unfeigned.

NÚÑEZ

You think to try me before the court of History!

JUANA

You have seen that your Church is dying--and grows more
dangerous as it dies.

And with it, your precious Order.

Because after seventeen centuries, they have forgotten the weakness in any order--divine or diabolical--
is our humanity.

Even you are less terrified of what they are *than
of what they might still make you become.*

It seems, Father, that we are all a house divided
against ourselves. But maybe that is not such a weakness, after all.

You are the flaw in their plan. And--who knows,
Father?--the strength in another.

NÚÑEZ

I have been party to terrible actions.

JUANA

You wanted so desperately to believe in their order,
yet even this could not extinguish your love.
    Reverend Father Antonio Núñez de Miranda, you are
a fraud.

NÚÑEZ

You are defying me to enter history as your Judas--

JUANA

You are not the man they would have you be.

NÚÑEZ

To be your judge.

JUANA

You are the weak link because you have loved me.

NÚÑEZ

Your executioner. . . .

JUANA

Yes, Father. So *choose.*
                    [long pause]
Might your God not learn to settle for a compromise
after all?
    New methods, Father, for a new age. More flexible,
more precise.
    It might help you to think of the soul as an inven-
tion, our greatest invention. A machine, or an
instrument.
    Imagine this instrument to be more substantial
than a hammer, harder than an anvil, though shaped from
ether, not steel.
    You yourself, Father, are its demonstration:
greater now than your fear of the Inquisition is your
fear that a soul you are not quite certain exists be
damned absolutely.

NÚÑEZ

It is as they have always said. You have a man's mind
in a woman's body.

JUANA

We are false converts to the Church of Reason, Father.
You and I both. Woman has been brought to this faith
of yours in bondage. Our minds master it but it does
not feed our hearts.
    But if it helps you with your oath of loyalty,
imagine that these convents can be made the observa-
tories of this new science of the soul.

For this new Jesuit science new instruments are to
be forged. To convert each woman into her own
Inquisitor. An auto-Inquisitor, who with saintly zeal
prosecutes the heretical hungers within.
   [rising to stand very close to him at the grate]
   As I say, imagine this if it helps.
   Or at the end of your life, have the courage to
face a simpler truth: that this faith of yours does not
nourish you, either.
   Instead, each day, it is you who sustain this
church of yours.
   By feeding it your heart.

PATIO--MORNING
Wearing a loose cotton shift, her body flowing softly
beneath it, Antonia serves a contented-looking Carlos breakfast at a table beneath a fig tree. She refills his cup of
chocolate, his hand reaches out and rests at her hip. She
looks down at him, smiling. Smile freezes as church bells
call the Sunday faithful to Mass. A loud deep tolling of
twelve.

PLAZA OUTSIDE THE CONVENT--MORNING
The old woman has replaced the flowers in the altar, and is
returning to her door. Sunday ball game played against the
convent walls. A group of boys--larger and even louder than
usual--begins to drift dangerously close to the altar
beneath Juana's windows.

The old man emerges from the house two doors down just as
the ball crashes into the altar, smashing candles, the
flower vase, sending flowers flying. He chases the boys
off. Bending down with difficulty, he begins to collect the
flowers.

The old woman is at his side now, helping him. He straightens up, flowers in hand. She stands to face him. He is
looking at her as though waiting for the answer to a question he has just asked. His lips have not moved.

INT--IN THE CONVENT LOCUTORY
Núñez enters. Leaves Gabriel to wait at the door. She is
still pacing. Maybe pacing like this since he left, minutes
ago, or days.

> JUANA
> [gently]
> Truly, Father, what brings you back to me?

> NÚÑEZ
> The anguish I have heard in your voice for twenty-five
> years. It is that anguish I still hear.

> JUANA
> I feel a loss, an agony, an absence, *in here*. It is
> real. It is true.

> NÚÑEZ
> You thought love was wisdom.

                    JUANA
I *believed* it.

                    NÚÑEZ
That if you could only know enough--

                    JUANA
. . . and know enough of this Love, I could overcome
doubt. Was this truly a sin against God? I ask you
again, Father: are we so different?
    Might not priest and poet share in the soul's care
and custody?

                    NÚÑEZ
Heresy.

                    JUANA
          [smiling gently]
    Will they call me a Manichean because of my fast-
ing? But a Manichean would not lie down with Satan.

                    NÚÑEZ
Then they will call you a Beguine.

                    JUANA
And say I refused to kneel in church?

                    NÚÑEZ
Or call you an adept of Valdés.

                    JUANA
Will they call me an Illuminist because I have sought
to know His Light directly? An Arian for finding my
Beloved too human?

                    NÚÑEZ
A vomiting blasphemer for rejecting the articles of our
faith.

                    JUANA
And for my experiments, a necromancer.

                    NÚÑEZ
A Vaudois for putting yourself above any human
judgement.
    Think of your friends if you are convicted. You
open them to charges of supporting and protecting a
heretic, trafficking in heretical tracts. . . .

                    JUANA
Am I a heretic?

                    NÚÑEZ
In reason of your celebrity and stature they will call
you a *heresiarch,* corrupter of princes. But you know
this.

                    JUANA
Have I sinned against God?

                    NÚÑEZ
They will call you a pseudo-apostle for claiming to
have brought down the floods.

                    JUANA
Am I a heretic, Father?

                    NÚÑEZ
The more serious the charge, the more inconceivable the
refutation. You will be given no opportunity to repent.

                    JUANA
Have I sinned against God?

                    NÚÑEZ
Heresiarchs are burned alive--

                    JUANA
Am I a HERETIC?!

*He pauses while echoes in the locutory die out, affects a
casualness.*

                    NÚÑEZ
Juanita, we are all heretics.
    Heresy is in our heads not our souls.
              [he shrugs]
    The soul is a shaggy, simple beast. It can be
taught a few simple steps--

                    JUANA
A tarantella.

                    NÚÑEZ
At best, Juana, at best.
    And now you must see that this way is best. With
your objections conquered and your confession taken
. . . you will be left free to pursue your negative
finezas in a new way by *not* writing, *not* studying, *not*
making a scandal for once. . . .

JUBILEE,
DAY 40:
CASTLE,
OR TOWER

EXT. PRESENT DAY MEXICO CITY--DAY
After a night of rain. On the convent's south side, the
eight lanes of Izazaga; across the street, the Vanidades
boutique. A car museum--*El Museo del Auto*--is on the corner.
Hawkers, pitchmen and vendors at the Isabel la Católica
subway entrance. A sidewalk market under red nylon
tarpaulins.

INT. LOOKING OUT THE LOCUTORY WINDOW
Part of a book lies in the dirt beneath the window bars. A
breeze ruffles its damp, sun-yellowed pages. Large red
paper wasps landing on the book. From close up, wasps are
seen rolling tiny strips from the page, ferrying them back
to a delicate pearl-grey nest in a copse of trees a short
distance from the locutory.

                         NÚÑEZ
    My superiors are considering your proposition. . . .
        So I am to make them understand you are no threat.
    I am to give them my word.

                         JUANA
    I will give them no further cause for discomfort.

                         NÚÑEZ
    I am the weak link in the chain, after all.

                         JUANA
    You knew this from the start. And trusted me to make
    you hear your own conscience.

                         NÚÑEZ
    It seems I have counted on you to be stronger than my
    conscience.

                         JUANA
    You would have heard it on your own. Eventually.

                         NÚÑEZ
    A few years ago, I would not have.
        But as I once said to you, old age does a lot of
    things.

                         JUANA
                     [tenderly]
    You have done everything humanly possible for me.

                         NÚÑEZ
    The inhumanities, then, I leave to younger men.

                         JUANA
I thought this would be easier--I thought it would be a
relief. Strange to see . . .
     It appears you are my last creation, Father. My
last work. We are each other's.

                         NÚÑEZ
You have said as much as the times permit.
     I am ready to believe you have this great hunger
in you for a reason. You have been given a great talent, a greater mind. Perhaps even a great soul. I am
in no position . . .
               [rises with stiff formality]
     So it is over. I can attend to my own ending.
Gabriel!

*Gabriel leads the hunched figure to the door, where they
pause.*

                         NÚÑEZ
Juana, one last piece of advice. Will you think of it
as from someone who once loved you?
     Stop thinking of your union with Him as a merger.
You are not equals. If He speaks to you, it will not
be because you have made yourself worthy, but by the
mysterious action of His Infinite Mercy and Grace.

*She has paused, too, at the locutory's inner door. She has
only half turned to hear, but turns now to answer.*

                         JUANA
You would accept a word from me in return?
     Though I doubt, I also *believe*. I believe that the
soul is the creation that shapes the world.
     God is a discovery, like fire. The soul is an
invention. It is the work of many, not one, and of
many generations. It is the greatest of our devices, it
is supple, it is strong. Like a castle, or a tower
with high windows, or a music. But this work of forty
centuries is not indestructible. There was a magic in
its invention, there is a science in its demolition.
And another in walling it in. . . .
     Look to your soul, Father, if you can believe you
are possessed of one. And if you cannot, have the
courage to invent one now.

PROTEST

(that, signed with her blood, the Mother Juana Inés de la Cruz made of her faith and her love of God at the time of her abandoning worldly studies in order to proceed, relieved of this encumbrance, along the path of perfection.)

I, Juana Inés de la Cruz, protest for now and for all eternity that I believe in one sole, all-powerful God, Creator of Heaven and Earth and all things; and I believe the most august mystery of the most Holy Trinity, that are three distinct Persons and one true God; that of these three Persons, the second, who is the Divine Word, in order to redeem us, incarnated and made himself man in the virginal womb of Mary, most Saintly, still virgin and Our Lady; and that afterwards He suffered death and crucifixion and arose from among the dead on the third day and now sits at the right hand of God the Father. I believe also that on the final day he must come to judge all men, to reward or punish them according to their deeds. I believe that in the Sacrament of the Eucharist is the true Body of Christ Our Lord; and finally, I believe all that believes and professes the Holy Mother Catholic Church, our mother in whose obedience I wish to die and live without ever failing to obey whatever she may stipulate, giving up my life a thousand times before betraying or doubting anything she may bid us believe; in whose defence I am ready to spill blood and uphold at any risk the holy Faith that I profess, not only believing and adoring it with my heart but also professing it with my mouth at any time and at any cost. . . .

And it grieves me intimately to have offended God, because of who He is and for which I love Him above all things, in whose goodness I find hope that He might pardon my sins by his infinite Mercy, and by the most precious blood that He spilled to redeem us, and by the intercession of his Mother most pure. All of which I offer in repayment of my sins; and prostrate before the divine observances, and in the presence of all the creatures of Heaven and Earth, I submit this new protestation, reiteration and profession of the Holy Faith; and I beg to serve all the most Holy Trinity that It might accept my protest and permit me to fulfil its holy commandments, just as It gave me by its grace the joy of seeing and believing its truths.

To this effect I reiterate the vow I have already made to believe and defend that the always Virgin Mary Our Lady was conceived without the stain of original sin in the first instant of her most pure being; and in this manner I believe that she herself has greater Grace and to her corresponds more glory than all the angels and saints together … and prostrate, heart and soul, in the presence of this divine Lady and of her glorious Spouse, Lord Saint Joseph, and of his most holy parents Joachim and Ana, I humbly implore them to receive me as their slave, and to whom I bind myself for all eternity.

And as a sign of how much I yearn to spill my blood in defense of these truths, I sign with it, this the fifth of March of the year one thousand six hundred and ninety-four.[32]

JUANA INÉS
DE LA CRUZ

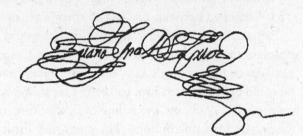

TRUE-CRIME
STORIES 2

"ROLL THE TAPE."

"You're done playing . . . ?"

"Roll it."

"Serious? No more preening?"

"Roll it now, Ms Stern. Or never."

She presses *record*. "Your lawyer's going to hate this."

"Fuck him."

"First say you're doing this of your own volition. Not under duress."

"None that you bring. . . ." He straightens in his chair. "No, I am not speaking under duress." Let it be read into the record.

"Professor Donald Gregory, what would you like to tell us about what happened between twelve and three A.M., on the night of . . ."

Portrait of a man drowning. Jonah. No, that would be another sodden prophet, another time. God but it feels good to speak of it. A night he has kept so tightly bottled up, the night someone showed him how far he could be led, ferried him to sanity's far shores and let him join her on the ledge. And now the telling of it, confiding in Petra Stern, murmuring into the microphone. The crazy new thrill of confession, how could a hundred generations of Catholics be wrong?

So by now you, his public, will have heard the story. Maybe you've forgotten it already, moved on to sub-Saharan drought. But he has not forgotten.

And it is not because he is drunk. He no longer needs that excuse.

As he spills his guts the reporter sits quietly nodding each time a piece falls into place. Much she hadn't guessed, so much she'd almost known. Petra Stern, eyes a shade of granite, sandstone frown, censorious. The jutting chin a rock of righteousness.

At last she interrupts. "Wait, let's get this clear. Two blood types on the floor—now you mention these deep scratches in your arm. You're telling us the blood was yours?" Anger gutters in her granite eyes.

You are so ambitious Petra Stern. Once he was like you. "It seems your friends at the police haven't told you much."

"Professor Gregory, *did you try to kill this girl—*"

"No—"

"But you attacked her."

"No it was—" *Convulsions.*

"A struggle, then. Maybe she provoked you."

"My arm, she gripped—Stop. Turn it off."

She watches him a moment through slitted eyes then turns off the machine. A moment of stillness. Neither of them speak.

"You had one chance, to let me tell it my way."

"If you've hurt her—"

"Oh I hurt her. Just—"

"Why haven't they *arrested* you already? A second blood type on the floor, the walls? Curtis would never have missed this! A woman calls me, implicating a man in some kind of blood rite. Two hours later a man calls 911 and flees the scene. He removes evidence then withholds it for *almost three weeks*—who's protecting you, Professor Gregory? Why won't they act? I want—"

"I *know* what you want."

"I want to see your wrists manacled."

"I told you, there was broken glass all over the bathroom."

"To see you leaving the courthouse in a van."

"I cut myself."

"You said you found her in the bedroom."

"I did. . . ."

"So you dragged her to the bathroom."

"Yes."

"With glass everywhere? Why? What would make you do that?"

"Now you'll never know."

"You think you can hide the truth. For how long?"

The truth, the truth.

"Show me your arm! We'll have your cuts tested—is that it, your sick game? Grandstanding with your lighter, telling me your story only now that your wounds are healed. Confessing only when the evidence fades—dramatic taped confession! But then when you're charged, you just say it was all a little fable, a bit of entertainment?"

We are all made part of the entertainment.

"Say something!"

"Petra, I've never disputed the blood was mine."

"All this sham self-pity and guilt's just part of the game, isn't it? For the man who holds all the evidence! Gloating."

"No."

"No *what?*"

No more.

"Interview over, Professor? All right then. You gave me lots here. More than you know," she says, reaching into her briefcase, casually extracting a little dictaphone, still turning.

Angrily he asks if machine number three is a suppository.

"So . . ." she says, ignoring the question, "I'm going to give you a little something in return."

"Tell me what she said to you."

"That's a part of the story that goes unfiled. I want you to know your little fable will always be incomplete—"

"What about your public?"

"Understand, Professor, that someone out there will always know—"

"And your duty to expose the truth?"

"What you never will."

"You've made this personal, Petra Stern, haven't you."

"Personal, you bastard? I heard her *voice.* She spoke to me. I could have gotten her help! She wouldn't tell me your name. Only that her prof would have the story, she'd left him all the evidence. You'd be able to explain. Everything. If I could get you to. She wouldn't give your name. She was standing in a phone booth. I could hear the cars. She had to go home now. . . .

"I could have helped her," she says, eyes boring into his. "The police needed something to go on. A name, an address. In the newsroom we sat up through the night, listening to the scanners for word to come in. Three A.M. . . . You know what that was like? To catch up just as the ambulance pulls away? Do you know how that *felt?*" She stopped the dictaphone. "To have wondered all along if it was you, and denied it to myself—for the two hours that might have made a difference? You're so fascinated by my name. Stern, Petra. Familiar, no . . . ?"

"I do know you, then." *The penitent's mortification deepens.*

"Twice a week for a semester, Professor. Check your lists for the class of '83. Your first year teaching, wasn't it?"

"But how, I don't—"

"Recognize me? But then, how the fuck could you? So many faces. So many students to do. So little time.

"You gave me an A if that helps—*does* that help? And I was at a cocktail party at your house five years ago. No? Don't remember that either. But you had so much on your mind back then. When she called, your face flashed through my mind. *That's crazy*—I told myself. Ten years ago *all* the profs were fucking their acolytes, it wasn't just you. Ridiculous to think. That you should cross my mind. . . . I could have phoned your house. I've met your wife. We might have found that girl. Found her before you. They say now she may have a damaged brain. How does that make you feel, Professor? This one really did go ga-ga over you."

She tucks the dictaphone into her briefcase, leans back, crosses her legs. "Maybe I'll take that drink, now. We can chat about old times."

"The bar is closed for the day."

"Women are attracted to you, why deny it?"

"Call it a paradox."

"No. *We like pricks.* Bigger they are, harder we fall."

He turns his head toward the wall of glass. The smoky light has fulfilled its promise. Violet clouds drift from the west, keeled in brass. Beneath, a dark blue shoal of hills. Lights flare on along the river. There, a phosphorescence. Another there.

"I think it's time you left."

"Maybe she'll wake up soon. When you go to visit, she'll see you but won't remember who . . . or why. Follow you around like a dog, drooling and sighing. She'll take you for a friend—idiots always think you're their friend." A voice quavering with rage.

She fumbles at the table in the half-dark of the room, then flicks on the lighter. The flame dances shadows across the planes of her face. "Or maybe not a dog. Vegetables have eyes too, don't they, Professor. Like potatoes." Her smile is a grotesque gash in the flickering light.

"Get out. Don't make me tell you again." He hears the words begin in threat and end in listlessness.

"Don't worry, I'm leaving." She leans forward, nodding towards the dim stacks beside the fireplace, "But I just have to ask you once, face to face. *How can you? Tell her story?* You have no *right.*" Still she makes no move to leave. "But you know that."

"It's why she picked me."

"How convenient for you." She uses the lighter now to locate her pad and pens, the dictaphone. She glances down, her face in shadow, as she puts them back in the briefcase. "You'll change the names to protect the innocent I suppose."

"The innocent have nothing to fear."

"Should be very popular down in Kingston, your book. I hear the prison there has a close-knit writing community. Though small." She waves the flame at the shadows surrounding him. "How many?"

"Many?"

"Copies. Of your book. How many will you pay them to print?"

He sits a while. After a moment, the flame goes out. She waits. He turns again to the soaring wall of windows.

He stirs finally. She thinks he will answer.

They sit another moment, together in the near dark. A moment more and she stands to leave, fumbling a little. She opens the door and pauses, silhouetted against the evening sky.

"These girls—women, young *women*—wanted so badly to give something of themselves. Back to you, Dr. Gregory. Our bodies were all we had. Or so we thought. Many of us were from towns out in the country. Small, prairie towns. Simple places. Plainspoken places. Not understanding any of it, you shared a gift most of us never even knew existed. It was never the beard, the blue eyes, the pipe. The *prestige*. You shared *a new world* with us. A passion—for ideas, for words—an enchanted space. A poetry. It was unlike everything we'd left behind.

"You were our guide. You had that once." *So very long ago.* "We gave that," she adds quietly, closing the door, "to *you*."

He had wanted to tell her the number.

The number of books was two.

But that seems just hours ago, not weeks. Now it is late. It is almost night. In the west just the palest glimmer remains above the chipped saw of peaks.

He sits out still on the curving porch as night draws on, the evening chill beckons from the grass, sound takes up the night's blind watch . . . A crow's hacking caw, a calf bawls in a pasture down the valley. A small plane makes for home. Its passage overhead bends from growl away to drone.

In the far distance a highway just within hearing. Endless exhalation, a river of sound . . . cascade that undercuts the banks of night in a raw, scouring fall.

He is beside you as you follow her to the end. He is with you, not before, not behind. Beside, abreast, to where she waits he walks with you, across on the other side.

TRUE-CRIME STORIES 3

The following bases its inferences upon facts in the public record.

ON APRIL 13, 1995, Petra Stern captured Professor Donald Gregory's rambling half-confession on tape. Her next few days were full as she sought corroborating facts and quotes from the other principals. Her intention was to present all of her material to the police, but only after it had been filed with her producer.

Whatever elation she may initially have felt must have quickly faded. She would come to wonder if she had not been set up, fed just enough disinformation to be made a fool of. On April 14, she called the Limosneros family and persuaded them to listen to the tape. For a victim's family, they had been unusually close-mouthed. She hoped the recording would jar loose an accusation or some item of damaging information or, better yet, earn her a look at their daughter's papers, which had been tantalizingly withheld from her by Donald Gregory on the previous day.

When she arrived at the Limosneros residence in Mount Royal, she was met at the door by the family's attorney and turned away.

On April 15, Madeleine Gregory agreed to a meeting, off the record. Mrs. Gregory had no interest in the role of bitter and betrayed wife. Useful background did however emerge, none of it strictly incriminating. As she was taking her leave of Mrs. Gregory, promising to stay in touch, Petra Stern was stunned to learn that Donald had flown earlier that day to England, for a research trip of indeterminate length. It was now apparent that by the time her exposé aired, Donald Gregory might well be beyond the reach of Calgary police. An interesting twist to her story but with unpleasant implications for her relations with Detectives Curtis and Green.

She was now a little desperate. She wasted much of Sunday, using the tape as a pretext for attempting to re-interview the professor's colleagues and former students. Petra Stern decided that a hostile reaction from the perpetrator in London would make an effective follow up once the story ran. She was briefly pleased with herself for so quickly locating Donald Gregory at a three-star hotel near the British Museum. She placed her call to London on the morning of Monday, April 17. It was her intention to take her material to Detective Curtis immediately after the call, and to incorporate his reaction into the final edit.

The police reaction was this: While the airing of a half-drunk ramble might make for sensational news, it contained in fact no evidence unknown to investigators, and no evidence contradicting the subject's own statement to police.

Two blood types were indeed found, but Professor Gregory had been kneeling in glass. The first officers arriving on the scene reported a suspected ritual assault. However, every piece of evidence gathered thereafter tended to disprove this. Fingernail scrapings and a rape kit were, in fact, routinely used to gather evidence in cases with ritualistic overtones. Although the victim was found naked, there was no conclusive evidence of sexual activity. Meanwhile Professor Gregory had not made even cursory attempts to wipe away his bloody fingerprints from all over the bath area. His tissue was found only under the nails of her left hand. If not the only explanation, convulsions were one that could not be disproved.

What reviving the story would accomplish, they assured her, was to embarrass Detectives Curtis and Green before a new police chief hungry for publicity.

The day after her report aired, Petra Stern was informed by a stone-faced Detective Curtis that Donald Gregory had checked out of his hotel two hours after her call and had taken the next flight to Mexico City.

What the detectives could not know was that April 17, 1995, was the three-hundredth anniversary of the death of Sor Juana Inés de la Cruz. A day earlier, Donald Gregory had been reminded of this fact at the British Museum where a display had been set up to commemorate the event, thereby drawing the attention of museum patrons to the passing of a great figure perhaps unknown to them. It now appears that Dr. Gregory, with no set itinerary for the foreseeable future, had the idea of prolonging the day of April 17th with a ten-hour transatlantic flight across eight time zones to Mexico City, where a month-long cycle of international conferences was underway.

What Detective Curtis did know, however, and took pains to stress to Petra Stern, was that Mexico City was one of the best places in the world in which to disappear.

A print version of Petra Stern's radio story was picked up by the Canadian Press wire service for national and international distribution under the headline, "Quiet Flees the Don—Again."

The only other item of note is that when these facts later became known to Professor Donald Gregory on his return from Mexico, Petra Stern's personal and professional discomfort gave him no pleasure.

This in itself should have served notice that things were no longer quite as they had been.

In truth, my sweetest love,

truly I do not overstate it:

that without you, even my words

sound foreign to me, estranged;

    because, to be in want of

you exceeds all the torments

that cruelty might invent

when abetted by genius.

    Who know the tyranny

of this beautiful device

use neither blades,

nor hooks, nor irons:

    idle were the knife,

superfluous the cords,

gentle the lash,

tepid the fires.

    Since these, to one put to torture,

at the sight of you bring glory,

when you leave,

purgatory . . .

JUANA INÉS
DE LA CRUZ

SERPENT LITTER

Beulah flies from Puebla to the ancient sacred seaport of Coatzalcoalcos. . . .

[16 Jan 1995]

I THOUGHT MAKE IT HERE, the last verse on loss. Draft the lost canticle of the three-chambered heart. For weeks in the cities, in the mountains—say the word, say them both out loud. Laughable. . . .

I hoped.

Coatzalcoalcos, 'abode of the serpent litter!' From here the FeatherSerpent sailed on alone to the land of knowledge and death, where even failure ends. Out onto the Gulf he stepped, and the sea matted with serpents risen numberless to bear him up, to carry him.

And he said he would come back—promised his dwarf retinue, told us Wait and gave us each a treasure map.

Horizon blot of supertankers twisting on chains. Styrofoam cups Jumbo cokefloats, bubble wrap, bottles of engine oil tapered like dunce caps. Even I could walk out there now—up and out on this litter of plastic. Stinking port of holy oil—mockery of the past. Of me. Oh look how far I've come from Calgary—straight to another oil boom.

Al estado de la Veracruz . . . to the true state of the cross.

And even so I still *believed*—I had everything I needed to finish this work—how could I fail? How hard can dying be? Every necessity in this hotel cell above the bus depot—cot, orangecrate nightstand, rough wooden cross, pitcher of Deuterium. Shutters for the window, darkness, a little desk—to light my path a Gideon's Bible, the traveller's friend in Spanish, English and Nahuatl. Nights of diesel in the sheets, in the dampness in the pillows in the dark. Rank solvent tang in the water and air. Does the whole city smell like this or just in here? in my *claustridium dificile*—abode of the cloistered insomniac starving for dreams. R.E.M. clockcrawl—I close my eyes on the blackness of shuttered day and see points of light beckoning. . . . If I could dream, just this one mercy—

But *no!* no quarter asked none ever given, sit tight little soldier hold your position, here in this Black Room above the steambath busdepot of holy Coatzalcoalcos, sit before these shuttered windows hapless barricade against the noise and smoke of endless motorcades. Refuse to rise! Hold fast against this CIA music treatment—mariachi brass from the lobby, speakers bolted to the *ceiling right under my desk*—give up give up little Noriega come out of there! Submit, surrender.

But no, I cling and cling to my numinous embassy.

So I work faster think harder look at the calendar can't you see the time? so little left the cursor blinking blinking its frantic mockery and I curse BACK. Laugh? I try I try—oh how I should *love* this irony that annihilates me:

Silence was once an agony; now I am drowning in noise.

How I hated it. But only at first. Because I didn't understand yet. I came for stillness and surcease. Now I tilt my face back in the cursor-lit darkness and suck at this noise so thick I can taste it SONIC OILBOOM *engine backfires cherry bombs, traffic whistles shrilling—flatulent blat of airbrakes jaunty hornblasts of pilot tugs pulling their silver ships into port under me. The pitcher on the nighttable quivers its welcome its gratitude / its bent-kneed meniscus under the cross by the cot—for each safe slide into dock.*

And I *am* grateful. I came for peace but have stayed for the din that drowns out the engine in my head. I have learned to submit. To everything here. To bank these my internal harmonics / combusted symphonies of white noise blasted to ash.

And I do submit—so cheerfully—to every sound but one. One sound drives me in the end from my Black Room. For an hour. For a little air. For a stroll down by the sea....

I walk out through the depot lobby, past the fat *taxista*, bloat-lip toad: *Oye muchacha*, I can take you to Lake Catemaco for thirty American dollars, okay twenty—ten—okay I pay *you* how much you want? Every day you say no. You are not here for the Tuxtlas, then why have you come to this hole?

Don't you think I wonder, stuffed Taximan, don't you think I ask?

I walk sticky-sided, sweat-slabbed, down to the running shore. Eyes stunned in sun ... face slicked with salt grime, lids cloaked in the pumice of moth wings, each blink a salt fan, folding. And each sticky step stokes this simmer of exhilaration that I can't prevent. Near the water, high winds toss and glitter in the fronds of dwarf palms—jesters dancing in silver-fringed jerkins.

At the sea a hot stink of brine, wet socks and rot. The wind blows faint relief in mirthless gales. Teases long windward plumes of tawny spindrift out over the waves till an agitate surf pounds out its brown foam like a fulling mallet. I tuck my boots under the same sandy bush, so good to be home. Stand in socks and glory at this my uncharted prospect! All along the grey-lipped shore a thin moustache of froth stashed by this Tropic of Cancerous tide.

Down barefoot now—over the burning grey sand—my fakirflail a hopped simulacrum—shallow flap / kneedip / heel and toeroll over hot grey coals. Each day the same grey fun. Bloodwarm surf embalming my soles.

Knee-deep in surf I walk up the beach to the broken jetty, a swayback skeleton gutted on surf. Lashed pilings of grey bone raked from an ash pit. Standing in its shadows the old Cuban man of the sea watches my sub-aquatic goosestep—lurching into potholes scooped in swirling sand. Lo the sea's ephemeral roadwork in progress eternal. How he shakes his white cotton head now to see the SeaCow pitch forward, clutch at her gluesoft hoof.

There—cunning-hid in sand is a rotted ship's plank . . . spiketips bated in rust, rust-wavered shanks. See the red rime dissolve at the wondering touch. Dull cold throb in the arch, I lift the plank to him, my show and tell, pedestrian.

It break the skin? the coolly curious fisherman has come for a gloat. Probes the arch redness with the sharkbit digits of a gnarled hand. Smile at the tickle of this stumpy nuzzling. I answer with a wisp of blood, its tiny thread fans into coral lace. You should get a shot—*una injeccion*—he doesn't say To the back of the head, but see its minnow-flash in his cataracted eyes.

What are you doing back here, *muchacha?* I told you one hundred times. No boat rides. No going out in this wind. With you, not ever. *Nunca, ¿me oyes?* No tourists.

He glares a cloud of marble down at my squat blur in surf. Call this yoga pose twenty-three: crane with punctured arch. Ask the old Hemingway cadre where else is there for me but here? Ask and hope for something oracular. Ask him is it alright if I cry, while he smokes and glares blunt daggers down. Hear his dislike in every chopped syllable: *Mira, m'chach,* I am going to try one time to make you understand. *De'pue,' no quie'o ve'te nu'ca ma,' ¿'ntiende?*

Understood, old man tell me a fish tale, then I go off for good. Study him, my fishy exegete: black wattle of turkey neck, corded arms, the stumpy spread of a scaly claw ups the smoke for one last draw—who rolls your smokes for you, stubfisher? I ask. One last glare—his glaucous skysearch for the story god, please give him strength to explain to this *gringa idiota*.

Go on old man, gonna tell me or not?

He smiles a white fence, three pickets kicked in.

You see *la piroga*—ahh, pause to admire the charred dugout dragged up, the battered visor of a raised outboard. When I got it from my father's dying hand there were twenty here. When he first got that boat—fifty. Coming home each night boats so full more underwater than over. Now I bring in one or two little fish—*¿te das cuenta?* Sometimes one has an extra eye or cheek. Fish cheeks in soup, this is a fine meal. But I have the easy job. My wife has to clean these. Then feed to our grandkids. She sits outside till they run out to play. We cannot look each other in the eye till then. She wonders if they have eaten even numbers or odd, of cheeks—each time, she cannot help asking.

For the last time, I am a fisherman. It is all I do.

I'm sorry.

Sorry for me or for you? But good you understand—why don't you get a bathing costume now and a straw hat and go to Cancún? Find a young black man if that's why you stick on this coast and have your experience. Or brown or yellow or blue. *Eso no me interesa.* Just go someplace else and leave an old man to what peace he has left. *Vete de aca, señorita.*

Remember, after . . . my little soldier's clayfoot limp and sway . . . rejected postulant, repellent pirate as she stumps back down the strand, through twisted streamers of kelp and stinking seawrack. See the salt grapes bunch under clouds of beetles that swarm up into her halt shadow—the serene dance of insects in a sheen of green and lavender . . . feel the fade of serenity as they settle back to roost. Tiny buzzards.

Under one kelp clump a doll—pig pink, socketed head. Naked, eyeless, crew-necked in grease. Its bent doll arm a signpost, a pudgy wave way down to a rocky point scarfed in spume.

See? it says, the blind seer, Miltonic eyedoll, See all this between, all this is yours, Daughter, you have it to yourself. Sea-tilled half-acres of dead smelt, skeleton crabs. A gaza of jetsam, driftwood, junk. Improvised squalor of yard sales, racked daily up and down the continental shelf.

Green starburst and fray of a driftnet's tattered end, braided over a buoy like a smoked glass lantern. Soft underfoot a million tiny balls of tar, of black salt taffy. Taste. Walk on past a sargasso stretch of medical waste bobbing like a little logboom. Sodden landings of dressings . . . crafty wink of hypodermics, threads of silk to keep you in stitches for a month.

Sit. Stop. On this oil drum . . . sandsunk rustpit. Sit and rest. Sun. Muddle. Slump.

Tired light, tired sun, I radiate its exhaustion, recycle its spent immensity, reflect it back across vast intergalactic gulfs. I answer, I correspond. . . .

Sit awhile, lulled by this gulf's exhausted middling plunge. Feel the champagne crush—swift push and slide, then slow hiss of ferment. See the seethe of disintegration, hear the rheumatic indraw of breath before a dive. . . . And again. Endlessly. I sit and stew here in the foetid heave and pant of this Gulf, this cavernous stench everywhere clinging and close like a meat mask. . . .

There now, see? You can still do this. A little doggerel at least. A line or two. See you are not finished, it's just a little slump, dear, cheer up.

Faraway down by the point I make for the cool shadow of the lighthouse. Into the sundial shade I step lightly into a *hot blue noon* of jellyfish streamers sinking a thousand quick hooks into one ankle. Time to rest again—right here in the sand. Doubled up in this grimy blouse, stink of black jeans bleached in salt . . . sickening cling at chest and and hip and knee. *Get a bathing suit a straw hat a beach blanket go to Cancún with all the other gringos.*

Sit for minutes, hours. Asphixiate eyes turned on a fixity. Open sea of writhing tin, brass sundog overhead. . . . I close my eyes to plumb the swells' deep boom—unchecked, unslowed battery of rams against the rock's shrouded jut. Beaten beaten again, unshaken obelisk unmoved. Point the way out. Or on, or up.

The little soldier has soldiered down to here, little toy all wound down. With this scream of silence in her ears. I tell and tell myself, little soldier you can finish this, your vast study in pointlessness. Make it here, since you can't follow anymore. Nobody knows where he sailed from here.

Last dwarf beating up her tambourine at the edge of the world, at its end.

So I crank and crank the handle, little drummer winding down her battery ever faster to exhaustion, avalanche of stone and drums. Wind her up, she really goes and hums. But something's wrong, this is not *music*—just the scream of gears, of an angry empty engine, bankrupt vacuum pump. The little coffee grinder is all used up.

Sound but no music but the silence is worse. Oh, much. It's why I try and try. But there's a spring now in the little soldier that can't be rewound, something in the clockworks cracked and sprung.

Give up.

Give up.

The little drummer says nothing in answer. After all the brave talk. Of a music of gaps . . . that has become this gulf.

Hop skip and trudge back up the beach, back into town, towards the sound I just can't learn to bear. That drives me from here. Hear it again from across the street.

I enter the busdepot lobby and feel it once more, as never before as never again . . . echoes of this new Arcady, the last Centaur fled. Cash register chimechime / barked karate KA!s, shell-shocked teens tensed over videoscreens. Electronic ball courts / bright mazes unravelling at insane velocities / simulate bomb-runs over Icaria—soft puppy sway / buck and twitch of thin hips. See the dark faces lit with thin rapture, then despair . . . suddenfaded in an ebb. Now *here* is a music box—Again! Feed the machine another token of cancelled will. Feed the whole. Feed the hole again.

And again!—renewed the fuedal duellings with alien polymorphs! renewed the camaraderies of a multi-racial Ninja society. Clatter of burst urns, gattle of gun / concertina of heretical wails, sobbed shouts-unmelodious . . . score the endless conquest of this last howling wilderness.

In us.

Stand fast little soldier, I tell myself, just another moment, here in the field tent where the maps are spread. Pick a destination. Scan the vast mural of Yucatán, pyramid cities painted across one whole wall, childlike as nursery clouds. Anywhere but here. Stand—eyes dilated fixed—stand it another minute if you can, under the television bolted to the sound-conducting ceiling tiles—miracle of acoustical technology piped direct to your room—and choose: Uxmal, Edzná, Palenque, Cobá, Tulum . . .

Deep Vadervoice *boom* of station identification: *This is CNN.* Call letters of the Death Star. I flinch but hold my ground as the Network tolls out its bellicose countdown. To the glorious four-year anniversary. Do not adjust your set. As we, united, free, mark this Olympian interval since the last jihad, hour of Baghdad. Remember '91?—remember the Gulf. Lest we forget, just four shopping days left to Armagedon, three two one: January 16th 1995, let's all sing auld lang syne. Hand out the duncecaps with the elastic chin straps, the *sambenito* lifevests. Slip them on just in time to catch the burst of Disney fireworks over the battlements. Holy Reruns of the Alliance Strikes Back. Against another Holy Land, coating another oily gulf in its extreme unction. While we, lion-eyed, lounged on couches like Persians.

Quick *choose*, what can it possibly matter now?—Uxmal, Palenque, Cobá, Tulum.

But I could have taken even this—that all the screens in this room look the same—wall to wall floor to ceiling. Boys with rayguns, even the salon of talking heads with cathode-ray tans. The same faces avid with despair. Same cheap last effects. Same bomb sites superimposed on an eye ever searching a lost centre . . . grainy steadycam of high-altitude death impending. I could have stayed and finished, but for this one sound, that again and again drives me from the Black Room.

It is these voices.

This cheap electronic opera of video moans, lobe death of attenuated souls . . . this choir rising up through the floor of my room in a long, expiring groan. Sobbed chorus of unending disenchantment. These breathless, despairing, unpausing moans.

Palenque, Cobá, Tulum.

This is why I can't finish here. This opera, that breaks my heart. Somehow, still, this miracle. . . . But how can it? How does it go on and on? What does it want that still it pipes and drums? Why won't it just stop?

This heart.

Palenque, Tulum.

Pick anywhere, Heart.

Tulum.

HE FLIES IN FROM LONDON. The taxi driver consults him on mat- S
ters of prosperity and international finance, seems to think he must be
an economist. The man in turn wonders if it is his bad Spanish.

At the conference welcome desk he appears only mildly angry to
have been omitted from the list of registrants, pays or repays the fees,
insists on eventual reimbursement. He asks for a tag please to be
typed, gives the name Professor Douglas (John) Gordon. He has been
to many conferences, attempts to blend in. He has been to too many
conferences, knows he does not. Within an hour he begins to wonder
why he has left London, flown ten hours to Mexico without a reservation, at a cost of two thousand dollars. The dollars are American, but
things back home are pointing towards a handsome settlement. Or
prison. As he strolls around the convent, it is not long before a purpose comes. He has come to find a woman named S and fuck her. It is
all he can think of, it is the least he can do.

In the first two days he meets dozens of women of the right age.
Registrants and presenters, employees and professors of the
University of the Cloister of Sor Juana Inés de la Cruz. He begins
to see the joke, or one. Sabina, Silvia, Serena, Stefana . . . But it is
not long before he finds her. There are few female lecturers on the
history of Medicine, only so many doctors S taking a turn in the
infirmary.

He sleeps in her house, on the couch one night, then in a guest
room, her bed. He stays through Holy Week. He likes the quiet
streets. She takes him to a district called the Countess, with restaurants of some refinement, elegant diners on terraces, before them
valets, bootblacks, strolling guitarists. On several occasions he has
seen one stylish client or other take food and drink, gingerly, careful of
a bulky cotton dressing just above the lip. It is perhaps a district of the
accident prone, he offers. Perhaps, but those are not accidents. *El bique.*
Nose jobs. Will she have one? Her eyes shine. She is beautiful, her
nose is ethnic, powerful. The man understands. A fine line, it might
leave her merely pretty. She corrects him, No, Professor Gordon. After
one of those, just whose nose is one to follow?

Her black eyes are bright and steady, slow to leave his.

They go to the Museum of Anthropology. Carvings, a calendar, sculptures unlike anything he was prepared to see. It is enough to make one doubt photography. Then the pyramids, then several such day trips. Once to a town in the mountains. He has admitted he likes mountains. At a restaurant in the market in the mountain town they watch a pair of young lovers having perhaps a first argument. He has seen them earlier, getting out of a new Jeep, spotless, red. The Spanish is too fast, the music too loud, but it appears her heart is being broken, the way they break in pop songs. He takes in the boy's angry arrogance, her pure absorption in the pain of the moment, of her commitment . . . to love, no doubt. But it is mostly the song he thinks of, there is something about it. S too is watching them, perhaps following the argument. After a moment, she tells him the song is quite popular among the students. An African man, he thinks, singing a duet with a woman, maybe American. Something about a quantity of seconds, then something incomprehensible, beautifully sung. Back in the city in the evening, the man and S buy a juice from one of dozens of vendors with a hand press and a shopping cart full of oranges. On a whim he asks to see the Auto Museum as he pays for her drink.

His Spanish is only passable. She asks in English, does he mean the Inquisition exhibit at the Museo de la Medicina. That is of interest too but no, he means the one for cars, the Nissan Museum. He can see the Vanidades boutique. It can't be far. He thinks it is finally this, but she has known who he was from the start. So S has fucked Professor D.J.G.

But he knows better, knows it is more than that. She is not ashamed or angry, she is curious and sad, has half-guessed why he has come, understands as much as he does or as little. She knew he could not help telling her when he was ready, and he has told her, with the museum. She hopes for good news, but does not expect it. He would not be the one to bring it. And though he tells himself they are even and that it is nothing to be so upset about, he goes back that night to the hotel between the cathedral and the convent, Hotel Isabel la Católica.

Over the next days he returns to places she has shown him, others he has only read of, sees the strangeness of the strangest of cities, alone. One day a dervish dancing blind across sixteen lanes of traffic. And a series of strange kindnesses. Another day an abduction on the sidewalk ahead, of a young girl who looks Mexican. Those who have also seen this walk faster. No one stops to take down the licence plate. He takes busier streets, the busiest, then only buses on El Paseo de la Reforma. The comforts of German engineering, the same AM radio as other places . . . tunes he recognizes, songs that stop when teachers enter lecture halls.

The buses roll on past the galleries, the theatres and jewellery shops, past the Angel of the Independence and the statue of Cuautémoc. FallingEagle. The buses are quiet, the air is cool inside, cleaner. The stops not too frequent. Museum of Anthropology, Chapultepec Lake, National Auditorium, Museum of Modern Art. Getting on, getting off, he rides switching seats so he can face the park. A uniform, an employee gets on, sits across from him, her back to the museum. Over her head he can see the Indian fliers whirling above the tops of the trees.

She watches him, seems about to ask the foreigner a question, asks it, but there is something in her accent he does not catch. She repeats it. The music is a distraction. He realizes it is the same song. He has heard it also a few hours before, popular with the students just now. He watches her fingertips flutter at her cheeks, thinks of rain. They play these things in cycles, playlists. Her face not unkind, she comes to sit beside him, an older woman, takes his hand. He feels her raise it to his own face, as with the fingers of her other hand she flutters little tongue-tips of rain, cool against his cheek.

The following morning he returns home, to his real home, a cabin in the mountains a friend has lent him. He settles in, prepares to write a prologue, looks for a way, a place to begin.

Awake sweet knight, your sister needs you.

Awake sweet Gavin, sweet Gawain, she needs you.

The hog-headed dragon is devouring the moon.

Kill your mother's lover—avenge my father's murder!

The hog-headed dragon is devouring the moon.

I am the Hydra-headed demon, your harpoon bearer.

He has robbed you of your pride, he has beaten me.

He covets his brother's wife, he has raped me.

He has blinded your eyes, he has filled me with his seed.

He is the Foreigner, the Storm-bringer resurrected.

The hog-headed dragon is devouring the moon.

Drive your harpoon into his body!

I will feed his bones to the cats.

Drive your thirty-barbed harpoon deep within him!

I will feed his fat to the worms.

Drive your blade of electrum up into him!

I will feed his suet to the crabs.

Blind his eye!

I will swallow his gore.

Cut off his testicles!

I will roast them in oil.

Sunder his vertebrae!

I will suck them clean of marrow.
Skewer his belly!
I will taste his kidneys.
Mangle his limbs!
I will cook you his foreleg.
Steep your shining weapons in his blood!
I will drink it.

Until his lamentations fill the southern sky.
Until his lamentations fill the northern sky.

We who are in the abyss have not forgotten.
We who are in the abyss remember the nights of his flood.
We remember the hours of storm and drunkenness and fear.

I sharpen my teeth in order to bite thy foe.
I whet my talons in order to seize his skin.
I am thy sister Savage Hippo.
I am Her-Speech-is-Fire.
I am She-loves-Solitude.
I am Death-in-his-Face-Loud-Screamer.
Bring me the Mutilated One.[33]

HORUS

(1–4 HORIZONTALS) THE ALL-LORD: Who prospers the Two Lands; the Two Ladies: [—] beloved of Ptah, l.p.h.!, who is called by the great name: [Ta-te]nen South-of-his-Wall, Lord of Eternity. [Joiner] of Upper and Lower Egypt.——who created the Nine Gods in the Temple of Souls.34

> Hail to thee, the All-Lord, from fist fucked-forth—
> himself, and all life gifted,
> to the Nine, to all the gods and their *kas*,
> through his heart, through his tongue,
> the Ennead, the Nine,
> through his semen,
> through his fingers,
> born of his fist,
> through his teeth, through his lips,
> jism issued forth from his own mouth and
> the mouth of his Anus.35

Re-Atum, this one comes to thee, child of thy seed, I, a spirit beyond destruction, return to thee, sown from thy fist through the first fist-twins, God Shu, Goddess Tefnut, through the cunt-twins their children, earth and sky, God Geb, Goddess Nut. I, child of thy seed, come to thee—may thou cross the sky united with the dark! may thou rise in lightland, forever where thou shinest!

I come, a spirit indestructible, second-born son after Osiris, and Isis, his fuck-twin, my sister. With Seth's own sister-wife Nephthys we are the Nine. Sky breaks! stars dim! earth quakes! planets still!—*to see Seth rise in his power.* A god—I—who lives upon the flesh of his fathers, who feeds upon the flesh of his mothers. Seth's glory is in lightland, like Atum my begetter. Through thy jism am I not bull-of-heaven, who rages in thy heart and feeds on the heart of every god, who eats their entrails and swallows their seed when they come, their bodies full of magic, from the Isle of Fire?

But if thou wishest me to die, I will die. And if thou wouldst that Seth live, Seth shall live.

I am master of cunning, whose own mother knows not Seth's secret name. I did all that majesty commands in bringing murder to my brother

Osiris, Foremost-of-the-Westerners—life, prosperity and health! I acted as his beloved brother, feasted the return of His-heart-is-weary. Osiris had travelled far to bring knowing to the Asiatics, to take learning to the barbarians in their stinking. In welcome and hospitality did Seth build for him then a fine casket, a sarcophagus of ebon and ironwood, worked with gold and lapis lazuli, in mother of pearl rimmed. Much feasting and beer, many toasts of his safe return. Seth offered then to the all-gathered-there the prize of the sarcophagus of Life in Eternity, awarded to him-who-lies-within-most-easily. All tried, none fit, much laughter, until His-heart-is-weary lay down in it. Good fit, good plan—swift my followers pushed down the lid, sealed it with lead! No laughter, no sound, no word from inside. Much consternation. No word from inside. MUCH CONSTERNATION. Seth clothed my brother's sarcophagus in its regalia, decked the breast of the casket with greenstone and turquoise, clear gems. Seth was pure of hand in decking the sarcophagus, like a priest of clean fingering. I made my allies to take up the *neshmet* bark, led the procession, champion of my brother, repulsed our attackers. Much death, much blood, sorrow. I cut down who would stop the launching of the Bark-truly-risen-is-the-Lord-of-Abydos. Seth hacked a path to the Nile shore, shielded the sarcophagus through the PANIC and consternation on the land. Then Seth set the casket in the Great-Bark-of-the-Nile. It bore his beauty, straight to the bottom. Cleansed is he who is cleansed in the Field of Rushes! Seth brought rejoicing to my followers in the eastern deserts, much joy also to the western deserts.

Though he was many-eyed, he saw not Seth's coming. Though my brother was the stronger I loosened the knot of his life—yet did not Seth leave intact all his beauty? Am I not great-in-cunning, loving-of-family?[36]

Seth will enter into the judgements with Him-whose-name-is-hidden, ever on the day of the slaying of the elder.

Seth is Lord-who-knots-the-cord that binds the sacrifice. Seth is who eats men. I feed on the lungs of the wise, I like to live on hearts and their magic.

But if thou sayest Seth should die, I will die. Yet if thou willst that I live, Seth shall not die.

Isis sought him everywhere. Isis, daughter of Nut and Geb, our parents. Isis, fuck-twin of Osiris, Seth's sister. She searched, left the throne, searched, left the Black Land to return to the Asiatics. Had I not been given dominion over the foreigners?—yet she too followed him to go among them! Had I not been given dominion over the Red Lands as had Osiris over the Black? To him the fertile, to Seth the barren. Isis found him in Byblos, the sarcophagus grown into a big green tree on the shore. Our sister brought him back in her moon bark to the delta, to the marshes. But there she hid Seth's precious sarcophagus not so well. It called to Seth from the rushes in the voice of my brother. I tore into the corpse like soft bread, shredded it in fourteen pieces. Smashed bones and marrow, seized the liver, pulled the long member from between the limbs. For is Seth not He-who-rends? am I not earth-tearer, life-in-disintegration? I fed up my ally Sobek, fed the fuck-member of my brother into the long gullet. Seth choked the crocodile on the dong-of-his-brother. For was I not then Seth-the-ungoverned, Seth-in-riot, Seth-in-bloodlust?

And was I not only acting as one with Seth's nature? Not fist-born, not cunt-born—but wild-fruit-torn-from-the-side-of-his-mother!

Deep in the Black earth and farthest corners of the Red Lands I buried the Thirteen—at night, when the black boar had hunted down the moon. For the sky-dwellers are to serve Seth—I eat their magic, swallow their spirits, and the pots are scraped for me with their women's legs. Seth seizes the hearts of the gods, as Khons, slayer of lords. I cut their throats, pulling up their bowels through the mouths of their anus. Like snakes from burrows. Seth has eaten the Red, swallowed the Green, licked clean the coils of the Red with abhorrence, yet felt delight in their magics in my gullet. The dignities of Seth will never be taken from me—I HAVE SWALLOWED THE KNOWLEDGE OF EVERY GOD.

But if thou willst my death, I will die. And if thou sayest that Seth should live, Seth will have life.

I went to console the widow of my brother, daughter of our mother-who-bears-the-scars-of-Seth-in-her-side. Seth brought the news of the defiling to where Isis sat on the throne. I sang.

> O One, the sister without peer,
> upright neck, shining breast,
> heavy thighs, narrow waist,
> the V of thy cunt
> like a brace of wild white geese
> trumpeting.

Spread wide those lips,
for the trumpeter,
split wide thy shores
for the bull of the Nile,
for the big reed-pipe of thy brother
not thy twin.
Joy has he whom she embraces.
He is like the first of men!
... My sister is angry.
No more will Seth cover his sister.
The gates to her mansion have swung shut.
The small door is bolted,
So Seth cannot enter.

Why did our sister send one dear brother's *ka* to sit in Orion?—while that day depriving Seth of the seat of Sirius, brightest among the stars.

After this, much sickness, heavy limbs. Well did she know how to cast the noose on Seth with her hair. Great-in-magic, she captured me with her eye, changed herself into a jackal bitch. Seth ran after her, lost seed on the sand. She caught it, took my potency. She mocked at Seth, branded me with her seal ring, made Seth's jism call out to him from her palm. Hail, fuck-brother, hail! Three weeks lying on my back in sadness not rising, while she sought out the hidden members of Osiris. Three weeks to the sound of Isis, weeping not for Seth. And Seth's own fuck-sister Nephthys helped her. My own consort also, the river-mare Taweret, helped THEM. Is Seth not copious-of-seed? Why did they covet His-heart-is-weary, why did my seed find in their moist gardens only barren ground?[37]

Seth is lord-of-thick-jism! who takes wives from their husbands!—whenever Seth wishes, as his heart wills!

Wherever Seth had buried the gobbets of his brother, our sister, finding them, raised a big temple. Thirteen gateposts to hedge Seth in, thirteen pyramids to fence Seth out. *Then, great was Isis in magic.* As a vulture she swallowed the Thirteen, each in turn, and in the fullness of the moon, vomited our beloved brother whole onto the Nile bank. Yet the dong-of-Osiris she found nowhere, nor even Taweret rooting in the slime of the Nile found it. The fatness of Sobek was not a clue to her. Out of Nile-bank clay, the great-in-magic rolled in her palms a thick member, wetted and made it to bind with the sallow yolk of Seth's own stale spittle. With the life-in-her-mouth made it slick, stiffened it to enter her. As a vulture she hovered over our beloved brother, on the perch of his member.

She had opened his eyes, she had opened his mouth. Now from his testicles she brought forth life-from-death—a half-dead-one who would contend with SETH for the White Crown. Within ONE MONTH was he born. Truly, who was spreader-of-disorder if not our sister? Confusion was *Seth's* nature not hers. It is SHE who had broken the Tablets of Destiny, cheated Death—such a thing has never been done—for love?

But if thou wouldst have me die, Seth will die. And if thou wishest that Seth should not die, I will have life.

Isis hid the infant-half-dead from Seth in the marshes. Nephthys and Taweret watched over them. The three, my rightful consorts, nursed it, guarded it from my allies in the swamps. Isis taught it much guile, took it to the Western Lands—more witcheries—to learn warcraft and sciences from our brother, the many-eyed, the weary-of-heart. The freak survived, the dead-thing was raised up—red-in-his-eyes, snot-in-his-mouth. Foul-of-breath, frail-of-limb, who-sucks-his-thumb. Horus the child.

It was thus he came with his mother to petition thee at the head of the Tribunal of the Nine, that he be given the White Crown. And then Thoth said it was a million times right. Horus should have it. I answered thee, to the All-Lord—life, prosperity and health!—the White Crown should be stripped from the stripling and thrown into the water, far from the Sun! True, that the Baba of Seth spoke then harshly against the All-Lord for even considering their petition. But is not unreason Seth's nature? True, that in unreason the Baba loud-shrieked from the small mouth of Seth's member that the shrine of the All-Lord was empty, UNTENDED, bringing unto thee much sorrow. All day the All-Lord lay down on his back in his hut. Until the Golden One thy daughter came to show thee her cunt, bringing thee much laughter. What daughter comes to Seth in my sorrow to show me her cunt? What daughter comes with joy and laughter? Is Seth not thus made covetous? Am I not loving-of-family-yet-barren?

Seth insulted, gave offence, but did not Isis THREATEN the Ennead?—to write Neith to bring down the sky! if the half-dead's petition was not heard. And then the Ennead placated her, very craven, the Nine made ready to hear Horus. Only then Seth threatened them. To the Ennead, to the council Seth said:

> Hail to ye, my kin gods!
> I know ye, your names are well known to me.
> Am I not then greatest-in-potency?
> By Him-whose-names-are-hidden,
> it is given me to ride foremost
> in the Bark of Millions,
> in the Sun-Bark as it rises,
> to fend off the Apophis serpent
> where it lifts its bowels
> at noon from the marshes—
> to drive off the Apep dragon [38]
> with my copper sceptre.
> For none of ye can do this.
> Not one can lift it.

I made them an oath to kill them, a god a day—slay each one with this my copper sceptre of 4,500 pounds, spit them like bullocks from the mouths of their anus to the mouths of their face. I showed to them the world come after their deaths—when bread shall be called for with blood and all shall laugh with a sick man's laugh and fast for death. When man turns his back on the killing of a friend, a son is a foe, a brother an enemy. When a man robs his own twin and kills his own father. When words are like fire issuing from the heart, and its words on the tongue cannot be borne. When the Sun rises but none can distinguish its shadow. Then Seth would strip their god-shadows from them, leave them naked, no-shadowed in a desert wind.

For is Seth not the red wind and Lone Star of Twilight? Am I not of those who rising are risen, who lasting, last?

And did they not listen? I refused to contend in court with Isis, for she was great in magic, greater in guile. Seth spoke movingly: Is the White Crown to be awarded to my little brother Horus while Seth the Elder is alive?

But she had changed herself again, into the figure of a buxom wench, unseen by the others, where we were eating bread together in laughter. I alone saw her and approached, spoke to her from behind a tree, of her beauty of a like unknown to this land. She begged a promise of assistance, telling Seth she was the wife of a cow-herd, but he died, and so her son began to tend the herd, when a foreigner came to live in her stable, threatened to beat the boy, take his father's cows, evict him from his father's house. Did not buxom-in-guile ask Seth's protection from the demon? Anxious to release my seed, very full of it, Seth's jism asked through me, very indignant: Is it while the son of a man is still alive that his cattle are to be taken by strangers? Here my dear sister revealed herself, and as a kite flew shrieking up to the crown of an acacia. Calling down to Seth: It is your own MOUTH that has said it, Seth's own deceit has judged you! What comeback have you?

I went before the All-Lord to tell of my deception, for thou hast been always my father, and wert well disposed toward Seth. Was Seth not created lascivious, am I not foolishness-in-rut? She is MOST guileful!

The Ennead would not award the White Crown directly to Seth but set the contenders a test. Three months Horus and Seth were sent as hippos to remain at the bottom of the Nile. AGAIN defying the Ennead, Isis cast her harpoon down into the river after us, seeking out the flesh of Seth but biting instead into the freakish one. Horus shrieked up: Mother beg the harpoon to let go. She did, it did agree. She cast it again—into Seth. But my cries were piteous: Could Isis prefer a harpoon of copper to her own dear brother? She was moved to tears, for Seth is tenderness-in-danger. The daughter of our mother Nut called to the harpoon of copper: See, it is Isis's own brother Seth, son of the Sky, and the Darkling. Let him go, Isis said, and the harpoon agreed.

Horus waxed furious, his-face-of-a-panther—and did he not cut off his own mother's head with a cleaver of 16 *deben*-weight in his fist? Thus she was made a statue of flint, headless. Only then he desisted.

Later I found him at a mountain oasis, asleep under a tree. And did Seth not then richly avenge the beheading of the daughter of my mother? As a red storm in the desert Seth seized him, threw the child down on its back. With the chisel of my loins, Seth fucked out his eyes, raped hard the freak with flame and the orbits ran fire. But was his mother satisfied with her brother Seth, was there gratitude? She sent the Golden One with spells to find the child in the desert, his eyes weeping pus. Hathor of Gold caught a gazelle and milked it, and rinsed Seth's own dear poison from the child's eyes and restored them. Then great-in-magic, Isis, great-ingrate, went before the Ennead to bring complaint: See the poor fatherless child left weeping in the desert. But had the

half-dead-one so much as met his father? and is not Seth bereft equally
of a brother?—and I knew him.

The Nine enjoined us to cease our contendings: Act with civility.
Upon whom the greater hardship, this? Was it not upon Seth?—was not
Horus weak at Seth's mercy, and civility an insult to my own true nature?

But Seth did make up with his nephew, in welcome and hospitality
made him a feast, as once was done for the father. So for the son did Seth
prepare him a place of rest, and after feasting and beer bade him lie down
with his uncle. The voice of Seth said then to the ear of Horus:

> How buxom thy buttocks seem to Seth!
> How broad are these thighs!

The mouth of Horus said: Beware, Uncle, I shall tell of this to my
mother! When the mouth had shut, its lips stopped, Seth took the
shape of a black pig—and performed the labour of a male upon the
child with the tusk of my loins. But his mother interfered even with
Seth's civilities! having taught the half-dead how to deceive me, making
of his fist a mouth between his buttocks. My dear nephew became as a
bitch to Seth and seized the spume of my testicles in his hand. Again
had great-in-magic CHEATED Seth, made my seed to fall on barren
ground.

She shrieked to see Seth's potency in the child's hand, with a copper
knife cut off the hand and cast it into the Nile water, never once letting
the Sun see, speaking spells against my potency, against the venom in
Seth's jism. Then the mother of Seth's nephew gave the half-dead a new
hand, chanting:

> Remember Horus, your hands belong to you. Your right hand is
> Shu, your left hand is Tefnut—they are the children of Ra. Your
> belly belongs to you, Horus—the children of Horus, who are in
> it, receive not the poison of the scorpion. Your strength belongs
> to you, Horus—the strength of Seth prevails not against you.
> Your phallus belongs to you. . . .

With sweet ointment she chafed it to a stiffness. With fist-love she
drew the semen down from its lips, with the life in her mouth collected
it, transferred it to a pot, many times until it was filled. Then the daughter of our mother Sky, wife of Seth's brother, mother of my dear nephew,
went to Seth's own hut, inciting there Seth's gardener to a betrayal.

Isis said: What food does Seth eat from this garden? *Only the lettuce,
the food of his potency.* Each leaf she smeared then from the pot until the

lettuce gleamed with the Horus-jism, taking strength from the Sun. Seth ate that night of the lettuce, a great salad, and in the morning went to the Ennead to tell of Seth's labours upon the half-dead-one, the freak: I have planted my seed high up in the bowels of Horus! Seth has defiled his sovereignty! The Nine hawked up their scorn, spat it as bile into the face of the child. But my dear nephew's mother had instructed him to deny this, saying: Horus has defiled the sovereignty of his uncle Seth! Horus has planted well and deep in the pleats of his intestines. Horus said then: Let my uncle's semen be called, that we may hear whence it answers.

So Ibis-head Thoth, script-lord, truth-scribe for the Ennead, called: Come out, semen of Seth! It called NOT from the mouth of Horus's ANUS but from the marshes. Then Thoth put his hand on the shoulder of Seth, calling: Come out, semen of Horus! And the semen talked from Seth's OWN bowels: Where shall I come out? Thoth replied: From his ear! But it answered: Am I to issue forth from an ear, when I am a divine jism? As a great Sun disk then it came from the top of Seth's head. Thoth, the swifter, set the disk as a crown unsteady on his narrow-bird-head. Seth loud-shrieked-death-in-their-faces—reached to seize and tear the disk. But seeing the Ennead turning on Seth—swiftly I called: Another test! Let each contender build a stone boat to race against the other. But she-is-greatest-in-guile taught the half-dead to build a boat of balsam, coat it with gypsum, in appearance like stone. In the morning Seth's stone boat went swiftly, straight to the bottom. So Seth became a hippo to sink the light swift boat! Horus drew back his copper barb, telling it—SLAY SETH! but the Ennead called out against this, Stop!

And Horus stayed his cast. Horus spared Seth.

Then Thoth prayed thee the All-Lord: Dictate a letter to Osiris, Lord of the Dead Lands, where he eats of gold and glaze—to choose between the contenders, who have been before the Tribunal now eighty years without a judgement. And did not His-heart-is-weary write back swiftly to the All-Lord of the Ennead?—causing thee insult, boasting of his accomplishments, of his gifts of barley and emmer and cattle to sustain the gods, without which all would swiftly starve, mocking the All-Lord's invention of the Tribunal, as the begetting of Injustice as an accomplishment. And asking: did not all the stars of the gods have to set beneath his feet in the Western Lands?

How Seth's dead brother vaunted then over the Tribunal! asking who among the Nine was greater than he in strength, that his son should be cheated of his birthright. And did not Foremost-of-the-Westerners, lion who hunts for himself, threaten the HEARTS of the gods? saying:

> In the land where I am
> are savage-faced messengers
> who fear neither gods nor goddesses.
> I have but to unkennel these demons,
> and they will seek out the heart of any,
> and return it to me
> for the weighing.

Craven, the Ennead said, the husband of Isis is right, the great-in-plenty and giver-of-sustenance is a million times right. But what need had Seth to fear the forty-two demons? Did not I know their names and have power over them? Seth-shrieked-death-loud-in-their-faces:

O Being-of-fire walking backward—yea, I have stolen a god's property! O Blood-drinker from the shambles—I have slain sacred cattle! O Bowel-eater from the Tribunal—I have extorted! O Pallid-one from On—I have prated! O Wrecker from Huy—I have trespassed! O Disturber from the sanctuary—I have wrought violence! O Accuser of Utjen—I have attacked and reviled a god! O Backward-facing from the pit—I have copulated with a boy! O Captor from the burial ground—I have cursed a god in my town. . . .

[——]
[——]

All these things Seth *had* done, but had he not been true to his own self, had he not been one with his *ka*? Seth's front is pure! Seth's rear is pure! Though others had lied and defied—though OTHERS had threatened and mocked the Ennead—yet the Nine found against Seth—even the All-Lord, who sent for Isis to bring Seth bound in shackles as her captive, in copper fetters to stand before thee. Why, thou askedst, does Seth evade the judgement of the Tribunal and defy it to take what belongs by right to Horus? But I answered thee—for is not Seth who-is-pleased-with-desertion and did I not then desert myself saying: No, not so, great Lord, All-Lord. I beg that Horus, son of Isis, pride of his uncle! be given the offices and titles of my dear brother, Osiris, his uncle.

Bring Horus, son of Isis. And set the White Crown upon him.

After eighty years.

Horus was vindicated in the One-are-the-Two-Truths court, vindicated in the Pool-of-the-Field court, *vindicated* in the Horus-with-Projecting-Horns court. Hearing of the judgement, Seth's followers took to the red desert in multitudes of rage—serpents, scorpions, crocodiles—the sky darkened. The Storm. But Horus was in possession of the Eye. It rose as a winged disk to rout the allies of Seth. Its wings were the breath of Kneph, its Ptah was the serpent's eloquence, its disk, the all-source without beginning or end. The winged disk of Horus filled the ranks of Seth's allies with madness, horror where it hovered over the battlefield. The allies of Seth were overthrown as by flame, turned back, driven out. Cutting and much slaughter were made of them, their names destroyed, their magics and their shadows stripped from them.

And the lamentations of Seth's followers filled the northern sky. And the lamentations of his *ka* filled the southern sky.

Then in procession throughout Egypt was Seth driven before the young king, crying: Horus has purified himself in the Field of Rushes! Horus, son of Isis, has arisen as ruler, l.p.h.! Horus thou art the good King of Egypt, of both the Upper and the Lower, Lord of the Two Shores, of the Two Horizons, good lord of all lands, the Black *and* the Red, even of the foreigners-in-their-stinking, forever!

Lo, the name of Seth reeks more than carrion, more than ducks smell. To whom am I to speak today?—brothers are unkind, the friends of today do not love. To whom shall Seth speak, when faces are blank and each turns his face from his brother's? To whom shall the *ka* of Seth speak today, when the *ba* of Seth cannot open its mouth?

To whom shall the *ka* of Seth speak today, whither shall I go now when I have been stripped of my seat in the dog star?

You who come after, you who are to come in a million years, Death is to me now like myrrh on the air. Like a sick man's healing. Like sitting beneath a sail spilling sweet wind. Like a bark beached on the shore of drunkenness. Like a sky, clearing. Death stands before me now like a mist lifted from a man's eyes to reveal what has gone unseen. Death stands before Seth like his longing for home, and reaching it from War.

There is One whose name I did not know, whose power Seth did not hold. He has crushed a million countries by himself. Before this name Seth is submitted. I am fallen on my side. Seth's heart was weighed, the *ba* of Seth was found wanting. It is as if my name never existed, and my words, my seed never were, and my *ka*. And to Horus has been awarded the White Crown.

Thou hast been vindicated against me. And if thou, O Horus, wouldst that Seth should die, his *ka* shall surely die.

But lo! Horus has been taught to bind and unbind the knot Tyt, of Beginning and Restoration! Horus does not kill Seth! but leaves to him the place of honour foremost in the Bark-of-Millions! Truly he who stands before Seth will pilot the Sun-Bark between the two sycamores of Turquoise, where it sails high over the lake of Qeb. Jubilate through all the land! let there be jubilation throughout all Egypt for Horus, son of Isis! And for Seth. Seth jubilates with the Tribunal, Seth is strife-kept-within-walls, Seth is strength-against-Apophis. Apophis is smitten, turned back, its snout is split! In the Bark-of-the-Dawn-and-Sunset, Seth is sent to the foremost to spill the blood of Apophis through the twilights.

For a million years.

Seth is mother of the Eye, is made its bitch and has suckled it. The *ka* of Seth has sucked the thumb of Horus. Horus is in possession of the uninjured Eye, Horus is in his power-of-the-Eye-Restored.

Horus, Falcon-of-Gold, is come from his egg, his wings are of green-stone. Child of She-who-wide-strides-the-sky, who sows stars from her seed-bag of greenstone, turquoise and malachite.

Horus is Falcon-of-Silence who walks the path of mystery in light-land, child who speaks in silences with the Hidden One. The potency of Seth's testicles fills the Eye of Horus. The potency of Horus grows silent in the bowels of Seth.

My cry is in the silence of the child.

> My cry is in the silence of the child.

>> My cry is in the silence of the child.

Phaëthon BOOK SIX

O you who enter the world and who leave it, God detests impudence.

EMPEDOCLES

And when you return, you shall have again been made a child.

CODEX
CHIMALPOPOCA[1]

CONTENTS

Ticket to Anywhere, Anytime Soon. First class yes—in this hell-heat what else. I board the bus, my silver-sided missile into the mysterious East. East across the Yucatán, peninsular swelter-states of steam called Tabasco, Campeche, Quintana Roo. Anywhere but here, the too-true state of Veracruz.

Chill exhalate of reconditioned air . . . black vents mould encrusted. Tubercular incubations, beware. Avert eyes. Look up, out, ahead. Every curtain drawn against the sun, the devastation, the road-kill of poverty. All Mexico reduced to this long tunnel of white curtains. At the tunnel's end a panel of sky blinding white, like a page of sun. Schoolbook bus-driver silhouetted in windshield. Mute flicker of television behind the silhouette head.

An old woman in the next seat is watching me from the corner of her eye as she crochets. An offer of headphones drawn from her knitting bag. *Si usted quiere*, I'm getting too deaf for these. Lilac perfume. Steady needle clack.

Diesel engine . . . gargle of pistons, breathless deathrattle that numbs and soothes.

Sleep . . . I sleep like never in weeks, lulled on this diesel song, garble of throttle, long mantra of ommmm. And I *can*—sleep if not dream. At the next steambath, terminal city of Villahermosa, I go to the counter. Another ticket, please. To anywhere. The next leaving south, east. The ticketman squints at this, my dubious quest. Hurry, nevermind keep it *keep it*—

All aboard the engine of rest.

Through a night a day another night, at depot after depot straight to the counter I stagger drunken gambler buying more bright chips. *Ya se lo dije, señor*—anywhere south or east—what does it matter? on these buses I can sleep. And sooner or later the wheel stops on Tulum.

Sleep-curtained screenings of silent shorts in Technicolor—Mexican slapstick, Hollywood drama. Jiminy Stewart crashed in the desert, a smash in an aviator's jacket. . . . What state is this? Quintana Roo? *Gracias*. Is this the road to Palenque? No *señorita* it's south of here. You're not lost are you?

Sleep, write, sleep. Wake every now and then to another traveller in the next seat. *Disculpa, señor,* are we near Tulum? No we are coming to the border with Belize. Tulum is north. You are not going to Belize?—you want me to tell the driver?

No matter, *no importa, me da igual.*

At the terminal a ticketseller hunched and squat says no—his head a fat brown orb socketed in necklessness. No more first class this afternoon. Tomorrow morning only, the Belize bus to Cancún. Ah *Tulum* . . . We have a very nice bus leaving in twenty minutes. . . .

All aboard this third-class rattletrap dipped in electric pink and green—gaudy parrot racket—cage without curtains or glass or screens. We barrel down the centre of our two-laned highway framed in low scrub and tall tree clumps. Foaming cascade of air, oblique riddling of light. Symphony of gears, gossip shouts, wind roar, furred howl of speakers of disembowelled cardboard—I sit, wide-eyed in this jetwash, more awake than in years. *Señora,* what is this music—salsa? No, CUMBIA, *te gusta?*

Sí, sí . . . I like I like. Acoustical caffeine. Seventy dark bodies sway to the rhythm, the whole bus rocks side to side—hysteria on helium tires—cowbells, coronets, bright hectoring of wind and light, heady concussions of oncoming trucks plunging south. . . .

Bent figures in evening fields of corn and cane, glints of scythe, burros half-hidden under tottering stacks like stalkingblinds. Palm tops lit gold, glimmers of eastern sea between the trees . . . Over the sea a litmus strip of umber dipped in slate.

Scabbed gaunt dogs / whippets of Sloth, slouch just clear of the giant shadow rush. Raw wounds scabbed in gorging flies that flinch and fluster in the last-instant hornblast. At every little town and crossing a grinding, screeching halt. Afterthoughts of dust catch up. . . . Child dervishes now, distilled from roaddust—sprite whirlwinds sprint to hawk bags of Coke and Fanta to go. . . . They hand up twist-tied baggies sprouting straws like potted palms.

At a gas station, vendors tiptoe on gaspump islands and press hot *elotes* through the window gaps—tender white corncobs with chilli and mayo. The parrot bus coughs—pitches forward as though shot. Haste of coins dropped to upcast palms or pitched, and on down this highway that roars and rattles we shriek past cemeteries—death's gaudy pantheons, mausoleums gay as carousels—right through front yards past lonely country shacks built to the road-side for company. House after house of unfinished second storeys, an endless spring of rebar sprouts . . . so many rusty hymns to optimism. On swayback porches, hammocks sag and gape their impassive freight of watchers.

Streaked in dust, naked toddlers stalk wary hens.

Elbow nudge. Toothless crone offers a stick of sugarcane—her own stick fiercely gummed and pulped. Defiant posterchild for tooth decay. Smooth black skin, whitewire hair, merry eyes, bright pink hippogrin. You chravel alone, fhar fhrum home? Where is your fhamily? Are you married?—no, thhhen soon? *¿tieneth nofhio, por lo menoth?*

Tropical nightfall's sudden blackout—theatrical bomb—my stiff-kneed stumble down. Welcome to Chetumal.

Warm coastal night . . . The blind lunge of a hundred thousand moths into floodlamps above the busbays. Strange mottling, freckled moth-shadow mosaic as through a crocheted lampshade, spun. The luxury bus in the next bay slides open its chilly window—Tulum, *señorita?* Cancún?

Every last passenger is asleep. Severed arms, heads, splayed feet dis-embodied in the aisle. One seat left, second row, lucky me spared this gauntlet run of snore and loll and drool. My wide-awake eyes still awash in the day's wind and light show. . . .

Bright morning. At last—Tulum of the pyramids on the sea!

No pyramid. No sea.

Along the highway a single scrawl of street under a white sift of flour dust. Strew of cinderblock cubes all missing their front, fourth wall. Two rows of open dollhouses, moviesets back to back, duel of musics across the dusty roadbed—west-side cumbia, reggae east.

¿Hamaca señorita, hamaca?

This is really Tulum? Sí sí, with a hammock you sleep not here but on the beautiful beach *a un kilometro*. Free, no hotels. Restaurants by the sea, bars discotheques. Everything you need, water fruit *mariscos*—fresh fish very cheap. The best *hamacas* in all México, made by my sisters. Here take a *Matrimonial* for the price of a *Doble*. How many only one? If you are on the beach tomorrow I will show you how to be comfortable. With hammocks there is a secret.

I limp down a whitedirt track through greygreen scrub. This heat, this airlessness. This bated breath, punctured arch. Limp on, ever on. Sun, seascent without sound . . . Ahead the shade of palms, a bend in the track—*the sea*. Lacquered tilt of a turquoise fan.

Blinding smear of sand, snow-white hourglass dust, uncanny coolness underfoot. Walk out and down into this pale impossibility of blue. Far far out, waves of indigo turn fleece collars against a shear of reefs.

Lean and strut of coconut palms prop puffs of cloud. An utter stillness seeps its white edges north, south . . . to each blank horizon. South through this still-life light I wade kneedeep into mindlessness. I wade past palm thatch parasols. Palapa huts. Under one or two a hammock droops . . . the chinstrap of a pith-helmet. Coolie hat.

Please in this stillness let there be rest.

[23 Jan. 1995]

Sameness, stillness, rest. I will not write this . . . her death. Each day fetches kindling to the new routine's cold ashes. Its flicker of pointlessness licks up as I get up hours before the dawn, walk the starlit strand north to Old Tulum.

Slip past the gate, the sleeping guard, weave through the serpent columns up the steps of El Castillo, clifftop Maya watchtower to the East. Look down. A gloam rises from the ground. Take a narrow ledge—shuffle round to the eastern face, seven storeys of tower and cliff straight down to the sea. Sit. Wait. Think of nothing. Not sunrises over distant cities, not other countries, not old lovers. Watch for nothing.

Slow turn of nothingness in its cage of stars.

Suffer now the dawn's blush deceptions, this sudden fetch of sun that kindles sea, kerosene reefs to molten gold. Glance left, north to the stone Temple of the Diving God—admire the brief illusion tricked in flame—the breakneck dive of stone into a shallow flood of fire. Look back now, west, back over precincts of old stone changed to rose . . . to dragon bones. Ruins charred on pure white light, to blackened blocks of chalky stone.

The dawn fades, the shallows turn the blue of glaciers. A long shelf of aquamarine spreading south . . . a shore of ice in a pale tremble of blue, as if melting under moonlight. Slow return to sameness, day.

In the distance the dapple of reefs, horseshoes of morning cloud stamped on sea. . . .

Insidious calm. Soundless sea I crave and dread. No wind. This breathlessness.

Figures stir back at the gates. I stop to buy a ticket on the way down and out. The guard shrugs at the ticketseller. Return for sunset. Rewind. Repeat in reverse.

[25 Jan. 95]

Each afternoon one guide finds me at the top. The others all give up, turn away in disgust. His beautiful little smile, deep black eyes unfathomable. Dear, cotton shortpants of an immaculate confection, brilliant like the sand, little pedal pushers hemmed mid-calf. He wears a white cotton shirt, yoke embroidered red and gold and green. Red cottonbraid overshirt, belted jerkin.

Will you let me guide you, *señorita*, last tour of the day? No, I did not think so. Quiet smile. *Hubiera sabido, ¿verdad?* You always shake your head. Perhaps you do not speak. Wait, I know—you teach me your sign language, I will teach you mine. We have been working on ours for two thousand years.

You should say yes soon. I am only here another day or two, I have stayed too long already. Maybe you have also.

Tiny little man, no taller than me, childlike, strong. White palms muscular at thumb and heel. Delicate ankles, feet sandalled in *huaraches*. His age utterly unguessable—twenty, fifty, a thousand years.

You may as well see something, since you come every afternoon. They say you climb up here each morning too. But only here, to El Castillo. Never the Snail Platform. Never the House of Columns, the Dance Platform. The Oratory. Why is that? Are you only here for the view?

At least you should go into the new Centro Interpretivo. It is why I have stayed some extra days. *Dioses de los Maya.* Travelling exhibit of the Maya gods. The best Maya art from all over the world. Together only a short time. Many Maya pieces I have only seen in books. They should be kept here, they have been taken from us. One day they again will be ours, I think. Not even this interests you? I am a very good guide.

Especially not this.

Ah, you do speak, but you have no curiosity. Tell me, do all tourists come here with their sunglasses and credit cards and rented cars only to be the stars of their own movie? You are disappointing, like the others.

Usually they just come once and stay half an hour. I did not see you wearing sunglasses. . . . He turns to go.

Is that why we come?

If I am wrong tell me. Let me share with you these things. The first time, you do not pay. If you like my work . . .

Bird bones, skin a softgloss mahogany. Pale full lips. Beautiful buddha man of an oriental elegance, features of a temple mask.

Do you even work here? Where's your badge and uniform, your rusty gun.

Ah, you are joking with me. I am not an employee if that is what you mean. I come once or twice a season to train the guides here and in Palenque. You should go there, have you been? From most pyramids it is with the sky we speak. But in Palenque the pyramids speak to the jungle all around. Some trees are much higher than the temple tops. Do you see the difference, does this interest you at all? You are lucky, I repeat the offer.

Yes why do you?—tell me. *Cuénteme.*

Pensé . . . No, have a good day, *señorita.*

Wait . . . Please. What is your name?

Jacinto Ek Cruz, *a sus ordenes.*

He makes a formal little bow. . . . Jacinto, do you mock me too?

Jacinto, ¿a dónde va, de dónde viene?

Now?

When you're not training guides.

I come from the South. You will not know it. My family home is in San Andrés.

San Andrés . . .

A village. But I lived in Mexico City for a time. Teaching white Mexicans and foreigners to translate Maya languages. Very free translations, too free for me. I live down the coast now. Not far from San Andrés, in our capital of Carillo Puerto. Do you know it? I am *Director General del Centro Cultural Maya.* It is small, but we do good works. You should come one day. Ask for me. Jacinto Ek Cruz.

I must be going now. They are closing soon. *Señorita, adios.*

I leave the ruins without the sunset. Already a crack in the new routine, its dead perfections. Splayfoot Chaplinwalk back through the shallows. Hemmed mid-calf in turquoise, herding minnows. Sit in the bloodwarm

water to cool the blackfunk jeans. Soak in this sinister beauty of late afternoon, doctored, hyperreal. Airbrushed postcard in the round, the flesh.

I sit in this stillness, in the light's icy shimmer. Sea birds. . . . I am
grateful for the sound. Sift the swift auspices of bird cries. Sit still for
this, their aerial *misericordia*. A curlew's frantic pipe and skitter—numen
cry!—its head-dip caesura.

Dart and spear of terns, blade voices shaped and turned on flight's
white wheel.

Descent of gulls. Feral howl, jackals of the air. Contemptible squabbles. . . .

Sunset. Moonless night. My subway penlight yellowing as I write this.

26 Jan
Endure another perfect sunrise from the stone tower. Mid-morning walk
back from Tulum. Mid-day bask in a dot of shade. Under my palm parasol of home, the last in a long scatter south. The secret of the hammock,
señorita, is to lie cross-wise. You see? It flattens everything. Makes it comfortable. Just watch . . . for scorpions in the thatch.

Two pairs of blond mirages waver down the beach. Towering backpack
cowls, glinting pack frames, blue bedrolls. Of course, take the two parasols
right next door a dozen others empty farther up. Company. Sororal littoral,
cozy row of sisterhood—stop! can you spell s-o-l-i-t-u-d-e? So I leave early
for the ruins, early afternoon. Four gold nods, bright smiles in quadru-
plicate. Upturned noses peeled and pink, dolleyes of palest turquoise.
Eight little windows on a beyond of bright shallows. Perpetual sea view.

I sit on the watchtower and listen to the last tour bus retreating north to
happy hour in Cancún. Sweet diesel croon that calls up my happy hour
in Old Tulum. The light ebbs. I look down between my feet. Seven
storeys down the dim foam rings the jagged stones like smoke. Still
Jacinto Ek Cruz has not come. Minor distraction, very minor. Study the
east for the first sign of dusk . . . a line traced in soft lead at the horizon,
a contraction in the sea's cooling skin.

Pale lemon glows in a far anvil of cloud. The sky's cobalt softens with
greens as if glimpsed through leaves.

Feel only a minor annoyance . . . the tiniest throb of hurt. He didn't
come.

Footscuff on stone—too late Jacinto, too bad, no guide-sale after all—
but no, a tall tall manboy, head down, gangle of arms—swift walk—furtive
/ mindless of the sheer drop of cliff, hungry rock-haloes of seafoam.

Recall it now so well so *sharply* under these stars—Shriek, Memory—as
I sit in cool night sand and write racing my subway penlight down to a
yellow death. Remember the fret of hightop laces, how it plumps like
string loosened on a spool, see the one big hand turn on its heel as he
swift/sits without quite touching me, not raising his eyes. Snailtrack of
mucous gloss trails into the soft black lipdown. Black T-shirt—guitarists
in clown masks. Dirty jeans, cracked leather belt . . . see the loose end's
skinny sprout and dangle. Still he doesn't look he cranes his neck, head
half-turned away—cringing hound abandoned to the cryptic future of
the master's hand—my brutal slap or mercy scratch.

Couldn't. One word. Repeated. Coul'nt? Warning, plea, accusation—
what? Still he won't look. Cou'nt. Is this English is he Cockney what is
he saying to me? Hangdog headswivel to look at my jeans, thighs, up.
What does he want IS HE GOING TO PUSH ME OFF? launch our
death pact without even asking?—wait wait I haven't signed yet—what
is he saying—'couldn't' *what*—jump alone? I scramble up shuffleturn to
take the ledge the other way, feel his hand—pigknuckle snout—root
between my thighs rooting in my ass.

Cunt.

Welcome to English class. Say *cunt.* Pronounce it clearly now. Rooting
with the back of his hand in my cunt why is this somuchworse than fingers? Cunt. He follows. Little pork grunts. Cunt. Cunt. Welcome to
Tulum let's tour the ruins. Up the Oratory steps. Cunt. Walk faster don't
run don't run. Cunt—Temple of the Diving God. Over to the Snail
Platform, is he still behind right behind me all root and snout past the
House of *Cunt* Columns. Temple of the Frescoes. *Cunt cunt cunt* feel the
taut coil winding winding up behind my eyes—hear it whisper into copper wire—comes a new word penny-bright to mind—*murder*—see
Jacinto at the exit oasis of calm talking to two guards.

Murder.

Walk don't run.

Murder.

Cunt.

You stalk ME pathetic dogboy braindead protosimian. I am not your prey—

*you stalk me? why didn't I slaughter you like a pig grunting cunt cunt—why
didn't I push you off—wanna get off PIG? here you want cunt? sticky your
skinny gristle into this—VAGINA DENTATA MOTHER CUNT TOOTH
God I want you dead. I AM NOT YOUR PREY I am the COBRA you are the
dimwit dream of a mongoose. What I hate—loathe more than anything in this
holewidesplayed world—it's the condescension / their PRESUMPTION—that
we are the flighty herbivores and they the great meateaters. Who made them the
fuckhunters? Drool from their noses snot drooling from their withering cocks / little testicular tear ducts all so quickfucked-out—so soon great hero of fuck? I could
have done a hundred like you and read a book—sucked your whole fucktribe to
dry salt tears—ground their little marble bags down to sand to glass dust—*

How could I let him herd me like a cow?

*I am not your meat you are MINE—protosimian dangling on the deadest
branch of the evolutionary tree. Dead as your dead eyes.*

I

       am

           not

              your

                    prey

FREAK.

Ah, *señorita,* I see you are curious after all. What did you think of the
frescoes? Maybe a little dark at this hour. Is everything alright you're not
ill is that one there bothering you? *Oye, muchacho, párate alla. ¿Qué diablos
estás haciendo? Ya te avertí. Vete a casa—¡ahorita mismo! Vete. . . . Hablaré con
tu padre.*

Get home boy. I will speak with your father.

You are trembling. He did not hurt you. No? I am surprised you have
not met him. He is here every day. Like you. You need not worry. He
hurts no one—but very annoying, yes. He is not like us.

Not *Maya?*—Mayans aren't like that—wouldn't *do* that?

It's true his father is Mexican, but no not that.

What, then.

Soft wave of Jacinto's small white palm in the dusk. Taps a finger to
the high-broad forehead. *Glue.* You have this problem too in your
country, no?

Wait, miss. Please. Do not leave our holy city this way. There is so
much here of beauty. I am leaving tomorrow. Let me show you some of
the treasures of the *Dioses* exhibit. You will not be sorry.

Quickflare glare of guards, We're closing up, as don Jacinto knows.

No te preocupes, Ignacio. I will lock up. Glares that fade, soft gutter of macho complicity. Yes, better stay with don Jacinto. *El loco* might still be out there in the dark. Waiting.

Come in please. Let's not stand out here with these idiots.

DEEP NIGHT. A breath of wind rattles high in the palms behind the beach . . . paring of moon between the shy fronds. There are patches of stardust over the night sea. Now and then a crab scuttles boneshadows across the cool pale sand. My subway penlight dances in the palm thatch, parasol turned petticoat of light.

Jacinto Ek Cruz, I'm sorry for how I acted. Why didn't you just walk away from me? I am such a *child*, I can hardly bear to remember. Write it. Take it all, get it all down. . . .

Deserted anteroom, ticket counter. Press clippings aflutter on a tackboard: *World Famous Dioses Exhibit!* come one come all. Follow the little guide in white, follow meek and mild. Simmering. He called him a *boy*. Twice his size, twice mine. Two-metre gluepot stuck on cunt. And this tiny animal tamer halts the madbull elephant charge with the soft wave of a whiteflag palm. Little traffic cop, mighty Maya hunter.

Part the theatre curtain. Prepare to Enter the Haunted House. . . .

Walls of deep blue midnight. Side-lit and from below a limestone serpent, jaws split wide. The head of a Maya prince emerging from the dragon jaws of night. Eighth century. Temple of the Magician, Uxmal.

Sala Azul, the Blue Room. Soft chirrup of crickets. Pools of tracklight. Glass cases. Statuettes of bare terracotta . . .

Draw breath.

You did not expect it to be quite so beautiful, *señorita*. I told you, one of the great art exhibits anywhere. How much money do you think the Mexican government spent. To bring such pieces from all over the world? But there is never much left for our Maya Cultural Centre down south. No . . . it is impolite to bother a visitor with all this.

But I want to hear. *Pass the hat for the Centro Cultural.*

The Mexican government understands this bond of culture and power. As have the Maya. I have been to conferences in Washington and Austin Tejas. They understand also, but not so well. For them money is power and culture is money. But this is not quite the same, I think.

We begin down the hall.

Spine of interlocking doorways. Past the Green Room. A little fountain. Another room, Wine-Red. Into la Sala Siena. Faint throb of drums . . . a long line of light-tables down the near wall, glow of frosted glass. Carved flutes, whistle figurines.

See the carving on this flute, here is one of the Hero Twins, Hunahpu. He pipes now to the Monkey Scribes, to entice them from the jungle. These instruments could be venerated as divinities themselves.

Like the Tecpatl.

Why yes, this is true, *señorita.* The FlintKnife is a very old god. But Mexican. Look, here—one of my favourites, this shell trumpet. Today it is kept in the Maya territory called Fort Worth Tejas. See where the surface of the conch is worn smooth by the trumpeter's lips. The carver of the king's image on the front has political opinions. Look how he has used the shell's taper to give the royal profile an overbite. See these traces of *cinabrio* they rubbed in, to bring out the lines. How do you say this word in English? I would like to learn more of this language one day.

Cinnabar.

Seenabal . . . *cinabrio.* Beautiful in either way. It is a pleasure to speak such words, no? Do you play an instrument?

What's this hole.

For a thong to hang from the trumpeter's neck. Some of these rites could last many hours.

What rites.

We see from the smoking *ahau* here in the king's chinstrap a connection to God K. Look, the same VisionSerpent in his headdress is also in this abalone shell over here.

Quickchange of subject to the concave shell, waxen sheen of palest blue, incisions traced rust-red . . . What was it you didn't want me to see?

I ask if you play an instrument because I wonder some days—what if the first meeting of Maya and Spaniards had been a *conferencia* of musicians?

Is this it, Jacinto Ek Cruz, your guide-style? Whimsy's dog and pony show . . .

The Maya, did they use obsidian or flint? For the heavy blows to the sternum—

A more musical History would be a very different one, would it not?

Obsidian shatters on solid bone, isn't that so? *Maya man, temple mask I will make you crack.*

But you too want to talk about sacrifice. For a tourist with no curiosity you know a lot about *los Mexica.* But think a moment—in this other History knives would be for slicing vegetables, and our mariners might have taken us to Europe during our Classic Period. To give concerts, for instance. In your Dark Ages they might have mistaken *us* for gods.

They'd have burned you in the ninth century too.

Come, let us visit the Sala Verde now.

Sala Verde. Burble of a fountain lit blue and green. Faint crash of NewAge waves on a primordial shore, synthesized, soothing. In the Beginning . . .

This is the room of our cosmology. Here on this stela is carved the World Tree, the axle on which everything turns. Its roots are in the underworld, it flowers in the heavens. Souls are its sap, they flower and fall.

For the Aztecs, there were nine underworlds. Nine levels. . . .

Yes, *señorita*, I know this.

So a question—

I am not an expert on the Mexicans. I am barely a student.

But you're my guide.

For a few minutes more, yes I will try.

They called the seventh level Place of Waving Banners.

They were not a people without poetry.

Sacrificed children were called waving human pennants.

We are not Mexicans, *señorita*.

But you sacrificed children, too. *So calm, so calm, Jacinto Ek Cruz, what does it take to make you walk away?*

I know you are still upset, but please do not say 'you' in quite this way to me.

The ancient Maya then.

We sacrifice them still. I think you have seen this yourself just today. I wonder if it so different where you come from. Or is glue only used to glue?

Waving pennants, like for a sports team—were they flayed, Jacinto Ek Cruz? Is that why they fluttered? *Show me how much you want it, Buddha man, just ask—not even nicely.*

Tell me, *señorita*, what interests you so much about the Mexica?

A lot of things.

Yes?

Los ixiptla, por ejemplo.

Ah.

You know about this don't you, Jacinto.

The god's substitute.

His stand-in, his stunned double.

How many did the Maya have? The disheartened the flayed the riddled with arrows—?

May I ask your name?

Lightly scorched then hooked from the fire while the heart still beats—*Fifty-seven ways of killing god.*

You are some kind of scholar. *Oh yes some kind of scholar.*

Yet you do not visit the site. You hardly look at these things I show you.

Here's a good one. Four Aztec warriors with flint axes, a captive tied by an ankle to the gladitorial stone. Armed with an axe of feathers to defend himself. *Beautiful sphinx in white cotton, what will it take to make you scream to make you leave just how great is your need? Show me your need.*

Is there something here you are afraid to see?

The captive's job is simple enough. Inspire his killers to kill. Beautifully.

Why are you so uninterested in the Maya, *señorita?* Are we not bloodthirsty enough for you? We were not pacifists—in barely a *year* the Spanish broke the mighty Mexica. Two hundred kilometres inland over mountain passes. Five hundred Spaniards. A dozen horses. No reinforcements, no food. Against some say an army of a million Mexica soldiers. Do not tell me about cannons. How many cannon balls could they have carried from the coast? *Pacifists*—the Maya hardly let the Spaniards ashore. Two centuries later they still had not finished us. To this day there are villages that have never surrendered.

Traffic cop, is that iron in your gloves?

Here. Look at this warrior figurine. So small it fits in one palm—but all the detail. His mask, we call the Mosaic Monster. The Maya king becomes this god when he goes to war. It is good we speak openly. I have wanted to do this for some time.

At last the real tour, authentic jungle cruise. Anything you ask, just take off the mask.

Why do you let me talk to you this way?

There are things, *señorita*, I wanted to show you.

But why?

Will you not tell me how you are called?

You should know I'm going to fuck you now no matter what—but no more kindness. This stranger kind of kindness. . . .

Beulah.

Yes?

Limosneros.

Is it only blood that interests you Beulah Limosneros? Is this the exotic film *you* came for? Come. . . .

Sala Morada. Room of Wine-Red. Pine-scent of burning copal. Dimness like smoke, darkened walls, a tracklit string of panels, white stone sculpted in swirls of flowing chalk. Seated figurines, zoomorphs. Limestone lintels captioned in cartoon glyphs. Intricate markings of a calendar carved in yellow rock. . . .

By 100 B.C. we had invented a system of writing. The Chinese had this also by then but were still busy perfecting paper. We had a calendar that used place notation, like your decimal system but never equalled anywhere, and no not even today.

Here. Has anyone seen a thing more beautiful and more terrible than this stone head from the eighth century and borrowed from Cleveland? Who were these Cleves, I hear there were Indians there once but what was their land? Why have I never seen *their* sculptures, *their* temples?

While this head was being carved in Copan, the Arabs were only just borrowing the Indian systems of decimals and numerals. Imagine the Romans counting barbarians at the gates using Roman numerals—perhaps they lost count, or only ran out of time. Do you know who this head depicts, Beulah? This is the Death God of the Number Zero. Carved before 800 A.D. By then we were the equals of China in printing, carving and calligraphy, of India in mathematics, architecture and medicine, of the Arabs in astronomy. And what was Europe's greatest invention by this time? No, not the wheel. Our children's toys had wheels for a thousand years. By 800, the best you could do was the water wheel. We have no rivers here, *señorita*. They flow under our feet.

Beautiful brown man, how gently you began. We should have met such a long time ago.

Ours is called a Stone Age civilization. Yet for five hundred years after our Classic Age began its *decline*, Europe does not have a single invention to impress us. Oh, I forgot. Steel. Our obsidian blades are still two hundred times sharper than the best modern scalpels. An edge one molecule wide. I am told you use them for brain surgery now, just as we did once. But you wanted to talk of sport. You see how his hair is bound, and his dress? The God of the Number Zero is a sportsman, a ballplayer. Captain of his team. And it is the captain who is taken captive once the outcome is decided. By the time Europeans first saw the Zero, Beulah, *we had been killing its god for a thousand years.* So it is a shame you are not

interested in the Maya. You want my favourite form of sacrifice? This.
They tore off his jaw. While he still lived. Is it because Zero has nothing
to tell us, do you think, or too much? *Señorita* Beulah Limosneros we
were never pacifists, but I wanted you to see my people were musicians
too, and architects, and poets. See these carvings of the Monkey Scribes,
their homely faces! Of all the gods, the ones we most admired—and the
Hero Twins, who always defeated the stronger enemy by guile. Once, we
worshipped creativity, genius, and especially its failures, mistakes guided
by the hand of god . . . who jiggles your elbow like a child while you
draw—I am sorry. I should not have touched you.

And I am sorry to be harsh. As I say, I have wanted to speak openly
with one of you for some time now. You cannot know us by comparing
us to anything. Not your *Aztecas*, not the Chinese, not the Egyptians.

There are lighter things I could have shown you, filled with laughter.
The Jester God, the royal dwarfs—court jesters a little like those of
Velázquez. Figurines taken from daily life. An old drunkard. A concubine
with a client. These erotic works are very rare today. A favourite target of
our Franciscan fathers. But I think that is enough tonight, *señorita*.

Jacinto how does this computer program work? I didn't know the
Maya had horoscopes.

This is garbage. We should go now.

What's your birthdate?

All your calendars are toys. Time is your disease.

What?

The guards will be waiting.

What did you mean?

The tour is over.

But there's one more room. *Sala Turqueza.* What's in there?

Only what the tourists come for . . . what is destroying our youth.

Jacinto wait, you asked why I came.

Destroying this coast.

Why I stayed.

You also, then. For drugs. The pretext the Mexican soldiers use to search
us for guns. Only three kilometres inland from here is a cave with an underground river, *so clear* . . . A secret cavern big as a cathedral underground.
A village hid down there for a week once while the Spaniards searched.
You should go there. It is better than all the drugs you will buy here.

I came to learn about a recipe.

I know nothing about cooking.

El vino de obsidiana.

Ahh. Now Mexican garbage. Obsidian wine, the recipe for disaster.

So you know it.

It is part of our work at the Centro Cultural to teach our youth how primitive this drug hunger is. To teach the difference between vision and escape. Yes we had these things. The dancing, the trances. Steam baths, fasts. Fish toxins, snake venoms taken as snuff, smoked with wild tobacco—or in enemas. Some visitors find this last one most exotic, and you would not be the first to ask me to arrange this. But none of these was sacred on its own.

Then what was?

The main hallucinogen, very exotic, was massive blood loss. The sacred ingredient was the blood of a king. Blood fed the VisionSerpent, but blood burnt, made smoke. On its slow black coils the VisionSerpent rose. As it rose when they burned our books. Señorita—

Beulah.

You are upset. I understand. The boy. You are far from home. These things are frightening. Please listen to one thing. I will be back in about three weeks. I hope I still do not find you. Tulum is not a good place to spend time with nothing to fill it. The boy earlier should convince you of this.

Tell me at least what you meant about time.

The tour is over.

About our disease.

The guards will already be angry.

Then tomorrow.

I am leaving tomorrow. Señorita Beulah I know many scholars who come here from the North, from Europe. They are all strange people, as I say, like the tourists. Stars of some exotic film running in their heads. You are maybe the youngest and the most unusual yet. And among the most beautiful, but my answer to you as to them is No.

We walk out through the doors between the smoking guards. Faces glisten with sweat and smirk. Crickets . . . sickle glint of moon. One guard goes in, throws a deeper lever of night.

Last ember glow of the last smoking guard.

Don Jacinto, you should walk the young lady back to her hotel.

She is not staying at a hotel.

And how would you know?

Los mosquitos. You look like you have chicken pox.

Your ancestors thought bloodsuckers were holy.

My ancestors did not get everything right. Good-night, *señorita.*

Why do they always call you *don Jacinto?*

Terms of respect are common here in Yucatán. *Buenas noches, Beulah. Ande con mucho cuidado.*

He fades down the walk of crushed white coral, beautiful brown calves like the flanks of deer clench unclench in the garden lights lining the path.

Don Jacinto?

Falters, turns. Eyes invisible in the upcast light. Yes *señorita* Beulah Limosneros.

How old are you?

Waits a moment, smiles, his inscrutable mask. Thirty of your years, *señorita.* Whatever that means.

Scrape and clatter of crushed coral. White cotton pedalpushers receding into gloom.

28 Jan [19]95

DEEP NIGHT. Peace. A whispering sea, milky light. At the shore, wavelets lap at their dish of hours. Night fades . . . muddles to grey. A quartermoon sets. North, four blondes stir. Match flare, emberglow. Giggles . . . a sliding scale, half-asleep to stoned. Two blondes swim out, naked in a sea of ink. Just before dawn a birdcry of ecstasy.

   Two dim figures come out, hand-in-hand, shimmering hides of grey silk, salt. They stand close a moment, looking out to sea. Murmur, share a small white towel.

Mid-morning. Topless frolic in ice-blue shallows. Sharp calls in German maybe Swedish. Mid-day cookout in coconut oil—eight pink eggs sizzling sunnyside up, coppertipped. Out of nowhere—the whole fucking beach just yesterday deserted—the sex jackals homing now to the cookout, flies to a butcherblock. More men skulking in the palms, sprawling in street clothes in the sand, watchful gun dogs.

Late afternoon mirage of a food vendor wavering south. Same skinny old stork as yesterday and days before. Red neckerchief, hat brim come undone—spill of plaid—a weave of straw and sea. Make a balanced meal of his random offerings. *Empanadas de piña.* Shark kebabs. Today he brings diced mango and lime.

   Señor, why is there no wind here?

   A good question, *joven.* This is the season of winds. Yet for days like this. Not a breath. Like in the season of storms.

   Feel the lime burn scurvy lips and gums.

30 Jan

No more walks to Old Tulum. For the new routine salvage the bare essentials: Think of nothing, look for nothing. Not the sails of a caravel, not old lovers. Stare out over a sea of bluest torpor.

   I have come for this. Exactly this. Silence, stillness. This breathlessness.

A biped bikinirack staggers up the beach ankledeep in sand, ambulant comedy. Fringed in pendulous cups and thongs—a tatterdemalion surge as she walks, this burly Maya lady in a comical hat of conical straw. All and only bikinis. She flutters to a discreet stop a few metres from the topless blondes, a stocky statuette of tattered decorum.

One takes the hint walks to the rack, all Yucatán her fitting room. She cups top after top over bare breasts of a goldpink perfection. The others join in, giggling, hooking unhooking straps, taking shy model turns. Four laughing gold towers above the Maya lady smiling now, walled in sisterhood.

Back from the beach the sex jackals quiver in their shade of fronds, throb in their palms to these intimacies neverglimpsed, beyond conceiving. Circle this day on your pin-up calendars, O scavengers, sing of this day at carrion feasts for generations.

All strain at their leashes. None approaches, not one.

The bikini lady flaps back up the beach eight pieces lighter, the blondes topless still. One pink bikini-top sprouts from a beach bag.

Study them, the golden ones. What movie are you in?

[2 Feb 95]
Pickup trucks coming and going. Each day more jackals arrive earlier, stay later. Earlyworm guts the bird.

Return of the bikini rack, but draped today over a rolling billiard ball—thick, muscular, purplish brown, the bikini lady's son, must be—it's in the genes, so very very enterprising. His long sparse hair kinked like the corrugated shanks of bobby pins. A thin moustache slips from the greasy corners of thick Tartar lips. Sleazesmirk—bikinis, *muchachitas*, bikinis? Two blondes fumble for sunglasses, turn face down.

Dauntless he comes, stands in the shade of my palm parasol. *¿Mucho calor, verdad?* He sweats out sincerity.

I don't speak Spanish.

¡Caray!—his call to the others. This one has *green eyes!*—*¡pero increíble!*

Of course you speak Spanish, *amiga*. Everyone hears everything here. No bikini? You don't like the sea? How about *yerba*—marijuana? Anything you like just ask me. You like mushrooms, *cocaina?* Yes you like *cocaina* I think all in black from the city.

3 Feb 95
Mermaid picnics up the high strand. Little palm parasols, fashion shows, sand for tea. We are all here to make believe. Stars of our own movie.

Rich and tanned healthy and thin. Learn to fit in. Study the tourists, not the locals.

Make a list:

    Buy straw hat.

    Sunglasses—myoptical purdah.

    Jackal repellent, one gallon.

    Long cotton dress, neck to ankles.

    Black one-piece, plastic sandals.

Two masked mermaids fin out to the reef, angelfish trawling spun-gold shawls.

Please—you speak Spanish—on the reef! Mariana stepped on something. Will you help us, eyes wide blue. She needs a doctor.

Pufferfish foot, red tendrils reaching up the calf, vines of poison ivy searching out a heart to grow in. Stay calm stay calm call out to the billiard ball lounging in the shade. He sits at attention, sniffing opportunity. Call to them. *Oigan, pisó algo en el agua. ¿No las quieren llevar al doctor?*

Billiard ball's slouch across the cool sand, casual.

So *señorita* you have remembered your Spanish. Let's see—*igua <u>puta</u>*, look at that!—a sea snake maybe. *¡Muchachos véngense!* Sudden yap-ring of diagnostical jackals. No no a sea urchin. *Idiota*, urchins are not poisonous! *Pues, tiene una alergia.* Or a ray, yes a stingray. All agree now. She stops crying. Whitelipped shock, laboured breath. . . .

Are you taking her or not?—just go. Let the doctor decide. *Apúrense por fav<u>or</u>.*

Sí sí por supuesto. Ya vamos. Anda mal, ella.

All clamber into an old grey pickup, pale swimmer in the truck box, head on a towel.

Won't you come with us please? I'm sorry I don't know your name. In case the doctor has no English? Please come.

Hypo squirt of clear bright drops. *Anti-histamina.* We will watch her for a couple of hours. Perhaps you will explain to your friends about these painkillers. . . .

My friends.

Two hours later, all bundle into the truck. Blondes encased in macho airbags, collision proof up to 50 k.

Don't you want a ride back? Shortcropped blond, wide mouth and teeth perfect as her English, asking me.

I have things to buy.

We could ask them to wait. Playful smile. They seem very helpful.

I'll walk.

Walk back from Tulum town on trembling knees. Have I gotten so weak? Sunset. Horizon of palest rose and lavender. Half-moon half-risen.

We wanted you to have some of this papaya. We wanted to thank you. May we join you? Just for a minute?

Mariana, Renata, Brigit, Margo. Golden opportunity to study the golden ones up close.

Beulah, would you like to do a joint with us?

Coughlaugh into a cloud of smoke. No, not sisters. Brigit and I are Dutch. These two are Swiss. We travel together because of the Mexican men—I mean, we are friends but with four of us we handle them pretty well. Long smokestream, joint tweezered between long pink nails. Well, Mariana and Renata can. Brigit and I don't handle men.

Not if we can help it.

You look beautiful in that dress. Did you just buy it in town?

Evening cook-outs on little blue gas bottles. Packaged soup all the way from Switzerland. Pork sausage skewered on a driftwood fire.

Will you eat with us?

I ate in the village.

Liar.

[4 Feb 95]

The sex entrepreneurs are bringing their ice chests. Yesterday's grey ambulance converted now into a delivery truck, backed up to a big palapa hut a hundred metres south. Bucket brigades of beer and ice and silver bottles. A generator sputters—blasts reggae in its first bawling breath. Welcome to Jamaica west.

One Samaritan ride breaks the ice, shatters the cool blue distances all around us. Smiling jackals are close among us everywhere now, muzzles in crotches, getting to nose us, one big happy family.

Tell your friends we have decided to open the bar for them. Same prices as Tulum. Fresh fish anytime, french fries, clean salads. Taxi service to the discos at night. We know they like marijuana, tell them I can get anything—*mescalina*, peyote, mushrooms. Very safe. For you free, if you translate. For you free anyway, *preciosa*.

The billiard ball is called Diego. Sex jackal #1. Alpha dog.

Practise new manoeuvre: slip black one-piece on under long cotton dress. Take refuge in the sea. Vamp Ophelia in a sea of aquamarine.

[6 Feb 95]
Hola, buenas tardes, joven.

Red neckerchief, bob of Adam's apple. Grizzled stork, bringer of random offerings. Feed your babybird, she eats only what you bring, only when you come to her. Yesterday you didn't or the day before, just so now I can forgive you absolutely everything.

Afternoon. Sheltering under my palm parasol, my veil of flowered cotton, purdah of mirror-shades. All watch this beauty of girls. Silver squeal and slap of a water fight. Mermaid naval battle at the shores of Valhalla. Duelling houris. Renata, skinny ribs, bladed hips, high little breasts. One blue eye, sleepy, skewed. Brigit all legs all day all angles. Mariana of the full-wide breasts, nipples pale sand-dollars, tiny paunch. Margo's wide-shoulders and narrow-hips, wide witchery of mouth, hair of cropped straw. A furious strawberry thatch presses out from her white g-string— crazed red wig of a balding clown as she runs past.

We are stars of our own movie, in an abandoned movie house. Ready on the set, stand by . . . 5-4-3-2-1. All lurch into action: Drawn down to the water fight, the sex pack flexes, vogues, beams white teeth. Pathetic pick up lines, beachboys in polysester pants, they call up to me, ask for translations.

8 Feb 95
Diego the purple-brown muscleman kneels in the sand, his dewy muscle-gut blocks all sea due east. What are you writing *amiguita*, are you a poet a journalist, what? Are you here to tell my story? Why do you buy food only from the old man? He has not come for two days now. Why do you not come to the bar with the others?

Why is the sea so clear here.

Compared to what?

Coatzalcoalcos.

Ah, el Golfo de Mexico, America's toilet bowl. Diarrhea of the gringo rio Mississippi. This here, *amiguita,* this coast is *¡el Mar Caribe!*

Long walks south down the beach. Floating for hours in my dress of red kelp, flowers. Write only after dark. Write at night if at all. Become a nocturnal animal. Write down to exhaustion, down to drugged calm.

10 Feb 95

Nights of bonfires in front of the bar. Reggae, seventies pop rock. Please more Jackson Browne. Turn up the Walkman, turn it up—to this blank tape hiss, my symphony of SSSSSSSHHHHH.

Each night they come back guiltier with offerings, each night drunker, more blurred. Brigit brings beer, Margo a joint, tonight Mariana a whole tinfoil meal of rice fish and beans. You should come with us, they're really not so bad. Diego, the one with the bikinis that day? Little giggles and groans. He gave us these mushrooms.

You don't have to sleep with that guy to get us free drugs.

Brigit's right, Mariana, we can pay.

It's safer this way. Besides he was very . . . primitive. Will you try them with us Beulah?

She means the mushrooooms.

Mariana is always with guys like him.

While Renata waits for her prince.

One even better than Diego?

We hate it when they fight.

They know each other since the first day of public school.

Tomorrow Diego is driving us to some clubs in Playa Del Carmen. You could come, Beulah, please come. Dancing under the stars, it's amazing. Don't worry about the men, if we don't like them we just pretend to be lesbians too.

Through Margo's wide lips a tight slipstream of smoke and hiss. Beulah they are very excellent pretenders.

Margo's always wanting us to try.

Might as well, the way these two touch themselves at night, listening to us.

Shut up.

We do the same things. You just do them to yourselves.

And you, Beulah, what about you? Like men?

None I remember.
Come swimming with us.

12 *Feb 95*
Bright celt of moon overhead.

Killing God, primitive trick I've almost learned it.

Nocturnal creature, the moon's lemur-eyed daughter she writes in her shroud of half-moon light. She can be just like you, Golden Ones. She will dress like you. We will eat the local food, write down recipes. We will stay medicated. Each day more sophisticated in the primitive. Once a year when we come here. We come for love, we say how it ends.

Shooting stars of our own tragedies—keep filming keep filming—tanned and rich and wealthy just three weeks a year. The show goes on and on, bright stars of our lives. We feed the sun our flayed skins, the crusts of our wounds, we feed the mites and the fleas of the Insect Prince. We peel, we flay. He makes us a film of us, a book, a lampshade. Stay medicated. We numb our pain. Make believe we can afford this, we are really alive. We could live here. This is our life. Please. Here on this coast we can be who we are really are, only here. Please, just a little while.

My alpha dog walks up to us stroking his Tartar moustachio. *Amiguita, ¿qué onda?* all these nice Colombians slaving for years to bring drugs for the gringos and you don't even know how to smoke a joint correctly—look at you. And now you want peyote? These prices you women pay are stupid. It will be the same with *el peyotl.* Let me arrange this for you.

So let him.

[13 *Feb 95*]
Slalom through tropical nights! blizzards of stars—honk and swerve of trucks without headlights—movie-lot hayrides in this grey truckbox, standing up way UP. Nights of flint, stippling of musks, orchids of road-kill and skunk.

Beulah sit *down* at least.

Hold on.

No hold me up I want to stand—what am I too heavy for you movie stars? Little visionary assumes the position / stands frisked and legsspread mouth propped wide / harrowed on nightwind—

Beulah please.

Open air disco, nightblood throb. Pass through the frond arches. Welcome to the Parrot Dance Academy.[2] Valentine Specials: Two for One. Remember Beulah, only reefers, only smoke here it's safer—the men can't put drops in your drinks. Over *here* Beulah, stay close to us.

Part the meat curtain, go in and get your fortune told. Rhythmically. A disco ball whirling under a nearfull moon, how novel how new. All sway—stutterstep—under this trash and scatter of costume-jewel light this endless changeless shorebreak of drumbeat.

Feel it, this doomed boombox tattoo feel it needle you stain you for life. Stand close, arms wide, let the speakers breathe for you.

Oye bonita, how old are you can't be twenty-two marry me I loave you. Oh I loave you too.

Recipe I've come so far for—found AT LAST. At a disco, end of the treasure map. Disco balls, swaying meat / foxglove and morning glory librium and allegories *Mescalina cocaina*—*teonacatl* togogo gogirl. *Peyotl, Ololiqui*, the sacred *octli*.   And the secret ingredient—the occultest, the last—

Massive blood loss, pale harbinger of Ecstasy.

This is the recipe for obsidian wine. Toast the brides.

Those men over there, *señorita*, are sending you this drink for free. They love the way you dance so do I. Come to a staff party after work with me, I want to be your boyfriend for life.

Hola we are Fidelio and Alejandro, filmmakers from the capital. Fidelio will go soon to Canada. Dance with us but give me first your address.

Hello meet Glenda of the piercing eyes, mellow Enrique of the oily pompadour. We are artists. I am a muralist, my wife does *artes plásticas*. Come dance with us.

Slowdance with the twisted pompadour. Glenda waltzes off to nowhere. Come for a walk with me. My friends will worry. Please just for a minute. What about your?—My Glenda? No need to worry she likes her men younger. Do you remember my name still, it's Enrique. And yours?

Xochiquetzal.

Goddess of love. So happy to hear it, with tomorrow our *Día de los Enamorados*. I want to make love with you now.

Slip through the palms under the moon. Underfoot, palmshadows of burst umbrellas. No not on the sand Enrique, not in the sea. Do it standing up, if you're really a muralist. Against this tree.

I don't want to make this like dogs.
From behind or don't do it at all.
Why this way—?
Shut up and fuck.
Ridged palm trunk—plant pots stacked in a column—warm and harsh on the palms at the first rough thrust.
So you don't want to see my face—or are you watching for something?
Yes, Enrique, my ship to come in. *On this thin white flux, sad little ebb. One last jerkpush deathrattle and throb.* Finished already back there pompadour, *¿ya terminado?*
Come back wait a minute I want to make it again for you. Properly.
Hey Enrique—you wearing a watch?
Two A.M.
Not the time, how long was that—we get the new record?
Now run off and swap trophies with Glenda, make wigs of our scalps.

Walk a way up the beach, stand alone in this magic. Feel the seed draining like pus from a wound. Feel the slickness cooling. Squat to watch it bead on the sand . . . bright bent pearls running out of me, a flowing baroque.
Happy Valentine's, Donald.

Quiet ride home in the truck cab. Diego's hot palm high on my thigh as he drives. Everyone hears everything here, *amiga.* You owe me now.

Take a long clean swim naked in the nightsea. Last refuge last stop. Night of obsidian, moon lost in cloud. Margo swims out alone, brings me safe to shore.
Her salt sex like a sea shell, my tongue lapped in candyfloss cloud. The festival of love goes on and on and on. Endlessly. Send in the clowns.

[14 Feb 95]
To do:
1) Apologize. To Brigit, about Margo . . . we couldn't help ourselves. We couldn't help me.
2) Walk to town.
3) Call home to Donald. Wish us a happy anniversary.
4) Wrap notes in red ribbons. Tie them in a bow, our correspondence on loss. Send it surface mail, send it slow very slow. At a snail's pace, crawling

back to you, Gentle Reader, Gentle Don, ready or not, here comes nothingness. Scarlet letter bombs with a two-month fuse.

Long walk back from Tulum town on trembling knees. Sun stuck high
overhead. All the blondes are packing. Things are getting too crazy,
Beulah. We were robbed last night—Margo and Brigit, anyway. Better
check your stuff.

My notebooks.

. . . Not you, Beulah? nothing lost? We can't figure this out. We two
have cameras, you a computer, your Walkman. Nothing touched.

Beulah you should come with us. *Sweet sweet Margo. Brigit's rocket red
glare.*

If you ask me, I think it's time she went home.

Maybe Brigit's right. You can be away too long.

*Brigit come back, there's something I wanted to say . . . Wait, wait. Please. Tell
Margo you love her still. It was meaningless, meaninglessness itself.*

17 Feb 95

RED LETTER DAY of days.

Wobble back to Tulum town. The last time. Too weak to walk it again.

Make a phone call. Post last message in bottle. Fill with kerosene and light. Little Molotov cocktail with festive parasol. *Soon we are done Don and if you concentrate, you may find that conquests no longer fascinate* . . . 3

Happy Deathday, Donald. Three centuries my joy is a cataract still fresh and bright, filling my eyes. You too can be brought to bleed, you too can be brought to see.

Near sunset the vendor comes. Too late old man.

The other young ladies, *las rubias*, have gone?

Yes old stork. No point in coming back. I am free of you.

Moonrise full from a pan of salt mist. Not full—its edge corroded, eaten through. Xochiquetzal has missed the full moon somehow. Learned Whore, how could you let this happen to you?

Night, a bonfire far up the beach. Here at the palm thatch parasol, my parody of home, our little family down to two. Mistress of flowers and alpha dog, her last new bestfriend. Fun for fetch and scavenger hunts. For wedding rites that rage on and in and up under this acid moon. *Collection time, Valentine, for all the free drugs, the sacred drink.* If you give it to strangers at discotheques, *preciosa*, you can give to me. If you won't tell your name if you say you only watch the sea—then take it like this. Feel the scorch and sear so familiar, nostalgia of fire. Up me. Hot skinny slide, enormous billiard balls, slapstorm of thrusts that lifts my feet off the ground makes me walk on my palms / wheelbarrow races of one—me the hod.

Scan scan furious scan the night sea for signs. Scanning the horizon. For her ship to come in. Rattling fronds, endless endless grunts, thud of falling coconuts in the sand near her head. And then again. When he's gone she squats to lick clean her bearclaws—curved, fastidious—from these battered hives boiling white amaranth. Ever ready for more she scans the night sea. Gently licking at the shore. All horizons narrow to this. Xochiquetzal is praying for oblivion, the Sacred Harlot prays for death. She writes She wants to die. Sacred Way #49—Death by Coconut.

She writes, If you cannot learn how to laugh here, *mi amor*, this place will kill you.

Hurry. I have laughed with you all I know how.

Bonfire ebbing down to coals. Empty bottles, music.

Ah good *amiga*, you have come for more. Meet these our new friends. María and Lydia. My friends have brought them from Cancún for this one night of *fiesta*.

Now watch miniskirted María and Lydia absent-mindedly fingered like peaches at a mini mart. Every now and then a disappearance back into the trees. A woman's laughter—see the sandjackal ears cock. But all eyes are on Xochiquetzal, dancing alone in her red flowerdress.

Billiard balls strokes his Tartar moustaches. *Amiga,* my friends say they are angry at me. We all buy our drugs together, we all share with you. They pay for prostitutes from the city while you give me everything for free.

To everything you must submit. Sacred harlot. To everything, Haetara. It is ancient, this work that you do, this sin of originality. Scared scarred nightslut of beauty, would you pull back now, so close to the end so far from Start? After all you've been through.

Slut, they know your name. Now they come for you.

§ *Saved by the infantry.*

Soldiers arrive at the bonfire, flames glinting sparks in buckles and gunbarrels. High boots still gleam at the tops—stovepipes dipped in flourdust—bakers with truncheons, beachcombing welders, their visors up. Six hungry young Mexican faces, eyes dull under beetlebrow helmets. An older Maya sergeant a little apart, helmet under his arm, tough face under a bowl cut.

Pale officer in a legionnaire's cap steps out of the shadows. *Buenas noches, compañeros.* No don't stop the fiesta for us. We were just on patrol. Making sure no one needed our assistance.

No. No trouble, *Capitán Offalitch.*

Lieutenant. As you know very well, Diego. Carry on. As you were. We will continue our work. *Hasta luego.* Yes, see you again very soon. . . .

Don't worry about them *preciosa*, we will protect you. Our boss knows their Colonel very well. They play golf together in Cancún. The Lieutenant was just letting us know they are in the area. To be *discreto.*

Only when you don't see them you must worry. Sometimes looking for guns they find drugs by accident. That is embarrassing to all concerned. About guns one must be careful. Very patriotic, the Mexican Lieutenant and his boss. Both from Monterrey—bunch of cheapskates. They would make their mother pay for her own cocaine.

I have had an idea. Tomorrow night all my friends will like to fuck you. Unless maybe the Mexican lieutenant instead. I could tell he likes you. Think it over. It would be easier for you. And a favour to me. I will explain to him carefully where and how you like it. Watching the sea. And not to ask your name. If you like you don't even have to see his face. . . .

SATURDAY

HER FIRST CALL came February 14th. Then February 17th, then nothing for almost three weeks. But by Saturday, March 18th, there were two calls a day.

The date's set for Easter dinner, Professor. A meal fit for an epicure like you, for a king. Know you love barbecue. . . . RSVP. . . . Everyone's confirmed but you. . . .

RSVP to what, to where? Where *was* she?

He tried to discuss it with Madeleine. She didn't want to hear. "Whatever it takes, Donald. Just make this go away." He could unplug the phone and answering machine and hide. He could request an unlisted phone number. Friends and colleagues and contacts would have to be notified, and ways devised to explain why. To explain how.

Yes, how.

He could call Beulah's family. The surgeon and the socialite. *Your daughter is having some kind of crisis, right out of the blue, apparently. All these calls—why me? Well there were some . . . complications back when I was her advisor. Yes, just before your prodigy quit school. Sorry, and good luck. If there's anything else I can do . . .*

Everything is different now. How the world changes in a week, a night, an hour. A month ago he was growing into the life he and Madeleine had made. It was something real and sane and solid for their daughter, for her future. Something he could take some credit for building.

How different everything is now. Brittle silences shattered by the jangling of the phone. It's never her. Never while they're home. The man and wife take turns finding excuses to run to the corner store, files forgotten at the office.

Saturday's forecast: High grey gauze of cloud, mercury falling, hard. Slow rise of tension to the breastbone, a blunt pressure.

In their daughter's eyes burns a bright anxious fever. Teething, probably, the paediatrician said yesterday. Catherine starts to cough. Once or twice. Soon more frequently. Teething does not make a baby cough. They spend supper time at Foothills Emergency.

"It's nothing, Dr. Gregory. Her temperature is not even 39—"

"How high is 39?" This is his daughter, he needs Fahrenheit. One hundred point two. Hundred and *two*? Sir, *point* two. . . .

As the troubled family comes through the door from the garage, the answering machine winks hello. They put their daughter to bed.

"She knew we were out, again," Madeleine says. "I'm telling you, that was not long distance. *Listen . . .*" She plays the call again.

"We can't be sure. Technology today . . ."

"She's *watching* us. Has a call come with us home—even once? How many times are we going to call that coincidence? Thursday I took Catherine for a walk. *Fifteen minutes.* Yesterday one came while I was in the shower."

"So she knows when you're showering too."

Madeleine stands before him in a full-length flannel nightgown. Tiny purple flowers on a cream background. It is unbuttoned at the neck. He sees the cords at her throat merge softly with her collarbones. He no longer looks readily into her eyes.

"We are being watched, Don. We are being *stalked*."

They are standing at the entrance to the kitchen. Madeleine moves stealthily to the living room window, parts the drapes with a finger. "She's probably out there."

"Where—in *this* cold? Show me a car we don't recognize."

"I want you to call the police."

"And tell them what? Somebody keeps calling? No, Officer, we haven't actually seen her. No, sir, no threats either—"

"She knows our schedules—"

"What does she *say*, Constable? Well, she wants us to do dinner."

"Knows about our barbecues—"

"*Everybody* barbecues."

They have been married for almost ten years. It comes to him that she is about to ask how much he tells his one-night stands. He thinks he will answer by asking how much she used to tell hers. He is thinking it might make everyone feel better if she hit him.

"She's studied you and now she's watching us. She's out there. I can feel it." Madeleine turns away from the window, faces him. He sees how tired she is. He must also be this tired. "What does she *want*, Don? What does she want from you?"

But he does not answer, he does not know how. He has withdrawn, an escape trick of his. She is already on her way up to bed. He has a lot on his mind. He too feels that she is near—how close? The sexual predator has become the quarry. The calls are not long distance anymore.

How long has she been watching? Planning . . . planning what? It comes to him, again, how much he has to lose.

His daughter is ill, his wife is exhausted. As he is, but he busies himself. He does not want sleep. He tends to his daughter, checks on her twice an hour. He sits in her room, or in the kitchen while the milk warms. Once, near four, he feeds her mashed potatoes and apple sauce.

At dawn his wife finds him dozing on the leather couch in the den.

She is covering him with a yellow woollen blanket. He sits up. "With Catherine sick and you not sleeping nights, I'm wiped out." She looks it. Her eyes hollow and blurred, skin drawn tight at her temples. "I need rest, I need to *sleep*. Just a few days. If you wouldn't mind . . . sleeping down here. Don, honey, I don't want you to misunderstand. Just for a couple of days. Just till we work this out."

"Won't it make things worse?"

"No. Not worse."

He is aware now of the one thing he has not proposed, has not offered to do. The one thing on his mind and Madeleine's. See her. *Go to her.* He has been telling himself he will not play into Beulah's hands. Emotional blackmail—we do not negotiate with terrorists. Not in our state.

It's over. She ended it. And anyway what would he say?

There is nothing to say.

But the truth is simpler. He is afraid to face her. The prospect fills him with dread. He has long harboured a dim idea of the minuscule events set to deflect the entire course of a life—a rotted rung, a film of ice, a quarrel in a parking lot. It is the butterfly of chaos theory, that flaps its wings in Canton, to trigger a typhoon in Madagascar.

He is exhausted but begins to see now what it is she wants. He thinks he understands at last.

She wants him to murder her.

He returns to Catherine's room, watches her sleeping, a sheen of fever on her cheeks, her face working, a restless furrowing of her brow. Her eyes make sidelong shifts beneath the petals of her lids, soft as moth wings. Everything moves him tonight, in his shallow way. Straining at the darkness, he senses, in the air around her crib, slippages, shadows, shapes of collapse. Tears threaten at any moment to scald him—hot, fat, sputtering gobs of mawk, painful in their superficiality, like burns in the first degree.

[18 Feb. 1995]

SWAMP OPHELIA, soggy manatee slipping out to sea, adrift under *el Peyotl's* hotstarred constellations . . . smear of prisms in a red dwarf shift. Tiny disk under the vast flaming stars far from shore she spins . . . weightless. Yardarms snapped little sailor drifting off the map. To wrestle with dragons, to swim with seamonsters.

She will not write it. She will not write this death. She has learned a new trick see she is never too old never too close to the end. *Listen* instead. To the breathless roar inside these seashell ears, a nightsea roar that pulls her down into a well of raven ink. Feel the stitches soften. Feel the hole reopening. Black oceans welling up, she is drowning in the hole in her chest.

Drift, then. Sink down on this gulfstream to the sea's deep trenches. Follow where it leads. . . .

But no . . . it only carries her in. Gently in. Mustn't hurry. Drowsy head bumping bumping on the hourglass sand, run aground on unknowing's vastest sea. Turn and kiss the grainy glitter. Claim this new shore for the Science Queen.

Lie and heave a bit. Try to keep the buttons down—retch a sear of bile, they said it would be bitter said take them with bread. But I am not afraid of bitterness, bile is my good-humoured friend. Watch the clouds slip in from the west, hitch a lift—now, little explorer. On. Up and on. To the bonfire, dead ahead, not far left. She has debts to pay, party favours to share. On Nanautzin, Scabby One. Ever on, *Bubosillo*, one last test.

The more she lets them touch the less she has to feel.

Call the night to fill her—darkfelt rag that plugs this emptiness. Walk on. The found must first be lost.

Lowering swab of cloud, soft hover of far off pulses, spectral colours—sheet lightning crackling. Over the sea a sheen of violet, faintest green. Pale sand a cream tickle of velvet underfoot. It crunches like fresh snow in new winter boots. Barefoot she steps, how chilly in this dress.

A soft whisper from behind—she turns to say hi—to the swiftshape rush of black hounds casting swirling without sound. Faintest whines that close to snap and chop riprending her flowerdress to allfalldown to hush. Hollow clop of jaws, pearlgleam teeth hideous but no pain no pain—is this how it happens how it ends—without pain? chopped down for kindling—

Hotmeat breath in face on thighs and knees.

Then gone. The sand is whispering. . . .

Try to stand try to stand. Judder of elbows, shuddering knees. Warm forehead propped in cool cool sand. Shooting streaks of violet, ear canals red coils of drybaked heat—little ear-ovens of solar energy. Only now the horror comes. A writhing up the back—churn and tumble of guts— hot clear scald of bile again over these hands of accident, into this sandy haircurtain in clumps.

Crawl then. Crawl, if you can't walk. Crawl to the rainbow fire.

Closer now. Flames flutter and start like jewels. All the wondrous shades!—blues and lemons, vermilion and rose. She will draw strength from this—from the holocaustic heat / flame's cauterous tongues— these cruel blasts of laugh for ambience. Stand, stand and greet your new oldfriends.

Muchachos, look! Our friend has been swimming out there in the dark with the sharks—all alone no man for protection such a crime—*¿verdad? ¿no están de acuerdo, hombres?*—and so very dangerous. *Ven amiga,* come- come to the fire, warm yourself you are shaking you are naked under- neath let us help warm you up. Are you hurt? your dress—who did this, dogs? you are sure? we are here to service and protect. Come I will pour rum on you. *Y un traguito para ti*—*toma, ándele. Otro.* Swallow it all at once there that's good. And once more for your wound. Turn to the fire—no not so close not so rumsoaked—here this way so I can see too. Ah, not so bad, maybe a bite, maybe not. Hold still.

This will only hurt a little.

You will be fine sit for a while then maybe you will dance with my friends. To warm yourself. You have been thinking about yesterday, what I said. You are ready right now? Good tonight we will all dance with you.

The Great Hunter cranks and cranks the handle. She is that music box all wound up. Watch her dance, dance nameless with her new friends.

Come for her now, sweet Xochiquetzal. All these men. She is still afraid of this. To go all the way to the end. But you, precious flower, she will follow you. Dance closer, please, slower for her, whisper sweetly in her ear. . . .

Ah, Captain Offlitch. She is here as you asked. As you see she has already started to dance with us.

Thank you, Diego. You and your people may go now.

Greet the smiling young masks of an ancient martial loathing—*slut*, they know her now. Hatchet faces glue-dead eyes. Remember they are only boy soldiers fighting for toys / all buckles and belts—boys with guns / running glue.

Now *señorita* I will dance with you.

Yes dance with the tall Captain—pulling rank in the rancorous swirl of feral revelry of soldiery and jackalry mingling so angrily now—no no cut in nicely don't quarrel one at a time there's enough to go round and round.

Off the tail-tucked jackals slink into the palms. The Maya sergeant not far behind.

Slowdance now with the tall blondbeard legionnaire / roaming shatter-hands over the ass / hike up the dress / put on a bravo tango show for the enlisted men. Well yes okay Captain if you want to impress let's show them your spectacular FIREDANCE. No we haven't practised yet but give it a whirl / till the flames lick up like jewelled birds to peck at this rumdrunk serpent skirt / till slim coral snakes lift from this seaweed hem in a green-wood hiss—too hot for you Captain even in boots?—her gorgonkiss.

Captain Slowdance stalks up the beach.

So we pull rank in reverse pull dress over head to entertain the enlisted men. Who needs a flowerscreen, *compañeros*, when we are all such good friends just us kids nekkid under nightshirts let her go first—*olé!* all the fireside boytoy soldiers laugh uproarious / stamp out the flameshirt weft specially for her. Liquid tar in their conscript eyes. Hardening. Well OK if you must touch her run your hands all over all at once—come rub your genie numb. Go on. Head to foot yes all the way down she feels it now a slowdance of fear thrilling her guts—so nice to be kneaded demi-urgently cupped / in the palms of new friends in boots dipped in ashtray sand and flourdust. The more you touch the less she feels. Dance closer dance harder—this is *cumbia*? Smell the musk of fuck gathering / feel its answer in her now netherly—oh yes she will eat your disease.

Feed the hole.

Leave them the body now. Like a tip. Just cast it aside, there look up at the bright night so wide *open*, spirals of sparks—smoke-dragons in diamond-back quilts, vision serpents writhing up—stare ever on ever skyward through these eyes brimming prisms—*stare on* as one final fiery

THOUGHT scales now the pyramid of the last First Cause—THIS IS HOW IT ENDS. Tomorrow these eyes will know what to do, when the last humpback firedance is done, at dawn she will burn these eyes blind to everything but you—track the sun from the kerosene sea up through the dawn's red palaces. Track it unblinking up to the nightsun's eternal noon, with eyes burnt cold as coals—for you jealous Apollo, for you. From now on she sees no one else.

Sweetest bliss of decision. . . . Savour the insightful moment, this last night of eyesight in gaza—so SEE! See the quartered moon drawn free of the sea, see the rent cloudbellies gleam—watch abalone figurines prance to the shore on slippers of pearl—to carry her on in the glow in the sand on the rocks in the sea. Carry her on to the altar of dawn.

So she can never write this death. So she does not have to go on.

No no friendly friends she is touched by you just enough just now. Come back at noon she'll see you then, to look deep in your eyes and find fellow feeling there. Stop. Hands off here let her show something new this is something else she can do—make angels in the sand for you.

This is her miracle.

Stand in a circle now holding hands bulging pants watch her skinny-dip backstroke in the cool coral sand. Arms and legs flailing out little wings and angel skirts.

One private-eyed tar with blackjack boots / with a lazy kiss of a pointy toe flicks a nudge of sand up between her thighs. A moment of pause, of tarry cogitation then all join in the tarpit fun / hysterical highkick—heap her high with sand only feet no hands all play bury your fallen comrade till she goes blind in a sandstorm of contempt.

Hear a bell's musical tinkle . . . *oigan compañeros,* watch this—this will put out her fire, eh?—hear the chorus of laughs, buckling chimes, answering. . . .

Hombres páranse. Ahorita mismo.

The laughter stops, the chiming stops the fountain plash—all stops.

Sit up and see, blink the sand from her eyes. Who is this now-and-ever more surprises, is her work never done will the end never come?

A tiny white vision walks to the fire, always room for one more, have you come for her? She must remember to remember this, write it in braille tomorrow at noon. On he comes tiny Maya man all in white wading through bloodsmoke trailing sparks—a comet train of glowing cotton that stops. Stands stonestill. Eyegouges of fireshadow, impassive

Maya face a soft brass mask. Its high broad brow *frowns the whole fuck carousel down.*

Their Maya sergeant surges out of hiding in the trees, the strain of shame in his face an urgency.

Good evening, *caballeros.* I am sorry to interrupt. *Compadre,* Sergeant, I wonder if you would shut the music off. The boy soldiers stand round all wound up all unbuckled—balled fists / fists in the balls—needing so bad for something good to kill. The little vision waits till the sergeant is done then the two Mayas speak—cascade of soft glots glissades / high clicks and glides.

Next Captain Slowdance strides back to stand TALL—spread-legged tripod—surveyor's hands parallaxed at his back.

Sergeant Dzul!—who is this person?

He is respected, Captain. *Un poeta, un maestro, un curandero.* With many friends in our region.

Just tell me what he said.

That you and your men are far away from your loved ones. He said this is not what we do with women here. Or in the villages where the mothers and sisters of these young men here still live. He asked that I explain how it is with us.

Ah. . . . Well, my Maya healer friend . . . it is good you are so widely known. *Y gracias por su comprehensión.* But understand also that it is not always healthy to attract so much notice. Too many friends might turn your head. Completely.

Thank you, Captain Hooflick. I will take to heart your advice. Now, with your leave, she will be coming with me. Beulah, I have your things. Pick your dress up. Now, there, that's good. Put it on.

SUNDAY   [*Sunday, March 19, 1995*]

CATHERINE IS FEELING much better. The sky is a soft, dove-grey.
The temperature has dropped to minus twenty-five. There is a heavy
snow warning for late evening. Make ready.

They have put away a hearty breakfast. Their faces are brave. They
are eager to leave the house, together, for a few hours. They bundle
Catherine up in layer upon layer of wool, the outermost a robin's-egg
blue. Casually, on the way out, Madeleine asks him to switch off the
answering machine. The car is warm after a night in the garage. At a
careful speed they make their curving way down one icy freeway
named after a vanished Indian tribe, and up one named after another.
The two meet at a river whose ancient name has been displaced.
Between upthrust crusts of ice, the river glimmers a deep, mint green
as they drive over the bridge.

Madeleine's parents live at the top of Coach Hill in an exclusive
condominium complex designed and built by her father. Though there
are still only a couple of inches of snow on the ground, Jack Cole is
out snow-blowing the driveway as the black Saab pulls up. A small,
solid man hunched over a thin plume of snow, puffs of steam issuing
from between his lips. His glasses are opaque with frost. He is bare-
handed and coatless. White hair pinches out from under a blue and
white woollen toque. He offers a stiff, ruddy smile of welcome. To
smile can be painful at minus twenty-five. With great reluctance he'd
traded his shovel in for the snow-blower, but only after the second
heart attack.

He and Madeleine's father started off tolerating one another but
have wound up almost friends. The proximity of a final heart failure
brought out a mellow sweetness in the man, a childlike pleasure in
simple things that Donald began noticing after Catherine was born.
Sunday drives up to Coach Hill have become a regular event.

The house is furnished in quiet luxury. The roast goose is a triumph, the Oregon Pinot a revelation, the brandy a *folle blanche*
Armagnac. The afternoon turns out to be just the tonic they all need.
Catherine, scaling furniture and grandparents like the baby primate
she is, appears almost completely recovered. She basks in the sunny

certainty of unclouded, unconditional love from every quarter, in every lap. After dinner, while the men sit hunched over snifters, the women load the dishwasher and tidy up. It is quietly agreed that Catherine will stay up on the hill for a few days, with Madeleine coming up for dinner each evening.

As they reach the bridge on the way home, the car skews slightly on a patch of ice. He slows.

"Mom's worried."

"She said that?"

"She was hoping we had put all this behind us when Catherine was born."

They stop at a traffic light, the only car on the road. Although it is not quite eight o'clock, it has been dark for two hours. At the spring equinox the sun sets in Calgary at about six-thirty, preceded, on days like this, by a long grey dusk. It is snowing more heavily now. Huge, wasp-paper flakes rare in weather so cold. A dry, fey beauty falls . . . flakes dropping out of darkness into the headlights. Flights of crystalline craft angle and bank to touch down on slant, molecular gear. All come to rest in a glinting, silica sea. . . . His wintry world has never been so lovely and precious to him.

"Did she ask what it was about?"

"She asked if she could help."

"Tell her not to worry."

And for the rest of the ride home they do seem not to worry. In the dashlight glow he sees her reach over, feels her hand, palm down, wedge itself snugly under his leg and against the leather seat. Over the years, how many miles have the two of them driven like this? He turns on the radio. Something by Haydn is ending.

He eases through the intersection and up the freeway home. The car gains speed through what seems an inexhaustible migration of moths on diamond wings, papery multitudes smashed without violence in the headlights.

Another traffic light. The freeway ahead curves up and away in a soft, orange strand of sodium lamps. As the car gains speed he feels through the steering wheel the shift in surfaces—slippage, stutter and grip—ice, packed snow, asphalt. In a news bulletin a provincial politician addresses the people of the empty ranchlands. His is the furry-tongued voice of repentant adolescence, austerity, alcoholism. He's had a belt or two again this night. It is the speech of a lackey, a quisling groomed for this common touch of his, for wrecking the common good. Man of the people, bred to turn on his own—a jowly, gimlet-eyed, half-pint cannibal in a Zellers suit. Another populist who despises democracy, fronting another government that hates government, a common-sense revolution backed by creationists.

At the wheel the driver has worked himself into a complacent pique. Forces are set to extinguish the world he has known. An extinction all the more devastating to remember for this day of reprieve. But his belly is full and the brandy flickers in him with a soft, certain glow. They drive through the enveloping night in a well-built foreign car.

He glances over at Madeleine. It is a long time since he has bothered himself about any of this, but he has been learning the price of turning one's back on the past . . . he knows this is why he hates this politician.

He thinks ahead to their destination, now five minutes away. Feels a flush of anticipation thickening in his groin. With Catherine out of harm's way, they will be more relaxed. They will fight back, push back the gloom invading the house. He will take down a fresh bottle of port from the wine rack in the dining room, throw a quick glo-log on the hearth, fill one goblet brimful with thick, dark grape. He will feel her lips, still chapped with cold, nuzzling his throat, release a warm slippery dram from his lips into hers. As husband and wife sink into firelight her slate-blue eyes will widen—once again the madcap tomboy playing Indian with the older boys. He will hear the sweet laughter he has heard so many times at the top of their toboggan ride—ohh, no-o- two drawn-out tones of complicity; they gather speed—precious peals of throaty laughter, so-o-o unlady-like. Then the long, smooth glide . . . his silence, her murmurings for each dip and rise. Like closed captions for the hard of touch. Never words, just her soft hum of ecstasy. She has given so much, these ten years. How much has been returned?

Where is she, is she laughing now?—he strains to hear her laughter as he writes. . . .

He has just seen how close he's come to falling in love with his wife.

The black car pulls up the driveway and stops at the garage door. He switches off the headlights. They sit for a moment longer, reluctant to break the spell. He rolls down his window. Snow continues to fall past the blue-green light at the street corner. A sovereign weightlessness falls from nowhere to nowhere, under a law more like whimsy than gravity. He angles his head out the window and looks up to catch a flake on his tongue. Overhead, a vast hopper of flakes tips through the dark in a soft hurtling of owls. . . .

He rolls the window up.

As he switches the car off, the announcer is introducing Bach, a fugue in D minor.

He starts to open the door and looks at her. She has not moved, has been watching him. He pauses expectantly. "Have we brought this on ourselves?" she asks.

"*No*. Don't say that."

"Something we did to each other years ago? Something still in this house?"

"Madeleine . . . let's go in—come on."

She looks just past him out the car window, begins again. "I shoplifted some clothes when I was thirteen. A white camisole and a pair of blue jeans. I had the money. For weeks I wore them everywhere, they became my favourite things. One night I lost my mind for five minutes and told Mom. The next day she made me take them back. I'd worn them already a hundred times. Can't I just pay for them? No. We're going to give them back together. She told me to wash them but I couldn't. I ran the washer and dryer empty. I remember inhaling the scent from the paper bag they were folded up in before we got out of the car.

"Then I gave them back, Don. I feel like that now, you know?"

He reaches over to take her hand. "We'll get through this."

"Maybe I didn't earn it, maybe I haven't paid enough . . ."

In her face it is clear how badly she needs to believe whatever he will tell her next. He walks around the car to her door. Opens it. Takes her by the hand. She follows him up the front steps, not letting go. He leads her through the living room of the life they have built. He feels there isn't much time. It is true. He does not take the time to light the fire, does not even turn on a light. A thin bluish glow falls between the drapes. He does not go to the wine rack, does not open port. He leads her to the couch, leaves her boots and long suede coat on, flakes dwindling to mist. He fumbles at her fly, pulls her jeans down to her ankles and kneels her on the couch. Their need is great, they have so little time, just enough light. There is no laughter tonight. He bends her like a bow. The melodic line he now plucks from her is of a woman toiling over a long, broken slope.

In the darkness, his own silence is intact.

Later, when much has changed, he will tell himself she was right, that there was something in the house, let in long before, a cruel spirit to be propitiated that cared nothing for reprieves. But at the time, for the briefest instant, his shame is intense. He burns with a black self-loathing. The moment passes.

Lovers are cruel sometimes. It's unavoidable, he tells himself. They find ways to apologize.

In the bluish light he glances across to the cold fireplace. He gets up and places a glo-log on the grate, turns on the gas, lights it and lowers the flame. Another candle's truth would be too much.

He brings over a glass of port. She is still on the couch, sitting now. She asks for her own glass. She has taken her boots off. Her jeans are stretched out on the floor. He is dressed, his belt unbuckled. A shiver, a deep swallow, she wraps her long tan coat tightly around her. She puts her white-stockinged feet side by side on the glass-brick coffee table, her chin on bare knees pressed tight together. With a quiet dignity she says they had better talk while they still know how.

"Okay."

"The truth."

"All right."

"Why you?"

"She's obsessed."

"There've been others. They never did this."

He has his answer ready. "I'm not sure, but she may have convinced herself I've stolen her work—some of her ideas."

"Did you?"

"She's confused."

"Confused? She's *nuts*, Don, crazy as a fucking loon."

"Is that a professional opinion?"

"As a loon. You heard her."

"Maybe I did," he says, "but that was a long time ago."

Her voice is very soft. "I said, *heard*."

He blinks.

"But she wasn't like the others, was she, Don."

"It wasn't all craziness back then," he begins. He is looking at her feet on the coffee table.

"Not like them at all. *Was* she."

"She was . . . *gifted*. But I would not stay on as her advisor. It's never easy to watch a career blow up. In a case like that, it was criminal. A terrible, sickening waste."

"Did you use her work?"

"*No*. I mean she got me started in a new direction, but no. Our approaches, our interests were completely different. You know how bored I was with what I'd been doing. . . ."

"How many dozens of times have we sat together on this couch and talked about work? You've read to me snippets from a hundred papers. Lazy ones, dumb ones, plagiarized, bright . . . Have I ever once heard you talk about this great prodigy?"

"Her name—"

"Don't . . . don't say it."

"Madeleine, you're acting like—"

"Don't say anything. Think how much easier that'll be for us both."

"I swear to God, I have had no contact whatsoever with this girl for over a year."

"I've never asked you to lie to me. I'm not asking now."

"Will you *listen?*"

"Christ knows, I've been no angel."

"It's *over*. I swore on Catherine's eyes. You never asked me for that, either," he says. Her eyes shimmer. "That much you know about me . . . Don't you?"

She nods, drawing her lips together, biting down.

"No more, I told you," he says. "I *love* our life."

He kisses away the tears that start down her cheeks when she smiles.

"I'm proud of us, Don. We found a way to give ourselves a second chance. How many people can say that?" she asks fiercely, her small chin lifting. "You know how rare that is?"

"First thing tomorrow I call the phone company—then her parents. Just ask them how she is, say we had a worrisome call. Leave it at that. If we spot her within a mile of this house, we call the cops."

"We can't take any chances. Not with Catherine."

"Never."

"I need to know you support me in this."

"Completely," he says. "In the meantime we leave the machine switched off—business calls be damned for a couple of days, if that's okay." She nods. "Unplug the bloody phone too."

"No, what if mom calls? About Catherine."

"Then let's bring her *home*. Tomorrow."

"I want to hear what the police have to say first." She sees his reluctance. "Why? Why do you keep avoiding this?"

"I just don't want to send the stormtroopers crashing in on her."

"After what's she's done to us you still want to *protect* her?"

"She hasn't done anything yet."

"How can you say that? Can you have the slightest fucking idea what she's got planned for us?"

"She said Easter—"

"That's weeks away. No, it *has* to be sooner. I can feel it," she says, her voice low. "I can't keep doing this. I'm afraid to answer the phone—every noise in the house. I can't sleep . . . and you can't either."

"I'll deal with it. Tomorrow."

"Fine," she says, voice flat. Getting up abruptly she takes one of the glasses off the coffee table and starts towards the kitchen.

He gets up to follow her, snatching up his glass from the table. Though she has rounded the corner, the kitchen light has not come on. "We can call them anonymously any time we need to," he calls after her.

Later, two months later, when it is much too late, he will wonder how they could be caught so devastatingly off guard by a thing they had thought about constantly for days.

He nearly collides with her in the darkness as he comes around the corner. She is standing still. Her glass gleams dully in one hand. He sees the blue clock readout on the dishwashwer: 11:46. Another light blinks red, a call counter reads: 1.

"How?" She has half turned to him as his hand touches her shoulder.

"I don't know."

"You said you'd switch it off!" Her eyes are wide in the darkness.

"I did. I'm telling you. . . ." But he does know how, if not yet why. "There's a feature," he says. "For emergencies. You can switch these things back on over the phone."

"You knew that?"

"It has to ring something like thirty-eight times." He hears a faint note of pleading.

The loose stone, the rotted rung, minute deflections of a life's chosen course.

He starts forward. She intercepts him, her small hands spread wide on his chest. Her eyes look searchingly into his face. "Erase it, Don. Let's just erase it."

"No."

"You *like* these messages—is that it?"

He feels something going tight within him. "It's probably not even her." He closes his hands over her wrists and steps by.

"Don't do this." She elbows past him and stands with her back to the counter. "What if I erase it?"

They face each other for an instant, chests rising and falling. He glances away. Through a window he sees snow falling, a dim gesticulation at the outer reaches of the backdoor light. Their eyes have adapted to the darkness. He is about to say he needs to figure things out—what she's up to. How to protect them. How to fix this.

"Not one fucking word. It's all over your face."

"I'll just listen. You go on up."

He will wonder, when he has lost the right to ask, whether it might have made the slightest difference—made it all less final, so much less inescapable—if they had not just made love, her hopes lying so near the skin. If she had not felt, just then, the stretched barrels of her vitals collapsing, the cold tracks down her thighs, her cries and his silences still in her ears.

"Just *call*, Don—get it straight from the whore's mouth. What are you afraid of? Call her! *Go* on."

He feels a whiteness fluttering up behind his eyes. He is afraid of the violence it contains. He feels it all coming to pieces. "Go to bed." It's all he can trust himself to say. How can he fix things, get it all back the way it was, if she won't let him listen?

She stands in the darkness in the kitchen of her house, her cheeks burning with fury, smarting at the indignity. In her house. "Don't forget where you're sleeping." She brushes past him and stops at the bathroom door beside the stairwell. She turns on the light but turns back to face him, light spilling over her shoulders, darkening her face. "You listen. Go ahead. But you get her out of our life, while we still have one. You get her out of your head. . . ."

He cannot see her face, but will remember until memory fails, the gesture like a dancer's plié, right knee bent, left out-turned, propped on the ball of an arched foot . . . the way the right wrist is flexed, the scooping, scouring motion between her legs as she hunches slightly forward. He will remember the light glistening on her fingertips as she raises them to him. Her voice rasps, breathless.

"You get *her* out of *me*."

He has not moved, he does not speak.

She closes softly, a bar of light under the door. He hears the water running, presses *play*. As he listens he does not notice the light go out and the door silently open. Hating herself, she too listens. When she has heard the end, she calls out a question, from the bottom of the stairs. He turns, startled to find her there.

"Donald . . . Those guests of hers, this party. Were they . . . *gods?*"

He sits in the living room until the fire burns out. He wraps himself in the yellow blanket and walks into the den. He puts on jeans and a T-shirt. The hardwood floor is icy under his bare feet. He lies on the leather couch but does not sleep. After an hour or two he gets up and listens again. The voice is coaxing, hushed. He will remember it more clearly than the precise order of the words.

He erases the message, unplugs the machine.

Diuturna enfermedad de la Esperanza,
que así entretienes mis cansados años
y en el fiel de los bienes y los daños
tienes en equilibrio la balanza;

que siempre suspendida, en la tardanza
de inclinarse, no dejan tus engaños
que lleguen a excederse en los tamaños
la desesperación o confianza:

¿quién te ha quitado el nombre de homicida?
Pues lo eres más severa, si se advierte
que suspendes el alma entretenida;

y entre la infausta o la felice suerte,
no lo haces tú por conservar la vida
sino por dar más dilatada muerte.

JUANA INÉS
DE LA CRUZ

Alan Trueblood, trans.

Hope, long-lasting fever of men's lives,
constant beguiler of my weary years,
you keep the needle of the balance poised
at the still centre between joys and fears.

You hover at the midpoint, disinclined
to move this way or that, lest your deceit
allow too free a hand to either state:
unbounded confidence, abject defeat.

Who was it claimed you never killed a man?
That you're a slayer anyone can tell
from the suspense in which you keep the soul
poised between lucky and unlucky chance.
Nor is it true your aim is multiplying
our days on earth: it's to protract our dying.

GOD'S WAR

A year after concluding his forty-day interrogation of Juana Inés de la Cruz, the Inquisition's chief censor is dead. Sor Juana's secretary, Antonia Mora, tries to persuade her to take up her work again.

17th day of February, in the Year of Our Lord 1695

FILLED WITH HOPE I come directly with the news, of Father Núñez's death early this morning. After an operation for cataracts the patient must lie absolutely still in a darkened room, avoiding the slightest strain or worry lest the eyes start oozing blood.

I hurry to bring her word, to be the first to tell her I stayed up all night crouched beneath his window, *whispering your name, Juanita,* so that he died, his ears filled with her, his eyes brimming blood.

After another night of heavy rain, the day dawns so calmly. In the morning chill, I pause at a street corner as a vast flight of swallows pulses overhead, like a liquid, seeping, blotting out the sky with their banking and wheeling—hysteria's emblem in the air.

But by the time I reach the convent of San Jerónimo, my ripe news of Núñez is half-forgotten. The streets are filling with the first whispers. People have gathered outside the convent of Jesús María, and again at the approaches to San Jerónimo—why do we come to the convents first?

The news is of a horrid pestilence that flared up on the coast a few weeks ago then disappeared, smouldering now in the Indian communities of Chalco and Xochimilco. Seemingly overnight, a grim market of tattered awnings and gnarled tent poles has sprouted in the shadow of each convent's walls. Stalls selling amulets to be worn as pendants: walnuts filled with quicksilver. Charms, poseys, and fragments of holy scripture copied out and tightly scrolled, to be placed beneath the tongue. Nosegays of spices and medicinal herbs. My eyes dart everywhere. I take note of everything, to make you explain it all to me. Talismans, crosses, images of Guadalupe. A row of copper palladiums engraved with the number 4. Xylographies in another row—small woodblocks inscribed with pious scenes—to be swallowed whole, the vendor tells me. At the next stall, an old woman sells phylacteries: pouches stuffed with sacred verses, or else the powdered flesh of scorpions, spiders and toads. Seeing my interest, she whispers that during the Black Plague in Italy, Catherine de Medici had her pouch made from the skin of a newborn infant girl. Only as I walk away do I think to ask the cause of death.

At the *portería*, they open the gate for me without a word, as though I had only been away on one of my trips to the market. . . . I have been away a year. It feels like centuries.

As I come down the long corridor, the mood in the *gran patio* is sombre, the figures there strangely seized, like statuary—all across the patio, sisters stand in tense clusters of two or three, as if the muscles of a single torso straining at a block. Many of the faces are familiar.

But upstairs, she is different. After the interrogation, after a year, should I have expected any less? She seems not at all surprised to see me, as if she'd been waiting for me to arrive. Her wide black eyes are grave, and in them the barest flicker of what I choose to see as pleasure to find me standing at the door of her cell. What is it that has changed? I remember that awful inward gaze, the blaze of tremendous energies focussed on the wavering tip of a flame, as though to still it.

You have stilled it. Should I be happy for you?

On the outside, people keep saying she has taken a vow of silence. Others, that after forty days of interrogation she can no longer speak. But the silence came first.

And now as we are discussing the plague she speaks freely to me. What does it mean, doesn't it matter anymore—what has happened? I can no longer restrain myself. "When did you start . . . speaking again?" I ask, feeling cheated. She tells me she never stopped.

"You know what I mean." Now no answer—*is it only me she does this to?*

"Because Núñez is dead, Juana?—or because I've come . . . ?"

I don't really believe this, but give her the opportunity to be cruel to me. The one who abandoned her here.

"No." She says this gently.

She waits for me to press her for more but I know this is all the explanation I will get. It's a relief when she turns away from me those black eyes that see everything. For this one moment I do not have to pretend to be still angry with her. She looks out the window over the rooftops. . . . Her chin is so small—the wimple, I know, is what does this, and makes her neck look so long.

"The Church has known for two weeks. It's been an open secret here, but no one is sure if it's one disease or three. One strain produces buboes. Another they call the Dragon, which can kill in a week or as little as an hour. Those two we knew. But the third may be new here. *La Flojera*, some are calling it. *La Flojera* likes her prey half-digested before she sits down to eat. . . ."

She turns finally to look at me. "Don't think I don't know why you've come."

"Juana—we can start *again,* now that Núñez is dead."

"You didn't expect the news to bring me pleasure."

"You didn't expect me to conceal mine!" Our eyes lock, then in her eyes the shadow of a smile.

"No."

"Carlos says the Archbishop has weakened."

"How is Carlos?"

"He wants to see you. He believes you *could* start again. With the Archbishop's confessor gone. . . ."

"We hear His Grace has ordered the building of an amphitheatre."

"The carpenters have already started."

"In the Plaza del Volador, I imagine."

"Carlos says the Archbishop wants you to write carols for the inauguration."

Finally I have the satisfaction of seeing a glimmer of surprise in her eyes.

The Mother Prioress enters as we're sitting by the window and without even glancing at me begins.

"Sor Juana, I've come to remind you of our understanding. Present circumstances notwithstanding, you are to continue to keep your contact with the others to a strict minimum."

Only now do I notice how the Prioress has been withered by the years. Her watery blue eyes stare out from a net of wrinkles. Liver spots dot the patrician face. Her hands are unsteady, but the voice is firm.

"Over these next days it will be difficult to keep order. Your presence here, now more than ever is an incitement to . . ." She searches a moment for the word, then continues. "If you have recommendations to make, if there are measures to be taken against the contagion, which is in all likelihood already among us, then you will communicate them to me only. We have no need of any heroism from you. It has been hard enough over these past months to reverse the influence you have had here. Your martyrdom would be a calamity for the order and spiritual well-being of this convent. This affliction, as with all things, must pass.

And for the survivors, things will go back to being as they were. I hope I have made myself clear."

Without waiting for an answer, the old wraith turns on her heel and totters dizzily out.

Juana stares after her a long moment. "We'll see how long their good order lasts."

Before very long the news comes from down in the kitchens that Concepción is dead. Dear old friend.

She had just finished making lunch. Feeling a little tired, she had gone to lie down. Vanessa was trying not to disturb her. She reached over her for a jar of flour. It slipped and came crashing to the floor next to that dear, grey head. She did not wake. She will not, again.

It is among us.

I tell Juana I'm staying. She does not argue. There's work to do, I say. She does not argue.

I tell Carlos, who has come to wait for me down in the locutory.

"We've been over all this!"

A flush spreads up from his collar to his cheeks. I know he has allowed himself the hope that she herself might come down. "We lost her a long time ago, Antonia. There's nothing more to do here."

I try to tell him there is, but he does not hear. He tells me they don't need me for this, that suffering is their vocation—what can one more person add but more suffering? More gently he adds, "Anyway nothing can be done. You have not worked in a hospice, no one even pretends to have a cure for *this*. And even if there were you'd still be doing it for her, and she for God knows what—do you think I've nothing better to do than pass my days waiting in the locutories of this *maldito claustro*—for her, now you . . . ?"

His face is flushed. "I thought it was Juana who was always leading me into these little tantrums. . . ." He cocks his head as if scanning the room. He is getting so grey. It makes his brown eyes look even bigger through the thick lenses of his glasses. "Maybe it's something in the air in here."

21st of February
I divide my time between her and attending to the sick. She is ever more frustrated to be confined to her cell. Her questions about what is being done have come to sound like criticism.

I ask Carlos to bring more news so I have something else to tell her about. After a year I thought I'd be grateful for any words from her at all.

In the street tonight beneath her windows and hers alone, the neighbours hold a silent vigil. I recognize a few faces, eerily lit by the upcast shadows—a candle held at the height of each chest. Hollowed eyes, a nose's triangle of shadow across each forehead. The look of silent, haunted carollers.

"Is it the same at the other convents?" she asks, standing at the window.

"They expect the convents to do their suffering for them," I answer. "You taught me that."

23rd of February

Carlos brings word that the Bishop of Puebla has refused to take over as viceroy for the Count de Galve, who has been recalled to Madrid. After demonstrating to everyone his political genius during the grain crisis, after having betrayed his friend Sor Juana Inés de la Cruz and leaving her exposed to her enemies and inquisitors, Santa Cruz claims to have withdrawn from worldly affairs. He must feel he has done enough.

Juana says it's his insane vanity. By retiring now he's punishing all of New Spain for his humiliation at not having been named Archbishop— instead of Aguiar—by universal acclaim.

Carlos comes every day. One of New Spain's most famous men. I know it's as much for me as for her. He endured a lot to let me stay with him. The scandal among his family and colleagues and neighbours—that a woman should leave a convent for a bachelor's house. Even if she was just an oblate and not a nun. At least they didn't know about my past.

He comes in the afternoon and waits in the locutory, waits till end of day then goes away again, to put in another long night working at the hospice. These past few days I've not been able to go down to him for even a moment. Yesterday from her window I watched him walking home, bent into the dusk as though into a stiff wind.

More and more I seek comfort in the learning that seems to allow Carlos and Juana to remain calm while the hysteria simmers down below, in the streets and the convent patios. I tell Carlos about the vigil, he tells me how it is in the city. With no trace of irony New Spain's finest historian says he's glad to be able to perform this small service at least.

After dusk the streets are almost empty. Few want to risk the miasmal airs that rise at night to spread the plague. Many in the surrounding countryside see visions in the pre-dawn skies. Each morning there circulate fresh tales of a flaming sword hanging over the city, dragons, giant black hearses . . .

Fly early, return late, the rich say as their coaches whisk them to lengthy retreats in Cocoyóc, the thermal baths Moctezuma once reserved for his personal use. Carlos describes the melancholy lethargy these flights provoke among onlookers too poor to leave. It echoes on long after each carriage disappears.

"And all the superstitions of Europe," he says in disgust, "are being dusted off now and retailed here. From normally reliable sources I'm hearing fantastic accounts—I hope they're fantasy!—of naked virgins being made to plough furrows around villages in the dead of night. . . .

"Now this talk again of an Indian uprising. Today any fool can see the Indians are too busy dying to threaten anyone."

We are sitting in the locutory. It is the one Juana used to use. There was once a rosewood grille here, but the room is divided now by an iron grate with barely room to slip a book between the bars. Carlos gets up and goes to the window, tall, barred, not much wider than his narrow shoulders. He stands looking into the little strip of garden. I am sure he is thinking of her. With almost anyone else he can be very short-tempered, and is not a little feared. Yet he endured no end of teasing from her in this room. Some of it wounded him, I think, more than he let on. But he told me once he would exchange the Chair of Mathematics for the privilege of her teasing.

"They've started in on the Jews again. I wonder if Juana was right . . . if our fear of them didn't start up again during the first great plagues in Italy. Soon they'll have Jews drinking the blood of Christian babies once again." I know he is speaking to her through me.

Juana listens carefully as I repeat his words.

"They're saying Jews are spreading the sickness to our drinking water."

She says nothing, eyes like coals. I've said this to make her angry. The old game I used to play to get her to speak. What kind of monster does this make me, that I played it then, that I should resort to it now?

25th of February
This morning there are two new red crosses of quarantine in the street below. But these are not the only signs.

Almost everywhere are hastily daubed 4s, and symbols I ask Juana to explain. One is the Greek *tau* wreathed in serpents. Another is an Egyptian trigram representing the *Animus Mundi*, though I am still not sure what this is exactly. Carlos says one of these was found painted in red on the cathedral floor. Juana couldn't say, any more than could he, who might have done it—unless someone from within the Church itself. What did interest her was to learn it took two days for the trigram to be removed from the cathedral.

This and other half-hearted responses to the tide of superstition give us the feeling the authorities are losing conviction, as though they fear God might be revoking the Church's magisterium on earth. It's true, everyone knows it: the Archbishop has lost his nerve, which more than anything feeds the malaise in the streets. This week he has had the fountain in his courtyard stopped, the basin drained. His mind was never stable. Carlos's devotion to him has always hurt and mystified her. I know that he brings news of the Archbishop's unravelling now as a gesture.

I find her sitting the window, gazing absently out. She listens to the latest without turning her eyes from the street. "How His Grace must fear this liquid inquisition, 'Tonia, like a woman's own flesh."

Does the *sound of many waters* trouble him so? Is it *la Flojera*, as Juana believes, that terrifies him? The old fanatic faces now the end of a life spent buying clemency with the charity of others. He has tried to purchase Grace. Now he finds nothing to preserve his body from its corruption. The Archbishop's palace is a fortress—walls thicker than the span of an arm, ceilings three times the height of a man. How it must trouble him now, Juana says, that his palace rests on the ruins of Tezcatlipoca's temple—ancient god of sudden reversals of fortune. The first bishop of Mexico, according to her grandfather, had a Mexica inscription carved above the main palace doors. An inscription since removed: *I leave you to the one whom I have seated on this throne; through him I renew all things.*

She is still thinking of him as, with a little smile, she tells me that to each Mexica god there corresponds a disease. To cure a disease, the healer acts it out, becomes it, in the guise of its god. A theatre of disease.

Old man, act out thine affliction.

Plague crones and plague maidens bring in the sickness. They enter through unlocked windows and unbarred doors. They exit the cracked lips of the dying as a tiny blue flame. They renew themselves each night from the earth herself, in the miasmal breath rising up out of the corruption of her bowels.

The man who spills his seed on the earth exposes himself to mortal danger.

27th of February
From the beginning, the rumours have held a special quality of unstoppable horror. Unnamed villages left without a living soul. Villages gone mad, thresholds and pathways strewn with bloated and blackened bodies. A vulture paradise. Fresh bodies, still warm, still moaning, reduced, by *la Flojera*, to the consistency of stew. They say it has followed the slaves out from Africa.

The War of God, they're calling it.

It should have come on crying panic and calamity. It should have spread like a forest fire roaring disaster. Instead it came quietly, as on the feet of mice.

JUANA INÉS
DE LA CRUZ

Alan Trueblood, trans.

Bolder at other times
my mind denounced as height of cowardice
yielding the laurels without one attempt
to meet the challenge of the lists.
Then it would seize upon the brave example
set by that famous youth, high-minded
charioteer of the chariot of flame;
then courage would be fired
by his grand and bold, if hapless, impulse,
in which the spirit finds
not, like timidity, a chastening lesson
but a pathway summoning it to dare;
one treading this no punishment can deter
the spirit bent upon a fresh attempt
(I mean a thrust of new ambition).
Neither the nether pantheon—
cerulean tomb of his unhappy ashes–
nor the vengeful lightning bolt,
for all their warnings, ever will convince
the soaring spirit once resolved,
in lofty disregard of living,
to pluck from ruin an everlasting fame.
Rather, that youth is the very type, the model:
a most pernicious instance
(causing wings to sprout for further flights)
of that ambitious mettle,
which, finding in terror itself a spur
to prick up courage,
pieces together the name of glory
from letters spelling endless havoc . . .

28th of February

THE PRIORESS takes to her bed with a fever.

The number begins to mount. Within two days the bodies are accumulating faster than they can be buried. Someone has the idea of dragging them into the cellars where it is cooler, but those of us bringing the bodies are more and more horrified by the swelling ranks of corpses in the semi-darkness. It was a terrible mistake to bring them there, compounded now several times a day. Soon no one is willing to go down. With a shudder, averting our faces now, we tip each litter's dead freight and send it thudding down the steps.

Then comes a night of terrible rain, and hailstones as large as fists. In the morning the cellars stand at least ankle-deep in a reeking broth.

4th of March

At mid-day, a minor earthquake, but strong enough to send a crack running up the column across from her cell door, and cause a minute or two of vertigo.

Over the past few years, such tremors seem more like a monthly occurrence. The conjunction of hail and comet and flood and quake should seem to us almost commonplace. Instead we're like children cringing before the next brutal cuff, a blow amplified by our fear.

It is said that in a town in Italy the plague was once averted by rounding up all the beggars, lepers, Jews and sodomites, then locking them in a big barn and setting it alight.

5th of March

Soon we'll all be saved.

In the Plaza del Volador the construction is nearly complete. The Archbishop's amphitheatre will hold twenty-five thousand. One of its chapels is dedicated to San Sebastián and another to San Roque, our intercessors against the plague. Open-air masses have been ordered said at the portals of the city, the five causeways across the half-drained marsh they say was once a lake.

Another order is circulated, that the head of each household must say prayers three times a day at the threshold of his house.

Barefoot processions wend their way through the city, as many as fourteen a day. Flagellants go dressed in sackcloth, nooses about their necks, lofting imprecations to the sky. Sometimes the Archbishop can be seen trudging ever more wearily in the vanguard, violating a health edict against public assembly that he himself helped promote.

In the first week after the outbreak, he was said to be everywhere—saying masses, launching pilgrims, blessing statues of San Roque, erecting rough crosses carved with the buboes of plague. Few claim to have seen him lately.

At the Archbishop's command a belt of wax is being laid that will encircle the city and be lit as a barrier against the pestilence.

I ask her how any plague could possibly stand against all this.

Faith should be made of sterner stuff, her answer.

Still Juana does not leave her cell.

From passing sisters and especially the novices, reproachful looks rise up to me on the second storey where I stand just inside Juana's doorway. They do not know about the Prioress's orders forbidding her to come out.

8th of March

Nine more bodies to the cellars. Tumbled down the steps through the swelling stench.

Within these walls, the body count rises; without, rumours spread unchecked. Almost every village to the east and south of the capital is said to be burning up with plague.

Like the Archbishop's belt of wax, she says grimly. A firebreak.

10th of March

Violent sensations batter my heart. Before the rage takes over I must write—or I am afraid it will never loosen its hold. I begin with the light that comes into their hopeless faces in the courtyard below as Juana emerges from the seclusion of her cell.

What did I *want?*—in one breath I am begging her not to come out, reminding her of the Prioress's order—yet my heart bursts with pride as she steps past me. In not a single face does there now appear even a glimmer of the usual resentment or scandal at her disobedience.

We stand at the top of the cellar steps. The scene strikes the eye like a vision called Despair. She is afraid, I know, if she does not do this now she will not be able to. I follow her down. I follow only her.

In the cellars, on the slippery stairs, in fluid halfway to our knees, I fight not to add my vomit to the putrid soup we walk through. How I would have fought to withhold my tears if only she had been able to stop hers. I watch them stain the pale fold of cotton she has wound about her face, another around mine. Thin shield against the reek clawing at our heads, searing our eyes.

How can he let this happen to his brides? Fury dims my eyes—is it so dark, can he not see? Can he not feel? This sacred heart of his, why does it not break? This? this is his sacred mystery—*misery?*

That's not what I see. I see bloated bodies swelling in the murk—a jumbled pyramid of meat. At its periphery rat corpses float like bloated little barges. I see this hallowed earth soaked in vomit and blood and pus. Out in the patio as we drag the bodies up, one of us stands guard to drive the carrion birds off—are these your dark attendants then, that we defend our sisters from? She accepts your silence. *I do not.*

Where has the light gone that once was in their eyes?

No one should ever have to touch what we touched, what our sisters have become. To feel unwilling fingers tearing through skin riven like sodden paper, sinking through the puttied, putrid flesh beneath, finding purchase only at the bone.

What have you done to us?

It's no use. There are no words to express the horror of those hours. There are no tongues for this.

Weeping, sliding, stumbling, we begin dragging the corpses from the cellars up into the light. She needed my strength, her lumbering Amazon. She needed my strength.

When I see how many have rushed to our aid—familiar faces, names for those hours erased—all my resentments for all the years of slights and spites and jealousies just fall away.

After, we stand together in the light ... slimy, fly-blown, sick with horror. And tonight I swear by all I can still find holy that for a moment I felt, we felt *clean.*

But he did not wash me. His hands never touched me.

The negroes in the sanitary detail sent by the city had been refusing— even on pain of imprisonment and excommunication, even under the lash—to enter those cellars. And no whip or cane or iron in the world could ever have forced me down there either. But now, out in the open, the bodies can be washed and blessed, taken away for burial.

A mass grave has been dug at the bottom of the orchard in ground greatly esteemed for its flesh-eating properties.

When night fell we rested in the darkness, unable to bear the world by torchlight. And while we rested, more died.

11th of March

I feel Juana jostling me awake at first light. Mind numb from a sleep like death, I still know, even before I open my eyes, yesterday was no nightmare, at least not one I will ever wake from. In every aching joint and muscle burns the memory of yesterday's heartsickening cargo. My back is a column of fire. As Juana's frail form precedes me through the dim passageway, I wonder how she can even walk.

Without a light, we make our way across the convent grounds towards the infirmary. At our approach a low droning fills the space between our footfalls, the space between my indrawn breaths. Just inside the door we pause as our eyes adjust to the room's near darkness. Two torches flicker weakly at the far end of the room. The drone resolves itself into the buzz of bottleflies and the low moaning of two rows of figures twisting in the gloom.

So many varieties of horror still to discover. Suddenly, that today might be worse than yesterday is no longer unthinkable. My pace slows as we make our way up the aisle between the rows. Juana has stopped a few paces short of a robed figure bent low over a bed, while above it, a novice I recognize holds a lantern over a woman's bare torso.

A blade flickers in swift descent to the woman's neck—darkness spurts from a swelling the size of an egg. As the robed figure straightens my blood runs cold—*is it all a nightmare after all?* A giant, beaked bird with glittering eyes turns and comes toward us. I hear a woman's strangled scream—the patient whose neck has been slashed?

Juana grips me by the shoulders.

The robed figure hastily removes the mask to reveal a young man's earnest face. "It takes some getting used to, I know," he begins, then falters as he recognizes who is with me. "Sor Juana? What you *did* yesterday ... I cannot begin to express my admiration." The mask dangles from one hand like a hunting trophy. "I've been trying for the past two days to get that vile mess cleaned up, but couldn't get a soul ..."

"There were several of us," Juana says. "Antonia, I imagine you've met our new chaplain, Father Medina?" By the way she says this I know she approves of him. The little gesture of an introduction amid the mounting misery makes me want to cry. I don't trust myself to speak.

"Our chaplain, as you see, is wearing the very latest in Italian fashion."

With a trace of embarrassment, he starts to explain. "Antonia, yes?— the robes here are of a waxed linen," he says, holding up the hem. "Quartz eyepieces. . . . The beak is stuffed with spices, to counteract the plague's miasmas."

"What they *may* counter," Juana puts in, "are the smells. Our next task should be to set out braziers to incense these rooms."

As the ill come in ever faster, Juana brings me to a grim appreciation of the chaplain's system for clustering the sick according to their symptoms. Those with only fever are held apart in case their illness is not plague at all. Those with buboes, who are the most numerous and the slowest to die, are brought to the main hall. If the swellings can be brought to suppurate within a week, some of these patients may yet live, though their hearts will be seriously weakened, the doctor explains.

"As will all ours be," Juana says gently.

Those in the clutches of the Dragon or *la Flojera* are confined together in the room nearest the chapel. Neither group lives long enough to catch the other's disease. And no one survives. The doctor almost never enters here to face his never-ending defeat, undisguised.[4]

> . . . so that they might concoct a healthful brew—
> final goal of Apollonian science—
> a marvellous counterpoison,
> for thus at times from evil good arises . . . [5]

12th of March
Today amid all the torment and darkness I am happy to be at your side, to do this simple, hopeless work. Our years together have come down to this. We will end here.

So little we can do to stem this sea of suffering. The kind chaplain's treatments are not just inadequate but seem almost to substitute one sort of suffering for another: man's for God's. Purges. Cauterizations. Emetics to induce still more vomiting, blood-letting to further swell the tide of blood, caustic vesicants to further blister the patient's blotched and burning skin, treacles of herbs to bring the buboes beneath to suppurate. Pain as an antidote for pain.

Still, the chaplain's energy and scientific presence bring comfort to the women who lie dying all around us.

Juana and I discover the finest treatment of all: cool water trickled across blackened lips and furrowed brows.

15th of March

Of the priests still courageous enough to stay among us, one spends most of his time among the victims of *el Dragón* and *la Flojera*, administering last rites.

I admire this bald little man for his gentle cheer. That he still finds the strength at times to smile. Sometimes I hold a lantern for him and listen to last confessions gasped over blackened tongues, feel shadowy pulse-beats at the neck or wrist flutter and still. I have seen him weep.

I never learned his name.

17th of March

Under Juana's supervision a few of us feed the braziers with spices, recharge the lamps, fetch water, tend the fires beneath great vats simmering in the courtyard.

The dead we lift by the corners of the sheet she died upon. We have neither the strength nor sufficient hands any longer to dress the dead nuns in their bridal costumes and shroud. But on each nun's head we still place the crown of wildflowers she wore at her profession. From the grave in the orchard, the sheets come back to be placed in one vat for boiling. From another, boiling water is drawn and the empty bed and floor beneath it are swabbed with lime.

To this work there appears no end.

Juana can be seen now all over the convent, among the nuns and servants equally. Lancing buboes with a skill she learned in dissections, applying hot and cool compresses, bathing the bodies of the dead.

Comforting the dying is the hardest thing of all, smoothing their tortured brows. As death approaches, she's the one they ask for. Most often it falls to her to signal to a priest and assist him in the ceremony I've come to detest.

My daughters, on your knees, pray to Our Lord God so that He may extend His mercy and His Grace to this sick woman, while I, His servant, give to her the unction of the holy sacrament.

Taking the oil from Juana's hands, the priest approaches the dying sister and anoints her, tracing the sign of the cross, first over the eyes—*close them, I bid thee*—then over the ears—*unstop them*—over the nostrils—*draw breath*—across the mouth—*seal it*—across the hands—*open them*—along the shoulders—*lay them bare.*

And so Christ's brides arrive before him, attentive, mute, blinded, barechested. Open-handed.

20th of March, Spring

In one room they die spread-eagled in agony, in the other they go quietly and quickly, blood rushing from their faces and secret openings. For many it begins with the mockery of a knotting pain low in the belly and the groin. What a black brood they are about to deliver.

Excruciating headaches, flashes of intense heat and chills. For some, the sudden gush of nosebleeds, a thin bloody fluid leaking from the eyes and ears. For most, the sinister rashes we call poseys, the wracking convulsions, the dry, black tongues. And the blood—vomiting blood, coughing blood, voiding bloody clay.

And the worse this madness gets, the harder it is to remember their names. They have names. We have names our fathers gave us. We have the names our mothers used.

We have names.

Tomasina, María, Asunción, Araceli, Candelaria, Concepción . . .

More terrible even than the agony is the confusion in their faces.

The horror, the prostration too, but worst is this anxious confusion. Their eyes glow with the purest humanity we see in the face of a suffering beast.

Who will explain this mystery? Will he? Will I? Will she?

28th of March

The second priest comes to the infirmary only when sent for. Father Landa. Yet at least he comes, unlike so many others. I try to remind myself of this to lessen my dislike of him, to not see the shadow of gloating in his fat, clean-shaven face. With such a beard he must have to shave twice a day. But how can that be—when is there time, and where . . . ?

It is late evening. I see him on a stool next to a cot, rounded shoulders hunched over the Bible in his lap, rocking strangely. I draw near, though I am reluctant to. Over the prone figure before him, he is reciting something. It sounds like Revelations:

And the Harlot of Nineveh was drunk on the blood of saints and martyrs. So He poured His hatred into the vessels of his judgement: that the horns of the beast should score her vitals, should eat her flesh and burn her with fire . . .

Can this really be Revelations? He isn't even *reading*.

He sent seven angels to pour out the vials of his wrath upon the earth, which broke out in grievous sores, and on the sea, the rivers and fountains, which ran blood, and into the darkness where they gnawed their tongues for pain—

He's making this up. It isn't like this—

And He tracked the dragon through the wilderness, where she hid from him in the swamps. He drove his sickle into the foetid earth and twisted, delivering her of the child she harboured there—

"Are you trying to frighten her to death?" I cry grasping at his shoulder, glaring into his mad eyes. "Get away from her!—Juana!"

She hurries over. The small, neat form beneath him is cool and lifeless. She's been dead an hour. Thank God, I murmur.

Vanessa . . .

This face we know. This name I have no trouble remembering. Vanessa.

I will remember your bright eyes, your graces, your body: small and slender and strong. Your mastery in the kitchens, Juanita's birthday party . . . I will remember.

I feel Juana's arms encircle me.

The next day, the little bald priest comes to tell us our fat Father Landa has been called away to duties at some monastery or other.

Our little priest, the one for whom I have no name, turns back to his work. I see a glint of satisfaction in his kind eyes.

2nd of April

Although the Dragon is more terrible, *la Flojera* more horrifying, it is the buboes I come to loathe. The very word . . . knotting first into clusters like tiny garlic heads, then swelling flower bulbs, then, ripe and soft and seedy. Huge, rotting figs.

Many of the corpses awaiting burial are so blackened that all distinctions of race are now erased. And so we go forth, hand in hand, equal before our God, waiting on his grace.

I find Juana in the infirmary, holding an old woman's hand. Her *name* . . . her name is . . . Ana.

The end approaching, Ana turns her face to Juana, a question in her eyes, in her face a century. "Is there something I can bring for you, Mother?" Juana asks anxiously. "Is there something you need?"

"No daughter. Only to die."

A minute or two later, the Prioress comes, roused from her own sickbed by the news of Ana's dying. Ana is the convent's most ancient nun, an old woman already when the Prioress first took her vows.

For a moment, Juana and the Prioress sit side by side. A moment of grace.

3rd of April

Juana tells me she too is losing the power to discriminate. At times the droning of a fly seems as loud as a scream, as terrible as a death rattle.

Sometimes, she says, I can think of no words as beautiful as *agua . . . gracias.*

5th of April

Carlos no longer comes every day, but when he can. His own hospice is filled to overflowing. With what time he has, he is experimenting with an idea Juana once had many years ago for making ice. To bring comfort to those with fevers. He has mounted a series of fans on a drum over shallow pans of water. If the rate of evaporation could be increased sufficiently . . . but he lacks the strength to turn the drum with enough speed. Perhaps something could be done with gears, he asks, beside a swift stream? Juana sends me back with the idea of driving the drum with steam. She tries to explain the mechanism to me, but I cannot follow.

6th of April

The chaplain has been urging the Prioress to permit that the corpses themselves be burned. Most of the bodies reach a sickening state of decomposition within hours, and there is little ground left in which to bury them. Juana agrees. But the Prioress cannot bring herself to issue the order.

"Burial in this convent's consecrated ground . . ." Mother Andrea de la Encarnación draws herself up and squarely faces him. Despite the strain in her face, her voice is calm. "This is not just a nun's most fervent dream, young man, it is her sacred *right*."

7th of April

A pause amid the carnage. Seeing the surgeon's young face filled with exhaustion and dismay, Juana teases him into a debate on disease transmission, a conversation he soon engages in with great absorption. Plague atoms, the reigning view, versus her champion Kircher's theory: living infective corpuscles he claims to have seen through a microscope in his laboratory in Rome.

"The waxing of our chaplain's linen, Antonia," she says turning to me, "is thought to keep the plague atom from attaching itself. A very sticky sort of atom, it seems. In my view, Doctor, the only thing those robes will keep out is fleas. . . ."

In a moment they will forget I'm even here.

We are sitting outside the infirmary toward the end of day. She and the surgeon had been discussing the possibility of laying the most feverish patients in a shallow water pan. But before he leaves they agree there are too many ill, too few hands.

A year ago I would have clung to my anger that she should speak so freely with the surgeon and have so little to say to me. But for the past quarter hour she has been talking swiftly, intently, only to me. And yet these stories of her childhood, which I would have been overjoyed to hear a year ago, I am suddenly afraid of.

" . . . I remember it so clearly, the day we arrived. There was such a light . . . Branches hung low over the road and the sun was setting red in the hollow beneath them. The *campesinos* were unloading the mule carts.

"How we loved the trees, Amanda and I. Once we spent a whole morning planting pines . . . in a churchyard—yes, *in Chimalhuacan*. I remember. How tall are they now, I wonder. . . ."

Juana turns to me to explain, but I know who Amanda is. She has told me before, though only once. Has she forgotten this?

Here in the courtyard tonight the light is so soft. We could almost forget what is going on inside. We sit on a stone bench at the edge of the orchard. Her face is pale, her round black eyes are lustrous with that intensity that still sometimes startles even those of us who think we are used to it. Her wimple is pulled back. Her black hair has grown back thick and straight, and above where it tucks under her robes, flares out like a satin cowl, framing her face.

At dawn from the colonnade above the courtyard I stare into the eastern sky. White smoke from Popocatepetl, though the mountain itself I cannot see. Is the entire world and heaven too now ablaze? Has your hero's bright chariot run wild, Juana, drying up the lakes and seas, scorching even heaven?

What was it in her stories yesterday that troubles me? Stone lovers cursed, demonic serpent children haunting mountain meadows, a lost tribe disappearing after the Conquest into an underworld, over whose entrance sits the smoking mountain . . .

The mountain is in each one.

I remember something in a poem. Evading another day of horror before me, I grasp at this glimmering . . . this sweet release of verse.

A poem of hers—the only one, she claimed, that ever really mattered to her. *First Dream*. I go to its hiding place in the archives, deserted these past weeks. I return to the cell with it, light a candle, find the passage.

> . . . Of a mountain next to which that very Atlas,
> which like a giant dominates all others,
> becomes a mere obedient dwarf . . .
> . . . of the loftiest volcano that from earth,
> a rearing giant, goads high heaven to war . . . [6]

I read page after page of these lines, the rhymes, the visions always too difficult for me to do anything but marvel at—and that in this prophetic Dream of hers she has seen so clearly, even down to the counterpoisons we have used against the plague. And suddenly I know why I am frightened by her stories. One after another with hardly a pause between. Not just that they should tumble out after almost two years of silence. It's how they come. They ramble. She has never been unclear in her life.

It is time to return to work.

I wake her.

8th of April

Some of the sisters have gone mad. Three run wildly about. I can barely bring myself to write. One stands outside the infirmary screaming in answer to each scream she hears inside. No one bothers to quiet her, what is one more scream?

The last shred of convent discipline unravels now, the vow of enclosure. Men everywhere coming and going. Here now in a convent, here in our dying, most know more easy freedom with men than ever while they lived. At last I have this to share with them.

And even as we still live, the last differences between us fall away. Old and young, poor and rich, learned and ignorant, sensuous and ascetic, talkative and silent. All engaged now in an unceasing inner dialogue of questions and silences. Look at these faces.

What have you done to their beauty?

If I could be granted the power to accomplish one thing, in this final hour, one single wish—O pardon me my wistfulness—*I would restore to them their beauty.* I would have them see themselves, some now for the first time ever in her life, as simply . . . beautiful.

Who dares call this a lie? This beauty of girls.

Does he—is our Eternal Author well satisfied with His creation now? With the grace of His loving union. . . .

> . . . utmost perfection of creation,
> utmost delight of its Eternal Author,
> with whom well pleased, well satisfied,
> His immense magnificence took His rest;
> creature of portentous fashioning
> who may stretch proud arms to heaven
> yet suffers the sealing of his mouth with dust;
> whose mysterious image might be found
> in the sacred vision seen in Patmos

by the evangelic eagle, that strange vision
which trod the stars and soil with equal step;
or else in that looming statue
with sumptuous lofty brow
made of the most prized metal,
who took his stance on flimsy feet
made of the material least regarded,
and subject to collapse at the slightest shudder.
In short, I speak of man, the greatest wonder
the human mind can ponder,
complete compendium
resembling angel, plant, and beast alike . . . 7

9th of April
A wind has been clawing all night at the shutters. In the morning I wake
to a sky swept clean of smoke.

Late morning. "I shouldn't say this," the chaplain offers, "but there were
only two new cases last night. With God's help, we may have this thing
beaten."

"A few more victories like this . . ." Juana murmurs.

"And we're finished. Yes, Sor Juana, I know."

11th of April
It should have come in like a hurricane, smashing everything in its path.
Instead it begins with a rash at her neck, a little cat's paw.

A mark I took no notice of. My mind would not open. All day long the
thought of her marred throat I managed to escape, but not the foreboding.

One day soon now, someone will say that the marks on your body
traced exactly the contours of the lake of Chalco. . . .

Thirteen hours we work without stopping, fed on green delusions and
false hopes. Night finds us still in the main hall of the infirmary, sitting
on stools, slumped against a grimy wall. A strange light in her eyes, face
flushed, Juana begins telling another story. A picnic beside a spring high
up on the WhiteLady. Cold *tamales con rajas.*

"I remember a cream made from honey, the women used to sell. We'd
spread it all over our bodies by the hot spring. Remember, Amanda?"
Her eyes are very bright and full as I look deeply into them and blush.

"All the wasps . . . ? How we stood naked, letting them land—then jumped into the brook to keep from getting stung! What is it, Antonia, what's wrong?"

"You called me Amanda just now."

The lantern guttering, rain falling into the hush beyond the windows, she starts to tell me about a sorcerer. A jaguar, whose friend is a bishop, or an Inquisitor. I wonder if it is a children's story. No, a story important to her grandfather, a story told to her the night he died. She wants me to take it down. He knows a bookbinder who conceals manuscripts by binding them into Bibles. Who does? *Carlos*. Write it?—write what, write which? She wants me to have Carlos bind it secretly under the cover of a Bible. It is a story that cannot be lost.

And so I write, but as usual only half understand what I am copying down. Other things I do not understand at all. Lies, false gods, twins of gods. Night, two prisons, three escapes. A jaguar vanishing, Night. The fulfilment of a prophecy—or else its reversal . . . a wheel, or a spiral . . . I cannot make it out, I copy it down. *Gaps will not be tolerated*, she says. Why does she say this to me. Do I not always *try?*

So I write it, to have it bound under the covers of Bibles. Gaps will not be tolerated, gaps must be filled. Under the covers of Bibles, between their contents and their covers. Her brow is damp, her smile strange. What did she mean? Juana, I don't understand. I write it anyway. Her copyist, her parrot. I write to fill the silences, between each breath. I write to save my own life.

Ever since I was little . . . the last honest man . . . the last sorcerer was . . . Who?

We had the most wonderful time.

I said it once, 'Tonia. One night . . . I think I said it, once. A wonderful time is gone. . . .

She is asleep.

I write this and feel my heart swelling within me, a grotesque thing that will no longer sit in my chest—sits *on* it, crushing the breath out of me.

> This dismal intermittent dirge
> of the fearful shadowy band
> insisted on attention less
> than it coaxed a listener asleep . . .

... while Night, an index finger
sealing her two dark lips—
silent Harpocrates—enjoined
silence on all things living ... [8]

... All was now bound in sleep,
all by silence occupied.
Even the thief was slumbering,
even the lover had closed his eyes ... [9]

Darkness. Silence. It is the middle of the night. Green hopes withered
on the vine, I hold her head to my breast as she sleeps her restless sleep,
full of dreams.[10]

In the morning word flies through the streets that Sor Juana has fallen ill.
    Several times that day, the Archbishop sends men to report back to
him on her condition. On the advances in God's War on the children of
the earth.

LAST DREAM

12th of April, 1695

BY FIRST LIGHT I KNOW: three days, five at most. We know the symptoms too well to waste a lie. She will not leave this cell again alive.

Carlos demands to see her. With so many people coming and going now, I know he can get in if he insists.

"Antonia please," she gasps, looking up at me, wide-eyed, "don't let him see me like this."

It should have come down like a comet, crying disaster, setting all the temples ablaze, like a sun summoned in the blackest night.

Instead it came quietly as on the feet of mice.

"Remember, NibbleTooth . . . ? Walking up towards the mountain, up through the pines . . ." She stops, shuddering with cold. The sheets and blankets are damp. She clutches at my arm as I turn to go for fresh bedding. "Antonia . . . ?" She makes an effort to concentrate.

"Find Amanda for me." Her teeth are chattering. "Ask Carlos if he will do this for me."

"But she's in a delirium half the time!"

"She knows what she's asking, Carlos."

"She is just sending me away. You just finished saying she doesn't want me to see—"

"She said you'd understand what this means to her."

"What if when I get back . . ."

"With a good horse you can be there and back in two, two and a half days." The coldness of the calculation shocks me. "There's still time."

"He agreed to go, even knowing . . . ?"

"Yes, he knew."

"When he returns, will you ask him one more favour?"

"Oh Juanita . . ." *He would do anything for you.*

"It will keep his mind occupied."

She tells me what it is. Yes, it will keep his mind occupied.

So tell me Juana about Nyctimene, this daughter of Lesbos—*shamefaced Nyctimene who keeps watch by chinks in the sacred portals.* . . . What last role would you choose for me: to desecrate the holy lamps, or top them up that no one die in darkness?

But it's too late to ask you this.

13th of April
I will not record any more symptoms. There are lies and slanders even I will not record.

Flashes of her old self, her clearness and irony. Like when she asks to be cremated so as not to have to lie next to Concepción and listen to her gossip for all eternity.

Just now as she opens her eyes I have the unreal sensation, almost of luxury, that she's just woken up from sleeping late. *We never once had the chance to sleep in, you and I.*

I reach for anger, anger is the safest. How can she make *jokes?*

"The question is not when but how. We are all dying, 'Tonia. How would you have had me go—breaking my neck slipping on the stairs? No, it is better to make a little comedy than die in one."

The sisters too begin to keep a record. A kind of recipe book. All now compete for miracles. To build a case for her beatification.

Did you see how the touch of her fingers healed sister Elena's sores?

Yes and as she kissed one of the slaves on the forehead I saw the pestilence leave the woman's lips like a blue flame. Sor Juana had no fear for herself . . .

They are half expecting the plague to lift when you die. And I cannot rouse myself to anger. Any day now someone will claim to have seen your breasts running with milk.

I pore over—pour through this, her great book of dreaming. I try to meet her in dreams, to follow her through mine. To make her see me again, where the light is clean, where there is no smoke, no cloud, no sun.

> The body in unbroken calm,
> a corpse with soul,
> is dead to living, living to the dead,
> the human clock attesting

by faintest signs of life
its vital wound-up state,
wound not by hand but by arterial concert:
by throbbings which give tiny measured signs
of its well-regulated movement . . . [11]

I wake startled, overcome with fear. In the darkness my fingertips find the faintest throbbing at your throat.

I sleep.

14th of April
Today a letter. A nobleman from Perú has written that he would like to come here, to make a life near her. A wealthy gentleman. He offers everything he has, without conditions, only that she might have the freedom to write whatever she wishes, whenever it pleases her.

More dreams, day and night, hers and mine. The cell is awash in dreams. It is all we have left to talk about. She tells me hers, still asks to hear mine.

I will not let anyone in. They bring fresh blankets, soup, oranges . . . and leave them at the door.

In a confused muttering she speaks to me of guilt—all the things and people sacrificed to feed her mind. Her hungers, her shame . . . something about a river, a face, or a hot spring called the Face. I cannot make it out.

What storm-tossed end would you have chosen for yourself, Juana, what tempest of the mind and soul?

. . . against her will was forced
to run ashore on the beach
of the vast sea of knowing,
with rudder broken, yardarms snapped,
kissing each grain of sand
with every splinter . . . [12]

I check on her. Her eyes are open. For a moment I . . .

"I had a dream, Antonia . . ." She pauses, closes her eyes, and after a breath opens them again. "There was a mountain spouting glyphs of smoke, ancient signs. An old dream of mine," she says forcing her cracked lips into a smile. "Good that it should visit me once more. Your . . . turn . . . now."

I'm not sure she even hears me. I have to speak loudly now. Her ears are leaking fluid. I shouldn't write this, but I can't help it. There is nothing else.

> . . . no rapid surging flight could ever reach
> of eagle soaring to the very heavens,
> drinking in sunbeams and aspiring
> to build her nest amidst the sun's own lights,
> however hard she presses upward
> with great flappings of her feathered sails
> or combings of the air
> with open talons, as she strives,
> fashioning ladders out of atoms,
> to pierce the inviolate precincts of the peak . . . [13]

It is not darkness she strives against but light, an all-conquering light.

"I was flying again," she murmurs weakly. "Before me the mountain . . . the sun at night. All human history stretched below, since before the Flood. . . . How we cling, each to our life." Her laugh is a gasp. "So real it seems, our little bit of clay. How stubborn we are."

She wakes, sleeps. One minute, two. She wakes, pauses an instant to swallow painfully.

"Just now, 'Tonia . . . I dreamed the whole of human history. From the first dawn down to our last day, last hour. How long have I been asleep—Antonia, are you there?

"How long would a dream of all eternity last?"

I watch her slip back into her dream of the sun at night, blood streaming from her eyes.

> At this almost limitless elevation,
> jubilant but perplexed,
> perplexed yet full of pride,
> and astonished although proud,
> the sovereign queen of the sublunary world

let the probing gaze, by lenses unencumbered,
of her beautiful intellectual eyes . . .

. . . .

The eyes were far less quick
to reel, contrite, from their bold purpose.
Instead, they overreached and tried
in vain to prove themselves
against an object which in excellence exceeds
all visual lines—
against the sun, I mean, the shining body
whose rays impose a punishment of fire . . . [14]

How could it have taken me so long to see that she was going blind?

The plague has broken. Or having eaten its fill, has gone away to sleep.
It is only hunger wakes the dreamer.[15]

16th of April, 1695

The day dawns bright, mocking us with its orderly distribution of the
gifts of light. There will be but one death today.

I can no longer keep her to myself. Fresh bedding, the braziers
charged with spices. . . . By late afternoon I've done what I can to scrub
the walls clean of their rust-red streaks, like a child's fingers run mad
with paint. In this stained nursery I am about to go insane. She has just
asked if the day is clear, if I can see the volcanoes. She has forgotten that
the new cell faces west, not east. I tell her yes. She asks about the flowers
blossoming in the trees.

The survivors gather about the bed. Someone asks if anyone smells
it, yes they all smell tangerines. . . . Is it only my own lies that can be
beautiful?

The Prioress comes in, unsteady, hesitant. I can see it in her face. This
final irony cuts even her, deeply: that the Archbishop has asked to see
you, has asked that you leave the convent for your protection. Or his.

The faintest hint of a smile caresses your dark lips. "Last night . . . just
now. I had the most beautiful dream." Your voice is a faint whisper. I bend
low and struggle to fill in the words. You feel my breath on your cheek,
the drop of a tear. "Ahh, Antonia, it's you. How good . . ."

Your eyes try to find me. "All my life I have been falling back to earth.

I would not look down, would not see. But hovering over me ..." She tries to swallow, shakes her head slightly as I try to press a *cántaro* of water to her lips. "... broken on the earth I looked up to the face of Ammon. *This bright dream....*"

"What did she say?" the Prioress asks. I do not answer. "I heard her say something," she demands, reddening.

"You must have heard her say Amen, Mother."

To be a liar can sometimes be a mercy.

At the end, in your beautiful blind eyes I saw a faint light turning in ... as if to sleep. The light I'd first seen last night. As though in a dream, I watched the Phoenix leave her nest of burning spices and take flight. ...

How long does the dream of all eternity last.

It should have come howling riot, crying havoc, on the thousand voices of the flood. Instead the end came quietly, as on the feet of mice.

Sor Juana Inés de la Cruz died an hour before the dawn, April seventeenth, in the year sixteen ninety-five.

WIZARDS *[? Feb 1995]*

EYELESS EN PLAYA....

Half-dark. Dirt floor. A bed. Light slants through a weft of wattle—fine strands of bright thread stretched on a loom. Bright activity beyond. Children. Chickens. Water's throaty run into a drum. A woman laughs, the slap of wet cloth.

I am naked, I am hurt. I am safe.

Please make it all a dream.

Where is the sea . . . ?

Sleep.

I wake to a shadowflow along the wattle wall outside. It cuts through the lightstrands like a scythe. At the door a blast of whiteness. He slides through, dressed in it.

How are you feeling, Beulah . . . ?

Feeling . . .

I was afraid you would not come with me.

And if I didn't want to?

I would have left you.

I didn't want to.

But you came.

You called my name.

Yes, Beulah.

How did you know?

You don't remember me at all?

No, how did you know *how*?

¿Cómo?

How to call for me. He doesn't understand, how could he?

The children are washing your dress. My cousin says she can fix the hem. Your other things are there beside you. Ah, I see you have found your notebook.

You knew where I was.

Everyone knew in all Tulum. I stay with a family not far down the beach.

Tell me what you saw. *Tell me please . . . how much.*

Later we can talk.

You're going?

To make a coffee. Espresso or cappuccino?

You have a machine, for espresso . . . here.

A real beauty.

He walks barefoot to the door, soles white as his palms.

I sit, sip, clean white sheet wedged under my arms. His onyx eyes. He sips to cover his curiosity. How is it?

Hot. . . .

Children at the door, shy faces peering round the bright frame.

All Maya villages have cappuccino I guess.

This is not a village, this is the capital. A friend with a restaurant went bankrupt. He owed some favours—

What capital?

Carillo Puerto. We are ten minutes' walk from the legislature. I can show you if you like. The seat of our democracy. You don't want to get dressed? Of course, your dress is not quite dry.

My dress is . . . filthy.

I can lend you something. We are about the same size.

It's good that you slept again. No do not worry, I can make you another later. You have a slight fever. If you would like to take that walk now we can get something for it.

Poultice, spider webs?

I was thinking of tetracycline. Here try these—or I can give you jeans. We call these pants ____. I just thought with the burn on your calf . . . the short cuff wouldn't rub. Do you like them?

Burns . . . but no bites. . . . What happened, what happened last night?

You can stay if you want.

No, you should have privacy.

See? A good fit, just as I thought. A bit loose in the waist of course. Meet the children. Ernesto. Rico. The toddlers Beto, Magy.

Little jesters. How do I say hello in Maya? Hello. Too excited to speak they chase chickens. Sprint-waddle pursuit, they toddle like ducks after hens, that spurt just out of reach. Many glances to check the effect—foreigners may be more difficult to please. They can do other things. Climb trees. Jostle and jockey and joust at the trunk of a little *limonera*. Beto stumbles, cries. Their mother comes out, shoos them into the house. Jacinto's cousin, Soledad.

Me da mucho gusto, Byula. I hope we did not wake you with the laundry. The water came.

We get water for two hours. Sometimes twice a week. Today Soledad and all the other women of the barrio do laundry.

Concrete basin, border of flowered tiles. Droplets glide from an iron pipe. Glitter and fall. The barrio a maze of cane fences chest high. Wattle huts. Dirt yards combed by brooms. Neighbour women kneel to spread prayer mats of laundry over washboards.

These are all fruit trees.

Yes each yard has a tree. We have limes, los Perera have mangoes. Pomegranate there, you know it? In each season we share what we have. One tree is too much for even half a dozen families. Papaya, this one everyone recognizes—a giraffe in a gourd hat, *verdad?* So much fruit it is ready to snap. A little heartbreaking, no? this bounty of trees.

That starvation is so . . .

Unnecessary? Yes, but the sheer *charity*. We do so little to earn. Come let me show you the rest of my neighbourhood.

You are different with me now.

How, different?

Not so polite.

You prefer rudeness?

It felt like dislike. Like the Captain.

Captain Höflich. They call themselves marines, trained by the Americans. The body armour is the latest American technology. Even the shields and visors are bulletproof.

Riot gear, out on the beach?

I think they call it *contra-insurgencia* now, this old work they do.

But there are no crowds.

It is mostly for effect. . . . My courtesy with you was only caution. It is a small moment of danger.

What is?

The moment when someone is no longer quite a stranger.

I'll remember.

Not quite a friend.

Buenas tardes, don Jacinto.

    Buenas tardes, don Jacinto.

    Buenas tardes, don Jacinto.

    Everyone calls you that.

    It is also courtesy.

    It seems like more.

    What is more than courtesy? Do you like chicken barbecued?—those women up ahead have a secret sauce. They are teachers, but sell chickens on their lunch breaks. The chickens earn more than their salaries. The little one teaches chemistry. I think the recipe is hers.

    Buenas tardes, don Jacinto. Won't you introduce us to your friend?

    All three have secret sauces for you, don Jacinto, if you only knew.

    We reach the barrio market. Over cinderblock pilings a tin roof incandesces sun. Foul flesh and bone shop of darkling meat, fat sallowing. Flystorms buzz a cyclonic fury, exasperated fizz. Cages of songbirds, lizards next door.

    People here can pay for these birds?

    No, he will sell them to anyone going to Mérida or Cancún. They can make a small profit.

    The lizards?

    Geckos, for insects. Especially scorpions, they say, though I have never seen them eat one myself.

    We walk past a flower vendor. A fruit stall. Baskets heaped with nuts, a weave of gore.

    This—what's that on her hands, blood?

    Cochineal. They are beetles.

    To eat?

    No to dye. For fabrics. They grow all over a kind of cactus, in a white cocoon. When they come out their bodies are filled with a deep wine red. We dilute it with lemon to get the right shade. Here crush one between—

    No . . . thank you, I see.

    If it is insects you wish to eat, come over here.

    Can we go somewhere else. Please?

    The cultural centre is nearby. We could walk there if you like.

    Ever the guide.

    It is my home I am showing you.

    Dusty streets, inland heat, each sunbeam a bright cudgel of reproof.

Smashed sidewalk tectonics all along a block-long wall, windowless, pitted, pale pink. Peeling posters of faded bullfights, political careers. We step from floe to floe, cement overthrust on roots of unseen trees— thirst as jackhammer. . . .

Here? In the middle of the block one door, cracked, sunsplit—and we step into the lush miracle of a courtyard. Sprays of bougainvillaea— pink, orange, red. Arcade of bleached columns and dim doorways, patio flagged in limestone, worn smooth, sprouting weeds. Rows of children's desks against a wall. Broken backs, warped plywood tabletops. At the far end a palm-thatch palapa over a desk . . . massive, battered, ceremonious.

My office. We needed the rooms for classes. During breaks the children use the desk as a football goal. Not impressive I am afraid.

It's big.

Mostly patio. The rooms are small.

Are those all mango trees?

In season the children sell them but in season most people here have mangoes. We do better with the pies. This is the library. When there is electricity you can even read in there. Half the time the power is out, half the time we do not pay our bill. Sometimes we only have power in half the centre. No one can explain why. Or half-explain. We keep the desks out here in the middle, move them to where there is light. Our classes are mostly evenings. Often we use torches. Very atmospheric. The children like it, the adults less. . . . Come let me present you to the sub-director. She is a whirlwind you may like.

Don Jacinto! I did not expect, I thought you were in Tulum this month.

Patricia, te presento a Beulah Limosneros. Una colega del Canadá.

Squat smiling matron rising from her desk, handshake crush, free hand to her heart. Wide oval face, almond eyes, puffy lips and lids. Friendly amphibian in her hollow of battered filing cabinets and AeroMexico posters of pyramids. One small window high in the cell, too high to clean. Dirty light drains in.

So you are a scholar. Welcome. We have a lot of research projects but little manpower. Are you staying long?

No.

A pity. Though we couldn't pay you anyway. The property taxes slowly kill us. They follow inflation, about twenty-five percent a year. Funding does not. Of course the government wants to build a new centre. They

are all the same—very happy to fund health and culture but only in construction projects. No kickbacks you see from nurses' salaries or teachers.
No fat contributions. They call it infrastructure development. It must be
very different *en Canadá.*

Her eyes glint with this.

But the authorities remember this city was once Chan Santa Cruz,
headquarters of the Maya resistance. They do not cut our funding altogether—they are afraid don Jacinto will become a *Zapatista*—

Have you?

No no that was only a joke but they know he is a friend of Commander
Marcos—has don Jacinto brought you for the play in San Andrés
tomorrow? It is classic agitprop, we are teaching the children about
dengue and malaria. How the little mosquitoes breed in anything that
holds rainwater—spare tires, styrofoam cups. I play an old drunk who
loses his cup. Don Jacinto can be our spare tire. Would you like to play
the sun, Beulah? The children have made a beautiful sun mask. You don't
have to say any lines—but you can of course. Do you speak a Maya language? I have not even asked you what type of *investigadora* you are—

Slow down please, Patricia. We will see. I am not sure about Beulah's
plans.

Cherryred pickup, cloud of percussion and dust. "Don Jacinto, *¿qué
onda?*—lift home?" Three black men in heavy gold chains, long fingernails for concert guitar and drag shows, three gleaming helmets of
straightened hair. Gold bracelets, gold rings. Gym shorts and watered
silk blouses, empty eyes. Voodoo dolls in marijuana cologne.

Another new truck, I see.

Got to keep up.

Thank you, we are not going far.

Another time.

The truck trolls off.

Who was that?

They may tell you they are musicians from Louisiana. Other times
Haitian priests. They are drug runners.

Can they be more obvious?

This is the texture of life here. People accept. It does not mean we
would want one to marry into the family.

Un negro.

Why are you always provoking?

It means I like you.

Like me differently please.

They seem to know where you live. Are you friends?

They think I am some kind of wizard—they think we are in the same sorcerers guild, or want to exchange recipes, or I do not know exactly. Maybe you want me to introduce you. . . .

My Temple Mask turns to me, eyes of blackest regret. I am sorry.

I can't expect you to just forget where you found me.

I do not know why I said this.

I'd like to go back now.

What are your plans?

Plans? You brought *me*.

Will you go back to Tulum?

No.

Why not come to San Andrés?

San Andrés . . .

Come, for the play.

No.

They will hold it under a huge ceiba tree. Did you and I not speak once about the Maya World Tree? It was often a ceiba. From there I could take you to Bacalar lagoon, one of the most beautiful places in all Mexico, perhaps anywhere. I have friends there.

You have friends everywhere. . . .

Or you can stay for free at the Hotel Laguna.

So many friends, so many places. Who are you really, Jacinto Ek Cruz?

I could ask you—

Guerilla poet secret agent drugman—shaman? Are you? It's what the Maya sergeant—

He said teacher.

He said *curandero*.

Which can also mean healer. We were very lucky he was there. You and I both. You are writing about us I think, but know only books. If you come like the tourists to take our souls, you should know us a little first, no? As a courtesy. Come to San Andrés and maybe you will solve the Maya mystery.

Why San Andrés.

It is as good as anywhere else. It is where my mother lives.

19 Feb, San Andrés, Yucatán

It's true, the ceiba is enormous. A thousand candles of shade, a menorah. The village arrayed beneath in a ring of sandalwood boxes. In the clear-ing between chapel and tree people make ready for the play. Sweeping, laying a pine needle carpet beneath the spread ceiba boughs. Small wooden tables dragged into a broken row, draped in embroidered cover-ings. Clay cauldrons, a griddle for tortillas. Off by herself Patricia arranges bright-lacquered gourds and cups on a solitary table.

Hola, Beulah. These cups we give the children after the play. We write their names on each with this paint. A cup to value and reuse and not throw away to collect rain. All this?—this is for the meal afterwards. I love coming into the country with don Jacinto but this is the hardest part for me, standing by while they do all the work. I am a guest here and a colleague of his so I am not allowed to raise a finger. At least that's what they say but it's also because I'm *mayera.*

Mayera?

A city Maya. Citified—they think I'd botch everything. Let me show you the village. I think I can manage that much. Don Jacinto's uncle lives over there, his mother back in the trees. . . .

A score of houses bend on an arc, roof thatch thick and neat. Mahogany beams. Beside each house is a painted cross, garlanded in pine. Inside the doorways little shrines, candles and Messiah. Dolorous virgin mother, but no Guadalupe here. Yards fenced in pale fieldstone— like chalk under lichen. We step into the little chapel of thatch, white-washed walls, red-trimmed. Floored in fresh needles that gleam green.

How far have they gone to find pine?

Don Jacinto could tell you, but maybe as far as Chiapas.

Does he really know Commander Marcos?

You should ask. I have heard that Marcos read some things don Jacinto wrote, but there are other rumours.

Like?

When he comes from his mother you can ask for yourself, if he feels like talking. Her attacks are smaller now. It's sad, such a beauty she was. Some people say it is a punishment. Of all the girls her age she was the finest weaver, the wisest, with the most suitors. Then she runs off with the grandson of a rich Mexican—the *chiclero* many of the village elders had been forced to work for. What would the gossips find to talk about if she hadn't come back to the village, I wonder? Just listen to me!—you must think *I'm* one.

Dusk gathers. Children in white cotton pile out of farm trucks. Dressed like adults but running, laughter soft and deep—no shrill and shriek of sugar in the blood. Children running hard running barefoot in the dusk . . . a deep river of joy flowing around us. Exhilarate hush.

How many children *live* here?

A lot. But half of these are from X-Cacal—this is new, very exciting. These are the purest Maya, or purist Maya as I call them. *Los Separados* . . . The separated ones have appointed themselves guardians of the Chan Santa Cruz.

You said that was the old name for the capital.

Named after the Speaking Cross of Maya rebellion. We hid it in the jungle after the city fell to the Mexicans. *Los Separados* think the rest of us are all *Mayeros*—fallen. Of course we don't have the Oracle to guide us. Even these people of San Andrés are too modern for their liking. But since don Jacinto came back from Mexico City last year . . .

Yes?

Things have become better.

Someone called him a *curandero*.

His grandfather was a healer. His mother was learning to become one before she ran off. But no. For don Jacinto, the old ones use an old word. Scribe. It is the highest praise. He is our foremost interpreter of the old texts and inscriptions. The Maya leaders come to him for help, just as the foreign investigators do. Someone so young. He has set many of our popular legends down, in a form that delights country people. And he has written *new* texts, new songs that even the purist Maya find beautiful. After he is finished playing a spare tire for the children tonight, he may be asked to recite. Watch the faces, of the old ones. They say he speaks as their own grandparents knew to speak once. Ah here he comes. It must be true that his mother is worse.

She would like to meet you, Beulah.

Why?

I am not the one to explain my mother. She wants to talk to you alone. Will you?

I don't see. . . .

Her reasons are her own. As usual. Maybe after you can explain her to *me*. Lately I feel a greater need. But I should warn you she can be harsh. Her speech is a little slurred. And her memory . . . It is a great frustration. And an embarrassment, since she was once admired for her wit. It is a trait we prize.

Small thatched hut shunned out of the arc. Behind lies a cornfield, vines of beans creeping up the stalks. A rocking chair tipped on its side. No shrines, no cross. A sweet smell of mildew or rot. Cardboard nailed over the windows, flattened boxes of pesticide—*Shelltox* again. Bags of grain are stacked to the ceiling poles. A backstrap loom tacked to one wall is the sole adornment.

Mother, this is my friend—

We can introduce ourselves ourselves, Jacinto. Two bright eyes gleam from a hammock slung along the sacks of grain. Come girl, sit down. She beckons to a little crate.

Your mother lives in a granary.

Thank you, *hijo*, you can go now. Sit. *Ándele.* Swing me.

¿Señora?

Swing the hammock. Call me Marta. And you are Beulah.

Fine weave of wrinkles, heavy cheekbones, sunken temples. Jacinto's toucan bill. Her hair is a turban, matte black, impossibly thick, braided with pink and blue ribbons. There is a slackening, a blur in the flesh from droop of lid to chin. Her right hand lies across the chest . . . a cutting of calla, a lily slowly withering. Petal fingers, she has Jacinto's white palms.

You have beautiful hair.

My downfall. My nieces help me with it now. So that it does not fall. This is the house of my brother. No, it suits me, it is perfect. He built it specially. Exactly where I asked. He said when I moved in, A house without a shrine is fit only to store grain. This suits me also. The corn is my shrine, no? What is yours girl?

You're a weaver.

Was. *Obviamente.*

You wanted to talk.

You can be direct. Good, it is best. Are you the one for my son? You are the first of his women he has brought here.

I'm not his—

Of course. No one is anyone's now.

Your blouse, did you—

I hope you are not changing the subject. I am already making an effort for you. No I did not weave it. *Huipil*, not blouse. Every true Maya must weave hers. It is a rectangle embroidered with the four directions, the four colours of the corn. Her head slips through the centre, like a noose. No matter how far she travels she is always there, where she has placed herself. Between the heavens and the underworld, woven into the centre. Hung like a spider. These threads are strong. . . .

They ask me why I lie here. Why I do not get up and hobble around. Do you want to ask me too?

No.

Good. Then you I will tell. I am where I have placed myself, am always. Three dead children, one beautiful husband with a stone for a heart. I am an old woman, almost sixty. There is only Jacinto holding me. Swing me. There . . . Again now, harder. Be careful with him, he is a smooth one. For his own good a little too clever, like his mother. But stronger. And his heart is good, though soft.

I should go, I don't belong—

Ah, you have noticed already. It only came to me later, after twenty years or so. No, do not go yet. Soon. That box there. Bring it. Open— go on . . . Do you know what that is, under the creases?

A *huipil*.

Obviously. That is the last *huipil* I wove. When I had come back here for good. The finest weaver in the village still and ever. How do you like the embroidery?

There isn't . . .

It is what they thought too. But this is my best work. Look more closely. The best embroidery they have never seen. I know it is dark. Look harder. Such detail, no? Of every colour, every shade. And every thread and stitch is *white*. When they finally saw, they said I was crazy. Then when I had my big stroke, they said . . . well, just think. But I was already sick when I came.

Señora, what do you want to tell me?

I want you to explain to my son.

About this?

No.

No entiendo, señora.

I want him to let go. So I can go.

He capers like a clown for a hundred children. This man, this famous Scribe. A spare tire, cheeks puffed out, fatman sway and swagger. Antic, comic is the serious face. He is the one they watch, eyes alight.

After, alone under the ceiba, he is the one the old ones bend their heads to hear. In such a sweet simple voice Jacinto sings—what lyric what lament? Two ancient sisters clutch at each other's wrists, eyes never leaving him. Patricia says they are granddaughters of a Maya poet dead a hundred years. How does this make them feel. . . . There is no way to ask this.

Patricia packs the panel van—No she insists, this is what she is paid for, just sit by the fire. An earthenware vat of corn simmers, banked low for the night, the women to rise in darkness, make fresh tortillas for the sleepy family.

Across the embers breaths of air glide shadow mantas. He comes to the fire. It is quiet for awhile.

Your father was a Mexican?

Not my father. Her husband. I was born much later. When I press her she says it was the gardener. It may be true. With her, there is no knowing. Our culture centre was once a depot for hemp and *chicle* for chewing gum. Her husband's family contested his will. The building was one of the things they could not take back. She gave it to me, and gave most of the rest away.

Is that why they think she's crazy?

In town, yes. But here, they understood her pride. She was widely admired. A kind of hero once, though people had different reasons. Some admired her leaving, some her returning. Everyone had thought she ran off for the money.

She didn't.

I believe she loved him. She kept only enough for her brother to build her house.

The granary.

Uncle has not touched the corn in there for months. He moved it in there after a fight. Then she would not let him take it back. It moulders now. The sicker she gets the worse he feels. He has begged her. He has begged me to beg her.

Have you?

With her, begging does no good. You have an expression in English— the good ones dying young? My mother has a harsher view.

That it makes no difference when.

Yes. You seem to understand each other.

He is beautiful in this light. Full lips, the oriental eyes.

How was she, Beulah? With you.

Not so harsh.

I am glad. Have you decided, about Bacalar? Or we could go to the village of the Chan Santa Cruz. I think that would interest you. It is a place the tourists cannot reach.

So different the nightroad. Bump bank stumble and swerve over the blond dirt. Shapes flit across the windshield. Green eyes blink in the dark-ahead. Washouts, potholes, seasick swells. The pale headlamps falter at each easing of the throttle. Creak of springs, torn tailpipe's tracheal hiss. No talk radio, no talk. Low sawtooth scrub . . . branches claw at the roof.

We enter the little city, shoals of light in the tropic dark. Patricia drops us off at the nearest street, returns the car to the Centro Cultural. In the barrio no lights at all. No streets. I follow Jacinto, paleshadow . . . warren of wattle. Mutter of hens. Meek and mild I follow into the hut, out in the yard of Soledad. Light a candle. *Will he fuck me now?* He pulls from his shoulderbag a little packet in butcherpaper. *My heart? Have you brought me my heart, Jacinto?*

My mother gave me this. For you.

What is it?

She did not say.

Wait, don't go.

It is for you to see, not me.

I'd like you to stay . . . *un momento.*

You know what this is?

A *huipil.*

But, it is not . . . complete. It is without embroidering. Does she want you to finish it?

Why did you take me there?

You came.

I don't belong.

You were expecting to?

Why I came . . . you asked. To San Andrés. My father's name was Andrés. My real father.

I did not know mine.

I can just remember him.

It is something, at least.

I'll come with you to Bacalar. If you still want me to.

IT SHOULD HAVE COME rising up, like the foul earth splitting, groaning chaos and ruin. Instead your death came quietly. To me.

Before the day was out, before the eyes had dried, the Archbishop came in person, to confiscate her savings from the convent accounts. I pitied the Prioress, then. She fought him like a lion.

I have asked to wash her body in the fountain. I have asked their permission, and they have not yet denied me.

I have asked your sisters leave to come down among them, though I have done nothing to earn their friendship, I know. I will take you to where the survivors are gathered murmuring down below. Let me be your Camilla once more.

Ahh, Juanita, how easily you lift.

See, see how light. I am not so strong. Will they give me leave to carry you down? Though I know it is dangerous . . . though the chapel is stacked with these like cordwood, who once floated in the cellars. Who once breathed with us.

And if the answer is yes, I will take you to the fountain's edge, under the trees and the black wedges wheeling in the smoke. And beneath the sun's dull glare, I will ask them if this is the woman they remember. Remember her—remember you? In the orchards and the classrooms, in the chapel and the choir. Do they remember you that day, striding through a pouring waterspout—just to make us laugh? Do you remember her, as I do? I will ask.

Then I will make our sisters listen.

Will you all give me leave to speak, to ask something difficult of you?[16]

You all have pity, I will say to them, if you but look for it. This, no one can take away, it must be relinquished willingly.

You loved her too.

But the fathers and the doctors will tell us she was impudent. They must be right, it must be true. Seventeen centuries must make it so. She defied an imperium of light.

I may say her death was unjust. But then, there was her *impudence* . . . and their cause was such a noble one: to build a kingdom for a second sun. But I will confess before you that I wanted a saint too, if of a different kind, and I lied to make her one.

I killed her too.

And now that I have bathed her body and shown it to you, confessed to you my capital crime, I ask you finally: how then do you find her? *How do you find?*

These are only words, and lack the power to stir your hearts. But our souls—may they only speak when spoken to? For Grace, must we only stand and wait?

Carlos arrives after nightfall. He has found Amanda's village, on the other side of the pass. But she had left the mountain thirty years ago. "The same year Juana came to the capital—she *must* have known. Even now she makes a fool of me!"

I know he does not mean this.

"She asked, Carlos, if you would deliver the eulogy."

His lean, weary face is stricken. I am sorry to have taken his anger from him. We cling to each other like children.

After a while he goes on. "The mother is dead now. She returned to the village a few years ago. Amanda, no one is sure about. Some say people have seen her in the South. Oaxaca or San Cristóbal, or even farther. . . . It's all I have. And this."

From a cloth bag, he takes a bundle of leather, sodden and stained, and begins to unwrap its layers of canvas and oilcloth, as though peeling a fruit, or unwrapping a jewel. And it is like a jewel, that which he holds up to me, luminous and bright, the size of an avocado pit.

He has brought down ice.

"Yesterday," he says, his face still streaked with road dust, "I could barely carry it."

I turn it in my hand. He sits quietly watching.

For an hour after he is gone, I run this cold jewel over her forehead, along her temples, across her lips. I know it cannot help, I know I cannot help it. So slowly now it melts.

You would have made Him speak. In the silence of the night at the bottom of the sea, drowning in the suffocating sufficiency of His grace, you dreamed of calling to the sun . . . calling him to answer!

And you called this dream cowardice.

Do not leave me with this work, Juana. He will not answer.

Do not leave me. He will not answer for his work.

Don't leave.

18th day of April, 1695

There is a vault where the flowered crowns are kept. It is entered only for a death. Inside, it is cool and dry. In the months of rain the walls are lined with sacks of rice to absorb whatever humidity they can. Two hundred bridal crowns from the day of vows. Once . . . Forty now. The scent of ancient wild-flowers is indescribable. I did not want to come, I never want to leave.

The Prioress has walked me here. She lets me walk back alone now with the crown.

As for the fountain, it is too dangerous. But I may have as much water brought up as I need.

Carlos tells me I am exhausted. I do not feel it. I ask him about the bookbinder. Yes, he will ask him, he will try. But even the sacrilegious, he says, have little appetite for sacrilege these days.

He tells me to rest a while and take some food. Tomorrow will be the most difficult, the funeral in the morning, the interment that afternoon. But there is one thing left to do, one last duty to perform, and when it's done—*wither this heart of mine filled with rancour and mutiny.* Blast these eyes that have watched you die. Void these lungs that breathed on after your last breath, burst this belly fired with bile and gall, that hungers on though I would make it stop, though I would stop it up.

Let bile and gall dissolve these stones now, bring down these walls that held you in. But oh, even then, that this black ink could raise the radiant dead. . . .

I have cleared the room to do this work. And into the middle of this empty cell I have dragged the desk where once you wrote and I have laid you out upon it.

I will return your body to you. I defy them to deny me this. I will restore you to your beauty.

How much water do I need for this?

I cloak your shoulders, replace your veil, fold your fingers against your empty palms. Cradle out these cool entrails with my own hard hands, pack your cavities with balm. And lift up your vitals in my hands and spread them through the sky, like ribbons.

Carlos comes afterwards, to tell me what was said. They should have come by the thousands, tearing their hair and rending their cloaks . . . and in truth the ceremony was a splendid one. Though many did not come.

But Carlos was there. He rose and came to stand before them. His closing phrases I record:

> There is no pen that can rise to the eminence that hers o'ertops. I should like to omit the esteem in which I regarded her, the veneration which she has won by her works, in order to make manifest to the world how much, in the encyclopaedic nature of her intelligence and universality of her letters, was contained in her genius, so that it may be seen that, in one single person, Mexico enjoyed what, in past centuries, the graces imparted to all the learned women who remain the great marvels of history. The name and fame of Sor Juana Inés de la Cruz will only end with the world. . . . [17]

There is a bird, born in Heliopolis, from a nest of burning spices, who lives but once every few hundred years. She is forged from fire in silence. She is the sun of night. To the first fire, does the firebird return. To the sun's first city, to Heliopolis.

And if you have a little time, together we will take her out across the plains and over the tortured hills, up through pines like bearded giants, where in the cold air her voice echoes still. Up and up across the snowy slopes to the cone's smoking brim.

I will make her long lived. I will make her live three hundred years. I will deliver her. From you, to you.

Here. I place the crown of wildflowers on her brow. There, now we start. This ceremony begins with the heart.

[March 20, 1995]

TEN A.M. He calls in sick. He has been up all night drinking port. Madeleine has already gone out. A whiteness flutters behind his eyes, a blizzard rages silently in his mind. He sits in the den staring at the phone he has brought in from the kitchen. The den once had its own phone. He removed it to remain undisturbed. He has not remained undisturbed.

He looks under 'Limosneros' in the phone book. There is only one. He realizes he remembers Beulah's number; it is not in the book, but it is not her number he is after. He leaves a message at her parents' home. His message now is something in a neutral tone. Have they spoken with Beulah lately? He's just received a disturbing call. Several calls. As he speaks, he knows this too will be a disturbing message to listen to. He is not displeased.

The phone company has promised him a new, unlisted number. By Wednesday morning at the latest. With the police, it goes as he expected. Delisting his number was a good idea. That should do the trick. If it didn't, if she came to the house or office—threatening calls, letters—anything, he should call again immediately. Constable Roberts. Call her police pager number, any time. He puts her card out on the kitchen counter for Madeleine. Their answering machine, unplugged now, is only a squat black box on a countertop.

He looks at the thermometer fixed to the outer frame of the kitchen window. It is almost thirty degrees below zero. A moment of certitude to savour.

It has stopped snowing outside. He begins grading term papers. He marks for almost seven straight hours, stopping only to brew more coffee.

When the phone rings his stomach plummets. Too much caffeine. He looks down at the desk. He is already on his feet. Still it takes him a moment to start towards the phone. It is Madeleine. She will go directly from work to be with Catherine. She'll eat at Mother's. He tells her about his calls, tells her about Constable Roberts. Her voice softens. Mom says Cate's fine. Won't be too late. The roads are icy. It's supposed to hit minus forty. Unbelievable, she says, tomorrow is the first day of *spring*. He tells her she should take care. Coming home. She chides him in return. Eat something decent.

He puts a TV dinner in the microwave, stands at the window. It is dark and very clear. Through the window he can see the stars. He turns on the kitchen light. His guts churn with heartburn and hunger. The microwave bell sounds. He takes his dinner out. Seven thirty-five. He takes the plastic tray back into the den. He is nearly through the stack of papers.

For five days he has hardly slept, since before the onset of his daughter's fever. Now, his belly quieted, he falls asleep.

Madeleine arrives home about ten, finds him propped face down beside an empty TV tray on his desk. She wakes him with difficulty. "You have potatoes in your beard," she says, her eyes crinkling. Bleary-eyed, he gropes at his chin. "Other side."

"Thanks." Though her face is gentle, her beauty tonight strikes him with the full force of mockery. A beauty too long neglected. She is sitting on the edge of his desk in a short black cashmere coat, thick-soled leather boots laced over black stirrup pants. A silver teardrop pendant gleams against a soft black turtleneck. A beaded vest to match the red felt pillbox over her short blond hair. As he looks up at her sitting there on the desk his eyes trace the strong bones of her jaw. Her cheekbones are wide, her blue-grey eyes thoughtful. It occurs to him her eyes look almost oriental. Her cheeks are flushed with cold or drink. Has she been out walking in this?

He is trying to clear his mind of sleep. He smells her perfume. She is wearing more make-up than usual.

"We've come a long way together, for Catherine—for us. We thought we could make our own rules."

"We were wrong."

"Don, let's not run from this too."

"I'm not running."

"Two years ago I would have settled for less." Her face has gone pale, just a bright pink spot high on each cheek. "Two *great* years." There is a fierceness in her voice.

"Best of my life, Madeleine."

"Call her, see her. If you want . . ." She looks down at her hands. "I'd go with you."

"You don't have to do that."

"Anything I ever had . . . my whole life . . . someone's taken back."

Noisy in love, quiet in heartbreak, his wife.

Ahhh, Madeleine. . . . *What have I done. . . . Hush. . . .*

It is dark. She has gone to bed. He is lying naked, covered with a blanket, on the brown leather couch in the den. The backdoor light folds shadows across the deck. Steam spills out from under the icy whirlpool cover. The phone is ringing. He cannot make his body move. The ringing seems to go on forever. He staggers to his feet, over to the phone, blanket bunched over his shoulders. Madeleine is standing at the bottom of the stairs in her long flannel nightdress. He can't see her feet. In the half-light, she hovers. His hand is on the phone. He hesitates.

"Answer it."

Three hundred years ago, a butterfly beat its wings in a convent cell in Mexico.

"Hullo?"

"Hello, Gentle Reader." The voice he knows so well, the voice he has been hearing in his dreams . . . soft, speech slightly slurred. He has never known her to drink more than a glass of wine. "Guess who?"

"Why are you calling me?"

"Because you're late, because it's the night of the equinoctial cocktail, night of shooting stars, night of the MorningStar—"

"Beulah . . ." He twists slightly away, hunches his shoulders to shield the phone. He does not want to see his wife's face at the sound of this name but he can see her shape.

"Please, *profe. Vente, por favor.* I have something here for you. Gentle Reader, please . . ." The voice is soft and faint.

"Why are you calling me that?"

"Because it's after midnight. Because it's tonight and I thought you'd know. Because it's already started and can't be stopped. Because you're late . . . and the best is left to come . . ."

"Beulah, what do you *want* from me?"

"You're the last guest. Everyone's here I'm all alone. . . ." Her speech is so blurred now he cannot make out the rest.

"I'll come tomorrow. Are you in the same place?"

His wife leans heavily against the stairwell.

"Beulah? Are you there . . . ? Beulah I can hear you—what are you *doing?*"

He flinches, and gently returns the phone to its cradle. He stands transfixed, as though it has changed into a snake before his eyes. He turns but cannot meet Madeleine's eyes.

"We can't get this back, can we, Don. We can't fix this. . . ." She looks from his face, to the ground, out the window. "We don't get to keep . . . us."

He moves away from her, walks into the den, begins to dress.

"You're not going *out* in this. . . ."

"You said."

"Not like this—not at this hour."

"It's tonight."

"You *can't*—the roads are *hell*—now *look* at me. *It's forty below zero.*" He pulls on the faded blue T-shirt he has been wearing for two days, something picked out for him in a Banff tourist shop. Beulah's idea of a joke. "*Say* something, for God's sake."

"I need to go out," he answers.

"I need to hear the words." Her lips quiver slightly. "You owe me that much. Are you still in love with her?"

"What . . . ?"

It was an obsession. A long time ago.

Only an obsession . . . no more. He is at the front door. He puts on his slippers, pulls a tweed sports coat from the closet.

"Go up to your daughter's room, Donald. Take a good look around. And you decide where your future is."

Instead he looks outside, thinks he sees a light snow falling.

"I will not let you do this to Catherine."

He opens the door. A burst of vapour rushes up past the eaves. She recoils from the blast of cold. Her hand goes to her throat. "I want your answer—first thing in the morning. One way or the other."

Something in his wife's voice stops him for a moment. He turns back. "She needs help," he says. As he speaks, steam slides between his lips, blurs Madeleine's face. He starts back down the icy steps. He must protect his family. She is ruining his life. He is responsible. This is his carelessness. She is ruining their life.

"I'm calling the police." Her voice is even. He hears the front door bang shut. He starts the car, drives away with the window down, a white fluttering behind his eyes.

By the time he gets back home, the police have come and gone. He is covered in blood. He should have worn dark clothes. His shirt is gone. His chest hair and beard are matted with rust. The quantities suggest a bloodbath. The taste of iron is in his mouth, his head throbs. From behind his eyes the fluttering of white is gone.

Dawn is breaking. His wife of ten years has her answer. An answer of a kind. She finds him standing barefoot on the cedar deck. There is a horror in her eyes. She asks him if he's hurt this girl. He thinks she's asked this before. *This girl*, strange formula for her to use.

Her name is Beulah. Of course he did.

White sun slants across the neighbours' back yards. Whiteness gouts from rooftop vents, trails away to wisps. He strips off his bloody clothes. Is he drunk? she demands. It's light, is he out of his mind? For a moment he turns to face her. He has a small cut on the bridge of his nose, another on his lower lip, gouges in one forearm. Deep slices ooze in his raw palms and knees. A matted track along the inside of one hairy thigh.

He climbs into the smoking whirlpool, scalds feet numb till then like frozen clay.

"Donald I need to know you haven't done something. Tell me you helped her. I need to . . ."

The water foams to iodine. To the tub walls there clings a winy froth, as from an injured lung. She has stopped speaking.

He finds he can look into her face now, straight through the steam into her blue-grey eyes. When he tries to smile, she looks away. She goes inside.

Gentle Reader, you have read the papers, listened to the radio. You think you know the story, maybe even why. It's not so simple. This is the last account of the one who ran, the one who saved himself. Roll the tape, run it again. Please. The facts are not all in.

GREEN AXLE

❧

... How could I fail to love you,
who have found you divine?
Can a cause fail to trigger its effect,
potential exist without its object?
    Since you are the acme of beauty,
the height of all that is sublime,
and all that the green-axle tree of time
ravels in its gyre,
    that my love sought you out, do you wonder?—
that I am yours, need I sign a statement?—
when your every glance and gesture
sets the seal on my enslavement ... ?

[28 Feb. 1995]

HAS IT ONLY BEEN A WEEK? A week out of time. How can I be feeling this? It's too late why now why now why now?

Jacinto Ek Cruz. There is such sweetness in his eyes. His beauty of a woman in a man. This body of a man in me. This body like a small brown flame. Who flickers in and out of me. White palms skimming, skimming ... the tails of startled deer.

Hotel Laguna, Room 22.

Dusk seeps into the room, powders the sheets with poppy seeds. I watch him as he sleeps. This face sophisticated in the innocent.

Eyes of gleaming onyx, flowers folded in a drowse.[18] Calyxes of epicanth, folded in the clasp of sleep. Curved nose, broad bridge—a dolphin fin, the tip a flowerbulb. Little buddha man, Temple Mask ... I watched you breathe. I took your hazel breath, into me. I spill it back over you, in almond dust.

This small man, hairless as a child, water strong. Cashew cock, salted curled, a bead of pearl—cornstarch on the tongue. My little lord of tender corn. Its slit a guppy pout, feeding me.

Vanilla.

You stir, murmur ... something spelled with Ks and Xs. Like ecstasy. I goad the proud little bull that roars, swelling now sweetly smooth unscarred from slot to sac of weathered teak. Greyish pouch, petal soft and ribbed. Testicle. Delicate, like the word. This small man, this delicate tide—who feeds my mouth, my lips on palindromes of moan.

Still I have not woken you.

Then sleep. This time, for you and for me. This time that is for mercy. . . .[19]

While I write.

For the first time in a week. Write *Bacalar!* This glut of beauty! On beauty I am glutted. On beauty he has gorged me. Lagoon of Seven Colours. I could be *happy* here in beauty's harbour. Where the sea has seven colours.

Here we were dragons.

Here we wore hearts.

Hotel Laguna, Room 22. Hooded in flowering trees. Jacarandas, violet pale. *Flamboyanes*, scarlet cardinals cowl. African tulips, their upturned palms orange—a flaming fall of votive wax. Hotel Laguna, Room 22. Rustic clean, built into a hill, every room a view of the lagoon. Feather whisk of a ceiling fan. Sea shells mortared in the walls. Our laboratory our bird blind our refuge our exile. Eat only fish and fruit. Eat only what we pick, only from the fisherman's hand. Wade out as he poles in. Buy before his feet touch land, or go without . . . wade hungry into loveliness.

My hammock on the balcony. The secret of the hammock, *señorita*. Is to lie cross-wise. Kidney pool, poolside bar. Stars of our own movie, drinks under parasols.

Jacinto they said seven. How many do you see?

Now? Only . . . three.

Turquoise, purple, green—*four*, red—

Where?

There, under the mangroves.

I have also seen deep blue and gold.

So only six.

And never yet all at once.

Let's file a complaint.

We saw a toucan yesterday. In the forest, Jacinto took me in through red mangroves propped on roots—each tree the squat of a titan crab.

Very rare now, *el tucán*, Beulah, there are many poachers.

Yellow throat black cloak—green keel-bill dipped in burgundy. Grave little sage, canoe on his head—my flying *portage*, all endurance and grace—make the hieroglyph for elegance the toucan bill.

Here was once a stand of mahogany, and other plants for medicines. . . . What is it, Beulah, why do you smile?

This small man, this Mayan scribe. It is the beauty of a toucan, in his face.

Jacinto, look!

A spotted drum on springs—a brocket fawn's startled leap—ears splay, its long tan neck a wrist of down. Then gone. . . .

On higher ground stand Maya watchtowers. Root-tangled vine-crushed crumble of mounds. A confused sea of striped butterflies that hic and dip and stumble and sway patting out tortillas on the way. Leggy zebras ferrying stilts—slinging girders to a tower of lace . . . somewhere in the trees. One alights on a bromeliad. Antennae drop like booms of hair like drawbridge steel like dowsing wands. Danger danger—*¡aguas!*—operator drunk on nectar, glutted on bromeliads. Yellow swabs of anther, blades of apple-red, rough like crepe—or wafer of meringue. A heart of purple shafts like bean sprouts tapering to the frail bloom tips of frosted flutes.

Bromeliad I drink to you, I drink you in.

But how can I believe? This is real this is me. Glutted on syrups on cornstarch on wonder. He has glutted me. Is this me eyes raw with colour? skin a harp of blasted glass . . . nails and teeth soft like caramels? Is this me making *love* in the trees on beaches and balconies? My body's every entrance a punished fruit, this hairy orchid where I walk bruised with ecstasy.

My tongue is a new animal.[20] It lives in my mouth. I have seen it looking back in the glass. Rawsplit tip, strawberry rough / in rawsugar dipped, the rest the pulp a oneleg squid—a lung a coral sponge—*muscle kite on a mango string!*

So how do I believe, how can this be me?

YESTERDAY I INVENTED A NEW COLOUR. A primary colour, I am sure of it. Beyond the farthest shore of purple. I see it in my head. Primarily. How do I show it? To anyone. I have seen the sea.

The sea has seven colours.

Last night we read our bodies, by the light of one firefly in a jar. The night before we swam in our new skins, in a lagoon as warm as blood.

It's safe Jacinto at night there are no sharks?

It is safe, Beulah. Here is where the dolphins come. To have children. Look. Look at the water.

What *is* this? This light—

A kind of plankton. Like the firefly. You shake it glows. Feel them? Like grit on the skin. I have not seen this since I was a boy.

Last night we swam through trails of green fire.

We dove and dove, eyes salt-scorched, watched comet tails stream from our hands our chins our hair. Over and over I traced with a fingertip the keel of fire between his thighs . . . proud barque, little dolphin fin.

Last night, with him, I plunged naked through a river of fire.

Jacinto how can this even be? Is it real. *Is it real for you.* . . .

Oh yes. And see this answer echo in his onyx eyes. Nights of fireflies. Nights of shooting stars. Nights that smell of cinnamon. Bacalar.

Jacinto tomorrow night we'll stay out—all night.

In the hammock? I am accustomed. But you—

We'll watch for another meteor shower.

Or lightning. Like last night, far out to sea.

Firefly storms like the night before.

Or just sleep, like never in years. . . .

Tomorrow Beulah we go farther up the lagoon. It was to be my surprise. A fisherman there saw manatees. You should see the tropical fish. They go by the thousands to feed. Where the underground rivers flow in. There are two of these. Who even knows where they flow from? Will that not be fine, Beulah? I have only heard of this, a thing I have never seen. We leave at dawn, we discover it together. I have arranged for masks and fins. . . .

Manatees.

Dawn. White and blue shrimp boats moored to red mangroves. A dog sleeps on a fishing net, white snout snuffling a reek of dogfish dreams. . . . Sunrise on the lagoon. The sea's seven colours are a spectrum fused to white gold. Charcoal shoals of kelp in the glare. Through them a lone fisherman poles to the sun, boat and man and shadow, a runnel of black wax. Offshore a fish leaps through the sea's gold mask, falls back.

Beulah—did you see?

Yes.

A tarpon.

Meet the fisherman. Make the mind blank. Admire the sturdy launch, the outboard twins by Evinrude. I have the masks and fins *que pidió*, don Jacinto.

Jacinto, let's not go today.

But the underground river. The masks. It is all arranged. . . .

Please, not today.

Pedro has taken a day from fishing.

There must be somewhere else. Ask. Please.

There are many places, yes.

Everything's packed, we have lots of water don't we?

Pedro, *la lancha* can make it out to Banco Chinchorro?

Claro, don Jacinto. I fish there every week. The bottom drops to a thousand metres. The grouper are big like pigs. But it will be two or three hours. Even with this calm.

Yes. I know.

One last day of make believe. For Jacinto, try. Expedition to Banco Chinchorro / Seine-net Bank, where flamingoes try to restart a colony, says Pedro, vendor of exotica—sorry all full up, suitcase stuffed. After an hour of sun and wind and spray look back to a coast all marsh and bays and bights and estuaries. Filaments of land in the sea. Land as lace—tresses strands scrolled banisters of land—green marbled in a march of blue. Out past coral quays—little chins that sprout toy scrub. Farther out, stunted lynx-tuft palms list on atolls of powdered glass. Smalltalk impossible over the Evinrude brawl of outboard twins.

Dry land at last, twin echoes fading, fading . . . two more engines in my head. Torment of smalltalk. Do not meet his eyes. Walk a shore of staghorn coral harvested by hurricanes. Musical chatter, carpet of femurs . . . a clearcut of chalk.

No flamingoes. So we dive we dive we dive into the mercy of silence, cross tan constellations of starfish in buckskin boots, skim a colony of conch—a cargowreck of smashed trumpets. Deeper. Two startled turtles with the heads of hawks, dear proud heads impossible hearts.[21] Slide through fish like storms of leaves—twitch and still, school and scatter—*hojarasca*, a thousand-headed ganglion. . . .

Side by side we glide past crests and combs, slabs of colour—spectral rhino hides in our underwater photographs. Come dive on a reef of pelts piled where dropped—drop in drive thru diveby extinction of the buffalo in Disney hues. Dive and drift, skim the brochure, take our underwater jungle cruise—but do not stay too long in this cartoon safari. In these dream gardens, in these palaces of bone. That beckon. Profuse, fluorescent . . . prodigal bouquets for the convalescent dead.

The tulips are too red.[22]

Evening. Sunset. Sea of painted glass.

Darkness. Crayons streak the fishing harbour—a string of coloured lights along the jetty. Thick smears of broken wax. We can hardly bear to look. At each other. Can barely speak with it. We measure off the distances, with lengths of silence.

The night smells of cinnamon.

Tomorrow, Beulah, what would you like to do. Do we go for the manatees? Or Fort San Felipe built in the 17th-century. *Sweet Jacinto, your turn to make believe.* Here is where the first Spanish ran aground. Two years before Cortés. They have repaired the bronze guns, the balustrade—

Jacinto . . . tomorrow I'm leaving. *Tomorrow I'm leaving Jacinto.*

But, we . . .

To Chichén Itzá.

But why?

For the equinox. To see the shadow. Of the serpent, moving down the steps.

Why.

It's what all the tourists—

Why.

Something I planned. For a long time. To see it for myself.

Why.

It's important . . . to me.

Why, Beulah?

The end of something. I need to see it end.

I did not ask where. I do not care why you are going *there*. I ask why you are *leaving*. Here.

Three weeks.

It is not three weeks. It is one Maya *month*. You can have no idea. What it can mean—I will go with you.

Don't you have work, important work?—how long were you planning to keep me—

I will go. *Contigo.*

No.

Why.

I need to go alone.

Why.

Because I can.

Why.

Don't. Please.

I know Chichén Itzá.

No more guides, Jacinto. *No more rescues.*

There will be thousands. In some years *a hundred thousand people.* Do you know what such a crowd is?—what kind of thing? It is like a god with no jaw.

He does not sleep in the hammock with me. He sleeps in the bed. He wakes me, stands by the hammock in the darkness.

Are you awake? Are you listening? Beulah we have something, I think. Do not throw it away. On a plan.

Three weeks. Why can't you just accept—

What you are doing is very dangerous. At the fire—with the men. The drugs.

You think I'm going back there. Chichén Itzá is so ridiculous to you?

This knowledge you want—

I didn't invent this, you did.

Who?

America—don't the anthropologists tell you people anything?

I am speaking seriously.

Synaesthetic sacred rites all across the Americas, the highest trans-ports—you're the guide you tell me.

Ahh, yes, five senses in one—a shopping flyer, a supermarket. Have everything at once, but something else first. This is not you speaking. This is your culture's sickness.

You said that before.

Time is your disease.

Now explain it.

Are you ready to hear?

Let's find out.

Our masterpiece was never drugs. And it is not a recipe. The Maya masterpiece was time. *Eres muy lista . . .* but you know nothing about us. A little about the Aztecs but only in books. By white experts. You will not know us through books or drugs. They are gone, but the Maya are here. One is standing before you. Here. Now . . .

Dear sweet Jacinto, pacing back and forth across the balcony. I climb down from the hammock. Sit in a cane chair. *The secret of the hammock, señorita, is to lie.*

Plans—this sickness of your culture. Going to the end of things. There is no end, Beulah. Or you do not get there, it comes to you. Whether or not you ask. So there is no need, to go alone.

I'll be back—*soon*.

How much has changed already in the one month we know each other? In this last week? *Soon*—you spend your lives in soon—so near so far. Your time is a caged animal. Your soon is the cage I walk in now. Look at me.

Silently, on bare feet, he swings back and forth—pendulum that strokes the nightsea gleam. My small eclipse.

Time is not a line, Beulah, time is not a ladder time is not a mountain side. Time is *Yaxche*.

Yaxche.

If you would put away your books and your experts I could show you, I could try. What is soon to you? Wait wait always first something else. A scientific culture—*how can you be so slovenly about time?* Your toy calendar—still no place notation for time even now. Time is your disease. I have read in five more years your magnificent computers may die of it. *A culture of wealth and property.* How much of what your parents now hold can they pass on to you? Of the items now in their house—that they do not really own yet anyway. How many of these objects will not fall apart, fall out of fashion, be repossessed? A dress, a car, a bowl, a tool?

One piece of advice that holds true for always?

My mother threw everything away, Beulah. Your parents will not have to.

Time is money you say. No, your money is time—how much is it truly worth Beulah Limosneros? I have seen them in New York in California in Tejas. Dishwashers, microwave ovens, running water—so much running and still you have no time. No time to cook. No time for others that you do not secretly begrudge. For family for friends. *A technological culture.* For every painful step your knowledge takes your ignorance runs back ten. Radio—can you explain it? What makes a toaster pop? Can you bake a bread of corn or wheat, light a fire without gasoline? Feed yourself for two days in the forest?—what *forest?* Name the hills the flowers the insects the plants all around you—even in your own country, your mother tongue, your home town? Do you have home towns? Can you tell what month—what day it is by looking at the constellations?—even *see* the sky at night? Draw a picture of what you see, without shame, or sing a song before others—without shame—play an instrument? How many of you ever wrote a poem? And, for those few, how long has it been?

What can you teach a child that you are sure of? One thing that lasts? Can you keep anything holy?

My pendulum stops. Stands naked in the dark. Between me and the sea. We had nights that smelled of cinnamon. . . . Long nights of want, nights of once. In a place called Bacalar.

You had to wait for the Mayans from India to give you zero. But still you have no concept of *zero time*. You cannot take time out of time. No true concept of both-and-neither. It is just a game for intellectuals I have read. You have no word for neverness. And it is this time out of time, this fusion of everything that thinks and feels and sees and is *and* time—you can just barely glimpse your ignorance. Except like a shopping trip like a duty free port like Belize. And this ignorance of yours is not bliss, it is your agony. Time you can cut into tiny fractions but time for you has no stop. Your physicists have barely begun to imagine it, how it might run faster or slower, yet you have sped it up without knowing what it was. You make it flat. You make it run on a line. Straight on and up. Like a train, like your progress rocket. But you cannot make it step off the rails. Walk across a field. Pick a mango. Sit. Rest. Look at the stars. . . .

The equinox, Beulah. In Chichén Itzá. Your March 20, 1995. Is this 1995 years after the birth of Christ or after his crucifixion? How many of you can say? And if it is the crucifixion was it done in the year zero or one? Thirty-three years' difference. Plus the uncounted months from Christmas to Easter. And why is your Easter always moving around? And why can't you decide when he died?

It is a kind of smoke in your heads. Time.

Months of 28, 31, 29, 30 days. How many of you even know how old you are? *How long is a month?* Do you count your age from conception or delivery? And what if you are born late or early? And when you turn twenty are you starting your twentieth year or ending it? How many *scientific* Americans still nod on Sunday to hear the world began in 4004? Is that 4004 years before his birth or 4038 years before his death . . . give or take a few months, and a few more days for Easter, and the count that begins at zero or one. . . .

It is a smudge, a greenwood fire burning in your minds. Time.

A month has 20 days, Beulah. Punto final. One *tun*. One year. Eighteen months of exactly twenty days. Five dog days each year. Time out of time, Beulah. Five days. Like our time here in Bacalar. *Katun*—each a decade of twenty. *Baktun*—twenty katun. Each cycle increasing by a factor of twenty. A simple system, Beulah. A stone age system. We have used it to make calendrical calculations. *142 nonillion years into the future*. To the day, to the hour. But here the smudge is growing bigger. It is now a forest fire. Your word nonillion, look at your dictionary. Any number followed by 36 zeroes ... or else 50. *Or else 50*. Fourteen zeroes difference, your dictionary cannot decide. Yet your Big Bang! happened *only nine zeroes ago*. This is becoming serious. An explosion, a holocaust, a fire that covers the Amazon. In Europe a billion is a million million. In America only a thousand million. Yes even today, in your information age. *A mathematical culture*. The zero, it still does not really count for you. Zero number, zero time. You still do not quite see, do you? Even after fifteen centuries—and fifteen new deserts. Time is like a mistake to you, the smear of an eraser. How can you bear to have this smudge in your heads? Is that why you have set the world on fire? It is your disease, Beulah. Like the first confusion of a fever, the clumsiness of the ill in the way you touch the world. And now your progress rocket burns out, like bad fireworks. Like bad time. Like a sun flaring out. It is why you smash and burn everything that is precious and precise.

Like a tree.

Your ideas of infinite time are even less interesting than of space. Your time is like the first geometry we teach a child. You have confused *time* with space—an infinite line running back and forth like a metronome. Then you confuse infinite time with *eternity*—a symphony so complex, that branches and leaves and dies like a tree, that swells like a seed. But time is not reason Beulah time is not a line, the tracks of a train. Time is mind, it runs how it will and where and why. And there is a mind of time out of time.

We were a people of the forest. Time, like the sky, was always green. Zero time is a living thing. Now it has come out of the forest to kill you. It swallows your dreams. It feeds where you eat. It feeds on what's left of your trees while you sleep. It is an abscess, an ulcer, an absence inside. It is a blur in your minds, a waking dream. It is the food that starves you.

And we were its wizards. Once. Once, there was a zero time.

Quédate, Beulah. Tomorrow morning I will borrow another car. There is a place I have been waiting to show to you.

I am begging *you* now.

CENOTE AZUL

COME SEE THE MANATEES. Stay one more day. Hear them sing like mermaids. Each to each.[23] Stay one more day in once, not soon. This is how they tempt you. The wizards in the road. Will you stay? We will bask in the sea. Singing each to each. Will you stay? We are all welcome here. Stay one more day in once upon a time. In a place called Xcalak. Take a boat from Bacalar. To places spelled with Ks and Xs. Like ecstasy. Like axes.

They tempt you with the world, the tulips are too red. They heal you, build you up. For more, for Never is enough. But the silence has reached here too. And it will spread. It follows you. In a slattern's slouch and sprawl.

Alright Jacinto Ek Cruz. One more day for what you have tried to do for me. Tomorrow, a place upstream. Of Cenote Azul.

Tomorrow is a place for divers, Beulah Limosneros. Like yesterday. I have seen photographs from underwater. Divers in a cave. Water so clear it looks like they are flying, like bats. . . .

Here, Jacinto? This is really it? It's the third 'Blue Cenote' sign we've passed.

There are a hundred *cenotes azules*, Beulah. It is the name we use when we have lost the old names.

Parched scrub, dusty parking lot, cardboard signs Cenote Azul fifty metres. Park the ancient Tercel, take a beaten path, follow the trash of drinking cups and straws. Dengue hatcheries. Through the last screen of branches I hear children's voices—laughter and shouts, deep splashes.

Turquoise!—colour as oasis of the eye!—a diving tank sunk in limestone a greenish blond. The water starts two metres down, jump from anywhere! A step of notches to climb back up. *Karst*, this rock is karst.

Cenote Azul. Here we are. In this water you can see sixty metres to the bottom.

Here? So many people. . . .

No, we go upstream. Two kilometres.

Upstream—what stream?

That runs beneath our feet. *Cenote* is where the earth falls, into the rivers that run under us. . . . Come. This is palmetto. This is *chechen*. If you sleep under this in a storm, it rains down poison. And this one, in a certain season when the sun shines hard it pops like popcorn. The whole tree, for hours.

An hour deeper into forest. We walk under taller trees, through a deeper green. Through a line of leaf-cutter ants.

Is it not like a picket-line, Beulah, tiny strikers waving signs?

Look, the iguana eating them, I haven't seen that kind.

Basilisco rayado, not quite iguana, but a cousin.

Banded basilisk. Chocolate brown, striped in lime. Stern-eyed, cowled, its throat a wimple of white. We wade deeper into green. Two green parrots flush—their broken faces a bob of apple-red, twin pugilists, little rams with bloody-brows. . . .

Jacinto stops. These tall ones are mahogany. This is ceiba. Their roots run down into the river here.

Where? Scan the ground the high canopy, filter the dappled light. . . . Clean muscular trunks, veined in heavy vines—calfed—*sandalled* they stride a lawn of giant ferns, elephant ears. Hush. . . .

We stand on the heart of a riddle, we dance in its palm. Paradox, a river that runs underground. Birdcalls in the hush, sun and shade, coolness in warmth, spaciousness as embrace. . . .

Come. He slips under a fern, another. Still I do not see. Another. Here.

A meteor has crashed to earth broken its crust of karst—scorched it lilac—veined it rust. Mintgreen wells to the wound—roots creepers vines start from the water in a shock of green wire I can't make sense of this. My eyes . . . make them slower, slower . . . see the ruined windings of an ancient motor, a clock. Broken trunks furred in a caterpillar moss crisscross the cenote five metres across. Stand stunned in a bower of tall ferns, in a blind of zero time.

On the crater's far side spreads a blistered skin of water lilies . . . Sprigs of shy orchids nestle in the vines. They hover just above the green water, their roots are strands of golden hair . . . that skinnydip.

I remember . . . this mint green, the Bow in winter. Wintergreen cracks in a river of ice. A breeze stirs the canopy—

Ohh—a shaft of sun—a turquoise wedge driven deep into green.

God.

I wanted you to see. Before you leave.

He undresses. In two stoops of white cotton. Two *huarache* shucks. He is naked, hairless as a child. Scentless as a fawn. We can swim. There will be no one. He stands at the edge, his naked back to me. A ray of light. A shadowbrand of perfect leaf in the small. In the small brown small of this back. He stands, watches the water. You see, he says, angel fish. He speaks without turning his face, half turns his shoulders. He is swelling for me or a shape he has seen in the water. Tropical fish, they come upstream in fresh water. The food is so rich. His nakedness . . . a slow wag, a little swing bridge of friendliness. My heart could break for this. He stands there so calmly, speaking to me, swelling still, so painfully now. This long sprain of cinnamon from a dove's swollen throat, petal-soft ruff. . . .

Will you swim?

He turns to face me. His large black eyes. He seems unaware. A length of anatomy, straining. A length of him, for me. To me. This small man. He clambers down the vines—little bum—pauses at the water, points—*That* one is an iguana. Clinging sideways in rigging, a lizard sailor.

Is it cold?

Same as the earth.

He goes in, lowers himself on the roots. Lowers himself to the brows, to the little bowlcut bangs. Crown dry, temples damp, scrolls down his neck, to the blades of his shoulders.

Will you swim?

I follow him to the edge. I make myself naked for him. For this small man, this scribe. I see his want. Now in his eyes. They follow me up. I stand for him. Naked in this air, in this blind space, in this zero time. I feel his onyx eyes. Their glow, their pause, their lingering. They follow me up. My thighs. I do not flinch. I let him in. This is me, this is real.

I follow him down, by the roots of trees. Down to the warmth of the earth to my chin.

This is making love. This silence, ankles wound into vines. Surges of water, this weightless angels' buck and plunge. Holding on. Hanging by roots, pushing back with white palms. Bucking like angels . . . we are mustangs with wings. We are mustangs with wings.

A whir, a hummingbird low in the orchids—lady doctor, dancing in her emerald sari. Her ruby veil tucked beneath her chin to work, a veil as soft as red as tulip lips. Jacinto, this is real, this is me. In this silence.

No . . . not silence.

In this small tide that rises and falls, in this breath before a moan before a sigh before the hush, in this lung of karst, this is not silence but the breath that quickens it.

Your hazel breath. I answer you with almonds—

Splashdown to water—our voyeur iguana, my startled laughter my breath moves in your mouth. I quicken you. We are in motion, in love, in the echoes of breath, in the warmth of the earth in a place off the map, where the lizard swims. . . .

It clambers out, drunken sailor, up the rocks. Breath, laughter—

Penny-echoes in a well.

Jacinto Ek Cruz, I have seen, I have heard. And felt.

I will remember. Now, I can write her death.

THE RED LAND, THE BLACK

[3 Mar. 1995]

THE BUS FROM CHETUMAL passes in less than an hour, or a lot more. The only one today. One A.M. It is never early, you can be sure. If he sees people, he will slow down. If we leave now, we can walk in plenty of time. You have so little, would you like to leave something behind?

Sweet lover, sweet friend . . .

As you say, I have so little.

I am becoming a little transparent no?

I'll be back—I promise. Now *you* have to learn.

Learn?

To trust *me.*

The dress looks very nice. My cousin did a good job with the hem. A few little scorches. Is it practical to travel . . . in a dress?

For peeing at the roadside or crouched on a toilet seat. Very.

Ah, I did not know.

Something else for you.

You see, you can teach after all. Here, I would like you to take my jacket. It is a light cotton but better than nothing. For the air conditioning on the bus. For the nights. . . .

Yes you are becoming transparent.

We walk north along the shore. A warm mid-night of cricket anthems, lightning far out to sea. We turn left to the lights of the little town. One main street, four streetlights, four storms of moths . . . blindness spirals down.

We wait here.

You're not angry anymore?

I am calm now. What does one say to someone who wants to leave.

I *don't*—

Who cannot see why she should stay, then. I have had a month to find the words. What does one say, *¿quién sabe?* Now I have said all I can. I have let the land speak for me. . . .

Jacinto . . . I have seen I have heard.

So not angry, calm. Sad, a little. As your friend, I should have done better. I have failed to understand you. There is some thing I am not quite seeing.

There are things I haven't said. About being responsible, about work.

But if we forget *all this*, even good work is a prison. And if it is service, I think our service goes nowhere if it does not lead . . . back here.

Sweet man, I want so badly for you to understand. I'll learn. I'll find the time in now. I'll fight for it, I promise. But first I need three weeks of soon.

Jacinto, there's something . . . I can finish now. This thing of five years, *yo tambien he andado buscando palabras.* And then I'll be back. But now I need you to trust me. Can you?

You can teach me.

I'll *write*.

Write if you want but come back. . . . ah, the bus.

With stops, five hours to Cancún. The road hugs the coast. Remember, the eight A.M. to Chichén Itzá. It arrives just as the tourists start to check out of their hotels. Close to the equinox the prices—

Go sky high, I know.

Driver, *un momento.* So what do you do?

Go to Valladolid and bargain a long term rate. I have your friend's name at the ruins.

No, Beulah, no more kissing until you come back to me. And no adioses. *Hasta luego,* is all.

I'll see you, Jacinto. Hasta la vista, hasta muy pronto, hasta la proxima vez. ¿Ves . . . ?

Jacinto—wait.

Yes?

I'll bring you back your jacket.

Queridísimo Jacinto,

I promised I'd write I am writing now, before the lights of the town die out. Four lighthouses, beacons back to you. We'll make a space together for this, the hardest thing in the world: to speak the simple truth to one another. And to speak of this greatness that runs in us, trapped in too few notes. Too many promises, too little hope. I'll learn, I'll try with you, to stop the engine in my head, let it run into the world like a child.

But for now I can write, that much I know how to do. Tell a complicated truth, begin with this. I will tell you about this work, for the sceptics who won't ask, for the believers who just can't anymore, for the others who won't let us. Who make forests into parks, while the sceptics build deserts for cynics to golf in. But how will I find words for you?

I'll start with what you've shown me. What can we hope for a people who every year sees fewer and fewer stars, less night in the sky? Each year more light, the combustion of what was. Ancient life forms turned to burning tar, light from younger stars. Each year bigger telescopes to show us still more of what once was. A sky of old news—out-dated by millions of years. The zeroes, we'll count them together from now on. Smudges in our heads—whole galaxies, Jacinto, not just Time. Little smudges of once and soon. We see stars *die*, like old home movies.

So why not a planet, a people, a language, a species—thirty thousand a year? Too many to name. And what's in a name but another kind of bias, of local perception. Of local affection. When a serial number would do. An order number in a star catalogue. Nothing really *is* anything else—no that would be a *metaphor*—admit one and the whole world starts sprouting tails and wings and horns. Again. Even numbers we make into trinities and pentecosts, octaves and hexes, the days of creation and the three names of serial killers. But all things are number, and number the first metaphor. We are the meaning machines, Jacinto, we make belief.

But more than that, through us, Being *means*—*believes*—and even *doubts*, who knows? Was our greatest invention ever and always our soul?

When we make these things meaningless—confuse myth with untruth—we sever the dragon twins and set them loose like storms, like only-children fighting over the world. Orphan twins riven at the ankle— dragons of rage and indifference, wonder and cynicism, Typhon and Apophis. Storming over the land while we sleep, swallowing the world, devouring us while we dream of certainties and shearing sheep.

But how do I explain? About the souldeath of accidie and these hands of accident? How do I explain that Phoenix and Phaëthon were twins? lone stars of dusk and dawn. How do I make a place in the world to speak of all this? Of the myths that are consuming us, even as we starve on transcendent unbelief. In an age of doubt, what is radical scepticism—the kind that asks the hardest questions over and over and will never stop—if not a kind of faith?

But how to make this into speech? I begin with what I've seen with you, and heard.

I have seen this beauty of the world with the Eye Restored, the eye that eats, to see through its swallowed adversary. And sees a world made still more beautiful through the knowledge of each new thing forever to be lost to us.

And I have seen your people. I've watched them bundle their lives into the streets. Like turtles. Seen this beauty of animals in their faces—the flashing black eyes and smiles. And I have seen them dying. I see them now at each stop. Climbing on, stepping off—the heavy bundles, the steps so tall. We ride together and rest a while. Look . . . the children, the ancients, the separate ones. Boys burning for the city, girls leaving home who hardly dare hope but, a little, do. I have loved them like you, and felt their courtesy. And I have seen how, quietly, they die each time we break a temple stone.[24]

Jacinto I know there is a life for me. Here and now. A place to be loved to be whole to be filled. With you, by you. For a time at least. You have shown me how, how almost belonging can be enough. I have seen our impossible love and loved it too. Hopelessly. Little turtle with the head of a hawk with eyes that see into me, I have seen into *you*, into your art of breaking hearts, so artlessly. . . .

With you I've heard the silence of the world between the heaves of breath. I've felt your breath of hazel on my neck—felt my heart quicken, felt the bellows in your soft chest / sough beneath my cheek.

I close my eyes. I go into you. With you, in you, I glimpse zero time, see the Great Year stop. Time lying on its side, lying down with us. Together we watch it turn on its green axle, spin to spin, irreducible paradox, spilling open now, spilling out. . . . spilling its bright child.

This holy terror, this stranger in the dark we've known all along.

Jacinto though I still worry and doubt—you're right, who knows what can happen in a month?—I can ask you to wait a little while. And then we'll tend our small fire. We'll plant and name, we'll remember and predict. We'll be determined. We'll have conviction.

There's no need to go alone. You've shown me now. The serpent writhing down the temple steps, this is not a one-way trip. Three weeks—how long is too much *soon?* Is that so long, to write this end, this death, and let the serpent into the rivers that flow under us.

One Maya month. To call the great holocaust by its secret name—four species that die for each minute of sun at the equinox. For the magic of that naming, for the magic that loves the hungry, is this too much to sacrifice?[25]

Three weeks of soon I dedicate to you, these journals, each day that remains. . . .

Dearest Jacinto, how did this get so grave?

The old man in front opens a window. Lets the warm night in. It rushes past my ears . . . The same night you hear now in the Hotel Laguna, Room 22.

You taught me a kind of laughter, too. And there is so much more to tell you. About the sweet bus driver who looked sadly at me as I left you. About his heart's complicity. About how hard I wish all the lovers in the world might find it all around them, this complicit heart. Co-conspirators—in bus drivers and flowersellers, in bakers and waitresses, in editors and executioners, in teachers and chicken vendors. In all the villages called San Andrés, in all the places that begin with Xs and Ks.

In all the dictionaries! As in excite, exalt, exhilarate exclamation, exquisite exhaustion—as in excursus, excuses, extenuating circumstances, ecstatic exhibitionists. But I can tell you all this tomorrow. I'll write every day—*sweet nothings*, sweet friend, you've taught me to sleep again, to laugh. Taught me too well. . . . I'm so drowsy now.

But wait . . . little turtle, world on his back, my flying portage . . . if you can't sleep yet, I send you a nursery rhyme, to hold and keep thee this night. These *berceuse* verses of *our* Time's great poet, Willy silly like this only very rarely. Could you make him for this one night an honorary Maya?

> . . . So they lov'd, as love in twain
> Had the essence but in one ;
> two distincts, division none :
> Number there in love was slain . . .
>
> Hearts remote yet not asunder ;
> Distance, and no space was seen
> 'Twixt the turtle and his queen :
> But in them it were a wonder . . .
>
> . . . Reason in itself confounded,
> Saw division grow together ;
> To themselves yet either-neither
> Simple were so well compounded . . . [26]

Good-night, sweet scribe. Enough for now. I throw you pennies down a well. . . .

Your Science Queen.

I thought it was a dream. At first. A bad dream. I start, awake—the bus
empty. It is pulled over to the side, tilted. *I am alone.* Same seat, driver's
side, third from the back. The old man in front is gone. The burning boy,
hopeful girl are gone. No lights, no town, no voices. The bus's emptiness.
Headlights, passing slow now . . . a cruising suspicion—skews a slow
ladder of light across the ceiling, the overhead rack, empty. Notebook in
my lap—your jacket over me, your scent—*my bag is gone.* I come to my
feet, to the front of the bus crank the handle, pitch down into the dark.
All the passengers are herded into a little clutch, huddled in bus shadow
and down into the black ditch. Beyond, two helmets, two machine-gun
barrels gleam in the moon. The luggage bays are open, bags in the gravel.
Two more soldiers, straightening up, the driver. Rushes over.

What *is* this?

Señorita, I . . .

My *bag*—you let them take it—*search* it?

I am sorry.

Why didn't you wake me? Why didn't anybody?

I was afraid the soldiers did not want me—

Did they pay you?

I was afraid.

The soldiers start forward, another calls from ahead. Wordless they
walk past, climb into a Jeep. Another Jeep pulls from the rear. Both drive
off. The driver scrambles up, turns on the interior lights—jaundicespill
of light into the ditch, the brush, over a dirt track.

If anything is missing, *señorita,* I will pay.

This is not a dream. It is the same dusty driver. Faded old photo-
graph of a young man, his universal driver uniform, dusty greys, blue
knit polyester vest, polyester tie. Little strip of moustache just along the
lip. This is not a dream, Jacinto. I don't dream of polyester. You need to
know this about me too, I dream in silks. The passengers mill, human
luggage carousel replacing bags in the bays. I find mine, open still. The
CD player, the music we listened to in the Hotel Laguna. Jane Siberry,
Annie Lennox, Jann Arden. McLachlan, Morissette. Gone, all my beautiful lyricists. But not the laptop at the bottom.

If you were here now, you'd tell me these things are replaceable, *son
cosas que pasan.* If you were here now.

Something is missing, *señorita? Sinceramente se lo pago el costo—*

No . . . No señor, olvídalo. Let it go.

But wait, where are you going?

For a swim.

But you can't—

How far?

Not far but it is not safe.

And this *is?*

There are patrols on the beach. We are near Cancún.

For the first time I've been robbed in Mexico, had something taken from me—*for the first time.* On your bus, *señor. Co-conspirador.* I'll take my chances out there. . . .

Soon it will be light. I follow my moonshadow up the dirt path. Yellowing moon at my back. Almost full. I am not alone, I am not afraid. I have the moon, and you.

Bonepale track I follow through dark scrub. One constellation emerges from this darkness that glows like black glass. Orion. We all know this one, frail in the moon. Long trudge, weary pony . . . finally my scrub blinders curl open to the sea—night sprawls above a deeper, liquid dark. I hook the straps of my sandals through two finger crooks, start the walk north. The sand is damp with dewfall. Under my soles it crunches like new snow.

North, Cancún's smudge and smoulder, east, the cool grey ash of dawn.

I stop here, there are so few stars, fewer with each step to Cancún. I sit on a log under Orion, tend its small fire, ours, wait for daylight to come. The coral sand still glows a little under me. I dig my toes in. My subway penlight a firefly winking off, winking on when I think of something to say to you. . . . Fading night that roars with crickets and stars. It's still our last night, Jacinto, the same moon, the same dark that held us both. Scents of sweet wild dill, if I close my eyes the faintest waft of cinnamon. You're not so very far. . . .

The moon sets a deep orange, its western edge of nibbled cheddar . . . dark orange of additives, mousetrap cheese . . .

After the moonset the stars flare, sharpen. Orion grows stronger in his hooded cage, straps on his sword. So softly in, the needles go, Jacinto, when we're not so alone. This too is beauty's harbour. The little bay, this glimmer of sand that curves east, out toward a low headland. Still not a breath of wind. Sea of still black oil, not the smallest wave laps the shore.

Slow Venus shakes herself free now of ash, bright pearl in a shell of cinders, in a char of coal and indigo. The last frail stars melt out, ice shavings on a *comal*. . . . Each minute ticks a notch on the spectrum . . . from royal purple to lavender to rawest pink . . . her soft, bruised blush to the dawn.

She wades now in a surf of faint pink foam. The tip of the headland is the gondola that has stopped for her swim. . . .

No, Jacinto, now there *is* a boat at the headland. A long rowboat pulled up on the sand. Its black silhouette curves under a bristle of oar handles, sharp under a sky gone furious crimson, the red of elements. The horizon as filament—tong-red Venus, soles roasting in the fire we tend.

The whole sea north to south is a pan of scarlet oil.

Now a slivering of sun splits the horizon—a new island a volcano a red continent nosing up from the seabed! Molten mass that will not hold, flares out a little skirt—a gather of glass tearing free of the sea— its lower edge stretches, a membrane, a winding sheet of taffy.

Behind the headland another sun reflects—iron-red, in the hull of a patrol boat at anchor. Little mast of thin sticks, that withers in this sun of pomegranate.

Closer in, a smaller sun wavers, cherry-red, the window of a beach house, a car . . . Oh, Jacinto I wish you could be here to see, this sky, this sea. Venus a hard red ruby now. Just as the sun pulls free—synchronized perfectly!—the first wavelet breaks on the shore, stirring a breeze. . . .

Today there will be wind. I get to feel the *tradewinds*—after how many weeks on this coast? I'M ON THE SHORE OF THE CARIBBEAN SEA! Morning star of my own movie.

A soft wind is blowing. The cherry sun is now two, unequal halves— so a beach house, not a car—wavering. Two dancers of fire. Jacinto did you ever stop in Cholula on your way to Mexico, see the *pulque* dancers, a temple mural? Intact from 2000 years ago. Have you seen them? Surrealism two millennia before Dali—wavering figurines . . . a liquid dance of drunkard reds and ochres. Let's go some time, together.

There are three red suns now, one large two small. Three copper figures from the mystical East, dancing out of a dream of fire. Guardians of the dawn's red palaces. . . .

Now four. One large three small. They have come from the valleys of Hinnom and Red Henna, where the fires are never quenched, where the wind flutes through the thighbones of children. They have come out of the Valley of Alders and Amber. Out of Phoenicia.

Jacinto, why have they come?

There are five red suns . . . in a wedge, sun glinting off their visors, their high-tech bucklers and targes that taper like kites. They march under a waving human banner—red sun glaring from heads of gold, arms of silver, bellies of brass. Beachcomber welders in splints, butchers and bakers widow makers—

We know these men.

Four hundred malevolent stars glint in their buckles and bosses and rivets and gussets, in their belts and guns, in the gleam of boots greaved in blood. Knees of copper, feet of porcelain dust. Sad death heralds they come to quell the insurgent Arab, make war on the doubting Ninevite. Scarab warriors of the beetling brows, umbrals of iron—roaches in russet armour I know you.

Bright Child, they have come for us . . . they have come for me.

They walk in ragged formation, they walk to me in fire and shadow. Fierce light off the water, in their long black shadows gouging trenches where they step. *Treble-dated crows of tyrant wing,* cast your sable pinions of murder west.[27] Foul forerunners of the fiend, augurs of the fever's end—

Captain Hoofleak where are your ponies gone? Commandant of the redshirts and black—my Blond Holocaust, *I name you.* Sun a crush of copper foil in his beard—a shower of sparks, rooster tails from a grinder of iron. I see the whites of his men's eyes—murrengers harbingers spites.

They have seen me now.

Jacinto just look at them! On they come in their breeches of bombast, vests of brass and buff, shields of Hephaistus and Ajax, hides of wild dog and ox. Scarabs! See the thighs slow in armour, the pea groins codded, queerbullies copped at elbow and chin. On each blunt head a little chapel of iron, burning down.

Beneath their beetle brows whole continents of red extinction, under brims ducktailed like turtle shells.

See their paultry shoulders—maxi-padded businessmen with cushy jobs / in their cladding of plate and property! Wearers of slaughter, turtle-crowned. *Property was thus appalled.*[28]

Good Friday to you, and a Happy Eastering, bargain hunters. They have come to make this a long weekend. They have come to place their order. They have come to read us their requirements. Welcome to a new world, wipe your feet on us, take whatever you want for free. We've been put here for you, all the fowls and the fishes that fly and swim, that smell like fish that taste like chicken. We are all here for you. You were expected.

But this time we're not alone. We wait for them together. They've come for me but we stand our ground. We go forward to meet them, barefoot on sand on scorched soles that crunch like new snow.

Little turtle we have had our time. Even here it catches up. Bit by bit, so softly, so Sothically. But once with you I saw such *wonders*—was made for a day your Science Queen. With you I heard America sing as it sang once, heard its thousand *wondering voices* echo through our long scorched fall [29]

down through a sky of such *sublimity* . . .

to this sacred ground.

Hurry.

Fall and then begin again, without assumptions, without end. With you I stood at the threshold and looked beyond, made love in the rivers that run underground, where the lizard swims. Hands of a deer, face of a temple mask—with this man, there was rest, there was breath—how I still hunger for it. How I do, I do. To this chastity was I wed on temple steps. With this man, simple and complicated, gentle and strong, there was life for a while. Hard and plain as flint. Opulent.

Hurry.

I go forward with him in a mutual flame, stars of our own love. In this wedding dress of fire, knit to fit like skin. Walk on. I am not afraid, I am not alone. Some part of him is here, some part of me is there with him. Together we once touched the inexhaustible all. Together we skimmed the painted books of black and red. Hurry now.

Side by side I walk with the turtle who carries the world. He has lent me his shield of tortoise shell. So now we pit scallop shells against scalloped steel, we clash clay flutes with fluted steel. We will fight them for our lives and *choose* this death. We have seen how it ends, so it begins again. We will make them poets, we will make them sing our elegies. We will make *them* make believe. Armoured in their hieratic technologies— let them stop the silver bullet of *poetry*. We go forth with our feather axes! We have put our bards on, we do battle with the sun. Walk on.

Fire up the engines of siege again. Repeat after me. We are not afraid. We are not afraid.

Feel the wind. See the pennants fluttering.

Little turtle this is the fight you *dreamed* of, duelling musics—cellos and log drums and barrels and chimes. Keep walking. Don't be afraid, they're not so tough—defunctive music, shields of glass! heads in salad bowls and bassinets! Men in gloves—hiding in skirts! We are not afraid of these. *Breathe*. Cuirasses in coy corselets and glancing visors—they're only brigands and goths, and they *drool* through their bevors.

Hear the breath of the sea—?

Please hurry up. Oh, little turtle just look at us.

Toy soldiers on a cereal box. Me in my cinderella dress and goose-flesh—chilly quills and raggy plumes. And you, your hawk's bill is only dipped in burgundy—my startled falcon, of soft sweet fruit.

No . . . wait here. You have done enough. Here, hold my cinderella dress. Naked is best. Don't come. For you it's dangerous.

They only want you when you're small.

So this is how it ends. You won't leave me then, you won't stay behind? Then say after me. Yes I am afraid. But I am willing. I have loved impossibly, I have loved heroically. I have faith in the fate that is this impossible love. We will fight and then choose, we will drink this death and swallow the worm. We will eat this death and vomit gods. We will make them write our epitaphs.

Feel the wind now, hear it howl. Bright Child, time to go now.

I will be your air force. And you can be my infantry.

Look at them in their turtle hats—scared of us already. They have pulled their visors down.

Sharpen up your feather axe. Stand tall.

Come on, little turtle, let's go get your shell back.

. . . ¡Qué milagro! We know this dress, do we not, *caballeros?* And how is our Canadian friend? *Vos queremos dar la bienvenida, señorita doncella honradísima.* And where is your Maya healer now?

He's right here. Can't you see? He walks beside me.

CONQUEST

THE FAR SHORE

SEE THE MAN. He drives with the window down as if to drive by ear. As if to clear his eyes. He is wearing a light tweed jacket, jeans, bedroom slippers. A T-shirt, faded blue. It is forty below zero. The point where centigrade and Fahrenheit collide.

Air shrouded in ice-fog . . . Muscular cuts of ice rut roads burnished now to a high gloss, like sculpted meat. At these speeds the ruts sometimes fling the car into slight fishtails. It is after midnight. He passes almost no vehicles. It feels as though he has been driving around for hours. It has been much less. Once, passing a phone booth, he thought to call her back, to tell her he isn't coming, he's never coming.

He finds himself following a tree-lined boulevard that winds along the river. It is not far from her house. He understands that this is where he has been heading for some time now. Sodium lamps flare orange up over the windshield and slip back into darkness. The river flows alongside, thickening with ice. It freezes where it pauses. Open water boils up its cold into the arctic night. The air is choked with ice, trees fog-rimed—a faeryland petrified in hoar. The car slews wildly sideways. The gut-clench of dread he feels is familiar to him now. He has time to swing the wheel into the slide before the car explodes sidelong into the soft-banked snow. A dream—weightlessness—then impact, very real.

He opens his eyes to a lap heaped with snow. Into it, slow, beads a string of rubies from a cut on the bridge of his nose. His left temple throbs. It is an ache more frail than bone. The door is wedged shut against the snow. He struggles out through the open window.

The black car's feathered track has missed the concrete pylon of a footbridge by less than a foot. He does not trust this hilarious urge to laugh that bubbles up in his chest. He clambers up to the footbridge for a better view. The steps before him are heaped with snow like high-risen loaves.

He looks back, down, grateful for the tracks. The facts so clear. He is fascinated by the scene. He sits down in the soft snow blanketing the bridge. He slips his feet over the side and swings them lazily back and forth above the water, through the steam. One foot has lost its slipper. He rests his elbows on the retaining bar and looks out over the river of smoke, across to the far shore. Clouds of sodium orange, sky of India ink, a glittering mist. . . .

He rests his chin between his hands on the frosted bar. He shapes smoke signals with his breath.

Hahh. . . . Huhhh. . . . Ahhhh. . . .

He feels a tender kinship for this small animal within, ally against the frigid night.

The arctic air claws at his nostrils, floods his eyes with tears. He lets the cold weld his lashes shut as children will. He feels the warmth of childhood memories he cannot quite recall, smells burnt toast . . .

To him, through a drowsy warmth comes the fabling croon magpies make to bait a cat. A slow pulse blooms in his head. He understands he is about to freeze to death.

His eyelids balk, flutter—crack the weld of lashes. From beside his face on the bar a shape flaps off, the feather rasp of its black-and-white motley still audible through the steam. A thought comes to him: that it has pecked out his eyes—he jerks his chin up, leaving the inside of his lower lip fused to the bar. White sear, trickling warmth, mouth filling with iron. He can't open his *eyes*. Panic rears in his eyelids, the delicate horror of moths. Both palms come away from the bar torn, flayed. Skinned fingertips scald as he wets them on his tongue to melt free the lashes of one eye. He scrambles to his feet, stumbles back along the bridge, one eye shut, one blind to perceptions of depth. At the car, in the rearview mirror, he glimpses nose and lips cased in ice the shiny red of candied apples. Oozing fingertips freeze now to the key as he turns it in the ignition.

But the car starts easily, pulls out of the snowbank easily. Everything will go easily now. If he can just get warm. Frost smokes the windshield glass as the heater fan blows powdery snow off the dash.

He pulls the car down a familiar side street, thrusts his head out the window to squint through the fog—on the glass, in the air—through the white flutter behind his eyes. To the freed lashes cling enamelled burrs, like tiny molars of ice. If he could just see, just get warm. . . . *Go to her.* The most natural thing in the world.

Snowy swingsets, slides, teeter-totters . . . stilled and silent, like agricultural implements wintering, idled. A harrow, a plough.

Bare branches, cracked trunks. Tiny tracks, wedges in the snow. His own tracks up the walk. Each step forward leads him further from what he's known. Thumb jammed to the intercom buzzer, unanswered. His speech rising, slurred, a thread of chill tangled in the jaws. No answer.

He goes back around to the front of the building, hauls himself up onto the low balcony though he has seen no lights inside. His raw palms again burn as they tear free of the railing. He is ready to break in if he has to, to smash the sliding door. He puts his face to the glass next to the handle. Through brush strokes he sees a faint light. He understands that the windows are not dark. They are painted black.

It seems so obvious that the door will be unlatched. He slides it open, stubs a numbed, stockinged foot as he staggers in. His back to the warm, black wall, he slumps to sit on the carpet, cradles the fire in his right hand. The whiteness that flutters behind his eyes does not feel like rage, does not feel like anything he knows.

For a long moment his surroundings do not register. Then another instant as if through a negative. The dining room is painted black beneath a film of condensation gleaming under candlelight. Black matted carpet, walls daubed in crude, red glyphs.

He thinks he can hear the thrum of water boiling.

On the cheerful tablecloth of red and white checks, three stub candles gutter—black wax pools on the linen. It is humid. He has begun to sweat.

The table is set for three. Oblong wicker basket. White linen napkin. Loaf of bread, heels cut off. Saliva floods his mouth. A pang of hunger. His lower lip throbs.

The plates are heaped with a red-brown mass like stew. Drawing nearer, he sees in the dim light that the pieces are not diced but halved or whole. He stands, hungry, sweating, staring down at the plates. But he has not moved to feed himself. It is not until he has stared for a moment at these strange vegetables that he understands that this is a heart.

This is a kidney. Heart, liver, kidney . . .

The room reeks of meat.

Over the kitchen's black and white parquet, the same red-brown mass flows. White fridge, a stove painted black. The fridge door is open just wide enough to slash a blade of light across the floor. He masters his need to look inside.

The floor is greasy underfoot. A stainless steel cauldron lies on its
side spilling stew. He feels the moisture through his sock, then the
warmth. It feels . . . good. He nudges off his slipper and warms the
other foot. He stands, anklebones pressed together. He wonders if
someone has knelt in the hot mixture, or fallen. Long muddy smears
streak the floor. The tracks of some incomprehensible dance. Partial
handprints, red, on the fridge door.

Two more pots of stew bubbling mud-thick, sloppy, flatulent, on the
stove. A kettle boiling dry. The fourth burner red, empty, fierce. Twin
sinks, piled dishes. A cleaver. Counters heaped high with raw meat. A
hundredweight of meat—ragged cuts—ribs, thighs, hocks, bone.

Pictoglyphs are painted on the kitchen walls. In yellow, white, blue,
red. Sun, snake, ox, dog . . . what might be a pig.

He touches nothing, walks out stiff-kneed over the greasy floor.

Two years before, the living room was already an office, its walls a
pale sky-blue. Red symbols now on the blue walls, red handprints in
the hall . . . The bookshelves are ransacked. In the middle of the floor
a pyre of books—filleted, broken-backed. The crumpled scrolls of
maps. A television lying face up on the floor. He sees now that it is
switched on. Figures slide across the upturned screen and up across
the ceiling. The effect leaves him dizzy, like looking deep into a face
wrongside up.

In the corner, the desk stands firm . . . island of order, wide rock
splitting a flood. Neat stacks of file folders, workbooks, computer
disks. White cardboard box, "Dr. Donald Gregory" printed on the side
in red felt pen. It is pleasant to read this name. His. A welcoming. The
box is almost empty, a few keepsakes . . . amber paperweight, amethyst
crystal, yellow key chain.

One sheet of paper is taped over the monitor. Underneath, the
screen is nearly blank, a cool dark blue, white cursor blinking after the
words, *Gentle Reader* . . .

The sheet between his sticky fingers also begins with these same
two words but is followed with the shingled shapes of paragraphs. He
begins to read. It feels good to read, even if the words make no sense
to him. His eyes trace the sturdy shapes of sentences . . . white mortar,
black brick. He hears from down the hall a rustling, like leaves.

It has never once occurred to him to call out. He does not want to
hear his voice now. Here in these rooms. He puts the paper in the

box. As he walks down the hall, he clutches a dull brass letter-opener in one hand. He smells starter fluid. The smell of a barbecue, he knows this well.

Smashed mirror . . . tiny obelisks spill rainbows on the bathroom floor. Across the hall, a door open on a darkened bedroom. This too he knows well. In the doorway he gropes for the light switch against the dark wall, turns his head, sees his own dim shadow traced across an unmade bed. The bedroom light is burnt out or broken. The solvent smell is stronger here. In the half-light by the bed he sees the body. He cannot tell if it is breathing, kneels beside it. He brings the brass blade to her lips.

He leans back toward the light, lifts the letter-opener to see if it has come away fogged. But the room is too dark. He hears the rustling as he shifts. It was not the rustle of leaves he heard but plastic. He starts, lifts a hand—it is wet, almost black. First he thinks this slick blackness is his, but there is so much.

She is lying on plastic bags spread out over the carpet. Her head rests lightly against the low night table. On this, the phone. As if she is waiting for a call. Or grown tired making them, has stopped to rest a while.

How long?

He has a simple thought, an easier thought. 911.

He dials, he grows cunning, thinks of fingerprints, recordings. He knows he does not need to speak, sets the receiver quietly beside the phone. The narrow-throated chatter chirps brightly on. He looks down at her, thinks of his daughter, tobogganing . . . happy children sliding down on a plastic sheet. Something he has seen or once done himself . . . something else he can't remember now.

He grips the bag. It is slippery. He forces his fingers through, clutches it between his fists, drags his burden towards the bathroom—dead weight, toward the light.

She is naked, the garbage bags are green. A black liquid pools and splits like oil on water. Black mercury on a plastic scape. The quantities are a surprise to him. Perhaps with blood there always seems more than there is. He finds in this thought a consolation.

In the hallway he lets go of the plastic slide, takes her under the arms, drags her into the bathroom. Hears a distant popping of glass under his stockinged feet. He lets her head down gently on the floor, stands over her. Studies her.

It has been so long. Has she changed? Has he? He thinks he has. Deep tan lines at her neck, elbows, calves. A sandal's brindling on little feet, out-turned. Her chestnut hair is matted. The body has become so frail. Pelvic ridge, soft declines of skin. A dressed hare's long, wasted thighs. Familiar tuft between the legs . . . a dark rabbit's foot. His eyes consume her. Bird knees, quill-boned ankles, rose-tipped breasts spilling back and up towards the throat, swelling their breastplate of hollow bone. Poetry . . . it is years since he tried this, it is good to try now. He kneels beside her as on a diamond shawl. He is pleased with the image, though its words have not yet come.

Thoughtfully his eyes follow the dotted lines traced in pink lipstick from her throat to her knees.

Afterwards he will think of a surgeon's pencil, now he thinks of meat, a butcher's diagram. Cuts of meat. He finds this thought dis-agreeable. He wants to cover this. He takes off his tweed jacket, drapes it over her, up to the wound. He finds it hard to cover this. He stares as into a dark well. Deep, jagged, barely oozing . . . a black, exhausted spring. From where belly meets breastbone, toward him it runs the full length of the first rib, shallower, more ragged at the lower end. Dull white bone. A membrane's sheen . . .

He rouses himself from this fascination. He must prepare the body. She has no one else. Who else is there for this? His eyes search the room. Flowered shower curtain crumpled in the tub . . . bare chrome towel rack, one chalked end pulled slightly from the drywall. On the toilet tank is a beige enamel basin laid with dried grasses and wild-flowers. Underneath the sink a stiff grey rag, scouring powder.

Basin in his lap, in his hands, he sits a moment, watching her belly's faint rise and fall. He seems to have forgotten his plan. He remembers now . . . he remembers everything. Memories, moments flood back to him in their tender rise and fall. He is grateful to have something now to do. Something solemn, necessary. At the sink he adjusts the tem-perature. Not too hot to burn her, not too chill. He adds the scouring powder, raises a blue froth with his bright-pink fingertips.

He kneels to wash her hands. The deep blade-cuts in her left, the scratches in her right. Swishing the grey rag in the basin, wringing it dry. He is enchanted with the flexibility of her hands, the bonelessness of a small child's. Again . . . left hand, right. He bathes her hands. Again. Each time he feels a little older with the popping in his knees, as he kneels close over her, across her, to the basin. Again. His head is bent low over the hand between his. He rocks again over warm, sticky knees.

His face is lost in thought. His face is lost to sight. Time is lost to him. He has reached a place he has never been. The twisted cloth unwinds as it hangs from his stilled hands. His body continues to mark a time . . . a slow sway back and forth, as though to music. Perhaps there is music. He appears now to be singing, murmuring a lyric. Perhaps there is music. Small parts of the story are lost. The music, the sight of his face . . . the look in his eyes as he shudders, once, and asks from a place far off, what do you want from me? Small parts are lost.

And still the white flutter behind his eyes, this confusion, this muted gesturing. There is something this flutter is concealing. Something hiding from him on the other side. He cannot keep her hands clean, though they are now more dear to him than anything. He cannot keep them clean. He has washed them many times in warm water. But now the left is bleeding more than ever. Something is very wrong with this bright, red blood, its rise and fall. She is alive. There is something else he should be doing. He has risen to a crouch.

She is alive.

She is bleeding to death.

No towels there is nothing—no, not his filthy socks—he tears his T-shirt off, balls it tight against the chest wound. He holds it there, remembers she gave this shirt to him . . . some kind of joke of hers. The wound bleeds profusely, hot, bright. He has broken something open in her. Again. She is bleeding to death. Tie it down, bind it tight—he is tearing at the green plastic sheet, trying to rip it into strips. It is slippery, it won't tear. It is strong, it won't tear. Brightness spilling over the floor. It won't tear . . . his weakness, its strength make him want to weep. He hacks away with a slippery shard of glass clutched tight in his fist. It is no good, it won't cut straight.

He is on her now, tamping the T-shirt down with the pressure of his own chest. It is tight. There will be less bleeding. Everything will be alright, he thinks this through the whiteness. . . .

It is warm here. The room is so white. Walls, tub, sink. He could fall asleep. He feels the smooth warmth of skin on skin. Remembers how it once was with them.

It is only later that his arousal will fill him with a mortal, scorching shame. Now it only stirs and deepens his confusion; he lies trembling slightly, like a dog half-trained. He pushes the coat down over her thighs. With one hand he fumbles open the button of his jeans. He arches his back, spreads wide the fly. He would love to take off his jeans, feel the full, swelling length of skin on skin, but he cannot do this without lifting the pressure from her chest.

He has taken her before in her sleep, more than once. This warmth, this whiteness . . . But it has been so long. A long time. He feels the need to ask. A kind of delicacy. He looks into her face, waiting, to see if she will wake.

She is having trouble breathing under his weight. But she is bleeding. She is breathing, she is bleeding. He must stop one of these. It is important here, he knows, not to be mistaken. He must stop one of these.

Relief . . . he feels a dizzy urge to write the answer down. He leans down to give her his breath, seals her lips, the prince's kiss, the kiss of life. She stirs. Under him. Now she will wake. Everything will be alright now. She stirs. He will ask if it's okay. Her eyes open, she smiles up into his. Warmth, reassurance . . . those green and amber eyes, so near. The light runs out of them. Three convulsions.

One.

Two. At the second the fingers of her right hand claw his forearm.

The third wracks her—the smiling face crashes into his then the head slams back against the floor. A low echo, muffled . . . sodden. He hears it still.

He hears a siren, wailing now. Far off. An accident somewhere, the roads are hell.

As at a switch being thrown pain hits him in a wave. A mix of voltages and frequencies. A raking—his *arm*, flame in his knees and feet, cold agony in one palm . . . mouth scorched, at his temple a dark bloom of pain.

His nose is bleeding again.

The siren is for him. He looks down over his hairy, blood-caked length. Run. He sees himself as he shall be seen, *run*. They will see him, they will know him *they will know*. He scrambles to his feet, does up his pants, turns—

In the hall an animal cunning stops him, the small ally within. He turns back for the coat draped across her thighs, does not look at her as he lifts it, at his lucky rabbit's foot. He remembers the phone. With a pillowcase, he wipes the receiver clean. Walks back to the living room. The cardboard box. *Take the box with the name.* His cunning is a friend to him, a small animal in the night. He lifts the box but pauses. It is nearly empty. A few keepsakes. . . .

He fills it with the things stacked neatly beside, slips through the sliding door and over the rail. He protects his hand with a pillowcase.

The air is less cold. A warm wind has stirred.

Into the pit of his stomach seeps an icy sensation. In the rearview mirror, as he turns back toward the boulevard, coloured lights flash gaily in the street.

He runs away. He saves himself. He is unmasked.

He runs.

Let the record show it. Let it show his face. By these works he shall be known.

[Equinox]
Gentle Reader, Gentle Don,

Come in. Come and dwell in me. I have prepared a place for you, I have opened a vein. Enter me quietly. Swim upstream, like a salmon, a virus, a bacterium. Come be my disease.

Your invitation—here I sign it, I sign with me. Come, sit down to eat. We will eat cool darkness. We will spew hot light. I am so tired now, I no longer believe. In this . . . it is so late for theories. But I have opened a way. Here, another. Hotter, brighter.

Will this make you come faster?

We will eat our deaths, we will vomit up our lives. We will become each other, the enemy of both sides. How I have fought to make you me, how I have fought to make me you. And now I make us both and neither.

This final test, it is exactly time. When I no longer believe, when none of this must be, when there is new life, new fire. Now, exactly now, a test of faith, when there is another way for me—here, I open one more to you.

Still you haven't come. So many times I have called. Do not be angry. Do not resent me, Gentle Don, that I have wished you other than you are. My other, the one you might have been. Have you ever seen your face? I have seen it. Here, I will burn your mask away. So you can meet him, too, face to face.

Together you will see such *wonders*.

I bring you fire. I have come to burn your house down, Don. To the ground, so you can build it new. I am so tired. I cannot wait much longer. Here, I open a new way for you. Wider, shorter, hotter. Hurry now.

Where are you? Your supper's getting cold. I have cooked meat for you, no fat no bone. Are you ever coming home?

Sheet after sheet, I have tended this small fire. To feed you my liver, baked fresh each dawn to make you strong. To feed you my heart, cupped wildly beating in your palms.

We too have loved an impossible love. Haven't we Don?

Where are you? Is that you—at the window?

Hurry please. We can go a little way together. I'll walk you to the door. Come, let's go see what's on the far shore. Of you, of me, of you and me. Do not be afraid. Bend, Don, you will not break. Bend to me. We are not made of glass. You have opened me. Now I open me to you. I am open to the future, can you be too?

You are so late now. I hoped we could talk. I have found new things for us to talk about . . .

But still you are not here, you haven't come. You will have to finish for yourself now.

You will be my clay. Bright Child, this is what I've waited so long to tell you. You will be my greatest art, as I am yours. We were always twins, we are ever other. We are made of dark and light, we rise to fall to earth again, through nights without end.

Bright Child, born of Night. Who are you?

You are not you, I am not I. Is it really true that two in one must die?

You walk to me through fire, through night. There is such a brightness in your eyes. That flows from us, that flows through you and me. Have you seen? See it on our hands—see? Feel it running through our hands, so *lightly*.

I hear you at the door. I call out to you.

And oh, Bright Child, *God . . . how I have loved you,* these long years.

Si los riesgos del mar considerara,
ninguno se embarcara; si antes viera
bien su peligro, nadie se atreviera
ni al bravo toro osado provocara.
 Si del fogoso bruto ponderara
la furia desbocada en la carrera
el jinete prudente, nunca hubiera
quien con discreta mano lo enfrenara.
 Pero si hubiera alguno tan osado
que, no obstante el peligro, al mismo Apolo
quisiese gobernar con atrevida
 mano el rápido carro en luz bañado,
todo lo hiciera, y no tomara sólo
estado que ha de ser toda la vida.

JUANA INÉS
DE LA CRUZ

Alan Trueblood, trans.

If men weighed the hazards of the sea,
none would embark. If they foresaw
the dangers of the ring, rather than taunt
the savage bull, they'd cautiously withdraw.
 If the horseman should prudently reflect
on the headlong fury of the steed's wild dash,
he'd never undertake to rein him in
adroitly, or to wield the cracking lash.
 But were there one of such temerity
that, facing undoubted peril, he still planned
to drive the fiery chariot and subdue
 the steeds of Apollo himself with daring hand,
he'd stop at nothing, would not meekly choose
a way of life binding a whole life through.

EPILOGUE

THE PLANE BEGAN its slow descent somewhere over Montana. From six miles in the air the blond earth was like a pelt, the matted flank of an elk in spring. I knew this country, searched it now for some sign of the season. Patches of snow in gullies, the faintest green on south-facing hills. At maybe two miles up, the patterns emerged. I'd forgotten this. No two fields ploughed or cut or seeded alike. Like a factory floor of shredded wheat; or microchips on some planetary circuit board. From lower down a twisted circuitry of coils and glints, of rivers in wooded draws. Then the sprawl and jumble of suburbs as we banked for the final approach.

On May 8th, 1995, I flew back to Calgary from Mexico City, after three days in London, three weeks in Mexico, thirty-six hours without sleep.

And after having known Beulah Limosneros little more than three years. It felt like ten. Ten years up the Amazon. Things I could not begin to explain even to myself. But I needed to, more than ever now.

It felt like lives. The life before her, the time with her. The slow time of forgetting. The lifetime since she called again on Valentine's. Another since the equinox.

I drove a rental directly to the Foothills Hospital. I'd called Dr. Aspen once or twice from Mexico. She was evasive about Beulah's progress, a little defensive. She seems to have been hoping I would be of more help. I would have liked that too, but before. When it might have made a difference. Before.

I found my way to Elsa Aspen's office.

She took a long look.

"Remind me never to vacation in Mexico."

That beautiful, reedy voice, so much richer than over the phone. Dr. Aspen was still receptive to our working together. Beulah had no friends here that either of us knew of. "Friendship," Dr. Aspen said, "can be a powerful thing."

I stood looking at her. "I'm the last person you should take for Beulah's friend."

"You're what we've got. It was you she called. Maybe not the best choice. . . . Anyway, you won't be alone with her."

"So—*what*, you take notes, while I sit at her bedside patting her hand—'Wake up, Beulah, wake up, it's Don, your old friend'?"

"You don't know, do you?" She frowned slightly. "Of course you don't. I'm sorry."

I sat a long moment across from her, looking past her desk, to the hills beyond her window. I thought about the many things I did not know, no longer knew, about not wanting to hear another.

"She's awake."

"Awake."

"For two weeks now. But hasn't spoken. No, her mind is fine, I think. She writes. Quite a lot, in fact. She's let me see a note or two. Her mind seems fine."

"But then you didn't know her before."

"Which is where you come in, if you're willing."

"She has family."

"That she refuses to see. Except the brother."

"And?"

"He has her trust. I don't want him to lose it."

"Which is where I come in."

"It's thankless, yes. . . . I had no idea you'd find good news so upsetting."

"Has she *asked* for me?"

"I'm not asking you to violate her trust, just general impressions. I've decided not to talk to the brother at all."

"So she won't wonder."

"She knows if you're here, it's because I've okayed it."

"And she'll know why."

"So if she talks to you . . ."

But she did not talk to me. I did not go in.

I got as far as glancing through the window panel in the door, where I was to wait while Dr. Aspen went in to prepare her. No farther. I had no business being there. I could not act the friend, though it was why I thought I'd come—why I did come. We had done enough to each other. She had her whole life before her.

Two beds, one empty. One name tag at the door. I didn't get a clear look at her in the bed under the window.

Stalling, I asked Dr. Aspen why Beulah didn't have her own room—her father was not short of money. No, it was a precaution, easier for the nurses to keep an eye on things. But never mind that now. I stopped the good doctor as she reached for the door, I told her no.

Elsa Aspen was straight about one thing: she didn't judge. Not a trace of irritation in her eyes. "I understand," is all she said.

I hoped, just then, she might explain it to me.

On the following day, May 9, Relkoff brought me a packet, sent from Mexico. Late for my birthday by just the one day. A slight imprecision in her calendar. The packet contained Beulah's last few chapters from the Yucatán, in a tone I'd never heard. But then there was a lot I had not heard.

I wondered if these chapters really were the last, though it said they were. I wondered how many more little packets of dread she might have sent, and which of those might still reach me.

And, small parts of the story were already lost.

In the afternoons, usually, I stop work on the manuscript to take drives out through the foothills.

Once, a long time back, this land was described to me as the undulation of an ancient breath, in one of my father's rapt disquisitions on geology. These were natural histories with the texture of myth, tales of alien chronologies and inscrutable motivations—vanished seas, and inexplicable returns. Rambling chronicles of titanic uprisings and eruptions. All the hecatombs—the vast dyings. Weaving from ditch to ditch, he'd especially loved to talk about oil, as *this rot that lights and warms the world.*

Lately I drive those same roads and wonder how he is. Still maybe in that motorhome in Arizona, the last time I saw him, exhibiting the first signs of his own father's senescence, the thing he feared most. Oblivion ahead, oblivion behind. Roaring, as he had for years, half-drunk, from the one to the other. Telling stories constantly now, afraid of forgetting, of some final interruption.

I'd gone down to find him, just after I married Madeleine. It must be ten years ago. To tell him, to ask if he would meet her. He sat in a recliner, arms on the velour armrests. Seeming not to have heard, he started in on the old stories of work accidents and sports and brawls, all with uncanny detail, as though the chemistry of a memory had just torn loose and drifted through his mind. Blocks of ice broken free of a floe, or dislodged sections of a puzzle. He would finish and start to

cry, sobbing like a small, inconsolable child, then fall asleep like a
child. And in a minute or an hour wake up talking, in the middle of
another story. Over and over for hours. Hundreds, I'd heard them all.
But never in this much detail, never all together.

For years, we'd driven everywhere together. From the time I was too
small to sit and see out. Instead I stood on the hump of the drive-
shaft behind the front seat and peered forward, my eyes just clearing
the seat-back. We drove for hours like that, we drove for years.

From the beginning he talked of the land. Maybe he was trying to
say he was sorry. For the role he had begun to play in all our lives, for
the figure he would become. Or maybe just once to say thank you,
son, for saving my life. And just perhaps, in the last years, we drove
once or twice together looking for my mother.

I drive these hills now, thinking about breaking old patterns, about
opening some new road into a future. Maybe going overseas. There is
a friend at a small college in Dubai. I imagine a curriculum of English
and horse-breeding. Falconry.

I drive a while longer, thinking about my daughter.

Yesterday morning Elsa Aspen called to say Beulah had something to
say to me. It was a very good sign apparently. June 19th. A good sign . . .
I was not so sure. Asked or *wrote?* She's stronger since my last visit.
That was not a visit, I said. Would I come? There was an urgency I
did not like the sound of. Would I come, please.

I have had time to think this question over. Exactly a season. I
drove to Big Hill Springs yesterday afternoon, walked up along the
creek winding through the wood below the grazed hills. My mother
took me there when I was a boy. I was not much older than Catherine
is now. I don't know where my father was. There were just the two of
us that day, as she walked me up into this wonder: a river starting
fresh out of a hillside.

I should take Catherine up there soon, I will go into town to see
her now. She'll be bigger. I have to brace myself for this. At her age,
one season is like forever.

It snowed last night. It began about three A.M., came down hard
until six through a long, grey dawn. June 20th. It has snowed in each
month of the past twelve. It is what we're known for. Calgary weather.
If you don't like it, we say, wait ten minutes. It'll change. The strange,
wild winters, every year a little stranger. Snow in June; in February,

powder skiers in sunblock and swimsuits. A kind of northern baroque.

I take the long way into town. First north through the wet snow then east under a wintry sun. Summer solstice, 9 A.M. I drive past the Baptist seminary. Up onto the tableland, then a right; the chipped saw-blade of mountains swings into the rearview mirror, dropping behind the deep swell of each hill as the car crests it.

The road rises and falls under a sky of cast aluminum, a pale rivet of sun. I drive past the Big Hill Springs turn-off and finally south towards the city. I follow secondary highway 722, through long prairie grass along the creek, smaller now, that begins at Big Hill Springs. I think of following that creek one day with Catherine, to see if it reaches a larger stream, or else runs dry somewhere to the east.

Fourteenth Street curves from south to west under the crown of Nose Hill, bald but for a little fringe of trees on the wetter, north side. Then curves back south, eventually, into Rosemont, one of the earliest suburbs, in what has become almost downtown.

I am glad to have taken the extra time. To figure out how to explain to Madeleine. Why I haven't called, where I've been. To decide I won't lie to her this time, I won't lie to her again. To think about how I will ask to see Catherine.

I read the shock in Madeleine's face to find me at the door. "How long have you been back?" In her eyes a flash of fury, at herself for asking this, at me for putting her in a position to. I see she does not really want the question answered. I think about not answering.

"Six weeks."

"Six. . . ."

I see her bite her lip, hard, bite back any comment. So as not to give me the satisfaction. But satisfaction is not what I would get.

I glance past Madeleine's shoulder as Catherine runs around the corner and into the hall. She stops dead as she sees me. Never do I want to live through a moment more painful. It is just an instant really, of shyness, of not recognizing me. 'Making strange' we call it. It is like dying. Let me die before the next time comes. Never let it.

Whatever is in my face changes Madeleine's mind. To let me in. To play with Catherine.

My daughter and I play outside, beside Margaret. White rabbit, hutched. We build a bunny out of melting snow to keep Margaret company. We build it where the barbecue used to be. While we work and talk, the summer sun burns the cloud to gauze, to mist, to blue. The snow melts off the sidewalks and then the green grass. It slips off droopy flower bulbs. We hold their heads up.

And everything is almost as before.

At lunch we eat two cheese sandwiches left on the table on the deck. Soon after, I leave and at the door Madeleine hands me one more little packet of dread.

"I don't know why I'm giving you this. I don't know why I kept it. Except to set it on fire one day and put it in your hands. I've been planning—rehearsing the moment, if I ever saw you. To hold Catherine up and as you reached out—to pull her back, to say, 'Take a long, *long* look, Donald. For the last time. *You will never see her again.*' I was ready to leave the country if I had to. And if you tried even once I'd make sure you never even knew where to *write* to her."

If someone, if a man, can imagine falling in love with a character, say, with a woman in the pages of a book, could it be so hard for him to fall in love with his own wife again? If only he had paid attention.

If someone, if a man.

I drive down Crowchild Trail to Memorial Drive, west to 34th street, then up to the Foothills Hospital, where it stands above the Bow.

I sit in the parking lot, in the heat of the sun, a remnant of snow melting under the windshield wipers. I sit, and see all the women I have failed to love and forgotten, or have loved and forgotten how. I feel them all now, as though rolled up into a ball in my chest. All rolled up into a single person, that person who is me. I sit, hands at ten after two on the steering wheel.

After a while I get out. I walk around the west side of the grounds. Past the roaring column of a medical incinerator, venting what it has killed and what it maybe hasn't. I sit a while at a scarred picnic table the maintenance crew appears to use for lunches, while they eat and talk and squint up the river valley.

I take the elevator to the seventh floor. I walk along the hall to the psychiatric nursing station. The duty nurse and a receptionist stand on either side of the Chief's open door. The receptionist holds a phone receiver out at arm's length in the doorway, the heel of her hand over the mouthpiece.

Dr. Elsa Aspen sits back, past that extended arm, behind an enormous cluttered desk, beside a fax machine sliding a message into the tray. Her own phone is wedged between shoulder and ear. The coiled cord disappears under a ragged line of straight red hair. She holds up a hand to keep her visitors at bay as she looks down, frowning in concentration.

Some kind of crisis it seems.

I walk past the duty station and down the hall. No need for note-takers, or chaperones. This won't take long. There is only this parcel to return. Beulah might be needing it, if she is writing again. Anyway, it's hers. For her to decide what to do with. Who knows how many more are out there. She should know I will be returning them all, all unopened. Like this one. I need to tell her this myself.

As I approach her door I feel my stomach lifting—a queasy solvent smell, and something like anaesthetic. The two slots beside the door are both empty of name tags now. Two beds through the window panel in the door. The one under the corner window is empty, newly made. On the other a woman's form is draped in a pale green sheet. A janitor's bucket and mop are pushed against the bathroom's closed door. Sunlight streams in over the bed. A southwest corner view. The mountains, the river, a peaceful view. Familiar. Peaceful. This is important now.

How can they leave a *bucket* in a room with *a dead woman?* I feel an irritation sliding up to anger, then to a fear I cannot breathe with.

I stand a moment, fighting for breath.

I hear a light step.

Before I can turn I feel a small hand, its warmth on my shoulder.

They said she was stronger. They did not say she was signing herself out.

It is hard to speak. I give Beulah the packet. She has it now.

The June sun is hot in the late afternoon. Hardly a trace of last night's snow as I drive back out west over the Trans-Canada, over deep swells of gold grass. In the troughs, stands of poplar are budding late, branches sharp through a faint spray of green. Ringing the sloughs are clumps of red brush, dogwood maybe, or alder. The hills are blue in the distance, below a line of white peaks.

I park beside the cabin, walk down to the Bow. Along the banks, among the alders and the poplars, are scattered still a few snow patches. Here and there, sprigs of Indian paintbrush, candles of vermilion against the white. Asters and goldenrod shaking their tops free.

If you bend low enough, look closely, right down on your hands and knees in the mud and the slush, you can see tiny wild strawberries, the palest pink. Not much larger than the pearl at the head of a tailor's pin, but bursting, in a couple of weeks, with the most intense flavour, almost unrecognizably strawberry.

I walk west along the north bank, steam rising off the snow. A silver braid trembles in the stream where it narrows.

If there are many rivers left among us as beautiful as the Bow, I have not seen them. One other, once, in New Zealand . . . the Clutha, I think, under a hydro reservoir now. I follow the Bow's baffled murmur, walk its passages. Soft tracts of a vague marble clatter.

Here and there in the stream glimmer highlights of an alluvial blue, a shift to mint as you turn to look, then to smooth jade in deeper water. The south bank winds in and out of shadow. Half in sun, half in shade, a flock of mallards gabble and preen in the shallows among the rocks. A drake, head of vivid emerald in the sun, spreads its glistening wings and shakes off a spume of rainbows—a whale's-breath against the shadows.

What do you say to someone who doesn't want to go on?

I have learned one answer is in the land.

Bundled in a blanket I sit out on the cabin's veranda until after dark. Around midnight a locomotive pulls into a siding somewhere up the valley and begins assembling a pull. Now and again the bang of a coupling. The engine like a bellows that rises and falls in the quiet. Soon just quiet and stars. For twenty minutes or more.

Then, as I stand to go inside, I hear a whistle-blast. One long, pure, organ-chord that rolls away up the valley.

I am about to turn away again when I hear its echo. Ten seconds after, at least . . . coming from somewhere far off.

Then another blast. I count off a slow, steady ten to the echo. Over the next minute or so, three more chords. As though the engineer can hear over the engines, hear the echo return to him in the sweet-spot where he finds himself parked. Or maybe they all know the spot, and another railway man tugs on the whistle-cord while he stands a way off from the rails to listen.

Then they are off. Two longs, two shorts, and the roar of several engines at once. Then they are gone.

I have been afraid of so many things, I almost lose track. But I have not for a moment lost track of this dread, long known to the lesser breed of scholar—of a finer version of the truth, of some revolutionary discovery that overturns an entire life's work. That makes of that life a sad jest. Or it is the forger's fear of being confronted by the master.

I had begun to think my fear was that one day I would have her answer. That she would see what I have done and in her eyes I would read her judgement. That it would be devastating and clear. On the work I have finished for her, on the ending I have made.

But today, I discover at last it's not quite as I thought, as I feared. It was not judgement there in her eyes today. There was a . . . kindness.

I have had my season here. Tomorrow morning I'll be leaving. In a few more hours. To where, I'm not sure, but a little closer to my daughter. I won't be going far. This is my place; my life is here. I love this landscape that has shaped me, I remember now. I remember how much.

And as the dread subsides, it comes to me as a sort of gift. That in all those drives, in all those years, my father was not trying to apologize, he was trying to say he loved me.

Until today I kept telling myself, reminding myself, that at the very end Beulah had after all found some reason to reach out to someone. Even if only to me. For these past months I have so wanted to see, to find what it was she found. And all the while I've felt I was writing, somehow, to keep her alive. Yes, to make believe. Until I could find it.

What do you say to someone who doesn't want to go on? But who knows, who can make *sense* of this. And just when did we start to presume some divine right to understand things?

The miracle is that we understand anything at all. In the end.

In her pages I have seen the Sistine Chapel made with Popsicle sticks, I have wandered with her ten years in the Amazon, to the ruins of the absolute book. I have tried to make sense of some small part of it. And now, maybe, I have.

You see, I always thought she'd called that night to ask for help. In all this time, in this season of thinking about nothing else, it never once occurred to me. It might have been the other way around.

What do you say to someone who doesn't want to go on? The man who would, the one who chooses to go forward is the man who lets himself be broken. So he can begin as new. That man begins in some small way as her creation, and sets out to make a life of his own. To make another start.

This ceremony, too, begins with the heart.

In recognition of the inimitable plumes of Europe, whose praise has so increased my work's worth

JUANA INÉS
DE LA CRUZ

When, divine Spirits,
gentlest Swans, when
did my carelessness
merit your cares?

Whence, to me, such elegies?
Whence, on me, such encomiums?
Can distance by so very much
have enhanced my likeness?

Of what stature have you made me?
What Colossus forged,
that so ignores the height
of the original it dwarfs?

I am not she whom you glimpsed in
the distance; rather you have given
me another self through your pens,
through your lips, another's breath.

And abstracted from myself,
among your quills, I err,
not as I am, but in her—
the one you sought to conjure. . . .

Timeline

*approximate dates

1321	Dante's *The Divine Comedy* is written not in Latin but in an Italian dialect.
1325	The Aztec capital, Tenochtitlán, is founded on the site of present-day Mexico City.
1428*	The Aztec poet-emperor Nezahualcóyotl creates the Council of Music, for the study of art, astronomy, medicine, literature and history.
1440	Cosimo de Medici founds the Florentine Academy, for the study of antiquity and the patronage of the arts and sciences.
1478	Ferdinand and Isabela receive papal approval to establish the Spanish Inquisition.
1492	Columbus discovers India somewhere near the Bahamas.
1517	Bartolomeo de las Casas, first Spanish priest ordained in the New World, begins a campaign against the oppression of the American Indians.
1519	Cortés lands on the shores of the Aztec empire.
1520	A guest of the Aztec Emperor, Hernán Cortés takes his host prisoner.
1521	The Aztec capital is sacked after a siege and naval blockade.
1532	A guest of the Inca Emperor, Francisco Pizarro takes his host prisoner.
1543	In Mexico, the apostolic Inquisitor Juan de Zumárraga is relieved of his position, for excess of zeal.
1571	The Spanish conquest of the Philippines is consolidated; Spain is a dominant power on four continents.
1577	Catholic mystic and poet John of the Cross is imprisoned in Toledo, Spain; composes *Dark Night of the Soul* subsequent to his escape.
1583	Examined at length by the Inquisition, *The Interior Castle* by Saint Teresa of Ávila is published following her death.
1588	First performance of Christopher Marlowe's *Dr. Faustus.*
1588	The Spanish Armada is destroyed off the English coast
1589*	The grandfather of Sor Juana Inés de la Cruz is born in Andalusía, Spain.
1600	Philosopher Giordano Bruno, author of *On the Infinite Universe and Worlds*, dies at the stake in Rome following an eight-year trial.
1600	Shakespeare writes *Julius Caesar* and *Hamlet.*
1615	Cervantes completes *Don Quixote.*
1618	Start of Thirty Years' War.
1624*	Sor Juana's grandfather leaves for the New World.
1630	Spanish playwright Tirso de Molina creates the character of Don Juan in *The Libertine of Seville and the Stone Guest.*
1633	The Holy Office of the Inquisition begins the trial of Galileo.
1634	An affair involving Cardinal Richelieu of France, the Ursuline convent of Loudun, demonic possession of nuns, priestly satyriasis and exorcisms, culminates in Pastor Urbain Grandier's being burned alive at the stake.

1648   Sor Juana is born Juana Inés Ramírez de Santillana y Asbaje in a mountain village near Mexico City.

1648   End of Thirty Years' War.

1649   Massive *auto de fe* conducted by the Inquisition in Mexico City.

1650   René Descartes dies at the palace of Queen Christina in Sweden.

1659   In Spain, the painter Velázquez is made Knight of the Order of Santiago.

1660   Peace of the Pyrenees: Louis XIV of France marries María Teresa, daughter of Spanish King Philip IV.

1661   Hunchbacked, mentally deficient Carlos, future King of Spain, is born to Philip IV and his niece, Queen Mariana.

1664   At the age of sixteen, the poetess Juana Inés Ramírez de Santillana enters the Viceroyal Palace in Mexico City as handmaiden to the new Vice-Queen.

1665   In the year of his death, Philip IV loses Portugal, his army reduced from 15,000 to 8,000 in eight hours of battle.

1665   A royal edict is issued forbidding unauthorized books to enter the Americas.

1666   Antonio Núñez, a Jesuit officer of the Inquisition, is appointed Juana's confessor.

1667   John Milton completes *Paradise Lost*.

1667   Juana Ramírez quits the palace for the convent of San José, and leaves three months later.

1669   Juana enters the convent of San Jerónimo, eventually choosing the religious name of Sor Juana Inés de la Cruz.

1680   Grandiose *auto da fe* in Madrid; the Queen Mother attends in the company of her dwarf Lucillo. Twelve burned alive.

1680   A comet, eventually to be named after Edmond Halley, appears over Europe and America.

1680   The celebrated poet Sor Juana Inés de la Cruz is commissioned to create *The Allegorical Neptune* in welcome to the incoming viceroy and vice-queen, an auspicious beginning to Sor Juana's most productive period.

1687   Isaac Newton publishes his *Principia Mathematica*.

1690   Sor Juana's published theological arguments attract the notice of the Inquisition.

1691   Inquisition proceedings are instituted against a priest defending Sor Juana.

1691   August 23rd, a total eclipse of the sun.

1692   Floods, crop infestations, famine in Mexico. In June, a revolt against Spanish authority.

1692   Salem witch-hunts. Nineteen women hanged.

1693   The Archbishop of Mexico publishes an edict condemning the scandal and disorder in the city's twenty-two convents. Sor Juana ceases all writing and study.

1694   Sor Juana's defender is condemned by the Inquisition. March 5th: Sor Juana signs a statement of contrition in blood.

1695   Plague enters Mexico City. Death of Sor Juana Inés de la Cruz, aged forty-six.

NOTES

⬧

Echo BOOK ONE

1. Ovid, *Metamorphoses*, translated and with a preface by A. E. Watts, with etchings by Pablo Picasso (North Point Press, 1980), p. 62.

2. The refrain of a poem by Sor Juana.

3. '*Siglo de Oro*'s latter, better half . . .' Evincing a certain editorial glee, I'd begun compiling lists of solecisms, errors of fact and anachronisms. But this one gave me pause. First, as a statement of personality it accorded well with widely documented instances of Sor Juana's bold self-awareness. In its devious way, the phrase was also accurate. Spain's *Siglo de Oro* was indeed its golden century, and Sor Juana was arguably the only great poet of its second half. Without her holding down the fort, as it were, it becomes merely a golden half-century. She is also, in the distaff sense, a 'better half,' being the only great female poet of both that century and that side of the Atlantic divide.

But then what of the anachronisms with which the whole manuscript is rife? Five categories have so far emerged.

i) Unintentional. These are legion.

ii) Deliberate. These are few. (For example, moving the date of a trip or trial from 1678 to 1693.)

iii) Misleading. These seem like anachronisms, but may not be; the intent is evidently to challenge the historical knowledge of someone who reads to debunk. A seventeenth-century reference to cancer, or to a shuttlecock, feels anachronistic even if it isn't.

iv) Aggressive. *Aggressively anachronistic* is a term one might apply to the work as a whole (diction, topics, themes).

Should characters sound *modern*, or instead carry what amounts to a heavy accent that they themselves would not have heard? Which is to say, they will sound bracingly modern to themselves, and we, antiquated, to readers of the future. (Passing over, for a moment, the extent to which 'modern' is a construct of modernism.)

Is this, then, an objective portrayal of the seventeenth century, or one filtered by our time? The trap here is plain enough: unfiltered, objective portraits are never available to us, and acting as if they were—in history or in fiction—is pretentious.

v) Chronic. (There was a temptation to call this category *meta-temporal* or simply *nonsensical*.) These anachronisms suggest a mission of historical fiction that is not just to lie by getting one's facts scrupulously straight, nor only to interrogate the concept of Fact as cultural artefact, nor even just to pose an alternative to history's account and thereby a challenge to it, but rather to mount an inquiry into time itself—its ultimate structure and our relationship with it.

After the digression, then, what to make of the 'Siglo de Oro's latter, better half'?

Misleading. Aggressive. Chronic—that is, the temporal knowledge of Sor Juana's early narration might include her entire century, or else both her time and ours. Indeed, it may be a voice speaking from the 'always' of myth; or a voice that begins at these Olympian elevations but ends by falling back to earth.

4. Sor Juana's own words, from her autobiographical *Response to Sor Filotea*, translated in part by Alan Trueblood in *A Sor Juana Anthology* (Harvard University Press, 1988).

5. The paraphrases from page 73 of Octavio Paz's seminal *Sor Juana, Or the Traps of Faith* (Belknap Press of Harvard University Press, 1988), translated by Margaret Sayers Peden, and are themselves taken from Sor Juana's autobiographical *Response to Sor Filotea*.

6. Translation by F. J. Warnke, to be found in his *Three Women Poets of the Baroque: Louise Labé, Gaspara Stampa, and Sor Juana Inés de la Cruz* (Bucknell University Press, 1987).

7. Two famous seventeenth-century anagrams for the angelical salute 'Ave Maria, gratia plena, Dominus tecum.'

8. Passage taken from a collection edited by Lewis H. Lapham, *The End of the World* (St. Martin's Press, 1998), pp. 21–22.

9. For a fine synthesis, see Algis Valiunas, "Commentary." (Print-out of an online document, original source unknown.)

10. The anagram of a 'mightier cry' is the two words 'mercy' and 'right' plus a missing 'I.'

11. Poems by Juana and Sor Juana in this manuscript fall into three categories: authenticated (most of these appear with her name in sections separate from the chapters); attributed (one or two poems are used whose authorship is contested); speculatively attributed. All of these will be identified in notes. This anagram poem falls into the third category.

12. About a year after this chapter was written (as closely as this can be determined), an article appeared in the Mexico City daily *La Reforma*, on the potential discovery of Juana's earliest poem. Composed by her at the age of eight, it was a *loa* of some three hundred lines on the occasion of the Feast of Corpus Christi. Among its many interesting aspects are these two: first, that at so tender an age Juana should have been writing on the Eucharist; second, that the poem was bilingual, one line beginning in Castilian and ending in Nahuatl, the next line Nahuatl / Castilian. A coincidence, I would propose, if an interesting one. Beulah might rather have taken it as a validation of her 'method' and of her investigations into the phenomenon of entanglement. Until recently, it has widely been supposed by Sor Juana scholars that she had help with her verses in Nahuatl; only recently have Nahuatl experts such as Patrick Johansson begun to assert that Sor Juana's fluency in the Aztec language might have been superb, given

that her verses over such a long period (even longer now, should the attribution of this new poem prove correct) are of such a high calibre.

13. Speculative attribution.

14. The translation is by Margaret Sayers Peden, and is found in Paz's *Sor Juana, Or the Traps of Faith*.

15. Translation by Thelma Sullivan, *A Scattering of Jades* (Simon & Schuster, Touchstone, 1994).

16. Our author appears to have had access to the lecture notes of a Professor A. Carson.

17. Plutarch, *Conjugal Precepts*, quoted in A. Carson, *Men in the Off Hours*, p. 147.

18. This may even have been the nominal purpose of a trip from Calgary to Mexico, for just father and daughter, when Beulah was thirteen.

19. Here was an apparent anachronism more difficult for me to categorize. By 1995 *quantum entanglement* had surfaced in the media because scientists felt they now had the means to begin validating the hypothesis experimentally. The problem for me was that Beulah's paper had been written in 1992, when, at best, it would have been a hot topic for only a small group of physicists. Certainly, it held no special significance for me and would have escaped my notice altogether, had I not had pressing reasons to be watching the back sections of the newspapers just as entanglement was becoming another tale of the bizarre.

20. I leave the dazzling, self-referential, self-promoting footnote to a younger generation of fabulist, having always found the endnote adequate to my purposes, and instead take the bold step of reserving the footnote for the reader's service. Papers and texts by Donald J. Gregory: "James Fenimore Cooper and the Negative Way"(1980); *The Liar Paradox* (1981); *Stratagems of Misdirection, Taxonomies of Falsification* (1981); *Truth, the White Whale: an epistemological poetics* (1983); *The Aesthetics of Ideology* (1984); *Ockham's Razor: God-Mind as Guillotine* (1985); *Constructivism and the Architectural Metaphor* (1985); *Up the Down Periscope: Metaphor as Logical Operator* (1986); *Truth and Aboriginal Reality* (1987); *Feldman and Ontic Dumping* (1987); *Metaphor and Knowing* (1989); *The Art of Approximate Knowledge* (1991); *Wisdoms and Constructive Paradox* (1993); "You Are Here: labyrinth and the postmodern minotaur" (1995, unpublished).

21. Quoted from Sor Juana's autobiographical "Respuesta a Sor Filotea." Adapted from the translation of Margaret Sayers Peden in *Poems, Protest, a Dream: Selected Writings of Sor Juana Inès de la Cruz*.

22. Phrase from Sor Juana's *The Divine Narcissus*.

23. A paraphrase of Sor Juana's autobiographical account, in her *Reply to Sor Philothea*.

24. Speculatively attributed to Sor Juana.

25. A similar placard from a poetry tourney of 1683 is quoted by I.A. Leonard in *Baroque Times in Old Mexico* (University of Michigan, 1959).

26. Miguel de Cervantes, *Don Quixote*; paraphrase of the translation of P.A. Motteux (Wordsworth Editions Ltd., 1993).

27. This following chapter derives its documentation from the accounts of the *auto grande* (the great *auto-da-fé*) of 1649 published by Solange Alberro in *Inquisición y sociedad en México 1571–1700* (Fondo de Cultura Económica, 1988), pp. 581–82; and a wondrously detailed chapter on that subject in José Toribio Medina's *Historia de la Inquisición en México* (Ediciones Fuente Cultural, 1905), pp. 196–208.

28. If Quetzalcóatl came to be the exemplar of the sage and priest and lawgiver, Tezcatlipoca was the shaman who 'walked backward' and dealt death with a sinister hand, the berserk warrior whose rages made things fly apart, the capricious sorcerer with an incomprehensible will, above law, reason or even fate. A valuable source in treating of the relations between Tezcatlipoca and Quetzalcóatl is the work of Burr Cartwright Brundage, particularly *The Phoenix of the Western World* and *The Fifth Sun*. In the former (p. 272) appears a chilling characterization of Tezcatlipoca by the Franciscan scholar Sahagún: "He is arbitrary, capricious, he mocks. He wills in the manner he desires. He places us in the palm of his hand; he makes us round. We roll, we become pellets. He casts us from side to side. We make him laugh. . . ."

29. It would seem that the Conquest and the pacification of Mexico drove the battle underground, unleashing a 'war of the syncretisms.' The first fathers were stunned by similarities between Aztec and Catholic practices, and the Franciscans, especially, built on these. The 'Indians,' meanwhile, worked to conceal and embed their differences within the edifice of Catholicism: a Native artist paints a mural of the Virgin Mother in Indian dress; an Indian stonemason works a pre-Colombian flourish into a cornice of Mexico City's great cathedral; on a Catholic holy day in the South, a procession of brown villagers carries at its head a cross too vitally organic to be the rustic cross of Calvary: they carry the Mayan tree of life.

30. While doing another edit of these notes, I recall something Beulah once said to me: Your Postmodern, Dr. Gregory, is just the Baroque with its blood sucked out.

31. Appears to have been adapted from the analyses of Alan Trueblood, *A Sor Juana Anthology*, and Octavio Paz in *Sor Juana, Or the Traps of Faith*, pp. 350–56.

32. Source the exact quote.

33. I'm not entirely unaware that my analysis of the Baroque has lost some of its balance. Under the circumstances, perhaps I can be forgiven. In the name of fair coverage, then, I give space occasionally to Beulah's champions: "Let no one forget them. Melancholy, old mawkishness impure and unflawed, fruits of a fabulous species lost to the memory, cast away in a frenzy's abandonment—moonlight, the swan in the gathering darkness, all hackneyed endearments: surely that is the poet's concern, essential and

absolute. Those who shun the 'bad taste' of things will fall flat on the ice." (Pablo Neruda, "Towards an Impure Poetry," Ben Belitt, trans.)

34. If that seems too easy a target, then imagine, instead, Ted Hughes acting like a changeling. Or a bird of prey.

35. The other Mexican to be so called was the god Quetzalcóatl, the 'plumed serpent' of Toltec and Aztec legend and D. H. Lawrence cult.

36. Someone will now argue that any regular stiff finding himself within five feet of Marlene Dietrich or Greta Garbo may indeed, in a fit of atavism, think of her as Aphrodite. I concede the argument. In such tight straits the gap between our two centuries is not unbridgeable.

37. Implicit in our modern awareness, I suspect, is the presumption that we must understand a past time better than it could understand us. In regard to our obsession with stardom, the Baroque might understand us better than we understand ourselves.

38. Modernity as the 'abolition of the past'—Terry Eagleton.

39. Also, some of her passion was of a political order. It was a reclamation project— taking back the night of myth, as it were, from the media ('hierophants'), politicos ('eunuchs'), ad agencies ('Madison Avenue classicists') and postmodernists ('toymakers').

40. Or in Beulah's notes the 'emotional technologies of myth, the sentimental craft of kitsch.'

41. Or as Beulah would have it: 'Puritan purges, pogroms and putsches—orgies of purity.'

42. The phrase and the insight are Andrew Motion's: see his *Keats*. And it is tempting if painful to wonder how many of the great myths might have been brought intimately back to life had that brilliant career been less brief.

43. Beulah would have added that these wilds of the imagination, however dangerous, revive and restore us in ways even the great museums and parks, especially, cannot. 'Especially' in that parks are precisely the 'virtuous virtual' we take for the real.

44. '. . . azure's crystal drift,' Alan Trueblood.

45. From Ovid, *Metamorphoses*, translation by A.E. Watts.

Isis BOOK TWO

1. This inscription was found, according to Proclus, carved at the base of a statue of Isis, most likely within the temple of Neith, at Saïs, Egypt.

2. This book reference is exactly the sort of thing that gives even the sympathetic editor fits. Although the book itself exists, I have as yet found no hand-sewn, leather-bound edition. Although Sor Juana is one of the three women Baroque poets, the edition I have

found bears no image of Sor Juana on its cover, though conceivably an errant dust jacket might have carried one.

3. The date corresponds roughly to the first of the CBC radio specials on Sor Juana, and marks the incept date of Beulah's formal research. Our national radio network is known, like the BBC, as 'the Corporation' (the latter has also been referred to by one wag as 'a Christian version of the Vatican'). Having heard my own name bandied about by the local franchise of the daughter corporation, I begin to understand how it must have galled Beulah to hear Sor Juana's name trumpeted in the public domain . . .

4. On the bottom of this page was scrawled in red ink: *See what you make of this, Dr. Gregory. I give you leave, a little ancient history.*

5. If I endnote this in passing and enlarge upon a point made earlier, it is not so much to congratulate myself as to round out the picture Beulah presents of me. The first time I read her journal entry for our night at the restaurant, I thought—Good, she *was* listening, after all. But in reading on, I discovered many other signs, few of them benign, that she had been listening to me very carefully all along.

Beulah and I had been to see a play at about this time. I thought she might enjoy it, a theatrical resurrection of Frida Kahlo. The evening was something of a success—precisely because the play was not, and for once we found ourselves largely in agreement. We took issue, or *umbrage* in Beulah's case, with the whole notion of actress X 'being' Frida Kahlo. A kind of 'time-travel tourism,' was Beulah's phrase, billing itself as authenticity. Certainly it ruined a brilliant performance by the actress, that she was being offered up to us 'as' Frida Kahlo with a very theek Mexican accent. Like most people there that night, we arrived aware Ms. Kahlo was Mexican. From the point of view of 'authenticity,' I doubted that she spoke a lot of English, and doubted that the way she spoke Spanish would make her companions think, without really noticing it, that Frida Kahlo sounded like the domestic help. So we decided that what the show had done was give us a transliteration, not a translation (the latter felicitiously defined as similar effects by different means). The one thing we did *not* experience—and most certainly not in our fetishized sense of the word—was authenticity.

Every time period has an accent, just not one terribly evident to itself. Cockneys have an accent alright, but they will never hear it the way we do. Historical authenticity could be defined in many ways, but rather than confusing it with 'accuracy' or 'facticity,' one might instead seek how a time sounded to itself, not how it must sound to the tourist from the twenty-first century. Or one might focus on what stood out as unusual or remarkable then—Sor Juana's worldliness, for instance, and how it might sound in our time. To our time, her intellectualism might be alienating, if untempered by an effort to translate it; to another time, that same trait might be inspiring, or erotic. When translating Homer, the modern translator may consider writing again like Chapman, but that would be translating Homer to the seventeenth century. We read Chapman today for the quality of the writing. But we continue to make translations that resonate for our times without necessarily making Homer a Londoner or New Yorker.

If these chapters really were written or dictated by Sor Juana, they would have been in seventeenth-century Spanish, and so would require a translation anyway. In the restaurant that night I missed a good deal, apparently, but what I now believe Beulah was announcing was not a factual representation, a resurrection or a possession: Beulah was not Sor Juana's entranced medium, not her 'voice.' The choices she saw herself as making in Sor Juana's name were not the creator's choices—but the translator's.

6. From Chapman's translation of Homer.

7. Either don Pedro's memory was faulty, or the day was preternaturally clear, or the mountain he took to be of the Atlas range (200 kms. away) was in fact the peak today called Tidirhine in the Er-Rif Mountains, some 150 kms. south of Gibraltar.

8. Also possibly an allusion to the Gallinero, a famed house of rare birds at Buen Retiro palace.

9. This is Augustine's phrase for a 'God who is remote, distant, and mysterious' yet one 'powerfully and unceasingly present in all times and places.' *Totus ubique*—'the whole of him everywhere.'

10. A reference to one of the great spiritual transports of *The Confessions*, Book 8, Chapter 12, "The Voice as of a Child."

11. Allusions to Hesiod, who wrote of both luck and preparation, and who said in praise of his own time: *When work was a shame to none.*

12. Axolotl, 'waterdog' or 'waterdoll.' My interest piqued, I investigated further, as I imagine Beulah intended (the reference to harlequins was meant to be the tip-off). Undeniably strange, the *axolotl* wears a ruff of gills bristling on stalks about its neck. Though outside the laboratory it is an endangered species, the *axolotl* is cultivated in large numbers in labs around the world, in part for its regenerative capacities. These include the regeneration of complex structures—limbs, spine, brain. The other qualities Beulah would have wanted me to know about (and I you, dear reader, and I you) were its three-chambered heart, blunt teeth, and neoteny: the ability to mate while still in larval form. Among the *axolotl*'s mythological attributes (by way of its association with Xolotl, the Feathered Serpent's double, usually represented as a dog): regeneration, deformity, twinning, dirty feet, a swamp life in hiding, cowardice and flight from sacrifice, death, especially by execution, and, oddly, playfulness or gamesmanship. Though it must be said that in the Meso-American tradition of the sacred ball court, such games were not necessarily of a sort we would call playful.

13. Roberto Calasso, *The Marriage of Cadmus and Harmony*.

14. The translation of the Hebrew Bible was, according to one Aristeas, the project of Ptolemy II Philadelphus, who wanted a Greek version for the library of Alexandria. Especially as concerns the specific number of translators (who were said to have been sent to an island, each to work in seclusion on his own version), the story may be apocryphal; but what is more certain is that the translation, considered highly skillful, was executed in Egypt during the reign of one of the early Ptolemies.

15. This light-hearted notion appears to come by way of an e-mail from the Canadian mathematician Chris Hermansen.

16. Translation of Nahuatl hearth poem by Thelma Sullivan, *A Scattering of Jades* (Simon & Schuster, Touchstone, 1994), p. 138.

17. From Canto I of *Cantar de mio Cid*, translated by R. Selden Rose and Leonard Bacon, and published in the year 1919, in Berkeley, California, by the University of California Press.

18. Speculatively attributed to Sor Juana.

19. Aside from the mention of magic, the concepts in this paragraph are a direct borrowing—be it tribute or theft—from Octavio Paz's *Sor Juana*, cf. p. 80.

20. English translation appears in Miguel León-Portilla's *Fifteen Poets of the Aztec World* (University of Oklahoma Press, 1992).

21. The scholarly Lucero, with his retinue of feminine companions, watches with growing horror the unfolding mystery of the Nativity, detecting in it the outlines of his final defeat.

22. Beulah's totemism: I lack the cultural equipment to even attempt to explain it. Not just the sea cow, but squirrels, seals, dogs and oxen . . . is it Egyptian polymorphism, the more stable hybrid forms of satyrs and centaurs? Is it some variant of shamanism / animism / zoomorphic fetishism I am unfamiliar with? I do not, frankly, know.

23. Much of the first part of this chapter draws exhaustively upon a section of *Giro del Mondo*, a seventeenth-century account of a journey around the world by an Italian gentleman adventurer, Gemelli Carerri. The three volumes in which Carerri chronicles his travels in the New World are rich in detail. Carreri was an acquaintance of don Carlos de Sigüenza y Góngora, and a good part of the Italian's information on Aztec lore and the Conquest very likely came from don Carlos himself.

24. Appears to be taken from a song lyric by Jane Siberry.

25. Speculatively attributed to Sor Juana.

26. Translation by Alan Trueblood in *A Sor Juana Anthology* (Harvard University Press, 1988).

27. Adapted from a translation by Alan Trueblood.

28. Translation by Alan Trueblood.

29. Two rich sources on this topic: Mario Lavista, "Sor Juana, musicus," and Ricardo

Miranda, "Sor Juana y la música: una lectura mas," in *Sor Juana Inés de la Cruz: memoria del coloquio internacional.* Instituto Mexiquense de Cultura.

30. Yet another translation that appears to take liberties with the original.

31. The fresco painter Luca Giordano did come from Italy to Madrid, did praise *Las Meninas* as the theology of painting, only he came in 1692, and at no time before 1667. The Vicereine, therefore, could not have been there or known anyone who had, could not therefore have lied or exaggerated about it, or even have been referring to a similar incident, 'the theology of painting' being so specific. If the anachronism is deliberate, its purpose is not obvious. Sor Juana, I suppose, could have heard this phrase and misremembered who'd told her of it, but only if she were looking back on her days at the palace at a distance of some twenty-five years. . . . But then this, I suppose, could be the point.

32. Probably an allusion to Galeano, *Open Veins of Latin America.*

33. For a detailed account of the *galanteos de Palacio*, the reader might begin with the Duke de Maura's *Vida y Reinado de Carlos II* (Madrid: Espasa Calpe, 1942), pp. 41–54. See also Deleito y Piñuela's *El rey se divierte.* Octavio Paz, in Chapter 7 of *Sor Juana*, admirably situates the *galanteos* in the context of the history of courtly love and analyzes their function in the sexual economy of palace life. Paz's image of a dance around a dying sun king has been lifted with a minor, if significant, modification: that Philip IV was the Planet King, and what was dying was not just the King but geocentrism.

34. It's likely that Beulah read something of this sort in Little's brilliant essay in Josep M. Sola-Solé and George E. Gingras, eds., *Tirso's Don Juan: The Metamorphosis of a Theme* (Catholic University of America Press, 1988).

35. If da Vinci has been held above all else and all others as the model Renaissance Man, today there is a tendency to see him as the illustration of a failed ideal. Athanasius Kircher, born in 1602, might be considered the model Baroque Man. But few have heard of him today. His reputation has suffered much more than the Renaissance da Vinci's, perhaps by becoming the unfortunate epitome of an age with an image problem, the Baroque. If anything, his reach was broader and more ambitious than da Vinci's. He proposed a system of universal knowledge, which was to become a powerful inspiration to Sor Juana, the poet of *Primero sueño.* Mystic, magus, humanist, geologist, linguist and (mis)interpreter of the Egyptian hieroglyphs, Kircher nevertheless found time to serve as one of the pre-eminent Jesuit theologians of his time even while becoming a encyclopaedist of music; he also designed magnetic toys and magic lanterns (and has often been credited with inventing the latter). None of his many scientific theories earned him the acclaim of a Newton or a Liebniz, though he did claim to have resurrected plants from their ashes. But over two hundred years before the discovery of the plague bacillus, Kircher's pioneering work with microscopes led him to formulate a theory that the bubonic plague was transmitted through invisible 'infective corpuscles. . . .'

36. This was no mere racist hysteria on the part of the Dominicans and others faced with explaining a much longer list of uncanny correspondences: notably the red and black crosses adorning the robes of Quetzalcóatl in the ancient codices; trials in the desert; a promised land; an Aztec network of monasteries and convents and an almost-Catholic priestly hierarchy; fasting and celibacy and moveable feasts; confession in confidentiality followed by prescribed acts of contrition; the association of baptism and naming . . .

37. Joseph Campbell, clearly . . . *1000 Masks?*

38. The family of Nezahualcóyotl ('fasting coyote') would continue to be associated with dissent and self-sacrifice. For instance, in a manoeuvre devised to prevent the Snake Woman Tlacaelel, a brutal general, from acceding to the Tenochca throne of the Triple Alliance. Nezahualcóyotl pledged to make himself and his people forever subordinate to the Tenochcas, who were then free to make Tenochtitlán the new imperial capital. Similarly, even as the Aztecs were being consumed by their fetishes for idols and blood sacrifice, Nezahualcóyotl was resurrecting from the Toltec tradition the possibility of an unknowable, unseeable god everywhere present—simultaneously near and far—and instilling all with holiness. Nezahualpilli, the poet-emperor's son, would one day visit Moctezuma II in his brooding solitude and foretell the calamities that would soon befall the Aztecs as a result of Moctezuma's misdeeds. Nezahualpilli's son, don Carlos Ometochtzin Chichimecatecuhtli, in 1539 was judged and condemned to death by the Inquisition as an apostate, idolator, libertine and predicator of the ancient beliefs. *His* son and the father of Juan de Alva, Fernando de Alva Ixtlilxochitl, would make it his life's work to preserve and make known the poetry and philosophy of his great-grandfather and the literature of his people. In 1692 it was this distinguished family's land titles that Carlos Sigüenza rescued, at some risk to himself, from archives set alight by rioters in Mexico City's main square.

39. The principal sources for this section on Guadalupe and Aztec sacrifice are (if the copiousness of Beulah's notes gives an indication) works by Clendinnen, Gillespie, Brundage, Carrasco, Lafaye and Neumann. Central here is Susan Gillespie's thesis of 'the women of discord,' whose violent deaths propel the Mexica toward their destiny.

40. In this connection the interested reader might profitably turn to Tzvetan Todorov's *The Conquest of America*, particularly the first chapter of a section devoted to the theme of love in the Conquest.

41. *Vino de obsidiana* or obsidian wine was not necessarily wine, or even a drink at all, but seems to have been a decoction administered to victims before sacrifice. The early Spanish sources believed its main function to be sedative.

42. Fredo Arias de la Canal, *Intento de un psicoanálisis de Juana Inés y otros ensayos SorJuanistas*, p. 22.

43. Arias de la Canal, p. 40.

44. Pfandl, p. 51.

45. The quote from Thomas Gage appears in Octavio Paz, *Sor Juana*, p. 122.

46. Pfandl, p. 51.

47. Octavio Paz paraphrasing Ludwig Pfandl.

48. Pfandl, p.51.

49. Ludwig Pfandl, after Carlos Sigüenza, in *Sor Juana Inés de la Cruz, Mexico's Tenth Muse*. Translated by Beulah Limosneros.

50. This entire chapter is almost certainly under the influence of the Robert Graves translation from Apuleius's *The Golden Ass*.

> Blessed Queen of Heaven, whether you are pleased to be known as Ceres, the original harvest mother who in joy at the finding of your lost daughter Proserpine abolished the rude acorn diet of our forefathers and gave them bread raised from the fertile soil of Eleusis; or whether as celestial Venus, now adored at sea-girt Paphos, who at the time of the first Creation coupled the sexes in mutual love and so contrived that man should continue to propagate his kind for ever; or whether as Artemis, the physician sister of Phoebus Apollo, reliever of the birth pangs of women, and now adored in the ancient shrine at Ephesus; or whether as dread Proserpine to whom the owl cries at night, whose triple face is potent against the malice of ghosts, keeping them imprisoned below earth; you who wander through many sacred groves and are propitiated with many different rites—you whose womanly light illumines the walls of every city, whose misty radiance nurses the happy seeds under the soil, you who control the wandering course of the sun and the very power of his rays—I beseech you, by whatever name, in whatever aspect, with whatever ceremonies you deign to be invoked, have mercy on me in my extreme distress, restore my shattered fortune, grant me repose and peace. . . .
>
> (Farrar, Strauss & Young: New York, 1951. pp. 263–264).

Sappho BOOK THREE

1. An introduction to the themes of science and exploration in Sor Juana's *Martyr of the Sacrament* can be found in an article by Héctor Azar, "Sor Juana y el descubrimiento de América."

2. As a reminder to the Queen, Sor Juana's use of *Plus Ultra* here might have been two-fold: When the first Hapsburg King of Spain, Charles I (1516–1556), sailed for Spain from the Netherlands to claim the throne, an armada of forty ships sailed with him. On his flagship was an image of the Pillars of Hercules and the young king's new motto,

Plus Ultra, which came to represent Spain's ambition to rule both hemispheres and proved to be an ambition that outlasted the Hapsburgs. Philip V (formerly Philippe, duc d'Anjou), grandson of Louis XIV, and the first of the Spanish Bourbon kings, had the motto stamped onto the Spanish eight-*reales* coin.

3. Apparent reference to the twelve labours of Herakles. The eleventh was to retrieve the apples of the Hesperides, the golden fruit given to Hera by Mother Earth as a wedding gift. The retrieval was actually performed by the Titan Atlas freed from the eternal task that was his punishment: to bear the world (or the celestial sphere) upon his back, a burden that Herakles offered to shoulder, proposing as a respite that Atlas grapple instead with the hundred-headed dragon guarding the golden tree. The Titan, having successfully retrieved the apples, very nearly did not take his burden back, and was only tricked into it by a Heraklean bit of table-turning.

4. As the story goes, according to one of Beulah's trusty sources, Robert Graves: For excesses committed on the banks of the river Heracleius, Hera visited upon Herakles a fit of madness. In a god-sent delusion, he mistook six of his children and two of a friend's for enemies and in a berserk fury murdered them. Turning to the Pythoness at Delphi for a way to expiate his blood crime, he was sentenced to twelve years of labour for King Eurystheus. The legendary twelve labours.

5. Beulah's oracle of preference, Robert Graves, lists three *daughters* born of Neptune to Amphitrite, the Triple Moon-Goddess: Triton (since masculinized), Rhode and Benthesicyme—lucky new moon; full harvest moon; dangerous old moon.

6. One might infer that by 'Ocean' the poet means Amphitrite, Queen of the Oceans, but finds it indelicate to say this directly, having already linked Amphitrite to the Vice-Queen.

7. In chapters of great general interest, Octavio Paz's discussion of triumphal arches is particularly satisfying to those averse to the baroqueness of the Baroque. As one such reader, I followed Beulah's research notes here with attention. In the seventeenth century, the absolute monarch's divine right to rule was promoted as never before, precisely when more human claims to legitimacy were becoming ever more plainly incredible: inherent nobility, wisdom, courage in the field . . .

Baroque art, largely sponsored by monarchs and by princes of the Church, for the most part actively colluded in the promotion of its patron's claims to divinity or sanctity. The equation being: beauty = divinity/sanctity = the right to wealth and privilege. (Arguably the equation still holds, if high-concept advertising, political campaigns and the vast majority of Hollywood movies offer an indication.) Much as the godlike beauty of actor-models in their Elysian settings serve today, countless examples of seventeenth-century art drew on the gods of pagan antiquity, already secularized by the later Greeks. Thus, even as the pope was God's Vicar, the king in the guise of Jupiter or Neptune might now be seen as His viceroy. So it was that Baroque theatre, painting and poetry made demi-gods of their patrons at a time when not a few were pushing the opposite threshold, of the sub-human.

Sor Juana participated in the norms of her time. As an artist dependent on her patrons she did at least her share of beautifying and sanctifying; nevertheless, as in so many areas, she diverts and subverts these norms to her own ends: she turns the canons and cameras of Baroque art, as it were, on herself. It is herself she beautifies, reifies and sanctifies, not so much for wealth (though she was not averse) or for power per se, but for the privilege to do as she wishes, for a woman's freedom of action and inquiry. As Paz points out, *Allegorical Neptune* is a riddle at the heart of which Sor Juana herself sits, on the throne of the goddess Isis, mother, widow, knowledge incarnadine, Man to the second power. Sophia, Ennoia, Athena (Wisdom, Thought, Mind) are all feminine for Sor Juana. This takes her well beyond even the tenets of Gnostic heresy.

8. Why Neptune? The incoming Vice-King was Marquis de la Laguna, Marquis of the Lake. Surrounded by floating gardens, Mexico was built on an island and was in need of protection from floods made worse every year by logging and soil erosion. Neptune was the Roman (and therefore less pagan) version of Poseidon, who turned Delos from a floating island into a stable one; was master of earthquakes and flood; built the walls of Troy; invented navigation and first tamed horses; fathered monsters but also water figures such as his granddaughters the Danaïdes. Sor Juana followed Pausanias in making him father of Athena, which is not completely far-fetched: Athena was without dispute sired on the sea-nymph Metis, was born along the river Triton, and was raised by Triton, offspring of Neptune and Aphrodite. Next, with a little quick footwork of her own, Sor Juana made Neptune the son of Isis—Horus/Harpocrates, god of silence and of wise councils. Just as significantly, Sor Juana's verses of welcome made the incoming Vice-Queen Amphitrite, Neptune's consort, goddess of the sea, mother of all waters, of all life, creativity, wisdom; and alternatively Aphrodite/Venus, foam-born daughter of the sea, beauty embodied, morning star, Lucifer rising at dawn, antebellum and antibellum, as it were, to oppose the bellicose fires of the Apollonian Sun. In sum, it is perhaps in this rather more dangerous context that we are to read the strange if beautiful fragment of *Allegorical Neptune* that Beulah has selected, as it veers away from the rising sun of Christian patriarchy and in doing so, towards Gnostic heresy, or *plus ultra*.

9. The line paraphrases Sor Juana's own lines on this topic.

10. In a footnote to his translation of Sor Juana's *First Dream*, Trueblood writes of Nyctimene:"For tricking her father into incest with her, this girl of Lesbos was changed into an owl, a bird believed to drink the oil of holy lamps in order to extinguish them." The oil, presumably, was olive oil, Athena's gift to Greece.

11. For past generations of translators, the challenge with Sappho was to fill in the blanks. In Davenport's translation, the square brackets reflect the gaps in the extant text. But here, too, to subtract is also to add, though not by human hand: inflections of contingency, mortality, earthbound process, time . . .

12. *Quise ayunar de tus noticias* . . . line from a Romance written for the Countess of Paredes.

13. *Discalza* was the word in the original, which has been replaced with 'barefoot' and this explanatory endnote: Roughly speaking, convents fell into two categories, and the *discalzas* were those convents conforming to the most austere rules of 'death to the world' and penitence. One such was the convent of the Discalced Carmelites, which Sor Juana quickly left before coming to San Jerónimo.

14. Machiavelli.

15. The story is almost certainly that of Sor Juana's contemporary and compatriot Sor María de San José, a nun and mystic eventually known throughout New Spain.

16. Many commentators have touched on the conjunction of the White Island, women and sacrifice in the Greek classical tradition. Beulah's principal source here appears to be Gregory Nagy's "The White Rock of Leukas." But the legendary home of the Mexica ('Aztlan') is also sometimes translated as White Island or Isle of Whiteness, their exodus from which was triggered by the Aztec war god's sacrifice of his sister. Curious (for her) that Beulah notes this fact but has made no discernible use of the parallel.

17. Though Sor Juana and Sappho were each called the Tenth Muse, there are only one or two direct mentions of Sappho in all of Sor Juana's surviving works.

18. Transit to Venus's gardens,
organ of marble, your songster's
throat imprisons even the wind in
sweetest ecstasy.
    Tendrils of crystal and ice,
alabaster arms that bewitch
fasting Tantalus's pendant desire,
banquets of sweetest misery . . .

19. Beulah's adaptation of an adaptation by Dusquesne and of direct translations by Davenport and Barnstone.

20. A wry allusion, perhaps, to one of the posts held by the painter Velázquez at the court of Philip IV.

21. Matins being the last prayer of the night, Lauds the first in the morning. Though the Divine Office may vary widely, the hours at San Jerónimo may reasonably be supposed as follows: Lauds—daybreak. Prime—7 A.M. Terce—9 A.M. Sext—noon.

Nones—3 P.M. Vespers—5 P.M. Compline—8 P.M. Matins varies the most, anywhere from 9 P.M. to, say, 1 A.M. at San Jerónimo, in particular.

22. Bénassy-Birling (p. 226) appears to have provided the basis for speculations about the Godinez affair.

23. In one of the great scandals of the early seventeenth century, the Ursuline convent at Loudun was reported to have been seized by mass visions of erotic congress with the Devil.

24. Núñez writes these injunctions to nuns in his *Distribucion de las obras del dia*. Cited by Wissmer in *Coloquio Internacional: Sor Juana Inés de la Cruz y el pensamiento Novohispano*.

25. The Council of Trent was convened to formulate responses to the Protestant Reformation. Among the reforms introduced: strict enclosure of nuns; no preaching except by approved ministers, especially not by women; institution of Inquisition Index of banned works.

26. As Queen Christina's tutor, Descartes was called to answer questions at all hours of the night. Unused to the Swedish climate, Descartes caught cold one winter night and died shortly afterwards. Or so the legend goes.

27. Probable source of the translation: http://www.windweaver.com/christina/.

28. Clytie/Clytia was an Oceanid said to be in love with not Apollo but Helius, designated in Sor Juana's phrase as 'father of lights.'

29. The ontological distinction between the written and the oral in New Spain, as illustrated by the Conquest's *Requerimiento*, seems to be one first offered by Margo Glantz.

30. The discussion of Aristophanes and Aeschylus appears to entwine observations made separately by Alan H. Sommerstein (on Aristophanes) and Richard Lattimore (on Aeschylus).

31. In another translation, Aristophanes has Lysistrata refer to these as Milesian Six-Inch Ladies' Comforters and to lament the wartime constraints on the importation of leather phalluses from Miletus that cruelly increased the dissatisfaction of the women who waited. . . .

32. Translation by Lattimore.

33. Translation by Sommerstein.

34. According to Ovid, the spring's waters changed the hitherto male offspring of Hermes and Aphrodite into an androgyne, thence 'hermaphrodite.' Hermaphroditus proceeded to put a more general curse on the spring: that any man entering it should emerge half-man. Therefore Sor Juana's reference has been thought a careless one, as regards her. But it may be a subtle way of suggesting that were one an androgyne already, the curse might be reversed.

Tarquin meanwhile, according to legend, committed the rape of Lucretia that led to her suicide.

35. *Sor Juana, Or the Traps of Faith,* a magisterial biography of one great Mexican poet by another, a book destined to become an instant landmark in both Sor Juana scholarship and the history of intellectual biography. All of the quotations remaining in this chapter are from Paz's work, notably from pp. 216–18, 482–84, 505–08.

36. Based on their content, I would be tempted to place these letters closer to the end of Beulah's descent into the underworld, but logically they must have been written much sooner, so I place them here. Yet again I find myself stunned that she could crash so hard, then within a few days pick herself up and keep going, keep working, keep the holocaust raging in her mind concealed from the rest of us, from me. I have not been able yet to determine which of these letters—if any, or in what form—she might have actually sent. I have found no evidence that Mr. Paz ever replied.

37. A discussion of Sor Juana's putative heretical quietism appears in Bénassy-Birling.

38. That Sor Juana was the first in her time to return to an ancient notion of Beauty as the Fourth Transcendental is the thesis of Tavard, fully developed in *Sor Juana and the Theology of Beauty.*

39. The phrase 'this white Eden' in reference to Canada was used in a valedictory address, by a recent arrival from Vietnam, to an assembly of graduands at Bow Valley College in Calgary.

Phoenix BOOK FOUR

1. Mexican cosmology is so complex that I undertake these few lines of gloss supremely confident of being fundamentally in error and in excellent company. Take a hard right at the Greeks. Abandon the concepts of monotheism and polytheism. Ponder instead a split such as numberlessness and multiplicity. Think not of a pantheon but of a palette—tones and hues, lights and darks. Think not of metamorphosis but of molecular biology, genetics, nuclear physics—valences and charges, base pairs and sequences of attributes . . . orbits. Imagine a series of masks but with no face behind them; the masks change and the constellation of attributes varies, depending on the context or season. Consider the metaphor of polarities, pairings of extremes— male/female, many/none, both/neither. One such pairing is Lord/Lady Two, the Lord and Lady of Duality itself, presiding over the highest level of heaven. Male/female pairings are common—it may be about androgyny, or it may be that this offers the most intuitive and natural emblem for the notion of elements in tension. Think hydrogen, think fission. The myth of the dragon twins may be an account of the forces unleashed when the pairings and constellations are broken, or may be an account of something else altogether. . . .

2. Variously translated as Plumed Serpent, Precious Serpent, FeatherSerpent, PreciousFeatherSerpent. Sometimes referred to as the Phoenix of America.

3. The kinsmen of FeatherSerpent appear to be guises and avatars of the broader constellation of powers attributable to Quetzalcóatl.

4. Precious Eagle Fruit: the human heart.

5. Again, little of this made any sense at all until Beulah's notes on *clostridium dificile* turned up: one of 400 species of benevolent foreign organisms colonizing the human intestinal tract in vast quantities (constituting a mass of nearly a kilogram) and, if present in the proper proportions, making digestion possible and preventing disease.

6. In keeping with our stated policy of giving critical air-time to Beulah's standard-bearers, a word on ambition from Italo Calvino: "Literature remains alive only if we set ourselves immeasurable goals, far beyond all hope of achievement. Only if poets and writers set themselves tasks that no one else dares imagine will literature continue to have a function . . ." *Six Memos for the Next Millennium.*

7. Paz, p. 367.

8. Margaret Sayers Peden's translation of Octavio Paz paraphrasing Sor Juana herself.

9. Sor Juana's frequent recourse to structuring her ironies in triangles was detected and discussed in detail using *romance* 43 by Alessandra Luiselli, "On the Dangerous Art of Throwing Down the Gauntlet: the Irony of Sor Juana toward the Viceregents de Galve," a close reading of Sor Juana's relations with the last viceroy and vicereine she was to know and serve before her death.

10. Although many SorJuanistas have noted the irony in Sor Juana's lines of welcome to an incoming archbishop who hated comedies and women in roughly equal measure, Antonio Alatorre and Martha Lilia Tenorio have developed the thesis (and imaginatively assembled the details) that a fateful enmity was set in motion that night. Indeed throughout this whole "Seraphina" chapter one recognizes their insights, on fencing, Camilla, the Seraphina letter and the Archbishop's enmity.

11. Margaret Sayers Peden's fine translation of Sor Juana's response runs to seventy-two pages in Penguin's bilingual paperback edition. It has been violently abridged here, with what remains only just sufficient to convey the flavour of a text that, as pointed out by Penguin, "predates, by almost a century and a half, serious writings on *any* continent about the position and education of women." One might add here that for roughly two centuries, say 1725 to 1940, the name of Sor Juana Inés de la Cruz went largely unmentioned.

12. "Several factors make Sor Juana's last years seem sadly 'modern.' The first is the theological—today we say ideological—nature of her personal difficulties and quarrels . . . Personal quarrels disguise themselves as clashes between ideas, and the true protagonists of our acts are not we but God or history. Reality is transformed into an enigmatic

book we read with fear: as we turn the page we may find our condemnation. We are an argument with which a masked person challenges another, also masked; the subject of a polemic whose origins we are ignorant of and whose denouement we shall never know. Neither do we know the identity of the masked powers who debate and toy with our acts and our lives: where is God and where the Devil? Which is the good side of history and which the bad? . . . Another resemblance between our age and Sor Juana's is the complicity, through ideology, of the victim with his executioner. I have cited the case of Bukharin and others accused in the Moscow trials. Sor Juana's attitude—on a smaller scale—is similar; we have only to read the declarations she signed following her general confession in 1694. This is not surprising; her confessor and spiritual director was also a censor for the Inquisition. Political-religious orthodoxies strive not only to convince the victim of his guilt but to convince posterity as well. Falsification of history has been one of their specialties." Octavio Paz, *Sor Juana*.

13. As an option slightly less inelegant than inserting dozens of citations throughout the chapter, the editor elects to acknowledge the principal and most likely sources for the ideas developed here. Two articles discuss Sor Juana as one of the great musical theorists of her age: Mario Lavista's "Sor Juana *musicus*," and Ricardo Miranda's "*Sor Juana y la música: una lectura más.*" Tavard in his *Sor Juana and the Theology of Beauty* presents Sor Juana as being the first thinker of her time to take up Saint Jerome's notions of beauty, treating it throughout her work as a fourth transcendental attribute of the divine, and in a sense the *plus ultra* of the other three. And one final source, Beulah's Octavio Paz, hovers over this chapter, very near, before she discards him too.

14. . . . and like a pregnant cloud, encumbered
by her gravid charge
condensed of earthly exhalations,
cloudbursts of agony perspiring
—terrible cloud serpent
whose trumpet is the thunderclap
that rends the airs of the empyrean—

15. Fisher of flocks,
Pastor of schools,
at times it is his crook
and shepherd's call we answer to,
at times his net that gathers us in . . .

16. Alessandra Luiselli.

17. The Persian mathematician in question might well have ventured an opinion on the Catholic Monarchs' expulsion of the Spanish Jews by edict and the Spanish Moors by force of arms. Of Christianity, Al-Biruni once wrote, "Upon my life, this is a noble

philosophy, but the people of this world are not all philosophers. . . . And indeed, ever since Constantine the Victorious became a Christian, both sword and whip have been ever employed."

18. Sweet deity of the air, harmonious
suspension of the senses and the will,
in which the most turbulent awareness
finds itself so pleasurably enthralled.
And thus:
your art reduces to what surpasses even science,
to hold the soul entire suspended
by the thin thread of one sense alone . . .

19. Sweet-throated swan, suspend the measures of thy song:
Chorister behold, in thyself, the master before whom Delphi bows,
and for earthly panpipes changes heaven's lyre . . .

20. See "The Woman/The Witch: Variations on a Sixteenth-Century Theme (Paracelsus, Wier, Bodin)" by Gerhild Scholz Williams, which offers an enchanting introduction to the topic.

21. Translation by Dava Sobel, *Galileo's Daughter.*

22. Verses by John of the Cross, something of a graveyard for translators, apparently, for encompassing Dante's depths and Sappho's intensities beneath a surface simplicity.
. . . Of peace and piety
it was the perfect science,
in profoundest solitude
the narrow way
was a thing so secret, yet understood,
that there I stood, stammering,
all sciences transcended . . .

23. This craft of knowing nothing
is of such exalted power—
even with all the sages arguing—
as never to be persuaded
that its own simplicity does not come
to encompass non-understanding . . .
all sciences transcending.

24. As mentioned briefly in Book Two, Susan Gillespie traces the theme of 'women of discord' through the Mexica histories and legends. Sacrificed, these women serve as catalyst—fuel, one would almost say.

25. Aeschylus, *Oresteia,* translated by Richard Lattimore.

26. Even the casual reader of Mexica histories is struck by the frequency with which themes and details recur in various narratives. Given that the storytellers and their audiences were influenced by the idea of Time as having a cyclical or spiral structure, it is not surprising that they should look for patterns, and therefore find them. But it would also appear that, in addition, the chroniclers planted them there: that is, the Mexicas revised the ancient histories, in inscribing themselves within a cycle of stories predating their own by at least a millennium; in highlighting those elements of new events corresponding to the older pattern; and, conversely, in drafting a revisionist version in conformity with what was seen to be the mythic structure of reality. In a sense, then, much of Mexica divination was not of the future but of the past, history being a form of prophecy. (Curiously enough, Carlos II, the last Hapsburg King of the Spanish Empire, had adopted methods at least superficially like those used by Moctezuma II, the last Emperor of the Aztecs.)

27. Don Juan Sáenz del Cauri is a near perfect anagram for Sor Juana Inés de la Cruz. What is one to do with little touches like these? The sensible editor notes them and moves on. The man does not. If Beulah were here she might have laughed. *Not everything's about you, Don.* But she is not here, will never be. How much could she foresee of what would happen to me in the aftermath of the train wreck she'd been planning for me? Was this anagram one of Beulah's little taunts? If so how am I to respond—by inserting myself into the story, by placing my own little persecutions in the balance against those of Sor Juana Inés de la Cruz? Or maybe I too am to see signs everywhere, patterns, and dismiss them as coincidence . . .

28. This excerpt from the sentencing request of Prosectur Deza y Ulloa, and the later one from the verdict of Master Examiner Dorantes, are verbatim translations from Inquisition records now in the Mexican National Archives, quoted in Castorena, pp. 297–300.

29. John of the Cross. From "I Live Yet Do Not Live in Me." It's not clear whether Beulah intended to translate these opening lines, as she had begun to do with other chapters. Roughly, " . . . *Living in darkest fear / And yet I hope and wait / dying because I do not die . . .*"

30. The Nahuatl phrase for 'Enemy of Both Sides' appears in a batch of e-mail printouts, this one from the distinguished scholar and lexicographer R. Joe Campbell. Other names for the Enemy of Both Sides: tenepantla motecaya, nezahualpilli (FastingPrince), tezcatlipoca, moyocoyatzin, chicoyaotl.

31. The phrase seems to be lifted from DeLillo's *White Noise*.

32. Toward the end of her life, Sor Juana began to sign documents with this. *La peor de todas,* 'the worst of all women,' 'the worst woman in the world.'

33. A more or less literal translation: . . . *and I stooped so low so low / as to fly so high so high*

/ that at last I caught the prey . . . The lines are from a poem on falconry *'a lo divino'* by John of the Cross. The theme, according to John Frederick Nims, is common in Medieval love poetry: the pursuit of the heron by the falcon was thought 'the noblest and most thrilling' form of falconry. The heron rises in steep almost helical rings, while the smaller, faster falcon gains slowly in a widening gyre. Traditionally the heron was female, the falcon male, but I imagine Beulah had the converse in mind.

34. This document, although undated (and perhaps incomplete), was undoubtedly written after Sor Juana's final poem, itself left unfinished. In all, three such petitions were written over the last two years of her life, constituting her last writings, and the only ones from this period. Depending on whether the "Plea before the Divine Tribunal" was the first or last of the three, it will have been composed not much earlier than February of 1693 and not much later than March of 1694. (The acclarative title was affixed to the text circa 1700 by the churchman Diego Calleja, her first biographer and the editor of a posthumous collection of her writings. For much of the next two centuries, her name scarcely enters the public record.)

35. *Prometheus Bound . . .* Aeschylus. Lines 514–520. [Paul Elmer More, trans.] From a scene involving Prometheus (PR) and Leader of the chorus (LE):

> PR: Not yet hath all-ordaining Destiny decreed my release; but after many years, broken by a world of disaster and woe, I shall be delivered. The craft of the forger is weaker far than Necessity.
>
> LE: Who then holds the helm of Necessity?
>
> PR: The Fates triform and the unforgetting Furies.
>
> LE: And Zeus, is he less in power than these?
>
> PR: He may not avoid what is destined.
>
> LE: What is destined for Zeus but endless rule?
>
> PR: Ask not, neither set thy heart on knowing.

36. Emperor of the Two Faiths: Alfonso VI of Spain. Lord Instructor of the World: a divine epithet used by the Inca. Lord of the Two Horizons: Ra of Egypt. Sovereign of the Two Worlds: the final honorific accruing to the throne of the Spanish Empire.

37. The spelling of this fragment of Chapman's translation of *Iliad* has been slightly modernized.

38. *Prometheus Bound . . .* Aeschylus.

39. John of the Cross, "La Fonte," translated by John Frederick Nims as *Bounty of waters flooding from this well / invigorates all earth, high heaven, and hell / in dark of night.* The final stanza is translated in Beulah's notes by Willis Barnstone as *O living fountain that I crave / in bread of life I see her flame / in black of night.*

40. A term of endearment of particular warmth, even among the many such to be found in Mexican Spanish, in this case denoting a fraternal twin; but the connotation

is perhaps soul-mate, soul-sister. (*Cuate* may or may not derive from Quetzalcóatl, or eagle, just as *cholo* might be from Xolotl, Quetzalcóatl's 'double.')

41. Bierhorst, p. 42. (The book title is not given. Possibly *Four Masterworks of American Indian Literature.*)

42. Bierhorst, p. 34.

Horus BOOK FIVE

1. Eliot, "Little Gidding." Beulah is not above citing this editor's preferred poets.

2. Paz, "The Poet's Labours."

3. Possible allusion to the Mexican glyph for gold: a god defecating a yellowish excrement.

4. Song of Songs, 2:5.

5. Such deprivations are not of course unique to the Baroque; so if the following cases are cited here it is because they were found among the author's diaries, not among her research notes. " . . . The best known of these saints, Catherine of Siena (1347–1380), ate only a handful of herbs each day and occasionally shoved twigs down her throat to bring up any other food she was forced to eat. Thirteenth-century figures such as Mary of Oignes and Beatrice of Nazareth vomited from the mere smell of meat, and their throats swelled shut in the presence of food . . . Somewhat later, in the seventeenth century, Saint Veronica ate nothing at all for three days at a time but on Fridays permitted herself to chew on five orange seeds, in memory of the five wounds of Jesus . . . Many medieval women spoke of their 'hunger' for God and their 'inebriation' with the holy wine. Many fasted in order to feast at the 'delicious banquet of God' . . . Angela of Fogligno . . . who drank pus from sores and ate scabs and lice from the bodies of the sick, spoke of the pus as being as 'sweet as the eucharist . . .'" From Joan Jacobs Brumberg, discussing *anorexia mirabilis* in *Fasting Girls* (Harvard University Press, 1988).

6. Appears to be a paraphrase, from Louise Bernice Halfe's *Blue Marrow*.

7. Observation made by Margo Glantz in *Sor Juana Inés de la Cruz: ¿hagiografía o auto-biografía?*

8. Beulah cut her hand in an accident at the museum erected at Sor Juana's birthplace in Nepantla.

9. 'Poor Mexico: so near the United States, so far from God.'

10. W.B. Yeats, "The Long-legged Fly."

11. Camille Paglia, *Sexual Personae.*

12. Based on a translation by Alan Trueblood.

13. Iain Sinclair, *Downriver.*

14. Beulah's hatred of what we call coincidence was unrelenting. Judging by all the red

exclamation points in her notes, it is safe to say she set great store by the following: "The primitive-religious mind sees itself enmeshed in a vast, shimmering web of coincidence, with God, or the gods, at the centre and in each of its skeins. The early Greeks preserved this in their reverence for the inescapable net of Ananke and the golden net of Hephaistos. The madman too perceives a great web of coincidence and interconnection. The difference is that he, or she, and not God, inhabits the centre . . ." Carla Alt, *The New Schismatics: a History of Schizophrenia, Multiple Personality and Dissent* (Atlantis University Press: Atlantis City, NJ, 1956).

15. At a young age one can get too much Jung. Arguably by mid-career even Jung had had too much Jung. The great Swiss Magus had by then found support for his theories of synchronicity in what he had gleaned from Chinese philosophy. In one of the first texts on synchronicity Beulah consults, she finds this gloss on the concept of the *Tao*: "The psyche and the cosmos are to each other like the inner world and the outer world. Therefore man participates by nature in all cosmic events, and is inwardly as well as outwardly interwoven with them . . ." (Robert Aziz, C. G. *Jung's Psychology of Religion and Synchronicity*.)

Jung and a patient are out walking. As they enter a wood, Jung's patient is telling him about a dream she'd had as a child, a dream of a spectral fox coming down the stairs of her parents' house. At that moment, not fifty yards from Jung and his astonished patient, a real fox comes out of the underbrush and calmly walks ahead of them for several minutes. It appears to be leading them. Their conversation does not cause the fox to appear, but in a sense its appearance reflects that the path Jung and his analysand are following harmonizes the inner and outer worlds. The *Tao*, then, is that terrain or that path where the inner and outer intersect, or rather superimpose themselves, and synchronistic events are its signposts.

Joseph Needham: "The key word in Chinese thought is above all *Pattern*. . . . Symbolic correlations or correspondences all formed part of one colossal pattern. Things behaved in particular ways not necessarily because of prior actions or impulsions of other things, but because their position in the ever-moving cyclical universe was such that they were endowed with intrinsic natures . . . If they [things] did not behave in those particular ways they would lose their relational positions in the whole (which made them what they were), and turn into something other than themselves. They were thus parts in existential dependence upon the whole world-organism."

Clearly then, our modern affliction, our great lie, was to have lost our relational position to the whole and to have become, therefore, other than ourselves. But for Beulah herself, more Jung now was the wrong kind of help. Eventually, Jung came to speculate that such patternings of mental and physical events indicated that they derived from a common psychophysical substrate, a *unus mundus* (a one-world). Robert

Aziz writes: "Through his study of the synchronistic patterning of events, the *unus mundus* thus became a living reality for Jung. What before were incommensurable opposites now linked. Opposites such as inner/outer, psychic/physical, symbolic/actual, and spiritual/worldly were now conjoined in psychophysical patterns of meaning . . ." Apparently Jung found himself becoming something of a lightning rod for such synchronistic events and began to keep a record of them. Aziz introduces the famous case of the golden scarab: "Seeking to circumvent the obstacle of his analysand's rationalism, Jung attempted to ' . . . sweeten her rationalism with a somewhat more human understanding' . . . [When this] also proved unproductive . . . Jung could only hope 'that something unexpected and irrational would turn up, something that would burst the intellectual retort into which she had sealed herself.' Reflecting later upon the synchronistic experience that served to do just this, Jung writes: 'I was sitting opposite her one day, with my back to the window. . . . She had had an impressive dream the night before, in which someone had given her a golden scarab—a costly piece of jewellery. While she was still telling me this dream, I heard something behind me gently tapping on the window. I turned round and saw that it was a fairly large flying insect that was knocking against the window-pane from outside in the obvious effort to get into the dark room. . . . I opened the window immediately and caught the insect in the air as it flew in. It was a scarabaeid beetle, or common rose-chafer (*Cetonia aurata*), whose gold-green colour most nearly resembles that of a golden scarab. I handed the beetle to my patient with the words, 'Here is your scarab.'"

To even this casual sceptic, Beulah's mentor's knack for finding unities—this passenger pigeon's homing instinct on the One—for all its scientific trappings, looks suspiciously like the beginnings of mysticism. But she was prepared to go Jung one vastly better. If someone must take the blame for what happened next, blame it on Jung. ("The objective event may be very distant in time from the subjective event.") Judging by their proximity in her notes, it is more than probable that, before she was . . . interrupted, she was about to try to connect the *unus mundus* of Jung, the *Totus Ubique* of Augustine and the *Tloque Nahuaque* of Nezahualcóyotl all in some vast mystical *holus bolus*. (Why try?— this is less clear. Because all things must be one? I am becoming unreasonable, but this makes me furious, this *waste*. How did she become so lost, get so hurt? What happened to her, that she should have so much, and throw it away?) On attempts to visualize the result: an Ur-reality tenuously anchored on an unstable poetics of sub-atomic physics and numbers as primal archetypes, quantum entanglements of subjective and objective events distant in place and time caught up in a shimmering synchronistic web.

Skimming through Jung, Beulah had allowed herself to see a synchronistic patterning with a periodicity of three hundred years and a radius of three thousand miles spreading outward concentrically from . . . what? The cannonball of some rough beast into a wading pool of Time? The passage of a great leviathan pulling three-hundred-year whirlpools in its wake? I struggle to understand this, that its Necessities had linked her fate with Sor Juana's, had linked Sor Juana's place and her time, at the dawn of the Enlightenment, with ours at its twilight. Or was even the end of an age grandiose enough? What was this apocalyptic moment—the death of an empire, a civilization, the end of history, of time itself? Or perhaps it was to be that instant, synchronistically sensed, in which the cosmic expansion pauses, on the verge of contraction? How big is big enough—*to make it worth it?* In the half-light of her room, Beulah seemed more or less to conceive of the anti-Christ as something like the degodding or disenchantment of the world, the extinction of wonder, the death of the Sublime at the hands of Transcendence. Whatever it was, according to Carla Alt's definition, Beulah was undeniably mad. But now the new logic of synchronicity impelled her towards another insane conclusion: that her role, her ultimate mission was to repair the web. To rehabilitate God. Or kill him.

16. Adapted from Fernando Benítez, *Los demonios en el convento,* and Glantz. Along these lines, Margo Glantz quotes at length from a sermon printed in Mexico in 1686 by the widow of Bernardo Calderón, for the edification of her heirs.

17. Plath, "Lady Lazarus"?

18. A concise statistical treatment of cases coming before the Spanish Inquisition appears in Gustav Henningsen's "The Eloquence of Figures: Statistics of the Spanish and Portuguese Inquisitions and Prospects for Social History" in *The Spanish Inquisition and the Inquisitorial Mind,* ed. and with an introduction by Angel Alcalá.

19. Henry Kamen, *Inquisition and Society in Spain* (London: Weidenfeld and Nicolson, 1985), p. 184.

20. Excerpt from Marturos's introductory remarks to an interdisciplinary symposium on Inquisitorial procedures and their legacy in modern settings. Published in *Inquisitive Minds* (Calgary: Crocus Press, 1993).

21. *The Art of War.*

22. This was a thesis developed by Octavio Paz.

23. W.P. Anderson, "Surrogates and Heroes: the Contendings of Hellads and Hellenes," in *Inquisitive Minds,* ed. Pedro Marturos (Crocus Press: Calgary, 1993).

24. Calgary: Crocus Press, 1993.

25. The structure of this and other scenes seems to have been cribbed from the work of Blake Brooker, resident playwright of Strontium Nanny.

26. These stanzas are the continuation and conclusion of "To the Triumphs of Egypt" from Book Two. The formulations developed here—linking the cross of Serapis to the crucifix; the crucifix to the axes of a circle; the circle to the hieroglyph of eternity—are shocking not merely because they appear in a carol written to be sung on sacred occasions:

Octavio Paz has pointed out that these are the very subjects Giordano Bruno was dabbling in before his condemnation.

27. "Dover Beach."

28. Jane Siberry.

29. It appears Núñez is quoting himself here, from one of his books of instruction to nuns.

30. From Dostoevski's "Grand Inquisitor," *The Brothers Karamazov, passim.*

31. Núñez is reciting the beginning of the Spanish *Requerimiento;* a legal requirement of the Conquest, it was read by the Conquistadors in Latin to the Indian populations about to be made war on.

32. There is every likelihood that the "Protesta" is the last thing written by Sor Juana Inés de la Cruz.

33. Lacks attribution: The verses are clearly based on a model—but where the did the model come from?

34. The principal translators traduced in this chapter are most obviously M. Lichtheim, W.K. Simpson and R.B. Parkinson. Beulah's correspondents, the Egypt scholars here identified as A and M, will almost certainly not want acknowledgement for what she has done with sources they had in good faith given her: the hieroglyphic Pyramid Texts of the Old Kingdom (c. 2500 B.C.E.); hieratic forgeries of priests in the Ptolemaic period (c.300 B.C.E.); snatches seemingly at random from love songs, royal inscriptions and funeral laments; the prophecies of Nefertiti and the Famine Stela; the "Dialogue of a Man with his Soul"; magical formulas of appeasement and propitiation. As for the resulting disorder, someone desperate to defend her might point out that a text narrated from the mind of Seth might, plausibly, be confused and chaotic. Perhaps the best that could be said for her methods is that Seth is a scavenger, and creates nothing on his own. The less-desperate-to-defend, however, might see this mish-mash as plagiarism-pretending-to-high-art-be, with the unit of plagiarism taken down to the level of meme. The obvious pomo dodge is that all texts draw on a constantly recycled fund of meanings; but this text seems almost entirely and perversely composed of phrases meant *not* this way by particular authors working with careful scholarship and seriousness to say something *else,* something *valid.* Or perhaps she does also, and I have understood nothing at all.

35. The problems of translating sexual content from ancient sources has met with a number of solutions, from metaphor and euphemism to poeticization (the gold standard of which is Sir Richard Burton's use of "lingham" and "yoni" in his translation of the *Kama Sutra*) to Bowdlerization, and now to what here seems its opposite. To be fair, among Beulah's notes there is an unattributed photocopy of a translated hieroglyphic text that indicates she is not the first to work in this vein.

36. It has been said that conflict in the Egyptian pantheon is relatively rare—relative for instance to the squabbles among the Olympians. Mentions of the murder of Osiris, while found in the very early hieroglyphic texts, are brief and allusive. Fuller accounts may have been lost, but it has also been speculated that the horror was too great ever to relate directly. So although the murder story forms the backdrop to the "contendings," no text integrates the two. And although fragments of the murder are more explicit, the fragments sometimes vivid, the one reasonably complete account of the *Contendings of Horus and Seth* is a meandering affair dating from a much later period. Of this version Simpson says: "Such a dichotomy between coarse humour, even about the gods, and seriousness in religion is an aspect of the Ramesside age . . ." (c. 1300–1000 B.C.E.) Arguably there have been other such periods: the age of Greek Old Comedy, ending with Aristophanes; the Baroque; and the Postmodern, admittedly short on seriousness.

37. While the hieroglyphic record of Osiris's murder is laconic, a very great deal is made of Seth's semen—no walk-on character this, but a speaking part. The rape of the child is handled uncomically.

38. Apophis/Apep being the primordial serpent or dragon lying in wait in the marshes to attack the Sun Bark. The serpent has been glossed as the figure of chaos, and Seth's special task of riding in the prow to fend it off, as a kind of homeopathy: 'Confusion' as an antidote to 'Chaos.' It is not then inconceivable that the Egyptians saw variegations in the colourings of the chaotic. The picture clouds further in that the Greeks, at least according to Graves, saw Seth as Typhon, 'stupefying smoke, hot wind, hurricane,' moreover connecting Typhon, dyslectically say, to Python, the great serpent of the Oracle. So two serpents: one of storm or smoke or darkling sky, the other perhaps of chaos. (Though in fact Seth in Egypt was more often an ass, a boar, or a jackal.) But taking a deep breath and a wild stab, one could suppose that Beulah saw this too in her own special way. She would see chaos as a dynamic principle, but not precisely primordial: before the first order, and before the swirling chaos preceding it, would have been a stillness, inert, inanimate. Conceivably influenced by the Mexicans, Beulah saw Apophis as a dragon of entropy, inertia, indifference, soul death. Her term was acedia. Originally it referred to the mental prostration of hermits, induced by fasting; but it was eventually used almost as the spiritual equivalent of Sloth, the fourth cardinal sin. Acedia or acidie, from *a-kedos*, uncaring. As a modern medical term it is lumped in with ennui, alienation, inner torpor. For Beulah, it might have been closer to a spiritual heedlessness, a going native, or rather 'going modern.' Here she had devised an extended etymology—from her notes:

> *Kedos*, yes, but *kerein* too—trouble, distress—and the Welsh *cas*—hate. But
> hatred of what? The synchronic God-mind troubles our torpor, disturbs our

slacker dreams, drags a nightstick across the bars of the Sloth Cage. The lobotomy that does not placate—and as the patient goes ape / slashes at the web of connection / grounds the numen charge—disconnects . . . us. Hail all hail! to the gory idols of Delinkage, Dissociation, Coincidence, Contingency . . .

Phaëthon BOOK SIX

1. The quote, attributed to J. Bierhorst, is most likely drawn from *Four Masterworks of American Indian Literature*.

2. Clendinnen, in *Aztecs: An Interpretation*, describes one of the effects of obsidian wine as a kind of parrot dancing, imitative movements.

3. Rilke, apparently, from "The Spectator." *Conquests no longer fascinate. His growth consists in being defeated / by something ever-grandlier great.*

4. A debt is owing here, obviously, to Camus' *The Plague*.

5. Sor Juana's *First Dream*. All translations of *First Dream* are by Alan Trueblood.

6. Sor Juana once wrote that *First Dream* was the only poem she had composed for herself. An exaggeration, no doubt, but there is little doubt that it was different—from her other work and from anyone else's. Octavio Paz argues that it is without precedent in all of Spanish literature. Again Paz (and here at least one cannot quarrel with Beulah's choice of sources, which for sentimental reasons I cite here at some length): "*First Dream's* break with tradition . . . is a sign of her times. Something ends in that poem and something begins. This spiritual departure implies a radical change in the relationship between the human being and the beyond. . . ." (Margaret Sayers Peden, trans.)

7. First Dream.

8. Harpocrates is sometimes identified as the Greek Horus, god of silence.

9. *First Dream.*

10. Edna Alford, *A Sleep Full of Dreams*.

11. *First Dream.*

12. Ibid.

13. Ibid.

14. Ibid.

15. This note fragment is marked "from page 97 as observed by Emilie Bergmann." The text in which this appears on page 97 is not specified. Emilie Bergmann has published widely on Sor Juana.

16. Antonia, it seems, draws upon devices used earlier in the century by William Shakespeare.

17. Attribution for translation?

18. Wordsworth.

19. Jann Arden.

20. Reference unknown.

21. For whatever reason, throughout this passage there appear references to and paraphrases of Shakespeare's "The Phoenix and the Turtle."

22. Plath.

23. Eliot.

24. From Ronald Wright, *Time Among the Maya.*

25. 'Magic that loves the hungry.' Leonard Cohen, *Beautiful Losers.*

26. "The Phoenix and the Turtle."

27. Ibid.

28. Ibid.

29. Camus, "The Myth of Sisyphus."

Debts of gratitude are owing.

To Fondo Nacional para la Cultura y las Artes (FONCA), Instituto Nacional de Bellas Artes (INBA), Feria Internacional del Libro de Guadalajara, Foreign Affairs and International Trade Canada and the Alberta Foundation for the Arts for financial and logistical support covering the *Hunger's Brides* theatrical tour to Mexico and a year or two of writing time. And, to the late, great Explorations program of the Canada Council.

To the staff and faculty of la Universidad del Claustro de Sor Juana Inés de la Cruz, for inviting One Yellow Rabbit to perform staged readings from *Hunger's Brides* in the Claustro's chapel and for hosting us afterwards. To the venerable magazine *Vuelta* for letting us crash the party in the *gran patio*. A special word of thanks to the staff, faculty and writers of the Writing Studios at Banff Centre for the Arts, '95 and '97.

To Sor Juana scholars Emilie Bergmann and Fred Luciani for their sources and support; to Teresa Castelló Yturbide, distinguished Sorjuanista, and to Patrick Johansson, Mexicanist and Nahuatl scholar, for inviting me into their homes in Mexico to share their latest research. To Dr. Salvador Rueda Smithers of INAH for giving me free run of the Castillo museum archives. To John Pflueger for his professional and poetic ruminations on geology. To the dozens of researchers who shared their expertise on-line, through scholarly discussion lists such as FICINO, Renais-1, Aztlan, Nahuat-1, historia-matematica, ANE. Perhaps never has a book relied so greatly on the collegial offerings of so many scholars. For their often multiple replies to abstruse queries, I would particularly like to thank Mohammed Abattouy, Evelyn Aharon, Anthony Appleyard, Christopher Baker, Kevin Berland, Luc Borot, Luigi Borzacchini, Thomas Brandstetter, Galen Brokaw, Paul D. Buell, R. Joe Campbell, Geoffrey Chew, Duane J. Corpis, Chichiltic Coyotl, Sarah Davies, Myriam Everard, Joan Gibson, Jim Gomez, Paul F. Grendler, James Grubb, Scott Grunow, Jack Heller, Peter C. Herman, Chris Hermansen, Helen Hills, Tom Izbicki, Tomas Kalmar, Frances Karttunen, Dan Knauss, Anu Korhonen, Heinrich C. Kuhn, Ray Lurie, Mary Ann Marazzi, Michael McCafferty, Katherine McGinnis, Leah Middlebrook, Mark David Morris, Steven N. Orso, Helen Ostovich,

ACKNOWLEDGEMENTS

Jack Owen, Dan Price, Francois P. Rigolot, Stewart Riley, Betty Rizzo, David Sánchez, Mel Sanchez, John F. Schwaller, Christoph J. Scriba, Jutta Sperling, Laurie Stras, Sharon Strocchia, John Sullivan, Roberto Tirado, Frank Young, Germaine Warkentin, Steve Whittet, the late Paolo Renzi and Linda Schele, and many others. And to Mata Kitimisayo, whoever you may be off-line, please get in touch; Random House Canada will know where to find me. A word of praise and gratitude, also, for the invaluable Sor Juana database created and maintained by Dartmouth University. And to the philosopher Terence Penelhum, for the first intimations of an ideal.

For publishing excerpts from *Hunger's Brides* years before the end was in sight, thanks especially to Andris Taskans of *Prairie Fire*, Natalee Caple of *Queen Street Quarterly*, Juan Manuel Gómez of the Mexico City daily *La Crónica*, and to the editors of the Banff Centre anthologies *Meltwater* and *Riprap*. To Linda Spalding of *Brick*, which does not publish fiction, for reading everything I sent, just for the hell of it.

For certain of Sor Juana's chapters, I drew directly from articles developed by Sor Juana scholars whom I credit in endnotes. Influential, also, were comprehensive works by Stephanie Merrim, Antonio Alatorre, Martha Lilia Tenorio, Fernando Benítez, George M. Tavard, Margo Glantz and Marie-Cécile Bénassy. And it was only years after reading it that I understood how much I had been affected by Diane Ackerman's *Reverse Thunder*. Alan Trueblood's translations gave me a first audition of Sor Juana's English music. Thanks to Harvard University Press for its extraordinary courtesy in allowing me to reprint at length from Trueblood's splendid *A Sor Juana Anthology* and from Octavio Paz's work as translated superbly by Margaret Sayers Peden.

Two writers and their works, above all others, fired and fed the genesis of this work: Eduardo Galeano in his *Memory of Fire* trilogy and Blake Brooker, in *The Land, the Animals*, a theatre masterpiece born in the same year as *Hunger's Brides*—two verses of one song, of an America that is lost. And there is a book without which this novel could not even have been imagined. Octavio Paz's magisterial *Sor Juana or, The Traps of Faith*.

To other writers and artists who gave comfort and blood: Kelley Aitken, Ken Babstock, Kevin Brooker, Gregg Casselman, Joan Clark, Bo Curtis, Chris Cran, Don Gillmor, Irene Guilford, Louise Halfe, Karen Hines, Lee Kvern, Richard McDowell, Dave Margoshes, Kirk Miles,

Michele Moss, John Murrell, Rosemary Nixon, Peter Oliva, Joanne Page, Mariko Patterson, Howard Podeswa, Paul Rasporich, Barb Scott, Anne Simpson, Dorothy Speak, Joy Walker, Rachel Wyatt. And to Jane, for the gauntlet in the teeth.

Special thanks to theatre angels One Yellow Rabbit, and to the crew of the *Hunger's Brides* road show. Blake Brooker (for who we were then), Grant Burns (for the ending), Ralph Christoffersen (great white bear, *explorador*), Denise Clarke (for the unbreakable commitment, the grace), Andy Curtis (who showed how deep Donald runs and, just perhaps, reintroduced Octavio Paz to Pablo Neruda), John Dunn (heart of the house), Michael Green (for helping make Núñez more than a special effect), Zaide Silvia Gutiérrez (brain-squizzer, comic, translator, theatre master, lexicographer, bringer of books and laughter), Richard McDowell (with such as these, one crosses deserts), Steve Schroeder, Elizabeth Stepkowski (for her journals and superb companionship, and for bringing Beulah to life in all her passion and yearning).

To the friends who always asked, so generous in their optimism: It's my fault if you don't know who you are. Cathy J., wherever you are, I hope you are well. The crew of Maiden Light (Andy, Hermann, Paolo), for the first big dream. To the friends who heaped material support upon the moral—a reading, a meal, a bed, a book, a name. Heather Elton, Warren Fick, Anne Flynn, Anne Georg, Anne Green, Emma Greenstreet, Shawna Helland, Michele Moss, Deborah Roth. And to Gerald Simon, gifted reader, gentle critic, fellow traveller on roads of myth.

My friends in Mexico form a category all their own: Alberto Ruy Sánchez, Guillermo Diego, Norma Chargoy, their son, Diego. To Amanda, thank you for the doll and the dances. I wish you love and health. And to *la familia* Rivera Morfín—Tey, Raúl, Raulito, Octavio and Fernando—thanks for so many things, for the introduction to Sor Juana and Nezahualcóyotl. And, of course, to Z.

From friends to editors and back again: Edna Alford at the Banff Centre, who believed before I did; Anne Collins at Random House, who believed when I had begun to stop. Surely no writer has been more blessedly mistaken in his prejudices about the editorial soul.

From editors to family: My father, for the stories and the drives, my mother, for the nursery books and nursery rhymes, my sisters, for glimpses of the exotic orient of women's lives. To the Ikeda-Cameron family and to Lil, for teaching me the Drabiuk house rules.

ACKNOWLEDGEMENTS

These books are written for Satsuki, for enfolding me in peace these long years.

Pale mountain flower . . . dancing mistress of my heart.
Who has the courage to face the hardest questions,
and strength to go on without answers.

The author would like to acknowledge the kind permission of the following rights holders to reprint from their material.

Guy Davenport: Translation of Sappho, from *Archilochos, Sappho, Alkman*, copyright © 1980. Published with permission of the author.

Constance Garnett, revised by Avrahm Yarmolinsky: Translations from Dostoevsky's *The Brothers Karamazov*, copyright © 1920, 1933. All selections have been reprinted with the permission of Easton Press.

Excerpt from THE GOLDEN ASS by Apuleius, translated by Robert Graves. Copyright © 1951, renewed 1979 by Robert Graves. Reprinted by permission of Farrar, Straus and Giroux, LLC.

Richard Lattimore: Translation of Aeschylus, from THE COMPLETE GREEK TRAGEDIES, AESCHYLUS I, copyright © 1953, reprinted by permission of the publisher, University of Chicago Press.

Miguel Leon-Portilla: Translation from Nezahualcoyotl, from *Fifteen Poets of the Aztec World*, copyright © 1992. Reprinted by permission of University of Oklahoma Press.

Miriam Lichtheim: Translations from *Ancient Egyptian Literature: A Book of Readings, Vols I-III*, copyright © 1973. Reprinted by permission of University of California Press.

Richard Livingston: Translation of Thucydides, from *The History of the Peloponnesian War*, copyright © 1943. Reprinted by permission of Oxford University Press.

Margaret Sayers Peden: Translation of Octavio Paz, reprinted by permission of the publisher from SOR JUANA: OR, THE TRAPS OF FAITH, by Octavio Paz, translated by Margaret Sayers Peden, Cambridge, Mass.: The Belknap Press of Harvard University Press, copyright © 1988 by the President and Fellows of Harvard College.

Margaret Sayers Peden: Translation of Sor Juana Inés de la Cruz's *La Respuesta a Sor Filotea*, originally commissioned by Lime Rock Press, Inc., in *A Woman of Genius: The Intellectual Autobiography of Sor Juana Inés de la Cruz*, copyright © 1982 by Lime Rock Press, Inc. Reprinted with permission.

Dava Sobel: Translation of Galileo, from *Galileo's Daughter*, copyright © 1999 by Dava Sobel. Printed by permission of Walker & Co.

Alan H. Sommerstein: Translation from Aristophanes, from *Lysistrata and Other Plays*, copyright © 1973, 2002. Reproduced by permission of Penguin Books Ltd.

Thelma D. Sullivan: Translations of Nahuatl texts from *A Scattering of Jades: Stories, Poems and Prayers of the Aztecs*, copyright © Rita Wilensky, 1994. Reprinted with permission.

Alan Trueblood: Translations of Sor Juana Inés de la Cruz, reprinted by permission of the publisher from A SOR JUANA ANTHOLOGY, translated by Alan S.

PAUL ANDERSON left Canada in his early twenties and spent years travelling in Asia, studying in Europe and teaching in Latin America, logging 25,000 miles of coastal and ocean sailing along the way. *Hunger's Brides*, his first novel, has been a labour of twelve years. In 1996, Alberta's One Yellow Rabbit theatre company toured a dramatic reading adapted by the author from an early manuscript of the novel, and performed in the convent where Sor Juana died. Anderson lives for the moment in Calgary.

To learn more, please visit Anderson's website: www.hungersbrides.com.